I0788176

THE FIFTH HORSEMAN SERIES

The Complete Saga

FREIDA KILMARI

Copyright © Freida Kilmari 2022
All rights reserved
First Published in 2022
The Horseman's Harem Saga: The Complete Collection

No part of this book may be reproduced, stored in a retrieval system, or transmitted in any form by any means without the prior permission in writing of the publisher, nor be otherwise circulated in any form of binding or cover other than that in which it is published and without a similar condition, including this condition, being imposed on the subsequent purchaser. All characters in this publication other than those clearly in the public domain are fictitious, and any resemblance to real persons, living or dead, is purely coincidental.

Cover: Amanda Matthews at AM Design Studios
Proofreader: Jutta Stiller at Square Peg Editing

❀ Created with Vellum

CONTENT GUIDANCE

Violence
This book contains scenes of graphic violence, including death scenes, and deals with this both physically and emotionally.

Profanity
This book contains excess profanity from all characters.

Sexual Situations
This book contains explicit sex, including MM, FF, MF, MMFFM, and MMF scenarios.
Kink list: DP, mild bondage, mild s/D, choking, and vampirism.

Dark Themes
This book deals with flashbacks, nightmares, and other PTSD symptoms that some may find uncomfortable. This book deals with war, anxiety, loss, and gender identity issues.

DEDICATION

To all the oddballs, misfits, and not-fitting-iners, this one's for you.

Elven Mall
Market Town
She

NORTHERN FOREST
HOME
THE ELVEN BARRIER
TA

FIFTH HORSEMAN SOUNDTRACK

Strangers Like Me - Phil Collins
Control - Zoe Wees
Invisible - Zara Larsson
Devils Don't Fly - Natalia Kills
I'm Still Here - John Rzeznik
Let it Go - Demi Lovato
Victory - Two Steps from Hell
Walk on Water - 30 Seconds to Mars
In the End - Black Veil Brides
Die for You - Starlet
Love is Gone - SLANDER
Someone You Loved - Lewis Capaldi
Uncomfortably Numb - Arrows in Action
Legends Never Die - League of Legends
Angel with a Shotgun - The Cab
Warrior - Beth Crowley
Battle Cries - Peyton Parrish
History Maker - AmaLee

PROLOGUE

In the year 2089, the Shifter, Fae, and Vampire communities banded together to expose themselves to the outside world, bringing about a new era of unstable human-supernatural alliance.

Now, after a hundred years of having no control over the supernatural community, of tentative peace and suffered silence, humans have decided to fight back, to rid the world of magic, and to bring back the old world of mortality.

With the world on the brink of magical war, the Four Horsemen of the Apocalypse are struggling to keep the balance they've maintained over the last two millennia. But with four supernatural communities tearing each other apart, and with the humans gearing up for a war against magic, they're going to need more than their usual team to handle this mess. They're going to need the Fifth Horseman of the Apocalypse: the Horseman of Magic.

VOLUME ONE

Gray light shatters my blurry vision, but all I can see are shapes as voices grate my eardrums. I can't make out any particular words, but a lilting sound flows its way toward me, a singing voice so beautiful in its cadence, I'm having a hard time focusing on anything else. Though there are other voices in the room, I can't stop my curiosity wandering around that lilt.

Where am I?

Who am I?

What's going on?

"Her eyes are opening . . ."

"She's practically awake, but she's still really weak."

"We're going to continue using this language, then?"

"It's only polite."

A thud startles my eyes open the final few centimeters, and four faces I haven't seen before meet my bewildered gaze. But now that I think about it, whose faces have I seen before? My memory . . . It's all a giant blur. And the harder I try to clear the picture, the blurrier it gets. I only remember a coppery smell, the feeling of drowning, and an ache in my feet.

Why?

"Miss, please don't be frightened." A woman's face comes into view, framed by beautifully blond hair—impossibly blond, actually, like the color of the sun chose her head out of billions of others to shine its radiance—that seems to trail all the way to the floor in two long braids. Save for the few strands of hair straying around her face, everything is perfectly in place, from the dimple on her left cheek to the deep green of her eyes and the feather earring hanging from her left ear.

"W-Who are . . . you?" My voice sounds so strange, as though it belongs to someone else and I'm stuck in a stranger's body.

"Name's Con, short for Connie." She grabs the pillow and maneuvers it into a more comfortable position. "Reckon you can sit up, hon?"

I nod, not wanting to hear my strange voice again.

She gently grips my elbow and half lifts me into a sitting position.

The other three faces—all male—sit patiently in the room, which I now recognize as some sort of bedroom, though it's like none I've ever seen before. The light filtering through the wall of crystalline window on my right is patchy from the forest dwelling just outside, while the room itself is covered in plush rugs and lounge chairs in all sorts of bright colors—some of which I've never seen before. From turquoise greens to burnt orange-yellows, it reminds me of peace. Of calm tranquility.

"Where am I?"

One of the men steps forward. His stubble just grazes the edges of his face, but he's an otherwise large man, towering well over six feet and carrying nothing but muscle. "You're safe."

"Where. Am. I?" The edge to my voice has a bite to it, and I can feel frustration showing on my face.

"Our home. We call it *Sheruta*. It's a realm separate from Earth."

"Okaaay." Clearly, I've gone insane. That or this is just some elaborate dream my stupid brain is concocting while I'm deep in a coma somewhere.

"No, sweet thing." Another one of the guys steps forward, and my eyes latch on to bright red swept-back hair sitting on top Asian skin, glinting in the sun. "You're not dreaming."

Did he just . . . read my mind?

"Yup." He smells like a bonfire in winter, and his hair's dirty bright red continues to flicker in the light, as though it were indeed a flame of its own.

A shiver escapes my body. That's right, I'm cold.

He looks to the muscular man from before. "Get a fire going."

I look down his slim form and chuckle at his t-shirt, which reads: YOU'RE ONLY A 10 ON THE PH SCALE BECAUSE YOU'RE BASIC.

While Muscle Man places some chopped logs from a wire basket into a fireplace at the other end of the room, the red-haired man sits by my bedside with a smile. "Name's Nine. It's nice to finally meet you, sweet thing."

I look to the only other man in the room, who sits in the shadows on the other side of my bed, as pale as death and almost translucent. "And you are . . . ?"

He steps forward, surprise etching his face as his black hair falls around his eyes in wafting waves of dark beauty that frame perfectly angular cheekbones, a chiseled jaw, and a snake-bite piercing both sides of his lower lip. "You are able to see me?" As the light catches his features, that translucence turns into an opacity of ungodly beautiful skin.

Is it weird? To like a guy's skin? Probably.

I realize then that I've been staring and haven't even bothered to answer his question. "Well," I start, "yeah. You're standing right there."

A smile reaches ear to ear, his raised eyebrows settling back down, and he leans forward to touch my forehead. "My name is Dea, and I was the one who reclaimed your life, little angel."

That smile is perfect, angling his jaw in all its chiseled lines and perfectly placed shadows, but his rugged hair and piercings gives him a messy, rockstar kind of look. I didn't know they make men like him. He's so beautiful it almost hurts to look. But what's most enchanting is his eyes; they circle in a swirling galaxy, whose pinnacle of golden starlight rests in the very center, where most people's pupils sit.

Nine chuckles. "You're distracting her, bro."

I can feel the blood rush to my cheeks. Damn telepath. I look at a smiling Dea, suddenly remembering what he just said. "Y-You saved m-me? How? When? Wh—?"

"That's enough," Connie butts in. "She needs to rest." She stands and ushers everyone out of the room, a dark look in her eyes that says she means business. "C'mon. Scat!"

Everyone practically runs out of the room, but Muscle Man still tends to the fire, slowly poking it and stoking the small flames into a roaring inferno. He gets up to leave once finished, not saying a word but following everyone else nonetheless.

"Wait!"

He stops at the doorframe and turns around with a scowl on his rough features.

Wonder what a smile would look like on that perfect face?

"Your name? What's your name?"

"What does it matter?"

"I just . . ." Fuck, I don't even know. Why do I want to know his name? "Would like to know your name." I look away and try turning over, only to meet a stabbing pain that has me whimpering before I can hold my tongue.

He sighs, and I hear his heavy footfalls getting closer before he gently helps turn me onto my side and places the pillows into a better position before leaving and clicking the door shut.

What a strange man.

"THE PATH TO VENGEANCE IS FRAUGHT WITH FEAR, DARKNESS, AND ICE-COLD DESPAIR." THAT saying echoes in the background of what I think is my new reality, what I think I have to suffer through for the rest of eternity.

The darkening alleyway leers against the setting sun as my head spins back and forth. I pull my hand away from the sharp pain, and it comes back bloody.

Shit. I've smashed my head on the concrete wall.

"Still think you can take me, hunter?"

The man standing in front of me wobbles on unsteady legs, his pale complexion only getting paler as the sun sets on the safety of daylight. His fangs glint in the orange glow, and if I were someone who found that kind of darkness beautiful, I would reach out and touch them.

"Yeah, I'm pretty confident." I shrug, not wanting to move my head too much. "You're just a turned Vampire. I've taken down born ones of your kind."

His face blanches. "Liar! No one can take down a highborn Vampire! They're the strongest creatures on Earth."

"A little egotistical there, aren't you?"

I love watching them freak when they realize what a mistake they've made by not running. I love the looks of horror etched on their faces before I turn my magigun on them.

And just like every other time I've taken down a turned Vampire, this one holds his hands up in surrender before I pull the trigger.

His scream makes me smile—a satisfying echo to match the beauty of his darkness.

I shove some magicuffs on him, immobilizing his Vampire strength—the only form of magic a turned Vampire has—and drag him to his feet.

"C'mon, big guy, work with me here."

He doesn't help, of course, because he's unconscious, but I hope some kind of goddess or deity takes pity on me having to drag his slumped body to my car and grants me temporary super-strength.

But alas, no such stupid prayers are answered because if there are gods or deities, I wouldn't be stuck in this shitfest of a life.

A FEW HOURS AFTER I FELL ASLEEP—OR, AT LEAST, I PRESUME THAT'S THE CASE, SINCE NIGHT has fallen by the time I wake—my stomach rumbles with a ravenous hunger as I fight off the sweat-soaked nightmare.

Shit. What was that? It felt so . . . real.

Another grumble of my stomach has me remembering reality.

Food! That's right, I haven't eaten in a while.

A knock sounds at the door before someone twists the handle.

Shit. Someone's coming in.

Fear wells for a reason I'm not too sure of. I'm in a strange place, surrounded by people I don't know, that is apparently not Earth . . .

I look around, frantic, searching for anything to use as a weapon, and only find a pair of tweezers on the nightstand. I grab them and aim toward the door as it swings open, preparing to throw if necessary.

"Whoa there, sweet thing," Nine says as he steps through the now-open door. "It's just me. Nine? Put the deadly tweezers down," he says through a chuckle.

He comes in carrying a tray of something steaming hot in a bowl, with some brown crusty stuff on a plate beside it, and a cup of something that smells like roasted heaven.

"Here." He hands me the tray once I sit up, and he cracks a smile. "No need to try to injure us, we're just trying to help." He gives me a smirk, as if my tweezers weren't even going to put a dent in this man—which they probably weren't—and I melt slightly at the sight of his smile lighting up that red hair.

"Sorry." Taking a large sniff, my belly rumbles once more, louder this time. "What is it?"

"Soup? It's just chicken soup. You're not vegetarian, are you?"

"Chicken soup . . . Right." I look at his confused face and let out a pained laugh of my own, my injuries getting in the way of me really enjoying the ridiculous moment of not knowing whether I'm vegetarian. "No, not vegetarian. I don't think."

"You don't think?" His amused smirk seems to make his hair a brighter shade of red, and it hypnotizes me for a long moment. "Shouldn't that be something you know?"

"S-S-S-Sorry," I stammer, "my memory . . . It's not remembering anything."

"Anything at all?" Concern etches across his features—genuine concern—a surprising change from his earlier smirking.

I just shake my head and put a piece of the brown crusty stuff into the soup—bread, of course it's bread—and take a bite. Taking a sip of the coffee, I exhale in relief as I remember the taste and smell of liquid life. Goddess, I need more of this amazing stuff.

What is wrong with me?

"I see." He leans forward, places a gentle hand on my forehead, and closes his eyes. He takes a deep breath and seems to concentrate, so I just continue to eat my soup while he sits there for a few minutes, continuously taking deep breaths now and then. Finally, after an awkward five minutes with his hand practically glued to my forehead, he opens his eyes. "Your memories, they've been damaged, it seems. I can't get a single read on them."

"Read? You can read my memories?"

"Yeah, along with other things. I can read your mind and look into your dreams. It's part of my gift."

"That's nuts. Cool, but nuts." I practically inhale the rest of the soup and wipe the bowl clean with the last chunk of bread as my belly rumbles a loud thanks.

The interesting room catches my eye once again. It's so colorful: The fireplace sits across from the bed and roars a gentle mix of green and orange flames, occasionally letting out a crack or pop as the dark wood splinters and burns. The rest of the room is full of turquoise-and-orange-shaded colors—a beautiful mixture of dawn and dusk. I raise my head and look over at the fancy closet to my right: sequins layer the side I can see, with white double doors and tassels hanging off the handles.

"Whose room is this?"

Nine chuckles and turns to look around. "Seems it's yours. The house is a little mysterious. It's magical, so it kind of has a mind of its own."

Mine?

Yes.

"Whoa. What was that?" I cough and splutter for a moment before catching my breath. "Did you just . . . ?"

"Speak into your mind? Yeah."

I see. Interesting. "Can the others do it?"

"No. We all have different gifts." He takes back the tray and places it on the nightstand next to a crystal lamp that seems to change color every few minutes. A hand lays gently on my left leg as he looks at me.

"So . . . err . . . What's going on? Who am I? What am I doing he—?"

He holds out a flat hand midair to stop my questions. "We'll answer your questions. Promise. But after you've recovered. You were . . . in an accident."

"Dea said he saved my life?"

Chuckling, Nine says, "Yeah, he's always had a flare for the dramatics, that one. But he's right in a backward sort of way. You'll get used to him."

The memory of Dea's smile flashes across my mind, but I push it away when I remember that Nine can probably see it.

Damn, that's gonna take some getting used to. I sigh. Time to see the damage, I guess.

My legs feel okay, and it doesn't hurt when Nine places his hand on the left one. I can wiggle my toes just fine, and my arms seem to be whole and functioning. Limbs are intact. My head pounds, but I can turn my neck without too much of a headache. But my chest . . . I can't really move it. Every time I inhale, my lungs rattle and a searing pain shoots through my left side.

I need to see the damage.

"Can I take a bath or a shower . . . or something?"

"Oh, of course. Your bathroom is just through there." He points to a door on the other side of the room, to the left of the now-raoring fireplace. "And the other door"—he points to a door on the right side of the fireplace—"is your study."

I nod slowly, not really understanding how all of this is mine. Do I have to pay rent?

"I'll get Con to help you bathe. Is that okay?"

I give another slow nod, not really sure what else to say, as I still puzzle over how any of this belongs to me.

This room is mine. How? Nine said something about a magical house. Maybe I've just been assigned these rooms to recover in? Maybe they'll send me home soon.

But now that I think about it, where is home?

I remember everything about the world: the countries; magic (Fae spells, Witch elements and charms, various Vampire gifts, and all the other random types of magic in the lower supernaturals); the different species (Vampire, human, Shifter, Fae, Witch, etc.); how to use a plasmascreen and all kinds of magical technology; history. But none of my personal specifics. It's as though my life has been erased—no memories of family, friends, what kind of food I like, what types of coffee there are . . . None of it exists for me anymore.

What do I even look like?

Connie arrives with a couple of towels just as that question flits across my mind, and she offers a gentle smile that breaks me out of my downward spiral into panic. "Bath?"

"Yes. Thank you. Sorry for troubling you."

"No trouble at all, hon." She goes to the bathroom door and swings it open on silent hinges.

What I can see of the room beyond takes my breath away. Well, I don't really remember any other bathrooms right now, but given the spa-shaped pool in the center of the floor and all the crystals and bright colors dancing over the semitranslucent tiles, I'm going to go out on a limb and assume this isn't standard.

But who knows, maybe it is?

She fills the pool—bath?—with steaming water from an array of taps on the side, and the room steams up as the tiles turn a bright blue crystal color, losing their translucent quality.

She adds various types of salts, crushed crystals, and a liquid that bubbles when placed under the running taps—bubble bath, of course—before turning around to me.

"Want help getting out of bed?" She comes over to the bed, hands at the ready to ease me up.

"No, I got it." I inch my way to standing and let the hem of my nightgown slide along the floor. It hurts like hell to put one foot in front of the other, and breathing through it is fucking hell on earth.

"Do I have many injuries?"

"Just two. One to your head, which we've stitched up, and the main wound to your chest, which is healing slowly with the aid of Dea's magic."

That explains the headache and chest pain.

I crawl my way forward toward the now-steamy bathroom and try to pull off my nightgown in the process, but I wince the moment my arms move above my head.

"Here," Connie says, "let me." She undoes a clasp at the back of the gown, then slides it down my body with ease.

"Thanks."

I cover my breasts, which are only just visible above the giant bandage wrapping my chest.

"Oh, would you prefer I waited outside?"

That's the question, isn't it? I would prefer that, yes, but I doubt I can bathe on my own, and I really need to feel clean.

It's amazing the dilemmas you find yourself in when waking up battered and bruised in a foreign world surrounded by magical weirdos.

"Ermmm, no. It's okay."

She lowers me gently into the bath, which sits into the floor in all its golden grandeur, and then brushes a comb through my hair that hangs in clumps down to the middle of my back—something about that seems wrong, though, but I can't quite place why.

I resist the urge to cover my whole body with the bubbles surrounding me, not wanting to seem prudish, but my cheeks burn a bright shade of red every time I feel her eyes rest on me.

Goddess, this is so awkward.

"So," I begin, trying to start some kind of conversation that isn't focused on my nakedness, "what kind of gifts do you have?"

She coughs in surprise.

Oops. Maybe I'm not supposed to know about that? "Sorry, Nine said you all had different gifts when I asked." Fiddling with my thumbs, I add, "Just curious."

"Ah." She stays silent for a while longer, and I don't think she's going to answer. But then I hear her take in a deep breath. "My skills are more practical and battle-focused. I'm a good archer, I can hit any target from any distance so long as I can see it, and I never run out of stamina, no matter how little I've eaten or how long I've been fighting."

"Wow!" So she's basically a warrior badass? A really beautiful warrior. "That's amazing."

She giggles, and I watch in awe as her blond hair sways with the movement, a perfect contrast to her reddening cheeks and dimpling smile.

She applies some shampoo to my hair and lathers it in. "I guess it's pretty cool. Sometimes I kinda wish I had more passive gifts. Ones that make me a little more feminine." She sighs.

"Eh. Screw being feminine. You're fucking badass. Roll with it." Somehow, that sounds more like me—a voice that a deep part of my consciousness recognizes.

This time, Connie lets out a loud laugh that echoes across the room. Even her laugh is damn beautiful. A hint of jealously creeps up my spine, but mostly I'm just awed and fascinated. This woman is incredible. As beautiful as she is deadly.

"What about the others?"

"Dea and Arrie?"

Arrie? "So that's his name! The fucker refused to tell me anything."

She snorts as she helps me sit up a little more to rinse out the shampoo. "Yeah, he's a bit of a brooder, but you'll get used to each other . . . Eventually."

"Doubtful. He's an ass."

"He's the most powerful warrior among us. Don't piss him off."

"Even better than you?"

She pauses for a moment, as if considering my question. "In hand-to-hand combat? Yes. I haven't once beaten him without cheating."

Fuck. Maybe I'll consider my words more carefully when speaking to him. Given that I'm already injured, I don't want to have another accident.

She rinses the shampoo out and works the conditioner into the ends.

Maybe she'll know what's going on? "Sorry, but I really want to know what's going on. I'm being really calm, all things considered, and I'm pretty sure I should be freaking out."

"Yeah, we were talking about that while you were sleeping. You're probably still in shock. This is a strange place to wake up in after losing all your memories. But honestly, we don't know that much about you either."

"Oh." Really?

I can't hide the disappointment, it seems, because she stops lathering my hair for a moment to look me straight in the eyes. "Chin up. It'll get easier. And you'll remember things over time."

"Really?"

"Yeah. That's what Nine thinks. But hush. Enough about that. Tell me, do you like popcorn?"

I laugh but quickly wince as it constricts my chest. "Don't remember," I groan, rubbing my chest. "Sorry."

"Well, let's try it out. Movie night? We're watching Church Bells and Doorknobs?"

That rings a bell in the back of my head somewhere. "I think I've seen that, but I can't remember."

"Well, Dea and Arrie hate it, but it's one of mine and Nine's favorites, and it's our turn to pick this week." She rinses out the conditioner and begins scrubbing my body with a soft kind of soap; luckily for my dignity, she doesn't wash anywhere private, just the other important bits.

"Sure. Why not? Might need some help walking more than a few paces, though. It's kinda hard to breathe."

"I'll help. Don't worry." She stands and grabs a towel. "Now, let's get you all dried off and wearing something better than that nightgown."

"Ugh. Finally."

Connie helps me towel-dry and then goes to the closet to see what she can find that won't irritate my injuries. She pulls out item after item—none of which I recognize—until she finally finds a nice baggy dress and leggings that will match and leave my chest free from tight-fitting clothes.

I stand in front of the mirror in the bedroom and take in my reflection.

I have long pink hair that lightens the farther down it goes and frames my Japanese features. My chest is wrapped in waterproof bandages that have small flecks of dark red in a semicircle along my left side. But what really takes me by surprise is the skull tattoo across my collarbone in a long triangle that reaches all the way to my shoulders and down to my cleavage.

"Interesting tattoo," Connie mentions as she comes up behind me.

"Thanks. It's pretty."

"You have another one on your back. It's a lion in splashes of bright color."

"Really?" I try to turn around to get a good look but wince and quickly give up when a sharp pain radiates out from my left side.

"Yeah. It's cool-looking."

I turn around to face the clothes she's picked out and laid on the bed. "Err . . . where did all these clothes come from?"

"They're yours . . . from wherever you came from. Though we will add to it when you're better, otherwise we won't be able to . . . Never mind. That'll just start too many questions. Movie time!"

They're mine? But . . . I don't recognize any of them.

She helps me into the clothes in silence—with the noticeable absence of a bra, I might add—and styles my hair so that it's dry and sitting well with none of the weird bed-head kinks it's prone to.

How do I know that?

Gah! This memory thing is confusing.

"C'mon!" She grabs my hand and leads me slowly out the door. I get the feeling she would have dragged me down the hallway running if I could move any faster than a damn snail.

The hallway outside my rooms is decorated with beautiful paintings, some of the guys and Connie in various historical periods, others of people I don't recognize, and sometimes the odd decorative piece. But what I do notice is the beautifully open-plan space the hallway is; each room coming off of it is separated by a set of double doors, with some rooms only having an archway opening. Every room I can see into has a different feel, from music rooms with heavy drapes and dark décor to lounges with bright open spaces and pops of color.

Connie leads me down a large winding double staircase that really is like a fairy-tale dream come true, with the golden patterns on the railings and a plush cream-white carpet that has my bare feet feeling like I'm walking on clouds.

"What kind of place is this?"

Connie laughs but shrugs. "It's a pretty impressive house, isn't it?"

I just nod, not really knowing what else to say.

Have I died and woken up in some weird kind of heaven?

2

I nod in agreement and step into my room, not even bothering to respond. My room. My new room, in my new house, with my new . . . friends? Something about this feels strange and makes my hands shake as I shiver. To the right of the downstairs and around a corner is another large archway, but this one leads to a chef-style kitchen with warm cream-and-grass-green colors threading throughout cream-white worktops and a stove larger than me.

"She's alivvvve!" Nine sings as soon as he sees me from his seat at the kitchen table. He throws his hands in the air and waves them around like some silly child.

"He's gonna be a handful," I mumble to myself.

Connie laughes beside me, guiding me into a chair. "Yeah, he's a special kind of crazy."

"I heard that!" Nine is sitting in the chair next to me, placing a gentle hand on my knee while scowling at Connie. "You doing okay, Sweetie?"

"Sweetie? I see you've upgraded my nickname."

"Well, if we knew your actual name, I'd call you that."

My name? I haven't even thought about it. What is my name?

My echoing silence seems to answer their unspoken question, and Dea steps away from making a cup of tea with fancy fresh leaves and asks, "So you remember nothing at all?"

I shake my head, trying not to let the tears fall as I struggle to take a deep breath. Why can't I remember anything?

"It doesn't matter." Connie opens a glass sliding door that leads to a giant set of stairs curling into a darkening pit that descends below ground level.

Where does that lead?

Is this where they kill me and bury my body?

Nine helps me to my feet with another gorgeous laugh.

Does he ever stop laughing?

"Don't worry, it's just the theater. We're not about to take you to some secret basement to murder you. So you can stop those silly thoughts right now." He jabs me in the arm and helps me descend the stairs.

The darkness is stifling, but somehow, I can still see where I'm going, as though the darkness has no effect on me.

Nine notices. "You can see in the dark?"

"I guess . . ."

"Interesting."

"Or totally freakish."

Arrie follows us all silently, his gaze boring a hole in my back as I feel every shift in his vision as he apparently takes me in. The whole thing puts me on so sharp an edge I almost can't breathe.

Light brightens the way the moment we step through the door at the base of the stairs, and a giant room with plush chairs, sofas, and beds takes up the space. They all face the same way, and I realize that Connie was being serious—this is a theater.

They have a freaking theater in their basement?! With beds?

"Yes, we do." Nine sits me on the couch in the centermost area of the room, facing the wall-length screen in front of us. "Hold on." He presses a button on the side of the sofa, and a circular platform rises from the ground, lifting us into the air.

"Fae magic." It reminds me of the smell of alcohol and a glowing room as an image of faceless bodies dancing in pulsing lights flashes across my mind.

"Yeah. It manipulates the air beneath the floating surface and thickens it so everything above it floats as high as you need. Just push this button to determine the height." He holds out a controller he plucked from the side of the sofa with a few basic buttons, but he points to the arrows. "Take it."

"Okaaaay." Instant unease shoots through me, though I'm not sure why. My hands shake, but I clench them tight enough to slow the tremor to a tremble.

Stop being so stupid.

Taking a deep breath, I hit the down button, and the platform lowers. "Ah, I see."

I experiment with the buttons until I get the height that I think is right while someone puts the movie on. To my left, the other three are cuddled on a corner sofa on another platform just below us, Dea with his arm around Connie's waist while she rests on his shoulder, and Arrie curling up between her legs.

Are all three of them together? Like, together together?

I look at Nine, hoping he'll answer, but he's busy arranging the cushions into their plumpest forms with the utmost concentration.

"Come here." He gestures for me to lie on the cushions, and I realize he's probably trying to make things as comfortable as possible for me, given my stupid injuries that seem to plague my every other bloody thought.

That's super sweet. I can't help but smile at him as I lay down on the bed of pillows.

"Just know"—he sits on the other side of the sofa, giving me a fair bit of space—"I'd totally cuddle you, but since you're still injured, I don't want to hurt you." He looks a little sad about that. Disappointed, almost. And the distant look in his eyes makes me feel a bit guilty. He probably usually joins the others.

Wait, why do I feel guilty about that?

"Come here." I mimic the tone he used earlier with a beckoning finger and lift my legs to lay them in his lap as I entwine my arm under his outstretched hand. "Better?"

He nods as a wide grin spreads across his face. "Much."

We fall into companionable silence as a movie with high-speed car chases and loud gun fights plays on the large screen, each scene clicking a fragment of memory into place for me.

I have seen this before, at the local theater, when I was a teenager with some friends . . . I think. The smell of popcorn brings a memory back . . .

"Taytay . . . C'mon!" A boy with rainbow hair and bright pink jeans ushers me forward, grabbing the Coke from the counter. "I don't wanna miss that hunk of a man on the big screeeeen."

I roll my eyes. I'm used to his antics but still find them funny. "Okay. Okay."

"You cannot deny his gorgeousness!" he sings as steps into the elevator, and I step in beside him. "Even your little virgin ass can appreciate those eyes."

"G, stop being a little ho. You know I'm not fuckin' blind."

He holds his hands up in surrender (while still holding the Coke) and smiles.

"How long is the movie again?"

He gives me a look I know to mean he isn't impressed with the question, but he answers anyway. "Two hours. Then you may get back to whatever stupid romance book you're currently drooling over."

"Great!" I hop on the spot and steal a piece of popcorn, before reveling in the salted caramel taste that echoes across my senses.

I've trailed off from the movie toward the end, too busy sorting through these new snippets of memory to bother concentrating.

What are they?

Who is the friend?

Where was I in that memory?

"Errr . . . Sweetie?"

I snap out of my thoughts and realize the sofa is back on the ground, and I'm lying here, staring up at the crystallized ceiling, as the others stand around me. "Yeah?"

"You dazed out on us there. You okay?" Connie kneels beside me, a look of concern plastered across her face.

"Yeah, sorry. It's nothing."

I stand up and walk out of the theater—crawling is more like it—and head up the stairs, but it isn't long before I have to stop to catch my breath halfway up as I clutch at my chest and wheeze like I've swallowed a dog's chew toy. Every breath rattles. When will my lungs finally collapse? I'm bloody surprised I made it this far.

Arrie sighs and grumbles as he comes up behind me, scoops me into his arms, and carries me the rest of the way to my room in silence. My face brushes against his chest as he takes me up every stair and down every corridor, his strong arms wrapping under my back and legs as he silently carries me to my rooms. "There," he says once we reach my door. "Would have taken you double the time."

"Would not." I cross my arms and turn my back to him, opening the door and stepping inside.

"So you're not injured and you didn't nearly die recently, then?"

"Nope. Not at all."

"Well, then you'll be okay to go on a run with me in the morning?"

Ugh. No fucking way. I can barely walk. "Fine. Thank you for helping."

He laughs. A proper full-belly laugh, and his face lights up in a way I've never seen before, softening those usually frowning eyes into pools of ice blue I instantly want to get lost in. "God, you're stubborn."

3

The shape of the woman in front of me, with her long blond hair and perfectly manicured nails, shrinks into the shape of a goat, her cute little horns protrud from the top of her tuft of white fur.

"You are cute, love. And honestly, I hate hurting animals. But you're worth twenty thousand dollars"—I shrug—"and I have rent to pay."

She lets out a bleating rally cry, and I almost cave—she is the cutest Shifter I have ever hunted.

Looking up, I stare at myself in the woman's lounge room mirror. Dark pink hair sitting at my shoulders stares back at me, alongside a look of pleasing terror, one that probably gives any surviving victims nightmares.

I shrug, not really caring. They're supes. I don't really care what happens to them. But this woman seems lovely, and she is cute, so I decide to show her mercy and stun her quickly.

In the time it takes to blink, I have my magigun in hand and fire two shots to her body and watch her go down without a single bleat.

Her body turns back to human, and I quickly shove a pair of magicuffs on her and drag her to the elevator.

"You . . ." she whispers, "are a terrible human being."

I just laugh at her. "Yeah . . . Yeah, I am."

A DISTANT KNOCKING WAKES ME UP, AND I SHOOT UP IN BED, MAKING ME WINCE IN AGONY. "Holy fuck!" I shout-whisper into the morning light of my room. What was that dream?

Dea walks in at what I can only assume is the asscrack of dawn, as pale yellow-orange light filters its way through the window I didn't bother to cover with the heavy drapes.

He interrupted a nightmare—but this time, I got a look at the person I was. It was me. But with short pink hair rather than the long pale pink hair I have now.

"You can draw those curtains, if you would like?"

"I think I prefer them open, but thank you." The morning sun makes me smile beneath its warmth, and the moon comforted me while I slept in a way I can't explain, like how the fire warmed me when Arrie first lit it. It just feels more . . . homely. Is that weird? That I feel kinda at home despite knowing next to nothing about this place or these people?

Yup. Definitely weird.

Dea nods as he rubs his hands together and helps lift me into a standing position.

"I'm so stiff. Fuck."

"I am not surprised, Angel. You really did nearly die when I found you."

"You found me?" I let him run his hands over my forehead and down the lengths of my arms. "Why? How?"

"We will have a meeting this afternoon, and I want you there. I think it will help if you know what we are and what you are destined to become."

I didn't even think about what they are. They have gifts I have never heard of, and their magic scares me a bit, makes me uneasy in an almost instinctive way I can't control.

Dea's hands give off a green glow, and I flinch away, taking an instant step back.

"It is okay," he whispers. "I am just going to analyze your injuries. I use healing magic."

"Sorry. Not sure what came over me." I step forward toward his glowing hands and peaceful eyes, and I close my eyes as a warmth tingles its way down my arms to my fingertips.

"You seem to be healing well. The head injury should be healed after another healing bath. I reckon another two weeks of daily healing with me should have you up and running them in no time."

"Healing bath?" How long was I out if they were giving me daily treatments? "How does your magic work?"

"I am able to manipulate a person's soul and encourage it to do what I wish, including to heal." His hands still rest on my arms as he looks at me with the warmest smile. "I have been doing that daily since you got here."

"Oh. I see." I take a deep breath. "How long have I been here?"

He flinches at my question. "Eight months."

"W-W-What?"

He nods, a solemn look overtaking his usually charming features. "It took a while to nurse you back to health, Angel.

Why do his hands feel so warm and gentle?

I'm still leaning into his touch. Fuck. I flinch back and sit down to change the subject. "Could Connie help me get dressed again? I still can't really lift my arms over my head."

"I will fetch her." He nods. "In the meantime, I placed some breakfast on the bedside table." He points a delicate hand toward the nightstand closest to the door. "You should eat something. You need your strength."

I smile a quick thank-you and watch as he leaves, still smiling like an idiot minutes later. Ugh, get yourself together, girl. Clothes. You need clothes. Let's see what you like to wear.

The closet is a fascinating insight into who I am—or was?—and I eventually pick out something I like that won't irritate my chest. A pair of dark red shorts, a baggy midi-crop vest I pair with a wireless bra I find at the bottom of the pile of underwear, and a pair of tights with a cat-ear pattern on the thigh. Just need to find some shoes and . . . There! Some makeup, too.

While waiting for Connie to come help me get into my clothes, I brush my hair out, apply some smoky eyeshadow and winged liner, and try my best to do something with my hair (not trying to think too hard about how I know how to do certain things and not others).

Eight months, though. Fuck. I've been away from whatever life I had on Earth for eight months.

Fuck, fuck, fuck.

It eventually becomes too painful to keep my arms raised, so I stop.

"I can help with that." Connie walks into the room dressed in a light blue dress that reaches the floor and cinches tight at the waist, displaying the delicious curves that catch my eye and make me blush. Her hair is in her usual two braids that trail down to the floor. "Pass me the brush."

I pass it over, and she gets to work brushing everything into place, even capturing a few lose strands that refused to do anything when I tried to tame them.

She turns toward the closet. "Now for the clothes . . ."

I point to the outfit I laid on the bed earlier. "Those, please."

"Wow. You have an interesting sense of style. Let's get those tights and shorts on first, ey?"

I remove my nightgown and step into the rolled-up tights she has ready for me. After bending my body this way and that, trying to find the least painful way possible to get all of my clothes on, we finally have me dressed (even if we have to pull the midi-crop up over my legs rather than down over my head).

"Feel free to lounge or explore the house. There's nowhere you can't go. Though there are a few places that might bring you more questions than you're ready to deal with right now. Just shout if you need one of us."

"Okay." She turns to leave, but I grab her arm and yank her to a stop. "Connie . . . thank you." She's been genuinely lovely since yesterday; they all have, really.

"Stop being silly. You're more than welcome. Wouldn't want one of the guys helping you into clothes, would we?" Her smile lights up her face as her giggle echoes around the room after she leaves.

I take one last look at myself in the mirror, once again noticing my pale pink hair and the tattoo that sits on my chest, and go to the only place in my rooms I have yet to explore: the study.

The door creaks open slightly, and what lies beyond has me standing stock still at the sight. I have paid no attention to this door until this morning. But I should have. I really fucking should have.

Books. Thousands upon thousands of books lining every shelf as far as the eye can see. This entire room is larger than the basement theater, and I can't see the end, no matter how far I crane my neck. The volumes sit on dusty, dark-wood shelves that seem to fill the room in no particular order or strategy, some piling on top of one another, some sitting in neat orderly rows, and others spilling over the higgledy-piggledy shelves.

This is all for me?

I can't help it—I squeal and inhale the scent of untamable knowledge and endless adventures at the tips of my fingers. It's all for me? I don't . . . understand.

Why? How?

Those seem to be the questions I keep repeating to myself. But Dea promised he'd do some explaining this afternoon, and I don't think I'm in any immediate danger, so I may as well explore my library.

My library! Wow. What an insane thing to be thinking.

Connie bursts through the open door, blond braids whipping behind her. "You okay, hon? I heard a scream?"

"Oh, sorry. It's just . . . Look at this place! It's really mine? All of it?"

Connie looks sheepishly to the floor, an embarrassed blush setting her face on fire. "Sorry. I have good hearing. Sometimes I panic. But yeah, it's all yours. None of us have been in here yet, but wow!" She spins a 360 to get a good look at the room. "The house must really like you."

"You've not been in here?" I make my way to one shelf near the door.

"Nah, we couldn't get the door open. Seems to only respond to you. You must be a really private person."

"Hmmm. Private, cute punk-style clothes, a bookworm. I'm a strange person."

Connie laughs another one of those beautiful laughs I like hearing so much as she rests an elbow on my shoulder—not enough to cause any pain, but enough to know she's there. "I'd say interesting. You seem interesting."

"Really?"

"Yeah." She walks over to another wall of book-lined shelves. "May I?"

"Yeah, sure. Help yourself."

"Eeeek! Thank you, thank you, thank you."

"No library in the house?" I flip the page of the first book I pick off the nearest shelf: DRAGONS AND WHERE TO FIND THEM.

"Not one this big, no. This is fucking insane." She sits in a comfy rainbow pouf in a reading corner by the door and starts devouring the book she picked. "I wonder if you're someone who likes a bit of fun and mystery?"

"Huh? Why?"

"Because I bet there are secret doors and hidden passageways in this thing. It seems like that kinda place, you know."

A part of me can't help but wonder how the house knows that I like this kind of room, but the other part of me can't help but get a little excited at the prospect of exploring. "That would be awesome, I'm not gonna lie.

4

We spend hours reading in the corner just beside the door, Connie on the rainbow pouf and me on the sparkly sofa (can't quite get down on the floor without feeling like a million knives are stabbing me in the chest).

Before long—when I'm halfway through my book—Nine walks in with a smile on his face. "Ah, so this is where I find . . ." He looks up and sees the room for the first time, his eyes glowing in amazement. "Fucking whoa. What did you do to deserve this kinda room, Sweetie?"

I shrug and give a noncommittal grunt, sticking my nose back in the book.

"Well, as great as this is, and as much as I want to watch you reading in that hot little outfit, Dea wants to chat with you. We all do."

The meeting. Fucking finally. I place the book back on the shelf and slowly stand up, but Nine runs to my aid and steadies me, before helping me walk out of the room. Not that I need the help by this point, but it's a sweet gesture nonetheless.

Wait, did he just call me hot? Like, sexy hot? The realization has my cheeks burning and my eyes looking anywhere other than at him, so instead my gaze lands on Connie, who stares at us with a knowing smile and raised eyebrows.

Oh, for fuck's sake.

I shake my head and hobble ahead of them, not even wanting to think about the looks they're likely giving each other.

Why are they all so damn hot?

Nine leads us into a small room down a hallway I've not explored yet, a few hallways past the kitchen. This place is like a maze; I really need to go exploring at some point or get someone to draw me a damn map. The room seems to be some kind of small, unique-looking study with a desk sitting in the center. And at that desk sits a black-haired god of a man with all the right angles it almost makes me jealous I'm not him. Dea.

Are they all amazingly beautiful in one way or another? 'Cause that's gonna get real old, real fast.

"Now we are all present," Dea starts, looking to Arrie, whose white hair stands out from the shadows in the far corner, "we can get started filling you in, Angel."

"Before we begin, Dea," Connie interrupts. "You should see her fucking library! It's insane. It's easily the biggest room in the house."

"Wait, what?" Dea turns to look at me, but I don't know how to hold his intense, stormy gaze. "Really?"

I nod, not trusting my voice to speak a coherent sentence. He continues to look at me expectantly, and I realize I need to answer him. "Finally explored my study today, but it's more of a library, really. How did you know it was a study if you've never been in there?"

"We all have one." He gestures to the room we're currently in. "This is the bottom floor of mine."

Hmmm. It's cozy and different, and I like whatever that amazing smell is. . . Smoked lavender. It permeates every drop of air around me, as though whatever makes that smell spends every waking moment in Dea's study. The desk we're sitting at is rather large, but the rest of the room is covered with overstuffed bookshelves, various maps, and weird objects I've never seen before, and piles upon piles of paperwork and unbound books litter the space.

Goddess, it really smells like heaven in here.

"Anyway." Dea snaps my attention away from his study and back to his face. "We have a lot to tell you, but we are not sure how."

Ugh. They're going to beat around the bush again? "Just spit it out. You'll never know how I'm going to take something if you don't just damn well tell me in the first place. It's not like I know where I am enough to run away, you know."

Nine laughs, and I even get a snort from Arrie and a giggle from Connie.

"Right. Okay." Dea spreads out his arms on his desk. "What do you know of the Bible? The Christian one? More specifically, the Four Horsemen of the Apocalypse?"

"That they existed. Well, according to the Bible. But religion isn't something that's overly practiced anymore, so I'm not too familiar, sorry. War, Death, Famine, and Conquest, though, right?"

Dea raises an eyebrow in question.

I shrug one of my shoulders and wince. "Went to church when I was little with Grannie." I rub soothing circles over my sore chest. "Clearly, it didn't stick. Wait . . ." How do I know that?

The image of my grandma sticks in my mind: her kind smile, her pink-gray hair that she kept in a rainbow of colors over the years, and her short, stocky frame that was never far from me when we walked anywhere.

Connie rubs a hand over my shoulder, trying to comfort my poor mind back into reality. "Things will come back to you over time, and often they'll be triggered. Try not to stress over it; let it all come back naturally."

Dea gives me a sympathetic look before continuing. "Well, they exist. And have for around two thousand years. They balance out the world and try to . . . keep the peace."

I can't help it—I snort my surprise. "Peace? That's what you call the state of the current world?"

I mean, seriously? What are these idiots smoking? The Vampires are months away from an attack on the Supernatural Council (otherwise known as the SC—the human government that deals with the supernatural) for restricting blood supplies—again—and the Witches still haven't come out of hiding; not to mention the Fae causing all kinds of issues in sex trafficking and human manipulation. And that doesn't account for the fact that humans are now growing complacent about magic, hating the side effects on society its presence has caused.

Arrie's giant frame enters my peripheral vision with a face like thunder that has me shrinking in my chair. "It could be worse."

"Errr . . . sure." His attitude rubs me the wrong way, and rather than continue shrinking, frustration edges my mind into retaliation. "The magical community could be heading toward war. Oh wait, they are." I fold my arms across my chest, not really sure why this line of conversation bothers me so much. "They should have just stayed in hiding."

Do I really mean that? Is that how I feel? Felt?

Dea's incredulous expression gazes at me, but he continues. "We are a group of magical beings as old as time. Ones that you have heard of. Apparently." I do not miss the scorned sarcasm in his tone.

"Wait a minute." The pieces are coming together faster than my mind can process. He asked about the Four Horsemen . . . "You're really the . . . Four Horsemen? That's what you're trying to tell me?" That's not possible. The magical community's mainly non-human, but ancient myth? No. There's always science to the magic. In fact, a lot of people resent the use of the term magic because it isn't factually accurate. Magic is just science we don't understand yet, after all.

Dea stares at me, waiting patiently for me to react. Probably for me to break down. Well, he's not going to get that. It seems Arrie was right: I am stubborn, and I seem to be getting some of my personality back, though I'm not sure I quite like the person I was. Am. Whatever.

He gestures to himself. "Death." Then points to the others in turn, starting with Arrie. "War." He moves on to Connie and says, "Conquest," and then points to Nine. "Famine."

Well, that explains their weird names.

Dea gets up and points to an old painting above his desk that depicts a traditional picture of the Four Horsemen in all their colors, with Death being a glassy translucent color. "We were all human once, until we died and were chosen by an old magic when our seals were broken." He points to each of their artistic depictions in turn. "And we woke up here, in this house, and have been trying to keep Earth peaceful over the years. Ending wars, pacifying political conflict, helping end world hunger . . . That sort of thing."

"So, you're not the cause of those things?"

"No," they all say in unison, each with a scowl upon their beautiful faces.

Seems that might have been an insensitive question.

Dea continues, however—without explaining why I was wrong—with his story. "We each have our own set of unique gifts. We have been alive for millennia, Angel, and not once have we come across the situation we have presently found ourselves in." He looks straight at me with a blank expression, one he's most likely forcing upon his face to hide his real emotions regarding what he's about to say. "There were seven seals, lost to history now, but only four were broken. Until recently. Now the fifth seal has been broken. And Fate has chosen a Fifth Horseman. You."

Nothing. My mind conjures nothing. No anger, no sadness, no confusion, nothing. I'm the Fifth Horseman, hey? So I get cool powers and get to live with my own personal library in a house full of hot and sexy people? Okay. I'm currently failing to see the downside.

But . . . why me?

"We don't know why we're chosen." Nine responds to my internal question with a smirk. "Sometimes it becomes clearer over time, as it might for you as you regain your memories." He steps out of the shadows from behind me. "But the magic will only wait so long before choosing someone, and it only has the recently deceased to choose from."

My mind gets stuck on that word. "D-Deceased?"

Connie looks at me with a guilty expression. "You didn't almost die. You did die. Dea was called to your location and whisked you back here."

So wrong place, wrong time, then? I see. Why am I not freaking out? I should definitely be freaking out. They could kill me any second they choose. I should most definitely be scared. At the least a little apprehensious.

"We're not going to kill you, Sweetie. You really need to relax about that."

"It's instinctive!" I snap and instantly regret it with a wince the moment I see his pained expression. "Sorry."

I get up and walk out the door in silence, leaving all four of them in the wake of my semi-calm exit. The only reason I don't run is because I fear what I might do to my already damaged chest.

The library (my library—eek!) is the only place I can go without being interrupted, since they can't seem to get in without me, and its gracious walls and comforting tomes of wonder greet me upon arrival.

"The Fifth Horseman? Fuck!" I just want to learn who I am and go back to whatever life I have. "Is that too much to ask for?" If I didn't value books so much, I would probably give in to the urge to throw things around right about now.

"Calm down, girl. This is probably still just a dream." I will probably go to sleep and wake up in my normal life again tomorrow. Whatever kind of life that is.

There are four main magical communities in the world, three of which came out of the supernatural closet a hundred years ago: Vampires, Shifters, and Fae. The other community is the Witches, but they haven't come out of hiding with the others. (Salem issues.)

And now I learn the Four Horsemen of the fucking Apocalypse are the real masterminds behind the world, the leaders keeping everything together (and currently failing).

But me, the Fifth Horseman?

Fuck no.

I take the book I was reading earlier and sit back down on the sparkly couch to finish it, absorbing myself into a world of words and sentences that take the very fabric of life right out from under my feet, along with all its craziness, and sweep me away on a dream-filled adventure. I read every word on every page and every sentence of every chapter until my eyes can't hold themselves open a moment longer, and then I doze off with thoughts of dragons and a book resting gently on my face from where it slid from my grasp.

5

"Angel?" A loud rapping knock jolts me awake. "Angel!"

Only one person calls me that: Dea. And it seems he's knocking rather loudly on the library door.

"What?" I half shout back as I get up to swing the door open, rubbing the stiffness out of my sore chest muscles. "What is it?"

Rubbing the haze of sleep from my eyes, I step into the doorway and am met by Dea's dark swirling eyes and bare chest, with his slacks hanging low on his hips and sweat glistening across every inch of his delicious skin.

Was he just working out?

"I wanted to know if you were okay."

"Is that all? You woke me up for that? Fucking christ, Dea, you scared the shit outta me."

"Oh," he says with a smile. He watches me stare at his tattoo—all golden swirls and stars on his left shoulder that trail down his chest to sit at the yummy V marking a descent lower than my eyes are allowed to go—with a bemused look on his face. "Enjoying the distraction?"

Most definitely. "Yeah . . ." I shake my mind out of the gutter it dragged itself into and force my eyes upward—not that staring at his handsome face with those dark swirling eyes that look like mini galaxies capturing my attention every time I glance at them makes me feel any less hot.

"Can I see it?"

"See what?" I ask with a squeak as I feel the heat rush to my cheeks. Eesh, I really need to deal with this sudden onslaught of heat rushing to places it has no business being.

He gives me a knowing smirk. "Your library," he says with a laugh.

Oh, of course he meant that. "Sure." I step out of his way and invite him in.

He steps into the room with a look of awe and jealousy, and I briefly wonder what the big deal is. Don't they all get rooms that suit them? Seems not.

"This is . . . astounding." He runs his fingers along the spines of various books as he examines the shelves. "What books do you keep in here?"

"No idea. There are fiction ones on your left and some nonfiction magic textbooks on the shelves over there." I point to the ones in the corner where Connie and I sat earlier. "I've not really explored much farther."

"Well, let us go, then." He pulls me to his front, propping my feet on top of his as he grabs my waist with a firm hand spread over my lower abdomen. I can feel the smile taunting his lips when he whispers in my ear, "Hold your breath there, Angel."

I take a deep breath, and we speed past a few rows of shelves faster than humanly possible, until he slows down enough for us to see what's in each section. We speed past nonfiction guides to the realms (plural?), more fiction books of every genre imaginable, and into a section that holds a few artifacts and maps. The place is incredible, and I really want to explore it in greater detail at some point.

Eventually, we stop at the back of the library, where a small desk sits with a laptop resting on top. My study, I presume.

"Ah, here it is."

He looks at the things surrounding the desk: more fiction books and magical guides sit behind on a set of overfilled shelves, every nook and cranny filled with some kind of book, stack of papers, or object. The plasmascreen laptop lies on the desk, ready for use whenever I need it; and a music dock sits on the edge of the desk with some kind of old iPod or something in the cradle.

"Seems you like music, books, and a place to collect your thoughts," he says as he hands me a black leather-bound journal he scavenged from the top drawer of the desk.

"Seems so." Flicking through the blank journal pages, I sigh. No clues as to who I am in here.

I sit in the chair, noticing how this is the one section of the library that isn't bright and colorful; instead, it's filled with deep browns and the scent of age-old knowledge.

Opening the top drawer, I find a translucent stone full of swirling mist I can just about see through that draws me to its gaze, and I turn it over and over in my hand, wondering what it is. Dea didn't pick it up, so clearly it isn't particularly unusual.

Maybe Dea would know?

I look up and see him sifting through the songs on the music device, frowning every now and then, but mostly in his own world of curiosity—probably trying to figure me out.

Wish I had the answers to his questions.

The golden swirling irises of those galaxy eyes of his scroll up and down as he pilfers through the playlists I assume are on there, and a smile catches his features on fire for a moment. Not a smirk or a teasing grin, but a genuine, heartfelt smile that highlights his angular face in a way that softens some of the hardened edges and makes his eyes seem a little darker.

Goddess, he's . . . I don't even have the words. His pale skin that seems more solid and less translucent today with the strange golden tattoo swirling down his torso stands out in the dark, brown-toned room, but the black choppy hair that falls from his head in short tufts and sits just at the crook of his dancing eyes frames his face in a way that brings out those gorgeous angles. And fuck, those lip piercings add an extra edge to his look, and I find myself wondering what kissing him would feel like. How I could roll my tongue over those piercings and feel them dig into my lips as I—

A small pop brings my eyes back to the desk, and a book sits in front of the plasmascreen that wasn't there a moment ago. What the—?

Dea grabs it and laughs, reading the title out loud. "PLEASURE ISLAND: AN EROTICA ADVENTURE NOVEL." He gives me a look I can't decipher, but there is definitely a hint of amusement behind those eyes. "Really?"

"Wait . . . What?"

He looks down at my hand still wrapped around the strange stone and lets out a laugh —a full belly-deep laugh that has him bending over slightly. "It is a Seeing Stone. It provides what you need by reading your emotions and thoughts. It seems you need some alone time." He raises his brows in a questioning gaze and bursts out laughing once more.

Well, him standing there half naked doesn't exactly fucking help. "Give me that!" I snatch the book away with a wince and quickly sit back down, rubbing a hand over my chest. "I don't even know what shelf this fucking belongs on." I groan under my breath. "Great."

"On a more serious note, Angel, if you need any questions answered, just think them in your mind and hold that stone, and it will do its best to give you the information you seek. Seems yours arrives in book form. Which makes sense."

"Oh." That is actually rather awesome. All these questions I have, I can get answers to them? Just like that?

"But unless you would like any help with that"—he gestures to the book still in my hands—"I am going to leave you to read it in peace."

"No. That's not . . . I don't intend to actually read it."

"Uh-huh. Sure. Well, you are immortal now. You have all the time in the world to experience life and live a little."

A memory shoots across my mind.

Live a little . . .

That phrase . . . It reminds me of someone. Someone I care about? Someone trying to persuade me to loosen up and live a bit more freely. But I couldn't—wouldn't.

"C'MON, TAY, LIVE A LITTLE. HE CLEARLY LIKES YOU. JUST GO DANCE WITH HIM." IT'S THE SAME boy from before, only this time, he has glow-in-the-dark blue hair.

We are in some kind of club, and this mysterious friend of mine is trying to get me to dance with a green-haired Fae eyeing me across the dance floor.

"But," I start, "I don't want to."

My friend sighs and turns me around. "Some day, Tay, you're gonna have to just take the plunge and get to know someone—anyone."

I sigh and turn back around, ignoring the stares I'm getting from the Fae man.

MY EYES GAZE OUT OF FOCUS AS MY MIND REELS WITH BARELY THERE MEMORIES AND FEELINGS of a past I have all but forgotten.

When I come to, Dea is kneeling at my side, rubbing my arm and trying his best to smile. "Are you okay? What did you remember?"

"Nothing important. But that phrase, 'live a little,' triggered some kind of memory. Similar one to the theater. But all I recall is the scent of alcohol and a glowing room. And someone important to me. It's all so . . . hazy." Before I can stop it, a tear escapes and falls in a singular lonely path down my cheek.

Dea raises a hand to wipe it away and lingers there a moment, resting my head in his palm. "If you ever want to talk . . . all you have to do is ask."

A coughing sound comes from somewhere nearby, and I look up to see Nine leaning over the desk, looking at us suspiciously but with amusement flaring in his eyes. And something else . . . something like a fiery heat. As though the sight of us makes him . . .

Oh. Oh no.

The last couple of days flood back to me in a rush of hot memories: the snuggling on the sofa, bathing with Connie, Arrie carrying me to my room like some kind of bride on her wedding day, and now this. No, no, no.

I can't seriously be attracted to all of these people after only two days!

Nine coughs again.

"Shit! Get out of my head, Nine!"

He smiles at me and sits on my other side, his sight caught by the book still sat on the desk.

For fuck's sake.

"What's this, Sweetie? Some nighttime reading?"

Dea chuckles, and I just know this is going to get out of hand. "It is what popped up when she held her Seeing Stone. Turns out hers gives her books."

Nine tries, he really does, to hold in his laughter, but the redder his face gets, the more hilarious he seems to find it, until he bursts out laughing and crashes to the floor, holding his sides as they probably split with laughter.

Dea stands and turns toward us. "Seems our little Angel is all flustered and having other problems right now that do not concern us. We should probably leave her be so she can read her . . . informative book." He winks at me—he actually winks at me—and walks around to Nine, who he helps up off the floor with a single hand.

Nine reaches over to me, whispering a gentle caress in my mind. *Or you could just fuck one of us and get it out of your system.*

"What? Don't be absurd!" Despite my best efforts at an honest refusal, my mind has other ideas, as the sudden urge to grab them both and shove my tongue down their throats swerves its way across my mind.

And by the look of Nine's embarrassed yet smiling face, he also got a frontrow seat to that little imaginative movie sliding across my mind.

"Just leave already! I have questions I want answered."

Dea and Nine both raise their hands in mock surrender, with matching sly smiles, and back out of the study area. I have no idea if they stay in the library or not, but they are at least out of my hair. For now.

Silence fills the air, and I can finally hear myself think. The Fifth Horseman, 'ey? Well, I could get really cool powers, live in a magical house, and have some new friends, but I bet it probably comes with some kind of catch, like saving the world in one of those hero-type books.

I roll my eyes as I place the wanton book on a nearby shelf of romantic fiction. What kind of questions do I have? What ones seem most important? Ah, I know.

I pick up the Seeing Stone and think about Dea, Arrie, Connie, and Nine, about the fact that they're the Four Horsemen, that they have magic, and wonder how old they are and where they come from. What are their origins?

A giant tome of well over a thousand pages lands with a thud on the desk. It is old, leather bound, and has thick parchment pages with bits of paper and corners sticking out at odd angles here and there. The cover is mostly blank—only some faded letters remain around the painted seal on the front.

Opening the first page, I gawk at the intricacy of the interior design—it's like something out of a movie. There are all kinds of deep colors decorating the frames of each page, with diagrams, illustrations, and curly titles littering the pages with ease. But the language isn't English.

I scowl at the Seeing Stone still sitting in my palm. "Fucking really? You're giving me the answers in a foreign language?"

Of course it is. What do I do now? Can I translate it? Do I know this language? Do any of the others?

Pop! Another book landed on the desk: GUIDE TO MODERN TRANSLATIONAL MAGIC. Aha! Perfect. Wonder if there's some kind of magic-enhanced technology that'll help? Since I'm pretty sure I don't have any magic yet, and even if I do, this probably won't be it. Seems silly for a Horseman of the Apocalypse, even for me.

The contents page lists everything from TRANSLATIONAL ABILITIES OF THE FAE, to SHIFTER SPECIES AND THEIR ANIMAL LANGUAGES, and to—bingo!—TRANSLATIONAL TECH-NOLOGY. Page 457.

From rare stones to enchanted glasses to various spells and potions, there are hundreds of ways to translate various types of languages, but all of this requires magic to be used by the person doing the translating. I am looking for a more passive approach.

Ah. There! TRANSLATIONAL BOOKSCREENS AND THEIR MANY USES. That's what I need. A translational bookscreen. Wonder if we have any in the house?

Grabbing the Seeing Stone, I ask, but nothing happens. Seems the answer isn't in the library—or available to me, anyway.

My stomach growls, interrupting my thoughts. I probably need to eat something, so I call it a day and go in search of food (and a translational bookscreen).

It takes me nearly an hour to get out of the library and find the kitchen from yesterday (my injuries and apparent shitty sense of direction being the main cause), but I find it empty.

Hmm, that's weird. It's usually filled with the team at this time, or at least, the last couple of days it has been.

Straining my ears, I pick up laughter coming from outside and head into the darkened night of the garden to an unusual scene. They have a bonfire going and are roasting s'mores and laughing with each other. Even Arrie.

Dea and Nine cuddle on one log placed as a makeshift bench while Connie and Arrie cuddle on another.

It is a beautiful sight in its own way, but if I go over there, I'll be intruding. So instead, I head in the opposite direction and sit at the edge of the forest, looking at them with wonder and longing. I'm not cold, as the fire's warmth reaches all the way over here, but a different kind of chill creeps up my spine. They're good together, all of them, in a way that seems almost natural.

You can join us, you know.

Nine! Fucking christ, you scared the shit out of me.

Sorry.

I'm okay. But thanks.

Why not?

I don't know how to answer that, but somehow, joining you is intrusive. You have a wonderful balance between the four of you, one you've spent thousands of years forming. I don't want to ruin it.

You wouldn't be. You'd be adding to it. But I won't force you.

Thank you.

I watch as Arrie lifts Connie into his lap and sends a trail of kisses up her neck. When he reaches her lips, she melts into him as her arms wrap around his neck. I probably should look away, give them their moment, but it's interesting and beautiful to watch. The way the team interact is . . . unique. I get the feeling they are all together somehow, but not like how normal couples do things.

Please join us.

Why?

Because you complete us.

I stop fiddling with the grass at my feet and stand up, sighing, aiming to go over there, but something stops me dead in my tracks. Something a little like fear. If I go over there, will they stop laughing? Will their smiles vanish?

"Sweetie!" Nine calls out the moment I step into view. "There you are. Come join us." He gestures for me to sit next to him. "We've just roasted s'mores, want one?"

Well, there's no going back now, is there?

I'm not even sure if I like s'mores, and the frustration of that fact crawls its way permanently into my mind.

Will I ever know who I am?

I shake my head. "No thanks."

Nine falls silent as the others continue to talk and debate what team they prefer and what players are better in some kind of magical sport they all watch. Connie is still sitting in Arrie's lap, but they've stopped their interacting, which confirms my suspicions that having me here is interrupting them.

"You know, you can always just try the food and see what you like now. You don't have to remain the same person forever. Live it up and try new things, see what kind of person you become. You've just been handed a giant reset button. Use it." Nine pats my knee.

Everyone falls into silence. My frustration and bad mood must have affected him, given that he can sense my emotions and thoughts.

Guilt edges its way into my mind.

"Sorry," I mutter. "Got a book as an answer to a question, but it's in a language I can't even read, and now I'm just frustrated. Could really use a translational bookscreen." I groan under my breath slightly, but everyone just sits here and listens with understanding; even Arrie doesn't poke fun or make a shitty comment.

A gentle smile graces Dea's face as he watches me. "There's one in my study. You're welcome to borrow it."

"Just show her how to use the house's magic properly," Arrie grumbles between a mouthful of marshmallow. I give him a questioning look, but he just grunts. "You can request things from the house, and it'll just give them to you. So long as you know what you want and it's a simple request."

Fuck, damn! This is the best house I have ever heard of in my life (not that I remember many right now, but you get the point).

Nine laughs. "That it is, Sweetie. That it is." He grabs a plate and starts piling a piece of food onto it from every container they have littered on the grass. "Here. See what you like. Enjoy."

I grab some random triangle thing with seeds on top and take a tentative bite. Mmmm. That tastes good. "What if I have an allergy to something or, like, an intolerance?" I'm a tad worried about puking my guts up in front of these people. (Friends?) It really isn't a good first impression.

Dea chuckles under his breath, blushing with hidden laughter. "Sorry," he says, holding out a hand in surrender. "I do not mean to laugh." He looks over at me with a serious expression. "We are immortal, Angel. We cannot die from allergic reactions, or from anything, really. Well, we can if we are killed in the right way."

"Right way?"

"Here we go," Connie says, still with her arms wrapped around Arrie's neck. "Way to scare her, Dea."

"I'm not scared. Just curious."

Nine smiles and gives me a pat on the shoulder. "She's really not," he says in a way that has me thinking he's a little impressed.

Dea shrugs, giving Connie a shit-eating grin I recognize as an 'I told you so' smile. "If someone deals a fatal blow after burning our seals, it can kill us instantly. No chance of reviving or anything."

"That's . . . intense."

"Now she's scared." Nine places his hand back on my knee, probably trying to comfort me, but it just confuses me further.

Is he being flirty? Just friendly? Is he embarrassed by my stupid dirty thoughts earlier? Ah, goddess, why did I have to remind myself of that? What if he finds me weird? What if they hate me? What if me finding them all stupidly hot is somehow weird?

Oh my goddess, I'm stuck with them for eternity!

"You're spiraling, Sweetie. Over something seriously silly." Nine leans down to whisper something in my ear, tucking a strand of hair behind it. His other hand hasn't moved from my knee either. "I'm just being nice, probably a little flirty, and no, there's literally nothing your mind can conjure up that will embarrass me. Much."

No one else hear him, given his quiet voice and close proximity to me, but Connie lets out a giggle, throwing me a raised eyebrow, and I'm suddenly reminded that she has great hearing. She heard my shriek when I first entered the library. (Then again, who didn't hear that?) Guess that's one of her gifts.

Nine looks at me and watches as my mind spirals once more. Does Connie think I'm weird? What if she has a thing going with Nine?

"Oh my god, just stop!"

He yelled. He actually just yelled at me. I've never heard Nine speak above a gentle lilt the entire past three days. It actually makes me put my food down and stare at him incredulously.

"Sorry." He pinches the bridge of his nose. "I've not had to deal with a mortal thought process for a long time. It's a little frustrating. Literally none of us care. We're all immortal." He raises his eyebrows in a way that I guess is supposed to mean something, but I'm drawing a blank.

"Ugh. You know what, I promise to come back to this conversation when we don't have other people listening in like we're the latest soap opera. Because that's not going to help and will only have you freaking out more."

I look around and see Connie smiling, Dea resting an amused face on his hand while his legs still entwine with Nine's, and Arrie looking utterly baffled. I nod at Nine and take another bite of the seeded triangle.

"So," I start, looking back at Dea, "nothing else can kill us?"

"No. We can be injured and fall into unconsciousness while our bodies heal, but nothing can actually kill us."

"I see."

Nine points to my food, encouraging me to try something else.

I take a forkful of noodles in some kind of sauce and shove them into my mouth, trying to give Nine what I know will be a gross but hopefully kind of funny grin.

His face is a picture. He looks a little shocked, and Dea looks almost disgusted, but they all laugh at my stupid antics anyway.

"They're good," I say once I swallow the last bite. "What are they?"

"Peking duck chow mein." Connie grabs a second helping of it. "My favorite."

"I can see why. It's kind of saucy and substance-y all at the same time."

Looking at my towering plate, I ask myself what's next. I pick up a crispy golden ball and dip it into the accompanying red sauce Nine pointed out goes with it. When I take the first bite, a small moan escapes my lips before I can compose myself. That's delicious! Like, I can easily eat that sauce all day.

By the time I open my eyes to the world again, they're all staring at me with surprised smiles.

Have I done something wrong?

Nine bursts out laughing the hardest from beside me, his fist slamming onto the ground from the outburst. "Just so you know"—he looks to everyone in turn (excluding me)—"you're all thinking the same thing right now."

Arrie grumbles something I can't hear, Dea just chuckles and gives Connie an interesting glare, while Connie goes bright red. What are they all thinking?

Honestly, my lack of good social judgment is starting to bother me. I get the feeling I didn't used to be like this, and it's only because I'm missing most of my memories that it's an issue. So far, the only ones that have come back to me are the ones in church with Grannie and a few with my mysterious friend, and honestly, they aren't much help.

"I'm going to eat this in my room, if that's okay?"

Not waiting for an answer, I grab my plate and glass of water and run into the house. Well, technically I hobble, since I can still barely walk, much less run, but in my imagination, I definitely run.

At least no one stops me.

I briefly hear Connie yelling at Nine about being inappropriate at the dinner table (even though they aren't at the table, which makes me smile despite everything) and making me feel uncomfortable, but my mind blocks it out, and before long, I can barely hear them as I get farther through the house and closer to my bedroom.

I spend the next day holed up in my rooms, with Connie and Dea having arrived earlier that morning to assist my healing. Turns out a healing bath is just a bath full of Dea's healing magic, which he swamps over my body, encasing me in a glowing green bubble for an hour.

Last night scared me, and more nightmares and flashbacks have put my mind on the edge of panic. I know I'm being silly, but it scares me nonetheless. I don't understand all the looks and other aspects of social interaction, as though I'm a toddler who doesn't understand how to share her toys yet.

I'm stuck with them for eternity. What if they hate me? What if they find me strange or annoying or too innocent now I've lost my damn memories?

Bloody fuck! I can't do this. I can't be the Fifth Horseman. I can't wield super cool magic or strength. I can't be beautiful and badass like Connie or calm and intelligent like Nine. I'm just little old me. And I'm not even sure who that is right now!

My lungs heave large gasps of air as I fail to breathe. In, out. In, out. C'mon, you can do it. But I can't. I can't catch my breath at all, as though oxygen has stopped doing its job, and my hands shake so badly I can't grip the glass of water on the nightstand. Sweat pours in rivulets down my forehead. Man is it hot in there. Why is it so hot?

"Sweetie . . . ?"

Nine barges in through the door, takes one look at my current pacing, unbreathing state, and charges into action. He takes a blanket from the bed and wraps me tight—despite my protests that I'm too warm—and helps me pick up the glass of water, presses it to my lips, and tells me to keep breathing as best I can.

"You're gonna be fine. Promise." He goes into the bathroom, and I hear the distinct sound of water running. "Just running you a bath."

"W-W-W-W-Why?"

"Because you're having a panic attack, and I need you to calm down before we chat."

A panic attack? Is that what this is? I can think clearly, and I know my body is overreacting, but it's like I have no control over what it does.

Why can't I stop shaking?

Why am I so irrationally scared?

Am I going to die?

Nine grabs me by the hand and helps me into the tub—still fully clothed in my pajamas, I might add—and starts rubbing circles on my shoulders.

"Relax, Sweetie. It's okay. You're going to be fine."

His voice lilts from my left ear to my right, and I realize that it's the same voice that woke me up that first day. The one singing the interesting song.

"Nobody expects anything from you, nor do we want you to be like us." He slides a leg either side of me from behind in the bath, each trouser leg having been rolled up at some point, and applies more pressure into his circling fingers, massaging the knots out of my shoulders. "I wish I could fight like Connie or Arrie, but if I even try to punch them in the face, I break my hand while their faces remains as perfect as ever. It's infuriating. Trust me. You're not the only one who wishes you were as badass as those two."

"Really?"

"Uh-huh." He leans down to my ear and whispers, "I'm sorry I scared you yesterday. I didn't realize social interaction was hard for you right now. I should have, but I just didn't think about it." He gently places his lips to the tip of my temple and gives me a light kiss, the warmth sending fireflies tingling throughout my body. "I'm sorry, Sweetie."

"I can breathe. I think."

The pressure that had welled up in my chest is lifting, and my hands aren't as shaky anymore. But goddess am I tired. And hungry. Really fucking hungry.

"We'll get you something to eat in a moment. Promise. But we really need to chat."

"Okaaaay." My suspicions rise, but I remain as calm as possible. I'm sure it's just about yesterday.

Correct. It is about yesterday. Listen, we're immortal, meaning things are different for us. We don't do relationships or love. He sounds a little disappointed by that, and part of me hurts for him. *And we've been around since early humanity. It doesn't matter to any of us who you find attractive. I promise. And no one is going to think you're weird. Or annoying.*

Really? But . . . but what if—?

Nope. There are no what ifs. We have all found each other attractive in some way or another at some point in history. We've appeared in all different kinds of styles and appearances over the years and have been stuck with each other for hundreds of years. But love? Relationships? They're hard for the Horsemen to have and maintain. There aren't any other truly immortal beings, so we've just mostly avoided it.

None of you have ever been in love? That's . . . insane. Doesn't that get kind of lonely?

Oh, well . . . errm . . .

Just spit it out.

Haha, okay, then. We've all slept with each other over the years at some point. It's just easier, I guess. And having flings with people is fine. But, as a general rule, we just don't let people develop feelings for us, because it's been a long time—and I mean a really long time—since any of us felt anything more than friendship with anyone. Any more makes everything harder for us.

They're likely all worried that if one of them falls in love with the other, it will break up the group.

That's not—

Save it. I get it, Nine. I do. But not loving just because you're afraid of the consequences is wrong. No one should have to live like that.

I shake the thought from my head and return to something else he mentioned.

They've all slept together? Like, even the guys? I mean, Connie I get, she's stunning and beautiful, and why not? But—

Nine chuckles. *Told you, we're immortal. Silly things like sexuality and monogamy aren't really our thing.*

Silly things? Wow. Way to shit on the ideas of an entire race there, buddy.

It doesn't work if you're immortal. Trust me on that one. None of us could ever be enough for each other—sexually speaking—for hundreds of years. A life that long isn't meant to be lived with that many social restrictions. Plus, we were around before sexuality was even a thing.

Makes sense, actually. So you're all in a weird, non-love relationship that you've been in for two millennia? I have just intruded on the world's weirdest relationship.

You're not intruding, and we're all just friends. Just stop feeling ashamed of your thoughts just because you're trying to fit into something that doesn't even exist here. You can find as many or as few of us as attractive as you want. We won't think you're strange. Believe me, we've seen it all over the years.

I bet. That doesn't bother me half as much as I thought it would.

"Why did you say all that in my head?"

"Privacy. Con has very good hearing and would have listened in because she's a nosy little shit. No one can hear me in someone else's head."

"Ah, I see."

"Let's go get some food. Arrie's making brownies, I think."

Arrie, cooking? The thought of him in an apron has me laughing so loudly my chest pangs in pain, and I hiss.

"You okay? Need me to fetch Dea?" Nine wraps his arm around me in an instant, worry etching his features.

"No, no. It's okay. Just need to stretch and eat some brownies."

"Okay." Nine leads me out of the bedroom with a smile and down the stairs, going slowly and carefully to avoid hurting my already injured body. "Seems you like food."

"And books. And have some strong opinions about magic. Oh, and I had a Christian grannie that I hated and loved at the same time."

Nine laughs while grabbing my hand and leading me into the kitchen.

The delicious smell of something sweet and delectable hits my nostrils, and I nearly cave with hunger. "What is that smell?" I sniff the air for a few seconds, reveling in the sweet aroma.

"Brownies," Arrie grumbles from the kitchen counter. He stands at the stove in black slacks, a loose black tee, and a white fluffy apron as he glides a knife through a tray of brown he's cutting into squares.

I stifle a chuckle at the sight but am more focused on the brownies, which smells of heaven.

"Arrie." Dea enters the room. "I need to borrow you for a moment."

Dea gives me a wave and another body-melting smile before grabbing Arrie by the arm and yanking him out of the kitchen, leaving me alone with Nine.

"Arrie likes to cook, even though the house will provide whatever food you ask."

"Why?" I take a seat at the kitchen table, eagerly awaiting my next foodie treat. If the house can provide whatever food you want it to, I don't think I'll ever cook.

"It's calming."

He brings over a plate and gestures for me to dig in.

A single bite into one of the squares has me letting a small moan slip free, and I flush bright red. That's what made them all uncomfortable yesterday. I don't get it, bu—

Oh, right. I'm such an idiot. It sounds sexual. Of course that makes them uncomfortable. They're all together (kind of).

"Sorry," I grumble between bites.

"It's fine. I'm glad you like them."

"Like them? They're the best things I've ever tasted!"

Nine smiles at me and grabs a brownie for himself. "You haven't eaten much yet. That you remember."

"Then I'll just have to stick around to eat more food." I grin at him, hoping it will make him smile again.

It works!

"How're you feeling today?" He looks a little uncomfortable, but I'm not sure why.

"Uhhh, not bad. Dea and Connie gave me another healing bath this morning."

I blush slightly, remembering what Nine said about them all having slept together at some point. Images of Arrie with Dea and Nine flash across my mind, but I shake them from my head. Does that mean even the guys have slept with each other? Part of me really wants to ask, but even I know that's inappropriate.

Those images do not do those men justice, trust me. And yes. Even us guys. Though Arrie does prefer women.

Get a grip, girl. Yes, it's slightly strange, but it makes sense. They're immortal, relationships with mortals are hard work if you're going to live forever. That'll just end in heartbreak, so what's the point? Everyone needs . . . attention. Even the Four Horsemen of the Apocalypse, it seems.

Nine doesn't interrupt my mind babble while I get my head around it, which I appreciate.

Wait a minute. "Are Vampires not immortal?"

"No, they're not. They do live a few hundred years and age slower than humans, but they're mortal. Like everyone else."

"Other than you—us. Other than us." Wow. That's insane. I'm immortal. I am going to live forever.

"Yes, other than us." He grumbles something under his breath and then shakes his head. "Wonder what you liked to eat when you were human? You know, some people say that senses can trigger memories. Like the taste of a particular food, the smell of a certain place . . ."

"Makes sense," I say between mouthfuls of my third brownie. "In the theater, I had a small flashback when I smelled the popcorn. It reminded me of the nachos I had when I saw that movie the first time."

"It seems your mind is having trouble remembering details of your life. If you like . . ." Nine looks to the ground, a flush reddening his cheeks. "We can cook you as much food as you like—all different types—and see if any of it triggers anything." He flushes redder—even his ears turn a bright shade of scarlet—and I can't help but smile at him.

"I'd like that. Thank you."

He relaxes and divides the last few brownies equally between us. "So what kind of powers do you want? You know, if you could choose?"

What kind of powers do I want? "I think I'd like to be badass, like Connie and Arrie, but maybe in a less violent way. I don't really know. Violence doesn't feel right to me."

"It never feels right." He looks a little dazed and distant, as though he's remembering some horrific detail.

"I think I have night vision," I say to bring him back to the present. "I could see in the corridor that leads to the theater." I point to the door to the right of us, the one we went through the other day.

"Ah! So maybe a ninja-type. Stealth and throwing daggers."

He mimics throwing daggers at me, and I feign an overactive death, making the gurgling noises and all. Goddess, we are both super lame.

"Want to come on a walk with me tomorrow morning? Arrie usually goes for a run, and Dea'll probably make you go along when you've recovered, but walking will help bring your strength up."

"Sure." That actually sounds lovely. "I don't know the first thing about this house or . . . realm. Would be nice to see it."

"Sure thing. Dawn, tomorrow. I'll come and get you."

Dawn? Like, first crack of light, dawn?

Ugggghhhh. Why?

7

"You going to actually talk to me?" A handsome blond-haired man sits across from me in the restaurant. "Or are we going to continue this farce of you deciding to hate me?"

"Are you going to apologize for ditching me afer my mom and dad died?"

"No." He folds his arms over his chest. "I was doing the best I could."

"Then, no." I shrug, not really caring about his feelings.

"We do these dinners every month, and every month since you were old enough to hate me, we've done them in silence." He growls low under his breath. "You're nineteen years old now, it's time you learned to grow up."

I blanch at his words. "Well, you'll be happy to know I have a job."

"Really?" He looks at me with a soft smile. "You gonna tell me about it?"

"I got accepted by the Hunter Society for the SC."

His golden tan face pales as he chokes on the mouthful of wine he's trying to swallow. "You . . . what?"

"I'm going to help the SC bring down rogue and criminal supernaturals."

"If this is about vengeance . . ."

"Don't even try to play that card." I give him a stern look, hoping it will stop him from asking questions.

"Fine."

"Heeeey." I hear a rough grumble somewhere in the distance, perturbing my dreams. "It's time to get up, Sweetie."

My eyes peel open, the remnants of that dream playing over and over in my mind as Nine's shadowy face comes into view. He's grown a bit of stubble since that first day I met them all, but it suits him. The rough, tousle-haired look makes him look like he just rolled out of bed this gorgeous from the beginning.

"Time for our walk. Get up. Get dressed."

"Oh, right." I wince as I sit up, and Nine helps me up off the bed.

The closet only really holds nicer clothes, and I'm struggling to find slacks or any kind of loose loungewear or workout gear, but right at the bottom of a pile of underwear, I find a pair of light brown slacks and a loose vest top. Looks like I'm going braless. Again. They just hurt too much, and most of my chest is wrapped in bandages anyway. But damn, I can't wait to not feel naked.

I carry the clothes to the bathroom, telling Nine to wait in the bedroom a moment. After cleaning my teeth, running a brush through my hair—which I can now just about do —I bend to lift my pants up and yelp as the action pulls at my rib muscles.

You okay in there?

"Don't suppose Connie is up yet, is she? Could really use some help getting dressed."

Nine sighs before he turns the doorknob and walks in.

I stand there, stark naked except for the bandages covering my upper torso—not quite covering all of my breasts—with no panties on, let alone having managed to pull up my trousers. "What do you think you're doing?" I shriek.

"Helping." He walks right up to me, not staring or doing anything too weird, and pulls up my trousers for me and grabs my vest.

Yes, I am going commando. (You have no idea how hard bending over with a stab wound to your chest is, so I only want to do it once.)

"Arms up." He rolls the vest top up to lift it over my head.

I wince the moment my elbows are above shoulders and shove my arms back down to my sides in a grimace.

"Wow. This is nuts." Nine puzzles over the problem for a moment, looking me up and down like I'm some sort of new toy he needs to figure out, before he unzipps his fancy top and reveals a completely bare chest beneath.

"What are you doing?" I shriek for the second time that morning.

Nine looks at my panicked face and laughs. "Relax, I'm just giving you my top. It's a zip up, so it'll be easier to get on."

"But what about you?"

"You know, you might find it hard to believe, but after two thousand years, this is not my only top." He unzips it the rest of the way, and I stand there speechless. I don't think I'll ever get over seeing these men topless. Every inch of his torso catches my eye—not a bit of fat in sight.

But he ate brownies!

Lots of working out, Sweetie. He winks as I blush at the fact that he heard my inner crushing.

"R-R-Right. Of course." I stretch my arms outward in a signal for him to help me into his top.

We walk a few doors down the hallway, probably heading to his rooms so he can put another t-shirt on, but I'm still mesmerized by this walking piece of popsicle in front of me.

Why, thank you very much. I do try. Though keeping up with Arrie is pointless.

Pretty sure they can both crush me like a grape. "Grapes! I like grapes."

Nine laughs once more and says, "Having you around is going to be the most fun I've had in ages. I can tell." There's a slight skip to his step after that.

We stop outside a door identical to mine just a few meters down the hallway but on the opposite wall.

"I'll be just a minute."

I wait outside, and in a couple of minutes, he returns.

What does his room look like?

Nine comes back outside with a new t-shirt on—a regular, less fancy one this time that has the phrase HANGING OUT written underneath a lost game of hangman. "Okay. Ready."

Wondering what my room looks like already, Sweetie?

"I, err . . . No." Smooth. Real smooth.

Nine laughs. "It's okay. Everyone has a room that suits them perfectly, so it's natural to be curious."

"Really?"

"Yeah, that's why everyone was so impressed by your library. You're already awesome enough of a person to know what you want and who you are."

"That's ridiculous. I don't even know my name." Even I hear the bitterness in my voice and wince at the impact it has on the conversation. "Sorry."

"It's okay. You're allowed to be angry and frustrated."

We walk through the kitchen and out the back door into a garden, the likes of which I'm blown away by. Almost literally, as a gust of wind nearly sweeps me off my fragile feet, but Nine steadies me.

"Careful there."

I didn't really see much of it the other night, just the edges of the forest and the bonfire.

"Thanks."

The garden is larger than anything I've ever seen before—probably even bigger than my library. The forest is to our left, the trees multicolored, from greens to purples to oranges. They all blur into a rainbow of colors that sparkles in the morning sunlight so brightly it's almost hard to look at.

Just outside the door and to the right sits a patch of burned grass from the bonfire, and I smile at the memory of seeing everyone together. They are all soooo cute.

We've been called many things over the years, but cute is a first.

We both laugh as Nine leads me onto a path that winds through the flowers and fields in front of us; a few well-placed fallen logs and vine trails make for a more natural look. This place is clearly managed, but it's so beautiful.

"We keep all kinds of creatures on the grounds. For potion ingredients and things."

"Really? Like what?"

"Well, unicorns, for example, were hunted to extinction hundreds of years ago, but we have a small herd in the forest. Their horns contain magical dust, similar to pixie dust."

I nod my understanding.

"People wanted the high, and they were hunted for it. But they're also useful in all kinds of confusion potions, some protection charms, and a whole host of other things."

Makes sense. "What other creatures?"

"We keep a flock of pixies in the flower garden. They tend to the flowers, some of which act as more ingredients, and the pixies provide us with a monthly supply of dust in exchange for a free home."

My eyebrows raise in question. They're using pixies to get high?

"Again, for magical ingredients. But pixie-dust highs are rather fun."

I give him another incredulous look.

He just laughs and continues on through a small field of grass and . . . horses. They have horses! My face lights up, and I can't help but smile.

"You like horses?"

"I think so. They have a specific meaning, but I'm not really sure what."

"Well, they're ours. We all have a horse. I'll take you out to the paddocks sometime. They're an unusual kind of horse."

"Well, if the Horseman of Famine is saying something is unusual, that must mean it's pretty fucking strange."

"Yup." He looks ahead to the sunrise and gives a deep sigh. "Listen, I know this has been a strange adjustment for you, but if you have any questions, now is a good time to ask."

"Yeah, it hasn't been easy. I guess being the Fifth Horseman isn't what bothers me, and I don't think the fact of being immortal has sunk in yet, you know. I just want to know who I am. Who I was. Did I leave family behind? What about friends, my job, my life? Did I have a pet?"

Nine reaches over and puts an arm around my shoulders, and I feel myself melt into it slightly. "I know. We all felt the same way. But we had our memories, so we knew what we were leaving behind. Most of us had a life, a family. It wasn't easy. Be we forged a new identity, became something more than what we were when we were merely human. In a way, not having those memories might be a blessing." He looks sad, but in a peaceful sort of way, as though the memory of his former life still holds pain, but he's at peace with those memories.

"I don't think I'll ever be at peace until I know. Someday, I'm going to have to find out. But for now, I have some questions. Actually, I have a lot of questions."

"I bet." He coughs and points to some pixies in the distance, flapping around some flowers. They have all kinds of colors painted throughout their wings, and their green bodies are no bigger than my forearm. "Ask away."

Where to start . . . ? "Where are we?"

"Way to start easy." He chuckles and gestures to the environment. "This is a realm separate from Earth. We call it *Sheruta*. The house is magical, as you've probably seen." He gestures behind him, and I get my first look at the house from the outside.

I stop walking, taking stock of the . . . house. "You call that a house? It's like ten mansions melded together and had a monster baby." Seriously, the thing is stupid huge. It looks around five times the size of the White House, and that's being stingy. Various windows line the house in no particular strategy or order; it doesn't really have a structure, as though they've added building blocks to it over time. Which, I guess they have. Their needs grew over time, meaning the house probably provided for them.

"That's correct. It's a little excessive, but we like to think it's Fate's apology for lumping us with this life."

"You don't like being immortal, do you?"

I bet that's why they sleep together and try to live it up as best they can, to make the most of a shitty situation.

"It's hard being this isolated. We can't really be friends with mortals because they just die, and hundreds of years of watching our friends die gets too painful to continue."

That's . . . Damn, that's hard.

"But you have each other, though. That's a . . . friendship that'll last forever." I hesitated. Why did I hesitate? Guess it's because I don't believe Nine when he says none of them have ever fallen in love with each other. We look for love, it's a part of being human —even for mythical beings; if all they have is each other, then they've probably fallen in love a long time ago, and they're just denying it to themselves.

Nine gives me a sheepish look, and I can tell he's reading my mind but also giving me space by not answering my unspoken thoughts.

"Yes. I couldn't imagine going through this life alone, without them." He turns back around to me and asks, "Next question?"

"Is it just the house here in this realm?"

"No. There's a town with residents, shops, and all kinds of things to the west, the beach with an ocean to the east, and all kinds of creatures roaming the mountains in the north. It's not as big as Earth, but we're not totally alone here."

Shops? There are shops? "I can go shopping?"

He groans as he wipes a hand over his face. "You're just like Dea. He loves shopping, too."

Laughter erupts from behind us, and I whip around, trying to calm my beating heart into submission.

"Relax. It's just Warro, our gardener. He lives in the town but works here." Nine puts another hand on my shoulder, the gesture growing more comfortable the more often he does it.

"Ah. Sorry about that."

"No worries, dear." He has a straw hat with a large brim shadowing his tan features and dark eyes.

"We'll let you get on, Warro."

Warro tips his hat to him, saying, "As you wish, sir."

He walks away as we continue toward the forest. "So, err . . . Does he know what you all are? Is he human? You guys have servants?"

"Stop. One question at a time. We have people to help manage the house and its grounds because the house is not, apparently, self-cleaning. And yes, we've asked hundreds of times. It never happens. So we employ the locals, who all know who we are and what we do but don't tend to get involved with us past that. We have around fifteen staff members on board, so don't freak out if you come across any of them. They're not allowed to enter our private rooms, except for the washing, and a few of the other rooms around the house, but they wander around freely other than that."

"I see. Makes sense."

"Oh, one more thing." He holds up a hand, as if mentally stopping himself. "House rule: don't fuck the staff."

I stop still and choke on my own saliva. "Why is that a house rule?"

Nine looks at my bright red face and laughs. "Because Con did that once, and it didn't end well. So, we made it a rule."

"Ah. So what happened?" I wag my eyebrows at him, kinda excited for some normal gossip.

"I'll let Con tell you herself. It's a funny story, but it's maybe a little unfair to the human staff member, hence why we don't allow it."

Oh. "Any other rules I should know about?"

"Clean up after yourself." He lists them off one by one on his fingers. "Help out around the house, don't bring guests round—ever—and don't fuck the staff. That's about it, really. We make them up as we go to make our lives easier."

No bringing anyone around? Ever? What if I make a friend and want to invite them over? Is that not okay? I know they said it will be easier if I don't make any friends, but I just don't want that. Everyone is really nice and super hot, but I don't want to live without interacting with others. How am I supposed to help protect the world if I know nothing of its people?

The ache in my chest is starting to get a little painful, and I can feel myself starting to wheeze.

"Let's stop for a bit, let you catch your breath." He gestures to a log just outside the tree line. "Sorry, I wasn't sure how far you could walk, so I just set out for a regular hour."

I wave my hand in dismissal. "Don't worry about it. I want to get back to normal, and I can only do that through exercise. Should probably work on eating right while I'm at it." I sigh. I really enjoyed those brownies.

"Well, then, we'll go on regular morning walks until you're well enough to start running. Then Arrie and you will run. I know Dea has a training plan for your fitness when you're all healed. So that'll help."

"He does? Do I get no say in this?"

"You're a Horseman. Until we know your gifts and what type of Horseman you are, we need to just work on everything, including your fighting skills, general fitness, and see if you can use any kind of magic. Things like that."

"No," I growl.

"No?"

"You heard right. No. I'll decide when I'm ready, what I want to work on, and what I'll be doing with my now-immortal life." I stand up, a new sense of determination coursing through me. "C'mon. I want to hurry and get back so I can yell at Dea."

Nine laughs a little but gets up and starts walking. We walk through the forest—along a trail that leads back to the house—in total silence, other than my occasional wheezy breathing and Nine's worried face that speaks loudly enough it's practically a physical noise. He's worrying I'm walking too fast, but I just need to let Dea know that it isn't okay to boss me around. I don't want him designing a training plan without even consulting me. Or asking if that's okay.

It's my life. It might now be immortal and belong to the Horsemen of the Apocalypse, but it's still mine.

The forest is beautiful, honestly, it is, but I'm too frustrated and angry to enjoy it. We reach the house in about twenty minutes and find the rest of them sitting around the table eating breakfast and laughing.

Connie stops what she's eating and looks at me, worry etching at her features.

"Dea!" Nine calls from behind me. "Sweetie's here to yell at you over something that I, for once, agree with." His bright red hair ruffles under the laugh he lets slip from his otherwise blank façade.

You're on my side, Nine?

Yep. He really needs to learn to talk to people before making plans. It's rude.

"You're right, it is rude," I say out loud so Dea can hear. "Dea?"

He looks up at me and gulps. "Yes?"

"What made you think it was okay to dictate what I do with my new life? You think that just because I'm not millennia old like you guys, I can't design my own training plan? That just because I've lost my memories I'm somehow less of a person?" I can feel my voice rising with each sentence, and Dea's face is reddening with each flinch of my words.

"No, I . . . It is my job to look out for us all. That includes you, now."

"Well, you can stop. I don't want someone ruling my life. I'm my own person—a woman from the twenty-second century—and I don't like people dictating what I do and when I do it. You have an idea? Fine. Run it by me. Ask me if I'd like to do that. Otherwise, keep your stupid male supremacy away from me."

"I-I am sorry. We will look at it together."

"No, we won't." I look toward the floor. "Look, I know it may seem stupid to you, but I don't even know who I am right now. I'd like to at least be able to become my own person, on my own terms. The last thing I need is someone telling me what to do with my whoever-the-fuck-I-am self."

Dea sighs, gets up, and brings his sexy, tight-chested, t-shirted self next to me.

Goddess, staying mad at him is hard.

"You are right. It was rude and inconsiderate. We have never had someone around like you before. And we did not lose our memories when we changed, so that is new, too. It is hard on us all. We can see how much this is bothering you—Nine even gets a direct link to your pain—but there is very little we can do about it, and that bothers us." He gestures to everyone in the room.

That's why they're being nice to me? Because they feel bad this is my new life?

Nine steps forward and joins us, putting a hand on my shoulder and the other around Dea's waist. "No. That's not it at all. We're nice to you because we're actually quite nice people, and we're trying our best to make you feel at home in this new world that you've just been shoved into. We've had millennia to get to know each other, and there's nothing we don't know about each other, but you're new. We don't know you. Meaning, interacting with you isn't like our normal interactions with each other. It's new for us, so please just give us time."

Guilt wells at Nine's words, and despite my spiraling thoughts that maybe I overreacted, Nine doesn't contest them.

"I'd like to take a look at that training plan with you tomorrow morning." I look at Dea and blanch at his smile. He isn't even angry with me. Goddess, it's hard to stay mad at this a-hole.

"Of course, Angel. Whenever you are ready."

Dea leans down and runs a hand from the top of my shoulder to the tip of my wrist and stops there. My whole body tingles under his touch, as though every crevice of his fingers has found every inch of my skin and set it on fire.

I want him to go further. I can feel the anticipation as my body tries to hold itself on the edge of a cliff, waiting for his next move just as I wait for my next breath. The rest of the world around us stops.

Nine's eyes glaze over for a moment, then flicker back to their usual golden brown.

Dea looks at me with smiling eyes, that mischievous glint shining in them once again. He lets his hand wander into my palm, his short nails lightly drawing circles over the sensitive parts, before grabbing it with his own. "Now, Angel, please try not to yell at us when we mess up. We are only . . . the Four Horsemen, after all."

A snicker of laughter escapes my lips, and he sighes in contentment. "That is better. Hearing you laugh is a much-desired improvement upon hearing you yell." He brings my hand up to his mouth and presses his lips gently against the knuckles.

I can feel his warmth spreading throughout my hand, and the heat of his gaze on my face sends a shiver of desire through my body, but something else comes with it, something darker.

The world shadows for a moment, leaving only Dea and me in the wake of the darkness, and something slithers over my bare arms and down to our entwined hands.

Dea jumps away, Nine right by his shoulder.

When my eyes focus on the world around me once again, I can see a shadowy mist forming at my fingertips, curling into a ball of energy connecting to every part of me. It wants something. I'm just not sure what.

"What is that?" I squeak.

"Magic," Nine says in wonder. "You're the first Horseman to have actual magic."

Panic broaches the surface of my mind, sending my hands into a shaking fury. What do I do with it? Can it hurt someone?

Nine is the one who answers. "It can't hurt us. Well, it could injure us, but we can't die. Stop panicking and start welling down those emotions. It was your desire that fueled it— I'm assuming—so stop thinking with your dick and start thinking with your mind."

"I don't have a dick, Nine!"

Connie chuckles from behind us. "It's just an expression. Stop thinking with your vagina and start using your head."

Right. I look at everyone in the room, roll my eyes, and turn around. As embarrassing as this is, I need to control this new magic, and that will be easier if I'm not staring at them.

Calmness. Tranquillity. Peace. C'mon, you can be peaceful. Think of the gardens, of the calmness of the forest, or the tranquility of the horses.

I breathe in through my mouth and out through my nose, attempting to calm my body into being normal again.

The darkness trickles back over my arms, back to wherever it came from, before disappearing completely.

Turning back around, I ask, "What was that?"

Dea steps forward, a smile twisting his features. "Magic. One we have not seen in hundreds—thousands—of years. It is Angel magic."

8

Angel magic. I have Angel magic. And it's black, which is a bit disappointing. I haven't asked what Angel magic is or how it functions or why it is black, and instead I simply sit and eat breakfast in silence, listening to their bustling conversation echo around me, lulling me into forgetting how much of a freak I've just become in the space of five minutes.

Grabbing the nearest newspaper—one Connie has just finished with—I open the first page and scan the upcoming headlines: VAMP ATTACK SERIAL IN MIDWEST US; INTERNATIONAL FAE PROSTITUTION RING UNCOVERED; PIXIE DUST FARMS UNVEIL CRUEL TREATMENT.

The list goes on and on the more pages I turn, and with each new headline, I have to hold back a gasp at some new unspoken horror.

On page forty-six, however, a headline catches my eye that sends all the others tumbling into dust: VAMPIRES VS THE SC. An article succeeds it, describing how the SC has lowered the Vampires' blood supply—again. (Humans donate to the program, the SC control the supply, and Vampires get daily rations.) But if the SC continues lowering those rations, it'll cause havoc. How long will the Vampires continue to starve for the sake of peace? How much longer until they fight back?

Breakfast is an assortment of rolls, cheeses, pastries, and other insanely tasty treats. I eat what little I can, but between the world's troubling affairs and the whole Angel magic thing, my stomach's doing somersaults the entire hour.

Finally, everyone leaves, and it's just me and Nine left at the table.

"If there's anything you need?"

I sigh. "Thanks, but I think I'm just going to spend some time by myself for a while. Maybe explore the house a bit."

He smiles and leaves me to my peace—whatever kind of peace I'm going to get, given the circumstances. But I wasn't joking when I said I need to explore the house a bit. This place is like a maze. Will probably take months to learn all of its nooks and secrets.

I start by going right at the staircase that I usually turn left at to get to the kitchen. It leads me down a smaller-than-average (not that it's small by normal standards—I think) corridor and peek inside many of the rooms, but most are just storage closets, cleaning closets, a washroom, and a few guest rooms.

"Hello, Miss, can I help you?"

I jump out of my skin for a second before turning back around and seeing a petite Fae woman handling a load of laundry, and guessing from the dark, gothic clothes in the basket, I assume the garments are Dea's.

"No. Sorry. Just nosing around. This place is like a maze."

"Ha, that it is, love. Well, down here"—she gestures to the corridor we're in—"are all the servants' quarters. We have rooms we can bunk in if need be, though most of us don't bother, as we live nearby. But we have cleaning supplies, laundry rooms, and all sorts down here."

"Ah, I see. So that's why none of the team comes down here." I roll my eyes. They don't even do their own washing. Eesh.

"It's nothing like that." She looks to the floor. "We're well paid, and it creates honest work for the *Sheruta* citizens; plus, when the Horsemen are really busy, they barely have time to eat, much less keep this mammoth of a house clean."

I sigh, giving in to the fact that I will just have to go along with it. "I guess you're right. But it wouldn't kill them to make things easier on you." I reach my hands out. "Here, let me help with that."

She has one hand on her back and winces when she moves.

"Have you asked if Dea could look at your back?"

Her face flames bright red. "Gods, no!" she squeaks. "We don't talk to them."

I giggle. "They're not gods, you know. You can say hi. They don't bite."

"Maybe not your hands, they don't . . ." she says. I look at her in horror for a moment, but she waves her arm at me in dismissal. "Was just joking, Miss."

"Please, call me . . ." I look away for a moment and collect myself, lest I fall into tears at this poor woman's feet. Will I ever have a name to my barely there identity? "Errr, in fact, never mind." I grab the washing basket from the lady. "What's your name?"

"Missandre, Miss."

"Well, Missandre, you just show me where to go, and I'll pop this in there for you. And I'll ask Dea to look at your back."

She gushes a humble smile at me.

"And next time, feel free to come to me with any issues. I'll help you deal with them."

"You're too kind, Miss."

She directs me to the laundry room I passed earlier, and I help her put all the clothes into the magically enhanced machines that wash, dry, and fold it all for you.

"I'm going to continue exploring, but if you need anything, come find me."

She nods and gushes another thank-you before I leave her to her work.

"They really need to take better care of their staff here," I mumble to myself as I continue down the myriad of staff hallways that leads to a wide-open foyer decorated in beautiful Morrocan mosaic tiles. In the center stands a fountain with a statue of a woman, and upon closer inspection I realize it's Connie—those telltale long braids seem to be a trademark for her.

Has she always been this beautiful?

Shaking the question away, I walk through one of many corridors beyond, and this one takes me into a black marble circular room with four shiny marble doors—each one a different color.

Which to choose?

The red speaks to me the most, so I go to that door, only to find it locked. Hmmm . . . Interesting.

It's like being stuck down a rabbit hole in here.

Those are our weaponry rooms. You'll need magical permission to get into each one. We'll need to build you one soon, too.

Weaponry rooms? That's fucking epic!

I now understand the significance of the colors: red for Nine, black for Dea, light blue for Arrie, and purple for Connie.

Goddess, these people are fucking nuts. Amazing, but nuts.

I spend all afternoon searching various hideaways and holes stashed all over the ground floor—hundreds of different rooms, all with various purposes—until I'm well and truly lost.

I end upin a small corridor of empty rooms, and I can't remember which way I came in or which way is backward.

Errr, Nine? Can you hear me from over here?

I'm tempted to stay quiet and see what you'll do, but even I'm not that cruel. What's up?

You don't already know?

I'm not constantly in your head, especially with how far away you are right now. Where the fuck are you, Sweetie?

I have no clue. I'm kinda lost.

I know he's laughing right now, but I'm really starting to panic. I hate being lost.

Hold up, let me just look through your eyes a sec.

I feel a slight uncomfortable presence in my mind, like someone's there with me but isn't.

Turn around and look down the next corridor for me?

I do what he says.

Ah! You're in the old east wing. There's nothing down there but empty rooms. I'll send Dea.

Thank you.

I wait all of five minutes, finding myself a comfy spot on the floor, before Dea whizzes past me and stops a few meters away.

"Got lost, Angel?"

"Just a bit." I keep my eyes on the floor. "Sorry."

"Do not be silly. It must be easy to get lost in here. I am forever saving servants when they go wandering around." He rolls his eyes when I look up, and his comment reminds me of Missandre.

"That reminds me . . . Dea, could you look at Missandre's back for me? I'm worried it's not helping her work at all."

He looks at me with a strange, puzzled expression on his face. "Of course, but she should have come to me sooner."

"They're a little scared," I say as he leads me back the way I came, and through some nearly recognizable corridors. "Of all of you."

"Really?"

"They look at you like gods, Dea. They wouldn't bother troubling you."

"Hmmm, well, we will have to change that, will we not?"

I smile to myself. Death is such a genuinely nice guy; that sounds strange, even in my head, so I don't do myself the embarrassment of saying it out loud.

Once Dea leads me back to the kitchen, I make myself a strong cup of coffee with plenty of sugar and head upstairs to read. I'm halfway through an interesting book on how to store magic in certain high-level charms—and I'm honestly rather intrigued by the prospect of potentially being able to keep smaller, less potent doses of the Horsemen's power in charmable objects—when Connie comes and gets me.

"Ready for a girly night?"

Connie and I have been arranging a girl's night for this evening that I've been looking forward to all day. Not sure what she's got planned, but it sounds like a good idea.

"Sure. Help me into my pajamas, and then we can go."

Connie helps me into my nightwear, packing a small bag of blankets and more of Arrie's brownies along the way. She drags me all the way down to the theater room, where the guys sit around the kitchen table.

"Oh, movie night?" Nine asks.

"Nope." Connie shoves open the door that leads to the dark corridor. "Not for you. Sorry, no boys allowed." She giggles as she leads us down the pitch-dark corridor and into the light beyond that signals we've reached our destination.

"Soooo," I start, "what you got planned?"

"Ohhh, it's a surprise. Well, not really, but I'm hoping you'll like it. And if not, we can just watch movies all night instead."

"We're not here to watch movies?"

She opens the door, and light seeps from within. I blanch at the room beyond. She's completely changed the layout and structure. Now the room is full of nothing but floating beds. It still has the big screen at the end, but it also has lots of floating food dancing around on various-sized plates. It's like some kind of supernatural slumber party.

"Nope. We're here to play video games and eat all the dessert we want. Figured you might want to find out what kind of things you like to do and eat, since you can't remember anything."

That's really sweet, and a part of my heart squeezes tight at her thoughtfulness. "That's . . . really thoughtful. Thank you." I can feel the prickle of tears threatening to spill, but fuck no, I won't cry over something so stupid in front of this goddess of a woman.

"C'mon! Let's hop into bed and start playing!"

I get the feeling this is one of her favorite things to do, which is a great insight into her person. She seems to not be much of a girly girl, but prefers keeping herself active and watching action movies. So she looks like a girly girl but acts more like one of the guys. She does, however, have a thing for beauty, and I really need to get some tips because I've never met someone with skin smoother than this woman's. Guess having a lifetime to figure it out sure helps.

"So," I say once she's lowered one of the beds for us to clambor on and raised us back into the air, "what we playin'?"

"Well, I wasn't sure what you'd like, so I grabbed a selection. We've got various RPGS, some shooters, a couple MMOS, and some platform adventures."

She lays them all out in front of me on the plasmascreen, and I select the one with the coolest front cover. Handing me a controller, she puts the game ANNIHILATION onto the screen. It's a multiplayer shooter, and by the way her face lights up at the loading screen, it seems I've made a good choice.

Time to see if I like it, too. The controller seems familiar, and I know the basics of what each button does, so it seems I've played video games before.

She goes through what each button does in the game anyway and sets up a practice run. "Soooo," she starts, and I internally groan. That's one of those dish the gossip *soooos*, isn't it? "What's going on between you and Dea?"

I raise my eyebrows in question, having found a good hiding spot in the game to wait out the fireball attack she's just thrown my way.

"It's not only super obvious, but we're also really in tune with each other. Plus, I heard some of your conversation with Nine, so I know he's clued you up. And that fucker, I am not nosy." She pouts in her cute little way, crossing her arms over her chest and grunting as she dies in the game. "Besides, I'm really just curious."

"I don't know. And honestly, I don't want to find out. Sex for the sake of sex just doesn't sit right with me. I'm not really too sure why, but it just doesn't. Since I have no memories right now, I have no clue whom I've previously slept with, so for all intents and purposes, I'm a complete virgin."

Coughing the sparrows away, she finally says, "Damn. Didn't peg you for the monogamous type."

"Not really sure I'd say I'm monogamous, I just want my connections with people to mean something."

She shoots me with a rocket launcher, and now I'm losing, so I playfully punch her in the arm, but it's like punching a mountain. "Ah!" I pull my hand back and wince at the red mark forming.

"Oh yeah, punching me and Arrie'll hurt like a bitch. Sorry. Nine still tries now and then with the aid of some strengthening potions."

"Noted. Would have been nice to know that before I punched you, though."

"Not half as much fun that way." She winks and loads a new game. Hopefully, I'll win this time. "And just because we're not all in love doesn't mean it means nothing to us. We all care for each other; we just don't want to complicate our already-complicated lives."

Hopping across the map, I snipe her minions down and run for where it says she is on the mini-map. "To me, it just seems like you're all scared. Do you think that if things ended badly, you'd all break up and go your separate ways and the world would be doomed? It doesn't have to be like that. You've all said it a hundred times: you're immortal. I'm sure you'd all get over it and learn to be friends again."

"And if we didn't?" She pauses the game to look me dead in the eyes. "You'd be willing to bet the world's safety on that?"

I look her up and down, noticing every inch of her curves that peek out of her skimpy tank top and shorts. She's wearing a lacy, red bra that pokes out the top of the tank, and I swear it's the perfect color on her. They're all amazing people. They honestly are. "Yeah, I would. You're all amazing, Connie. You've sacrificed millennia of love for the world. Live a little."

She blushes a bright shade of red, and I know I've gotten my point across when a few different plates of dessert fly over. I pick a few things from each one, intending to prove my point, too. I try each of them and love them all. "What are these?"

"Custard slices, chocolate profiteroles, and raspberry muffins."

"They're all amazing!"

"Well, the house serves good cakes, but I got these from town earlier. The baker has some serious skill, and the house can't get anything from this realm, just from Earth."

"C'mon, let's play some more games." I point to an odd-looking RPG called IN THE MOMENT OF DEATH. "I wanna play this one!" I bounce slightly on the bed in excitement and gleam when I realize that reaction feels a lot more like me.

We spend all night playing various video games, stay up way past midnight, and eat more desserts than I can possibly stomach. It's an amazing night, and she's even more awesome than I originally thought.

We fall asleep in the floating bed, sharing the duvet, and for the first time since I woke up here, I feel like I really have a friend.

The next morning, we're both rather bloated and still sleepy, but we crawl out of the bed and go into the kitchen for breakfast anyway.

"Which one was your favorite?" she asks as we sit at an empty table.

"Ermmm, maybe that weird gothic RPG. It was kinda cool. The one with the girl who has cat ears."

"Ha! I love that one, too." She looks around, confused. "Where is everyone?"

Dea enters the room looking a little frustrated but mostly amused. "Well, given that it is four in the afternoon, Arrie is out in the forest getting some training in before dinner, Nine is trying to get this new piece of Fae tech to work somewhere, and I was researching something."

I gulp. "It's really four pm?"

"Uh-huh." He nods. "Guess you ladies were having too much fun to bother telling me you would miss our morning meeting, Angel." He smirks at me and looks all smug at our disheveled clothing. "You've only just woken up, 'ey?" He winks at Connie and turns to leave.

"Wait! Dea, I'm so sorry I missed our meeting this morning. I'm free whenever you are."

"It is fine, Angel. I was just teasing. I knew you were going to miss it when I asked Nine to mentally check on you this morning, and he found you cuddled up in bed, still in the theater."

He gives me a knowing look, and I know exactly what direction his thoughts have traveled in, but I don't call him out on it. Instead, I smile and let him think whatever he wants.

Ugh, I really need to stop flirting with this guy. I have no intention of sleeping with him, and I really don't want to lead him on. I'm not really hungry, so I get up and go back to my rooms.

"Could you stop flirting with her, Dea? It's really not going to happen anytime soon," I hear Connie say in the background as I leave.

I don't really know what to do at this point. Everyone is busy, I don't feel like reading, and I have no questions I need answering right this minute. Looking out the bedroom window, the green side of the forest calls to me. I can go for a walk. I did miss walking with Nine this morning, so fitting one in now sounds like a plan. Besides, I want a chance to get to see the forest again—in a less angry mood.

With a plan in place, I get into some more appropriate clothing—sweatpants and a loose tee—and make my way out into the gardens. The winding paths that leads through the front of the gardens takes me past fairy ponds, over carefully placed fallen logs, past bright blue mushrooms and shrubs with glowing leaves, and under an afternoon sun that glares down on all the garden's splendor. It truly is a sight to behold, and the instantaneous peace that settles over my heart and mind has my thoughts lulling with ideas of ways to stay calm in this new world of uncertainty.

I know I should be freaking out, throwing some kind of tantrum or having a meltdown, but something about this place just feels like home. I belong here. A relationship, even just a friendly one, with all the Horsemen scares me, and the suddenly large expanse of my future makes me apprehensive about everything I'll see and lose along the way, but despite the insecurity, I have the potential to really exist here. I can't remember my past, and I know I've left people behind on Earth, but maybe one day, I'll go back to see what my life once was, but right here and now, this is my present, and it's time to learn what that really means.

This new power, the Angel one that presented itself yesterday, isn't normal, even for a Horseman of the Apocalypse—and that scares the shit out of me. Like, put me in a coma and make me skip a few centuries, because I can't be bothered to deal with the drama of that kind of magic terrifing. But the Horsemen of the Apocalypse have their place in this world, an important pedestal of power, and for a reason I'm sure will become clear at some point, they need me.

I reach the forest's edge, and the gentle glow of the rainbow-color leaves on this side create a haze of multicolor shadows that flit around like dancing pixies and their everchanging wings. It really is fucking awesome.

Has it always been this way? Or has it changed at some point to someone's preference?

I log that away in my list of questions to ask either the team or the Seeing Stone. For the time being, I wander off the beaten track and weave through the trees, always keeping an eye on which way leads back to the tree line connecting to the part of the garden I know, and just let my mind wander through the maze of beauty I've found myself in.

My mind worries over so much, creates so many questions I need answers to, and wonders over the infinite possibilities of what my powers could be and the things I could do now that I have an infinite number of years to experience life. It feels good to just let my mind go, not holding it back or letting fear stop me from simply thinking.

The phrase, live a little, echoes in my mind in a voice that isn't my own or any of the people's I've come to call friends over the past few days. Whose is it? And why is it so important to me?

Grunting in the distance penetrates my peaceful mind babble. "One. Two. Three. Four," the voice repeats in some kind of ritualistic chant.

What is that?

I follow the voice and discover a topless and sweat-sheened Arrie in a small clearing running through some kind of dance-like flow of movements. They all move in to one another, from lunges to spins to jumps, they're expertly executed, and his eyes never open. Not once. It's amazing to watch; his muscles ripple under every movement, and the way his slacks hang loose on his hips has my eyes glued to him. An all-too-familiar heat rushes through me, making my core ache with a desire I'm not yet ready to quench. But there's no harm in watching (I hope).

He's tied his shoulder-length white hair up into a knot out of the way, and I get a clear look at his not-frowning face for the first time. It's aged with years of trouble. I can tell from the frown lines and shadows beneath his eyes, but his face also speaks of an experience the others don't seem to grasp so heavily. Something about this man draws me in, something dark and twisted. I want to understand his pain, to revel in that darkness with him, to understand what kind of horrors this man can inflict.

I lean against a nearby tree and watch for the rest of his repetitive routine, and with each passing round of maneuvers, the curiosity within me grows.

What kind of workout is this?

What's the purpose?

How long has he been practicing this?

A part of me knows that he probably does this every day, because inner peace seems like a big deal to him, and ritualistic habit often helps with peace.

He finally stands still in the clearing, his arms hanging loose by his sides, feet relaxing in the soft, slightly worn grass underfoot. He turns. His ice-blue eyes meet mine in a shiver as he scowls me up and down under the falling sunlight. A growl escapes his lips as his brow creases, and his mouth turns into a sneer that has my hands shaking and my body wanting to flee.

Shit. I need to get out of here.

I stand straight and turn around to walk back to the house, embarrassed, but with a lighter mind and an even lighter soul, one etched with determination. It's time to start learning who I am and what I can do.

His blood seeps into a puddle at my feet, covering my knees and bare toes as I shed a single tear. I've never cried on a job before, but this has pushed me past my moral point of comfort. I bring in criminals, rogues, people who are then prosecuted by the Supernatural Council. Not kids. Not children.

No one told me my mark is a child.

"I'm sorry."

And no one told me that this child had a cyanide pill under his tongue. One he triggered the moment he saw me.

"I'm so sorry."

I've never been responsible for anyone's death before. Imprisonment? Sure. Maybe even a broken family or two, but they should have thought of that before they commited their crimes.

But death? I'm not a killer. At least not until today.

I WAKE UP DRENCHED IN SWEAT AND WITH MY FACE COATED IN A SLICK FILM OF TEARS AS MY stomach roils, and I have to run to the bathroom.

"Fuck," I say through clenched teeth as I brush them with more vigor than required. "Need to get a handle on these fucking nightmares."

My meeting with Dea is in a minute, and I walk downstairs to sit in his study and wait, but I find him waiting for me. "So you don't know what I am yet?" I ask as I take my seat. "What type of Horseman I am or the skills I possess?"

Dea sinks his face into his hands and lets out a long sigh. "No, I do not. But we can assume that because you are the only one of us to really have magic that you were called upon to deal with the turbulence within the magical community and what that will later lead to."

His eyes turn stormy with the thoughts of the potential future. The potential for war among the main magical forces of the world and the human population. This is clearly something that plagues his mind frequently of late.

"Right . . . about that. What do you mean the only one to possess real magic?" I don't get it. Dea can heal. That's magic, right? And what about Nine's telepathy?

"Our abilities are based on Angel and Demon powers, and because of that, we have inherited particular types of powers, rather than magic itself. Connie, having angelic powers, and Arrie, having demonic powers, both have passive abilities that allow them greater strength and focus in battle situations; Nine's abilities, which are demonic in nature, while a type of magic, aren't active types; and I, having angelic powers, can manipulate souls and persuade them to move and change their course of action." He gestures with his hands to each of their biblical depictions in turn on the large canvas above his desk. "None of us can use spells or have any sort of active magic. You are a shiny new toy, Angel."

Angel? That cannot be a coincidence. "Is there a reason you call me that? I didn't think anything of it before, but since my magic seems to be Angel-based, I'm now starting to wonder . . ."

"Hmmm. That is a good question. I nicknamed you that because when I found you, it was the night of Halloween, and you were dressed in a costume of the Angel of Death, which we all found highly amusing." He looks up at me with a small smile. "You looked great, by the way. Killer outfit."

"Dea, focus. Please." I can't help but smile, though; he thinks I looked good in my Halloween outfit. Wait, why does that make me giddy-happy? I don't even remember wearing the fucking outfit!

"Right, sorry." He takes a sip from his cup of tea and continues. "I am not really sure of the significance. Could just be a coincidence, and probably is, if I am honest."

He's hiding something, but if he's hiding it from me, there's probably a good reason. He's been so upfront about everything from day one. Whatever he's hiding, he isn't sure about yet.

"So we're not sure what I am, what I can do, or who I was, but we can explore more about my abilities when I'm fully healed, right?"

"Yes." A genuine smile graces his features, and my professional businesslike resolve melts as I trace the line of his jaw along his smile with my eyes. "And that should only be another week at most. For now, you just need to hold tight and try to recover as fast as possible."

"Okay. Then, can we up the healing baths to twice a day? They really help. I can breathe and move now, and I can stretch my arms above my head, meaning the wound isn't such a problem anymore. Plus, I can walk for about a half hour without getting wheezy and being in pain, so the inside seems to be healing well, too."

"Good. And yes, I can do that. I will do one bath in the morning and one in the evening. Sound good?"

"Perfect. Thanks." I pick up my plasmascreen, and bring up a timetable-like feature. "I plan to do some yoga at dawn and then spend the morning in the library doing some research."

"Okay. For now, I will do the healing baths after your morning yoga, and when you begin training, I was thinking of having you do some early physical combat training with Arrie."

"Then some study time, right? I have loads of stuff to catch up on, and it's really bugging me that I can't remember some vital details about the world." I put the cup of coffee to my mouth and sip.

"Sure. Then you will have me and Nine for the afternoon, working on your abilities and magic." He pauses then, looking up at me from the schedule. "Is that okay?"

He's trying to be considerate. That's soooo sweet, I coo in my head, but I don't want to say that out loud, so I just nod for him to continue.

"And then some weapons training with Connie in the evening."

"Ohhh, I get weapons? Oh my goddess, I could totally be a ninja with all the dark shadow magic and night vision. Can I get throwing stars? What about daggers that strap to my thigh, like in those sexy movies?"

Dea chuckles as his eyes light up a pale golden color. "We will let you and Connie decide. She is best at that kind of stuff. Arrie is pretty good, too, but we need to divide their workload somehow, and he is better at hand-to-hand combat."

I nod my understanding and bury my excitement over what kind of weapons I'll be using. It can be anything, can't it? Completely my choice. Yay! I mentally clap my hands like a child on Christmas Day morning.

"Oh, before you go . . ." Dea rifles through a massive pile of paperwork in the top drawer until he finds something and hands it to me. It looks like a thin black pen but with two buttons on the side. "A translational bookscreen. Keep it."

"Thanks!"

I shoot out of my chair and walk to my library as fast as possible. I can't wait to be able to run again, so I can run around in my crazy, excitable moments. It feels a little withdrawn to simply walk everywhere, like it isn't really me. At least not this new, immortal me.

The rest of the day, I'm holed up in my study, using my new translational bookscreen to translate that mammoth of a book, and it's amazing! You just press a button to open the screen, which descends from the pen-like thing, and it glows a faint blue as it resizes itself to match the page underneath; the words then magically translate into the programmed language—English, in this case.

I have read half the tome by the time lunch comes and goes, where I forget all about bothering to eat, but I have learned the complete origins of the Four Horsemen:

THE FOUR HORSEMEN OF THE APOCALYPSE, ONCE HUMAN, WERE CALLED UPON BY AN ANCIENT MAGIC TO PROTECT THE WORLD FROM ITS OWN, SELF-CREATED, EVIL. A MORTAL MAN, CONCERNED ABOUT THE STATE OF THE THEN-CURRENT WORLD, WENT LOOKING FOR ANSWERS. STUMBLING ACROSS THE SEVEN SEALS IN AN OLD TOMB DEVOTED TO A GOD LONG FORGOTTEN TO THE REALM OF MAN, HE BROKE THE FIRST FOUR, BRINGING FORTH A MAGICAL FORCE SO POWERFUL, HUMANITY WOULD FOREVER LIVE IN PEACE.

THE REST OF THE SEALS, WHICH REMAINED UNBROKEN, HAVE SINCE BEEN HIDDEN BY THE MAN-MADE COURSE OF TIME. THE FOUR HORSEMEN—CONQUEST, DEATH, WAR, AND FAMINE—ARE THOUGHT TO HOLD THEIR OWN SEALS NOW, AS THE ONLY WAY TO KILL A TRULY IMMORTAL BEING THAT POWERFUL IS TO BURN THE SEAL THAT HOLDS ITS MAGICAL LIFE FORCE INTACT. DOING SO WOULD THEORETICALLY PURGE THE WORLD OF THAT HORSEMAN, CREATING AN IMBALANCE TO THE STATE OF THE WORLD AS WE KNOW IT TODAY.

JOSHUA, THE MORTAL HERO WHO BROKE THE FOUR SEALS, WAS WORSHIPPED AMONG MANKIND

FOR HAVING BROUGHT AN ERA OF PEACE TO AN OTHERWISE WARRING, STARVING WORLD. LEGENDS WERE CREATED, STORIES WERE WRITTEN, AND FROM OUT OF THE ASHES, HE WAS REBORN AS THE LEGEND OF JESUS.

Wow. Jesus really broke their seals? That's . . . insane.

They're just like me, called upon to help with some state-of-the-world nonsense, and they've been doing that ever since. All right, wars break out now and then, and some countries starve during periods of poverty, but they always ebb and flow over the course of time, and that's because of them. They do that. They keep the world safe. But they won't be able to fix a world at war with magic because none of them actually have any real magic. At least, whoever broke my seal doesn't seem to think so.

Wonder who it is, and why?

No matter how many times I ask my Seeing Stone that question, no answers are given. It seems that's something I need to find the answer to myself.

Sweetie, dinner's ready if you're hungry.

Ah, food. The rumble of my lunch-starved belly penetrates the silence—it's probably best to refuel so I can come back to my questions later.

Entering the kitchen with renewed vigor, a familiar sight catches my eye—everyone in their usual spots around the dinner table, but with some kind of food I haven't tried yet.

Taking a large sniff, I recognize it in the recesses of my misted memories. "Italian."

Nine turns around, a smile on his face. "You like Italian food?"

I nod, a little unsure.

"Well, we have lasagne, garlic ciabatta, tossed salad, and a good white to wash it down with." He points to a bottle of white wine on the center placemat, and I can't help but grin.

Taking a seat, Dea asks, "Did the bookscreen work?"

"Yeah. It's an awesome piece of tech. Thanks!" I grab my plate and start loading a slice of lasagne, some of the ciabatta, and a little salad. "Been reading all day."

Connie pinches a bit of the tomato I left on the side of my plate, having discovered I don't like it much. "What were you reading?"

I gulp, unsure if they're going to be weird about the book. "The origins of the Four Horsemen."

They all put their cutlery down and stare at me, but it's Dea who speaks up. "You managed to find a book with an accurate telling of that story?"

Accurate? "I hope so . . ." Now that I think about it, how accurate is the information my Seeing Stone provides me?

"It has to be accurate, otherwise it wouldn't provide that book to you." Nine's palm rests of my thigh, which is becoming a habit at the dinner table, and each time, it sends a tingle of heat up my leg, and the smirk he always gives me tells me he damn well knows it, too. "Mine gives me website addresses to look up, and it's the same kind of deal. It only provides ones with accurate information. But sometimes, if information is scarce, the accuracy is limited to a few particular facts on any particular webpage."

Sometimes I forget how much of a nerd Nine is, but I love it. It's . . . refreshing.

Nine smiles and returns his gaze to his plate, his cheeks and ears blushing a gentle shade of scarlet. Our little resident nerd isn't used to compliments, which equally amazes and frustrates me.

10

The next two days are full of note-taking, morning walks with Nine, and shutting myself indoors to finish reading that book. In the process, I learn the complete origins of the Four Horsemen and all their gifts and powers—well, the ones in the book anyway. I make hundreds of pages of notes summarizing various facts about the people I now share my eternal life with:

DEA, DEATH, CAN ACCESS THE ENERGY WITHIN SOMEONE'S SOUL AND MOVE IT OUT OF THE BODY OR PULL IT BACK IN, INCLUDING TO PERSUADE IT TO HEAL. THIS IS KNOWN AS SOUL MANIPULATION AND IS UNIQUE TO DEATH. HE CAN ALSO MAKE SOMEONE'S DEEPEST, SOUL-DEEP DESIRES CHANGE, PERSUADING THEM TO DO AS HE WISHES. HE PREFERS TO WIELD DUAL DAGGERS IN BATTLE, AS HE IS THE FASTEST OF THE HORSEMEN DUE TO HIS FAZING ABILITY, AND HE USES STEALTH-BASED SKILLS TO FIGHT. HE IS INVISIBLE TO EVERYONE BUT THE FOUR HORSEMEN UNLESS HE CHOOSES TO EXPEND ENERGY MAKING HIMSELF VISIBLE, AND EVEN THEN, HUMANS ONLY SEE HIM AS SEMI-OPAQUE.

CONNIE, CONQUEST, HAS MORE ABILITIES, BUT THESE ARE LIMITED IN THEIR USAGE. SHE HAS EXCELLENT SENSES TO HELP HER IN BATTLE, ESPECIALLY HEARING, AS WELL AS NEVER-FALTERING AIM AND STAMINA. SHE COULD BATTLE AT ONE HUNDRED PERCENT FOR WEEKS AND NEVER TIRE. SHE DOESN'T NEED TO SLEEP OR EAT MUCH BUT CHOOSES TO DO BOTH ANYWAY. SHE IS A SKILLED ARCHER, AND HER THOUSAND-YEAR-OLD BOW IS HER WEAPON OF CHOICE.

NINE, FAMINE, HAS THE ABILITY TO READ MINDS AND EMOTIONS, COMMUNICATE VIA TELEPATHY, AND ACCESS SOMEONE'S DREAMS. THIS ALLOWS HIM TO UNDERSTAND A COUNTRY OR PEOPLE'S DESIRES AND PROBLEMS, THEREFORE USING HIS GREAT INTELLECT TO FIX POLITICAL ISSUES. WHEN IN BATTLE, HE USES MAGIGUNS AND A SHORT SWORD SWORD FOR A DEADLY COMBINATION.

ARRIE, WAR, IS A SKILLED WARRIOR, WIELDING DUAL BATTLE-AXES FROM ATOP HIS WARHORSE. HE HAS A BATTLE-MODE ABILITY THAT ALLOWS HIM TO SOLELY FOCUS ON THE BATTLE AT HAND, SHUTTING OUT ALL OTHER ISSUES, AS WELL AS A STRATEGY GIFT, WHEREBY THE BEST AND EASIEST WAY TO WIN A PARTICULAR FIGHT WILL PRESENT ITSELF TO HIM.

The more I learn about them, the farther my jaw drops. They all sound amazing, and I can't wait to see them in action. It's going to take me at least a few hundred years to be anywhere near their level. Hopefully, the world won't need that anytime soon.

Footsteps interrupt my note-taking, and Dea rounds the corner, quickly followed by Nine. It's eleven in the morning, and my lunch-starved brain is dawdling and procrastinating, so they're a welcome a distraction.

Nine rounds the desk and grabs the thick leather-bound notebook I've been using for my notes and casually flips through the hundreds of pages of squiggles. "Wow, Sweetie, you've really been working hard. You practically know all our skills and abilities inside and out, probably more than any other person in the world." He hands my book back and rests a hand on my shoulder.

Dea picks up the book for inspection. "Would you like me to read it over and add some extra notes for you?" He looks at my raised eyebrows and shrugs. "You cannot learn *everything* about us from a book. Some things we never wrote down. Like the location of our seals, for example."

Of course, they probably have them hidden so no one can kill them. It's been rumored in several texts that they hold their own seals nowadays, but Dea practically just confirmed it.

"You're all so . . . fascinating. You've been around longer than any other species and have abilities I can only dream of." I can't help the niggling doubt that creeps its way into my mind—the feeling that has made a home there over the past few days.

Nine tries to interrupt my oncoming mind babble, but I hold out a hand. "I know. It's okay." I get up and put my notebook in the top drawer, closing the latest reference book I had open with a bookmark. "So what did you guys want, anyway?"

Dea smiled. "Well, we were just headed into town and thought you might like to join us. It is about time you started learning about life in this realm."

"Ohhh, yeah! Oh my goddess, tell me I can go shopping."

Nine grumbles, but Dea laughs and says, "Finally, someone who understands. Yes, we can go shopping. It is a great place to shop, trust me." He threads his arm through mine and guides me out of the library.

I can walk for about an hour now without getting too out of breath, but I'm worried about shopping all day. Will carrying everything cause further harm?

Nine takes my other arm. "Don't worry, we're going to walk slowly, and then we'll get any stuff you buy sent to the house directly. Minimal walking and carrying. Promise."

"Okay." I blush slightly, a little embarrassed they even have to do something so stupid for me, but I wave it off when Nine tries comfort me about it.

Once more appropriate footwear has been donned—booty flats—we head out the front door (which I didn't even realize existed until now). Turning around, I stop to admire the building's front exterior. Much like the backyard, the front yard is like a fairy garden, with the house having a very Japanese feel. My Japanese ethnicity and the style of the house and the Zen style of the gardens is way too much of a coincidence, surely?

"You're right." Nine's arm wraps around my waist and gently pulls me closer. "Before you got here, the house changed to suit what it presumed was your style."

"Damn." I whistle my appreciation. "But why?"

Dea wraps an arm around my shoulders and lands a hand on Nine's neck. "I have a theory about that." They seem particularly close, even for the Horsemen, but I just give Dea a look that I hope says go on and not dish the dirt. "Well, since you are the most magical being here, we are assuming you can wield more magic than us, and therefore, you may have a stronger connection to the house."

Makes sense in a sort of fated way. Has the house been magical this entire time because it waited for me? No, that doesn't make sense. The others have magic, too, just not in the same way. Has it been existing for everyone, no matter who or what came along in the future, then? Something doesn't add up.

Turns out the town is about a half hour's walk away, which is great because I'm getting out of breath from all the walking and talking.

"Let's grab some tea before starting." Nine gives me a long, side-eyed look, and I know instantly the decision is for my benefit.

Thank fuck, because I seriously want some coffee.

Ahead of us is a cobblestoned street that reminds me a little of medieval Europe with all the red brick and gray stone each side of the street, with signposts swinging in the light, afternoon breeze.

There are a few people meandering around, all of who give us a wide berth and a small bow aimed in Dea's direction. Wait, isn't he supposed to be invisible to others? At least, that's what I've read. Maybe the book is wrong.

"I can make myself visible for a few hours at a time, but humans still see me as slightly permeable. Luckily, there are no humans in this realm."

He still has his arm around me and resting on Nine's neck, and I'm pretty sure this particular fact will garner some gossip with the locals. Ah well, who really cares? We're immortal, we'll outlive them anyway.

Wow. Never thought I would think that cold-heartedly. True, though. But does that mean I should not make an effort? I mean, people still matter. Yup. Turns out my brain needs to put more effort into being morally centered.

The café we end up at is on the corner of the first street, and the first thing I notice are the plates of desserts flying around—just like the ones from mine and Connie's gaming night. A sudden image of Connie in that bloody skimpy tee and short-short pajamas flashes across my mind, making my breath hiccup and my core ache with an unstifling need.

Nine looks at me with raised eyebrows, trying his best to stifle a laugh. "Yes, this is where Connie got those desserts for you both."

Dea grabs us a table, but Nine's still giving me a knowing look and obviously trying to hide his obvious amusement, which doesn't go unnoticed by Dea.

"What is so funny?"

"Oh, nothing. But I have a feeling our little sweet thing over here"—he wraps his arm around my shoulders and squeezes slightly—"is going to create an interesting dynamic in our lives."

Interesting, huh? Is that what he thinks I am, interesting?

A waiter comes over and takes our orders, and I ask for an extra-large coffee and some of the cream puffs I had the other night.

The café in question is an interesting mix of magical and normal. It looks like so many cafés I've been in on Earth—a few now flitter across my memory—but not. The ones I can remember are plain, boring, normal. A few have some fancy décor, a few have some interesting themes, but none are like this. There's Fae magic at work here. The plates float over to the tables, along with trays of traditional Japanese tea (another odd curiosity), rather than being brought over by the waiters, who just run around cleaning and taking orders using various types of magic. The walls are deep red and plum in color, creating a mystical vibe that, if I wasn't sitting in another realm entirely, I would have assumed was due to tourism. It certainly has that traditional magical vibe going on.

By the time I turn my attention back to the table, everyone's orders have arrived, and Nine and Dea are locked in a mental conversation—I assume so anyway, since they're giving each other raised eyebrows and gestures. I just hope they aren't talking about me.

"So . . . err, I have a question."

They both stop their silent conversation, which makes me feel a little guilty (what is the proper etiquette for interrupting conversation when you can't hear it?), and look my way with warm smiles.

"How . . . How do I buy things?" It hadn't even crossed my mind before now, but I don't actually have any money. I'm not even too sure what money is used in this place or how to earn money as a Horseman of the Apocalypse that no one even knows exists.

Dea dismisses my concerns with a wave of his hand. "We have a group fund, as it is hard to earn money when saving the world. We have various investments on Earth, which the house turns into derra, the currency used here."

Makes sense. "But don't I need to chip in? I mean, I feel kinda bad that you're doing everything for me, and I haven't been doing much." I keep my eyes on the table, nudging my cream puff and eyeing the coffee, waiting for it to cool down.

"Nah. Don't worry. Dea usually handles it for us all anyway." Nine smiles, giving Dea a fist to bump, which he does so with a roll of his eyes.

There is more going on there, more than just general intimacy between immortal friends. But broaching that topic is a no-go right now because it still confuses the fuck out of me. But at least money is one less thing to worry about.

Dea chimes in after sipping his chai latte (of course that's what he ordered). "I will give you access to the team's account in a few days, plus the house account. We use the house account for things like today, and the team account when out on jobs. The only person not allowed anywhere near money is Nine. His Famine nature drains it every time he is upset or experiencing any kind of negative emotion. In a totally magical, only-Famine way."

Giggling, I give my coffee a swirl before drinking as Nine crosses him arms and lays back, silent (for once). "Okay. Thanks." It still feels weird to have access to these people's money, but I guess I'm one of them now, and I don't really get a choice in that.

"Look, Angel." Dea grabs my hand from across the table, clearly having been filled in on my inner thoughts from Nine (who I give the stink eye). "I know this has been a rough adjustment, especially since you have no memories, but today, you can just relax. Spend however much you like. Consider it a sorry-you-are-stuck-with-us-forever-now gift."

"Okay. But if anything is too expensive, just let me know."

"Fine." Dea laughs, his face the picture of amusement.

"I get the feeling she'll freak when she sees the accounts." Nine also looks amused by my cluelessness. The fucking ass. "C'mon. Hurry up. Let's get this over with."

"Not a shopping fan?"

"Not with this one." He points to Dea with his thumb, who shrugs and feigns innocence.

But I'm excited. The thought of shopping and seeing what I like and dislike both thrills and terrifies me. I quite like Connie's beautiful dressed-up style, but I get the feeling I'm more of a quirky, gothicy kind of girl. Definitely fits with the whole tattoos and pink hair I'm currently sporting.

"C'mon, then!" I drain my cup, and, noticing they have also finished, grab them both by the hands and walk us as fast as I can out of the café. "Oh, wait a minute!"

I turn on my heels and walk back toward the small desk in the back corner. "Excuse me?"

The purple-haired, pointy-eared Fae looks me up and down with a frown. "We donnat get many visitors here on *Sheruta*, girl. Who are ya?"

"Oh, right. I'm . . ." Damn it. Still don't have a name. "That's not really important. I'm staying with them." I point to the guys in the doorway, who stand waiting for me with smiles reaching ear to ear. Nine has probably filled Dea in on my intentions. "I just wanted to thank whoever made the desserts Connie ordered the other day. They were amazing and made for a great night. Thank you." I bow slightly, lowering my head.

"Oh." The guy blushes. "No need ta thank me, deary. It's always a pleasure doin' Miss Connie's orders."

"So, you're the fantastic baker? Oh, how wonderful." I clap my hands and give him a smile. "You have quite the talent, sir. Again, thank you very much."

"It was my pleasure, Miss." He looks at me, then gives the boys a strange, questioning look and looks back at me. "If you donnat mind me askin', Miss, what's your business with the Horsemen? They donnat 'ave visitors these days."

"Oh, I'm—"

Tell him you're just visiting.

"I'm just visiting. Hanging out with Connie for a few days."

"Ah! Well, it's good to see 'em makin' friends outside of their circle again."

"Indeed. If you'll please excuse me?"

"Ah, o' course. Have a good day, Miss."

I nod, give another small bow, and exit.

Dea grabs my waist this time, with Nine's arm over my shoulder. The intimacy is nice, if I'm being honest. I know it isn't sexual or anything, but the caring nature makes me feel a little less alone.

"Sorry," Nine says. "Not ready to announce you to the world yet."

"That's okay. I should have asked. Sorry."

Dea shakes his head at me, his hair falling out of place. "Do not be sorry for what you are. We should have mentioned we were trying to keep you a secret until you are all trained up."

I nod, feeling a little . . . ashamed. Part of me, the logical part, knows they're just trying to protect me and ease me into this world gently, especially given my memory loss and strange gifts, but the other part of me can't help but worry they might be ashamed of me or trying to hide me because they know I won't fit in.

Nine whispers in my ear, "You fit in perfectly. And I get the feeling that you'll be the one to bring us all together in the end."

Bring them all together?

I give him a questioning look, but he ignores me and continues walking down the next street.

The few streets this side of town have that same medieval Europe feeling mixed with a more magical approach, and the stores are all posh and tailored, with store clerks offering to help the moment you step through their door. I don't really know how to act, so I just roll with it. It's fun pretending for a day.

"Soooo . . . I looked through my closet before coming out with you guys, and it's a little on the small side. Even for necessities."

"Well, what do you need?" Dea smirks in excitement, and I realize that he really does love shopping.

"Workout gear, running shoes, everyday outfits, underwear, and pajamas—which I only seem to have a single pair of."

Nine smirks. "You probably weren't much of a pajama girl, but the house does only bring stuff it thinks you like, so it probably didn't bring everything."

"Right." I point to what I hope is a general clothing store. "I need general clothing, underwear, and workout stuff."

Dea grabs my wrist and pulls me into the shop while Nine laughs it up behind me.

"This is the best place for casual wear, but we actually have a special exercise clothing store here in town," Dea says.

"We probably keep it open, for fuck's sake." Nine looks at me and says, "There's a fancy underwear store around town somewhere." He winks and goes off into the men's section.

"Damn." Sighing, I sink my head into my heads. I didn't think of it like that. I just really need some damn panties and bras, since the house seems to only have brought over a handful of each. "Shoulda brought Connie along."

"She loves shopping but tends to prefer the downtime of doing it alone." Dea comes up behind me, frightening the fuck out of me. "Sorry."

"You're terrifyingly silent, you know that?"

"You are pretty light-footed yourself, Angel." He has a handful of things in his arms in all the colors of the rainbow. "Try these on." He points to a changing room at the back of the store and guides me in that direction.

Flitting behind the satin curtains, I try on the first item: a bright pink crop top with a black dead-eyed unicorn image. "Where did he find this?" I mutter to myself.

"I have my talents. Shopping happens to be something you get good at over time. Come out and show me. I want to see!" The excitement in his voice does not go unnoticed by me or Nine, it seems, who groans under his breath, having apparently rejoined Dea.

Swinging the curtain open, I show him, and the delighted grin on Dea's face makes me smile. Yup. Definitely getting this one.

We continue in this fashion for a few stores, Dea paying each clerk and ordering them to be delivered to the house, which everyone is happy to oblige. Dea seems to have a penchant for shopping, picking out various styles he thinks I'll like, from Japanese kimonos to gothic punk tees to shorts and skirts to match all kinds of outfits. I have all kinds of styles now, and even a few dresses I don't know if I'll have the opportunity to wear.

By this point, we've spent a couple hours shopping, Nine's complaining, and Dea's visibility is starting to wane, so we decide to head straight to the exercise shop and pick up yoga pants, sports bras, sweatpants, vests, and sneakers—everything I will possibly need for any kind of exercise they might throw my way. The store clerk is familiar with them both and gives us all warming smiles, even flirting with Nine a bit. Dea tends to stay out of flirtatious situations, which confuses me slightly, as I thought they're both open with their romancing.

Ah! The more I think about all that, the more confused I get, so I ignore it and continue.

Last stop of the day is underwear, and I really want to do this one alone. "Stay out here. I won't be long." I give them a don't-fucking-disobey-me glare and walk into the fancy boutique as the store's bell chimes.

"Hello, sweet pea!" A young woman comes out from behind a curtain in the back, her long blond hair flowing around her waist like a jeweled curtain. "Anything I can help you with?"

"I'm staying with the Horsemen for a while but didn't bring much stuff with me, and now it looks like my stay will be longer than expected. I just need to stock up on some basic underwear."

Her eyebrows rise at the mention of the Horsemen, and I get the instinctive feeling she's a little jealous, given the odd glare and smile she's giving out the window at the guys, who, now that I've turned around, I notice are staring in like two kids in a toyshop window.

"Just basic stuff."

She gives me a knowing smile. "I can help. Trust me." She starts walking around the store, picking out various bras and matching panties that I think are far too fancy for everyday wear, but what do I know? I just go along with it.

"You know . . ." She gives me a smile and looks me up and down. "Nine prefers darker-laced underwear in the bedroom." Winking, she picks off some fancy black-laced underwear and adds it to growing pile.

"Oh, I'm not—"

"Please. He's rather flirtatious, that one. No one avoids him forever. You won't be the first. Or the last." Her tone turns bitter at that last note.

"So, you and Nine have . . . ?"

She giggles and waves a hand. "Yes, yes, yes, sweet pea. But nothing to worry about. Nine never sleeps with the same person twice."

Except the team.

"Our relationship isn't like that in the slightest, but thank you for the advice anyway. I'd best be on my way now. If you could charge Dea's account and have them delivered to the house, that would be great."

She looks taken aback by my statement, but she nods and takes everything behind the counter to box it all up. "Should be at the house before you get back, Miss."

"Thank you."

I rush toward the store's exit like my life depends on it, even getting a bit winded in the process, but I trip on the doorframe on my way out and nearly tumble to the floor.

"Careful there." Nine catches me before I hit the cobblestones. "Don't run if you can't walk."

"Are you okay, Angel?"

"Just fine," I say through gritted teeth.

Nine throws me a weird look, but I stare at him and say, "Stay out of my head."

Taking a deep breath, I grab both boys by the arm and head for the house, hoping to get back to my library where there are no snooty, judgmental women trying to get me to hook up with the Horsemen. I'm there to help with a possible magical war, not fuck my way through the team.

This isn't some weird fantasy romance novel.

11

Boxes upon boxes of fancy clothing are on my bed when we finally make it back. The journey took almost an hour this time as I struggled and wheezed back up that hill. I'll be damn happy when I'm fully recovered.

I plan to fit in morning yoga sessions first thing tomorrow, hoping to regain some level of fitness before training really begins. Connie and Arrie look like they can sprint all day and not break a damn sweat, so working out with them will be painful if I don't prepare first.

Looking at my small closet in the corner and then back to the boxes and bags, I wonder if I truly have room for it all. Oh my goddess, a walk-in closet would be fucking awesome! Wonder if I can ask the house to adjust? Is it that simple?

Placing my hand on the wall and feeling a little ridiculous, I take a breath and mentally ask, Can I maybe get a bigger closet? Something a little more me. I like looking stylish, and having somewhere to do that each day sounds like a great idea. Love the original color scheme, though, and the general style.

I open my eyes, looking at the original closet, and let out a breath I didn't realize I've been holding. Of course it isn't that simple. That would be ridiculous.

I turn back toward the bed to unpack some of my new clothes when I hear a deep rumble from behind, shaking all the walls and floor like an earthquake.

What the—?

I turn back around to look at the cause and am astounded by the lack of a closet that's been replaced by a door to the right of my nightstand

Where did my closet go?

Opening the door, I take a nervous breath, wondering if the house really is connected to me that much. Inside is a lavish set of connected areas, each one serving a separate purpose: shoes and bags, jewelry and makeup with a large dressing table and mirror to match, everyday wear, party and evening wear, and even a section for my new workout gear.

"Whoa."

This is fucking nuts. Great, but nuts. I can just ask the house for anything I want? And it'll just expand and renovate itself to accommodate me?

Footseps thunder into the room, and the entire team tumbles through the doorway, looking ready to throw down at the first sign of an intruder.

"What the fuck?" Arrie is the first over to me, peering through the open door. "Did you just ask the house for a walk-in closet, and it gave you this?" He gives me the stink eye, and I can't help but stifle a giggle at his obvious jealousy. The Horseman of War is jealous. Of me.

What a life.

Connie walks over next, marveling at the space in the room. "It's just like mine!"

"Really?" She has one similar? Makes sense; she is a woman. An immortal woman, but a woman nonetheless. And she always looks impeccably well-dressed. Even in pajamas, which is just ridiculous.

"Wanna help me put everything away?"

She gives me an excited smile.

I go to grab everything and take it into the closet. "I mean, you don't have to. I just thought—"

"I'd love to," she whispers. "Let me help grab some of those." She shoos the boys out with a wave of her hands and a mean look I know means business—as do they, clearly, as they scamper.

She bounces into the closet with all the boxes and bags, closes the door, and gives me a look. "So, Nine tells me you met Claudia and have been a little standoffish ever since. I just wanted to take the time to apologize for her fucking attitude."

"Claudia?"

"That shitty excuse for a woman at the fancy underwear boutique?"

I nod and start unpacking the workout gear into the otherwise empty section of the closet.

"Yeah, I know. She has this weird obsession with Nine after sleeping with him, like, three years ago, and she's been a petty bitch with me ever since, too. I try to do all my underwear shopping on Earth to avoid her."

So Nine has slept with her then? But only once. That seems . . . strange. "You shop on Earth?"

"Of course, but I feel that's not the question on your mind." She raises her eyebrows and stands with her hands on her hips. She's clearly not moving until I spill the beans. "Ask away."

"I really don't want to talk about it. I just want to learn who I am, learn about my magic, train, and be useful to you all. Nothing else matters."

"Oh, hon . . . That's not . . ."

I wave a hand at her and turn around, trying not to let the tears brimming at the edges of my eyes spill over. I really am interrupting them, aren't I? I mean, I know they've all slept with each other over the years, but it's like Connie has her own personal harem, and I'm the only other woman to live with them. Ever. And I have just interrupted them.

"Let's just get this stuff unpacked. I have more research I want to do before bed."

"Okay. But, listen, if you ever want to chat about us all and the weird kind of family we all have, it's totally okay. For us, it's as natural as breathing and goes back centuries, but for you, it's like a whole strange concept. We get that. We want you to fit in here."

I can hear the desperation in her tone. They don't want me to fit in. They need me to. Because what happens if I don't? We all have to work together, no matter what.

I'm starting to understand Nine's point of view: What happens if I don't fit in? Will I be able to stay? Will I stay living with people where I'm not wanted just for Earth?

We unpack everything other than the last couple of ribbon-tied boxes, which I assume hold the underwear. Connie grabs them and peeks inside. "Ohhhh, these are fancy. And tell me . . . who are they for?"

I roll my eyes at her antics. Everyone here is completely insane. "Me." I'm not sure I want to start seeing anyone right now, especially not any of the team.

"Whatever you say." She holds up a purple lacey bra-and-panties set to my body. "But I think you'd look super hot in this."

My cheeks flame into two burning balls of heat, and man, is it hot in here. "Really?"

What the fuck? Why would I let that slip out?

Connie looks me up and down and smiles. "Yeah." She steps closer, holds the set up to my body again, and says, "Yup. Definitely hot in this."

"T-T-Thanks. I . . ." Why can't I get a single word out? Just the thought of her seeing me in that kind of underwear makes me hot under the collar, nervous in a way I've never been before.

She goes to put them in the fancy drawers in a section I didn't know was dedicated to underwear and comes back to me and wraps her arms around my body in a tight embrace. "You're doing great."

The warmth of her body seeps into my limbs as I inhale the musky, rose-tinted scent of the perfume she wears that mingles with the mango scent of her hair. Her entire body presses close to mine as she backs us up against the nearest wall so I can lean on something to take the edge off our now-joined weight.

"Really, you're going to be fine here. Nine and Dea really like you, and I think it'll be great having a girlfriend around the house."

I snort my surprise—girlfriend?—but try to hide it with a comforting sigh.

She's taller than me, not that it's a great accomplishment given my five-foot-four frame, and my head rests lightly on her shoulder. Slowly, my arms tangle themselves around her waist as I pull her the last few inches flush against me.

We stand like that for a few moments, listening to each other breathing, and I rejoice in some kind of nice touch that makes me feel a little less lonely.

She pulls away slightly, and a small moan of protest escapes my lips before I can stop it, and I'm pretty sure I can't be more embarrassed by this point. But she doesn't break contact; instead, she keeps her arms wrapped around the small of my back and pulls her head and chest away. Her lips are inches from mine, and I can feel the gentle caress of her breath on my face. Everything slips away from me in that moment. Nothing matters. Not the pang of loneliness I've been trying to fill with studying, not the confusion of my feelings toward the team, and not the pressure of finding my place among the Horsemen.

It's as though something pulls my head in toward hers, and I can see her leaning in, too. Oh my goddess, she's totally going to kiss me. But just as heat floods my core in a way that makes me almost want to try on that underwear for her, panic sets in.

Heart racing, I pull away. "Connie . . . I—"

She pulls back and holds up a hand. "It's okay. I didn't mean to make you feel uncomfortable. I just meant to show you that this"—she gestures to the two of us—"is okay." She smiles and unwraps both arms from my waist.

She knows? Seems I'm pretty fucking terrible at hiding my feelings, which does not bode well for the rest of the team. Do they know, too? Well, Nine knows everything, but that's okay. He generally keeps it to himself. Wait. Does he? Did he fill the rest of the team in?

"Hon, I can see you spiraling. I'm not Nine—I can't tell what you're thinking. You have to actually use words with me." She smiles that beautiful smile of hers, and I know she isn't trying to be horrible.

I look sheepishly to the floor, finding something in the large closet to look at besides her. "Is it that obvious . . . or . . . Or did Nine say something?"

"Ah. That." Connie grabs my chin in a slight pinch and forces me to meet her eyes. "Nine likes to tease people, but he never tells us what's on each other's minds unless necessary. So, no. I just . . . have been watching you."

Watching me? That sounds . . . creepy.

"Oh, fuck. That sounded creepy, didn't it?" I nod but can't help the laugh that escapes. "You're the first girl on the team besides me, and I'll admit that I'm intrigued by you. I can't help it. You try spending two millennia with those three and then have a girl come along."

"Fair enough." That actually makes a lot of sense, and the dread in the pit of my stomach starts unknotting itself.

"Tell ya what. Why don't we make a deal?" She holds out her hand to shake. "We arrange some kind of girl-chat evening once a week, and we just tell each other how we feel no matter how embarrassing it might be."

"So . . . like a girly sleepover?"

"Oh my fuck, yes. A sleepover!"

I shake her hand as firmly as possible and smile at the prospect of having someone to chat with—another woman who will likely understand some of the challenges of being here.

"So anything else you wanted to chat about? You must be worried about a lot. And confused."

"Let's have a sleepover tonight, and I'll dish all the dirt. Promise."

She lets out a girly squeal. "I'll come get you at six!"

12

It's five thirty, my sleepover with Connie starts in thirty minutes, and my nerves can't be more shot. It's just a friendly sleepover, I keep telling myself. But no matter how many times I repeat that phrase, the idea of this being a date has my nerves in a damn tumble. Connie said that it's important I feel okay with everything, so why doesn't this feel okay?

"Because you're worrying about what she'll think and forgetting that she just wants to spend time with you."

"Ah!" I jump to the other side of my bed and nearly fall off in fright.

Nine stands in the doorway, a bemused look plastered upon his smug face as he leans against the frame.

"Fucking Christ, Nine! You scared the shit out of me."

"Sorry." He puts a hand to his mouth, covering yet another laugh (that's becoming a habit, it seems), and I finally notice he's wearing swimming shorts. And nothing else.

Fucking hell. Living here is creating a whole new set of issues I never thought I would have to deal with. No tattoos like Dea and not as many muscles as Arrie, but the definition is still there in a very swimmer-like way, and is that a . . . nipple piercing? Part of me really wants to reach out and run my hands over that chest and through that wet red hair, but I stay put, lying on the other side of the bed, trying my best not to clench my thighs too obviously at the sudden need thriving there.

Nine clears his throat, and I realize I've been staring too long, and he's probably just read my mind anyway, so there's no point hiding my desire.

"You need to have some alone time. Your thoughts are worse than the rest of theirs put together." Nine laughs some more and comes to sit on the bed next to me. He bends toward me and mentally whispers, *But honestly, I kinda like it.*

I angle my head in question, hoping he'll explain.

Being in someone's head is really interesting, and although I try not to pry, it's hard. It's in my nature to read surface thoughts, and I don't like hiding myself away and pretending to be something I'm not. The problem is that usually people don't like that—Arrie especially. But with you, your surface thoughts are either panic and worry over your new situation, which is completely understandable, or wondering what it would be like to fuck one of us. It's kind of refreshing to see someone so . . . hot.

"Oh."

Your mind, that is. Sorry. It's really hard to explain. I tend to judge people based on how they think, since that's how I communicate and see.

I nod, kinda getting where he's coming from. But the one thing that sticks out—he thinks my mind is hot? I scoot closer, wanting nothing more than to reach out, but I hold back. "So, you don't think I should be nervous?"

It's not really a date anyway. I don't even know why I thought that.

Well, it is kinda like a date, but Connie's just as nervous, if that helps.

Really? She's nervous? That does make me feel a little better.

You should wear the new underwear she likes. Nine winks at me and gets off the bed.

We're not gonna sleep together, Nine.

I know. But just because you're not sleeping together or planning on being a real couple, doesn't mean you can't tease and have fun. It's kinda the whole point of living, Sweetie.

Oh my goddess, I really need to be more relaxed and chilled. It's just all this damn pressure: new friends, new house, new powers, new identity. It's . . . a lot.

I know. But hanging with us should be easy. Just go with the flow. Stop worrying so much.

Right. Okay.

I take a deep breath (well, as deep as I can without causing pain), get off the bed and go into the closet to change, choosing to take Nine's advice (not sure how good of an idea that'll be) and wear the new purple underwear, and match it with some sparkly, skull-covered pajama shorts and vest. The lace of the bra pokes over the low-cut vest, and, testing my chest and general flexibility, it seems like my wound is healing enough to wear wired bras. Fucking finally. I can see my actual cleavage in the mirror for once.

I'm going to get Dea to check on my wound tomorrow morning anyway. Haven't actually seen under the bandage myself yet, as the baths Connie's been helping with have been completely un-mirrored.

By the time I exit the closet, Nine has left, and Connie's sitting in the rocking chair in the corner. I haven't sat in it yet, but it looks comfy with all the cushions and blankets draped around it.

"Ready?" Connie stands up, wearing a matching set of pajamas to the other day, except these are pale blue and have tiny kittens on them. The Horseman of Conquest wearing pajamas with kittens on them is pretty funny, and I can't help but let a small hiccup of laughter slip at the thought.

I can't imagine these people being deadly. Well, maybe Arrie—he's pretty cold and grumbly—but I get the feeling he's got a lot on his plate, and his Horseman of War magic must make things hard for him.

Connie grabs my hand and drags me out of the door. "C'mon! This'll be fun. We're gonna eat pizza, I got Arrie to make us some of those brownies you liked, and we're just gonna listen to music and chill."

"Okay."

She leads me down a mind-boggling number of hallways and around so many corners I'm pretty sure she'll have to drop me back off at my room later.

"I have a room farthest away from everyone else because of my hearing. I never sleep otherwise."

"Do you even need to sleep?"

"Yes. But less so than the rest of you. I have more stamina, and we regenerate because of our immortality, so I only sleep once or twice a week."

"Whoa." Once or twice a week? She must be really useful on longer missions.

"You'll have cool abilities, too. Trust me. I have a good feeling about it. And Dea already thinks you're interesting; it's taking a lot for Nine not to study you like some kind of pet project." We walk down a final hallway and end up in front of a plain white door. "He's a bit of a nerd when it comes to magic."

"Really?"

"Yeah, he creates all kinds of new magical tech, various potions, and spells we use for both household things and on missions."

"What kind of missions do you guys go on exactly?"

"Hmmm. It varies."

Since she doesn't elaborate, I assume it's something she either doesn't want to really chat about tonight or something Dea prefers me not know just yet. Either way, I put the worry to the back of my mind and focus on the room that now stands in front of me as she slowly opens the door.

It's rather old fashioned, but it has a few modern touches. The high ceiling has a golden chandelier with actual candles lighting the room, and the floor-length window-wall on the far side overlooks the distant mountains to the north, and the town with its twinkling lights under the setting sun is situated not too far in between.

I really need to start looking into this realm and understanding how it works. I'll start that tomorrow.

But what's most impressive is the size of her bed. It could easily fit us all in (which is presumably why it's that big in the first place). It's a four-poster, with white silk drapes cascading down each side and a mountain of pillows arranged neatly at the head.

"Closet's through that door." She points to a door beside her bed and then to the one on the other side. "And that's the bathroom." While pointing to the double doors on the other side of the room, she says, "And that's my study and training room."

"Training room?"

"Well, my magic is more practical than the others', so my study has a desk in the corner, but it's mostly a private workout space. We do have a massive gym next to the kitchen as well."

Oh, a gym. Really? "Is there a pool here?"

She chuckles. "Yeah. One in the gym and one in the gardens." She gestures to a cute little set up of tea and pizza on a couple of poufs in the corner. "Shall we?"

"Sure." She's being more formal than usual, and I'm about to ask why when I remember what Nine said. She's nervous, too. "Err, Connie?"

"Huh?" She looks up from the pizza.

"Just be yourself and chill with me." I wink and sit on the nearest pouf, then pour myself a cup of what smells like peppermint tea.

She just laughs and takes her seat, looking a little more relaxed. "I also have other types of tea on the boudoir, if you'd like to try others."

"Oh, really?" I have become quite obsessed with the different types of tea I notice Connie drinking and am starting to feel like a Japanese cliché, what with my obvious Japanese descent to my love of tea, and how I'll be starting meditative yoga in the morning. Essh.

"Yeah. Let's get through this one first." She pours herself a cup with perfectly manicured hands. "I also have some dusted tea, if you want to really have fun."

I look at her in shock. Dusted tea, really?

"Oh my fuck, you should see your face." She snorts with laughter so hard that some tea dribbles out. "I do have dusted tea, but we won't have any today."

Oh, phew. Dusted anything is supposed to be quite bad for normal people and has severe side effects on humans. But I wonder . . . "What kind of effect does dust have on us?"

"Same as most of the magical community, but we do have to continue drinking to retain the high, since we have regenerating capabilities."

"Ah. Makes sense."

"Soooo . . . gossip. Remember. You get to unload all your problems and concerns, no matter how small, and I get all the juicy gossip in return."

"Well, Nine knows most of this stuff anyway, but sure. What do you wanna know?"

"Hmmm . . . Let's see. You obviously have a thing for Dea, which I totally get, but what about Arrie and Nine?"

"Errrm. Not really sure. Nine's really flirty, and I like the playful banter, and he looks great shirtless."

"They all do. Trust me. But not Arrie?"

"I dunno. He's a little . . . gruff with me."

"He'll melt eventually. He has a hard time handling his abilities and doesn't take change very well. But I don't really like gossiping about the others without their permission, so it's best if he tells you himself."

"That's okay." I've drained my first cup by this point and pour another while asking, "Can I ask questions, too?"

"Of course."

"It's just, you've had millennia to get to know the others. What kinds of relationships have you all had over the years? With each other, I mean. There have to be preferences, right?"

This feels weirdly easy. Like talking a good friend.

"Fair question. Feeling out of the loop a bit?"

I nod, snuggling in to listen as though she were my new favorite show.

"Okay. I'll get the obvious one out of the way. Nine and Dea have a rather sexual friendship. Dea seems to prefer men to women but has slept with both over the centuries. Because of Dea's invisibility, he finds it hard to sleep with people outside of the team."

"How so?"

"He has to concentrate to make himself visible, so it kinda ruins the vibe for him. Nine sleeps with quite a lot of people and has no preference. We all prefer magical species to humans, and Dea has never slept with a human. Nor has Arrie, I don't think."

Makes sense, since humans only partially see Dea. That would be kind of weird. I'm starting to see how the relationships work between them all.

"Arrie prefers women," Connie continues, "but Arrie and I have an . . . understanding."

I waggle my eyebrows for her to continue, which makes her giggle.

"We're both really strong and have to hold back, which is something Arrie's not great at. But with each other, sex is easier because we're pretty well-matched in strength. Also, Arrie never sleeps outside of the team."

"Ah, makes sense." Wonder why Arrie doesn't have sex with anyone outside of the team? I'm betting it has something to do with his abilities.

"We've all slept with each other at some point and will probably do so again in the future. Though we keep our relations with each other on the side. We don't really talk about them much, and we've not had group sex. I actually don't think all four of us have slept together at once before." She shrugs while in thought, as though that hasn't occurred to her before. "At least, not with more than just the two of us and other species."

"Why not? You've lived for centuries. And you're all having sex with each other anyway. What difference does it make?"

She sighs and puts her cup down. "We try to avoid anything that would cross the line of friends with benefits. The world relies on us, and if any of our drama affected that, it could have devastating consequences."

Hmmm. There's something not quite right about that to me, but I don't bother mentioning it. Dea and Nine have something more than just sex going on, even if they won't admit it to themselves, and Arrie has other issues forcing him to be more wound up.

I wonder if . . . "Can we have children?"

"Your mind works in the strangest of ways." She smiles. "But yes, we can. I haven't, though. The guys have over the years. Especially before contraception was really a thing. Not in the last couple of centuries, though."

"Did they, you know . . . stick around?"

"Sometimes. Depends. Sometimes they didn't know, in their defense. But if they could, then they did. We have a very demanding job."

"Why have you not had any children?"

"Wow. I didn't realize you had so many questions."

"Sorry." I look to the floor, embarrassment coloring my features. "If you'd rather not answer any of my questions, you don't have to."

"Nah, it's all right. With the guys, they don't have to actually have any of their children live here. If I had a child, it would be raised here. With all of us. That would be . . ."

"A bit strange?"

She nods but looks away.

"Would you like children?"

"I dunno. What about you?"

"Not sure either. Maybe. Someday." I get up to browse her tea collection. She has over twenty different types of tea on a shelf above the boudoir behind us, all lined up perfectly in a neat little row. I browse past jasmine, rose, and caramel, and land on citrus blast. Holding it up, I ask, "This one?"

"Sure." She grabs it and starts putting the leaves in the silver pot's strainer and pours more hot water from a steaming jug that I'm not sure how stays hot.

Grabbing the pizza, I try a few slices—all different flavors—and groan when I find one I love. Pepperoni.

"Any other questions?" She smiles at me, and I get the feeling she's genuinely happy to answer them.

"Not sure." I have a ton of inappropriate ones, like what they are all like in bed, but I think better of asking. She's been generous so far.

I'm suddenly reminded of Nine's rule—don't fuck the servants—and think to ask but also don't want to intrude.

"What is it?"

I give her a look of confusion, wondering how she knew.

"It's written all over your face," she says through a smile.

"Well, Nine mentioned something but told me to ask you."

She raises her eyebrows. "What's the ass-rat been saying about me now?"

I smile. "Well, he mentioned the rule of don't have sex with the servants, and—"

"Ugh, that story." She rolls her eyes. "Okay. Okay. It's a fair one, I guess." She settles into the back of her chair and begins. "About three hundred years into living here, we began to employ servants to help keep the house clean, and I took a fancy to one of the Shifters—tortoise Shifter. His name was Manfred. He was really sweet." She sighs for a moment on a pause before continuing. "We had a summer fling, and I thought that was all he wanted, but I was wrong. Since he was around the house all the time, it was . . . different than usual."

"He fell for you, didn't he?"

She nods with downcast eyes and bright pink cheeks. "I didn't mean for it to happen. So I sent him away, made sure he had enough money for a while, and sacked him to make things easier. But he refused to leave. In the end, Dea had to have him escorted off the premises by the local army—no police back then."

Nine was right; it is a little funny. But that poor man . . .

"Well, then . . ." Connie places her hands on her knees, clearly wanting to change the topic. "Now that I've told that humiliating story, I have another question for you."

I nod while sipping my tea.

"If you're so attracted to them, especially Dea, then why not just sleep with them? Nine is actually a really loving person."

"Really?" I shake my head, feeling stupid for even asking. "I just . . . It doesn't feel right."

"What doesn't?"

"Sex for the sake of it. If I slept with one of you . . . I don't know. It just feels wrong to me. The way you live your emotional lives doesn't feel right. I can't really describe it, since I don't have any values or even a moral standing. Sorry."

"It's okay." She kneels next to me, her braids being pushed behind her in the process.

"I get it." She leans over and whispers in my ear, "I heard what Nine said. And since you're taking his advice on the underwear"—she leans down, taking in my new cleavage-on-show look—"I don't mind the teasing and the games." She winks, and to prove her point, she lightly brushes her lips just below my ear, sending a shiver throughout my body.

I turn my head and want nothing more than to press my lips to hers and see if they're as smooth as they look, but instead I settle for a lingering kiss to her cheek, watching her blush slightly.

She leans back and smiles at me, clearly pleased with herself for some reason. "Let's put some music on."

"Sure."

She presses a button on a control panel in the wall that I didn't notice earlier, and a light piano tune trickles over the soundstrip running around the room's ceiling perimeter. An electric-blue strip lights up the system's soundstrip, and I sway along to the pleasant tune.

"C'mon!" She grabs my hand and places my tea back on the table. "Let's dance."

The music changes to a more upbeat pop song with a click of a button, and she gets on the bed and dances and jumps around like a teenager. Her braids fly everywhere, and her smile grows wider when she sees me laughing.

"You look ridiculous!"

"Only because you haven't joined me!" Her braids fly in the air as she jumps. "I've never done this before!"

The volume turns up via the controller in Connie's hand, and she helps me onto the bed, where I try to keep up with her antics, jumping around and dancing to the silly pop music. It's the most relaxed I've been since I got here, and maybe this friendship is something I need. Something normal. Well, normal isn't really a thing here, but normalish.

In true sleepover style, I actually sleep over in her room—which, yes, is as awkward as it sounds, but is actually kinda fun, too. We dance, talk, eat pizza, and do each other's hair —a totally girly night. She gives me some great skincare advice and even lets me borrow her special conditioner. Mango scented. Just like her. Mmmmm.

Light creeps through a crack in the curtains, and I groan. It's already dawn. Shit. I wanted to start yoga today.

Grumbling, I untangle myself from her arms, which have wrapped themselves around my waist in the middle of the night. I'm careful not to wake her, but a knock at the door makes all my efforts in vain.

"Whaaat?" Connie complains.

"Have you seen Angel? I wanted to check on her healing progress. Hoping to take off the bandages today and clear her for training."

Connie looks at me, and both of our faces flush with embarrassment. "Err. Yeah, she's in here." She gives me an apologetic look but shrugs. "Don't worry about it."

Dea opens the door and stands there smiling. It's so similar to Nine's usually smug face that I almost want to punch it.

"What do you want?" I'm tired. Grouchy. And hungry. So sue me. We stayed up late chatting last night, and although it was fun, I'm now seeing the downside.

"To check on your healing. But if you ladies are busy, I can come back later." He waggles his eyebrows at us.

Connie chucks a pillow at his face. "Stop being a rat-assed bitch!"

I get up, smiling at him, and lift my top. "Well, you wanted to check."

He stands there for a moment, a little dazed, and comes over. "I will need you to remove your top and bra. Sorry. It is important, though. If I can see how the damage has healed, then I can clear you for training."

"Well, I can do everything normally now and can exercise for short bursts." I carefully take my top and bra off, noticing both Connie's and Dea's eyes stuck like glue to my every movement.

I stand in front of them, naked from the waist up, while they stare at my chest, and I would be lying if I said I didn't feel terrified, but I'm also a little excited by the slight hint of heat in both their gazes.

"It is completely healed." Dea sounds astounded. "You have remarkable healing capabilities, Angel." He places a hand on the spot where the wound used to be and allows his magic to suffocate the area, sending a warm tingle through that side of my chest. "I will keep doing this twice a day until the inside is completely healed, but that should not take more than a couple of days. You are cleared for light training." He points a finger at Connie. "Light."

"Yes, boss." She mockingly salutes him while standing to attention. "Light."

"Training today or tomorrow, Angel?"

I shove my bra and top back on. "Today." I don't explain to them that I want to feel useful and powerful, like I belong on the team, but I get the feeling they already know.

"Okay. We will all meet for lunch in a couple hours, then Nine and I will start magic training with you in the afternoon."

We all stand here in silence for a moment, Connie and I looking at Dea, waiting for him to leave. It takes him a second to get the message, but when he does, he leaves with a chuckle.

"Ugh. Is being just friends such a big deal around here?"

Connie walks up to me, a smile lingering in her blue eyes, and grabs my hands in hers. "We're all friends."

"I meant—"

"I know. I'm just teasing, silly." But she doesn't move.

I get the feeling she's waiting for something . . . But what?

She moves her hands around to my lower back and embraces me in another hug, this time a little tighter. "We promised to always be open and just chat about things," she whispers in my ear. "So, I kinda want a kiss goodbye." She isn't looking at me, but I just know by the inflection of her voice that tries to cut off before she can finish the entire sentence that she's embarrassed.

Would it be that big of a deal? Nine said fun is fine, even if it leads nowhere. Well, Connie and I nearly kissed yesterday anyway, so I don't think it would be a big deal if things progress. She knows I don't want a friends with benefits kind of relationship. And Nine said fun and teasing is okay. He said that, right? I'm not just making that up.

Clearly, I don't decide quick enough for Conquest, because she grabs my wrists and pulls me to the bed, spins us around, and lightly throws me onto the mattress. "I'm not used to waiting for others to make a move. So, if you really don't want me to kiss you, then just say no."

Her sudden dominant nature shines through those usually gentle eyes, which are now a deeper shade of green, and I think this might be how she is with Arrie. The thought of her with any of the others has me squirming to release the tension building up at my core, and she notices, too, as a wide, predatory smile leaps across her face.

She straddles my waist, and my heart rate speeds up. Nine's words echo in my thoughts: Isn't that the whole point of living? To have fun. To take what we want. Especially from a group of friends who understands and doesn't mind either way.

Taking a deep, shaky breath, I grab her thighs and run my hands up the insides, tracing fingertips against her smooth, creamy skin and watching her shudder, hopefully showing her exactly what I want.

Her smile turns sultry, those delicious corners of her lips turning up enough to make her dimples appear, and that breathtaking beauty turns into a heat that flares her eyes a deep sea green. Leaning down and placing her hands either side of my head, she traces a finger along my jaw, making my breath hitch, before her thumb brushes across my lips, and I blow out a frustrated breath.

Is she going to kiss me or not? Goddess, I just want her to touch me.

The patience she's using and the time she's taking are killing me. I'm a bundle of nerves and heat and molten puddles, and I'm pretty sure I will have to take a cold shower after this.

She's really going to kiss me. She leans closer to my face, but then she pulls back, looking down at me with a genuinely curious smile and whispers, "You're beautiful."

I can't take my eyes off of her pink lips, wondering when they will reach mine. Impatience bubbles closer to the surface, and before I know it, the need to kiss this beautiful woman overtakes every rational thought, and I grab a fistful of her pajama top and yank her face to mine.

Our lips connect, and that tingling sensation her every touch has caused since I got here explodes throughout my body, making me want to feel every inch of her smooth skin against mine.

Her lips move slowly with mine, in tandem with my uncertainty, but that insecurity flies farther out the window as the seconds tick by, and her lips press harder against mine. I want more—more of her, of our lips together, of her breathes mingling with mine—and a frenzied urgency fills me as I crash harder into her, nipping her bottom lip open in a gasp.

She rips my hands off of her thighs and yanks them above my head, pinning me beneath her.

Her lips steel everything from me—my breath, my rationality, my worry over whether this is a good idea—and I meet her with equal fervor. Her hips shift against mine, and I can't help but respond. I wiggle my fingers free from her grip, return them to her thighs, and inch my fingers closer to the edge of her shorts, feeling her skin cool against the heat of my touch.

She groans against my mouth and breaks away, gasping for breath, and whispers, "Fuck. I've wanted to do that since our moment in your closet."

"Me . . . too," I say between heaving breaths.

Now the moment has dissipated, that worry and anxiety creep back in, and a million concerns shoot across my mind at once.

Is it weird now?

Was the kiss okay?

Does she hate me?

What will Nine and Dea think?

Oh my goddess, I have morning breath!

"Relax." She releases me from her impossibly strong grip and sits up. "I'm happy to spend the next millennia stealing nothing but kisses from you. Especially if they're like that."

Relief washes through me.

"I get that casual sex isn't your thing. Everything we do, as friends or otherwise, is completely up to you."

Suddenly, everything clicks into place. She held back because she wanted me to be sure. She wanted me to take what I want and just admit it to myself. And goddess damn it, I want her. I have no idea if I was lesbian or bisexual or something else in my human life, but in this life, this woman drives me damn crazy.

Lunch is an assortment of sandwich stuff; simple, but it allows me to try lots of different sandwiches and ingredients. Simple ham and cheese is sooo good, but so is egg mayo. (Have you ever had a marshmallow sandwich? They are divine. If there's a god, he definitely created marshmallow sandwiches.)

"Here, Sweetie, try a PB&J." Nine hands me a single-slice sandwich with ingredients I barely recognize.

"A what?" I ask as I take it from his hands.

"Peanut butter and jelly. It's an American thing. They're pretty tasty."

Taking a bite out of the fluffy white bread with a gooey filling, I don't have a weird immortal allergy to peanuts. But I don't, and that sandwich is the king of all sandwiches, evident by the fact that Arrie and Nine are smiling while Dea and Connie are frowning. Seems we have a PB&J battle on our hands, and I've just tipped the scale.

Making myself another half sandwich (only halves so I can have four or five different fillings), Dea coughs to get everyone's attention. "I have cleared Angel for training, but she needs to take the physical stuff easy for another couple of days."

Connie smiles.

Nine practically bounces in his seat, hands slamming down on the table. "Ohmigod, does that mean I get to watch and see what kind of magic our sweet thing has? I wonder if you'll be able to do something similar to Dea? Oh, or maybe you'll have actual power over life and death? No, that seems a bit op, even for us . . ." He speaks for, like, thirty seconds without taking a breath.

Dea shoots Nine a look, and he snaps his mouth shut. "I have another announcement, one I have kept quiet until now because I did not want everyone freaking out." He pauses, looking a little unsure of himself.

It's a look I haven't seen on him before, and I'll admit it unsettles me enough to put mysandwhich down (I know, I'm shocked, too).

"I cannot find Angel's seal."

Silence fills the room as everyone stops eating and stares at Dea as though he's announced the end of the fucking world, then the table explodes into a flurry of questions, shouting, and flying hands all at once.

I don't get it. "What do you mean?"

Nine looks at me with worry creasing his eyes, and I know this isn't going to be good. "Remember, our seals are the only thing that can actually kill us. We all have ours hidden away, as they turned up here in this house with us. But yours—"

"Is missing," I finish for him. Fuck.

"Well," Dea starts, "not missing. Missing implies we lost it. It actually just never turned up."

But that doesn't make sense. "So, it could be around somewhere? Right?"

Dea looks at me and grins. "Yes. And I wanted your permission to check your library. It is huge, and it could be in there somewhere."

Nine frowns. "But . . . all of ours just popped up in our faces. They weren't hidden anywhere." His fists clench and unclench as his skin turns paler.

No one seems to have any more questions, and we all sit in silence, finishing lunch, as the danger of the situation wells the tension in the room. Now and then, one of them looks at me with worry or confusion, and I just know they're thinking about my seal.

With a small tap on the table, Dea breaks the silence. "I want Con to ask around on Earth. Few people know about our seals. Ask if they have seen one. Do not mention it is Angel's or even bring her into conversation."

Connie frowns at him. "Why not send Nine? He's much better at interrogation."

Nine shakes his head. "Nope. Not happening. I want to be here for her initial training, so I know what magic she possesses."

Dea chuckles in that deep, throaty way of his. "Yes. I doubt I could get him out of the house while she is training."

"Damn straight!" Nine slaps the table and grabs the last slice of bread, most likely to make another PB&J. "Think of all the cool notes I can take, all the new groundbreaking magic she'll probably possess . . ."

"Okay, okay." Connie raises her hands in defeat. "Looks like it's me, then. I'll leave this afternoon." She looks at me and smiles. "Try not to freak out over anything while I'm gone."

The emphasis on the word anything tells me everything she's trying to imply: do not worry about the kiss.

The memory of her lips and the glimpse of her desire brush the edges of my mind, causing my face to heat like an inferno and Nine to choke on his sandwich.

I laugh and place a hand on his back. "Sorry. I'd say don't choke, but what's the point? It's not like it'll kill you."

Dea raises his eyebrows at me. "Did our Angel just make a joke?"

I shrug and get up to fit in some yoga before Nine and Dea probably spend the entire afternoon pissing me off. It's inevitable. They'll try to get me to use my magic, I'm not going to be able to, and I'll get frustrated with their pushy, excitable nonsense.

I just know it.

Half an hour later, yoga mat in hand, workout gear on, and hair pinned back, I'm ready to find the perfect spot. Somewhere in the sunny garden would be nice—breathing in the fresh air, overlooking the tranquility, inhaling the scent of grass and flowers and beauty . . . Somewhere relaxing.

It's time I take a leaf out of Arrie's book and aim for peace, just like his odd dance/yoga/stretch workout thing.

The sun shines brightly on the fairy garden, and I briefly wonder whether it does anything more than be sunny in this realm. Surely food would have difficulty growing? Ugh. I really need to learn more about *Sheruta* when I next get the chance.

I wander along the paths, hopping over toadstools and ducking under rose bushes, careful to avoid any fairy dens that might suck me in with their curiosity and exquisite magic. People have been known to lose their lives in those dens, forever breathing in the dust that permeates a fairy's air until they wither and rot.

I'm looking for a perfect place to relax, somewhere that overlooks the garden and brings me peace—but what in particular I'm looking for, I don't know. The curse of not really knowing yourself, I guess.

It's getting a little old and confusing, and I'm starting to feel like I'm in Wonderland. *Sheruta* is amazing, but I feel like one wrong footstep or one misplaced word will get me killed—forever doomed to look out at the beauty I can never be a part of.

Connie's words echo across my mind—I'm happy to spend the next millennia stealing nothing but kisses from you—and I smile. It doesn't matter if I want friendship, something more, or something in between because she just wants to spend time with me.

A familiar deep rumble fills my ears and splits across the ground, and my thoughts of Connie in those sexy pajama shorts all but dissipate into the depths of my subconscious. I run to follow the sound, hoping beyond hope that the house really has done what I think it has.

I reach the edge of the rainbow forest, with the horse paddock in the distance, but in front of me lies a hill I'm pretty sure didn't exist before.

Damn. The house really listens to me. On top of the hill is a small *Shinto* shrine. This one doesn't look to be used for the normal sacred purpose, but it overlooks the entire valley.

Climbing up the hill, I eventually reach the top and step inside. Cushions of all different shades of gold line one side, while the gaps in the walls all around the shrine allow me to look as far as the ocean, mountains, the local town, and back of the house. I can see everything from here. The whole of *Sheruta*.

Turns out I don't need the yoga mat after all, so I set it down at the entrance and grab a cushion instead. I want to start with breathing exercises, to ease myself in and make sure I don't cause any further damage. I'm pretty much healed, but I know if I push too hard it could set me back weeks.

Breathing in, breathing out, all I think about is my new life. I'm supposed to be thinking about nothing, but that is unlikely given the circumstances.

I spend nearly two hours running through various stretches and poses, losing my mind down one rabbit hole and into the next. But I let it wander wherever it wants to go, allowing it to worry, cry, and laugh at the insanity of my new life, and by the time I finish, I feel calm again. Like a refreshed version of me.

Yup. Definitely doing this every morning. Especially if my life will be crazy for the next few thousand years. I mean, I guess I have a magical war to diffuse somehow.

That is not a good thought, so I shove it to the back of my mind as I head to the kitchen for another cup of coffee. That shit is the best stuff ever. I don't care how addicted that makes me. I'll take all the positive stuff I can right now.

"Ready, Angel?" Dea stands in the doorway as I stand at the kitchen counter drinking my coffee. He's shirtless—again—and that swirling gold tattoo catches my eye.

"Dea?" I involuntarily step toward him, forcing my hands to my sides so I don't touch that swirling, gorgeous body of his.

"Yes?"

"What's your tattoo about? I mean, I've never seen one like that before. That I know of."

He chuckles and reaches to grab my hand. Placing it on the top of the tattoo that swirls around his shoulder, he says, "It is actually a Shifter tattoo, and I got it after a good friend of mine died."

"Wow. I mean, er . . . I'm sorry."

He shakes his head. "Do not be. It was a long time ago. He died in battle, as a Shifter should."

Part of me wonders if this person was just a friend or something more, but I refrain from asking anything that will sound too pushy. Connie will probably know, but she doesn't like gossiping about the guys so probably won't tell me.

"Well," I start, "let's get this over with."

Dea leads the way to my room and asks me to open the library door, carefully observing me from the corner of his eye. "Nervous?"

"No shit." We enter, Nine having followed once we passed his rooms, and start searching for a good magical space. "So, we should find somewhere perfect, right?"

"I am hoping so," Dea says. "Both Arrie and Connie have training rooms in their study because their abilities are so active."

We go to my study area, hoping to find something nearby, but come up empty.

"Oh, there's an artefact room somewhere over there and a door at the end. Haven't had the chance to look in there yet."

Nine smiles, jumps to his feet from where he sits at my desk, and says, "Let's go!" He grabs my hand and drags me down aisle after aisle, occasionally stopping to ask me directions.

"Here we are." I let out a sigh, glad I don't have to continue running, and look around. There are objects on pedestals, behind locked glass doors and on various shelves, none of which I recognize. Unlike my study area, this is a lot like the rest of my library—full of color—but it has a certain old-world feel to it that the rest doesn't have.

What are all those artifacts?

We really do need to do an inventory check of this place at some point because some of those items are valuable magical artifacts that are pretty powerful.

I'm beginning to suspect what kind of Horseman I am. But rather than voice it in my head, giving Nine the answer, I keep it quiet.

The door at the back of the artifact section is locked, and I'm not really sure why. Only

I can get in there, right? Why the fuck would it be locked? Stupid library of wonders. Nothing's ever simple around here. I try the handle a few more times and groan in frustration. "What now?"

Dea steps up and places a hand on my shoulder. "It probably recognizes your magical signature. The door to the library does the same thing, but it looks for you. This time, you need to send your magical signature into the door."

Oookay. Cause that doesn't sound like something out of a fairy tale at all. I'm not sure what I'm doing, but I place my hand on the door and take a deep breath, imagining my energy and life reaching out of my palm and layering itself around the door. That's what they do in all the storybooks, right?

A clunking sound snaps my eyes open, and shock takes hold of my mind.

"Whoa."

I'm not sure which one of them says it, but it makes me my breath hitch in my throat, and for a moment, I fail to remember how to breathe. The door swirls in blue, red, green, and milky-white tendrils of magic, with a spiderweb of inky blackness threading through every strand.

"Wh-what is that?"

Dea doesn't touch me, but he steps into my peripheral. "It is your magical signature, and I think I know what you are."

"Really?"

"Yes. But let us all get inside."

I open the creaky door to find a cold, dark, stone-like room beyond. It isn't anything special.

Nine flicks a switch behind me, and the room lights up with those strange, annoying buzzy lights you find in hospitals and other corporate buildings. Safe to say, this is not my favorite room. The light is too bright, hurting my sensitive eyes, and the buzzing is like a drill in my already busy mind.

Spinning around to get a good look, I nearly trip over my own feet in shock. Weapons. Targets. Dummies. This place is a murderer's playground. There are racks of varying types of knives in the corner, matching a set of targets on the other side of the room. Dummies and swords lie in the other corner, with punching bags and weights dotted around the room at various intervals. Gray stone slabs the perimeter wall, and the floor consists of the same grubby-looking grayness. "What kind of room is this?"

Nine goes to look at the various swords and knives on display, while Dea looks in a set of drawers and then on the shelves dotting the room.

"This stuff looks used. Not brand new." Nine brings me a knife and shows me the scuff marks and scratches.

"Stun guns. Magiguns. Magic-dampening cuffs. A magic blocker," Dea lists as he rifles through various objects. "All with some kind of wear and tear." He turns to me with curious eyes. "Seems this is your stuff. From when you were human."

I stumble, and my jaw hits the floor. How is that possible? What did I do as a human? "I-I-I . . ." I don't know what to say.

"There are magic blockers in this room's walls, meaning we can practice here and not risk burning down the library." Nine comes up behind me and wraps his arms around my waist, pulling me into him. "It's okay. It doesn't matter who you were, only who you will become."

But it does matter! How many people . . . things . . . have I killed?

"None. Because you aren't human anymore. You died and were reborn."

But-but-but—

"But nothing, Sweetie. We're not going to judge. Though I am curious. I'll admit."

"That makes two of us," Dea adds, coming to stand in front of me.

"Three." I want to know. Even if I hate it, I have to know. "So, Dea, you said you might know what I am?" Change the subject. Fuck! Please change the subject.

"Yes. I have a feeling you are the Horseman of Magic. Those colors on the door are indicative of a particular type of magic: elemental. Strong Witches possess elemental magic—"

"Right. They usually have an affinity for just one, though." This is information I already know somehow, and it makes me question who I was on Earth because knowledge of Witches is not common among humans, or anyone, really. They stayed in hiding, even after the other three main supernatural species came out of the closet.

"Uh-huh. But those black bits were the Angel magic we saw the other day."

Nine pulls back and gasps. "It kinda sounds like . . ."

"I know," Dea says.

"What! What does it sound like!?"

"Sorry, Sweetie. It looks really similar to an Angel-descended Witch."

That . . . makes a lot of sense. Thought it would freak me out, but it doesn't. Or if it does, I'm still in shock and will likely freak out later. Seems to be my thing. "So, what does that mean?"

"When an Angel's power mixes with a Witch's, a unique form of magic occurs. Witches can use the magical essence in the atmosphere given off by the leylines. Angels have power over life and death at a single touch. When mixed, they can, in rare cases, form a sort of death-wielding magic, where the Witch can use magical essence to create a literal tendril of death, killing whoever it touches."

Nine continues Dea's explanation, "Most species can mix, and their magic forms a collected kind of supernatural. The only reason they don't is because it's frowned upon to mix bloodlines by most supes, so they usually only breed with their own species."

"But what about the genetics of it all?" The main communities of magic, I have learned recently—Witches, Vampires, Shifters, and Fae—are all opposites and sit as the four main supernatural communities, keeping the balance of magic in place. How they interact is really specific and follows an annoyingly complex set of laws and inter-species rules.

"Right," Nine continues. "I did say most can mix. Not all. The four main communities can only mix in certain ways: Witches and Fae cannot breed together to form a mix, for example, and if they do breed, it forms one or the other because of how they use their magic."

I throw him a questioning look. I haven't gotten this far in my reading, and it seems I didn't know this when I was human.

Nine sighs and rubs the back of his neck. "Fae use leylines to charge their magic, then use it in all kinds of ways, but they need to stay near the leylines or regularly revisit them.

On the other hand, Witches can access the magical essence given off by the leylines. It's a weaker form of magic, but it's so ingrained in Earth's atmosphere that they never run out."

"And Vampires use magic to enhance their external form." Dea grabs my shoulders, clearly trying to steady my spinning mind. "In turned Vampires, this is done in the form of super strength and speed, but in royals and highborn Vampires, this also gives way to their various abilities. On the other hand, Shifters use internal magic to change their internal environment, causing them to shift. It does give them some enhanced strength, but it is nothing compared to a Vampire."

I nod, absorbing all this information. "So, theoretically, a Vampire could breed with a Witch?"

Nine nods but looks a little put off by the idea. "Only born Vamps have the ability to breed, but yes. I'm unsure if anything like that exists, though. Vampires usually inbreed, and if they do mix up the genetics more, it's usually to create some kind of unique ability among the highborns."

Remind me not to get involved in Vampire politics. Sounds like a whole other world.

Nine claps his hands behind me, causing me to jump. "Let's get started."

"Right." Dea steps back, handing a plasmascreen to Nine. "Nine is just observing, offering his expertise in the theory of magic, but I will do the actual training."

Why is Dea always shirtless? That golden swirling tattoo is the most distracting thing I've ever witnessed. Fuck. Remind me not to have both Connie and Dea in their pajamas in the same room as me, because I'm pretty sure I'd melt into a puddle.

Nine snorts from behind me. *Tell me about it.*

I giggle at his antics as Dea looks at us with suspicion. "I want to know what kind of magic you have access to. Clearly death and elemental magic, but what else?"

"How do we find that out?"

"You need to release your magic so we can see for ourselves."

Even if I knew how to do that, wouldn't that be potentially dangerous?

"We can't die," Nine so helpfully reminds me from his spot at the only desk in the room. "So, no. No danger here."

"I don't know how to do that. Before, I was just angry or trying to show what I am, like with the door." I look to the floor, hoping not to see their looks of disappointment at my failure.

Dea steps forward, grabbing both my hands in his, and looks me straight in the eyes with those dancing galaxy eyes of his. "When we are accessing our magic to do something more active, like when I am moving a soul or Nine is delving deep into someone's mind, we are entering a deep part of our mind, a part we do not use otherwise."

Kind of like meditation, then. Okay. I can do that. Taking a deep breath, I sit on the floor with my legs crossed and my back straight. Relax. Access a part of my mind I would otherwise ignore. But what part?

I know so little about myself. There's the part of my mind that loves trying new things, that loves books, that has trouble sleeping, that is reminded of her past in horrible ways, and then there's the part of my mind that gets stuck on things and worries about everything, that unhelpfully ogles a bunch of people—friends?—I have no intention of getting involved with . . . But what part do I not access?

"You're thinking too literally, Sweetie." Nine comes up behind me, passing the plasmascreen to Dea and places both hands on my shoulders. "Relax a little and just explore. Where does your curiosity lead when you think of your magic?"

My magic? Like when I nearly hurt Dea in the kitchen when I got mad at him? Well, that just leads me to self-loathing. How can I see in the dark? What about the door? I have all four types of elemental magic then, but that's not possible for any known Witch.

Not a Witch, I remind myself. A Horseman of the Apocalypse.

"Ugh! I just don't know." I slam my fist on the concrete floor in frustration and wince. "I'm sorry."

Dea sighs and kneels in front of me. "It is okay."

"Err, guys?" Nine stands at my side in shock. "What's that?"

"What's what?" I ask as I look to where his eyes fixate—on my fist punched into the floor. The concrete floor. I have created a dent in the concrete floor. "That . . . that was me?"

Nine smiles triumphantly "Strength. You're strong. Arrie'll freak."

Dea smiles at something I'm clearly out of the loop with while Nine makes various notes on the plasmascreen he steals back from Dea. "Nine," Dea says, "you will have to help her access her magic for the time being. We just need to see what we are dealing with. Then we can work on helping her access it herself."

Nine nods. "Sweetie," he says as he turns to my front, stepping in front of Dea, "this won't be pleasant. I need your permission to delve into your mind and search with you."

"Of course," I reply without hesitation. When did I become so trusting? Will he see the nightmares and flashbacks?

Nine gives me a puzzled look, like he heard that thought and it's news to him.

Well, I've been trying hard to hide them.

"C'mon," Nine says as helps me into a standing position.

He grabs my hands and takes a deep breath as I let out a pained gasp. I can feel something putting pressure on my mind, like an odd weight squeezing at my emotions as it shifts around my thoughts and memories. He pauses for a moment on the hot make-out session with Connie, and then again on the way I stared at a shirtless Dea when he came to the library for the first time, and I briefly think I hear a chuckle in the distance, but before I can grasp onto that sound and decipher what it is, I'm dragged away again into distant thoughts and memories I have all but forgotten over the past week.

We sail around my mind, past so many misted sections I can only assume are memories from my human life, before stopping.

"We're here, I think," I hear Nine's voice echo across my mind in a weird, almost-cosmic way.

Here is an empty space, somewhere only bright magic permeates. In the center, on some kind of mental pedestal, sits a ball of power; I can feel its magical essence and powerful strength pulsing through the space.

Everywhere is pitch black, with rivulets of red running around in various ribbonlike streams across the space. "What are those?"

Nine remains silent, and for a moment, I think he might not even be here with me, but a quick glance to my right tells me he is. He stands there in all his usual geeky hotness and just stares at the space. "I've not seen this before."

Great. The magic expert is stuck.

Nine jabs me in the arm and looks mockingly offended. "Put your hand on that ball of power."

I do as he says, assuming he likely won't let me out of this mental space until I do, but as I touch it, relief flows through me in such bounds I can feel the tears flowing freely down my cheeks and my shaky arms reaching out to grab at something that no longer exists.

We're back in the dank training room, and Dea sits watching us with equal shock and amazement on his face.

The first thing I remember feeling is excruciating pain, as painful as it is wonderful, an odd, heady mixture that sends my body spasming to the ground in a rough heap.

"Angel!"

Screams pierce my ears, so intent on their journey into my soul that I only vaguely recognize them as mine, and I realize that pain can be felt in every inch of my body.

Opening my eyes, I see Dea in front of me, his body pressing up against mine in an effort to cuddle me, and I briefly feel Nine doing the same from behind, though I have no idea why.

What are they doing?

"We're trying to comfort you," Nine says with amusement.

"Oh," I think I try to say, not really knowing if it comes out as intended.

The pain is subsiding, though, and I can feel the pulse of magic in its place, a power threading throughout my body that I can tap into anytime I want.

"Whoa . . ." Dea steps back, propped up in the air by some kind of wind current.

My wind current. I'm doing that.

"Aha!" Nine exclaims from behind me. "Air magic. Excellent." He lets go of me, presumably to write more notes down, and I fall to the floor once more, weakness engulfing my every limb.

Exhaustion clings to every part of me, and I can barely keep my eyes open. "I just need to rest for a min . . ."

Strong arms pick me up and cradle me against a strong, bare chest. A brief glimpse of swirling gold strikes my vision as I let out a sigh of contentment. Dea. One day, Dea will be mine. But until then, I'll just bask in his radiance as he carries me to my room.

Just as that insane thought flits across my mind, I droop into the drowsiness of sleep, and emptiness suffocates me as not a single dream or nightmare plagues my mind for the first time since waking up immortal.

In a cruel twist of irony I don't see coming, everything hurts the next morning. I just healed from my injuries, and now I'm back to aching all over—again.

I fucking hate that stupid Horseman of Famine right now. I bet it wouldn't have hurt so much if I did it naturally. No one told me it would be quite that painful. Fucking a-holes!

"I heard that," a familiar, traitorous voice calls from the doorway as I struggle to do up my boots.

"Good." Let me make it easier for you to understand my current mood, Nine. You're a lying, pig-smelling, ungrateful, son of a—

Nine grabs my arm and pinwheels me into a bone-crushing hug, forgoing the laces that are only half tied. "I'm so glad you're okay."

I look up at him to see genuine relief in his eyes. He's really been worried? But why?

Because I like you. You're family now.

Family . . . The word sounds so unfamiliar. I try to roll it around my tongue, but it gets stuck.

"Come, let's get some breakfast."

Breakfast, it turns out, is a rather grand affair. Even for this strange, magical household. Platters of cheeses, breads, biscuits, cakes, and what can only be . . . bacon. The smell reminds me of a breakfast bar I used to visit, and I smile at the familiarity.

Pancakes, bacon, and maple syrup—best breakfast yet.

"So," Dea starts, "elemental magic, most likely all four types given the rainbow color of her Witch powers. And Angel death magic."

Nine shifts uncomfortably in his seat, like he's avoiding bringing something else up, and I suddenly remember what he said in my mental landscape thing: I've not seen this before.

He hasn't seen anything like my magical landscape, meaning I'm something different, but so far, my magic is something that already exists.

Something's not adding up.

Dea interrupts my spiraling—as the team have so lovingly taken to calling my mental chatter—but Nine stops him with a quick wave of his hand.

"Training's at one, right?" I look at Dea, who just nods and gazes a hole in my back my entire journey out the kitchen archway and up the stairs.

The familiar scent of broken pages and endless knowledge greets my nostrils, and I feel an inebriant sense of calm upon walking into my library. The longer I spend here, the more at home I feel, and that terrifies me. But for now, I take the long journey to my desk and start asking question after question about *Sheruta* and the house, about what kind of people live here and how this strange realm works.

It's the most complete I've felt in mind and soul in a long while, as every question is answered with some kind response and I learn more than I ever thought possible in a single few hours of study.

Seems I'm pretty good at the whole studying thing, which surprises even me, but I'm less great at the whole using magic thing, which doesn't surprise me.

Half an hour until Dea and Nine are due to show up, I find myself trying to manipulate the air to create a cool breeze—but to no avail. I do manage a quick flick of the wrist to bring a book toward me, though, which is some kind of progress, I guess.

Sighing, I stand and make my way to the murderer's room (that's the only way I really catalogue what's going on with my human past right now), once again noticing how stupidly dark and dank this one room is compared to everything else I've been given by the house. It's like a literal representation of the darkness behind the colorful persona.

One day, that darkness is going come into the light.

One day, I'm not going to be me anymore.

Three knives in my left hand, four in my right, one sailing through the air for the twentieth time—and like the other nineteen times, it hits dead center.

Flashes of memory upon memory feed my naked mind—knives buried in various body parts, a hundred different types of targets, all with bullseyes stabbed dead center, and I can't help but whimper as I look over all the weapons once again. "What am I?"

Two. Three. Four. Five. Five. Six. Seven. Dead center. From every angle, from every maneuver I can think of. Not one is even an inch off the mark.

"Well, well, well . . . Seems we have a trained killer in our ranks." Arrie walks down the steps, his words making me wince. "You know, we've been a part of the supernatural community before the term community was even coined, and I'm finding it hard to believe Fate gave us someone who is so obviously trained to kill us."

"I can't kill you, Arrie, so fuck off." I don't even know what else to say to someone like him. He's so . . . Arrie.

"The magical community, I mean."

"You could just as easily kill them, you know." I pick all the knives out of the targets and return to my throwing position.

Arrie grumbles something unintelligible under his breath—something I'm pretty sure isn't English—and leaves.

One. Two. Three. Four . . . Fuck! He's right. Of course he's damn right. Why did Fate choose me? I'm clearly not the best choice here. I bet the magical community will hate me when I try to prevent a war, not to mention how many of them I've probably killed in my time as human.

Nine winces as he comes into the room, watching me throw the daggers perfectly every time. Great. Another Arrie reaction.

"What did he say to you?" Nine's fists ball into spheres of tension as he barely moves from the spot.

I don't dignify him with a response.

"What. Did. He. Say?"

I shove the memory at him, not really caring to repeat it out loud.

Nine gasps and throws himself out of the door, running to some unseen goal he has in mind.

Me? I honestly don't care what he does. I stop and look around the room for a moment, noticing Dea leaning up against a wall. "Can we just get this fucking over with?"

He nods, coming forward to meet me in the center of the room. "Concentrate on that wind element for now. Try to grasp it and move the air a little."

Since I practiced grabbing books earlier, I'm fairly certain I can manage that. And it's a great distraction from my spiraling thoughts.

Imagining I'm grabbing something nonexistent in the near distance, I try moving the air to create a ripple, but for a moment, everything remains static, as though I have no magic whatsoever.

Whoosh!

Dea's hair is suddenly askew as a gust of wind bats his face, and he makes a surprised yelping sound I didn't expect.

"Good." He moves behind me, redoing his hair and facing us both toward the targets. "Now try grabbing a knife and throwing it at the target."

My eyebrows rise in surprised excitement. I can see where he's going with this; he wants me to combine my gifts to create various skills and maneuvers. Combat maneuvers.

Excitement bubbles through me before I can even begin to question why I'm excited about something so violent. Being able to defend myself, actually having some skills to do the job I've been summoned for—even though we're not totally sure what that is yet—and being useful to the team . . . It's something I didn't realize I wanted so badly. Until now.

I throw myself into training that day. I use air magic to throw daggers at targets (much harder than doing it by hand); alter my aim trajectory to better hit my target, especially moving ones; hurl spears and swords across the room; and generally enhance the skills we know I already have (which aren't many, I admit). But it's a start.

Nine doesn't return, though, and I'm starting to get a little worried. The team makes it sound like he's obsessed with magical theory and wants to study me—I honestly don't mind, and his knowledge and expertise comes in handy—so where has he been all afternoon?

Dea and I eat dinner in silence, mostly because it's only the pair of us; Connie is still out on a mission, and Nine and Arrie are still missing from earlier. The worry grows until I can't take it anymore, and I slam my plate down so hard it cracks in two, marring the perfectly polished table.

"Where are they? I honestly can't live with knowing I'm causing problems between the team."

"Angel, this is Arrie's problem, not yours. Nine showed me what you showed him, and Arrie was . . . out of line. He of all people should know that our human pasts do not define our immortal futures."

I'm not sure what that's supposed to mean, but it isn't particularly comforting. I want to go talk to them, see if maybe I can have some semblance of a conversation with the Horseman of War.

Please don't be fighting just because of me.

I run around various hallways of the house—ones I know my way around—and listen for any hint of voices or sounds I can make out. They have to be somewhere . . .

"She doesn't belong here!"

A sickening crunch echoes down the hallway that leads to Arrie's rooms.

"She . . . was . . . chosen." Nine's voice sounds so faint, like he's failing to keep himself conscious.

I round the corner and peek through a crack in the just-open door. Arrie stands tall in the center of a surprisingly beautiful room while Nine lies crumpled on the floor at the base of the wall. The whole room is covered in flowers and indoor trees and has its very own spa-like pool in the center. Guess Arrie likes the outdoors. There's a bed low to the ground on the far side, with two floor-to-ceiling windows, like the ones in my room, that open up to the forest behind the house.

The sound of water trickling around the room and birds flitting between trees dotted in various corners makes my head swoon. It really is beautiful. He seems to value peace and relaxation, which is odd as shit given he's the Horseman of War. But maybe that's the point.

Nine's body slumps farther down the wall as his eyes hang heavy.

Oh goddess! Please, no. "Stop!" I run in, hands in the air, ready to try to do something —anything—to prevent this fight. "Please, stop."

Arrie turns to me with a snarl, fighting stance at the ready. "What do you want, Killer?" He growls that last word like it's the worst thing in the world, despite him being the Horseman of War. Something tells me he's killed his fair share over the last two millennia.

"I want you to stop fighting. You're a team. A family."

"We were."

Arrie fully turns around to look my way, and I get a full glimpse of Nine's condition— blotching bruises, cracking and splitting purple skin, and hair ruffled from where he hit the wall.

"You still are. Look, I get it. Change is hard, Arrie. And honestly, I think I'd rather still be human than here."

Nine looks at me with sad eyes, but understanding dawns behind the disappointment.

"Being immortal, alone forever, and stuck with a kind of magic I don't even under-stand, let alone know how to control . . . I don't want any of that."

"Then leave!"

"I can't!" I step forward, refusing to give up just because Mr. Strong and Moody is having a temper tantrum. "I can't just leave the world to die."

"Think you can stop a war, Killer?"

"Not alone, but yes, I think you'll need me. Otherwise, why would I be here?"

Arrie stops snarling and sighs. It's more of mix between a groan and a sigh, but at least it's not a snarl or a growl. He clearly understands what's going on here, but he seriously dislikes it.

"We don't have to be friends, and you have thousands of years to learn to be okay with this, but you can't hurt the people you love just because of me." My voice cracks at the end, and Nine shakes his head, as if trying to tell me in his half-conscious state that it isn't my fault. But it is. This would never have happened if I didn't turn up.

"I'll never be okay with this," Arrie growls. "You'll always just be a murderer."

Anger boils beneath the surface, a raging sea of frustration I've been tamping down ever since he found me in the training room, but something about that sentence just snaps any lasting control I have.

I sprint and reach Arrie in less time than it takes to inhale and connect my fist with his nose.

He flies backward, arms flailing as a surprised yelp escapes his usually perfect facade. He lands in a heap beside Nine, who lies there staring at me in shocked silence.

I look at my fist, whose knuckles are a bright shade of crimson red—ugh, those are gonna bruise tomorrow—and wonder who the fuck I am.

Dea's beside me in the blink of an eye, looking around the room at Nine and Arrie lying next to one of the many serenity ponds. "What happened?"

"I-I-I-I punched Arrie in the face . . . and he landed over there."

"You . . . punched him? And he actually fell backward?"

I nod, vaguely understanding that this is a big deal.

"She broke my nose," Arrie grumbles a little less murderously than before. "My nose is actually . . . broken."

Dea goes to take a look at them both, sees the stupidity of the situation, and walks straight back out again, not even bothering to heal them. "You can heal on your own!"

I help Nine up, who looks at me gratefully and directs me to his room. It takes an agonizing twenty minutes, but we make it to the room just down from my own. We walk through an open door and into a dark room with lots of computers and gadgets dotted around and a plasma wall set up in the corner where various plasmascreens are embedded into the wall.

It's very Nine. And I start to get the feeling that everyone has a room that suits them—somewhere they can relax and just be themselves. Connie has a suite that suits her beauty and chilled-out persona, Arrie has a set of rooms that suits his need for inner peace, and Nine has a room that suits his inner geek.

Wonder what Dea's room looks like?

I lay Nine on a chaise that lounges next to a corner bookcase, its black velvet a stark contrast against the white shelves and red cushions.

"I'm sorry, sweet thing."

He looks at me with guilt-ridden eyes, and I kneel next to him. "No. Don't be. It's not your fault. I should be thanking you for trying to keep the peace."

"I didn't really do very well." He sighs and sits up slightly, wincing the entire way. "Connie's usually the one to talk some sense into him. But with her gone, I thought maybe . . ."

"You could try? You could have been seriously hurt. Arrie's not the type to hold back, or so I hear." That gets a laugh out of him, and we both relax slightly. "I could probably persuade Dea to heal you if you wanted me to campaign on your behalf?"

"Persuade him, huh? And how would you do that?"

The suggestion in his tone has me blushing. "Not like that! I was going to simply ask him. I mean, you were trying to do the right thing."

"Yeah, but I should have just waited for Connie to get back. She'll only be gone a few days." Nine gruffs and scowls. "I was just so angry at him. He can't treat you like that. Any of us."

"He's right to be suspicious. I'd be lying if I said I wasn't also concerned about it." Nine raises his eyebrows in question, and I sigh. "I mean, why pick someone to stop a magical war who has clearly already picked a side? It just doesn't seem logical."

Nine looks at me with those sad eyes from earlier, clearly sensing the general tone of my thoughts. "You know, when I was human, I was kind of like a priest in my town."

I snort in disbelief. Yeah right.

"It's true."

"Really?"

He rests a hand on my arm, his thumb rubbing circles in slow, comforting movements. "I shunned anything magical, never took a wife, and died a virgin. When I came to in the house, and we learned more about what we were, I spent so long in denial. Suddenly I was this powerful magical being who was immortal? It went against everything I'd ever believed in." He takes a shuddering breath, and I raise the blanket up to his chin as his eyes start drooping. "We change when we become a Horseman. We have to be who the world needs us to be."

His eyes close, and I feel his chest rise and fall in even breaths, leaving me alone with his words of dooming wisdom.

The person the world needs me to be . . .

But who is that? And how do I become her?

Two days I spend my mornings doing yoga in the garden's new *Shinto* shrine, researching the Four Horsemen and *Sheruta* in the library, reading up about magical theory, and discussing with Nine how I seem to have all four elements as my magic.

Turns out *Sheruta* was created at the same time as the Horsemen—or that's the theory, at least, since they were the first ones to settle here—but eventually, more and more species discovered the portal, some of whom were shown here by members of the Horsemen, and the realm grew. The realm itself is completely self-managing, from having its own four-season cycle to various creatures, ecology, and culture. The most interesting part, in my opinion, is learning about the various ecosystems, and I want to make it my mission in the future to explore everything *Sheruta* offers, log all the various plant and animal species, and see what ones can be useful in various magical spells and potions.

Not even Nine has bothered to make a list, just mentally cataloguing the ones he's found useful over the centuries. For a science and magic expert, and resident nerd, he's rather lazy with going out in the field.

I spend my afternoons learning to use my new air magic in various ways under Dea's instruction while Nine makes notes. Once I gained access to the magic, it came naturally, and it feels good using it, both for myself and in training to help the team.

I have since perfected my aim with my air magic, and have for moving targets, too; I can use air to both throw a dagger and make its course more accurate when thrown by hand.

Dea and I are sitting down to breakfast early on the third day, waiting for the others.

"Eventually, with some field experience, you will learn to adapt your magic to specific situations and use it fluidly without placing limitations upon yourself," Dea says.

Arrie has said nothing since the incident, but I occasionally catch him watching me, and today I'm going to try to break that thick layer of ice, or at least chip at it a little. It's been awkward tiptoeing around him recently, and I'm ready to move on from that, like yesterday.

Nine and Arrie enter, both since healed from their stupid man-headed injuries, and sit at the breakfast table, as Dea asks the house to prepare a spread of toast and condiments.

Dea and Nine chat about something and laugh about old times while Arrie and I sit in silence.

"So, Arrie," I say, causing everyone to stop eating and talking and to look at me, "want to come join our training session today?"

Nine smiles at me, clearly seeing what I'm trying to do, but Dea looks at me with doubt.

"Why?" Arrie grumbles between bites.

"Well, it would be great to get some pointers from all of you, and you must have some killer knife-throwing skills, but I thought you might feel more at ease if you came and saw my magic for yourself." I pause, watching him stare at me with a blank face while he continues to chew. "I mean, I can only use air magic right now, but we've done some cool things with it, and—"

"Whatever." Arrie gets up and leaves, abandoning his plate on the table rather than washing it like usual. He grumbles something under his breath in another language as he heads back up the stairs with heavy footfalls.

"Well, that went well." I roll my eyes and sigh, dragging a hand over my face in frustration. Why won't he just quit with the stupid attitude and try to get along with me?

Nine places a comforting hand on my knee while Dea gives a gentle smile. "Just keep trying, Angel."

I nod, determination filling me, and head to my library. Research. More research. And today, I will look into Witch magic.

Wonder how Connie's doing? Is she all right? Shaking my head, I try to tell myself not to worry about her. She's the Horseman of Conquest, for fuck's sake, she'll be fine. It's silly of me to worry. But still, that niggling doubt persists in raising my hackles as I walk by shelf after shelf, brushing my fingertips along various spines and mentally cataloguing where they are.

Witch magic. Witch magic. Witch magic, I tell myself over and over, trying to focus my mind on the task at hand, but I fear it's going to be one of those days of mental disparity: Arrie is still angry with me for existing, no one has heard from Connie in a few days, I can still only use air magic, and I still have few memories of my past.

Did I have any friends?

Family?

People who cared?

Did they mourn me?

Did I cause them suffering?

I can feel my emotions spiraling down one of those familiar black holes of insanity, with questions being asked that I have no hope of getting answers to, and emotions being challenged that I have no place feeling. Maddening. That's what this life is. Utterly fucking maddening. And if I have to live another damn week in this stupid immortal body with no answers to any of my questions, I'm going to explode.

Standing up in a huff, I bang my fist on the desk, releasing a growl of frustration, and pace around the library in random directions. I'm not looking for anything, not really, but my mind needs to wander so it can find its way back to its usual maddening, if slightly okay, normality. The brief thought of being immortal and part of the Horsemen of the Apocalypse being my new normal has a laugh leaking from my lips. How ridiculous my life has become in such a short space of time.

A break. That's what I need. A damn break. I go to the nearest shelf that holds some deliverance of escapism and breathe a sigh of relief when, a few seconds later, I sit on a turquoise pouf with a fantasy book in hand. I don't even deliberate over the title, just see it's about some random female hero saving dragonkind—something so far from the troubles of my own reality—and sink into peace.

I have no idea how many hours have passed or when my training session is due to start, and that lack of timekeeping is the most blissful few hours I've spent since Connie left. But voices in the distance break my fantastical haze and bring me right back to crushing reality.

"Not sure where she is?"

"Around 'ere somewhere. This place is huge."

"It's fucking awesome, and you know it."

A familiar grumble ruptures the air around me and sticks to my ear like cheese to a grater—Arrie.

I get up and try to find where the voices are coming from—probably the study—and watch from a corner as Nine, Dea, and Arrie poke around my little nook of knowledge. Dea places my research notes on the desk—he must have finished going through, annotating them for me. A little surge of joy sparkes my insides at that; he's really taken the time to add details to their story.

I know it's silly, but they've got two millennia on me. They know everything about each other: their gifts, their personalities, their past, their worlds. I'm just supposed to know it all straightaway? I hate being out of the loop, and they're one large fucking loop.

Nine hasn't spotted me yet, or maybe he has and just doesn't want to tip the others off. Who knows? That guy is an enigma. A really hot puzzle I need to figure out. He's the nerd, the one to sit down and explain everything to me about their lives (even small parts that probably doesn't matter to them), the one who knows more about magic than the rest of us combined. Probably the rest of the world.

Arrie sits in my chair and flicks through the leather-bound book I use to make notes on them. I have a separate one for magic, *Sheruta*, and Earth, all packed into that top drawer. He flips through the pages, his general scowling expression morphing into one of surprise and dare I say it . . . admiration.

Have I impressed him with my notes?

I've found I'm naturally studious, and the more I let my mind become more active, the more I find myself being more like Nine. A nerd. But at least I have the potential to be magically badass, too.

Nine sits with Arrie, perching his ass on the end of his knee—the fact that doesn't weird me out is more bothersome than I care to admit—and flips through the pages with him.

"Ha! Look!" He points to something on the page I can't see. "Seems she has made correct assumptions about all of our gifts and how they relate to our personalities. Look, Arrie, she has your grumpiness down to a tee."

Arrie shakes him off his knee, his usual scowl plasters back across his face, and he slams the book shut.

Damn. I thought I made good progress for a moment there. Oh well, guess I'll keep trying. I have all of eternity, after all.

I step out of the stacks.

Nine looks my way, Dea sends me another one of those panty-melting smiles that makes my knees tremble, while Arrie doesn't even acknowledge my presence.

"Ready?" I walk past them head toward the area of the library that holds my training room.

They follow behind, or at least I assume they do—I can only hear Arrie's footsteps and Nine's endless chatter. Dea is as silent as ever.

Stack after stack, I take them through the shelves, never stopping to look back, and soon arrive at the training room door that only opens when I let my magic seep into it, lighting it up like some kind of magically darkening rainbow.

Would have been cool if I wasn't so pissed off that I could only access my air magic. There are three other elements . . . Why can't I fucking use them?

We all step into the dark room, and I walk over to the knives and start laying them out on the table next to the start line in front of the targets.

"You really can see in the dark, 'ey?" Nine says as he flicks the old-fashioned lights on, sending those irritating flickers of humming lights right into my eyes.

A small hiss and groan escape my lips. "Really need to change those fucking lights."

Dea walks up behind me. "Why is that, Angel?" He places a hand on either shoulder and gently rubs the tension out of them.

"Cause they're really fucking irritating. Hurts my eyes, and their damn humming hurts my ears."

"I do not hear anything, Angel."

I stop preparing the blades and turn around. "What?"

Nine comes up to us. "Yeah, I don't hear anything, either. They're just . . . lights."

"Okaaaay." At this point, I don't care. I'm already a freak, stand out even here among the Horsemen, and just really want to throw something. Preferably at someone, but I'll settle for a moving, inanimate target.

Nine grabs Dea's hand and pulls him away, shaking his head.

Breathing in, I line up the knife in my hand with the target against the far wall. Breathing out, I let go, using my air magic to zigzag it around the room before hitting the target. Okay, so I'm showing off a bit. But who cares? I'm stuck with this, so the least I can do is show off to the asshole who thinks I'm some kind of murderer.

But what if I am? Was?

My head shakes violently for a few seconds before I can regain control and stop it.

No, I don't think so either.

Picking up a sword from the area outlined in white tape off to the left, I look to Dea, who steps forward. "Ready?"

His chosen sword in hand, he merely nods.

I rush left, aiming for a spinning, behind-the-back shot, but he turns at the last second and counters.

The ring of metal on metal clashes around the room as he feints right but jabs left. I spin out of the way, using my air magic to push me a little farther than my legs can take me, but Dea is on me in a flash. His speed is something else. And I have yet to think of a good counter for it.

For now, I simply try to stay on top of it by keeping a close eye on what direction his feet are facing. I really hope he doesn't let on to that little trick.

We both stop for a moment to catch our breath, and I briefly have a terrifying thought of what it would be like to spar with Connie, given that she never runs out of energy. Damn. That must be insane.

Nine laughs a little from behind his plasmascreen. "She breaks every fifteen minutes for us. But yes, we're all a little terrified of her inability to tire."

Dea chuckles, clearly seeing where my thoughts have gone. He seems a little out of breath, and I think that maybe his ability costs a lot of energy for him to use. That is interesting.

With his shirt now noticeably absent—the cheating fucker—he stands, ready to continue. "Ready?"

I nod, taking a deep breath.

Dea moves first this time, coming in for a straight shot, which I quickly counter by leaping backward and meeting his sword midair.

Another clang of metal, and Dea is already pushing me back against the wall, his sword against my neck. I don't even have time to blink.

He's been holding back this entire time—fuck, damn him.

Dea drops his sword as mine clangs to the floor and my hands raise in surrender above my head. I let out a frustrated breath. "If I could use the other elements, I might actually be able to fight."

"Shhh." He holds a finger to my lips, gently stroking his thumb across my lower lip.

Seriously? He's shirtless, stroking my lip, and has me pinned to a wall. The golden glimmer of his tattoo distracts my eyes, though, as they wander over the spiraling shoulder. I remember him telling me it's in memory of his Shifter friend. I think it's a beautiful memento.

He told you that?

Looking over at Nine, I can see his head still stuck in the plasmascreen—he's trying to hide this conversation and that it's even taking place.

Yes. Though he didn't tell me the story. Just that it's in memory of a Shifter friend. I did ask. Not everyone has to keep things hidden, Nine. In fact, Dea's a . . . really open person.

Not with just anyone he's not.

I can sense the humor and insinuation in his tone, but I elect to ignore it because honestly? Nope. Not even going there.

I realize then that Dea still has me pinned to the wall, and I've been staring off into space for the last thirty seconds while talking to Nine. Damn. I'm trying to be as inconspicuous as Nine.

Dea looks at me with a sexy smirk on his face, and I can't help but smile like a stupid teenager with a crush. He really is beautiful. Even more so up close. Part of me wants to reach out and run my hands through his hair while seeing what it would be like to meet those delicate lips with my own. I've already made out with Connie, and I doubt adding Dea to that brief list will really matter.

But it will. And part of me knows that. Connie knows the deal and understands, and she's willing to be patient with me and build something, even if it ends up just being a close friendship. So I push Dea back, and he lets me, as I step out of the intense position.

Shaking off the feeling of need that settled and the intense desire to turn right back around and pin him to the wall, I instead look at Nine, who's no longer burying his head in that plasmascreen but staring at me with a longing look.

What does he see when he looks at me like that?

Beauty.

I blush at his almost romantic compliment and walk back to the knives.

"No." Arrie stands in the doorway, and this is the first time I've taken note of him. Honestly, I try my best to ignore him most of the time. "Spar with me." He waltzes down the room toward me, pinning me with those eyes of burning anger, and picks up a different sword from the rack—a heavier one.

Spar with the Horseman of War? I think I would rather keep his angry, moody self as my newest pet. I'm going to regret inviting him along today, aren't I?

Probably.

I hold in the laugh about to squeeze out of my throat and turn toward Arrie. "All right. Let's fucking do it." Bouncing on my toes, I mentally prepare myself for a sparring match with the Horseman of War. Pretty sure I'm about to lose. But I will do so with dignity.

Arrie stands in the center of the taped circle, sword drawn at his side, eyes closed.

Do I just go?

Yes.

Okay, then. I grip my sword tighter, tip my foot forward to charge, and run.

Arrie's sword meets mine while his eyes are still closed, and I'm momentarily shocked still.

I shake myself out of the unprotected statue position I've found myself in and use some air currents to propel me to his left and around to his back, aiming to strike from behind.

A clang of metal on metal meets my ears, so I knew he's countered it, even though it happens so fast I can barely keep track.

Fucking damn it. He's too fast. Too accurate.

Arrie turns so his back is to me and then makes his first offensive move: he spins in a quick 360 and meets my throat with the tip of his blade.

My feet dodge backward, but I'm pretty sure in a real fight I'd be dead. I use my air magic to make me weightless and flip effortlessly over his head—mentally, I'm praising myself for looking so epic, but I don't have time for the vocal ego boost right now—then spin and meet his wide blue eyes as my blade presses gently to his stomach.

"Yes!" Totally got a hit on the Horseman of War. How cool is that?

But, looking at him, I get the feeling he isn't really trying, as he stands there with those wide eyes, not even trying to retain a defensive position, and that deflates my new confidence just a little. (Okay, a lot, but who's counting?)

"That was . . . interesting," Arrie says. Not a grumble. Or a complaint. An actual sentence. Said to me.

I'll take that as a win. Score one for the Horseman of Magic.

"Indeed," Dea adds. "You used your magic intuitively and flexibly to adapt to your scenario. Well done."

Wait . . . I did? I just did the most logical thing to try to surprise Arrie. I didn't realize that's what Dea was on about yesterday.

Arrie stays silent, then breaks my mind babble by saying, "I'll train you."

I mean, Dea says that I will eventually adapt my abilities to suit my environment, but — "Wait, what?"

"I'll train you."

"For real?"

"Yes." Arrie puts the sword down and leaves without saying another word.

"Okaaaay."

Nine strolls up and shows me the plasmascreen. On the faintly blue, non-physical screen is a tally chart: one side labelled MAGIC and the other WAR. "I'd say that's two points for the Horseman of Magic."

We high-five, and I can't help but grin a stupid, girly smile at the nerd. I've really convinced Arrie that I'm okay. Well, okay enough to train. I'll work on the rest later.

16

I spend the rest of the afternoon doing the research into Witch magic I meant to do that morning—before Arrie ruined my good mood. The research involves the history of Witches, how they didn't come out of the closet with the rest of the magical community because of the whole Salem thing, and how together with Shifters, Vampires, and Fae, they created the four pillars of magic.

That is the first time I'm hearing this reference (since it isn't triggering any further knowledge), and despite asking my Seeing Stone about it, no other books come up in my search. I don't know why, but something about that seems awfully suspicious. I mean, this damn library is huge. Why is the only mention of the four pillars in this one book? It's a pretty thin-looking book, too. Doesn't have much in it.

Can I ask the others? Maybe they've heard of the reference before? I'll bet my movie night choice that Nine'll know. The nerd knows everything. I kinda love that about him. It's hot, and I rely on him for any kind of question, (bonus, I can just ask internally if I don't want the others knowing) no matter how silly or embarrassing it is.

To dinner it is, then. It's seven pm anyway, and that usually means someone's thought of dinner. Good, because I'm starving. All this training has really increased my appetite.

The four of us sit around the table in our spots: me and Nine on the left side, Arrie opposite, and Dea at one of the heads. Connie's empty space bothers me more and more as the days go by, and I'm getting anxious enough to ask how they reckon she's doing, but it really is silly.

It's not silly to worry. She's probably fine. Dea was thinking about checking on her in a few days if she's not checked in by week's end.

Phew. I feel myself audibly exhale in relief, and Dea raises an eyebrow at me. I shake my head, trying to dissuade him from asking out loud.

Dinner is pizza. I fucking love pizza! Ohmigod, pizza and coffee. Now that is the stuff of dreams. From pepperoni, to Hawaiian, to Greek feta, to fancy mozzarella . . . I love them all.

But I need to stop gorging myself and actually ask Nine my question from earlier. "Nine?"

"Hmm?"

"Have you ever heard of the term 'the four pillars of magic'?"

Nine looks off into space for a moment before coming back and looking at me. "There was this guy . . . Dr. Oscar Walzto, I think. He released a theoretical paper on how the four largest magical communities kept the balance of power."

"Oh. That makes sense." Dr. Waltzo is the author of that paper-thin book I read. "Do you have a copy of that paper I could borrow?"

"Probably." He takes another bite of his pepperoni pizza. "Why do you ask?"

"Well . . . I saw the reference and went to ask the Seeing Stone, and nothing. There were no references in the library."

Dea chimes in, obvious confusion etching across his face. "None at all?"

I shake my head. "Nope."

Nine and Dea share a knowing look and then glance back at me in this freaky unison thing they have going on.

"What?"

It's Nine who answers. "He's a particularly influential research doctor within the magical community. It's a little odd your library has nothing more on that reference."

Oh. Well, why doesn't his name or that term ring any bells? Maybe human me didn't really know much about magic. No, that makes little sense because I know all about Witches.

The all-too-familiar question raises its ugly head again: who was I? Nothing about the facts of who I was makes any sense. I know loads about specific things, but not a lot about the magical community as a whol—

A scream pierces the air, and we all snap to our feet and turn toward the source.

Connie.

She half stands, half crouches in the center of the kitchen as blood leaks from her mouth and multiple wounds across her torso. Her feet are bent in a way I'm pretty sure isn't natural, and tears streak down the side of her face in screeching agony.

Her usually perfect visage of beauty is a tangled mess, and worry shoots its way through my system and forces me to rush forward and place a hand on her shoulder.

As I get closer, I inhale an intoxicating scent, one of honey with a salty, metallic tang that has me hungrier than I've ever been before.

Stopping dead in my tracks, I sniff the air, drawing in as much of that sweet, sweet scent as possible as I lustfully scoop large gulpfuls of air with my lungs.

I want to be near her . . .

I lean closer, still sniffing the air, trying to gorge on that sweet, addictive scent. My hands tighten on her shoulders, and Connie winces in pain as she tries to pull away.

But I inch closer until my nose is flush against her cheek and my mouth centimeters from hers.

"Sweetie?"

I can hear Nine in the background, but his voice is a faded record, calling out but not quite reaching me.

Connie gasps when she pulls away and looks at my face, and a vision of pure terror crosses her eyes. "Ahhhh!" She scrambles to get away, but I grab her other shoulder and hold her in place.

Someone grabs my arms and yanks me backward, flying me off my feet.

I hiss and scramble, kick and punch. "Let go!" I need to get to Connie. Now. There's something about her scent that I need.

Breaking free of the grip that holds me, I run to Connie, but not before Arrie stands in front of me, a mixture of concern and confusion plastered across his face. "Stop."

He holds my arms in a viselike grip as Nine grabs me from behind, arms wraping around my waist. "Please," he whispers.

The plea in his voice breaks me out of my reverie.

Wait . . . What happened? What am I doing?

I wanted to . . .

Ohmigod. I wanted to eat her. To taste her blood and see what it's like. I needed to . . .

"Shhhhh," Nine comforts. "It's okay."

"No!" No. It isn't okay. I could have killed her. How is he saying tha—?

"We can't die, Sweetie."

Right. Even if I drained her dry, I wouldn't have killed her. Drained her of . . . blood.

Oh my goddess, I'm a V-Vam . . . ?

Dea pushes us out of the way and crouches on the floor, where Connie slides to meet him. "This might sting a little."

She nods, silent tears racking her body.

Dea gathers himself onto his knees and places a hand either side of her temples. Green light shines from his hands, healing her internal wounds, and I watch as she grimaces in pain, but the blood pouring from her mouth stops trickling and dries almost instantly, but my need to go to her and . . .

Goddess, it's so intoxicating.

"Lay down." Dea moves himself out of her way.

Arrie lets go of me and comes up beside her, laying her head on his lap as he strokes comforting hands over her head. I've never seen him so caring. It surprises me.

Dea heals the rest of Connie's wounds while she shakes from the pain, and before long, she's all healed and wrapped up in Arrie's arms like some kind of fragile princess. Even through the blood and torn clothing, she still looks beautiful.

"Hon . . ." Her eyes flutter open, and she looks at me with a mixture of friendliness and . . . fear. "Can you p-please get me some f-food?"

"Er . . . right." I jump up, happy to have something to do to help distract me from the obvious. I fill a plate with various flavors of pizza and kneel back down to hand it over. "I'll grab you a tea."

She loves tea.

"Peppermint."

"Okay, one peppermint tea coming right up." I get to work brewing her request while Arrie takes her into another room, followed by Dea.

Nine wraps an arm my waist from behind. "She'll be fine. She's just tired. She probably didn't sleep on her mission, and then she got wounded. She needs a good night's sleep is all." He remains where he is, and although I know it's slightly intimate, the comfort is warm and aids in stopping the shaking of my hands.

He doesn't seem to be afraid of me.

I stay silent while I pour the hot water into the teapot. My hands are shaking slightly, but not as badly as before.

"Hey." Nine holds the water jug over top of my hand, connecting our fingers. "It's okay." His voice brushes against my neck, and I revel in the comfort of his gentleness. He nuzzles my neck as his spare arm wraps tighter around my waist. "I promise she's fine. You're fine. We're all okay."

"Okay."

Nine won't lie to me. He and Dea have been upfront from the beginning, but Nine has been the one to fill me in and try to guide my spiraling thoughts into something that resembles tentative calmness.

"Bet she'd love to hear all about your new developments, Horseman of Magic."

He used my actual title rather than Sweetie, and it makes me melt against him as my hand drops from the jug's handle and comes to rest at my side. The way he says my title sends shivers down my body.

He wraps both arms around me in a tight embrace, and I inhale his cherrylike scent and let it wash away my concerns.

New developments? There are a lot of them all right, but we'll figure it out. Hopefully.

"C'mon, let's get Con her tea."

"Mmmm-hmm." I can barely form functioning thoughts at the minute, let alone words. He's so . . . relaxing.

Nine grabs my waist once more and walks me down an empty corridor to the last room on the left. As the door opens, I see Dea and Arrie in a heated discussion. I can hear them, too, but I choose to ignore Arrie's words right now. They aren't particularly nice.

"Sit here." Nine gestures to a plump armchair in the corner. He grabs the tray from me, places it in Connie's shaking hands where she lies on the couch, and comes back to me. He sits next to me, scoots me up, and sits me in his lap, nuzzling a comforting face against my neck.

I expect Dea to say something. Hell, if not Dea, then Arrie. But no one says a word. We all stand and sit in silence, Dea and Arrie's heated words long since faded the moment I stepped into the room.

The room itself is a slightly bland but large lounge. A smattering of brown sofas and armchairs line two walls, a large plasma TV takes up another, and a fake window with an artificial seafront setting displays along the other. There's a small chandelier hanging from the ceiling, and in its holders at regular intervals sit candles that are all alight and glowing the room in a soft yellow blush that makes the situation seem a little less daunting than it is.

Taking a deep breath, I break the sience first "I'm sorry." Even to me, it sounds pathetic. As though sorry is going to cut it when I nearly drained Connie dry not moments ago. "I . . . er . . ."

"No," Connie says, sitting up. "Don't." She stands and walks over to me. "You're new.

We don't know the extent of your powers yet. I just . . . have an innate fear of Vampires." She mumbles that last part, and I have to strain to hear it.

"R-Really?" She's scared of something? Like, actually scared? And that something is me.

"Yes." She gives me a gentle smile. "Maybe someday I'll tell you all about it, but for now, I really need to update you all and get some rest."

I nod, knowing that her understanding is about the best I'm going to get right now, and I don't even deserve that.

She turns around and sits back on the couch. "Thanks for the tea, by the way." She raises the cup to me, and I smile. "So." This time she faces Dea and Arrie. "I have no idea who broke the fifth seal or where it is."

"What?" Dea stands, dumbfounded, a look of incredulity on his face. "You were gone for days and found nothing?"

She nods. "Yup."

"I . . . I don't get it," Nine adds.

Connie laughs slightly. "Took me a while to track a few of our informants down, but everyone came back with the same thing: no one has heard anything about the seals in centuries."

"Okay." Dea sits on the couch next to her, lifting her feet in the process. "So what do you need to update us on?"

Connie looks to the rest of the team and grimaces. "The magical community are heading for war. If they aren't already, they will be soon."

We all stare at her, dumbfounded. I thought I'd have more time. To train, to practice, to learn who I was and am. My head spins, thoughts barely forming before they flutter away to make room for new ones. War. So it's finally happening, then.

Nine rests a head in the crook of my neck. *It's okay. We're in this together.*

"You don't seem very surprised by this news."

Dea shakes his head. "We are not. While you were away, we discovered what type of Horseman Angel is. Though we still know very little about her powers."

Connie grins. "Oh, c'mon . . . Don't leave me hanging!" She sits up and looks at me. "Tell me!"

She's like a kid in a candy store, and for a moment, it reminds of the all the dancing and fun we had last Friday. So much has changed since then.

"I . . ." I take another deep breath. "I am the Horseman of Magic."

A smile creeps up Connie's face, looking a little stunned, but a happy kind of pride takes over her features. "Well, well, well . . . Look who's got the potential to be the strongest now?"

Strongest? Ha! Hilarious.

She's right, Sweetie.

I pull away from Nine and look at him blankly. "Don't be ridiculous." My eyes pull toward Connie. "Both of you. I'll be an equal member of the team. Someday."

Dea smiles at that, and Arrie . . . Well, he just grumbles something in an unintelligible language under his breath that has Connie throwing him a scary-as-fuck look.

"I went to see Milila but got ran out by her pack before I could even get close. Hence" —Connie gestures to herself—"this."

Her pack? Who's Milila?

Milila runs the hyena pack in Ueno, Tokyo.

"Why were you run out, Con?" Concern etches onto Dea's features.

"No idea." She shrugs. "Never got the chance to ask."

Dea looks even more concerned from the lack of information and leans back into the couch, deep in thought.

"I need to sleep." Connie gets herself up off the couch.

Arrie crouchs down next to her. "I'll take you to bed." He scoops her up in his arms, and I watch as she rests her head on his shoulder, and it reminds of the time Arrie carried me like that back to my room.

Damn. Stop it! He clearly hates you. Now is not the time to be getting hot over some asshole who has barely said a nice word to you . . . ever.

Well, he is an attractive man with all that muscle.

Shut up, Nine! And get out of my head.

It's hard when your thoughts scream as loud as yours. He just chuckles from underneath me and wraps his arms tighter around my waist.

And for a moment, I let him wrap me up in a pretend ball of comfort, as though the world isn't at war and dependent on me to save it, as though I'm not in a house full of teammates I'm weirdly attracted to. As though I belong.

17

"Hon . . . You're . . . just wow!"

Connie stands in the doorway of my dingy training room the next day, observing my new skills, and so far, I seem to be impressing her. And I refuse to admit how like a giddy teenager that fact makes me. Nope. Nuh-uh. Not happening.

"Like what you see, Con?" Nine sits at the desk—his usual place—and has spent the entire afternoon teasing me about that kiss. Inside my mind, of course, because then no one else understands why I'm suddenly blushing after she whoops for the hundredth time when I hit the bullseye. Again.

Connie stands behind me and adjusts my position slightly, placing her hands on my hips. "This way, you'll be able to pivot more in the field when attacking moving targets. Keep your weight on your back leg."

"Oh." That seems to be the only word my brain can come up with because it's far too focused on her warm fingers clenching my hips and her breasts now pressing against my back.

Seriously? You're crushing hard, aren't you?

Shut the fuck up!

Nine chuckles in my mind. He actually mentally chuckles inside my head. The fucker.

I can feel the heat rising to my face, but Connie doesn't move. Instead, she wraps her arms around my waist in a backward hug and whispers against my neck. "I missed you."

"Me too," I whisper back. "It's good to have you back."

She seems to be back to her normal self today, but there's a part of my mind at the very back that niggles with uncertainty. Will she still feel the same way? I'm a . . . a . . . Nope. Still can't say it. Not even in my head.

Despite my mental spiraling, Nine's remained silent on the matter, and I get the feeling that Dea is ready to call a meeting soon and has purposefully asked him to keep quiet.

We'll all chat soon, Sweetie. Promise.

Well, that confirms that.

Connie peels herself away from me as Dea coughs from the doorway, having returned from grabbing bottles of water for everyone. He sneeks a questioning look at Nine, whose gaze goes blank for a minute as Dea's eyebrows shoot to the ceiling.

"Really?" Dea asks as he looks straight at me, then at Connie. "You two really kissed before you left?"

"Well," Connie answers, "it was more like a hot make-out session, but sure. Yeah." She winks at me and shrugs a shoulder.

I admittedly want to die on the spot. Magic, kill me now. This team is going to murder me with embarrassment before I can even do my job.

Dea gives me a heated look and walks on up to me in purposeful strides. "I did not know you were . . . bisexual?"

"Really? You guys do the whole labeling thing? You're like . . . what? Two thousand years old?"

Nine chuckles from behind. "She's got a point, bro. Let 'em be."

"Oh, I am not complaining." And to prove that point, he grabs my waist and yanks me against him, his dark glowing eyes turning golden for a split second before returning to their usual galaxy greatness.

Usually, I try to get out of his hold, but between Nine's affections yesterday, Connie's closeness even after the whole blood thing, and now this . . . My control is decidedly slipping through my fingers like sand.

"Dea . . . I—"

"Shhhh." He places a finger to my lips, and I have to resist the urge to kiss it; instead, I remain as motionless as possible. "It's okay." He pulls my waist tighter until I'm flush against him and can feel everything hidden from view. From his rigid, muscular torso whose defined lines I can feel beneath the thin material of his t-shirt, to the growing hardness pressing against my lower stomach. He's . . .

Fuck, damn it, he's gorgeous.

Uh-huh. Don't need to yell it, Sweetie. I know.

I'm not yelling it for your benefit, asshole.

Well, the mental picture you're conjuring is not giving that man enough credit. Trust me.

I-I-I . . .

Nine throws me a mental picture—memory?—of a mostly naked Dea propped up against a wall, still in his underwear but otherwise available for perusal.

Great, now my imagination has decided to take a road trip to the bedroom, and I'm keenly aware of both pairs of eyes boring holes in us—a little hot but mostly curious (I think)—and Nine's knowing smirk.

Breaking Dea's hold on my waist, I pull away. I have to swallow the whine of disapproval as he, too, steps backward.

"So I have a plan for this afternoon's training." He steps away farther after noticing my gaze is still stuck to his lips. "Connie, why don't you help Arrie with Angel'sphysical training plan?"

"Sure." She smiles and gives a brief wave and a wink before exiting. "Keep up the great work, hon!"

Dea spins to face me. "I want to see your Vampire powers."

I stop dead in my tracks, all the fun, sexy thoughts fly out of the mental window, and stare, slackjawed, up at him. "Wh-what?"

"You cannot avoid it forever, Angel. We need to see."

I know that. I do. But . . . But I—

He's right. We need to understand. We don't have a lot of time. Nine throws the memory of Connie telling us the war is coming.

They're right. Of course they're right.

"Okay. How do we do that?"

"You need to gain some kind of control, and we need to understand what abilities you have. It's natural to assume your strength comes from your Vampire side, as well as your ability to see in the dark."

"But I'm not affected by sunlight. And I don't need to drink . . . To feed."

Nine steps into view beside Dea. "I have a theory on that. I think because we don't really need to eat, you don't need to feed. But if you did, you'd be more powerful. Just like we're more powerful and have more strength if we keep up a healthy diet."

"We really don't need to eat?" That is news to me. "You guys need a handbook: BEING A HORSEMAN OF THE APOCALYPSE 101."

They both chuckle, and it breaks the tension for a moment.

"We eat because it increases our strength, and we get a bit . . . sluggish if we don't. But it won't kill us or make us lose any weight." Nine blinks as he mentions something internally to Dea, and I look around, feeling a little lost and out of the loop.

"Just tell her, Nine."

Nine grimaces. "I don't think you'll be fully up to strength unless you feed. And if we're ever in battle, you'll need to feed to access your full strength."

Hmmm . . . I wonder. "Is it possible that's the reason I can't access all of my magic? I mean, could they be affecting one another?"

Nine blinks in surprise; clearly the thought hasn't occurred to him. "Maybe. But . . ." He gives me a look I hate, one I instantly abhor.

"We'd need to test it to find out," I fill in the blank for him.

"And I don't think it'll work like that anyway. I think it'll make your magic stronger, but I don't think it's blocking it."

I nod. "Still need to work on that access, then."

"Yes. But for now," Dea says, "I want to fight you in your Vampire state."

"Vampire state? That's what you're calling it? I'm just me!" I can feel the frustration boiling beneath my skin. "I'm not some freak of nature!"

"Sorry, Angel. Of course." He picks up the nearest throwing knife and nicks his finger, drawing a single droplet of blood.

The heavy scent of liquid honey with that familiar metallic tang hits my nostrils, and my fangs descend in response. It smells . . . like the first piece of food I've been offered after months of starvation, as though I haven't eaten in years and this is the only smell suffocating my senses throughout the involuntary fast.

Mine. Looking at Dea's galaxy-swirling eyes, watching the slow drip-drip-drip of his essence staining the concrete floor, I know it instantly. He's mine.

I leap from my position, covering the two feet between us in an instant, and toss him to the ground with a grunt.

My fingers fly to his lips, where they keep his silence and bring a smirk to his face.

"So," he says, speaking from behind my fingers, "you are stronger than me now. Interesting. But you were not stronger than Arrie yesterday." He looks to Nine, who scribbles down the information. Dea doesn't move, not an inch. He just lies there and accepts his fate.

I run my fingers, still lingering on his mouth, down the side of his throat along his jugular, where I feel the pounding of his blood, and I sniff closer.

"Angel?"

I look up at him, irritated by his interruption, but curious about what he wants.

"What does it . . ." He looks sheepishly to the ground. "What does it feel like?"

I don't know how to answer that. What deoes this feel like?

Like I won't be able to continue breathing if I don't taste him. Like if I don't drain every last drop, my body will crumble into a million pieces.

"Remember," Nine says, "we're immortal. If you don't drink the blood, nothing will happen. You cannot die."

Right. Immortal. No need to feed: food or blood. But I want to. "I feel like I'll die if I don't just . . . taste you."

But why am I so hot? I'm straddling Dea's waist and can feel every delicious inch of him beneath my jean shorts. I want more than just his blood, it seems (well, more than normal).

"She's also incredibly turned on. Which is pretty normal for a Vampire," Nine says in a formal reporting tone as he scribbles more notes onto his plasmascreen.

It is?

Yep.

"Okay," Dea whispers from beneath me, the vibration of his deep voice doing nothing to keep me calm. "Calm down." He raises his bloody finger—the cut on which has now healed—to my lips and smears what's left of the blood over my bottom lip. "Go ahead." His voice has turned raspy, a tone I haven't heard from him before, and I get the feeling this thing between us is making him as hot as me.

But that doesn't matter right now; all that matters is the scent of the honey-filled, metallic-tasting blood left on my lips like an offering on a silver platter of desire.

I dart my tongue out, just a little, to get a small taste, curiosity and need overcoming my better judgment. A small moan escapes my lips as my head tilts back and the taste coats my tongue. My fangs descend farther as the need to lick my lips clean becomes an itch I need to scratch.

Two and a half seconds.

That's how long it takes me to savor the taste of Dea's blood. That's also how long it takes for him to use the distraction to throw me off and pin me to the ground, his legs and arms pinning all my limbs as his torso restrains every inch of me he can.

I could lift him off and throw me clear across the room, but I don't want to. I like the position he has me in. I can clearly bite him from here, getting more of that sweet life that has my center on fire, every sense heightened and every thought amplified. More. I want —need—more.

My vision blackens as the need to feed confuses every thought, overcomes every other instinct.

Calm, Sweetie. Stay calm. You're going to be fine. Come on. Come back to us.

Nine's voice in the distance of my mind pierces the darkness I've succumbed to, but it's faint, as though I were deaf and having trouble hearing him. But that doesn't make sense; my hearing is better than ever right now.

That's right. You're strong. Stronger than us. Please. Movie night's your choice tonight. Remember?

Movie night? Right. I want to watch some fantasy superhero movie with the promise of a great love story. I want to watch it with the team. My friends.

Friends. That's right. We're your friends. Your family. Come back.

Family?

I open my eyes and see Dea's worried gaze on my face loosen slightly as I start waking back to reality. For a moment there, all I could feel was the bloodlust. I would have done anything to drink him dry.

It's okay. We'll work through it with you.

I let Dea get off me and quickly jump up, feeling my fangless face rise to stand on top shaky legs. Physically, I feel better than I have since arriving here, but mentally, I'm weaker than ever.

What would have happened if Nine didn't bring me back? If I couldn't control myself?

"Don't ever do that again!" I raise a hand and slap it across Dea's face. "I could have seriously hurt you! You fucking dick!"

Dea smiles, not even reacting to me slapping him. "As the Horseman of Death, dying is not something I am afraid of, Angel."

I shake my head and storm out, seeking a place of peaceful tranquility to store all this new insanity. The *Shinto* shrine.

18

"I have a theory," Nine mumbles between bites of spaghetti. I requested Italian again, since I loved it so much last time. We all stare at him expectantly. "Sweetie, you mentioned the four pillars of magic, and I found that paper this afternoon. You can borrow it later."

I nod my thanks.

"I think, given your access to Witch and Vampire powers, that you might also have access to the other two pillars of magic: Fae and Shifter."

I stare absentmindedly into his brown eyes.

"It would make sense," he continues. "Since you're the Horseman of Magic."

"Is there any proof of that, though?" I ask, denial edging my tone.

"Of what?" Dea asks. "You being the Horseman of Magic?"

I nod.

"Well," Dea continues, "we were all summoned when our powers were needed most. Mine to open the blocked gate to Hell, to allow souls to pass, Arrie and Con to help solve the world's conflicts and wars, and Nine to distribute provisions and aid countries in times of famine. Together, we brought about the modern world.

"So, given that Con proved the magical community is on the brink of war, and you have two of the four main communities' powers, it is a pretty safe assumption." He smiles, but this time it's sincere and not flirtatious, like he's trying to imbue a sense of self-confidence I don't have into every fiber of my mind.

Once again, I just nod. Turning to Nine, I ask, "But aren't the four pillars of magic opposite each other? So, you can't have a half Shifter, half Vampire?"

Nine smiles at me, a smile I'm beginning to realize is his wow-she's-a-nerd-too smile. I can't help it; his excitement over magical theory is addicting.

"Yes. Typically, Vampires and Shifters don't breed, and Witches and Fae don't breed because they each use magic in totally opposite ways. And even if they do breed, hybrids won't form; they will always be one or the other." He grabs another slice of garlic bread before continuing: "But you can have hybrid Witches and Vampires, or Witches and Shifters, or Fae and Vampires, or Fae and Shifters, et cetera."

"I see. But . . ." I've never heard of those kinds of hybrids before.

"The Treaty of Magical Crossbreeding prevents it. So, if there are any hybrids out there, they're likely in hiding."

"Ah. Makes sense." I look to Dea, who just smiles and silently chuckles to himself while watching us. "So, do you reckon my body could hold all four? It just sounds a little unlikely, even for a Horseman."

"Yes, it does. I guess, until your other powers come into play, we will not know."

"So we wait. Again?" I can't keep the irritation out of my voice; all this waiting and training is driving me crazy. I want to get out there, to do something useful.

Dea seems to sense the problem. "How about a group mission to Earth? To assess the problem, hunt for your seal, and see why the Shifters attacked Con?"

Earth? Me? With the rest of them? A silly grin escapes my usually stoic defenses, and I let out a little squeal. "Yes!"

"That sounds like a plan." Connie smiles and turns to the dishwasher, where she stacks the plates as we each finish. "But"—she points at me—"you must be with one of us at all times. You're not fully trained."

"Pretty sure I could throw a dagger at anyone who tried anything, or at least blow them a couple miles downwind," I grumble. There is no way she's playing the you're-not-strong-enough card on me. "Besides, I'm pretty badass myself now, you know."

"Oh yeah?" She stands behind my chair, where I'm just clearing the last of my plate. "Wanna put that to the test, little Vampire Witch?"

The fake venom in her voice lights me up, and I'm itching to go. I stand, forcing my chair to drag across the wooden floor in a squeal of wood on wood.

"Bring it on, Conquest." My arms fold over my chest.

She chuckles and shakes her head. "Maybe another time."

"After a few more centuries of training," Arrie grumbles.

His entire being pisses me off. All his grumbling, all his deep-voiced complaining . . . Argh!

Can't he just be nice or shut the hell up?

"Fuck you."

I storm through the open door to the cinema, slamming it shut behind me (which shakes the entire hallway, as I forget my strength is a little more than usual).

"Asshole."

Superhero fantasy. The cinematic world of fiction. Sweet, sweet escape. Pulling out the plasmascreen from the front of the room that connects with the large 4D screen on the wall, I select the movie and wait for the others to join.

I choose a bed this time, wanting nothing more than to snuggle under the covers in my pajamas and lose myself in another world. Up, up, up I send the bed, and watch with a smile as I realize no one is going to bother me this high in the air. A sigh of contentment escapes my lips.

I wait for the others to join me, and before long, they all stumble in, grim looks on their faces.

Not fair, Sweetie. I wanted to watch the movie with you.

The pout in Nine's voice and the sad puppy-dog look on his face makes me feel instantly guilty. For fuck's sake. I lower the bed, knowing I won't enjoy the movie if I've made someone upset by a simple choice.

Come on, then.

I can get Dea and Con to join us, if you'd like?

I do not miss the suggestion in his tone, but I shake my head. Not fair to Arrie. He's not too sweet on me at the moment, and his attitude pisses me off, but he doesn't deserve to be alone.

That's actually really sweet. Fine. Just Dea, then.

After a quick exchange of who's sitting where—and Nine getting his way—both Dea and Nine climb into bed on either side of me, Dea on my left, Nine on my right, and we raise the platform to the right height.

"Soooo," Dea starts, eyebrows raising, "that kiss with Con . . . ?"

"Is that really what you want to talk about?"

"Yes." He stares at the screen as the intro music starts, a small smile on his face. "I guess," he starts, a more serious look taking over, "I wanted to know if it is just her you harbor affection for?"

Ohmigod, ohmigod . . . Is he really asking that right now? When Nine is here and can read my mind and Connie can hear the entire conversation? "I . . . er . . ."

No.

But how do I tell them that?

Nine looks at me strangely, clearly a little baffled by my inner predicament. *Just say so. It's not like we're monogamous or anything. We're immortal. That would be . . .*

Impossible. I'm beginning to see that. Or maybe it's just my stupid attraction to this entire fucking team. It's not like I've been attracted to anyone else since I've become a Horseman.

"No, it's not." I sigh. "But she knows that."

"Oh." Dea's smile grows.

"Now shut up and watch the movie."

"Yes, Angel."

Nine slips an arm over my shoulders, and I quickly find myself snuggling into his shoulder as though it's the most normal thing in the world, and I guess, in some ways, it is (at least in this world). Dea nudges up to me from behind and curls around my back, trapping me between the two.

Connie says to tell you that we'd make a good sandwich. Wink-wink.

Did you just mentally wink at me, Nine?

I roll my eyes, feeling the heat of Connie's suggestion penetrate my cheeks—and other, more heated areas—while I try to shut the idea down. But that stupid, crazy bitch's idea has ignited a random flame of desire (well, maybe not quite so random) as I resist the urge to kiss both men beside me. Having them both in my bed . . . at the same time . . . would be insanely hot.

And they clearly have something going on, meaning they would also enjoy being together. Just the thought of their hands running all over me has me swallowing a gasp of desire.

You need to stop with that fantasy, Sweetie, or this might turn out to be quite the show for the others.

Then get out of my head.

I can't. You draw me in. And your thoughts are really loud, too. Especially those kinds of thoughts.

"Oh," I say out loud before realizing it.

"Hmmm?" Dea asks from behind me.

"Nothing," I mumble before moving to get more comfortable. I hear Dea swallow a grumble behind me, but I ignore it while Nine laughs, and we all settle down to watch the movie.

The movie turns out to be pretty good, actually, a story about finding love across the galaxy while a universe-ending event tries to rip them apart. One day, I hope I get to find love like that.

"Ugh," Arrie grumbles, "I hate love stories."

"Well, get used to it, cause they're my favorite." I skip up the hallway, choosing to walk myself to my room this time. Since I'm no longer a fragile little thing, and I seem to have gained some ass-kicking powers, I think I can manage to walk around the house without Arrie carrying me everywhere.

Arrie grumbles something behind me as I leave, my legs practically running to my room (because I can now). Seems the blood has healed all of my internal injuries, because I'm not even out of breath. Bet it would have helped speed up the healing if we knew about it earlier.

"MOMMY! DADDY!" I SCREAM AS I WATCH THEM RUN FROM THE CRASHED DOORWAY, WHERE A group of men wearing all black and carrying guns rush in.

Mom bends down and grab me, shoving me into the closet at the end of the room. "Shhhh. Please stay quiet. I need you to be quiet right now, okay?"

I nod.

"Good. Now stay here and stay hidden." She takes her necklace off and wraps it around my neck. "This will help." The bead I spent hours playing with every evening is torn off the chain that now wraps around me. "Just stay quiet, baby."

I let silent tears fall as she leaves me in the dark all alone. But a small crack in the door is just large enough for me to see through.

Mommy and Daddy fight against the men, but the men's guns loosen from their sides and aim at my parents' heads.

"Remain still!" the front man shouts. "Where is she?"

"Please!" Mom begs, now on her knees with her hands pressed together in prayer. "Please just let us be!"

"Sorry, but we cannot let a danger like her risk the safety of our world."

One of the other men whispers in his ear and points to the closet I'm in.

He growls and looks to Mommy and Daddy. "Silence them."

Two loud shots echo across the room, and I watch Mommy and Daddy fall to the floor in puddles of dark crimson blood. I want to shout out, to scream at them to get up, but I can't. I promised Mommy I'd stay quiet.

The men walk straight to me and open the closet door.

I stay stock-still, swallowing a whimper as they look straight at where I'm sitting.

Are they going to kill me?

"It's empty!" the leader growls. "It's fucking empty!"

"What?" The man that whispered before barrels past the leader to look for himself. "That's . . ."

"Let's go! Someone's probably taken her. Some friends, maybe. Let's regroup with HQ."

A HOT SWEAT OF FEAR SHOOTS ME AWAKE FROM A NIGHTMARE I CAN'T QUITE PLACE; I WAS IN A place I barely recognized, surrounded by people I didn't know, and they were all dying. Everyone around me was dying. Could this be a memory? Or just a random dream? It was much more real than the other nightmare fragments.

I try to forget about it and go back to sleep, but as the minutes tick by and my mind stays as wide awake as ever, I realize I need to know.

Nine will know. Plus, his rooms are only down the hall. I get out of bed, throw on a thin nightgown, and tiptoe down the hall. I have no idea what the time is or if he'll even be awake.

Maybe waking him is a bad idea.

What if he'll be angry with me?

It must be exhausting mentally babysitting me all the time. Maybe I'll try to give him more of a break from it in the future. But right now, though, I really need answers. Can I dream of a past I can't remember? Who are those people? Are they my . . . family?

Nine's rooms are only a few meters away, and I soon find myself in front of a slightly ajar door with a small amount of light creeping through. A familiar pair of voices are talking beyond the door, and I know it's rude to eavesdrop, but I'm ashamed to say their conversation intrigues me.

"You can't complain about that! You're not the one living her every fantasy and dirty thought, bro."

A few small moans follow, along with Dea's response. "But . . . she is just so . . ."

"Yeah," Nine sighs. "She is, isn't she?" They shuffle around a bit (well, I assume that's what they're doing) and resettle before Nine says, "I can help."

"That is why I am here, lover."

Lover? Right, they have something going on. I already know that. Dea's voice sounds so husky, like he and Nine are. . .

Oh! I turn to walk away, realizing I've eavesdropped on the wrong kind of conversation.

Come in.

Wait, what?

Come in and join us.

But . . .

I can hear your mind wondering. Want to see what we're doing?

Do I? Will that be okay? My mind says yes before I can stop it and say something more appropriate. But that would be rude.

Then I invite you in to come and see.

Will that make anything weird between us? Maybe just a peek . . .

I open the door farther and am thankful Nine's hinges are well-oiled. I intend to just have a quick peek out of curiosity (he did say it's okay) and leave, but what I see has me frozen to the spot.

Dea stands by the edge of the bed, eyes closed and head rolled back, his feet on the floor, and kneeling in front his legs is a head of bright red hair—Nine's hair—moving up and down on Dea's cock.

Nine chuckles in my mind, clearly amused by my stooped curiosity that has my feet firmly fixed to the spot.

Dea fists Nine's hair and commands, "Harder."

Nine says nothing; he just picks up the pace, using his hand to massage the base of Dea's cock to the same rhythm his mouth has set.

Dea stands the entire time, his knees buckling now and then, his usual galaxy eyes glowing shots of gold as he opens them. He starts gently moaning as Nine seems to change the pace to something else he likes.

I need to leave. This is private between the two of them. But, fuck me, it's hot as hell, and my entire body wants to jump into the mix and see what happens. But I don't. I can't leave, my eyes darting between what Nine is doing and Dea's face of pleasure, but I can't join in, either.

I still don't want the whole casual sex thing, even as every inch of me cries out for attention.

Dea tries to say something, but Nine sucks harder, his cheeks hollowing out, and Dea instead lets out an audible moan that has my insides squeezing in pleasure.

"Nine," Dea growls as he grips Nine's hair tighter and meets his mouth's every stroke with a few thrusts of his hips. Every thrust is harder than the one before until he's fucking Nine's mouth so hard Nine's gone still to let Dea use him and take his pleasure.

I want to look away, to give them their moment of privacy, and I finally make my feet turn around when Nine interrupts my thoughts.

Keep watching.

But—

You'll miss the finale.

I've never heard Nine be so incorrigibly filthy-mouthed before—well, filthy-minded.

And, goddess dammit, I want to watch. No idea what that says about me as a person, but so long as I have permission, I refuse to feel guilty about it.

I turn back around as Dea cries out with his head tipping backwards and his hands keeping Nine's head firmly in place.

Nine pulls away slightly with a wince, and if I didn't know any better, I would say he's giving me a better view. I watch Nine swallow every last drop of Dea's release and give me a cock-filled smile afterward.

My head lifts from Nine's face to Dea's galaxy-filled eyes once more, and, shit, they're staring right at me. I've been totally caught in the act. I have no idea if Nine told him I'm watching.

Nope. But he's fine. Promise.

Well, that's good news. Kind of. I mean, I'm still kinda peeping.

I don't know what to say, and every time I try to open my mouth to let any kind of defensible words come out, my voice dries up. Shit. My legs take me out of there as fast as they can before I say something stupid.

What was I thinking?

I just watched Nine sucking Dea's cock and chose to stay. "Grrr," I grumble to myself. Connie's gonna get a laugh out of this on Friday when she asks me all about my week.

I roll my eyes in exasperation as I climb back into bed, the essence of my previous nightmare having all but fled my mind as I lie there in a mess of sexual frustration while the image of Nine's lips wrapping around Dea's cock refuses to leave my mind.

I leap out of bed with a frustrated groan and run a bath, hoping it will help relax my body into sleep and make me forget about Nine and Dea—fat chance of that.

Once the tub is full, I dip my toes in and edge the rest of my body into the bubbly water, sighing in relief once I sit up to my neck in the warmth.

Dea's eyes were like shining gold when he . . .

Stop thinking about that! Think of something else instead. Like that romance I was reading the other day: they sure were perfect for each other.

A bit like Nine and Dea in a way; they're perfect for each other, too.

For fuck's sake.

The memory of Dea's comment about some alone time flitters across my mind, and maybe he's right. Even Nine said I have a sex-filled mind, and he can read everyone's minds. If I want to continue working with this damn team, I need to take care of all this pent-up frustration and need.

Lowering my hand down my stomach, I take a deep breath and let the memory of earlier play over and over like a stuck record as my fingers brush the outside of my core, teasing the entrance until I'm a mess of need. I thrust one finger, then two inside, hooking them slightly and finding that perfect spot as I continue thrusting.

My breaths come quicker as I spread my legs wider and graze my clit with the heel of my hand, causing a small moan to escape my lips.

Before I know it, my imagination slips out of my control, and I'm imagining myself on that bed in Dea's place, with Nine's tongue working me into a frenzy that matches the speed of my own hand. Imagining Dea joining in is what pushes me over the edge, though, and I'm suddenly thankful for the size of this house.

I can't stifle the cry that slips out before I sink my head under the water and feel every muscle in my body switch off as I rise to the surface and lie there for a moment in a pool of unworried bliss.

19

The next day is beyond awkward. I do my usual yoga routine at dawn and then sit down to breakfast with everyone. Connie immediately knows something's up, as Nine, Dea, and I keep exchanging awkward glances and returning to our breakfasts in silence.

Every time I glance over at them, all I can picture is them together on Nine's bed, and I get the feeling my memories are making Nine uncomfortable, as he looks more and more frustrated as breakfast goes on. He even grumbles something under his breath in a true, pretty accurate mimic of Arrie's usual nonsense attitude.

I can't stay there a moment longer in the awkward silence. "I'm gonna be in the library."

"We will be continuing from where we left off yesterday," Dea announces to my back.

It takes me a moment to realize he meant with training, not my midnight escapade. Fucking great. I'm gonna spend another evening bloodthirsty and turned all the way up. Ugh. I thought some time to myself would fix all this pent-up need, but I was wrong. All it did was fuel the flame.

The library invites me in with its usual airs and graces of knowledgeable silence, a state I find myself mimicking every time something gets a little difficult. Fiction for a few hours, I think. Research can wait. I go in search of a new book down the various aisles and corridors of towering shelves. Maybe a romance? I flick my finger across a few titles and pick out one that sounds interesting: THE DRAGON SHIFTERS OF ANCIENT GREECE.

The nearest reading nook is a few corners away (I have most mapped out by this point), and I settle in and quickly devour page after page, and before I know it, I hear voices interrupting the character's badass battle with the evil dragon hunter asshole. I consider putting my book down and trying to find the intruders, but fuck 'em. Let them find me for a change. I have a climactic ending to finish.

It only takes a few more pages before Dea's whizzing form rushes by, and I catch a brief glimpse of galaxy eyes as he rushes past. He slows, and I hear him turn back around and come to a stop.

"What delectable book are you reading today?"

I hold up the cover as I continue to read, not bothering to respond. He can fucking wait a minute.

"Hmmm . . . You seem to have a thing for dragons, don't you?"

I nod, turning the next page.

Dea chuckles and sits on the bright orange pouf next to mine, leaning his arm over my shoulder to read with me.

I don't bother slowing down for him, though, I just keep reading, wanting to know if the characters inevitably beat the villain and finally mate for life in the end. Will he take her as his dragon bride after all?

"You read some utter drivel, Angel," Dea mutters close to my ear. "Mating does not really exist."

Again, I don't answer. I just keep on reading.

"Okay!" Dea steals the book from my hands, stashes it spine-up on the nearest small bookshelf, and grabs my hands. "You are ignoring me."

"Nope. Just trying to read."

"Oh, so you not saying a single word to either of us the entire morning has nothing to do with your little perverted escapade last night?"

That familiar, charming confidence is back, and I know Dea isn't going to let this go.

"I'm more concerned about other things right now. Like winning a magical war with next to no magic."

"That is why you are reading fiction rather than studying?" He tugs on my arm, and I sigh, letting him guide me into standing. "I know you read when you want to escape. Quit trying to escape this."

"Escape what?" I look up at him, mere inches from his face, and give my best stony exterior.

He sighs. "This conversation." He grips the tops of my arms. "Neither Nine nor I care that you were watching. Okay? It just took me by surprise. You are rather . . . innocent." He blushes at the comment, clearly feeling a little awkward.

I can't help it—I let out a giggle. "So Nine doesn't tell you all of my thoughts, then. That's nice to know."

"Nine does not tell anyone the private thoughts of another. Well, he does if it is important." Dea waves the comment off, as if to say it doesn't matter, and continues. "Look. Just quit feeling embarrassed and come to training?"

"Fine. But you should know that Nine asked me to watch. I wasn't being some kind of weird pervert." Well, to begin with I was, but Dea doesn't need to know that. "I was invited."

Dea stands still as I turn and head toward the training room. Realizing he isn't following, I look back. "What?"

"He . . . He really invited you?"

"Yup." I smirk, knowing I have one up on Dea and am using it to be as confident as possible in the moment. I grab his elbow, link my arm through his, and drag him along with me in silence.

The training room is warmer today, and I realize Nine is placing some logs in the burning fireplace, heating the room.

I am gonna fucking boil alive in here.

Nine?

Yes?

I'm sorry I've been ignoring you.

I sheepishly look to the ground, arm still locked around Dea's. But, as Nine turns, he's smiling his happy smile.

It's okay, Sweetie. I was just giving you space. Last night was fun. We should do it again sometime.

Blushing, I get the feeling that Nine is more confident when speaking telepathically than vocally, like it somehow makes him feel more comfortable; in a way, I kind of understand. It's a private connection between the two of us.

"We need you to fight with your Vampire strength," Dea interrupts. "So we wanted you to feed, then take on Arrie in hand-to-hand combat." Dea doesn't even flinch as he says that; he just stands there all stoic and shit, looking like a lit candle by those sparkling flames in the otherwise boringly dull room.

For fuck's sake. This is going to be impossible. Even more so once someone bleeds. I remember the feeling of tension and heat radiating from my core yesterday, and I'm equally as terrified as I am eager to repeat the experience. On the one hand, being a . . . you know, thing, is weird, and it feels awkwardly intimate when feeding, but it's also desirable in a way normal food just isn't.

"Do not be scared," Dea says as he wraps me in his arms from behind. "We are both right here. We can give you anything you need to help ease the process."

Damn him. The fucker. He knows very well what I want when feeding, but I'm just not prepared to give it. Not yet. Color me old-fashioned, but I'm just not ready. That doesn't mean his words don't set a new flame alight in my body, making my nipples harden and my thighs clench.

I pull out of his embrace and turn to face him. "Fine. But if you're stuck in bed for a few days recovering, you ain't fucking complaining about it. This was your idea."

Dea smirks. "Deal."

I'll be right here to help.

Thank you. "So, how do we . . ."

I look nervously at Dea, who smiles gently and offers me his wrist.

Guess I'll need my fangs out for this one. It doesn't take much focus; all I have to do is concentrate on the memory of his blood from yesterday, and I can feel that familiar tickle and ache in my gums that signals the extrusion of my fangs.

I catch myself, shocked for a moment there. My fangs? How ridiculous my life has become. Though, you never know, my life may have been just as insane before.

But the moment doesn't last long, as that familiar hunger that comes as an almost-comical side effect explodes through my body, forcing my foot forward and causing my neck to crane toward Dea's offered wrist.

Dea still smiles at me, but it's a little weaker this time, and I can see the nerves settle across his eyes. He's also worried about this, but he's doing it anyway.

Yeah, because he's a fucking idiot.

Dea, Arrie, and I will always offer to help with this; any one of us will willingly feed you to keep you strong and healthy. You're family.

I do not miss the exclusion of Connie in that sentence, or the small amount of warmth I get from Nine's surety that Arrie would participate despite his obvious disdain toward me.

Dea's wrist rests in the palm of my hand, and my fangs inch forward, itching to sink in and taste him once more. But if I do, will I stop? Will that black hole my mind always goes to become more permanent? I'd be lying if I said I'm not scared. This is it, though. There's no going back after this. But it doesn't matter because I can't go back to being human; I haven't been human since the moment I woke up in this house, and that isn't going to change just because of this. I am a Vampire—or at least part Vampire—and this is my new normal.

With that last internal pep talk, and the slight reminder that Nine is there at the edge of my mind ready to help, I sink my fangs into Dea's wrist and draw a few mouthfuls before pausing to savor the taste. This isn't just a drop, where I can taste the honey and metallic scent that pervades my senses and tries to lure me in; this is like my every need is being met. From all things physical to mental to emotional, I'm sated. Completely and utterly whole.

After the initial bliss, my mind returns to my body as I swallow another mouthful of Dea's blood, and the fire that has been a small blaze since my perverted escapade (as Dea politely put it) last night, is now a roaring inferno, setting every crevice of my being on fire. The thin tank top I chose to wear today is doing nothing to hide my hardened nipples —neither is the thin lacy bra, I might add—and I can feel every raw need pulsing through my entire body.

I need this man. In so many ways.

Before I know what I'm doing, I shove Dea back against the wall, pinning him in place, and look up at his face. His eyes are a slight haze, as though he's enjoying this, too, and I'm all too aware of his every muscle that tenses, every artery that echoes a gentle rhythm in my ears, and the feel of his erection against my body.

I want it all. His blood. His body. His soul. I want to devour every part of him.

Wait . . . what? Sudden awareness lights up my mind like a fairground. I don't want to devour him at all. That's just the bloodlust.

You need to stop feeding now, Sweetie.

Huh?

I blanch and tear myself away from Dea's wrist, not even realizing I was still latched on. Still drinking his . . . blood. Oh no! I nearly . . . I was just . . .

Shhhh. It's okay. Dea's fine.

I look up at my willing victim (because, let's be honest, he was prey for a minute there) and watch as the desire slowly fades from him.

One minute, Dea looks like he wants to yank me back against him and for me to drain him dry, and the next, awareness hits him like a freight train as he stumbles forward on shaky legs.

My arms go out to steady him, and Nine and I slowly sit him on the floor. All Dea says, though, is, "Time to fight Arrie."

Seriously? That's what he's thinking about right now?

"I will be all right in a few minutes." He looks up at the doorway. "All right, Arrie. Now it is your turn."

Arrie? He's been there the whole time? How much has he seen?

Everything.

Oh. Well, shit. He's sure to hate me even more now.

Arrie steps forward, a heated, angry glare on his face, and gets himself into the center of the room. "Fangs out, Vampire senses on." He cracks his knuckles. "Time to train."

I nod, trying to focus on my senses and the newfound strength coursing through me. Just like with the fangs earlier, it's instinctual, and my fangs descend easily. I'm not sure how strong I am right now, or how fast, but I am eager to find out. But I really don't want to hurt another teammate today.

Throwing a look over at Dea, whose color has returned to his cheeks and looks a little less weak, I grimace.

"Ready?" Arrie grumbles.

"Yes."

Arrie brings his arms up to his middle, protecting his vital organs that I can hear thrumming away, and closes his eyes briefly. Upon reopening them, his gaze is different; his eyes take on a more focused, battle-ready color. It's a little hard to describe, but this is not a man you fight against willingly.

I speed forward and raise a fist, hoping to get a right hook in before he's prepared to defend, but he jumps back, and I fall to the floor on two balanced feet.

Vampire senses rule.

I'm a little weightless so try using that to my advantage by spinning around Arrie and kicking him in the back. I catch him with my toe, but he mostly dodges.

So close.

Is he gonna fight back?

Just as the thought crosses my mind, Arrie spins on his heel and throws me to the floor. He has me pinned, his hands on my forearms and his knees on my legs. Pain radiates from his weight on my pressure points, but it isn't enough to cripple me; I can still move.

Arrie pierces me with his battlemode-hazed eyes, and I should be scared—this man (if you can even call him that) is far stronger than me, even after my feeding, and has the ability to magically figure out the best strategy for winning any fight—but I am not. Color me stupid, but I find his ability fascinating. He plays on my inability and unskilled body in terms of fighting, knowing I can outrun him if it comes to it.

Also, his battlemode is supposed to be an all-encompassing thing, and supposedly he struggles to come out of it until he's killed his opponent. So why can I still move?

He doesn't kill us in his battlemode.

Ah, okay. That makes sense. Guess it would be pointless anyway, because there isn't a strategy that can kill us in battle, so the two likely cancel each other out.

But, still, he's going easy on me in a mindset that's plagued him for years—centuries. I bet he doesn't go easy on the others. So why me?

"Arrie?"

I lose all pretense of this fight (we can go again in a moment); right now, I want to figure out why I can still move.

I wriggle my wrists free from his grip and grab his shoulders as his palms slam down on the floor. He groans under his breath before whispering, "Feed from me next time."

"Huh?"

"Do not hurt my family." He climbs off of me and walks to Dea, placing a hand on each shoulder. "You okay, dude?"

Dea wobbles from his now-standing position, and I fight back a gasp. He's hurt, isn't he? I did that? Me?

I can't . . .

Worry creeps its way through my mind, and although I can hear Nine's soothing words in my head, I can't actually hear them above my own anxiety.

Dea collapses to the floor, pale from blood loss, and Arrie catches him just before his head hits the concrete. "I'll take him to his room."

I can't breathe. I try hard to inhale and gather up oxygen, but I just can't. Air. I need air.

My feet run from the room before I can do anything else or warn Nine, who's halfway to reaching me when I zoom out of there at Vampire speed, leaving a windtrail in my wake.

I'm not really sure where I'm going, I just need some air. I run down the stairs, my feet finding the kitchen, where Connie sits reading some magical newspaper, and I exit through the back door and sprint into the forest. I don't stop until I reach a clearing in the middle that has Arrie's scent dotted around, teasing my Vampire senses and making me hungry in a way that makes me crave blood instead of food.

"Argh!" I cry out in frustration.

I don't want comfort right now, and I'm pretty sure that's why I came here, because Arrie's scent reminds me of something I can never have.

Family? Nine's a bigger idiot than me. I can't have a family here; even among the Horsemen of the fucking Apocalypse, I'm a freak. I just want to be normal!

A memory rushes across my mind.

Smoke pours from my hands in a simple backyard as I scream at a familiar man. "I just want to be normal!"

He looks at me with pity, understanding, and his blond hair and handsome features school my attitude as he scowls. "But you are not."

Tears stain my face as I sob, not really sure if it's the past's or present's fault, but in that moment, it all molds into the same pile of crap my life's become and seems to always have been.

My mind comes back to the present, and I find myself crouching in a ball in the middle of the forest clearing I've run to. I can't wallow in regret like this; it isn't like my life will change and I can wake up human tomorrow. But the memory of Dea collapsing replays itself over and over in my mind, like a stupid broken song that I can't quite jam to but keep playing anyway.

Arrie's face. He really hates me. If not before, then he definitely does now. I'll never fit in here, and part of me really doesn't want to stay in a house full of people I put in danger. Not to mention all the stupid dynamics that I've completely ruined just by being myself.

"Arrghh!"

I jump to my feet, frustration curling my hands into fists, and begin pacing in a circle around the clearing. I need to think myself out of this. Somehow. But no matter how many circles I think around, I'm stuck, because the world needs me; no matter what I'm doing to the four people I've come to call friends, the ten billion people on Earth are about to head into a war only I can stop (supposedly).

"Looks like I have to stay." I need their training, no matter what it puts us all through, no matter how torturous it might be.

As great as it is to come to some kind of conclusion about my life, the conclusion itself frustrates me beyond belief. I need to do something. Something to let all this pent-up energy out. Between the frustration and the blood I drank, it's like my anger has a fire fueling it.

I stand in front of a tree and do the first thing that comes naturally to my regret-addled mind. I punch it.

Yeah, I know. It's stupid. Even for me. But you know what? It helps. And since my skin heals as fast as I punch, it seems like a good stress reliever.

Left. Right. Left. Right. The skin on my knuckles breaks again and again, and eventually blood stains my hands, but nothing. No thoughts stop the anger from taking control.

Dea could have been seriously hurt.

Left. Right.

If he were human, I would have killed him.

Left. Right.

I'm breaking this team apart.

Left. Right.

I'll never belong anywhere.

Left. Right.

Who am I?

Left. Right.

It continues this way for an hour, until the sun starts to set, lighting pieces of the sky I can see through the trees in a beautiful pink blush. I must have been playing over that memory and drowning in my sorrows and guilt all afternoon.

That is so not like me.

But . . . who is that man in the memory?

What was that smoke?

Was I not human in my mortal life?

That question is enough to throw all the day's infuriating events out the window and force me back inside the house.

Connie, Nine, and Arrie sit around the kitchen table eating various types of giant sandwiches, and they all look at my bloodied hands with shock and sadness in their eyes, but it's Connie who breaks the silence.

"Hon—"

I hold up a hand and shake my head. "Tell me when Dea wakes up."

She nods, and I grab the sandwich waiting for me and leave, working my way toward the scent of age-old knowledge and musty pages that I can smell, even from down here.

20

Nothing. A big fat nothing. That's what I find when I ask my Seeing Stone about black smoky magic. There's no record in this library about that type of magic. Either I was someone insanely special with a unique type of magic when I was human (if I even was), or this is another one of those stupid times when the library is purposefully hiding things from me or not stocking them so I can't learn important pieces of info on my own.

Either way, it's frustrating as hell.

My hands are bleeding slightly—seems my Vampire healing, which speeds up even my Horseman healing, has started to wear off—but I leave them be. I want to be reminded of the reason for the pain. Dea's in his room somewhere, unconscious, because I nearly drained him dry. He looked so damn pale—

Nope. Stop thinking about that. It's not helping. You need to work on control, find out who the fuck you are, and fix this stupid magical war.

My sandwich lies untouched on the desk. Honestly, I only took it because Nine or Connie would have bothered me for hours if I didn't. But now, after a few hours of nothing-research, my stomach grumbles, and I take a bite.

It's made of some kind of meat, but I didn't bother to ask what it was in my foul mood, and it tastes damn amazing. It's salty, smoky, and melds well with the fluffy white bread and butter surrounding it.

"That is a pleasing sound," a familiar, overly flirty voice says. "Seems you like bacon. Not that I have ever met someone who does not."

Dea.

"Bacon? Ohmigod, of course. I used to eat this at a particular café in Akihabara; they served the most amazing dusted tea with their fucking rainbow cupcakes."

"Rainbow cupcakes? You have lived quite the colorful life, Angel."

"Hilarious." I roll my eyes to the floor, trying my hardest not to look at him.

"Angel . . ." Dea walks up to me and sinks to kneel beside my desk chair. "You know it was not your . . ." He notices my hands and sighs. "Fault." He grabs my hands and takes them in his, using his green-glowing healing magic to clear up the last of the cuts.

"Dea . . . I . . ." I don't even know what to say. What do you say to someone you drank dry in a Vampire-feeding frenzy? "I'm sorry."

He shakes his head with a smile. "Arrie should not have said anything to you. I knew the risks. I knew you were not likely to control your feeding this early."

"Then, why—?"

"Because I wanted you strong and using the magic available to you. You are a half Vampire, Angel. You need to feed. It will make you the Horseman Fate intended."

That phrase reminds me of Nine's eerie words of wisdom the other day: You must become the person the world needs to you be.

Is that who the word needs? A blood-sucking Vampire?

"I just . . ." I sigh. "I'm sorry." Tears threaten to break the banks of my tenuous hold, and I bat them away. "I just don't want to hurt any of you, or break up the team, or let the world down, or never discover who I am—"

"You have a lot on your plate right now. That is okay. You should get some sleep, and tomorrow we will go to Earth to start seeing what the problems are."

"Earth? Really?" That perks me up. Finally. Going back to Earth.

Dea chuckles. "Yes. So get some rest."

I should tell him about the flashback. "Er . . . Dea?"

"Yes, Angel?"

"I had a flashback while in the forest."

He looks at me with raised eyebrows.

"I-I-I . . ."

"Take a deep breath."

Heeding his advice, I take a deep breath and force the words out of my mouth at a louder-than-normal volume. "I wasn't human!"

"Wh-what?"

"I wasn't human. In the flashback, I was using the Angel magic just like in the kitchen. I was screaming at some man that I just wanted to be normal, and it leaked out of my body."

"You . . . You what?" He looks genuinely taken aback. "You were an Angel-descended Witch in your mortal life? That . . . that is not possible."

"Why not?"

"Because the last of them were destroyed twenty years ago."

THE NEXT MORNING, WE'RE ALL DRESSED AND EATING BREAKFAST IN THE KITCHEN TOGETHER AS though nothing went wrong yesterday. They avoid talking about it. Arrie doesn't speak or look at me, and Nine's back to helpfully flirting. All in all, a pretty standard morning for the Horseman of Magic.

Dea fills them in on the flashback, saving me the job, and Nine could not be more excited by the magical possibilities.

But there's something they're not telling me. Something they're keeping quiet about. I can see it all in the silent looks they give each other, the occasional heated mental conversation between Nine and Dea, and the way Connie's constantly smiling sweetly at me. It's driving me nuts.

"Enough!" I slam my spoon down on the table—bending it in the process—and get everyone's attention. "Spit it out!"

"Are we that easy to read?" Nine asks sarcastically.

"Yes."

Connie's the one who comes forward with the answer, though. "You need to feed before leaving."

The spoon I try to pick back up clatters to the table. "No. No way. Forget it. You can take my Witch magic or nothing." I fold my arms over my chest and shake my head.

"Then nothing," Dea whispers through clenched teeth, then sighs. "You need to move past this, Angel. You are a half Vampire. You are at your fullest when you feed regularly."

"Half Vampire means I don't need to feed."

"Fucking christ," Arrie says in the loudest voice I've ever heard him use, and even then, it's barely above normal volume.

He picks up the knife he was using to cut the bread with and slices his palm. Blood drips onto the table in a steady stream that makes my gums tingle and my teeth ache as that familiar hunger returns.

Connie gasps and turns around, and I can't help but be a little hurt. She's clearly gone through something involving Vampires, and I should try to help her past that—the moment I can fully control myself because I have to fight every instinct not to rip Arrie's throat out right now.

Arrie grabs a glass and holds his squeezed palm up to the rim, letting the blood steadily fill the glass. He has to make a few more cuts, but he eventually fills the glass to the rim as I watch every drop land in my new favorite glass.

"Here." He slides the glass across the table and holds his hand, waiting for the last cut to heal.

But I don't care about that—he's a Horseman, he'll heal in a moment—all I care about is the delicious smoky, metallic scent wafting from that glass. It smells different from Dea's blood, which is like smoky lavendar, and that fact alone has me curious enough to drink it.

I tip the glass up to my lips and take a sip, trying not to bang my fangs on the side of the glass (yes, I'm aware of how odd an issue that is to have). When Nine notices my struggle, he hands me a straw from goddess knows where, and I down the entire glass in one, not even noticing my surroundings.

In that moment, I don't care that Connie's terrified of me, that Arrie looks at me with equal measures of disgust and fascination, that Nine probably thinks I'm some kind of strange science experiment he can probe whenever he wants. All I care about is the taste of foresty goodness lapping along my tongue asI swallow every drop.

Once the glass is empty and the straw is making that weird, empty-cup sucking sound, I frown. I want more. Looking up at Arrie, I can almost see the artery in his neck pulsing, and I can definitely hear the beat of his heart if I concentrate. Right now, it's faster than it should be.

Is he scared?

My fangs snap back in an instant and my hand grabs the glass to go and wash it —thoroughly.

"Thank you," I say to Arrie once I sit back down and tap Connie to turn back around. I give her a sweet, understanding smile, hoping one day she'll open up enough to talk to me about it. I take a deep breath, wanting nothing more than to just be my normal self for the moment. "So," I say as I turn to Dea, "where are going? How are we getting there? Do we split up? What exactly are we—?"

Dea's laughter fills the air. "It has been a while since one of us had our first mission. You are staying with me and Nine, and we will be taking the Witches and Vampires, while Connie and Arrie will handle the Shifters and Fae."

"Handle?" That doesn't sound good.

Nine smiles at me. "We're going to talk to the leaders of each community, generally sniff around, and be a group of nosy shits. See what's going on. That kind of thing." He looks up at me. "Oh, and ask around about your seal."

I nod, understanding finally settling in. "Sounds good. Let's go." I stand up quicker than lightning but stop. "I can't believe this question hasn't occurred to me sooner, but how do we get to Earth?"

This time Arrie laughs a deep, belly-filled laugh that escapes his throat, and the sound surprises me so much I jump and nearly fall flat on my ass, but Nine catches me last minute.

"Thanks."

"You'll see, Sweetie."

We leave out the front door a few minutes later, after packing all the weapons we need (I'm carrying more knives than I know how to handle and a few sealed bottles of blood Dea prepared earlier), and head down the trail into town.

The town is only thirty minutes away, and it's awesome to get there in that time instead of the hour it took previously due to my injuries.

It's just as I remember, a combination of Victorian England and modern-day science magic. It's beautiful in a way I can't really describe, as though the best bits of Earth got together and called a truce to coexist peacefully. It's just . . . nice.

I breathe in the fresh air of people, shops, and flowers as we walk toward a tall building in what looks like the center of town. Inscribed on the front is a sign that reads: TOWN HALL. So we're getting to Earth through the town hall?

I hear Nine chuckle next to me, and I have a funny feeling he's keeping a closer mind's eye on my thoughts after yesterday. It's a little invasive, but I'm kinda used to it by now (since I think so loudly anyway), and besides, it's nice to know he cares enough to keep an eye out.

I don't think the old me really had that, at least not fully. I'm not sure how I know, but I just do. I briefly wonder who was in my life, and my mind latches onto the memory from yesterday, of me wielding black, smoky magic and shouting at some random guy that I wanted to be normal.

Even though I can be anything I want now, and can probably change my mind every fifty or so years, I still want that. To be normal. Human.

You might not be able to be human, but you could live out a human-spanned life as normally as you wished. You're not trapped here with us, you know. If you wanted to spend a few decades on Earth without us, you can.

But after we've dealt with this.

Yes, sorry, but the world does need saving.

And you'll rightfully have to call on me anytime a crisis that needs my attention comes along. I'll still be a Horseman, Nine. That won't change.

Secretly, or at least I hope I manage to keep it a secret, the very thought of spending time semi-permanently away from the team is a painful notion. I need them. Maybe that won't always be the case, but for now, I need people who understand what it's like to be me.

We walk through various hallways and past a whole host of office doors with all sorts of names and positions written on their respective plaques, until we reach a door at the end labeled: EARTH PORTAL.

"Portal magic?" But that's—

"Not around anymore, yes. We know. But this was created the same time as this realm, which was when we were born, so it was back in a different time," Nine explains.

There's going to be a lot of Nine explaining my questions today, isn't there?

Probably.

That was rhetorical, Nine.

He chuckles before opening the shiny black doors and clearly takes immense pleasure in watching my jaw drop at the sight beyond.

It's a room full of trees and brightly glowing flowers. From tall pines to small, glowing blue fairyroots, this place is like a snippet of the fairy garden back at the team's house—or how I imagine it looks at night.

I would love to capture it in some kind of painting or image.

We all enter, and Nine takes it upon himself to explain how the portal works. "It's a combination of Witch and Fae magic that takes your magical energy and distributes it on Earth. It's actually really clever. Portal magic doesn't exist on Earth because there isn't a Fae alive today who can use it."

"Hmmm. So, hypothetically, if I could open up my hypothetical Fae powers, I could hypothetically create something like this by combining my magic?"

Nine grows a wide smile and nods excitedly. "Exactly."

Arrie rolls his eyes. "C'mon nerds. Let's get going."

I look around, not really sure where to stand.

"Over there." Nine points to a section in the center with five chairs. "Seems the portal has already adjusted to your presence."

He gets lost in thought for a moment, and I catch myself wondering what it would be like to see the inside of his mind, see how his thoughts work, how his process happens when figuring things out. How much knowledge must he have, being two thousand years old?

"Oh god, we really do have two nerds to deal with now." Connie smiles, pulls me by the arm, and drags me to one of the chairs before sitting in the one on my right.

Nine plonks himself down on my left, and Dea and Arrie take the remaining two.

"Now wha—?"

My question is cut off by the sudden feeling of losing every part of myself to a weightless void of space, my body barely hanging onto its own limbs as I crash down into a random place full of scents and sounds I don't recognize.

"Wh-where are we?"

"Denver, Colorado, US."

Looking around, I notice we're in a sort of office-looking room surrounded by the same type of fairy garden as the portal on the other side. But on this side, there're tables and chairs dotting the foliage and doors on the side of the perimeter wall.

Dea gets up first, followed by the rest, but my stomach feels like it's going to fall out of my body, and I swear that my breakfast is going to come back up.

Nine senses my predicament with an amused expression, but Arrie just grunts and walks toward the door.

"A little heads up next time, please."

"Sorry." Connie winces once she's noticed me half huddled over in my seat. "Let me help."

Dea wanders off somewhere to do goddess knows what, while Nine and Connie help me to my feet. Arrie's already exited the room, but I have no patience right now to deal with him.

"Here," Dea says, handing me something in his hand. "Eat this."

Eat? Like, now?

Seeing my confused face, Dea explains, "It is a ginger biscuit. Helps with nausea." He points to a desk by the main entrance in the distance. "They hand them out free over there."

I blush, feeling a little cared for with all the attention he seems to pay my needs. Between Dea taking care of my physical needs, Nine taking care of my mental and emotional wellbeing, and Connie helping to lighten things, they're my personal balance right now.

That makes Nine smile wider than I've ever seen, and that's saying something, because his neutral facial expression is smiling. Or at least, I assume it is; he never does anything else unless he's puzzling something out, and even then, he looks happily confused. Like he enjoys being as confused as other people are frustrated.

I nibble on the gingersnap for a moment, refraining from correcting Dea's comment about it being a biscuit (he obviously learned his English in England, or maybe he is originally from England?) But really, if you have a ginger snap in America, it's a fucking gingersnap. It would be a biscuit if it's something from the UK. Right? Maybe? You know what, I feel like I've gone off on a tangent here, and I should be focused on something else.

Nine doubles over in laughter. "Oh god, Sweetie. I can't wait for you to bring that up with Dea!" He can't control his laughter and has trouble breathing for a moment, wiping his eyes from the tears that spill. Then he corrects himself and dusts off his black jacket as he strides toward the door, the rest of us following on his heels.

"Bring what up?" Dea asks.

"Oh, nothing." Nine skips forward with a sly grin in the best mood I've ever seen him in.

Connie links her arm around mine and whispers, "Nine loves Earth."

"Ah. That explains his child-in-a-candy-shop attitude, then." Though part of me wonders if it's also due to my earlier thought.

"Uh-huh." She winks, and we follow the guys out the front door and onto Earth.

We step into an empty parking lot. I guess not many people use the portal, at least not regularly enough to need a permanent car here.

Nine fills me in with his usual fact-of-the-month voice. "Most people only use the portal for business, but none as frequently as us."

"Does the portal only open to here?"

"Yes," Dea says on a sigh. "It is a little annoying, actually. Takes ages to get anywhere, and I cannot tell you the stress of moving a horse across the ocean, even magical ones."

"You take the horses through that monstrosity of a mode of transportation?" I gesture back to the portal building, which I have decided to put on the top of a new list in my mind: places I want to spend as little time in as possible. So far, it only consists of two places. The portal buildings and alone with Arrie.

"Yup," Nine adds. "But only Dea really needs to on a regular basis. We rarely need them these days."

I look confusedly at Connie, who explains, "We only use them in battle, but Dea uses his when dealing with dying soul issues."

"Right, Horseman of Death. Almost forgot." It's hard to think of Dea as the Horseman of Death; he's just so . . . normal.

Right? I keep saying he needs to act the part more.

I internally chuckle. Are you going to stay in my mind the entire time we're here?

Sorry, he cringes. *But Dea asked me to. Your first mission, your first time here on Earth with not many memories, and yesterday . . . We just feel it would be best to know if anything upsets you.*

Right, because I'm a powerful Vampire Witch with untapped power and can probably level a country if I have a bad mood swing. Remind me not to spend time around other people when on my period.

Do we still get periods? Cause it would be a great perk if we fucking don't.

You do. Sorry.

Nine doesn't say anything else on the matter and gestures to Connie as if to say this is an ask-the-female kind of question.

Men. I roll my eyes. It's nice to know immortal men are just the same as the rest, though. It's also nice to know that I can start making those internal comments as my non-conscious memories of my Earth life settle in.

I'm looking forward to this.

Arrie waits for us at the road-side entrance to the parking lot with his usual scowl beside two amazing cars. Aperta 9000Xs. One is white, one is black, and I swear I nearly stop in my tracks. They run on a combination of magic fuel and leyline power, meaning they can travel off leylines if need be. They're top of the line, only released in the last year or so (I think), and the most ridiculously expensive vehicle I've ever seen in my life.

Nine, tell me I get to drive one of those?

Haha. They're Arrie's. Sorry, Sweetie.

Fuck my life. Well, I have all of eternity, I will get my hands on one of those bad boys one day, even if I have to send Arrie into a mini-vacation of unconsciousness to do so. The ass cannot have all the toys and not share.

But you can ride up front with me if you like?

I can?

Yeah. Ours is the white one.

"Shotgun!" I run up to the white car's front passenger door and refuse to move, my hands on my hips as I bob up and down on the spot. I'm so ready to ride one of these fucking cars.

Connie and Dea laugh while Nine silently smiles. Arrie, however, looks conflicted, as though seeing my love of his cars confuses him. Wait, am I breaking down some kind of barrier here?

Let me roll with this a sec.

"So, Arrie, how fast can they go?" I just look at him expectantly, a little giddy with excitement.

"Up to 900 mph with the G-Zone safety function engaged."

"And . . . how fast can we go today without getting a speeding ticket? Wait, can we get speeding tickets? Do we even have ID chips?"

Arrie briefly smiles before covering it with his signature scowl. "I'm sure Nine will take you however fast you want to go, Killer." The way he says killer is . . . different to usual. Usually it's with a scowl, but this time it's almost endearing, and, dare I say it, even a little flirty.

But Fate must have a different kind of shit power-up item installed into my cosmic karma-meter because Arrie then looks me up and down with disgust and then huffs, turning and throwing a set of keys at Nine before storming off.

What the hell?

You know what, that was progress. I don't get what his fucking deal is, but that . . . that was the closest thing to a conversation I've ever had with the guy. So he likes cars. I add that little snippet of info to another list I've started: conversation starters for talking to Arrie.

I buckle up and sit eagerly in the front seat as I watch everything Nine does, analyzing his every button press and manual set-up process. One day, I'll be in that seat. Arrie will have to kill me to stop me (you know, figuratively speaking).

When Nine gets the engine going (almost silent, by the way), I squeal in excitement, genuinely happy for the first time in days. This is the best distraction ever. Doing shit like this forever? Sign me up!

As I said when I first learned about being the Fifth Horseman, there are pros to this; it's about time I start living some.

Nine drives onto the nearest highway just off the road the portal building's on, and shoves us into a steady 100 mph drive up the highway, following closely behind Arrie and Connie.

I'm giddy with excitement in this fucking car. It's awesome. Like, way more awesome than pepperoni pizza, and that's saying something.

"More awesome than your library?"

"Ummmm . . . no. But definitely a close second."

We drive for a couple of hours up the highway before taking an exit for a small town somewhere here in Colorado and finding ourselves navigating the annoying leylines of the small town that barely has more than a car's width of road in most of the main streets.

At the end of the main road, however, is a small cottage-like that looks out of place amongst the regular houses lined up beside it. But that's the exact place we stop in front of, right behind the black car that holds Arrie and Connie.

Dea gets out and grabs my door. "Welcome to our Colorado base, Angel."

I step out, thanking him like a lady should, trying to refrain from thinking of myself as a lady and totally spoiling the moment with a snorted laugh. "How many bases do you have on Earth?"

Dea answers. "Too many to list, but one in each state here in the US. Since most of the magical community's headquarters are here."

Nine interrupts. "Well, the Vampire and human division's HQs are here. Along with quite a few Shifter colonies. And they're the ones we deal with most. The Shifter's HQ is in Tokyo, the Fae's is in Paris, and the Witches's is in South Africa."

"South Africa? That's a bit of an odd place to have a HQ."

"Yeah," Nine adds with a sigh. "But the Witches move theirs to wherever they're least likely to be found."

I nod. Makes sense. Clever Witches.

The front door is a simple storm door with the usual white-painted wood behind. It's so old-fashioned. It's kinda cute in a way. The windows even have shutters, just like in those old movies. I catch myself stifling a giggle, not wanting to insult anyone. Keeping each base updated without the use of a magical house must be a nightmare.

The inside is so normal that, for a moment, I'm pretty taken aback. It's a standard four-bed house, with a lounge, kitchen-diner, and a bathroom. Damn. A regular family could live here.

We are a family, Nine reminds me.

If you guys are your definition of regular, I've got some bad news.

Fair point, he said through a laugh.

"I'll order some food in," Connie says. "Hon, preference?"

"Er . . . I haven't tried Indian yet?"

"Indian it is."

I give her a smile before she walks off into the kitchen to order some food, watching her ass all the way through that door in those tight black jeans. Sighing, I sit on the couch, watching as the guys give me a weird look.

"What? Those are some killer jeans, and trust me, she knows it."

"Damn straight I do!" Connie calls from the kitchen. I even hear her smack her own ass as though confirming that fact.

Right, Conquest hearing. Oops. I shake the worry from my mind, determined not to let anything get in the way of this awesome road trip.

Mission, not road trip.

Shut up, Nine. We're not missioning until tomorrow. For now, it's a road trip.

"Right," Dea says once Connie returns and we're all sitting on various pieces of matching floral furniture. He pulls a bag from his shoulder I didn't realize he wore and digs through it. "Standard equipment." He hands each of us a stun gun, some kind of purple crystal, and a regular pistol. "Angel, that crystal is vital. Do not lose it."

"What is it?"

Nine, who's sitting next to me on the rose-patterned couch, rests a hand in his usual place on my knee. "They're teleporters. If we're in danger, they can teleport us back to *Sheruta* instantly."

"But why not just use those rather than the goddess awful portal?"

"They're expensive and difficult to make and take a high Fae Lord to create."

Riiight. Makes sense. Hopefully, if I one day master my powers in all four supe types, I might be able to create them for the team. That would be useful.

"How do I use it?"

Dea looks at me and smiles. Clearly, I'm asking the right question. "Smash it on the ground at your feet and think of home."

"Really? That's the most cliché magical thing ever."

"We know." Dea settles into the armchair. "Do you understand everything else? Have any more questions?"

"Yup and nope."

"Good."

Not long after that, dinner arrives, and I gorge myself on various curries, stealing a bit of everyone's order (including Arrie's, much to his annoyance), and finding that spicy food is soooo good. Then again, we haven't come across anything I don't like yet. Except tomatoes. Yuck!

"You really like food, hey, Angel?"

"Seems so." I look to the ground, suddenly reminded of why I can't really answer that question. "Wonder if anyone will know me at the Witches's HQ?"

"Still can't believe you weren't human," Connie says.

"Me neither," Nine adds.

Dea, ever the conversation-interrupter, interrupts. "Angel, you will have to share with someone tonight. We only have four bedrooms here."

I look briefly at Connie before realizing that probably isn't a good idea right now. "It's okay, I'll just take the couch. We're only here one night."

"If you are sure? Nine and I can always share, if you want to take my room?"

My mind flies back to the time when I caught Dea in Nine's room, and I can't help the ache that burns between my thighs, causing me to shift on the couch. "Ermmm, it's okay. Thanks, though."

Really? Is that memory ever not going to come to mind?

Probably not.

If I knew it would make you this happy, I would have invited you in days ago.

I barely knew you. It's weird now, Nine, much less a week ago.

We all sit chatting, with me interrupting now and then to ask a random question about something I either didn't know or have forgotten, while finishing up dinner.

I really like medium-level heat, but anything more than that and I find the spice over-powering, so I mainly stick to my own food, occasionally pinching things from Nine's plate, too. I fucking love samosas, as it turns out, and practically eat half the bag, leaving the rest to the others.

Everyone slowly heads to bed, but I have to wait until they all go upstairs to hit the hay, since I'm crashing on the couch. Eventually, just me, Nine, and Dea, are left, and it can't bemore awkward.

"So, Con's likely going to overhear this—sorry—but I just wanted to put it out there," Nine starts. He fiddles with the hem of his shirt while his eyes never leave his lap. I've never seen him look so nervous. "I'm sorry I didn't ask your permission for her to watch the other night, Dea. And I'm sorry that you made you feel awkward, Sweetie."

Both Dea and I look at each other and give sheepish smiles. Nine's clearly been worrying over it. Sometimes, it can be easy to forget that only he can read our minds, not the other way around. He has feelings and stuff, too.

Fuck, how bad is that to forget?

"It's okay, Nine." I rest my hand on his knee. "I shouldn't have stayed in the first place." I look briefly at Dea. "Sorry."

I can feel my cheeks burning and just hope none of the others' eyesight is as good as mine in the dark.

Dea sits on my other side, sandwiching me between them. "Do not be sorry. I . . . liked it. Well, I like the memory of it, since I did not know at the time."

We all laugh a little.

"Me too," Nine adds, now lifting his face to meet our eyes.

I don't know what to say to that. I enjoyed myself that night, but if I admit that out loud . . . I don't want to give them the wrong impression.

Say it out loud, Sweetie. It's important.

Sighing, I acquiesce. "I enjoyed it, too. But I don't want to give you guys the wrong impression. I really don't like the idea of casual sex. I'm sorry." I shake my head slightly, staring at my hands fiddling with the hem of my vest tee as though it's suddenly the most important thing in the room.

Dea puts his hand on my shoulder and whispers in my ear, "That is okay. I have an entire lifetime to persuade you otherwise." He winks at me, and I just know he's going to spend the next couple of centuries torturing me.

"For now," Nine adds, "feel free to watch anytime you want." They both stand, wink at me, and walk up the stairs in perfect unison, leaving me dumbfounded and stunned silent

21

The next morning, we split up and head our separate ways at the nearest airport. Connie and Arrie are on their way to Paris to meet with the Fae Council. Apparently, they called ahead, and apparently, they know we exist—well, they know the others exist. I'm still trying to stay in the closet (for now). We, on the other hand, are on our way to New Orleans—Vampire central and home of the Vampire Royal Council. Sounds like fun.

Honestly, the thought of dealing with Vampires right now is less than thrilling, but I do get to ride shotgun with Nine again, so bonus! Everything's a little more serious than it was yesterday, given we have actual work to do, but I'm still excited. I'm part Vampire, after all. Maybe we'll learn more about me while there. Or maybe they'll rip my head from my shoulders and I'll have to somehow grow it back. Sounds painful.

"Dea?"

"Mmm?" He's half napping in the backseat, but I have a nagging question.

"Why don't you drive?"

I feel him looking at me from behind and then hear him sigh. "Since humans cannot see me unless I stay corporeal for them, driving long distances is tough; when we get pulled over, they do not see the driver unless I focus. I cannot go corporeal for more than a few hours at a time, and it is draining."

"So," Nine chimes in, "I drive on missions."

"And when you're here on your own?"

"I bring my horse and we can travel at my usual speed everywhere while invisible to everyone. Only ocean travel is annoying."

Our flight is only an hour, since Fae magic is used to buffer the engines, but it's still an hour I have to fill with something other than the million questions running through my brain. I fear if I'm left to my own mind right now, I'll go insane.

You're going to be fine, Sweetie.

You're sure?

Absolutely. Firstly, we can't die. Secondly, we can crystal out of there if needed. Thirdly, you're with us, and we've dealt with these idiots for centuries.

Goddess, he's right. I need to get a grip. Everything will be fine. I breathe a sigh of relief as I repeat that over and over again until my mind eases.

I can do this.

Dea promised to go over the plan once we land and get to the motel (apparently, no safe house in New Orleans because the Vampires won't allow it), so, until then, I just have to sit tight.

"Here," Nine says and hands me a plasmascreen. "Do research, read a book, play some games, go online . . . Whatever. Just please distract yourself and try to relax."

He grimaces at me, and I realize he's also getting frustrated with my internal thoughts; they're probably screaming at this point, and he's been told to stay in-tune with them. Poor Nine.

I take the plasmascreen and open an app that lets me download books. Searching for something romantic, I download the first thing that promises a lot of romantic suspense. Anything to get me engrossed at this point.

Not dragons this time, but werewolves. Honestly, I like reading other types of fiction, but nothing melts my mind more than fantasy romance, no matter how unrealistic or stupid it may be to other people.

An hour later, Nine taps me on my shoulder, pulling me out of the book. "Time to go."

"We're here?"

He nods and grabs Dea, who's fallen asleep on his other side. We leave the plane, grab our luggage, and hail a cab, and arrive outside a small, rundown motel not an hour later.

"Really?" This place looks like I might get infected just from standing in the parking lot. "This place?"

"We like to keep a low profile on Earth." Nine grimaces but tries to smile. "That's why we stay in regular houses and rundown motels."

Makes sense, but I don't really understand why they prefer to stay under the radar in the first place. Guess that's a question I'll have to ask later. For now, we're trying to get two rooms from the stingy man manning the front desk.

"I've only got one. Sorry, dude."

"C'mon," Nine urges. "You must have something available?"

"Look, it's one or nothing. Take it or leave it."

Dea stays behind us, letting Nine take the lead, and I assume this guy is human because he never looks Dea's way once, and Dea is someone you don't just ignore. He makes a whole room turn toward him like he's the bright, shiny new kid.

I grab Nine's arm and turn to the man. "One room will be fine. Thank you." I snatch the key dangling from the man and hand the signing pen over to Nine.

I don't really know what name to sign, so I just let him handle it. He uses a fake name anyway (which makes sense), so I guess it doesn't matter.

I bow slightly before leaving toward our assigned room. The room is at the farthest point from the desk, at the other end of the motel, and has a single double bed, a dingy sofa I assume no one wants to sleep on given the mold creeping up the sides, and a small, pretty unsanitary bathroom attached.

Sorry. It's just for a few nights.

It's fine. I'm a grown adult, Nine. I can handle sharing a bed for a night.

But even just the thought of us all snuggling up in that bed has me quickly moving to place my bag down on the floor to remove the building tension between my legs.

It's going to be a long night.

"Right," Dea says as he sits on the edge of the bed. "Tomorrow, we have a meeting with the Vampire Royal Council. In that meeting, I am going to do the talking. Angel, I need you to remain silent, as though you are just someone working with us for the time being." I nod my understanding. "Nine, I need you relaying messages between us so the Vampire Council cannot throw curveballs at us." Nine also nods. "We are going to ask them how they are doing, have a general catch-up, and drink tea. We are not interrogating them or doing anything to piss them off. Clear?" He looks straight at us, as if daring us to challenge him.

"Clear," I say.

"Clear."

"Angel, no matter what happens in there, please be careful. They are going to be drinking blood and offering you humans to feed from. Just so you are aware."

Wow, I could be really dangerous in that room. I'm likely more powerful than most of the Vampires individually, but I'm hoping that'll go unnoticed given that only half of my powers are vampiric.

This is gonna to be a pain.

"But tonight," Dea continues, "we are going to a party."

"A party?" I didn't pack party clothes. What the hell?

"Seems," Nine says with a sigh, "we'll need to go shopping first." He flicks his head toward me while looking at Dea, who gives an immediate smile.

We head out to a nearby shopping mall, and Nine escorts me through a few shops to find a party-style dress, but nothing's really popping out. Dea trails behind us, mostly staying out of people's way so they don't bump in to an invisible him. He stays completely invisible at this point, not even letting himself be semi-translucent to supes. Why is that? Dea's been a little more restrained here on Earth than back at the house, so maybe it's best not to mention anything.

I've already walked in on them in a rather compromising situation, I don't also need to go poking around in their private thoughts.

"Nothing's sticking out at you?" Nine asks as he holds up a black dress in a silent question.

"No, not really. Everything's just so . . . meh." I shrug.

The real issue is that I know this is Vamp central, and now I am a Vampire, I don't know what to wear around other Vampires. Is it expected of me to dress a little more provocatively to fit in with the usual slutty attire of Vampire kind? Is there any kind of Vampire dress code I should be aware of?

Nine doesn't answer any of my questions—he's probably leaving me to my private thoughts on the matter, given that this is one of those situations where I need to make my mind up for myself.

I growl under my breath in frustration. "Do I need to fit in with the other Vamps tonight?" I look at Dea, then quickly to the ground, remembering that staring at a fixed point no one else can see looks rather stupid.

Dea stops and looks at me for a moment with a curious smile. "You just need to be yourself tonight. Tomorrow might be a different story, but tonight, we are just scanning the area, getting into conversations with random supes—preferably Vampires—and seeing where the community's opinions lie."

"Okay. Okay." I can do that. All I need for that is a dress and an attitude that speaks open and chatty.

Nine grabs my arm, gestures to Dea to follow us, and leads us to a small boutique a few blocks over. "This might have something more you."

A little bell chimes in the fresh, rose-smelling store, and we're greeted by a young woman in a short yet flowing pink dress with blonde and pink-highlighted hair. Her smile seems genuine as she waves. "Welcome to Cathy's. Anything you need, just gimme a shout." She can't have been older than mid-twenties as she turns around and continues furiously tapping away at the cashier's plasmascreen on the desk.

"Thank you."

I stop to peruse the store briefly; it's small but looks beautifully laid out with lots of large mirrors and well-styled decor. It has a range of bright colorful clothing that instantly catches my eye, and I find my feet pandering to the nearest rack, which seems to hold a range of cropped and shortened tees.

"You can buy anything you like, Angel. You can always bring it home with us."

I nod, my eyes still focusing on the cropped tee they unharmoniously landed on moments ago. It's short, stops a couple inches under the boobs, and is a deep red with black slashes plastering through it. My current dark, confused mood likes its equally dark presence, and I find myself grabbing it by the hanger and handing it to Nine.

"I wanna try some things on."

He nods and hops away, seemingly excited that he's picked out a store I like.

We both spend around an hour picking out various items of clothing, holding them against my body, and selecting the best ones to be tried on.

The changing room is a single block with heavy, dusted violet curtains. "Wait out here." I open the curtains to find a larger-than-average changing room dotted with mirrors, a stool in the corner, and various hooks.

Oh, and Nine? Stay out of my head while I'm getting changed.

Haha. Okay.

I can practically hear him winking, and I have to repress a laugh. It's easy to flirt with Nine, especially with the telepathy making it private. But with the others, it's always more nerve-wracking; Dea makes me stumble over sentences I would otherwise speak perfectly while Connie makes me feel like a teenager again. It's all like walking on lava, trying to hop onto the right stones before you drown. And that thirty seconds of flirting with Arrie in the parking lot? Well, I don't even know what to make of that.

The first item is a potential dress for tonight, and I have to admit it looks rather flattering. Okay, it makes my boobs look fucking epic. But that's still flattering, right?

Stepping out of the changing room, Dea smiles and nods his head (which is pretty good for him), and Nine makes a motion with his finger, asking me to twirl.

"Looks good, but I've got my eye on a different one for the winner."

He isn't usually a shopping kind of guy, but since Dea can't use all of his energy on being visible right now with tonight looming on our calendar's horizon, I guess Nine's taking over shopping duty.

I return to the changing room, hoping to get a better reaction out of some of the others. Four dresses later, we have a potential winner, with a pile four-high of nopes.

This is the last one, and it's another black dress, but this one has a light-pink glow to the sparkles that light up the entire thing. I have to say, it matches my long, light-pink hair perfectly. But looking in the mirror behind me, I realize why this is the one Nine has his hopes on—the back is open and has a draped effect right down to my middle. My lion tattoo, which is a mixture of pink, blue, and violet, is on show, and I'm suddenly reminded of how it glowed in the dark under most club lights. My front neckline tattoo is hidden, but it doesn't matter.

"This one. Definitely this one," I say from behind the curtains. I swing it open and jump out, eagerly awaiting their reactions.

Nine smiles, obviously happy, while Dea stares for a moment and asks me to turn around. A couple of low whistles follow.

"I did not know you had such an amazing tattoo, Angel?"

"Oh, really?"

"I have seen the skull on your front, but this is . . . Wow."

"It glows under the typical lights clubs use."

"Damn, Sweetie." *Can't wait to see.*

"So, this one it is, then?" I ask.

"Yes," they both say in unison.

I go back into the changing room and sift through the rest of the non-dress pile, trying things on, showing some to the guys, some not, and by the time I'm done, I have a pile of about ten items I want.

Guilt races through my mind when we step up to the cashier, but I shake my head. Dea said last time we went shopping that it's okay if I spend some money. But, really, I want my own funds. I bet the others have their own money and don't rely on Dea.

I'll show you how we make money when we get home.

Okay. Thank you.

I genuinely mean it, too. I really hate scrounging.

I AM JUST FINISHING UP MY HAIR AND MAKEUP IN THE BATHROOM MIRROR WHEN I HEAR THE guys chatting from the bedroom. We've gone back to the grubby motel to chill, which seems to have lightened Dea's mood, and I've spent the last hour showering and getting ready.

"She's doing great in training, but I really want to know if she'll have the other pillars of power as well."

"I am sure it will come with time, Nine. Just give her time."

Nine hushes to a whisper, probably hoping I can't hear, but Vamp hearing and what-not. "We might not have time, bro."

I hear Dea whisper something back but can't make it out, so I shake my head and look in the mirror one final time before declaring myself pretty enough to party with

Vampires—and I have to admit, I scrub up pretty well for someone who barely has an identity.

The bathroom door clicks shut behind me as I walk out, and I face the guys as they look the other way. "Ahhhmmm," I cough, trying to get their attention. "I'm ready to go."

I avoid their gazes when they look at me with stunned smiles, especially Nine's, and push the memory of their conversation to the back of my mind. Do not want to think about that right now.

Dea steps forward, grabs my hand, and raises it to his lips. "You look beautiful, Angel."

"Mmm, I have to agree. That dress really was made for you." Nine reaches for something in his back pocket. "One more thing." He hands me one of the sealed bottles of blood. "Drink up."

I look at them both with annoyance, but their stony faces remain insistent. Fucking damn it. I chug it down in one, trying to ignore the coldness of the blood and how it makes it taste stale and dry. "Ugh."

Dea grabs my right arm while Nine grabs my left, and they escort me out of the shitty motel and to the nearest, busiest club they can find.

I have the room key stashed in my bra, but the guys have everything else. I'm not even armed tonight, which seems a little stupid to me.

You have magic, remember.

Right. I don't need a weapon.

That is the fact I remind myself of as we walk through the main door, past a few security guards, and into what I can only describe as a club of debauchery and insanity. There are supes everywhere, including a few Shifters in animal form (there's a panther curled up on a sofa in the corner a few feet from the door); Vampires are dancing and seducing all kinds of people on the dancefloor, from supernaturals to humans; and every few feet stands a topless dancer on top a small podium. There's an upper floor you can see from the ground, where runway-like floors crisscross and hold more topless dancers, but this time dancing with the public.

But the most obvious part of the club? The Vampires feeding in the darkened corners of the large space. I can see in the dark, but the others can't, so it's blindingly obvious when one male Vampire in particular has a party of three human women dancing around him in the far corner beside a main stage as he alternates feeding from each one.

As much as I hate it, I can smell the blood permeating the air, and the only reason my fangs don't come out is because Nine made me feed before leaving.

Thank fuck.

You're welcome. Got another bottle in my pocket if needed. Or you can, you know, go be a Vampire.

He gestures to the club with a wink, but I know he can't see in the dark, so he looks at me confused when I scowl at the joke.

I send him a mental picture of the Vampire frenzies going on all around us, including all the dark, hidden places, and he visibly recoils.

I . . . err . . . sorry.

It's okay.

I get the feeling this place is supposed to just look like a hot human-supe club. That's why Nine can't see all the feeding.

"We should blend in, have a few drinks, and go dance." Dea makes himself visible as he says this, and I can see the strain on his face the moment he does. He eventually rids his face of the signs of his discomfort and smiles, but it's clear he's more comfortable in his invisible form. "Basically, let's have fun."

He sounds almost modern as he says that, and I almost laugh at the attempt but manage to keep it hidden. Not from Nine, though, who sends me a mental laugh while remaining externally stoic somehow.

I turn to take another look at the club, and as I do, Nine and Dea gasp.

"Angel . . . your tattoo is glowing!"

"I did say." I show them my full back and hope like hell it looks as cool in real life as it does in my memories.

It does. Nine throws what he's seeing into my head, and the image of a glowing lion greets my mind.

Wow, it really does look cool.

"Well," Dea says, "Con will definitely want to see that in the dark." He winks and leaves, heading toward the stage.

Nine and I, on the other hand, go to the bar.

What you want to drink?

"A dusted vodka soda, please."

He raises an eyebrow at me in question, and I just shrug. It's an instinctual answer, and something I know I liked from when I was mortal. Haven't really had time to try alcohol yet, what with all the training. Connie said dust doesn't have as large of an effect on us anyway, so I'm hoping it just make's me happier (goddess knows I can use the pick-me up).

We'll spend some time getting you drunk and trying all the alcohol you want some day. It takes a lot to get us drunk anyway, so we should be able to look the part all night here.

That sounds oddly inviting and . . . fun.

We can be fun. He frowns at me in mock hurt, but I just laugh.

Our drinks are poured quickly once Nine orders them from a cute Fae bartender with pink hair like mine but short. The Fae winks at me as he hands mine over, and I turn to see Nine staring at him with the same appreciative glance.

"Like what you see, Nine?" I say, mimicking his mockery of Connie from last week.

He looks at me and smiles, eying me from head to toe. "Definitely."

Wait, is he talking about me or the bartender? I don't want to embarrass myself by asking, so I laugh and tell him to stop being so cliché.

"I'm going to go this way." I point to the area near the back where the most Vampire activity is, thinking I can probably get one or two to chat if I flash my fangs.

"Okay. I'll go the other way and we'll chat later."

I walk away with my drink in hand, but, just as I get a few feet, Nine says, *I was talking about you, Sweetie.*

Oh. Thank you.

He's probably laughing at my stupidity, but I don't have the time to ponder over it as I weave through the left-hand side of the dancefloor and attempt to fit in somewhere.

My drink still in hand, I start dancing with a woman who comes over and offers a smile; but she's human, so I need to find a way of ditching her and moving on. Honestly, I need a little more alcohol before I really get into this.

I dance for a while, only really bumping into humans and Shifters, but I eventually come across a Vampire seducing a female human. Please let me be able to say hi without getting my head ripped off.

Least it'll grow back.

I sidle on up, hoping to dance with them, but his fierce blue eyes stare at me as his fangs drop in warning. I raise my free hand in surrender, trying to show I'm not there to steal his . . . meal (ugh, what a crass way of putting it), and he relaxes a little.

I drop my fangs in defense anyway, just in case, and see the human woman smile in fascination. She grabs my hand, and I let her pull me forward. She's pretty, but she has nothing on Connie and isn't really my type (not that I know what my type was before), but I act interested for the sake of getting closer to the other Vampire.

Just one conversation, that's all. We both dance with her—him from behind and me in front—and she laps up the attention in sultry looks and giggles. I take a deep breath and step a little closer, pressing my body to hers.

God, this stuff is easy with Connie, Dea, and Nine; heck, even Arrie is easier to enjoy than this. But I'm not here to enjoy myself, I'm here to gain general opinions and intel. But I don't even know how to start a conversation, given that I know next to nothing about the current goings-on in the community. I really should have looked up some general news articles on the plane.

Live and learn.

Is he going to be in my head with little insults all fucking night?

Probably. This Vamp I'm talking to is a little boring, so thought I could probably hold two convos at once.

All right for some.

You're not talking right now.

Not with words, no.

And, to prove my point, I run my hand up the woman's shoulder and along her neck, lifting her hair out of the way of her pulse as I drag a nail alongside the gentle thrum. Her face lights up, and the other Vampire meets my eyes. I give him a smile, hoping it's at least slightly sexy.

Damn. You make one hot Vampire, Sweetie.

The other Vampire lands a hand on her other side and mimicks my movement.

She shudders in front of me, and whispers, "Do Vamps share?"

I don't know how to answer that. Do they? Instead, I look to the other Vampire in question and just hope it's a personal choice.

"Sometimes," he answers in a French accent. Seems he's a quiet one, which doesn't really bode well for me. "If we like the other Vampire enough."

"Well?" she asks, looking me in the eyes.

"I've only just met the guy, sorry."

She looks a little disappointed, and I go to walk away, but the guy grabs my wrist and flings me back around. "Doesn't mean I don't like you enough to share. You're new, aren't you?"

I just nod, and he shakes his head in laughter.

"You're doing fucking well for a newbie."

So, he's a talker . . . when you can get him talking. Time to keep him going.

"Yeah?" I giggle at his compliment, trying to act a little flirty. "Well, I've had a good mentor."

"It's nice when the person who turns you actually stays to show you the ropes, ain't it? But it's not common, unfortunately."

"Really?"

He shakes his head and resumes dancing. I don't actually plan to share this woman with him since I don't want to feed on anyone at all, but if I can hold a conversation while dancing, that might work enough to grab some useful intel. And I can use this newbie Vamp angle.

"He's been great, but it's nice to chat to others. Get to know the real community."

"God, it's been a while since I've been in your shoes."

The woman seems content to dance with us, not really contributing to the conversation, and I get the feeling she just wants to be fed from—probably a hoster (humans who enjoy being fed on by Vampires on a regular basis).

"Is it rude to ask a Vampire's age?"

"A little, but I'll answer. I'm 142."

I do a double take. He's how fucking old? I'm dancing with someone six times my age!

Really? Because Dea and I are over two thousand years old, and I distinctly remember the thought of you wanting to fuck him multiple times over the last few weeks. If age gaps are a problem for you, I've got some bad news.

I internally laugh at that. He has a valid point.

But you seem so . . young.

Hardy ha. Get back to flirting information out of that Vamp.

Yes, sir!

Not my kink, but you might have some luck with Dea there.

Ohmigod, shut the fuck up!

He, thank fuck, stays silent.

"I didn't realize we lived quite *that* long."

"You don't seem to know much for someone who has a mentor."

"Oh"—I scramble for an answer—"he passed away recently, so I've only had a bit of time to adjust."

"Oh, my condolences. Well, if you have any questions, I'd be delighted to answer."

"Really?"

"Sure."

The woman in front of me ups her dancing game by running a hand up my front and cupping my boob. I let her. This conversation has real promise, and for some unknown, beyond the depth of my thinking, reason, being touched by someone feels so good. Okay, so it's probably because I'm so pent up from all the non-interactive flirting with the team; so, shoot me, I like the attention. I'm only hu—

A Horseman of the Apocalypse.

I roll my eyes and dance a little more with the woman, not wanting to lose the only reason I have a connection to the Vamp standing behind her. She grabs my waist and pulls me flush against her, pressing her lips to my neck.

It gives me a small shudder of surprise, and my head lilts to the side, giving her greater access. The Vampire in front of me, however, has his eyes on us like a lust-filled prize and reaches down to press his lips to mine.

Shit. I don't want to kiss him. I pull away slightly, hoping it won't deter him too much. "Lesbian?"

Oh. Oooo. "Yeah. Sorry."

He shakes his hand in the air as if to say no worries, and I feel kinda bad for him.

You're playing the lesbian card. Really? That poor guy.

I ignore Nine, hoping he'll go away.

"Still up for sharing?" I ask through nervously chattering teeth, and I think he might've noticed my nerves.

"Sure." He smiles. This guy actually seems kinda friendly. Not sure what I was expecting, but this isn't it.

"Soooo, what's the latest gossip in the Vamp community I've just joined? Any surprising lovers? Shock horror deaths? Who killed their husband in blind blood rage? You know, the good stuff."

I hope that's subtle and comes across all gossip-y, but I doubt it.

We need to work on my social interrogation skills, Nine.

Yup. I've put it on my mental list for training.

But, luckily for me, Mr. Nice Vampire decides to answer anyway. "Well, there's the usual stuff: the SC limiting our blood supplies, making these places more popular." He gestures to the club. "I hear one of the royal princes pissed off the SC recently after they killed someone, and it's causing a bit of turmoil between the SC and the Vampires."

Oh really . . . ? "How did he piss them off?"

"According to the rumors, he went behind the Royal Council's back and submitted a formal complaint about the misuse of their Hunter Society."

The Hunter Society: the Supernatural Council's way of bringing in criminal rogue supes. Basically, they're a human group of bounty hunters for supernaturals.

"What? That's insane!" I have very little idea of the magnitude of the info here, so I'm just playing along.

"I know. He's a fucking idiot. But he's actually a pretty decent guy. Partied with him a few times."

"Partying with a Vampire prince? Damn. Sounds . . ." Like a fucking nightmare. "Intriguing."

He shakes his head. "God, you girls are all the same. Even when you're not into men you find royalty alluring." He rolls his eyes and laughs a little.

"A Vampire prince?" the woman says.

"Vampires have a whole royal family, with three princes total," Mr. Nice Vampire answers. "One of whom is a little bit of a partier, but he can be a bit hot-headed."

"I've never met a prince before," the woman says.

"Me neither," I respond.

We both laugh, and I find myself having fun. Well, what do you know?

"Hey." The guy grabs our hands. "After we've had some more fun, I'll tell you where you can party with him." He gestures to a free sofa in a dark corner behind us—one used for feeding, going by the general scent coming from that direction.

Shit. I don't actually want to follow through with this. But finding this prince will be helpful. He'll know more about the problems between the SC and the Vampires.

Nine?

Yeah?

Keep an eye on me.

The Vampire pull us toward the sofa, and we all sit down, the woman in between us Vampires. This is it. I'm actually doing this. Here's to hoping I don't kill her.

You sure about this?

Nope.

I'll help.

Thank you.

I place my arm on her thigh, trying to be as gentle as possible, and my other arm slides around her shoulders as I move her hair away from her neck.

"So," she says, "you said I could party with the prince?" She looks pleadingly at the other Vampire.

"I'll give you the address of the party afterward."

She nods, and I have no choice but to go along with it if I also want the address. She looks at me and smiles. "Bite me."

My fangs descend, and I find myself naturally drawn to her neck, where I can hear the blood rushing through her.

She lets out a small moan as the other Vampire bites her other side, and she grabs my hand on her thigh and tries moving it up, but I don't let her.

I run my tongue along her neck, eliciting another shudder from her, and sink my teeth in, drawing a few mouthfuls of blood that I quickly swallow, trying not to taste it. Just like when feeding from Dea, I want more than just blood, and I can feel that familiar ache pooling low. My hand on her thigh slips my control, and she finally manages to pull it higher, where I meet his hand fiddling under the hem of her dress.

The feeling isn't as strong with her, though, I notice, and the blood doesn't taste anything like Dea's or Arrie's; in fact, it isn't that pleasing except to satiate the hunger that comes with being a Vampire. But still, I want more.

"Angel," a voice beside me says, and a hand gently lands on my shoulder. "Stop. The other guy has stopped."

I gasp, pulling away instantly, the need to stay in character and get that address tearing to the forefront of my mind.

Dea sits on the sofa's arm, invisible again, and looks at me with a pained expression.

He looks a little jealous, if I'm honest, but that's stupid. The Horseman of Death is not jealous of me.

Realizing I'm staring at someone no one else can see, I turn back around, and find the other Vampire smiling at me gently.

"You really are doing great for a newbie."

"Thanks." I smile a genuine smile. Because, although I may have lied about my magical status, I'm still, technically, a new Vampire, and it is kinda hard.

He turns to the human woman and gives her a handkerchief from his pocket. "It's the house at the end of Addler Street," he whispers into her ear, then turns to me. "Name's Ryan. It's nice to meet you." He turns and leaves in a rush of Vampire speed.

I let Dea guide me off the sofa as my mind dazes off a little. Why is drinking Dea's blood so much more attractive? Why does it taste sweeter?

Nine stands a few feet away, and I grab his hand, steadying myself. "You did well, Sweetie. We can check that address out after tomorrow's meeting."

"We should head back for now," Dea says. "Regroup our information and get some sleep."

I let the guys guide me out of the club and back to the motel

22

We decided to share the double bed last night after we got back and crashed—all fully clothed—so this morning, as I lie in the middle of two sexy as hell men (how has this even happened?), I don't bother moving right away. Because, let's be honest, who wouldn't lap this shit up? Nine's fast asleep on my right, his arm wrapping tight around my waist, so for once, he can't hear my thoughts. Dea's curled up asleep on my left with his chin on my shoulder.

These two men have woven their way into my life more than I can even say, and lying here with them, even though it isn't sexual, just feels so . . . right. It feels like home. I mean, Connie being here would make it one hundred percent perfect, but it doesn't take away from this moment.

I can feel Dea's gentle breaths tickling my shoulder and chest as Nine's arm swings low over my stomach, gripping my hip lightly; between that, the blood yesterday, and the memory of my midnight escapade running through my mind on repeat, I've practically had my thighs shifting gently all morning, and I can feel how wet this is all making me. If it wasn't for sharing this small room in a skanky motel, I could fix the unbearable ache between my legs, but, alas, I'm going to have to suffer until we return to *Sheruta*.

Or you could just ask nicely.

"Nine," I gasp under my breath. "How long have you been awake?"

Long enough to know the awkward predicament you're in.

His hand wraps tighter around my hip before loosening and traveling lower.

"Nine . . ." But rather than the sharp tone I was going for, it comes out as a breathy moan, and I lose all credibility that this isn't affecting me.

"Yes?"

His hand continues to press lower until he's no more than an inch from my clit, and I hold my breath, waiting for him to move lower and touch me everywhere I've dreamed of. "I—"

"Fuck, you two are killing me," Dea complains, his cussing taking me by surprise.

"Dea!"

How long has he been awake?

Longer than me.

What?

Nine laughs, and I groan in frustration, causing them both to shift closer and align their bodies flush against mine.

Dea's hand trails up my stomach, drawing light patterns that send sparks to my core, and are just about to dip under my pajama top when my mind remembers why I haven't slept with either of them.

"Guys, I can't do this."

The moment snaps as they both stop and look at me.

Dea looks confused but stops his hand from going any higher. He also doesn't remove it from my body entirely. "Explain it to us, Angel."

"I . . ." Goddess, I really don't want to have this discussion, but being open and honest, like they've been from day one, is how they seem to run the team, and that's important. So, pulling my big girl pants on, I take a deep breath and force the words out. "I want more than you're prepared to give." My voice comes out as a frail squeak, and it surprises even me. "And, if we go there, I won't . . ." I exhale my held breath, unsure how to finish the sentence.

"You won't what?" Nine asks. He's purposefully not reading my mind right now, or he's asking out loud so that everyone can have the conversation together. Either way, I'm grateful.

"I won't be okay with that. It'll hurt me." Maybe that's silly of me, but the thought of them sleeping with me and then just sleeping with anyone else outside of the team makes my chest feel like it's going to implode.

They both stop breathing as they look at me, and I get the feeling they're having a conversation without me. I won't lie and say it doesn't bother me, but they already have some kind of relationship, and I can't expect to just barge in on that.

The silence that follows my admission drowns me in wave after wave of guilt, confusion, and terror, so much so that I try wriggling under the covers to hide my flushed face, but they both hold me in place.

Dea speaks up first. "We do not want to hurt you, Angel. We just know how much you need to release this tension, especially since you started feeding. Vampires usually feed and have sex together, or at least keep up a healthy diet of both."

"And we also know, as do you, the growing tension between the three of us. We just thought we could help." Nine sounds actually hurt, his voice a little broken, and I'm beginning to see a real problem in the future if one of us doesn't cave.

Me not sleeping with them, given that this is their normal, hurts them, but them not being committed will hurt me. Goddess, this is such a fucking mess. I don't even care about them being with just me (I can't break the team apart like that), so long as they're committed to the entire team.

Nine looks at me with surprise, choking slightly in shock. "You'd really be into that?"

"Be into what?" Dea's out of the loop, and for once, it's bothering him.

Ha, serves him fucking right!

I shake my head when Nine looks at me expectantly, not wanting to say the words out loud, so he does for me. "She was thinking about a polyamorous relationship between the entire team. Freedom within but no sex outside of."

Dea looks at me with a smile touching the corners of his lips. "We have never considered that before, but it still poses the same issue. What happens if we all fall out?"

With that question, I'm done with the conversation and wriggle out from between them and off the bed, speeding into the shower.

I don't understand. I know duty comes first, and above all else, Earth must be protected from itself, but that doesn't mean they don't get to fucking live. They deserve to live and love. Just like anybody else. It's clear Nine and Dea love each other, but they won't do anything about it. And for what? The fear that something could go wrong? That's utter horseshit. What if nothing goes wrong?

I run that frustration under the hot water, knowing we have to meet with the Royal Vampire Council soon, and watch as the water washes it all away. Here, I can just be. No expectations to be someone specific, no blood making me crazy, no hot as hell Horsemen making me irrational with need I have no business feeling. Just me. And whoever that is, she is standing right here.

The Vampire Royal Council is housed in a giant, modern office building a twenty-minute drive from the motel we're staying in. I'm not sure what I was expecting—maybe something more underground and castle-like—but this isn't it.

The entrance is guarded by at least a dozen guards, all of whom are armed Vampires. I shudder at the thought of needing to make a quick getaway through them.

They'd need an army to stop us, and even then, they'd still likely lose.

It occurrs to me in that moment that I've never really seen any of the team fight. I have no idea how powerful they are. Not really.

Dea makes himself visible, and the guards blink in shock for a moment before some blond-haired woman dressed in a tight skirt suit and clippy heals and with perfectly polished nails walks out. "Death. Famine." She looks to Dea and Nine in turn. "Please, follow me."

They both nod, and I follow.

Nine? What kind of story do we tell them about me?

That you're a newly turned Vampire we rescued and have taken under our wing. No one's gonna try to go through us to get to you.

Are you sure?

Yes.

We walk through the halls, and the deeper we go, the fewer windows and less open space there is, until we end up outside a large set of ornate double doors with gilded silver inset into the intricate pattern of roses.

"The Vampire Royal Council is waiting for you inside." The secretary—I assume she's a secretary, she never introduced herself otherwise—walks away, and I listen as her clippy heals fade into the distance.

"Remember your story, Angel. And just as a warning, these meetings can be tense and boring and last hours."

"Also," Nine adds, "there will be live feeding and normal Vampire oddities ongoing, remember."

That has me stopping in my tracks. "But doesn't the SC outlaw all live feeding? Why would the Vampire Council break the law?"

Both Nine and Dea look at me with raised eyebrows, but it's Nine who answers in his usual fact-giving tone. "Vampires don't like the Supernatural Council and have always flaunted their rule breaking whenever possible."

Dea opens the doors, and I just hope my question hasn't been heard through those doors. But, boy, am I disappointed, because beyond these doors is a room full of plush velvet sofas with various Vampires and hosters lounging around, and every Vampire in the room is looking right at me with a menacing growl. If I wasn't secretly a Horseman of the Apocalypse and didn't have a teleportation crystal in my back pocket, I would have peed myself a little.

They're an intimidating bunch, I'll give them that. But the number of old Vampires and high-ranking officials just feeding on humans in the presence of guests bothers me. It just doesn't seem right. And, no matter how hard I try, I can't completely wipe the disgust off my face, though I wheedle it down to a grimace.

It's the best they're fucking getting, they'll just have to deal with it.

We sit on a sofa at the front, facing the whole room so we can address everyone. Well, so the guys can address everyone; I'm simply observing today.

Nine, any princes here?

If you're thinking about the one mentioned last night, then no. There are a couple, though. The pink-shirted, camp-looking one on the sofa closest is Prince Villané, and the dark, imposing one at the back trying to hide unsuccessfully in the shadows is Prince Phillipe. He's next in line for the throne.

Hmmm. Interesting. You'd think they would have someone with more presence next in line.

Lineage is based on strength.

Oh. So he's the strongest? Interesting.

"Death. Famine. It is good to see you again." An imposing man with a white beard and half-moon glasses approaches our sofa and holds out his hand to shake.

Nine gets up and shakes his hand, but Dea remains seated.

"Who, may I ask, is your friend?" The man gestures to me.

Nine, sitting back down and placing a hand on my knee, says, "This is Sarah. She's a newly turned Vampire we saved from a troubling situation a few months ago and have taken her under our wing since."

"That is saddening to hear, Famine. I apologize for the Council not being able to protect every newly turned Vampire." He falls back into a seat with all the grace of a Vampire.

Nine nods. *That's the king.*

Fuck me, he looks so . . . normal.

"No one expects you to be able to take care of every one of your kind; no Council can do that," Nine says.

Seems Dea's going to sit this one out, which I find perplexing given he's the most well-spoken of the Horsemen. But I trust they know what they're doing.

"You called a meeting with us, Horsemen. Why?" A lady from the front sitting with Prince Villané stood.

"Nothing ominous. We're just checking in on all the councils. Things have been a little tense recently, and we are just looking to undertake a general assessment of things."

She nods and sits back down, seemingly satisfied with the answer.

"You expect us to believe that?" another Vampire at the back stands and spits out. His fists clench, and he puts one foot in front of the other; clearly, he doesn't like us.

This time, Dea raises a hand with a stoic expression on his face. His hand glows green, like it does when he heals someone, and the Vampire screams in pain as he falls to his knees. His screams pierce the air as every Vampire in the room, including me, flinches. Dea lowers his hand, and the screaming stops. "Yes," he grinds out.

"V-Very well. I apologize." The man sits back down.

Nine stands back up, ready to talk once more. "We understand the animosity between the Vampires and the Supernatural Council has been somewhat increasing of late, and we were wondering if you could explain why?" He sits back down, clearly following their 'you must stand to speak' rule, as though they were a bunch of children in a school classroom.

The king stands once more, stepping forward. "It is true, I'm afraid. They keep restricting our blood supplies, which is causing problems when trying to control the amount of live feeding. The SC have long since overlooked the live feeding, so long as we don't slaughter an entire species or kill anyone important. But since the supplies have been restricted, there are many Vampires choosing to ignore the live feeding restrictions we place on our own kind."

Well, what did the SC expect? The Vampires just to willingly starve?

"Blood supplies have always been up and down over the years since the Supernatural Council was formed. That is nothing new," Nine responds. "So why the problem now?"

Jumping straight to the issue at heart, I see.

They're not that political here. Vampires value openness in the modern world, since it's illegal and frowned upon to live feed without permission from the hoster. Feeding is their entire world, after all. It's created a more open atmosphere than we've ever seen among Vampire kind. The Witches, on the other hand, are an entirely different matter. We'll have to be more tactful with them.

I would have thought the Vampires would have been the problematic ones. But if the only issue is blood, then that's just one problem for an entire race, rather than the potential for multiple problems, like I expected.

"If you could negotiate with the SC for less restricted blood supplies, we could sort this whole mess out without hindrance."

"We'll take that under advisement. Thank you for your openness, Your Majesty."

The king nods and sits, avoiding answering Nine's actual question, I notice.

Dea stands, and everyone in the room ceases all kinds of small conversations that may have been ongoing. "There is the matter of succession. Since Vampires live a long life, we take the succession of the Vampire throne seriously. It is only once in a century you gain a new king, after all."

The king stands, nodding his understanding.

"We understand Prince Phillipe is next in line. Is everything prepared and ready for that?"

The room visibly bristles. Seems Prince Phillipe is not liked among the council. I can see the king trying to avoid answering Dea's question, but one scowl from the Horseman of Death and he caves.

"There are many who do not believe he would make a good king. He is a strong and good leader but not well liked. Not here on the Council, and not among the Vampire population."

"I see," Dea says and sits back down.

Nine stands. "That could pose a problem. If you're already having issues controlling the population through a blood restriction, won't having an unfavorable king make things harder?"

The king nods, his eyes falling to the floor.

Nine sits, clearly not having anything left to say.

Prince Phillipe in the shadows, though, simply smiles. He's also aware of this situation, but his eyes are not fixed on Dea or Nine, they're fixed on me. He steps out of the shadows, and everyone turns to look at him. "I have a question for your friend. Sarah, is it?"

I nod, standing to follow protocol. I purposefully place my hands behind my back to hide their trembling.

"Although we have always worked alongside the Four Horsemen—their power far exceeds our own—your king is the person you answer to. You are loyal to us, not them." Shit. This is going to be a problem, isn't it? "So, why do you sit over there? On their side?"

Their side? So he has a grudge against the Horsemen? Ballsy stance to have.

"They were good to me. I was ill for weeks after my poor treatment at the hands of the person who turned me. I will always be grateful to them."

"Yes, and being indebted to them is something I understand. Yet Famine over there has his hand placed on your knee as though he owns you. Does he own you, Sarah?"

"Own me? I'm sorry, I wasn't aware anyone owned me." Venom laces my voice as I try to calm the rising wave of anger.

Careful. We need to save face here. We can't lose their support. He is the next king. We need him on our side so he'll listen to us, especially if war is coming. And Dea already pissed him off once a few decades ago, please don't make it worse now.

What did Dea do, fuck his Vampire bride or some shit?

Nine doesn't say anything.

I turn to him in surprise, looking at Dea with an accusatory expression. Fucking really?

Yell at him later.

Right. The Vampire prince. "Nobody owns me," I say as I return to Prince Phillipe. "I am a woman of the twenty-second century. I am not a pet, or a tool, or a thing to be used. I recognize my Vampire Royal Council, as they are my own kind, but I am, and will always be, indebted to the Horsemen."

"I see." He steps back into the shadows at that, but he continues to watch any and all interaction between me and Nine the entire time.

"One more thing," Nine stands and says. "We heard a rumor about one of the princes aggravating the SC. Is that true?"

"Yes," the king says, though he doesn't stand this time, since he has his fangs deep in the neck of a human girl on his lap. He pulls his fangs away momentarily to further clarify. "We are currently in the process of dealing with it."

"If you value your blood supplies as much as you say you do, I would advise you not to piss them off any further. Save face, Your Majesty. You'll need it for the future."

Nine walks away after that, and Dea and I follow, not really knowing what to do other than complete his dramatic exit.

"Well," I say once we get outside, "that was . . . underwhelming."

"Yes, I did say they were a little boring. Sorry, Sweetie."

Dea walks beside me and places an arm around my waist, causing me to flinch. "Sorry," he says as he takes his arm back.

"No, it's okay."

What's going on?

I've never seen Dea use his power like that. It was a little scary. I'm a half Vampire, remember. They are kinda my kind.

No, they're not. You can relate to them, which is probably Fate's point, but we don't have a kind. We're the Horsemen of the Apocalypse. We're our own kind altogether.

Nine leaves me with that little pearl of wisdom, as he so often does, and walks ahead, linking his arm through Dea's as I follow behind them in thoughtful silence.

I wear the same dress as last night to tonight's party, and as we walk up the stairs to the mansion with solid stone pillars and verandas and the whole I-have-more-money-than-sense look, I regret that choice.

What if someone sees me in the same dress? Will they think that's gross?

Seriously, the world is on the brink of war, and that's what you're worried about? Goddess, get it together, I mentally chastise myself.

My internal voice sounds distinctly like Nine's, but I just shake off the worried feeling and continue up the beautifully kept front yard.

Seems you don't need me anymore, if you're mentally chastising yourself in my voice.

I ignore that comment, because I'm not really sure what to say. He's right, it is weird. But, honestly, I don't really want to dwell on it right now. I'm oddly looking forward to the party beyond those doors, but I know we have work to do and that I can't really enjoy it.

When we get home, we'll go out properly. Sheruta has some great party life.

Really? Never really pegged it as the partying kind of place.

We've only taken you to the upper-class kind of areas. There's an entire shopping mall, a nightlife district, a supernatural zoo, and everything. It's really grown over the years.

Fuck me, there's a mall? And you never bothered to take me?

Nine laughs. *Sorry, Sweetie. I will next time. Promise.*

That sounds an awful lot like a date, so I cut off the conversation and head inside, arm linking through Dea's despite him not being visible to others this evening. He used up the last of his visibility for the boring Council meeting. Seems a little unfair on him if I'm being honest, missing the good stuff and remaining visible for the boring shit. I kinda feel bad for the guy.

"I'm going to stay with you tonight, Angel. So you and Nine can split up like yesterday."

"Okay."

There are three floors to this monstrous party: two dancefloors with different types of music, a relaxation area with minimal music, and a Vampire den. I stay away from the latter. Not repeating yesterday. One risky feeding session is enough for me. Well, figuratively speaking, of course.

There's also a pool party out back with the best swimming pool I've ever seen. It has lots of sections interconnecting with mini-waterfall style latches. It's actually quite pretty, and someone has clearly put a lot of time and effort into designing it.

"So," Dea starts, "where would you like to go first?" Nine already wandered off somewhere on the second floor, and I'm left with an invisible Dea, both of us trying to work our way around the first-floor dancefloor.

"Dancing, I guess. Best place to meet people, right?"

"That it is, Angel."

I walk us to the main dancefloor in what looks like a half-ballroom, half-lounge, with lots of gold and red drapes dangling around, making the whole place seem fancier than the actual party, which is closer to a frat house than an actual ball.

Dea dances behind me, being careful not to touch me, as I dance in the center with a few women in front of me. We've formed a sort of semi-circle and are all just having the normal kind of fun. None are Vampires, and I hope I don't come across as one in this moment, as I really don't want any hosters hanging around me. Just a nice, normal evening. I'm not quite as pale as a normal Vampire, nor am I as graceful on my feet, so unless my fangs are out, I probably just look like a pale-ish human (or supernatural, if you can distinguish us from humans).

"You know," Dea says from behind me, "this is not information gathering."

I resist the urge to respond, since that will look weird, but seriously want to give him a good solid right hook. Can I not just have a half hour to myself? Since coming to New Orleans, I've fed from a human to gain information, been kissed by a random Vampire I don't know, sat in the world's most dangerous room, had my loyalties questioned, had to keep up a lie about who I am, and am now fishing for information about a Vampire prince I couldn't care less about. Just thirty minutes really doesn't seem that much to ask for.

But fuck it, I can't be asked to deal with Dea grumbling behind me all night. If I didn't know any better, I would say he's channeling his inner-Arrie. Grumpy as shit. So I move along to find a few Vampires to chat to.

I try dancing toward lots of Vampires, but none of them give me the time of day, and it's frustrating. "They seem a little more ageist than the guy last night."

"Welcome to normal Vampires, Angel."

I sigh, deciding to find Nine and reconvene for a different strategy. We just have to try to find this Vampire prince.

"Do you know what Vampire prince we're looking for?"

"No. I just knew the two from yesterday would not have done something so stupid."

"Well then, let's hope this one's the only one that's here."

"Hmmm. Let's." Dea grabs my wrist but leaves it by my side so as not to look weird, and walks me up the stairs toward where Nine headed earlier. "Let's go and find Nine."

"That's what I was doing," I grumble.

"What has you all grumpy this evening?"

"Ugh." I don't bother answering him. I'm simply frustrated—with everything. With my growing feelings for a group of people who will never feel the same way back, with the brewing war caused by stupid people doing stupid shit, and with not being able to actually use all of my supposedly perfect powers.

Everything about my current situation is pissing me off, and, as much as I'm trying to not let it show, it seems to be affecting my ability to do my job.

Searching through crowds of people on the second floor, scouring various dancefloors, seating areas, and crowds of people on the edges of each room, we eventually find Nine with his arms around two Vampires with bouncy blond hair, wearing next to nothing as they're clad in bikinis way too small for them. He laughs and smiles at their every flash of fang.

Dea stops in his tracks for half a second before continuing toward him, which is the only indication I get that it bothers him. He smiles as he approaches, though, and Nine catches his eye briefly as something unusual passes between them.

"Hey!" I say in a way too cheery smile as I walk on up. "Fancy seeing you here . . ."

"Sarah, I didn't know you'd be here tonight." He smiles as he releases one of the blondes on his arm to grab my hand and pull me in, tightening me around his waist in a warm hug. "It's so good to see you."

What are you doing up here? Dea says you're having problems?

Ugh. Vampires are avoiding me like the plague. Like, seriously, they're ageist as fuck in here.

I see. Let's tag team then.

I nod, pulling away from him and sidling backward to grab each blonde by the arm, feigning being human (hopefully) by whooshing my hair back and exposing my neck.

Bingo. They each wrap an arm around my waist, still including Nine in our little circle, and zone in on my neck.

"You know 'im?" one of them asks as she nods to Nine.

"Yeah, we go way back!" I give her a raised eyebrow, hoping to convey exactly how close we are, and she gives me a questioning look.

"Really? That's so cute!" She flashes a fang at me, and it takes everything in me not to return the threat. I could blow her to the Pacific Ocean if I really wanted to.

Nine seems to sense what's going on, even as I try hard to block any active thoughts from leaking, and steps out of the blonde's arms and guides me away from them.

What was that?

I don't answer, but Dea gives me a sad look of understanding and also remains silent. And in that moment, I'm certain: Dea's in love with Nine.

I try hard to keep that thought to myself, but it seems to come out of my mind loud and clear, because Nine stops in his tracks and throws me an angry look.

Sorry. Didn't mean that to be so loud.

It's fine, he snaps.

He schools his features as we arrive at the nearest dancefloor, hoping to once again find this stupid, elusive prince.

Dea joins us, and although we all have smiles and dance with a bunch of humans and Vampires, and even a few Shifters, we can all feel the tension. None of us looks each other in the eye, and we all stay well away from touching each other.

"You looking for Prince?" a foreign-accented voice sounds from behind me.

I turn around to a pair of golden eyes (a Shifter) resting a few feet above my eye level. He's a big guy, probably some kind of wolf or bear Shifter, with black-and-white-peppered hair, a graying beard, and a fallen expression.

"What of it?" I'm done with pleasantries for this evening. I just want to grab the nearest cab and head to the Witches's Coven so we can be one step closer to returning to *Sheruta.*

"Follow." He turns and walks off the dancefloor.

I eye both Nine and Dea, who shrug and nod. Guess we're following Mr. Weirdo. We follow him down the stairs, across the first floor, and out the front door. The grand front yard looms in front of us, having since been lit up by various fairy lights dotted around.

"Where are we going?" I ask Mr. Weirdo.

"To Prince."

Okaaay. He could also be leading us into a trap. And, honestly, that seems more likely.

Stay alert. It's a trap. But he doesn't know who's laying it. He's just a hired man.

Right.

Dea says to use your air magic and your Vampire strength and speed in any kind of fight, but try to avoid any armed opponents; we'll take care of them.

And how exactly do you plan on doing that?

Dea has his sword on him, and I have my pistols.

Where the fuck are you hiding them? And why am I not armed?!

Quit complaining. Pay attention.

He sounds stressed, and I get the feeling it isn't because of the current situation.

Nine . . . I—

Not now. Later.

Okay.

We continue to follow Mr. Weirdo around the corner of an otherwise silent part of the front yard that's hidden from view. Only a Vampire would be able to see here (which could pose a problem for us).

We're just on the other side of the mansion when I hear footsteps. "Stay where you are, Horseman!"

We all stop, but Dea and Nine don't look worried. I gather a ball of air in each palm, readying for a fight.

"What do you want?" Nine asks in the emotionless tone he uses when trying to hide how he really feels. He's nervous, and that doesn't bode well.

"Nothing but your heads."

Dea yells at us both, "Now!"

We leap into action, and I suddenly realize that Nine can also see in the dark because he can see through the minds of the other Vampires. Dea, on the other hand, can't, so I stay near him, just in case. He's invisible, so no one even knows he's here, but still.

There're eight Vampires in front of us, all carrying some kind of weapon, and a few lurking behind bushes surrounding us.

You take those, I'll take these.

You sure?

Just do it.

Okay.

I leave Nine to it and leap into action toward the nearest bush. It's a small, low-to-the-ground thing with a few thorny roses sticking out, and the guy crouching behind it is trying not to be seen, but his bright blue hair gives him away. I use my air magic to send a gust his way, knocking him to the ground.

He flies to the floor, his head smacking against the ground—not hard enough to knock him out, since it's grassy, but enough to make him a little dizzy as he stumbles to his feet.

"Who the fuck are you?"

"No one." I send another gust of air, which this time, sends him to the concrete, and watch as his head splatters on the ground, knocking him unconscious (or killing him, but I'm trying not to think about that).

I hear a few screams from the direction of the other side of the fight, and I see Dea backing Nine up as he sends three Vampires to the ground in wailing agony.

So that move doesn't kill them, it just incapacitates them.

I move along, using the same method on a further three hiding Vampires, sending each one flying to the concrete, where they hit their heads hard enough to knock them unconscious. Or kill them.

I crouch on the grass, trying to discretely look around for other Vampires, but seem satisfied there are none left. Nine and Dea still have two opponents left, so I run toward them.

"Angel, look out!"

A loud thump hits my head from behind, and I stumble to the ground. Dea and Nine react almost instantly, but they're pulled back by their own opponents, who have them pinned to the wall in seconds as they use the distraction to their advantage.

I can feel blood dripping down the side of my face, and my vision is a little hazy, but I manage to make it to my feet, only swaying slightly.

Have. To. Save. Them.

Thoughts are barely coherent at this point, and I fear we might be about to lose to a small group of Vampires all because I missed someone.

For fuck's sake.

But just as a hand wraps around my throat, a loud gunshot goes off, and the hand loosens enough for me to stumble out of its grasp.

"Shit. Fuck. Shit," I mumble to myself.

Someone moves from the shadows beyond with a gun in hand, and I half run, half stumble toward Nine and Dea to try to help them escape so we can run.

But the gun sends off another two rounds, and the Vampires holding them to the wall collapse to the ground.

The shooter, however, runs forward, and the shock of blond hair and blue eyes has my memory doing twists and somersaults, but my mind is too foggy right now. I can't pinpoint the memory enough to relive it.

"Little hunter? You . . . you're a-a-alive?"

Nine and Dea stand beside me, Dea holding me up.

"Famine. And is that you, Death? But, hunter, what are you doing here? And how are you alive?"

I realize, after a moment of confusion, that he's referring to me. "You . . . know me?"

He laughs. "Of course I know you. I gave you a heads-up about being on the SC's hit list nine months ago. But . . . you died. They had a funeral and everything."

The SC killed me? I was . . . assassinated?

"But you were with the Horsemen all along?" He looks genuinely perplexed.

"Thank you for saving us, Prince Lucien. It truly has been a help," Dea says.

"Well, I could hardly let my own kind kill two of the Four Horsemen, could I?"

It's Nine's turn to laugh this time, and he puts an arm around my shoulders as he does so. "Sweetie, this is Prince Lucien. And I get the feeling he's the prince we've been looking for."

"Indeed I am."

"And Prince Lucien, this is Sarah. A recently turned Vampire we saved from a difficult situation."

"V-V-Vampire? So you're a hybrid?"

"You know what I was?"

He nods, not really sure of himself. "An Angel-descended Witch, yes. It was I who accidently let it slip to the SC."

Dea looks at Nine quickly, grabs us both, and speeds us out of there faster than any Vampire could manage to keep up with

23

Dea holds me and Nine on either foot, holding us in place with an arm around our waists, and races us back to our motel faster than I think possible. But even as the world speeds by us, I can feel the anger boiling beneath.

What was he thinking? That was my chance at answers!

As the motel comes into view, Dea puts us down in front of our door, letting us catch our breaths, and in my case, curb the nausea currently threatening to bring up what little I've eaten in the last few days.

Once inside and the door firmly shut behind us, Nine steps back, giving me a look of concern as I face Dea with a look of what I hope is scathing fury.

"What. The. Fuck. Was. That?"

Dea looks at me and steps forward, reaching his hand out to touch me, but I bat it away with some force, causing it to swing and slap his side.

"The more we talked with Prince Lucien, the more issues we were creating."

"That . . ." I take a deep breath, trying not to explode every ounce of frustration I've gathered over the last forty-eight hours toward Dea. But, ultimately, I fail. I push him so hard he flies across the room and lands inside the exterior wall.

He winces as he steps out, stretching his limbs.

"That was my chance at fucking answers, Dea! Why would you do that? You absolute, motherfucking piece of shit!"

My fangs have descended in my rage, and I'm pretty sure my eyes are now bloodshot red as I can feel them pulsing.

"Sweetie, maybe you shou—"

I hold up a hand to Nine, really not wanting to yell at him, and take my eyes off of the Horseman of Death. "I need answers. He is the only person I have met over the last few weeks who knew me before I was this . . . thing!" I gesture to myself.

"Angel, I—"

"Don't even think of calling me that." I turn away and pace the room, trying to vent some of my anger. "I can't even look at you right now. You took away the only chance I've ever had of getting answers." Facing the wall so I don't have to look at either of them, I whisper, "How could you?" The tears finally fall, and I let them, hoping they'll stress the seriousness of Dea's actions.

"If I had let that conversation continue, our mission to keep your true identity hidden until we are one hundred percent sure of what Horseman you are and who broke your seal would have been compromised in an instant."

"I don't have an identity to keep secret."

I storm out of the motel's door, slam it shut behind me, and stride down the path of rooms, aiming to just get anywhere away from them.

Don't go too far. It's not safe now.

Goddammit, Nine's right. So instead of finding the nearest bar and getting flat-out blind-drunk, I settle on punching a hole through the nearest vending machine and grabbing as much caffeine and sugar as possible. At least this way I won't be as tired by the time I'm finished. And if the manager has an issue with that, Dea can fucking pay for it.

I sit on a wall in the parking lot, downing cans of liquid energy and packets of sugar, causing my body to need to expel the overdose. I could Vamp-speed around the parking lot, but I think it might attract too much attention, so I settle on pacing. Something that's becoming a bit of a habit.

How could he? I need answers, and part of me wants to run right back to that party, find Lucien, and ask him. But instead, I'm walking in a dingy parking lot following the orders of a fucking a-hole!

I've never actually been angry at any of the team before (other than my frustration at Arrie, but that doesn't count), and it doesn't feel good. We shouldn't be at odds with each other. But why did he do it?

To protect me? I don't need protecting.

To protect Earth? Maybe everyone should do a better job of getting along, rather than expecting us to clean up their petty messes.

You're right. They should. But it is our job, nonetheless, and whether they deserve our help isn't the point. Earth is ours to protect. Even if that isn't what Fate intended, that's what it's become.

But what's the point? I don't want to live forever, protecting Earth, if I can't even live. I want my memories back. I want to know who I am.

By this point, I've stopped pacing and sink to the ground against the wall. The tears won't stop flowing, and I can feel the start of a breakdown oncoming, so I wrap my arms around myself and focus on breathing.

In, out.

In, out.

I don't want to breakdown like I did in the forest the other day and cause the team more problems.

Ugh. Why do I even care at this point?

Because you're an amazing person.

No, I'm not. I'm a stupid little nobody who can't even use the powers granted to her by Fate, for fuck's sake. I don't even have a name!

Then pick one.

Huh?

We picked our names afresh, and they all correspond to our Horseman type. So, pick one for yourself.

I don't want to. I want my actual name.

Nine doesn't respond, so I let him be.

I don't want a new name or a new life (though I did get one). Maybe one day I'll like that, but I would like to know who I was before moving on and becoming someone else. I want to close the door on my old life first. What if I left someone behind? What if I caused the war?

I lay on the concrete path for a while, staring up at the pollution-filled night sky, trying to name as many constellations as I can. I manage five before giving up and walking to the motel for some sleep. Besides, we still have Witches to see; any excuse to get out of this damn city. I can always come back and ask Prince Lucien questions later. But I'm still mad as fuck.

I take my time walking back and manage a few laps around the block first, hoping that isn't too far for Nine's telepathy to reach. If it is, they don't bother coming to find me, which I assume they would if Nine can't reach me. The door to the motel is open slightly when I arrive, I assume to let me in since I didn't take a room key, and I lock it behind me as I enter.

The bedroom is empty, but I hear the shower running and murmurs coming from the bathroom. They're showering together?

Sitting on the edge of the bed, I place my head in my hands. They're really having sex while I'm having an internal crisis? But I can't be angry—I've drowned all of my anger in candy and caffeine—so I kick back and lay on the bed, assuming they'll likely be respectful since Nine will know I'm here.

You know, part of me doesn't want to be. I can hear the smirk in his voice. *But since Dea feels guilty and doesn't want to cause you more mental anguish, yes, we'll be respectful, as you so politely put it.*

Then be respectful to him, too, and stop talking to me while you're fucking your boyfriend.

He's not my boyfriend.

I don't answer that. I try to keep my mind on something else so as not to accidentally respond, and I succeed when I start doing some yoga on the dirty floor. Not my first choice of places to relax, but it'll have to do.

I manage multiple positions and flowing changes with an empty mind before curiosity gets the better of me, and, damn it, I have to actually resist not walking into the bathroom.

What is wrong with me? When did I become such a pervert?

When you realized you wanted to be where Dea is now. Nine sends me a mental image of Dea bent over, hands splayed against the bathroom tiles as the shower pours down his back.

I try to shake the image free, but Nine keeps it there.

Seriously, Nine, stop it.

That didn't sound all that convincing.

Ugh. You're impossible. What do you want?

Well, I know you're attracted to both of us, as you frequently refer to us as being 'hot as hell,' so I want you to indulge. To live. And I will continue trying to push past that barrier of yours until I succeed. Or until you stop finding us attractive.

Well, that last one is not likely to happen within the next couple of centuries, so I refocus on my yoga routine and ignore the blazing heat threatening to engulf me.

But, as I continue blocking him out, Nine ups game. He does something I didn't know he could do: show me what he's seeing. Not just a still image in my mind, but like a personal, live movie. And honestly, I would complain, but it's the coolest power I've ever seen.

It's like I can see everything from Nine's point of view, including their new position, with Dea on his knees sucking Nine's cock.

Am I going to be privy to all of your sex life?

Just the stuff you'll enjoy.

The personal movie is silent, but my Vampire hearing is pretty good—I was just trying not to use it until now.

"Is she watching?" Dea asks.

He knows? Well, that makes me feel a little better than last time, at least.

"Yes," Nine says on a moan. "She's listening, too."

"Really?"

"Vamp hearing."

"Hmmm. Angel, I am sorry for earlier. Let me make it up to you."

With my own personal porno? That's ~~fun~~ . . . extreme.

Extreme was not the word your mind came up with first.

Shut up and enjoy the bloody blowjob Dea is so expertly giving you. I would not watch and continue to do my yoga routine to block you out, but that doesn't seem to be an option you're letting me choose.

This one was Dea's idea, actually.

Really?

"Yes," Dea says. "I want to make it up to you. And technically, you are not having sex with either of us."

Well, that's just . . . cheating. Works. That works is what that does. Does it make things weird? Probably. But it means I'm not connecting to them, right? That I won't fall into a relationship with two people who have no interest in being in one? But still, I can indulge slightly. I mentally chastise them for not allowing themselves to love because they're afraid, but I'm doing the same thing.

I lay on the bed, having forgone my attempts at yoga, and focus on watching my own personal pornographic movie, trying to forget about the weirdness of what I'm actually doing.

Maybe I'm not ready for casual sex, but that doesn't mean I can't join in, right? I can't mentally send anything to Dea, but Nine can.

What are you planning, Sweetie?

You'll see.

I conjure up the first image, the memory of my kiss with Connie, thinking to start it off light.

Send what you're seeing to Dea.

I hope to convey everything I'm feeling in the moment, but it's hard to do while watching them, so I try a different tactic and send them the memory of the last time I watched them.

"Fuck, Angel. That is how you saw us?"

Dea picks up his pace slightly, and I hear Nine cave under his skills, his breathing becoming heavier. "Dea, fuck me."

Dea releases Nine's cock and spins him around, bending him over into the same position he was in not ten minutes ago.

I don't have anything else to send them, but the fact that my nipples have pebbled and my clit is throbbing for any kind of attention makes it very hard not to touch myself.

Do it.

You'd be into that? Watching me?

You can't really judge about watching people, Sweetie.

He has a point. A really annoying but good point. But I don't want to masturbate to their ridiculously hot fucking, as that feels too much like connecting, but I do get a better idea.

Instead, I send them the memory of my alone time in the bath, hoping it'll be a good contributor.

And it works! Dea speeds up his pace as Nine's fingers try clenching onto a solid surface but slip under the wet tiles.

Nine yells in pleasure, throwing his aim of being respectful out the window. *One of these days, Sweetie, you'll be in here with us. And it'll be because you begged to join in.*

In your dreams.

"Angel," Dea moans as he thrusts harder into Nine, his fingers digging into Nine's hips hard enough to leave bruises.

Send us that last memory again.

I do as asked, lapping up the attention and the fact that they find me as hot as I find them. My core's burning by this point, and I need some kind of release, so I shove all my worries to the back of my mind and slide my hand lower to my clit, hoping that Nine can see and equally hoping he can't.

I hear Nine and Dea's releases as I see them, Dea's grip on Nine's hips growing hard enough to bite into his skin.

Moving my hand faster, I chase my own release as Nine shuts down the movie and I'm left with nothing but the sweet memory. I never thought in a million years I would find watching two men as hot I do, but I'm past the point of caring as my orgasm crashes over me, and I have to stifle my own cries by biting my lip.

"Damn, Angel," Dea says from the doorway. "I wanted to be the one to make you look like that."

Technically, they are the ones to make me look like this, if you think about it, but I don't give him the satisfaction of saying that thought out loud. By the time I look up at the pair of them walking out of the bathroom in towels, a confident smirk has settled across Dea's face, and Nine just winks at me.

The fucker betrayed me.

I'm not mad, I'm far too high in post-orgasmic bliss for that. Instead, I roll over and get under the duvet, not even bothering to change into my pajamas, and fall asleep the moment my head hits the pillow.

24

The next morning, I wake in a surprisingly good mood (well, it's not all that surprising, but it's welcome) and pack for South Africa. I didn't bring much with me, so I just shove all my things into my backpack and wait for the guys to finish.

"For a couple of guys, you take ages to pack."

"I have weapons to pack," Dea says as he carefully places a variety of guns, swords, and daggers into a suitcase specially designed for weapons. "And you did not pack that much."

I shrug. "Figured we could get anything we needed on the go. It's only recon." I snack on a giant fluffy pretzel Nine brought back from his breakfast trip a half hour ago, and it's one of the most delicious desserts I've ever eaten. The sugar, the cinnamon . . . Fuck me, it's honestly making my stomach grumble.

"True for most things," he says. "But our weapons are ours, and we hate losing them. Nine spends a while designing them for us."

I look to Nine with raised eyebrows. "You design weapons?"

"I design a lot of things, mostly magical things."

I can picture him in a lab somewhere in one of those white lab coats, designing all kinds of fun and weird shit with all kinds of magic they've picked up on over the years. "I'll make you some daggers soon."

He's a little preoccupied trying to fold his clothes in that little precise way of his to really hold a conversation, so I let him be and wait patiently for them both to be done.

"Call us a taxi if you are bored," Dea suggests.

"I'm not bored, just shocked I was packed and ready to go before you guys."

Dea rolls his eyes and looks at the phone on his nightstand and then at me, as if he's giving me an order. Well, I guess he kinda is.

Sighing, I grab it and dial the local cab number we've been using since arriving in the city. And in thirty minutes, we're off to the airport once again, heading to South Africa.

. . . .

Fourteen hours on a flight with Nine and Dea is torture. If they aren't purposefully pissing me off, they're snoring, invading my personal space, or generally being a couple of fuckwits. Getting off that plane and into open space cannot come soon enough, and when it does, I bound down the hallways of the airport, listening to Nine's and Dea's laughter in the distance as they watch me twirl my arms around just because I can and shout at the top of my lungs because I no longer have to be considerate to all of the people stuck in a small enclosed space hundreds of miles in the air with me.

I do not like flying, it turns out, but apparently no one does. It's a universally accepted hatred for everyone, unless you can afford your own jet, which sounds like it would come in real handy for the team. I make a mental note to bring it up with them later.

Grabbing the guys' bags from security, I wonder how Dea gets all those weapons through airport security.

We have a free legal pass given to us by the SC.

So they do like you?

Like is a bit strong. They tolerate us.

We manage to get out of the airport without too much hassle and hail a cab from the front entrance. "So," I ask as I get in the back with Nine, "where are we going?"

"To Howick Falls, please," Nine says to the driver.

Dea sits between us, completely invisible to the driver, and remains silent.

Dea says to hide your Vampire nature here. Be a Witch. One of the benefits of having both types of powers is that you can fit in with both communities, but Witches famously hate Vampires.

What should I expect of this place? Of the Witches?

They're . . . unusual but generally kind and humbling to most. Unfortunately, we're not most. They can be a bit hostile toward us. We're a little worried they'll know what you are straight away, since some of their clan are seers.

Seers?

People who can look into the future and heavily examine their surroundings. They often experience time in a less linear way. They also always know who we are, even when disguised.

Oh, shit. What if they do suspect?

Hopefully, they'll keep quiet.

I don't answer him after that, thinking that hopes are not something to base a plan around.

It takes hours to get to our destination, and the stifling silence all three of us have fallen into is suffocating. I can't stop thinking about last night, and not in a good way.

Are things weird now? They don't seem weird, but maybe everyone's putting on a brave face?

Goddess, they totally watched me come from the bathroom doorway; that is so beyond my nice, pretty line in the sand.

You ever make a massive mistake you can't take back, and then are left to steam in a pool of regret for days until you finally manage to mentally calm down? Well, this is like that, but I'll never calm down from this—and I'm immortal, so that's a long regret.

Okay, yes, they're both hot and insanely attractive, and I like them both. I'm not ashamed to admit that. But honestly, it's more than that. Without them both there to help over the last few weeks, I wouldn't be okay right now. Between Dea's guidance and

Nine's assistance in almost everything, I'm slowly becoming the Horseman of Magic, a member of the team that maybe one day I'll consider family. And last night has put a giant wrench in that.

Dea has his head back and his eyes closed, so I assume he's asleep, but Nine has his head in his hands and his thinking expression on; that doesn't seem promising.

Nine's . . . sweet and caring and flirty in a way that's just fun. He's never made me feel awkward or strange (maybe a little embarrassed from time to time, but since he can read my mind, he knows exactly when it's too much). I love the way his face scrunches in concentration when he's figuring out some kind of puzzle, and the way he's nearly always touching Dea when they're in the same room together. Even now, Dea's hand is on Nine's leg. They try to hide it, but I know they entwine their legs under the dinner table, take every opportunity to sit next to each other, and probably spend more nights together than apart. Nine's a mind-reader (literally), so he must know how Dea really feels, and yet he's always considerate and has never backed away because of it.

And the fact that I can list all that after only a few weeks with these guys scares the shit out of me. How in the world will I manage centuries without falling . . . ? I don't want to say the words, not where Nine can hear them.

Fuck.

Last night was such a mistake. What was I thinking?

Both of you, shut the fuck up! You're giving me a headache. He audibly groans from his seat as he rubs his temples, and both Dea and I lift our heads to look at him. *You're both thinking too loudly. If I knew last night would cause you both so much fucking anguish, I would never have followed through.*

Sorry.

Hearing Nine shout with a frown on his perfect face puts me in my place rather quickly. It's such a surprise I sit up straighter in my seat and pull out the plasmascreen I used to read on the flight and delve into a book so quickly, I hope no more thoughts leak from my mind. But just before opening the book and settling down, I ask myself one last question.

Why is Dea so worried?

25

When we arrive at what looks like the end of a well-worn path just before a field, I get out, cross the field in an instant of Vampire speed, and look out over the clifftop. The view takes my breath away; for hundreds of miles, all you can see is the expanse of country as the waterfall rushes below, thrumming against my ears in a way that blocks out my worries. Greens and browns paint the scenery before me in a wash of color you'd never find in the city, and I find myself staring at the expanse of nature in a trance of awe and admiration. The Witches have chosen a beautiful location for their coven.

I can really do some good yoga here.

I pivot back around, realize I've probably taken way too long staring at the world, and find Nine and Dea gazing at me with gentle smiles.

"Beautiful, is it not?" Dea steps forward and grabs my hand. "Let me show you the rest of what the Witches call home."

Nine looks at us with a curious expression and grabs my other hand, dragging us away from the cliff's edge and toward a path I didn't notice earlier that must lead to the bottom of the valley below, next to the waterfall's base.

Dea carries most of the bags, which I think is stupid given that I'm stronger than them both, but I let him have his chivalrous moment; I'll smash that stupid chivalry later, but right now, I'm still a little awed by my surroundings.

Sure, *Sheruta* is amazing, and this still has nothing on the team's home, but that doesn't take away from the beauty currently surrounding me. It's all just so . . . peaceful.

It's because you're a Witch. Eventually, you'll be able to use earth magic, and being in places like this helps earth Witches feel more grounded.

Curious, I try swaying some trees and shrubs without using my air magic, but they either remain stationary or flutter in a fake breeze I accidentally let slip. I keep trying as we descend the narrow path, but by the time we've gotten to the bottom, I'm well and truly frustrated. Again.

"Looks like I'm an air Witch for the time being."

"Indeed," Dea says. "And as much I hate forcing people to hide who they are, you are going to have to not let your Vampire magic slip while here. That would really put a wrench in our plans of trying to talk to them."

I sigh, knowing he's right but hating the idea of struggling through the next few days. They should have sent the others here, for fuck's sake.

"You'll be useful when trying to connect with them. They've always been difficult to work with, trying to stay out of the world's issues as much as possible."

"When they finally find out what you really are," Dea adds, "it will be easier to deal with them. They will finally have a Horseman they can relate to. Even with your Horseman magic, you were once a Witch."

"That would be great, if I could remember being one."

They both still hold my hands, and Nine begins stroking his thumb across my fingers. "It'll come to you in time."

"I'm not sure that's what I want anymore."

They both stop walking, and Dea puts the bags down and turns toward me. "Why not?"

I put my head to the ground and yank my hands out of their grip. "I don't wanna talk about it." I pick up the bags in one hand and descend the last few hundred meters to the base of the waterfall.

In truth, the more I learn about who I was, the more horrified I become. And, honestly, what's the point? No one cares enough to let me find out anyway.

I wait for them at the bottom, hoping they'll just meet me there and go on pretending like I'm not mentally falling apart.

No luck.

Dea steps up next to my perch on a rock and places a hand on my shoulder. "Talk to us, Angel."

"No."

Nine stands below us with a grimace. "She doesn't want to talk to us because she thinks we don't care about her finding answers. So, she's trying to block out caring about it, too, thinking that's what's best for the team."

Dea blows out a frustrated breath.

I'm being difficult, I know that, but I don't care. I could have gotten answers from Prince Lucien, but that isn't important enough to them to stop and consider how we could have gotten them without causing too much damage to my cover.

Dea grabs the top of my arm with a growl and yanks me to my feet, forcing me to face him. "For someone so good at reading the inner workings of this team, you are incredibly stupid." He takes a deep breath, as though he's trying hard not to explode in anger at me, and I recoil slightly from his tightening touch. "We do care. Not only because we care about you, but because without you knowing everything about yourself and becoming the Horseman you are meant to be, we cannot fix this war."

I don't know what to say to that, so I remove myself from his grasp and turn around to jump off my rocky perch.

"Arghh! You are the most infuriating person on this fucking planet, Angel." Dea grabs the back of my t-shirt, pulls me toward him, and throws me into the lake below.

The waterfall thrashes me around, battering my limbs in a tangle of mush, but a few powerful kicks have me breaking the surface, gasping for air as I try hard to stay afloat in the tumbling current.

Dea's in the water in front of me, a stony expression on his perfect face. "Sorry." He helps me swim to the edge and pulls me out.

"Now that you've had your tantrum, can I go back to sulking, so we can meet the Witches?"

He sighs in exasperation and storms off.

"Come on, Sweetie," Nine says and follows Dea along a treacherous rocky path toward the waterfall.

"Where are we . . . ?"

Dea falls behind the corner's edge of the waterfall and disappears beyond.

Nine smiles at my inner shock. "They really do have a beautiful home here. You'll like it." He grabs one of the bags, so I can better balance with only one in each hand, and jumps off the last rock to a little ledge just beside the thrumming water.

He probably won't hear me if I speak, so I don't bother, but I can hear him just fine given my Vamp hearing; I just have to focus on separating the sounds.

"That's kinda how Connie's hearing works. Or how she controls it, rather. Otherwise, it gets a bit much and gives her a headache. So she zones in on things and blocks out the rest."

At the sound of Connie's name, a pang of longing throbs through me. I really hope we get back in time for our sleepover in a few days. We have so much to catch up on.

I love your feelings for Con. I know you won't talk about it, especially not right now when you're still mad at us, but I just wanted to say that you two are great together.

I can feel my face blush hard, and I have a hard time forming any kind of sentence, so I settle on not saying anything, verbally or mentally.

When we work our way behind the waterfall and into a massive cavern, we meet Dea, who gives me a pained look but smiles nonetheless. He really is trying, bless him.

He's mostly hurt you don't trust us, but he's also a little annoyed last night didn't make up for it.

I blush again, but this time I have an answer.

I'm not some sex-starved idiot like you find in books. I'm not going to get laid and then everything be okay again.

I know that. So does he. But he was hoping, that's all.

Why are you telling me this?

Because he asked me to.

Wow. You're like a telepathic intermediary. That must fucking suck.

A little. But I'd do anything for the team. Even act the mediator for petty tantrums.

My tantrum is not petty.

No. But his is.

I laugh at that, and Dea turns around to face us in a scowl, obviously aware of what we were talking about. "Don't worry, Death," I say, annunciating his title, "all in good fun."

"If you are going to sulk, stop having fun about it."

I can't really argue with that logic, but his grumpy, childlike face is really funny. I didn't realize the Horseman of Death could throw tantrums.

He's good at it, too. Beaten only by Arrie.

Ugh. The thought of dealing with an Arrie-Dea tantrum has me recoiling in emotional horror.

It's not pretty.

We're standing in the cavern—not really anything special—when I hear the sound of thumping feet in the background.

"Heads up," I say, catching Dea and Nine off guard.

They each grab a weapon out of their bags.

I form balls of air in each palm, ready for anything.

"Death, Famine," a male voice echoes around the cavern. "State your business."

It's Dea who does the talking this time, and I notice he doesn't drop his sword. "We are checking in on all the larger magical communities for an in-person update. We request to speak to the full Coven. We would have called ahead, but staying in touch with your kind has proven difficult."

"For good reason." The owner of the deep male voice steps out from the shadows I didn't bother looking in earlier, and I recoil.

He has on satin and leather pants but is otherwise topless, and patterned in the marks of a whip all over his body are scars inches thick. Even across his face. "I'm afraid you may have to wait a while; the full Coven is not present at the moment."

"Then, if it is okay, we will wait." Dea drops his sword and picks up the weapons bag. "If you would prefer, we can wait in a hotel somewhere nearby."

"That won't be necessary. Follow me." He disappears back into the shadows, but this time I focus enough to notice a tunnel.

Dea and Nine look at me, and I nod, letting them know it's all right to follow. Neither of them can see in the dark, it seems.

Dea can if he's not using his powers to be visible.

Being visible is a real vice for him, and I hate it. Maybe we can find a way to use my Witch magic to create some kind of charm.

We follow the man, me taking the lead as I use my Vampire sight to see where he goes. I hope that won't make them suspicious of me and they don't think too hard about it.

Walking down dark cave tunnels, I wonder where we're heading, but as we get deeper into the cave, it becomes more and more habitable as signs of life start forming, from moss and plants to glowing mushrooms and fairylights lighting the way.

A giant light blinds me from up ahead, and I have to hold back my gasp of surprise as the set of tunnels we've spent the past half-hour walking down opens into a large cavern with a skylight pouring daylight down onto one of the best sights I've ever seen: a hidden world.

Trees, houses, small pockets of buildings, ponds and fountains are all mapped with semi-natural pathways crisscrossing the entire cavern. Lots of doors line the edges, and I bet they probably lead to more caverns like this one.

They use their elemental magic together as one whole unit to create homes like this. They've been doing it for centuries to stay hidden from the human world.

They use their elemental magic to create this? That is. . . incredible.

We're staying in an elaborate hut—which I know sounds insulting, but it's actually rather charming. It's a small two-bed apartment-like thing that sprouts straight out of the ground and looks like it's been carved directly into the cave itself. Knowing this whole place is created using elemental Witch magic, I assume this is all via using earth magic. And I'll be damned if I'm not jealous right now.

I can do this? Well, I can do this when I can access my earth magic.

This is so fucking cool! Think of all the houses I can make when—

"I know this is like a Witch's wet dream, but we really need to make a plan about how to handle the Coven." Nine sits with his feet on the coffee table, lounging on the couch that looks like some kind of moss-covered log in the shape of a couch. He has a smirk on that pretty face of his, and I have the distinct urge to wipe it right off.

I sit on the chair handily placed in front of the couch and lean my head on my hands, half-sulking, half-interested in their plan. "Why do we even need a plan? You just walked rightinto the Vampire Royal Council?"

"This is not the Vampire Royal Council." Dea paces the small lounge, occasionally bumping into corners of furniture but refraining from the usual cursing I would be doing if I stubbed my toe that hard.

"Okay . . ." Color me curious. "What kind of plan do you have in mind?"

"Well, for starters, we can't reveal your true nature," Nine says. "That would be devastating. The only thing they would think is that you're a hybrid, and they usually execute any they come across."

I laugh lightly, but Nine's face deadpans. I sit up a little straighter. "Wait, you're serious?"

He nods. "And even if we were to tell the Coven what you truly are, they would either not believe us or just add you to the hostility they already show us. So that's not helpful either."

"Also," Dea adds, "we want to tell all the community heads at once, so no one can argue over favoritism, and it would be best if we waited until you gained your Fae and Shifter powers, so if they ask for a demonstration, you will be able to acquiesce."

"Right, show monkey. Got it."

Dea rolls his eyes, a movement that seems very me, and I have to resist the urge to smile at him. Damn him. Even when I'm mad at him he's sexy.

Nine smiles in that flirty way of his, not needing to say anything else for me to know he picked up on that.

Of course he did. Why does he always pick up on the dirty thoughts?

Because those are the ones you shout the loudest, alongside the emotional ones, of course.

Sure. Because that's obvious.

"What do we need from these people?" I ask, trying to get this little meeting on track.

"Information," Dea says.

"Honest information," I correct. "They could lie."

"Right. Nine has to physically invade someone's mind to read it. It is only ours he can read so freely. And the Coven usually use charms to protect against telepathic attack, lest it give their location away."

"So, you read the Vampires' minds, then?"

"Everyone but the king. He also has telepathic powers, and we can block other people out." My momentary look of panic has Nine smiling again. "He can't read our minds, of course."

"Of course." Actually, that doesn't make any sense.

"It is because we are not actually alive," Dea supplies in answer. "Plus, most powers work better against people weaker than them."

There's so much about how magic at this level works. It's really simple when considering it from a human perspective, but from a Horseman perspective, it's really fucking complicated.

You have an immortal lifetime to figure it all out.

No. I don't. I have until Earth destroys itself.

Nine's smile pales as my attention turns back to Dea, who's still pacing. "We need to manipulate them into talking about the SC, their relationship with the Vampires, and their continued closeting." He sighs. "And your seal."

"Okay. I think I can handle the closeting," I say.

Dea raises a single eyebrow.

"I'm a Witch who knows nothing about how her Coven works. I can just ask."

Nine nods. "Should work. But the other two will require some effort on our part."

"I hate politics," Dea grumbles. He heads to a mini-fridge and grabs a can of beer, pops the cap, and downs a large mouthful as he falls beside Nine.

"I know." Nine places a hand on his knee, and I internally giggle at my correct assessment from earlier. "But we can do this. We always do."

"There has never been a magical war before. This is new territory, even for us."

I didn't think about that, and hearing him say it has my heart rate racing. They're right, this isn't normal. If we push these people in the wrong direction, we could kickstart this war.

Fate chose me for a reason, and I honestly have no fucking idea what that reason is, but surely this is part of it. Otherwise, why pick me so early? Why not wait until the war has already begun, like with the rest of the team?

"How long are they gonna take, d'you reckon?" The thought of sitting here stewing in my nervousness has my knees shaking and my hands sweating.

"No idea, but that is a good question." Dea stands and paces again, this time not bumping into any furniture. "We should get some rest. Then we can take Angel on a tour of this place."

That helps ease some of my concerns, but not all. At least I won't be stewing in nerves the entire time. Maybe they can help me take my mind off things.

I shake that idea out of my mind before it can even fully form, lest it go in a hot, sexy direction that I have no place desiring.

"I'm taking the room on the right." I point in the general direction of the bedroom I scouted earlier and grab my bag and head that way.

"Guess we're sharing, bro," Nine says in a tone that can't hide the suggestion if he tried.

THE NEXT MORNING CONSISTS OF A BREAKFAST OF FRESH FRUIT, MEATS, AND BREAD, AND I HAVE to admit, the freshness has me thankful. I really want to eat a bit better. I mean, I'm immortal, and I can't really die from heart disease or anything, but that doesn't mean it doesn't matter. Plus, I want to look good. The rest of the team look fucking godlike all the time.

"Ready for your tour today?" Nine asks, clearly trying to break my thoughts away from their self-depreciating hole.

I appreciate it.

"Sure," I try to push out in a cheery tone, but even I notice it's a little lack-lustre than usual. "Let's go."

I'm excited to see how the world down here works, but I'm super fucking nervous about everything else.

"I am going to stay here and try to hurry this along." Dea turns away from the table and takes his plate of food into their bedroom.

I heard nothing from them last night, and can only assume they were back to being respectful, or they were as tired from traveling as I was. I can't decide if I'm relieved or disappointed by that, but either way, I try not to think about it while in the vicinity of Nine, as I don't want to have that discussion.

Nine and I leave the house at dawn and walk around the town, popping into shops and watching children playing, but my lack of enthusiasm does not go unnoticed.

You okay?

No. I'm not. But I'm trying to forget about it.

That does not seem to be working.

You think? Look, I know you don't see it this way, but I am a part of these people, just like I am with the Vampires, and it would be nice if at least one magical community likes me.

I'm sorry. I hope so, too, but it's unlikely to be the Witches. They really hate us.

Why?

He hesitates, and I get the feeling I'm not going to like his answer.

We tried to force them to come out with the rest of the magical community, and they didn't receive our meddling well.

You think?

I know. It was their decision to make, but having this unbalance of power is as dangerous as we thought it would be. There's more Fae, Vampire, and Shifter magic in the world now, and so very little Witch magic. I'm not certain, but I bet it's causing all kinds of trouble for them.

Did you support the outing of the magical community?

Yes. As did Connie, but Dea didn't think it was such a good idea. Arrie didn't really have an opinion. He hates politics. Tries to stay out of it.

Bet Connie's having fun with him. Then I remember that Arrie and Connie frequently sleep together, like Dea and Nine, and have to backtrack my own thoughts.

You know we can talk about anything, right? Even that.

I don't want to talk about me and Connie. Not that there is a me and Connie, of course. Argh, you know what I mean.

Nine laughs, and the few people around us stare like we're crazy.

I understand.

We stop outside what looks like a park for the children, and I stand and watch. A group of five children, all under the age of six by the looks of things, play on the grass, throwing balls of air at each other and shouting and face-planting the grass—all the while laughing. The parents stand off to the side, chatting and occasionally shouting at the kids to be careful.

It seems so . . . normal.

I'm never going to have this, am I? It hits me like a truck. Immortality takes away my chance to be a parent, have a real family, worry about money and my career. The tears roll down my cheeks before I can attempt to stop them, and I turn on my feet and look straight at Nine, who's staring at me with an expression I don't recognize. Maybe pity? But it seems more solemn than that.

Familiarity.

He wraps an arm through mine, and I let him guide me away as the tears continue to fall in a hiccuping mess.

As much as I want to live and try life—and I have all the time in the world to do just that—immortality also takes away other aspects of a mortal life I didn't realize I wanted until the option was taken away. A family—a real one—is something I can never have.

I unwrap myself from Nine and sit on a nearby bench, just letting myself be for a moment.

I don't know who I am, what kind of powers I will have, how to stop this stupid upcoming war, or how to be in this new world, and it's all so overwhelming.

Was it like this for all of you?

No. We were clueless together, and although it took a while, we worked together. We had our memories; we knew who we were. That changed over the centuries, and some things were hard, but we changed and evolved together.

Why me?

Likely because you were the most powerful supernatural on the planet at the time.

It's my turn to laugh. You're serious? That's insane.

An Angel-descended Witch is nothing to scoff at. You could literally bring death to anyone you touched if you so wished. And we're pretty sure you were the last of your kind.

Wiping away the tears, I get up. "Can we just head back? I kinda want to rest for a bit."

"Sure thing." Nine grabs my arm once more, and we head back, our tour not even extending beyond the hour.

When we enter the house, Dea's sprawled on the couch, staring up at the ceiling, and sits up faster than someone caught stealing a porn magazine. "Why are you back so early . . . ?" He trails off as he looks at me, probably noticing the puffy eyes and tearstains left on my cheeks. "What is wrong, Angel?" He stands up and heads over to me, wrapping his arms around my waist and pulling me into a hug.

"Nothing." I unwrap myself from his arms and head back into my assigned room, hoping to just wait out the Coven and potentially pull myself together before they arrive.

No such luck. It takes three days for the Coven members to convene, and in those three days, I read five books while locked in my bedroom, only coming out to eat, use the bathroom and go on the occasional walk. I even do my daily yoga routine in the bedroom.

Both guys have tried to talk to me, but I've blasted music in my ears from an earstrip I found in Nine's bag and borrowed. Okay, I stole it. But I'll give it back when I get my own.

I haven't figured out how I feel about anything, and quite frankly, I can't be fucking bothered. They're just going to have to deal with my bad mood for a bit. Maybe I'm coming on my period? It's not like I know what my cycle is, but it's been a few weeks . . . Do immortal periods occur monthly? Or are they less regular given we live longer? Because that would be some good news—

A knock at the bedroom door startles me out of my train of thought, but I don't bother answering, hoping whichever Horseman it is will go away after trying to coax out a conversation.

Again, no such luck. "Angel, the Coven is meeting in an hour."

I sigh. Can nothing go my way?

"I'll be there in a moment."

I get out of the pajamas I've stuck myself in for three days and get washed and dressed into a formal dress that's very not me, but Nine bought it me for this specific occasion, so I can't really avoid it. Apparently, formalities are a thing around here.

In the lounge beyond, a place I haven't ventured to in the last three days, Nine and Dea sit on the couch, each with a beer in hand, watching something on the plasmascreen —it's an oddly human sight that has me doing a double take.

I shake the surprise out of my system.

"Where? How long will this take?"

Nine and Dea look up at me, probably both surprised that one of the first things I say to them in three days is work-related.

Dea's the one who answers after turning back to the plasmascreen. "A chamber just off of this one. No idea. Hopefully as little time as possible."

You need to be calm in there. I'm being serious.

"Okay."

I sit on the armchair next to the couch and continue reading with the earphones in until we have to leave.

The chamber in question is exactly that: a chamber. I'm expecting something more grandiose, but it really is just a giant, excavated room with a hand-carved six-pointed star stretching across the floor. At the head of each point sits an elderly lady on a simple wooden chair, each wearing old-fashioned robes from the stone age, and each wearing a scowl on their face at the sight of us.

Each point represents a different type of Witch magic: fire, water, earth, air, charm, and seer.

Three chairs line the wall closest to us, and we sit in them, with me in the middle.

"Death, Famine," a Witch at one of the points says, "what is it you require the full Coven for?"

Dea handles this straight from the start, which does nothing to calm my nerves. "We are checking in on each of the four main communities and trying to get a feel for the current atmosphere of the magical community, given the rising tensions of late."

Another elderly lady snorts. "Shouldn't you already know the state of the magical community, Death? You are, after all, the reason it exists."

Okay. Now I understand what Nine and Dea tried to tell me. They openly hate us. I was expecting some kind of undercurrent or social decorum.

"Nothing like a little visit to all the councils to gain good first-hand experience of the problems. We want to explore everyone's viewpoint before taking any kind of action."

"I'm sorry," I interrupt. Nine and Dea give me scathing look, but I ignore them. "May I know why you're holed up in a cave in the first place?"

The Witch at the top point, sitting directly in front of us, stands and crawls over to us. "Who, my dear, are you?" She gives me a gentle smile, and it makes my nerves sit even further on edge.

She's the lead seer of the Witch community.

"Sorry. Of course. My name is Heidi. I'm an air Witch. The Horsemen took me in after a rough start to life. They just wanted me here to help smooth this conversation out."

She inclines her head. "So you're an air Witch?"

"Yes." Didn't I just say that?

"Well," she starts as she sits back down, "we remain in hiding out of choice. We do not feel comfortable letting the world know of our magic, lest they exploit it."

"Or start burning us on modern-day stakes," the Witch from earlier adds.

"So, you don't think we've moved past that by now? I mean, look at the other magical communities, they're all out of the closet and doing well."

"If by well you mean on the brink of a human-versus-magic war, then sure."

Dea steps in. "Human versus magic? What do you mean?" She remains silent, and it clearly annoys Dea, who schools his features quickly enough that not many notice his frustration. Except me. "Please. This is important, or we would not here."

She looks to the other Coven heads, who all nod, and she continues. "The Supernatural Council, as you know, is human-supernatural run, and they've been using hunters to bring in and arrest rogue supes for some time now. Those arrested are never seen again. We believe, as do many other groups, that they're being executed."

Nine recoils in horror. "Why?"

The seer stands once more and speaks. "Because that is what I have seen, Famine. I myself had that vision, and we have been trying to find more information. But mostly we've been staying out of it."

"The number of Witches arrested has been less than ten in the last hundred years, so it doesn't concern us."

They're staying out of it despite other magical beings being executed? That's sick.

That's Witches for you.

But they've seen it, unlike other members of the magical community, who are only guessing.

"This bothers you, young Witch." It wasn't a question.

The horror is written all over my face.

"No. Everything is fine."

"You cannot lie to a seer, child. Please, explain."

"I . . . I can't believe you'd sit back and watch the magical community be tormented by humans when you have the power to help."

"Only Witch problems concern us. We cannot be held accountable for other races."

"But we're all magical beings. We all exist together. Shouldn't we fight together, too? If it comes to that?"

She smiles. "I admire your comradery, young one, but it simply isn't possible."

"Because you're scared. Of being outed to the world. Right? You're leaving them to die because you're scared."

Sweetie . . . Nine warns in my head.

Instead of listening to him, I stand. My fists clench. "I know what it's like to be scared of being yourself. You're worried people will shun you, that they'll never understand who you are." My mind goes to Connie and how she'll probably fear me, on some level, for all eternity. "But that shouldn't stop you from being yourselves anyway. Is living in hiding really living?"

"Stop your foolishness!" Two of the Coven members stand in abject horror. "You're being ridiculous. We don't live in some fantasy world. We can't come out and hold hands with humans while we magically cross the rainbow together."

"That wasn't—"

"Who are you really?" the seer asks. She remains seated this time, but eyes me with curiosity.

"An air Witch, ma'am."

"No. I feel the presence of air in your soul, but I also feel the presence of fire, water, and earth, as well as the potential for harnessing seer and charm magic. You're not a normal Witch, are you?"

The other Witches look on in surprise as gasps fill the room.

She didn't mention the Vampire part, so keep it quiet.

What am I supposed to say?

That you're a Witch.

"I've only managed to harness air magic. I'm sorry if that answer disappoints you."

She contemplates me for a while before smiling and returning to her seat. "No, young one. That is fine."

The Witches murmur amongst themselves while we wait for them finish.

You would have done well among the Fae. They forbid you from lying in their court, and it's a real pain. You just managed to answer truthfully without giving away what you are.

It's a gift. I hate lying.

Nine rolls his eyes at me while I give him a smile, and he smiles for the first time since we arrived here. I didn't realize just how much my mood was affecting him; he can't escape me here.

I'm sorry. I'll spend some time alone when we get back, so you can have a break from my mind.

It's okay. It's not usually an issue, I just have to actively be in your mind while on this trip. Dea's orders.

Is he the leader?

Yes.

Why?

Because he saved the world when we were first born. We helped, but it was he who opened the sealed gate into the next world so supernatural souls could pass and magic would once again be a safe practice.

Oh. I see.

Impressed, aren't you?

Maybe a little.

He's incredibly powerful. I would be surprised if you weren't impressed. He's certainly reaped the benefits from that fame along the years.

"Is there anything else you wanted to discuss?" one of the Witches asks.

Dea stands this time, clearly getting to the meat of the reason we're here. "What is your current relationship with the Vampires?"

They all recoil at the word Vampire, and I'm left questioning where his tact had gone.

They seem to be less frustrating than usual. He's just going with it for now.

"As hostile as ever. Why those vile, evil cretins still walk the earth is beyond me."

It's my turn to recoil, feeling a little personally attacked. But, really, after the last few days, all I'm feeling is fed up, and if I let that fester too much, it'll turn into anger, and that will let my fangs slip, and we don't want that. So I try to remain upset about it.

"They're unnatural, and they love Witch blood and often hunt us down."

Dea nods and sits back down. "Thank you for the honest answer."

They're an awful lot like the Vamps. They wouldn't appreciate that observation, though, so I keep quiet.

"We're quite tired, Horsemen, Heidi, so if you wouldn't mind, we'd like to go to bed. Unless there's something else?"

Dea asks the question I've been waiting for. "I have another question, but I need your secrecy. It has become an important matter for us, and we will not take kindly to anyone using this information against us."

The seer Witch walks forward to meet him. "What is it, old one?"

"Have any of you heard anything about a Horseman's seal?"

The seer's eyes stretch wide. "You've lost one?"

Dea looks her straight in the eyes and lies. "No, of course not. We are tracking down a rumor is all."

"I see."

I get the feeling she does indeed see—all the way past Dea's lie and to the truth.

"I'm afraid none of us have heard anything about any of your seals." She takes a deep breath before returning to her seat. "Anything else?"

Dea and Nine shake their heads, but I stand up. Taking a deep breath, I ask, "Why do you not like the Supernatural Council? Other than the prosecution of supes?" My gaze drops to the floor, hoping they notice the sign of respect and not bite my head off.

"They support the Vampires. Even supply them blood. It's sickening."

"So, you hate them just because they try to keep peace between supes and humans?"

"Do not be ridiculous, child. Peace is but a farce."

"There's been no war and nothing but peace for two hundred years since they outed themselves—I'd call that peace. No matter how tentative."

"Then you're as childish as you look."

"I am not childish. You're the ones practically letting the SC murder innocent people just because you're afraid; you're not even bothering to make peace with other species because of a centuries-old spite. So, tell me, who are the childish ones?"

Stop speaking.

I seal my lips, realizing how angry I let myself get at their non-action.

"You are no Witch if you do not see the danger and horror of the Vampires," the seer says.

"I. Am. A. Witch." Of all the things I've been through this past month, that much is clear. I can feel my frustration over everything boiling over, my rage seeping into the top of a pot of bubbling fury. "And, as a Witch, I would like to openly practice magic and be a part of the new world."

"You are forbidden from ever doing so, as per the rules of our world."

"Yes," I say between gritted teeth. "I am aware. And it pisses me off more than I can say. I'm not allowed to openly be myself because of you!"

Nine places a hand on my shoulder, but I shrug it off. "This isn't going to go well," I hear him mutter to Dea, who agrees.

"Hold your tongue, child!"

"I am not a child!"

Air rushes around me, and it takes everything in me to keep my fangs fully retracted. Instead, my anger turns into a mini-tornado, sending the seer and the angry Witch (who I can only assume is the head fire Witch) flying across the room.

Gasps of audible horror echo across the chamber.

"Arrest them!"

Well done.

Can we not just leave?

No. We like to work with the councils, not against them.

For fuck's sake. I hold my hands up in surrender, despite the burning desire to rip out the throat of the Witch who binds my hands using a pair of magicuffs.

The air Witch. How fucking fitting.

It can hardly be called a prison, really. A hole in the ground is more accurate, slightly larger than the lounge of the guest house we've been staying in previously, with shackles attaching us to the mud-caked walls. They think they can hold the Horsemen of the Apocalypse with simple iron shackles? Are they that dense?

"No, these are spelled. You could try breaking out of them, but it will simply drain your magic," Nine informs me with a hint of irritation.

I guess I've given him the right to be pissed off at me. I did land us in here.

"Not why I'm pissed at you."

"Huh?"

"I'm pissed at you because, despite the shitstorm you've caused here, you're still upset over something you can't change. And that is still the one thing on your mind right now."

Dea slumps against the wall, arms above his shoulders, eyes closed. He doesn't seem to want to be a part of this conversation.

"Dea's not part of this conversation because he doesn't know what upset you the other day."

I look up at him, shocked.

"I don't tell the team what's on anyone's mind, ever. Not unless I really have to."

Somehow, having Nine angry at me rather than Dea is something I don't like. When it's just Dea, I can brush it aside because he's done something genuinely wrong (no matter how logical the choice might have been at the time); but with this, it's all on me. I fucked up. I let my anger get the best of me in a sensitive environment.

"I want a normal life," I mutter, hoping he'll hear me.

"I know—" Nine starts.

"I wasn't talking to you." I turn my face toward Dea, who opens his eyes. "I was crying because I realized that I would never have a normal life. A family, with a husband and children. I never thought I wanted that until the choice was taken away."

He nods, not saying anything. But eventually, he sighs. "We get it, Angel. Believe us, we understand." He blinks and scoots closer. "You may not be able to live a completely normal life, but you are not bound to the team. Maybe solve this war first, but you are allowed to live anywhere, with anyone. We are not holding you captive."

"Wait . . . But I thought—"

"What?" Dea asks. "That we would force you to stay?" The indignation in his tone can't be more evident. "No. We would never do that. We might occasionally pop in and ask for your help with something, since you will always be a Horseman and have that duty on your shoulders, but you are free to live your immortal life however you see fit."

"But . . . that's not . . ." That's not what I want.

Then what do you want?

I . . . It doesn't matter.

We have a fair amount of time before we can find a way to escape using Dea's tentative command of language. You might as well tell me.

It's fucking stupid. And lame. And you'll just cringe or laugh. Probably both.

"I would like to be a part of this conversation, please," Dea says calmly from where he sits.

I sigh. "That isn't what I want. Nine asked me what I wanted then, and I said it doesn't matter. He then said we have a lot of time to kill, so we might as well chat about it. But I don't want to chat about it. You'll both find it stupid. Even I think it's stupid."

"We would never find your pain stupid, Angel."

"You say that now."

"We won't," Nine reiterates.

"I want some kind of a family with all of you." Okay? There, I said it.

And now I've said it, I can't stop the rest from tumbling out.

I just want sex, I don't want some kind of weird relationship where I'm the only not getting sex, I want . . . I don't even fucking know! But damn it, I can't say it out loud. But I don't want it with anyone else! I . . . I can't explain it. I haven't been with you all very long, and I'm not in love with you all or anything, but I just . . . I want the chance, the option. I want the freedom to feel without having to hold myself back."

"She wants all of us to be the kind of family Arrie wanted us to be in the early years."

"Huh? Arrie wanted . . . ?"

"Yes," Dea said over a sigh. "He was the only one who, like you, thought it was stupid to not let each other be in love with any member of the team."

"The rest of us saw reason."

"We cannot give you that, Angel. I am sorry."

They both look to the floor, tears brim, and this is honestly the last fucking place I want to cry about not being able to be in love with any of them, despite how hard I seem to be falling for three out of four of them.

"I knew that saving the world would come at a price, but I didn't know it would cause this much heartache." And the tears fall.

We spend three days holed up in this prison, and I conclude that I'm just a really shitty teammate. Really, what I want is to be able to let myself fall in love without holding myself back. I like them, I do, but I don't know if I quite love them. Yet. But I really want that future possibility, the one where my new feelings for Connie, Nine, and Dea are allowed to grow. Instead, I have no choice but to taper them down (if that's at all possible).

And I have three days to spew over this nonsense while Nine listens to all of my thoughts, which I'm sure I'm shouting despite trying to whisper, and I can't stop myself from crying, either. It's torture. I'm crying because of them, and they're both in the same room, listening to my awkward tears as I try to cry as silently as possible.

It's pathetic. Even I know I'm crying over something pathetic. A love I don't even yet feel. I guess I'm mourning the loss of a possible future, rather than something I already have. I can't stay living with them all, knowing they're right there and I can't let myself have any of them. I could try being just friends. But really, when is that ever possible?

"This is all my fault," Nine says. "I'm so sorry." That has my ears perking up. "I should never have let Dea's plan continue the other night in that motel. I knew your true feelings and hopes for the future. He didn't. I'm sorry."

"Stop being so fucking stupid."

He looks my way.

"You're not responsible for my happiness, Nine. None of the team is. This is just the way my life is right now. I have centuries to get over it. I'm sure I'll fucking manage."

Dea sighs. "When we get home, Angel, I want to talk to you about this. Somewhere private."

Nine doesn't say anything, but the message is clear: somewhere Nine can't hear.

"Let them go!" a familiar voice in the background shouts. "Or I'll shoot you all, you fucking Coven-driven crazies."

Connie. A really pissed off Connie.

"Great," Nine mutters. "Another emotionally driven female come to make everything worse."

"I heard that, you ungrateful ass-pig!" Connie shouts from a distance.

"Good. Then maybe you'll stop attacking the Witches and try to debate our release instead. While remaining on their good side."

"If you wanted a . . . Oof . . ." I hear her fall to the floor in a scuffle. "Politician, you should have me swap places with Dea. I barely managed to chat to the Fae without spilling all our fucking secrets."

Dea looks at me in question, and I repeat what she said.

"Look, Con. Now isn't the time for this. Just get us out of here."

I hear a set of rumbling footsteps coming our way, and Arrie suddenly appears, yanking the gated doorway (did I mention it's made of six-inch steel?) out of the hole and then breaks Dea's chains with a single hand.

"Damn, Arrie! You've been holding out on me." I can't help it, he's stupidly strong. Even with my Vampire strength, I couldn't break those spelled cuffs.

He smiles at me but quickly shakes his head in a normal scowl. "Easier to break when you're not trapped in them, Killer."

"Ugh, could you not call me that? Especially where other, less than liking of me, people can hear."

"Do you want me to help you escape or not, Killer?" He emphasizes the nickname, drawing out every fucking letter.

"Fine! But hurry the fuck up. I'm hungry. It's been a really shitty mission."

Connie bounds toward the opening, looking shocked at the surroundings. "What happened here?"

Dea stands up, then helps Nine to his feet and looks hard at me. "Ask her."

I sheepishly look to the ground, but Connie lifts my chin, looking me dead in the eyes. "What did you do, hon?"

"I may have air-blasted the seer and fire Witch Coven members into a wall," I mumble.

She tries to hold back her smile, but she ultimately fails. "That's more like it. Maybe a bit of fear will help them listen."

"Ugh. Women," Dea groans. "Let's just get out of here, shall we?"

"But don't we need to make peace first?" I question as we run out of the prison cells and into the shadows of the main cave town.

"Well, ideally, yes, but you pretty much ruined all chances of that when you attacked the single most important Witch in the entire international community." At my questioning look, he says, "The seer."

Oh. "So, they're unlikely to forgive me after that, 'ey?"

"They are more likely to remove your head from your body."

"That's a bit fucking grim."

"They're a bunch of Witches completely removed from modern society, what did you expect? Flowers and chocolates?"

Nine's attitude is really starting to piss me off. I already have to deal with one Arrie, I don't need two in my life.

We run around the outskirts of the main cave town, everyone with their weapons drawn—Connie even hands me a couple of daggers (mine are back at the house we're staying in)—as we try to sneak to the exit without attracting too much attention. We nearly make it, too, but then we round a corner and have an army of Witches standing in front of us with menacing scowls on their faces that could rival Arrie's.

Fuck. "Now what?"

Connie smiles, and Arrie grimaces.

"Arrie," Dea says. "Your turn."

I look confused, but I watch as Arrie steps forward, his gaze having fallen into a gray-slate color I recognize.

"Dea, go invisible and take out the fire-throwers at the back; Nine, stay with Killer, try to stay out of this; Connie, you and I will go in frontline style."

"Okay," we all say in unison.

We rush out, but Nine grabs my arm just as my foot steps forward to help Connie avoid an oncoming ball of compact earth.

"Nope," he says. "Arrie's instructions are absolute in battle. We follow him, or we usually spend weeks in recovery from decapitated limbs or some other horror."

"Okay," I say meekly as I watch Arrie and Connie go to work. They move together, working as a single entity to dispatch enemies two each at a time. They don't have to communicate, they just know how to act.

Connie pulls two arrows from her quiver and fires them in rapid succession, felling the guy with a mini-tornado about to rampage through Dea's general area and some woman with a ball of water about to suffocate Arrie. She dashes to her next target and takes them down with solid punches to the shoulder, resulting in resounding cracks that echo enough to make me wince.

Arrie is his usual self, spinning and cutting down anyone in his way. That doesn't surprise me at all. He's the Horseman of War, after all. But it does not fail to impress. He ducks, spins, pivots, and leaps at all the right moments, never taking a scratch, let alone a real hit. No one touches him, and he looks just as beautiful as he did before the battle started.

The difference? His victims are dead. Connie and Dea's were just down for the count or knocked unconscious. I shiver at that thought but don't mention it out loud, knowing how much Arrie tortures himself over it.

"Okay, Nine, Angel, come along," Dea says once they've taken down the army of twenty or so Witches in less than five minutes. "Time to leave."

We're leaving and heading back out of the cave system when it dawns on me. "I've just screwed everything up, haven't I?"

No one answers, but that's answer enough.

Fuck.

29

We go back to *Sheruta* two days later, and I couldn't be more pissed off with myself and the world if I was actually trying. Nine, Dea, and I aren't speaking, which has become painfully obvious to the rest of the team on the trip back; and believe it or not, the person I feel most comfortable with right now is Arrie. (Yeah, I'm just as shocked as you.) But between Nine and Dea's anger, and Connie's weirdness ever since the whole Vampire thing, Arrie is the only one treating me like usual, and it's comforting.

So when we're all sitting around for breakfast the next morning, I ask Arrie what he's doing that day.

He just stares at me like I've lost my mind as the rest of the team choke on their fried eggs and bacon.

"Blowing off some steam in the woods, then probably tending to the horses. Why?"

"Mind if I join?"

"Err, sure." He huffs as he puts his face back into his breakfast, but I just smile. It's nice to have some sense of normality in my world of team turmoil.

The rest of them continue to stare at me.

"What?" I ask, exasperation filling my voice. "Am I not allowed to speak to any of you anymore?"

"It's fine, just not what we were expecting," Nine says. His leg is wrapped around Dea's under the table, despite the others not noticing, but the small gesture nearly brings a smile to my face. Nearly.

"I'll see you out there, then. Maybe we could start some of that physical training you were planning before we left?"

"Okay," he says.

I make myself my fifth cup of coffee that morning, filling this one with pixie dust to give my magic an extra boost—I'm likely going to need it against Arrie—and then head to my room to get changed.

Dressed in yoga pants, a sports bra, and a loose tank, armed with daggers, dust-boosted magic, and blood-fueled Vampire strength, I head to the clearing in the woods as prepared as I can be.

Arrie is running through some kind of weird dance-yoga combo thing when I approach.

Not wanting to disturb him, I sit cross-legged at the edge of the circle, nursing my sixth cup of coffee as I watch him gracefully move from one pose to another; some moves are fluid like a dance, never staying in one place for even a breath, but others he holds and focuses on his breathing. He's even doing some of my regular yoga poses, and I briefly wonder where he got them from.

"Stretch and warm up." His low, gruff voice reaches my Vampire-fueled hearing.

Placing my mug down on the nearest fallen log, I do as instructed.

"If you came to chat about your feelings, that's not—"

"I wanted to join you today so I didn't have to talk to anyone at all."

Arrie nods, seeming to understand what I want from him. Whether he'll give it to me is another question altogether. I've done enough reading between my time sulking with the Witches and the last few days locked in my library. This is my change of atmosphere.

Arrie stands in the middle of the clearing, arms resting by his sides, not holding any kind of pose for the time being. Once I meet him in the middle, he says, "Copy."

I nod. Placing my left arm in a warrior pose, I follow his yoga-dance routine for a half hour, getting a light sheen of sweat on my skin from some of the more difficult poses. Arrie, on the other hand, doesn't break a sweat. But I guess he has two thousand years on me.

"You favor daggers?"

"I can use them best with my air magic."

I love this particular aspect of Arrie. He isn't a talker, and right now, that is perfect.

"Okay. For now, we'll start with hand-to-hand combat until you've experimented with more weapons. Con will probably have you master a few over the years."

"Right." I strip off my daggers and throw them to the side, returning into a basic defense stance.

"Good. Always protect your middle and head. It's a bitch to heal."

I nod.

"Defend." He comes at me with a few basic jabs, the third knocking me flat on my ass. "Defend," he says again. And once again, he comes at me with more jabs.

I try to block them but don't really know how. "How do I best block a jab?"

"With your clenched hand and arm meeting the punch."

Another nod, and we are back at it, with me blocking a few but mostly getting knocked on my ass. It doesn't deter me.

Arrie never bothers to help me up, and I don't complain at the forming bruises that aren't healing with their usual gusto.

We go at it for a few hours, me learning a few different ways to block a jab while Arrie remains as impassive and stoic as ever while giving basic instructions when I ask questions, until we're both a little breathless and ready for a break.

"Here," Arrie says as he passes me an empty glass. He slides a blade over his wrist and bleeds into it for a few minutes until it's full.

"Thanks."

There's no straw waiting for me out here, so I struggle to not spill any down my front, but eventually down every last drop. Arrie, however, seems to find my struggle amusing and has to hold back a laugh the entire time.

"Bring a straw next time." I roll my eyes and place the glass next to my empty coffee mug. I don't need a longer break after having fed, which, when I look at Arrie, is obviously the point, as he doesn't need a moment longer either.

We continue training basic blocks for basic types of hand-to-hand combat all morning and well into the afternoon until Arrie calls it a day and goes to tend to the horses.

"You coming with?" he asks.

I hesitate. I don't want to overstay my welcome here, and bonding with Arrie really isn't the purpose. "Nah. Thanks." I wave and walk away, heading back to the kitchen to make myself a salad.

"Training with Arrie to avoid us?" Nine's voice penetrates my peace the moment I walk into the kitchen.

"I'm not avoiding anyone, Nine. Just getting some training in and trying to be the best Horseman of Magic I can possibly be. It is why I exist."

Nine sighs and puts the newspaper down on the table. "Not my question."

"Best answer you'll get right now."

"Why is your mind blocked off to me?"

That takes me by surprise. "Wha . . . What?"

"Your mind. I can't read it now. Not even when I go probing."

"Good." I continue making my chicken salad and put a lid on the leftovers before popping them in the fridge while continuing to ignore him.

"Play with me tonight?"

I stop dead in my tracks as I raise an eyebrow at him.

"I don't need to read your mind to know what you thought I meant, but that isn't what I meant. Play some of my new magic gaming systems with me? Tonight."

"Er . . . I don't think—"

"Ugh! Fine. I won't force you to hang out with me." He raises his hands in defeat and storms out of the room.

"Fine!" I call. I can't stand to see him miserable because of me. It's quickly become my Achilles heel, and I'm starting to hate its effect.

"Nine pm. My room," he shouts back down the stairs with a smug smile.

"Date with Nine?" Connie's insinuating voice echoes from the kitchen door that leads to the garden.

How long has she been there?

"Er . . . A date might be pushing it."

"Fair enough. This Friday, girl time. Still on? Since you're back to talking to us now."

Ugh. "Sure." I try for a smile, but it comes out as more of a grimace.

"Look, hon, we need to keep talking through things. Especially now we're a team."

"I know." I sink against the kitchen counter behind me in defeat. She's right, it's just hard to think of myself as part of the team. I don't know where I fit anymore. Not that I really had a place before the mission.

Connie places a warm hand on my bare shoulder, and I give her a genuine smile. She's trying, and I can't ignore that.

Maybe I can work it out with all of them.

Dea chooses that moment to walk in, forcing a grumbling moan to escape my lips.

Well, maybe not all of them. I'm still pissed at Dea for denying me answers. And I don't think I'll get over that soon.

Connie must feel the tension in the room rise, because she quietly leaves us alone and heads upstairs, probably to her room so she doesn't have to overhear the inevitable argument.

Dea sits at the kitchen table and picks up the newspaper Nine left. "Have something to say?" he asks once I stand staring at him for a good solid minute.

"No." I turn to leave, but Dea is at my side, grabbing my wrist.

"Come with me." He runs into the garden, and I sprint at top speed to keep up. Eventually, we stop on top of the hill created for my *Shinto* shrine. "May I?" he asks as he stands in its entrance, gesturing to the rug and cushions beyond.

I nod, not really even sure why he's asking.

"Please sit, Angel."

That nickname has some of the anger daring to leave my tense body, and I hate that he has that kind of effect on me. All of the team do—even Arrie in his own way.

"I wanted to chat about what you said—what Nine said that you said—when we were in the Witches's prison."

I look to the floor, not ready for this conversation. I can feel the heat blushing my cheeks, and I want nothing more than to run away and hide from the embarrassment of this moment.

"Do not do that. Not with me. You have no reason to be embarrassed. You want something that is so natural to want. Eventually, it might become something you have to explore."

I give him a questioning look, not fully understanding.

"Just because we are immortal does not mean we are an exception to normal, sentient needs and desires. Like the desire for love. Or to have a family."

"Please, I can't . . ." I hiccup, feeling the tears breech their usual bloody wall. I spent weeks here barely crying over a thing, and this one damn thing I can't seem to stop crying about.

"I know it is hard, Angel. I know what it is like to love and not be able to actually be in love."

"You're talking about Nine, right?"

He nods. "He knows. I am sure of it."

"He does."

"But we both know nothing can come of it. It is harder for me since I rarely sleep with people outside of the team. Meaning my more intimate affairs are with the same few people. I bet Arrie has the same issue."

And I guess that would make it more likely to fall in love with someone. "You could just not have sex, you know. It's not a requirement for living."

Dea chuckles. "Sometimes, I forget how innocent you are. I will ask you that again in ten years' time and see if your answer remains the same."

Fair enough. I have no idea if I had any kind of relationship when I was alive, and I don't now, so I have no idea what abstinence is like.

"I know why you made your choice, Dea. I do. And I understand it. I just don't agree with it. It's not right to cut yourself off from love just because you have a duty to the world. You are still allowed to live. You are still allowed a life."

He stares at me, as though that notion has never been said to him before. Perhaps it hasn't. But either way, there really is nothing left to say.

"I am not sure if this will make things harder for you, but you should know, I would have loved the chance be in love with Nine openly and pursue something with you, too. Having a relationship with you both while maintaining the team and our current relationships would have been beautiful. I have not had the pleasure of dating, falling in love, or courtship for some time."

That insinuates he has done so before. I throw him a questioning look, but he just says, "A story for another time, Angel."

I get up and run back to my room as fast as I can, shutting the door behind me.

He would have liked to dated me? Maybe even fall in love, if that's how it went down? Damn. He was right. That does make things harder. Because now I know that my feelings are spot on, and he's trying as hard as I am to keep it together.

He's just had more practice than me.

30

Tonight is going to be awkward as hell, isn't it? I ask myself as I get dressed in some basic pajama shorts and a tank, ready for my friend-only date with Nine.

What's he expecting? Me to just roll over and forget that his stubborn, idiotic self is hurting Dea, and potentially me, too, if I can sort through my feelings enough to decide whether I like him in that way.

Here's to hoping that mental block Nine was talking about earlier is still there, because otherwise, I can't promise my conversation with Dea will remain private. It's all that's running through my head. I still can't actually believe he's into me. He . . . loves me?

No. That's not what he said. He said he would have liked the chance if it was something we could have. I didn't realize it until he said it, but it really isn't the happily ever that after I want (though, that would be nice); it's the dating, the awkward first kiss, the romance of it all. I want to feel the butterflies and know that they're being returned. I want a romance like the ones I read about, but you know, more realistic.

I want my own romance.

Nine o'clock is in five minutes, and I decide that being a few minutes early will look best (not that I care about how it all looks), so I leave my room and walk the few paces to Nine's rooms and knock on his door.

It opens slightly, and Nine yells, "Come on in. I'll be right there!"

It's weird to hear him yelling. I'm so used to him talking to me in my mind.

His room is the same as the last time I was here: a massive four-poster bed with black drapes, a reading corner with a small bookshelf, and a corner full of various screens and gaming machines. I wonder which one we'll be playing today?

Nine comes out of the bathroom with damp hair, slacks hanging low on his waist with no top on, and from here I can see his nipple piercing glinting in the artificial light. Damn, he looks good just coming out of the shower. The few droplets of water that are left run down his shoulder and onto his abs, making my eyes travel lower as they stop at the waistband of the underwear poking out from his slacks.

"Enjoying the view, Sweetie?"

"Flirting out loud? Well I never," I say in my best Dea impression.

"It's been known to happen." He smirks that famous smile that always makes me melt and give into whatever it is he wants.

And, for a moment, I forget everything and go back to the old me, the me that never quite understood what it meant to be immortal. My smile quickly fades, not unnoticed by Nine, whose face also drops.

"So," I try for a distraction, "what are we playing?"

"Well, I've been trying to hook up older systems to newer power sources, so we could play some retro games that were cool back in the day, and I finally managed to get it working."

He walks over to the corner of computers and screens and turns on a series of thelining the desk. His hand pats the other chair as he holds out a controller for me. "Come, sit."

I sit and take the controller, forcing my eyes to one of two screens turned on in front of me rather than the very topless Nine on my left.

"We're gonna play some of the most successful games of the 20th and 21st centuries."

"Really?" I ask, a little sceptical. "Aren't they a little . . . old-fashioned?"

He raises an eyebrow at me. "I don't know if you've noticed, but I'm pretty old."

Smiling and holding back a laugh, I manage to not laugh at his age as we start with something called MORTAL COMBAT on a controller I have no idea how to use. I eventually manage to get the hang of it, and we spend a few hours hopping from game to game, spending longer on the ones I enjoy the most. But at some point in the night, when I've forgotten all about the awkwardness, something in my mind latches onto a previous memory.

"Nine?"

"Mmm?"

"Could we perhaps create a charm that could control Dea's visibility better? You know, something that holds the magic and turns him visible rather than using his own stores of magic?"

Nine pauses the game we're playing and looks at me with raised eyebrows.

"I was just thinking about how much it holds him back when on Earth," I explain. "But with my Witch powers being able to most likely use charm magic, I could probably help create a charm that channels a Horseman power and works on one of you, right?"

Nine looks shocked, taken aback, and nearly falls off the chair. "Oh my god." He chokes on nothing, and I have to ask the house for a glass of water lest I lose Nine for a few minutes while he chokes to death. (You know, kind of.) "You're right," he says between gulpfuls. "That could work. But you'd need to master charm magic first."

I grimace at his words, unsure if I even can. I still can't master more than air magic, so it's likely I won't be able to, but you never know. Maybe? "I want to try."

Nine nods, a smile taking hold of his face.

"For Dea."

Nine looks at me with a curious smile, and the memory of my earlier conversation with Dea runs through my mind. Can Nine see it? I'm not sure if I want him to.

Yes. I could see that.

I wince. "He asked me not to show you. But I don't know how to do that."

You can't.

"Really?"

He nods and goes eerily silent. Pensive, almost. Looking over, I see him brush a tear from his left eye and try to act normal, but, clearly, he's hurting.

I put the controller down and turn to face him. "Come here." I open my arms and stand, pulling him into a hug. "It's okay."

Nine's tears grow heavier as I hold him in my arms, and he cries for a while in silence. I just continue to hug him, not saying anything—not really needing to—and let him just be himself for a bit. Not someone who constantly rebukes his love's affections for the benefit of the world, not someone who barely holds it together after sex knowing they can't actually be together, and certainly not someone who cries over the fact centuries later.

"I-I'm sorry." Nine sniffs.

"Stop being stupid. Everyone's allowed to cry."

"You don't help. Your emotions are so raw."

I wince. Sorry.

He sighs. "That's not fair of me. You're just a normal person, Sweetie, and we're really not."

I can't help but laugh at that. He thinks I'm normal?

"You're more normal than us. I can promise you that."

Sighing, I pluck up the courage to bring it up. Goddess help me if this ruins all the progress we've made. "I'm only going to say this once, and then we can go back to not talking about it. But you know you guys can change your minds, right? You don't have to continue with an agreement you made two thousand years ago. Things change. People change. Situations are allowed to change, too."

I stop talking after that, knowing it isn't something he's open to, and I really don't want to continue to bleed over those wounds. Lest I make them worse.

Nine nods and turns back the game. "Bet I can beat you with just a knife."

"Against dual pistols, a semi-automatic, and a rocketlauncher? You're fucking insane."

And that's how the night goes. It feels good. Really good to be normal and not have to think of magical communities and war and other shit I honestly couldn't give a shit about right now.

At the end of the night, when I'm walking toward the door ready to head to bed, Nine reaches out and grabs my hand. "I . . ." He takes a deep breath. "Stay the night."

This has me pausing and staring at him intently. "The night?"

He nods. *We don't have to do anything. Just . . . stay with me.* He looks so lost, as though he no longer knows what to do with his life, and the puffy rims of his eyes tell me he probably didn't stop crying while we were playing.

How can I leave him like this?

I nod. "I am already in my pajamas."

He smiles in relief and yanks me into his arms, inhaling the smell of ny coconut shampoo as he crushes me against his rigid, still-naked torso and wraps his arms tight around my body. I try hard not to think about it, I really do, but even though I know he needs me emotionally, I still have to tamper my stupid, not-helpful thoughts back.

"C'mon," he says as he drags me to bed. "It's late. Your training continues in the morning."

"Ughhh," I groan, causing him to laugh.

I let him drag me to his bed, where we lay underneath the red sheets next to each other, his legs curling around mine, and his arm wrapping around my waist as I wait for him to fall asleep. And, just as promised, we do nothing but cuddle. When he's halfway to the land of sleep, I place a gentle kiss to his forehead, hoping he won't notice, and close my own eyes.

Fat chance of that, Sweetie.

I can't believe I slept in Nine's bed last night. The fact that nothing happened makes it infinitely worse; that means it was an emotional thing, the exact type of bonding I'm trying to avoid. I'm starting to understand their no-love rule—doesn't mean I agree with it, though. Nine simply smiles at me in the morning and gets dressed, heading to his computer as I head to my morning yoga.

Halfway through my hour of attempting to relax, I give up. No matter what I do, I can't get my night with Nine out of my head. The more time I spend with the team, the deeper I fall. As if my body is working in tandem with my mind, I fall out of my hand-stand at that thought.

"Shit." I'm really falling in love with them, aren't I?

But honestly, what can I really do about it? I spent days trying to ignore them, just living with them because I have nowhere else to go; but even if I want to live elsewhere, I still need their help. I'm not trained enough to save Earth right now.

I give up trying to be peaceful and head to breakfast early, deciding I'll make everyone some toast in order to stay preoccupied. I have a full morning of research ahead of me before a whole afternoon with Nine and Dea, where Nine will be able to sense my every thought (since that stupid block has apparently come down), and where Dea will inevitably feed me to do more Vamp and Witch training.

"Making breakfast, hon?"

Connie joins me as I am trying to create as many slices of toast as possible and place all the condiments on the table, fully removing those pesky thoughts from my mind.

"Finished yoga early. Thought I'd help for a change. Think I can handle some toast." Just as I say that, I smell the start of burning bread from under the grill. "Fuck!" I yank it out and realize I caught them just in time. I sigh in relief.

"Uh-huh. Totally able to make toast," Connie says around a laugh before joining me at the table and starting on breakfast.

Nine, I mentally called out. *Breakfast's ready.*

Five minutes later, the guys are all accounted for and eating with us.

"So," Dea starts, "I have a plan to put by you all."

We all perk up, curious.

"We have received a number of complaints from the Vampire community as well, given that we had to defend ourselves against their ilk." He looks to Connie. "And what happened at the Fae Court? We have a letter from them saying they would be happy to dance with the team when we are free to do so?"

Connie blanches at his words and turns a dark shade of red. "Sorry, Dea. But we wanted information, and they weren't willing to give it, so I bargained them for it. One night of dancing with them—the whole team—and they gave us everything we needed to know. I'm still wrapping up the report."

Dea sighs. "Fine. At least one of the four pillar communities went okay. The Shifters seem to have a wealth of information for us. And the Vampire Council went well, it was afterward that fell apart."

"What happened at the Shifter and Fae councils?" I ask.

"We usually do a massive meeting following recon once all reports are in," Nine informs me.

Avoiding his gaze entirely, I say, "Okay."

"Ugh," Connie complains. "Are you two still not talking, even after your date?"

My cheeks flame bright red, and she just gives me a knowing smile.

"What date?" Arrie asks, suddenly and randomly interested in the complicated dynamic that has become my love life. Or lack thereof.

"It wasn't a date," I correct. "We just hung out while playing some old video games. Nothing untoward."

"So, you staying the night in his bed classifies as 'not a date' then?" Connie asks. And I swear, she's about to be kicked to the curb, Vampire style.

Nine looks to Dea, who looks at me with a bit of hurt, but eventually smiles. I can't tell what he's thinking, but Nine can, and he looks confused and then happy. Which doesn't make any sense to me.

Is he okay?

He thought we'd slept together, I corrected him, and now he thinks he's one step closer to having that poly-romance shit between the three of us you were thinking about the other night.

He wants that?

You and him both, apparently. I can almost hear the sigh of exasperation in his voice.

I look over at Dea and smile, realizing I may have someone on my side if I can play my cards right. Wait, what am I thinking? I can't manipulate them into a relationship. For starters, I don't think I can actually do that; they're much wiser than me. And secondly, I don't want to.

Stop stressing. It'll be interesting to see how think you can manage that. Game on.

Nine throws me a flirtatious look, and I have a feeling that bargaining him into any kind of exclusive relationship will involve sex.

"Er, guys?" Connie interrupts our weird, three-way conversation. "I asked if you'd slept together?" She looks at me and points to Nine with a flushed, flirty look in her eyes.

"Oh, no. No, not at all. Just a harmless sleepover between friends," I stammer, embarrassment flooding my features.

She looks a bit disappointed at that, as though she wanted me to sleep with Nine.

Well, it is Friday, I'll ask her about it tonight.

Arrie's back to being silent, as though he likes to observe conversations more than be a part of them. It's uniquely him in a way. Kinda cute.

I clear my throat to get everyone's attention. "Anyway. Dea, what was your plan?"

"Ah, yes! I think we should publically announce Angel to the magical community."

Connie drops her slice of toast and looks shocke.

Arrie growls in protest. Like, legit, he actually growls. "Why?" he squeezes out between clenched teeth.

"Because everyone is curious and angry with us. Besides, we need to know where her seal is, and for that, we need to draw out the person behind this. We can pacify the councils all year long, but she would not have been summoned if that were all that was required. We could manage that alone."

Arrie seems pacified with that answer and continues eating.

"I think we should host a ball," Dea says.

Connie's face could not be more child-in-a-candy-store-like if I placed a dead Vampire's head in her lap. She lights up like a child at Christmas. "When? What theme? Ohhh, what do we get to wear? Wait . . ." She holds up both hands, pausing by taking a deep breath. "Why?"

Nine chips in with the obvious explanation. "So we can tell everyone at the same time."

"Could draw out the person who broke her seal, too. That way, we might actually have some leads on the things going on behind the community's senseless bickering without causing ourselves to be the sole opposition in this war."

"You think someone's pulling the strings?" I bite into my toast, genuinely curious as to his thoughts.

"Yes. It seems odd that the SC are being so restrictive to supes all of a sudden. They have always been at odds with the magical community, but the blood supplies are below the minimum necessity. They would only do that if they wanted to cause trouble."

Nine rests a hand on my knee, a familiar gesture that sends heat straight to my core; I forgot how much I like his gentle touch while purposefully avoiding it over the last week. "And the Witches knew more than they were letting on, too. They're hiding something."

I nod. "What about the Shifters? You said we got some good info?" I look to Connie.

She swallows her last bite of food and stares down at Nine's hand on my knee and smiled. "Yeah, but honestly, it's a little complicated. Can we chat about it over dinner, once I've finished that report?"

"Sure," Dea and I say together, causing me to blush.

"Sorry."

He shakes his head, not appearing too bothered, but I notice the frown underneath the facsimile of a smile. "Right," he says, shaking his head slightly. "Con, finish that report. Nine and Arrie, get the guest list together and send out invitations and do the planning nonsense Con usually handles. I want the ball as soon as possible. This cannot wait any longer. Angel, you are with me. More training. Let us see if we cannot unlock more of those powers of yours."

Everyone clears the dishes away and resets the dining table like we're on a mission, then heads off in their own direction. Arrie doesn't look too happy to be on party duty, and the thought of him doing invitations is almost laughable, but otherwise, it seems like a solid plan.

Dea and I head to my training room in the meantime, and I seriously hope he has a plan in place, because I'm clueless as to how to unlock these so-called powers.

"So," Dea asks the moment we're alone in the training room and has clicked the door shut behind him, not wasting a second of time. "What really happened with Nine last night?" He raises an eyebrow in accusation, but I know Nine's told him we didn't sleep together, so that playfulness I see on his face is probably genuine.

That doesn't mean I want to talk about last night, though. I look to the floor. It isn't because I'm embarrassed, it's because I'm not sure if Nine wants Dea to know. "I . . . Please ask Nine. I'm not sure if I should tell you."

"Huh?" He looks confused all of a sudden.

"Well, it's not embarrassing for me. But it might be for Nine." Does Nine care about other people knowing he cried over Dea? Especially Dea himself?

Dea looks at me with his arms crossed over his chest expectantly as he leans against one of the concrete walls. "Tell me."

I sigh. We're going to get nothing done if I don't spill it, and they tell each other everything anyway, so Dea will find out at some point. "Nine wanted to smooth things over between us, so he had me help him test some retro gaming consoles he got hooked up to a new magical energy system. Everything was going fine until he saw our conversation in my mind when I accidentally thought about it."

Dea flinches.

"I'm sorry. I couldn't help it. He would have found out eventually. And it—"

Dea places his hands on my shoulders. "It is okay, Angel. Just go on."

"It made him cry, Dea. Like, proper, full-on sobbing."

He pulls away from me, nearly tripping over himself. "He . . . what?"

"You both feel the same way. It's hard to watch. We both played games all night to distract ourselves from this"—I gesture between us—"but he continued to silently cry all night. I stayed with him last night because he needed a friend."

"I-I-I . . ." Dea stutters. I've rendered him speechless—a state I haven't seen him in before. "I have not seen Nine cry in some time."

Ugh! That's it. "All right, both of you meet me in the library this evening at nine." I've fucking had it with them.

Nine! I mentally yell as loud as possible.

Fucking ow, Sweetie.

Sorry. I wince. Meet me in the library tonight at nine.

Okaaay. May I ask why?

No.

"Sure. But why?" Dea asks.

"Goddess," I moan as I run my hands down my face in frustration. "You're as bad as Nine. I'm not dealing with your emotional issues a moment longer. I'm fed up of being stuck in the middle of you two. I'm going to play Nine's role of mediator while you two have an actual conversation about this."

Dea looks at me in surprise, gets himself up off the wall and saunters over, wrapping me in a bone-crushing hug—or it would have been bone-crushing if he were stronger than me. "I am positive you will not manage to change anything, Angel, but thank you anyway. And you would love to be stuck between the two of us, our time in the motel taught me that little fact." He grabs my ass in one hand and flattens me against him, causing me to feel every rippling muscle under those low-hanging jeans.

I let out a small whimper, his words lighting up every nerve across my body in anticipatory need. "Dea," I moan, intending to tell him off but causing him to run a hand up my side and cup my breast over top of my vest. "Please . . ." Goddess, I hate how needy I sound.

"Yes?" he asks as he runs a harsh thumb over my nipple. How has my choice to wear a thin bra this morning suddenly become my main problem?

"Please st-st-stop."

He leans down and tucks a loose strand of hair behind my ear, leaving his lips brushing the edges of my ear. "You sure that is what you want, Angel?"

I nod, not trusting my voice. "Please."

He sighs and gives in. "Okay. I will leave you be." He lets me go, and I stumble backward, my knees barely keeping me upright as I struggle to grab something—anything—for purchase and find Dea's waiting arm. "For now."

"Tr-tr-training," I stammer out.

"Right." He rearranges himself in those sexy-as-fuck loose jeans and shakes his head. "I want to see if we can unlock those potential Fae and Shifter abilities before the ball."

"You're really banking on that, aren't you?"

He shrugs, clearly not wanting to put any extra pressure on me, but the message is clear: if we want to pacify the magical community and show them that I'm a part of all of them, I need to show off every ability to some degree or another.

"Okay," I say. "Explain to me how Fae powers work."

He raises his eyebrows, as though shocked I don't know much about them.

He's wrong, of course, I know all about them.

"Yeah, yeah, yeah. I know how they work. Just repeat the basics to me for a minute."

"Well, unlike Witches, who can use the small amounts of magic in the air, Fae need direct access to local leylines on a regular basis. This does, however, mean they can use greater amounts of power. A leyline runs straight through town and under the house; it's what powers the house's magic. We think."

"Okay, so I should have a fully topped-up power by now. So that's not the problem. How do Fae learn their magic?"

"When they are young, their parents teach them spells, but they have always been able to use magic, once exposed to the leylines, in small ways. Like moving objects, for example."

He closes his eyes for a moment and exhales a deep breath. Before my eyes, Dea's appearance changes. His skin glows and his cheeks hollow, but the most startling change is the black feathery wings that now reach from one wall to the other.

Dea plucks a feather with a wince before inhaling another deep breath and changing back to his normal form.

"What . . . What was that?"

"My Angel of Death form."

I wince without meaning to.

Dea hands me the feather and changes the subject. "Make it move without Witch magic."

I wince again, unsure if I can actually do this. "But . . . how?"

"I do not know. None of us has ever had to study magic like this before. But I think it might be easier if the thing you are trying to move is connected to one of the Horsemen."

"Great," I mumble.

I hold the feather in my left hand while raising my right and trying to focus on the feather and getting it to move. But all I manage is blowing it out of my hand with a gust of air.

"Ugh."

"Try again," he says as he hands it to me.

Okay, Horseman of Magic, you can damn well do this. The team are counting on you.

I try again, this time not raising my hand so I don't blow it away, but nothing happens. Nothing. I feel no tingling magic brushing along my arms like I do with Witch magic, nor do I get that exhilarating rush like when I go Vamp-mode.

Dea sighs. "This might take some time. I have asked Nine to search in everyone's library to see if there are any Fae Magic Starter Guides or something."

"Like Fae Magic for Dummies. Cause that would be brill right now."

We both laugh slightly, but it's tight and restrained, both of us understanding how crucial it is to show equal powers at the party.

"Wait," I say, "does that mean Arrie is left on party duty on his own?"

Dea stands there for a moment and thinks about it. "Yes. But Con is joining him once she is done with her report."

I nod, checking back in on my feather and trying again.

Nothing. Fucking nada.

It's starting to grate on my every nerve that I can't just manage something. Even a small lift of one of the feather's veins. Anything!

"Still nothing?" I hear Arrie's grumbling from the doorway.

Great. Just great. That's all I need. "Fucking obviously."

Arrie holds up his hands in defense, one of which is carrying a binder full of paperwork. "I'm going to finish my work at the desk in here. If that's all right? I might be able to help. And this is fucking boring as shit."

Dea chuckles under his breath slightly, and I just raise my eyebrows.

"Sure, come on in. Let's all stay to watch the freak show of the Horseman of Magic with no fucking magic!" I stomp my foot a little harder than intended and crack the concrete, but I don't care.

"Being angry ain't gonna help, Killer."

"And since when have you cared about being helpful?"

"Since this war is as much ours as it is yours. So stop being a judgmental prick and start focusing."

Gah! He's right, and that pisses me off more than I can say. Arrie, Horseman of War, resident pain my ass, is fucking right.

I take a deep breath and wait for Arrie to sit at the desk before focusing on the feather once again. Still nothing, but at least Arrie has stopped moaning at me.

"You know," he starts. Too late, he's about to start again, isn't he? "If you wanted to learn Fae magic, you should have come with us on Earth. Would have helped more."

"You know what would help? You being quiet unless you have something useful to say."

Arrie grumbles something under his breath, but I relax when a sudden thought comes to mind: he's being more talkative since our little flirting session with the cars and then our training session.

Maybe he's warming up to me? Or maybe he just realizes that I'm stuck with them and is trying to be neutral.

"It was a useful suggestion. You should go see the Fae."

"No time for that," Dea responds. "Nine planned the ball for three days' time."

I stop all of my concentration, drop my feather, and stare at him. "Three days?" I shriek. "Three days? Are you fucking nuts?"

"Calm down, Ange—"

"Don't tell me when to be calm. You've given me three days?" I cough, choking on the realization. "Even if I manage to use both Fae and Shifter magic, I have no hope of controlling either enough to present to the magical communities on cue."

"Killer—"

"Shut. The. Fuck. Up. I don't need your stupid comments and arrogant grumblings right now. Because, just like Connie, I have supernatural hearing and can hear all of your mean words!"

"But, Kille—"

"What part of—?"

Sudden tingles spread over my body in a way I haven't experienced before. It's itchy, not like the beautiful tingles I feel when using Witch magic.

"What the—?"

And then comes the instant of pain. It's like every cell in my body has a knife slicing it into a million microscopic pieces, like a fire spreading throughout the entire inside of my body, but I don't scream because as soon as it starts, it's over.

My head feels light, and my vision is a little dusty. The dizziness lasts a few moments, but the nausea settling in my stomach lasts for a fair few minutes more before I throw up my breakfast on the concrete floor.

When I lift my head to look around, Dea and Arrie stand together, looking at me like I'm some kind of amazing freak of nature. "Angel . . . You changed."

"Yeah," Arrie says, "you're a . . ."

"A what?" I ask, but jump when I hear the masculinity of my voice. Looking down at my body, I'm suddenly naked, but that isn't the most shocking part. My boobs have vanished, I suddenly have abs, and is that a . . . ?

"WHY DO I HAVE A PENIS?!"

32

Connie and Nine rush into the training room and stand alongside the others, both looking confused.

"Who is that?" Connie asks, pointing at me.

"Sweetie?" Nine asks. "Is that you?"

"What?" Connie steps forward. "No way. That's . . . impossible. Nine, that's . . ."

"Insane?" Arrie supplies.

"Oh my fucking god!" Nine exclaims. "That's how your powers work."

Everyone looks baffled, including me most likely, because I have no idea what he's talking about.

"Don't you all see?" Nine looks at us with a wide smile. "You can't mix Witch and Fae magic in a single person, or Shifter and Vampire magic. They don't even create hybrids. But you could if that person had two forms. Like Dea's Angel of Death form. It's Sweetie, but it's a different body."

"I'm a . . . a guy?" I can't help it—tears burst from my eyes. "But . . . I don't want this!" My knees sink to the ground, followed by the rest of my body. "I'm already weird and strange, I don't need this. As if I didn't have enough of a non-identity before, now I don't even have a static fucking gender—sex. Argh! I don't even know!" I stand up, brushing myself off, and stamp my foot—this time not breaking the floor. "I can't do this anymore."

I don't want to live a life this confusing. I'm not straight, or gay, or anything; I'm attracted to more than one person, possibly falling in love with them; I have all four types of magical abilities from each pillar community, meaning I'll never have a home; and now I have two genders or sexes or whatever. What the fuck is wrong with Fate?

I just . . .

I'm not sure if I want to continue living like this. If immortality is going to be this hard, then what's the point? But even if I wanted to end it all, I couldn't. Because no one knows where my seal is.

"For fuck's sake."

The tears have vanished, as have my emotions, and with it, my body tingles all over, flitting into another moment of pain. But this time, I don't change back into my female self. I grow fur, go down on all fours, and change into . . . a panther. I think?

I try to ask, but it comes out as a roar.

"Yes, Sweetie, you're a panther. Interesting choice of shift."

I didn't choose this!

"No Shifter does."

Another tingle-defining shift, and this time I grow feathers. A bird? Am I a bird now?

"More like a fucking falcon. That's kinda badass, Sweetie."

Great, even my Shifter side is uncertain. This fucking blows.

"Try to turn back into your male form."

If I knew how to do that, I would be back to my female self by now, Nine!

"Okay, okay. No need to snap."

Seriously? If there was ever an excuse for yelling, it was when I literally grew a dick!

That has Nine laughing, but everyone else just looks confused. Nine waves a hand at them, as if to say it doesn't matter. "I know. But I wanted to see if your male form can use Fae magic?"

Oh. That's actually a good idea. I focus on my body, think about what little of my male form I can remember, and quickly shift back—minimal pain this time.

"Okay," I say, still shocked at my voice. "Could I have some clothes, please? In whatever size I currently am now?"

The house does its gentle rumbling thing, and a pile of neatly folded clothes appear on the desk on top of Arrie's paperwork.

I pick up the underwear, jeans, and t-shirt, followed by the socks and sneakers. At least dressing as a man—male, guy?—isn't going to be too hard. But I honestly have no idea how I am supposed to put my new penis in these pants. Is there some kind of man protocol I don't know about?

Goddess, the things I didn't think to ask as a woman.

Nine laughs again but doesn't answer out loud, thank goddess. *However is most comfortable.* "Our internal conversations are about to get a whole lot more interesting."

"Oh my goddess, how do guys pee?" I ask out loud, feeling the comings of my third mental spiral in as many minutes.

"In a toilet," Arrie grumbles.

"If you suddenly grew a vagina, would you know the ins and outs of bathroom etiquette?"

He shuts up at that, hopefully mentally thinking I'm right.

I try to air-blast the feather that fell on the floor earlier into my palms, but it doesn't move. Right. No Witch magic in this form. Goddess, that's gonna take some getting used to. I bend and pick it up by hand.

Trying the same exercise from earlier, the feather floats a couple of inches above my hand, and the team claps, clearly impressed.

I, on the other hand, am not impressed. Not in the fucking slightest. Not caring that I'm still in my male form, I ask the house for a mop and bucket, clean up my vomit (not something I recommend doing by the way—totally gross), and leave.

"Where are you going, Angel?"

"To bed!"

And that's exactly what I do. I snuggle up in my duvet and blankets, ignoring the world and everything in it for the entire afternoon. No one comes out of the library—that I know of—but someone does come to light the fire for me. Sleep takes me for one of the best naps I can remember, and I wake to all four of the Horsemen sitting in various chairs they've pulled from the library and scattered around my bedroom.

"Afternoon, Angel," Dea says from a chair on the left of my bedside.

Talk about déjà vu.

I don't answer. Instead, I look down, feel my body, and sigh. "Seems I can keep this form indefinitely."

"Yes, it would seem that way." Nine bellows the fire a bit, helping to coax the flames into a larger fire after they died down during my nap. *By the way, since your body is a Fae form, just remember that Fae forms are supposed to attract people to you.*

I groan at that. "Great."

"What did you tell her now, Nine?" Connie complains. "She's already got a lot to deal with."

"Just reminding her of the allure of the Fae."

Arrie snorts. "As if you need help with making that aspect of your life more complicated."

"Ugh, tell me about it." Am I casually chatting to Arrie about my not-quite love-life right now? Goddess, this day is crazy. "So," I start, "any chance any of you know how the fuck I change back? Call me crazy, but I love my boobs."

That has everyone laughing, but eventually, a solemn, tense air settles around us, and I get the feeling I'm not going to like their answer.

"No," Nine answers. "How did you shift into this body in the first place?"

"Arrie pissed her off," Dea supplies.

Everyone's eyes turn to Arrie, as if expecting him to make me angry.

"Well?" Connie asks.

Arrie sighs and folds his arms. "I'm not a dick on purpose. I can't just do it on cue."

Despite everything, laughter fills my chest and spills out of my mouth. "Great, Arrie." I look him straight in the eyes. "Give me back my boobs."

Nine snorts from behind me as Dea and Connie stifle laughs. They can laugh it up all they want, but I'm pretty sure I have an erection right now, and I have no idea what to do about it. I want my usual problems back.

That's it. That's what does for Nine. He falls off his chair laughing, his hand holding his splitting sides for dear life. "Oh . . . my . . . god. These are the stupidest thoughts I have ever had to deal with in my life."

"What? I don't know how to be a guy!"

It'll go away on its own. Luckily, you're still clothed under there.

"I feel so out of the loop here," Connie grumbles.

I shake my head at Nine, begging him not to the let the others know my little predicament.

Nine sighs, hopefully sticking to his no-telling rule. "It's nothing important."

Connie pouts. "No, but it sounded funny."

"Arrie!" I yell. "Please piss me off. I really want to go back to my previous self."

"I told you, I can't," he growls.

"So, you be an asshole every time I don't need it, but the one random moment I need you to step up, you won't?" I growl. "You are such a fucking dick!"

The frustration wells inside me, bubbling and boiling. Ohhh, maybe this'll change me back? My hands clench into fists as I ball the sheets under the duvet and focus on how unhelpful Arrie's being. But as frustrated as I get, I don't tingle, and I can still feel my male body betraying any sense of decency I have left.

"All right," I say eventually. "Everyone out. I'm gonna have a shower, look in the mirror to see the damage, and get changed." I sigh. "What's the time?"

"Four," Connie answers. "Still doing girls' night?"

I raise my brows at her. "Really?"

She stumbles over herself and looks uncertain and maybe a little embarrassed. "Riii-ight. We might need to change the name. Still hanging out tonight?"

"Sure," I sigh. Might be a good distraction. "Can we stay here tonight, instead?"

Connie nods, a smile taking hold of her features and lighting up her beautiful, flawless face. I enjoy making her smile.

Nine coughs, breaking us out of our trance. "We'll leave you be, Sweetie." He gets up and gestures for everyone else to do the same.

"Why did you all stay in the first place?"

Nine looks at me and blushes. "To make sure you were okay."

Oh, he probably heard my less-than-happy thoughts from earlier. I hope he didn't share them with the team.

No, I didn't. But . . . please be okay.

The airy seriousness in his mental voice stops my heart for a moment. He's worried about me, so he got the team to stay while I napped off my frustration.

Damn him, that's amazingly sweet and caring.

After everyone leaves, I have the unfortunate job of getting acquainted with my new form in the bathroom. The crysal-inbued flooring glows at me, as though the house is trying to give me some encouragement. The mirror across the room grimaces at me in all its reflective glory, and I sigh. Time to see the damage.

I edge closer to the mirror, eyes squeezing shut, until I reach the sink's rim and grip tight. Deep breaths. Deep breaths.

My eyes peek open, but I snap them shut again at the first sight of my reflection. Short blond hair. I have blond hair. A Japanese woman—man, male—with blond hair. How unusual.

Another peek, and I stare in horrorified amazement, taking it all in. Chisled jawline, no facial hair, ash-blond hair, and I'm taller by like five or six inches. A little more musclar, but mostly I'm slim, slimmer than Dea. I lean in close until my breath fogs up the glass and smile. My eyes are the same brilliant shade of purple, and, looking into them, it's like I haven't changed. I can see my soul in those eyes. The fear of having to save the world, the confusion over my love of four people, my hatred of magical predujice . . . It's like I can see it all staring back at me.

I'm still me.

I think.

Peeing as a guy is not fun, let me tell you, and I'm so afraid of touching my penis (goddess, that's an insane thing to say) that I spend my entire shower avoiding it, until it's time to wash and I can't avoid it anymore. At least my new penis has stopped being so hard by this point; Nine was right, it does go away on its own.

It's like a newly wrapped and unwanted Christmas present.

Nine's going to spend the next few months in stitches of laughter being inside my mind while I get used to my shifting.

By the time six pm comes around, I'm showered, dressed, and ready for a night of fun with Connie. She'll want to know all about the two moments with Nine and Dea, what my tantrum was about, and how I feel about my new . . . form. It's going to be a long night.

"Can I come in?" Connie asks from the open doorway, where she holds a dress bag in her arms.

I nod. "What's that?"

I lounge in the corner where I've set up a tray of peppermint tea and ask the house for some fancy types of cakes I have yet to try.

Gesturing to the seat in front of me, I put some music on as she shuts the door and sits down in front of me. "So," she starts and gestures to my body, "this might not be the best time to give this to you, but I bought you something while in Tokyo."

"Really?" I blink in confusion.

"Yeah." She hands over the bag. "Since you're Japanese, I thought you might like it."

I stand and unzip the bag, pulling out what is the most beautiful *kimono* I have ever seen. It's a dark, dusted-pink, buttons up all the way to the neck, and has long sleeves that puff out at the forearm section. It wraps around the middle and hangs down to what I think might be my mid-thigh at the front, and passing my knees at the back is a cream drape with a light pink and gold hem.

"Wow!"

"It matches your other hair perfectly." She wraps her arms around me from behind. "Thought you might want to wear it to the ball. But I'm not sure if you'll want to now."

"I'll find a way," I say as I turn around in her arms and wrap her in an embrace I hope lets her know how grateful I am.

She rests her head on my chest and breathes me in.

I don't want to break away, but I find myself managing it nonetheless.

Sitting back down in the corner, Connie gestures to me. "Fluidity, huh?"

"Ugh. Yup. Just another puzzle piece to add to the mess that has become my life."

She raises her eyebrows. "Gonna fill me in on everything that's happened since we last chatted. These are supposed to be about gossip and hanging out, after all. Male or female, you're still my friend."

"Well," I start, getting ready to launch into an update on the weird three-way relationship I've found myself in, "things got a little . . . interesting between me, Dea, and Nine."

"I figured as much. I overheard your chat at the safe house on Earth. So, have you slept with them yet?" She bounces slightly in her seat, eager for the juicy gossip.

"No."

She frowns and is about to ask why, but she cuts herself off. She knows why.

"But . . . we've done . . . stuff."

"OMG. Tell me everything!"

So I do. I tell her about the time Nine asked me to watch them in his room, then about the time I nearly slept with them the morning in the motel, then about the stupidly hot not-quite-sex we had the next day.

"Damn! You're really holding out, aren't you? But seriously, I've never slept with any of the team together, just individually, so this is like the hottest piece of team gossip I've had in centuries."

"Really?"

"I know it's weird, but it always feels a little strange to me."

I shrug. It isn't really any of my business.

"Doesn't mean I haven't slept with two guys at once, just not any of these guys."

"Right . . ." That makes more sense. "So, what about Arrie?"

Connie smiles a knowing smile. "He's . . . a tough one. He prefers to just sleep with me. But he's dabbled outside of that, too."

Why is that? Does he love her?

The cake is soooo good. I can't stop eating it, and I find that I prefer different things in my male form, which is interesting. For example, coffee isn't as decadent in this form.

"Connie?"

"Yeah?"

"I . . ." I really want to chat about the whole not having a family thing. But I'm not sure I want to bring it up. I can feel the sting of tears threatening to break the banks.

"What is it?" She puts her teacup down and shuffles next to me, putting a hand on my shoulder.

Taking a deep breath, I exhale and tell her all about what's been wrong over the last week, including the moment in the Witches's coven.

"That is quite a lot of emotions. You've had a tough week, huh?"

I sniff, and I can feel the tears threatening to break the banks. Shit! I can't cry in this form. Can I? I've never seen the guys cry before—other than Nine that one time, I guess. Won't that look ridiculous, though? Oh, goddesses. "Understatement."

Connie sits on my lap and smiles up at me. "Don't do that." She places a gentle hand on my cheek. "Don't hold back tears because you're worried over how it'll look. You're allowed to cry, no matter your anatomy. Your sex or gender does not change that."

She's right. Of course she's right.

I shake my head and laugh, letting a few tears spill over. "It's just so hard, you know?"

"Well, no, I don't know. But I can only imagine how confused you must be right now." She kisses me so softly I barely feel it, but it's enough to send a warm tingle dancing across my body. "You know, just because your form has changed does not mean you have. You're still a woman."

"Huh?" I looked confusedly at her. "How in the world is this"—I gesture to myself— "a woman?"

"Firstly," she says, tapping me on the nose, "you are a person, not an it, this, or a that." She takes a deep breath and reaches both arms around my neck. "And secondly, gender is not the same thing as sex, you know. They're totally different things."

"So, I'm trans?" Does that even apply here?

Connie leans in and whispers, "I think you need to stop trying so hard to fit in when you are so obviously meant to stand out."

The tears start up again, but this time I let them fall, knowing that this amazing, beautiful woman in front of me is not going to judge. "But I don't want to stand out." I sniffle. "I just want to be like you guys."

She chuckles as she tucks a piece of my blond hair behind my ear. "We're not so great. Just look at Arrie. You really wanna be like him?"

We both laugh for a minute before she gets up and moves back to the other chair. "You know," she starts, "all you have to do is tell us what you want from us, and we'll comply." She looks at me with concern, as though she isn't sure how I'll take that statement.

It's a bit of a loaded sentence.

"I . . . I don't know what person this makes me." I take a deep breath and wipe the tears from my face. "I still don't remember much from my mortal life, I don't understand my sexuality—if I even have one—and now I don't even have a static form."

"But you're still you, even if you don't know who that is yet."

I shake my head. I don't get it. How can she say that? Everyone else can conform, even if that isn't their at-birth assigned identity. But I physically can't do that. Does this make me less of a woman?

I might still be me, but I'm not sure who that is anymore.

"Oh," Connie says, "and regarding the having children thing. I don't know what to say about it, really. I've never had children because I don't want them—I think it would make things complicated—but that doesn't mean you don't have to. I mean, if you wanted to start a family by having a baby with or without the team, you're free to do so." She falters, finger halting mid-air. "Assuming you can." She gestures to my body, and I suddenly get what she means.

Can I have a baby when I can change sex? "How can I still be a woman if I can't even have a baby anymore? Isn't that one of our greatest purposes?"

Connie sighs and puts her cup of tea down. "So elderly women aren't women? What about children? Are they less of a woman just because they can't have babies? What about people without reproductive organs?" Connie looks at me with stern daggers in her green eyes. "We're more than just baby-making chambers, you know!"

I flinched. "Sorry, I didn't mean to offend your choices." Sighing, I pick up my cup of tea and take a sip. "But . . . I want . . ."

"A mortal life?"

I nod.

"I know. It took us some time to adjust, too."

"Really?"

"Yeah. Arrie took it the hardest. But you'll have to ask him about that." She turns the music up and jumps me to my feet. "Enough serious talk for now. I want to see that hunk of a male form you have hidden under that t-shirt. C'mon! Off with the shirt!"

"W-W-W-What?"

"Oh, c'mon . . . I'm curious."

"You saw me butt naked just a few hours ago."

"Yeah, but I wasn't paying attention then. I want to revel in the fact that I get to drool over a Fae body whenever I want. Well, whenever you're not looking." She winks at me.

"You're just like Nine," I groan.

"We're the most openly flirtatious, yes. Now. Off with it!" She grabs the hem of my t-shirt.

"Okay. Okay. Okay." I laugh. It's just a t-shirt. She isn't asking me to strip naked or anything. I yank it over my head and lean against the wall, trying to hide my embarrassment from Connie, who just stands there and stares.

She traces a hand over the ripples of my slight abs that I don't fully understand how I even have and sighs. "Damn. Nine was right. It is alluring."

"You've never seen a naked Fae before?"

She nods. "Yes, but . . . It's just that our magic is always more potent. I would refrain from being naked in this form around anyone other than the team. Dea might break necks." She stifles a laugh before she tears herself away from me.

I pull my t-shirt back on and put the TV on, hoping we can catch some movies. "What you wanna watch?"

"Ohhh, we could binge a new show: SHIFTERS IN SHIFT. It's supposed to be good."

Connie lays on my bed, and I grab extra blankets from the ottoman, ask the house for some male pajamas, and change in the bathroom before settling down with her.

We snuggle, and it feels a little weird in this form, like the fact that maybe we're more than just friends is a little more obvious. But she doesn't seem worried, and honestly, I have bigger things to worry about. Like trying to shift back. So I try to relax and enjoy myself.

CHAPTER 32

The next morning, I wake with my arm around Connie's waist and her curved back against my middle. I have no idea what time it is, but given that I have training for the next two-and-a-half days, I assume someone would have woken me if it's particularly late.

Connie stirs. "Mmmmm. Morning." She stretches, and her back straightens. "I like your male form. It's bigger and makes for a good big spoon." She's delirious with sleep, clearly, but I find it adorable nonetheless.

"Yeah? I like cuddling you like this, too." I wrap my arms tighter around her waist and give a gentle squeeze.

Connie stifles a laugh, and it takes me until she wriggles her ass against my groin to realize why. Fuck. I have to deal with morning guy problems now? What has my life become?

I groan and pull away. "Sorry."

She grabs my arm and yanks me back. "Don't be." Her ass wriggles some more, pushing back into me, and just the feel of it has my newly discovered cock twitching slightly.

"Ugh. Don't do that."

"Why? Like it?" She doesn't stop, and I have to admit that I don't want to pull away.

I groan in her ear, and she shudders from head to toe. But if I'm not ready to have sex with the team as a woman, I'm definitely not ready to have sex with them like this.

"Connie?" I ask as I pull away. "Does this change anything? You know . . . between us." I cough, trying to hide my embarrassment. "I mean, I know there's no us, but—"

Connie turns around, hooking a leg over my legs, and puts a finger to my lips. "No. Not at all. I like both your forms. Promise."

I kiss her finger in return, hoping it sends the right message.

"But I will admit, your male Fae form is hard to resist. But then, it's supposed to be.

Fae struggled to breed with their own species, so over the years, their attractiveness grew in hopes to outbreed to other species. It worked. But the Fae can only do strong magic if they have two Fae parents."

"Really?"

She nods and wraps her arms around my waist, pressing her lips to my cheek. "Yup."

She's so warm, I find myself melting into her embrace.

Someone knocks on the door, and I grumble a little like Arrie. "What?"

"Angel, training really is important right now." Dea opens the door.

Neither Connie nor I bother to move. She's too warm, and I missed spending time with my . . . friend.

He takes one look at us and rolls his eyes. "Seriously? Did not take much to seduce you, did it?" He points daggers at Connie.

Connie blanches at his words and flies out of bed and across the room quicker than I can blink. "Dea! I have not slept with him—her—whatever." She looks at me apologetically, but I just shrug her off. "But we are good friends and enjoy spending time together. So . . ." She grabs him by the scruff of his shirt and throws him through the window, which shatters as he lands on the other side. "Fuck you."

Connie stands there looking furious. I don't bother to do anything—not even get out of bed. She has every right to be pissed off; he practically called her easy. Might as well have called her a whore.

Nine and Arrie rush in and take one look at the scene and just stand there. I can feel Nine looking through my mind, but I save him the trouble and send him the memory. He freezes, clearly surprised by Dea's words, but doesn't say anything.

I give him a questioning look.

Yeah, he's jealous.

Oh. That actually makes some sense. But I snuggled with them both and did more while on Earth. Maybe I should try to spend some more time with just Dea? I have spent some alone time with both Connie and Nine recently. I even did some training with Arrie (not an emotional thing, but still time spent alone).

"Dea," I call out as I get out of bed, ignoring my hard-on that was so obviously pitching a tent in my pajamas. "You should apologize to Connie, and then we can begin training." I walk toward the broken window and hesitate when I notice his blood, expecting a Vampire reaction, but get nothing.

Right, not a Vampire right now. That's actually kinda handy.

Dea stands up and looks sheepishly. "Sorry, Con. I did not mean it." He climbs through the broken window and stands outside the entrance to the library.

I open the door for him, and he strolls on through.

"Could I maybe help with the party plans today, Arrie?"

Arrie nods and follows Dea into the library.

"Looks like everyone's working in your library today, Sweetie."

"Well," I say, "there's enough room. Besides, I think I'll need everyone's knowledge to help me learn how to shift back."

Nine nods and goes into the library. "I'll ask the house for a breakfast spread in the training room."

Connie and I are left standing in a breezy room in our pajamas, her face depicting a clearly pissed-off woman.

"Hey," I say as I wrap my arms around her shoulders. "He was just jealous of all the time I spent with Nine and you. He didn't mean it." I whisper into her ear, "I'm sorry."

She pulls away. "You really need to have that talk with them. This is getting out of hand." She smiles up at me, letting me know she isn't angry with me.

Right, I forgot about that yesterday. Oops.

I nod, hoping that changing back into my normal female self will make me feel better. We both get changed—myself in the bathroom and her in the bedroom—and head to the training room, where there's a table next to the desk with muffins, pancakes, maple syrup, bacon, and waffles spread out.

Connie stays a little temper-sensitive all morning, occasionally snapping at the rest of the guys when they ask something obvious or want to know if she's okay. The only person she is okay with is me, and I would be lying if I said it wasn't the cutest thing ever.

I, on the other hand, have spent the morning getting pissed off at everyone because I can't do fuck all to change back. Yesterday we were worried about me only being able to show off Witch and Vampire powers, but now I'm starting to have the opposite fear: what if I can only show off my Shifter and Fae abilities?

"Angel, stop getting so flustered and concentrate."

I growl at him. "Have you ever tried to relax, Dea? It's fucking impossible!"

"You seemed pretty relaxed this morning," Arrie comments in a huff.

I punch him in the arm as hard as I possibly can in this form—causing him to shift in his seat and me to cringe in pain as red marks begin forming on my knuckles—and go back to ignoring him.

Connie also grunts at him with glowering eyes. "Stop it."

Everyone's a little tense, and Nine seems to be suffering the most. He can leave if he wants, and I've told him multiple times to do so, but he seems adamant on staying.

I need to help you.

He looks at me with understanding eyes, and the mental anguish I see on his face tells me just how much being around all of us in bad moods is affecting him.

Don't worry about it.

But I do worry about it, and I continue to do so well into the afternoon, where I have still made no progress whatsoever.

"What did shifting feel like?" Nine asks.

"Like . . . a tingle all over, but a painful tingle, not like the kind I get when using Witch magic. And then it started to hurt so badly I nearly screamed, but it was over in under a second."

Dea steps forward, surprise etched on his face. "So it feels like a Shifter's shift, then?"

I think for a moment, trying to remember what it felt like when I first shifted into a panther, and nod. "Guess so. But that started to hurt less the more I shifted."

"It does. The more you practice, the easier it becomes." Dea holds up a hand and runs out of the room, pulling a phone from his pocket.

I raise an eyebrow at Nine, who tells me to wait.

A few minutes later, Dea comes back in with a smile on his face. "Tomorrow, a Shifter friend of mine will be coming to the house to help. Your shifting sounds like a form of actual shifting, or at least something similar. We cannot help because it is something we cannot do; our magic is different to yours."

I nod, understanding what he means. "So, until then?"

"We wait. But we might as well try to see if we can get some control of your Fae magic and produce something more than flying a feather."

Connie stands, then smiles to everyone. "We're done. Fuck yes. Ball's on Monday night. Japanese-themed, in celebration of our new Horseman, and everyone who knows about us is coming, and I've made it an open invitation to *Sheruta*. I've organized the caterers, bartenders, and an entire supply team for the decorating, all of whom will be arriving tomorrow to set up."

Dea smiles. "Great work. Pretty sure that is a record." He steps up to her and looks her straight in the eyes. "I am sorry, Con."

"I know, Dea. Just . . . promise me you'll all have that chat this evening."

He wraps his arms around her, embracing her much smaller frame as he plants a kiss on her cheek. "Okay."

The whole thing makes me grin, and Nine notices, a smile of his own creeping across his face.

You're all already more polyamorous than you realize. This should be easy.

You think?

Yup. I'm allowed to be who I want when I'm immortal, right?

Of course.

Then I have made my decision.

I'll try to get this team together in a way that none of them fears and all of them have wanted for centuries. It doesn't have to be forever, and when we're talking immortality, preferences and tastes are bound to change, but that doesn't mean everything has to vanish. So long as everyone's okay with us all changing and growing over time, including our love and sexualities, then it should be just fine.

Nine smiles at me, as though he's already committed to losing this battle.

I plan to be the Horseman of Magic, friend and girlfriend/boyfriend to the entire team, and I plan to romance them all into place.

All I need now is to make some devious plans.

Woman power for the win! Well, sort of.

33

Nine pm comes quicker than I would have liked, and my confidence from earlier has all but vanished; what if they're too scared? What if they don't like me the way I think they do? What if—?

Stop spiraling.

Looking to my left, I see Nine walking among the book stacks toward me, his red hair bouncing as he walks with an upbeat brisk to his step.

"Where's Dea?"

"Not far behind. Just wrapping something up with Arrie."

I didn't train physically today—we've been too worried about managing my shifting—but I'll start again tomorrow.

"Tell Arrie I'd like to resume training at dawn tomorrow?"

"Sure thing."

"Sorry," I wince. "Does it annoy you if I use your telepathy like that?"

He shrugs. "A little. But I'm used to it."

I shake my head. "You shouldn't have to be. I'll stop." I'll just get a phone and communicate that way. Phones are pretty old-fashioned nowadays, since Earth uses datachips to communicate, but we don't have those, otherwise we would be trackable by anyone, so we have to adjust.

"I'll make you one like ours. Should have done it already. Sorry."

"Cool. Thanks."

Dea walks up to us and sits on the couch to the right, one nestled in a reading corner I particularly like. "So you wanted to chat?"

I nod. "Sit," I order Nine. C'mon stern mindset. "Nine, please stay out of my head as much as possible. Dea, I need you both to listen and be honest."

I sigh. I'm not prepared for this.

"Watching you both is the most painful experience I've had since being here." They both blanch, clearly understanding my meaning. It's more painful than not knowing who I am, thinking I have no hope of a normal future. "I see the way you look at each other, the way you always touch under the kitchen table, the way Nine finds Dea's smile sexy as hell —which it is, by the way—and the way Dea finds Nine's nerding out adorable."

They both look at me, clearly uncomfortable, like they want to run.

But I shake my head. "Absolutely not. Neither one of you is leaving. I might not have my Vamp strength in this form, but Shifters are still pretty strong. Wanna test that theory?"

"Con and Arrie are both stronger than you in this form, by the way. Just a little tidbit of—"

"Shut up, Nine. Now's not the time."

I have to do this for them. They need to clear the air. "Even if, after this, you decide to go straight back to the way things were, that's totally fine. But lying to yourselves and each other isn't healthy, and you guys have the rest of time to be in pain, so that isn't really fair. Is it?"

Goddess, I feel like a mother hen.

"So?" I ask, expecting them to take it from here.

They both raise their eyebrows.

"You've never done this, have you?"

Nine shake his head. "Feelings aren't really the Horsemen's thing, Sweetie."

"Ugh! Oh my goddess, you both feel the same way. Trust me on that."

They both look at each other, and I can see the tears welling in Nine's eyes, though he chokes them back.

"Really?" Dea asks.

"I'm sorry," Nine says. "I've known how you feel for a while. And I knew that you wouldn't have that same surety as me."

Dea shakes his head. "That is nothing to apologize for. You are always surer of things than the rest of us. But staying silent . . . That is not okay. I have been thinking you just did not feel the same way."

Nine straightens at that. "What? How could you think that?"

I lean against a bookcase and listen. It isn't my job to talk for them. Just to be here and help.

Dea stands, hands balled into fists. "You rarely ever stay the night, you sleep with a lot of other people, and I am not telepathic, Nine!"

"We've been together for two millennia, Dea! You fuckin' moron. How could you not know that I'm in love with you?"

"Because you never said!"

"I shouldn't need to say it!"

"Maybe not to you, you always know. I do not!"

"Death. Famine!" This is my cue to step in. "Sit back down and talk like adults." Goddess, this feel a lot like mediating toddlers. You would think immortal beings over two thousand years old would understand emotions more.

Dea sits, but I notice a significant amount of tension between them, visibly represented by the entire person-sized space on the couch between them.

Ugh.

I take the seat between them and place a hand on both of their knees. "I can't stay in the middle of you anymore. I just can't. You both love each other, and you're displacing that onto me because it has nowhere else to go since you refuse to experience a regular emotion." They both go to speak at the same time, but I cut them off. "I know you're not ready for this, and I get that. I'm not asking you to be together exclusively or in any other way. I'm asking you to recognize each other's feelings, and maybe, someday, you'll find a way to be happy as a part of this team."

They both look at me in surprise, as though their happiness isn't even something they considered until this point.

"Your happiness matters just as much as the safety of Earth." I get up and leave, thinking I can probably hear them if things get out of hand anyway.

The next morning is a weird time for the team. Nine and Dea are smiling at each other, but both make no announcement that they're together, so I just assume they worked things out and are remaining in their no-love relationship they've got going on. And everyone at the table has noticed their good mood.

Goddess, this team is going to kill me. I'll die of emotional exhaustion before I ever manage to win the fucking war I was summoned by Fate to fix.

Dea tears his gaze away from Nine and looks at me. "My Shifter friend will be here at ten o'clock."

I nod and look to Arrie. "Training until then?"

Just as Arrie opens his mouth, Connie claps. "Can I join?" she asks.

I shoot a questioning gaze at Arrie, who nods—again, in silence. But I notice the smile underneath the stern frown.

"Yay!" Connie bounces in her seat and grabs my hand. "You're going to be exhausted by the time Arrie and I are done with you."

I don't think she intended that to be sexual, but that is exactly how I take it, and my blush clearly lets the whole fucking world know it.

"Oops," she says. "My bad." She winks and gets up, taking her plate to the sink to wash before she heads upstairs.

Nine laughs. "She's playing a game, too. Seems things will be interesting around here."

Nine doesn't look at me and instead focuses on his breakfast.

"Half hour. Woods," Arrie grumbles and gets up to follow Connie.

By the time I finish my breakfast, get changed into some workout clothes, and walk to the clearing in the woods, Arrie and Connie are already sparring.

Loud clangs meet my ears as they sprint at each other full-throttle, Arrie growling and Connie smiling. They whizz around the clearing, trying to draw some blood from the other, bouncing over rocks, flipping through the air, and I'm mesmerized by the sight in front of me.

If I'm ever that awesome, I'll have no problem impressing anyone.

"Hey, hon!" Connie waves me over from where she stands, Arrie panting beside her. Connie doesn't even break a sweat, of course, her everlasting stamina being the reason she outlasts him.

"Hey!" We have three hours of training to go before I need to meet this Shifter who's supposed to help me with my shifiting problem. "What's on the dossier today, Arrie?"

"More self-defense. After the ball, Con'll add in weapons training. But mastering your shifts is the priority for the moment."

I note his businesslike self is back the moment he starts talking to me. With Connie, he's effortlessly himself—he even smiles during their sparring match. But with me, he's his usual gruff self.

It's going to be a bitch bringing him on board, isn't it?

"Blocking various types of attacks today, not just the basics."

Connie steps up to me. "Show me what you got so far."

Her businesslike attitude matches Arrie's, and I have to admit, it has me feeling a little better about his mood.

I run through the basic blocks from the other day, Connie making some personal suggestions as Arrie attacks in a variety of jab combos. So far, so good. But as Arrie attacks in more advanced ways, I start taking more hits, bruises and broken bones healing fast, but not as fast as usual. Stupid lack of Vampire healing.

"I was thinking," Connie says as she attacks and gives Arrie a break. "We're going to have to split your physical training across both forms for you to stay in shape. You're taller in this form, meaning you'll need to adjust your attack and defense styles for each form. You should spend half of each of our sessions in each form."

Oh my fuck, I'm going to have to do two lots of yoga and exercise if I want to be fit and flexible in both forms, aren't I?

I groan as that realization hitt me, and Connie manages to get a lucky shot straight to my face, making me fall backward and land flat on my ass.

Arrie laughs, and I shoot him a dirty look. "Glad someone finds this amusing."

"Your drama is the most fun I've had watching in years, Killer."

I bristle at the comment and decide to put him in his place, Vampire strength or not. Anger forces its way through my usually perfect façade of any-emotion-other-than-anger mask. "You fucking asswipe." I swing a right hook to his face, but he blocks with ease. "My life is not a drama for your entertainment!" I try to take a jab at him, but he moves, and I stumble.

"Well, your attack needs some work. We'll work on that later."

"Argh! You. Are. The. Most. Infuriating. Person. In. The. World!" I launch myself at him and feel that familiar less-painful-than-last-time tingle reshape my body as I connect my paws with his shoulders, my panther form taking him down with ease.

I roar in his face, not stopping until the frustration is out of my system. Lifting my paws off his shoulders, I stride away and sit by Connie, not really sure how to turn back into a man.

She rests a hand on my head and scratches behind my ears. It feels . . . good. Kinda relaxing and tingly, but in a good way. I lean my head into her hand and purr, and she giggles and gives Arrie an I-told-you-so look.

But now what? How do I change back? How did I do it last time?

"Luckily," Connie says, "the Shifter is here."

Ah! Perfect timing.

Connie leads me out of Arrie's clearing, explaining that he doesn't like many people using his space, and to another part of the forest.

Nine, Dea, and a dark-skinned woman I don't recognize walk toward us. Dea's eyebrows raise in question when he sees me.

Pointing at me, Connie answers Nine's unasked question. "She's stuck, I think."

"Yup," Nine confirms. "She can't remember how to shift back."

The woman with them laughs and walks up to me. "I hear you are the new Horseman?"

I blanch at her words. They told her?

"Don't worry." She holds her hands up in surrender. "I'm sworn to secrecy. I'll be at the ball anyway."

I nod, my whiskers bouncing and tickling my face, causing me to sneeze.

Connie finds that hilarious. "Oh my fuck, that's so fucking cute!" I growl at her, and she holds up her hands in defense. "Sorry." But she remains smiling.

"Okay," the Shifter woman says. "Just think about your human form, visualizing the details, and want to shift back."

Sounds easy enough, and it is. In a matter of seconds, I'm a fully clothed male me standing next to Connie in the forest.

The Shifter holds out her hand to shake. "Name's Kally. I manage the Shifters here on *Sheruta.*"

I shake her hand but remain unamused by her so far. She seems nice enough, but I've become wary of anyone not a member of the team. I haven't met many nice people so far.

"You have unlimited shifts?" she asks, looking a little dubious.

I shift back into my panther form using the same technique as before, and then move into a falcon, owl, horse, and bat with ease. Anything I can visualize, I seem to be able to shift into easily.

I shift back into my male body. "Shifting is the easiest power to manage so far. It's instinctive."

She smiles with wonder and awe in her eyes. "The only thing Shifters have to worry about is control. We shift under intense emotion."

"Makes sense. So, how do I turn back into a female?"

She looks at me confused. And one look at Nine and Dea tells me they haven't informed her.

"I have a male and female form. Male for Fae and Shifter magic, female for Witch and Vampire magic," I explain. "I turned into this"—I gesture to myself—"yesterday and haven't been able to shift back since. But I need to so I can demonstrate my powers at the ball."

She nods and cirles me, a hand scratching her shiny black hair in thought. "What makes you think I can help?"

Dea steps forward, gesturing toward me. "She explained it a lot like shifting in the young, so I thought you may be able to offer some insight."

"Okay. Explain it to me."

"It hurts, like every cell in my body is tingling with a fire I can't control, and it made me puke my guts up. Fucking sucked."

"Okaaay." She puts her hand on her chin in deep thought, and we all stand and stare at her. "It sounds like when a wolf cub first shifts. They're stuck like that until they get used to their wolf, then they naturally shift back and gain control over time. Usually happens around sixteen-to-eighteen."

"We don't have time," I remind her.

"I know. I know. Hmmmm." Another painful few moments pass before she turns around and says something that nearly knocks me on my ass. "Have you fully explored your male form yet?"

"Fully explored?" I look at her confused.

She means have you done everything you typically would as a man. Food, emotions, sleep . . . sex. Wolves usually shift after having sex for the first time, so long as they've experienced puberty and stuff.

"Oh. Ummm . . . no. But I'm not having sex with anyone. The magical communities can fucking suck it if they think I'm doing that just to pacify them."

Kally smiles. "Of course. Have you done everything else?"

I nod. "Think so."

"Okay, well then, we'll just have to keep working on your shift and hope it comes to you in time."

She spends the rest of the morning and the whole of the afternoon coaxing me through various shifting methods, none of which work. We find a few more cool animal forms (a few more birds, insects, and even a housecat) but no female me.

Arrie comes along at some point but remains silently observational for now. Thank fuck, because I don't think I can take his sarcasm right now.

Gah! This is so frustrating. How am I supposed to do anything to help this war if I can't even shift between my human forms?

Arrie chooses this moment to step up and annoy the shit out of me. I assume that's what he's going to do, as he has that usual scowl on his face he seems to save just for me. "Killer, come here." He pulls me to him and turns me around, away from the ears of everyone but Connie as I face away from everyone else and have my back to him.

"I used to be friends with Dea's old Shifter friend, too, and he once told me something about his young Shifter days."

This is the closest I have ever come to a normal, pleasant conversation with the man, and honestly, it's nice.

"He told me that, sometimes, when we're trapped in our emotions, Shifters tend to get stuck in their shifted form." He places his hands on my shoulders and kneads the tense muscles into relaxation.

I have to refrain from moaning out loud. This man knows how to give a good massage. Despite my extra height in this form, he still has a good few inches on me, and it reminds me just how sexy as hell this damn man is.

"I know you have a lot to be worried about right now, and I haven't made that any easier on you. But right now, you need to let all that go. Dea, Nine, and Connie are going to spend the rest of eternity being completely enamored by you." He sounds almost annoyed but also slightly amused. "And, eventually, you'll get what you want from them."

"And you?"

Arrie breathes a sigh of tension. "I don't know, Killer. But I'm trying."

I nod and feel the tension leave my body as he continues to massage my neck and shoulders. "But that's not the main issue . . ."

"Then what is?"

"I . . . I want a normal life, Arrie. Marriage, children, growing old, friends, getting so drunk I can barely walk in a straight line, and not having the world on my shoulders."

"You can have all of that. In time. We've had some great years together of complete peace."

"Really?"

"I promise."

Some of the weight of my uncertain immortal future lifts from my shoulders, and with it, that painful tingle comes back, quickly turning into an inferno that inflames my entire body in a million pounds of pain. As I feel my body change back to female, the nausea comes with it, and I once again puke my guts up.

"Ugh," I say, wiping my mouth after. "I have to get that under control."

Looking down at my body, I notice I'm shorter, have curves, and . . . boobs! I grab them in excitement. "I have boobs again."

I spin and fling my arms around Arrie's shoulders and murmur, "Thank you," into his ear before letting go and skipping around the clearing, reveling in the fact that my boobs bounce when I jump.

Boobs! I have actual boobs! Goddess, I didn't know I would miss them so much.

You are really fond of your boobs, Sweetie.

Shut up. You would be, too.

Nine chuckles from his spot against a tree just behind Dea. I've noticed since being here that no one even looks curious when Nine laughs at something someone's thinking or when he appears a little strange as he jumps into mental conversations.

It's just the way I am. They've spent two thousand years living with this. You'll get used to it.

It's actually kinda sweet.

The faintest hint of a blush reddens his cheeks.

"That was great," Kally says, "but now we have to focus on you being able to switch between the two at will. Hopefully, in time, you'll be able to do it mid-fight and with no side effects."

"I'm going to spend a lot of the afternoon throwing up, aren't I?"

They all stare at me with grimacing smiles, Arrie also holding in a laugh at my future pain. Fucking asshole.

And that's what I do: Arrie pisses me off enough to make me change forms while Nine calms me down enough to change me back. Back and forth we go as I vomit up every last scrap of food in my stomach until I'm retching bile every time.

"There has to be an easier way," Connie say. "We're not going to be there every time she needs to change form, and we're not always gonna have the time to anger or calm her enough to manage it."

Kally looks at me—currently in my male form—with a sort of painful wonder. "Did it take you all this long to manage your abilities?"

Nine flinches. "It took us years to manage them enough to do our jobs. We've just honed them perfectly over the years."

"Great." I wipe my mouth, trying in vain to rid myself of that acrid taste etched into the back of my throat. "I don't have years."

"Neither did we," Dea says, coming forth from the hours of silent observation. "The world went to hell while we mastered our skills."

"Things were different then," Nine says. "The world was already hell, we just needed time to fix it. Nothing got worse because of that. But if Sweetie takes too long, things will get worse, and I don't think any of us can live with that."

"Let's just keep going. The more I practice, the more it'll sink in." I need to be useful. I need to help. I can't let the team down.

I stand on shaky legs, nearly tripping, but catch myself before I face-plant the forest floor.

"You can barely stand, hon. Let's get you som—"

"No!" I stand straighter, trying to look more confident than I feel. "I need to get this. We only have another day and a half."

"But—

"Just shut up, Connie!"

She flinches, and I instantly feel guilty. I didn't mean to snap, and the look on her face tells me I've made a mistake. She looks a little heartbroken before she takes a deep breath and replaces it with her usual resolve.

"Sorry," I breathe. "Just stressed."

"I know. It's okay."

I put that aside for now. I can always find some way of making it up to her later. This is my priority right now. Getting this right.

Taking a deep breath, I sit on the forest floor, away from the steaming pile of vomit I've managed to produce over the course of the afternoon, and inhale the familiar scents of those around me: Connie's mango shampoo, Arrie's tangy metallic scent mixed with whatever the hell amazing shit he uses as body wash, Nine's page-and-ink scent that never fails to excite me, and Dea's lavender, heavenly smell of home. I let them encompass me and ride my mind into peace.

I hear them trying to talk to me, but Nine hushes them, telling them to be silent while I concentrate.

I don't mind my male form so much, if I'm honest. I need more time with it, to get myself properly acquainted, but it seems useful; especially if I'm going to try to bring people together. But right now, I need to be in my female form because that way I can wear the amazing *kimono* Connie bought me from Japan (cos there's no way that'll fit on me now), and I can dance with the guys at the party, try to mingle with some of their friends, meet people of power and make face. I can do all that better in my female form. Right now, I need to be female.

I try to picture my own body in my mind, from my light pink hair that trails down to my waist, to my five-foot-six frame with small curves and clunky feet. If I picture my body enough, I can even produce fangs with the image, blood-red eyes, a pale complexion, with air magic streaming from both hands. That's me. Or part of me, at least. Half of who I am.

That's why I felt so . . . not myself before. Because that isn't me. I'm both male and female. I'm all: Witch, Vampire, Fae, and Shifter. It allows me to blend in with the world, become something of a glue that will hopefully allow them to celebrate their differences and similarities alike.

Goddess, I sound so whimsical, like some kind of soothsayer from one of my books. Although it's a cliché, it's true.

I don't want to win the war. I want to prevent it.

"You did it!" Someone exclaims from a distance.

Opening my eyes, I notice they aren't speaking from a distance, my mind is just far away. They're a few feet in front of me, bouncing around in their typical excited fashion. Connie.

"Reckon you could do that on cue at the ball?" Dea asks, ever the planned one of the team.

"I reckon I need more fucking practice, but yeah. Hopefully."

Nine looks at me with some kind of prideful smile on his face.

I want to ask what it means, but Connie grabs my arms and yanks me to my feet. "C'mon!" she shouts. "Let's grab some food and have a movie night. All of us."

I look around at the people in the forest and have a sudden warm feeling I can't quite put a name to. I've only known them for a month, and two of them have spent that time confusing the hell out of me, while another has spent it trying their best to break my calm resolve (and succeeding on several occasions), but all four of them are amazing. Maybe one day I will call them family.

"You gonna join us, Kally?" Connie asks.

I totally forgot she was there. "Thank you," I say, stepping up to her. She has on a nice smile, and I think she might be the first non-team member I've met and actually like. "You saved the day today."

She laughs and shakes her hands. "Nah. You guys are the heroes, right? The rest of us just help when we can." She turns to look at Connie. "Thanks for the offer, but I'm gonna head on home. Got a few hungry wolves to feed before bed." She gives us all a little playful salute and heads back through the forest.

"Soooo." I thread my arm through Connie's. "What we watching?"

"Well, it's Arrie's turn to choose tonight."

I look over at him, and he shrugs. "I think Killer should choose. She's earned it." He strides off through the forest ahead of us.

I stop still. "Did he just . . . compliment me?" My head rushes in dizziness for a moment, but I steady myself and continue back to the house. "Goddess, the world's gone fucking topsy turvy." And now I'm starting to sound as English as Dea.

Fuck it all to hell

34

I choose a Disney animated feature for the evening, a movie that speaks to some long-forgotten memory of mine. No one complains, and even Arrie seems to enjoy some of the jokes and singalongs. We all curl up on one of the larger corner sofas. I'm tucked in the corner between Nine and Connie, with Arrie lying across Connie's lap on my left and Dea in the crook of Nine's shoulder on my right.

Compared to the last time I was here with them all, when I cuddled with Nine and Dea and the others sat on a separate sofa, this feels more . . . right. More like home.

The final song comes on as the credits roll, and Nine and Connie burst into song and dance, leaping off the sofa and dancing around the floating platform, performing a terrible rendition of one of the movie's main songs.

"You'd think after two thousand years, you'd be able to sing better." I shrug and smirk at them, even as Connie throws a pillow at my face using her full strength (which hurts like a bitch, by the way). "Remind me not to piss you off. You could do some serious fucking damage to my face." I throw the pillow back to her.

"You'd just heal anyway!" she yells as she jumps off the platform and lands on the floor below without a scratch, leaving me momentarily speechless.

"You're a Vampire, Sweetie. You could probably jump that easier than her."

Really?

Putting it to the test, I jump off the side (not like I can die anyway) and land on my feet, not even feeling a tremor as my feet hit the floor.

"Nice jump." Connie puts her arm around my waist and pulls me away as the guys lower the platform and get off. "Next movie night's on Arrie, right?"

He rolls his eyes. "Fine. After the ball, I'll pick something." He walks off, probably heading to bed.

I have other ideas. "Connie, come with me."

Nine smiles at us as I grab her hand and drag her out of the theater and into the kitchen, where we head back outside. Night has fallen somewhere between dinner and the movie, but that isn't stopping me. I have an apology to give for snapping. It isn't her fault; she's just looking out for me.

I walk us over to a small clearing in the fairy garden and have her stand in front of me. "Ready?"

"For what?"

"For the world's best apology." I wave my hand in the air and lift us both a good twenty feet off the ground, above the trees of the forest and high enough to look at the whole of *Sheruta*.

Flying myself closer to her, I grab her from behind and wrap my arms around her waist. "C'mon, let's go exploring."

I fly us toward the town and over the fancy section Nine and Dea took me to, and then above a more modern street with clubs and bars and various entertainment facilities. "What's in that direction?" I ask her as I nod ahead of us. In the far distance, I can see the coast, but the bit in between us and that has a large circular building.

"That's the mall."

"Mall? We have a fucking mall?" That's right, Nine promised to take me.

"Yup."

I grab her hand and whisk us through the air, reveling in her laughter as I twist us in corkscrew motions and fly us in circles toward the ground before flying us back up into the air last minute.

When we get closer, the mall looks ridiculous. It has at least ten stories and is lit up like a Christmas tree.

"Nine and Dea didn't take you here?"

"Nah. We couldn't walk very far because I was still healing."

"Dea doesn't like it, says it's too modern. He probably just wanted to avoid it."

"He doesn't seem to like public places. Probably because of the visibility thing."

Connie grabs my hand once more and pulls me toward her. I use the air to bring us closer together as she wraps her hands around my neck. "Wanna see the coast?" I nod, and she points to the edge of land ahead of us. "It's that way."

I fly us over there in less than a few minutes and land us straight on a pure-white sandy strip of coast that is as beautiful as the starry sky above us.

The moonlight reflecting off Connie's blond hair enraptures me for a brief moment, before I realize I'm staring.

She gives me a quizzical look.

What the hell. Might as well. "You really are beautiful," I murmur.

"Thank you," she says as she steps in front of me, our bodies pressing together as her arms wrap around my neck. "But so are you."

I blush and look away from her bright green eyes, not really knowing how to take a compliment from this woman.

She gently grabs my neck and forces my eyes back to hers. "You are beautiful. You shouldn't be ashamed of how you look."

"I'm not. Just . . . I now have two bodies to worry about; two sets of confidences to deal with."

"It's all the same. They're both you."

"I freaked out to begin with, but you're right. I kinda feel whole now. Like I've gained something I've been missing this entire time."

She smiles that perfect smile at me, flashing the dimple that makes her face adorable under the single light of the moon. We barely talk in whispers, being so close, but when she presses her lips to mine, I sigh in relief.

Kissing this woman feels so right, and I couldn't care less what people think. She's amazing, beautiful, powerful, and strong, and I'm lucky to have my interest in her returned.

She deepens the kiss, encouraging me to open my mouth by swiping her tongue across my lips, and then she delves deep, connecting our kiss and exploding my mind into stars. Her hand slides up my t-shirt to rest on my lower back, pressing me flush against her, and I find myself tiptoeing up to her, getting as close as possible to the Horseman of Conquest, someone I have come to call my friend.

Maybe a little more than a friend, but labels aren't really something I'm interested in right now.

As she raises her hand higher up my back and brings it round to the front, she grazes a thumb over my nipple.

I gasp against her lips before pulling away, breathless.

She looks at me a little disappointed but smiles. "Maybe next time."

The sudden memory of Nine's comment this morning brushes itself across my mind: *Looks like you're not the only one playing a game.*

Is she trying to get me into bed? Is that her end game?

I smile at the thought; although it isn't something I'm ready for, the feeling of being wanted—needed—floods my mind, and I find myself sighing in comfort. "We should head back," I whisper. "Got lots more training tomorrow. And I'm sure the party décor needs arranging."

She grabs my hand. "You're right. You need some sleep."

I raise us both into the air and fly us back to the house, where we land on the backyard porch and share another melting kiss goodnight before I head off to bed with another cup of coffee.

THE NEXT DAY IS AS FRUSTRATING AS THE LAST, AS I SPEND IT TRYING TO SPEED UP THE PROCESS of shifting forms, but I have about as much luck as a leprechaun born on a Friday the thirteenth.

"One more time, Angel."

We're back in my training room this time, Arrie sitting just outside the open door with a book I don't recognize in a language I didn't even know existed. Nine is sitting at the desk, taking diligent notes while Dea coaches me through each shift. Arrie's taken to joining us recently and dragging me off for physical training every time I get too frustrated to continue. The balance is nice, but what would be nicer is managing an effortless shift.

"Dea, how do you do it?"

"Hmmm?" he asks, turning around from his examination of my weaponry contents. "Oh, you mean shift?"

I nod.

"Took me a while to get it right, but I just imagine my soul's power and let it fill me up, and I just shift."

"Right. Makes sense." And is completely useless to me. I don't have soul magic, so that won't work.

"Sorry, I know that is useless. That is why I have not bothered to tutor you based on my own shift."

"The party's tomorrow. This is as good as it's going to get, I'm afraid. Everyone's just gonna have to stare at me meditating for a solid five minutes before seeing anything." I cringe at the thought. Meditating in front of a crowd almost sounds like a paradox. How is that going to be relaxing? "Sorry."

Dea waves off my concern. "We will make do."

Nine stands. "Let's all have some dinner and get an early night. We'll all be needed by Connie's drill sergeant orders tomorrow, I'm sure," he groans.

I laugh, but they just look at me, deadly serious. Damn, she's going to be bossy tomorrow, isn't she?

Yup. Good luck. Though she'll likely be easier on you, given your date last night.

I roll my eyes. It wasn't a date, just an apology for snapping at her.

Uh-huh. Whatever you say. But it's been loudly playing on her mind all day.

This is what I get for apologizing? Nine's annoying commentary? But it's kinda normal by this point. It's a refreshing change from Dea's politeness and Arrie's silent, grumpy attitude. Though, since our moment in the forest, Arrie seems less grumpy with me. Maybe we've made progress?

That thought goes completely out the window when we're all sitting around the dining table—Nine teasing Connie and I about our not-date last night, Dea raising his eyebrows in that annoying way of his, and Arrie . . . Well, he just gets up and storms offce.

I get the feeling there's more to his feelings for Connie than I originally thought. They don't seem as close as Nine and Dea, but maybe I misjudged.

Dea sighs, Connie practically sinks into her chair, and Nine looks stoically at the table (probably trying to remain impassive).

Back to square one.

35

The following morning, I wake up a bundle of nerves, but as I get downstairs, I realize the entire team have started preparing for the ball without me. My Vamp hearing leads me down a wide hallway (I can probably sprawl across its width twice lengthways) with a gilded arch at the end, leading into a vast open space with higharched ceilings, a window wall on one side leading to a fancy balcony, and walls painted in an intricate golden detail. It looks like something out of a fairy tale.

Dea and Nine wear gray aprons and hold feathers dusters, Arrie is helping a bunch of people I've never seen before put up decorations, and Connie is barking orders at the caterers on how and where to place all the food. All in all, it looks like everyone is busy.

"Sweetie," Nine calls, "Con wants to see you." He barely looks over his shoulder as he says it, but the moment he does, Dea turns around to give me a wave.

I run over to Coniie and watch as she carefully moves the giant cake in the center of the table two inches to the left. "You wanted to see me?"

"Er, yeah. Could you help Arrie with the decs, please? Your air magic will make it much easier."

I look at her with raised eyebrows, but she doesn't even bother turning around to greet me, so she doesn't notice.

Arrie's working in one corner, layering pink and gold drapes along the ceiling edges and letting them hang in sweeping arcs halfway down the wall. He seems to be struggling on a ladder to reach each point, and I see him stumble.

"Here."

I wave my hand and air-lift him off the ladder so he can drape the fabric more effectively. After he's pinned that one into place on the wall, I set him down on his feet, where I watch him take a deep breath.

"Want me to handle this?"

Arrie frowns and hands over the next pink and gold drapes to be placed on the next section of wall.

I don't waste any time getting them pinned up, using my air magic to stick the pins, drape the drapes, and swing the arches. All in all, it's pretty easy. Arrie hands me all the material, tells me how low to hang each one by giving me a faraway point of view, and I do the heavy lifting (magically speaking). We're done in no time, and the almost-silent routine we have going on feels . . . peaceful.

"What's next?" I ask as I spin around to meet him.

He shrugs. "Ask Con." He spins around and heads her way, and I watch as he has the same kind of discussion I had with her, before marching back my way.

"She says we should take a walk into town and make sure the guild is sending over the correct number of staff for the event and that there are no problems."

"Could we not just call them?"

Arrie shrugs. "She said to go there in person."

"Right."

I go to grab my shoes from my room and then meet Arrie by the front door, and by the time I've come back down, he's dressed in jeans, a tight-fitting t-shirt that shows off his muscular form underneath, and boots.

"Ready?"

Everything is so simple with this man, and I love that. There's no guessing what he's thinking, no weird flirting that promises something I can't obtain, and no secrets or hidden thoughts. It's so . . . relaxing.

"So," Arrie says in what I can only assume is supposed to be suggestive, "you and Con went on a . . . date?"

Ah, so that is why he's acting all moody today.

"Yeah, about that . . ." I look at him, not really sure what to say. "I'm sorry." There, I said it.

He stops halfway down the trail we're walking and looks at me. "Why?"

I sigh, walking straight past him and continuing on our way. "I'm not really sure." He jogs to catch up, and we end up walking side by side. "I didn't realize you had feelings for her, and I'm sorry if that's upsetting you."

He laughs. Like, legit laughs. And I forot how magical it sounds. To make someone laugh who doesn't usually loosen up enough to feel humor is a challenge I can spend the rest of my life puzzling out and always be fulfilled when achieved.

"I don't have feelings for Con."

"But—"

He holds up a hand. "I'm just a little off-put by her interest in you. It's not normal for her."

"Oh?"

"She's usually a sex-only kind of girl, just like the rest of us. Kind of our thing. And it's weird to see her actually falling for someone. Especially someone on the team."

"Falling?" It's my turn to laugh. "Goddess, Arrie, she's not in love with me. Stop being so stupid."

I walk a little bit ahead, trying to hide my flushed cheeks, but he grabs my arm and pulls me back into step with him. "Maybe not right now, but she looks at you differently." He gruffs and goes back to silence.

She does?

I get the sense that he doesn't want to continue talking, which is fine by me, so we walk the rest of the half hour it takes to get to the *Sheruta* guild in the center of town in silence. Not the uncomfortable kind of silence one often finds themselves in and wonders how on earth they're going to navigate an attempt at conversation, but the amicable kind two people often find when comfortability succeeds mindless conversation. And while I love Nine's endless chatter and Dea's artful communication, the peace that comes with being in the presence of this silent man is something I haven't found in the other members of the team, and I find myself rather enjoying it.

Maybe we can be friends after all.

The center of town holds the guildhall, and just behind that sits the portal building; Arrie explains that the guildhall is how the Horsemen communicate with the residents here, both when looking for new workers around the house and when needing the assistance of the magical community. The guildhall is all stone and copper plating, looking like a fancy steampunk designer got all modern with the Victorian-esque natural look of the town and settled on some fancy in-between that I have to admit looks rather quirky.

The inside is everything you would expect of a guildhall in a realm you never thought existed: grand and fantasy-like. Its interior stone buttresses that reach to the arched glass ceiling are simply phenomenal in design and remind me of the kind of architecture you find in Europe in grand, medieval buildings; each one depicts a different scene with all kinds of magical creatures showing off their powers.

Various high desks dot the scene in front of me, each one labeled so you'd have no problem distinguishing one from the other, and the one Arrie stops in front of says COMMUNITY AFFAIRS on the golden plaque. The man sitting at that desk is small, smaller than I think I've ever seen before, and he wears a brown top hat with a floppy open top that would have me laughing if I didn't catch myself in time.

"Mr. Handser." Arrie speaks in the most dignified way I've ever heard from him. It barely even sounds like him. "Just checking in to make sure all thirty-eight workers are prepared and ready for this evening. It's an important event."

The small man waves a hand at Arrie and then holds up a finger telling him to wait while his eyes, that so far have not looked up from the papers he's signing, lift slightly and startle at the sight of us. "Ah, Arrie, sir. I do apologize."

"No apologies necessary." Arrie tips his head slightly in way of thanks and stands straight.

"I spoke to the team lead for this evening this morning, and he personally assured me all thirty-seven of them will be . . ." He pauses, just noticing his error. "Thirty-eight?"

Arrie nods his head once. "Yes, thirty-eight. That is what Connie said when I left."

"You're sure?"

I step a little closer. "Yes. Thirty-eight. Heard it myself, and I have good hearing, like Connie."

The man gives me a confused look, as if to say who are you, but then backtracks on whatever he was about to say and sits back down. "I've scheduled you thirty-seven workers, as I have on the paperwork you submitted three days ago."

Arrie sighs. "Please don't make me go back to Connie with that message."

"I'm sorry." He holds up his hands. "I can't do anything this late. But you could always take a look around town and see if anyone wants some paid work for this evening?"

Arrie grumbles but concedes, and we find ourselves taking a walk around the same area of town I came shopping in all those weeks ago. It almost seems like a lifetime ago. We knock on a few doors, but most people are so startled by Arrie they can't even think, let alone offer up their evening to help us out.

I sigh as we turn our back on the fifteenth closed door. "Let's take a break." I lead us to that café from last time and order two ice-cream cakes (they sound amazing) as we sit down in the window seat.

Arrie sighs over a cup of his usual pumpkin latte, and I breathe a sigh relief over my extra-large cup of coffee. We continue our silent afternoon in the usually pleasant fashion, but Arrie seems a little tenser than earlier.

"Something wrong?"

He grumbles but doesn't say anything.

"C'mon, you might as tell me. You know I'll just annoy you until you give in."

He sighs (again), but is that a hint of a smile I see breaching the corners of his mouth? "Do you not find my company . . . unpleasant?"

I balk. "What? No. Why?"

"Most people feel the need to fill silence with conversation, and you're usually so chatty with the others."

"I like the silence with you. There's no expectation to talk or even think much of anything. I can just be. It's peaceful." I blush as I say those last words.

Arrie places his cup back on the saucer. "You find me . . . peaceful?"

"Yeah, I guess I do."

He smiles and then laughs, and I get that familiar sense of self-satisfaction I always get when I make him laugh. "Sorry, but finding the Horseman of War peaceful is . . ."

"Ridiculous?"

He nods.

"Then maybe people don't know you as well as they should."

Arrie seems to relax after that, and I'm really hoping that today and yesterday means I'm getting on the guy's good side, and we can start working on being friends.

The ice cream cakes are amazing, as is the mutually comfortable silence that ensues while we devour them.

At the counter as I go to pay, Arrie by my side with the payment chip ready, a friendly face says, "Still stayin' with the Horsemen?"

It's the baker from before, the one who made all those scrummy cakes for me and Connie on our gaming night.

"Indeed."

"What brings you out 'ere rather than exploring their mansion? Bet you haven't seen all it has to offer yet."

Arrie hands over the payment as I laugh.

"Well, we need an extra worker for tonight's party, and we were sent on an errand run, so here we are." I gesture to the two of us.

"You really need more workers?"

I nod.

"Me nephew is lookin' for some extra work to help pay for 'is wedding. I could ask?"

I look at Arrie, who smiles reassuringly in a way that I assume isn't supposed to look like a grimace. "Sure. That'd be great, actually."

The baker winks in my direction and loads up his chip's communication device before heading out back. We move aside to make way for the rest of the queue when some assistant replaces the baker. A few minutes later, he comes back out with a smiling face. "He said he'd love to 'elp. The usual party stuff, I assume?"

He directs that last question at Arrie, who nods. "Five pm start. Late finish. Working with a team of thirty-seven others."

"He'll be there. And thank you."

"Always happy to help," I call as we turn around to leave.

"You have more friends here than I do, Killer." Arrie smiles at that.

I just shrug. "It pays to have a chat with people now and then, you know."

He grumbles, and we head back in silence, satisfied that we fixed a problem we now don't have to report back to Connie. That would have been terrifying.

36

Turns out, Connie's hired us a hair and makeup stylist for the afternoon of getting ready so we can look our absolute best. The guys are doing their own thing, but this lady is extravagant to say the least. She's a Fae, so that's their way, but she's a little extra. And that's putting it nicely.

"Soooo, Connie, who's your little friend here?" she asks for the hundredth time. We keep trying to evade her question, because we a) don't know my name, and b) aren't supposed to discuss who I am.

Connie sighs, and I can see by the tense set of her shoulders that she's getting tired of this conversation. "She's just a new friend, Treeb. Now please drop it."

"A new friend you haven't taken your eyes off since I started doing her hair?" She raises her painted-on eyebrows up to her gold—literally the color of gold—hairline.

Connie smiles at that, clearly satisfied that this is a conversation she can at least navigate. She looks my way with questioning eyebrows, but I do and say nothing. "We're just friends."

Ah, so she's going with completely anonymous when it comes to telling people we're slightly more than . . . friends? Okay. I'm a little disappointed, but it's hard to ask the team to admit to themselves they want more out of their relationships, much less to others. This is probably just a standard line of answering for Connie.

"That's what you always say!" Treeb removes her hand from my hair and waves it in front of Connie's face.

"And that's what I'm going to continue saying." Connie sits on the edge of the bed, hair and makeup done but otherwise in her underwear. She wants us to show off our dresses together.

I'm just thankful I've managed to learn the whole shifting thing in time, otherwise I would be navigating a suit right now. Ugh.

A knock sounds at the door, a knock neither Connie nor I hear coming (which is the most surprising part), and I startle, causing Treeb to curse and yell at me to stay still.

Connie goes to answer it, saying, "The room is spelled to keep any and all sound out so I can sleep. Only Nine's telepathy can get through."

I go to nod, but one warning look from Treeb tells me I probably shouldn't if I value the current length of my hair. She held those scissors to Connie's hair with some force, and therefore, I don't let her anywhere near mine with them.

Dea comes in, not the least bit perturbed by Connie's underwear look (he's probably seen it all before; probably even taken it off a time or two), but stops dead when he sees me in a chair in nothing but my thin silk bathrobe. "Er," he stumbles, clearly not really sure what to say. "This is for you." He holds out a beautiful suit, and I sigh.

"I'm going like this, Dea." I roll my eyes.

"Yes, but when you change, you want to fit in, right?"

He's being cryptic, and Treeb clearly gets the not-supposed-to-know-anything message, as she blatantly ignores the conversation and continues working on my hair.

"I guess."

Connie grabs it from him and ushers him out of the room. "I'll make sure she looks great in both. Now get!" She shoves him a little harder than I would have expected, and he lands on his ass outside the bedroom door, where she slams the door in his face.

She hangs the suit on the back of the door, and I guess I will be navigating a suit after all. Fucking hell.

By the time Treeb's done and left and Connie and I have helped each other into our gowns, I have to change form and start the styling all over again.

Connie sighs exasperatedly. "God, you're lucky Fae look good anyway. Otherwise getting you ready for anything would take all bloody day."

She's applying some gel she stole from Nine to my hair, and I just let her get to work. We can't ask Treeb to do it without raising suspicion.

"Time for the suit." She grimaces, noticing how many golden buttons the front has. "This is gonna be a fucking nightmare, ain't it?"

"You're two thousand years old and you don't know how to put on a suit?"

"I know how." She folds her arms across her chest in defiance. "But I'm not the fluid Horseman here. I've never put one on myself."

"Good. Because I have no fucking clue."

She sighs and starts picking apart the suit, piece by piece, placing each section on me from the underwear up. Eventually, and after about half an hour of cursing and prodding, I'm ready to go.

"Change back and forth for me."

She steps back, and I focus on relaxing and changing my form, managing to turn back into my female-self with ease (well, with about five minutes of concentrating). As it turns out, my look from earlier has survived the shifting. Must shift into whatever look my other form had on previously.

"Good." Connie holds out her arm, and I tuck mine around hers as we head out of her room.

We descend the fancy stairs, where all three guys wait for us, and I manage to have my first fairy-tale ball moment as they all stare at us—me in particular—with open mouths.

Even Arrie's eyes linger on my face without a scowl longer than usual, but it isn't long before he rips his gaze away and rests it on Connie's beautiful smile beside me.

Arrie whisks Connie off, muttering how beautiful she looks into her ear so no one can hear it—though I clearly can—and I'm left with Nine and Dea, who wait on either side of me when I get to the bottom of the stairs, both holding out their arms.

Dea wraps his left arm underneath my right while leaning in and whispering, "You look beautiful, Angel."

Nine, on the other hand, wraps his right arm underneath my left and mentally whispers, *You'll be turning heads tonight, Sweetie. Even Arrie stumbled at the sight of you.*

"He was probably stumbling at the sight of Connie, Nine. Trust me on that."

He gives me a look that says he's not believing a word out of my mouth. Dea, thankfully, stays out of the conversation, as he often does where Nine and I are concerned. It's nice that he gives us time to just be . . . friends. In fact, they're all pretty good at sharing time with each other. Guess practice makes perfect.

Nine and Dea are both dressed in suits that match them perfectly. Nine's wearing a dark brown suit with a red tie and an off-white shirt, while Dea is sporting a Victorian-style black suit that has a floral design in black silk covering its entirety, matched with a top hat, pocket watch chain, fancy black cane with a gold head, and a frilly vest-y neck thing that matches his pocket's hanky thing.

Goddess, this suit nonsense is ridiculous. But he looks very Dea-like, and only he can pull off a suit like that. Being around him, especially dressed like this, is like being around someone pulled straight out of a Victorian romance novel. It's all very swoon-worthy, and by the smug look on his face, he damn well knows it.

"What do you look like in yours?" Nine asks, a slight blush creeping across his cheeks.

"My suit?" I turn my head his way, making sure I understand the question.

"Yeah." He scratches his head in befuddlement and adjusts his suit jacket for the third time since walking down the hallway. He clearly hates wearing suits.

"You'll see later. I'm most likely going to be changing back and forth all damn evening. So, if you wanted to hang out with any particular version of me, just watch out for the magically sex-changing person in the room." I roll my eyes, trying not to let my sarcasm drown my voice.

While I'm comfortable in both forms—a comfortability that came surprisingly quickly —and I know the team have adjusted well so far, I have yet to see the general public's reaction. Historically speaking, the general populace are not ones to be well-adjusted to categorical things such as this.

"Try not to let it bother you, Angel. We like both your forms." He gestures to Nine when he says we and gives me a wink.

Ah, I see where he's going with that. I wonder which form they prefer? I mean, I can really use that to my advantage if I'm serious about bringing the team together.

That's just mean.

Using every tool at your disposal is not mean. It's just being clever. You use your telepathy to flirt with me all the time.

Fair point, he says in an amused tone.

We get to the archway that signals the entrance to the ballroom, and I pause. The room is full of people—not too full, just enough to make it look like a fancy ball without it being too crowded. Some make small talk on the fringes, some hide out in the shadowy corners the candle flames don't illuminate but my Vampire eyesight can identify, but most of the crowd are dancing. And not just any kind of dancing, but ballroom dancing.

I . . . er . . . don't think I can dance.

"It's okay. We didn't expect you to."

"What is the matter, Angel? You looked perturbed?" Dea spins me around to face him, and the sight of those galaxy eyes lit by the iridescent candles makes me take a gasp.

Nine comes up behind me and sandwiches me between them, and I'm acutely aware of a few people near the entrance watching us.

"I can't dance. I don't think. At least not like that."

Dea ponders for a moment. "Hmmm." He brings a hand to his chin in thought and leans in closer. "Then, I will just have to teach you."

"Wha—?"

But before I can finish the question, he whisks me away to the center of the dancefloor and stops. "Place your left hand on my shoulder and your right on my arm."

I do as instructed, hoping no one can hear us—well, no one but Nine and Connie.

He places a hand on the small of my back and another on my shoulder. "Just follow me and try not to step on my toes."

I restrain a laugh, but he smiles anyway. "For future reference, you guys should tell me when I need to do stuff like this, so I can practice and not make a fool of myself."

"Duly noted."

He moves us around in circles on the spot for a bit, before he moves to the center of the dancefloor, weaving in and out of other couples who apparently know exactly what they're doing, and I only step on his toes a few times. Mostly, I use my Vampire speed to keep up with his fancy footwork.

I don't take my eyes off of his, though, and by the time the music's changed, I find myself not wanting to let go of this beautiful man.

"Could we dance some more?"

"Of course." He smiles at me, and we continue in a different style of dance that suits the new song.

The music's being played by a group of fairies and Fae who each hold different types of instruments, switching them between songs so they can get the right texture. This one is more of a stringed song, and is being played by some violins, a harp, and cello, with a beautiful female singer at the front whose voice holds magic within her notes. Or, at least, it sounds that way. But I'm pretty sure no such magic exists.

Someone comes up behind me when we stop and coughs.

Turning around, I notice Nine holding out his arm. "May I have this dance?"

"Of course." I look to Dea, who looks at us both and turns to walk away.

Nine watches him leave and says, "He's an amazing dancer. Not quite as good as Arrie, but he fits the mood more for these types of things."

"Wait. Hold up. Arrie can dance?"

"Sure." Nine smiles. "He even incorporates it into his morning workouts, I believe."

Oh, that's right. He did seem rather flowing and dancelike when I watched him that time. It'd be great to dance with him sometime.

He'd ask you if you ever let him.

"No, he won't. But that's okay." I take a deep breath and let Nine waltz me around the dancefloor, careful to avoid any of the other dancing pairs. "We've managed an amicable, working friendship, I think. That'll do for now."

"Friendship, 'ey?"

"I damn well hope so. At the least, he doesn't seem angry with me as much."

"Well, that's progress."

We continue to dance for a few more songs, and just like with Dea, the attractive man in front of me dazzles, but unlike with Dea, Nine knows it. He knows that I find the way the light bounces off his red hair to be enrapturing, and so he circles us more toward the candlelight, and he knows that I enjoy being pressed up against him in some of the closer sections, so he presses me flush at every chance he gets.

He knows exactly what I like about him, and it makes it hard not to fall into his every step and move, to become enthralled by his presence and send myself into a daze of lust and . . . feelings.

Just when I think the evening is going great, Dea steps up behind me and places a hand on my shoulder. "It is time, Angel."

I wince and step away from them both, nodding. It's time to show the world that the Fifth Horseman really exists. I can do this. Right? I mean, nothing bad is going to happen this night? No one's going to try to attack me for simply existing?

Dea takes me by the arm while Nine follows, and we head for the stage. Connie and Arrie join us moments later, and we send the musicians off the stage while Dea takes to the microphone. He's been visible for all of one hour, and he doesn't have much time left to enjoy it. The sooner we get this part over with, the sooner he can enjoy the party.

"Thank you for joining us here tonight," Dea announces.

Everyone turns toward us and crowds around the stage.

"You might be wondering why we gathered the heads of the magical and non-magical communities together in one place, especially since it has not been done in quite some time." Dea gestures to me, and I come to stand by his side, the rest of the team forming an arc behind us. "We have an important announcement to make."

Everyone's silent—even I hold my breath. But looking over the crowd, I can't recognize many faces, other than the ones I met on the mission and Kally from earlier in a bright orange dress that perfectly matches the color of her lips. I recognize most of the Vampire Royal Council, including the three princes I've met, and I recognize all the Witch's Coven, but I note that the seer is missing.

"Nine months ago, the team was made aware of a special someone who recently died. We would like to introduce you to the Fifth Horseman, the Horseman of Magic."

Everyone's stunned silent for a moment, but the whispers and gasps erupt seconds later, and before we know it, everyone is shouting questions. The biggest being why did we lie to them all recently.

Dea hushes everyone and continues. "We apologize for lying on our recent travels, but we wanted to get a feel for things before people made the connection. Horsemen are only born when there is a need."

What few whispers there are die instantly.

"That is right. War is coming. A war requiring the Horsemen of the Apocalypse—all five of us—to fix. We have been keeping things steady for years, but for some reason, Fate decided we needed extra help."

"How do you know she's the Fifth Horseman?" someone from the crowd shouts. By the looks of his golden eyes, I would say he's a Shifter.

"That," Nine says as he grabs the microphone from Dea, "is why we waited to have this ball. We wanted to her to be able to show you her powers for herself."

Everyone nods their agreement, clearing seeing the logic, and I get the impression it's time for me to do my thing.

Dea and Nine step back, allowing me to take center stage. I don't want to give a speech, so I don't. Instead, I produce my first power: air magic. I can't access the rest of the elements yet, but I can still create a whirlwind that sends the room into darkness and start a mini-tornado above the crowd's heads.

The candles are quickly relit—I assume by some fire Witch—and I focus on the memory of blood and feeding to produce my fangs.

The audience gasps, and I know I look like a less-pale Vampire hybrid.

I sit on the floor, cross-legged as much as I can in this dress, and breathe. I hear the crowd growing restless as they wait for something to happen, and murmuring conversations start up a couple of minutes in. I want to yell at them to shut the hell up, but I know it won't help. What will help is changing form.

Eventually, after minutes of insufferable inner-peace finding, I feel the familiar tug of my magic changing my form. I don't vomit (thank the goddess), but I do revel in the gasps and audible what-the-hells from the audience.

Using Fae magic, I bring a few of the candles from the wall to me in midair and dance them above everybody's heads. I hope that's enough and that the lack of wind will distinguish it enough from my earlier magic. But it's the next display of powers that has them leaping back and shouting yells of surprise.

I first shift into a wolf, then my preferred form of a panther, then into a couple of birds I've mastered, and then into a few insects—of which, Nine gathers me into his palm to demonstrate I haven't just vanished into thin air.

Coming back into my male form—and then returning back to my female form—the questions begin.

"So, she's . . . he's one of us? All of us?"

"Do we refer to her and a she or a he?"

"She belongs nowhere, then?"

"Does she have an allegiance?"

Dea steps forward with the microphone once more. "Please, enough. We understand this is troubling. We understand that having someone who is clearly meant to balance you all is a threat to quite a few ways of life in this room." He takes a deep breath. "You know us. We would not threaten you or your way of life unnecessarily. We have served and helped you for two millennia. That has not changed."

A few heads nod, clearly agreeing with Dea, but a few look disgruntled, angry almost, and it's those faces I try to memorize. Those are the people we have to worry about.

Half an hour later, Dea takes me by the hand and leads me out of the ballroom and into the house—the part of the house guests can't enter. The team's home.

He takes a deep breath, and I can see the physical exertion being visible for so long has had on him: he's donned a light sheet of sweat on his forehead, and his skin is paler than usual.

"Dea?" He looks at me from his place on the kitchen chair. "You can go back to being invisible for a while here. Please, don't exert yourself."

He chuckles lightly. "Do not worry yourself over such an insignificant problem, Angel. I am fine."

"Don't be a fucking idiot. Just relax for a moment." I place a hand on his shoulder and squeeze hard enough it causes him to wince but light enough that I don't actually cause any serious pain. "Turn. It. Off."

He sighs. "Fine." Taking a deep breath, he exhales, and the color returns to his cheeks almost immediately, and his eyes sparkle brighter. "There."

I give a firm nod and remove my hand. "That's better." Taking the chair beside him, I place a hand on his knee. "You okay?"

"Just needed a moment."

Then why bring me?

It'll probably be best to give him his moment and remain silent, hoping he'll appreciate it as much as Arrie and I do.

"You were amazing this evening, Angel."

"Thank you."

"Are you enjoying yourself?"

"It's . . . amazing." I smile. "I never thought I'd be in a scenario like this."

"When all this is over"—he lowers his gaze to me—"I am going to show you the world, show you a life worth living forever. It is not all doom and gloom."

"That sounds nice. Can the others join us?"

He chuckles. "Yes, of course. If you would like."

"I would."

"Even Arrie?"

I sigh. "Assuming our current peace keeps up forever, then yes."

"Is he included in your so-called plan Nine mentioned?"

I wince. "He told you about that?"

Dea stays silent but grabs me by the hand and leads me through various hallways; clearly there isn't a destination, but we continue walking nonetheless.

"If I am honest, the thought has crossed my mind before. But I was not sure it would work." We stop outside my bedroom door, and he pins me where I stand with those wanderlust eyes and pushes me up against the door. "But everything is different now." His voice turns husky, and it makes me shiver in anticipation.

He has me locked between his two arms, palms spread out on the door beside my head.

"How?"

"Because we have you."

He leans closer, and I can't help but lean out to meet him halfway. His presence is overbearing, and his smoky lavender scent has my head spinning in various directions; logic is all but evaporating from my brain, leaving just the curiosity and building need for a man I've wanted for weeks but couldn't have.

His lips crash against mine, and I sigh in relief. All of my need and desire spilling over. But this isn't a quick or gentle kiss, this is Dea full of need and passion that I didn't realized he held for me unleashing all at once. He pins me to the door with his body, his hips trapping my lower torso to the wood behind me, and trails one hand down my waist, where he slips it behind to rest on the small of my back, and presses my body against his. His other hand rests behind my head, pulling my lips closer to his until we're a tangle of passion.

When he slips his tongue across my lower lip, tingling need shoots through my body. Dea takes advantage of the distraction and slides his tongue into my mouth to meet mine, and I can't help but buckle slightly, feeling weak at the knees. Dea catches me, of course, and pins me to the door once more.

I groan, making his hand in my hair grip tighter.

But I need more. I can feel his growing erection pressing into my lower stomach, and the hot need growing there matches my own. I need more. More of him. More of this. My thighs shift, trying to gain any kind of friction to release the growing tension.

Dea notices and lets out a small chuckle as we break for air. But the spell doesn't break with it; instead, I grab his shirt and yank him forward, slamming my mouth against his once more and lifting my hands to tangle in his hair.

He groans into the kiss, causing my hands to travel under his shirt and trace all the lines of his muscles, gently raking my nails down his front to the hem of his pants.

His hands travel south to my ass, and before I know it, he's lifting me up against the door and wrapping my legs around his waist, my core lining up with that delicious heat of his.

"Dea," I warn, breaking the kiss suddenly.

He places a finger on my lips. "Shhhh. Relax. We are not going there today. Just enjoy the moment with me."

I nod. Honestly, I'm done holding back with this man. Everything about him draws me in, and he currently has me backed up against my bedroom door, legs wrapped around his middle as he holds my weight with a single hand on my ass, leaving the other free to roam. He well and truly has me pinned.

I can feel his cock pressing against my clit gently, not moving but creating a whirlwind of pressure I need to release lest I explode. I buck my hips against him, and he groans in response, pulling away from my face slightly as he looks at me in question.

"Dea . . . Please."

I've lost all sense of the plan, all sense of what I feel is wrong and right in that moment, and am driven by something far less logical.

My hips continue to grind against him, and I watch him struggle to retain control; what I wouldn't give to watch this man break that carefully mastered control, to watch him come undone by my hand.

He places needy kisses along my jaw and down my neck, landing in a sensitive spot on the crook of my neck that has me moaning his name on a gasp of air.

"Dea . . ."

"Angel . . ." he gasps. "I want nothing more than to hear you moaning my name all night, but I know that is not what you want right now."

Lowering me to the floor and pulling away, he looks at me with pained restraint. I'm disappointed but thankful one of us is able to use our brains in a logical manner.

"I . . . I'm sorry." I look to the floor, embarrassment flooding my features. I can't believe I just did that.

Dea grabs my chin and lifts it to meet his eyes. "Do not apologize. You are amazing." He bores those galaxy eyes into mine, and I understand what he means; he wants me to know that he enjoyed himself, too.

He grabs my hand and leads me back to the party, where we quickly break apart and rejoin the fun.

I stand at the edge of the ballroom, Dea having vanished the moment we entered the first thrall of people, where I'm hidden in the shadows only few can see. I change into my male form as I watch the party—specifically, I watch Connie and Arrie dance the night away. I've never seen her smile so brightly, nor have I seen Arrie so relaxed. I have to wonder if it's Connie causing that reaction or the dancing. Maybe a bit of both?

"Hey, Sweetie. Watcha doing way out here?"

"Observing." I have a glass of champagne in hand, though I'm only drinking it because everyone else is—have to at least try to fit in.

Nine stands beside me and looks down my line of sight. "Ah. Observing Connie?"

"Observing them both, really. Not in a bad way, just in a curious one."

"What's so curious about them that has you hiding in the dark to observe them?"

He grabs my champagne and downs it in one before leaving the glass on a server's tray that floats past, courtesy of Fae magic.

"Nothing I want to voice. Nothing to be concerned about."

"This about your plans for the future of the team by any chance?"

I look at him and have to quickly look away. "Maybe." I cough out the tension in my throat. "It's just a fantasy. But an entertaining one."

"I don't know. You have a way of just existing that's intoxicating. The way you think so freely about emotions and love is almost beautiful. You're also annoyingly stubborn. Don't peg it as a fantasy just yet."

That's saying a lot more than normal for Nine. He knows everyone's thoughts and feelings, usually before they know them themselves, so, if he thinks I stand a chance in the long run—of making myself and the team happy—then I have an honest chance.

"Besides," he continues, "I like the effect you're having on us."

I look at him confused, but he doesn't elaborate, and I get the feeling he's referring to his private conversation with Dea. I wonder what the damn hell they talked about after I left, but I don't want to ask and ruin anything, and if Nine wants me to know, he'll tell me.

"Let's get some air, shall we?" Nine takes my arm just like he did when I was in my female form and leads me through the edges of the crowd and out onto the balcony that leads to some stairs I didn't noticed before.

We descend with ease and enter a secluded section of the garden I've never been in. "Where are we?"

"It's just a cute, cut-off section of the garden. You can only get here through the ballroom."

"Ah, I see."

"There are more nooks and hiding places in this house than you'll be able to fully explore in the next hundred years, trust me."

"It's like a child's hide-and-seek dream."

He laughs and slips an arm around my waist. "That it would be."

I raise an eyebrow. "Never once had a child here? Not even a child of one of the cleaners or servants?"

"God, no. Children are . . . difficult."

Now it's my turn to laugh, and I stop us at a water fountain shaped like a pair of doves to do just that. "Seriously?" I wipe a tear from my eye. "You're the Horseman of Famine, and you're uncomfortable around children?" I can't stop laughing, and I kinda feel bad, but the scenario is ridiculous. "It's just so . . . You fight wars and basically run the world, but children are a step too far?"

Nine smiles, clearly finding my amusement funny. "They're just not something I have an awful lot of practice with."

He turns away from me slightly, and I get the feeling he's a little offended by my laughing, so I turn him back around and make him face me. "Is everything okay? Did I upset you? I'm sorry—"

He holds up a hand. "No. You didn't upset me. Sorry."

"Then, what—?"

He doesn't let me finish that question, as he leans forward and presses the gentlest kiss to my lips, hard enough to leave a slight tingle that has me brushing my thumb over its shadow, but light enough that I would have barely felt it had I not known what he was doing.

Grabbing my arm once more, he continues walking us around the garden, past more fairy patches, glowing flowers, singing vines, and a few more fountains shaped like various pairs of mated birds, and I have to admit that this is turning into the perfect night.

Dancing with Dea, then Nine, showing off my powers was nerve-wracking, but making out with Dea was something else, and then watching Connie and Arrie having a good time and coming out here. It's all so . . .

Romantic?

"Yes."

"These things are supposed to feel like that. It was the main form of socializing for the upper classes at one point. Romances were made, flings were had . . . They were a thing of the time, I guess."

"Do you miss it?"

"The time?"

I nod.

"Yes and no. Time moves on, and each new era is more interesting than the last."

"It's something I'm looking forward to. Being able to see how the world evolves and moves." I snake my arm around his waist and move closer (a little more confident now I know for sure he likes this form, too). "There will be things that are hard"—my mind instantly goes to having no family and being alone for so long—"but just for this evening, I want to focus on the things I'm looking forward to. I'll deal with the rest later."

"You have all the time in the world, Sweetie." Nine shuffles on his feet and looks from me to the fountain. "Erm . . . sorry to change the subject, but how are your nightmares?"

I blanch and take a step back. "Ho-how . . . ?" He taps his head, as if to remind me he can read minds, and I sigh. "They're okay," I whisper. Now that I think about it, I haven't really had any since before we went to Earth. "They've stopped. For now." But I get the feeling they'll come back, and when they do, I'll have to deal with them.

"When they do," Nine says on a low whisper, "I can help."

I look at him with a puzzled expression, silently asking him how.

"I can enter people's dreams and help guide them through. Eventually, we might be able to pinpoint the problem and try to stop them altogether."

"Entering people's dreams?" That's . . . absurd. Out of all the things I've seen this team do, that is the most insane. Well, it's definitely up there.

Nine nods. "I don't often do it because it's so invasive, but I can if you ever need my help." He grabs my hand and looks me in the eyes. "Don't hide your problems because of some sense of duty to the world. I care." He gestures to the house, where the team are probably still dancing away. "We care."

I don't know what to say to that, so I just nod. Hoping to convey my gratitude with a kiss to the cheek rather than words.

38

"Well, well, well. Look who we have here," someone's deep baritone voice penetrates the darkness. Out of the corner of my eye, I see a trio of people dressed in fancy suits walking toward us—armed with magiguns (because of course).

Nine grabs my arm and pushes me behind him, causing me to roll my eyes. "Really?"

They're from that same Vampire clan that attacked us in New Orleans.

Wait, what? They are?

They descend a few feet to stand in front of us as more than a dozen other people—Vampires, I now realize—come out from the shadows.

How did I not see them?

I step out from behind Nine to stand at his side, wishing like hell I had some kind of weaponry in this bloody suit. If it's gonna restrict my movements, I should at least be able to kick some ass with a few throwing knives.

"What do you want?" Nine asks, going to step forward once again and in front of me, but I stop him by yanking his arm backward.

"Her." The Vampire in front jerks his chin toward me. "Or him." Waving a hand in the air, he says, "Or whatever it wants to be called."

"It?" I ask, surprised I've been deemed less than human already. "I am not an *it*, you overgrown bat."

Nine snickers beside me, but his face remains serious. "Yeah," he says, "that's not happening."

I've alerted everyone else.

Good. Now be careful and move out of my way.

He raises an eyebrow at me but steps to the side just in time to avoid me shifting into a panther.

The Vampires balk but stand straight and face me. They're brave, I'll give them that. But bravery is often stupid.

I leap off the ground and swipe a paw at the leader's face, gouging an eye out in the process. We tumble to the ground, but he manages to get off a shot from his magigun in time to send me sprawling backward and crashing into Nine.

"Get off!" He shouts from beneath me.

When I move, he sucks in a deep breath of air and jumps to his feet in a quick jump.

Stay out of my line of sight.

Okay.

I stand behind him, with every Vampire in front, and he raises his hand in the air and mutters something under his breath I can't hear.

Every Vampire in front of us stops dead in their tracks, but the leader just looks at Nine and smiles. "Not gonna work, Famine. Sorry."

"What?" I hear him gasp. "Ho-how?"

The leader pulls out a silver leaf from his pocket and crumbles it into dust to let it fly in the wind.

"For fuck's sake," Nine grumbles. "Should never had told them that."

"Silver Vine. Telepathy blocker," the leader answers as he looks at me, clearly responding to my confused face.

Telepathy blocker? Wow. That must really piss Nine off.

You have no fucking idea, Sweetie. I'm unarmed, you can't change back into your other form to use your air magic while under attack, and your Fae magic is too untrained to be useful.

Ah. We're fucking screwed, aren't we?

You'd think two of the Five Horsemen couldn't go down like this.

We're not going down, stop being ridiculous.

I shift into a falcon and swoop toward the back of the Vampires and claw out a few more eyes, hoping if they can't see, it'll give us some kind of advantage. The leader only has one eye now, and honestly, seeing the socket bleed all down his face is more satisfying than I expected.

Dea, Connie, and Arrie are on their way, so we just have to hold them off long enough. But where's Dea? Why hasn't he fazed here?

No idea. But it can't be good. He's not responding.

I grumble but shift back into human beside Nine, hoping for some kind of princess rescue from Connie. She'll slay these fuckers into pieces if they even try to mess with the team, and I'll laugh alongside her.

Damn. You two are dark.

We have seventeen Vampires in front of us, each of them armed with magiguns—although my last wound healed when I shifted—the leader only has one eye left, and a few of the others are blind, but otherwise, we're still where we started.

The leader steps forward, aiming his magigun straight at me. "This won't kill ya, but it will cause some damage. Hopefully you'll come along quietly after."

The rest of the Vampires crowd around Nine, and between them all, they have him pinned against the fountain.

Fuck! Run!

But if I turn around now—in my non-Vampire speed form—I'll likely get shot.

I stand with my hands in the air for a few moments, trying to think of what to do. But, really, there's only one thing I can do. Fight.

I spread my arms wide and imagine my body turning into a bear. I've never tried it before, but desperate times and all that.

A roar escapes my lips as my body twists into its new form, and I have no time to check if I managed it because I have to jump out of the way of the Vampire's magigun, and I barrel into him from the side.

The Vampire goes sprawling with a twist but quickly gets back up again. Vampires are fast healers, and they're pretty strong, so it'll take a lot to bring this guy down. If I were in my other form, I could just blow him away or rip his throat out, but in this form, I'm limited to Shifter abilities.

I need to fucking work on my Fae powers when this all blows over. Would be great to know a few destructive spells right now.

"You fucking bitch!" the Vampire snarls. A few of his cronies step forward to try to help, but he holds his hand up. "Nah, I got this."

Raising his magigun once again, I shift into a bird and flit around his head, hoping to minimize my target size and stay on the move.

"C'mon, bitch. Fight like a man. Stop being a coward!"

Does he really think that'll work? The whole world can call me a coward if it saves my life.

He takes a shot and clips my wing, sending me spiraling to the ground, but I shift back into a panther just in time. The wound heals almost instantly, and I leap onto the fucking asshole, hoping to do some damage with my claws.

"Taylor!" someone shouts from the distance. "Taylor!" A man leaps from the balcony and shifts midair into a panther, landing right beside me.

Who is he?

I can see Nine slumped on the fountain with blood trailing down his face. Nine! He looks unconscious, and likely has been for a few minutes, but that's ridiculous considering the rate at which we heal.

The new panther snarls and leaps at the Vampire, and I follow suit. He takes down that Vampire leader with a single swipe to the face, clawing his head clean off his shoulders.

Fuck me! I'm glad to have this guy on my side. His panther form is three times the size of mine, and right now, I'm glad for it.

I leap into the fray of the dozen or so Vampires guarding Nine and snarl, swipe, and claw at as many of them as I can. None of them go down, and I realize just how fucking untrained I am. But a few of them step back, leaving themselves open for the new panther to dispatch.

If Nine were armed, he could help.

As if my wish has been heard, Nine leaps to his feet and steals a magigun from one of the Vampires and takes out three in a row quicker than I can blink.

Damn. You're amazing.

Thank you, he winces. He slinks to the ground beside the fountain.

He's hurt.

Why aren't his wounds healing?

I shift back into human form and crouch beside him. "Nine?"

The other panther shifts into a man, and I concentrate enough to shift into my female form so I can at least try to help heal Nine with my semi-Vampire blood. I rip open my wrist and let it pool into his mouth, watching as it slides down his throat.

Please, please, please let this work.

Nothing happens.

"What isn't it working?"

"He's been shot with these bullets," the man says as he holds one up to the moonlight to it. "They're made with Silver Vine leaves. Toxic to Famine in particular. Seems this was planned."

I take a good look at the man's face as he holds up on of those bullets and recognize him, but I can't quite place where from.

What? I almost shriek but refrain.

"Taylor?"

Is he speaking to me?

"Who's Taylor?"

He looks at me with surprise. "You are."

My breath refuses to come out, but one more look at a struggling Nine and I know I have to take him to Dea. "C'mon," I say as I scoop Nine up and carry him bridal-style back into the ballroom.

I'm met with gasps and murmurs as I walk through the double doors, but nothing is more shocking than Connie, Dea, and Arrie stopping their dancing to turn around in shock.

"You've been dancing?" My outrage clearly takes them by surprise. "We needed you!"

Arrie is the first to understand what's happened. "Everyone out! Go home!" His voice carries like nothing I've ever heard, booming across the doomed room.

Guests clear away in a hurry, leaving the ballroom empty except for us five and my mystery savior.

"What happened?" Dea asks as he takes in Nine's body slumped in my arms and tries to grab him from me. But I refuse to let go. "What. Happened?"

Eventually, I let his body go to Dea. "We were ambushed by the same Vampires from New Orleans. They're all dead in the garden."

Arrie raises an eyebrow at me in question.

"Not me. Him." I jerk a thumb back to the mystery savior and kneel beside Nine, who's now lying at Dea's feet.

Everyone looks up at the Shifter behind me and stands stock still.

Connie steps forward with an outstretched hand. "Mr. Compton. We are in your debt."

He shakes his head. "Anything for Taylor." He gestures to me, and everyone immediately shuts up.

I stand, really needing some answers from this guy. "You keep calling me that. You . . . knew me?"

"Very well." He grabs a glass of champagne from a floating tray nearby and comes back to join us. "You are Taylor Angelis. You are—were—last of the Angel-descended Witches. And my goddaughter."

I balk, my eyes going wide. "No."

Connie comes to rest a hand on my shoulder. "It's oka—"

"No!" I shrug her hand off my shoulder and walk up to this Mr. Compton guy. "Tell me everything." I grab him by the shirt collar and yank him to me. "Now."

He nods.

Dea's healing Nine as best he can while Connie stays by my side as I sink to the floor, needing to feel the stability of something solid.

He's about to tell me everything.

"Taylor Angelis, last of the Angel-descended Witches. You were born twenty-five years ago to your parents, who loved you dearly. Your powers grew stronger and stronger by the day, and before everyone knew it, you could kill with a single touch. Your parents were both Angel descendants, too, but they didn't possess your level of power. Unfortunately, word got out in the magical community, and the SC sent a hit out on you. But when the hunters came, they killed both your parents. You alone survived."

"How?"

The man looks to Dea, but Dea's so focused on Nine he isn't even listening to the story. "Your mother gave you an invisibility charm, one of very few in existence. It hid you until it was safe."

That grabs Dea's attention. He looks to me and then to Mr. Compton, and just shakes his head, uttering, "It's a small world."

"That was your charm, wasn't it?"

He nods and continues working on Nine. He needs a lot more healing than usual, and I can see it's taking a lot out of Dea, who's starting to sweat and go pale like earlier.

"I took you to a Witch community and set you up with some friends of mine. They looked after you, loved you."

"Why do I get the feeling there's more to this story?"

He grimaces. "You had a difficult start to life. You hated magic with a vengeance. You refused to use yours, despite the good it could do, and grew up a normal human, for all intents and purposes. But it didn't stay that way. One day you came to me with some news I didn't like. I didn't say anything back then, but now I wish I had."

"What aren't you saying? Just spit it out!" My hands ball into fists, shaking and clenching in the cooling air.

"Taylor . . . You were a hunter for the SC. The only supernatural in their employ."

I laugh, not really sure if I should be upset, infuriated, or if this is a joke. "There's no way I was a hunter. They take people to the SC for prosecution, often to be killed."

He nods.

"You're serious?"

He nods again, his eyes looking straight at mine.

No. It can't be . . . "I killed supernaturals—my own kind—for a living?"

Arrie grumbles something that sounds like, "Told you you were a killer."

I throw myself at him before anyone can stop me. I ball my fist and throw a right hook to his face, sending him flying across the room. "I am not a killer."

Connie takes one look at me and flinches, turning around. Ugh. Great. Between Nine's blood and the anger, my fangs have come out.

"Sweetie . . ."

"Nine!" I turn around and run to him. "Nine." I grab his hand, holding it to mine. "Are you okay?"

He nods and places a hand on my cheek. "Oh, Sweetie, what you were isn't relevant. None of us cares."

I flick my gaze toward Arrie, and he flinches and storms out of the room.

"Even him." Nine coughs as hesits up, and Dea holds his weight. "Promise."

I'm weak. I haven't fed in days, and the scent of Nine's blood is everywhere. No one's in the right shape to help me with that right now, so I take a shuddering breath and try to rein myself in, trying—in vain—to retract my fangs so I can turn back around and smile at Connie.

But it isn't enough. I've used lots of magic in the fight, and unlike when I first started using my powers, I'm now used to the extra power blood gives me. It has, without me realizing it, become my new norm.

"Fuck it," I mumble as I sprint to my rooms, away from everyone else, where I lock myself in my library, vowing to stay until I can be bothered to come out.

"Fuck!" I kick a stack of books and watch them fall to the ground in a splutter. "I was a hunter."

PREQUEL SHORT STORY

1

The soul of the young child in front of me fizzled as it left her body, a black matted mess of incorporeal tethers knotted to the base of her lifeline. Stuck. Some magical souls were like that, determined not to let go. But that was what I was here for.

Reaching forward with the scythe gifted me from the otherworld upon birth, I tore the last remaining holds of humanity from her grasp. The scream that ripped from her soul reverberated through the air and pounded at my ears, but I didn't flinch. Two thousand years and dealing with the stuck souls of children never got any easier.

Her small lifeless body rested in frozen terror on the harsh rabbled concrete of the shopping center's parking lot while her mother screamed at anyone to help. But it was five am, and there wasn't another living being in sight, magical or otherwise. Her bloodied hands fumbled with the datascreen hovering in front of her trembling face, trying to phone for help, but it was pointless; the young girl's datachip imbedded in her wrist had been flashing red for the past thirty seconds, and her soul now held on to one of the feathers of my angel wings with a placid face that gave no emotion.

"Come on, little one." I sighed. "Let me take you to the gates."

She didn't nod or smile or let any sort of sign of acknowledgement slip, but as I turned to fly away, her soul's hand gripped mine, and she came willingly. They always did.

We flew up past the atmosphere and into the stratosphere, where the clouds below looked like small bundles of candy floss that had lost their flavour, and where it was airless and cold, to the point where the tips of my feathers had started to freeze. But still we travelled on.

Following the familiar prickling feeling in my chest, I led us both to the pair of floating black gates that to anyone else would look ominous and foreboding. But I knew better. Because I was the one being who had been beyond and returned safely to the land of the living. As the Horseman of Death, it was my job.

The gates opened for us without a sound in the near-vacuumed space, and I looked to the little girl still holding on to me with a smile. "Go on now." Her color had started to return on the journey here, and she looked less like a ghost and more like the human child she once resembled, with rosy cheeks and one front tooth missing amongst a splatter of messy blonde hair. "This is where you belong."

She nodded and let go, letting the magical current tethering her to the beyond float her soul across the gate's boundary and into the afterlife.

"What a day," I said on a sigh—or tried to. Talking didn't really work this far up. "Time to go home and—"

Pain shot through my entire body as my wings shook. My magic flew out of me in a rush of red so bright I had a hard time keeping my eyes open. My body flared hotter and hotter until my wing feathers started to fall off and my skin started to burn.

I loosed a silent scream as I tried to control my magic. Reign it in.

What was happening to me?

My magic usually glowed green, but in my Angel of Death form, it had always glowed an evil shade of red that I detested. Nothing made a guy look more terrifying that feathered black wings and sparking red magic. Trust me.

A white pulsing ball of magic floating in front of my face made my heart beat faster, no matter how controlled I attempted to keep my breathing. It grew in size until it floated to the size of a football in front of my chest. I would be scared, since this had never happened in the last two thousand years of existence, but that ball of magic felt so . . . warm. As though I could grab it and let it guide me home.

Reaching out, my hand hovered above its warmth for a moment before it tapped my palm, like a scared horse giving me permission to pet it, and engulfed my hand. It tingled, though not painfully; rather, it was like a pleasant relaxant that made my muscles unclench after a hard day's work.

As it worked its way up my arm, slowly encasing more of me, I felt more and more like this strange use of my magic would guide me home. To safety. So when it pulled me in a singular determined direction, I didn't struggle. I went willingly. Knowing no harm would come to me.

I flew back to earth with ease, air finally gulping into my lungs in heave-full breaths. I didn't need to breathe, considering I was immortal, but it felt bloody good to inhale that sweet oxygen anyway. It was just brokering morning when I landed on the streets of Tokyo—the first place my new magic guided me—and people were already up and starting their days. No one saw me, of course, because I was the only Horseman to be invisible, but it was nice to mingle with other beings anyway.

In the corner of a nearby alley, four shifter children (foxes, I believed) played a racing game on their datachips while waiting for more of their friends; on the only occupied table outside a cute new-age café sat a pristine-looking woman and a young man who both looked to be on a breakfast date; and walking down the street beside me were countless school children and businessmen in uniforms and suits on their way to school and work.

But the magic pointed to one woman in particular. One woman, I hastened add, who would catch anybody's eye with her short, bright pink hair and her zombie-rabbit t-shirt with cut-off shorts and knee-high boots that sculpted a well-muscled body.

It was her my magic was pointing to. But she was still alive.

2

I tried to walk in the other direction, to get away from this woman and go home, but my magic flared red hot again and redirected me toward the pink-haired girl. Curious, and more than a little a stuck without knowing how to turn off this new radar feature that had glued itself to this girl, I followed her through back-alleys, over fences, and around the shadiest parts of Shinjuku as she kept her eyes and ears alert, clearly worried someone was following her.

I kept an eye out, too. Just in case.

She looked paranoid—looked the type, too. But you never knew with the world nowadays. Maybe she was being followed.

She looked Japanese, so she couldn't be far from home, but I was more than a little curious as her behaviour got odder the longer I watched. She had a magigun attached to her belt, hidden behind her bright pink jacket that perfectly matched the shade of her hair, and I caught myself wondering what in the hell a girl like her would need a gun designed to kill supernaturals for.

I looked her over once more as she walked down the street beside me and found her species identity even curiouser. She wasn't a Shifter or a Vampire, and she definitely wasn't one of the Fae, but her soul didn't feel quite human, either. Maybe a Witch? They were harder to detect nowadays after all the showy magic supes had used since their coming out. Of course, she could be a lesser species, which would make her identity that much harder to figure out, since it could be one of a thousand inconsequential things.

There was a small shambles of a café on the street corner, and she took a seat outside as a menu flew overhead. Fae magic. She pinched it out of the air.

"Hmm, must be Fae owned," I muttered to myself.

She stuck her head in her menu and pulled up her datascreen after a single tap to the chip in her arm.

She muttered something to herself, but it was too quiet for me to make out.

None of the other chairs were pulled out, so I hovered over her and imagined me blocking out the sun; I couldn't actually do that because I wasn't visible, but it was a fun piece of imaginative play that made me smile and sigh at the same time. She brought up information on an American man named DESMOND ARROW: 52, 2 children, assassin for hire. With a gray-speckled hair and a chiselled jawline covered in a black-and-white beard, he was quite handsome. Shame he was such a terrible person.

"Ugh." I groaned. "Why do scum like that even exist?"

I caught myself murmuring obscenities at the state of the world, as I so often did, when the girl flicked off her datascreen, pulled the menu down, and peeked at a familiar-looking man sitting over the way.

Desmond Arrow.

So she was following him. Why?

The white light encasing me dulled and flickered for a moment before fading, and I returned to my regular, still invisible self. Testing the boundary, I stepped away from the girl. No pain. I stepped farther away still. No pain.

"Thank heavens," I mumbled. I could finally leave this girl and go home.

But with every step I took away from the mystery girl whose name I never managed to figure out, my heart beat harder. Faster.

Why was it so hard to turn away from her?

I got to the corner before I returned my attention to the little white café seat she was perched on just moments ago, only to find it empty and devoid of my pink little lifeform. The man she had been following had vanished, too.

"So much for my last glimpse."

3

I took the nearest flight to Colorado, US that I could, paying extra for a private room in first class so I could manage the use of my two hours of visibility a day my powers enabled me. Luckily for me, most flight attendants left me alone when asked, so I only had to use those two hours in two one-hour intervals: once when boarding and once when disembarking.

My wings snapped open in the warm weather, letting the sun heat up the feathers and send tingling shivers down my back. I flew from the airport to the portal, exercising my wings as much as possible—who knew when I'd next be needed. Most people didn't need help crossing over; only those stuck needed my assistance, which, given I had opened the otherworld's gate to magical souls two thousand years ago, was almost never nowadays. I mostly helped the other Horsemen with their problems and lead the team when we were all needed.

The portal in Colorado was just up ahead, so I landed firmly on the concrete a block away and walked the last few minutes. It was a building that looked like any other in this small, hokey village: run down, with cracked walls and a broken rooftop. Until you got closer and stepped onto the entryway path, then it changed into a shining corporate building with a hidden secret.

Entering the building, the two sandy-haired guards stationed there saluted me and coughed. It still took me by surprise when I made myself visible for them using the few minutes of visibility I had left. "Death," the first one with the scraggly beard said. "Heading back today?"

"Indeed, Bernie. Thank you."

"Not a problem, sir."

I sighed. "What have I told you about the sir thing? Just call me Death." I shrugged. "Everybody else does." Well, everyone but the other Horsemen, of course, who nick-named me Dea.

"Of course, Death. I ap-p-pologise." His hands shook as he remained in salute form.

I waved him off and walked down the single corridor this building had and into the portal room. The room in question was covered from floor to ceiling in trees, flowers, and animals—looking for all the world like a mini rainforest—but the center clearing had four chairs, one for each of the Horsemen, made of solid wood.

Taking a seat, I took a deep breath.

The portal whirled around me, sending my stomach reeling and my mind spinning, but after a few calming breaths, I was home. *Sheruta.* A realm for the Four Horsemen of the Apocalypse to call home, and also home to a variety of supernaturals who had found their way here over the years. Some were invited, while some stumbled across the portal, but so far only supes were permitted to inhabit our realm.

It was separate from Earth; at least, that's what Famine says. Nine's a rather geeky Horseman, but he's our resident nerd, and I didn't know what I would do without him.

The walk from the portal building in *Sheruta* to our magical house on top of the hill was only a thirty-minute walk, but I found myself strolling and putting it off.

Whatever had happened with that girl was new. My magic didn't work that way. I was pulled to the dying who were struggling to let go, like a magical string was pulling me, but I was never pulled to the living. Perhaps she was going to die soon and my magic had upgraded? But even so, she was likely to never need my help. Only one in a million did nowadays, and they were mostly people with traumatic lives that wanted to carry on and make it better.

What would the other Horsemen think of this? "Ugh." Just thinking about telling Arrie, our Horseman of War, that I was having problems with one unknown supernatural and my magic made my head spin. He'd be angry, frustrated, and jealous that my magic had upgraded. I feel for the guy, since he has one of the worst magical abilities of the Horsemen, but could he not be more . . . accepting? Understanding?

I ran a hand through my hair and watched the various citizens of *Sheruta* go about their business, unknowing that I was there. Whenever we were around, the citizens of *Sheruta* were either in awe of us or terrified, so it was nice to watch people without the social mask or the barrier of fame. Like Shamus, for example, who owned the bakery Connie, our Horseman of Conquest, loved so much. He was always polite and friendly whenever we were around, but he had actually been rather depressed since his wife died a couple of years ago and almost never smiles when not working.

The town's new-age Victorian vibe made most people feel like they were walking through a book's pages or across a movie screen, but not me. The entire realm had always just felt like home to me. From the brown-brick buildings to the shiny silver embellishments, to the neon blue of the magic that permeated the realm and kept all the lights glowing, the shops' sign floating, and the rain trickling down its specific pathway.

I enjoyed being able to walk around without being seen. Sometimes. Often it made my life more difficult, and I stayed at home where I could always be seen by my fellow Horsemen. Being ignored certainly gets old. But sometimes it's nice being anonymous.

Walking up the hill, I was trying to come up with some way to tell the team that my magic had connected me to some random girl living in Tokyo. But I was coming up short. If I focused on that feeling of heat, that familiar tingle of new magic that stuck me to her like glue, I could spark it to life and feel the tenuous connection still.

Who was she?

How was she connected to me?

The house came into view, and I stood in a frozen gasp as I took in what our house looked like. Its bricked Victorian architecture had been swapped for an ancient Japanese look, with the swooping roofs and screen doors and bamboo wall structures. First the girl and now this.

What was going on?

I turned up the speed and fazed the rest of the way home, making the final few hundred meters in half a second as I blinked into existence outside the front door, which I yanked open. A sigh of relief escaped me. The inside was the same, with the same grand circling staircase and golden chandelier and plush cream carpets that always welcomed me home.

"Thank heavens."

"Dea?" Connie's voice rang out. "Is that you?" The Horseman of Conquest herself ran down the stairs with all of her usual gusto and threw her arms around me. "Welcome home."

Untangling her arms and wiping her long golden hair from my face, I gestured to the house. "Care to explain?"

"Well . . ." she began.

But Nine walked in and beat her to it. "We were hoping you could tell us, bro."

Nine's red hair was gelled into his usual swept-back style as he leaned against the kitchen doorway topless, his perfectly etched and tanned abs tantalizing my eyes, causing my hands to clench and my body to heat up.

Later, bro, Nine mentally sent me, then winked and walked up to me.

I wiped a hand down my face and refocused on the moment. Right, the house. Japan.

"I do not know," I half lied in a grumble as I made my way to the kitchen.

I really didn't know, but I suspected it had something to do with the girl my magic seemed attached to. I tried to keep that thought to the back of my mind and away from Nine's telepathy, but I doubted it worked. He can't shut us out like he can with the rest of the world, so he always reads our surface thoughts involuntarily.

My stomach grumbled, so I laid my hand on the kitchen table and asked the house for some sandwiches. With a quick rumble and pop from the house, a plate of small sandwich triangles appeared beside my hand.

Thank you.

Nine and Connie joined me, each pinching a sandwich, and while Connie chatted away about her latest battle with Arrie, Nine stared at me with a confused expression.

Please don't, I mentally begged him. I'm not ready for everyone to know yet.

Alright. But we need to talk.

Sure.

"I mean, I nearly had him," Connie went on, "but he fucking slammed me into a broken tree branch that skewered me right through my middle." She sighed. "The fucking asshole."

"Let me see."

Connie lifted her tank top and revealed a gaping hole that had started to heal in the center of her stomach. Given our supernatural healing capabilities and the whole 'we can't die' thing, I suspected this was a wound she'd gained earlier today.

Placing a gentle hand over the blood-soaked bandage, I flowed my healing energy into her soul and directed it toward the broken tissue and muscle sinew, instructing them to repatch themselves, my magic now its familiar green glow. A few seconds later, she was good as new.

"There."

"Thank you, thank you, thank you." She punched me in the arm and ran off, probably back to training.

Rubbing the bruise forming on my arm, I turned to look at Nine. "Sorry. I do not understand what happened to me today. I am not sure I am ready to tell the others."

"It's alright, bro." Nine wiped a frustrated hand over his face. "I just think you should always be honest with us. We're a team. A family." He leaned over and grabbed my hand, running circles along my thumb. "You shouldn't feel the need to hide from us."

I smiled at him and whispered, "Well, then how about I show you exactly what I think of my *family*." I emphasized the last word and looked him up and down, admiring his topless, lightly sweating form—probably just came from the gym.

We weren't always like this—there was a time when our entire relationship was nothing more than a close brotherhood—but things had changed over the last two hundred years; though, neither of us would admit it.

That sounds like a promise.

Think of it more as a threat.

I clenched his hand harder, pinching at the sensitive place between his thumb and forefinger, and watched him hiss and try to hide a groan. No doubt trying to hide it from Connie's supernatural hearing. Though, she'd probably heard it all over the last two thousand years.

That thought had us both chuckling, and Nine stood and closed the distance by sitting on my lap, purposefully making it hard not to run my hands over his thighs.

God, he knew just how to push my buttons, this guy. He knew control was something I relished, so he had spent the last few hundred years making it his mission to try to break it. So far, it hadn't worked.

Might have to start getting more people involved in our little trysts, bro. Not sure I can manage breaking that control solo. He winked and got up, readjusting his own struggle for control that was not at all hidden in those slacks. *I don't struggle. I give in and enjoy.* He smiled before walking back to the gym.

I watched his ass stroll all the way through the door, unashamed of being attracted to a member of my family. It's not like we were actually related; more like brothers in arms.

All four of us had dinner on the veranda under the stars that night, and while Nine and Connie were their usual chatty selves and Arrie poked in and out of the conversation, I sat in the corner deep in thought. What if there was a reason for my magic evolving now? It could have been a freak accident, a one off. But how likely was that? It'd never happened to any one of us in the last two thousand years. Could something be coming? I wondered as I gazed up at the same starry night I regarded the first night I woke up here in this house an immortal Horseman of Death. Was Fate dealing us a new hand?

"Do you think Fate really exists?" I asked no one in particular. "Or is it just an imaginary figure we have conjured to better explain our existence?"

The conversation fell silent at my admission as everyone looked at me with a sad smile.

"I don't know," Connie admitted. "Maybe Fate exists. Maybe it doesn't. Who knows. But it doesn't make our life any less valuable." Her blonde hair glowed under the moonlight, and I momentarily lost focused in its brilliance.

"We just exist," Arrie grunted, his usual scowl ripping across his face.

Nine looked at him, curiosity peeking through his playful exterior. He was a nerd at heart, and he wished to understand the non-understandable in a way I'd not seen in anyone else. "I think something must be in control of the Four Horsemen's journey."

His honesty took me by surprise. "Really?" I scoffed. "But isn't that a bit . . . magical, Mr. Magic Is Just Science." I mocked his usual stance on magic not being like we see in books, and that it can all be explained if we look to understand hard enough.

But Nine just scowled at me. "You really think this"—he gestured to us all—"is a coincidence? That somehow we were summoned into immortality to make us an ancient magical mantle just at the time Earth needed us? That we've been summoned and guided for the last two thousand years by some kind of magic to keep humanity and all the supernatural community safe just by chance?"

"That is how evolution happened," I bit back, frustrated by his response.

He couldn't honestly believe we were just Fate's puppets, could he?

"True," he argued. And I just knew he had a comeback. He always bloody did. "But this is too coincidental. Too much has happened in our pasts to have been left to chance. Every time we needed information or knowhow to complete some kind of mission, we've already learned a lesson before that helped or guided us somehow." He took a breath. "Every. Time." He hands were clenched, and I knew this line of questioning had started to go too far for Famine.

He was a thinker, and he couldn't think his way to the right answer. It bothered him.

You're right. It fuckin' does.

He shot out of his chair and stormed off into the night, his fists clenching and unclenching as he took the longest path around the gardens.

"Well done," Connie grumbled.

I smiled. "I know it bothers him, but . . . it has been grating on me of late."

Connie sat up straighter. "How so?"

The words were on the tip of my tongue: 'Because my magic's evolved.' But I couldn't release them. Not yet. None of us had evolved our magic in the last thousand years. I had no idea what would happen to our fragile team if I admitted that now.

"No reason." I stood and went to the kitchen door. "I'm off to bed."

Connie and Arrie wished me goodnight, and I went off to my hideyhole of a bedroom in the far corner of the upper floor.

The small wooden door I hadn't had changed since its inception in 1344 greeted me, and I couldn't keep my sigh of contempt from escaping its masked prison. Our rooms were designed by the house upon arrival, but we could change and update them as we went by asking for adjustments, so long as we didn't ask too much of her. And my bedroom was a small corner room painted black, still in its original brick work, with a roaring fireplace in the far corner opposite the four-poster bed. My lab table was in the corner, which was where I did all of magical experimentation and where Nine created a lot of our potions and spells. It was piled high with various text books, ingredients, and empty spellbeads and potion vials; it looked for the all the world like something out of a wizard's book or one of those old movies we still watched now and then. My study was through the door on the left while my en suite was through the door on the right. It was simple and old-fashioned but updated. For example, a soundstrip wrapped around the ceiling that played music and was voice activated.

"Soundstrip, play my metal playlist."

"Playing metal playlist," it responded in the usual robot voice I was pretty sure hadn't been updated in the last half a century.

Falling on the silky black sheets in a huff, that familiar surge of white-hot magic pierced through me, and my Angel of Death form popped into existence. Urgh. Why couldn't I get this nonsense under control? I tried to shift back but couldn't. My wings were far too big for this bed, but I tried my best to lay comfortably, eventually ending up on my face with my wings hanging over either side of the bed.

Knock knock.

You never have to knock, Nine.

You seemed a little . . . busy.

Just come in, you idiot.

Nine swung the door open and burst out laughing. "God, this looks even more hilarious in real life." He swung the door shut. "So, you're really stuck?"

I groaned. "Yes. Obviously."

He sighed and sat on what little space was left of the bed. "Show me what happened today."

I groaned but opened my mind to his telepathy. It wasn't really possible to shut him out completely, but you could hide things if you tried hard enough. If he really wanted to find out, though, he could just probe around and find the memory or thought. But this was Nine, and he didn't like doing that.

It's a horrible thing to do to someone, he echoed inside my head. Louder than usual because he was already inside my head watching me follow Little Miss Mysterious around.

"Who is she?" he asked out loud.

"Does it look like I know?" I sighed. "Sorry." I wiped a hand over my face. "It has been a long day." I sat up, shuffling my wings to try to fit inside this room. "What I want to know is why my magic seems drawn to her. She is not even dead yet."

Nine shrugged. "I've no idea, bro." My surprised blinking must have caught him off guard because he went on to explain, "I don't know everything."

"You usually do," I mumbled.

He laughed. "I know. But two thousand years of being a nerd creates a large internal library of knowledge." He shrugged and laid back on the bed next to me, resting on one of my wings. "Wanna talk about it?"

"No."

"You're starting to sound just like Arrie." He ran a hand up my naked back—courtesy of my Angel form—and I shuddered as he touched the tips of my wings where they connected to my shoulder blades. His legs tangled with mine as he placed small kisses along the sensitive seam.

Heat teased my senses from his warm breath along my back, and let out a calming breath, expelling the stress of the day. That could wait.

"But I think I can handle a little grumpiness."

I lifted my head up off the pillow and smirked at Nine. Flipping over and pinning his hands to the bed, my legs landed either side of his thighs. Leaning down, I whispered in his ear, "You think so?"

Nine groaned beneath me as his usually perfect red hair ruffled across the black sheets, forcing my eyes to his face. "I know so." He shifted his hips upward, grinding against my cock that was already hard from earlier, causing my body to tense with need.

Now it was my turn to groan. "We will see about that."

Nine wriggled beneath me, trying to break my punishing grip on his hands, but I just smiled. He thrashed a little harder, letting a moan slip from his delicious lips when I tightened my grip on his hands.

I watched his face scrunch and his eyes close, and it was clear to me that he might need this more than me today. Makes a change, I thought to myself. I leaned close to his ear and whispered, "Something tells me you enjoy this submissive play with me?"

He smiled and winked. "Just with you, bro." He was usually more of a flirtatious tease with everyone else, but with me he was happy to play at submission from time to time.

He writhed once more, his back arching as he thrusted into me, and this time, I could feel the hardness beneath his jeans giving away just how much he enjoyed his time in my bedroom.

My lips threw themselves against his in a sweeping need that caused him to both gasp and groan beneath my punishing kiss. I caught his needy groan between my teeth and nipped at his lower lip, then assaulted his tongue with my own—a battle of wills I knew he would lose.

He never wins. I never let him.

The battle raged on long enough to have us grinding into each other, his arms thrashing against my grip as he tried to free himself, and I relished the needy, panting look on that usually smirk-ridden face.

Eventually, Nine broke and gasped for air, smiling in that dazed, heated way of his that always made me squirm. "What do you want tonight, bro?"

"I think you already know the answer to that." I broke away and tried to sit at the end of the bed, but my wings kept getting in the way and catching on the bottom two posts. "Grab the rope."

Nine slid out of the bed and opened the chest at the bed's foot, grabbing some black nylon rope. "Is that all today?" His eyes met mine in a mischievous sparkle, but I just nodded.

"For today."

Nine grinned and walked back to bed, handing me the rope.

I could see it in his eyes: he wanted me to ask for more. Maybe next time.

I worked in silence as I sat Nine on his knees facing the headboard, his back to me, and bound his hands to the top posts using a simple single column tie and hooking the loop over the hooks already attached to the bed. All the while stroking gentle hands across his shoulders and back, teasing the crook of his neck with gentle scratches, relishing every caught breath and muscle twitch.

I pushed him forwards slightly so he was bent over, his ass against my groin. "There," I muttered. "Perfect."

"Always with the perfect tying."

I couldn't help it. I enjoyed watching him squirm, knowing he was only like this for me. Knowing that no matter how often we slept with other people in our centuries' long lives, the only person who saw this side of him was me. I tugged his slacks down and helped him out of them, grazing my fingers along his gentle v lines and down the impression his cock was making in his underwear.

"You know," he said, "I've never fucked you in your angel form."

I blinked. Now that he'd said it, I didn't think I'd ever had sex in this form.

Really?

"I do not think so, no."

I traced a hand over his bare back, a light finger teasing the skin as it trailed down his spine, resulting in a shiver. Kneeling behind him in my jeans, I watched him struggle not to shift backwards, to stay in place and behave. But heavens, I wanted him to misbehave.

My hands wandered beneath his waist and down his back to his ass, where I stopped and rested for a moment, relishing in the breathy groan of impatience that slipped from Nine's mouth. I followed the rim of his pants around to the front, where his breath hitched the moment I descended.

His cock twitched as my hand found his shaft and wandered upwards, tracing lazy circles over the head.

"Dea . . ." Nine's entire posture was rigid, from the tension in his neck to the rigidity of his legs. "Stop playing around."

I didn't respond, I simply slipped a hand beneath the waistband of his underwear and tugged them down and off, leaving him naked and tied to my bed.

A chuckle escaped my lips. Heavens, I loved watching his smug, teasing self be completely helpless.

My own cock strained against my jeans, and they were starting to feel uncomfortable, so I shrugged them and my underwear off and kneeled behind Nine's ass. Lube in hand, I spread his knees apart with my legs teased a finger around his hole, watching as he arched his back and groaned.

"Bro, please . . ."

"Begging already? Didn't last long, did you?"

We laughed together, but his chuckle was cut short when I pushed one finger in up to my knuckle, and the moan he released without meaning to was enough to have me holding back the involuntary thrust of my finger.

I wanted all of those breaths, moans, and involuntary thrusts of his hips. I wanted to keep collecting them for all of eternity and never let them go. They were mine.

He was mine.

I pulled out and pushed two fingers in, finding that spot that made his knees buckle and his cock twitch as he struggled against his restraints. Burying my fingers to the hilt, I stretched him ready for me.

"Bro, if you don't fuck me soon, I'm going to come early." He tried to laugh it off, but I could tell he was struggling this evening.

When was the last time you . . . ?

You.

My fingers stopped moving and my cock twitched with lust. Me? The last time he'd let anyone top him was with me? But that was nearly four months ago.

I pulled my fingers out and spread more lube over my cock, relishing in the tight fist and the sight of Nine still struggling to contain himself. "Ready?"

In answer, his thrust his ass back as far as he could against the restraints, and I watched as the knots on both his wrists and the bedposts tightened and strained. *Fuck me. Please.*

Grabbing his hips, I lined my cock up with his ass and inched forward, relishing in the tight feel of him as he gripped the head of my dick with more force than usual.

"Fuck, Nine," I hissed.

Impatient and lusting, Nine didn't wait for me for be ready; he pushed his ass back and buried himself to the hilt. "Fuck yes," he groaned.

I smacked his ass, hard, and my hand left a nice red imprint on his left ass cheek. "Who is in charge here?"

Nine's body slackened as neither of us moved. "You are." He sighed.

"Good." I rubbed a gentle hand over the red mark, soothing the sting.

Sweat dripped in a delicious trail down the center of Nine's spine, and I couldn't help but run a finger through its path. "You're so beautiful."

Nine stopped squirming and turned his head as far as he could to look me in the eyes. "I'm the one sleeping with an angel." He smiled.

I gripped his hips and thrusted softly at first, but I soon picked up the pace as Nine's impatience bled over into mine, and soon we were chasing the familiar high as Nine's moans got louder and I struggled not to come too early. He had let me stay in control so far, my earlier reminder of the rules keeping him in line, but with every thrust of my hips, he got more impatient and my control slipped further.

Fuck, Dea. C'mon, stop fucking around.

My hand found its way around Nine's hips and grasped his cock in a tight hold, but I didn't move it. Nine's resulting groan of impatience had me chuckling before I thrust into his ass harder.

His cock pulsed in my grip, and I couldn't help but move, fucking his ass and dick at the same time.

His body tensed further, and soon he was throwing himself back on my cock with reckless abandon, meeting the punishing pace I set.

Bro, I can't. I'm gonna—

"Do not worry, Nine. You will come apart multiple times this evening before I am finished with you."

His back arched as he thrust onto my cock and into my hand, and I let him. Gone was the control I relished and lived for; instead, I fell into the pit of human pleasure with the man I most cherished screaming my name into the small black bedroom I called mine.

We both panted and fell apart in the post-orgasmic high, and I just about managed to pull out and muster enough energy to untie my lover, clean up, and pull him into my arms under the ruined sheets. That night was full of carnal pleasure, and luckily, Nine didn't bother asking about the girl or bringing my magic up in conversation. We ate, we watched old-fashioned movies, we chatted about his latest magical theories, and we fucked some more until neither of us could keep our eyes open.

"It couldn't have been that bad," Nine said the next morning while we both searched for any traces of who this girl could be.

"Bad? Nine, it was awful." I took a deep breath to center myself. "I was stuck to her like glue until my magic unleashed me. Like some kind of magical thread attaching us together."

Nine coughed a surprised splutter. "Like, stuck stuck?"

"Stuck stuck."

We were both sat on his bed, surrounded by various magical bonding books and trying our hardest to match a sketch I'd drawn up to some database—any database—Nine had hacked into.

Nothing.

Nine sighed. "Witch database is empty, too."

"So she is not a Vampire, Shifter, Fae, or Witch?"

"Appears so." He rested a hand on my knee. "You could have been wrong, bro."

I shrugged him off. Wrong? Could she have been human the entire time?

"Well," Nine said, "I'm checking the human database anyway."

I growled under my breath in frustration, but I walked it off by pacing the black-and-red room covered in books, datascreens, and various pieces of tech and parts. It was so perfectly . . . Nine. "Fine," I huffed. "But you will not find anything." I walked up behind his hovering chair and whispered, "She is not human." I rubbed my chest—the center of our magical connection, it seemed. "I can feel it."

Nine didn't answer, but I knew he could feel what I was feeling because I could feel his presence in my mind (years of practise), and it was currently centered around that burning sweet feeling in the center of my chest.

The datascreen in the wall in front of us glowed blue, where it hovered in mid-air in all its transparent glory. Damn, technology had come a long way in the last two hundred years. I remember when the first telephone was invented: a stupid two-piece wired thing that people shouted down.

I was chuckling to myself when Nine's search pinged.

"Got a hit," he said.

But the screen in front of us couldn't be right. DATALOCKED: SECURE FILE.

"But . . . that is impossible," I whispered underneath my breath. "What kind of file gets locked away from your hacking?"

Nine's face was scrunched up in concentration as he banged his fist on the desk. "None." He sighed as he scraped a hand through his ruffled red hair. "Until now."

"Thank you for trying." I tapped him on the shoulder and went to shower.

"Wait," Nine said. "Are you going to track her down?" He pointed to the burning feeling in my chest. "Do you . . . I mean, do you need any help?" His eyes avoided mine, and his hands shook, but he shoved them behind his back before my eyes could linger.

I walked up to him and grabbed his chin. "Everything is going to be okay, Famine." I stared into his brown eyes and sighed. "You . . ." I trailed off, not wanting to even think the words. "Would be off better here."

He looked up at me and sniffed.

God, please don't cry, Nine.

He chuckled. "Cry? Over you?" He made a sound of indignant nonsense. "Fuck off." He pushed me away and out of his room. "Let me know what you find out?"

I nodded and headed back to my room, my hand attempting to rub the tension out of my neck as I went.

What was I going to do about him?

I shook my head. Now was not the time. Later. I'd figure it out later.

I showered and packed quickly, not needing anything but my wallet, and headed back to Earth for the second time in as many days. "This is going to be a nightmare." I could feel it.

6

On a plane. Really? She was on an airplane right now? For heaven's sake, girl. I growled under my breath and frowned at the metal contraption I glided above. I couldn't get inside of the plane, either, so I couldn't do anything but wait to see where it would land. If Nine were here, I could get him to look up the flight path and see its trajectory, but he wasn't here because I had told him to stay at home because I didn't want to stare at that hurt face.

Was he really going to cry?

Over me?

Not the time, Death. Not the time.

I focused on following the plane, which was somewhere over the Pacific Ocean heading for the US, if my sense of direction was anything to go by, and it usually was. So, Little Miss Mysterious was heading to the US. Why?

I shrugged and continued flying for the next five hours it took to get to Louis Armstrong New Orleans International Airport. Yes. Little Miss Mysterious was heading to Vampire central.

New Orleans was home to the Vampire Royal Council, the entire royal family, and most of the noble, born Vampires; though there were Vampires all over the world, most of those were colonies or families of turned Vampires. Only certain lineages could procreate, and with those lineages come extra abilities. The current king, for example, can read minds, like Nine. Only, he's nowhere near as powerful. It's really more of a parlor trick.

I stayed invisible as I wound my way around and over airport security, following the little pink-haired girl the entire way, but so far, the only thing of note was that she had a permit from the Supernatural Council (SC) for her weapons. Only a few personnel were able to obtain those. I cannot express how difficult it was for us Horsemen to get a hold of four of them.

We are not exactly liked by the SC.

Seemed she had no problem, though.

She hailed a cab from the airport's exit and headed into the heart of the city with a beautiful frown upon her face. I got the distinct impression she was not here willingly, or at least not happily. She looked too grumpy for a tourist and too wound up to be a human looking for a Vampire date.

Maybe she was here on business? Or to see a relative?

For a few hours, she did normal activities: checking into a motel, scoping out the area, and getting dressed for a party. If I didn't know better, I'd say she was here as a regular tourist, but there was something about the way she went about her business. It was cold, calculated. She looked behind her at regular intervals, constantly checked to ensure her weapons were still in place, and checked her datascreen for messages and to look New Orleans up.

She was here on some sort of mission.

I just had to figure out what.

With a practised smile plastered across her face, she entered the vibrant world of New Orleans, partying with the supernaturals that frequented the area: Shifters and Vampires, basically. This place was any human with an obsession over paranormal fantasy's wet dream; and so it was often filled to the brim with hosters (humans who willingly let Vampire feed from them), fanatics, curious wanderers, and partying college kids looking for a good time. It was not my favourite place in the world to be, but Connie rather enjoyed it back in the day.

Little Miss Mysterious took a deep breath before venturing into a few pubs at the edge of town, only just managing to hide her shiver at the sight of so many Shifters.

So she was afraid of Shifters? Maybe all supernaturals? It's unfortunately common to find supe haters among humankind. Perhaps she was looking to start a war or was part of a dangerous group, and that was why my magic seemed obsessed with her.

Maybe she was a terrorist?

I looked at the cute, pink-haired girl in front of me whose body swayed toward the bar and shook my head. Terrorist? Her? No. That didn't fit. It must be something else.

I watched as a Shifter walked up to where she had sat on a barstool and gave her what I assumed was supposed to be a charming smile. "Hey, cutie." He placed a hand on her shoulder. "What's a cute little human like yourself doing so far from the party life?"

She looked over the middle-aged man from head to foot and removed his hand from her shoulders. "Just looking for something a little more . . . authentic."

I froze.

Her voice. It was . . . soft. Melodious. As though a million stars had graced her body and expelled in a soft stream the moment she opened her mouth.

The lion tattoo on her back painted in various colors shifted as she laughed at something the gentleman said, and I bristled. What the fuck was this man doing? It took all the effort I had to refrain from sending this man flying across the room. He'd made her laugh? What an arse.

I shook the tension from my body and told myself to stop being such a fopdoodle. I had no claim or right to this woman, and she was more than welcome to flirt with whomever she chose. But just as I said that last part, her hand rested on his thigh as she laughed at another one of his ridiculous jokes.

Blind rage shook my entire being, and my form snapped out of place as my angel form took over, wings spread wide. Luckily, in this form, only the dying could see me (and the other Horsemen, of course). The only reason I didn't stay in it full time was because it felt . . . off. As though my body was ten times heavier and wider than it should be, and I often found myself bumping into doorways and catching my wing feathers on everything. But, right now, I didn't care about any of that.

My hands trembled, and I had to force my arms to stay by my side before they found their way to this loiter-sack's ugly face. I breathed a heavy exhale as I practically force-fed myself peaceful thoughts. Eventually, the frustration subsided, but by then, Little Miss Mysterious' conversation had flowed from casual to flirty, and it didn't take long for me to recognize what she was doing: gleaning information.

"Soooo, what kind of Shifters live out these parts?" She smiled at him and practically begged with her eyes. "C'mon, a girl's gotta know." She winked.

Ugh. Tell me this guy was not falling for this?

His alcohol-laden smile slipped at the question, but she quickly picked herself back up. "I just wanna know how many Shifters I can *meet* in one weekend."

The double meaning was not lost on the guy, who smiled once again and leaned in close to her ear. "Well, there are a few wolves and a bear pack, but the prominent Shifters to live out 'ere are werepanthers."

Her eyes sparkled with interest. "Werepanthers?" she whispered. "Like big pussy cats?"

Her forced giggle made me smile and sigh as I shook my head, but it made him melt like ice in the summer heat.

"Yeah. Our pack is huge. A good one hundred strong." His shoulders threw themselves back as pride filled his features. And to be fair to the man, the pack was pretty impressive for a Shifter pack nowadays, but they had nothing on the kinds of packs that used to run around here. Thousands strong. They used to be bigger before supernaturals came out of the closet, so they could protect themselves and stay self-sufficient. Now, though, it wasn't as big a need. "Best pack I've ever been in."

Her purple eyes sparkled with interest. "How so?" she mumbled around the rim of her glass.

He huffed. "The rules here in New Orleans are a little looser than in other parts of the country. We run with the Vamps here, rather than stay away like so many other packs. We're pretty close, actually; all helping each other out." Not entirely true, I thought to myself with a chuckle. "Plus, our leader, Desmond Arrow, never kicks anyone out. He's so chill." He leaned back and took a deep breath. "Treats us all like family, you know."

Her hair swayed as she brushed it behind her ear, trying to take his eyes away from the lump in her throat that she just swallowed.

Wasn't Desmond Arrow the name of that guy she was looking up at the café back in Tokyo? The one who was conveniently sat across the veranda from her?

Curious.

Was she here because of him? Why?

The guy smiled at her and caught her hand. "You okay, darlin'?"

She nodded. "Thank you, but I . . . err think I should start heading back. It's been a long trip here."

The guy looked disappointed for a minute, but he let go of her hand with a sigh and got up to walk away. "Have fun this weekend."

She bowed her head slightly and stumbled out of the bar on a heavy breath. "Shit," she mumbled the moment she almost fell through the door. "Fuckety fuckballs."

I followed her around the city as she walked past block after block, mumbling various things to herself and generally looking a little odd, but the moment anyone came in to view, she walked with her usual confident swagger that I was starting to realize was all for show.

Who was this girl really?

She took a deep breath and headed back to her motel for the night, where she spent her time laughing at some videos on her datascreen before falling asleep to the bustling sounds of the nightlife outside her ground-floor window.

I didn't know whether to stay and keep following or head back. If I headed back now, I would only be returning with more questions and an even bigger headache. I still didn't know who she was, what she was doing here, why my magic seemed weirdly attached to her, or why I was in this mess to begin with. If I could just find out who she is . . .

Her datachip glowed a faint green on the inside of her wrist, where everyone's chips were held. It was against most country's laws to invade someone else's chip for any non-emergency reason, given that they hold all the person's personal data: address, medical history, ID, etc. Everything that made them themselves was imbedded in those chips. When a person died, it flashed red before blinking out of existence, but while the person was alive, it flashed green. If that person needed any assistance and hadn't acted upon their stress, it will flash yellow and call the person's emergency contact. The only people allowed to access them are certified scanners, such as medical professionals and identification checkers, and even they only get what information they need.

If I could just access her chip, I could grab her basic information and be gone. Easy peasy. Once I knew who she was, I could . . .

What then?

I still didn't know if I was attached to her for a good or bad reason, so I couldn't murder her or stop by and have a chat. Could I? Maybe if I just asked her who she was, she'd tell me, and then I could decide from there.

Shaking my head, I laughed and muffled the sound with a hand over my mouth. What was I thinking? I'd never ignored my magic and Fate's warnings before. I couldn't start now. There was a reason I could find her anywhere, and that reason would reveal itself eventually. I just had to be patient.

7

For the next two days, I followed her around New Orleans, listening to her conversations with various supernatural strangers as she got closer and closer to Desmond Arrow. Eventually, she would track him down—or he would come find her—and the reason for her trip halfway around the world would be revealed.

I just had to hang in there.

I could do this.

Eventually, Little Miss Mysterious found her way to one of the most popular exclusive parties in New Orleans, hosted by none other than the Vampire Prince Lucien. He's . . . Well, he's Lucien. He's not overly political and is the center of every social circle, but he's a nice guy. Better than his brother, anyway. I chuckled as I thought about her meeting the prince. She was going to hate him.

If there was anything I've learned about my stalkee, it was that she hates parties and speaking to people in general. She was everything he was not. He will likely see that as a challenge, however, and drag her to whatever party corner he was currently occupying.

She walked through the front door with a deep breath, her long pink hair swaying in the open door's gentle breeze, and froze. By the looks of the party in front of her, it was in full swing: People were grinding on the dancefloor as built-in lights flashed in a blinding sequence no one else seemed to mind, and various slips and spills of alcohol washed the once-shining mahogany floor in a layer of sticky grime that had us both wincing upon our first step. Silver netted drapes hung from floor-to-ceiling open windows all around this room, and electronic pop music poured out in a wall of sound that also had me wincing, but she seemed to reluctantly enjoy it as her foot bobbed to some cheesy lyric.

My eyes rolled.

Typical.

She shook the tension out of her limbs and walked through the throng of people in front of her with that familiar fake smile notched in place. She used that face like a well-oiled mask she'd managed to master for every possible occasion. I wonder what her real smile looked like? She danced with a few people, not really getting much conversation out of them as every third person attempted to get a hand up her dress.

She was gorgeous. But she was having none of it as she turned every guy, and a few girls, down and moved on.

Interesting.

"Hello, love." A blonde-haired familiar, annoying face entered my vision as Prince Lucien sidled up to her on the dancefloor and grabbed her arm. "Enjoying yourself?"

She sighed. "Eh. Could be better."

He laughed. "My party that bad, huh?" His laughing smile faded as he took in her serious expression. "Wow. Okay."

She winced. "Sorry. Not usually my scene. Just trying to live a little."

She continued dancing, but he didn't make her stay where she was uncomfortable. He guided her through the chef-style kitchen and out the backdoor, where I knew the garden party awaited.

It was more relaxed out here, with people lounging to more casual, quieter music as they chatted in groups of two or three. Some lounged naked in the various pools that all linked together with small waterfalls to create a cascading effect down the center of the expansive yard. But that was not what caught her attention.

"Ohhh, a hot tub," she said with a breath of excitement. "Can we, can we, can we?"

Lucien laughed but guided her in that direction. "We may." He grabbed her hand, and, once again, I had to hold myself back from throwing him to the ground.

What was wrong with me?

This was . . . strange. I shook my head. Stranger than normal, anyway. I could not stop my hands from shaking and forehead from sweating, and no matter how hard I tried, I couldn't push that irritating, clogging emotion down. Jealousy? But . . . that was insane. I didn't even know her name!

I followed them to one of a few hot tubs they had behind the back of the pool—the one she had pointed to earlier—and stopped dead. There, lounging with two naked blonde women in his lap, sat Desmond Arrow.

She had found him. Wonder what she'd do next.

"You're not hiding a bikini under that slip of material you call a dress, are you?" Lucien flashed his fangs with this smile, and I grinned at her shocked reaction.

She gasped. "You're a Vampire?" But there was a hint of a smile underneath all that fake concern. She knew. She had to know. Between his pasty palor, his location, and the ethereal tone to his face, it was hard to miss. Vampires didn't blend well with humans. "Well, I am shocked."

Lucien smiled, and I had another sudden urge to wipe it off his face.

"But," she started, "I do want to know who that is." She raised her eyebrows in that suggestive way of hers she'd used on every man thus far.

"Oh, really?" he said as they sidled on up to the hot tub. "More into Shifters than Vampires, huh?"

She shrugged. "Never really been with either." She looked at Desmond with longing, and part of me wondered if it was real or fake. She was a good little actress. "But he turns into an actual animal!" She squealed under her breath as she pressed her hands together in excitement.

Lucien harrumphed but took it in good stride. "Well, you could always have both." He slipped his t-shirt, pants, and underwear off until he was stood in front of her naked. "Shall we?" He gestured to the hot tub once more.

By the flashing look of surprise on her face and the uncomfortable shuffle she tried to hide, she didn't expect to get this far. I could practically see the pep talk she was giving herself before she slipped her dress off and folded it neatly on top of her clutch beside the hot tub's rim. She slipped her heels off and slid into the bubbling tub in her underwear.

Desmond watched her with rapt interest, paying little attention to the two blondes beside him the moment he eyed the tattoo on her front chest—the skull design was enough to catch anyone's attention. Also, being a Shifter with better-than-human hearing, I was pretty sure he'd heard their earlier conversation. "So," he started, shooing away the other two as though they were nothing more than accessories, "what's your name?" He shuffled to her right, on the opposite side of Lucien, who had wrapped an arm around her left.

"Candy," she giggled, looking to her thighs and uncomfortably avoiding his gaze.

"Candy?" He wrapped an arm around her right, laying it just behind Lucien's. "What brings you here? And with Prince Lucien?"

Her eyes widened. "Prince?"

Ah. That was a real reaction. She didn't know who he was.

She gave Lucien the stink eye, and he laughed. "Not the first thing I tell someone."

"Prince Lucien over there doesn't like his station," Desmond mumbled. "He just likes to live it large and have no responsibilities." He chuckled, his dark eyes throwing shade at Lucien.

"So," she said, "you don't want to be the next Vampire King?" She snorted in disbelief. "Really?"

He looked at her as though he wanted to rip her throat out for a moment, but he quickly covered it with a flash of mock hurt. "I have a strict no shoptalk policy at my parties." He coughed. "I don't ask for your real name, and you don't ask about my royal station."

Desmond chimed in with, "And I don't talk about pack politics."

"Yup," Lucien said. "He's head of the local werepanther pack, by the way. Desmond Arrow."

Desmond rolled his eyes.

She giggled again, but this time she put on an act of fake courage and turned her head his way. "Wow. Look at me, hot tubbing with a Prince and an Alpha." She fanned herself.

Desmond caught her hand and trailed his fingers up her arm and to her shoulders, where his hand brushed the outer edges of her black lace bra. "Well, it can't be that surprising. You're stunning."

Well, he wasn't wrong, but that did not stop my hand from itching to fly at his face. Who did this Shifter think he was? Right, Alpha of the biggest pack in the area. So he thinks he's the bee's knees.

Rolling my eyes, I refocused back on the scene in front of me with a steadying breath.

Candy, or whoever she really was, straddled Desmond's lap, her hands running up his chest and landing on his neck. Prince Lucien moved in behind her, closing chilled kisses down her neck, and despite her resolve, she shuddered. Whether in pleasure or fear, I couldn't be sure, but if the flush of her cheeks was anything to go by, I'd say it was the former.

"How about . . ." Lucien started in between kisses, "we find somewhere a little more private." He gestured to the top floor of the house, and I repressed my growl of protest.

I knew all about the traditional layout of Vampire parties, and the higher floors were typically used for feeding dens. Clearly, she knew this, too, as her hand clenched behind Desmond's neck—out of sight of the others.

"Oh, that sounds . . . perfect."

Lucien stood up and stepped out. "I'll go find us a room then." He looked to Desmond. "Meet me there in five minutes."

Desmond chuckled. "Sure thing, Prince."

Lucien's smile faded as he pointed to the werepanther. "Don't start without me, Alpha." The bite in his voice couldn't be ignored, and I watched Desmond's throat bob as he swallowed his defiant reaction.

I bet those two would be a fun night in the bedroom. What with all that macho man nonsense they've got going on. Shaking my head out of the gutter, I refocused on Little Miss Candy Mysterious.

"Sooo," she whispered in his ear before kissing his neck. "What are we gonna do for the next five minutes?"

Did she really stalk this guy across the Pacific Ocean just get into his bed? That seemed . . . far-fetched at best. There had to be an ulterior motive I wasn't seeing.

He looked at her with such adoration that, in the moment, he was besotted by her. Even I could see it. He wanted her, even if that meant sharing. "Well, before I share you with a friend"—he ran a hand up her torso and snuck a finger up her bra and grazed her nipple—"how about we take a walk." She looked taken aback. "Get to know each other a bit better?"

She giggled. "Wasn't really looking for a chat, Desmond." She looked him in the eyes and saw how serious he was. "But if that's what you want, I'll be happy to have you to myself for five minutes." She winked.

"Promise to make it worth your while," he growled while pinching her nipple hard enough to make her moan. She nodded as he pulled his hands away and lifted her off of him. "C'mon." He grabbed her hand and pulled her out of the hot tub.

She shimmied into her dry dress, leaving wet patches where her underwear was that you could barely see over top of the black, and followed Desmond across the lawn and around the side of the building. "So, Alpha, huh?"

He shrugged. "Yeah. Guess so." He rubbed a hand over his neck. "Was never really meant to be me, but shit happens." He took a deep breath. "What about you?"

"Human," she replied a little too quickly. "Work in Tokyo with a friend of mine at a club. Just took a trip here to vacay to Vampire central for a little supernatural tourism."

He chuckled.

Supernatural tourism was all the range now that three of the biggest supe species were out of the closet—Vampires, Shifter, and Fae—but most young people used it as a euphemism to mean sleep with supernaturals. It had become something of a modern phenomenon. There were even dating apps where you could pair up with a local supernatural for one night only; and that didn't cover the number of escort services now specialising in the supernatural. The way supes were treated nowadays by the human population made my skin crawl, but there was little we could do about it.

"Supernatural tourism," he said on a sigh. "Really?"

She shrugged. "Don't most girls my age do that at some point in their lives?" she asked almost innocently, but I understood the undertone. She was checking to make sure she was on target for his experience.

Perhaps she didn't usually do this after all?

"Yeah. Yeah, they do." He looked at her. "And the guys. Though they're quieter about it."

"Really?" That peeked her interest.

He wrapped an arm around her shoulders as they reached the front yard. "Yeah, you'd be surprised how many propositions I've had from young men doing the same." He shook his head. "Flattered, but I'm more of a girl kinda guy."

"So, there's no chance of getting a show tonight?" She wiggled her eyebrows, her intentions clear.

He snorted but shrugged. "Never say never."

They eventually reached the front of the front yard, and she grabbed one of the metal fence posts outlining the property. "Wanna get out of here and go solo?"

"You don't want a threesome with a Shifter and Vampire?" He laughed. "Thought you were touristing?"

"I've had Vampires before, and I gotta say, I wasn't impressed. The whole blood thing?" She shook her head with a shiver. "Not my thing."

He laughed. "Fair enough." He grabbed her hand and dragged her toward the front gate. "If you really wanna get out of here, we're not far from the pack's main house. We could go there and have some one-on-one time?" He leaned in to her body and bent down to kiss her.

She met him halfway with fervor, passion flaring in her eyes for a split second before she pulled back and led him off the property.

I kept following, but I wasn't about to stay for the show if that's really what she was up to. But something about this situation felt off. If I took her at her word—like Desmond was doing—I would have left already; but something about her actions screamed fake. Like she wasn't really into this. But why would a human put herself alone with a Shifter if she didn't really enjoy it?

Nothing made sense.

I followed them through various streets and around a couple blocks when they ventured down a dark alley that had me shaking my head. Did she not watch movies? Why was she letting herself be led down a dark alley by some random stranger who's stronger than her?

Stupid girl.

When they were fully shrouded in darkness and random passersby couldn't notice their actions, he pinned her to the wall and shoved a tongue down her throat, not waiting for permission.

She lapped it up like a kitten and its milk, savouring every last drop of Desmond's passion. He growled at her and let her hands go, which she used to stroke a finger down his front and palm his hard cock tenting the slacks he'd put on before leaving the hot tub area. Her hand snapped to the bag beside her as she drew her magigun and snarled. "Get the fuck off me."

He stepped back, a sympathetic apology written all over his face. He was worried he'd gone too far. I, on the other hand, was enjoying the real-life movie.

"Desmond Miles," she said in a calm, detached tone, "you're under arrest." Her hand flickered in the moonlight, and I watched as she let a familiar emblem flash: an eagle with its claws out. The symbol of the Hunter Society. "I'm tasked with the job of bringing you to the Supernatural Council for processing."

He turned to run away.

"Please, for the love of the goddess, don't make this harder on yourself."

He barely placed one foot forward when she pressed the trigger, and a bullet of magical energy shot from the barrel of the small handgun and hit him firm in the sternum. Blue crackling energy snapped around him, forcing his body into a rigid standpoint before collapsing to the ground in a deadened heap.

"So," a familiar voice echoed from the shadows, "little hunter, what are you going to do next?" Prince Lucien exited the darkness, a sadistic smile shrouding his usually charming features. "Because I'm not sure your puny body could carry that hunk of Shifter down this alley to whatever getaway plan you have."

She was a hunter. I couldn't believe the thought was even crossing my mind. A hunter for the supernatural was basically a bounty hunter for supes. The Supernatural Council send out a hit to their database, and one of their many employed hunters picks it up, accepts the job, and cashes in when they've caught their target. No assassinating, but god knows what they do with them once prosecuted. It was an issue that was on our radar but low on the priority list.

Nothing about this made any sense. I couldn't apply the label of hunter to this girl who was barely in her mid-twenties. Most hunters were ruthless, cruel supernatural haters. But she seemed so . . . innocent.

Prince Lucien was still smirking at her, and I wanted to strangle the stupid—

"You knew?" she asked, genuine surprise in her voice.

He huffed. "Of course." He walked out of the shadows and closer to her, wrapping an arm around her shoulders tight enough that she had to be feeling it start to crush her bones. "We at the Vampire Royal Council know all of the hunters." He eyed her as though she were his next meal, and she shivered; this time, I doubted it was in pleasure. "Especially the ones operating in our hometown."

She laughed. "Oh, the moment he said you were a prince, I knew you were going to be a pain in my fucking ass."

"No, that was what I planned on being, until I realized Des was your target, and I watched you work your feminine magic on him like he was putty in your hands."

"You didn't help him?" she asked, sounding genuinely curious. She went to move away but winced as his pressure on her shoulders increased.

He shook his head. "Can't afford to piss off the SC, so I decided to let you have your bounty."

"Decided?" She snorted. "You have zero control over me, Prince." She snarled his title at him.

He winced but chuckled. Like him, I could see he had the upper hand. Born Vampire versus a human? Even an armed human, that wasn't an equal fight. She would lose if he decided that was what he wanted.

"Perhaps." His voice was barely a whisper, but the threat oozing from his lips was louder than the echoing silence surrounding us.

Should I intervene? Was that my purpose here? I trembled with indecision. For once, could Fate not be specific? I was so fed up with all the cryptic nonsense and following this girl around.

"So," she said, "what's your choice?" She sighed and stepped out of his hold, him letting her. "Because I'm tired and need to cash in my target"—she nodded to Desmond— "before morning."

"All business and no play." He looked at her and frowned. "You're just no fun." He waved her away. "Go. But Taylor?"

She winced, and her eyes widened.

Taylor? That was her name? Her real name?

"Don't come hunting here again." Liquid poison dripped from his lips, and if I didn't know any better, I'd say he was using his abilities to influence her mind. It was always hard to tell, since his magic didn't work on my invisible form.

She nodded and rushed to Desmond's body. He was still alive, just unconscious. She dragged him by the arms to the end of the alleyway and sighed. "Shit. He's fucking heavy."

I watched as she walked up to the nearest magicar and used an illegal hacking device to unlock it and hardwire it to her chip.

This girl was good.

She grabbed Desmond by the legs and pulled him into the back of the car and slammed the door shut, most likely banging his head. "There," she whispered, "job done."

Nine looked at me like I'd presented him a ghost from a thousand years ago. "Your magic is attached to a hunt-t-ter?" he stuttered. "Like, a real-life hunter?"

"Yes," I ground out. "Fucking yes, alright."

He flinched at my cuss, but he smiled underneath it all. He liked it when I cussed, though he never admitted it. "Well, we kinda know who she is now. That's a start, right?"

"Yes." I breathed a sigh. "I guess it is." He was right, but I was more twisted than ever. "But why? How?"

He shrugged. "No idea, bro." *Maybe it's something a little less world-ending and little more . . . personal?*

"Personal?"

He nodded but shrugged, refusing to give me anything more.

"Come on, Famine. Do not hold out on me now." I punched him in the arm a little harder than normal and watched him grimace. "Sorry, but I need answers."

"I know." He grazed his hands up my arms and placed a soft kiss to my lips, which I returned. "But sometimes you need to let things fall into place. She's not ending the world, nor is she in any imminent danger, so let things lie."

Let things lie? Seriously? That was his worldly advice?

Don't knock it till you've tried it. "Stop trying to be in control of everything and just relax for a moment." He wrapped his arms around my waist and smiled up at me. "I'm sure everything's fine."

So, for the following six months, that is what I did. I ignored her. I ignored the heat in the center of my chest every time it flared, and I ignored my curiosity every time it wandered to that pink-haired beauty, until eventually it stopped hurting and I forgot all about her. In fact, when Nine asked me if I was okay one morning, I honestly answered yes without even remembering her name.

For some reason, she was slowly vanishing from my memory, and now, when I tried thinking about that burning heat that flared up every now and then, I couldn't for the life of me remember what it was. Or why it was there. Or if I ever knew the answers to those questions.

When I asked Nine about it, he shrugged. "Sorry, bro. I don't know."

He couldn't remember either? That seemed unlikely. Dealing with dreams, thoughts, and memories was his magical forte, after all. That he couldn't remember anything bothered me more than I'd care to admit, but what if there was nothing to remember? What if that burning feeling in my chest was just some bad heartburn?

Yeah, Death, because we Four Horsemen can come down with heartburn. I laughed at my stupid reasoning and went out for a walk through the house's wonderful fairy garden, saying hello to all the different fairies that crossed my path. From the glittering blue ones that harvested the magical poppies to the dark brown ones that kept the garden tidy. They all smiled at me when I passed, and with the sun glinting off their sharp, needle-like teeth, I remembered that they could cause some serious damage in a flock.

Shivering from a bad memory of the last time they had attacked me, I rushed on ahead in a quick flit of speed and took a deep breath. I laughed at my stupidity for a moment before continuing my walk past the rainbow forest and through the pixies' section of the fairy garden. I reached the lookout hideaway at the edge of the forest that allowed us to see the unicorn flock and hissed as a sharp, stabbing pain shot through my chest.

"What the—?"

A tingle of heat spread through my chest, and some part of my memory rang with familiarity at the feeling. Something about this was . . . so familiar. But I couldn't put my finger on it. The heat spread from my chest to my limbs, and before I knew it, my entire body had an ethereal glow to it that burned white hot.

"Ah!" The scream left my lips as I collapsed to the grassy floor of the garden in a body-convulsing huddle. "Nine . . ."

Footsteps thundered through the garden, and before I knew it, the rest of the team were leaning over me, shouting, swearing, asking what was wrong. But it was too painful to open my mouth for anything but screaming.

"Help him!" I heard Connie say. "Fucking do something!"

"He's the healer," Arrie grumbled.

And he was right. This was my area of expertise. I had to do . . . something.

I took a deep breath, but as I did, my wings ripped from my back as my angel form popped into existence, the usually golden glow to my angel skin smothered by the white-hot glow of whatever was happening to me. My body floated in the air, my wings flapping despite me not consciously controlling them, and I screamed into the afternoon daylight.

The fairies and pixies scattered as my screams echoed, all thoughts of beauty flying with them.

My chest tugged, but for the life of me, I couldn't figure out why. It yanked me around on the spot for a bit, spinning, until dizziness overtook my insides and I spewed vomit in a wide circle.

Steadying, slowing, colors now appearing, my eyes focused on my surroundings, but I was no longer in the garden or anywhere on *Sheruta* that I knew of. My wings flapped behind me, keeping me ten feet above the highest building of the city below.

Taking deep breaths, I planted both feet on the ground and steadied my erratic breathing and shaking hands. Deep breaths, Death. Deep breaths.

No one seemed to notice my freak out in the middle of a busy city street.

At least I was invisible.

I lowered myself to street level and paced a couple blocks until I saw something: a sign written in Japanese. So I'm in Japan, I thought to myself while I flew around another few blocks and tried to make sense of where in Japan I was.

My chest still burned like I'd eaten a thousand ghost chillies and vomited them back up, but that magical husky feeling at the base of the pain seemed to know where I was going despite my otherwise wandering directions.

Black feathers fluttered at the corners of my vision, and I sped up, my magic eager to get to whatever destination it had locked on to.

I flew for who knew how many hours, but it was long enough for my wings to start aching and my body to need a rest. As I passed various buildings and landmarks, I knew where my magic was pulling me: Tokyo. But Tokyo was a huge place. Where specifically was I going?

All I knew was that I needed to get to wherever my magic wanted me to go because if I tried to resist, it felt like I was being burned alive. So despite my wings burning from the effort of flying so far, so hard, I kept going. I whizzed past people leaving for work and getting ready for their evenings, past school children hanging around on their way home, and past clubs just opening for their evening customers, and by the time my wings slowed down and my magic stopped yanking me around, the sun had set and people in various costumes—from skeletons, to werewolves, to devils—were walking around half drunk.

Halloween.

"For heaven's sake." I sighed.

I hated Halloween. It was just an excuse for everyone to get drunk and be annoying. I still remembered a time when Japan didn't celebrate the pathetic excuse of a holiday, before globalisation really took hold of the human population.

My wings slowed to a stop outside of a large mansion of a house whose party was in full swing already. The white columns and silver-purple Fae lights created an ethereal look that certainly made the place look spooky, but it was the supernatural personnel guarding the door that took me by surprise. By the looks of the guests, they were all under the age of thirty and mostly human. So why would they need supernatural guards?

I waited for a good gap in the crowd, looking for entry, and slipped inside, shivering as I passed some kind of magical barrier. More Fae magic.

My magic still had a small hum in the back of my chest, and I followed where it was leading me until I stopped behind a pink-haired girl ordering drinks at a ghoul-infested bar—the ghouls were fake, but it was a cool piece of plasma tech.

"A dusted vodka-coke, please." She leaned against the bar as the bright blue-haired Fae bartender went to mix her drink.

I stepped up beside her, remaining invisible for now, and watched her pay the bartender with a swipe of her datachip and turn to lean against the old-fashioned wood of the bar with a sigh.

But one look down her body had me holding in a laugh: She was wearing a tubed tank top that stopped just inches under her boobs and was wrapped in some kind of mummy-like material and spray painted black and light pink. Her ass was only just covered in the world's shortest skirt as her legs sported some knee-high pink-and-black boots. But behind her back were wings; and not just any wings, Angel of Death wings. Yes, this woman my magic seemed attached to and had dragged me halfway across Japan for had dressed up as a female me for Halloween.

Hilarious, Fate. I rolled my eyes and tried—again—to hold in my laugh. As she sipped at her drink and watched the crowd drift by, I found myself itching to touch her.

No, Death. Touching someone while invisible is the right way to go about sending someone insane. Even in the new magically-outed world, invisibility still wasn't normal.

"Hey, TayTay!" A rainbow-haired man dressed as a rainbow unicorn waltzed up to her in all his brightly-colored swagger. "Come dance, girl."

She shook her head.

"Tay, if you don't do something fun this evening, I'm gonna throw you into the pool." He winked. "Never know, all those wet clothes might finally get you laid."

"Ugh." She sighed. "Georgieeee . . ." she whined.

"I know, I know. You don't like hooking up." He whipped an arm around her shoulders and guided her to the air-lifted dancefloor. "I just don't get why."

"Because it should mean something more than that," she shout-whispered to be heard over the music.

The Fae in charge of the air-lift mechanism brought the dancefloor down for them to step on to, and then he lifted them into the air.

I flew up beside them and perched on the edge of the now-floating platform, not wanting to get in anyone's way. Luckily for me, they danced at the edges.

Georgie threw his arms around her waist, and they began dancing—well, he danced and forced her to move a little. "Tay, live a little, would ya?"

She smiled, and with those words, I could see the tension drop from her shoulders. She grabbed her drink, that she'd used a Fae charm to make float in the air, and downed it in one, then spun around and used Georgie like a dancing pole.

For someone so against 'living it up,' she sure knew how to act it all out. Georgie kept up, though I was pretty sure he wasn't into women—or just her, perhaps—as his eyes kept wandering to the two guys making out a few feet from them.

When she noticed, she smiled and said, "Go!"

"You sure?" He grabbed both sides of her face. "I don't wanna abandon my fav girl."

"Stop being such a goof, and go get laid." She removed his hands from her face and signalled the nearest free air-lifted one-person floor to bring her to the ground.

"Finally free," she murmured to herself the moment she was out of earshot.

I only heard her because I was so close. Seemed I couldn't be farther than a couple feet away, or my magic started burning again.

She travelled out of the main atrium, where most of the party was, and up the stairs that had been cordoned off, but just one swipe of her datachip gained her access past the magical barrier.

Seemed she lived here. But why throw a party she obviously didn't want?

I flew behind her stumbling body as she took a couple of left turns and walked into a grand library with floor-to-ceiling shelves that held so many books, it was a wonder they didn't crack the wood.

She was different in here: more alive, less tense. Her shoulders drooped as her hands brushed various shelves, and she took deep breaths of the ink- and page-filled aroma of what I could only assume was a centuries-old collection. Whoever owned this place must have had volumes and tomes handed down to them; or they could perhaps be a great collector.

After searching a few shelves of fiction, she grabbed a book seemingly at random and curled up on a couch by a massive window and sank into the pages.

I read over her shoulder and smirked at her choice of reading material: romance. Of course she'd be in to romance. I stifled a chuckle.

A couple of hours passed before someone entered the library, and she flinched her eyes up to smile at her guest. "Marty," she whispered. "Hi."

Marty's red eyes softened at the sight of her curled up with a book, his messy black hair toppling down his pale face in all its pristine glory. A turned Vampire. "Hey, Tay." He sat beside her. "Care to share?" He gestured to the book.

She chuckled. "We haven't done this since we were kids."

He shrugged. "Nothing like the good old times." He looked off into space for a moment before coming back to reality.

"Sorry," she winced. "I didn't mean to—"

"It's okay." He took a deep breath and laid an arm around her shoulders. "Really."

"Well, I ordered a cab for half one, which is in an hour, so I have time to kill."

He rested a head on her shoulder and snuggled into her neck. "Okay, bestie, read me a romance novel."

"Okay, but I'm skipping any sexy bits."

They both laughed, and before long, she began reading out loud, her voice a mimic of perfection as it rang out across their little corner in all its hiccups and cadences, her imperfections echoing her perfections to create a rise and fall that had me enraptured from the first note.

Her pink hair swayed with every laugh, her eyes creased with every sigh, and watching her was like watching a painting come to life, like someone had taken each and every brush stroke with the utmost care to create their masterpiece.

Her datachip vibrated in her wrist, and as she swiped her datascreen into the air, the alert rang clear: her cab had arrived.

"Sorry, Marty," she whispered.

"S'okay." He yawned as he stretched. "I'm gonna head to bed anyway." He got up and helped her up off her seat. "Thanks for coming. I know you hate these things."

"Wouldn't miss it for the world." She smiled, and I swear my knees buckled. "Besides," she continued, "I'm not sure I'd live through Georgie's punishment if I skipped out."

They both laughed, and she left to grab her cab that waited patiently outside the main gates.

I flew above the cab, still not being able to step away. Every time I tried, my chest felt like it was burning from the inside out, and I didn't know if my immortality would survive something that had never happened before. Besides, I was intrigued by this mortal. Her species was a mystery, but she was . . . alluring. I wanted to at least make sure she got home safely, and then I'd worry about trying to detach myself.

The cab drove her right across town to an estate that was neither great nor terrible, but the contrast between this and her previous destination could not be more obvious. Her friend was rich, it seemed, while she was not.

But just when I thought the cab was going to a housing estate downtown, it took a left and headed to a small industrial estate that manufactured human resources. The walls were barely standing in most places like this, and this one was no exception. The smell alone was enough to put even the homeless off of living in these parts, and rats ran rampant on street level.

"Hey!" she shouted, just as the cab driver threw her out and onto the street. "This isn't where I asked you to go!"

He shrugged, slammed the driver door shut behind him, and stalked toward her.

She scrambled to her feet, steadying herself on the nearest wet, moss-covered wall, and shivered. Her outfit was less than covering, and I watched as the man's eyes roamed the skin on show as his tongue darted out to wet his lips. "Ah, don't worry, girlie. I'll make your hit quick."

Her eyes widened. "Hit?" She stifled a gasp. "The SC put a hit out on me?"

I froze, not knowing what to do. This guy was a supernatural hunter, and that meant he was here to drag her to the Supernatural Council for processing. She was going to either be arrested or executed if I didn't do something, but the moment I tried to grab hold of my magic to help, my wings froze in place. I couldn't move.

Why? Why couldn't I help her?

"Please, don't!" she screamed. "I don't want to hurt you." She turned hysterical, holding her hands out in front of her, trying to stop the man from moving forward.

"Hurt me?" He laughed. "You're just a dumb little girl. What could you possibly do to me?"

She grappled with her handbag and pulled a magigun out, aiming it at his body.

"Now, now," he said, "let's not be hasty." He took a careful step forward. "If you do that, the next thing they'll do is send out an assassination contract, and we both know you don't want that."

Her finger itched over the trigger, and he ducked seconds before she pulled it back. A shot of pure Fae magic hit the wall on the other side of the alley, and she screamed in frustration.

Magiguns had to recharge, so she was out of weapons for the next couple of minutes.

The hunter laughed, and I struggled against the magic holding me back as I growled under my breath. Let. Me. Help. Her!

The hunter threw a knife at her chest, and I watched her scream as it pinned her to the concrete wall.

She scratched and clawed at the wall, but she couldn't move. Every time she inched her chest forward, she hissed. She had to be in agony.

And I couldn't do anything to help. Gah! "For heaven's sake!"

The girl in front of me, seemingly small and frail, took a deep breath as best she could and stared intently at the hunter in front of her. "I'm sorry." Her arms lifted off of the concrete as her fists clenched, and a black mist fell out of her entire being, surrounding the air in a cloud of Witch magic I hadn't seen in some time.

Death magic.

She screamed as it took the form of a horse and galloped down the alley before turning and charging straight for the hunter.

"No!" He sprang to his feet and ran, but it was no use. The death magic swallowed him whole before he reached the road.

By the time the girl had yanked the knife out and fallen to the cold hard floor, he was nothing but a pile of ash.

The magic holding me in place vanished, and I flew to the ground, turning myself visible in the process. I could heal her, I just needed a few minutes. "Please be okay."

I crouched beside her body and took a shuddering breath. Her pulse had vanished, but if I could just grab the last vestiges of her soul, I could pull them back together and save her . . .

My thoughts trailed off as a blue glow glinted above her forehead. It swirled into a familiar symbol of a reared flying horse carrying a knife between its teeth. I gasped.

"No way." I took a stuttering breath. "It cannot be."

Fate had chosen a new horseman: the Fifth Horseman of the Apocalypse.

VOLUME 2

I stay in the library all night and all of the next day, ignoring everyone's knocks on the door, every annoying mental probe from Nine, and I haven't even bothered with food. I can ask the house for some if needs be, but since I can't die of starvation, I don't really see the fucking point.

A hunter. So my nightmares are real then.

Fuck.

That means . . . All those people . . . I killed them.

That little child who killed himself rather than be dragged to the Supernatural Council; the Vampire I cornered in the ally; the rabbit Shifter I darted six times to keep unconscious. They're all . . . dead.

By my hand.

I don't know how to feel; I don't even know what to say. Fate chose me—a killer—to be the Fifth Horseman of the Apocalypse. It's sick. Disgusting. Almost laughable if the situation wasn't so dire. But above all, it's fucking ludicrous.

How?

How could Fate have chosen me? Me of all people? One of the few responsible for one of the largest turbulent situations in the magical community?

Supernatural hunters are a group of humans working for the Supernatural Council (otherwise known as the SC) to bring in rogue and criminal supernaturals for legal processing. Basically, they're bounty hunters for the magical community. Every one of them is human; every one of them, that is, except me. Apparently, I was some weird Angel-descended Witch wielding death magic. But what the hunters don't know, including me until recently, is that 'legal processing' means execution—or, at least, that's what the head seer of the Witch's Coven said she saw in a vision.

I didn't know they were being executed when I was mortal, before I was chosen by Fate to become the Fifth Horseman of the Apocalypse upon my death, making me immortal (yeah, immortal; crazy, right?). But that didn't make me a good person: I still hurt people. Still mercilessly dragged them to the SC. Still killed that little boy.

His face as blood poured out of his mouth upon swallowing the cyanide pill still haunts my every nightmare—and quite a few daymares, too. His adorable, cute, pale face that'll never know another sunrise.

I take a deep breath and release, freeing the trapped memory alongside it.

I know I need to come out of this library at some point, and many of the team have tried to encourage me with varying tactics: Nine tried encouraging me out with food and the promise of yoga; Connie tried chatting to me for hours on the other side of the door, just talking away about various memories, funny stories, and that one time someone accused her of being a dirty, unmarried twenty-year-old virgin (when she was really 422), so she had a public orgy in the town square and had to be dragged away at the hands of Arrie as they were all kicked out of town for public indecency; Arrie hasn't bothered trying, of course; but Dea's been there, unmoving, not talking—doing nothing, really, just standing there in some kind of presence of comfort.

It's lunchtime two days after the ball, and I'm pacing near the door, waiting to see who'll try next. Honestly, I'm eager to see what Arrie'll do but too scared to ask in case he does nothing.

Am I attention seeking? Hell yes.

There are piles of books everywhere, since I've been spending my time cataloging the library (well, trying to), and I've had a hard time avoiding the stacks, even with my Vampire-nimble feet. I've kicked over so many stacks this morning that my toe now has an actual bruise forming that doesn't seem to go away with its usual gusto. Humph. Instead, it stays there, looking ugly and purple, reminding me of how thirsty I am. I haven't fed in my Vampire form since the morning of the ball, so I've spent most of the time in my male form to avoid the problem, but I'm still more comfortable in my female body, so I torture myself until I can't stand it any longer.

I'm just lifting a stack of non-fiction dragon books and placing them on their new shelf when a familiar sweet smell hits my nostrils that has me dropping the pile on my already-bruised foot and running to the door handle.

Sniffing once more, I detect brownies, lasagna, and . . . blood. Fuck, damn him! Arrie has decided to bake and play on my Vampire weakness on the off-chance I'm in this form.

Maybe he had Nine check?

Nine's ability to read someone's mind usually amuses me to no end, but over the past couple of days, it's been nothing but irritating. The fucker keeps telling ridiculous jokes to make me laugh, trying to encourage me to talk, and randomly dropping in on me whenever he feels like it. So far, I've managed to avoid responding, and I feel pretty damn satisfied about that. Some of his awful dad jokes are hilarious, and they take effort to not laugh at, even in my current mood.

I'm just being stubborn now, and I need to come out, continue training, and help the team try to prevent this war (hopefully). Assuming I even can, given my mortal history.

Ugh.

Don't think about it. Don't think about it.

The door handle is cold under my slender fingers, and as much as I know I need to pull it down and open the closed door, I hesitate.

What if they now hate me? I mean, I would. A killer on the team is just a silly idea. What if I turn out to be some crazy psychopath?

We're all crazy around here, Sweetie. You try living two thousand years and see how sane you are.

I mentally chuckle, and then chastise myself for laughing at Nine's silliness after doing so well avoiding it.

Yes! Score one for Famine.

I pull the handle down with a deep breath and push the door open. I can do this. Any day now courage? I can do this. People always say that if you just act confident it'll naturally imbue you with its gloriousness, like some kind of magical ego bath. But they're wrong. Real insecurity doesn't magically go away just because we're trying to ignore it; it sticks to you like ever-lasting glue you can't seem to burn off.

My bedroom still looks the same. The same burnt-orange and yellow colors dotting the room, and the same floor-length windows still letting the midday sun trickle through the various shades of green that paint the forest outside in an insulting attempt to retain normalcy while I'm having a breakdown.

I can do this.

I tiptoe out my bedroom door, down the hallway, down the stairs, and creep into the kitchen doorway to a familiar scene: Arrie wearing a fluffy apron while the others sit around the table in their usual spots.

"She's gonna be fine, Nine. Stop worrying." Connie sits drinking a steaming cup of what I assume is peppermint tea while Nine nurses his usual cup of coffee, looking more troubled than I've ever seen him.

"You don't see what's inside her mind, Con. She thinks she's some kind of killer. A murderer." He scowls at Arrie. "And we all know whose fault that is."

"Alright." Dea raises a hand. "Enough with the arguments." Dea looks my way and smiles.

Everyone else follows his line of focus and looks at me with varying smiles: Connie beams at me, Dea gives me a charming smile, Nine tries his best but he's clearly worried, and Arrie gives his usual grunt of a hello but otherwise remains with his back to me as he continues with lunch.

Nine gestures to the chair beside him—my usual place—and I follow his hand and sit down.

I don't know what to say, so I elect to say nothing at all. All I do know is that I need some kind of distraction, so I want to ask about my training from here on out, but every time I open my mouth to speak, no words come out.

Want me to ask for you, Sweetie?

I nod.

"She wants to know about her training from here on out."

Dea looks at me with surprise, and I try for a comforting smile, but it probably looks more like a grimace.

"Well," he begins, "we have no deadline now, so back to normal. Combat with Arrie in the morning, magic with me and Nine in the afternoon, and weapons with Con in the evening."

"Can I add some studying with either you or Nine in there somewhere? I have questions, and I want an actual person to answer them."

Even I'm surprised by my blank voice, by the lack of tone and cadence I'm used to hearing.

"Sure. We can do lessons late morning and over lunch, if you would like?"

I nod.

I don't want to speak more than necessary. I don't know what's wrong with me, but I just feel so broken. So empty. If I thought not having an identity was bad, finding out that my identity is a murderer is worse.

"Lasagna and brownies are done," Arrie calls from behind us as he walks around the table and places both dishes on top. "Here." He shoves a glass of blood in front of me with a silly straw sticking out the top with a genuine smile—albeit a small one.

One sniff and I know it's Arrie's; I can't miss that sweet, woody fragrance if I try. "Thanks."

I take my time drinking it, trying to not let my fangs slip and scare Connie. I don't think my heart could handle that right now. Turns out, I can handle small sips without going full-on Vamp mode, and that actually serves to cheer me up a little.

No one brings up the obvious elephant in the room the entire time lunch is ongoing, and I'm grateful for it. I don't want to talk, not to anyone—not even to myself. Though I seem to end up doing it a lot anyway.

The need to burn off this inner frustration and anger penetrates my thoughts, but I don't know how. What would I have done in the past? Before I learned who I was? What would I have done when I was mortal?

The image of a gym passes across my mental eyes, and I know the answer: work out.

Okay, that I can do.

Nine mentioned a gym on the other side of the kitchen. Behind me is the kitchen, to the left is the door to the gardens, and to the right is the cinema. So do those double glass doors in front lead to the gym?

Yes. Feel free to use it however you like.

Thank you.

Digging into my brownies, I swallow a heavy sigh. Fuck me, they really are amazing. How does he make these damn things? I mean, hook a sister up with the recipe, damn it!

With two thousand years of practice.

Well, at least one of you has put those years to good use.

Nine scoffs. "You're internally joking now?"

"Might as well make someone laugh." I shrug.

Besides, Nine's smile still makes my insides all gooey, and don't even get me started on Dea's charming grin he probably still practices in the mirror every morning.

Grabbing my plate of brownies, I get up. "I'm going to work out for the rest of the afternoon."

"Hon, wait a minute," Connie says. "Here." She shoves a folder in my hand. At my questioning look, she says, "It's my write-up from the last mission. I was supposed to finish it ages ago, but things got a little crazy. So I finished it up this morning for you."

I nod, still confused, and glance over the few pages of notes within the flimsy file: THE

Fae appeared fine, with the usual grievances of rules and restrictions of their magic usage and dust supplies. The Shifters are having some problems with packs warring over political issues, some adhering to the SC laws and human interference and some not. But the Shifter Council seem on top of things. I received a full apology for the state Tasha and the hyena pack left me in after my last visit; I had interrupted them during a pack run and meal. No one has seen a seal, no one seems to know about Magic, and all is its usual on-the-edge feel.

Relief rushes through me. "At least the Fae and Shifters aren't causing problems."

"Indeed," Dea says.

Everyone smiles at me—well, tries to—clearly glad I've progressed past the shutting-myself-in-my-room phase and moved on to the sulking-around-the-house phase. Childish, I know, but I'm, like, two thousand years younger than them, I think I can get away with being a little childish. Maybe. Just a little.

(Hey, I won't tell if you don't.)

I open the doors to the gym and do a double take. As with everything in this damn house, it's not a gym, it's like ten gyms had a baby and produced the world's most insane fitness arena for gladiators. Everything from cardio machines, to acrobatics areas (including trapeze equipment), to the largest weights area I've ever seen, including some of the heaviest weights I've ever seen, to a jungle gym in the far corner that looks like I can get some serious shifting practice in.

I walk through and notice a sliding door to the right that has a pool beyond. Swimming sounds like a good idea. I slide the door open and inspect what I have to work with. Looks to be about a hundred-meter pool with a diving depth at the far end. Pretty standard. But then I guess pools don't have to be fancy, just functional.

Flick the night switch on the panel to your right.

Err, okay.

The panel to my right is a bit like the one in Connie's room, and after flicking the big red night button, the entire room goes dark for a moment before flittering lights fill every inch of the previously blank ceiling like the night sky. The pool has lights in the bottom that light up a deep lilac color, and a hot tub I didn't notice before bubbles away on the far right.

Fuck damn. This would make one amazing pool party.

Fiddling with the panel, I turn off the night switch and figure everything back to normal, but the aquatic gym is calling my name, and I'll be honest, I'm a little impressed, and for a moment there, I forget all about my mortal life and the horrors I've caused. It's just me and the pool shifting into something that resembles an aquatic jungle gym, with various balls of water hanging suspended in the air to mini pools embedded in raised platforms that dot the airspace of the room.

Wonder who this is for?

The door behind me opens, and the rest of the team stand behind me and gasp.

Connie grabs my shoulder. "What did you do?"

"What?"

Nine steps up next to me. "How did you make it do that?"

"Turned on the aquatic gym setting on the panel thingy." I shrug and gesture to the gray wall panel. "Is this new?"

Nine nods, looking a little speechless.

Dea examines the panel and nods in concentration. "Probably changed when she arrived, or when her Shifter abilities manifested."

I look at him in baffled confusion for a moment before it sinks in—this is where I can train my aquatic Shifter forms. Oh my goddess, I can be a dolphin! I internally clap with excitement before I temper it down in guilt. I don't deserve to be excited while other people have to live in grief because of my actions.

Nine flinches.

Ugh. This is gonna be so hard on him; he has to sit through all of this mental shit with me.

I'm sorry.

Don't be.

I spot some changing rooms in the corner and head on over. I'll have to ask the house for swimwear in both forms, I guess, but it'll be worth it. I end up asking for some kind of modest swimwear in my female form, and it gives me a tank top and shorts (which is better than a skimpy bikini) and then some board shorts. I change into both and step out in my male form, ready to check out my aquatic Shifter abilities.

The team are still standing on the side lines, waiting for me to do something.

I look at them with raised eyebrows.

"Can we watch?" Connie asks on bouncing toes while eying my mostly naked Fae form.

Right, Fae body.

Usually, I would find that funny, maybe even a little hot, but right now I just find it annoying. I don't want any more complications, much less any that would affect the team.

"Sure." I shrug and step into the pool.

I stand in the shallow end for a moment, thinking about what kind of shift I can try. I've never tried a water Shifter before. Picturing a bottle-nosed dolphin in my mind, I force my body into a different form and enter a whole other world of insanity.

Suddenly, my head's underwater, and at first, I panic, but then I remember that dolphins can hold their breath for quite a while, so I take a deep breath from the surface and dive. My tail is powerful, moving me meters in a single flick, and my fins and body allow me to change direction in a flash.

This is pretty cool. Probably not particularly useful on missions, but you never know. Right?

How do dolphins jump?

I engage my body muscles and flick my tail downward, leaping myself out of the water and back in, in what I hope is an awesome-looking dolphin jump.

My ears don't pick up on much below the water other than the gentle rolling of the waves I create, but when I poke my head up out of the water and change back, I hear the team clapping away.

I get out of the water to grab the towel left on the bench for me.

"That was awesome!" Nine runs over, his usual magic-geek self bubbling over the surface of misery I've put us both in recently. "I bet the air bubbles of water are for you to jump in and out of in various aquatic forms, and you can fly between them if you can time your shifts right, and . . ." He trails off.

But I stop listening. I understand the point of the gym, and it's great, but shifting isn't really taking my mind off of anything.

I head over to the panel and switch the pool back to its normal function, change into my female form, which takes an agonizing four minutes of concentration and awkward silence, and head back into the pool.

Lengths.

That's what I need. To feel the burn of a hard day's workout. And I'm going to achieve that through swimming lengths—as many as I can fit in between now and dinner.

I don't bother telling the others to get out, I don't even really acknowledge their presence, I just dive into the deep end and swim.

One.

I could have been normal in my death.

Two.

I could have just died and moved onto wherever the hell the afterlife is.

Three.

I could have not been stuck with these stupid gifts in the first place.

Four.

Why did I join the Hunter Society?

Five.

Why did my parents have to die?

Six.

Why was I alone?

Seven.

Why didn't Mr. Compton take me in instead?

Eight.

Gah! I have so many questions, but I'm really not prepared to find the answers. There's a niggling, however, somewhere in my mind, that in order to understand this war, I'm going to have to find out everything about my life, including the people I left behind.

By the time I've done well over a hundred lengths (and taken many breaks in between), Nine calls for dinner.

My body aches—there are parts of my body that ache that I didn't even know have muscles—but it feels good. So fucking good. And I can't help the smile that creeps across my face as I walk into the kitchen with my wet chlorinated hair, my swimwear still on but covered by a gold-colored slip that falls to my mid-thigh, and my eyes stinging from my stupid decision to swim without goggles for hours.

"You look happier?" Connie is sat in her usual position, looking me up and down as I sit next to Nine in my not-so-dinner-appropriate outfit.

"Yeah, not bad."

"So, you like swimming, then?" Nine's hand rests on my knee, like usual, but he pulls it back with a smirk. Probably because I'm not clothed like normal.

"Seems so." I grab myself a glass of water and chug it down. "So, what's for dinner?"

"Tacos," Arrie grumbles from the kitchen.

Is he cooking again? Why?

Because he thinks it'll cheer you up.

That's . . . adorable. I'm sure he'll piss me off again before I can thank him, though. He usually does.

Sighing, I grumble under my breath before turning to Connie. "What does weapons training involve?"

"Fighting with weapons." She shrugs and smiles to hide her laugh. "Nah, just training you to fight with all kinds of weapons. I reckon it'll be a challenge to find weapons that'll shift with you, though."

"I'll probably have to have weapons for both forms. Not sure about my Shifter abilities, though." Would my weapons stay on my person when I shift back? My clothes do.

"I'll look into it," Nine says from beside me. "Should be fun."

Arrie places the tacos on the table, and everyone digs in. I'm surprised Dea has stayed silent up until now. He hasn't mentioned plans, what happened at the ball, or anything. Maybe he's trying to be considerate?

Well, that's stupid. I look at Dea to get his attention. "What's next?"

He sighs a lazy smile. "I am not sure, Angel."

"Oh." He doesn't know what to do, either. Maybe it's time I start making some suggestions, given that this war is mine to solve after all. Somehow. According to some mysterious Fate figure. "I think we need to investigate this rogue Vampire faction, see who they're working for?" I raise my voice into a question so as not to sound pushy or order-y. "They seem hell bent on us, for some reason. And I'd like to deal with them before they become a bigger problem."

Dea nods. "That sounds like a swell idea." He leans back in his chair and goes back to being silent.

Why is he being so weird?

He's letting you lead.

Fucking why? I can barely aim my dick at the toilet bowl most mornings.

He thinks it's the right call to make.

But I don't even know the team all that well, or the world, or fucking anything! I'm clueless.

You won't always be. And you have us.

I take a deep breath and look at the people around me. Nine's right. I might not know everything, but I bet the team's collective knowledge far exceeds anything I could have alone. So even if I did remember every detail of my mortal life, I would still be outmatched in knowledge.

"Okay." I look to Dea. "Shall we leave for Earth next Monday? Give everyone a chance to recover from the ball and for me to get in some kind of weapons training so I don't have to rely on being unarmed."

Dea nods. "Sure. Sounds good."

3

The training structure I've found myself in is grueling, and I'm only halfway through day one. I'm not sure I can keep this insanity up. Arrie's combat session went much the same as last time, with us both staying as silent as possible and him teaching me how to block a variety of hand-to-hand attacks, all with varying degrees of strength and technique. My gym session consisted of a mix of cardio and plyometrics and a half hour swim session to cool down.

Now, however, I'm finally sitting in my study, with Dea on a chair beside me that I dragged (begrudgingly) from another section.

"Do you know what you would like to study, Angel?" He places a hand on my knee, stroking his thumb over the soft spot on the inside, and I swear my insides melt.

"I . . . err . . ." Damn. All this does is bring back memories of that stupid kiss. Stupid hot. Stupid hot kiss. Goddess, I could really use more of that in my life.

"Angel?"

"Oh, errm . . ." My face heats a familiar shade of red, and I dart away from his gorgeous galaxy eyes and shift my attention to the suddenly interesting floor. "I wanted to . . ." What did I want to learn about again? Oh, yeah! "I wanted to learn about the SC." I cough my throat clear.

"Ah, I see." He removes his hand from my knee, and I have to swallow the whine of disapproval that threatens to break free from my sealed lips. "Why not ask your Seeing Stone?" He points to the milky-white crystal ball on my desk in front of us.

A Seeing Stone, I learned recently, is a stone that, if you hold and think about your emotions, problems, and/or ask your internal questions, will provide you the answer in book form. Well, mine provides it in book form.

"The Seeing Stone is great, it really is, but I wanted to get some opinionated accounts. You know, from real people who were there."

He nods, shaking a strand of hair away that's fallen into his eye. Goddess, he's beautiful. Like, seriously, insanely stunning. There's not more than an inch of space between us as he sits there in his black jeans and white tee that shows the edges of that delicious golden swirling tattoo inked on his shoulder, chest, and torso, and from here, I can see the ridges of his abs beneath the thin material.

My hand reaches out before I can stop it, and I find myself tracing the edges of that tattoo. I really want to ask what it means, but I know the story is probably a painful one from the dark expression that passes across his face whenever I ask. But I can't stop myself from touching it, tracing its pattern around his shoulder.

Dea watches me with a smug expression, and I gaze at his relaxed eyes in somewhat of a trance until he clears his throat and snaps me out of it. "Angel . . . ?"

"Yeah?" My hand's still resting on his shoulder, but I'm reluctant to remove it.

"About that kiss . . ." He looks away from me, breaking eye contact. "I just wanted to offer my apologies if I was too forward—"

"Stop." I place my finger to his lips. "I . . . liked it."

"Oh," he replies, kissing my fingertip in a gentle breath, "I know." Aaaand there's that famous smugness. Damn him and his confident attitude. It's sexy as hell. "But I know that you would rather wait until you are ready, and I just—"

"Dea, please stop."

He stops talking, thank the goddess.

"I'm not sure what I want. I mean, what I said before still stands, I want a life, a future, a . . . I don't know, life partner? Whatever you'd call it when you're immortal. A family. But I can't stay away from you all forever. Eventually, I . . ."

Eventually I'll what, exactly? Cave and give in? There are plenty of men and women in the world I can casually sleep with that would create far fewer strings.

"Yes?" He opens his mouth and slips my finger inside, gently rolling his tongue along the sensitive tip. "You will what, Angel?"

"I . . . don't know," I whisper between gasps. Just the thought of other places his tongue could be doing that has me squirming in my seat.

His eyes bore into my soul as he watches me wrestle with my own mind, but in the end, I'm too weak to resist those soft lips of his; I remember their sweetness and their urgency, a hot mix of syrupy heat that buckles my knees and makes my head spin.

Dea leans forward and places a commanding hand on my waist, letting my finger go and inclining his head toward mine.

He's going to kiss me again, isn't he?

"What about Nine?" I mumble before I can stop it. I cringe the moment it comes out. "Sorry."

Dea smiles. "Do not be sorry. I like that you care about him too. But I already told him about our kiss, so there is no need to fret."

I sigh my relief, but before I can rethink my choice, Dea sweeps in and catches my sigh with his lips. His hand travels under my top to stroke gentle circles on the small of my back, the pace of his hand matching the rhythm of his tongue.

As heat pools in my center and I can't help but arch my back against his touch, my body takes over, knowing what it needs and letting nothing stand in its way. I pull away and climb onto his lap, straddling his legs and recapturing that kiss.

Warm hands run up my back, tracing patterns up and down my spine as I run my hands over his chest, tracing my fingers over the delicious ridges of his torso. I inch my hands lower and soon find the waistline of his jeans and underwear. I hesitate. I want this. Fuck, do I want this. My hands fumble with the button, eager to take this further and wrap my hand around his—

His hands catch mine and pull them away. "No, Angel. Not right now."

Is he being fucking serious?

"Sorry, but I do not want to be a mistake."

I flinch. I didn't even consider that. Would sleeping with Dea right now be a mistake? I sigh. Yeah, fucking probably. I'm not ready. I mean, I'm soooo ready, but I'm still not sure what I want in the long run, and any mistake I make with the team is permanent. And an immortal's permanent is pretty fucking lasting.

"Sorry."

Dea captures my chin in his hand and forces me to look at him. "Stop doing that. Stop being sorry for being yourself." He smiles.

Footsteps echo from behind us as someone coughs. "What kind of lessons are you teaching her, bro?"

I fly off of Dea's lap and back into the chair next to us, my face redder than a tomato.

Niiiiiine. Could've given me a heads up, asshole.

Wouldn't have been half as fun.

Dea and Nine just laugh at my flushed face, but I quickly recover.

"What did you want?"

"Just to see what lessons you were learning today, but I had no idea they would be this exciting. I would have joined earlier." He winks at me and grabs another chair.

"Err, well, I was just asking about the SC before we got . . . distracted."

Nine chuckles. "What would you like to know?"

I look at them both with a serious expression (well, I hope it's serious). "Everything."

Dea clears his throat. "A history lesson, then."

Nine leaves to browse the stacks of books I've spent the last few days organizing and cataloging (not getting very far), while Dea stands and paces on the other side of my desk.

"A hundred years ago, we helped organize the outing of the supernatural community. As you know, the Witches did not join the other pillar communities in this plight. Nor did a few lesser species."

At my questioning eyebrows, he explains, "Dragons and unicorns, among other things, are still vastly regarded as myth, a few demon creatures we let live after the original war, such as hellhounds and succubae, never came out of the closet, and there are probably lots of hybrid species we know nothing about."

I start taking diligent notes, making a list of things I want to look up, such as demon species and how to recognize them, whether dragons really are extinct, and what the hell succubae are.

But Dea continues with his lecture, and much to my pleasant surprise, he's a natural lecturer. But then, he would be, wouldn't he? His voice is so . . . dreamy.

Focus.

Right.

"When we planned the outing of the supernatural world, we told the human leaders first. This allowed them to conduct counter measures to rebellions, control the media of the mass public, and more importantly, to create the SC."

"So, it really was human created then?"

"Yes." He clears his throat and continues. "The three main pillar communities—Vampires, Shifters, and Fae—negotiated with the human governments to have some say in how the Supernatural Council was run, given that it will be looking after their people."

"Makes sense," I add. "Couldn't have any unfair laws just because humans didn't understand the culture of the other races."

"Right," Dea adds. "And it was, and still is, run by a council of twelve individuals, three from each race: Vampire, Shifter, Fae, and human."

"No Witches?"

"No. They chose to stay in hiding, and they aren't ever prosecuted by the SC unless it is something extreme and a threat to the general public."

So that's why the Witch Coven aren't worried about the SC intervening in Witch politics. Because they can't.

"Yes." Nine comes back around the corner he went down earlier with a stack of books piled higher than his face. "It would be a violation of the Species Protection Treaty, created at the time of the supernatural outing to protect the integrity and survival of each species."

Dea takes half of the pile from Nine's grasp, and they both place them down on the desk.

"Here," Nine says as his half-pile slams the desk, "start with these."

I grab a couple off the piles and read their titles:

Supernatural Policies and Laws

Supernatural Council: The Formation

Supernatural Treaties and their Protections

"Damn, Nine." I cough at the dust one of the books chucks up as I open the front cover. "This is some reading list."

"I'm sure you can fit it into your schedule, Sweetie."

Yeah, along with dying from sleep deprivation. My muscles twinge at the memory of my schedule, and I stand up to stretch.

"You okay?" Nine walks over and looks at me with a worried expression. "You seem . . . tense?"

"Do I?" I laugh. "I didn't notice."

"Don't be snarky with me just because you chose a stupidly intense schedule."

"Not like I have the time to relax. Might as well train as much as I can." I reach down to touch my toes, and my back pangs. "Ah!" I hiss.

"Stop." Dea steps up with his glowing healing hands at the ready. "You need to slow down. Day one is not even complete yet. You will not be able to keep this up."

I look at them both, their annoyingly worried gazes, Nine biting his lip in concern, and Dea with his glowing hands, ready to heal me.

"Watch me."

I sit back at the desk and ask, "How are the SC run now?" I open the book on supernatural policies and laws and begin flicking through. "Is it still the same kind of council formation?"

Dea and Nine exchange glances and then sigh in unison.

"Technically," Dea starts, "yes. But there is a lot of underhanded playing, tied loyalties, and blackmailing behind the scenes."

I grunt. "Great."

"Well," Nine says, "everyone was present at the ball, so at least no one's been assassinated yet."

"Real helpful." I yawn and look at the time. Fuck. It's already 1:30. "Ready for magic study?"

Nine looks at me and smiles. "Always."

My training room flashes an ugly shade of heated gray due to the fireplace in the corner flickering against the cracked concrete walls.

"So far"—Nine wraps his arms around me in the otherwise empty room—"we can access all your abilities."

I nod in agreement.

"I think I'll leave your shifting practice to your gym sessions and ask if Arrie and Con'll include it in some of the later physical stuff. That way we can work on everything else."

That's actually a good idea. That way we don't have to work on one of the four sets and can instead focus on the other three.

"I'm also pretty happy with your Vampire abilities, using them to enhance your other powers and be useful in less active scenarios. So, really, I just want to work on your Witch and Fae powers."

Ugh. I groan in frustration. Witch powers means working on unlocking my other elemental abilities, mastering charm magic, and tapping into my seer powers, while Fae magic means learning spells. Honestly, both of those things already hurt my head.

"Hey, quit complaining!" Nine pulls back with a smirk. "This way, you don't have to do anything physically stressful. You can sit down for the whole afternoon."

I raise my eyebrows in disbelief as an overwhelming urge to kiss him confronts me. No moving for the whole afternoon? Bring magic lessons on!

That really all it takes?

Shut up!

"C'mon! C'mon! C'mon!" I yank him into the middle of the room. "I want to try to unlock some more of my elements. I can use air pretty well and am still practicing in what few spare moments I have to use it in unique ways."

Nine chuckles. "Okay, okay."

Nine's Chinese features glow in the firelight, and for a moment there, his brown eyes catch ablaze and glow an intense shade of orange, but it's gone the moment I blink. He really is beautiful in this light.

I watch his cheeks blush. *Thank you.*

Laughing at his formality, I yank his arm once more and sit us both on the concrete floor. "How do I unlock my other abilities?"

He shrugs. "No idea."

Well, great.

"How did you unlock your air one?"

I think about it for a moment and remember how Nine went into my mind and forced me to engage with my magical center. "It was after you went into my mind."

He cringes. "I don't want to do that again."

"Why not?" Is there something wrong with my mind? Is it a bad place to be?

A hand caresses my upper arm, and I gaze at Nine's grimacing face. "No, not at all. It's just . . . I hate being in people's minds like that. I end up seeing more of them than I would ever like." He looks away and gazes into the fire. "Even with people I care about."

Oh. "Nine, I'm s—"

"Don't do that. My life is nothing to be sorry about." He turns back around and smiles. "Now, how do we unlock those other elements?" He mumbles to himself.

"Out loud, Nine. I want to hear your thoughts."

He stops mumbling and looks at me. "Really?"

"How else can we figure it out together?"

His usually casual smile reaches ear to ear. "I was just thinking that me forcing you to engage with your magic shouldn't have just unlocked a single element. It should have unlocked them all."

"I could just be an air Witch, you know."

He looks at me and blinks in indifference. "Nope. You're designed to engage with the entire magical community: Vampires, Fae, every Shifter . . . and every Witch." He sighs. "You can't just be one type of Witch any less than you can be just one type of Shifter."

I nod. It makes sense. There's so much about my identity that doesn't fit into one pocket of society, from my gender, to my sexuality, to my magic. "Is that how it's meant to be?" I look to the floor. "Fitting in everywhere so that I fit in nowhere."

Nine tilts my head up and meets my eyes in a blazing heat. "I think there's a point to it. I think . . . that maybe you're meant to bring about magical and societal change so that the world remains in peace."

I blink. "That's . . . a tall fucking order."

Nine chuckles and drops my gaze. "I know." He stands. "I have an idea." He walks over to the fireplace and grabs the spade.

"What are you doing?"

"Testing a theory." He opens the glass door to the fireplace and shovels out a piece of lit coal, keeping it carefully on the spade. "I want you to touch it."

But . . . that'll hurt.

"Even if it does hurt, which I don't think it will, Dea can heal you if you don't manage it yourself."

I nod. "What's your theory?"

"I think your first power was air because it was the first thing your magic latched on to. Air is all around us. If we were in a pool at the time, I think it would have been water." He inches closer to where I sit on the floor, the spade hovering at head height.

I know that fire can't hurt me that much, and even if it does, I'll heal in no time, but that doesn't stop my hands from shaking, the sweat from billowing across my forehead, and the ever-quickening breaths my chest heaves over.

It's going to be fine. It's going to be fine.

Goddess, stop being so stupid!

"Go on." Nine pushes the spade to an inch from my nose. "Touch it."

I raise my hand, and Nine pulls the spade back, giving me room to move. Inching my hand closer, the heat bores down between my fingers. My hands get clammy as I flick my fingertip across the flame.

I snatch my hand back, cradling it in my other palm against my chest, but . . . it doesn't hurt. I expected the familiar feel of burning, the sting of bubbling skin, but nothing. I feel nothing.

Nine holds the spade out still, expecting me to try again. So I do. I edge my finger into the flame all the way until my palm grabs the coal and lifts it off the metal.

Wow. "I'm doing it!" I'm holding fire!

"Well, kinda. You're holding already created fire, but you haven—"

"Shut it, Nine! I'm holding fire." I can't keep the grin off my face. Okay, so I'm not actually creating the flame, and holding a burning coal hasn't magically unlocked my fire powers, but it's a start. And a start I can do.

"There's all kinds of uses for that power alone. You could throw flaming daggers, walk through fire, not be affected by fire magic . . ."

He's right. This can be useful. My powers are growing at such a rate, it's a little unsettling. Do I have any limits? Will I ever stop growing?

Eventually. None of us have gained new powers in centuries.

Oh. Well, that's hopeful, at least.

"Life will be more relaxing one day. Promise." Nine places the coal back into the fireplace and the spade back on the hook on the wall and sits beside me. "You doing okay?" His hand sits on my knee again, and I can't help but be comforted by the familiar gesture, as though his warmth flows into me.

"I don't know." I really don't. There's so much to unload. So much new information I have to unpack.

"You don't have to unpack it all at once."

"But it's not information I can do anything with. It'll just sit there, stewing."

He nods but remains otherwise silent.

"I just wish . . . Gah! I don't even know anymore. I was a murderer, I'm now the Fifth Horseman: I have to deal with all of you, I have to save the world, I have to figure out what's going on in order to save it, and all the while . . . we're just waiting for some war to happen when I would rather prevent it in the first place."

Deep breaths heave my chest as I cling to Nine's hand like it's a life raft in my new crazy world.

"It's okay." He strokes his spare hand up and down my back, and I feel the tears coming before I even have a chance to stop them.

But what am I crying about?

I try to make sense of it, but heaving sobs wrack my brain before I can use even a cell to make a thought.

How could he reject me? The fucking asshole!

Ugh. That's what I'm crying about? But that makes sense. He made the right call.

"Wait a minute, who rejected you?"

I look at Nine through tear-stained eyes. "Dea." Sniffling, I try to pretty up my face and stop looking like an insane victim of heartbreak.

"He did . . . what?" he asks through gritted teeth.

"Please don't be mad at him. It was the right choice."

Nine looks at me questioningly.

"It would have been a mistake to sleep with any of you when I'm still not sure what I want given . . . everything." Given that I can't actually have any of you, I say mentally, fearing the words enough to not say them out loud.

Goddess, I sound pathetic.

Nine chuckles. "You should ask what Dea and I talked about after you made us have that chat."

"Huh?"

"Nope. Not gonna tell you now, Sweetie."

"Nine!" I whine. "Come on!" I swat him on the arm.

He jumps to his feet and holds out his hand.

"Noooo, you promised I could stay sat."

He rolls his eyes and drags the desk chair to where I now sit. "There."

Huffing, I get up with a wince and sit in the chair.

"Let's see if we can replicate that fire with your own." He calls the house for a bucket of water and throws it over the fireplace. "Relight it."

The rest of the four hours I'm stuck in that ever-colder room I spend in magical exhaustion, up to the point where I nearly faint off the chair and Nine forces me to take a break. Still, though, no fire.

Frustration could not have been more evidently plastered across my sweat-sheened face when I sit down to dinner.

Today so far: Arrie's still a god in combat, the SC are assholes (no surprises there), and I'm still a fire-less Witch. If I don't make some kind of progress with Connie this evening, I might just burst.

Arrie is still cooking for me and being . . . nice, and I'm still utterly baffled by his intentions. "So, what you girls working on this evening?" he asks in an attempt to make conversation.

I just look at Connie in bewilderment, as though I can't understand why he's talking to me in the first place.

She, of course, just laughs it off and answers, "See what weapons she likes, introduce her to ones I think she might be able to use, and then spend a few hours putting her on her ass." She shrugs.

Hope she can dodge my knives, 'cos I'm gonna stab her if she doesn't give me a win.

Nine laughs at my inner turmoil, and clearly it's written all over my face because she looks at me with red cheeks and a warm smile.

"No one's good at weaponry straight away. It takes time. Training. Effort."

"I'm sure." My eyes roll of their own volition, and everyone laughs at my own personal world of training pain. "So, err . . ." Breathe, Horseman, breathe. "When was the Hunter Society formed?"

Everyone's heads turn my way, cutlery gently placing themselves down on the table. They all start talking at once, and I can't hear any of them, no matter how much I try to focus on one person's sound.

"Stop worrying and just give me the fucking answer!" I am so done with their tiptoeing around my feelings. I'm a grown-ass woman, I can handle bad news. I'm still here after Mr. Compton's bombshell, aren't I?

Nine's the one who steps up after everyone remains silent for more than a single breath. "About ten years into the supernatural outing and the SC's formation, we had a problem with public supernatural criminals. It was causing bad press for the magical community as a whole, and the SC wanted to change that. So they created the Hunter Society. Humans could take back some semblance of control by bringing in rogue and criminal supes in exchange for money. Not only did it reduce crime, but it helped balance out the new world."

"Thank you."

5

Connie meets me in the gym, an assortment of weapons at her feet, as Arrie sits on one of the many weight machines, working away, and I would be lying if I said my eyes don't linger a moment longer than would be polite.

"So, what weapons are you most excited about?" Connie asks, snapping me out of my daydream.

"Errr . . . what weapons are there?"

"Wow. Okay."

She looks far too surprised for my liking, and I suddenly feel seriously underprepared for this session. I should have done some prep.

"Wait, sorry. No. Not what I meant." She shakes her hands. "Just surprised that mortals don't really get weapons these days."

Doesn't really help make me feel better, but I'll take it. Some tension between us will be good for our . . . relationship (goddess, that sounds ridiculous); it'll put some distance between us.

"Well," I say as I peruse the many—did she bring the entire armory?—weapons on offer, "I'm good with knives, so maybe smaller ranges might be good?"

"Good thinking." She picks up a pair of dual blades, shorter in length than most here, but not as short as the various daggers at her feet. "Try these."

I grab the blades from her and hold them by the hilt at my sides. I look at her in question, and she tries hard to suppress a giggle, but clearly, I'm not knowledgeable about all this stuff.

"Okay, widen your stance, like you would when throwing."

I follow her instructions.

"Good. Now hold them out in front you, but ensure your elbows are tucked in, protecting your center." She claps when I have the stance right. "These are dual shamshirs, but they're slightly shorter than what is common to allow for their dual nature. This type of sword isn't usually dualized, but it works well for fast soldiers, and given your Vamp nature, speed is gonna be your friend."

"Especially against her," Arrie grumbles from behind me.

I don't look back; I don't want to be distracted again. Instead, I nod at her. "Now what?"

She grabs a fancy-looking longsword with some Celtic writing on the hilt that glows a faint gold against the bronze wrapping. "We try it out."

Like, right now? Eek. I don't want to fight the Horseman of Conquest ever, much less right now, after a full day of exhausting training.

"Ready yourself. And try to block."

I nod, hands shaking.

"Don't look so terrified, I'm not going to kill you, silly."

"Right."

Connie runs at me with her sword, slashing it in front of her, aiming for my torso.

I manage to put both swords up in time to block the attack, but they fly out of my hands.

"Grip harder next time."

I pick up my swords, readjusting my stance back to normal. "Right."

She attacks again, this time slower, in a timed attack I manage to predict—somehow. As she brings her sword down on my head, I duck and move out of the way.

"Good." Her arms do some fancy flailing I can't see; they move too fast for me to understand where she's going to strike next.

It works, because the sword nicks my shoulder, and I hiss at the paper-like cut now oozing a thin trickle of blood down my arm.

"Okay." She puts her sword back in its place on a nearby table. "Let's try another weapon."

We spend the next few hours exploring how well I naturally use each weapon, no matter how silly and untrained my form is. A few of them are clunky, difficult to manage, and are a clear no-go for me, so we put those to the side, and we are left with a few options.

"Does it have to be a sword?" I ask.

"Huh?"

"My weapon, does it have to be a sword?"

"Well," she hesitates, "no." She shakes her head. "What were you thinking?"

"No idea. But something less . . . aggressive."

Arrie laughs from behind us, still working out. Probably just trying to watch us and wanting an excuse. "You want something that won't instantly kill someone, don't you?" He walks up behind me and places his hands on my shoulders. I don't respond, not wanting to give my inner thoughts away. "You know," he says, "every weapon is dangerous in the right hands. No matter how sharp its edges might be."

"You can be really wise when you want to be, Arrie."

Connie laughs and steps forward, sandwiching me between the two of them. "Shame he's usually such an ass."

That has us all laughing—even Arrie, who punches her in the arm hard enough for her to have to step back.

They're both standing close enough for me to feel their body warmth, Arrie at my back and Connie at my front. And damn, I don't need this level of sexy from these two (I have enough threesome issues with Nine and Dea).

Heard that.

Ugh, go away.

He mentally chuckles at me, and I sigh.

"You know," Connie says, "you need to slow down."

Arrie grabs my waist from behind in a surprisingly hot grab to press me flush against his front. "She's right." He grumbles something in a language I don't understand, but Connie does, because she blushes.

She steps forward, and I find myself pressed between the two of them in an embrace I did not see coming.

"What is this, see who can make me break first?"

"We did have that bet, yes, but only in a playful way." Connie smiles at me and whispers in my ear, "Though I'm not certain someone hasn't already won."

What? How does she know about earlier?

She blinks at me in surprise. "Wait, what?"

"You were just teasing, weren't you?" I sigh. Damn. I actually wasn't going to tell her about Dea's rejection.

"What happened?" Arrie asks from behind.

"I don't want to talk about it. It . . . didn't go well."

"What. Did. They. Do. Now?" Connie says through gritted teeth.

"Nothing."

Arrie tightens his grip on my waist. "Not leaving until you tell us."

Sighing once more, I grunt. "He said no."

Connie growls. "Which one of those pretty fuckers rejected you after everything you've been through in the last few days?" She looks at me with expectancy.

"Dea."

That answer seems to surprise them both, as they step away from me and glare at each other, clearly having some kind of secret conversation.

"Stop worrying." I start a run on the nearest treadmill. "He was right. It would have been a mistake." Not wanting to cry in front of either of them, I push to a faster pace and run using my Vampire speed for a solid thirty minutes before I stop and turn back around.

They're both nattering away on the floor, waiting for me to come back to the session.

"Okay"—I step up to the weapons—"what's next?"

Connie points to the next few we need to try, and we go at it again; she pushes me to use each one naturally as Arrie makes sarcastic remarks from the side lines. In a way, it's kind of perfect. Almost like home.

The bed that night feels better than it's ever felt. I'm off in mere seconds.

Unfortunately, my mind is not, and clearly, it's not done with these stupid nightmares.

I'm in a room with no windows this time, a concrete room with knives, swords, guns, and all sorts littering the edges and dark corners. I'm in my training room.

"Can't believe I lost that fucking mark," I grumble beneath my breath. Throwing a dagger at the target, I hit dead center and laugh under my breath. "Fucking stupid dog."

A bell sounds in the distance.

Fuck.

It sounds again before I make it to the doorway of the training room. Once outside, I hit a button behind a book on the nearest bookcase and watch as a magical spell activates and a shimmering disguise of wall covers the door.

The bell sounds again, and I realize it's the doorbell.

"Coming!"

Running through the hallway, I answer the door to a pale, smiling face. "Marty! Hey." I move out of the way to let him in.

"Hey, Tay." He smiles at me in a way that's almost charming, but if mortal me realizes that, she doesn't react.

"Want anything to drink?"

"Hilarious, Tay." He flashes his fangs, and I internally panic. I'm not sure whether it's mortal me or dream me that gasps, but it's internal nonetheless.

"Just keeping things light."

So I was friends with a Vampire? Seems unlikely.

"Was just wondering if, maybe, you wanted to grab a coffee this evening?" He fumbles with the collar of his shirt, and I notice his distinct lack of confidence despite seeming familiar with me.

He likes me. He's asking me on a date?

Dream me hesitates, grasping her coffee cup with more force than is necessary. "Err . . . I'm not sure . . ."

"Oh," he says, disappointment filling his features. "That's okay. Maybe next time."

"Yeah, I guess." I don't turn around; I just stand with my back to him like a coward.

Just tell him straight, you asshole! I find myself yelling at . . . myself. (Odd experience.)

"Listen, Taylor. Would you"—he steps up to me and grabs my hips—"like to go out with me properly? You know, one day?"

"I-I-I . . ." I stumble through several reiterations of this sentence starter before I finally turn around and look him in the eyes.

Before I can get out my answer, though, Marty places his lips on mine and kisses me. I gasp into his mouth, and Marty takes his opportunity to deepen his show of affection, and now I find myself making out with someone I'm pretty sure I don't like. No, I'm absolutely sure.

Finally, I peel myself away. "Marty, I'm sorry. But . . . I don't like you in that way."

"But the kiss?"

"You took me by surprise is all. You've never been forward before."

"Thought I'd try a different strategy." He looks to the floor, and I can see the tears rimming his eyes.

Goddess, how horrible could one mortal have been in their life?

"Well," he starts, "I'll just be going. But still friends, right?"

"Always."

. . .

My eyes shoot open in the pitch black of my room (I closed the curtains for once), and I try—and fail—to catch my breath.

"What the fuck was that?"

6

Nothing quite like throwing up first thing in the morning, and that's how I find myself leaning over the toilet basin at five am the next day. What a way to start a Friday.

Ugh. All that training yesterday really wiped me out, and not to mention the severe lack of sleep all this dreaming and nightmare-ing is causing my already tired body.

Need to be at my morning yoga session in half an hour. Need to get up. Get out. Start my day.

I throw on some clothes after rinsing my mouth out as best I can and head to the garden, where I'm met by a surprisingly peaceful face.

Dea is waiting for me in my *Shinto* shrine, legs crossed and arms resting peacefully on each leg. His glossy black hair falls into his eyes, but he makes no effort to move the stray strands. He looks peaceful.

"Err, Dea?"

"Hmm?" He doesn't open his eyes; instead, he keeps them closed and continues audibly breathing.

"What're you doing?"

"Joining you." He opens his left eye. "Is that okay?"

"Err . . . sure."

I scoot him back slightly so I can have more room, and I begin stretching through my urge to yawn. Goddess, I'm tired. This is going to suck. This whole day is going to suck. Just the thought of Arrie's hand-to-hand combat training in an hour makes me want to crawl back into bed and hide under the duvet until sunset.

Nope, I tell myself, you need to train. You need to be better.

Okay, I can do this.

Stretching into my next pose, Dea interrupts. "About yesterday . . ."

Ugh, that's why he's here. Great. More humiliation.

"I am sorry." He steps up to me and pulls me to standing. "I might not have explained myself well, and now I feel like you might be feeling a little rejected."

He looks shy all of a sudden, and that cute look does nothing to quell the crazy tumbling of my insides; he's so damn gorgeous . . .

"Fucking damn it, Dea! Why are you so fucking hot?"

He blinks and chuckles. "What?"

"I can't ever be mad at you, you're just too attractive. It's annoying as hell." I bunch my fists at my sides. "Nine, too. He gives me that sad puppy-dog look, and I just melt. I swear, he could make me take a literal trip to hell with that look."

Dea's choking with laughter at this point. "I had no idea you were so caught up in us, Angel." He rests a hand on my cheek, and I find myself leaning into his warm touch. "I am not ashamed to admit that I want you. I just want you to be making the right choice."

I nod, swallowing back the tears. "I know. And you're right." I sigh and hiccup. "I don't know what I want anymore."

"What happened to your plan?"

"What? The seduce-everyone-onto-my-side plan?" I laugh. "It was just a cute fantasy. It's never gonna happen. I don't need my own harem of lovers, Dea." Sighing, I roll my eyes.

He looks at me with a serious expression, all his usual charming smiles and warming eyes vanishing. "To live, to really live, you need to go after what you want and not just suffer with what you need." He brushes the tear that's fallen astray and leans in to kiss my forehead. "If you want us, come and get us."

Stepping back from him, I can't think straight. Is he saying he wants to . . . what? Be one of my lovers? That's . . . crazy. I can't have all of them, can I?

Dea turns to walk back inside, but at the last minute, he stops and turns to face me head on. "For the record, you already have me."

"I . . . I . . ."

Before I can think of anything to say, he fazes back to the house, leaving me standing in the center of the shrine on a misty Friday morning, tears running down my cheeks as a warm sort of nervous relief washes through me.

He . . . wants me? He wants this? All of this? To help me bring the team together and give everyone what they really want?

To give me what I want?

Yoga. C'mon, focus on the schedule. No time to ponder over Dea's declaration of . . . fondness. There're only a few days until our next mission, and I want to be able to actually help this time.

Hopefully, we'll stay together.

Once I'm halfway through my yoga routine, I change into my male form and complete the other half. I'll admit, my male form is much less flexible than my female form; it means I have to dumb down the second half of my routine.

"This is a pile of shit," I mumble to myself as I walk to Arrie's forest clearing.

The sky is cloudy today, and I remember reading that *Sheruta* has a rainy season in between each dry season. Must be coming up to a rainy season.

Arrie's waiting for me in the middle of the clearing and looks at me with surprise. "You gonna train in that form today?"

Oh. I look down at myself and remember that I can't be bothered to change back. "Yeah."

"Why?" He looks genuinely curious, but I can't ignore the accusation in his tone.

Lie: "Need to train both forms at some point. Why not now?" Truth: I'm exhausted and can't be arsed to change back.

Arrie nods and gestures for me to join him in the center. "I'm going to show you how to block better today. Now that I know what kind of stuff you're capable of."

Nodding, I walk on over to him.

He turns me around so that my back is to his front, and it reminds me of the precarious position he and Connie put me in yesterday.

Focus.

Right.

Arrie places his hands on my waist and turns my position so that I'm half side-on, half front-on. "Pull your elbows in, like Con showed you yesterday, and use your fists to protect your middle." He moves my hands into the right places and steps back. "There."

Turning around to my front, Arrie matches my stance. "Block."

And that is how we spend two hours, him trying to punch me, and me trying to block as best I can. Occasionally, he'll adjust my position or alter what I'm trying to do, but mostly, I learn through practice. The more I try to block his attacks, the more I find myself actually doing it.

Arrie isn't a talker, but that's okay because he's a good trainer. I'm actually learning under his instruction, and hopefully, all of this will come in useful on our mission.

Just three days to go. Then, I'll be ready. We'll be ready.

"Enough." Arrie wipes the sweat from his forehead with a towel, then throws it my way. "Breakfast."

I decide breakfast that morning doesn't apply to me. I just grab some buttered toast and run to the gym. Connie tries to protest, but I ignore her.

"She's gonna work herself to death at this rate," she says as I close the door.

"She needs to learn that for herself," Dea adds.

"Oh, don't you start with that wise old shit. You're adding to her problems!"

"Con, could you keep your voice do—" Nine tries to interrupt.

"Stop defending him. If you weren't prepared to actually fuck her, you shouldn't have led her on."

Dea interrupts her ranting. "I will have you know, I fixed that this morning. I apologized and explained myself better."

"Oh my fuck, what did you say to her now? Every time you open your mouth, you confuse her further!" Connie doesn't take any shit from the guys, and now she's extending that protection to me, it seems.

But I can't take any of them getting an ear-full just because of me, so I reopen the door and glare at her. "That's enough, Connie. It's fine. We have more important things to worry about."

She nods but still sits there glaring daggers at Dea, much to my pride. A girl's gotta have some female backup against these gorgeous-as-hell guys. And Connie is some seriously sexy back up.

After a day of training with sore limbs, torn muscles, and magical exhaustion permeating every second of Nine's study session, I can't wait to get into bed and go the fuck to sleep.

I didn't realize training would be this hard. Like, seriously, who the hell decided this is the way to get more badass? Whoever the fuck it was had terrible taste.

I crawled through my earlier gym session, with even the thought of Connie protecting my ridiculously delicate emotions from the guys not helping; my study session with Dea was awkward as hell for us both, his earlier declaration hanging over every second of learned knowledge; and now, with twenty minutes to go, I have still not managed to unlock a single other element.

Blowing out the frustration at my lack of progress in most areas, I ask the house for a glass of water and down it in one. I changed back into my female form earlier, having need of my Witch powers for magic study, but I'm itching to change back. Something about being female just doesn't sit right with me today. I don't even know what it is; it's like an unsettling feeling in the pit of my mind that I'm not who I'm meant to be right now.

"Okay, change back." Nine sighs. "I can't handle your inner frustration any longer, and I hate that I'm making you uncomfortable."

Relief floods through me.

I concentrate and manage to return to my male form in just under three minutes—a new record for me—and have both Nine and me smiling as we walk to dinner.

Today's dinner is pork ramen, and fuck me, it's amazing.

"Sooo . . ." Connie starts, and I can already tell what direction she's planned this conversation to go. "How was your afternoon?" She looks at me, then at Dea, and raises her eyebrows in a not-so-secret question.

Sighing, I answer, "Still a virgin, Connie."

Everyone splutters their food.

Oops, may have forgotten I said that only to Connie on one of our Friday night sleepovers. "You know, immortally speaking. I think."

Dea looks at me in shock while Arrie tries his best not to laugh. But Nine? Well, he just mentally says, *I can help with that,* and winks.

Internally, I sigh.

"You know what, Connie," I say as I turn to her, "let's do something fun tonight. Something without those three." I thumb-gesture to the others and smile.

Everyone pouts, even Arrie looks a little left out, but Connie smiles. "Yes! Training break!"

She loses herself to thought for a moment, and the entire table falls into a strange silence while Connie's internal wheels turn. But it isn't long before she bursts out laughing, and I have to ask her what's so funny.

"Nothing. But I have a great plan for this evening."

Nine looks at her in horror, and suddenly I'm worried. "Con, please don't. I don't think she'll—"

"Nonsense. She's spent enough time *with* you two that it'll be great fun."

"What's going on?" Nerves shoot through my system, and I can't help but be terrified by what the Horseman of Conquest might have me doing this evening.

"It's a surprise," she whispers and stares daggers at Nine.

Nine motions zipping his lips and looks at me with a facial apology. *Sorry. Don't murder me later.*

Err . . . okay.

"Meet me in your room in half an hour." She shoves the last bite of noodles into her mouth and runs off to goddess knows where.

"Okay." I look to Nine, expecting him to spill it. "C'mon, out with it!"

I hear Connie shout from somewhere in the house. "Don't you dare, you pretty little fucker!"

That has me laughing.

"I don't want to ruin the surprise." Nine leans over and whispers, "Just be prepared for anything."

Ugh. I'm not going to like this, am I?

Nine gives me a shrug, as though he doesn't really know if I'll like it or not.

Half an hour later, though, I'm sat on my bed after Connie has just come through the door, but it's what she's wearing that's worth note. A skin-tight, fake leather, strapless dress that barely comes down to her mid-thigh, with her hair loose and falling past her shoulders, landing at the floor in golden strands of beauty I'm still jealous of.

"Damn, Connie, you look . . . err . . . amazing!" I can't help the pooling of heat between my legs and the sudden urge to pick her up and kiss her that flies through my mind.

"Thank you." She turns to me and then looks at my closet. "Your turn."

I'm too busy staring at her to notice what she said, but when I do, my mind stutters. "W-Wait, what?" I rush over to her and grab her hand. "I don't think I can—"

"Nonsense. Male or female?"

I'm not sure which would be appropriate, so I shrug. "Which do you think?" I'm currently still in my male form, but I'll change if she prefers a girly night out. Doesn't really bother me.

"I think you'd feel more comfortable as a female, but honestly, either could work. Your choice."

Okay. If she thinks whatever this is will be better in my female form, then that's what I'll go with. Might as well trust her, 'cos I'm gonna kill her if she's taking me to some weird BDSM club or some shit.

"Okay, female it is. Though, I'm not sure I have something like"—I gesture to her outfit —"that."

She waves her hand at me, as if waving away my concern, and enters my closet. "Can always ask the house for it if you don't like any of my choices."

"Oh," I say, remembering my shopping trip, "Dea did make me pick up a couple of sluttier dresses, just in case they'd come in handy. Maybe one of those?"

Connie looks at me and smiles. "Yas! One hundred percent yes!"

"Over there." I point to the section of the closet I put them away in and grab the three I own. "Here."

Connie snatches them from my hands and runs out of the closet, holding each one up to the light, assessing them, and placing them against me, until she settles on the one.

The one in question is a thin, strapless piece of material that I seriously hope will stretch when on because as it is now, it won't fit past my ass.

Sighing, I grab it and go back into the closet to change, shifting into my female form in the process. It does feel good to have my boobs back, but something about my tummy feels odd in this form right now. I can't put my finger on it. Oh well, it's just for one night.

Stretching the material (it is indeed stretchy, thank goddess) over my boobs, down my waist, and past my ass is easier than expected, and since it falls just past my ass by a few inches, I can safely assume I'm dressed appropriately for the occasion—given what Connie is wearing. The difference between her dress and mine, however, is that mine is made of something stretchy, and definitely not fake leather; plus, it shows my front tattoo off with its plunging neckline. I match it with some sexy underwear I'm hoping no one will get to see (hey, a girl's gotta feel sexy every now and then), and step out of the closet.

Connie wolf whistles upon my arrival, and I blush hard at the compliment.

She thinks I look good?

"You look amazing, hon. Truly." She comes over and asks me to spin for her, so I do. "Your tattoo is looking awesome, too."

"I know, right?" I beam at her, glad to have some regular, girly moments in my ever-complicated life. "So, can I get a hint?"

She shakes her head.

"Anything?!"

She laughs. "Okay, okay. We're going to a show."

That's it? Why is Nine so worried? I've been to shows before.

She's not telling you the whole truth.

Figures. Of course she would do that. There's gonna be something odd or unusual about this show, isn't there?

Nine doesn't answer. Of course he doesn't. But I take his not answering as a sign that, yes, it probably has something different about it.

But what?

"You hate not knowing, don't you?" Connie looks at me as we descend the stairs.

I nod. "I hate feeling out of the loop."

She laughs. "This is a sucky time in your life for that."

"Tell me about it."

Nine and Dea's wolf whistles reach my ears before we even make the turn on the staircase and come into view. All three guys stand at the bottom of the stairs, just like at the ball, and just like then, they're all staring. But this time, Arrie does not hide his appreciation for how I look. He eyes me head to foot and gives me a flirtatious smirk I haven't seen before.

We've really made progress since we talked during the ball preparations, and so far, we've managed to be friends. I love how caring he really is behind all that grumpiness.

"Damn, Sweetie, Dea was right, that dress is fucking amazing!" He asks me to twirl like Connie did, and I oblige.

Strong hands grab my sides, ones I would recognize anywhere. Dea leans down and whispers, "You look radiant, and a prime article of splendor, Angel."

He twirls me around on his foot and places me gently next to Nine, who grabs me in his usual bear-hug kind of way and squeezes tight. Well, he tries.

Arrie comes up to me next and looks down at me like I'm going to be his next meal, his tongue flicking across his lips and his eyes piercing mine. My heart flutters and skips a beat as I melt into his ice-blue eyes, and a cool smirk flits across his face. "You do look nice, Killer." He leans down and whispers, "Keep it up, and you might melt the rest of my stony exterior."

So he can be flirtatious?

Connie grabs my hand before I can force the big guy into a hug, and she drags me off into the night beyond the open front door. She laughs as we walk down the pathway that heads into town and teases me non-stop the entire way.

"And you thought you couldn't have us all. Look at those three back there. They were practically drooling over you."

"Us," I remind her with a shiver against the cold evening air. "They were drooling over us." I grab her arm and link mine through it. "And I wouldn't have it any other way."

"Really?" She seems uncertain, and I think I might understand the reason why.

"Connie, I don't want you to feel like I'm stealing them away from you. If they're paying you less attention because of me, please just say so. I'll kick their asses. We're a team in this, remember?"

She smiles at that. "It's not that, but thanks for caring. I just . . . I've never been in a relationship with any member of the team before. And what you're doing to the team, to all of us, is feeling more and more like a relationship every day." At my confused face, she explains, "We were just friends with benefits before—maybe a bit more family-like and a few feelings between Dea and Nine—but nothing more."

Ah. "So now I've added feelings and romance into the mix, you're feeling a little uncertain?"

She nods, looking oddly shy for someone of her confidence.

"We're in this together." I squeeze her hand. "All of us."

She nods and speeds up. "C'mon, the show starts soon."

"What show?"

She just laughs and drags us to the center of town in half the time it would usually take. Once there, though, I can see the Witch lights illuminating the streets like Christmas, and the Witch marks on the ground lighting the way around the most populated areas of town.

"Wow! This place looks amazing!"

"I forgot you haven't been here at night yet."

I shake my head but smile at her. When I turn to look at her, however, I'm dazzled by how her eyes now seem to glow a brilliant green-orange in the Witch lights, the nearest one clearly being the effector—it glows bright orange.

"Hon?"

She breaks me out of my reverie, and I find myself blushing. "S-Sorry. What were you saying?"

"We need to go that way." She points down the main street but looks at me with a smile. "You okay?"

I nod, not trusting words to come out okay right now. This is like a . . . date. Like? This is a date, isn't it? I . . . err . . . kinda like it.

"What's going through your mind?"

We walk toward the entrance of a grand building with old-fashioned theater strips around the upper ceiling of the front stoop. In bright lights, the show listing tonight is: FORBIDDEN MAGIC. A dancing man and woman sign flashes next to the words, and my mouth drops open.

We're going to a sexy strip show?

"Hon?"

"Oh." I shake my head, trying to remember what she said. "I was just thinking that this is like a date."

"Well, I hope so, because that's exactly what this is." She rushes us to the queue forming at the ticket booth. Once in line, she turns and asks, "This is okay, right? Not too much?"

I frown at her in confusion for a moment, before I realize she must be talking about the show. "Oh, that. Yeah, this should be fun."

"Sure?"

I lower her head to whisper, "Nothing can be as hot as watching Dea and Nine." I let her back up as we approach the ticket booth.

"Too true." She laughs. "Lucky!"

"You've never watched?"

"No one has. They're really private about their relationship." She shrugs. "We all are, actually."

I stand there, dumbfounded, as I suddenly realize why Dea was shocked Nine invited me to watch that day. They'd never done that before.

I'm gonna kill that nerdy fucker!

"Next!" the young ticketer calls from his old-fashioned booth.

We skip forward, Connie with a cash chip in hand, and pay for two front-row tickets to what promises to be a sexy show.

"So, are the people in the show locals or a group that comes to *Sheruta* every now and then?" I ask as we make our way inside.

"They're locals, but they tour everywhere and are hardly ever in *Sheruta* anymore. They've gained a little fame over the years. You'll see why."

The entire theater is old-fashioned, with large red drapes covering a Victorian-looking stage, upper balconies gilded in golden-looking ornate designs covering its architecture, plush red chairs and sofas dotting everywhere in some semblance of structure, and the ushers dressed in red three-piece suits from a whole different century. It's like I've stepped back in time.

"C'mon." Connie takes hold of my hand and rejects the usher's offer of assistance in finding our seats. "Let's get seated. I don't want you to miss a moment."

I giggle at her and am off, the usual girliness overcoming me like it usually does when I'm alone with Connie.

"Have you seen this show before?" We find our seats pretty easily, given that Connie knows exactly where she's going.

"Yeah. It's one of mine and Nine's favorites. We come and see it together every time they're in-realm." Guilt floods me, and it's clearly written all over my face because she waves away my concerns. "I got Dea to bring him tomorrow. They're here for two nights."

Relief washes over me, feeling slightly better that Nine wouldn't miss the show but still a little guilty because I bet one of the reasons he likes coming is that it gives him some time with Connie without the other guys. It's like a them thing.

"Maybe next time we could go all three of us together?"

Connie smiles. "He'd like that. I'd like that."

"Me too."

The curtains raise, and a steady beat rings out from the soundstrip all around the arena. "And now . . . the night you've all been waiting for. This year's Forbidden Nights show!"

Everyone erupts into a chorus of cheers, whoops, and claps, and I can't help but join in; their joy's infectious, and I can see how much Connie enjoys this, as momentarily she forgets I'm there and rises to her feet to holler along with everybody else.

Yup, I can see Nine here. Clapping along and being his usually excitable self alongside Connie. They would make a cute couple, but I don't think either of them sees each other that way.

The announcer walks on stage, dressed in nothing but a white pair of sweatpants glowing in the club-like lights shining from the ceiling. He clearly works out, and although I can appreciate him, I can't keep my mind from thinking that he has nothing on any of the men back at the house.

Connie clearly sees exactly where my thoughts have gone. "You'll spend your entire immortal life disappointed if you constantly compare every man to the other Horsemen. Trust me." She sighs. "They've been working out for two millennia and have it down to an art."

The show, much to my surprise, is milder than I anticipated. I'm not sure what I expected, but they stay covered (albeit, in a tantalizing way) where it counts. Everything else is on show, though, and nothing is left to the audience's imagination.

Connie spends the entire time drooling over one of the men in particular, who puts on an amazing strip show with full-body paint that glows various colors under the fancy lighting. He's a Fae. She must have a real thing for Fae.

"He's your favorite, huh?"

"Yup! Aaron is my fantasy piece of cream pie," she whispers in my ear at the part of show that's silent.

"He is dreamy."

"So," she starts, "who's your favorite?"

"I'm not sure." I think back to the duo performance at the beginning; they were twins, and they both looked hot as hell, and I'm not ashamed to admit that particular fantasy played on my mind the entire show. "The twins from the beginning."

She looks at me a little shocked, as though she didn't expect that answer. "I think you'll fit in with Nine and Dea brilliantly."

"Why?"

She looks a little shy all of a sudden, something she's been doing all evening. Why is her confidence not its usual self this evening? "Because apparently they threesome well. They know each other really well and can work together without verbal cues given Nine's telepathy."

Right, she's never threesome'd with any of the guys before. Maybe I could persuade her someday?

I give her a questioning look. "How do you know that?"

She points to her ear.

"Right. Hearing." I laugh. "I forget about that a lot."

"I know." She smiles at me suggestively. "It's brilliant."

What has she heard? Goddess, I hope not anything too embarrassing.

She laughs at my spiraling thoughts and puts her hand on my shoulder. "Don't worry. Nothing I won't hear and see for myself eventually." She returns to the show.

I give an exasperated shake of my head and laugh.

By the time the show ends, I've sat through so many naked and topless men dancing to various routines and putting on special performances that I'm well and truly worked up.

Damn, I can see why Connie and Nine like this show.

"Sooo," Connie asks in her usual gossip-y way, "did you like it?"

"Oh my goddess, yes! It was awesome!"

"Hah! And Nine thought it might be a bit much. I knew you were more like me than Dea."

"Not Dea's thing?"

She shrugs. "He's more into private, behind-closed-doors kinda stuff."

"What kinda stuff?" Okay, so I'm fishing. Sue me. I have tempered my curiosity long enough.

"Nope. Nuh-uh." She crosses her arms over her chest. "We are not doing that."

"Doing what?" I feign innocence.

"I'm not telling you what it's like fucking the guys because then a) it'll ruin the surprise, and b) you'll get all jealous and shit."

I stop mid-step, causing her to have to step back to meet me. "I'm not the jealous type. Especially with the team. You could have your own orgy, and I would be content to watch and have fun."

Damn, I cannot believe I just said that out loud, nor how true the words are. What's wrong with me? Fuck, fuck, fuck.

Connie sees my surprised expression and laughs, then hugs me tight. "Don't be horrified, that's kinda hot."

"Really?"

She nods. "Definitely."

We walk back to the house hand-in-hand, chatting endlessly about the show and generally having a fun time, but we're met by three thundering faces upon arrival. We took our time walking home, taking almost a full two hours rather than the usual thirty minutes.

"What time do you call this?" Dea asks as we step into the foyer.

"Err, hi guys, we're home?" I say in a questionable tone. "We're home from the show. Sorry it's dark. We're not children." I list off each item on my mental to-do list and walk past them all to the kitchen.

"You were gone for hours!" Nine whines.

Connie's getting just as irritated by them as me because she snaps, "You've been before! Countless times. You know exactly how long their show lasts. And we took a slow walk home." She sighs. "If you're that jealous, arrange your own dates."

I nod in agreement. "It was fun. Deal with it."

Arrie seems the least jealous of the three (which in itself is a miracle) and leans against the doorway, more at ease now he's seen we're both okay.

I go about making myself my nightly cup of coffee when Dea fusses from behind, checking me over, making sure I'm okay. "Fuck off, Dea! I'm fine."

"Yeah," Connie says from behind, "she was with me for crying out loud. What did you think would happen?"

He shrugs, suddenly looking to the ground in a bright shade of red. "We were just . . . worried. The last time you went anywhere alone with one of us, a rogue group of Vampires attacked."

Connie meets my gaze, and equal looks of guilt snap between us. Shit, of course they're worried. The ball was only a few days ago.

"Sorry," I mumble, "I didn't think about that." I dust myself off and give a twirl. "But I'm fine." I grab Dea's hand and place it on my cheek. "Promise."

He sighs into my touch when I place my hands around his neck, and suddenly the rest of the team's staring doesn't matter. It's just us, and I really want to kiss him, to feel those soft lips against mine—decidedly, I want more than just those lips, but that's probably all the tension from the show.

Before I can decide what to do with that thought, he leans down and places a gentle, chaste kiss to my lips before pulling away.

Smiling, I return to my coffee, stirring in a heap of sugar, and head to bed, trying to ignore the knowing smiles all four pairs of eyes send my way as I walk out of the room.

Halfway up the stairs, Nine interrupts. *You really enjoyed the show?*

Yeah, it was fun. Now, if you don't mind, it's left me needing some time away from all of you. You're all way too hot to be around right now.

He mentally chuckles, and I can picture him shaking his head at me.

Saturday and Sunday consist of more training—with a break Saturday night for Nine and Dea's date to the FORBIDDEN NIGHTS show—but it's easier with the lightness of Friday night on my mind. Somehow, having fun makes everything easier.

Should do it more often.

Nine stands opposite me in my training room—topless—the fire glowing against his tanned skin as he tries to show me a way of relaxing my magical center, hoping it'll entice a calm element out of hiding, like water. But so far, all it's doing is distracting me. (I mean, have you tried relaxing when a hot as hell Horseman of the Apocalypse sits opposite you with no top on? If not, then let me tell you, it's distracting as fuck!)

While Nine clearly finds my predicament funny and a great ego boost, he's frustrated with my lack of progress.

"Can you not think of sex for a single minute?"

"Says the not Vampire," I mumble under my breath. "I'd change into my Fae form, but we really wouldn't be able to access my Witch powers that way. Plus, it'd distract everyone else."

Fae forms have evolved to be particularly alluring; since their species almost died out, their magic has evolved and stepped in, making them more appealing to breed with. I still find the entire thing ridiculous, but hey, who am I to argue with magical biology?

I'm starting to think Dea and Nine are right, up keeping a healthy diet of blood while not having sex is difficult. I've read in some of my research that it can send mortal Vampires crazy if it goes on long enough, and there hasn't been a recorded case of anyone lasting longer than a month without starving themselves of blood.

You'll need to feed properly eventually, Sweetie.

I ignore him, trying not to think about it. I'm a Horseman, immortal, and we don't need to eat, meaning I don't need to feed. I'll be fine.

You don't know that.

"Oh my goddess, Nine, shut up!" I take an attempt at a calming breath but exhale in frustration when it doesn't work. "Just leave me alone!"

"You need to feed properly. Eventually, it will leave you too unstable to function."

"This is all your fault to begin with. I should never have started drinking blood, and this would never have happened."

"You know that's not the point," he growls.

"What's going on?" Connie stands in the doorway, clearing having heard our argument and brought Dea along with her—probably for a faster trip.

"Nothing." I growl, forgetting I'm not in my male form with Shifter magic, so it comes out as more of a pathetic mewl. "Study my magic without me."

I hear Nine sigh, but I don't care.

Deep down, I know he's right, but I don't have an answer, so I remain as frustrated as ever. Storming out of the library, I grab my coat—it has started raining as the rain season began—and slam the front door shut behind me.

Cake. Decent cake. That's what I need. Then I'll be right as rain. I internally chuckle at my joke given the season and speed in to town at top Vampire speed, getting there in under a minute.

The café is empty when I arrive, and that's when I realize it's probably close to closing, given that it's four in the afternoon.

"'Ello there." The baker stands at the cash register and waves at me upon entry. "Can I 'elp?"

I walk up, trying to smooth my hair down to resemble some modicum of normality. "Cake. Cake and coffee." I gasp lungfuls of air as I bend over to catch my breath.

The baker laughs. "That bad a day, Miss . . . ?"

I grunt my frustration at my lack of a name. "Don't have a name yet."

He looks at me with sad eyes but nods his understanding.

"And yes, my life has become complicated in the last few weeks. To say the least."

He nods as he gathers a collection of pastries and cakes onto a mini platter. "I can only imagine, Miss. Being the Fifth Horseman and dealing with the upcoming war . . . Must be awful work."

"Ha. That's not even the problem. That I can deal with." Hopefully. "It's . . . never mind." I wave off my words, hoping to get out of talking.

"They can be difficult, can't they?"

I take my cake and sit in a comfy-looking armchair in the corner of the café.

I . . . I don't even know where to start. Nine's right. All I think of recently is sex and war, and it's driving me nuts. I can barely focus on anything, and it's probably my Vampire nature reacting to the blood. Dea did mention Vampires need a healthy lifestyle of both to remain functional, just like Witches need nature. I just didn't think that would apply to me. You know, given that I am immortal.

But it's not like they help. They're all so . . . Argh!

"Wanna talk about it?"

Startled, I look up to see Connie standing above me.

"How did you get here so quickly?"

"Dea gave me a lift."

She points to Dea, who stands outside the café in the rain, and I laugh as how appropriate he looks standing there all sopping wet in his black jeans, black tee, and boots, his face a solemn frown as his lip piercings dull in the rain.

She grabs a chair and sits opposite. "C'mon, spill."

"I'm really not in a gossiping mood."

"Not gossiping this time. Real talk." She looks at me with raised eyebrows.

I sigh. "I couldn't focus in magic study, since Nine was sat there topless like it was fucking nothing. He got frustrated that I couldn't keep my thoughts straight, and it reminded me of what Dea had said about Vampires, blood, and sex."

She seems to piece the puzzle together from there. "It's starting to affect you, huh?"

"I think so."

She grabs my hand and squeezes it. "You know we're not your only options, right? You can sleep with anyone."

I laugh and shake my head. I . . . don't want that. But if it comes down to it, what choice do I have? The guys are being difficult, I don't want to ruin anything between me and Connie, and Arrie . . . I haven't even let myself the luxury of thinking about it.

"I just want . . ."

Connie sits there patiently, not pressing or laughing, actively listening.

"I want it to be special. To mean something." I sigh. "I think it's something I wanted as a mortal, too." I down the rest of my coffee. "I want it to be one of you."

She smiles, a slow blush creeping up her face and neck. "I don't know what to say."

"There is nothing to say. I want something I can't have. Again." I want to wait, to do things right, but unless I can fight this war without feeding my Vampire side, I won't get that choice. "It's fine. I'll deal."

"That's not—"

"It's fine, Connie."

I get up and go to pay, using the payment chip Nine gave me a few days ago. "Thank you," I say to the baker. "Your deserts always cheer me up." I do my best to fake a smile, but it doesn't seem to work.

He gives me a sad smile in return. "One day, you'll have peace, Miss."

"I sure hope so."

9

The next morning, we're all getting ready when Nine knocks on my door, a bag in hand. "Here." He chucks it on to the bed and unzips it.

He pulls out a set of throwing daggers. "They're hollow, so they'll fly better." He then pulls out a chip. "Use this when buying anything on Earth." I nod as he pulls out an old-fashioned mobile phone, but this one looks more modern. "Use this to stay in contact with us over long distances."

I grab it and fumble with various buttons, trying to find which one turns the display on.

"You do know how to use one of those, right?"

I shake my head. "No one uses these anymore. We just use our datachips for communication and a plasmascreen for research."

He grumbles something about kids these days and spends twenty minutes showing me what buttons do what, how to phone people—phone people, like in the movies!—and how to use all its basic functions.

He goes to leave, but I grab his hand and pull him back. "Nine, I . . ."

He holds out his hand, but something about the look on his face tells me he really is hurt. "It's fine."

I shake my head. "No, it's not. I shouldn't have snapped at you. You were just trying to help." I've already decided how I'm going to make it up to him, so I yank him into my arms and hug him as tightly as possible without causing him too much harm.

I try to hide my thoughts, and hopefully I succeed because he seems surprised when I pull his face to mine and press my lips to his.

Kiss me. Please.

He melts under me, his shoulders loosening and his hands beginning to wander up my back and into my hair. As our tongues slide together and I sigh into the relief of finally being with Nine.

Breaking away, he gasps. "Sweetie, why?"

Because I like you.

But . . . I thought, Dea—

I do like Dea—he's alluring in a way I haven't seen in anyone else—but you're the most amazingly caring person I've ever met. Watching you be your amazing self and not kissing you has been like walking through a desert with no water.

I grab him by his shirt, yank him the rest of the way toward me, and tumble us both onto the bed.

What are you doing?

Enjoying you.

His smile beneath my lips holds the promise of long summer nights spent under the stars, the guarantee I'll always be taken care of by this man, the security of knowing he will never hurt me. I can't help but smile back.

Always.

I would be lying if I said I didn't want you, but I want it to be right. The moment, the time, us . . . I want it to be . . .

Loving?

I cringe at his use of the L-word but sigh my acquiescence.

Yes.

Let me help you.

He climbs from underneath me and rolls us so that he's on top, his arms resting on the pillows beneath me. One arm lifts, and he shifts his weight onto the one elbow as he moves his hand down my body, grazing gentle thumbs over the thin material of my t-shirt and bra.

I gasp into his mouth, and he groans in response.

I've always wanted to know what you sound like for myself.

As his hand travels lower, brushing over the hem of my shirt and reaching the skin beneath, I lift my hips to meet his and feel his hardened cock beneath his jeans rub against my clit.

Not holding back, I groan into his embrace.

"Nine, I . . . I . . ."

"Yes?" He trails a gentle finger along the rim of my trousers.

I can't handle his teasing anymore and buck my hips to gain some kind of friction— anything. I need him. "Please . . . Help me." At the thought of his cock in my hand, the familiar ache of my gums signaling the descending of my fangs overtakes my body.

He chuckles. "You shouldn't have left it this long, Sweetie."

He's right.

His hand delves deeper, underneath the material of my pants and panties, and trails two teasing fingers along my clit, making me gasp.

Kiss me.

He places rough lips against mine and trails needy kisses along my jaw, all the way down my neck, before coming back up and licking my fangs.

Need pulses all the way from my fangs to my clit, and I give an involuntary thrust of my hips as I hold in a light moan of pleasure. Fuck, those are sensitive.

Don't hold back.

The echoing sounds of footsteps outside of my bedroom door meets my ears, and I grumble.

"I . . . err . . ." I'm honestly caught between some sense of modesty and the insatiable need coursing through me. I want him—need him. But I don't want to be caught naked by the others if we continue.

Let them catch us. They all want to fuck you anyway.

At that, Nine moves his fingers in slow circles, massaging my clit, and I swear I can hear the blood rushing through the artery in his neck.

"Dea," I hear Connie warn from outside the door, "I don't think that's a good ide—"

Just as Nine presses harder, easing another moan from my lips, Dea bursts through the door and stands frozen at the sight of us tangled up in each other on the bed.

My moaning echoes through the silence, and heat flushes my already red features.

Connie and Arrie stand behind him, both looking awkward.

"We were . . . looking for you both."

I jump up from underneath him and readjust my clothes. "Knock next time!"

"Bro, seriously?" Nine looks just as pissed. Even his lack of fangs doesn't take away from the menace on his face. "I was helping her!"

Helping? He was only doing that to . . . help me?

Nine sighs. "No, obviously not. That's not what I meant."

I growl under my breath and storm into the bathroom to straighten up.

Nine sighs as I shut the door. "Seriously? Now she's mad at me again?"

"Then don't say stupid shit!" Connie yells at him.

As I pull my panties down, I totally understand why I'm having tummy cramps. Period. Ugh, great. I don't even have anything here to help. No tampons. Nothing.

That's why I'm preferring my male form right now. No cramps, less hormones, etc. Wait a minute . . .

Concentrating for a few minutes, I shift into my male form and the cramps are gone. Like magic. I laugh at myself. I'm still frustrated but not nearly as hormonally charged. And bonus, no cramps, blood, or other period nonsense.

I come out of the bathroom to everyone's surprised faces, but they quickly shrug and roll with it.

Only Nine laughs, knowing the truth behind my choice. *Connie is going to be so pissed.*

Why?

After two thousand years of periods, she's fed up of them, and you just come along and manage to avoid them.

Oh. She's gonna kill me, isn't she?

Nah. She's totally falling for you. She wouldn't lay a finger on you. Well, she might if you ask her nicely.

We all head to the Earth portal packed and ready to kick some Vampire ass. I'm going to make them pay for what they did to Nine. The portal in question is just as shit as last time; and just like last time, I nearly hurl my guts up upon arrival.

"You have a weak stomach in both forms," Nine points out in his usual nerd tone.

"Gee, thanks for that assessment." I bend over my chair, trying not to cover the pretty foliage covering the floor in vomit.

Dea hands me another gingersnap, and I thank him. Aren't anti-sickness spells a thing nowadays? And if not, then why the hell not?

If I'm going to have two sexes, can I at least not puke my guts up in one of them? Ugh. For fuck's sake.

After having stood up with the help of Connie and Nine and devouring my gingersnap, we head outside, where I'm reminded of one of the greater things in my immortal life. The cars!

Fuck yes, I forgot about those.

"Shotgun!" I start humming some song from one of my playlists before I add, "I don't care who I'm riding with."

You should ride with Arrie. He's a great driver.

"Nine says I should ride with you," I say as I walk on up to Arrie to where he stands beside the beautiful black Aperta 9000X.

Arrie looks at me with a scowl—oh, how I've missed those scowls—and crosses his arms over his chest.

"Oh c'mon, big guy." I laugh. "It'll be fun!"

He smirks and gives in, looking at Connie with an apology.

"It's okay," she says through a chuckle of her own. "I'll ride with Nine."

And so, I get into the passenger seat of Arrie's car while the others get into theirs, and off we go, racing down the highway at ungodly speeds, a giant smile on my face.

"You really like cars, don't you?" Arrie manually changes gears, his shirt sleeve rolled up to his elbow as he shifts the stick. "You never smile like you are now."

I blush. Did he just compliment me? "Arrie . . . can I ask you something?"

"Sure."

"Why are you being so nice to me?"

He quickly looks my way with raised eyebrows, then turns his attention back to the road we're going down at over three hundred mph. Sighing, he answers, "I had a change of heart, I guess."

"Was it because you heard of my fantasy plan?"

"W-What?"

Aha! Got him. "Nine mentioned it's the kind of relationship you wanted with the team back in the early days . . ."

He groans, and if he weren't driving, he probably would have placed a frustrated hand through his long white hair. "He shouldn't have told you that."

"Sorry, but I know lots of things about the team." I wink at him. "If you wanted to get your own back, now's the time."

He smiles but shakes his head. "It's okay. Maybe one day." I can see the wheels turning in that pretty head of his and wonder what his plan is. "You're an amazing person, Taylor."

I flinch at the use of my mortal name, and I can feel the pinpricks of tears edging my vision as I remember all that name symbolizes—all the death, the lies, and the destruction.

"You manage to get along with all four of us because you fit perfectly in this team. It's like you were made for us."

That has my wheels turning. "You think Fate intended it to be that way?"

He shrugs. "Dunno. Never really been a big believer in Fate. Not like the others. Maybe?"

Goddess, watching this guy drive is making my cock hard, and the faint echo of Nine's fingers running over my skin ignites the memory of where that would have gone.

"I'm gonna kill Dea later. The fucking wet drip," I mumble under my breath.

Apparently loud enough for Arrie to hear, as he looks over to the very noticeable bulge in my pants and laugh.

"Con mentioned you were starting to have problems . . . ?"

He's fishing, and I'm not even mad. I just nod. "All the blood is making my female form insane. But in this form, I feel fine, if a little flushed at the memory of Nine."

"We're pretty open people, you can just chat to us about it, you know."

"We're not the chatting type, Arrie. I think this is the longest conversation I've ever had with you."

He laughs at that, and it sends those familiar bubbles of happiness through me. "Driving makes me a little more . . . me, I guess." He shrugs.

"Well, I like you." I backtrack. "This you." Sighing, I give up.

Foot, meet mouth.

But Arrie isn't laughing, he's . . . blushing? "That is why I like you."

"Why, because I actually like you?"

That doesn't make sense.

"Because you cared enough to look beneath the surface in the first place."

We turn off at the same junction as last time, heading toward that familiar quaint cottage in the familiarly quaint town. With the stupid leylines.

"Ugh, who the fuck designed these lines?"

"I know." Arrie growls, the deep rumble echoing through the tense air, and I can feel my cock throb in response.

That's . . . unexpected. Wonder what kind of things this guy can do while driving? Damn. Should have asked earlier.

He could probably fuck you and drive at the same time. He's got serious driving skills.

Damn. I have a new appreciation for those skilled hands that're parking us just outside the Colorado safe house. And driving while having sex? Something I really want to try in the future.

Not like I can die, right?

You're gonna be a handful, aren't you?

10

"So," Connie asks once we've all sat down and ordered take out, "what's the plan?"

She directs the question to Dea, but he looks at me expectantly. He wants me to plan this? I don't think that's such a good idea.

"I, err . . ." I cough to clear my throat. "We find the rogue Vampires, fight to the top, and interrogate him?" I shrug my shoulders.

Dea sighs. "Okay, so strategy might need to be included in our lessons." He stands and hands out the same equipment as last time: teleportation crystal, stungun, and a regular pistol. "We will hunt down the rogues, get them to take us to see their leader, or whoever, and then we will chat with him. Or her."

But I want to fight them . . . Oh well, guess there are more important things to worry about. Like who's controlling the rogues, who they're partnered with, and are they working for the SC?

My muscles ache from all the training, and the thought of sleeping on this sofa has me swallowing a low growl.

I'll sleep with Dea. You can have my room.

Thank you.

After endless chatter, me staying mostly out of it, and a few yawns, Nine's had enough. "Of to bed with you." He yanks me off the sofa and scoots me out the door.

"I'm not a child!"

"Then stop acting like one. Go to bed when you're tired!" He shoves me up the stairs and leads me to his bedroom. "It's this one." He points to the first door on the left.

"Thanks," I mumble through a yawn.

"Go to bed, Sweetie." He wraps an arm around my waist and pulls me in for a hug. "We'll regroup in the morning."

I nod and leave to go to bed, but he pulls me back last minute. He grabs my shirt collar, yanks me forward, and pins me to the nearest wall. When his lips meet mine, I'm transported back to my bedroom at the house, his hands running all over me, and the amazing orgasm he would have given me . . .

I can finish what I started, if you'd like?

My cock throbs at his words, and he damn well knows it, as he rubs his hand over the tip through my pants, causing me to let out a groan.

Even your male form is affected by your Vampire needs. Fucking you is going to be my life's greatest pleasure. However, I'm going to wait.

A groan of protest slips through my lips, making him chuckle.

Sorry. But what you said earlier about wanting it to mean something? I . . . I'm going to make it mean everything.

He pulls away, running one last stroke down my stiff erection, sending an impulsive shiver up my spine, and goes back downstairs.

I, on the other hand, go to bed.

THE NEXT MORNING, WE ALL HEAD TO NEW ORLEANS—HAVE TO START SOMEWHERE, AND NEW Orleans is Vampire central. On the plane, which is even more annoying now the entire team are here and I have more than just Dea's mindless chatter to contend with, I start to formulate some kind of plan.

It'll be a good idea to at least ask the Vampire Royal Council what they know, therefore working with them and keeping good ties, and at the same time they might genuinely be able to help. They seem to listen to Dea, so maybe sending him might be a good plan. I want to find that young Vampire Prince and grill him about the end of my mortality; plus, he's the one who started everything with the Vampires and the SC to begin with, so he might be a good person to chat with.

But what to do with Nine, Connie, and Arrie?

What are the main objectives?

1. To find the group of rogue Vampires who attacked us at the ball.
2. To speak to their leader (with Dea's help).
3. To learn who they work for and/or with.

But how does one achieve that?

By causing a scene.

Seems I'm going to be particularly useful on this mission after all.

When we land an hour later, I've finalized my plan before the wheels touch the tarmac.

"Dea?" I look his way, waking him up from whatever thought trance he's in. "Where are we staying?"

He grimaces, but Connie steps in. "Nope. We are staying in a proper hotel. Not some cheap, rundown motel." She sighs and looks at me. "Unless our plan requires us to be covert?"

She has such hope in her eyes that even if I did need us to stay hidden, I'm not sure I could have stood my ground.

"No," I say, smiling at her.

"Thank fuck." She grabs my hand. "In that case, I have a great idea." She drags me along and hails a cab from outside the airport once we've grabbed our luggage.

The cab ride's tricky, since Dea can't go visible yet and there aren't enough seats. I make him sit on Nine's lap, much to Nine's annoyance, since Dea keeps purposefully wiggling around, giving Nine a very obvious hard-on that everyone who isn't us can see.

Connie and I find the whole ordeal hilarious, hiding our snickering behind coughs and hiccups the entire journey.

It's upon arrival, though, that I have to really cough at my choked surprise. "We're staying here?"

Connie nods while Dea groans.

Here—the hotel in question—is not what I expected, even given Connie's more flamboyant nature. The *Lucifer's Devil* hotel is well-known throughout the world as one of the more openly-minded hotels. Okay, so real talk: it has a Vampire live feeding menu, a menu with your personal choice of on-staff hookers, and various sex-themed rooms.

"We're really staying here?"

"Con, are you serious?" Nine steps up beside me. "What if that's not what Sweetie wanted? Did you even think to ask?"

Connie stops in her tracks, her smile falling into a frown. "Oh, well, no . . . I didn't. I just assumed you might find it fun?" I don't think she meant it as a question, but it came out as one.

I shrug and walk on in.

Nine? Own rooms or are we sharing? Tell me what to do so I can walk up to the desk all confident and swagger-like. C'mon, help a guy-girl out.

He chuckles and says, *Own rooms.*

I walk up to a posh-looking lady with blonde hair, red-polished nails, and a lip-line to die for. Like, seriously, I would die for those fucking lips.

"Hello," she says with a sickeningly sweet smile. "What can I do for you?" She looks up from her plasmascreen and notices me, eye fucking my entire body from where she sits behind the desk.

Ugh. Stupid Fae form.

"Five rooms please. All on the same floor, as close together as possible."

Dea makes himself visible and places a card on the desktop—it's gold and has the logo for the SC on it, which I guess gets us into more places than I can manage on my own.

She coughs to cover her surprise and looks in the system. After a few seconds, she smiles at me and hands me five separate keys. "They're the only rooms available that are all next to each other. Any preferences on who goes where?"

I shake my head.

"Very well. I'll book you all in now. Names?"

We all give fake names, and she gives us each a random key, mine with a dangling handcuff keyring. Using keys is a bit old-fashioned nowadays, but I guess it adds to the general feel of the place. The black-and-red décor theming this hotel definitely gives the devil's vibe, and it gets me thinking if this at all offends Nine and Arrie, given their demon-descended powers.

Nah. We got over that a long time ago.

Oh. Well, I guess you would learn to move past things when you're that old.

I'm not that old, he jokes.

I don't give him a response, just in case he's age sensitive—but the very thought has me holding in a laugh so hard I end up snorting and making Nine laugh harder. An immortal who's age sensitive? Ha!

Arrie grabs our wrists and drags us, I assume, to our rooms. Dea looks at us with a scowl and mumbles something about stupid children while Connie just smiles at me in a way that suggests she might find me and Nine adorable.

We all head up to the top floor, where there are five rooms in this wing of the hotel. How convenient. I find my room, which is sandwiched between Connie's and Nine's (not a bad sandwich if you ask me), and enter, dragging my bag behind me.

My bag tumbles to the floor with a thump upon entering, however, as surprise shocks my system. I didn't know they made hotel rooms like this!

The whole room is black and pink, with the wall behind the biggest bed I've ever seen striped in a hot pink, matte-black combo that has me jealous I don't have the personality for a room like this back at the house. The bed is the black cashmere kind with silver jewels studded along at various intervals and has attached metal bed poles on the ends of the headboard. I can take a pretty good guess what those are used for.

The room is bigger than any kind of bedroom I've ever seen (including Connie's, and that's saying something); it has a sunken hot tub in the glossy back floor opposite the bed with pink rose petals scattered around the rim. The room has a loving, feminine, light BDSM vibe going on that I actually rather like. If I were in a romantic relationship, this would be kinda cool, but I'm not, so it just kinda sucks.

I empty the contents of my bag onto the bed and start carefully putting away my clothes, shoes, weapons, and assortment of things. Although I'm in my male form, I really need to go and buy some lady things, just in case my Witch or Vampire powers are needed.

Nine?

Yeah.

Just popping to a shop quickly, then I'll be back and want to run through my plan with everyone.

Okay.

There, I've let the overprotective men of the team know where I'm going; now, I just have to find a shop and be back before anyone freaks out.

The shop I find myself in is one of those massive grocery stores, with the plasmascreen shelves where you can scan each item that you require using your datachip, or a chip card in my case, as you shop, and then you go to the collection point, grab your items, pay your total, and leave.

I head down the sanitary products aisle in search of tampons and eventually find what I'm looking for. A few women surround me, looking at other related products, and I don't get it at first—why they're giving me strange looks—but then it hits me. I'm in my male form.

Shit. Is it weird buying tampons as a man? Should I be doing this in my female form? I consider switching, but that's gonna freak them out even more. Goddess damn it.

I scan my chip card over the nearest tampon screen a few times and rush down the aisle, heading toward the collection point.

The collection point is run by a lanky Fae woman with scraped-back red hair and freckles that would have been cute a hundred years ago. Her scowl before I even get to the desk is enough to make me want to turn around and go back to the hotel empty-handed. Is she going to be weird about it too?

"Please scan your chip," she says in that sullen voice everyone gets after working in retail for too long.

I scan my card.

She briefly frowns at the plasmascreen in front of her before masking it and continuing with her usual frown. "Your products are at door three, sir." She gestures to the numbered door behind her.

I walk up, scan my chip card again to pay, and rush out of there like the devil is on my tail.

Turns out, no one freaks out about my absence because Nine lets them all know where I've gone, and by the time I come back, they're waiting for me in my room on a set of comfy black and pink sofas in the corner by the bed.

I shove my shopping bag in the bathroom and join them. Connie looks kind of tired, and I wonder when the last time she got some sleep was.

She's been freaking out over the mission.

Right. Vampires. Well, I'm going to help with that.

"What's the easiest way to find a group of murdering a-holes that probably don't want to be found by their council?"

Dea smiles at me but stays silent while the others look at me in befuddlement.

"You draw them out." I grab Connie's hand. "Wanna help me punch some Vampires in the face?"

She shoots up straight with a wide grin. "Oh my fuck, yes!"

"Thought so."

Arrie chuckles and Dea smiles appreciatively.

"Dea," I say, "I think you should go to the council to ask for information. And take Arrie with you because he'll be useless for the other part of the plan."

"Yes, Angel."

"Connie and Nine, we're going to stage a coop."

Everyone smiles, and I can't help it, I beam with pride. I've come up with a plan everyone agrees with. "You know this could put us in danger of exposure, though, right?" You know, just in case that's a big deal to them.

Dea is the one who answers. "We are not going to be able to hide forever now the community is out and on the warpath."

Thank goddess he sees reason.

Arrie speaks up, because of course he would be the Debby downer on all this great planning. "Do we really want our first public appearance to be an anti-Vampire fight?"

Grrrr! (Pretty sure I do that out loud, too. Oops.) Why is he always fucking right when he complains? We need to draw them out somehow, and clearly, they're all for Vampire freedom and against the SC's controlling BS.

"What if the Vampires we fought knew what was going on? Like, volunteers?" Nine raises his brows in that sexy, nerdy way of his, and I melt.

Seriously, does this guy just ooze sexy nerd? Is he the reason it's a thing? 'Cos I could get behind that. OMG. What if he wears glasses?

Nine just looks at me with a smirk, blushes, and shakes his head. *Focus.*

Right. Back to planning.

Dea's speaking. "We do not know any Vampires who could help—outside of the council."

An idea sparks, and I shoot to my feet, accidentally scaring the shit out everyone. Oops.

"I know a Vampire who owes me a favor." I look to Dea, hoping he'll get my meaning.

"No, absolutely not." He stands to join me. "That could be dangerous! He is the reason you were killed in the first place."

Connie gasps. "I'm with Dea. We shouldn't use that contact."

I wave them both off, going ahead with my plan anyway. Who the hell do they think they are, my keepers? I'm a grown-ass adult. An immortal adult. What the fuck could happen?

11

"Oh, c'mon . . . please!" I place my hands together and beg the Vampire Prince in front of me to help.

I find him at the last place we saw him—partying, feeding, fucking . . . generally living it up.

"Nope. Nuh-uh. Not happening, little hunter." He crosses his arms where he lies on the couch—stark naked with two women curled up on either side. "I'm not doing that. That's insane."

I blanch. "I am not a hunter anymore."

"Riiiight, sorry." He shrugs. "Little Horseman?"

I growl, frustrated this is the place I have to be—in my female form of all things. Turns out, he doesn't recognize me in my male form, so here I am, standing in a Vampire den (with no help from the others, I might add), hungry, horny, and on my period.

Turns out, things can go pretty badly.

"Can we talk somewhere else?" I mumble, knowing he can hear me. I seriously can't take the crazy directions my thoughts have gone in while in this room. The things my Vampire side wants to do to those women . . .

He creases his brows and sighs. "Fine." He shoos the girls away, downs the last sip of blood left in his glass, and gets dressed. "Where to?" He turns to face me.

"Follow."

I Vampire speed out of there, waiting to see if he can follow me at this speed—he can— and continue all the way to our hotel.

"You're staying here?" He looks at the hotel in front of us with an amused smirk.

"We're all staying here, yeah." I shrug, and we head on in. "Listen," I say once we reach the elevator, "please behave yourself. They are not your biggest fans."

He flinches ever so slightly, but it's enough for me to notice.

"Scared, little prince?"

"Of the Four Horsemen of the Apocalypse? Yeah. Yes, I fucking am."

"I won't let them kill you, don't worry." I clap him on the back.

The ping of the elevator signals we're on the top floor, and I gesture for him to follow me to my room.

Here's to hoping no one's doing anything sexy in there. It might just pop the last lid on my mental pot of crazy right now. Seriously, how long can one stay permanently turned up to eleven?

Luckily for me the room is empty.

"Sit," I say as I stroll to the lounge area. "You don't mind if I change form, do you?"

He sighs once more. "What do you have against being a Vampire?"

"What?"

"It's obvious you're not feeding properly. What's the problem?"

"That is none of your business." I huff and fold my arms.

"C'mon"—he smiles—"just tell me. I have a little experience when it comes to being a Vampire, little Horseman." He flashes his fangs and laughs.

He isn't going to let this go, is he?

"It's not the feeding that's the issue. I feed at least once a day, sometimes twice, and carry extras everywhere I go."

He smiles in approval.

"I don't need to feed, I only do so because it helps keep me healthy."

"Then, what's the problem? Why do you look like you're starving yourself . . . ?" He trails off, realization hitting him like a storm. "You're not having sex, are you?"

I shake my head, blood rushing to my cheeks. Goddess, kill me now. Please, I can't sit through this conversation.

He doesn't laugh; he doesn't even smile. "It's not funny or embarrassing." His voice has turned stern, and he looks . . . disappointed. "When a Vampire doesn't feed and mate, or keep up a healthy lifestyle of both, it can kill them. It's how our biology works, just like how Witches need the outdoors to settle their magic." He sighs and sends an order of blood through the e-ordering system. "You can't die, so all it'll do is send you crazy, and that's how you'll stay."

"I know!" I snap. Taking a deep breath, I try again. "I know."

"You going to tell me why you're so adverse to something so goddamn normal?"

"I'm not adverse! I'm just . . . waiting."

"On what?" He leans forward and smirks. "It's not hard. Rod A goes into slot B."

"I know how sex works!"

"Clearly." His sarcasm knows no bounds. He grabs my hand and yanks it toward him. "If you want, I can help?"

The suggestion in his tone does not go unnoticed, and even though I'm not particularly attracted to this guy, the thought of feeding and having sex at the same time still sends a thrill through me. But . . . I'm waiting.

What am I waiting on again?

The pounding in my head matches the blood rushing through my body, making it hard to think.

Why does it matter?

All rational thought flies out the window, and I find myself leaning into the Vampire Prince. "Lucien . . . I . . ."

No. I shake the haze from my head. This isn't what I want. I want the team, my home, my family. I want to wait and finally find my place. I want to be with the ones I love.

I pull away. "I can't. Sorry. You wouldn't understand." I sit back down and focus on shifting while he complains in his usual drama-queen tone.

As the magic tingling sensation washes over me, I force the urge to vomit down and refocus on the task at hand. "We've gotten off topic."

He leans back, but as he does, the doorbell rings. Yup, this hotel has doorbells for each room. "Ah," he says through an exhale, "dinner's arrived."

I roll my eyes and sit back.

Nine, get the team in here please. I'm having issues with my guest.

What guest? Where did you go? You said you were going for a walk?

Ugh, just get your ass in here.

He siphons the other Horsemen, and they all run, but not before he takes a long look through my memories and grumbles the entire time. Until he gets to the part where I nearly kiss Prince Lucien, and then he just remains silent.

Shit, did I piss him off? Does he hate me now? What if I messed everything up?

Stop being stupid. I was just surprised that you actually admitted your feelings to yourself rather than burying them. And you've never called the house home before. It caught me off guard.

Oh . . .

Connie, Nine, and Dea barrel through the closed door, weapons ready, after Lucien sits back down, and they all stop dead upon noticing my guest.

"What were you thinking?" Arrie growls.

"Woah," I say, getting up and walking over to him, "calm down, big guy. I'm doing my job."

"No," Dea interrupts, "you were being reckless."

Says the Horseman of Death with his whole I-do-not-fear-death bullshit.

I roll my eyes at him and gesture for us all to sit. "C'mon, we need to persuade him to help us. He won't budge." I growl under my breath at him. "It's starting to piss me off."

I'm seriously tempted to just go all bear on him and growl in his face, but I manage to restrain myself from threatening the little Vampire Prince.

Little?

I shrug. He calls me little Horseman. Who knows, maybe he's small.

That has Nine laughing. *You should have found out.*

I . . . err . . . didn't want to.

I know. I'm just messing.

Oh.

Back to the task at hand. "I swear I'll bite your ears off if you don't at least listen to me—to us." I add a bit of a growl to the end of my sentence, hoping it'll add to the effect. I really don't want to have to put anything of his into my mouth, even in animal form.

"Okay, okay." He raises his hands in social submission and smiles. "What kind of a stupid plan did you have in mind?"

Well"—I step forward—"we want to draw out the rogues. By doing so, we'll hopefully be taken to wherever they're based and get to speak to whoever their leader is. But we need to gain their attention first. They're not going to just attack us again after losing so spectacularly last time."

Nine steps in, all charming smiles and blinking innocence. "We want to stage a fake fight: Horsemen vs Vampires."

"Ah, so that's where I come in. You need Vampires willing to 'go down' at the hands of the Horsemen?"

"That's about it, yeah." I shrug.

"Sorry, can't help you."

Arrie growls behind me.

Lucien stiffens ever so slightly. Smart man.

"Why not?" Arrie asks as he sits beside me on the couch.

"Because I'd need to explain who you are, and even then, people wouldn't believe me." He raises his eyebrows. "You guys are a myth. The only reason I know about you is because I'm on the Vampire Royal Council."

"Yeah," I say, "about that . . ."

He raises one eyebrow at me.

"We're not staying in hiding throughout this war. We won't be able to. Might as well start coming out of the closet sooner or later."

Lucien blanches. "Really? You're all on board with this?"

Everyone shuffles their feet.

Clearly, they don't like it, but honestly, I'm past caring. It doesn't matter. We can't win a public war against magic while remaining hidden. It isn't fair to the humans we're asking to put their trust in us. They have a right know what's out there.

"When everyone figures out who I am, do you think they'll like me?" I ask. "Do you think they'll like a previous supe hunter hunting her own kind being the one to bring about peace?"

Arrie visibly tenses beside me while Nine places a hand on my shoulder—which does not go unnoticed by Lucien, who smirks at the gesture.

"Because they won't. We need to come out to the public eventually, and we need to do so in a way that is beneficial to the balance of power."

That was pretty well spoken, Sweetie.

Thanks. Channeling my inner Dea.

Lucien opens his mouth to say something but closes it again, as though reconsidering. "Okay." He shrugs. "How long do I have?"

Dea answers this time. "As long as you need, Prince Lucien. But try not to make us wait too long. We do not like being stuck on Earth longer than necessary."

He nods and gets up to leave. Just before he turns to walk out the door, he smiles at me. "Just so you know, that offer's still on the table. If you're too scared to deal with"—he gestures to the team—"that."

I wave him out and rake a hand through my hair. "Well, he's a handful," I mumble to myself.

"Your choice of contact, hon." Connie just has to pick that moment to turn into Arrie, doesn't she?

"I know." I look at her and smile, hoping to be as dazzling as Dea, but I probably still have a few hundred years to go before mastering that look.

She blushes nonetheless, and I'm thankful I don't look like an idiot.

Can't we all stay together this evening, just for one night?

But even I know that's asking too much of them. I just want to feel less . . . alone. Just for a few hours. One night with no nightmares, no concerns, surrounded by . . . family.

Nine looks at me and nods, a smile forming on his face. *You just have to ask.*

It doesn't matter. I'm just being stupid. "I'm going to bed. It's been a long day, and I'm tired."

No one speaks for a moment, but Dea and Connie smile while they all have an internal conversation with Nine.

I can't be arsed with it all, so I go into the bathroom to get ready for bed. Ten minutes later, two sets of teeth all sparkly clean, two bodies freshly showered, and guy-me dressed in nothing but a pair of sleep pants—hey, it's not every day I can sleep half naked and not have to worry about flashing my boobs everywhere (#maleperks)—I step out of the luxurious bathroom and freeze in the doorway.

Nine, Connie, Arrie, and Dea are all in my huge bed, all wearing pajamas (and the sight of Arrie in pajamas is enough to have me stifling a laugh), with a clear and defined space for me between Nine and Connie in the center.

Are they serious? They want to keep me company just because I feel lonely?

"Yes," Nine says. "Now come to bed." He pats the empty space beside him, and Connie smiles.

Connie looks tired, and I'm glad she's choosing to get some rest before the mission—she looks like she needs it, which is saying a lot for her (she always looks pristinely beautiful, even when injured).

I smile as I climb into bed, Nine lifting the covers and Connie snuggling into the crook of my shoulder once I've gotten comfy. Arrie snuggles into her back beside her—the big guy looking almost cute as he wraps an arm around her waist—while Nine entwines his hand in mine as we lie side by side. Dea lies on his left with a peaceful smile on his half-asleep face.

This is nice. Warm. Surprisingly attractive. And it feels like . . . home.

12

We spend three days in the city of New Orleans, waiting for Lucien to get back with some more info for us. We party, hang out and watch movies in my suite, go shopping, and just generally act like tourists. Dea is his usual quiet self, but even he enjoys the shopping trip he's visible for. Today though, I've had enough of waiting and send Dea and Arrie to the Council, where they're planning on extracting information at any cost (hence Arrie tagging along). We need to know who these Vampires are; they're the only lead to the oncoming war we have, other than tabloid nonsense and the Witches being . . . well, Witches.

That just leaves me, Nine, and Connie to find Lucien and see if he has an update. Fuck this no datachip bullshit and relying on mobile devices—no one uses those anymore. When we come out of the supernatural closet, we're getting datachips. That way, I could be calling Lucien right now. The fuckwit.

"What we gonna do today?" Connie asks as she steps out of my bathroom in a towel, exposing her upper thigh.

All of them have slept in the same bed with me every night, and I would be lying if I said it wasn't the best feeling in the world. None of us are having sex or doing anything remotely sexy, but it warms my heart to know they're doing it just for me.

I get the feeling they wouldn't usually sleep all together like that.

You'd be right. But everyone is enjoying it more than they're letting on.

That is an interesting tidbit.

"I'm not sure. I wanted to track down Lucien to see how he's doing." I shrug. "What would you like to do?"

"I really wanna go dancing with you in your female form." She shrugs. "But I totally get why you don't want to do that right now."

Is female me still on her period? I change and go into the bathroom to find out. It's only been four days, but between the lack of blood and the calming of the insanity in my head, it's safe to assume that I can remain in this form if I want.

There's still the whole crazy Vampire no-sex issue to work with, but that's much calmer off my period. Okay, I can do this. I can do this for Connie.

I step out of the bathroom dressed in the last thing I wore in my female form—combat gear from when I planned to go on this Earth mission—and jump out of the doorway. "Let's do this!"

Connie smiles, then falters. "You sure?" She walks up to me. "I mean, your male form is seriously hot, but there's something about you like this that I just like. But I don't wanna be the reason you spend the day all crazy."

"It's okay. I'm good."

She raises an eyebrow in question, as if doubting me. The bitch. But I can't stay mad at that pretty face. Grrr. I swear, they all have me wrapped around their little fingers. I can never stay mad at any of them. Well, maybe except Arrie.

"I'm good. Seriously. No period, so less crazy Vampire me."

She scowls. "That is so fucking shit!" I step back as she clenches her fists. "You get to just magically avoid your periods for the rest of time while I'm stuck with them?" She laughs in that crazy way of hers, and I get really worried for my pretty face for a second. "How is that fair! What did I ever do to Fate to deserve this bullshit?"

I rest a hand on her shoulder. "Sorry?"

She takes a calming breath and looks me in the eyes. "It's okay. Just a little . . . annoying."

"Hey, I get it. Two thousand years of periods must be seriously sucky."

"You have no idea." She rolls her eyes and turns away to get changed.

I rummage through my wardrobe to find something more appropriate to wear and settle on a simple look of black ripped jeans, sparkly pink knee-high boots, my punked-out denim jacket (pink sequins and skulls included) and a black tee. Oh, and don't forget the black choker (what even is an outfit without one?).

Okay, so maybe it isn't a simple look, but I swear that's what I was going for to begin with.

Scout's honor.

Okay, so I wasn't a girl scout, either. But, hey, a girl can only go so long without pink sequins in her life—trust me—and this is a pink sequin kind of day.

"You girls done?" Nine asks, exasperated from watching our antics and having to turn around from us getting changed.

"Yeah!" we both say in unison and giggle like a couple of teenagers about to go out drinking for the first time.

So far, the partying hasn't really interested me that much. Maybe it just isn't my thing? It all seems so . . . over the top. Like each club is trying too hard to be something they aren't.

Goddess, I sound so old.

Ha! Good one.

Oh, right. Partying with two-thousand-year-old beings; I am not the old one in the room.

It's two in the afternoon, Dea and Arrie left three hours ago, and none of us have heard from them, so we have time to kill. If Connie wants to party, then I guess we're partying.

Weirdly, I feel more comfortable partying in my female form. Wonder why?

I shrug my shoulders, grab my handbag (also black with pink sequins), shove my stuff in, grab my room key, and shove everyone out of the door. "Let's go!" I wrap my arms through Nine's and Connie's and drag us all outside.

It's on them from here; I'm not exactly filled with a map of the area, nor do I know where all the best afternoon bars and clubs are, so I let them guide me.

Nine seems to have some kind of idea, so he drags us girls behind him with fervor, past blocks, streets of tourist insanity, and onto a quieter back alley path that leads to a wide street with low-key parties, no through traffic, and a wonderful-smelling food place on the corner that I nearly drag us into before Nine promises some place better.

On the corner end of that street sits a wonderful-looking, café-style eatery with an attached bar: DISASTER CAFÉ. Apparently named after their famous Disaster Vodka Shake—drunken shenanigans are likely to ensue. (Please look away now if you do not wish to be embarrassed alongside me.)

"C'mon!" Nine grabs our hands as we look at each other and shrug. Seems Connie hasn't been here before either. "This'll be hilarious!"

What's he up to?

You said you wanted to live life a bit? Get drunk and stumble home. Well, their Disaster Shakes are a good way to go! C'mon, live a little with me . . .

Well, when he puts it like that . . . Why not?

When we get into the café and sit down on the food side, me being starving (as usual) and Nine wanting me to try one of their Death-Defying Donuts, I instantly take a liking to the place. It's cozy, but at the same time it has a unique, dancing kind of atmosphere.

Nine smiles at me once he's ordered us three donuts, clearly enjoying my approval of his choice. It's so easy to please him—I love it!

The donuts are as big as my face! Oh, and dripping in chocolate. Two donuts later (I go back for seconds, they're fucking great, don't judge me), Connie is ready to party, so we head to the other half of the floor where they have a mild club atmosphere going on, complete with small dancefloor, a couple of pool tables in the back, and some tables dotted around.

A few people are here but not many. That being said, it's only five in the afternoon.

"Okay," Nine says, "I'll get the drinks, you two go off and . . . do whatever it is girls do on nights out." He winks and heads toward the bar.

Connie grabs my wrist and heads over to a pool table. These are a little old-fashioned nowadays but really add to the cultural, cozy vibe this place has going on.

"Wanna play?"

She gives me such a sweet smile, I can't say no. Despite having no memory of this game or any real experience. Here's to hoping my Vampire nature might help. Or I could cheat using air magic. (Shhh, don't snitch on me.)

"Sure." I grab one of the digital cues and act as though I know what I'm doing, but I think Connie sees right through that, as she laughs and rolls her eyes at me.

"Need me to explain the rules?" She doesn't even wait for me to put on a fake load of confidence and shrug off her suggestion. "Yeah, whatever. Here it goes."

She goes on to explain the basic rules, and I think I kinda get it: just shoot my color balls into the pockets using the cue's aiming feature and don't pot the white or black. Got it.

Halfway into the first game—I'm losing, by the way—Nine comes back with our drinks: one Disaster Shake for each of us. Connie downs half before her next go while I try to compete and fail miserably, spluttering half the foam all over Nine's shirt.

He just laughs it off and whacks me on the back, trying to get me to stop choking. "Easy there. Drink slowly." He eyes Connie with a scowl. "Don't challenge her. Milkshake's hard to chug, you know."

She shrugs. "Age has its perks." And downs the other half.

Damn it, I'm not going down like this. I take a deep breath and chug the entire two-liter vodka milkshake in one, hoping my immortal system will save me from getting too drunk too soon.

Neither, I think to myself, am I losing this game. I bring my attention back to the pool table and pot a ball by coaxing it into the hole using a little bit of air manipulation.

"Oh, so we're allowed to use magic, are we?"

Nine watches and laughs. "You shouldn't have done that. She has magically perfect aim, remember?"

Ah fuck. I forgot about that.

"She's won hundreds of thousands of piles of gold over the years hustling poor folks at pool, darts. Anything with an aim." He shakes his head. "Fun while it lasted, but it usually got us thrown out of town."

"Hey, it ain't my fault they can't keep up."

She was seriously high maintenance back in the day, wasn't she?

You have no idea. She was such a fucking handful. Mellowed out since men and women have become equal, though.

Damn. Would have been fun to see.

You might get lucky.

Connie goes ahead and pots every ball of her color in under a minute, and I sulk on the nearest chair.

"That's not fair! I was just using a little magic!" Part of me wants to go all out and stomp my feet, but I manage to restrain myself. One point to adult me.

Nine wraps an arm around my shoulders. "Told you so." He pulls me into a hug and runs his hands up my back, dipping his fingers under the edge of my vest tee.

Connie walks over and coughs, interrupting the moment. "May I?"

Nine lets go of me, and Connie moves in, placing a hand to either side of my face and tilting it up. "Let me make it up to you." Her voice is huskier than usual, and I recognize the movement of her head and the half-lidded haze of her eyes. She's about to kiss me.

Closing the distance, I grab her lips with mine and make out with the sexiest woman on the planet in a bar half-full of people.

Nine stands next to us and furiously blushes.

But she isn't done. She's not letting me go. Not this time. Especially not after seeing how far Nine and I got before we left for Earth—at least, I suspect that's the direction her thoughts have gone.

She grazes her tongue along my bottom lip, and my lips part on instinct. She uses the opportunity to slip her tongue in my mouth and tangle it with mine, deepening the kiss. Her hand leaves my cheek and brushes the edges of my vest and bra, teasing the sensitive skin there and flaring a heat I've been ignoring into a blaze of passion that has me running my own hands under her top and creeping under the edge of her bra.

I can feel my panties getting wetter by the second, and the only thing that stops me from taking things further is Nine's mental reminder that we are in a public place and lots of people are staring at the two hot women making out in the corner.

Before I can pull away, however, Connie dips a finger into my bra and brushes it over my nipple. I groan into her mouth and feel her satisfactory smile press across her lips.

"Connie . . . not here." I pull away and look around, noticing Nine smirking at us as he casually watches the show, along with a lot of other people who've started to file in for the evening.

She just smiles and plays it off, but I know she wants to go further with me, and I would be lying if I say I don't find her struggle to hold back hot as fuck. This woman is going to be the death of me. When I get her home to *Sheruta,* I am going to spend a very pleasant afternoon with her sprawled on the bed, discovering exactly what she's imagining right now.

Nine blushes at the direction my, probably very loud, thoughts have taken, but I just re-challenge her to another game of pool.

"Another drink, ladies?"

We both nod, and he goes off in search of more alcohol. He's right, it does wear off quickly for us; I'm already feeling less light-headed.

I lean forward and whisper, "Don't worry, I'll give you everything your little heart desires when we get home," into Connie's ear.

Watching her blush as she fumbles with setting up the pool table is an absolute delight. For all her confidence, I sometimes forget that she's as nervous as I am about taking this further. At least with me she is.

I wonder . . .

"Connie?" I walk over to her so we can have a more private conversation. "I have a question, though it's a little . . . personal?"

"Well, it is a Friday." She laughs. "Ask away!"

"Have you had relationships with women before? I mean, I get the entire team is more fluid than other people, but . . . I was just curious . . ."

She sighs, as though expecting my question. "I've had a few threesomes with women before, when trying to please the guy or whatever." She groans. "But I've never had sex with just another woman." She tries to shrug off her blushing, but I can tell this is actually a semi-serious topic for her. "You're the first woman I've ever really been attracted to, I guess."

Really? "I just assumed you'd done it all."

"Oh, don't misunderstand, I've done a lot with other women over the years during group sex, but that's not a frequent thing for me. Nor is it something I've really wanted to do. Until now." She raises my hand it to her lips. "I really want to explore things with you. It'll be new for us both, which I know is something you'll look forward to."

She's inexperienced in this area, too. Well, kind of. As inexperienced as you can be after two thousand years. She's right, that does make me smile.

Nine comes back with two more shakes each and a series of shots. We down them all, play a hilariously drunken game of pool where we both lose miserably while Nine distracts us, and then we start dancing.

Nine takes over DJing from the guy after he refuses to play anything recent, and once that happens, everyone in the bar area, and a few from the café, too, dance with us.

By the time ten pm comes around, we've each drunk over a dozen of those Disaster Shakes, more shots than I know how to count, and I can't keep from stumbling around the dancefloor like an idiot.

"Okkkaay," Nine says, "I think I should get you two home." He seems pretty sober, which is a total bore.

"Nooooooo," I scream a little too loudly. "More dancing . . ."

He chuckles. "One more song. Then we're off. We have work to do tomorrow."

"We do?" I'm struggling to think straight.

"Uh-huh, but don't worry about that just now." He kisses my forehead. "Keep having fun."

He lines up another song and joins us on the dancefloor, and I soon find myself dancing between them, Connie in front and Nine behind. And I would be lying if I say I don't find this hot as fuck. This would be a legendary way to lose my immortal v-card, and the more I think about it, the better an idea it becomes.

Not while drunk. I'm not fucking either of you until you're sober. And before you even think about it, neither will Arrie or Dea.

Boooo! Buzzkill.

He drags us off the dancefloor at the end of the song (well, as much as Famine can drag Conquest and Magic anywhere—which is to say, barely anywhere). He sighs and mumbles, "Fine."

Three songs later, Dea and Arrie arrive, and we're finally being dragged out of the cool shake club and down the winding cobble-stoned paths toward our hotel.

Connie and I sing and dance down every street, getting strange looks from all three sober men behind us as they each find our antics hilarious as we trip over every possible thing in our way. (No, I didn't trip, the floor rose up to say hello.)

Connie grabs my hand and drags me along, both of us singing that nursery rhyme about the spider's water spout and the ring of roses. Or is it the one with the sheep? I dunno, I think I get confused and sing a mixture of both.

"Just call me the nursery rhyme rapper and bow down to my glory! Mwuhahahaha!"

Nine bursts out laughing while Connie tries to pull me into the nearest club to dance some more.

"Nope." Arrie grabs us both by the waist and throws each of us over his shoulders, Connie on his left and me on his right. "Let's get you to bed."

"Yessss! Take me to bed. Grooooup orgy time!"

Dea and Nine give each other a look that clearly means something, but I have no idea what, while Connie just laughs and agrees, and Arrie mumbles something in a foreign language.

"Stop mumbling prof-f-fanities under your breath, big guy."

"I wasn't," he whispers. "I was saying how much of a great idea that would be if you both weren't flat-out drunk."

"Yes, three votes for the orgy. I win. I win. I win."

Everyone's cringing at my stupid antics, but I'm having the time of my life.

That is until Arrie drops us both off at our hotel rooms and I have to run to the bathroom to throw up all of the evening's happiness.

Ugh. More vomiting. Yay.

13

The pounding of my head wakes me up with a groan of complaint to an empty bed; everyone must have slept in their own rooms last night. Makes sense, since I was pretty drunk.

Memories of my stupid antics—losing epically to Connie at pool and dancing like a weirdo—flash through my mind. And did Connie and me . . . ? Yup, we made out and had some less-than-innocent fun in public. Great.

On the plus side, it was a fun night.

My stomach turns upside down and I sprint to the bathroom before I vomit all over the floor.

Horsemen get hangovers? How is that even fair?

Because we're still human (kind of).

Ugh. Fuck off, Nine. You're making my headache worse.

Tough, because we have a meeting this morning with your little Vampire Prince.

Really?

Uh-huh. Come to breakfast in Dea's room, and we'll all chat.

Be right there.

There's only one way I'm getting through my work day and dealing with Lucien: cheating. I focus for a few minutes and change forms, stepping out of my bathroom as a male like some kind of weird sex-quick-change magic act.

Sigh.

I get dressed, genuinely dressing down this time in jeans and a plain, white tee, and head to Dea's room. His door is glossy black and seems to fit him perfectly, and upon entry, I realize I may have the better room.

The entire suite is a glossy black-and-white monochrome with pictures of less-than-child-friendly women dotted around. It has a sexy, black, boudoir feel. But when I notice Dea laying on his four-poster bed with black satin linen, I notice that he fits right in with the décor, as though the room were made for his emo-style, and his style alone.

This room is smaller but has a seriously awesome built-into-the-floor lounge area with strip lights and a cinema-style screen on one end.

"Damn. These rooms are awesome."

"That, Sweetie," Nine says from behind me in the doorway, "is cheating." He grabs my hand and drags me to the lounge area, where Dea joins us. "When Connie gets here, she's gonna take one look at you and punch you in the face. She's spent the past two hours throwing up in her bathroom."

I chuckle and laugh him off, but true to his word, Connie plods in half an hour later and looks around the room for me with a smile. That smile falters, however, when she notices I'm in my male form.

She storms over and stands in front of me, arms on her hips. "What the fuck is this?" She gestures to me.

I shrug. "You'd do it if you could."

"Fuck you!" She sits on the couch opposite us, glaring daggers my way until Arrie walks in and laughs at her obvious problem with me.

"Damn, Killer, you wind her up better than anyone with that trick."

Trick? Is he being serious right now? "My sex changing ability is not a trick!" I mean, how dare he? As though I'm some weird magician with some basic magic tricks? As though this doesn't make my life one giant comedy?

I shift back into my female form instantaneously, form a clenched fist, and punch him in the face, sending him flying backward into the couch with a surprised look on his face.

Nausea overtakes me from all the jostling around, and I have to run to Dea's bathroom. But upon exiting, I feel better, and I manage to stay in my female form without coloring the black-and-white décor in vomit.

Everyone stares at me with smiles on their faces when I sit back down, taking my place next to Nine. When no one says anything and they all continue to stare, I begin to wonder if I have some vomit left on my face.

"What?"

Nine chuckles. "You just changed instantly."

Thinking back to Arrie's now-black eye, I smile. "I did, didn't I?" Ha! Take that, Fate. The Horseman of Magic is growing up.

Arrie grumbles in the corner next to Connie.

I give him the stink eye. "My sex changing ability is as much a trick as your battle-mode focus."

He flinches, sensing where my agitation has come from, but he doesn't say anything, choosing to remain sat there with his eyes avoiding mine at every turn.

Ugh. (Told you my good relationship with Arrie wouldn't last.) Well, I'll work on it later. Right now, a pretty little Vampire Prince is knocking on the door.

"Come in." I don't raise my voice, knowing he'll hear me and equally knowing the door has been left ajar in preparation for his arrival.

Little Prince Lucien waltzes into the room and sits opposite Connie and Arrie, smiling a flirtatious smirk Connie's way. If I were in my male form, my Shifter side would likely have growled at him, but as I am in my female form, I settle on glaring at him in the most menacing way possible.

He can stop flirting with my girl . . . friend. Friend who is a girl? My bestie?

Lucien takes one look at my descended fangs and smiles, backing off, hands raised in surrender.

"What have you got for us, little Vampire Prince?"

He raises an eyebrow at my nickname but smiles and crosses his arms over his chest. "A team of twenty Vamps willing to be beaten up by you four in exchange for payment."

Payment? Seriously?

Just agree.

"Very well. How much?"

He laughs. "You misunderstand me. They want to be the first civilians to see your powers for themselves."

I stiffen. I'm not sure that is such a good idea. What if they use it against us?

Don't panic. We'll only show them a bit of our powers.

I nod at Lucien, who smiles and holds his hand out to seal the deal. I shake it, disgruntled I have to be a show monkey. Again.

"And," he says, "you'd do well to show them what you showed us, otherwise the discrepancy could cause an issue. No?"

"Yep. Already on it." I sigh and stand. "When would they like this payment. In advance, I assume?"

"Nice assumption."

A knock at the door interrupts our conversation. "Breakfast, as requested."

Oh, right.

I answer the door and dismiss the teenage waitress, wheeling the silver tray in myself. I place it just above the lounge area and sit back down.

"Breakfast, Lucien?"

He frowns. "No. But thank you. I have someone more appetizing in mind." He strolls toward the door. "This evening in council room 3B. Be there." He leaves, creating a breeze that billows his long white hair behind him with his dramatic exit.

He really is a show pony, isn't he?

I sigh, honestly not comfortable with the direction this agreement has taken. Something about showing off our powers doesn't sit well with me. But we need to get their attention—we need to get to the top.

I need to get to the person sitting at the top.

Nine grabs my arm with a worried gaze. "What aren't you saying?"

I shrug. "I don't know what you're talking about." I yank my arm back with a little too much force and grab a sweet-smelling pastry on my way out.

What I really need is blood, but the thought of asking more from them right now makes me nauseous. I could order from the hotel menu, but my one experience with human blood was . . . less than satisfying.

Ugh. I can feel the crazy lust permeating my mind, my body, every cell on fire like it is trying to force me to turn around and drag one of the team back to my room with me.

I ignore it and open the door Lucien closed, aiming to drag my Vampire ass right out of that room whether I like it or not. But something stops me, something sweet, honey-like, with the faint aroma of smoky lavender hidden beneath the tresses of the metallic tangs permeating every breath.

Blood. Dea's blood.

I turn around, run to him faster than the others can blink, and sink my fangs into the part of his neck he made bleed for me.

He staggers a step backward, but I catch him with one arm as he lets out an audible moan of pleasure as I suck a little harder.

I know where everyone in the room is: Nine still by the breakfast tray, watching with intent, his ever-annoying presence in mind ready to intervene if need be; Arrie staring daggers in my back with his usual glaring hatred whenever I feed from someone other than him; and Connie who . . .

I gasp my surprise at where Connie is in the room. She usually turns away, scared of my glowing eyes and blood-red fangs, but she creeps closer today, peering around the corner of my back I purposefully put between me and her.

What does she want?

To watch.

Ah, she wants to confront her fears. Give me just a moment—one last lick of the spilled drops—and I turn around to face her.

She gasps at my face, her hands trembling as she balls them into fists while frustration crosses her scrunched-up face. I make no move to hide my eyes or fangs, not bothering to concentrate on tempering it all down. At some point, she needs to move past this. We need to move past this.

I don't really think today is that day, but if she wants to try, I'm not going to deny her.

My body doesn't move. I stay stock still, like a feather caught between two different breezes, not really sure which way to go: to back off or get closer.

Everything in the room freezes, everyone holding their breath—even Arrie remains silent, not a single hard line on his face as he looks on with curiosity.

Connie takes a single step toward me, making an effort to close the distance separating us despite every instinct screaming at her to run. "I . . . Can I . . . ?" She raises her hand toward me, wanting something, but I'm not sure what.

What does she want?

To touch your fangs.

I give her a solemn nod, prepared for the sensual response of having them touched this time, prepared not to react, lest I frighten her away. This is progress. (I hope.)

She closes the distance in a single deep breath and lowers her hand to my face, tracing the lines of my glowing eyes down my cheeks and across my lips.

Fuck, it really does heighten everything being in this state. I can feel every ridge of her thumb as she brushes it over my bottom lip a second time, and it takes every ounce of strength to swallow the gasp of pleasure that rolls up my throat.

I don't know if I can hold back when she reaches higher and touches my fangs. Don't know if I can not react. Would that frighten her? I feel as though any sound I make might terrify her, even otherwise pleasurable ones. She's like a deer caught in headlights, stark and terrified of every movement I make.

Slowly, ever so slowly, I raise my hand—palm up and non-threatening.

She flinches at first, but then she relaxes when she realizes I'm just as terrified of this moment and am trying not to scare her away. Eventually, she wraps her fingers through mine, and I sigh in relief as I smile and she smiles back.

Progress. Fuck yes, Fate! Take that, you crazy bitch.

She brings her other hand up and raises it questionably to my mouth, as though asking my permission. I nod, and she goes for it, stroking a single light finger down my fangs.

I can't hold back the moan that escapes my lips, but it thankfully doesn't scare her, just gives her a playful smile as the guys laugh.

Fucking assholes.

"I didn't know that felt good," she whispers. "Sorry." But by the look of the smile plastered across her face, she isn't sorry in the slightest. I'm right, because she uses her other hand to stroke them both at the same time, and fuck me, I don't want her to stop.

Just like last time, it's like my fangs are directly linked to my clit, and I can feel every wave of pleasure pulsate through me, every throb of need that has me arching into her.

Connie giggles and grabs my waist, holding me tight, and I can't help the slight rocking of my hips as I look for any kind of friction. She delivers. She drops one hand to the button of my shorts and undoes them before slipping a single finger below the waistband of my panties. That one finger is enough to have me moaning all over again as she continues stroking my fangs in tune with the gentle circling motion she strokes along my clit.

Fuck, I can't breathe. Every part of me is on fire, as though she's lit my skin with a torch and never intends to douse me in the cooling aftereffects of water.

I want to say something—anything. But I don't know what. Words fail me.

Connie gives a final giggle in that girly way of hers that is so defiant of her kickass powers and general badassery and pulls both hands away. She lifts her finger to her tongue and licks it dry, drawing groans from all the guys, even Arrie, and turns away with renewed confidence as she skips out of the room.

Fuck. Shit.

What am I supposed to do with that?

There is only one thing my body does do, and that is buckle and slide to the ground, needing something solid to ground me.

That woman is such a tease. She is going to be the death of me. If she wasn't terrified of my Vampire nature, I would have pinned her to Dea's bed and taken everything I wanted. But . . . no.

That isn't me.

"Angel?" Dea's voice penetrates the fog in my mind, and I look up to see all three guys sitting on the floor around me with worried expressions.

Nine, is Connie okay?

Yeah, just a little shaken at her own confidence. She just needs a moment.

I nod.

Dea and Arrie continue looking at me with worry, until Arrie asks, "Is there anything we can do to help?"

Nine and Dea laugh, knowing full well there are lots of things they could do to ease the molten puddle of need Connie has left me in. But I'm so shocked by Connie and reeling from her interactions that I don't think I could do anything right now.

I shake my head and focus on changing back into my male form, hoping it'll take the edge off. It only takes around ten seconds this time, but I'm not in the right mind to enjoy my success.

I lift my downcast head and run my eyes across all the guys' faces and down their more-than-pleasing bodies. Seems I am not the only one enjoying Connie's show, as I can see three very prominent erections bulging three very tight-fitting pairs of jeans.

I had to persuade Dea to leave you both alone. Nine chuckles out loud, making me laugh. *He wanted to jump into the fray and fuck you both into oblivion.*

14

"So, we're agreed?" Nine asks for what feels like the hundredth time.

"Yes," I growl. "I'll do the same demonstration from the ball, Connie will show her archery skills, Arrie his strength, Dea his Angel of Death form, and you your telepathy." I sigh.

He's been so worried about all of this, as we all have, but Nine's consistent pestering is getting on my last nerve.

"Are you sure this a—?"

I growl at him, edging my voice toward a roar, and cut off his question.

"You had that coming," Arrie says on a chuckle.

Sorry.

I shake my head. "Just stop being so pestering about it. I'm aware this is a shitty idea. But what other choice do we have? We need to come out of the closet sooner or later. When doesn't really matter." I shrug.

"I agree," Arrie rumbles.

I cannot believe the person on my side in all of this is Arrie. He's seemed a little off with me ever since I fed from Dea this morning, but he isn't being openly hostile, so I can comfortably respond with, "See, even Arrie doesn't seem worried."

Arrie raises his eyebrows at me. "I do not worry about most things, Killer."

I laugh. "We both know your moodiness comes from worrying. Don't worry, I won't spoil your precious bad boy attitude." I slap his arm and walk ahead of the group slightly, wanting to get a glimpse of the Vampire Council building we'll be entering soon to be a group of show monkeys.

Arrie grumbles something in a foreign language behind me, but I shrug it off. Well, I try to.

For once, though, I'm curious.

Nine, what did he say?

He remains silent.

Nine?

Nope. Not getting involved in this.

N'awww, c'mon. Please, help a guy-girl out?

He sighs. *It's always something dirty or offensive. Do you really want to know?*

Yeah.

Fine. He said he'd like to slap your pretty ass into next week.

That is not what he said!

I wouldn't lie about something I didn't even want to translate in the first place.

I suddenly have the urge to slap Arrie on the arm again just to see how far he would go. But I shake that crazy thought from my head. I know he doesn't hold back during sex, Connie eluded as much, but with her refusing to tell me anything about the guys in the bedroom, I don't have much more to go on.

I suddenly find myself wondering what each would be like in the bedroom, and I find myself in a rather compromisingly tied-up position on Arrie's bed in a fantasy I would very much like to try one day.

Please stop.

I look over to Nine, who's trying to discreetly rearrange himself, and I laugh harder than I have in a while.

"Sorry." I pat him on the back, rubbing the tears from my eyes. "Didn't meant to turn you on, too."

He blushes at me. "Kinda hard not to be around you." He smiles, trying to be charming, but he just looks like he finds the whole situation awkward.

Dea looks at me with a raised eyebrow, and I nearly melt on the spot. "What were you thinking, Angel?"

I just wink and shrug. "Guess you'll just have to use your imagination."

Dea pouts and looks to Nine, who shakes his head. "No way. I'm not translating that fantasy to anyone. Sweetie can imagine whatever she wants between Arrie and her female self." He shrugs, suddenly gaining confidence in his ability to manipulate the team around his little finger.

"You little shit!"

He runs forward, and I go to chase after him, knowing I'll catch up to him with ease, but Arrie grabs me by my waist and holds me back.

"What were you thinking?"

He doesn't seem put off by my male form; in fact, the entire team seems to find my sex changing ability less than weird. Accepting, even.

I shake my head. Not the time to get lost in my non-identity issues.

"Don't lose confidence now, Killer," he whispers in my ear. "I want to know."

Shaking my head again, I look to Connie for a rescue, but she laughs and walks beside Nine. Traitor. What happened to girls always stick together?

Dea follows, leaving Arrie and me alone in a less-than-innocent embrace with my ass pressed against his groin.

He growls softly in my ear, and I shiver, my animal side calling to his gruffness. He nips my ear, sending more pleasant shivers down my body, and now I'm the one sporting a hard-on in public. Great.

"Tell me."

"I had Nine translate what you said." I can't look him in the eye as he stiffens. "Not that I know if he gave me a true translation, of course. But it had me wondering what it would be like. You know . . . with you?"

Arrie chuckles, his chest rising and falling with the delicious sound. "What did you imagine?" He lets me go but walks by my side as we chat a few feet behind the others.

"Err . . ."

"Come on, don't go shy on me now, Killer. I'm just curious. Promise."

Goddess, that nickname melts me every time it escapes those bright red lips.

"I thought about being tied to your bed and left at your mercy."

He licks his lips, my eyes tracing every swift movement of that tongue as he leans in to whisper, "If that's what you want, all you have to do is ask."

I shake my head. "I don't think taking you"—I gesture to his giant of a body—"as my first time is wise." I mean, the guy is huge. Not just he-works-out-a-lot huge, but Horseman of War massive. Like, I wouldn't want to be anywhere near him when he's really angry. Pretty sure I wouldn't live through the endeavor.

Arrie chuckles again, that sweet, melodious sound caressing my ears. "All right. Once you've deflowered that precious little body of yours with someone less . . . me, we'll come back to this discussion."

"We will?"

He nods.

Taking a deep breath, I ask my next question, the one that's been playing on my mind for the last few minutes. "So, does that just go for my female form?" The words rush out in a mumble before I can stop them, and I can't help the red blush that creeps over my neck and face, making my ears hot with embarrassment.

Arrie looks at me with a serious expression before leaning back and whispering, "I guess you'll just have to wait and find out.".

It never even occurred to me that I could sleep with Arrie in this form; I always just assumed sex in my male form would be with the other three, but I'm trying to learn not to be so presumptuous when it comes to them. They're a surprising bunch of people.

"There it is!" Connie yells, her voice traveling to my ears without much resistance.

I have good hearing in both forms, though my Vampire hearing is the better of the two.

The council building looms in front of us in all its modern-day glory and un-Vampireness. Like, seriously, it isn't at all what you'd expect a Vampire Council building to be. It has bright open windows, a white-and-gray-slated design, and plasmascreens built into the sides displaying all kinds of graphics. No castles. No dark, dingy corridors, no loud wailing or pitchy screams that'll keep you up at night.

(I know, I was disappointed too.)

"Can we just go inside?" I ask the rest of the team.

Dea makes himself visible, and the guards suddenly notice our presence and step aside, allowing us entry.

"I'll take that as a yes."

We enter through the glass double doors and walk right on up to the receptionist.

"Excuse me?" I say, getting her attention.

She lifts her hand and looks me over, leaving her red-eyed gaze on my torso a few seconds longer than what I'd consider comfortable. "Can I help you?" She practically purrs at me, making me internally grumble.

"Yes. We have an appointment with Prince Lucien in council room 3B."

She recoils, and I don't have the damnedest why. "Oh, you're that appointment. I . . . err . . ."

Sighing, I lean in and smile. "If you could just point us in the right direction, I'm sure we can make our own way there and be of less inconvenience to you, ma'am."

She giggles at my use of ma'am, waving her hand to cover her blushed cheeks. She really isn't all that special; or at least, I don't think so. She has manicured hands with long, pointed black nails, badly dyed hair, and far too much makeup. But she points us toward the elevators anyway. "It's on the basement floor, sir." She winks.

I turn around and walk away, waving her goodbye with a small thank you as I roll my eyes. "I'm ashamed to be female right now," I mutter under my breath.

The others find it hilarious, especially Dea, who prods and pokes fun at me the entire trip downstairs—with Nine's help, of course.

Upon exiting the elevator, Dea says, "Is that how you lured all of your hits in when you were a hunter, by flirting them into a corner and then, bam! Taser them?"

That is it. His jabbing has finally crossed the line. Before the doors fully close, I grab him by the scruff and shove him back inside, closing the doors and sending him back upstairs.

"I cannot believe Arrie is not my biggest problem today." I turn to Nine. "What has gotten into you two?"

He shrugs and continues walking down the corridor we've found ourselves in. It is, contrary to the rest of the building, a little rundown; the walls are less pristine, with flaking paint here and there, and the whole hallway smells of a musty kind of rust I have no intention of smelling again.

Connie walks on ahead, muttering, "3B . . . 3B . . . 3B." Until she stops outside of a metal door and shouts, "Found it!"

I wince. They can hear everything through that door, as I can hear everything beyond it. Muffled conversations, a few laughs, and Lucien's voice silencing them all flutters through the doorway cracks.

I hold my hand up to stop the team as Dea rushes toward us. Shushing them, I ask Nine, Anyone have any questions, concerns, or problems? There're twenty-one Vampires through that door, all of whom sound as though they don't believe we exist.

After a couple of seconds, Connie comes up to me and wraps her arms around me, hugging me tight.

I hug her back, knowing how hard this must be on her. "You'll be okay," I whisper so low I know only she can hear it.

She nods.

Nope. Everything's fine.

I step forward to open the door.

What greets me beyond the door is not what I expected; twenty Vampires stand around Prince Lucien, none of whom I recognize, except one.

Mr. Nice Vampire from the club walks forward with a quizzical expression, clearly not recognizing me in my male form, and smiles. "Welcome."

Essh, he is nice. I should probably change and inform him who I am.

Why ruin the surprise?

You are evil, Nine.

But he's right, it will be fun to see his face. Bonus, he isn't the grumpy or angry type, so hopefully he won't try to punch me in the face for tricking him.

Dea turns himself visible and smiles that charming smile. "Thank you for hearing us out and for agreeing to help should you like what you see."

Prince Lucien steps in front of everyone as Mr. Nice Vampire steps back into the ranks. "Well, well, well, little Horseman"—he turns to face me—"you showed up."

"Of course. A deal's a deal, little prince."

"That it is." The smile vanishes from his face as he turns around to the group. "These are the Five Horsemen of the Apocalypse. I'll let them demonstrate their own powers. Step back in line against the wall." He steps back, too, but remains a little forward, introducing us one by one. "Horseman of War."

Arrie steps forward, pinches his thumb and middle finger together, and flicks the wall no one is leaning against. It cracks from floor the ceiling, leaving dust flying around the room.

Everyone murmurs, but from what I can hear, they aren't all that convinced, so I step up to Arrie and whisper, "Punch me."

He blanches. "I don't want to do that."

"Just do it. And make it a good one."

He sighs and nods. He lifts his arm up with a clenched fist and throws a right hook to my face, sending me through three walls as the entire team wince and rush to my rescue.

Every bone in my back hurts, but I wait patiently for my body to heal. Crack after crack, my back rights itself, and I manage to get to my feet without crumpling back to the ground.

Dea rushes over and looks at me with love in his galaxy eyes. "Are you okay, Angel?" His eyes flash gold for a moment before he reaches over to touch my arm, his hands glowing a bright green, and smiles. "You healed okay."

I nod. "Let's get the rest of this over with. Next time, someone else can be the assistant." I rub soothing circles around my lower back but join everyone in the other room.

Most of them are talking, but one conversation stands out. "Only Princess Alberta could throw someone that hard, and no one has lived to talk about it. Not even a Vampire."

Interesting piece of information. Wonder who Princess Alberta is?

"Next," Prince Lucien says, "the Horseman of Famine."

Nine steps forward and looks to the audience. *I'll need a volunteer.*

By the shocked looks on everyone's faces, he sent that to everyone in the room. Vampires included.

Mr. Nice Vampire steps up, cautious after Arrie's display of brute strength. "I'll help."

"This won't be pleasant," Nine says. "But it won't hurt."

Mr. Nice Vampire balls his hands into fists in an attempt to control his nervous shaking.

Cute.

Nine focuses on the man stood in front of him, hand raised in concentration. "Jump."

He jumps, eyes going wide.

"Stick your tongue out."

He sticks his tongue out, much to the hilarity of everyone around us.

But we stay silent, knowing how much Nine hates using his powers like this. He defends himself and the team, but without permission, he wouldn't enter someone's mind like this—not even ours.

"Pinch yourself."

He pinches himself lightly on the arm.

Nine releases his mental command. "I can use it to make someone do anything, even kill themselves."

I wince. Really?

Yes.

The solemnness of his voice takes me by surprise. He really doesn't like what he can do, does he?

Nine steps back in line.

It takes Prince Lucien a moment to announce Connie as he processes Nine's statement. "Horseman of Conquest."

Connie jumps forward, lightening the mood. "I can shoot any target I can see, no matter the distance." She takes the bow off her back and shoots a couple of arrows between people's heads.

They shout in shock but aren't impressed.

Well, they're about to be.

Arrie lifts Connie above his head and throws her into the air. She shoots an arrow mid-spin into the ceiling above her with ease, not even breaking a sweat, then she lands and splits the arrow with another shot with her eyes closed.

That has everyone murmuring their surprise.

"I can also hear, taste, smell, and see better than any species on the planet and never run out of energy in battle."

We weren't going to announce all of our powers, Connie, I complain in my head.

She didn't want to have secrets with the world. If we come out of the closet, she wanted it to be honestly.

Damn. Self-righteous bit—

"Horseman of Death."

The team take a step back as Dea steps forward. He changes into his Angel of Death form instantly—much to my awe. He is beautiful. His golden skin shows off his tattoo—which I think is odd he has in both forms—and his black-feathered wings reach wall to wall in this empty, cellar-like space.

"This is my Angel of Death form." He voice is like silk, drawing a lot of the Vampires forward in a trance-like state.

I can feel my mind turn to mush, and I just know I would do anything he asked in that moment. My feet try to move, but Arrie grabs my arm and Connie grabs the other, a smile on her face.

I briefly hear her say, "I didn't know that would affect her."

Arrie grumbles his agreement, but I don't care. I just want to go to Dea, to run my hands over that beautiful golden body.

Dea turns around in shock as he looks at me, ignoring the Vampires now on their knees (a few are still standing unaffected), and walks toward me. He places a hand on my cheek, relieving the ache in my chest at not being able to touch him. Like the world was all topsy turvy but is now the right way up, the blood rushing back to the rest of my body, and my lungs finally inhaling that sweet, sweet oxygen.

He turns back into his normal self.

Relief floods through me, like a tidal wave of tension has finally ebbed, but my shore has been left ever changed.

What was that?

"It controls the dead," Dea says.

So that's why it affected me? Because I'm technically dead?

No, otherwise it would affect the rest of us, too. You had a different reaction to him. One I don't understand. We'll think about it later.

Dea turns back around. "I can also heal almost any wound or injury, persuade your soul to have different desires and grievances, and can open and close the gate of the dead at will."

Also being honest. Interesting. It seems only Arrie and Nine have been semi-dishonest with their powers. But everyone gets a choice; it's their existence, after all.

I, on the other hand, do not get that choice. I step forward at Lucien's command: "Horseman of Magic."

"I'm new. Arrived a few months ago. These guys"—I point to the team behind me—

"are two thousand years old. But I'm barely even a year old in my immortal life. You're all here today because of me."

They look at me with confused expressions.

"Horsemen are only born when there is a need for us. The Four Horsemen fought the ancient war, ending most of Demon- and Angel-kind and lifting the gate to the afterlife, allowing magical souls to pass through. But now, we're fighting a different war, one that hasn't fully started yet." I cough to clear my throat. "The war against magic."

Everyone gasps. Questions fill the room, and most of them are the same kind of questions I had when I first woke up in the house.

"I have the powers of each pillar community: Fae and Shifter in this form." I lift various Vampires and swing them around the room gently, then place them on the floor. I then shift into my panther form, bear, swallow, eagle, cricket, house cat, wolf . . .

They get the picture.

Turning back into my male form, it's time to shock the hell out of Mr. Nice Vampire who has so far leaned against the wall and watched with vague curiosity.

I blink and change. "But in this form, I can use Vampire and Witch powers."

Mr. Nice Vampire gasps. "You? You're . . . ?"

"Uh-huh. Sorry for the deception." I shrug and step up to him. "And thank you for being so nice. Balancing all these powers isn't easy."

He chuckles. "You're welcome." He has another question on his mind but is too afraid to ask or is too embarrassed. It's written all over his face.

I leave it be for now, choosing to turn back to the audience. I leave my fangs come out and hope that's enough. A mini-tornado rips through the room moments later, sending everyone flying and making me laugh. Goddess, it's good to be stronger than everyone in the room at something. For once.

Alright, asshole.

Shut up. You'd be just as happy as me right now if you could be this awesome.

You are awesome.

I blush, letting my air magic slip and allowing everyone to right themselves.

"That about covers it." I momentarily consider being honest like Dea and Connie and telling them about my Angel-descended Witch powers, but it's pointless because I have no control over them and can't be of use that way anyway.

"So," I ask, "will you help us?"

Everyone steps forward and, one by one, gets down on one knee. Eventually, Prince Lucien and Mr. Nice Vampire join them. "Always, Horsemen."

I turn back to the team, who look at me and smile. We did it.

Now to stage a coup.

16

Back at the hotel, we all crash on the couches in Dea's room and exhale our sigh of relief together.

"We . . . did it."

Dea smiles at me. "We did indeed, Angel." He scoots closer and wraps me in his arms, pulling me into a hug as we lie on his couch.

I breathe in his smoky lavender scent and curl up on his chest. Nine joins us by resting on my stomach between my legs, while Arrie and Connie lie behind us. We stay like that all afternoon, watching movies and eating junk food.

So far this has been a much better mission than the last, but I get the feeling the hard part is still to come. The coup is set for tonight, then we'll hopefully be taken by the rogue Vampires and I can murder their leader's fucking ass.

Flashes of Nine's lifeless, bleeding body cross my mind, and I bristle.

I won't let them get away with that.

My fangs slip in my anger, and I have to control my breathing for a couple of minutes to calm down. Not to mention the slight breeze I'm causing. I hope no one notices.

Well, no one but Nine because he knows everything about me.

Everything you know about you. And only because you think so loudly.

Right.

Arrie, however, interrupts the blissful afternoon in the only way Arrie can. "We should talk about what happened this morning."

Nooooo. "Or we could not." I don't want to talk about why I'm so physically attracted to Dea, almost magically, in his Angel of Death form. It's . . . embarrassing.

Connie laughs. "C'mon, it can't be that bad?"

Nine snorts. "She was magically drawn to his essence and wanted to lick every part of his body. Not touching him physically hurt."

Dea gasps. "Really?"

I just keep my head on my chest and nod. I can't look anyone in the eye right now. Goddess, it's so embarrassing. Why? Why is it always me?

"It really is, isn't it?" Nine asks.

I just whine.

"So," Arrie asks, and I internally shudder, "what was it?"

Nine shrugs. "No idea."

Everyone looks at him in disbelief.

"What?" he asks. "I don't know everything. I've never come across anything like that before."

"But . . ." Arrie trails off.

I'm pretty sure I have some vague idea, but I'm uncertain. "I think it's my Angel magic calling to his." I sigh. "I just don't know why it only works with Dea and not Connie."

"Because my magic doesn't work the same way, hon. Although it is Angel magic, I don't transform into a literal Angel."

Ah. "Makes sense."

"And that theory works with how your mind was at the time. You weren't in control. Connie and Arrie had to hold you back, and I'm pretty sure if Dea was naked they wouldn't have managed that." Nine laughs, and I throw him an irritated scowl. "Sorry. Sorry."

"Can we see it again?" Connie asks. "Just to make sure. And this time, we don't have to hold you back or anything."

"See where it goes," Nine finishes. "I agree. It would be useful."

I don't want to become some mindless magical slave to Dea's Angel form.

Dea must have sensed my hesitation because he grabs my chin and lifts me to eye level. "Do not worry, Angel, I will not let anything happen against your freewill."

I nod. "Okay." I trust him.

He stands and pulls me to my feet. "Here it goes." He closes his eyes and transforms, his wings reaching the floor in a wide arc of beautiful darkness.

Does this have to be in my female form? I mean, why can't my Angel powers be in my non-Vampire form. This is gonna be a bitch.

I look up at Dea, now even taller than before, and am struck with the same sense of mind-melting awe as before. His golden skin shines brightly in the afternoon sun, and his wings look like I could soar on them for hours.

Damn, this man is beautiful.

His tattoo swirls over his chest, which always seems to shift with him topless, and I can't resist reaching out and touching it.

He lets me, thank goddess, because my mind and chest hurt not touching him. I follow his tattoo down his shoulder and onto the ridged lines of his abs, following it through to the edges, where I run my hands along the boned ridges of his wings.

Dea groans and leans into my touch.

He likes it. Maybe it's like my fangs. Speaking of fangs, they slipped out at some point during this experiment.

His wings encompass me as he yanks me into his arms.

He's so warm, so comfortable, so . . . him. The lavender scent I always associate with him envelops every sense, and I can't help but take a deep breath as he leans down and places a gentle kiss to my lips.

A caress of his lips against mine, like a gentle brush of *I love you* that scorches its way into my heart. He sighs into me, then presses his body against mine and forces his tongue into my mouth, causing me to moan at the sensation of his mouth on mine in this form and all the various areas of his lips and tongue grazing my fangs.

I can vaguely hear the rest of the team shouting in the background, but I ignore it in favor of tasting more of the man who has his wings wrapped around my torso.

"Bro," Nine says as he intrudes past Dea's wings and into our space, "change back. She doesn't want this. Neither do you. Please. We'll have her together one day, or you can have her alone, but when you're both yourself."

Dea snaps out of our trance and stumbles backward as Nine catches me and steadies me on my feet. His wings vanish, and with it, the foggy haze I've found my mind in.

"Fuck," Dea swears. "That was . . . intense."

"I need some time in Sweetie's library to confirm, but I think I have the answer."

We look at him expectantly, but he remains tight-lipped. "Later." He waves off our concern. "Not an immediate concern, and I don't want to worry you both without getting all the facts for your no doubt endless list of questions."

I nod, understanding his reasoning, but the lack of immediate answers bothers Dea, as he begins to protest.

Nine cuts him off with a quick kiss, though, and then blushes when he realizes the entire team are watching. "Trust me."

Connie smiles at them with relief while Arrie stands with his arms across his chest, like usual, but there's a hint of a smile underneath that resting scowl face.

Dea sighs. "Very well."

The next thing on our dossier is the coup, and I can tell we're all a little nervous about it. Fake fighting Vampires is gonna suck, especially with Arrie not really being able to hold back and Connie not wanting to.

"Errr . . . Arrie?"

He turns toward me with a smile, and I cringe. He isn't going to like this conversation. He frowns and sighs. "What is it?"

"Ummmm . . . Are you able to hold back in a fight, or should I bench you?" I wince, knowing it's a sensitive subject.

His brows furrow for a moment as the room holds its breath. "I'll stay on the side lines as back up but hop in last minute so I'm with you when we're caught."

"Thank you." I can't help it, between Dea's Angel issue and everyone being so nice to me since the whole 'I was a murderer' thing, I need to comfort him. I run right up to him and throw my arms around his neck—having to jump to reach that high.

He chuckles and holds me in place, and we sort of hug. I think.

I'm hugging the Horseman of War. Goddess, that's a strange thought. But it feels so . . . nice. He's strong—stronger than anyone I've ever met—and it makes me feel safe. Protected. More so than with the others, since I'm stronger than them in my female form.

He nuzzles my neck and breathes me in as I do the same. He smells of that familiar metallic twang mixed with the scent of the pine forest outside the house. It smells like home.

I eventually release him and jump back to the floor. Turning around, everyone is smiling at us, even Dea, who has been frowning since the whole incident a few minutes ago.

"What?"

They say nothing, but Nine goes ahead and answers, *We rarely see him like this. It's . . . beautiful.*

Oh. "Ready for the coup, then?"

Everyone grimaces but nods.

"Remember, we need to hold back and not seriously hurt anyone, but it does need to look realistic."

"Yes ma'am," they all say in unison, causing me to grin.

17

The coup is to take place on a busy tourist street with lots of attention, so the rogue Vampires will hopefully notice in time to step in once they realize it's us causing the problem.

Rule number one: do not attack or harm innocent bystanders.

Rule number two: do not kill the volunteers.

Rule number three: be as disruptive and annoying as possible.

Arrie would have been great at this had his mind not been so focused on battle that he accidentally loses control every now and then. Not that I could say much when it came to control. We should be able to make do with us four, especially with Connie and her hatred of Vampires.

The 'enemy' Vampires are walking the street as innocent civilians, and we're all stood on the corner looking as menacing as possible in all-black hoodies and combat boots.

Guess it's up to me to make the first move. I see one of the volunteers and Vampire speed up to him, throwing a light punch. "Bloodsucking a-hole!"

There, that should start everything up beautifully.

He fights back, struggling to get a good grip on my arms as I flail in his hands, pretending to struggle. Truthfully, he's weak as fuck, but I don't want to make the poor guy feel bad.

His brown hair and mundane features wash into my vision as I punch him in the stomach, causing him to bowl over. "Where are they?"

"Where are who?" he yells back.

"Your little friends, the rogue Vampires that tried to murder me!"

He slides to his knees and begs for his life. "Please . . . please, I know nothing."

"Pfft." I wave an arm and send him sprawling to the floor. I watch until I'm sure he's okay before moving onto my next 'victim.'

Nine's interrogating another Vampire while Connie is spending a fair deal of her time punching another in the face.

Tourists have started videoing with various plasmascreens, and I'm sure it's everywhere by now. The whole street has erupted into terror and screaming, with humans and other innocents running away.

We could catch them if we want, but that isn't the point.

I run up to Mr. Nice Vampire and swing at him.

He smiles and blocks my punch, sending him flying backward. "Why, hello there. Can I help you?"

Seriously? He's playing nice even now?

"Tell me where they are?"

He scowls and screams, "Never!"

Sprinting at full Vampire speed, he rushes me, taking me by surprise and throwing me off balance. "Ha, caught you by surprise, newbie."

He punches me in the stomach, and I double over in pain for a moment before pulling my air magic back and flinging it at him, sending him flying a few feet away from me.

I transform into my male form and then into a lion before roaring down the street at him. Everyone stops screaming and turns my way; even Nine, Connie, and Dea have turned around to see the commotion with amused yet surprised looks on their faces. Connie, of course, is sporting a proud mama-hen look, clearly delighted at my show of violence.

I run at Mr. Nice Vampire as he looks at me in terror—real, edging terror—and pin him to the tarmac as I roar in his face. Transforming back into a man, I yell, "Where are they?"

You are surprisingly good at this whole bad guy thing.

Thanks. I think.

"I-I-I . . . I don't know. I swear." He sounds genuinely terrified, and for a moment I think he's being real with me and I feel bad, until he uses that to his advantage and throws me off, sending me flying through the air.

"Fucking friendly asshole," I mutter as I land in a heap on top of a magicar, groaning at the pain spiraling through my back and ass.

That's going to be a bitch to heal later.

I really hope they're coming soon, as I have figured out this evening that I dislike being the bad guy more than I do reliving my nightmares of actually being the bad guy.

Fuck it all to hell. Time to kick it up a notch.

I lift my female self into the air, hair splaying backward in an attempt to look as cool as possible, and use air manipulation to stretch my voice along the entire street.

"Where are the rogue Vampires?" I demand of everyone in the nearby vicinity. "We'll keep killing your kind until you come here and pay for your mistakes!"

I pull a car up to my level and smash it in the general vicinity of one of the volunteers but nudge him out of the way just in time to save his life.

He gives me a grateful smile before schooling his features and running to help a 'fallen' Vampire to safety.

Just at the end of the street, I see a flock of Vampires marching our way through a thick shroud of fog, and my breath hitches. Finally. I was wondering how much more public chaos I was going to have to cause before they decided to actually show up.

"Enough!" a voice I barely hear above the carnage shouts down the street. "They're innocent Vampires. Leave them be, you monsters!"

I fly toward them and go to attack, Nine, Connie, Dea, and Arrie following suit. I swing a punch at the leader as I descend toward the ground faster than I knew I could fly, but he ducks out of the way, causing my fist to land in a crater hole I punch into the tarmac.

We're gonna have to pay public damages, aren't we?

Don't worry about that.

Right. They have lots of money.

Focus.

"So," the man at the front of the army of Vampires says, "you've finally decided to fight back. Show the world what you really are." He raises his hand to the army and closes his fist.

Everyone descends on us, penning us into a circular army of Vampires, each one with their fangs out, eyes glowing red, and a menacing scowl on their faces.

I grab hold of Connie's hand and rub soothing circles in the center of her palm before I drop the knife I've drawn from my collection on the floor and get to my knees.

No point in fighting if we're going to be captured anyway. "Take us to your leader."

The man laughs. "You don't want that, monster." His sickening smile mars his otherwise handsome blond features.

I shiver. "Take us to your leader."

He sighs. "Well, you're in luck, because we have orders to bring you straight to him."

Thank fuck. For a minute there I was worried this plan had been for nothing and they were going to kill us on the spot. Not that that would work, of course, but it would certainly ruin the whole 'get to the top' part of the plan. Luckily for us, villainous leaders are predictable.

They strip us of all our weapons—much to Connie's annoyance—and stuff us in the back of a van in magicuffs. This time, however, I'm prepared for not being able to get out of them and don't even bother trying.

"Well," Connie says, "this fucking sucks."

I grumble under my breath, suppressing the growl that threatens to erupt from my open mouth. "Yes, I know. Don't worry about it."

Our weapons are in a locked storage chest beside us, tantalizingly out of reach.

Dea huddles in the corner, his visibility wearing off now he's in the cuffs; Nine sits next to me, his shoulder pressing up against mine; while Arrie sits next to Connie, trying to provide some modicum of comfort despite the fact we're trapped in a van by Vampires with no magic or weapons.

Yup, this part of the plan sucks, but at least it's expected. We won't be stuck like this for long. I hope. At least I had the decent decision to change into my male form before they put us in handcuffs, so I don't starve into insanity in the process; goddess only knows how that would have gone down.

Nine squirms uncomfortably beside me. "I fucking hate these cuffs. It's like being blind."

Right, he wouldn't be able to use telepathy like this, since it's a form of magic. Wow, that would suck. I shimmy around on the spot a bit before grabbing his hand with mine and squeezing. "It won't be for long."

"I know." He sighs. "It's just like having my main way of communication and seeing taken away. I hate it." I can hear the tears he's holding back; this really bothers him.

I shouldn't have put him through this.

"I don't need to read your mind to hear that, Sweetie. Stop being silly. This isn't your fault. It was the right plan to make."

"He's right," Connie says through a sigh. "I mean, I hate this plan, but we need to see who's at the top."

"They can hear everything," I say. "You know that, right?"

They all nod.

"As if they didn't know we had some sort of plan." Arrie scoffs.

It takes over two hours to get to wherever their headquarters are, and by the time we get there, I seriously have to pee. They yank us out of the van, and I squirm. "I gotta pee!"

Nine chuckles while Arrie sighs.

The Vampires just scowl at me and roll their eyes. "No."

I growl under my breath at the pair of them. "I. Need. To. Pee." When they look at me with disdain, I sigh. "Look, I really gotta pee, I can't be arsed to punch you in the face—which I couldn't do anyway given these." I wave the cuffs and jangle them in front of me. "And my plan won't work if I fight now. So please let me fucking pee."

They give each other a silent shrug and drag me through a door down the alley the others all stand in, waiting. Through the metal door, I find myself in a bathroom. A public bathroom. The guy who dragged me in here doesn't make a move to leave.

"You're gonna watch me pee?"

He shrugs.

"For fuck's sake."

There are two other guys at the urinals, and I look at me and shudder. Shit. I wish I could speak to Nine right now. Isn't there a bunch of rules about peeing in a men's room? I'm gonna fuck this up, aren't I?

Luckily they cuffed my hands at the front; this way, I can undo the zipper of my jeans and actually pee without sending piss everywhere.

Walking up to the nearest free urinal, next to the guy with the blond hair, I unzip my pants and pee. Ugh, and I thought peeing as a guy was hard when I wasn't handcuffed. (Let me tell you, it's not fun.)

The blond-haired guy looks at me funny with a heavy amount of side eye, but I have no idea what's wrong.

"What is your problem, dude?"

He coughs his surprise, rushes to finish up, and runs away to the sink.

Did I say something wrong?

The Vampire guard snickers at me, and the two men run out of there like I'd served them my shit on a stick at a hotdog bar. Seriously? I'm just trying to pee.

Once I zip back up and turn around, the guy stares at me with slight disgust. "What? I seriously needed to fucking pee!"

He shakes his head and drags me back outside to the team, who wait patiently for us to return.

"Peeing as a man while handcuffed . . . Not fun."

Nine laughs, but Arrie just grumbles something I actually can't hear for a change. Thought I would be relieved about that, but I find myself feeling out of the loop, instead, and desperately wanting to know what he said.

Our two escorts lead us down the alley and out the other side to stand before a large derelict building. It has at least four stories and looks like it could all come crumbling down at any moment. My thoughts are clearly written all over my face because the escort standing next to me laughs.

Huh?

They push us toward the half-broken door with pieces of splintered wood jagging out at odd angles. But the moment I step onto the broken pathway that leads to the front door, the light shimmers and everything changes. The once derelict building shines a brilliant white and pale blue—an office building with heavily shaded windows.

A Vampire building. A seriously expensive, well-funded Vampire building.

Everyone stands aghast at the sight of the building and the surprise of the whatever-the-hell magic conceals its real appearance.

"C'mon," one of the guards says. "She's waiting."

So the leader is a woman? Interesting. Wonder if it's anyone we know?

They lead us through doors, corridors, and hallways that all looked hauntingly like the ones of the official Vampire Council building; seems they want to create a new government, if this imitation is anything to go by.

Up ahead is a small office door—no grandiose framing or other over-the-top frills, just a simple door—leading to a simple room. But the person standing in front of the desk in that room is far from simple. Her every facial move is calculated, from the vague twitch of her eyebrow feigning surprise at seeing us, to the gentle smile feigning delight at having to deal with us.

"Horsemen." She gestures to the seats lined in a row on the far wall a few feet from the desk. "Please, sit."

18

We all sit without fuss. It isn't as though she's really more powerful than us, so the whole sitting versus standing power play isn't going to work here.

She doesn't look at Dea, so he probably can't be seen right now, but she looks at the rest of us and frowns at the cuffs. "Remove those. They won't be necessary."

The guards who escorted us here unlock the cuffs with a spellbead of some kind (would be good to have one of those on hand in future) and when he undoes Nine's, I hear him release a gratifying breath.

I grab his hand and smile. "Better?"

He nods, then returns to his stoic, not-caring-about-this-bullshit expression he was sporting before.

Right. Stoic. Play the long game.

Is she really their leader? That's the first question I need answered.

Dea knows her.

I glance Dea's way. He knows her? How?

Nine stays silent, and I just look at him and know instantly how he knows her.

He's slept with her, hasn't he?

Nine nods.

Great. Just what we fucking need. Tell Dea I won't hesitate to remove her head from her shoulders if she pisses me off. I don't care where his dick's been.

I change into my female form and step in front of the woman trying to look as scary as possible. It isn't working.

If she's responsible for this Vampire group's actions, she's the one I need to have a little chat with. The team aren't going to like this, so I keep them in their seats using an intense increase in air pressure so they can't move.

Refocusing on the annoying-as-fuck piece of Vampire shit in front of me, I tighten my fist.

She starts choking as the air surrounding her disappears. Her hands grasp at her neck, trying desperately to stop what probably feels like being strangled.

Good. Let her suffer a few seconds longer.

I unball my fists as she inhales large gulps of air, swallowing them down with eager abandon. "So, tell me, who are you working for?" Because she has to be working for someone; Vampires don't take war-level grudges against the Four Horsemen without a serious grievance, and since no one has pissed off anyone that much, I'm guessing they're working for or with someone.

"No . . . one." She coughs as she leans against the wood of her desk. "We work . . . alone." Her voice croaks and cracks the more she tries to talk.

The more her denials are voiced, the more pissed off I become. I would ask Nine to look, but I don't want him to feel any more uncomfortable today. That isn't fair.

"Nope." I shake my head. "Not the right answer." I remove her air supply once more, thinking about nothing but Nine's bleeding body on the floor of the garden, Dea's face when he realized Nine was seriously injured . . . "You wouldn't know enough about us if you weren't working for or with someone."

Her lips turn blue. Lucky she's a born Vampire, or this would be harder. And messier. Born Vampires are born, live, and die. Turned Vampires, however, really are undead—though, the magic that keeps them undead dies eventually. We got lucky, or I would be totally ruining these clothes.

"Stop." It's Nine's voice. I can hear them all pleading, but I don't care. We need answers, and this is the best way to get them.

I let her breathe once more and catch her by the arm before she collapses to the floor. "Gonna tell me what I want to know?" I sigh. "Not a fan of torture, would rather you just tell me."

"You're crazy," she says. "Get off of me!"

"Yeah, probably. Immortality'll do that to you." I pick her up by the scruff of her perfectly-placed shirt and deposit her scrambling body on the desk chair.

Her surprised face and uncomfortable posture gives me a revelation: she doesn't sit there often. Sighing, I wipe a hand over my face. "Who's the real leader?"

She blinks at me and smiles. "You're as good as they say." She stands up. "But I can't answer that."

I release the team behind me, but they don't move. Only Arrie comes to stand next to me, placing a hand on my shoulder. "What now?"

I look up at him and nod, hoping he will understand my meaning.

He grimaces slightly but understands, because he grabs her body and throws it through the nearest wall. It isn't enough to kill her, but it is enough to shock her into a new sense of talkative, as she realizes we are all a little crazy.

It's a good act, but I don't know how long I can keep playing the bad guy before my moral compass spins in the right direction. I need answers, and I need them now.

There is one thing Vampires don't like, and that's more powerful Vampires. I don't want to scare Connie, but answers are more important.

I sprint at the female Vampire with full fangs, red eyes, and hopefully looking a tad scary. Scratching a gash on the side of her neck, I let the trickle of blood wash over my finger before raising my hand and licking it off.

"No, please!" she whimpers. "I can't tell you anything. He'll kill me."

"He?"

She nods. Her shirt slipped in the fall, and I notice finger marks surrounding her neck. Ones not created by me given the width of the fingers compared to my tiny ones.

I trace the bruises with a finger and ease up on the whole scary interrogation thing. "Who did this to you?"

Tears spill down the side of her face, and that's it, all my fake, mean-faced bullshit crumples to the ground.

Sighing, I help her to her feet and offer a small sip of my blood to help her heal. Least I could do. "Take it. It'll heal you in no time. I think."

She raises an eyebrow and licks it off my finger.

I watch, astonished for a moment, as her cuts, scrapes, and bruises vanish, her pale Vampire complexion returning to its normal color.

"C'mon." I grab her hand and guide her to the desk chair she was not so comfortably sat in earlier. It's designed for someone taller than her, by the looks of it. "You know," I say, "we could always bring you back to *Sheruta* with us."

We can do that, right Nine?

Yes.

"Listen, we need to know who the leader is so we know who he's working with. We can't prevent or stop this war without the right info."

She nods. "I know. I just . . ."

"Look, I know you're scared, but this isn't about you. The world is in danger if we let war run rampant through the streets. Thousands of innocents of every species known to man—and probably some unknown—will get injured in the crossfire. Not to mention what this'll do to the humans. I don't want that. Do you?"

"So, you're not crazy?"

"I'll do whatever it takes."

She looks to where Dea sits, not quite meeting his eyes. "It's him. He's leading this."

Dea stands and pales, going visible so she can see him.

Her eyes meet his with affection, and I recoil in annoyance, spending a split-second of my time reconsidering the decision to let her live.

Relax. You know Dea's obsessed with you.

Nine's right. I really need to relax. I'm not a jealous person, so where is this coming from?

Focusing on the task at hand, or trying to, I turn to our new informant and ask, "Who is he?"

"My husband. Prince Phillipe."

Well, shit. The future Vampire King is working against the SC and has some serious beef with us. Just fucking great.

19

"Now what?" I ask Dea. "This was not what I imagined when I planned this fucking trip."

"What did you imagine, exactly?" He looks straight at me with exasperation, then steps toward the perfect-looking Vampire and wraps an arm around her shoulder. "Come on. Let's get you sat down."

"This isn't going to end well," Connie mumbles.

I shoot her a please-shut-up look and stare daggers at Dea. "I imagined being able to end the existence of whoever's plan it was that nearly got Nine killed." You know, figuratively speaking, since he would just come back from whatever death he would have suffered.

Dea turns my way with a shocked expression—his arm still wrapped around that Vampire's shoulder that I can't seem to stop staring at.

"What? Were you expecting some kind of nice Horseman of Magic with aims of peace and dropping candy off to poor children's houses?" I shift into my male form and growl. "I'm only one person!"

I can feel the anger well beneath the surface, ready to explode. I'm not feeding properly, Vampires and Shifters are known to be territorial over their loved ones, and he's intentionally making my life harder!

My body flits back to my female self of its own accord, causing everyone in the room to step back with a gasp.

I mean, could he be any more inconsiderate right now? I'm sure if I wasn't so strung out, come off my period not two days ago, and starving, I wouldn't be having a problem, but clearly I am, and I really wanted to rip her throat out because of it. I can see her main artery pumping away underneath that delicious skin of hers. I could easily peel that pretty, delicate skin off of that pretty, delicate neck.

Dea steps back from the Vampire whose name I still haven't bothered to get with raised hands. "Easy there, Angel. Calm down."

What's going on? Why do I feel really hot all of a sudden? "What's happening to me?" Sweat beads down my forehead in washes of desert-inducing sweat.

The Vampire on the chair looks horrified, and I turn to see the rest of the team with similar expressions, though admittedly less shocked.

Nine steps forward, though he still doesn't come near me. "You're on fire."

Wait, what? I look down at my body and scream.

Flames engulf my entire being from head to toe. My instinct is to try to bat the flames out—somehow put the fire out—but I'm not in any pain, I can just feel the intensity of the heat with every breath and every slight movement.

Err . . . Calm, Magic, calm. Remain calm. You can think your way out of this. The others can't help without getting burned, so it's up to you. Triggers? Jealousy. Definitely jealousy. Maybe anger. How to turn those emotions off?

Ha! That's like asking me not to want brownies. Or at least, it feels that pointless.

Come on, Magic, you're not the jealous type. You barely reacted to Dea and Nine's flirting on the last mission; and he's not even flirting. This is just some kind of heightened Vampiric response because of my lack of a sex life.

Dea steps forward, but I hold up a hand. "Please don't open your mouth and make things worse. Just . . . gimme a minute."

He nods.

He loves you. I know it's early days, I know we have all of eternity, but he thinks about you differently to anyone else. Even me.

That . . . He . . . What?

I've rendered you speechless. Who knew that was possible?

I smile amidst the tears leaking from my eyes and look back down at my body. No fire. But I can feel the simmering of heat just below the surface, ready to burst the moment someone pisses me off.

Male form. Male form. Male form.

I feel the switch come over me, and before I know it, we're safe from me bringing the building down to a pile of ashes.

Deep breaths—and promptly avoiding Dea's eyes—has me walking over to the Vampire. "My name's Magic." I help her to her feet and grasp her hands. "If you need anything at all, come and find me. The moment you change your mind and want somewhere safe, a real life, call me."

I ask Nine to pass on some kind of contact information to the poor Vampire bride and walk out of the room, practically running out of the building. My skin itches in a way I can't explain, like it's crawling with a deep sense of uncomfortableness; I need to be outside right now, some place where I can't hurt anyone.

Shift. I need to shift. The moment I get outside, I shift into the first instinctive animal I can think of and pace outside the building while waiting for the others to join me.

What's wrong with me? Why have I gone from semi-innocent and wanting to wait and be myself to this sex-obsessed, jealous girlfriend? That's not me. At least, I don't want it to be. I just want to go home. I want to go back to my library, back to family dinners, back to watching Arrie get annoyed every time I feed from someone else.

Normality.

The others stalk toward me with serious faces. They all stand around me, stopping me from pacing and caging me in place.

Connie crouches down to my level and runs a hand through the fur on my head, eliciting a purr from me. "You okay, hon?"

I nod my panther head and stalk off in some other direction, hoping to grab a cab so we can get back to the hotel. I shift into a small tabby housecat the moment Connie hails a cab from the nearest busy road, allowing me to rest in her lap as she strokes comforting hands down my back and scratches between my ears.

I won't lie, that feels like a brilliant massage, only better. I purr the entire way back, content in my own little cat universe as I ignore all my problems and the pending doom of the upcoming war.

Connie carries me back to my room in the hotel, where we have to sneak around to avoid all the stares and whispers from everyone who saw us attack Vampires earlier this evening.

"Are you going to shift back?" Dea asks as we all sit on my bed in silence. "Because we need to make plans."

Internally sighing, I shift into my male form and then female form. "I'm done with plans. You make them." I walk into the bathroom and run a bath, adding in generous amounts of bubble baths, salts, and other smelly, relaxing liquids I don't recognize.

I can hear them all chatting in the bedroom but decide to ignore them in favor of sinking into the best moment I've had all fucking day.

Sweetie?

I sigh. Yes.

Dea's worried you're mad at him.

I'm not.

I know.

Tell him to come in but with his eyes closed.

Nine chuckles, and two minutes later, Dea walks in with his eyes closed, taking small but measured steps into the bathroom.

"Give me a minute." I yank the curtain across the bath and lay back down. "There you go." He can see my silhouette but nothing else. That'll do.

Dea remains silent for a few minutes, and I worry he might bail and run away. "I am sorry, Angel."

I sigh. Again. "Don't be. I'm not mad at you. You helped an innocent woman into a chair." I grumble some non-words and start again. "I don't know what's wrong with me. I'm not usually a jealous person."

"I know." Dea sits on the floor by the bath, his back to the tub. "I cannot change the past. She was so miserable, I just wanted to show her what it should be like. Just for a night."

"Stop." I sniff, trying to hold back the tears. "You don't need a reason or an excuse. You could sleep with whomever you wanted. It doesn't matter to me." I creep my wet hand around the curtain and rest it on his shoulder. "I care about what you do now."

I can feel his shoulders rise a little at that, and he turns to grab my hand and place a gentle kiss on the palm. "Do not be too angry at yourself, Angel. Your powers are new, as is this . . . link between our Angel powers. It will take time to figure out."

I nod, hoping he can see.

"We'll be waiting in bed for you."

The sleeping arrangements are a little different this time, with Dea and Arrie on either side of me and Connie and Nine on the outside. Dea's gentle charm to Arrie's gruff warmth is a perfect combination of . . . contentment.

One day, you'll be brave enough to say it. One day you'll be ours as much as we've become yours.

20

A loud knocking disturbs the five of us early the next morning, merely four hours after we all fell asleep. Grumbling, I get up to answer the door.

"Huh?" I ask as I open the door to a servant holding out a letter. An actual letter. On paper! I don't think I've ever received one.

Grabbing it, I sprint back into the room to find everyone awake and sitting up in bed, a space still left for me to re-join them.

"What is it?" Dea asks.

"A letter . . . I think."

"You think?"

"Well," I say, as I sit back down between Arrie and Dea, "I've never received one before."

Dea chuckles as Arrie rests a hand on my shoulder. "I do not feel this is going to be a good first." Dea grabs the letter from my hand and frowns. "It is from the Fae Council."

"How do you know?"

Connie leans over Nine and points to the fancy symbol on the front. "That's their emblem."

Ah, so the Fae want us for something. I groan. "What now?" I rub my eyes to try and wake up, but nothing I do makes a difference.

"Here," Arrie says as he holds out his wrist but keeps his eyes on the letter.

I take his hand in mine and rub circles over his knuckles, making the big guy shiver. Breakfast time. The moment my fangs slip and I bite down on Arrie's wrist, he stifles a moan—well, he tries.

I haven't fed from him directly before. His woody, metallic scent trickles down my throat as I suck harder.

"Fuck, that's . . ."

"Intense," Dea finishes for him. "More so than other Vampires."

That vaguely registers in the back of my mind as I focus on the task at hand and not getting lost in the moment, accidentally draining the Horseman of War dry.

I lean over his body slightly and can feel his erection pressing into my thigh that rests between his legs. Resisting the urge to reach down his pajama pants and help myself takes an impressive amount of effort in my current state; one I am rather proud of.

Dea comes up behind me and trails lavender-scented kisses down the nape of my neck, forcing my body to arch into his, and I'm lost in the sensations for a moment before snapping back to reality.

I unlatch from Arrie and look up at him, giving what I hope is a thankful smile, but realize I am probably covered in blood. "Thanks."

He looks at me with a glaze over his eyes as he runs a hand down my side and settles it on my waist. "You're welcome." Shaking his head, he tries to readjust himself, but it's pretty pointless in those loose sweatpants.

I realize in that moment that they would have let me continue if I wanted. That this is something they're prepared for. Goddess, that actually scares me a bit.

We've talked about it.

Really?

"Yes," he says out loud. "When we saw the direction this was going to go back at the beginning, we talked about all of this. Don't worry." He winks and grabs the letter from Dea's hand. "Now," he says, "about this." He waves the letter and opens it. Quickly scanning the words, he chucks it onto the bed with a groan and glares at Connie. "Why did you have to make that agreement?"

Understanding dawns on her face as she blushes and whispers, "Sorry."

"Huh?"

Nine grabs my hand. "We have to dance with the Fae Court. It was the bargain Connie made for answers in the last mission. They saw the fight online and know we're on Earth."

I sigh. "Better get going then." I have no idea what dancing with the Fae means, but since I'm part Fae, I gather it won't be as hard on me as the others.

"We should definitely tell her," I hear Connie say.

"Yeah, but Con, she's gonna freak." Nine's ever-annoying words of wisdom.

"What lollipop of sucky shit do I have to deal with now?" I throw on some clothes, not bothering with a shower if we're going to spend the next ten-plus hours on an airplane.

Dea winces. "Dancing with the Fae is dangerous for humans. They become entranced and dance until they die. It is an extreme event. One you will not like."

"You don't know that." But by the looks on everyone's faces, I get the feeling I really won't like it. "Okay. Can we just get this over with?"

Arrie stands. "I have a question for the Fae Court anyway." At everyone's confused faces, he explains, "Who among them are working for Prince Phillipe?"

"Right," Nine says, "they had to have some Fae magic to create that illusion spell to hide the building." He looks at Arrie in surprise. "Nicely deduced."

Arrie grumbles something in another language, and for once, it's aimed at Nine; that fact alone has me smiling.

I can do this, right? Dance with the Fae, not die, tell the truth while avoiding the juicy bits to a court famous for its flaunting of the laws surrounding lower paranormal life-forms. The Fae are in charge of the world's dust supply, and rumor has it they cage pixies in giant farms and bleed them dry until they eventually die.

Yeah, Dea's right, I'm not going to like these people.

Everyone is dressed and ready to go in little over an hour, but it's me who seems to think of the politics in our decision. "Can one just pop in on the Vampire Council? Is that, like, a thing?"

Dea looks at me with furrowed eyebrows. "No. Why?"

"Because I think updating them on the fact we really weren't attacking their Vampires is a good move."

"If it's just an update you want, we can screen-message them." Nine's busy repacking the clothes in the small suitcase he dragged in not twenty minutes ago.

"We can do what to them?"

He lifts his head to smile at me. "Right. You were unconscious still when they brought it out."

Arrie gruffs as Connie mumbles, "Here we go."

Nine abandons his clothes folding—which shocks me enough into a standstill—and stalks toward me. "I invented a type of video message you can use via a telepathic spell the Fae helped me utilize. It was released a few months ago."

"Video messaging? But that's so . . . 2000s."

He laughs. "Yes, but this is more like a holographic video than a recorded image." He grabs my hand and sits me on the bed. "Here, I'll show you." Nine rummages around in his bag and pulls out a small black disk that he sits on the floor.

Okaaaay. I am officially weirded out.

He pushes a button on the side and says, "Vampire Royal Council." The machine sparks to life in a series of blue flashes and beeps like straight out of a science-fiction movie.

"It uses telepathic linking magic to connect two separate devices, similar to how our magiphones work, but this device scans the people and sends a holographic image instead of a video."

The device glows a deep green for a moment before it announces, "Vampire Royal Council member, Prince Lucien."

"Ah! Little Horseman."

I hear the little prince's voice crystal-clear through the device's speaker strip running around the outside. Or, at least, I assume it's a speaker strip.

The green glow beams toward the ceiling as a faintly-glowing image of Prince Lucien appears, looking like he's standing on the device.

"Wow!" I jump to my feet and walk around it, but the image stays the same. "This thing is awesome, Nine."

"Stop stroking your boyfriend's ego and say what it is you want."

My . . . boyfriend? Shaking my head, I reply, "Just wanted to make sure the Council were aware of our plan and they don't want us dead."

"Updated them for you this morning, little Horseman. No need to worry."

"And, err . . . who was present for this update?"

Prince Lucien blinks. "The entire Council, other than my father, he was busy. Why?"

"Nothing you need concern yourself with. Thank you for your co-operation, Prince Lucien." I bow lightly and look to Nine. Turn it off.

He flicks a button on the side, and the image goes dead, the lights dimming as the device shuts down.

I sigh. "To the Fae Court, then."

21

New Orleans to Paris is the longest piece-of-shit flight I have ever been on (that I can remember, of course). Feet firmly on solid ground and my stomach back where it should be, I can finally breathe easy.

"Nine, when we get home, please remind me to help you invent easier, cheaper, Earth-to-Earth teleportation crystals. I'm sure I could do it with my Fae magic."

"Noted." He wraps an arm around my shoulder and directs us to the nearest cab outside the airport. At least, that's where I think he's taking us, but just as we get to the cab station, we keep on going until we stop in front of a limo.

An actual limo!

"We're getting in that?"

Connie smiles. "We are."

"Unlike the Vampire Council, who are terrified of us," Dea starts, "the Fae like to flaunt their excessive wealth and power to intimidate us."

I laugh. "Hilarious."

"We think so, too."

We all fit inside the limo with room to spare—much to Nine's delight after the last cab fiasco—and Connie decides that the offered champagne is the best way to start this trip.

"Gonna drink with me?" She offers me a glass.

I look at the glass with some trepidation. I don't trust the Fae, especially not with the possibility that they could be working with the rogue Vamps. What if they've poisoned it with something like Silver Leaf Vain?

You're too paranoid. Just drink the champagne.

I change into my male form and grab the offered glass. Waving a hand over the rim, I check to see if there are any spells or enchantments present. I might not be able to do anything to get rid of them, but detecting magic is as easy as breathing.

Clean. To my untrained magic hands, anyway.

I take a careful sip, not really confident in my abilities to detect Fae magic, even in this form, and sigh with contentment as I lean back and relax.

"You really thought they might poison us?"

I shrug. "Don't know what to think right now. Just making sure none of us have to expel poison in the middle of the Fae Court." I raise my eyebrows to her in challenge. "You're welcome."

Nine laughs. "Sweetie does have a point."

Dea and Arrie nod, but Connie just frowns.

I want to say not all of us are obsessed with the Fae, but given how little I know of Connie's background, it could be insensitive.

That gives me an idea. "What's the craziest thing you've ever done?" I direct the question at everybody, hoping they catch on.

Nine does, obviously, and answers, "This should be good."

Connie laughs, but Dea and Arrie grumble, as though sharing their massive amount of past is a chore, rather than a good way to get to know each other better.

"Oh, err . . . don't worry about it." It's not that important. I don't want to inconvenience them or make them uncomfortable. I change back into my female form and huddle over my plasmascreen to read a new book: mystery thriller this time. (I know, I'm shocked too.)

Dea gets up and sits beside me, placing a hand on my arm. "Sorry, I did not mean to upset you."

I shrug, wanting nothing more than to sink into my book and forget things for a few hours. I'll work on getting to know them better later. For now, life is too . . . Horseman of Magic-y. And everything little thing is bothering me, but I'm trying hard not to snap.

Instead of interrupting me, however, Dea merely lifts me into his lap and wraps an arm around me while I read. I won't lie, I melt a bit on the inside. Okay, a lot—my insides are a puddle of molten feelings right now. He can be so sweet when he wants to be.

Ugh. No. Still mad.

Arrie joins us—not wanting Dea to take the apologetic spotlight, I assume—and lifts my feet onto his lap, sending gentle strokes up and down my legs.

The book is good, or would have been if I could get past page five; being in Dea's and Arrie's laps is more than a little distracting. But mostly it's just comforting. They run hands over the small of my back, my shoulders, and my thighs, soothing any wayward thoughts that they don't really care, or that it's too soon to care in the first place.

They avoid any too-sensitive places, thank the goddess because I don't think my Vampire-self could take that right now, but everyone is seemingly comfortable with each other, despite group intimacy not having been a thing with them in the past.

"Err . . ." I start as I put the plasmascreen down. "I . . . umm . . ."

"Just ask," Nine says in his no-nonsense, factual attitude.

"How are you all so comfortable with"—I gesture to Dea and Arrie—"this?" I can barely contain the blush that creeps over my face and neck. "It's just so . . . unusual, and you're all so comfortable with it."

Dea sighs behind me while Arrie tenses—something about his reaction bothers me. I grab his hand from my thigh and stroke comforting circles over his palm.

Arrie sighs this time and opens his mouth to speak. "I think we're all at different places with this, and for different reasons." He looks at Dea with a questioning look, and he nods.

"We are all okay with it but for different reasons." Dea points to himself. "I like that I could be in a relationship with you both." He gestures to both myself and Nine.

"And I, Sweetie"—Nine grabs my hand—"like the freeing nature in the way you think about it. I would be free to explore any relationship with any of you. I like that level of family between us, and you make it complete."

Connie goes next. "I've never wanted this before. Not with any of you." She looks to the floor. "But I like you, even . . ." She shakes her head, her blonde hair spilling out of its bun slightly. "Never mind." She walks over, hunches to avoid the roof of the limo, and grabs my hand as she sits on her knees. "I like you, and I would never restrict you. Besides, what if one day I didn't want to be restricted with any of the guys?"

"You'd be free, of course."

She nods and smiles.

I look to Arrie, but he shakes his head and sits up, getting out from under my legs and returning to his original seat. He's hiding something, and one day, he'll be comfortable enough to share. But until then, I'll smile at him and do my best to be a good friend.

I hope.

None of us deserve someone as naturally loving as you.

Where are these compliments coming from?

I just . . . Sighing, he says, *it doesn't matter. We'll talk about it when we get home. Besides, I've got a surprise in the works for you.*

"Ohhh, a surprise? Really?" I bounce on the spot, my spirits lifting almost instantly. Okay, so call me basic, but it's been a tough few months, and a girl can only have so many love interests without wanting to be spoiled every now and then. (You would if you could.)

He nods. "You'll just have to wait and see."

The others look at Nine and smile, catching onto something I'm missing, but I don't mind; they know me well enough by now that I'm sure I'll love anything Nine surprises me with.

We ride the rest of way in moderate silence, the occasional question from me breaking the tension; seems everyone is worried about this visit to the Fae Court.

"But I'll be fine in my Fae form, right? I mean, what harm could they really do to me?"

Nine nods. "You'll be fine. We're not worried about that."

Huh?

He sighs and says, "You're just not going to like the Fae Court. But it'll be easier to show you rather than explain. Just promise not the murder the Fae Queen, alright?"

Connie chimes in. "Yeah, don't go all crazy on her. They're a very particular type of people. We can work with them, we just need to be a little open minded."

That sounds ominous at best.

Another hour in the limo, drinking a second glass of champagne and finally getting past the fifth page of my new book, we're finally ready to get out of the moving vehicle.

Goddess, I hate all modes of transportation that don't involve my feet on solid ground and my stomach where it fucking should be.

Upon exiting the limo, I come to a halt—my thoughts, actions, reactions, and feet all coming to an abrupt standstill.

This is the Fae Court?

It's . . . beautiful. Old-fashioned. Rustic. Peaceful.

We're pulled onto the sidewalk of a wide, cobble-stoned street with red, gray, and white-bricked buildings surrounding every inch of our view of the city. There are no magically-enhanced displays, no modern magitech, and no cars. It's so . . . dated. But in a way that makes me release a sigh of contentment.

We're in a courtyard, and every building is like it's stepped out of the twentieth century; it's like stepping into one of my textbooks. Like I've gone back in time and can't quite catch my breath at the tranquility of the past.

"Is all of Paris like this?"

Connie shakes her head and grabs my hand. "No, just the Fae Court. They prefer limited technology. They're old-fashioned like that."

One day I want to see the rest of Paris. The city of love, of beauty, of upstanding technological advancement. It would be . . .

"Breathtaking," Nine finishes for me. "Paris is breathtaking."

I look at him with a smile as the limo drives away. "Maybe we could go see it one day?"

Dea steps up to us and wraps an arm around each of our waists. "Maybe we might all have time to go together after this."

He looks at me, and I understand: this is him making good on his promise to show me the world, the reasons to live, the benefits to being immortal.

"I'd like that."

Connie joins us and stands in front of me, grabbing my hand. "Me too."

Arrie doesn't say anything. He's lost in thought, it seems, as he looks into the distance without really looking at anything in particular, a hazy gaze covering his eyes.

I wonder what he's thinking about?

The past.

I flinch. I never really considered that their past might be as sucky as mine. Goddess, how selfish of me. I should make more of an effort to ensure they're doing okay.

Arrie still gazes into the distance, so I run up to him and wrap my arms around his neck, simply hanging there until he looks at me. As his gaze turns to mine, the look of solemn hurt forms tears in my eyes. So I do the only thing I know to do in that instance, I wrap my legs around his waist and my arms around his neck while my head buries into his hair.

I don't talk, I don't use words, I don't try to eke out a conversation I know he doesn't want, I simply hug him, trying to show him that I'll always be here. And eventually, he wraps his arms around my body and buries his own head in my neck, breathing me in.

"Thank you."

I can hear the tears in his voice, and I really want to know what kind of pain is in his past that makes him suffer like this, even after two thousand years. Maybe I can help?

"I'll always be here," I whisper into his hair.

I climb down the big guy's body and grab his hand. "C'mon, let's go deal with this stupid Fae Court and then go see Paris."

He walks beside me, not letting go of my hand.

I need to change into my male form while here ideally, but holding his hand feels too good, and I don't want him to let go.

Arrie leans in and whispers, "You should change form while here."

I nod and try to pull my hand away, but he keeps hold of it firmly. A few quick blinks and I'm in my male form, my hand actually large enough to not be engulfed by his. But still, he keeps holding my hand.

I look at him in confusion, but he smiles dazzlingly. "You're still you. I'm not too stubborn that I won't hold a man's hand." He rolls his eyes and moves us forward.

The others surround us with smiles that reach ear to ear while Nine mentally says, *Thank you.*

I don't think I've done anything of note, but appreciation is a girl's—guy's?—best friend. Damn it, I really need a neutral pronoun for my self-absorbed internal ramblings.

We walk down a stone corridor that has wide, empty arches looking out into the center of the courtyard where a grand statue of an old Fae Queen stands.

"That's the first Fae Queen, Titania, and inside the other courtyard is the first Fae King, Oberon." Nine sighs. "They were king and queen of the summer court, the first court of the Fae. Now they're all a single court, united a long time ago, but once upon a time, they were all separated. It was Oberon and Titania that brought the courts together and created the Fae we know today."

I nod, thankful for the info.

"She's beautiful."

Nine chuckles. "That she was."

"This was in your lifetime?" I ask in surprise, my eyebrows raising in shock.

He nods. "I wrote the entire thing down once in a lore book; I'll lend it to you when we get home."

"Oh, yay!" I almost clap my hands but refrain.

Connie groans. "Could you two stop geeking out every two seconds." But she has a smile on her face that lets me know she's joking.

"Puuuhhlease, if I were geeking out over you, you'd love it."

She winks. "Yeah, but instead you're geeking out over some long-dead beautiful Fae Queen." She pouts.

"Don't worry. You're way more beautiful."

She blushes, and Arrie laughs. "That you are, Con." He squeezes my hand slightly, and I squeeze back, letting him know that I don't mind. She is beautiful. I would be more pissed at him if he didn't think so.

We walk through all kinds of ancient stone corridors: some with armored statues, some covered in vines and roses and other flowers I have no idea how to identify, some with nothing more than grand-framed paintings of lewd and beautiful images. The entire place is breathtaking.

It extends into the buildings surrounding that courtyard and beyond. Nine tells me that most of the Fae live in relative seclusion, other than the ones who prefer the outside world; in that sense, they're similar to the Witches.

That's why you see more Vampires and Shifters in the world.

We reach a set of golden-brown doors with intricate roses worked into the wood, twirling into one another like lovers under the moonlight. I pause to admire the handicraft. "Whoever made those doors is talented."

Arrie, who is still holding my hand, huffs and hides a chuckle.

"Who made them?"

He shrugs but looks to Nine, laughs and shakes his head. "Arrie did."

I turn to Arrie with shock and admiration to watch him blush.

He shrugs. "I loved the original Fae Court. The one created by Titania and Oberon. It meant something. It was my gift to them."

So Arrie likes the Fae Court, too.

It's changed over the years, especially since the outing.

Ah, so they used to like it.

The doors open, and Arrie tightens his grip on my hand. I squeeze it, telling him I'm okay, but I get the feeling he keeps hold of me for more than just comfort. The fucker is keeping me on a leash, and I growl at the prospect of even needing one. I'm a free, independent woman—man—dammit!

The hall beyond is more eloquent than anything I've laid eyes on, including our house. The ceiling is so high I can barely make out the intricate design work painted onto it—but I manage with the help of my Shifter eyes—and the buttresses and arches trailing down to the stone columns covered in rose vines stand out with their stone artwork of more lewd images.

The whole room screams 'look at me' in the most attractive way. Even I can appreciate the time and effort that must have gone into the making of this room, especially before magical technology.

"Before technology altogether, actually."

"Really?" I ask Nine.

He nods.

"Damn."

A gilded throne sits on a singular dais at the end of the room, trailing roses in every color imaginable drape in waterfall designs behind, and sitting on that throne is a lady I can only assume is the Fae Queen. Her beauty exceeds anyone's I've ever seen—other than Connie's. She has pointed ears, just like me, glowing green eyes, and white hair that lands in a heap on the floor. Her smile is warm but obviously fake. These people can't lie, but they can act however they want. Luckily, my Fae form is not restricted in the same way.

Still shouldn't lie here. It's seen as disrespectful.

Noted.

"Ah, the Horsemen of the Apocalypse. It is good to see you once again." She smiles at everyone, including Arrie, which is unusual, but stops when she sees me. "And the new Horseman. It is a pleasure to finally meet you."

Her voice is melodic, and I can tell she uses it to charm most of her subjects, or at least foreign diplomats. Probably both. She raises herself from the throne and floats down the dais' stone steps to meet us in the center of the room.

"Horseman of Magic, charmed." She holds out her hand, but I'm not sure what's expected of me.

Kiss it.

Ugh. Fine. I grab her hand and raise it gently to my lips, much to the surprised smile of the queen.

"My, it is a pleasure." She smiles at me. "Someone of Fae heritage is always welcome in my court."

I bow my head slightly. "Thank you."

"Queen Darianne," Connie starts as she steps forward, "it is a pleasure to be welcomed once more into your court. We are most looking forward to your party this evening."

Queen Darianne sits back on her throne and waves Connie's compliment away. "Dancing with the Fae is a grand gesture, but one you have all received before." She pauses to look at me. "Well, everyone but our new guest, of course." She laughs, and her pleasant tones dance across my ears. "I assume you will be wanting to take part in the festivities on offer this evening, too?" She raises her eyebrows.

What is she talking about? Goddess, why do the team never give me a heads up?

All members of the team tense, but it's Arrie who steps up, a smile on his face as fake as the pleasantries on offer by our fancy-looking queen here. "Actually, Your Majesty, we will be retiring after the party. We are rather busy of late."

Her scowl darkens the room. "My court does rather enjoy your presence at the festivities. You are all much practiced in the arts of lust and love."

Oh, those kinds of festivities. Nine, you guys can participate if you'd like.

He shakes his head slightly—enough for me to notice—and returns his attention to the queen.

We all stand in solemn unity on the matter, and the queen sighs. "Very well. If that's all, you can be seen to your rooms." She dismisses us with a wave of her hand, and we follow a servant out of the room.

The servant is a small, wispy type of girl with the same pointed ears as all Fae, but her skin tone has a subtle green tint to it, and I wonder why that is. I've only ever seen pale, white-skinned Fae. Do they have different skin colors to match what would have been their old season court?

Yes. Green is the old summer court. Pale-skinned Fae would have belonged to either the winter or autumn courts, while the blue-skinned Fae would have belonged to the spring court.

She guides us down singular corridors and multiple hallways, all made of stone, and all as beautiful as the rest of the court. "There are five rooms prepared for you down there and to the left. We have taken the liberty of—"

Nine interrupts. "We'll just be needing a singular room for our stay. Which one has the biggest bed?"

The Fae girl blushes and says, "The first one." She smiles at me and says, "We have taken the liberty of acquiring fresh blood for our new Horseman. I'll have it stocked in the room you choose."

I bow my head and walk past her toward the corridor she referred to. Five doors lie alongside the roses and tulips brushing the walls and ceilings, each one wooden with the same kind of decoration as the main door to the throne but not quite as elegant.

"Not your work, I assume, Arrie?"

He shakes his head. "How can you tell?"

"It's not nearly as beautiful." I enter the first room on the left and stop to take a breath at the beauty of the room. "Will we always be staying in beautiful places?"

"When we can, Angel."

The bed is the biggest I've ever seen, and that has to be a coincidence. We'll all fit, assuming that was what Nine had in mind when he requested a single room.

"It was." He smiles at me.

I just blush. "I . . . I'm sorry."

He frowns. "Why?"

"Because you're all going to so much effort just for me."

He walks up to me and wraps me in a hug. "It's not just for you. Everyone in this room prefers sleeping this way. It was one of your better ideas. But even if it were just for you, it would be worth it."

I blush once more and feel weirdly uncomfortable with all of this in my male form. Bushing as a man isn't normal, is it? I mean, I never catch any of the other guys doing it. Maybe I should just change into my female form for a while.

"No." Nine steps up to me once more and wraps another arm around my waist. "Don't do that. Just be you."

"But—"

He silences me with a finger to my lips and whispers, "Your sex does not define who you are. It is merely an aspect of your biology, of the way you work. You can be whomever you choose to be."

He's right. Fuck whoever thought being a single sex was a good idea. I get the best of both worlds this way, and I am going to damn well use that to my advantage, starting with Nine.

He raises his eyebrows at me, but I silence whatever remark he was about to make with a kiss. I grab his shirt in both hands and yank him flush against me, his body flat against the panes of my torso.

Groaning into my mouth, he runs his hands up the ridges of my body and around to the small of my back, hooking a thumb under the waistband of my jeans and underwear.

Before I can progress things any further, a knock at the door interrupts us. It's my turn to groan, and I pull away to answer the door. "What?"

The young girl from before flinches. "I'm so sorry for disturbing you, Mr . . . Mrs." She flushes. "I'm so sorry." She bows. "Please forgive me."

I sigh. "It's okay. Just call me Magic."

She nods. "Magic, I have been informed to supply you with garments for this evening's festivities." She bows her head as she thrusts her hands forward, and out of nowhere, a large pile of clothing forms on her hands.

"Thank you." I grab the clothes from her petite hands. "Is there anything else?"

"No, Magic. I will leave you in peace."

"Thank you."

I bow back to her, and she smiles, hiding a laugh. Seems she isn't used to respect from people above her.

She closes the door as I turn around, and the others all look at me with gentle smiles. It's Connie who says something, though, as she walks up to me and wraps her arms around my shoulders. "It's so nice to see you be . . . you."

"Huh?"

She laughs. "It's just beautiful to watch the person you're becoming, and to have a hand in that."

The others nod.

She brushes a kiss across my lips and walks away to finish unpacking, which they all started to do while I made out with Nine.

Goddess, they are all so okay with this. I don't get it. I thought it would take longer for them to adjust, but here I am, romantically engaged with them all to some degree or another, and they're just acting like it's a normal average Tuesday.

Nine and Connie are locked in an intense internal conversation, with Connie shaking her head in disgust at something Nine is saying. "C'mon," he says out loud, "it'll be a good test, and I'm sure Sweetie will be fine with it."

I think I know what they're talking about. "Connie?" She looks my way. "It's fine. If Nine needs this as proof that I'm seriously okay with all of this"—I gesture to me and the team—"then go ahead."

She raises her eyebrows but nods.

I'll be honest, I want to watch. I want to see them all together as much as I want to be with them all together; just the thought has my cock twitching in pleasure.

Nine laughs but shakes his head and walks slowly up to Connie, who wraps an arm around his neck and leans in, lightly placing a kiss to his jaw. Nine angles himself so she can get better access to his neck, and she continues trailing kisses along his jaw until she meets his lips.

Dea and Arrie join me, both with an arm wrapping around my waist, all three of us leaning against the wall, enjoying the show. Dea leans down to my ear and whispers, "Someone's enjoying the show."

I look down to see my cock straining against my jeans and blush. For fuck's sake. "Sorry."

"Don't be," Arrie says, "you're in good company."

I look down at both the guys standing beside me and see them having the same issue.

Nine runs his hands under Connie's top, grazing the edges of her bra with his thumbs, and she moans into his mouth. Fuck, just the sound of her moaning has me hardening further. I wish I could be in my female form without going all Vamp-crazy right now because this would be easier to deal with.

"Nine," Connie gasps as he grazes her nipples, "just how far were you planning on taking this?"

"I've already got my answers. I'm just enjoying myself."

She giggles and runs her hands down his chest, but eventually she pulls away and looks at me. She flicks her eyes from my crotch to my heated face and smiles.

Arrie and Dea inch their hands closer to the rim of my jeans, but I pull away before they can do anything.

"Four cold showers it is," Arrie grumbles, and we all laugh.

22

The garments, it seems, barely cover anything. In my male form, all it does is drape down my chest, leaving not much to the imagination, and then hangs from the waist and glides along the floor, a slit going up the side for leg exposure. Nine helps me use a magical body hair remover potion to look all sleek and shiny, but thank the goddess I don't have to shave, because apparently facial hair isn't a thing for the Fae.

Lucky me.

In my female form, however, I wear what I can only describe as a belly-dancing outfit. You know, one of those things with layers of cloth that shows your legs with sexy splits and your belly with a sexy crop top that pushes my boobs up to maximum effect. If it wasn't so bright and colorful—and totally barf-worthy—I would have liked how it makes my curves flaunt a little. But it's bright and colorful and therefore yuck.

I step out of our bathroom in my female form, wearing the barf-outfit, and my displeasure is clearly written all over my face because Connie smirks and Arrie laughs. This is one of those occasions where Arrie's beautiful laughter is not worth the trouble it took to get him to laugh in the first place.

"Stop laughing, asshole. This isn't funny." I cross my arms over my chest. "I look like someone's seamstress threw up on me."

Nine comes to stand beside me, barely containing his laughter. "Well, what about your male form?"

I change, and everyone stands still, mouths agape.

"Damn, that's . . ." Connie seems at a loss for words.

"Hot," Nine answers for her.

Dea steps up off the bed and says, "Insatiable."

Arrie grunts but gives me a smile.

Seems they all like it. "It really looks that good?" I twirl around in front of a huge mirror beside a vanity, trying to see everything about this look.

"Hon, you look fuckable. Like, seriously fuckable."

Nine and Dea agree with confirming nods and stand either side of me, both in their own barf-clothes, but I have to admit, it looks good on them.

Nine? Guy question.

Go for it.

How the fuck do you hide an erection in this thing? It's just so . . . flowy.

You don't. The Fae are . . . highly sexual.

"Ugh. Great." Is there a magical species that's not sexual?

Witches. Shifters are a little more enclosed depending on the individual species.

Connie looks at me in confusion, but I wave her unasked question away.

I turn to face Arrie and really look at him for the first time in this stupid get up. The soft material hangs off him in waves of bright colors that contrast his skin, and his hair is pinned back into a low bun so I can see his edgy jawline and cheekbones more prominently. His entire top is empty of clothes, and my mouth momentarily waters at the sight of all that muscle. He . . . he looks . . . damn! Like, seriously, hot damn. It looks good on him.

"Just noticing, are we?" Dea chuckles from behind me, wrapping his arms around my waist. "Looks good, right?"

"Yeah, Arrie, you look . . . good in this stupid get up."

"Thank you." He's still a little off from earlier, and I'm worried tonight might be a bit much for him, but he smiles at me nonetheless.

You should stay with him this evening.

Good idea.

We're escorted to a ballroom just south of the throne room, and upon entering, I have to admit that I kinda like this party. Okay, so everyone is involved in flirting, playing, or fucking of some kind, some hidden in the shadows at the edges of the room, some on display, some on various couches and chairs dotted around the space, but it's mutual, consenting, and kind of beautiful. Towering flower cascades are dotted every few feet, circling a large, empty area of floor space—a dancefloor, I presume—and there is a champagne fountain, naked waiters with small canapes walking around, and lots of non-Fae supes, even some humans.

What are humans doing in the Fae Court?

"They're used as dancing partners," Nine leans in and whispers.

"But you said—"

"Yes, I did."

"Oh." I grab Arrie's hand, hoping he'll steady the growing rise of unease in my belly. "I can do this," I mutter to myself.

Connie leans in from behind me. "Yes, you can. Just ignore the bad and focus on being a Fae."

I can do that. I hope.

Just as we enter the party, the lights dim and the queen strolls into the center of that empty space. "Now that our guests are all here, let's begin."

Stringed music plays, and some tall, muscly Fae steps up to the queen and grabs her hand. They start twirling around the dancefloor in no particular pattern or form, and I realize that I will have to dance.

Shit. I'm fucking terrible. And I'm in my male form. I can't lead, I don't even know what I'm doing.

Arrie leans down to whisper. "Don't worry, sexuality isn't a thing here, either. Come on." He pulls me by the hand I'm holding onto the dancefloor. "Just relax." He pulls me flat against him, resting one hand in mine and the other on my waist.

I take a deep breath and follow him around the dancefloor, trying to keep my eyes on his so as not to freak out about everyone staring at us.

"Just focus on me, we're doing fine."

I nod.

Soon the other Horsemen are all on the dancefloor, Connie dances with Dea while Nine dances with a pretty green Fae girl, twirling her around and making her laugh.

"Arrie," I start, not sure whether now is really the time, "I know you don't want to talk about it, but I'm here."

He darts his eyes away from mine.

"Hey." I grab his chin and force him to look at me. "It's not the end of the world. You don't have to be a part of us, you know. If you don't want to." I sigh, hoping he'll get my meaning. "I still wouldn't stop you from being with the team."

He blinks, catching onto my meaning. "It's not that." He sighs and brings us to a standstill. "Sorry, no, I do want this. It's just . . ." He looks away from me and blinks tears from his eyes. "I'm the only one of us who had a family before we died and were chosen. The others? They all lost people, but I had a wife and children. It's hard to do this again."

I stiffen. "Really?"

He nods.

He had a family? Children? A wife?

"What was she like?" I smile, genuinely curious.

He has this wispy smile on his face that lights him up in the most gorgeous way. The reality of his situation is starting to sink in, though, and I can't help the growing pity on my face. He had a family, one he could have very well returned to via the Earth portal, but he held back. Couldn't have been an easy transition.

"She was beautiful. Stubborn, like you." He laughs. "I couldn't get her to do anything I wanted. It was most frustrating." He starts dancing again, dragging me around the dance-floor after him.

I don't have my Vampire speed and precision in this form so step on his toes a few times, but I hope it goes mostly unnoticed by anyone else.

"She was an amazing mother, but she was a warrior, too. Much better than human-me."

That surprises me. "Is that why you mostly keep your interactions within the team?"

He shrugs and nods. "Partly. It's also 'cos holding back is hard for my magical abilities, so Con just makes that easier, I guess. Believe me, you wouldn't be celibate for two thousand years, either."

"Not judging." I laugh at his embarrassed face. "Just curious."

He nods and returns to focusing on the dance.

I catch Connie staring at me from across the dancefloor a few times, breaking her visual contact with Dea momentarily to flash appreciation my way; at least, that's what I think that expression is. Hard to tell while being whisked around the dancefloor by the Horseman of War.

He's good at dancing. Like, really good. We waltz, swing, and leap through the people with no care for anyone else around us. Over the past few weeks, Arrie has become a . . . friend, and I can't wait to explore what that means.

Arrie looks down at me as he slows our movements, boring holes through my soul with those ice-blue eyes of his, and I nearly melt. He's so beautiful, it hurts. Now would be a great time to kiss him, but I'm still in my male form. Quickly changing, and internally grumbling about the shitty female outfits for this dance, I wrap both hands around his neck (while standing on my toes to reach him) and meet his gaze.

He sighs and leans down, inches from my face, inches from closing the final bit of distance between us and finally becoming something more than friends. Completing the final piece of my familial puzzle.

The moment his lips connect with mine, I internally exhale a metaphorical breath I didn't realize I've been holding. He really is perfect. His lips brush mine in gentle waves of affection, like the sea caressing the sand amidst a storm, and calm envelops me.

He lifts me into his arms, and I wrap my legs around his waist as my arms entwine around the back of his neck.

I pull away to take a breath. "Arrie, I—

He silences me with eager lips—all pretense of gentleness gone in the blink of an eye— as a small growl vibrates his throat, awakening that pesky lust-starved part of my Vampire brain.

I meet his kiss with equal fervor, biting his lower lip so he'll open and entangle our tongues in equal amounts of passion. He doesn't hold back this time and crushes my lips against his, his fingers digging into my hips where he holds me up.

Pulling away slightly, he puts me on my feet with a smile. I notice the other Horsemen are not still dancing and look a little out of breath—everyone except Connie, of course, who just stands on the side lines watching us with a smile.

How long have we been dancing for?

About an hour.

An hour? But I don't feel exhausted.

Arrie is starting to tire with all the Fae magic draining us. Though, you aren't affected by it.

Okay. Time to drag Arrie off the dancefloor.

We meet up with the others, all smiles and no judgment. "So," I ask, "they extract the energy of those dancing to fuel what, exactly?"

"You felt that, huh?" Nine wraps an arm around my waist while Arrie holds onto my hand. I nod. "It's like a drug. An ancient spell. They use the energy stored later to create an atmospheric drug. Plus, it's a pretty traditional part of Fae culture."

Makes sense. "But what kind of drug?"

He shares a look with Dea, who shrugs and answers for him. "They harvest the energy of those around them to create a drug that stimulates a sexual high."

"Sexual?"

Nine nods. "See the queen dancing in the center?"

I look at her.

"She's fueling the entire thing, having all of the energy flow through her and into the vent below her small dancing circle."

I bristle. They're harvesting magic, sometimes at the cost of human lives, so they can get high? My gums tingle, and I cover my mouth, taking calming breaths.

Male form, Magic. Male form.

In a quick, imaginary poof of fancy magic and an intense bout of nausea, I return to my male form. I shrug to the team. "Best not to be angry in that form right now."

Nine nods, but Dea snickers. At my questioning eyebrow, he says, "I would pay good money to see you rip out the queen's throat."

"Dea," Connie warns and points to her ears. "They're not deaf."

I shrug. "They're not going to care what we think of them." They clearly think enough of themselves. But what Dea said gave me an idea.

In my male form, I'm taller than Nine and the others, except Arrie, who towers over everyone, so I lean down to whisper in Nine's ear. "I think I have a plan."

He throws me a questioning look, but I don't bother explaining. I can't do anything until we're home anyway. And away from prying ears.

Connie pulls me toward her and embraces me; the randomness of the act takes my breath away a little, and I pull away, hoping to take a look at her face. But Dea swings me around in his arms and pulls me into him.

What are they up to?

"You're not going to be able to do that all night," Arrie grumbles.

"Do. What?" I huff and yank myself out of Dea's grip.

"Distract you every time a human dies or faints or something else tragic happens."

I growl at Dea and Connie, who both back off.

"I am more than capable of not getting involved." They both raise their eyebrows. "In this form." I gesture to my male self.

My female form is a little more irrational right now; though, it has nothing to do with my sex and everything to do with my lack of proper feeding.

I want to see, to make sure I really can handle this, but I don't want to look overeager.

Nine saves me from my predicament by grabbing my hand and pulling me onto the dancefloor. "There's one behind me."

I briefly gaze over his shoulder and watch in horror as a human falls to their knees and is scooped up by a Fae guard, one of many dotted around the perimeter. Is she going to be okay? I shift to my female form and hone my hearing in on the body, listening for a heartbeat.

Nothing.

She's dead. The blood quickly running from her cheeks as her arm dangles from her Fae coffin's hold.

Dea and Connie were right, I can't handle this. She died for nothing!

Deep breaths. Male form.

I shift back—reluctantly—and take a deep breath. I can do this. Just stay dancing with Nine.

I'll keep you distracted.

I look back to his face as I rip my gaze away from the Fae guard's retreating back and notice Nine's playful smirk.

What do you have in mind?

Sooooo, you and Arrie?

Ugh. He's going to girl-talk me into distraction.

Arrie and I are . . . more than friends?

I can see that, he says through an audible laugh.

Well, I'm just trying to see where I am with you all, and it's difficult given that I have two sexes, four species, and a huge destiny that sucks donkey balls.

You're doing great. Promise.

He waltzes us around the dancefloor, me taking some lead every now and then, wherever I'm comfortable enough.

I was thinking of distracting you with this.

He sends me a mental image of a very naked Arrie on his back lying on a low-lying bed. The viewpoint is Nine's, obviously, since this is most likely a memory, and I watch as what looks and feels like my hand shoots out and caresses Arrie's cheek.

His stubble grazes my hand, and it sends shivers down my spine.

Nine, stop. I don't want a hard-on in the Fae Court.

Too late.

I groan but watch the scene play out before me as I let Nine guide me around the dancefloor. I probably look ridiculous right about now, but oh well. Nine's mental abilities are rather fun.

Nine's hand moves down Arrie's chiseled frame, smoothing over creamy skin, and wraps around his cock. Its silky smooth skin slips beneath my—Nine's—hand, and I groan as Arrie groans under Nine's tight grip, but Nine just grips harder until Arrie grabs his hand and guides it down in one smooth motion.

Memory Nine gasps, clearly turned on and hard, and one look down his body tells me that is very much the case. "Dude, are you sure?"

Arrie leans his head back and groans. "Yes. Fucking do it, Famine."

Nine nods and bends over, ready to swallow Arrie's cock. He takes a breath and wraps his lips around the tip, and the salty, perfect taste hits my tongue like a firecracker, causing both me and Arrie to groan once more. Nine smiles and lowers his mouth as far as he can, his hand covering the rest.

Arrie's hips buck underneath Nine's moving head, and Nine's hand works in tandem with the rhythm Arrie sets.

I can feel my own cock pulsing with need in time to Nine's hand. "Fuck." This is different than watching, this is like I'm experiencing it with Nine—through Nine.

Nine sucks a little harder as they move a little faster, both moaning in pleasure.

I look up in the memory to watch Arrie's face as his brow furrows and his eyes close. His hand grabs the back of Nine's hair tight, and the sting sends a lightning bolt through me, but that doesn't deter Nine, it just spurs him on.

"Come here," Arrie mumbles, pleasure taking hold of his every syllable. He reaches his hand out beside him. "Let me help."

Nine swivels around and allows Arrie to grab his cock, and I can feel the punishing grip of his massive hand stroking Nine's cock—my cock—and I buckle. Nine pauses a moment when Arrie brushes a finger over the tip, causing him to move his hips gently and me to groan.

As they both continue sucking and using their hands to please each other, me feeling everything, they speed up, the crescendo building, their moans growing louder, and my own dick begs for release.

"Nine . . ." I gasp.

Change.

I do as he asks and change into my female form just as I watch—and feel—Arrie thrust his hips frantically.

"Nine," Arrie groans, "I'm going to . . ."

His sentence ends on a moan as Nine sucks harder.

Arrie's release explodes into Nine's mouth, and Nine follows soon after while swallowing. It hits the back of my throat (Nine's throat), and I swallow his scent, his essence, and the sight and feel pushes me over the edge, my own orgasm ripping through me. I collapse into Nine's waiting arms, burying my head into his chest to at least attempt to muffle my own scream.

I stand back up, the memory having left my mind, and heave air into my lungs. "Why would you . . . ?"

Thought it would be fun. Didn't realize it would be that fun, though.

He escorts me off the dancefloor into Connie's waiting arms.

Oh goddess, Connie probably saw and heard the entire thing. My face burns red as she wraps her arm around my waist and pulls me into a hug.

I don't want to come back up and face Nine and Arrie, but I have to at some point. First, I pull away and change into my male form; I really don't want to be dealing with this horseshit of a party in my female form. I'm too easily agitated. And that mind-blowing orgasm left me a little hungry, too.

"So," Connie says, "have fun?" She grabs me a glass of something pink, fizzing, and tasting of raspberries.

"Uh . . . yeah."

Nine laughs out loud. "Better than Arrie's dance?"

I raise an eyebrow at him. "Not going to let you guys be in competition, especially considering none of the rest of them can do that." I cross my arms over my chest.

"Do what?" Arrie asks. "I'm confused."

Oh my goddess, I don't have the straight face to answer him. Luckily, I don't have to because he goes bright red the moment I open my mouth.

Yeah, I told him for you. You're welcome.

I throw Nine a grateful smile and just avoid Arrie's eyes.

Dea laughs from behind me, and I spin to see him watching our exchange with mild humor in his eyes. "Seems you are enjoying this party more than I anticipated, Angel."

"Well, it's hard not to with this lot." I thumb the team and walk into his arms.

He wraps me tight in his arms and whispers, "I know. I was watching."

I blush but keep my head resting on top of his. "Oh."

"Do not do that. It was . . . seductive watching you. What memory did Nine show you?"

"He didn't say?"

Dea shakes his head, and I turn around to find Arrie shaking his, too.

"I can not say, if you'd prefer."

Arrie just sighs. "He put her in Nine's shoes on that night in Japan a few hundred years into our immortal life."

Dea coughs. "Oh, that." He leans up and whispers into my ear, "Well, that is good to know."

I shiver at the feel of his warm breath on my ear and his hand moving slowly to the rim of my flowing skirt.

"You're all impossible." I move away and stand on my own for a minute, catching my breath. Are they always going to be this . . . persuasive?

Probably. Nine shrugs.

Arrie is still blushing—which is weird in itself—Connie is laughing, Nine just stands there looking innocent, and Dea has his arm around Nine's shoulders.

You ever get those moments when you step outside of your own little bubble of reality and realize how blessed you are to have such amazing people in your life? Well, this is one of those moments. It's like watching them in slow motion, and I'm able to take each and every ounce of the moment in, etching it to memory. It's then, however, that I realize I might totally be in love with them all.

Nine smiles at me and blinks hard, trying to hide the tear that threatens to escape.

The rest of the party passes by in much the same fashion, with me trying to ignore the ugly, evil parts and enjoy some relatively good downtime with the team. They each take turns dancing with me in either form, but we mostly keep me in my male form; not only because I'm a Fae in that form, but because I'm less likely to explode in anger when a human drops dead.

Is it wrong of me to enjoy this? I don't enjoy the things around me, but we rarely get to spend time together, and this entire mission has included lots of bonding.

The queen interrupts my inner ramblings with a halt to the music and an announcement. Seems we're here for more than just a dance. "My people, and the people of other species present tonight, it has been an honor to have you all in my court for another wonderful evening. But now the dancing part of the night must come to an end and the entertainment come to fruition. Everyone is invited to the after party, of course, where we will share our spoils and come together, no matter the species."

She grabs an old-fashioned piece of paper wrapped in a bow off a silver tray dangling in mid-air beside her and reads from it.

"But now we have an announcement to make. We, the Fae Court, have teamed up with the future Vampire Royal Council to create a new world of supernatural order. A new leadership. And a new force where the Supernatural Council will have no jurisdiction."

The crowd cheers, especially the Vampires and Fae, but turning my head to the team, we all stand with our mouths open.

"Well," I start, "that answers your question, Arrie."

The queen continues, of course, and then addresses us directly. "We understand that this goes against the wishes the Four Horsemen of the Apocalypse, who have always worked hard to keep the peace. But your war is over now, Horsemen, and it is time we learned to govern ourselves."

I clench my fist and watch as Connie does the same, but it's Dea who steps forward and gives a nod.

"Please, my fellow people, enjoy the rest of the festivities."

"C'mon," Nine says as he drags us all off to the side, "we need to leave."

"Agreed," Dea says. "The new Vampire Royal Council do not like us and have tried to kill us on multiple occasions. This is not the safest place for us right now."

Arrie grumbles something under his breath. "Hopefully they'll just let us leave and be done with it."

Connie remains silent but eventually speaks up as we enter our room. "I liked the Fae. I can't believe they'd do this."

"Like them?" I gasp. "They're murderers for pleasure. No better than Vampires who kill for blood."

She flinches but doesn't respond.

The Fae Court might look beautiful on the outside, but it's rotten at the core.

23

We pack quickly, all of us throwing things into our bags, even Nine, and run out the door and down the corridor. Everyone is armed, me with the throwing daggers Nine gifted me before we left, Connie with her bow and arrow, Arrie with a massive sword hanging from his belt, Dea with a pair of dual black daggers, and Nine with a series of magiguns.

Dea leads us out of a maze of silent corridors and up into the main entryway. We pass no one, there are no sounds coming from any of the closed or open doors we pass, and even the servants are mysteriously absent. Just as we are about to exit the building, and I'm about to jump for joy at our easy exit, an army of Fae surround us, magiguns and swords drawn.

"They're going to have the same technology as the rogue Vamps, most likely, so . . . yeah. Sorry guys." Nine steps back, not really sure how to help beyond basic fighting. They're likely using Silver Leaf Vain to block his telepathy and mental abilities—just like last time. But hopefully, not like last time, Nine won't nearly die (you know, 'die').

Arrie draws his sword. "Go."

"Nope." I draw a couple of daggers, ready to throw them.

Arrie places a hand on my shoulder. "Go."

Dea, Nine, and Connie join us, weapons at the ready, supporting my decision to stay and get us all out.

Connie drags me back so I have a better vantage point, both of us having long-range weapons, while Arrie directs himself, Nine, and Dea around the room using his strategy ability.

Clangs of swords, bangs of guns, and the sizzle of magic erupts around us. Dea moves faster than I can see but is invisible to the Fae so manages to get a few on their knees before the fight really begins.

"Back up the guys, I'm gonna shoot some of their long-range defenses down," Connie orders me.

"Right!"

She runs off to the sides and shoots arrow after arrow into the back of the head of every archer and long-range spellcaster around the perimeter of the room. Most are in the air, using air magic to keep themselves above the fight.

I change into my female form and wave a hand at Connie, lifting her into the air on a small board of compressed wind I hope she can quickly learn how to use. I designed it like an airborne hover-board, so hopefully it shouldn't be too hard.

Meanwhile, Nine is struggling against four Fae with longswords, so I throw a couple of daggers and hit two in the eyes, reducing his opponent count.

Thanks.

"Argh!" Dea flies into a wall, having been hit by a flying lightning spell.

Shit.

I fly a dagger toward who I think the spellcaster is, but I have to dodge an oncoming fire arrow in the process and miss.

"Killer, help Con!" Arrie shouts as he rushes to Dea's side.

I look up and see Connie hanging from a buttress and give her a lift to the ground.

"Thanks!" she shouts.

I don't answer as three Fae rush at me. I shift form and then again into a bear, roaring them to an abrupt halt.

My feet thunder forward as I swipe. Swipe again.

They all duck and dodge with ease.

This form is too slow. I shift into a panther and sprint at them, taking one head off with a powerful swipe.

I pant, already getting out of breath with the force of all this shifting.

Some spell hits me in the back mid-shift, and I tumble to the ground with a whine. Three thunks follow me to the stone floor, and I look up to find three Fae with familiar arrows in their backs.

Connie.

I jump to my feet and change form again, feeling my energy reserves faltering with every change, and look around to see where I might be most helpful.

Connie is caught between a group of five Fae, all with shorter weapons, and is doing her best to outmaneuver them, but she didn't come with short-range weapons and is relying on just a dagger.

I have to help her.

I grab my last dagger from my thigh and throw it, shifting the air to make it hit the one about to slice her face in two. It pierces his shoulder. He cries out as I force the air around it to push deeper until it flies out the back of his body.

Connie turns to me and smiles, pride smothering her features. But the other Fae seize the moment and grab her arms, yanking her to the floor.

"Connie!"

I sprint forward in a burst of Vampire speed but am not quick enough. They have her in magicuffs before I can rip their heads off.

Four more Fae rush out of the corridor beside us and step in front of Connie. "Stand down, Magic."

"No." I create two small balls of air in each palm, hoping they'll be enough.

The sounds of fighting can still be heard behind me, but all I'm focusing on is the one in front. The sight of Connie on her knees struggling against two Fae pushing all their strength onto her magic-less body makes my blood boil.

"Let her go." I don't yell, I just force the words through gritted teeth, trying my hardest to hold on to my anger and not let it fluster my decisions.

The Fae laugh and pull Connie to her feet.

She grunts, and a trail of blood trickles down the pale skin of her neck and adds to the mess of colors painted onto those hideous clothes.

Every Fae draws their sword at me, but the sound of Nine and Dea screaming behind me has me turning around.

I stop dead. One of the Fae has managed to sneak up on Arrie and put some magicuffs on him, rendering him useless.

Shit.

That's it for me. I flip the lid on my anger, my crazy Vampire lust making me frustrated that I've been holding back, and my hunger for not having fed yet today. It seeps into every movement as I rush to sink my teeth into three Fae, one after the other, freeing Arrie's immediate vicinity.

I yank Dea off the ground, throwing him and Nine toward Arrie so I can better protect them all in one place.

Heads fly off bodies, ears rip from heads, and bones snap and pop as I tear limbs from joints. Blood coats every inch of my skin, but eventually an army of dead bodies lies before me. Despite all the blood I've drunk while ripping throats with my teeth, I'm still hungry.

Seems I need the team's blood specifically.

I turn to make sure everyone is okay but only find Arrie, Dea, and Nine huddling on the floor, looking at me with a mix of fear and amazement on their faces.

I probably look like a monster.

"Where's Connie?"

They shake their heads.

"Why didn't you help?" I roar.

None of them speak, but Nine says, *We're all in cuffs.*

I turn around and look at their hands. They're all indeed in magicuffs.

Ripping them off one by one, I yank them all to their feet and drag them to the front door. "We need to find her."

Arrie nods. "Why did they take her?"

Dea shrugs, but Nine shivers. "You don't think it was him, do you?"

Dea and Arrie go stiff, but I just sigh in frustration. "Someone's going to have to fill me in, but for now, we need to leave."

Dea leads the way, yanking out one of those holographic phone devices Nine invented. "I will get us a jet."

Nine yanks us all down the courtyard and to a back alley. "You can't walk around like that. You'll likely be arrested."

I look down at myself. Most of the blood is on my torso, but even my legs look tortured. I turn to Arrie. "Shirt."

He sighs but throws it my way.

Yanking these stupid clothes off, I strip in the middle of an alleyway in Paris in the middle of the night. None of the guys look my way, but I can see them all hiding pained smirks.

"Now isn't the time," I snap.

"She'll be fine," Arrie says.

"I'm not worried about her life."

He flinches.

But it's true. She'll live. Of course she will. Her seal is back at the house. But will she be okay? She's been through something truly horrific with the Vampires, and I fear that whatever it is has come back to haunt her.

I look down at myself and sigh. I need a shower. It isn't great, but it'll have to do. Arrie's shirt falls to my knees, so at least I'm covered. For now, I'll stay in my male form, but at least I can change without looking like a horror movie.

Dea walks up to us and says, "Let's go." He throws Nine over his shoulder. "We need to run."

He gives me a pointed look, and I shift back into my female form, grab Arrie and cradle-carried him as I run after Dea, who fazes through the streets of Paris faster than I can run. He slows for me, but it isn't much use; I'm exhausted, hungry, and have depleted most of my magic reserves.

"Okay." Dea stops. "Arrie, come here."

Arrie steps up to him as Dea draws one of his daggers and cuts Arrie's wrist open. I watch as the blood drips onto the paving stones beneath us, spilling all of the glorious life onto the dead concrete. No one is around, and my control isn't solid right now, so I yank his wrist and drink. I don't stop, not even when Nine asks if I'm okay, and certainly not when I know I should. His blood is my only focus, my singular drive, as though without it I'm nothing spinning into a void of empty pointlessness.

I'll carry Arrie to the jet, and he can recover there. Right now, Connie needs me. I'm too focused on her to feel the full effects of feeding, but a distant throb pulses low in my body, one I'll have to deal with later, I guess.

Arrie slumps on my shoulder, and I steady him as I pull away. "Okay." I pick him back up and turn to Dea. "Lead on."

Dea fazes at top speed, and this time, I'm able to keep up with him. We speed through street after street, down alleys and past midnight drunken assholes, and on toward a small country estate whose name I don't recognize.

MORT MONTANTE.

"Where are we?" I ask Nine and Dea, who open the gates and walk on through.

Arrie is still passed out in my arms, so I carry him for the time being until we can get him to a bed.

"We, Angel, are at our Paris safe house."

Nine looks over his shoulder at me and Arrie and smiles. "Top level security in this one, so we came here instead of our townhouse."

"I will continue getting us a jet for tomorrow. We should rest."

"Rest?" My hands tighten around Arrie's body as I my blood pumps faster at the ridiculous suggestion. "Connie needs us. We can't rest now!"

"Shhhh," Nine says. "I know. But we can't help if we're tired and drained." He looks to Arrie. "And he needs to rest for a couple hours."

I flush. That was my fault. If I didn't need their blood in particular, this wouldn't have been a problem. "Why is that?"

"Why is what?"

So he doesn't always pay attention to my thoughts.

"I drown it out when you're angry or upset."

I wince but quickly get back to the question at hand. "Why do I specifically need blood from you four?"

"Probably due to the level of power you get from it. The blood is fueling a Horseman, after all. Vampires gain power from blood, not just sustenance. They cannot use their speed or strength if they have not fed."

Dea opens the grand double doors, and we all enter into the main entrance foyer.

"Other people's blood has no effect on you other than basic sustenance because it doesn't hold enough power."

I huff. Talk about a pile of Vampire shit. What happens if I need blood and they aren't around?

Nine goes to say something, but I cut him off. "Not now." He nods. "Just show me where I can sleep."

Dea smiles at Arrie's limp form in my arms. "We can sleep in the larger bedroom upstairs."

"We?" I can't stop the gentle smile that curls my lips. "Like, all of us?" I just assumed that would stop the moment our bubble was popped.

"If that is what you want, Angel."

"It is."

The bedroom is two floors up, and the stairs are stone concrete like the Fae Court—and huge. I'm not having problems carrying Arrie other than the fact that he's huge and bulky to hold, but if I were human, these steps would be a pain.

"That's the point," Nine says. "Not many people could reach us, other than Vampires."

"And they are unlikely to attack us here in Paris and risk pissing off the Fae." He takes a deep breath. "Well, usually."

Right. Their alliance. Vampires and the Fae, both working toward a world they can be themselves in without SC restrictions. That places the SC as their main enemy. Right?

"We need to talk to the SC." I turn to Dea. "How do we do that?"

He grumbles. "I will arrange a meeting if I can. But they are not fond of all meeting in the same place."

"Then tell them war is on their doorstep." I yank Arrie and me up the last step. "That should get them moving their asses."

Dea leads us through a huge door and into a room with a bed bigger than I've ever seen. Seriously, it could fit five Arries. Which, I guess, is the point.

"Whose room is this?"

Nine shrugs. "No one's. Was just here for guests."

With a bed that huge?

Vampires and Fae tend to live in groups rather than monogamous pairs.

Oh. Well, I guess that makes sense.

I don't bother with pleasantries, I just dump Arrie onto the bed and throw the covers over him, then take off my bra underneath Arrie's shirt I'm still in and get in next to him. Anything else can wait until morning.

"Well?" I ask Nine and Dea, who are looking at me in amusement.

Dea strips, and I can't help but stare, but my usual fun reaction is marred by the possibility of where Connie will be sleeping tonight. He grabs some spare clothes out of the bags he was carrying and throws on a pair of sweatpants and comes to bed.

Nine does the same, sleeping on Dea's other side.

Curling into Arrie, sleep takes hold quicker than I realize it could, but before I drift into unconsciousness, I hear Dea and Nine kiss each other goodnight and smile. Just a little.

They're perfect for each other. I'm glad I could bring them together.

Some big, muscly, grumbling thing awakes me hours later, and I open my eyes to find Arrie chatting to the guys.

"She's going to be fine, Arrie," Nine says. "Con's strong."

"They've probably taken her to that piece of Vampire scum. I should have killed him decades ago."

"You cannot murder everyone that wrongs one of us." Dea sighs. "We are better than that."

I move my head to speak. "Not all of us care to be better."

Arrie squeezes my shoulder and lets me go. "You're awake?"

"Yup."

I shoot up and hop out of bed. Or, I tried to, but Arrie grabs my thighs just as I'm climbing over him. "You're still tired, Killer."

"Hmmm, tired. What a revelation. Wonder what bad things Connie is feeling right about now?" I shoot him a death-by-Magic stare and watch him flinch.

He lets go of me, and I climb out of bed. "Clothes," I mumble to myself.

"In the bags over there." Nine points to the pile of bags in the corner.

I mumble some semblance of a thank you and go in search of clothes.

"You know," I hear Arrie say, "I could get used to seeing you in my shirt."

I'd totally forgotten I was wearing it. Looking down, I also remember it's all I'm wearing. Heat creeps up my face as I bend over to grab more clothes, hoping I'll find something at least clean, and equally hoping my ass will stay covered given the lack of panties.

I turn back around and am about to ask where the bathroom is before I bump right into Dea. "You have no need to be embarrassed about anything with us, Angel." He grabs my cheek and brushes the tear threatening to break free. "It is rather alluring watching you walk around a bedroom in nothing but Arrie's t-shirt." He looks me up and down, checking me out, and I fight hard not to blush.

Arrie and Nine join him, ganging up on me on either side, a wall to my back, so that I'm now trapped between three very hot guys, and my mind is doing all kinds of things to my body.

Arrie grabs the collar of the shirt and yanks me toward him with a growl. Pressing up against his body, I can feel just how good he thinks I look before he leans down and captures my mouth in a heated kiss that has me moaning the moment he parts my lips with a forceful lap of his tongue.

I pull back to take a breath, but Arrie just stands there with a smile on his face. "Good morning."

"Oh, right. Good morning." I turn and see the other two watching us. "Good morning."

Dea smiles, Nine smirks, and I nearly lose my virginal shit and pull them all back into bed. But it wouldn't be right, not without Connie home safe and with us.

"I want to rescue Connie," I whisper.

Dea pulls a hand through my messy bed hair and whispers, "I know. And we will."

I nod. "Then I want to shower." I shoot raised eyebrows at Nine, who points to a door on the left I didn't notice before. "Thank you."

I shower, brush my teeth with one of the numerous unopened brushes on the side, and get dressed. Black sweatpants and a white t-shirt: nothing fancy, just simple clothes I can move in. Then I switch forms and do it all again in my male form. What to wear, though? Guess the same. Right? Sweatpants and a plain t-shirt.

Upon stepping out of the bathroom, hands in the middle of tying my hair back, all three guys stare at me as though I pissed in their morning coffee.

"What?" I mumble beyond the hair elastic hanging from my teeth.

"The clothes . . . They're not very you, Sweetie."

I shrug. "T-shirt's from my guy wardrobe, and the sweatpants are something I would usually wear to bed." The plain white t-shirt in question hangs from my frame, so I tie it into a knot at the front, having it clinched at the waist and therefore out of the way. "Happier?"

Dea nods. "Much."

I roll my eyes. "You don't see me critiquing your choice of clothing."

"And what would be wrong with what I am wearing, Angel?"

I look him up and down—past his fitted white-and-black jacket, hover on his studded cross earrings and then again on his snake bites, and fly past those ripped skinny jeans that make his ass look fantastic—and mumble, "Absolutely fucking nothing."

He looks smug and goes back to grabbing a few things from his bag before entering the bathroom.

The other two are in equal states of undress, so I lay on the bed and watch as Nine pulls a shirt over his head and Arrie wiggles into sweatpants (still shirtless, and still looking like a god).

"Having a good time there, Killer?" He winks at me, and I melt, my mouth opening and closing multiple times before it gets itself under control.

"Yes." I cough to clear my throat. "You're all looking gorgeous. Carry on." I gesture for him to continue with a smirk of my own, and he just laughs as he yanks a t-shirt over his head. Similar to me, he's going for comfortable and practical. Probably because, like me, his magic is active, and we'll likely have to fight and move in whatever we wear today.

"So," I ask the moment Dea steps out of the bathroom with his hair all brushed and gelled into place, "where is Connie, d'you reckon?"

Dea shares an ominous look with Arrie, and I sigh.

"I get it." They all look at me. "I don't need the details, but I'm not going in blind just to protect her secrets. She wouldn't want that. So tell me who you think has her, who we're likely up against, and where she probably is."

Nine nods. "You're right." He sits down next to me on the bed and pulls me into a hug. "Given that they took only her, and they're working with Vampires, we're pretty sure The Diamond has her. He's a Vampire who controls all the black-market blood supplies, and recently, we also reckon he's the reason for the increase in black-market Fae magic supplies."

I wince. "The increase in pixie dust. You reckon that's 'cos of him?"

He nods. "Last we heard, his base is in a remote part of the Andes Mountains. Not sure where, though."

Dea sits on my other side and places a hand on my shoulder.

"Well, is there any country the mountains go through that has a special connection to Vampire blood or pixie dust?" They all shake their head. "Okay, so we get a plane and fly over. My Vampire vision should be able to see down to the ground if I try hard enough, assuming there's no clouds in my way or some shit."

Dea smiles. "Good plan."

"That jet?"

He nods. "Got one while you were in the shower, Angel. Coming to get us in one hour."

"From here?"

He smiles. "We have a landing strip through the forest behind us. And a helipad in the garden." He shrugs.

Of course they do. "Do all of your houses have insane levels of shit?"

He smiles. "Just the ones Nine's in charge of."

I look at everyone confused for a moment, but they all just laugh.

Nine answers. "There's a lot of safe houses. So we divide them between us. So long as I'm having a good day, I can make money and resources increase just by being near them." He laughs at my mouth hanging open. "Famine, remember?"

"Riiiight." I shake my head. "But if you're having a bad day?"

Dea laughs. "Then we let him nowhere near our finances."

Arrie laughs alongside him, and I can't fight the giggle that escapes my mouth at the sight and sound of Arrie laughing. It really is melodious and surprising. I don't think I'll ever get tired of making and hearing him laugh.

Nine coughs, and I realize I've been staring at Arrie like a freak while the room filled with silence. "Errrr, sorry." I shake my head.

"What were you thinking, Killer?"

"It was nothing sexual. Not this time, at least." They all laugh. "I really like it when you laugh."

I just said that out loud, didn't I? Ohhhh, no. No. Nope. I did not just tell the Horseman of War that I like his laugh. Gah! What is wrong with me?!

"Stop freaking out." Nine snaps me out of my thoughts and brings me back to the present. "You're fine."

I look at him with raised eyebrows.

"Promise."

Arrie looks at me and blushes. "It's . . . err . . . fine." He shrugs. "Just not used to it."

I place my hands around his waist. "Well, get used to it. Because you are adorable."

He laughs and I melt—again. What are these guys doing to me?

"Only someone as crazy as you would find the Horseman of War adorable, Killer."

I shrug. "Then everyone else is blind."

"Come." Dea walks to the door with a smile on his face. "It will take twenty minutes to get to the landing strip, and I want something to eat first."

"Ugh, nope. Not eating if we're flying. Not unless you want me to blow chunks all over you."

Nine laughs. "Yeah, maybe not for you."

Arrie wraps an arm around my shoulders. "We'll get you something when we land."

I miss his cooking. Nothing is as good as Arrie's food. Nothing.

"Don't you have one of your restaurants in Argentina, Arrie?" Nine asks. "We should land there and get her something to eat."

"Restaurants?" I look to Arrie.

He grumbles and shoots Nine a 'shut the fuck up' look before turning to me. "Yeah." He scratches the back of his head. "Opened an entire line of them back in the 1980s, and they've just kinda stuck around."

"Which chain? What's the name? What do they serve? Tell me everything!"

Arrie chuckles and grabs my hand. "Kappi Matur. It's Icelandic for Warrior Food." When I look at him with a questioning gaze, he explains, "Icelandic is the closest thing we have to the Old Norse language—my native tongue."

"Why not just stick to using Old Norse?"

He shrugs. "Felt more appropriate if someone other than us four knew what it meant."

We sit down to breakfast, where I eat nothing, and leave via the grand backdoor into the overgrown gardens. "So, Nine, isn't this your job?" I gesture to the uncared-for garden around us. It's a couple of acres, and honestly, a costly job for very little outcome, but teasing him makes me smile. He just looks at me with a mimicking death stare, and I laugh. "We'll work on that death stare when we get home."

Dea stops dead, and I walk right into the back of him. "Hey! Watch it."

"You called it home?" he asks.

"Err, what?"

"*Sheruta*. You just called it home."

Arrie and Nine are smiling at us, but eventually, Dea turns around, and Arrie lets go of my hand so he can scoop me up into a massive hug.

"Is it really home to you?" he asks as he squeezes me tight—not really causing me any pain, but bless, he tries.

I nod. "Of course. All of you are there." I sigh as I take in his lavender scent, nestling my nose into the crook of his neck. "Besides, who the heck would give up that house?"

Nine laughs. "She is magnificent."

"She?"

He shrugs. "Just feels . . . right."

Dea puts me back on my feet and continues walking, him on my right, Arrie on my left, both holding my hand as we walk.

Seems I didn't have to fight very hard for my little harem fantasy after all.

Don't speak too soon. We haven't talked about it yet.

I look at him. You don't want to?

I didn't say that. I'm just saying it's not all tied off with a pretty ribbon until we all chat.

He's right. He's always fucking right. I swear, being surrounded by two-thousand-year-old assholes twenty-four seven gets old.

I heard that.

I shake my head at him. "Nope. You didn't."

Connie, I tell myself. Stop flirting and save Connie. Then you can flirt with them all in sexy bikinis the next hot season in *Sheruta*.

"So, where's this airstrip?"

"Center of the forest," Nine answers. "It's about two miles that way." He points in front of us, right toward the dense tree and foliage in the distance.

Gah, I could just sprint there in, like, ten seconds, but I have to be social and walk with these goons. I bet Dea has the same problem.

We walk through the forest, ducking under branches and hopping over roots, and I have to admit, it's a beautiful place. The light filters through the trees at just the right angle this time of morning, and it lights the fall leaves up like a cinnamon-roasted latte; divine, tasty, and made of the only real goddess we should worship. Coffee.

Yup, nature is like coffee. Kind of smells similar, too, when you take in all the scents through a Vampire's nose. Strong, slightly bitter, smooth, but mostly just relaxing.

I hear Nine chuckle at nothing beside Dea and can only assume he is listening to my nature-coffee comparison.

"Your mind is the best place to be, I swear." He grabs Dea's hand and walks a little faster. "C'mon, we can't be late."

Another plane, another flight, another piece-of-shit few hours in the air. I consider seeing if I can fly myself that far, but considering the vast expanse of ocean beneath us for most of the trip, I decide not to. You know, wouldn't want to drown. That would be an awful afternoon if I couldn't die.

The pilot is an odd man, someone who looks as though they shouldn't be flying an airplane, let alone carrying out a rescue mission. "So," he says, "where we off to, Death?"

"He knows who we are?"

"Not until recently," Nine adds.

"Everyone knows who you all are, now. Though, no one really knows you, darlin'." He looks to me with a smile plastered onto his rough, bearded face. "No one really understands you."

I roll my eyes. "Join the club."

The airplane in question is a small, sleek-looking black jet with room for ten passengers at full capacity. It's posh but practical, with white leather seats in a fancy wooden interior, magitech screens glowing all over the place, and every seat has a cup holder.

"Can I get coffee?"

Dea rolls his eyes. "How addicted to coffee are you, Angel?"

"Ah yes, as opposed to my less murderous addictions, I guess coffee really is the devil." I point a glare at him, and he shrinks into his seat.

"There's a coffee machine over there." Nine points to a tea and coffee station just in front of the front two seats. "It's basic but decent."

I hop to my feet to grab a cup before take-off.

I read two small books between Paris and Argentina; oh, and I finish that gruesome mystery. Her lover kills him! What a shocker. I internally roll my eyes and read the last few lines of my newest romance.

"Sweetie, we're about to land."

I just nod.

Dea laughs at me. "Does she ever not read on a flight?"

"She gets travel sick in both forms, so it distracts her."

Dea smiles at me, which I only just about catch above the screen, but my Vampire eyes seem to have the ability to zoom in on my peripheral vision and bring it into focus without losing sight of my normal circumference of sight.

That could be useful.

"I can zoom in on my peripheral vision without losing my central line of sight," I shout to Nine.

"Really? That's quite cool."

"Ohmigod, I could totally pull off one of those super sexy ninja moves where the person throwing the dagger doesn't realize the cool, hot-as-fuck superwoman character can actually see with her back turned, and then bam! She catches the knife mid-air." I internally high-five myself but remember why we're on a private jet in the first place.

Connie.

Not a time to be smiling.

The guys all smile at my stupid antics—like usual—and even Arrie cracks a smile in his usual stone-wall façade.

The plane starts its descent just after we all buckle ourselves back in, and I try hard not to throw up on these lovely cream-white leather seats while my stomach tries to persuade me otherwise.

I just about make it as the wheels touch the ground, but I have to run out of the plane (whose door mechanism is like a thief's worst nightmare, by the way—totally unnecessary) to throw up nothing but gross yellowish-green bile that has me wishing I'd eaten breakfast to at least have something to throw up.

I am seriously sick of being sick.

"Here." Nine hands me a gingersnap. "Started packing them when I realized this was going to be a continuous issue."

"Thanks," I say as I take slow nibbles.

"That's really some travel sickness, Killer."

I death-glare him. I wish he would pick me up and carry me to wherever the hell we are going because just walking is making my tummy tumble.

He sighs and wraps an arm around my waist. "If you want help, just ask."

"Traitor," I whisper to Nine.

He shrugs, not really caring.

"Would you like me to carry you?" Arrie asks.

I look to the ground, embarrassment flushing my features, and nod. "Please."

Goddess, I sound so pathetic, but seriously, travel sickness sucks eggs. Ugh, eggs. That thought alone nearly has me vomiting again, but I manage to hold back as Arrie sweeps me into his arms, bridal style.

"Anti-sickness charm. Add that to my list."

Nine smiles. "Added." He taps his head and smiles brightly at the sight of me in Arrie's arms, probably finding us adorable.

It's kinda hot, too.

Nine! Now is not the time to wake up the crazy Vampire side.

Right. Sorry.

I promptly ignore all the crazy, sexy thoughts Nine's words elicit in my mind, which in turn has me noticing just how close to Arrie's jugular my mouth is, and instead focus on the current disaster.

Connie. Need to find Connie.

25

"So, where are we going?"

Dea turns around to us and smiles. "To dinner. Well"—he looks at his watch—"lunch-dinner."

"Good." I am kinda hungry. "But I want to take off again to find Connie asap."

Arrie grumbles, "So do we."

I flinch. Right. They care, too. I run a calming hand along Arrie's shoulder and whisper, "We'll get her back. And we can kill that son of a bitch together."

Arrie grins from ear to ear, a menacing look that makes me shake a little in his arms. He laughs at my reaction and whispers, "Don't worry, I won't touch you." He pauses and looks down at me with a wink. "Unless you ask nicely."

I can once again feel my cheeks heating. Damn it. Are these guys trying to make me lose my immortal virginity in the most public of places? Because I really want them all right about now.

Maybe back on the plane would be a good place to—

"We're here," Nine announces over the top of my internal chatter. Maybe a little too loudly, because Dea and Arrie look at him like he's crazy.

"Thank you." I climb out of Arrie's arms.

Here is a high-class restaurant with a red-and-black interior that speaks volumes about the type of people who usually eat here: rich people. People who could afford to eat at a place with windows for walls, who never have to worry about when their next meal will be or if they'll continue to have a roof over their heads tomorrow; people who usually look down on the rest of the world with their immortal stupidity.

Arrie coughs loudly behind me. "Shall we?"

That is when I realize this is Arrie's restaurant. Shit. So glad he isn't the one who can read my mind. That would have been aaaawkward.

Nine ushers us inside, and Dea turns visible so he can eat in public.

"Don't worry about that, dude," Arrie says in Dea's direction. "I called ahead. We're eating in one of the empty VIP rooms."

Dea exhales loud enough for us to all be thankful he isn't too uncomfortable and turns back to his usual self.

When we reach the front desk, where we're met by a handsome waiter whose name I can barely pronounce with swept-back hair and tattoos on both arms, I take a second glance around and feel even guiltier. It seems to be full of regular people; not rich but not poor, either. So just a regular restaurant, then, but with a very five-star feel.

Arrie likes to have his recipes actually eaten.

I roll my eyes to hide the embarrassed flush that has settled on my face red enough to let everyone around us know how flustered I am behind the social mask.

The restaurant itself has black circular tables, encouraging families to talk, eat, and chat with everyone, with a few two-person circular tables lining the large window wall on the right by the entrance. The plates fly around the room on a type of invisible air conveyor system, latticing the entire roof of the room in various plates, glasses, and cutlery. Fae air magic.

Waiters and waitresses sit people to tables, take orders, and then send them to the kitchen via their plasmascreens; all the while, you can see the cooks making the food in the far corner, all dancing along to the music playing over the soundstrip.

It's all very . . . fancy.

"Killer?" Arrie walks up next to me and stares at me with a questioning gaze.

"Sorry, huh?"

He smiles. "I said are you coming?"

"Oh, yeah."

He gestures to a deep-red velvet curtain in the far back, and we both step beyond into a corridor of other heavy curtains, some closed, some held back by thick black ties, and Arrie leads us into a closed one at the end. A massive circular table is beyond, surrounded by high-end décor and a few waiters waiting for us to get settled. Dea and Nine sit at one end, both having made room for us either side of them.

Nine pats the spot next to him while looking at me. *Sit next to me?*

I scoot across the long seat bed circling the table until I reach the place his hand rested. He places a plasmascreen in my hands, one with the menu on, and I scroll through until I pick three courses: sushi for starters, pasta al pomodoro for mains, and chocolate mountain lava cake for dessert (because who the fuck wouldn't order that from the menu?).

"So," Dea says, "what is the plan from here?" He looks to me, and I gulp.

None of my damned plans ever work, but here's to one last try. "We're eating, then we're getting back on that jet and finding Connie. We're going to break in, break her out, and then go the fuck home."

Arrie smiles his approval.

"How do you plan to break in, Sweetie?"

"I'm gonna wing it." I wink. "I could plan all day long for that, but I don't even know what a base in the Andes Mountains could possibly look like, so we might as well just be cautious and play it by ear. Carefully." I look to Arrie as I say that last word, knowing he'll lose his shit the moment he sees Connie in whatever awful condition she is likely in right now.

He raises his hands in surrender. "All right. All right."

"I mean it. I'm not losing any of the rest of you just because you've decided to be an idiot. I'm also not saving anyone else if they get caught because of their own stupid choices." I look to everyone. "Am I clear?"

They all nod, and I get immense satisfaction from being the one whose orders are being unquestioned. Mwuhahaha. We could make a leader out of me yet.

You've already gotten us wrapped around your finger, Sweetie.

With that, we finish our food—which is all fucking delicious—and head back to the jet.

"So," I start as I buckle myself in, "we're flying over the Andes to see if I can spot anything that looks suspicious?"

Dea nods. "You should be able to zoom in with Vampire sight."

While the take-off procedures are ongoing, I practice using my Vampire sight. I've used it a few times, but nothing on this scale. The coffee station comes in and out of focus as I concentrate, and if I try hard enough, I can zoom in on the buildings and people milling around outside the plane. But looking a few hundred feet out of the plane and down a mountainside? That is a tall order. I don't know if I can do this.

Arrie sits beside me, probably sensing my torrid emotions from the other side of the plane, and brings my hand to his lips, placing a delicate, soft kiss to my knuckles; it's so soft, in fact, that it takes me off guard, and I find myself melting into the warmth of his lips and the cool ice of his blue eyes. "You've got this, Killer."

His rugged voice meets my ears, and I snap out of the reverie.

I nod, a little shaky but determined. "I know."

He remains beside me, his hand in mine, the entire flight. Once in the air, however, we all unbuckle and stand by the big window on the right; I'm in front, using my enhanced sight to try to see anything below us.

It takes about half an hour to hit the mountain range, and once we do, I get myself comfortable on the floor as the guys supply me with various cups of coffee—Arrie even spikes his with a bit of blood.

We fly in a zigzag fashion around the mountain range from south to north, and I spend hour after hour looking for something—anything—that will lead us to Connie. I can zoom all the way down to the ground if I have a good supply of blood on hand (which Arrie is happy to supply), and I find myself looking at what is probably a very beautiful landscape, with all kinds of animals roaming, natural wonders beaming, and nature at its best, but I can't get the image of Connie being tortured out of my head so don't really take much pleasure in the task at hand.

"I can't spot anything!" I slam my hand down on the jet's red carpeted floor. "There must be something . . ." My voice breaks at the edges. I don't want to leave her there a moment longer than necessary.

Someone rubs a hand on my shoulder while someone else, probably Nine, places a hand on my knee. "We will find her, Angel."

Taking a deep breath, I get back to searching what seems to be an endless supply of mountains. Rock . . . more rock. And even more rocks. It's all I can see for miles. By the time another hour has sped by, we're a quarter way through the mountain range and are just about to enter the Bolivia-Chile air space.

"Nothing in Argentina, and so far, nothing in Chile."

"Noted," Nine says and probably notes it down. "Bolivia, Peru, Ecuador, Colombia, and Venezuela left to go."

I sigh. "Does someone have some sugar or something?" I roll my eyes. I am going to need as much sugary goodness as possible to get through this. My eyes are itchy and sore, and I can feel fatigue starting to set in. Zooming in this far with my enhanced sight is as straining as using my Witch powers, it would seem, and it's beginning to make me shake and feel queasy (though there is no telling if that is the crazy movements of this jet).

A donut appears in my lap. "Thanks," I mumble around a mouthful of sugary sweet goodness that has me moaning. It's like I can feel the food fueling my magic reserves.

"Here," Arrie grumbles. He bites his wrist the moment I finish my donut and offers it under my nose.

I shake my head. He goes to complain, but I hold up a hand. "Not a stubbornness thing. I need you conscious. I know it's been you feeding me this entire time." I meet his eyes for a brief second before peeling them away and readjusting my focus to the mountains below. "If I need blood, it'll be from the others."

He groans and wipes a hand down his face, but he sits beside me in resolute comfort nonetheless.

Nine's bleeding wrist is the next underneath my nose, and I briefly take a moment to wonder. I've never had Nine's blood before. Dea's tastes just like he smells: lavender and smoke. Arrie's taste just like he smells: forest and fresh laundry. Nine doesn't really have a scent, not like the others, but that doesn't mean his blood won't have a particular taste.

The plane slows down to a crawl as I take a break and focus on Nine's bleeding wrist. Blood trickles down the side of his arm, and his fingers twitch on his other hand, as though he wants to pull his own arm away.

I look to him. Are you sure?

I was going to force your head forward not bring my arm away. Yes.

Okay.

I allow my fangs to descend and run my tongue along the trickling line of blood before sinking them in.

Nine gasps and moans beneath me, his hips thrusting upward desperately while Arrie and Dea aren't stupid enough to come close to a feeding Vampire who is also tired and sex deprived. Smart men.

"Damn," Nine says on another gasp.

I look up with a smile—which probably looks menacing and insane—but he just looks at me with wide eyes that briefly shine with a promising amber glow for a moment before he blinks, and they turn back to their normal brown color.

It turns his magic on.

Yes. It's . . . fuck. I can't even explain it.

I know.

No wonder you're going insane. This is how you feel every time you feed?

I think so. Never been on the receiving end.

I take another mouthful, then detach from Nine's wrist and return to the window with a swipe of my mouth on my jacket sleeve.

Dea places a comforting hand on Nine's shoulder while Arrie sits back down beside me, but not before throwing a jerked smile Nine's way.

Men.

"You can all chat about sex later. Connie." I don't even need to attach a sentence to the end of that—they know what I mean.

Arrie rests an arm around my shoulders and pulls me into him. "You're doing great," he whispers into my ear. "But it's fun to see Nine come undone." He winks.

That has my head reeling with sexy possibilities, but I shake them clear and focus back on the task at hand. Connie. Mountains. Enhanced vision.

I spend hours kneeling by that window, gazing out at nothing but mountains and regretting even bothering to help the guys instead of Connie. I mean, they were three, she was alone. What kind of stupid idiot makes that decision? Every minute that ticks by has my emotions reeling further and further out of control. Pretty sure my fangs haven't retracted at all in the last half hour.

She could be screaming out in agony right now, and I'm not there to help. I'm just sitting here doing nothing! Every second of conversation without her frustratingly sexy sass is agony, every lack of a sex-related response to every stupid scenario we find ourselves in is like a breath of ice, and every interaction with the guys I have without her reminds me of how important just her existing in my life is. She completes us. She might not be a guy, and maybe that makes everything between us stranger than what most other women would be comfortable with, but without her, this relationship between us all will never be the same.

I have to find her.

Jumping to my feet, I grab each guy by the arm and drag them to me. I grab my empty coffee cup from the floor and hold it out to them. "Blood please. Mixed, from all of you."

Nine looks at me with a quizzical expression, but I just shrug. "Trying out a theory and seriously hoping it works."

He nods and bleeds first, filling the cup a third of the way. Dea goes next. And then Arrie. Soon, the cup is full of all three of my . . . team's blood, and the smell is a heady mixture that almost scents like home.

I grab the cup from Arrie and sniff with caution. My lips edge over the rim of the cup, and as the first drop hits my tongue, my fangs extend and I down the entire thing in a few gulps. It's . . . intense. Usually, I can feel the blood filling an internal need, but this is like the blood is filling almost every need.

Complete. That's how I feel. Well, almost. Something is missing . . . Connie. Her blood would complete this. Wonder what that would be like? Eh, now's not the time to wonder.

I sit back down by the long window and zoom in. "Wow." I can see every detail of every crevice, crack, and inch of the mountain range beneath us. "It's like I have telescopic vision."

Nine chuckles behind me. "Well, you just got a power-up from three of the most powerful supes on the planet. What did you expect?"

Arrie grumbles, "Do not use your powers right now in this plane."

I chuckle. "I don't like flying, either. Remember?"

Turning back to the task at hand, I have no problem seeing, and it doesn't seem to upset my eyes or magic supply. This is awesome.

"We're heading into Ecuadorian airspace," Nine kindly informs me.

"Noted." I keep my eyes peeled, hoping this might be the place.

A few minutes later, something in the air around us shimmers, like someone has turned on a switch in the energy surrounding the plane.

"What's that?"

"Huh?" Nine asks.

"The air . . . it shimmered." I take a deep breath and zoom my vision in, but nothing. It doesn't look any different than the other countries' section of the mountain range. "It's a Fae spell," I realize. "Like the one on the Rogue Vampire Council building."

"Where?"

I look around us, peering through as many windows as possible, and change into my male form. I can feel the magical pressure of the spell. "Everywhere."

Nine looks to Dea. "They can't do a spell that powerful without some serious magical supply."

"Let's worry about that later," I offer. "I need to get out of this plane. Now."

I run into the captain's cabin and shout, "Can I jump out at this height?"

He nods. "Parachutes are in the back cabin."

"Thanks!" I run back out of there.

Nine follows me. "What are you doing?"

"Disabling the spell."

"You don't know how to do that!"

I reach the back cabin and look through boxes and shelves before I find the parachutes. "I can feel the magic, the intricacies of the spellwork at hand. I should be able to pull at a crucial point of the spell and watch it all crumble."

"That's just theoretical!"

I turn around to face him. "Theories are what my life is currently based on, Nine. I have to do something."

He sighs and grabs the parachute next to me. "Then I'm coming with."

"We're all going!" I shout loud enough for Dea and Arrie to hear. "Worst comes to the worst, I'll change form and fly us all to the ground. We'll be fine."

The other guys run into the cabin and grab a parachute each as Nine nods at me.

"You're going to hate this, Killer." Arrie smirks at me.

He doesn't need to tell me that. Just the thought of hurtling to the ground at goddess knows what speed after jumping out of a plane has my stomach in knots.

I can do this.

And I will do it without puking everywhere.

C'mon, Horseman of Magic, time to woman up . . . or man up . . . or WoMan up. Yup, going with that. You can do this, I keep chanting to myself.

"Okay," Nine says, "the back of this plane opens and we're gonna jump out. You got that?"

I nod.

"I will signal when we're low enough to pull the parachutes. They're air assisted, so we should be able to guide them where we want to go."

"Okay." I try my best to ignore my stomach's somersaults and all the dangers I am about to put us all in.

Don't worry, if you do this and we all get out 'alive,' I'll make sure to reward you handsomely.

Reward me? I look up and see him winking at me. Oh, that kind of reward. I just smile like an idiot and blush, fully aware the other guys are watching me blush at nothing, probably figuring it's something Nine said.

"Okay," Dea says, "open the hatch, Fawn!"

A whirring sound fills the air around us, and I can feel some kind of spell opening the back hatch of the plane wide enough for us to jump out.

Fuck me, this is insane.

I am sooooo going to die today.

Arrie runs first, headlong into the air, and jumps as far away from the plane as possible. Dea goes second, following the same strategy as Arrie. Which leaves me and Nine, and there is no way I am jumping last.

Go. Nine pushes me forward, and I run full-sprint into mid-air with a scream, and whomph . . . I jump out of a fucking plane.

The air rushes past my ears at such speed, I can't hear anything around me—not even the guys signaling me to form a circle with them. But their hand gestures are enough for me to get the message, and soon I am holding hands with Arrie and Dea, who still have one hand left spare each—for Nine, I presume.

Yup.

Nine hurtles in front of us and grabs Dea and Arrie's hands, completing our little circle.

Time to disable that spell.

Now? In the air!?

Before we land into unknown chaos would be lovely, Sweetie.

Oh, right. Don't want to land into trouble we can't see. That wouldn't be a good plan. Time to learn on the job.

Again.

I let go of the guys' hands, and they shimmy me into the center of the circle—where I can work while they protect me from any unknown threats. Something tells me I'll need some concentration for this.

Closing my eyes, I reach out to the spell with my Fae magic, sensing its form, shape, and how it was created. It seems to be coming from a powerful energy source that is constantly fueling it—day and night—which makes me think it might be an object. No person can sustain a spell this complex over this large an area indefinitely.

I can see the spellwork in my mind as I trace my magic over it: the patterns, words, and ingredients that make up the building blocks of the magic at work. Hopefully, if I can find a way of removing some of those blocks, it'll all come crashing down.

I can't get rid of any incantations because that would require knowledge of reverse cantations, and I don't know any yet, so it'll have to be based on either the ingredients used or the patterns created. Ingredients will take too long, and I'd need to pray and hope we find the right ones upon landing; and besides, that wouldn't fix this damn issue before we land.

Patterns then.

It's intricate, like the caster (or casters) weaved together a giant circle surrounding the entire Ecuadorian Andes mountain range. Well, it's more of an oval. Kind of. It stretches the length of the entire country from north to south along the mountain range and is some of the most complex spells I have ever seen before.

This is going to suck.

Parachutes!

I pull the lever without really thinking, my mind still trying to find a way to change the spellwork to our advantage. Maybe there is a way I can write us into the spell, so we can see beyond the glamour designed to keep us out. Speaking of which, how did they even manage that? That would take something more powerful than the Four (Five) Horsemen.

Not the time. Spellwork. Focus, Magic.

There's a section of the spell, repeated at each compass point, designed to keep us out —specifically—so we could fly through the air space and never notice. Seems they underestimated my ability to sense Fae magic.

I mean, hello, Horseman of Magic . . . Does that mean nothing to some people?

Okay, Nine, I'm going to redesign the spell in four places, and each one is going to take me around ten minutes. How long till we hit the ground?

He flinches. *About ten minutes with these parachutes. They're designed to make us descend a little faster.*

I sigh. Well, disabling that air spell would make good practice, I guess. I reach out with my magic, testing my own chute's spell first. It seems to be a simple Fae spell to displace the air around us and only uses a small circle pattern. I fling my own magical energy at it and rub some of the pattern away, rewiring it to a halt.

My parachute slows down, and I descend with the wind rather than with magic. Perfect.

I quickly do the guys' and ask for a new time analysis.

Don't really know. Maybe thirty minutes.

Still not perfect, but at least it buys us some time. I'll have to do the last one on the ground.

Using my hands as guides, I start on the nearest compass point—south—and get to work. I throw my magic left, right, and center, disabling pattern points, rubbing out sections of runes, and generally trying to rewrite it all to fit us into the spell. Once I am satisfied, I move on to the next one. Each takes about eight minutes—which I am pretty proud of—and after each one, I whoop and yell as I manage to beat my previous record. The more I practice, the easier it gets.

I have just finished the northern part of the pattern when I look down and realize I am a few feet off the ground. Damn. So much for getting it all done in time.

I brace my legs in front of me for the landing, hoping I don't break anything in this form because healing will take longer than in my female form, and I have to rush this last eastern pattern point.

My ass hits the ground with a thud as I drag along the dirt, my parachute ripping on the mountain edges around me.

The guys are just behind me, all coming down a few meters away. I unclip myself and run over to Arrie, who wraps me in a warm hug before I clamber out of his arms.

"I still need to disable the eastern point. Cover me."

He draws his weapons and turns his back to me.

I stand behind him, my back up against the mountain edge as Dea and Nine come to help, effectively forming an arc around me as I close my eyes and get to work.

"Fae incoming," I hear Nine say from what sounds like far away, but opening my eyes, he's right in front of me. "About a dozen."

Arrie steps forward. "Stay there."

Nine and Dea confirm his instructions and form a tighter arc around me.

"Hurry up!" Dea shouts at me over his shoulder.

Following his instructions and trying to ignore how dangerous fighting alone will be, I start rewiring the eastern point of the spell.

Goddess, I hope this fucking works. If it doesn't, and I get it wrong, I'm going to have to start all over again, and that will mean everyone being in danger.

Five minutes in, and Arrie is still fighting in the distance, with Nine helping from the side lines by trying to use his mind control magic on anyone not under the influence of Silver Leaf Vain.

It is kind of working, and I am nearly done.

But even when I am done, the most that will happen is we will see our surroundings properly, probably showing us more enemies we'll have to fight.

"Dea?"

"Yes?"

"If this works, I am about to raise the barrier for us. What do we do now?"

"We fight, but knowing our true surroundings."

Right. We could literally be anywhere right now, and we wouldn't know. I don't bother taking down the entire spell; there is no time for that (and I wasn't sure I could), so the rest of the world won't be able to see the truth, but we will. And right now, that is all that matters.

I move one last rune around, changing its meaning, and bingo! I open my eyes and watch as the shimmer around us folds and vanishes. What was once natural, open mountains, shifts and changes into a more manmade path that forks, potentially taking us to Connie. Or perhaps away from her.

Arrie is fighting the last three Fae standing; the others lie dead at his feet, blood pooling around them and sinking into the dirt-filled path. Arrie turns and looks at me with a smile, clearly proud of my progress. "Well done, Killer," he whispers, my Shifter hearing just picking up on it.

I shift into a panther and leap into the air, tackling one of the Fae to the ground and ripping his head from his shoulders in one swift movement.

Arrie swings his sword one last time, skewering it through the two remaining Fae in one move. "There." He sighs.

Nine walks up. "Five minutes? Dude, you're lacking."

Arrie punches him in the arm. "I'm tired."

Dea laughs. "As are we all." He gestures to the two paths before us. "This is like some kind of fabled nonsense. Which path do we take?"

Still in panther form, I sniff the air in both directions but don't scent Connie in either.

"She wasn't brought in this way," Nine translates for me. "Sweetie can't scent her."

Dea looks at me. "Try your Vampire sense."

Right. I'm all hyped up from the mixed blood.

I shift back into my male form, then into my female one, and immediately take a step back and wince. All the surrounding scents and sights are playing havoc on my mind. Too bright. Too many scents. Too much . . . everything.

I wince and cower to the ground but continue sniffing nonetheless. Eventually, I pick up on a faint scent of Connie coming from the north. "She's north," I whisper.

Dea nods and goes to lift me up, but I shift back into my male form with a relieved sigh. "This way." I point to the pathway that leads toward the northern point of the spell (the only way un-navigational me can sense any kind of compass point).

With no more Fae around, we relax slightly. I will likely pick up on anything close by, with Nine picking up on anything within a ten-mile radius, so we all walk down the path a little—away from the blood and dead bodies—and relax into a heap on the floor.

"That was . . . fucking intense." I hold my head in my hands.

Dea sighs. "That it was, Angel. But you did brilliantly."

"Yes, you did," Arrie grumbles. He sounds tired, and I wonder how much sleep he's gotten over the last few days. Between being drained dry by me, fighting with his battle-mode focus, and running around with the rest of us, he probably hasn't had time to rest properly.

"Rest a little," I say to everyone. "We need to be in full strength for traveling and fighting later."

"I agree." Dea nods. "We should rest. Connie cannot be saved if we do not have the energy or magic supply to do so."

Arrie thumps his head to the ground, falling asleep almost instantly, while Nine and I slump against the nearest rock and close our eyes.

"I will take first watch," Dea says.

"Wake me for the second," Nine mumbles as he falls asleep, but Dea just sighs at him and smiles.

27

The sun is beginning to set when we all start heading north. I try suggesting Dea and I carry us all north because it would be faster, but everyone wants to conserve energy.

"So," I start, "what do we know about this organization?"

Nine grabs my hand as we walk. "They're in charge of the legal and illegal blood supply for all Vampires across the globe. They work for the SC, but they also undermine them whenever they can. And since Fae are here, and there has been an increase in pixie dust distribution, we're pretty sure they're also helping with that global stream, too."

"Great," I mutter. "And how are we going to get Connie free from an organization like that?" I sigh. "They must be huge!"

Dea nods from in front of us, where he walks solo—Arrie is bringing up the rear. "They are. Their leader, Sanio Bontanos, is a right mumbling cove."

"A . . . what?"

Nine interrupts. "It means a deceitful and unpleasant person."

"How many people work for him?" I ask. "Will it be a hundred or an army? How many will be here at the base? How big is the base?" I resist the urge to stomp my foot like an impetuous child and instead growl out, "Info!"

Arrie catches up to us and wraps an arm around my shoulders. "We don't have all of that information, Killer. He's an ass, but he's kept to himself up until now. The blood supply was going well, and everyone knew the illegal supply was happening, so we just let it slide."

Makes sense, I guess. Why fix something that ain't broke?

"Nothing to do but follow Connie's scent for now." But I swear, I am going to bring her home the moment I damn find her, no matter how many heads I have to roll to make that happen. I pick up the pace a little and catch up with Dea, who shifts beside me and grabs my hand.

"Are you doing okay, Angel?"

I nod, not really knowing what else to say. "For now."

• • •

THE ROAD NORTH IS LONG, WINDING, AND TIRESOME; EVEN FOR MY VAMPIRE-LEVEL STAMINA, the entire trip is tough. It takes us three days to trek through the mountains enough for Connie's scent to get stronger, and we spend the entire time dodging groups of Fae, skirting well away from any Vampires at night, and not one of us has had a decent night's sleep since the battle at the Fae Court. We are tired, exhausted, and hungry. But mostly, we're all pissed off.

The guys all takes turns babysitting my high-strung emotional state, and it's starting to take its toll on them. I can tell by the exasperated looks they try to hide whenever they think I'm not looking. I appreciate the effort, but I think it's best they just leave me alone to sulk and growl in my own ball of stewing nonsense.

I just want Connie back, and then to go home to my books, my comfy (so very fucking comfy) bed, and Arrie's homemade brownies. I didn't realize basics are so luxurious—or that brownies count as basics—but boy doesn't this shitty trip prove me wrong.

Halt, Nine calls out to us all. *We're heading toward a large group of Fae and Vampires.*

Okay, we're probably at some sort of gate. Nine? Feed me into the other guy's heads.

Done.

I'm going to fly up and see if I get a better vantage point. Dea, sneak around as much as you can, try to gain some credible info. Nine, try to poke around in their heads. See what we're up against. Arrie, find somewhere we can make camp.

They all agree, echoing a chorused *yes* into my mind that leaves a ringing bell effect in my ears, as though they all just shouted loud enough to partly deafen me.

Shaking my head, I start climbing the nearest mountain ledge in my female form— promptly ignoring the overload of sensations whirring my senses—and use my flying ability to climb and glide up the side with ease. I don't want to shoot straight up into the air, in fear of being shot out of the sky or spotted, but I can climb in among the mountains, using them and the clouds as cover while I try to get a better look at whatever is in front of us.

Maybe I can see the base from here.

I never thought I'd say this, but climbing the mountain's edge is easy. With the use of air magic, it's . . . a breeze (get it?). Laughing at my own internal dad joke, I focus on the task at hand. It takes me all of fifteen minutes to reach some kind of high up ledge long enough crouch on and high enough to see a few miles into the distance, and with my Vampire sight, I can zoom in all the way to anywhere I can see.

Handy.

Mountains surround us. No surprises there. But in front of us, around the path and a couple miles west, stands a giant metal gate in the middle of a wasteland; it honestly looks like something straight out of a medieval fantasy movie, and I'm caught halfway between an impressive snort and rolling my eyes. Of course this Sanio Bontanos guy has a gate like that. Seems Connie's enemy has a god complex—an evil one. But whatever, I think as I shrug my shoulders.

The gate is armed by rampart crossbows, ballistae, well over a hundred archers, and various Fae dotted around the upper gate's ledge. And that doesn't account for the army behind the gate.

This is gonna be a pain.

Nine? Tell me you were serious about needing an army to take you guys down?

No answer. Great.

Slowly, I ease my way back down the mountain's edge and land firmly on a spot of soft grass. Now I need to find Arrie. Taking a big sniff, I seek out his scent. The effect of the mixed blood is starting to wear off, because I can actually look into the sky without wincing into a ball of pain.

I follow the scent that leads me to a cave large enough to make a mini home in. "Arrie?"

"Over here." A light flickers around the corner, and I walk over. He's started a fire, grabbed some logs, and unpacked our meager supplies. "That expression does not give me hope of good news."

I shift my feet. "I think we should wait until the others are back."

He pats the spot next to him, his arm raised in question. He wants to cuddle?

I hesitate slightly, my foot not quite hitting the ground as I pause.

"Unless you'd rather not," he says, and I don't miss the disappointment in his tone.

Damn it. I can't upset him like that. I scoot over to him and plant my ass next to his. "I'm just not used to you being so . . . cuddly."

He chuckles, and damn if that doesn't do crazy things to my insides. "I want this to work." His voice is barely above a whisper, but I catch the hesitation in his tone.

"You don't have to try so hard, Arrie. I like you for you."

He leans down and places a gentle kiss to my temple. "I will always try for you."

I shiver at the warmth of his breath. "I . . ." I don't know what to say to that. It's far too close to a declaration of love for my personal level of comfort, and I don't think I'm ready for that. "Thank you, but just be yourself. Please."

His smiles ever so slightly. "Okay."

I turn around and wrap my arms around his shoulder, only just managing to do so, and kiss him. Not hard or urgent like last time, but soft and gentle, with enough need to let him know that he matters, that I'm telling the truth.

But Arrie has other ideas. He grabs me by the waist and hauls me onto his lap without breaking the kiss, and suddenly I find myself straddling his lap as his hands wander up the edges of my top.

I break the kiss to gasp at air and watch him smile at me.

"We can stop," he whispers.

I shake my head, afraid that if I stop us now, it'll ruin the moment.

"It's just . . . Connie . . ."

He puts a finger to my lips. "She's going to be fine. We can't do anything more without a plan, and that requires waiting for Dea and Nine." He takes a deep breath. "She wouldn't want you being miserable and upset for days. Especially when we are going to rescue her either way."

He's right. I can't just fall into a stupor every time one of the team is hurt. We are all immortal; it's not like her life is in any danger. "I just don't want her to hate me."

"Oh, Killer." Arrie places both hands on either side of my face, forcing my gaze to his. "There's nothing you could ever do to make Con hate you. She's totally in love with you."

I flinch but smile. "In . . . love?"

His face turns a deep shade of red. "We all are."

"B-b-but . . . it's still really early, and—"

"We know. We have all the time in the world to make cheesy declarations and be honest." He rolls his eyes. "There's no need to freak out over normal evolving emotions. Just enjoy your new immortal life." He leans in and places a needy kiss to my lips, parting them with a forceful sweep of his tongue. "Besides," he says between breaths, "you wanted romance."

I smile. He's right, I did. It means something to me that they're willing to be slow, go on dates and do silly, non-sexual things before we all get too entangled, and do everything at my pace.

I kiss him back, hard, pushing us both off the log we were sat on and onto the floor, where I straddle his waist and pin his hands by his head.

He groans into my mouth as I shift my hips to meet his rapidly hardening cock, and his tongue moves more fervently, his hips shifting to grind into me. He grinds against me, his control slipping as he struggles against my hold.

I laugh under my breath, but it strangles into a moan against his decadent lips, my lust-crazed mind coming back into the driver's seat.

Someone new enters the cave and coughs. "Can't leave you two alone for two minutes."

I break away from Arrie's mouth and growl in the direction of Nine. Way to ruin the moment.

Not sorry. I have plans, and he's ruining them.

I get up off of Arrie, holding out my hand to offer him some help off the dirty cave floor I pushed him onto. But he doesn't take it and instead glares daggers at Nine.

Nine shrugs at him and sits down. "Stop ruining my plans."

Arrie huffs. He stomps out of the cave and into the rain, leaving me alone with Nine and a crazy libido.

Damn it.

I concentrate for a moment and change forms, exhaling a sweet sigh of relief at the immediate change in bodily functions. The need is still there, but without my Vampire senses, it's dulled.

"So," I say as I sit next to Nine, "what are these so-called plans of yours?"

Nine chuckles. "Nope. Not telling." *You'll just have to wait and see. I've told the rest of the team already.*

I'm the last one to know?! I internally growl at him, hoping it translates.

I wanted you to have something to look forward to. He crawls over the log and sits behind me, placing me between his legs. His hand travels over my shoulder, tracing the outside of my ear and down my neck and stopping to stroke my collar bone. He dips his head low to whisper, "You'll like it. Promise," in my ear.

I shiver.

Dea fazes in and sits beside Nine, placing a hand on my shoulder. "Everything okay, Angel?"

I clear my throat. "Yes," I squeak.

Nine chokes on a laugh, and Dea smirks while shaking his head. "Cannot leave you two alone for two minutes."

A laugh bubbles out of me before I can stop it. I am beginning to think it might just be me that can't be left alone with any of the team for two minutes.

"Where is Arrie?"

Nine groans. "He went off in a strop."

Dea raises his eyebrow in question.

"Nine interrupted us," I explain, hoping he'll get my drift.

"Ah, I see." He turns toward the fire and smiles. "He will come around."

"I hope so." I rest my head on my knees as Nine wraps his arms around my torso.

Half an hour later, and just as my stomach starts to complain it's hungry, Arrie stomps back into the cave carrying an alpaca carcass on his shoulders.

I have to resist the urge to vomit.

It's no different than the meat on your plate every evening.

It's not that. And it truly isn't. Something about my Shifter senses goes into overdrive; it feels wrong. Seeing its blood dripping onto the cave floor like it's nothing . . . Like its life means nothing.

I can't hold it in anymore and run off to vomit in the corner.

"Change form, Angel."

At this point, I'm used to changing on command and just decide to follow his instructions rather than argue about being bossed around. When my female senses are back in control, everything flattens out. My nausea vanishes.

"That's . . . weird."

Nine looks at me with recognition in his eyes. "Some Shifters are sensitive to seeing dead animals. Kind of like seeing dead kin." He rubs soothing circles on my back. "Most of the Shifter world are vegetarian."

Arrie mumbles something in what I am starting to recognize as his native language and begins laying out the carcass to gut. And although it is kinda gross, it isn't sending me into a weird vomiting state of depression, so I just turn my head and watch the flames flicker against the cave wall.

"They have an army behind their gate." I break the silence. "At least a thousand soldiers. Vampire and Fae."

Arrie curses, and I turn around to see he nicked his thumb, but the blood has no effect while mixed with the alpaca's scent.

"Be careful," I huff.

Arrie laughs while Nine and Dea stifle giggles, and I realize I have just told the Horseman of War to be careful.

"Sorry." I shake my head.

Nine breaks the following silence. "No Silver Leaf Vain in the regular troops. But should probably expect some in the higher-ups."

I nod. "Archers, ballistae, and crossbows . . . The place is like a fortress. Not to mention the strategic pockets of Fae dotted along the outer gate walls."

"They will have spelled traps everywhere." Dea sighs. "It will be like dodging a minefield. They have probably also noticed your interference with the cloaking spell by now."

He places some more wood on the fire, causing it to snap and crackle. "The troops are loyal. We will not sway them. They agree with the cause of destroying the control the SC has over the magical community."

"Ugh." I sigh. "I don't even know what to do about that. They're right, the SC does have too much control. There's no balance."

Nine looks at me with surprise. "Explain."

"Well, if the SC control everything and the individual councils have no legal room to move, what do you expect? Them to just roll over and ignore how they've ruled their people for centuries?" I cough, clearing my throat, and Nine taps me on the back. Stupid smoke is hurting my Vampire senses. "But the councils can't just run in, weapons drawn, and hurt innocents in their plight."

I sink to the cave floor. "Can I not just take the entire system down and start from scratch?" I laughed.

Nine, ever the voice of literalism, says, "Sorry, but probably not."

"Rhetorical question."

"Right, sorry."

Dea grabs my hand. "I did not find anything of interest. Just a normal army guarding a gate."

"Right." None of that helps. It all just reaffirms what I already know: we have no hope of winning.

"We could win," Nine says, "no army could truly defeat us if we were going all out, but it would be a waste of energy. We should find a better way in."

All out? What, have they been holding back this entire time? 'Cos I won't lie, that shit ain't cool. But alas, my sexy nerd is right. We need a better way in.

"I could fly us in. Clouds would provide some coverage if we didn't freeze that high up." I shrug.

"We would need to know where Con is being held for that plan."

"We just need to get behind the gate, Dea. And either me or Nine getting a good grasp of where to head." I smile, a plan coming to mind. "Ohmigoddess, it's time to be ninjas!" I laugh. "Connie is going to be so proud of this plan."

Nine laughs and rolls his eyes at the image of me and the guys dressed in black trying to blend in. "We'll just steal some army uniforms, Sweetie."

Right, of course. That makes sense. But I can't hide my disappointment at not being able to wear any ninja clothing.

Damn it.

I will get my ninja fantasy!

"All right, get some sleep. We'll go when it's dark. More cover that way. At least from the Fae." Vampires can see just as well in the dark.

28

It's midnight exactly, and we're all crouched just outside of the cave we made camp in. All of us are armed to the teeth, and I have so many sets of knives strapped to my body that I might as well be a walking kitchen appliance. The set Nine gave me before we left *Sheruta* are strapped to my thigh, but I'm only going to use them in tricky situations, since they fly faster and more accurately than my regular ones.

I'll get him to make me some more when we get home.

"Okay," I start, "I'm going to fly everyone over the gate under the cover of the clouds. I've never flown this many people before, so . . . err . . . sorry if I drop you all a hundred feet on your heads?"

Nine chuckles but rests a reassuring hand on my shoulder. "You'll be fine, Sweetie."

Dea and Arrie nod when I look at them, and that's all the reassurance I need.

"Brace yourselves."

I raise my hands in the air like some kind of weird magician (hey, it looks cool and helps me focus) and we all lift into the air. I test everyone's balance; everyone has a different airflow and current around them because everyone is a different shape, size, and weight. Arrie takes three times the amount of air displacement than Nine, for example, and is harder to maneuver around. Eventually, after fiddling and nearly dropping Arrie on his head (oops, but I did warn them), I get the hang of managing this much air.

"I'm going to fly us up and over the gate, and then I'm going to drop us somewhere less crowded as close to Connie as I can get. I can't keep this up forever, it's difficult to manage, so I can't have us fighting in the air."

Dea nods. "That is okay, Angel. Just get us there as silently and as close to Con as possible."

Everyone nods their affirmative, and off we go. I take us up beside the mountain's edge to provide some cover, just in case any of the enemy are looking up. We aren't exactly inconspicuous.

Once we reach the top, I drop us on the ground to catch my breath and practice trying to wrap the clouds around us by using the air.

This would be so much easier with my water element unlocked! I internally grouch to myself as I let the clouds slip the moment they reach us, and I watch in frustration as they float away like the shitty pieces of water vapor they are.

"Fucking clouds."

Taking a deep breath, I focus on just moving the cloud itself, rather than trying to float it this way. Luckily, clouds aren't too scarce this high up. The guys are all in various states of shivering, and I could have created a fire for them, but I'm worried we'll be seen, so they'll just have to be cold for a while until I figure this out. Not like they can die from hypothermia anyway.

"C'mon, c'mon . . ." I beg the cloud in front of me, trying to persuade it to move.

I'm hoping the presence of air in the cloud might make it easier for me to move the water, therefore moving the entire thing.

"C'mon, c'mon . . ." I gradually move my hands closer, the cloud following inch by inch. "You can do it, cloudy cloud, come here."

I can hear Nine trying hard not to snicker at me treating the cloud like a cute puppy, but I don't care. Anything to get this fucking thing to bloody move. I can bring down a building with fire, kill dozens of Fae in a fit of Vampire rage, but I can't move a fucking cloud?

Eventually, I have it surrounding us, and moving it while I am inside seems to be easier than dragging it from afar. "Okay, huddle up!"

The guys rush to my side, careful not to displace the cloud too much in their hurrying.

"And up we go."

Since we are inside the cloud (clouds are soaking wet and freezing cold, I might add, so don't try this at home) we can see out of it, so I only hope no one can see in.

We rise as fast as we can without garnering too much attention from the army below us. Nine keeps an eye on their minds (all one thousand of them at once, which I hasten to add is the most impressive thing I've ever seen) to make sure.

"If this is what you find most impressive about me, Sweetie, then I have not been flirting hard enough."

Dea and Arrie chuckle.

"You're looking into the minds of a thousand Vampires and Fae all at once? That's just . . . insane."

He blushes as much as his skin will let him at this cold height.

"Don't distract him," Arrie grumbles.

"Right." I look away and watch in my peripheral as Nine goes back to the task at hand.

"I don't want to take us much higher, lest we freeze and I have to manipulate fire in a controlled enough way to defrost out frozen bodies without getting seen."

Dea points down and to the north. "Okay, then head us in that direction." He sighs. "It seems to be where the rest of the army is."

"Sure, let's just walk right up to an army and say hi." I laugh at my joke, but Dea frowns at me. "All right, all right." I throw us in that direction slowly.

Ten minutes later, when we're all a little warmer from being at a lower altitude, Nine winces.

"You okay?" Dea asks.

He winces again, and I stop us. "What's wrong?"

"Nothing. Just a headache."

Arrie grumbles and Dea sighs. "Nine gets headaches from overuse. We have been up here for an hour already, and he has spent the entire time flitting through a thousand of minds."

"We're nearly ready to land, just hang on."

I speed us up as much as I can, frustration easing out of its familiar hole in the pit of my mind where I tried to bury it with the lid glued in place. Looks like I need to invest in some stronger mental glue. A growl escapes my lips, which causes Dea and Arrie to flinch.

"Just give me a minute." I take a few deep breaths and descend us. "Keep an eye out for a good place to land without being seen."

Sniffing the air, I search for Connie's scent. I can't really get anything this far up, but I keep trying.

"Here." Dea holds out his wrist.

I need everyone fighting fit for this, so I hesitate.

"I will be fine, Angel."

I sink my fangs in and take a little while Arrie has to place a hand over Dea's mouth to keep him quiet. (I'd be lying if I said it isn't the hottest thing about this new existence.)

After just a couple of mouthfuls, I start to smell Connie's scent in the air and stop. "Got it." Looking down, I notice Dea is hard, and I am damn curious what my bite feels like, but I'll never fucking know.

It's more potent than a normal Vampire bite.

But the human in the club wasn't affected?

It might just be a Horseman thing. I don't really know.

Hmmm. Something to think about later. Right now, I fly us as fast as I can toward Connie's scent. A few minutes later, I've found a good place to drop us down: a small pass between two mountains.

Using the cover of the clouds, then the mountains' edges, I dump us on the ground in an exhausted huff. "Did it." Mini celebration for me.

Honestly, that was exhausting, but at least now I only have to focus on ninjaing around while tracking Connie's scent. Hopefully, it won't come to an all-out war. I am trying to keep the peace, not purposefully break it.

Connie's scent heads west, so that's where we go. "Can you not extend your invisibility into a charm or spellbead of some kind, Dea?"

"It's super hard to do, actually," Nine chimes in. "I can place it into a spellbead, but it only lasts around twenty to thirty minutes."

"So that's what my mother used on me?"

Dea nods.

Is now the time to ask? Oh, to hell with it. "Dea, how did you know my mother?"

He flinches. "I really do not think this is the time for that question, Angel—"

"Just answer her. It's not a bad answer, bro."

"Very well." Dea takes a deep breath. "I knew all of the Angel-descended Witches. We all did. They were powerful, so we wanted to stay friends in case we needed them. Mostly, they stayed out of everyone's way and off the radar." He falls back to grab my hand. "Your mother and father were the last ones left. I only really knew them as acquaintances. They did not know what I was, of course, but they knew me as Derek."

I snort in laughter at the chosen name.

"Do not judge me. It is hard coming up with a name on the spot. I gave them a few spellbeads, just in case."

"It was just coincidence," I mutter to myself.

"A fucking huge one," Arrie grumbles just loud enough for me to hear.

For once, we're on the same page; that is a stupidly huge coincidence, and I am starting to not believe in them. Maybe Fate designs it that way.

But that poses the question of whether Fate really exists, and I'm not sure I believe in that level of magic. After all, magic is just science we don't understand yet. Not some mystical force of nature no one can quantify.

We exit the pass to a worn path, and Nine holds up his hand. "Soldiers, a few hundred meters that way." He points left. "Heading this way."

His telepathy has a wider range than my Vampire hearing, so he's on lookout (hearout?) duty, but my sense of smell is the best on the team, so tracking Connie is down to me.

"She's to the right."

Nine nods. "We're going to steal their uniforms and head right."

Arrie steps forward and draws his longsword, a hardness setting to his features I haven't seen before. He's being serious this time. He'll do anything to get Connie back. Just like me.

I step up next to him and draw a few knives as my fangs descend. I nod when he looks to me. "Stay here," I order the other two. "We'll be right back."

We run—well, he runs, I jog—and before long, we see five soldiers walking down the path. Other than those five, it's silent. We need to do this quickly and silently, so it doesn't raise any alarm.

"I can probably take two before they realize what's going on, then maybe throw some daggers on the way to take out a third."

"I'll handle the other two."

I sprint at full Vampire speed toward the group, who don't see me coming, and rip out two throats before anyone even breathes; two daggers later, four Vampires are on the floor before the one Fae in the group has any time to react.

He goes to scream, opening his mouth in terror, when Arrie jumps from his spot a few meters away and moves his sword in one giant swing. The Fae's head comes clean off and tumbles to the ground beside my feet, blood spurting out of the man's body like a fountain until it slows to a dribble down the side of his neck.

"What happened to leaving me two, Killer?"

"Got a little carried away, sorry." I shrug and realize I probably look a little crazy with all the blood over my mouth.

I go to wipe it away, but Arrie grabs my arm and yanks me to him. He spins me around into his arms and presses a kiss to my mouth. I flinch and pull away. "Doesn't that bother you?"

He laughs. "If blood bothered me, I probably wouldn't be a very good Horseman of War. Besides, it's not like it can kill me." He looks me in the eyes and winks.

He actually winked.

I'm going to melt. I'm going to die right here while my body is on fire from the heat caused by this man. I wrap my arms around his shoulders and kiss him back. Hard this time.

He groans and presses his body flush against mine.

A coughing in the background has us pulling apart. "Now is not the time," Dea says while placing Nine on his feet after fazing them here. "We need to wear these clothes to blend in better."

"Right. I really would rather not start a war. Already have one to deal with."

"Soooo . . . who's gonna . . . ?" Nine gestures to the bodies with a cringe that matches Dea's.

"Seriously? How many dead bodies have you guys seen in the last two thousand years?"

They both shrug.

My sigh matches Arrie's, and we get to work stripping the soldiers of their uniforms. I just pray that something here will actually fit Arrie.

"Ugh, I'm gonna have to change twice, aren't I?"

I tell you, this sex changing business makes my life stupid hard. Like, who the fuck has time to get dressed twice every morning? Not me, that's for sure.

By the time I've taken all of the clothes off three of the five soldiers, Arrie has managed the same with the other two, and we lay everything out.

"Arrie, you take the largest stuff."

He nods and grumbles, "You should take the smallest."

I nod and grab it, then leave Nine and Dea to sort through the other three. Luckily, their uniforms aren't difficult, and I manage to get dressed without needing to ask for assistance.

"Here." Dea hands me the last uniform. "You should put this on in your other form."

"Right." I sigh and roll my eyes.

You'd think being naked in front of these guys would be an issue, but it isn't. Firstly, I have nothing to be embarrassed about, and they'll all see me naked eventually anyway, but it is also really not the time. Weirdly, though, I do have an issue showing them my penis, and I catch myself thinking this is a strange thing to be worried about for someone who primarily identifies as a woman and seems to have no issue showing them my boobs.

I turn around and get changed with my back to them—much to Nine's amusement.

We walk up the worn path toward Connie's scent, and I just hope we find where they're keeping her before nightfall, because otherwise we'll have to hide out in enemy territory overnight. Nope, not happening. We'll have to work through the night.

"I'm going to use the crystals to take us home the moment we find her. That way, we won't have to fight our way back." I look to Nine, hoping it's a good idea. "We just have to get to her."

He nods and smiles.
"Good plan, Angel."
Yay me!

Three hours later, and we still haven't seen anyone else on our travels through enemy territory. It's all seeming a little too easy. Part of me is waiting to be ambushed by a thousand Vampires and find out just how painful this immortality shit is.

We're all chatting harmlessly, but keeping our voices to hushed whispers considering the good hearing of our enemy, when Nine holds up his hand.

"Hush."

We left the bodies hidden in a small crevice in the side of the mountain, but I get the feeling that won't last forever once the Vampires scent the blood, so despite our camouflage, we are all wary of bumping into others.

We kinda stand out.

"Another five-person group."

I sniff the air and catch on to the familiar scent of Vampires and Fae. "Three Fae and two Vampires."

Dea steps forward. "We will take care of this." He looks back and gives me a smug smile. "Stay here."

Arrie laughs, but I stamp my foot like the petty child I am. "Doesn't feel good when someone else does it."

Arrie wraps an arm around my shoulders. "We should move to the edge of the mountain. Stay out of sight."

I follow him to the edge. There aren't many hiding places at this point of the path, and we have to strain hard to fit into a small crack in the stone.

Arrie wraps an arm around my waist.

I suck in a breath at being this close to the Horseman of War. This close, I can feel *everything*, and it makes me tense.

He chuckles, clearly sensing my dilemma. "Sorry, Killer," he whispers in my ear. "We can move soon."

I just grumble, *"Kutabare,"* and shift against him. If I'm going to 'suffer,' so is he. Mwuhahaha!

He groans behind me as I arch my ass back into his groin after standing on my tiptoes. "Stop that." His voice is strained, and I love that I have that effect on him.

"Why?" I place a hand behind me and go straight to the buckle on his pants. "Scared?"

"Of letting the entire army know where we are by fucking you senseless? Yes. Very much so." I sigh and move my hand away, but he grabs it and yanks it to his mouth. "Later. When we're home."

My head nods of its own accord, and I am getting slightly fed up with how pliant I'm becoming with these stupid Horsemen (and women, because let's not forget how wrapped around Connie's finger I've become).

I swivel around as best as I can and look Arrie in the eyes. "You are not the boss of me. In this instance, you are right, but goddess damn it, none of you are escaping me when we get back." I have to whisper, but I hope my whisper shouting works to get my point across.

He grabs both arms by their wrists and pins me to the rock wall. "Who said you were in charge, Killer?"

Goddess, my entire body melts and arches into his—much to his amusement—and if he wants me to be submissive, I know he'll have no trouble persuading me. Instead of an answer, however, I just let out a pathetic mewling sound and internally beg him to do something—anything—to help rid me of this need driving me insane.

I drop my hands to my sides when he lets me go and walks out of the crevice. I take a moment to breathe, but then I follow and see why he left: Dea and Nine are back, watching us from afar, and Nine has the world's largest smirk on his face.

"We dispatched them," Dea announces with a smile at my flushed face. "Time to keep going."

"I want to run there." They look at me like I'm crazy, but I shake my head. "We're taking too long. None of us want to be here when night falls and the rest of the Vampires that are too sensitive to sunlight to wander the day come out and say hi and scent that blood. Plus, I don't think anyone can see us run, anyway."

Dea sighs but nods reluctantly. "Very well. You carry Arrie, I will take Nine."

Arrie grunts his dislike at being carried by me (someone half his fucking height), but he walks over nonetheless.

I sweep him into my arms bridal style, and he wraps two arms around my neck; the entire thing looks hilarious, and I have to stifle many, many giggles to keep him from punching me in the face.

Once Dea has Nine on his back, we both take off as fast as we can, making much better progress than earlier. I'm all for slow and steady and careful, but it'll all be for nothing if we're caught here at night now.

The only thing that matters now is Connie.

About an hour later, Nine tells us all to stop, and we hole up in a small cave Dea spotted nearby. "Okay," Nine says, "there's an entrance to the mountains just around the corner and about a hundred soldiers posted outside."

I sniff the air. "All Fae."

Dea grimaces. "That means heavy spellwork."

"There's a heavy spell going on inside somewhere, I can sense it," I inform them. "Also, Connie's scent is much stronger here."

"We're close," Arrie says in surprise.

"No one expected us to get past that gate," I say. "Hence the lack of patrols on the main path."

"That ends here," Dea says. "From here, we are going to have to fight to get inside."

He looks to Arrie, who grumbles but smiles. "At least we're killing assholes this time."

I am not going to point out that they're only doing their job for a cause they believe in, because that would make him feel bad, and we really need his magic right now.

Drawing my daggers and letting my fangs descend, I prepare alongside everyone else. Dea has his dual blades, Arrie his longsword, and Nine his magiguns and dual daggers.

Time to fuck some shit up.

We run around the corner and immediately stop dead in our tracks at what the entrance looks like: a massive spell circle.

Damn it. I'm going to have to break that to get in.

And surrounding that spell circle is at least a hundred Fae warriors.

"Fuck," I mumble under my breath. I turn to the guys. "I'll disable the spell; you guys take the army."

They run ahead while I hang back and change into my male form. I still have a bunch of knives on me, just not my special ones, but I mostly rely on my magic and shifting powers in this form anyway.

Nine and Arrie are back to back in the center of a circle of enemies while Dea whizzes around the group and thins the numbers from the outside. Nine's abilities are working well, so he's managing to join the fight properly.

Might need him to train without his mental abilities when we get home, and see if we can't stretch them further.

The sounds of battle rage on around me while I stand in horror and watch. We've killed people before, sure, but only ever small groups or individuals, and those at the Fae Court were only a couple of dozen. This . . . this is different. They're dropping like flies, a body count piling up in a ring of death.

Movies don't do enough justice to the sounds of people screaming, of bones snapping; to the smell of death, blood, and piss that permeates the air; and the sight of everyone around you dying and the light leaving their eyes. It's harrowing. As though it'll be the last thing you ever see in this world.

How do people live like this?

I don't move, I just stand there, my mouth hanging open and my ears ringing from the clash of swords and the sounds of exploding spells.

Snap out of it! Yes, it's horrible, but Connie needs you. None of us can break through that spell circle.

I shake my head out of the dark hole it's creeped into and raise my arms to try to feel out the spell. Luckily, it's not nearly as complicated as the concealment spell. It's simply there to keep anyone out in the event no one is guarding the door or the army are defeated. It's made purely of runes, so all I have to do is magically rub them out.

Three, two, one . . .

And the spell is down.

Once the spell releases with an almost silent pop of air pressure, the guys look my way and smile.

I run to them and leap over the army in my panther shift, joining Nine and Arrie in the center.

Back in my female form, I arm myself with the knives and aid the effort.

"No point. We're just wasting time. We can outrun them," Nine says.

He's right. "Get Dea in here."

I watch Dea struggle to break through the mass of bodies attacking us, so I airlift him to us and place him gently on the ground.

He looks at me with a questioning eyebrow.

"We're gonna run. They won't be able to keep up."

"Right." He grabs Nine by the scruff and shoves him over his shoulder as I grab Arrie and throw him over mine. "Now!"

We run full-sprint, knocking over dozens of Fae, and I blow the rest out of our way.

The cave tunnel is dark, dank, and smells of rotting mushrooms. I nearly vomit, my Vampire senses taking the brunt of the vile onslaught, but I can't change forms because I need to run Arrie and me to Connie.

We pass plenty of Vampires on the way, but none of them can keep up with us at this speed. Pretty sure we have a full army chasing after us like some weird cartoon scene, but oh well, it's working.

We'll have to stop at some point to get Connie out.

I smell the air and adjust our speed to slow down. She's close. Like, a few hundred meters at most.

"Stop!"

Dea and I come to an abrupt halt at my order, and I place Arrie on the ground as Dea does the same for Nine.

"She's close."

Arrie perks up at that and moves forward.

Just around the dark corner no one but myself can see is a hollowed-out cavern a few meters across. It forms a square with a lab table in the middle with all kinds of torture instruments laid out in a surface nearby. The smell of piss, shit, and sweat permeates the air, burning death and decay permanently into my nostrils, but I don't care. Connie is in there somewhere.

I shiver. "What the . . . ?" I don't need to voice my question because the guys all take one look at that table and stand still in horror.

"Really?" Dea asks. "He did not stop with his experiments after we rescued her last time?"

Last time? This . . . this is what happened before?

At the sides of the room stand multiple prison cells, and I sprint around the room and tear each one off its hinges. Whoever is being kept in here is now free; I don't care who it might be. No one deserves this.

A meek voice in the back of one cell in particular has me rushing forward, barreling past pixies, Witches, and all manner of creatures.

"Connie?"

"Ma . . . gic."

She lies in a heap in the corner, barely a reflection of the person she once was. Her skin is gray, her hair is covered in so much grime it's turned a dark shade of brown, and there are bite marks that haven't healed all over her.

I have to keep my fangs from slipping in anger, and instead change into my male form when approaching. "It's me." I raise my hand slowly, asking permission to touch.

She nods her head with a smile, barely a whisper of happiness, and I crouch and grab her hand.

"We're gonna get you out of here. Take you home."

She shakes her head. "No."

"Connie, you can't stay here." I don't understand.

She points behind me, and I turn around to find the guys in a heaped pile on the lab table, all in those stupid magicuffs, and all screaming through their gags.

I must have been so focused on Connie that I didn't hear their struggle.

Standing at the head of that table is a man I instantly know not to fuck with. He has a scar the length of his face, eyes a piercing bright red color, and is almost as stocky as Arrie. His buzz-cut does nothing to ease the edge of menace in his eyes. "You must be the Horseman of Magic. You've done quite a number on my army."

I stand to attention and block Connie from view. No way am I letting her go again. "You must be the piece of shit I've heard so much about." I grin at him, trying to make it as menacing as possible, but next to this guy, I probably look like the Easter bunny.

I don't care how mean and villain-like this piece of shit looks in the dim light of this cave-hole, I am going to enjoy tearing him apart.

Boss fight, bitches!

"I'd love to see you in action. Come on at me." He doesn't move to defend himself, nor does he look even an ounce afraid.

"They trained me." I point to the pile of men on the lab table. "And you're not scared at all?" Sue me, I'm curious. But I also want to get him talking. He looks like the monologue type, and I am going to use every advantage I have; this is the real world, after all, not some video game with dumb rules.

He laughs, and the maniacal that rises and echoes around the cavern makes me shiver. I try to tamper that shit down, but I can't help the small shaking to my hands that escapes my control. The bastard notices, of course. "Scared, Horseman?"

I shrug and move forward, worried about leaving Connie behind me but not really having much of a choice. If we want to leave, we have to get past the dungeon boss first.

I'm in my male form, and I know that one of the first things I need to do is test this guy out. How strong is he? How fast is he? Does he have any magical abilities? To do that, I'll need to be in my female form.

Okay, I can do this. Breathe, Magic, breathe.

If I strategically use my magic, I can take this guy easy.

Flipping into my female form, I charge him faster than I can blink.

He flies across the room in utter silence.

No screaming. No maniacal laughing. Nothing.

It's more horrifying than the sounds of battle from earlier, if I'm honest.

He crumples a few feet into the wall but gets to his feet and walks out with a confident swagger, as though I didn't just use supernatural-level strength to throw him *into a wall*.

Freak.

"Hmmm, Conquest was right. You *are* strong. Perhaps, when properly fed and trained, stronger than my old friend, War, over there." He smiles at Arrie, and I nearly throw up.

Please tell me they weren't actually friends?

I don't bother waiting for an answer, since Nine can't give one anyway, and I fling my air magic at him, hoping to do the same thing as before but in a different way.

It works, though not as effectively.

He flies to the ground in a skidding halt. This time, he jumps to his feet with renewed vigor. "Your air magic isn't as strong as your Vampire strength. I see."

Is he observing me?

Shit. I don't want to give this guy all the knowledge in the world about my powers. That would be stupid. But I guess it won't matter because he won't live through the day to do anything useful with the knowledge gained.

I hurl a fireball at him, taking a few extra seconds than before given my lack of practice with the volatile element.

"Not as well practiced?"

I growl. Nothing slips past him.

Use your brain, Magic. Think.

Aha!

I twist an air current in a continuous circle to create a mini-tornado (don't want to bring the mountain down), and ad fire to the mix. Double usage!

Take that, asshole.

I throw it at him full-force, holding nothing back.

This time he grunts and has to suppress the squeal of fear that escapes his lips; but nothing gets past my Vampire hearing at this close a range. I hear it. And it is all I need.

Fueled by the image of Connie weak and fragile, and the guys in a pile completely useless with their cuffs on, I sprint through the fire tornado and leap onto his writhing body.

"You," I grit through a heavy breath, "are going to regret the day you ever decided to deal with me." I punch him in the face harder than I've ever punched Arrie in training, and the satisfying clunk of his cheek bone breaking under my knuckles draws a smile from my pained expression.

The man beneath laughs as he takes a few quick breaths. "You're doing so well, Magic. You are a force to be reckoned with, for sure." He throws me off his body with a flick of his arm. "But you haven't bested me yet."

I let the fire tornado diminish and watch what he's about to do. My hands instinctively protect my middle, and I internally thank Arrie and Connie for all the repetitive drilling of basic fighting stances over the past month.

His fangs descend, and he walks up to me with a calm demeanor and a placid expression on his face. He's trying to exude calm and collected, but I can see through it. He's worried. You can see it in the occasional twitch of his fingers and the widening of his eyes with every step he takes.

Fear races through him.

He looks me straight in the eyes and flicks a finger.

I wait for something to happen—anything. But nothing does. The room remains silent except the guys' breathing over their gags and Connie's pained mewling in the background, and I remain conscious and in control.

"What?" he asks, looking baffled. "Why isn't it affecting you?"

I look at him confused, baffled. Whatever power he has, it isn't working on me. That's the best news I've had all fucking day. I smile, making sure to show my fangs, and leap at him.

We fly to the ground in a crash as I push his body into the dirt about an inch, creating a villain-sized hole in the ground.

Punch left. Punch right. Uppercut. And he is out like a light. Unconscious.

I run to the guys, uncuff them, and yank their gags out. "What was his magic supposed to do?" I ask Nine.

"Control your body."

I shiver. "That's . . . awful."

"It works on the rest of us." Nine looks to the ground and then up at Connie with tears in his eyes.

Shit. Connie.

I rush to her aid and help her up, simultaneously ripping off her magicuffs.

She heaves a sigh of relief as magic flies through her again uninhibited. But her wounds don't heal instantly like they usually do, and it causes my brow to crease in worry.

It'll take time. Dea can help.

I scoop her into my arms and watch in tearful joy as she loops hers around my neck with what little strength she has. "Let's go home." I place a kiss to her forehead and walk out of the cell to the guys.

"What now?" Arrie asks, looking frustrated and on edge.

I don't blame him. I'd be just as pissed if I was left out of the fight.

I hand Connie to him while I look around the other cells and think about what to do. In the other cells are various creatures that have been experimented on: pixies, fairies, Witches, Shifters, humans . . . You name it, this sick creep has it. We can't take them all back with us, but we can't leave them here. The army'll be coming any minute. Goddess knows what they'll do to them when they find their leader unconscious.

Speaking of whom. He lies on the floor still breathing, and I want to put a swift end to that. "Best way to kill a Vampire, guys?"

"Decapitation," Arrie responds on autopilot as he tries to be gentle with Connie's body.

I grab Arrie's sword and swing it above my head, ready to swing down and—

"Wait!" Nine runs up to me and grabs my free hand. "Are you sure you want to do this?"

I don't bother answering him. I swing the sword down and take off the bastard's head without a second's hesitation. "Yes."

Nine shudders and Dea grimaces.

"I'm not some innocent, lollipop-sucking child. I'm the Horseman of Magic, and this guy is fucking up my destiny." I shrug at their looks of exasperation. "Deal with it."

For good measure, I set his body and head alight, hoping to get rid of the evidence before anyone enters and notices. It'll give us a few days at least before people start to worry.

That just leaves the other cells. "Break everyone's cuffs off. Check to see who's still alive."

Dea, Nine, and I go to work, systematically ripping off cuffs and asking for names. Most of the people here are female, I notice, and all look a little like Connie; or, at least, would have if they weren't looking so grim and damaged.

"Nine?" He looks my way as he helps an elderly lady out of one of the cells. "Were you serious when you said you'd need an army to defeat you all?"

He looks to Arrie with a questioning grin, and they both turn to look at me with matching nods.

"Then I want you three to stay behind and get these people to safety. Get them on whatever transportation you can to their nearest council or whatever. Get them home."

I grimace as I give the order, because I don't want to leave the guys behind, but Connie is in no condition to help fight, and she needs to get home to rest and recover.

I guess I could stay and help, and someone else could take Connie? But I'd rather not—

"No," Nine answers. "You take Connie home. We'll handle this."

I look at him with doubt, and he feigns insult.

"I just . . . don't want to lose any of you again." I look to the floor in a whisper of fear, hoping no one really sees it, but who am I kidding, I'm practically opening up my friggin' heart right now.

All three of them walk up to me and smile.

Dea places a hand on my arm. "We are going to be fine, Angel. We have nothing to worry about now. We can just kill the army and leave."

I nod, but I'm still worried about them. I know they can't die, but still . . . They can get injured, or be tortured, and what if I'm not there to—?

"Hey"—Nine cups my cheek with his hand—"stop that. Dea's right. We've been doing this a lot longer than you. We'll dispatch the enemy and get these people home. It's the right call."

Looking around at the half-dead people, I know he's right. I can't be selfish and leave these people here. "Okay." I sniff to clear the tears threatening to spill over my tentative barrier. "Then use the teleportation crystals and come straight home."

"Yes, boss," Arrie says, and I laugh for the first time in days.

I yank the crystal out of my pocket and look at it in question. "How do I use this thing again?"

Dea answers, "Smash it on the ground and think of home." He rolls his eyes. "You'll need Connie's, too. They only take one person each."

I nod and search Connie's person for hers but can't find it.

"On . . . the . . . table," she whispers just loud enough for me to hear.

I walk over to the lab table with gritted teeth. Honestly, I've tried to ignore it until now, but all the blood on the various instruments and vials and bottles of goddess knows what makes my stomach boil and vomit rise to the back of my throat. But sitting on the corner of the table is a purple glowing crystal that matches the one in my hand. Seems Mr. Freak-a-zoid didn't have a need for it.

Thank fuck.

Arrie hands Connie to me, and I smash the two crystals on the ground and think of Connie's bedroom, the way the afternoon light plays well with the crystal chandelier.

The familiar rushing sensation of teleportation overcomes me, and I might have vomited somewhere in the ether of wherever. If it lands on anybody in the process, I'm not even the least bit sorry.

This shit is an awful way of traveling.

30

We land in an unceremonious on a heap on Connie's bedroom floor, Connie's landing having been softened by landing on me. But fuck if I don't want to throw up again. I gently nudge her off me and run to the bathroom.

Goddess, Connie needs me and I'm stuck with my head down a toilet bowl. Great friend I am. Okay, Magic, calm down. The more you think about it, the worse it'll be.

Five minutes later, I walk out of the bathroom to find Connie unconscious on the floor. I sprint to her side and check her pulse on reflex. Yeah, I know, it's stupid considering we can't die, but it's concerning how little she's healing: her bite wounds are still fresh and bleeding, and the bruises all over her are an ugly shade of purple.

"Connie?" I rub her cheek before scooping her into my arms and laying her on the bed. "You're home now. Safe." A kiss to the cheek has her stirring a smile.

"Ma . . . gic?" Her eyelids struggle to stay open. "I'm . . . sorry."

"Shhhh," I whisper. "I'm right here." I blink away the tears and take a deep breath. "Everything's going to be okay."

I need to heal her wounds before doing anything, so I get to work taking her clothes off and seeing just how bad they are. She has bite marks all over her, some in various states of healing while others are fresh as daisies; I have to suppress the growl that escapes my lips lest I scare her.

Okay. So I don't have Dea here to heal her (goddess I hope the guys are okay), which means I have to do it some other way. Vampire blood has healing properties, right? I mean, mine would. Right?

It's the only plan I have.

Sitting myself underneath her head, which I lay in my lap, I make sure her eyes are closed before ripping my own wrist open in a hiss of pain with my fangs. "Here." I force my wrist to her mouth. "Drink."

Connie tries to fight my arm away, but I hold her down. "Please." My voice trembles in a desperate plea. I don't want to force her, but I will. I can't keep my hands from shaking as I hold my wrist firmly to her mouth.

She goes slack in my arms, and I watch as her throat bobs up and down with the gentle swallows of blood.

Please work. Please work. Please work.

I have to break open my skin a couple more times before I start seeing any results, but eventually, her bite marks start closing over and scabbing. A sigh of relief hisses out of my lips.

"Thank the goddess."

Okay, now I can work on everything else.

I have already torn her clothes off, so now I want to give her a bath and clean her up a bit. She'll appreciate that. Throwing a blanket over her body, I go to run her a bath.

Her bathroom is just as huge as mine, but her bath is smaller, though still inlaid into the floor. Crystals matching her chandelier surround hers, though, and I wonder if they mean anything to her.

Once full and appropriately bubbly, I carry her into the bathroom and lower her into the water. She's half-conscious, as she'll smile and sigh and whimper every now and then, but she's mostly out of it. I scrub her body, going gentle over all of her wounds, which makes it a slow process, but I eventually have all of the blood, dirt, and goddess knows what off of her body so her skin glows its normal beauty, if slightly pallid in complexion.

Next is her hair. I ask the house for a jug to help me pour the water and get to work washing the blood and dirt out of her hair. Everything below the waist is pretty matted, and I can't detangle the strands.

"Shit. I'm going to have to cut them, aren't I?" She's going to murder me when she wakes up.

Fuck. Fuck. Fuck. Well, there's nothing to it.

I grab a pair of scissors from her vanity and get to work. Her once floor-length hair ends up falling to the middle of her back, and I cringe with each snip of the scissors, but I hope waking up to her usual appearance will help her mental recovery. Hopefully, this doesn't put all of that at risk.

"Okay, Connie," I say once I get onto using her special mango-scented conditioner, "please don't murder me, but I had to cut your hair. I'll try and create a growing charm for you before you wake up."

That'll soften the blow a bit. You know, hopefully. And, hopefully, I'll escape that day with my own hair intact.

Once done, I towel dry her and her new hair and then carry her to bed, snuggling her in three duvets once she starts shivering.

A kiss to her forehead and I am out of the door to my own shower.

She'll be all right, I keep telling myself. She will be just fine.

I check on her every hour, like clockwork, and every time I go to see her, she stirs a little and smiles at me before drifting back off to sleep. I know I have to get her to eat something at some point, but I don't know what or how. She hasn't been conscious longer than two minutes at a time, so how I am supposed to get her to eat something?

Maybe some soup would be all right? Or a smoothie? That way she can have a little every time she wakes up. Yup. I'm going to make her a smoothie, some cookies, and anything else that's easy to eat in under a minute. Hopefully she'll be strong enough to keep it all down.

Best not make too much.

I navigate the kitchen with a little clumsiness and realize that I seriously need to stop relying on Arrie and the house for my meals. I don't even know where the blender is, for goddess sake.

I use as much good stuff from the fridge as possible: apples, kale, pears, kiwis—all the healthy stuff I know Connie likes—blend it all together, add some water, and get the tray ready to take up to her room, complete with cookies and mini pastries (okay, so I ask the house for that last item).

Her door creaks open, and her body shifts as her eyes blink in the dwindling daylight. We've been back for six hours, and I still haven't heard from the guys. I'm getting worried. I assume Nine'll send me some kind of message to update me, and the fact that he hasn't only tells me one thing: they're still fighting.

"Hey, Connie . . ." I keep my voice low and happy, trying to encourage her to wake up in a good mood—goddess knows she deserves it.

"Mmmmm . . ." Her eyes are open, and she turns her head to look at me with a smile. "Hi," she whispers, her voice raspy and distant.

"Hey." I walk over and place the tray on the nightstand. "I made you a smoothie and grabbed some cookies and pastries. Try to eat something every time you wake up, okay?"

She goes to sit up but winces.

I rush to her side and lift her into a sitting position, then take a seat on the stool next to the pillow. I push the silly straw her way, and she smiles.

"Tha . . . nk you."

Light from the floor-length window filters through, and I can't help but feel a melancholic happiness—a slightly broken peace. I've gotten her home safe, and she's on the mend, but the guys aren't back yet. I know it'll be a few days, but I still miss them.

Damn. When did I go from wanting to be part of a family with this team to actually having them and missing them? Goddess, my life is crazy.

"It's . . . Friday," I hear Connie croak. "C'mon, spill." Her voice is barely a whisper, but she knows that's all she needs with my Vampire hearing.

I laugh at her. She's right, it's Friday, and I have so much to gossip about. "But . . ."

She shakes her head as she continues to sip her smoothie. "I'll be fine." Her eyes distance themselves as she says it, and I get the feeling she won't be fine at all, not on the inside.

But I indulge her. "Well, you were there for most of it. You saw me kissing Arrie, you probably heard me . . . you know, when I was dancing with Nine in the Fae Court." I wince as I remember the rest of that night, but I shake my head to clear the memories. "After you were taken, we raced to the Paris safe house, the Mort Montante."

She raises her eyebrows in surprise.

"We slept in the guest room with the big bed." Her face blushes at my comment, but she smiles. "No, nothing happened. I'd drained Arrie to have enough magic to Vampire speed all the way there, so he was unconscious, and I was kinda . . . out of it."

"You were worried about me." Her voice is getting stronger now that she has something in her system and some water to parch her dry throat. It's so beautiful to hear, like fresh lilies after a rainstorm.

"The next day we flew on a private jet to the Andes." I smile. It was a nice jet. "Oh, but we did stop at one of Arrie's restaurants."

She laughs, and I join her. "He's fucking brilliant in the kitchen, truly."

"That he is." I smiled wistfully. "He's been . . . different since the moment in the Fae Court."

"Different how?" She's moved on to the pastries and cookies, and I can't help but smile at my genius idea of nibble food.

"He's been nice. Flirty. Kind." I sigh. "It's disconcerting. I asked him about it when we landed in Ecuador, and he said he was worried about messing things up. So I told him to stop being so stupid and to just be himself."

"C'mon . . ." she whines. "The good stuff." She waggles her eyebrows, and I know what she wants.

"I've still not slept with any of them."

She complains and pouts.

"We've been a little busy saving you."

She sighs and lays back down, clearly done with the conversation if I don't have any juicy gossip.

"But . . ."

Her ears perk up, and her eyes snap open.

"Arrie and I did have a few hot make-out sessions along the way to your rescue." I fake-fan myself. "Got a liiiitle carried away there."

Her eyes beg me for more details.

"It was just a kiss."

"Arrie doesn't just kiss." She spears me with her green gaze. "Spill."

"Nine and Dea had gone on ahead to take down a patrol after Arrie and I had taken down the previous one and stole their uniforms. So we hid in a crevice in the mountain, and there was not much room in that slither of space, let me you tell you." I could feel myself getting carried away. "He pinned me to the wall and, fuck, it was insanely hot."

I blush furiously as I realize how much detail I just gave away. Thank goddess I chose to tell her that story and not the one of us making out covered in enemy blood. That would be hard to explain.

Connie coughs to get my attention, and I realize I've slipped away from the conversation. "If you need some alone time, I'm going back to sleep."

31

Four days since I transported Connie and myself back to *Sheruta*, and the guys still haven't returned. Nine sent me one of those holomessage thingies on the second day, saying that they had defeated the army and were transporting everyone to their nearest council or home. But that doesn't stop me worrying about them.

Connie is making great progress, though, and is up and about like her usual self. She thinks I'm not watching, but occasionally she gazes off into the distance with a fearful frown in her brow, and it's during those times that I'm reminded just how fragile we Horsemen can be; we're still alive, after all.

We aren't just Horsemen of the Apocalypse.

We are people, too.

Connie has spent most of the time in the gym and outside, trying to regain her strength, while I've spent most of my time training with her in the evenings, practicing my new-found fire magic (outdoors), and studying in the library. We've fallen into a routine since we've been back, with me making breakfast and lunch and Connie making dinner at the same three times every day. We could have asked the house, but I want the practice and Connie wants to have something to do. I suspect to take her mind off of the torture she must have endured.

On the morning of the fourth day, she clears her throat at the breakfast table and asks, "Did you kill him?"

"Huh?" I swallow my mouthful of French toast. "Who?"

"Sanio. Did you kill him?"

I blanch at the name, not realizing they were on a first name basis, and nod. "Decapitation, then burning."

She nods slowly, visibly digesting the information. "I see." She gets up and goes into the garden, leaving half a plate of French toast behind.

I can't help my curiosity from wandering. How did she know Sanio Bontanos? Why was he so obsessed with her?

I can't help it, I follow her outside. Even if she doesn't want to talk about it, making sure she's okay is paramount; the rest of the team aren't here right now, so that duty is mine. It'll always be mine.

The previous mini rain season came to an end while we were on Earth, and the sun is back out in all its glory, beaming waves of heat onto my bare back and stomach (I'm wearing a bikini and shorts today).

"Hey, Connie! Wait up." I jog after her and go to walk by her side. Her cheeks are stained with tears. "Wanna talk about it?"

She takes a deep breath and lets it out through a strained jaw. "Maybe . . . I dunno."

I've never seen her like this, withdrawn and folded in on herself, and it scares me. Will she be okay? I loop my arm through hers and guide her around my favorite spots in the garden.

"You don't have to talk. We can just walk."

We walk along the edge of the rainbow forest, through a few pixie gardens and past a fairy's nest I'm still wary of, until we reach the *Shinto* shrine I usually do my morning yoga in.

"This," I say, "is my favorite place in the entire garden." We climb the hill slowly, me helping her up when her knees start to shake. "You can see everything from up here."

She breathes a sigh of relief when we sit on the grass outside one of the arches. Her hair shines like the sun in this light, and the usual golden glow of her skin, though dimmed slightly from recent events, has started to peek through the dull pallor of pasty white it's been over the last few days.

"About fifty years ago, not long after the magical community came out of the closet, I had a boyfriend."

I raise my eyebrows in question.

"I know. I know. We've all dallied in relationships in the past, but they're always fleeting, and we know that, so we just don't do it often." She smiles at me. "Well, I guess that's all different now."

Blushing, I lower my head to the floor, but Connie grabs my chin and forces me to look at her. "I like it."

"I . . . Err . . ."

I don't know what to say.

"I like what you're doing to this team. You're bringing us together, circling us around you so you can better lead us in the future." Her cheeks swell into peaks of pride. "We want you. All of us."

I still don't know what to say. "Thank you."

"Anyway, his name was Anthony. He was . . . very caring." I watch her vision go off into the distance again, and I wonder what memory she's reliving. "He once told me that it didn't matter who I was—despite never being told the truth—that he knew I was someone important but didn't want to pry."

"You never told him you were a Horseman?"

She shakes her head. "It just . . . didn't feel like the right time." She sighs. "I should have. If I did, it might have saved his life." Her eyes meet mine again, and I see the tears glistening in front of those bright green eyes before they escape. "If he knew what I was, he might have asked for my help, and I might have been able to save him."

"You can't know that—"

"Please don't." She shakes her head. "He wasn't anyone more special than anyone else I'd dallied with in the past. It gets a bit lonely, immortality, so sometimes I liked to seek something semi-permanent."

She looks like she doesn't want to tell me any of this, so I place a hand on her knee like Nine always does to me, to let her know that her past boyfriends aren't anything to be ashamed of.

"But he was abducted by a blood trafficker one night on the way home from a gig." She waves my curiosity away with a flick of her hand. "He was a small-time musician."

Nodding, I wrap an arm around her shoulders and squeeze gently.

"Anthony was allowed a single phone call to say goodbye, but he tried to use it to call for help, and rather than call me, he called his brother—a police officer—who died trying to save him." She shudders. "I ran after his trail, but by the time I'd tracked him down in the Andes Mountains, it was too late."

Her tears are flowing openly by this point, but I just let them fall. If she needs to be sad for a while, then I'll sit with her while she cries.

"I was foolish. I should have turned back and asked the guys for help, but I didn't. I wanted to free him like one of those superheroes from the movies and watch his awe and fascination as I dramatically revealed who I was . . ."

"So you broke in?" I ask.

She nods, her eyes far away, her tears still falling. "Killed half an army before I was finally captured. Magicuffs weren't a thing back then, so it was harder to capture us."

So magicuffs are a recent thing? Interesting.

I store that away to unpack later.

"But they did capture me." She shudders. "Took the guys four-and-a-half years to find and rescue me, but by that time, the damage had been done."

"Four-and-a-half years?" That's . . . fucking nuts. "What did he do to you?"

"He experimented on me, quickly coming to the realization that I was unique and didn't fit into any known species. He tortured me for information on the Horsemen for years. Eventually, I'm ashamed to say I cracked." Her voice breaks at the end. "He used Vampire venom to force an addiction, using a mixture of pain, horror, and pleasure to confuse my senses. It's an effective form of torture."

Decapitation was waaaay too easy an out for that cunt. I should have left him writhing in pain. I have to resist the urge to growl with my fangs as they descend. Luckily, I hide that fact from Connie by burying my head in my knees.

"When the guys rescued me, it took months, years, before I left the house."

"That's why you're scared of Vampires," I realize, my voice still muffled from where it lies buried.

Connie lifts my head into her hands and stares intently at my fangs and red eyes.

"Sorry." I try to pull away and give her the privacy she needs.

"It's okay. You don't scare me, Magic."

Fuck, I love the way she says my name, and the fact that she isn't scared of me nearly makes me kiss her, but I resist. That might be too soon given the reliving she's undergone recently.

But Connie has other ideas.

"Can I kiss you?" she asks.

At my nod, she grazes her lips against mine, trembling her pain across my broken smile, her smooth lips across my fangs.

Pleasure shoots through me, even at the softest of touches, and I stifle a whimper. This is about her, not me.

Her face scrunches, a moan slipping free from her mask, and she plummets her mouth against mine, crushing my fangs, and forcing us to the grass. She forces her tongue past my lips and tangles ours in a dance of sorrow and ecstasy.

With pain and passion all intermingled, I can taste her grief on my lips from the tears that continue to flow freely down her cheeks, and I can feel the fear racing through her erratic heartbeat as she presses herself up against me. I grab her waist in a desperate grip, doing anything to hold on as she throws wave after wave of life at me. The good and the bad. The memories and the dreams. Everything that makes her alive. Everything that makes her . . . her.

Goddess, does this woman know how to kiss. They all do, but Connie's are the best. (Shhhh, don't tell the others.)

Far too soon, however, she pulls away. At my moan of complaint, she laughs. "Nine wants to be the first."

"First . . . ?" Oh. Realization dawns on me. "Why the fuck does he get to decide?"

It should be my choice. No one elses.

"That's what I said, but he made a sound argument."

"He did?"

"Sex with Nine is different than with anyone else. He knows exactly what the other person needs or wants at any given moment." She looks at me. "He's the perfect choice. Trust me."

Oh. I suddenly understand. And I do trust her.

I'm going to lose my immortal virginity to the Horseman of Famine.

32

That evening, after a beef pot roast, we train in the gym together; more weapons. Cue eye roll. I am legit terrible with fucking weapons.

Connie stands back watching my stances and movement with the twenty-fifth sword/dagger/knife combination we've tried to date. Nothing seems to work.

"Oh my fuck, of course!" Connie yells from nowhere and runs out of the gym like her ass is on fire.

Least she's gotten her spark back.

I continue with the drills she set me—no way am I disobeying her—and twenty minutes later, she runs back in with a stick of carved wood nearly the length of her body in hand.

She holds it out to me. "It's a bo staff."

"A what?" I ask, baffled.

"A bo staff. Originated in Okinawa, Japan in the . . . fifteenth century—I think." She moves her hand along the carved light wood with grace. "It's not as deadly as other, bladed weapons and should work well with your elemental magic with a few protection charms ingrained into the wood."

Realization dawns on me. "You mean, I could use this to assist my air and fire magic? Like a goddamn wizard in the movies?" I can't help but bounce on my feet a little.

"Pretty much."

"Ohmigoddess, this is awesome." I twirl it around in my hands using my air magic, trying out a few basic magic-staff movements. I might have fumbled a little, but I'm doing much better with this than anything else we've tried so far.

"This one is a little too big for your height, and they're usually created personally for the wielder, and you'll need some fire protection magic on the wood, so we'll have to get you one made, but . . . you can practice with this one, if you like?"

I hesitate. "Whose is it?"

She sighs. "Nine's."

I get the feeling there's a story there, but I don't pry. There is always a story with this lot.

"He won't mind. Not for you, anyway."

She grabs the nearest sword, one she isn't massively familiar with, and lowers into her usual protective stance. "Ready?"

I stand a little higher than usual, ensuring all of my enhanced knives are attached to my thigh, and smile. "Bring it on, Conquest."

She smiles that delicious grin of hers that makes her cheeks rise and her dimples deepen before attacking first. Her arm comes in for a jab.

I reflect it with an air-enhanced swipe of my staff. "Damn. This thing is cool."

Her laugh brightens the room, and I find myself distracted momentarily by the smirk on her face. She's planning something, isn't she? Of course she is. The bitch.

I smile as though oblivious, but when she twirls and tries to attack from the right while feigning left, I block with a flick of my wrist, extending the staff outward as though my arm were four-foot long.

"Nice," she says with surprise.

"This staff is easy to use with my magic."

She grins and goes for another attack, which I go to block, but I get there a little too late. "Just think what you could do with it when you unlock your earth magic."

Right, because it's made of wood. "Ohmigoddess, I could extend it, mold it, shape it . . ."

I get distracted by the possibilities, and Connie throws the sword to the floor and leaps at me, arms outstretched. I catch her, and she wraps her legs around my waist.

"This," she says as she kisses me, "is what I've been missing in my life." She showers my face with small kisses that tickle, and I have to fight to get her off of me.

"Stop," I say through a laugh. "I'm . . . going to . . . pee myself."

I push her off and look up, finally able to move my neck, and gasp as Nine, Dea, and Arrie stand in the doorway, looking a little worse for wear, but all are safe.

"Guys!" I run to Dea and jump at him, just like Connie did to me, and he catches me mid-air and twirls me around.

I feel like a princess for a moment, and I won't lie, it feels amazing. Every one of the guys embraces me and lays a small kiss to my lips, and Connie just hangs back and watches us with a smile on her face.

"You're back!"

"We are, Angel. That we are."

"Well," Nine says through a smile, "as great as kissing you is, I'm going to shower. It's been days since I've had a shower."

I wave them all off as they go to their own rooms to shower and rest. Goddess knows they need it. Maybe I can make them all some late-night dinner and bring it to their rooms? Yes, that'll be good.

Or is that too clingy? Too much? Not enough? What if I get their favorite food wrong?

"Stop," Connie says from right beside me. "Whatever spiral your mind has entered, stop." She hugs me. "What you thinkin'?"

I blush. "That I could make them some food before they fall asleep. They're probably hungry."

Starving.

I laugh, and Connie looks at me quizzically. "Nine's hungry."

My favorite food is pizza.

"Pizza for Nine." I think for a moment. "What about Dea and Arrie?" I look to Connie for help.

She looks at me and smiles. "You asking me for advice about how to woo the guys through food?"

Thinking about it for a minute, I nod. "Yes, yes I am. Now woman up and help me." I widen my eyes as much as possible and stick my bottom lip out (yes, I am pleading with the Horseman of Conquest, and yes, I'm also quite shocked at how my life has turned out).

"How can I say no to that?" She sighs. "Arrie doesn't have a favorite food, he just likes variety. Dea likes cheese a lot."

"Fancy cheese pizza, a mixed pizza, and spicy meat pizza. Got it."

She looks at me with a chuckle.

"What?" I sigh. "I only have until they finish showering."

I pick my plasmascreen up from the kitchen table where I left it earlier during dinner and look up fancy pizza recipes. After a couple of minutes, I find a nice-looking one on ciabatta rounds.

"Fancy mini pizzas!"

I ask the house for all the ingredients we don't have and get to work. In twenty minutes, I have three trays of various pizzas, OJ, and coffee/tea.

Connie sits back and watches me work, finding my antics hilarious, and probably checking to make sure I don't burn the house down. Which is fair. Last time I was in here doing anything difficult I nearly burned toast.

"I'll be back," I say to her.

But she shakes her head and says, "Chill with them. I'm going to play some games and head to bed."

She seems solemn, and I wonder if maybe dividing my time between them isn't such a great idea right now.

She needs me.

"You sure? We could play together?"

She frowns at me and turns away, storming off down to the cinema room.

What is that all about?

The trays of food are steaming heat into the otherwise cold kitchen, and I honestly don't have time to go after her. I'll pop down and see her after I make sure the guys are okay.

Yup. That's a good plan.

Right?

I carry the trays on top of one another using air magic and try my best not to trip up the stairs at the same time.

We're all in Dea's room.

Right.

I get to the top of the stairs and don't know which way to turn. It's then I realize that I don't know where Dea's room is.

I'll come get you.

Two minutes later, Nine bumbles down the corridor I explored my very first day out of bed. It's down the other side of the staircase, rather than the left I'd usually take to get to my, Nine, and Connie's room. This corridor eventually leads to Arrie's room, but along the way we enter a small door I haven't thought to check in. It's just a foot taller than Nine and solid black with those large fancy hinges you see in movies based in medieval times.

It's so . . . Death.

That thought has both me and Nine chuckling as we enter the room. The room is . . . not what I expected. It's an odd mix between medieval, gothic Victorian grandeur, and modern-day technological.

I expected the black chandelier and the four-poster bed that has black netting draping down each side, but I didn't expect the workbench in the back that looks like a potion master threw up all over it; nor did I expect the small, hole-in-the-wall feel the room gives me.

Dea clears his throat, and I realize I've been staring at the room while the guys stare at me. "Sorry," I mumble.

"Never been in here before, Killer?" Arrie's tone is slightly suggestive, but he also looks curious.

"No. I've seen everyone else's but not Dea's."

Dea looks at his feet, and if it were possible, he probably would have blushed.

"What's the matter?" I ask as I give each guy their tray of mini pizzas.

"Errr . . ." Dea rubs the back of his neck with his hand in that sexy way all three of these guys do, and I have to focus to stay on track. "It is just . . . the room is always a little surprising to people. It is not what people expect when they look at me."

I sit down next to him on the bed and smile. "It's perfect." It really is. Dea is a down-to-earth kind of guy, and this really reflects that. Sure, he's vain when it comes to how he looks, but he's practical and realistic.

He pulls me into a hug.

"You made pizza?" Arrie asks. Surprise etches at his voice, and I wince.

"I tried." I look to the floor. "The last time I cooked anything I nearly burned toast, so . . . I won't be offended if you ask the house for a decent replacement."

Nine chuckles and looks at me with a strange expression I haven't seen before. It almost looks like . . . love.

No. Nope. Definitely not.

I shoot up from Dea's bed and say, "Err . . . So, goodnight. See you all tomorrow." I rush out of the room.

But Nine grabs my wrist just as I rush out of the doorway and drags me back in. "You're not doing that."

"Doing what?"

"Running away the moment someone cares."

"I don't . . ." I don't know.

Nine turns me around and pulls me into a hug.

"Sorry," I mumble, "it's been a tough few days."

Arrie pipes up at that and asks, "How's she doing?" through a mumble of mini pizza.

I shake my head and let Nine lead me into a chair that he sits on first so I'm sitting on his lap. He wraps his arms around my waist and takes a deep breath.

"She was doing great until . . ." They look at me expectantly. "Until she asked if we killed him. Obviously, I told her the truth."

Nine flinches beneath me. "Well," he says, "she would have found out eventually." He rubs circles along my back. "You haven't done anything wrong."

"That's not the point."

"No, it is not," Dea says. "The point Angel is trying to make is that Connie is unhappy, and she does not know how to fix it."

"Time," Arrie grumbles. "Give her time."

I think about Anthony and how if Connie didn't give him some time, he'd probably still be around today and old enough to have gray hair and grandchildren.

"She told you?" Nine asks incredulously.

"Right after I told her we killed him." Looking around, we all wear matching expressions of concern. "She'll be fine," I say, more to myself than anyone else. She has to be.

Nine reaches for my shoulders and rubs them, placing gentle pressure in all the right places, and I nearly moan—I just manage to hold back before I take this rather sweet moment in a whole other direction.

"You need to stop worrying about everything all at once."

Dea nods. "Take things one issue at a time. Connie will be fine." Dea comes over after finishing off his last mini pizza (he ate them all, woo!) and wraps his arms around my waist as he entangles them in Nine's. (Two-way cuddles are great, by the way—in case you needed to know.)

"These weren't half bad, Killer." Arrie smiles at me. "We can make a chef of you yet."

"Really? You like them?" I shoot out of my seat and run over to Arrie. "They were . . . nice?"

He laughs. "Yes." He stands and wraps me in his arms. "Now stop making me all gushy and start being annoying again. It's much easier to deal with."

Now it's my turn to laugh. I tickle him and, just when I have him writhing on the floor, I kick him in the ass. "Good enough?"

He growls, so I take that as a yes and leave to head to bed. I'll check on Connie in the morning.

33

"What now?" I ask over breakfast the next morning. "We've lost the entire Fae Court and half the Vampire population. We officially have an enemy."

"We do not have anything, Angel. Humans have an enemy, and it is our job to ensure balance is kept."

Connie's been quiet all morning, but she chooses that moment to participate in the conversation. "They're trying to replicate Horseman blood."

The room falls cold and silent as everyone digests her bombshell, but it seems I'm the only one who doesn't understand the implications, because Nine looks up at me and says, "When a Vampire feeds off of someone more powerful, their magic gets a big boost. The more powerful the donor, the more magic they get." His eyes plead with me to make the connection.

"So when they feed off of a Horseman . . ."

"They're never more powerful," Connie finishes for him. "They'd be unstoppable with a Horseman-fueled Vampire army."

"But they can't even synthesize human blood," Nine says with a frown. "What makes them think they can synthesize Horseman blood?"

Connie's eyes fall to the floor as her hands start shaking.

"What is it?" I ask as I grab her hand in mine.

"They were experimenting with using magical properties of different species' blood to try to recreate Horseman blood, but to do that they had to extract a lot of blood from me."

"That's why you were so weak . . ." I realize.

She nods, still avoiding our gazes.

"Just how much blood did they take from you, Connie?" Dea comes over to rest a hand on her shoulder.

She flinches at his touch, and he pulls his hand away. "Enough to fuel an army for a few days."

Nine's jaw drops. "They know that we heal quickly?" She nods. "So they used your ability to quickly replenish your blood supply to bleed you dry."

It wasn't a question, but she nods anyway.

Arrie grumbles something in his native language, and for once, I'm not curious as to what it means because I whisper my own expletive in Japanese at the same time.

"*Kuto.*"

I stand and place my dish in the dishwasher. "We need to alert the Vampire Royal Council. Bring them here." I direct that at Dea, who nods and clears his own dishes before walking off to follow my orders.

"Nine?"

He looks at me in question.

"Meet me in the library, and bring your genius mind with you."

He follows Dea out the kitchen.

"Arrie?"

"Yes, Killer?"

"I need to know where the Shifters and Witches stand with this new development." I turn to Connie. "Feel up to going with him?"

She nods and smiles. I thought having something to do might help. Something far away from Vampires.

"Right, wait until tomorrow. I might have something to help."

I REALLY, REALLY, REALLY WANT TO WORK ON SOME TELEPORTATION CRYSTALS THAT'LL WORK backwards, and take us from *Sheruta* to anywhere on Earth. That way, mission times will be shorter, we can portal straight to councils, and I won't have to deal with the portal-vomiting situation.

Racing to the library, I find Nine in the stacks, pulling various books on Fae magic, charms, and teleportation. He's heard my idea.

Yup.

"Good. I'm going to start researching by using the Seer Stone."

Okay.

The Seer Stone has trouble answering my questions:

1. How do I create a teleportation crystal?
2. Teleportation Fae magic
3. Can you mix Witch charm magic with Fae spell magic?

It doesn't even give me an answer to that last one. I guess they wouldn't usually try. Goddess, what I wouldn't give for a Witch-Fae hybrid. Ha! If only that were biologically possible.

"Okay," Nine says from behind a shelf to my left. "I've got some good resources on creating teleportation crystals so you can see the theory behind it for yourself, though I'll teach you how to make them anyway." He pops around the corner and smiles from behind a stack of books that reaches his chin. "I've also got resources on charm magic, and thought if we looked at the basic building blocks of both Witch and Fae magic, we might be able to find a way to combine them."

"Sounds like a plan."

He places the books down on the desk with a thud, and we get to work. Nine has a penchant for remembering details while I like to take notes and flip back through when necessary; I find more links that way. But there is one thing we share: we both leave books open on various pages, spine up, so we can come back to them later. The floor is littered in various books, papers, and objects, all in complete disarray to anyone not included in our system, which we started piling onto after the desk creaked with the ninety-second book I placed on it.

We've been at it for ten hours, and dark has finally descended. No one has bothered us, so we assume they are all okay, but I'm getting hungry and frustrated with our lack of progress.

"There must be something somewhere!" I growl, mirroring the growl of my stomach. "We can easily create transportation crystals that use a mental-magic link to take us anywhere on *Sheruta*, so why can't we just reverse the spell?"

Nine runs a hand through his hair. "Because that would require reversing an ingredient there is no cure for. Not one person in history has ever managed to reverse the side effects of the gugi plant."

"I know, I know." The question is rhetorical.

Nine huffs at me, and I can tell we are seconds away from having an argument over something stupid. We need a break.

"Dinner!" a familiar gruff voice rings out from behind us. Arrie stands there with a tray in each hand.

It smells like . . . ramen!

"Fuck, yes," I mumble and run over to him, dodging various stacks of books along the way. "Thank you." I place a quick peck to his cheek and take the tray to a relatively clear spot a few meters from the desk.

Nine follows me, and we both sit in exhausted silence as we eat our ramen and drink our smoothies. Goddess, I've never been so thankful for food before.

Arrie stands there and stares at our mess in astonishment. "What are you trying to do?"

"Create a teleportation crystal that can get us from *Sheruta* to anywhere we want on Earth."

His eyebrows shoot to his hairline. "You can do that?"

Nine and I look at him and shake our heads. "We've come up with most of the theory, but we've been stuck for the last four hours on how to reverse the effects of the gugi plant used to stabilize the Fae magic's direction."

"Why would that need reversing? Surely you can just use it the other way around?" He sits down where I've just been and starts rummaging through my pile of useless papers.

"Could you . . . not?" I whisper, afraid he'll mess with my system.

"He can't mess with your system," Nine says, "he's literally a strategist."

Arrie nods. "I can see what strategy you've used and am only picking things out of your discard pile."

"I didn't realize that applied to non-battle scenarios," I say, and then wince. "Sorry."

Arrie shakes his head. "I don't use it outside of the battlefield often, I just didn't want you mad at me for ruining your strategy."

"Good shout," Nine says.

I punch him in the arm. "I'm not that scary."

They both look at me like I kicked a pigeon—dumbfounded—and laugh.

"We both know you would have punched him in the face if he ruined that system of yours, Sweetie." Nine's red hair dances in the light as he continues laughing.

"Would not."

Arrie comes over and sits on my other side. "Yeah, you would have, Killer. But that's okay." He wraps an arm around me. "Think I can handle a little temper tantrum."

Nine scoffs. "None of us can handle yours, and it's going to be the same with her. She's stronger than any of us. And when we've trained her up properly, she'll beat us all in a fight, one versus four."

Arrie slumps his shoulders and agrees.

"I don't think that's—"

"He's right."

But . . . that could be dangerous, couldn't it? One bad day and I could bring down a fucking country. I don't want that kind of power or responsibility. I just want some ice cream, some more of Arrie's cooking, a good book, and some great sex. Is that too much to ask for?

"Stop spiraling!" Nine shouts. "It's fine." He grabs my hand. "You're not alone."

Arrie grabs my other hand. "He's right."

"You say that a lot."

Arrie shrugs. "He's right a lot."

Nine chuckles and lightly taps Arrie on the arm in that way guys do to show affection that I'm not sure I'll ever get used to.

I'm a hugger, what can I say.

"Ugh. Guy nonsense."

"You know," Nine says, "you're a guy, too."

I groan. "Don't remind me."

"Does that . . ." Arrie begins and pauses, looking for the right words, "bother you?"

"What? Suddenly growing a dick every time I want to use my other magics?"

He grimaces while hiding a laugh but nods.

"Yes."

"I thought you'd come to terms with that, Sweetie?" I get up to leave the conversation, but both Nine and Arrie grab a wrist each and hold me back. "Nope. Nuh-uh. You're going to talk about it so that you don't freak out and melt down about it three days from now after your mind has overthought it."

Gah! This fucking shitty asshole.

"I'll have you know," he begins, and I can tell by the smirk on his face that he's about to say something inappropriate. "I have a fantastic asshole."

Arrie tries hard to hold in the laugh but is unsuccessful, and he barrels over in a fit of giggles I didn't realize he had in him. Goddess, that laugh melts me every time. I hoard every little chuckle, every snort that slips his defenses, but this, this is just gorgeousness on a silver platter.

You have a real thing for his laugh, don't you?

I don't give a shit how insane it is, it's the most beautiful laugh I've ever fucking heard, and the fact he doesn't laugh a lot just makes hearing it all the sweeter. Quit judging me!

He holds his hands up and backs away. "No judgment." He runs a hand through that gorgeous red hair. "But seriously, what's so wrong with having two sexes?"

"Seriously?" I give them both an incredulous look. "How many things are wrong with being a guy? How many times have you been looked at funny when you smile at a child in the street? How often have women crossed the sidewalk to avoid you for just being a guy?"

They both look to the floor.

"Now times that by two, because I also have all of the sexist issues of being a woman, and you might start to see the problem!"

Arrie huffs and continues sifting through my piles, careful to put them back in the same order and place he found them.

"You get both the good sides, though, too. Like, you get to be the only person on the planet who knows if childbirth or being kicked in the balls hurts more." Nine smiles handsomely and angles his face toward the light the moment he notices me staring.

He's such an egomaniac.

Yeah, but you love me really.

That I do.

He freezes. I freeze. The entire room falls silent. And I just want the earth to open up and swallow me whole.

I . . . what? What have I done? Oh my goddess, I've ruined everything. He'll never want to sleep with me now. What if he doesn't even want to be friends? Oh shit, what if I've ruined the tea—

SILENCE! Nine shouts louder than I've ever heard him shout before.

Once my mind has officially stopped spiraling, which takes another few seconds, if I'm honest, he grabs me by the waist and yanks me to him. But rather than slap me stupid or tell me to pack my things, he gently grabs my lips with his and tells me just how much he loves me back.

It's a sweet kiss, one full of promise and passion; not the kind of passion you fall into a melted puddle over, but the kind that leaves you questioning your very existence because the person who's sharing their heart with you in that moment has just changed your entire being in one simple second. In one second, you've gone from, perhaps, maybe having feelings for someone and being in denial, to knowing for utter certainty that what you share with them is indispensable—crucial to your happiness—and that you'll do anything to protect it.

It's the kind of kiss that changes your world.

I love you too, Sweetie.

I sniff and feel the not-so-familiar tingle of tears run down my cheeks. Damn it. Now I'm crying.

Nine swipes them away with a gentle brush of his thumb. "You know, you've ruined my plan slightly."

"Oh, that." The memory of Connie spilling the beans ripples across my mind, and I feel instantly guilty. "Sorry," I say through a hiccup.

Nine sighs and pulls away from me. "Never mind. At least she didn't you tell you the deets. Because I never told the team."

"Soooo," I say, trying to be suggestive, "you have it all planned out?"

He nods. "Just need some time to get everything ready." He leans down to whisper in my ears, but in true Nine fashion, he mentally says, *Don't worry. You'll love it. Promise.* He pecks me on the cheek and sits by Arrie, who is still flicking through my research notes, oblivious to my world changing before his very eyes.

"I just . . . err . . . need some air." I run out of the room like my life depends on it and race to the kitchen door—past Dea, who's sitting at the table reading the news—and into the garden.

The stars are bright tonight, and I briefly wonder if that's a coincidence. Suddenly I'm able to see, and I don't even know why I didn't notice before. I'm totally in love with them all, and fuck if I don't want to wrap them all up in a Christmas cracker and keep them to myself. Does that make me selfish? They're sharing me, why shouldn't they be allowed to be shared?

Well, I guess they are in a way—with each other. I would never stop them from being together as more than just friends; what happens in the team stays in the team.

"Hey," Dea says from behind me. "Are you okay?"

I turn around, fresh tears on my face, and he fazes right up to me and wraps me in his arms. Yup, I'm definitely in love with this one, too. But we have a lot to work out. Like why I'm weirdly addicted to his Angel form, and what he and Nine talked about when I left.

"Tell me what the matter is . . ."

"Oh." I sniff. "It's nothing. Honest."

He looks down at me with a look that says, 'yeah, right.'

"I might have just told Nine I love him, and now I'm scared, and I'm totally in love with the rest of you, too. I'm confused and concerned, and I have such bigger issues to be dealing with right now than my love life, and—"

Dea places a finger to my lips and sweeps me up, placing me gently on the grass. We gaze up at the stars in silence for a while, finding comfort in his presence in a way I don't with the others, and it gets me thinking.

"Why is it different between me and you?"

"I honestly do not know, Angel."

"Whenever I'm around your Angel form, it's like I've come home. Like I can't get enough of just touching you and knowing you're mine . . ." I gasp. "Sorry, that sounded crazy, and you're totally not mine."

"I am yours. Always." He turns to me and kisses me on the forehead. "Just not yours alone."

"I would never get between you and Nine."

"I know. That is one of the reasons I love you, Angel."

I shiver. "You too, huh?"

"I think you will find the others feel the same way."

"But I don't get it . . . How? You've all known each other for so long, but I've barely been here a year."

Dea shrugs. "Love is . . . unpredictable. Sometimes it just happens, and you cannot do anything to stop it. My advice? Just go with it and enjoy yourself. Life gets a bit tedious if you stop to ask every question before jumping in."

Can he be not wise and all-knowing for, like, just a minute? But goddess, he's right, isn't he?

"So you're saying I should do everything that makes me happy that I can? Just in case I live a depressing immortal life?"

Dea nods. "Mortals do the same thing because they have a short lifespan, but for us, it is not about dying and not living life, but about making sure the lives we do live make us happy."

So far, I've tried to put my former life behind me, but I don't think that made me very happy. Maybe I should be trying to find a way of doing both: having my old life and my new one together.

But there's one thing I want to do first, and luckily, the man in question is lying right beside me. "Dea?"

He moves his head to the side in question, and I press my lips gently to his. His hands grip mine and yank me over him so that I'm now straddling his waist and leaning down to continue the kiss. "Yes, Angel?"

I take a deep breath, gathering all the courage I can, and say, "I love you."

A smile lights up his face, and his eyes that are usually that amazing galaxy color turn a bright gold as he gazes up at me. "I love you too, Angel."

"C'mon," I say after one last quick kiss, "maybe you can help us."

"With what?"

"Teleportation crystals that take us to Earth."

34

Turns out Dea knows the answer and that Arrie was on the right track all along. Rather than try to reverse the effects of the gugi plant, we can just use it in the other direction if we modify it with a Witch charm. So the theory is down, it's three am, and we're all more than a little exhausted, but I still have to figure out how to combine Witch charms into a Fae spell. I'm hoping it'll come naturally to me, given that I'm the Horseman of Magic, but so far, no luck.

I asked the house for a large bed in the library about an hour ago, and so far, Arrie is sprawled in the center looking oddly peaceful as he snores away, while Dea, Nine, and I are still brainstorming over how to manage this bullshit.

"Tell me again how you managed to rewrite the Fae spell in Ecuador?" Nine asks.

I sigh and repeat myself for the fifth time. "I found the key points of the spell circle, which were at each compass point, and reworked each section to include us into the spell."

Nine sighs. "That's not helpful."

"No, because that approach will not work here."

"Well . . ." I smile as an idea comes to me. "Maybe it will." I look at Nine and Dea, who both look at me with matching confused expressions.

"Your thoughts are running too fast to see, Sweetie. You'll have to explain."

"We've been attacking this with magical theory in mind, following rules of magic, because that's what everyone has to do." They nod. "Well, I'm the Horseman of Magic, I don't need those rules. Why can't I just write the charm into the spell?"

Nine frowns. "Because no one can do that," he grumbles. "You can't just rewrite a spell to suit your needs, you have to write it with the rules in place otherwise they won't work."

"What happens if the spell does not work?" Dea asks.

"It could just be a dud and won't activate, but at worst, a spell like this could scatter the user's existence all over the ether."

It's my turn to look confused. "What the fuck is the ether?"

Nine waves my question away with a quick answer. "It's what magical scientists theorize is between two pockets of space. What we travel between to get somewhere when teleporting."

Oh. So that's the 'wherever' I vomited into. Cool.

Nine chuckles and nods.

"I'll try it first, then."

Both Dea and Nine groan in protest, but I hold up a hand. "I'm the one most likely to be able to put myself back together if it goes wrong."

Nine responds reluctantly, "She's right. If anyone can pull their particles together again, it's a Horseman of Magic."

"I still think that idea is awful." Dea sighs. "What if you cannot achieve that?"

I shrug. "Then we get to see just how much Fate needs me." They both frown. "Look, it's the best chance we have, and I really want this to work. It'll be so advantageous to our work that it's worth the risk."

They sit either side of me and each place a hand on my knee, looking at me in complete adoration, and the attention is too much. I have to look away.

"We are with you, Angel," Dea whispers.

Nine kisses my cheek and whispers, "Always."

I assume they've had some kind of internal chat during the last few hours and are both up to speed on . . . everything. Goddess, I can't get my mind around it.

Errrgh, I'm gonna have to spill the beans to Connie on Friday.

Yup. Don't worry. You don't need to talk to us about anything. We're all on the same page.

"Definitely," Dea adds.

"Okay then." I take a deep breath and remove myself from between them. "Time to try writing a Witch charm into a Fae spell."

"Yes." Nine looks like a kid in a candy store, and I briefly wonder if he's tried this before.

"Yup, and with no results other than a few blown-off fingers."

I look at him with fear. "Blown-off fingers?" I don't want to blow off any of my fingers, goddess damn it.

"Don't worry, they grow back pretty quickly."

"Not the point!"

Dea chuckles behind me and places his hands on my shoulder. "You will be fine, Angel. I promise."

He doesn't know that for certain, but I'm thankful for the attempt at comfort nonetheless.

Right. Time to attempt this magical bad boy!

I can do this.

Taking a deep breath, I focus on the spellbead in front of me. At the moment, it lies there completely see-through, but as I pour my magical intent into the bead (which are specially created to hold magic for a limited amount of time), it turns a silvery-white color.

"There," I mutter, "a reversal spell with directional intent."

Stage one complete.

Fae spells are a little harder, as I have to apply all of the ingredients and runes to the crystal first and then include the incantation. So far, I just add the spellbead to the ingredients and hope that works. Yes, this looks a lot like a Witch's cauldron as I dip a glowing crystal with runes etched into the side into a pot of liquefied ingredients. (I am just as surprised by the lack of magical-looking voodoo as you.)

Incantation time.

This is the kind of magical voodoo you see in the movies, and I can't help but bounce on my feet a little. (And guess what? This you can do in any language, so I choose Japanese.) It feels right. Using my first and native language for something as powerful as this.

"With this crystal, I imbue,

the power of Fate and magic anew.

With this intent, I enspell,

a way to travel and keep us well."

"That should do it."

I open my eyes and look at the crystal. It just looks like the usual purple crystals Dea hands out at the beginning of missions. Guess we won't know until we try it.

Grabbing it out of the potion bowl (which Nine frequently reminds me is not a potion bowl but an ingredients bowl—cue eye roll), I grab it in both hands and assess the magic. All the runes are in place, the ingredients seem to have worked, and I can tell the intention is right.

With no reason to be concerned, I smash it at my feet and think of somewhere I know on earth, somewhere I can picture easily but not get into trouble when I pop in. Unfortunately, I can't really think of anywhere good, since my experiences so far have all been in official buildings, hotels, and dangerous places. The safe-ish place I think of, however, is that party house Prince Lucien frequents.

At least I won't be arrested or stabbed. Hopefully.

Best of a bad bunch and all that jazz . . .

It takes a little longer than I experienced going the other way, but I eventually pop up in the front garden, which is empty because there's no party being had.

Strange.

I seem to be in one piece: all ten fingers and all ten toes wiggled just fine, and I have them attached to all four limbs. Reaching my hand to my face, I feel two eyes, one nose, two ears, and a mouth with all my teeth still intact. Boobs and dick are firmly in place, and I can still switch between forms just fine. Oh, and my favorite feature—my pale-pink, waist-length hair—is fine, too.

So far, so good.

Now I need to get back, but the blackness of the atmosphere here is making me curious. Why is it so quiet? Now I'll admit, I didn't really pay attention to the news over the last week after we turned the world on its head, but I had every plan to begin all that nonsense again the moment we start getting back on track tomorrow. So I haven't seen anything about New Orleans or the Vampire Royal Council having problems.

Maybe I should have been paying more attention? I mean, Dea was reading the news, so he would have said something. Right?

Well, maybe not. He could have been trying to shield me while I was taking a few days and we were all recovering. Especially Connie.

Dammit, Dea!

I expand my Vampire hearing as far as possible, but nothing other than a gentle breeze and a few rolling cans echoes back.

Strange.

Cities are usually full of sounds that I have to block out as background noise, but New Orleans is . . . silent.

Should I investigate before heading back?

Ugh. I have no idea. And I didn't think to take one of those cool contact pods with me before I teleported here because I am supposed to be going right back.

The guys will worry, so I should be quick.

At a full Vampire sprint, I run through a few streets to find nothing but empty houses and rubbish strewn across the equally empty streets. What the fuck?

It's like the apocalypse or some shit.

I run toward the Vampire Royal Council building and see lights still on through the shaded windows, so they must still be up and running. But what about the city's general population?

I race through a few more streets to find a couple of back alley bars open and a few Vampires lurking around. But no humans. It's empty except for Vampires. Even the Shifters have vanished.

Okay, I should head back.

Just as I think that, a group of four Vampires walk out of the shadows I noticed them lurking in earlier and smile at me.

A slimy, greasy-haired blond man leads the group, and by the looks of his cruel smile, I'm not going to like whatever he has to say. "What do we have here?"

"Horseman of Magic, isn't it?" one of the Vampires on the left asks.

"What do you want?" I ask, more confidence in my voice than I feel, as I try to suppress the shaking in my hands.

I'm here alone. No backup. No weapons. Only my teleportation crystal to get me back home. And I know I should use it, I do, but I am soooo curious. I need to know what happened here.

"What happened here?"

They all stop walking and look at each other. "It's been a week since you and your Horsemen friends came here and started a human-Vampire war, and you're asking how?"

"W-W-What?"

Shit. All the pieces are coming together. The fake fight. The video recordings of it going live online. Shit. Shit. Shit. I turn to run away, ignoring the calls of the other Vampires wanting to goad me into a fight, and find an empty backyard to activate the teleportation crystal in.

I land back in the library to Dea and Nine fussing over me. They both check me for injuries, but I wave them off.

"Shit, Sweetie, are you okay?"

Turning sternly to Dea, I ask, "What has been happening in New Orleans?"

He flinches. "I did not know that is where you would go." He gives me an apologetic smile. "Humans have evacuated the city."

Nine looks at him. "What the hell, bro?"

"I did not want to worry Angel until we returned to work fully."

I punch him in the arm with a little more force than necessary, and he stumbles backward. "It could be the middle of the night and that shit should have been mentioned." I poke him in the chest. "Never try to protect my emotions again." I sigh. "Not at the expense of the war."

Dea nods. "I was just trying to help."

"I know." Rubbing my hands up and down his arms, I lay a gentle kiss to his lips. "Just don't let others suffer because of me. Please."

He nods.

Well, no one says a relationship this . . . multifaceted would be straight forward.

I can see the sun peeking over the horizon out of the nearest window and sigh. I look over to where Arrie is sleeping on the bed and decide that he looks like the perfect place to curl up and sleep. His body is so warm as I crawl up next to him and wrap an arm around his chest.

"Killer . . . ?"

"Shhh . . . It's just me. Go back to sleep."

He looks so cute, I have to suppress a giggle.

(But shh . . . don't tell him that.)

35

"All right," I say to Dea the next morning after breakfast. "Come on. Spill it, Angel dick."

Connie splutters a laugh, and the sound is music to my ears. Dea shoots her a 'what the fuck' look, but she just shrugs. "She's right. Sometimes you can be an Angel dick."

He sighs as he finishes shoving his plate in the dishwasher. "I just did not want to worry you, Angel." He places his hands on either side of my arms. "But New Orleans was evacuated three days ago. Humans left. Only Vampires stayed, but there might be a few other species left, too."

I shake my head. "Just Vampires. Hungry ones."

This is all my fault. Not only is this the worst possible response to us going public, but we also took out the main blood supply outside of the SC's restricted supply. "If we don't do something, they'll starve."

Nine clears his throat as he walks up to me. "We should split up. Take on different missions."

"Good plan." I look to Arrie. "Go to the Shifter Council and ask for their aid, then pop in on the Witches and update them. Get a feel for where they're at now the world's gone to shit."

Arrie doesn't really say anything, but his face tells me he doesn't mind going alone.

"Dea," I ask, "did you manage to get the Vampire Royal Council to meet us here?"

"Yes. They will be here this afternoon. They seemed eager to speak, so I assume they will ask for some assistance."

"We'll make a plan about the blood supply and New Orleans after we've spoken to them."

Connie steps forward and grabs my hand, not meeting my eyes. "What about us?" She looks to Nine. "Am I not going with Arrie?"

"No. Because I have a special project I want you to help Nine with." She looks at me with those beautifully puzzled green eyes, and I could have kissed her there and then and never stopped. "How much experience do you have with the Hunter Society?"

She flinches. "A bit. A few contacts."

"Good."

Nine asks me what I'm thinking, which is weird in itself, but I just wave him away. "Later."

I turn to Arrie and give him the two crystals, one to take him to Earth and one to get him home. "At some point, I will work out how to teleport within Earth, but right now, that's the best I've got."

"You really managed it?" Arrie asks, surprise etching his voice.

"Yes, asshole. No need to sound so surprised." I cross my arms over my chest and have to resist the urge to pout.

Fucking dick.

Arrie just grumbles something under his breath and goes to smash the crystal at his feet, but I rush him last minute and try to wrap my puny arms around his huge body.

"Don't get injured. Be quick."

He nods and smiles at me as I let go, and he's off in a plume of red smoke.

Damn those things really are cliché.

"Okay, Nine, Connie?" They both look at me with a gentle smile. "Meet me in the library."

They nod and walk off to the library, probably both curious as hell about my secret plan. I'm trying not to think about it too much, lest Nine overhear, so I instead turn to Dea.

"When is the meeting scheduled for?"

"Three pm in the conference room in the east wing."

"East wing? Conference room?"

Dea smiles and chuckles at me, but he eventually offers me his hand. I take it, enjoying the sense of mystery this house provides. "Let me show you."

I prepare myself for a nice, small adventure as Dea carries me bridal style through the kitchen doors and down the servant's hallway. We pass many rooms I haven't seen before, and soon I'm lost and dizzy from all the twists and turns we've taken, but eventually we come to a more professional-looking section of the house that's clearly designed for formal meetings with important people.

"This is . . . what exactly?"

Dea puts me on my feet. "This is the meeting wing. We hold important meetings with important people here."

The whole place feels like an office, from the clinical smell to the pristine white-washed walls. Ugh. Not to my taste.

"You do not seem impressed, Angel?"

"It's just very . . . office-like. You've seen one office, you've seen them all." I shrug and turn to go back the way we came.

But Dea grabs my arm and spins me back, wrapping his arms around my waist. "Then maybe I should find a better way to entertain you." He lifts me off the ground and pulls me toward him, where I wrap my legs around his waist and sit there staring into his amazing galaxy eyes.

"Your eyes are beautiful."

"Thank you." He walks us over to the couch in a small lounge area of the waiting room and lays me down. "But you're definitely the most beautiful thing in this house."

Goddess, damn him. I'm a molten puddle of feelings all over again, and this time I can't escape them because he knows I love him.

"It wouldn't be a mistake this time . . ."

Dea leans over me on the couch and rests on his forearms. "No, with you it would not. But with Nine, it would."

Right. I forgot about that. He wants to be my first, and the others all agreed. Doesn't mean I can't enjoy the moment.

Having allowed myself to relax around the team more of late, especially Nine and Dea, I relax into the moment and grab his lips in a crushing kiss that I hope portrays everything I'm feeling in this moment—from the love and happiness of being accepted, to the ease of sharing them all and seeing them smile. It's all perfect.

Dea pulls away and looks at me with tears in his eyes. "I love you too, Angel."

I brush the tear that threatens to escape away and give him what I hope is a questioning look.

He sits up, pulling me with him and into his lap. "It is nothing of importance, but I will tell you anyway."

"Story time?"

He smiles weakly. "Story time, Angel." He clears his throat. "About five hundred years into our lives, we met this group of lion Shifters who were being hunted for their manes in what is now the plains of Africa."

"Wow. Lions?"

He chuckles. "Yes. They were . . . impressive, to say the least. But they were struggling against a local Witch Coven who used their manes as an ingredient in some potion that made them stay young. It became popular all over the continent and provided many riches for the Witch Coven."

I know exactly where this is going.

"Their Shifter pack was being decimated, but no one knew what to do about it. We passed them in the area while on another mission and decided to stay and help. We tracked down the Witches and scared them into stopping their cruel hunts. Instead, Nine encouraged them to pay the lion Shifters for wads of their manes."

"Clever Famine."

"It is his job, after all." Dea leans back, and I can see him shutting himself off from the world.

I don't want that. So I turn in his lap to face him and grab his face between my two hands. "It's okay. It's just us right now."

He takes a deep breath. "The plan worked, of course, but it started a war between Shifters and Witches, and we felt semi-responsible, so we tried to help."

"Did it work?"

He shakes his head, no. "We tried, but . . . nothing worked. Eventually, they fought themselves to extinction. Both sides."

"The Witches and the Shifters?"

"We do not always win, Angel." He coughs. "But anyway, while the others left when they saw no point in helping a defeated cause, I stayed."

His eyes avoid mine, and his cheeks are a slight red color, but I just sit there and smile at him, encouraging him to continue.

"There was this Shifter. Haji." His hand traces the tattoo underneath his black t-shirt, and I realize this must be *the* Shifter. "He was . . ."

Dea doesn't have the words, so I help. "Perfect?"

He looks at me and nods. "Perfect."

"How long were you together?"

Dea looks at me with surprise etched all over his face. "Six years, until he died in the final battle between his people and the Witch Coven."

Tears flow down his face freely now, and I don't make a move to catch them. Sometimes, crying frees the soul. This feels like one of those moments.

"I—"

"Please, do not pity me. It was a wonderful six years." He wraps his arms around me. "But that was not the point of this story. Ever since then, I have never . . ."

Wait a minute. "You haven't been in a relationship in 1500 years?"

He shakes his head. "We are immortal, Angel. Loving a mortal can only end one way."

"What about Nine?"

Dea chuckles. "I knew you would ask that. But Nine and I have only been a relatively recent . . . thing. Two hundred years, at most."

I smile. "It can be scary to love without knowing what the future holds." I lace his fingers through mine. "But how about we try together?"

"I would like that."

36

I walk into the library an hour later, trying my best not to cry at Dea's pain and be a blubbering mess, but these guys make me feel so many emotions, it's crazy. (I swear I'm not a crazy mess all the time. Pinkie promise.)

"Sweetie?" Nine wanders around the corner of the bookcase and frowns at my tears before rifling through my mind. He instantly sobers any facial expression and opens his arms for a hug. "Come here."

"Hon?" Connie walks around the same corner and runs to me the moment she sees me crying. "What's wrong?"

Nine chuckles. "Nothing's wrong. But Dea told her the story of Haji, and now she can't stop crying, and she hates that it's making her cry in the first place."

Connie giggles and pulls me into her arms, and I just let her, absorbing every modicum of comfort I can get.

Goddess, why can't I stop crying? I have a really cool idea, plan, and stuff to put in place.

"You have a plan?" Nine asks. "A secret plan that you're not letting me see?" The curious look on his face is enough to stop the hiccupping tears.

"It's . . . a . . . surprise."

"And I'm supposed to help with this? You realize how un-nerdy I am, don't you?"

I laugh. "Relax. There's two parts to the plan, and I need someone to do the non-nerdy bit."

Connie cracks her knuckles. "Let's do this!"

I lead them both to the pile of paperwork in the study area and yank out the giant A1 sheet of paper I was doing planning on before Arrie woke up the other morning.

"Meet Operation Anti-Hunter Society."

The schematics before me are pretty basic, and mostly consist of a mindmap with several main branches for the initial stages of development, and then of smaller things to consider.

"I want to develop a quest society. You know, like in all the fantasy games?"

Nine laughs, clearly not taking me seriously, so I frown at him, and he shuts up. "You're serious?"

"Yes." I cough to clear my throat. "The issue with the Hunter Society is that it was formed with only one purpose in mind. But what if anyone could ask for help? What if a family of Vampires needed some new complicated Fae spell to help build them better daylight control for their new house? What if the Witches needed some help guarding the change for their new coven location?"

"You want to create a digital help board? Where anyone can apply their skills, no matter their species?" Nine looks at me in awe for a moment, and I go a little shy. "That's . . ."

"Brilliant," Connie finishes for him. "That's brilliant."

"I just thought that it would help bring communities together: magical and non-magical, higher supes and lower supes . . ." I pause, taking in what Connie just said. "Wait, you think it's a good idea?"

Nine grabs me by the waist. "I knew there was a reason you were the new Horseman, Sweetie. And this"—he gestures to the basic schematics of my plan—"is why."

Connie joins us with a smile. "So where do we start?"

"Well, we need a data-app that people can download to their personal chips and access whenever. That way, they can look for and/or post new jobs on the go."

"It should match to a website, too."

I nod as Nine's mental cogs turn; he has that faraway look on his face matched with that curious smile that's a dead giveaway.

"And we'll need backing," Connie says. "That's where I come in, right?"

"Right." I sigh. "Leave the Vampires and Fae for a minute and just focus on preparing a pitch for the SC, Shifter council, and the Witches. We probably won't get the Witches on board, but it will be good to include them anyway."

She nods. "I'll help Nine plan the data-app so I know what it's going to look like, and then I'll get to work."

"Sweetie," Nine says, "the Vampire Royal Council are starting to arrive."

I groan. "Right. Gotta go. I'll be back later." I wave as I run out of the library and to the office wing of the house Dea showed me earlier.

"Ah, Angel, there you are," Dea says from behind me.

The foyer is starting to fill with the members of the Vampire Royal Council, and having this many Vampires around after we just spent a whole week trying not to be seriously injured by many of their kind is more than a little unnerving. But I spot Prince Lucien in the background, trying his best to blend in and not stick out.

He smiles and waves at us before sprinting over. "How is my little Horseman?"

"Ugh. I hate that nickname." I sigh but laugh, brushing it off. "Things are not good, Lucien. Not good at all." I turn to Dea and ask, "Did you invite . . . you know, him?"

Dea shakes his head. "I told the king we would like an audience with the Council without him present. He was none too happy but obliged."

"Ohhh, and the drama unfolds. Who are we talking about?" Prince Lucien's white hair ruffles as he laughs at our seriousness.

"You'll find out, little Vampire Prince." I smirk at him and watch as the doors open and the king walks in. "Here he is."

"Indeed," Dea mumbles before turning to the nearest member of staff we hired last minute for this event and says, "Please open the meeting room doors and start ushering people in."

The small, mousy-haired man bows his head and hurries to do as asked.

"Time to yell at bunch of Vampires," Dea whispers in my ear as we watch everyone filter into the room beyond the foyer.

The room is a pretty standard meeting room, but the chairs are loungers and the seating is arranged to mimic the Vampire Royal Council's hierarchy, with a couch at the front for the king. Prince Lucien, I notice, sits at the far back, away from everyone. He must not be favored among his kind.

Wonder why? Sarcasm laces my thoughts.

I walk to the front of the room and decide that I want to do this in my male form so I can avoid all the Vampire-ness of the situation. I stand at the front, a snarl on my face as I try to look as menacing as possible, and face the king.

"This is not a pleasant visit. I have bad news, and quite frankly, I couldn't care less if you believe me or not."

The king sighs and goes to stand, but I hold out my hand to keep him sat.

"I'll take questions and debates later. You need to listen first. I'm done playing politics. I'm tired."

He nods, allowing me to continue.

"The Rogue Vampire Faction have teamed up with the Fae Court and Bandio Bontanos. They're being led by Prince Phillipe of the Vampire Royal Council." I hold out a hand to silence everyone's gasps and rising fury at the accusations. "You're going to ask for proof, and I have nothing concrete, but we're pretty sure they're working against the Supernatural Council and are wanting to start a war."

I wait for the gasps and rising tide of whispers to die down before continuing.

"Now I know Your Majesty has a telepathic ability, so I will allow you to read my mind, but only of the facts of our last mission. Nothing more."

That earns a stunned silence. I don't think anyone expected that, but I want to be honest with them.

"I want to always be honest with you. I'm not someone who likes lying or playing games of deceit, but the world's peace rests on our shoulders, and your time as ruler is nearly up."

The king rises at this and looks at me with a smile. "Very well, Horseman of Magic. Please allow me to examine your mind and see where your claims are coming from, then we can all discuss this rationally."

Dea steps down from his place behind me to follow me to the king's couch. I don't think the king will try anything stupid with Dea present, given his ability to persuade the soul to feel pain.

Eesh, even just the sound of it has me wincing.

"It might be a little uncomfortable," the king says as I sit next to him. "Just focus on your last mission and where it started. If there's anything you don't wish me to see, just skip ahead to the next part. Like a movie."

I nod and take a deep breath.

A shiver runs through my brain, like when you suddenly realize you're cold and a shiver runs through your body involuntarily. It's like that but inside my head, and I can do nothing to stop it.

Memories flit past my closed eyes so quickly I have a hard time stopping to process them, but eventually I find the moment we were 'attacking' the Vampires and staging a coup.

I think I hear the king chuckle at my villain attempt, but I can't be sure.

He keeps sifting through, watching us get caught and entering the derelict building that suddenly pops into full development the moment I step onto the path (I do skip past my bathroom break, though—don't want the king seeing my dick).

He watches the entire conversation we have with Prince Phillipe's wife, and I feel the king stiffen beside me at the sight of her bruises. He is none too pleased about my treatment of her, but he understands my pain; I just want answers.

I skip us ahead to the Fae Court, the announcement, and then Connie being stolen and our plight to get her back.

Finally, after what seems like forever, he leaves my mind and I open my eyes and sway a little.

"Easy," Dea whispers beside me. "You are okay, Angel."

The king grimaces at me. "I am reluctant to agree with Magic, but agree with him I must. There is no way anyone but the future Vampire King could motivate the Fae Court that way. The queen might be a little cruel at times, but she loves her people. It would have taken some persuasion to put them in harm's way."

"What kind of persuasion?" I ask.

"The alliance kind. Marriage between firstborns, maybe. It is hard to say. But something substantial."

I bristle at the idea of forcing two people into marriage, but now really isn't the time. Standing back up to my position, the king stands and announces his thoughts to the council.

I watch the room react in horror, and then chaos ensues. Everyone is shouting, everyone is arguing, but one little voice stands out beside me. Prince Lucien has walked up to the small stage I'm stood on with a smile on his face.

"Thank you," he whispers. "Now they might believe me."

"You knew?" I ask.

"Yes. I have always wanted to work alongside the SC. It is for the benefit of everyone, after all. But he has always been against their ruling."

"He is not the only one by the looks of it." I gesture to the room's growing debate about which side they should be on. "And you are not the only council to be having this problem. Loyalties are dividing everywhere we look."

Prince Lucien places a hand on my arm and smiles. "You'll do fine, little Horseman. You've got this."

I address the room. "May I have your attention, please?"

The room gradually grows more silent as the seconds tick by, and eventually, I have the whole room's attention once more.

"My advice to your council is to pick someone else as the next king. Someone whose loyalties are not as divided, someone who is more liked, and someone who is more willing to work alongside other Courts and Councils." I clear my throat. "We need to improve our solidarity over the coming months and form a solid unit of peace. If possible, I would like to set up an embassy for each species willing to work alongside us; the embassies will come together to motivate and communicate with the outer reaches of our people. That means that anyone involved will have to get along with each other: Vampires and Witches, every Shifter species, and so on."

I'm kind of making things up as I go here, but our team can't keep up with this complex level of communication.

"I will oversee everything myself and arrange monthly meetings to hear any complaints direct from the councils. The embassies will be set up here, in *Sheruta*, and will work as a go between for us and you. Any and every species will be seen as equal, and we will set up as many embassies as needed."

That is all I have to say. I'm sure they'll argue for hours over it, so I intend to let them at it and walk off the stage and out of the room.

Dea excuses us and gives them the use of the room until sundown, then follows me.

"That was amazing in there, Angel. You really caught their attention."

"Really? Because it felt like I was trying to herd a bunch of deaf sheep."

He chuckles. "Welcome to politics. But I think you have just made things easier for us in the future."

"I damn well hope so. I don't want to keep having to video message every Council and then send one of you to chat. It should be easier than that."

Dea rubs circles into my shoulders, and I the stress leaks out of me. "You should get ready. Nine's surprise will be waiting for you at sundown."

Get ready. Get ready for sex with Nine. How in the hell does one 'get ready' for that? What do I need to look like? Ohmigoddess, I need a shower and to de-hair. In both forms. You know, just in case. Not that I plan on losing both immortal virginities in a single night, nor am I particularly comfortable with the thought of sex in my male form yet, but I want to be prepared for all eventualities.

Currently, I'm pacing the floor of the bedroom, trying to make a mental list of everything I need:

1. Pick out underwear and clothes
2. Have a shower
3. Wear deodorant and perfume
4. Put some makeup on

"Fuck, fuck, fuck. I'm soooo not prepared for this."

What if everything goes terribly? What if my vagina feels weird or something? What if I sound stupid? What if I don't know what I'm doing?

"Oh dear." I hear a familiar female voice in the doorway and have never been happier to see Connie in all my fucking life.

"Thank the goddess!" I yank her inside and slam the door. "You have to help me."

Connie smiles and sits me down on the bed. "You need to stop freaking out and trust that Nine knows what he's doing." She takes both hands in hers and looks me in the eyes. "He knows you. Better than any of us. Trust me, he has this down. Just turn up as you."

"But I want to be a more confident me." I sigh. "Like you."

Connie smiles. "Thank you, but I'm not confident. I'm just old and know that being worried about every little thing in life is a pointless way to live." She leans in and plants a small kiss to the corner of my lips. "Just go have a shower and pick something nice to wear. Nothing else matters."

"Right." Okay. I can do that. "Shower and nice clothes."

"Tell you what," she starts with a grin. "You have a shower, I'll pick out something for you to wear. I know parts of his plan." She taps her nose, and I pout.

"That's so unfair," I mumble as I plod to the bathroom and get the shower running. I usually bathe, given the size of the damn bath, but I want to be quick.

By the time I've washed (twice), shampooed and conditioned my hair, and de-haired everywhere else, I have been in the bathroom for forty-five minutes and am starting to have a butt-ton of questions I need a fellow woman to answer. Unfortunately for her, Connie is the only woman around, and really, the only woman I know.

I walk out of the bathroom wrapped in a towel, letting my hair dry naturally. "Connie? If I have questions, may I ask . . . ?" I trail off at the sight of the scene in front of me.

Dea and Connie both sit on various items of furniture around my bedroom and are mid-discussion when they suddenly stop talking to look at me.

Dea blushes at the sight of me in nothing but a towel that barely covers my ass, but Connie just smiles.

"What are you doing here?"

Connie coughs to get my attention and thumbs toward Dea. "He wanted to tell you to stop freaking out and just enjoy yourself." She gets up off the bed and grabs my hands. "And yes, you can ask me anything."

I look to her and then to Dea. "This is definitely a woman discussion."

"Right," Dea says. He walks up to me and nudges Connie out of the way before wrapping me in a hug. "Remember, you wanted it to mean something. To be important. To be a memory you can look back on. He is just doing what you asked, Angel." He places a gentle kiss to my forehead and unhooks my towel, which I let it fall to the floor, not really caring about them seeing me naked by this point. "Besides," he says as he brushes a wet strand of hair behind my ear, "you are perfect. And Nine thinks so, too." He trails a single finger down the side of my jaw and neck, going ever lower as he traces the outside of my breast and rests a single hand on my waist.

Goddess, damn it, that feels . . . surprisingly hot. He doesn't really do anything, but I feel the light, feather-like touch all throughout my body, and now it's shaking to be touched more by this man I'm slowly coming to realize I'm in love with.

I stand on my toes and wrap my arms around his neck. My lips crush his in what I hope is a forceful, heated kiss, and I grin in delight when he stumbles backward and has to steady himself on the wall.

"Angel . . ." he groans beneath our kiss. "You are making it hard to leave."

I'm vaguely aware of Connie watching us from somewhere in my bedroom, but in that moment, I don't care. Everyone knows the score by this point. All I want is for someone to take away the nerves and fill me with heat so I don't go to Nine a mess of anxiety.

"Good," I say as I pull away, "then I'm doing my job well."

"A little too well." He grabs my legs and lifts me off the floor in one smooth motion.

I wrap them around his waist, vaguely aware that I'm butt naked but not really caring.

He pulls away from the scorching hot kiss and takes a deep breath as he smirks at me. "Feeling better?" he asks as he puts me back on my feet.

I nod, not embarrassed in the slightest. "Much. Thank you."

"Now leave." Connie pushes Dea out of the room and slams the door in his face. "Now that," she says as she turns back around, "was hot."

"Oh, I . . . err . . . just . . ." Now I'm embarrassed. Goddess damn it. I was doing so fucking well with the whole modern female confidence thing.

Connie walks up to me with an expression I only recognize from our drunken night out and heated make-out session. A sultry smirk that lights her eyes on fire and makes me squirm. She's turned on. A lot.

"You like watching?" I ask, genuinely curious.

She shrugs. "It's kinda hot." She wraps an arm around my waist and pulls me flat against her. "Promise you'll let me watch one day." She looks embarrassed by her request, but I just smile reassuringly.

"You can do more than watch, babe." I lean in and kiss her, aiming for something hot but ending up tumbling us onto the bed in the process. "We can threesome any time you like." I wink at her, and I climb on top, straddling her thighs and leaning down.

Connie looks surprised by my outburst of confidence, but somehow it feels so . . . right. So me.

I've only become unconfident because of recent pressures, but I am a naturally confident person it seems.

"R-Really?" She seems unsure, and I can't help the feeling of the tables turning here.

"Yes," I say as confidently and full of adamant emotion as I can. "I want to see Dea come undone." I gasp in surprise at the filthy words coming out of my mouth, but I resign when I realize they're all true. I really do want to see him come undone. To lose that control.

Connie chuckles. "I've never seen him lose control. Not once." I can't hide all of my disappointment at that, and Connie notices. "But," she says, "if anyone can do so, it's you and Nine."

Fuck. Just the thought of being the one to make him lose control has me fighting the urge the bite my lip in anticipation.

"Like the idea, don't ya?" she asks.

Who the hell am I to care if she knows about my fantasies? She's in a lot of them anyway.

"Come on," she says, shoving me off her, "we need to get you dressed and ready."

I go silent, the confidence oozing out of me with every step we take to get closer to my closet.

What is it about this one time with Nine that has me so worked up? Is it just because it's my first time with any one member of the team? Or is it because it's with Nine in particular? Maybe it's because I said I loved him?

Gah! I don't know the answer.

Connie holds up an outfit I'm having trouble associating with sexy. It's nothing more than a pair of dark green jeans, a black vest tee with matching studded jacket, and a pair of worn combat boots.

"Why that?"

Connie looks at me and says, "You'll be going to *Sheruta's* western forest. So you can look great underneath the clothes, but you should definitely wear something comfortable for walking around in out there. Just in case."

Makes sense. "Okay . . ." I grab them from her and put them to one side, awaiting her choice of underwear.

She turns back around and grabs the matching set of bra and panties she laid out for me. They're simple black lace, but with enough detail to make it a little more than just plain.

Her smile falters. "You look disappointed?"

"Err . . . Not disappointed, just surprised."

She chuckles. "I was being serious when I said you should go as yourself." She puts the underwear down and walks over to me. "I don't want you worried about looking a certain way or acting a certain way; you should just be you."

I agree with her, I really do, but it's just . . . "I guess I want to be someone more . . . sexy."

"There's time for that in our immortal future, but right now, I think Nine wants you to be yourself. And yourself is already pretty fucking hot, hon."

"Okay. If you say so."

"I do." She shrugs. "Now put the outfit on!"

I salute the fashionable drill sergeant in front of me and put the underwear on first, then the outfit. Connie leaves me in peace to do so, so I get to look at the underwear in the mirror before covering it. I have to admit, it does have a certain charm. Especially with my pink hair. It all looks so . . . me. I quickly put on some casual clothes in my male form, hoping Nine doesn't have a plan quite that big.

Walking out of the closet, I watch as Connie gets a few makeup supplies ready. "I assume," she says upon seeing me, "you can manage your own hair?"

I nod and quickly whip a little wind around it, drying out the final bit of water, then flatten it in place and let it hang naturally from my shoulders. "Done."

"Damn. That's fucking efficient."

I sit on the stool she's prepared for me. She puts on some light foundation, some awesome smoky eyes that I'm jealous of not being able to achieve by myself, and then finishes it off with some clear, cherry-flavored gloss.

"Done." She pulls me up and nudges me out the door. "Now go!"

"Where?"

"To the western forest."

"Right, the blob of green to the west near the mountains on the map?"

"That's the one!" She pushes me out of my own bedroom door, and I'm off, sprinting down the hallways and out the back door of the kitchen in a flit of Vampire speed.

I fly there—because who the hell would walk when they can fly?—and notice a small firelight in the distance straight away. I really hope that's where he is and I'm not about to interrupt someone else's night.

Yup. Come on down, Sweetie.

Oh, err . . . hi.

Stop being so nervous, he says as he filters through my memories of my evening with Connie and the brief encounter with the guys. He pauses, however, on my hot kiss with Dea and takes particular note of the confidence it seemed to give me. *That's . . . fucking hot.*

Do you all like watching? Is that a Horseman thing?

You're going to lecture me on watching? You, whose first sexual encounter with any of us was watching me suck Dea's cock?

Well, he has a point. A really damn good, sexy point. So I leave it be and fly down to the fire. As I get closer to the ground, I notice it's a bonfire, but one contained by stones and lifted off of the forest floor so as not to cause permanent damage to the area.

Once firmly on the ground, I look around and gasp. He's created a clearing in the forest (or made use of one) and set up an actual low-to-the-ground bed at the top, complete with duvets, rose petals, fallen leaves, and a small table to the side with snacks and drinks. But the rest of the clearing is just as beautiful: String lights hang from tree to tree, making use of the witchlight bulbs they use in the town square at night, and cast an enamored light around the clearing. A clear path has been made around the fire, outlined with leaves and decorated with vines that hang from the trees. It's all so . . .

"Perfect. It's perfect, Nine."

I can feel the sting of tears threatening to burst the banks, and I have to sniffle them back before I look like an idiot.

"You could never look like an idiot, Sweetie." He walks down the pathway to meet me and stops just in front of me, taking me in. "Connie did a wonderful job persuading you to just be yourself."

Really?

Yeah, you look beautiful just as you are. "Come on." He grabs my hand and guides me toward the bed. "We can have something to eat or drink if you like? Or we can just chat?"

He's fiddling with his fingers, I notice, and I wonder if he's nervous.

This is different than with anyone else. This—he gestures to the decorated forest clearing—*means something. I've never done this before.*

Oh, I see. "Well, let's make our first time special then, shall we?" I grab his hand and move us onto the bed, where I just lie there and snuggle into his side, making the most of our unlimited time together.

"So," Nine says, "I saw your concern about your male form. I just wanted to say that we don't have to do anything you don't want to do." He goes to say something else but stops.

"Go on."

"Well, I know the others want to share some of your first times, and although that is completely up to you, it would be unfair of me to leave them out."

Goddess, he's right. And honestly, that's a load off my mind. I'm just not ready for sex in my other form, and there isn't a pressing magical need for it, either, like with my Vampire nature.

He grabs my chin and leans up to me. "You need this. I'm making it special because I love you, but this is more than that. Your Vampire side needs to feed properly, and this will help." He sighs. "Even if you still choose to take your time with the others, you'll have me to keep you stable."

I laugh at the thought of trying to persuade Arrie to go slowly.

Nine laughs alongside me. "You're right. You two are quite fired up recently." He raises his eyebrows in question, but I don't know what to say.

"His . . . err . . . roughness, I guess, speaks to my Vampire nature. It . . ."

"Turns you on?"

I nod. "Yeah."

"Don't worry," he says, "we'll go as slow as you like. Or not at all." He adds a wink to the end there. "There's something we need to chat about first, though." He rummages around his side of the bed and brings out what look like a potion bottle. "This is a contraceptive potion. It's made by Witches. The issue is that I have no idea how effective this will be on you, but they're the same ones Connie uses."

I take it from his hands.

"You just need to take it before you have sex. Connie takes one every morning, just in case." He shrugs. "They don't have any side effects or anything, so if no sex is had that day, then they're harmless."

"Good to know." I pull the cap off and down it in one. "Tastes like strawberries," I say as I lick my lips. I look to Nine and know I can just ask the question on my mind. "No diseases with us, right?"

He smiles. "Right. Diseases don't even infect us in the first place."

"Good." No need for anything else to get in our way. "I'm a little . . . nervous."

"Don't be," he says on a sigh. "We can spend the entire night here with no expectations and wait until morning if you like. There's no pressure."

And, he adds in his mind, *if you like, I can help take away those nerves?*

You can?

He smiles in that devilish way of his.

Whatever he's about to do, it's going be his usual cheekiness. Relief floods through me that we can spend the entire night just being ourselves and that there's no pressure.

He grabs my hand and lifts me onto the pathway. He must have clicked a button on some kind of sound system because music dances to life all around us.

"Dance with me?"

I nod, already liking the idea of dancing around the bonfire with Nine. It's all so . . . beautiful. I really don't have another word for it. He's put in so much effort, it's crazy. This wasn't what I was expecting.

Nine wraps his arms around my waist and guides me along the makeshift dancefloor, dipping me at all the right moments, kissing me as often as possible, and never saying a word. Eventually, the song ends, and I'm a little disappointed we can't keep dancing, but Nine puts on another tune, so we keep going.

This is a good distraction from my nerves.

This is not the distraction. This is just the warm up.

What?

This is the distraction.

He closes his eyes and lowers his mouth to mine, his lips molding perfectly against my own, and I gasp in surprise when he places a picture in my head of him and Dea, both naked, in the middle of a field. Given the lack of clothes and buildings, I have no idea of the time era, but they look perfectly content.

They're chatting away as Nine rests on Dea's bare chest and traces his golden tattoo. Dea laughs at something Nine says and then flips him onto his back and kisses him with reckless abandon in that way that makes your heart melt and your knees shake. Eventually, though, the kiss deepens and becomes more desperate, more needy, and Dea's hand lowers down Nine's body and wraps around his cock in a tight enough hold I can practically hear Nine's groan from here, despite this particular memory having no sound.

As if Nine is reading my mind (which he probably is), sound filters through, and I can hear them both moaning perfectly.

"Brother," Nine asks, "are you sure?"

Dea grips him tighter, causing Nine to groan louder. "Yes. Now lie there and take it like a good boy."

"Yes, sir," Nine says through a laugh. But that laugh is quickly cut off by Dea's lips wrapping themselves around the head of Nine's cock, and I get the pleasure of watching Nine come undone for a change.

Nine takes the memory away before Dea can finish, and I moan my disappointment before I can stop myself.

Nine laughs and whispers in my ear, "Not to worry. You'll get to see me first hand later."

I shiver with pleasure as I feel my core ache with a familiar tingle of need. "Fuck, Nine . . . Why is that so hot?"

He shrugs. "Probably the same reason why guys find it so attractive when two women have sex."

"Soooo," I start, and he giggles, "you find me and Connie . . . attractive?"

"I find you and any of the team attractive. I don't really have a preference when it comes to gender, but yes. You and Connie together is rather hot."

"When was that memory?" I ask as I pepper kisses down his neck and graze one of my fangs along his neck, making him shudder.

He clears his throat. "Year 623. It was one of our first times together. Before we were anything but friends, of course."

That's why Nine asked if Dea was sure. Makes sense.

I continue kissing Nine, having grown more than a little needy since that hot memory, and Nine roams his hands under my tank top, grazing the underside of my bra.

"I want to see that underwear first hand," he says, a little breathless from my attention. "I looked away when I was looking through your memories of this evening, so I didn't ruin anything."

I chuckle. "Lie on the bed then."

He looks at me in surprise, but he smiles and does as I say anyway.

I slowly walk over, trying to at least be semi-sexy, and shove my jacket off and let it fall to the floor.

I thought this would be nerve wracking, but it's not; Nine doesn't care either way.

And with that final thought of confidence, I lose all of my inhibitions and worries and just go for it.

Tucking a finger underneath the hem of my tank top, I inch it up and over my breasts before throwing it to the floor.

Nine's breath hitches when he watches me go to unbuckle my jeans, and the heat in his eyes spurs me on.

I slowly shimmy out of them, having taken my boots off earlier, and stand there in nothing but a thong and bra.

Nine's eyes practically salivate at the sight of me, and although I don't see what he sees, I understand, because as he stands up to meet me, he also removes his clothes one article at a time; he matches my semi-sexy tone and goes with it, bless his soul.

You look . . . pretty fucking tasty, actually.

My face heats into a flame as I think of the right words to say, but Nine grabs the back of my neck and leans me into a kiss before I can scramble together a sentence. He kisses me as though we have all the time in the world to savor every moment of this night, and I guess, in a way, we do, but I'm eager to show him just how ready I am to be his.

Tonight isn't about the team or our group relationship; tonight is about just the two of us. Tonight, I am just his.

His hands roam up my back and trace gentle patterns up and down my spine, but I need more. Want more.

I lean into the kiss and deepen it, hoping to convey what I want, and boy does Nine deliver.

He pushes me onto the bed and climbs on top, straddling my waist. We're both still in our underwear at this point, but I do not miss his hardening cock straining to be free of those boxers. With a gentle caress, he grabs my hands and lowers his grip to my wrists, where he shoots them above my head in a fierce shove that has me whimpering.

"Not wanting to take things gently, Sweetie?"

I shake my head, no. I don't think gentle is my thing right now. Maybe later, but right now, with my Vampire nature edging further over the edge of lustful insanity, I just want this man to fuck me.

Fuck, you're hot like this. Lying here and allowing me to restrain you.

I giggle, understanding his hidden meaning. He can't ever truly restrain me because I'm stronger (much stronger), but I'm letting him do what he wants, purposefully taking the submissive role with ease.

"Don't worry," I whisper in a huskier tone than I knew I could pull off, "I'll take control later." I go to lift my head, but I find myself slightly restrained by his weight pressed into my wrists.

"Nuh-uh," he says with a shake of his head. "Don't make me tie you up, Sweetie."

I shiver at the thought, the growing heat pulsing through me only grows hotter with the idea of being tied-up with any member of the team.

Maybe another day.

I whimper as he peppers kisses down my jaw and along my collar bone, taking his time to lick, nip, and tease his way farther toward my breasts. The moment his tongue first flicks over my nipple, I arch into him, wanting more.

He flicks harder, caressing each nipple in turn with small circles of his tongue until I can feel the effect pooling in my soaked panties.

Bucking my hips, I beg for more. "Nine . . . please."

"Let me see your fangs," he commands, and I nearly moan but manage to hold it back.

My fangs descend, and the smirk on Nine's face could not have been more devilish. What is the nerdy fucker up to?

He releases my wrists, so he has two free hands, and uses one to palm my breast as the other runs fingers up and down the sensitive peaks of my fangs.

"Fuck," I whisper, not holding back the moan that leaks at alongside it.

My hips move of their own accord this time, and I can't help the needy whine that escapes at the sight of Nine's cock now poking out of the top of his underwear.

Nine doesn't say anything, mentally or physically, and I revel in the teasing perfection he's managing to do to my incredibly needy body.

Connie's right, he's good at this, I think to myself as the hand palming my breasts shifts lower, stroking the skin of my abdomen before delving deeper. Low enough that I squirm underneath him and move my own hands down his chest and along the gentle ridges of his abs.

I want. Now.

"Nine, can we—?"

"No," he says in a more commanding tone than I've ever heard him use before. "I'm not done with your body yet."

His tone sends a pleasant shiver down my body, and I can't help shifting my thighs to create some kind of friction.

Nine frowns and rips my legs apart with a knee, clearly wanting to be the one to bring me pleasure.

His fingers finally reach the apex of my thighs and tease my opening.

"Come on, Nine . . ." I beg as he refuses to give me what I want most. "Please."

"God, I love hearing you beg." He slips one finger in, and it's enough to have me writhing all over again.

Fuck, he's good at this teasing shit. But seriously, I want to fuck him. Can't a girl just get fucked?

He chuckles in my mind and whispers, *You'll get me soon, Sweetie. Just let me have my fun first.* He smiles before slipping another finger inside and lowering his head to my navel.

Trailing kisses down my body, he takes his time getting to his destination, but when he does, fuck am I glad he waited. He laps quick, forceful strokes of his tongue against my clit in time to the rhythm of his fingers, and it takes everything I have not to scream out in pleasure.

Don't hold back. There's no one out here to hear you but me.

He slides a third finger inside and curls them slightly to hit the world's best part of my body, and I convulse around him as I let out a half-stifled scream and bite my lip, accidentally drawing blood with my fang.

"Fuck," I say between gasps, coming down from the amazing high. "You're good at that."

Nine chuckles but says a simple, "Thank you."

I sigh a breath of relief as a peaceful calm washes over me; the type of calm I haven't felt since before drinking blood. "Wow. I didn't realize how on edge I was."

Nine's hands travel up my body and graze my nipples on the way to trace the outline of my lips as he leans over me. "Yeah?"

I nod but stay otherwise silent.

"Don't worry, we're not done."

My breath hitches. I never considered multiple orgasms before, but more of this man? I'll take it.

Got any preferences on how you want your first time to be, Sweetie?

Ummm . . . I haven't really considered it, if I'm honest. I shake my head, a little shy at having to make any choices.

Nine settles himself between my legs. He rubs slow, lazy circles over my clit until I'm writhing beneath him and begging him to fuck me properly, and finally, after more pleas than my dignity cares to admit, he lines his cock up and slowly enters.

He goes slowly, allowing me to get used to the feeling of being stretched and filled. It's so different to using my own fingers, or to Nine's fingers, for that matter, but fuck, it feels so good.

"You doing okay?" he asks.

"Yeah," I reply on a breathy moan. "So good."

He slowly goes deeper, burying himself to the hilt, then stops and looks at me.

I try to shift my hips to encourage him to move, but he stays steadfast. "Nine . . . ?"

Yes?

My hips buck and shift as much as possible, but he refuses to help. Instead, he rests on his elbows and smirks at me like the cruel fucker he is.

"Please, I want . . ."

What do you want?

"Fuck me. Please, for the love of the goddess, fuck me."

He chuckles and begins moving. Slowly at first, and I can feel the familiar pleasurable tension building already, but soon he picks up the pace and is thrusting higher toward release.

Fuck. Shit.

It's only been less than a minute, and I can feel my release there, just over the edge of the cliff. Is this too soon? If he continues, I'm going to—

Nine thrusts harder and presses a thumb to my clit and begins rubbing small circles. "Let go, Sweetie."

My head falls back onto the mattress as I arch into him.

He takes one nipple into his mouth and sucks and nips while he rolls the other between his fingers.

I can't hold on any longer, and another toe-curling orgasm overtakes me. I cry out, louder than I thought I would, and hear Nine groan.

"Fuck," he whispers. "You're so . . ." He's watching me with rapt attention and looks to be struggling to hold back his own release.

Grabbing him by both arms, I flip us over and pin his arms to the bed above his head, just like he did to me. At first, I shift my hips in a slow, circular motion, getting used to the feeling, but the moment I feel his cock hit the right spot, I lift myself up and down and watch his expression go from wonder to scrunched up in pleasure.

Nine's moans get louder as I move faster, finding a rhythm that makes his hips buck beneath mine and his eyes go wide in surprise.

Fuck, Sweetie. I can't keep holding back if you . . .

I crash my hips into him harder, trying not to hurt him, but my concern was ill-founded, as his eyes glow a bright orange and his lips snarl with a hiss.

He likes being dominated, it seems.

It that what Dea's like with him?

Yes. Even Nine's thoughts sound breathless. *Dea likes to tie me up, spank me, and make me do whatever he wants. He's a control freak, but it's fucking great in the bedroom.*

Fuck, I want him to do that to us both.

"Fuck, yes." He grabs my hips and lifts me a few inches above him, giving himself enough room to fuck me. And boy does he fuck me. *I want him to tie us both up and watch him spank you with your ass in the air.*

His control snaps, and I watch him buck, writhe, and thrust beneath me with reckless abandon, all the while hearing his delicious moans getting louder. "Yes, yes!" His cock stiffens further inside me, and he screams his release into the night air.

His body quickly goes slack, as though all the energy leaked out of him.

I roll off him and curl into his side.

We lie for a few minutes after the waves of tension subside (hell, it could have been a few hours and I wouldn't have noticed), me lying on top of his sculpted chest as I run gentle circles over his collar bone in a haze of sexual high.

Nine? I ask mentally.

Yeah?

Thank you.

He chuckles beneath me. *No need to thank me. That was amazing.*

That it was, but I mean thank you for everything else. For being you. This night has been amazing. I love you.

I love you too, Sweetie. How about we get some sleep?

"Mmmhmmm . . ." My eyes are beginning to close as sleep takes hold.

The last thing I remember is Nine lifting me off of him and placing us both under a duvet as he holds me tightly in his arms.

39

Morning comes far too quickly for us both, and I wake with a groan at the amount of sunlight piercing my peaceful sleep. "Why is it so light?"

A deep chuckle resonates from beneath me and vibrates my head. "Morning, Sweetie."

"Morning, Nine."

Flashes of the previous night enter my mind, and I smile. I did it. I actually slept with a member of the team. And it was fucking amazing.

More laughter sounds from beneath me. "You are welcome."

"How much longer do we have?" I mutter, enjoying one of the only peaceful nights sleep I've had since waking up immortal.

"Only until lunchtime I'm afraid. I need to get back to that data-app design for your big plan."

I groan. "Right." I flop off of him and lay on my back under the duvet. "And I need to start making plans for the embassies."

"Huh?"

Right, I didn't tell anyone how mine and Dea's meeting with the Vamps went or my on-the-spot decision.

I quickly fill him in, showing the entire afternoon in flashes of memories.

He whistles. "Wow. Big plans, hey?"

"I guess. You think it'll help?"

"I think it's a big political move, Sweetie." He rubs a hand over my shoulders and leans in to kiss me.

I take the kiss and go with it, wondering how much more fun we can have before we have to leave.

Knew you'd be a handful, he groans. *It'll take more than just me to keep both your forms satisfied.*

"Lucky I have four of you then."

Speaking of . . . They're going to be all over you now you've popped your immortal cherry. They've been holding back.

"That was them holding back?" Eesh. But really, I like the idea of having three—four—people wanting to sleep with me. (Color me basic, but it feels good. Remember? No judging. I have a world to save. I'm allowed to indulge.) "So, err . . ." I cough to clear my throat. You and Dea?

What about us?

What did you talk about when I left you both alone in the library?

Ah, that. He climbs on top of me and rubs a thumb down my cheek. "We talked about you, actually."

"Me?"

"Yeah." He rubs a hand across the back of his neck, and I can see the twitch in his smile falter and can tell he's nervous about whatever this was. "We agreed to try to make us all work together. Like, all three of us."

I look at him confused.

"You make us complete, Horseman of Magic. We know you're going to pursue something with Con and Arrie, and that's okay, but between us three, we want it to be . . . together. Like, all three of us, rather than a weird, unbalanced triangle."

I just smile at him like an idiot. "Oh . . ."

"It's totally okay if you'd rather be with us separately. We don't mind, it's just—"

I shut his rambling up with a kiss I hope conveys everything I'm feeling. The heat, the love, the all-encompassing feeling of rightness. Eventually, I pull away. "Yes, I'll be your girlfriend. Both of yours."

He smiles. *I love you.*

"I love you too."

Unfortunately, we have to head back. So there's no morning fun after all, but hey, the night was amazing. I couldn't have asked for a more understanding partner, and by the time I walk into the kitchen at eleven am, I'm practically glowing. Much to the delight of all three members of the team waiting for us at the kitchen table.

They look at me with those smug smiles, and Connie puts down the magical newspaper to look at me with raised eyebrows.

I just nod and look away, too embarrassed to actually talk about it in front of everyone.

"Hey," Nine says as he turns me around, "don't do that. None of us care. You could sleep with all of us separately every single day, and we wouldn't judge. Not ever."

Okay.

You okay?

Yeah, actually. I'm doing great.

And I really am. For once, I feel good about the prospect of my future. I'm surrounded by people I love. What's there to be worried about?

40

The fate of the world. Right. Forgot about that.

While Arrie is due back this evening with news from the Shifter Council and Witch Coven (of which, he's been updated regarding the embassy idea), Nine and Connie are still busy creating my wonderful stamp on the new world.

That leaves just me and Dea, and I'm hoping he can help me with something. We're sat at the tail end of lunch together after Nine and Connie disappeared twenty minutes ago, and I'm dying to ask for his help, but I don't really have a plan, so have kept quiet for now.

"Is there something you wish to say, Angel?"

"Errrm . . . maybe. Actually," I say, thinking back to Nine's comment about us three being together, "there are lots of things I have to say, but maybe now isn't the best time to address them all."

I shuffle around on my chair, trying to see if any part of my body actually feels different; it doesn't. And that fact makes me feel somewhat disappointed. I'm not sure what I thought I would feel like after finally sleeping with a member of the team, but I certainly expected to feel something. But oddly, it feels just like before: like I have friends, boyfriends, a family, a home, and I'm still exploring what that means.

"Perhaps you should start with the important things first, then."

"Right." Clearing my throat, I begin. "I want to try to work on some Fae spells, see about playing in water to unlock my water Witch magic, and then do some research about our Angel magics connecting."

There. The important stuff.

"I guess we also need to make plans with the *Sheruta* Council about building embassies and see if they will allow more free passage between here and Earth, too."

Dea nods. "I will send a message to the *Sheruta* Council with an update of our plans and see if they can do anything to assist." He gets up after putting the newspaper down and walks up to me, offering me his hand. "In the meantime, maybe we should go for a swim in the lake. It is certainly warm enough for it, and you can see about your water abilities and perhaps try out some water-related Fae spells." He gently pulls me to my feet and wraps his arms around my waist. "But right now, I want to remind you that I exist."

"Huh? What does that mea—?"

He cuts my question off with a searing kiss that would have melted any woman's panties clean off. Including mine. It sends my knees buckling and my breath hitching, but luckily, Dea catches me and lifts me onto the kitchen countertop.

"It means I want you to remember that you have more boyfriends—and one girlfriend—than just Nine to juggle."

His fingers trail themselves down the side of my neck and dip underneath the edge of my tank top, slinking close to my nipples but not close enough.

My heart flutters a million miles a minute, and I swear I'm ready to drag this man back to my bed. His lips are still pressed firmly to mine, with enough pressure to know exactly what he thinks about the idea of me and Nine fucking in the woods, but he delves deeper when he slides his tongue past my defenses and tangles it with mine.

He slides me to the edge of the countertop and places himself between my open legs, and fuck, he's hard as steel beneath those jeans.

Gasping for breath, I break away and whisper, "Had a hard night?"

He does not miss my innuendo and groans. "Yes, very." He doesn't give me time to respond and, instead, returns to kissing the life right out of me. But this time he thrusts his hips against my center, and I groan against him, my fangs descending in the process.

Fuck, I forgot to feed this morning. I can feel the pulsing of my arteries like a suffocating cloth around all my senses.

Dea, not missing a beat, turns his head to expose his neck. "Help yourself."

I don't hesitate. I snap my head toward his neck and slam my teeth into his artery, and shit, fuck, shit . . . that feels so good. I thought sleeping with Nine would help balance me, and it absolutely did (I'm no longer crazy), but it's just made me want more . . .

And right now, Dea is offering himself up on a sexy silver platter. My hand slides below his waist and to the buckle of his jeans, which I make quick work of undoing, and then delves below his underwear to grip his cock.

He groans against me, and I can't help but take one final mouthful of that smoky lavender nectar before unlatching and looking up at him. His eyes are swirling a bright gold, brighter than I've ever seen, and I'm curious . . .

I grip him harder and stroke a couple of lengths from base to tip, then watch as his knees buckle and his breath gasps and those beautiful, golden galaxy eyes of his glow so bright I look away.

"What's gotten into my Angel of Death this morning?" I smirk at him. "I've never seen you this worked up before?"

Dea looks straight at me. "I have just spent the entire night imagining my two lovers in all kinds of compromising positions and not being able to join in. It has been one torturous twenty-four hours, Angel."

I chuckle to myself as I think of the effect just the thought of Nine and I have on this man. "Well then, next time, you'll just have to join us." My hand speeds up as I test his reactions, and I can't help but swirl my thumb over the tip.

The moan he lets out is music to my ears.

I grip harder and speed up once more, hoping I'm doing a good enough job, but one more look at Dea's face screwed up in pleasure tells me I'm managing all right.

The bite marks on his neck haven't quite healed yet, so I lick a teasing tongue over them, putting as much pressure on them as I can.

Dea's hips jerk forward as he gets himself off using my hand, and I watch as the moment he loses control overcomes him. He buries his head in my neck and bites down in a sensitive spot between my neck and shoulder, causing me to squirm and moan, but Dea doesn't notice because he's too busy muffling his own moans of pleasure as he speeds up and explodes into my grip.

And fuck, I would pay to see that control snap. Even when coming he's controlled and polite. One of these days, I'll shatter that control into a million pieces.

"Now can we get on with magic for the day?" I ask as I pull my hand free and go to clean up at the kitchen sink with a satisfied smirk.

Dea walks up behind me and places a hand on my waist as he whispers in my ear, "Thank you, Angel. I am more than happy to return the favor." His hand skirts the waistband of my jeans, and I shudder.

At the sound of those words, my body betrays just how much it wants that cock all to itself, and I involuntarily arch backward. "I would, but I really want to get something done today."

He pulls away and grabs my now-dry hand. "Another time, then."

"It's a date."

41

The lake, it turns out, is a beautiful, serene piece of the garden I've yet to explore, or it could be a new feature. Who knows? It's tucked away in a copse of trees that allows the perfect amount of smattering light to filter through and sparkle off the water. The lake itself is large enough to fit a small swimming pool in but intimate enough to be a great outdoor area. The large rock and mini-waterfall on the right side of the lake creates a picture of tranquility as it perfectly matches the pond lilies and various flowers scattered around the water's edge and the lake bank.

"This place . . . It's beautiful."

"I am glad you like it, Angel." Dea leads me by the hand toward the lake. He removes his jeans and socks, but remains in his underwear and t-shirt, and wades into the water. Turning back around, he smiles. "Are you joining me?"

Right. Water. Need to be in the water for it to work. Most likely. Why didn't I think to grab some swimwear before we left? Oh well. Might as well join him.

Removing my own jeans and socks, I wade in after him. Luckily, my tank top falls past the top of my ass, so I'm not showing much.

"How did you intend to try this out, Angel?"

"Ermm . . . I really was just hoping I could splash about a bit and it all just come to me."

Dea chuckles. "I doubt it will be that easy, Angel. Air was the first, and fire came to you when you were angry." He swims up to where I'm sitting just off the bank up to my waist in water. "Maybe we need to incite a great need for your water abilities first."

Hmmm. "You know, that's not a bad idea." I punch him gently on the arm and swim out to where I have to swim to stay afloat. "Now what?" I mutter to myself.

What kind of emotion does water make me feel? Is it calm like the gentle, tranquil placidity of this lake? Or is it angry like the lashing of ocean waves against an unforgiving cliff of dirt and stone?

Eugh. This is starting to feel a lot less science-y and lot more hocus-pocus-y. How is water supposed to elicit emotion?

"What is going through your mind, Angel?" Dea's behind me quicker than I thought possible, making me jump and choke on water. "Sorry," he says through a laugh.

I get the feeling he isn't sorry at all.

Rolling my eyes, I say, "It's hard to think of magic in this way. In a non-scientific way. How can water cause emotion?"

"Well, that depends on how it is used."

I turn and look him in the eye with a questioning gaze.

"If one were drowning, then the water would cause fear, no? If one were thirsty, then relief."

"I see. So there is logic there."

Dea grabs my waist and spins me around, pinning my back to his chest. "There is logic underpinning everything we do, if only you look hard enough to see beneath the human surface." He cups water in his palm and lets it trickle out of his hands.

See beneath the human surface? Maybe if I think about it from a new angle?

I take a deep breath and dive underneath the surface of the water, peeling my eyes open and looking around. My Vampire sight allows me to see even the darkest of crags in the lake's bed; every creature, plant, and stone can be zoomed in on and examined. And for a while, that's all I do, examine the underneath of the lake beyond what most people can see, but it doesn't really help me gain any new perspective. So I break the calm surface of the water and inhale sweet oxygen.

I don't really need to breathe, but it's sweet heaven when I can. I take lungfuls of the candy the world offers so freely and promise to never take its honeyed goodness for granted again.

"Any insight?" Dea is still lounging in the water where I left him.

I swim up to him and shake my head. "None."

"Okay. Well, for now, let us work on some Fae spells involving water."

I nod. "Good idea. If I get any clever ideas, I can always change back and try them out."

I get out of the water and change into my male form, taking off my trousers in the process, and wade back in. Our clothes lie on the crest of the lake bank, and I can't help but smile at our clothes mixing on the floor.

Swimming back up to Dea, he grabs my hands and floats me in front of him. "I know a few water-based Fae spells, so we can start there if you like?"

"Sounds good."

"First off, moving water should be easy. You should be able to do whatever you like with the water pool here, for example." He gestures to the entire lake, and I smile.

I can feel the power rippling underneath my skin, and it itches to be let free and utilized. I can't help the maniacal smile that lights my face as I gently push the water around me like a kid splashing about in the local swimming pool.

"That is good." Dea lies on the bank near our clothes, sunbathing in nothing but his underwear.

It's more than a little distracting.

Nine, are you seeing what I have to work with?

Nine groans in my mind. *That's just mean, bro.*

Dea chuckles. "I could always make it worse, you two." He moves his hand lower and grabs the hem of his underwear.

Since I had hold of the cock beneath that material earlier, I know exactly what he's hiding underneath, and I'd be lying if I say I don't want to see what I could only feel before.

I have things to concentrate on here, and so do you two. Behave!

"Easy for the man who actually got some last night," Dea mumbles under his breath.

I know you got some earlier, bro. Quit complaining.

"You do?"

I was watching.

He would have winked if he were actually with us.

Con's yelling at me to focus, and I don't want to have my feet chopped off like last time. Gotta go.

"Feet chopped off?"

Dea laughs from where he lies, his hands firmly on the ground beside him. "She got stabbed in the chest by three swords like fifty years ago because Nine was too busy mentally flirting with me, and she cut off his foot as penance."

I struggle to contain my laughter but fail miserably. "Goddess, that woman," I groan.

Dea just nods in agreement and goes back to explaining different techniques of how the Fae use water in some of their spells. Some are just used as an ingredient in a larger spell while others are full-on attack spells. But one is pretty fucking cool: a water weather spell.

"It is only supposed to be used by multiple Fae at once, and controlling it can be tough, but I do not see why you should not be able to at least accomplish it."

"Controlling it?"

Dea looks at me with slight concern but shrugs his shoulders. "Might take some practice."

"So what does it do?"

"It raises the water from a particular source into the sky and forces the clouds to become heavier, therefore making it rain. On its own, that is not particularly useful, but it can be the smallest detail that turns the tide of battle. Plus, it could be useful to cast the spell with a time limit and then change into your female form and use the rain as a weapon via your Witch powers."

I stare at him dumbfounded. "My powers really are limitless, aren't they?"

"That is probably the point, yes."

The thought kinda scares me, if I'm honest. But I don't have the time to waste on such pointless thoughts, so I turn around and try to lift the water into raindrops.

"So how do I do this?"

"You need to lift drops of water into the sky, and as the temperature increases, it'll take less energy to bring those water drops to boiling point, therefore creating water vapor to increase cloud capacity."

"Cloud capacity? That's a thing?"

"Yes." Dea takes a breath. "It will require you to hold the rising water spell while you perform a heating spell. It will also require you to practice how much water you will need to raise on any given day based on the initial cloud coverage available."

"Okay, so today, for example, I will need lots because it's a clear day." The sun beats down in rays of heat, and I'm thankful for the refreshing cool of the water I'm treading.

"Right."

Okay, I can do this. I raise as much water as I think it'll take to create some kind of heavy cloud (though truthfully, I have no fucking idea how much water that'll take) and mutter the spell in Japanese under my breath.

"Water rise,

beyond this earth,

and beyond my sight,

to the heavens

and in to the night."

I repeat that spell over and over again until I have a giant ball of water in the sky I'm struggling to hold.

"Okay. Time for some heat." I look to Dea expectantly, but he's looking at the sky in a look of wonder. "Dea!"

"Oh, right." He looks to me and tells me the incantation and circle for the heating part of the spell.

The circle I create with pure magic power pretty easily, but I'm struggling with the wording of the spell. As I tumble over the words in Japanese, I manage to finally get it right.

But it's too late. My hold on the giant ball of water thirty thousand feet in the air cracks, and I watch in awe as it crashes to the ground.

"Angel!"

I vaguely hear Dea's scream as an entire ton of water dumps back into the lake with such force it throws me out and into the air.

"Angel!"

The sound of the water meeting its brethren back in the lake is like a crash of thunder against my ears, and they go deaf as the water encompasses me.

Shit, shit, shit.

"Transform!"

Right. Female me can handle this better.

I am about a hundred feet in the air, the water having splashed back into the lake already—though splash is down-playing the tidal wave that soaked Dea and would have put a human in real danger—as I change into my female form in an instant and fly myself to the mud-soaked ground.

I look up at Dea and smile. "Sorry."

He scoops me into a hug and squeezes tight before putting me back on my feet. "You okay?"

"Yeah." I take a deep breath and laugh at his reaction. "You remember I'm immortal just like you, right? I couldn't have really been seriously injured . . ."

"But, but . . ." He trails off, not really knowing what to say by the looks of things.

The adorable moron. He really is cute.

Bro, that was such an overreaction.

I laugh out loud so hard I cough up what I think is more water, but it turns out I'm choking on air. (Me, an air Witch, choking on air. Yeah, I know, right?)

"Shut up, asshole," Dea mumbles as he sulks where he stands.

I wrap my arms around his waist and place a sweet kiss to his cheek. "Thank you for worrying."

He smiles down at me and kisses me back. "You are welcome."

"Right, time to try again!" I shift back into my male form and run into the lake once again.

But one look around tells me I'll need to raise the water level. Oops. May have made too big of a splash. I use intention and a basic water rune circle to pull all of the leftover water from around the lake back into its intended hole.

"There."

I SPEND ALL AFTERNOON REPEATING THAT SPELL AND EVENTUALLY MANAGE IT, BUT IT DOES TAKE some insane levels of concentration and more tidal waves than I care to admit to creating.

"Fuck, I'm starving," I groan as I lie by the side of the lake panting for breath after finally having managed to do the spell correctly. "Food time?"

Dea chuckles. "Yup. Arrie's not back yet, so we should get dinner ready."

At the thought of Arrie not being back yet, I flinch. I hope he's okay.

"He will be fine, Angel," Dea says, as if reading my mind.

42

We make an extra helping for Arrie and have to put it in the fridge because he doesn't get back in time, much to my disappointment. Nine sends him a message using the video-screening technology, but I don't hold out hope.

I have a bad feeling. Something is very wrong.

"Where would Arrie be at this point in time?"

Dea is the one who answers after swallowing his mouthful of spaghetti. "Most likely at the Witch Coven."

Nine rubs my knee in his usually comforting manner, but it goes in vain because I'm constantly reminded of the lack of Arrie every time I lift my head, given his empty place at the dinner table is right in front of me.

"We did not leave the Witches in a very humble fashion on our last visit, Angel, so I am sure things are . . . tense. But he will be home and well soon, I promise."

Dea's right. He's the Horseman of War, for fuck's sake. Who in their right mind would go head-to-head with that tank?

"You're right." I rub the back of my neck, trying to get rid of some of the tension. "Just got a bad feeling, that's all."

It's okay. You're allowed to worry about him.

Just feels strange worrying about someone who two weeks ago made a career out of hating me.

Nine laughs. *He's a big softy really.*

Clearing the table (using some fancy air magic rather than doing things the boring way), I don't really know what to do with myself.

"Update?" I turn and ask Nine.

"In the middle of creating the data-app, and Con has a plan for getting backers and people to use it."

Connie puts a hand on my shoulder. "I'll start putting that plan into place tomorrow. Have any more of those teleporting crystals?"

I nod. "I'll make some more of both, and I might try and see if I can make some Earth-to-Earth ones, too. Should be useful."

Connie smiles and whispers, "You're always useful."

Nine yanks a piece of paper out of his pocket and hands it to me with a kiss on the cheek. "The list you asked for." He walks out of the kitchen and, I assume, to my library, where he's creating my masterpiece.

I don't think I asked for a list, but I unfold it anyway and smile at the contents.

1. Anti-sickness charm
2. ~~Teleportation crystals~~
3. More throwing knives
4. Unlocking beads

I fold it into my pocket for later. For now, I need a distraction from my strange worry over Arrie. Why has he been gone so long? It's supposed to be quick. If it were anything minor, like a flight delay, he would have noticed Nine's message.

Goddess damn it, Arrie, you're such an ass for making me worry.

"Hey," Dea whispers in my ear, making me jump, "let's watch a movie."

"Okay."

There's a butt-ton of stuff I should be doing, like mastering the bo staff, working on unlocking my water or earth Witch powers, practicing more Fae spells, quickening my shifts, creating more charms—

"Stop." Dea places both hands on my shoulders as he guides me down the corridor to the underground cinema room. "Arrie is going to be fine, and you have worked hard all afternoon. Do not overdo yourself. You need to rest regularly."

I just nod, not trusting my voice to work.

"What would you like to watch, Angel?" he asks once we've gotten through the doors at the end.

"Not fussed. You pick."

He picks something or other (I'm not really paying attention) and lowers the couch. "Come here." He pats the space in the very corner and grabs a blanket from the stack behind the couch. Tucking me in like a burrito, he kisses my forehead and wraps an arm around my back and starts the movie.

Romcom. He picked a romcom for me. N'awwww . . .

Fucking softy.

Dea groans beside me. "Shut up. Just trying to make her smile, and romance seems to distract her."

Nine laughs inside our heads and goes back to whatever he's doing.

"Thank you," I whisper.

The movie is good, honestly it is, but it isn't distracting enough. Where is that Horseman of War? And why isn't he back yet? Why hasn't he responded to Nine's message?

"This is not helping, is it?"

I shake my head. "Sorry."

"Do not apologize. If it were you or Nine not responding to my messages and being gone longer than logically expected, I would be as worried as you."

His admission takes me aback. "Really?"

He clears his throat and looks at me with a light blush coloring his features. "Yes." His eyes avoid mine after that, and I can't help but smile at his embarrassment.

It's cute as hell.

"Hey," I say, turning his chin back toward me, "don't be embarrassed. You are allowed to feel and have emotions. Please don't hide them. Not from me."

He wraps an arm around my shoulder. "Then in that case, you should know I would like to sleep next to you tonight. If that is okay?"

"You are all always allowed. No need to ask permission."

He smiles, and we watch the rest of the movie in relative peace, his admission easing the concern for Arrie.

Arrie is on his way back, Sweetie.

"Really?" I jump off of the sofa and nearly fall off the floating platform, or I would have, if not for Dea catching me. "Thanks," I mumble.

Yup. He just messaged me back. He's just flying back to Colorado and is only a few hours out.

Relief floods my system, and I have to sit down. "Thank fuck for that." Now that I'm not worried, a new feeling overtakes me: anger. "What the fuck took him so long?"

He said he lost the teleportation crystal. You can grill him when he gets in.

Tell him to come find me straight away.

Will do.

"Now what would you like to do?" Dea says from beside me, his hand resting on the small of my back, inching just below the waist line of my skirt.

I do not miss the suggestion in his tone, I just choose to ignore it. Instead suggesting, "Let's hit the gym? You can help with my bo practice?"

Dea groans but grabs my hand. "Fine. Come on then." He smiles, though, to make sure I know he isn't being serious. He'll wait for me to be ready—without being butt-hurt, I hope.

The gym is a peaceful place by this point; a place I can vent all my frustrations without hurting myself or the others. It allows me to just be me. And tonight is no exception. Concern for Arrie has left me edgy, and that didn't vanish when I learned he is indeed okay. The fucking asshole. If he is injury free, he will not remain so when he fucking gets home.

"How far have you gotten with bo practice?" Dea asks as he grabs a practice sword from the rack and changes into more comfortable attire: sweatpants and a loose-fitting tee.

"I can pull off a few maneuvers without falling over, and I can handle the basics pretty well." I also change, and then grab the bo I left beside the sword rack.

"Well then, Horseman of Magic, show me what you have got." His adorable Victorian English accent makes that phrase all the more hilarious, and I have to stifle a laugh before mirroring his ready stance.

I make the first move, swiping left with a whoosh of air, knocking him back a step before he regains his balance.

"Nicely done." He looks impressed, and damn if that doesn't make me giddy.

Death is impressed with me.

Score one for me!

Dea lunges at me, trying to aim low, but I sidestep and speed around him, going for a gentle tap to his back. He quickly spins, however, and rolls out of the way.

Damn. So fucking close.

Try again, Magic. Try again.

This time I use my Vampire speed to outmaneuver his spin attack, and he smiles with a wicked sort of glee, one of the corners of his lips higher than the other. I know that smile. He's about to up his game.

With one foot to the left, he dodges right and fazes circles around me, too fast for even my Vampire eyes to catch. But he isn't too fast to sense.

One circle.

Two circle.

Three circle.

Four—

I hold my bo out, and he smacks right into it, flipping over and falling on his ass. "Bet that's the last time you'll be trying to out-speed me, asshole."

He jumps to his feet with a grimace and probably a sore ass with the momentum he hit that floor with. "That is what you think, Angel."

The wooden sword drops to the floor with a thud, and before I know it, he yanks the bo staff out of my hand and wraps me in an embrace so tight I'm worried I might actually feel it, but he lets me go pretty quickly. He smirks at me, and I'm about to ask what the cheeky smile is for, until he sweeps his leg out and sends me flying to my ass.

"Payback is sweet."

He smiles down at me and offers his hand, but I ignore it and get to my own feet. The chuckle that escapes his lips has me smiling.

"Come here." I hold out my arms. He looks at me with dubious concern for a moment, so I say, "I'm being serious. No tricks. I'm not the asshole here."

More laughter fills my ears as he walks toward me and wraps both arms around my waist.

I place a lingering kiss to those delicious lips, playing with his lip piercing as I ease my tongue into his mouth with sweet and tender strokes.

"Angel?" he asks as he pulls away.

"Yeah?"

"Can I tell you a secret?"

I nod, tension suddenly filling the room.

"I prefer your male form in terms of sexual attraction." He looks to the floor with a sheepish layer of sweet-red embarrassment heating his cheeks. "I know that might not be okay, but—"

I grab his lips with my own and try to convey everything with that simple kiss. It isn't deep or hot or anything more than a tender peck, but he smiles once I pull back.

Changing to my male form, I smile at him. "You mean you prefer me like this?"

"In terms of sexual attraction, yes. But everything else does not really rely on sex. I love you. And you are you no matter your form."

I don't know what to say to that. Am I? Do I really not differ form to form? Am I still me like this? All these pesky questions I never have an answer to pervade my mind, and the spiral it sends me into makes me dizzy beyond my ability to stand.

Dea steadies me with a questioning look, but I just wave his concern away. "Talk to me," he whispers as he leans closer to my ear.

"I just . . . It's hard, you know. Never just being one solid person, never knowing what to expect from those around you. But you all make it so much easier. Thank you." Tears creep into the rims of my eyes, and I swear I'm so fed up of crying that once this whole war thing is over with, I'll never fucking cry again.

The door behind us slams open, forcing me to quickly wipe my eyes, and in walks a face so familiar it hurts.

"Arrie!" I run to him and wrap my arms around his neck. "Arrie," I whisper, snuggling my face into his neck. "Where. The fuck. Have you been?" I say through gritted teeth. Yanking my head away and putting my feet to the floor, I take a step back and glower at him. "Huh?"

He sighs and runs a shaky hand through his hair. Mumbling something in his native language under his breath, he finally takes a breath and explains, "The Witches. They were challenging. Tried to lock me up for your crimes. Then I lost the crystal." He sighs. "But the Shifters are helping the Vampires as much as they can. Taking in strays, offering up empty homes in the Shifter Underground, and feeding them."

I flinch. "That does not excuse the lack of messaging! Do you know how worried we were?"

Arrie exchanges a glance with Dea, who I hear chuckle behind me. "You were worried about me?"

Damn. Fuck. Shit.

"Really?" He tries to grab my hand, but I yank it away.

"Still mad at you."

He chuckles, the pleasant kind of laugh one makes when they're happily surprised by something, and fuck damn it, I'm lost. All the anger floods out of me as I run and jump on him, forgetting all about that control I'm supposed to be showing or the angry frustration I was feeling not a minute ago. This man makes me crazy, and that laugh weakens my defenses every damn time.

I smother him with the longest kiss I've ever been a part of, and I revel in the feeling of completeness I feel now that I finally have my entire team here. Home. Safe. And I'm going to remind him exactly why that is such a good idea.

Shifting my body down slightly, I press myself against every inch of him, and the groan that escapes his lips has his hands clenching my ass tighter.

Your team, 'ey?

Groaning, I mutter, "Way to kill the mood, Nine."

Arrie grumbles beneath me but tightens his hold on my ass even further, where he helps keep my legs wrapped around his waist. "I'm gonna kill that *fjandinn*."

Dea's in stitches of laughter behind us, content to watch our reunion from the side lines, it seems. "Come on, you two. Let us go to bed. It is late."

I climb down from Arrie's hold and drag them to bed but when I get there, there are dozens of boxes, wrappers, and other gifts on the bed. "What's all this?"

Arrie runs a hand behind his neck. "I thought, since you didn't have much, I'd pick some more clothes up for you." His eyes dart away from mine.

But I force his face back to mine with a smile. "Thank you, Arrie." I place a gentle kiss to his cheek.

Dea blows out a breath behind us, and I scowl at him.

They help me put it all away, and the moment my head hits that pillow, I'm a goner. Asleep in the land of nod, snuggled between two amazing men, and sometime in the night, Nine and Connie join us, creating a familiar snuggle pile that always keeps the nightmares away and makes me smile uncontrollably.

43

The next morning, Connie leaves for Earth, where she's arranged a meeting with all four pillar communities (I know, I'm shocked too) in the heart of Colorado, meaning she doesn't have to travel too far. Apparently, the Fae are holocalling in, as they don't trust the other communities. Plus, Arrie managed to persuade the Witches to at least hear us out. So, all in all, it's a win-win, if slightly compromised. Connie made me prepare a speech, which I had Dea's help in creating, and she's to read that on my behalf.

The rest of us are in the library, researching various things to help tick items off my list; also, creating Witch charms and Fae spells helps harness my powers, so I'm doing two things at once.

Horseman of Magic for the win!

"Dea?" I ask, suddenly remembering something else we should be doing, "have you managed to get hold of the SC?"

He groans from a couple of book stacks back. "No. They are ignoring my calls." He peeks around the corner of the shelf and grimaces at me. "I am sorry, Angel."

I sigh. "That's okay." How can I get them and the magical communities to communicate if they aren't even talking to us? "Why aren't they talking to us?" I mumble. "They came to the ball." Goddess, all these politics are so confusing.

"Ah!" I hear Arrie gasp from beside me. "Medical charms." He throws a book at me, which I catch, and continues looking. Arrie's helping me create anti-sickness charms, which I'm still surprised haven't been created yet.

"Maybe I could open up a magic shop after the war is over. Unique charms and spells . . ."

I'm just muttering to myself, but Dea looks over and smiles. "That sounds wonderful, Angel."

Arrie grunts but smiles and returns his eyes to the stack in front of him.

Awesome plan. Should totally do it.

"I was just joking." Goddess, could you imagine it? Me, owning a magic shop? Hahahahahaha. Hilarious. I'm nearly giggling at the ludicrous idea.

"Why not?" Dea asks.

"Because that requires responsibility, and thought, and customer services, and . . . Just no way."

"Right," Arrie says, "because saving the world is just a lazy person's job."

I huff at him and search through another shelf, content to mull in my own thoughts for a while. Me, a magic store owner? As if anyone would buy anything from someone the world hates.

Shaking those pesky self-doubting thoughts from my mind, I focus on the task at hand: referencing sections, chapters and pages from all the books the guys are handing me. We can then read them and make notes later.

"Found it!" Nine yells from several stacks back. He hasn't handed me a single book the entire time we've been here and instead has been off looking at something on his own. He runs over with a massive volume that looks a thousand years old and is bound in black leather with faded gold lettering on the front.

The lettering is in some ancient language I can't read, so I pull the translational bookscreen from my pocket and grab it from Nine's hands.

Angels: Myths and Facts.

"What is it?" I ask, curious as to why this is what he's been looking for.

"Well," he says, scratching his head, "I said I'd do some research into the whole Angel magical connection thing, and I have. I was searching for a book I'd read a long time ago. Sorry, it took me a while to find a copy." He hops on the spot, clearly nervous about something.

I raise a questioning eyebrow, and he sighs.

"Look, it's complicated. Can you just read the section on Angel mating toward the end, please?" He sighs at my sound of surprise. "It'll help. Promise."

"Fine." I huff and go over to my desk. Dea follows, eager for an answer as much as I am. "Let's see."

I place the bookscreen over the old-fashioned contents page and the flicked to the right page: ANGEL MATING AND MAGICAL BONDS.

"Fucking Christ, this is gonna piss me off, isn't it?"

Dea chuckles. "Probably. But know that I do not care what it says, it does not change anything."

Sure. As if.

I skim the page and can already feel my blood boiling beneath the surface. This can't be the answer, surely?

"One of the common myths of Angel lore is the concept of bonds between different Angel magics," Dea begins reading out loud. "It has only been seen in full-blooded Angels, and the effects are mostly seen only in Angel form . . ." Dea's voice trails off, coming to the same realization I did two minutes earlier.

I sit there, staring at the page, well aware of all three guys staring at me. I don't know how to feel. On the one hand, I'm already in love with Dea, so it doesn't really matter, but on the other, I am sick of magic controlling my life. What gives it the right to decide who I'm attracted to? And does this mean I'm only attracted to him because our magics bonded? Does he not really love me?

An arm yanks me back from the book. "Watch the book!"

Looking down at my arms, I notice they're on fire. "Shit." Quickly changing forms, the flames puff out of existence as quickly as I grow a dick. "I'm going for a walk," I whisper.

Dea calls after me and Nine tells him to give me some space, but I can't deal with them right now. There's a part of me that knows talking to them will help, but right now, the thought of talking to the very person I'm magically bonded to scares the shit out of me.

"Why didn't it happen the moment I first saw him change?" I mutter to myself. I'd seen his Angel form a few times before that moment in the Vampire Royal Council room. It doesn't make sense.

I wander the corridors of the house, walking past empty rooms, used rooms, the servants' quarters, and doors I have no idea of the contents, if any. "This place is like a maze," I mumble for the thousandth time since I woke up in this house.

It's been months since then, and I'm practically a whole different person; it seems like it was just yesterday when I was worried about who I was and who I'll become. I'm still worried, but it's different now. I have a home, a family, friends, boyfriends, a girlfriend, and most of my memories are coming back.

Sighing, I come to the decision that it's time. I need to speak to Mr. Compton and learn everything there is to know about the old me. Plus, he's with the SC, so he can take a message back to them.

Nine? Where I am? I look around a strange-looking corridor made of wood and stone.

Wow. You're in the original layer of corridors. We haven't been there in some time. Hang tight. I'm sending Dea.

The brick, stone, and wood are layered to create compact walls that've stood the test of time for nearly two thousand years, it would seem. This must have been the original house, before it got upgraded over the years. There are rooms with no doors littered down the hallways, but every single one is bare of life. Empty. Cold.

"Angel?"

"Dea," I say under my breath as I turn around from peering into another vacant room. Standing in front of me is the man in question.

"Angel, I . . . I am sorry." He looks to the floor, his cheeks redder than a tomato, and the tension in the corridor could not be thicker.

"It's nothing to apologize for," I say. "It's not any more your fault than it is mine."

"I did not know Angels mated. I thought mating was just a myth."

"I know."

He runs gentle fingers up my bare arms and finally looks me in the eyes; his piercing gaze never fails to take my breath away with those sparkling galaxy-like eyes unlike any other I've gazed into. "It does not change anything."

"I know."

He frowns, confused at my acceptance, no doubt.

"I'm not concerned about us, Dea." I grab his hands and step into his arms, which he wraps around me. "I'm concerned that magic rules my life, and I'm just supposed to go along with it like it's nothing. As though I control it. But I don't." Tears creep along the edges of my eyes before they finally fall. "*Chikushou*," I grumble.

Swiping away the tears with a fury usually only reserved for Arrie, Dea laughs at my silly antics. "You are allowed to be upset."

"Just feels like I'm always upset these days."

"If you count the number of laughs as well as the tears, you will likely find they even out. We just tend to only see the tears."

There he goes again, his never-ending, well-spoken wisdom that makes him sound like a poet.

"C'mon." I grab his hand and drag us down a corridor.

"It is this way." He pulls us in the other direction.

"I knew that."

44

Back in the library, we all fall into a rhythm as the guys search for books and online information that might help, and I tag, highlight, and reference them for later. By the time we have a pile taller than male-me, we stop for dinner and return.

"Ugh. Reading," Arrie grumbles.

"Get used to it!" I punch him in the arm and watch him smile as he goes to rub it better. "Baby."

Arrie grumbles something in what I can only assume is Norse, and I sigh.

"C'mon, we need to start going through this information and putting my magic to good use." I run to the desk, my pink hair flying behind me, and pick up the first book on creating Fae-spelled objects.

"Still reckon it would last longer if you put the Fae spell into a Witch charm." Nine wraps an arm around my shoulders.

"I concur," Dea says. "It would be a more solid spell, too."

"Okay, let's try it."

After creating a charm bead, I change form and imbue a basic Fae spell to make someone forget the last five minutes for an hour.

"That was easy." And it was. It's similar to the Witch charm I put into the Fae-spelled teleporting crystals the other day, but the other way around.

We spend the rest of the evening playing around with my powers, learning that joining my Fae and Witch abilities is pretty simple, but I can't use them at the same time (obviously), so it has to be planned; I can't, for example, create an attack spell using both unless it's imbued into an object first.

Earth-to-Earth teleporting crystals are also pretty simple, as are anti-sickness charms (turns out medical spells aren't doable for the Fae—something about the Fae magic not reacting well with the internal body of any Animalia).

"What next?" I ask, right before the doors to the library, which have remained open these past few days, slam closed, right behind a walking blonde beauty who smiles at me in a way that has my insides melting and my eyelids fluttering.

"Connie!"

I sprint and leap at her, throwing all of my female weight at her body, but she catches me with ease and wraps my legs around her waist as she holds me up with a firm two hands on my ass.

"Hey, hon. You doin' okay?"

"Much better now."

She laughs and leans up for a kiss, which I happily answer with my own slightly steamy kiss that lasts longer than I think she anticipated. When we finally break for air, she smiles and places me back to the floor. "C'mon." She grabs my hand and takes me back to the guys and our heaping piles of books.

"Hey Con," everyone greets at once, not even looking up from their books.

"You soooo have them whipped, hon." She motions a whip crack and laughs at her own joke.

Goddess, it's good to have her back.

Nine looks up from his book. "Have much luck?"

Connie nods and shakes her head at the same time. "Kinda."

I wince. "Explain."

"Well . . ." She takes a seat on the floor and sifts through the volumes in one of the piles. "The Vampires and Shifters are on board, the Witches don't really care either way, and the Fae are against it."

"Well, that was about the outcome I was expecting," Nine says. "It doesn't really effect the Witches either way. If they wanted to ask for help or post jobs, they can do so without having to reveal their species, but they probably won't be taking jobs until they finally comes out of the closet."

"Right. That makes sense." I nod.

"And the Fae don't want to make peace with the humans. They want turmoil so their less-than-savory practices can continue." He sighs. "But they probably won't stop their people from using it. But don't expect many Fae users."

I sigh too. "And the rogue Vampires are probably going to cause mayhem too." How do we stop people from misusing it? "It's a great opportunity for communities to work together in all kinds of ways. Why can't everyone just see that?" I groan.

"Hey," Connie soothes, "they will. It'll take time."

"Yup," Nine adds. "We're going to have to show them ourselves."

"What does that mean?"

"We'll have to take the jobs and make them public, film some of them, get promo going, and make people see the use of it."

"Filming? Us?"

Dea coughs. "We are being hounded by media mongrels for interviews as it is. The world wants to know who we are. We are going to need to do some media control at some point." He puts his head back into TALES OF ANCIENT WITCH CHARMS.

Ugh. Great.

Hey! This was your fault to begin with. You made us go public. Remember?

Ugh. Stop being so right all the fucking time.

Nine laughs, and the others just look at us with weird adoring smiles and giggle under their breaths.

"What?"

"You are both adorable, Angel," Dea says.

Adorable? "I. Am. Not. Adorable. I'm a fucking lioness. Don't make me shift into one to prove my point!"

Arrie bursts into a fit of laughter, dragging Connie down with him, and soon we're all just laughing in the library so hard I have to hold my sides and dry my tears.

Goddess, it's good to laugh.

I spend the rest of the evening practicing various Fae spells and Witch charms until I'm exhausted with all the back-and-forth switching of my forms. I mean, seriously, could my Fae and Witch abilities not be in the same fucking form? Ugh.

I'm running out of energy.

"Okay," Nine says as he stands up. "It's past midnight and you're exhausted. Let's go to bed." He grabs my hand and looks to the others. "You lot coming?"

Dea looks away, Arrie awkwardly coughs, and Connie just looks to the ground.

"What's going on?" I let go of Nine's hand and walk up to them.

"Well," Connie begins . . .

"Just spit it out." I hunch my shoulders and sigh. I'm tired, hungry, and magically exhausted; give me a fucking break. "Please?"

She nods. "You sure you two want company? We could sleep separately if you like?"

"Oh. Ohhhhh." I look at their awkward faces and sigh. Again. Sitting on the floor, I make them all face me while I prepare my speech. "No. We're not doing that. Just because I've had sex with Nine does not make our relationship any more valuable than the ones I share with all of you. I know we haven't really figured out the details . . ." Goddess, damn it, this is hard. "But I still"—I look away from their piercing stares and to the floor—"like all of you. We're still, you know, like a thing, right?"

Goddess, I haven't ruined everything, have I?

I can handle the silence that ensues. What I can not handle is the snickering Connie is trying to hide and the awkward cufuffling laugh Arrie is trying to swallow.

"All right! I get it. I'm shit with words. Just stop making it harder." I get up in a huff and go to take my magically exhausted ass to bed.

But Connie runs to me and grabs my hand. "No, wait. We're sorry." She spins me around and wraps her arms around my waist. "I'm sorry. That was mean of me." A small smile creeps onto her face and makes her eyes sparkle. "But you were just sooooo cute." She pecks my cheek and whispers, "Yes, I'll be your girlfriend." She unwraps herself from me and walks away. "But I'm not tired." She shrugs. "Need less sleep than all of you weirdos."

Right. Of course.

"I'll keep working on some advertising plans for the app and see if I can't get ahold of the SC for you. You wimps go to sleep."

"C'mon, Sweetie." Nine grabs my hand. "Let's go."

Arrie and Dea follow us into my bedroom in silence, and I worry my lip until Nine tells me to stop.

They're both fine. They were just a little worried about interrupting us.

"Oh . . ."

Dea looks at me in confusion, but I wave him off.

I'm too tired to deal with my relationship drama. It can wait until tomorrow.

Stripping down to my pants and vest tee, I crawl into bed. I could have sworn this bed was smaller earlier. Hmm. Never mind.

The guys join me, with Dea and Arrie either side of me, and Nine on the opposite side of Dea.

"Night guys."

Arrie plants a gentle kiss to my temple while Dea grabs my hand and whispers, "Goodnight."

Goodnight, Sweetie.

"COME ON YOU LOT! TIME TO GET UP. YOU'VE ALL SLEPT ENOUGH."

Whaaa? Sunlight pours through my bedroom window, and heat from either side of me trickles sweat down my front and back. But when I remember whose heat it belongs to, I smile. Totally worth it.

"Come on!" Connie jumps on the bed, and all four of us groan.

"Fuck off, Con!" Arrie grumbles from my right.

I could have just air-lifted her off the bed, but I'm enjoying the havoc in a weird, my-version-of-perfect kind of way.

"What's up?" I sit up and rub the sleep from my eyes.

She crawls up from the bottom of the bed and places a leg either side of me as she straddles my waist. "I finalized the advertisement plan, organized some safe, low-key media control, and have worked out twice. I'm bored!" She pouts and grabs my hand. "Come on! Wake up and cause more fun."

I giggle and lean into her.

"I could get used to waking up like this," Nine whispers just loud enough for us all hear as he watches Connie and I embrace in a less-than-innocent kiss that takes my breath away.

Like usual.

"Mmm," Arrie moans from beside me, struggling to keep his eyes open. "Definitely."

"Okay, okay." I push Connie off and hop over Arrie to get out of bed. "Let's hear these plans of yours."

We all get showered, dressed, and ready while Connie rattles off a schedule of advertisement that could run without any input and media meetings, interviews, and goddess knows what else to keep us in a positive public light.

"So," Nine says as he steps out of the shower in nothing but a towel wrapped around his waist. "I was thinking we should hire an agent to deal with all of our press appearances?"

He strips down to his birthday suit while Dea and I openly ogle his lean form and gets dressed into sweatpants and one of his geek-shirts; this one has a picture of a t-rex drinking tea, with a caption saying TEA-REX.

I can't help but laugh when Nine smiles at the pun in the mirror.

"Sure. Seems helpful." I turn back to Connie. "So, we have a group interview this afternoon, right?"

Connie nods. "And we need to make our profiles on the app to actually get it started before we go live this evening."

"You know," I start as I pull a fresh pair of bat tights on, "you're better at this lifestyle management than I thought you'd be. Remind me to have you organize my training schedule in the future."

Connie pecks me on the cheek and winks. "You don't want that," she whispers, "I'd just organize an orgy every time you got stressed. That would make the stress drop right off."

I laugh as I blush.

Nine just looks at me with a knowing smirk. *Could totally be arranged.*

Stop distracting me. Lots of training to do today.

Nine laughs and directs me to breakfast, where we basically all eat toast while we try our hardest to keep up with Connie's energy levels. Seriously, she's like a bunny on dusted steroids.

Does she ever calm down?

Not when she's happy. And you're her first partner in a long, long time, so she's pretty happy.

Looking at her radiant smile as she bites into another peanut-butter and marshmallow-fluff toast sandwich, I can't help but be happy for her. For us. Things aren't perfect, but maybe this weird relationship could work.

It's about time something went my way for a change.

Now I just have to figure out how to save the world before there actually ends up being a war.

45

We all sit in an office in the official meeting foyer of the house as Jeremy Bouler sits in front of us with a scowl that matches his defensive posture and stupid floor-length cloak.

He doesn't want to be here.

"Drew the short straw, Mr. Bouler?"

Dea shoots me an irritated glance, and Connie groans. "Behave," Connie warns. "He's probably anxious about meeting five supernaturals he didn't know existed until a week ago."

"That assessment would be correct."

"Well," Dea starts, offering him a hand to shake, "I can personally guarantee your safety during your stay here in *Sheruta*, Mr. Bouler."

"Thank you." He shakes Dea's hand. "That is most appreciated."

"I'm sorry," I interrupt, "but who do you work for?"

He smiles at me—or he tries to. Bless him. He isn't very good at dealing with my randomness. "Of course. I'm one of the head reporters for the Supernatural Council. It's nice to meet you . . . ?"

I bristle at him being with the SC, but I force a smile nonetheless. "Magic."

He raises an eyebrow in question.

I sigh. "This is Death, War, Conquest, and Famine." I point to each in turn. "And I'm Magic. Dea, Arrie, Connie, and Nine have all nicknamed themselves, but I haven't had the brain space to think about it recently."

"Right." He writes some basic notes down. "So," he starts, "the four—five—Horsemen of the Apocalypse?"

Dea takes point—thank the goddess—and explains their backstory. Leaving out the details, of course, but he gets the main point across. A small recording device hovers around us, flying to each of us as we fill in some of the gaps in Dea's story. Well, the others do. I don't come in yet. Obviously.

I'm not that old.

Yet.

I grimace.

"So, it's been you guys all along? Like some kind of behind-the-scenes kings—and queen?"

Dea grimaces. "That is not how I would describe it. While we help and have the power to do what we wish, we usually just advise. The magical community tends to do what it wants either way."

I remember the Fae being a pain in our fucking asses. "He's right," I say. "We can advise all day long, but keeping the peace is challenging. Being separate from all of the magical communities and not being human allows us a unique vantage point."

Nine chimes in with, "Plus, we have respect in the magical community. We've helped solved many issues, and even smoothed the coming out process a hundred years ago."

The interviewer, who's gained some degree of confidence over the last hour, nods and asks, "So, you just advise and step in when things get out of control?"

We all nod.

"Okay. So, where do you come into all this?" He looks at me as he asks his question.

I don't know what to say. What am I supposed to say? I don't want to worry the human community.

Dea says to explain that your seal was broken by an unknown party and you've been training here ever since. Don't bring up the war. It'll cause panic.

Right.

So that's what I do. I tell my story, minus the war part.

"Have you ever left *Sheruta*?"

I nod. "I've visited each pillar court and council."

Mr. Bouler looks to Dea. "And the SC were already aware of your existence?" He looks doubtful.

"We helped form the SC, so yes, they know of us."

Mr. Bouler's mouth hangs open in shock. "This is not going to go down well."

"How can we help?" I ask.

He looks at me with a soft smile. "The public aren't going to like the governing factions keeping things from them. Especially humans. They're going to ask what else is out there." He sighs. "Heck, they already are."

"I see." I rack my brain to think of a way out, but I can't. "It might help for them to know that the magical community didn't know about our existence either. Just the leading councils and covens."

He nods and writes it down. "It might help do some damage control." He worries his lower lip and picks at his fingernails, eager to ask a question he isn't sure he should ask.

"You can ask us anything, Mr. Bouler." Dea looks at him with a reassuring smile. "Though I will not guarantee an answer."

Mr. Bouler smiles and sighs in defeat. "Why now? Why come out of the closet now? After two thousand years in hiding?"

We all fidget slightly, shifting in our seats. I really don't want to lie to this man; he seems sweet. But reporting on the real reason isn't an option.

"Mr. Bouler," I start, "I don't want to lie to you. But public knowledge of everything we're doing isn't an option right now."

Mr. Bouler nods.

"It became necessary for a recent problem we are trying to solve."

"Is this problem something we humans should be concerned about?"

I look to Dea, who nods at me, before I turn back and say, "Yes. But rest assured, we will do everything in our power to help."

A small Fae serving girl in a casual dress enters the room after knocking, air lifting a dozen trays of tea, cakes, and pastries. "Dinner, as requested." She curtsies and places all the trays on the tables in the far-left corner.

Food! Finally. All this talking and worrying is sending my stomach on edge. Looking over Dea's shoulder, I zoom in and see my favorite cake from the café and airlift one my way.

Mr. Bouler gasps, surprised. "You . . . just lifted it to you . . ." he sputters as I bite into the cakey goodness.

"Yeah, air Witch magic."

"Right." He still looks confused, bless him. "Witch magic. Something I'm not allowed to put into my report."

I snort. "Right. Witch closet."

Mr. Bouler laughs, and I can't help but feel happy that this guy was sent to us and not some snotty woman determined to cross every fucking line in the sand.

"So," Connie says, "you're coming back every day this week, right?"

Mr. Bouler nods over a cup of jasmine tea. "Yes. Each day has a different agenda. Today was an introduction. Tomorrow is about your powers."

"I hate being a show monkey," I complain.

"Stop complaining!" Connie yells. "This is all your fault in the first place."

I poke my tongue out at her and return to our interviewer, who looks at us with a thoughtful smile.

"You all must be really close?"

Dea coughs and looks to me in question.

Do I want the world to know about our relationship? Well, I certainly don't want to hide it. I'm not ashamed. I just . . . maybe now isn't the right time?

Before I can make up my mind, however, Arrie stands and walks to the food table. "We're just friends. But yes, we're like family."

My face pales and my heart goes a mile a minute.

Just friends? But . . . I thought . . .

Looking to Mr. Bouler with my best attempt at a neutral expression, I nod my agreement amidst holding back tears. "Like family," I choke out. I change form and take a calming breath.

Don't burn the human. Don't burn the human.

Mr. Bouler looks stunned again, and I get the feeling I'm going to continue surprising him all week.

"Thank you for being so patient with us, Mr. Bouler," Connie says. "I think we're about done for the day."

He nods and gets up to shake all our hands. "It was nice to meet you all."

After he leaves, everyone looks at Arrie with an accusatory scowl.

"What were you thinking!?" Connie yells. "Just a friend?" She walks up to him and swings a left hook to his face, but he blocks with ease. "Did you not sound that out in your head first!"

Nine steps up to them with his palms out flat in surrender, clearly not wanting to get involved in the fight. "Yeah, dude. That wasn't cool. It was her call to make."

Arrie looks at him in confusion. "It was our call to make, not hers. You act as though her opinions are the only ones that matter. That her feelings are all that counts." He clenches his fists and storms out of the room.

He didn't even look at me.

Why didn't he look at me?

I stand in the wake of his exit, dumbfounded and confused. The others all turn to me with gentle, comforting looks, but I don't want their pity. I don't know what I want.

"I'm going to, err . . . go somewhere else." My legs take me out of there as quickly as they can, my male form not being as fast as my female form.

I can hear Nine and Connie talking about it if I strain my ears hard enough. They're all on my side, it seems. But in this instance, there isn't a side to take.

46

We all spend the following week showing Mr. Bouler our lives, powers, and what we do; starting some ad campaigns on my sparkly new app and gaining as many profiles as possible from allies and friends; and we're all dodging around Arrie's bad mood and my current drama. Before I know it, it's Friday and the first job request comes through.

"Guys, guys, guys, guys . . . Look, look, look, look!" I shout as I run through the house at top Vampire speed to collect everyone.

"Huh?" Nine asks as he steps out from his bedroom with tired eyes and a yawn on his face. "What's up?"

"We got our first job request!" I jump up and down and cause Nine to smile with pride at me.

Connie and Dea stand behind me, both looking happy my plan is starting to work.

"Well," Connie asks, "what's the job?"

"Oh, right." Need to actually look at the job posting. "Japan, $4,000, removing a spell from an old magic book. Posted by the Magical History Museum of Tokyo."

I go silent for a moment while the others patiently wait for me. "Tokyo?" But I'm avoiding going back there. If I go there, I'm sure I'll get a million flashbacks and visions of my time living there. "Fuck."

It has to be me. No one else can disable a spell without dragging a Fae along. And that's un-damn-likely.

"I can go with you, Angel. If you would like?" Dea places a hand on my shoulder. "We all can."

I shake my head. "Too much to do here. I want someone managing the political nightmare of creating the embassies, and I need you to contact Mr. Compton for my return."

Nine nods, but Connie looks at me in shock. "Mr. Compton? Really?"

"It's time. I have questions I need answers to. Before another reporter arrives and starts asking questions about my mortal life."

"If you're sure, hon." Connie yanks me into a hug. "But you can do it at your own pace."

"Con's right," Nine says. "We spent a long time exploring our pasts. You don't need to do it all at once."

"But yes, Dea," I add, "you can come along."

He smiles behind me. I don't need to turn around to know that because I can tell by the hazy look of love on Nine's face. That man is an open book.

I am not.

Whatever you say.

"What's going on?" Arrie's familiar grumble echoes down the hallway. "Meeting?"

Dea shakes his head. "Got our first job posting on the new app. Angel and I are going together."

I accept the job request as myself and attach Dea's profile to the listing, so they know it'll be both of us.

Arrie grumbles something in Norse under his breath and walks away. Again, without even looking at me. Has he changed his mind? Maybe he doesn't like the idea of sharing? Or maybe he thinks I'm taking away his family? Goddess, there are so many options for things I could have done wrong. Maybe—

Stop. Stop giving him exactly what he doesn't deserve. Enjoy your trip with Dea all alone, and come back and deal with him then.

Right. First day on the job. Eeeeek!

"Gossip night before you go?" Connie looks at me all excited. "Your turn to pick something for us to do!"

"Sure."

Shit, shit, shit. I totally forgot. I have to do something, but what? Fuck, fuck, fuck.

How about going to a bar in Sheruta town? You've not been, Con loves going out . . .

Great idea!

Mwuhahaha! Conquest and Magic are going out drinking. Goddess, I hope she doesn't get me too drunk.

AN HOUR LATER, I'M IN MY CLOSET STRESSING ABOUT WHAT TO WEAR. THIS IS BECOMING A regular occurrence. What the fuck do I wear to a bar? Maybe some jeans and a low-cut tee? Maybe something with sparkles? Ohhh, what about that sparkly dress with the low-cut back—that'll show off my back tattoo. Nah, that's too slutty.

"How about you just wear some jeans and a nice top, hon?"

"Ah!" I jump around with my fists raised and notice Connie's shock of blonde hair dazzling in the setting sun seeping through the open closet door. "It's just you," I say, relief washing through me.

Her laugh echoes through the small room, and I feel my cheeks blush crimson. "Relax. Just me." She raises her hands in mock defeat. "And jeans and a slightly slutty top would be great for the bar I've chosen."

Even though tonight's date is my choice, I left the details up to someone who's actually been to the bars in *Sheruta;* lest I take us to come crummy shithole.

"Err, right." I grab my trusty pair of black skinnies and shimmy into them. "What top?" I whisper to myself as I search through the rack of them.

I've gained quite the collection over the last few months, with every member of the team helping me fill it.

"Oh!" I yank a shimmery purple crop top off the rack that I've yet to wear. "Let's give this one a go."

"Isn't that the one Arrie got you when he went to see the Shifters last week?"

Ugh. Just the reminder that this top is only here because of that dickhead is enough to make me put it back on the fucking hanger.

"Hey, no. Don't let him do that. You can look fabulous without him." She throws it back at me. "I think it'll go great."

Connie herself is sporting a fabulous miniskirt in a dark, grungy green color paired with a long-sleeved orange top with a relatively modest neckline for her. And she finishes it all off with a pair of bright orange heels that make her look even taller than usual.

After finalizing my outfit, we're off. "Want me to fly us there? Or do you want to retain your hairstyle?"

She giggles, and I can't help but thread my arm through hers. "Don't mind," she finally answered, "but I'd rather drag our date out as long as possible."

She has a point. If I fly us there, we'll lose an hour between traveling there and back. Walking in the setting sun it is. Not a bad start to a great night.

"I know this is a sore subject, but I'm sorry Arrie's being such an idiot."

I wince as she says his name. "It's . . . fine. Not your fault."

"Still . . ." She avoids looking at me.

"Hey!" I stop us halfway down the main road from our house. "You are not his keeper. He's capable of making his own choices. And certainly capable of making his own mistakes." I roll my eyes. "So he can make his own apologies."

"I know," she says through a sigh. "I just wish he would open up to you more. Maybe there was a reason, you know."

A reason? Yeah, like he doesn't want to be tied to me while I make a fucking mess of this entire relationship. Not to mention while I destroy the damn world.

"Stop spiraling." She gets us walking once more and holds my hand. "It should be a fun night. And if you need to unload any of your drama on me, I'm all ears." She gives me knowing eyes.

I know what she wants: the dirty deets of my night with Nine. "Sorry, but I'm not talking about that." Not yet, at least. Who knows what I'll say if she gets me too drunk.

Her evil smirk tells me she's come to the same conclusion. The fucking bitch.

An hour into our date, and we've downed enough shots to have us fully dancing without a care in the world in a bar that had some cool air darts I rocked at. It's a small, rustic place with good company, smiles, and familiar faces. Seems *Sheruta* is finally getting used to me. Or I'm getting used to them. Either one.

"Soooo . . ." Connie begins as she grabs my waist and presses her body flat against mine. "Your first time with Nine . . . How was it?" she whispers in my ear just loud enough for my Vampire hearing to pick up on.

"It was . . . perfect." And it was.

"He can't hear us out here. So don't hold back on me now!" She runs her hands under the hem of my crop top, and every touch sends a sizzling fire under my skin, spreading to every crevice of my body. "C'mon, help a girl out, hon."

I let my hands roam over her waist and ass, and I eventually give into her pleading eyes. "It was . . . as romantic as it was hot. He'd created a witchlighted clearing in the forest and had a bed, rose petals, and a bonfire set up so we could enjoy ourselves no matter what we chose to do."

Connie pulls back to look at my face and smiles. "Really?" She swears under her breath. "Damn. That fucker makes it really hard to be romantic."

"Well, we had sex, and then we cuddled all night and came back the next morning." She looks upset at my lack of details, but I go on to say, "Oh, and then I got Dea off in the kitchen. I told them both I loved them a few days previous. And I'm somehow mated to Dea's Angel form."

Connie coughs and splutters. "Hold up. That's a lot to unpack." She takes a deep breath. "Let's start with getting Dea off. In the kitchen? That's where we all eat!"

"We cleaned up! You wouldn't be complaining if it were you."

She shrugs. "Probably not." She takes another deep breath and moves to behind me as she wraps her arms around my waist. "Now, about the whole saying you love them. Really?"

"It just sort of slipped out when I told Nine. I panicked and then told Dea when we were chatting about it."

She chuckles behind me as she peppers kisses down my neck. "I can just imagine your internal panic."

I spin and throw my lips against hers so hard she stumbles back and has to catch us both. Her hands roam to the hem of my crop top, and I let her slip them underneath and roam wherever she wants.

We have great fun dancing on the barrier of inappropriate behavior all evening. Eventually, when we can barely walk anymore, much less dance, we decide to head home. I don't trust our ability to walk so elect to fly us there.

Turns out, flying drunk is just as dangerous as walking drunk, if not more so. At least when walking, the only directions you have are forwards, backwards, sidewards, or downwards. When in the air, you have every direction imaginable, and the potential of me flying us into a wall or the ocean is pretty high.

"Weeeeeee!" Connie spreads her arms out on either side of her body and is pretending to be some kind of a superhero. "Hero of Conquest to the ressscue!"

I concentrate on trying to get us home in one piece, and eventually, after losing the way multiple times and nearly smacking us into the ground more times than I have fingers to count them on, the house comes into view.

Connie laughs and points out the garden.

Now to land without beheading us. Hmmm. Concentrating on the ground rapidly rising before us in all its spinning glory, I try to slow down when noticing the porch but only serve to speed us up.

The porch, made of some kind of glass, smashes as we crash through it and land in a bloody heap on the floor. We're both bleeding, I can smell it, and when three pairs of feet rush to us, we can't stop giggling.

"What the fuck?" Arrie groans.

"Did you fly drunk?" Dea scolds.

"What were you thinking?" Nine asks behind an obvious laugh.

I try to stand up, but I can't. Something is keeping me trapped to the floor.

"Shit, your leg is pierced to the floor with glass." Nine runs over and yanks the glass out while Dea heals me up in no time.

"See, all good!" I spring up like a bunny rabbit and go to walk to my room, but I stumble and fall into Arrie instead. "Oops, sorry."

Arrie sighs and picks me up, then goes to grab Connie, and deposits us both in my room before walking away. Still, he doesn't look at me once.

"One day, I'm going to punch that f-f-fucker so hard in the balls, he'll forget his own gorgeous ref-f-flection."

"Yas, girl! You go for it. Heeee . . ." Her face pales as she hiccups. "Shit." She runs for the bathroom and slams the door behind her.

Well, it was fun while it lasted. I focus hard and change into my male form so I can take care of Connie. It's my choice of date, after all. But when she doesn't come out of the bathroom for over fifteen minutes, I go in to investigate and find her passed out on the floor by the toilet.

Scooping her up, I tuck her into bed and ask the house for a bucket (just in case).

47

"You are the one that got so drunk you crashed through the porch ceiling, Angel," Dea says as we rock up to the museum that hired us. "Deactivating a Fae spell may require your female form's Witch powers."

Ugh. Even the thought of being in my female form sends a wave of nausea through me. "Let's just hope that's not the case, or I might vomit all over the ancient book." So far, I've stayed in my male form to avoid the hangover.

Dea chuckles but quickly hides it behind a frown. "You should be more responsib—"

"Bite me, Angel of Death."

Dea stops us at the front of the museum steps and yanks me to his lips. He devours me in front of at least twenty people coming and going through the front door, and I do nothing to stop him. Just when I think he'll pull back, he nips my bottom lip and smirks. "Do not make threats you do not intend to keep, Angel."

A shiver runs through me from the small tingle of pain he caused, and the need to bite him back echoes around every inch of me. "Shouldn't start something you don't intend to finish." I push him away and turn back to the front doors.

Dea grabs my wrist and flips me back around, however, as he presses a lingering kiss to my lips. "Who says I do not intend to finish what I started?"

Damn this man. He's so . . . candy-like. Like I could eat a shit-ton of what he's dishing out and still need more. An addiction. That's what this man is. A gothic addiction.

I smirk at him and press a kiss to his cheek before turning back around.

Get your head in the game, Magic. C'mon, you need this.

We have small cameras attached to our shirts to record real-time footage for promo purposes, and I click mine on and signal Dea to do the same. It's time to get this show started.

The museum is huge. So huge, in fact, that I have a hard time navigating us, even with the Japanese signage. "This way?"

We've been instructed to meet our employer at the gift shop, but I have no damn clue where that is. Goddess help me, this is ridiculous.

"Maybe we should stop and ask for help?"

I scowl at Dea. "I am more than capable of navigating, Dea." So help me goddess, I am going to strangle this man.

"Hmm? Then maybe a map might be of use?" He points to a display of maps on one of the many information desks littered throughout the displays; this one focuses on navigating tourists through the Hall of Shifter Fame.

Every type is represented here, and I find myself smiling at the equality shown; from war-winning tiger Shifters to an HIV cure-finding pelican Shifter, no one is exempt from recognition here. It's . . . nice.

"Shifters are some of the most balanced magical species in the world. You would like them."

"Maybe we should meet them before we leave?"

"I could introduce you. They are, after all, the only pillar community you have yet to meet."

I nod with dwindling enthusiasm as we walk past the next statue, and I stop to read the plaque. "Defeater of Invaders?"

Dea bristles. "Not all of their history fits with the modern worldview of peace. There have been numerous wars and fallings out over the centuries. This one celebrates the day Theobrim slayed the leader of a human pirate fleet that continuously wreaked havoc on his local fishing town."

"Hmmm, I see."

I don't see. Not really. Why would they celebrate senseless violence that does nothing to connect to the modern world? It's not even important anymore.

A voice interrupts my musings. "Horseman of Magic?"

I turn to meet the face of a handsome young man with piercing blue eyes and dark hair. His badge catches my eye—he works for the museum. "Yes. I'm here to complete a job your company requested." I gesture to an invisible Dea beside me. "And this is the Horseman of Death."

He nods toward Dea.

"I hope you do not mind, but we are recording the job today so we can create a real-time promotional video."

The man hesitates before pressing a hand to his ear and nodding. "Of course not. We're not dealing with anything sensitive today."

Someone else is pulling the strings. Strange.

I shrug and walk past him, gesturing forward. "Shall we?"

"Of course." He turns and walks ahead of us. "Please, follow me."

He leads us through a set of staff doors and down winding corridors to a room that has my eyes widening in amazement.

"Where are we?"

The man turns around and says in a gentle voice, "The back room. It's where we keep our stock before putting it on display, and it's where experts do their studying."

"Cool." I've never seen the inside of a museum before. It's . . . more corporate than I expected.

Eventually he leads us through a door at the back and into a plain-looking office, where a squalid man sits in a grand desk chair and pours over an old tome's front cover that has dust and dirt still imbedded in its leather.

"Ah," he says, looking up, "Magic. Death." He looks to each of us in turn. "It's so lovely to meet you. Please, do take a seat." He gestures to the two seats in front of the desk. "Thank you for taking our request."

I nod. "It's our pleasure, sir." We both sit, and I move to touch the book. "May I?"

The man nods and scoots it my way.

The moment I touch the leather-bound tome, I can feel the magic seeping around it, suffocating its knowledge. Preventing me from opening its pages. But why?

"Excuse me, sir, but do you know why this book is sealed?"

The man sitting behind the desk frowns. "It's rumored to contain dark magic. Magic forbidden by the Fae."

Forbidden by the Fae? What on earth could be insi—?

"Death magic," Dea whispers, somewhat taken aback. "This book contains death magic spells."

The Shifter behind the desk bobs his head side to side. "Supposedly. But death magic? Really? I doubt it." He scoffs, not believing.

"Sir?" I grab his attention and wave the book in front of me. "Whatever is in this book is contained by a powerful Fae spell. It will take a few hours to break it."

The man considers for a minute before he looks at me with a smile and says, "Well, then get on with it." I sigh as he continues. "It's what I'm paying you for, after all."

"Very well."

Dea places a hand on my shoulder. "Angel, I do not think this is the best use of your magic."

I turn to look Dea right in his galaxy eyes, imploring him to trust me with a small smile and reassuring nod that I know what I'm doing.

Roaming my hands over every crevice of the book, I quickly disarm the spell, but what I'm attempting to do next will take me quite some time. "May I get a glass of water, sir?"

"Of course." He motions to some guard behind us by the door, and a glass of water appears in less than a minute.

Good staff.

After a couple hours of sweat-inducing spellwork, I finally lay the spell I want over the book and hand it back. "It's done." Everyone's waited and watched with apprehension as I worked—which was a little unnerving, if I'm honest—but the look on the director's face is worth the extra effort.

"It's able to be opened. No side effects?"

I smile. "None whatsoever." I gesture for him to go ahead.

He opens the first page and pours over the inscriptions in some ancient language I don't recognize and has the look of a child with a brand new toy to put together on Christmas day.

"Come on, Dea. I want to meet the Shifters of Tokyo!" I yank him out of the room.

Turning both our cameras off, Dea turns me on the spot as we get on the subway and pins me to the side of train. "Are you insane?"

I laugh. "Maybe a little, but trust me. No one is performing spells from that book without some serious consequences."

He looks at me in befuddlement before smiling. "You spelled it?"

"I did." My smug smile says it all. "Removing the spell was easy, but it took time to create a spell that would nullify the effects of any spell attempted from that book."

"Nullification?"

Nodding, I say, "Yup!"

He runs his hands over my shoulders and gently rubs the tension out of them. "Knew there was a reason I love you, Angel."

The words still take my breath away, and for a moment, I stand stunned, before I turn around and kiss the ever-loving-fuck out of my boyfriend.

He chuckles before turning visible ('cos that would look weird to everyone looking on) and returns the kiss with equal need.

Feeling my cock harden beneath my jeans is still a surreal experience, and if I can help it, I try to sleep in my female form so I don't get that particular problem in the morning. Groaning, I lean into Dea, who presses me flush against him with a single hand flat on the small of my back.

"Dea . . ." I gasp between kisses.

"Shhh, Angel. Do not worry, you will have to wait until later." He pulls away and winks. "Much later, because you wanted to meet the Shifter Council."

I groan under my breath and mumble a few choice words in Japanese before turning back around and putting some distance between me and the Angel of Death.

"As if that is going to help," Dea whispers from behind as he wraps two hands around my waist and grinds into me from behind.

Peeking over my shoulder, I notice he isn't visible anymore. That fucking asshole!

He trails breathy kisses down my neck and across my bare shoulders until we come to our stop and I can finally run away and breathe again. Damn that man.

Dea runs after me with a few hearty laughs before dragging me down a few streets and into a local park.

"The Shifters live in a park?"

Laughing at my curiosity—like the fucker he is—he yanks me into the nearest copse of trees and pins me to a tree. "No, but I needed some privacy for this." He pins my hips to the tree as he undoes my belt buckle and reaches for the waistband of my boxers.

He hesitates. "If you would rather do this in your female form, I understand."

Letting out a breath I didn't realize I was holding, I hesitate. What do I want? Right now, my cock strains my jeans and I want anything to release the pressure, but I don't think I want to have sex in my male form yet.

But . . . does it really matter?

What's the difference, really?

Dea smiles and pulls his hand away. "I know you want it. What is holding you back?" He does up the button of my jeans and frees me from the tree.

I shrug, not knowing how to answer his question. "I dunno." Thinking about it for a moment, I add, "It just feels a little . . . uncomfortable to think about."

He frowns at me, and I can tell I've hurt his feelings.

"Not being with you," I rush, trying to defend my previous feelings, "just sex in a body I'm not used to. Like, it's somehow not really me."

"I see." He frowns still, but he's lost the insulted expression and grabs my hand, running soft circles over my thumb. "Maybe you should spend more time in your male form, so you can become more comfortable with it still being you."

"I guess."

"You know"—Dea stops our walk to look at us—"you never have to use this form this way. If you would rather stick to sex in your female form, that is okay with all of us."

I shudder at the thought of spending eternity uncomfortable being half of who I am. "No." I'm more stern than I intended, and it seems to take Dea by surprise, too. "That's not what I want. I want to feel comfortable being me. It just might take some time." I turn to face him and ask, "Go slow with me?"

I can feel the embarrassment heating my cheeks as I ask something so unfair of my boyfriend.

He just smiles and pulls me into a hug. "Always."

48

Turns out, the Shifter Council is under the park, and it expands to underneath the city, too. It's . . . weirdly breathtaking; as beautiful as it is rugged. Moss grows up stone walls in beautiful murals while wooden benches litter the underground alley we walk down, escorted by two tiger Shifters in their animal form.

"So," I whisper to Dea, "are they going to hate me too?"

Dea chuckles and whispers, "No. They are a lot more flexible and open minded. We have always liked them, even before all of"—he gestures around us—"this."

Nodding, I continue following our escorts down twisted paths and across stepping-stone ponds (this place makes the house look like a simple two-story) until we reach a room with an earthy table and chairs set up in the center that's bigger than most rooms in the house back home.

"Damn, what goes on in here?"

"They hold their tribal meetings here. It is a place where any and every species can be represented. Though, they tend to stick to the main mixed packs and a few older pack lines."

Packs? That sounds so . . . old school.

"Yes, we do," a deep rumbling voice booms through the chamber, echoing all around us. "It's also where we convene to meet important people, like the new Horseman." A man steps out of the shadows, taller than anyone I've ever seen, and beaten in muscle mass only by Arrie (that isn't really a competition, though). His eyes glow a silent silver that pierces the dark room with an echo of moonlight I feel the need to shift beneath.

It's like an itch under my skin that has me wanting to claw it off and run under the moon.

"Nice to see you have some Shifter instinct, Horseman." He relaxes as he lets out a breath and his eyes turn to a dark brown that I can only see because I can see so well in the dark with my Shifter eyes.

Dea laughs beside me in that gentle Victorian manner of his, and I could have punched him square in the face if I wasn't so worried about making a good first impression. Instead, I step forward and hold out my forearm. "Magic. It's nice to meet you."

The man grasps my forearm and shakes. "Cal, head of the Shifter Council here in Tokyo."

Whoa. This guy is like the guy. *The* guy. Equal to the Vampire King, Fae Queen, and the Witch Coven. But he's so . . . relaxed. Normal.

The man sighs. "I get that a lot. People look surprised to see us Shifters being so regular."

"In my defense, I met the Vampire Council first, then the Witch Coven, then the Fae Court. I had stick-in-the-mud expectations."

His laughter booms throughout the room, and he clasps my shoulder. "I saw you demonstrate your powers at the ball. I have to admit, I'm impressed, young one."

"Thank you."

Shyness clearly outlines my features because he removes his hand and says, "We know how to chill and party like the best of them. It's part of our charm. Isn't that right, Death?"

Dea nods. "That it is, Cal. That it is."

"The Shifter Council will convene in two hours, but in the meantime, why don't you let us show you around?" Cal offers me his arm.

I look to Dea in question, who smiles and nods for me to go ahead. Taking a deep breath, I wrap my arm through Cal's offered one and step up beside him. "Well then, Cal, looks like you're my escort for today."

I figure since I'm in Shifter territory, I should remain in my male form; plus, Dea's right, I should spend more time male so I can get more comfortable with just being me.

"So, err . . . I hope you don't mind, but I have a question." Cal avoids my eyes, and I find myself curious what he's worried about.

Nodding for him to go ahead, I pull my arm out of his and walk by myself.

"You have both a female and male form, right?"

I nod.

"Isn't that a little . . . tricky?" He coughs to clear his throat and looks awkward as fuck. "Sorry."

I wave away his concern. "It's okay. It is hard. It's not easy having the downsides to both sexes, but it's also helpful." He looks confused for a moment before he goes to ask how, but I cut him off. "I understand the plights of many being in this non-conforming form. I understand how important shifting is to you Shifters, how important a sex-positive lifestyle and the blood supply are to the Vampires, how important being surrounded by a natural environment is to the Witches, and how important respect is for Fae spellwork considering their culture."

He looks surprised for a moment before smiling. "I guess that makes sense. You were brought to keep the peace."

I scoff and look straight ahead—anywhere to avoid his eyes. "Yeah, somehow."

Cal laughs but takes my arm again. "You have a tough road ahead of you, young one. But you'll do great. You have the Horsemen behind you, after all."

I look back at Dea and smile.

Cal shows me the entire underground area within a five-mile radius, and I have to admit, I'm impressed. They have a fucking brilliant system. Shifters are welcome above and below ground; they can live happily among humans but will always be welcome and have a safe space here in the Shifter Underground.

The Shifter Underground is as large as Tokyo itself, and far too large for us to explore it all in a single day; they even have forests and spaces for pack runs for species that need the space, hiding spots for smaller Shifters that need hibernation spaces and hidey-holes, etc. It's impressive. They're so inclusive.

This is what the rest of the world should be like. Making some small adjustment or addition to their lifestyle and environment to help others feel more included and considered.

But eventually, our tour comes to an end as we're expected back in the Council Chamber for me to officially meet the Shifter Council.

Nervous. Excited. Apprehensive. Terrified.

I'm a ball of emotions I can't untangle for the life of me, but Dea rests a hand on my shoulder and whispers, "You will do fine." Making my nerves calm somewhat.

I can do this.

I think.

Taking a deep breath, I step into the room with the giant table from earlier; only this time, those seats are filled and others spew out across the room, looking for any place to stand where they can see.

Cal pulls me to his side and announces me on some kind of stone stage I swear wasn't there before. "The Horseman of Magic has come to meet the Shifter Council."

Everyone cheers, hollers and hoots, and I find myself smiling. This is the warmest welcome I've had so far. And it is indeed welcome.

"All right, all right. Settle down. Settle down."

Quiet hushes over the room in a wave of eager silence as I step forward to say hello. "Hey!" People smile at my lack of formality, but I just continue. "I just popped in to say hi, since I haven't formally met you yet. Thank you for welcoming us." I bow low and step back, allowing Cal to take over once more.

"Okay, all non-council members, please leave."

The standing crowd ushers out in moans of disappointment and disapproval.

"I am sorry," Cal whispers, "I couldn't keep them away now you've gone public."

"It's okay. It was nice. Made a change."

Cal laughs with some gusto while the stragglers exit the chamber, and we're left with the filled seats, a mixture of smiles, laughs, and a few frowns.

Seems even the Shifters are divided somewhat. Never mind, I can't be liked by everyone.

"Horsemen," an elderly man says from the closest council seat, "it's good to see you once more and meet your newest member."

I bow my head and cough to speak. "I have to ask, and I'm sorry for doing so, but why isn't everyone Japanese if you're based in Tokyo?"

Cal smiles but hands the question off to a weedy-looking man halfway down the table. When he opens his mouth, he speaks in fluent Japanese, which takes me by surprise considering his Chinese features. "Once, the Shifter Council was solely Japanese, but as globalization took place, more and more Shifters came here looking for sanctuary, to be a part of our new open world. Now we have a massive mixture, with not a single race taking dominance in terms of figures."

"It sounds like you are a very loving species," I reply in Japanese. "Thank you for answering my question, and sorry if asking was rude."

He waves off my concern. "You were curious. There's nothing wrong with curiosity."

The council seem pleasantly surprised with me, and I can't figure out why. I'm just having a conversation with a fellow nerd.

"While you're here, Death, Magic," Cal starts as he takes his seat at the head of the table, "we would like to officially pledge our support to your cause."

I falter in my stance, and if it wasn't for Dea holding me steady, I may have fainted. "Wha—?"

Cal laughs and asks, "You're surprised? That does not bode well for our fellow supernaturals then."

I look to Dea, asking permission to give them an update, and he nods. "It's been difficult. Everyone has their own issues, problems, and things that make our job harder. The Vampire Royal Council are with us, too, but the rogue Vampire faction have been causing mayhem at every turn. Now the Fae have joined them, we don't know what to do. And the Witches are still staying out of things, as usual."

My disgust doesn't go unnoticed, because a few of the council members grimace.

Cal looks concerned. "Well, that's half of the pillar communities' official governments helping you. If you can get the Witches on board, it'll be the world against one."

He's right. All isn't lost just yet. Since they're so willing to help, I might as well inform them of my plan to create embassies for their representation on *Sheruta*. And boy doesn't that go down well. A few are a little apprehensive, but mostly, it's met with warm applause.

"We want a triad running every embassy so representation is equal. One member chosen by yourselves, one member chosen by us, and one chosen by *Sheruta*."

Everyone looks at us in confusion for a moment, but Dea steps in. "*Sheruta* would like to have their own representation, given that their Shifters are run outside of your council."

Cal looks to the men and women around him and nods. "Very well. When you're ready for us, we'll send over the two members chosen."

49

"Well?" Dea asks as we walk back to our hotel. "What do you think?"

I jump forward and yank him to me. "They're amazing. I'm so glad I could meet them." I take a breath and whisper, "They're so . . . peaceful."

"We get along with them, and they actually like us. Though, they get a little antsy around Connie and Arrie."

I laugh. "They're Shifters. They're used to being the physically strongest in the room, which is okay if the strongest is one of them."

"Right. They aren't too fond of Vampires, either, but they get along well enough."

"Makes senses. Vampires are pretty strong too."

"Ready to call it a night and go back to the hotel? Or we can go back home?"

Right, with the new crystals, we can return whenever we want. Ha! Knew they were a good idea. Woo, go me!

"Can we stay the night and return in the morning?" I ask, trying desperately to avoid anyone—Dea, specifically—noticing the blush burning my cheeks. "It would be nice to spend some time together."

"Of course. I would love that, Angel." He hesitates. "Just promise me something?"

"Hmm?"

"That if you would prefer to spend the night in your female form, then you will do it?"

Damn this man for being so fucking considerate. "Okay," I whisper.

Dea grabs my hand and pulls me to the side of the street out of people's way. He wraps his arms around my waist and smiles. "I love you for you, and that does not change based on your gender. I have a preference for your male form, since I prefer men to women, but I also like your female form." He sighs. "I am sorry if I am confusing you further. Con mentioned I do that a lot." He mumbles something under his breath and looks away, flustered.

"Don't you fucking start with the whole mumbling thing too. I get enough of that shit from Arrie." Ugh. Just saying his name frustrates me. Don't think about him right now,

Magic. "And I understand. You wouldn't be disappointed if our first time was in my female form?"

"So long as it is you, Angel, I will never be disappointed."

The hotel is a luxury hotel Dea splurged on, but it's not, unlike Connie's choice, sex-related. Nice, simple, fancy hotel.

We order room service, I have a shower in both forms, and we have a few drinks over a dinner of steak ramen. And fuck don't I love ramen. How can anyone not like this stuff? I thought I'd be too scared to enjoy the evening, too nervous, but so far, we've spent it joking, messing around, talking, and chilling together. It's almost perfect.

"Angel?" Dea asks from his spot on the bed beside me.

"Yeah?"

"Would you prefer our first time to be with Nine?"

He looks a little concerned about my answer, but I'm not. "No. I don't want to have my first time with Nine mean more than anyone else's, you know. So I want to conquer the Horsemen of the Apocalypse one a time." I wink, and that serves to make him laugh.

"Okay. Well, I am going for a shower." He gets up off the bed and turns back around to me. "Would you like to join me?" He holds out his hand in offer.

And I take it.

I thought I would be scared, like I was with Nine, but I'm not. This man, this sexy-as-sin Angel of Death, is mine. I might share him with Nine, but he's mine. And tonight, I will show him what that means.

As Dea suggested, I'm in my female form, and I'm trying not to feel guilty about it. Like, really trying. But in my male form, I'd be hard as steel right now, and the fact that is my comparison shocks me a little. And then makes me smile.

Maybe I'm more comfortable with my dick after all.

We walk into the bathroom, and as Dea turns on the shower, I slip my clothes off and strip down to my underwear. It's not like I've never been naked in front of this man before, but it means so much more now.

When he turns back around, his eyes smolder under the soft lighting, and I shrink under his intense gaze. But he doesn't let me. He grabs my chin and whispers, "You are not allowed to avoid my gaze tonight."

I smile and try to nod, but his harsh finger forces my head to stay in place.

He smirks and brushes his lips against mine, never letting his finger slip. "This should be fun, Angel." He kisses me again, deep and sensual, until we're both out of breath and have to come up for air. "Nine told me a bit about your time together. I hope that's okay."

I try to nod again, but I can't.

"And you sound . . . perfect." He says that last word on an exhale, as though he's been dreaming about this moment for forever.

Dea unclips my bra and removes it, folds it, and places it neatly on the pile I'd thrown my clothes into earlier, then he goes to remove my panties, sliding them off my legs with gentle fingers and small caresses over my smooth skin. He hums satisfaction against my thighs, his breath tickling pleasure across my skin, causing goosebumps and shivers to break out.

"May I please undress you?" I ask, breathier than I'd intended.

He looks up at me with a smile, his eyes a gentle gold. "Yes, of course, Angel." My name shivers off his skin as I run my hand through his hair.

I help him up, kiss his lips, skimming over his piercings, and breathe a sigh of relief that I can finally let go of this building pressure to be with this man. This need boiling inside me . . . It hurts.

I need him.

I brush his t-shirt off, undo his jeans and slide them off his legs, until he's standing in front of me in nothing but his underwear. His tattoo glows under the soft lighting, and it shimmers beneath my touch, as though alive and responding to my unanswered question: May I?

I know it's been 1500 years since Dea's last lover, other than Nine, but it's important that I understand their history, their roots. They've lived such a long life, had so many memories and deaths on their doorsteps, made so many friends, and I want to understand all of that. I want them to know that I'm okay with that.

Dea smiles down at me, tears in his usually stoic eyes, and slams his mouth to mine, slamming me against the cold bathroom wall. He doesn't stop, lashing his emotions at me with every forceful swipe of his tongue, breathing me in with every gasping breath, before diving right back in, like I'm some pool of life he can't escape.

"Dea," I whisper, "are you okay?"

"I am more than okay, Angel." He gives me a small kiss to my cheek and checks on the shower. "It is warm enough for us."

I walk up behind him and wrap my arms around his waist, reveling in the muscle, the skin, and the overall feeling of touching him without restraint.

Dea slides his underwear off and gets in, offering me a hand to follow.

The water beats down on his body, his hair falling in elegant waves down his face, and I trace the mini waterfalls outlining his chest and abs with my eyes, not able to look anywhere else.

"You're beautiful," I whisper.

Dea chuckles. "Thank you, but you are exquisite, Angel. Like an ocean I cannot help but jump into on a scorching hot day in the middle of the desert." He runs his hands up my sides, trailing a finger around the edges of my curves and down my thighs. "I will never get enough of you."

Hands trace patterns all over my skin while his mouth meets mine under the shower stream, and we bathe in one another's presence, sinking into each other's scent and memorizing every ridge, curve, and dip on our bodies as we wash each other, kissing trails of love down thighs, washing care and caresses into hair, and staring meaning into eyes where there wasn't any before.

This is different than with Nine. Connecting to Dea is more physical, more shown, because we don't have that mental connection to rely on. So I need to show him how much he matters.

With the intention of doing just that, I kneel and run my hands up his thighs.

"Angel, what are you—?"

My hand wraps around his gorgeous length, wet from the shower, as my tongue licks the head, and he bucks.

"You do not have to do that, Angel . . ."

I wrap my lips around his cock, easing a moan from his lips before he can protest any longer. I want this. I want to taste every inch of him, every gorgeous, chiseled inch, and I'm going to start right here. I want to make him look how he did that night with Nine, with his head thrown back, his hand in Nine's hair, and moaning his release down Nine's throat.

Fuck, that was a good night.

I take more of his cock until I can't any longer, and I wrap my hand around the rest, squeezing and twisting, moving up and down.

And Dea's knees buckle as he groans. His hand twitches toward me, but he pulls it back. Restraining himself.

I know what he wants. So I stop and look up at him. "You can do whatever you like, Death. I'm not fragile."

He looks down at me with those golden galaxy eyes and pins me there, a scowl ripping across he features. "You want that?"

I nod. Fuck yes, I do. I want this man's control. To feel those hands on me that usually work so well on Nine. "Yes, please."

"Shit." He grips a firm hand on my head and guides me back to his throbbing cock. "Then sit there and suck my cock, Angel. Kneel and please me."

I want nothing more.

So I wrap my lips around his cock again, and this time I suck harder, hollowing out my cheeks and squeezing a little tighter as I move my hand faster.

"Angel," Dea moans.

Is he going to beg? Is his control finally slipping?

"Fuck this," he growls. His hand rips me from his cock and yanks me up by the hair, before he slams my body against the tiled wall face-first. "No way are you making me come first."

No. No he's not going to beg.

How did I ever think otherwise?

He smooths gentle hands down my back, kneading tension from shoulders, and trails tender fingers down my stomach and lower, until he reaches the apex of my thighs and the source of my uncontrollable need. "You are going to come first, Angel," he whispers in my ear as gently as he declares his love. "You will always come first with me."

The inside of my thighs are ticklish, and as he starts tracing patterns upwards, I giggle and squirm.

"Ticklish?"

I nod.

"How about here?" He traces a line up my entrance, dipping his fingers inside an inch before removing them.

I shake my head.

The cold of the bathroom tiles on my breasts has my nipples pebbling, begging for attention. But I don't know how to ask for that.

More ticklish patterns trace as he breathes deep breaths into my ear, and then he presses one finger gently inside, refusing to move.

But I want it to move. Need it to. "Dea . . ."

I shift my hips, trying to build friction. Anything.

But he pins me in place with his body. "Do not even try. You will moan and scream when I let you, Angel. And no sooner. Is that clear?" He punctuates his question with a thrust of his finger, curling it to graze just the right spot.

"Yes," I moan.

He moans into my neck, tickling soft breaths into the crook between my neck and shoulders. "God, you sound delicious."

He adds another finger, moving them faster, growing the pace with my moans. "Dea, I . . ." I want him to move faster, to make me feel good. "Faster, please." I shift my ass backwards, into his cock, and feel him thrust involuntarily forward.

For once, he does as asked, and moves his fingers faster, grinding his palm against my clit in the perfect combination of pleasure, like he's done this to my body a thousand times before and knows exactly how to get me off.

"Yes," I breathe. I shift my hips against his hand, riding the rhythm he's set. And I'm so close. So nearly there already.

But Dea screams in pain, echoing across the tiled room.

What the . . . ?

I spin, trying to see what's wrong, and gasp.

Dea's Angel form. He turned into an Angel while fucking me. Christ almighty, we have some seriously unique problems.

But the concern and confusion wash away as I look into those eyes, those gorgeous eyes that have captured me from day one, like a fish in a net, and I'm helplessly drawn in. He's reeling me in, and I can't stop. I don't want to stop.

"Dea," I whisper as my hands trace his skin.

"Magic." His hands grab my hips and slam my body against his.

I wrap my legs around his waist as he wraps his wings, damp from the shower, around my body, the feathers like silk against my skin. His cock is inches below me, and I want it. I want him inside me. Now. "Fuck me."

I watch the moment his control in this form snaps, and it's beautiful. His eyes pierce me with gold light as he steals my breath with a hard kiss, one that makes me gasp and hiss as he shifts his hips against mine, desperate. Pleading.

"Yes, Angel," he moans when I throw my tongue into his mouth. "Yes."

He slams the shower door open and fazes us to the bed, where he throws me onto the sheets and flies on top of me, wings spread out across the room, his gaze drawn to mine like a moth to a flame.

"I want you, Dea." My voice is a dreamy, hazy and off-kilter. But I mean every word. "I want you inside of me."

His hands grab mine and pin them above my head, while his knees hook beneath my thighs and push them up.

I want to run my hands down that beautiful golden skin, up the ridges of his abs, and around the hardness of his cock. I want to touch him.

But he doesn't let me. Instead, he lines his cock up with my entrance slams home with a grunt, forcing a scream out of my throat that quickly turns into a series of unintelligible moans and words that I'm pretty sure should have been a sentence.

"Angel . . ." He seems to be struggling for words, too. And he hasn't even moved yet. "You feel so good." He catches my response in a kiss before the words can form, and fuck if it isn't the best kiss of my life. "You are perfect, my love."

My hips beg for him to move, to create some kind of friction, to give me what I've wanted since I woke up in a magical house and had to deal with this out-of-reach man and his insistence on torturing me with his beauty. Eventually, I can't take it, and I scream, "Move!" at him. "Do something. Anything. Please."

Dea chuckles.

Great, even his Angel form is a dick. What a surprise.

"You want me to move?"

I nod, my face scrunched up in some kind of tortured form of pleasure.

"How much?"

How much? Is he kidding right now? I bend my head and nip at his nipple, causing him to groan and shift his hips ever so slightly. I nip at the other one, and his control slips with a growl and a snarl.

His hips pound against mine. He doesn't start off gently like Nine did, he takes me body and soul, his eyes never leaving mine as he slams into me with enough force to have my head hitting the headboard. "Fine." His hands squeeze mine, still pinned above my head. "You want to be fucked. Then I will fuck you."

He pushes my knees higher, and the angle deepens his thrusts, hitting new places and stealing new moans. "But you are still coming first, Angel. I will not stop until you are screaming my name and begging for release."

I'm already begging, I want to say. But just as the first word reaches my tongue, he slams harder against my hips, causing a lance of pain to spin through me, spurring the pleasure on, higher, until my clit is bursting with need and my body's demand to orgasm is too much.

"Dea, for fuck's sake, please . . ." He's pleasing me, but it isn't enough, and he knows it. His smirk says it all. He's keeping me on the precipice. Never quite hitting the right places. Never quite letting me come. "I just want to come."

The smile that graces his features is beautiful and menacing, and I'm both enthralled and nervous about what's going on in his mind. What's he planning?

"You want to come, do you?"

I nod.

"Then," he says with another harsh thrust of his hips, "beg me for it." He kisses me, long and hard. "Lie there with my dick inside of you and beg me to let you come."

I have zero dignity, it would seem, because his words please me, like the gentle caress of a tidal wave against my ears, and I have no issues with begging. Not from him.

"Please, sir," I try out, watching for his reaction. Nine once mentioned Dea might like it.

His face lights up, his eyes glowing brighter. "Yes?"

"Please, sir. May you please make me come?"

"Hmmm . . ." he says, "since you asked so nicely." He releases my hands and shifts my knees into a better position, higher, more comfortable, and then tweaks and pinches my nipples.

"Dea, yes!" My moans turn into screams, my hips slamming upward as much as possible as I run my hands down his chest, grazing his nipples along the way.

"You like that, huh?" He pinches them harder, my breasts thrusting out toward him, and then he reaches down and pinches my clit with the same harsh fingers.

Pleasure shoots through me like lightning, lighting me up from the inside out. And I'm so close to tumbling over the edge, my fangs slip and my eyes burn bright, causing Dea to gasp.

"You can feed if you'd like," Dea whispers, a slight pause in his dominating ministrations from earlier. "I do not mind."

I shake my head. "I'll feed later. Just fuck me, goddess dammit."

That makes him laugh, and he pinches my clit in small, harsh circles as he thrusts harder, his hips bruising mine with every pleasure-damning kiss of his cock.

"Shit, yes," I scream. My orgasm rips through me, and I thrash, my strength slipping free as I yank Dea into me. "Dea . . . Fuck." I can't hold back any more, and I flip us over, straddle his waist, and ride it out. Wild and free.

My hair spills out around me, and Dea's wings fan beneath him, a gorgeous pattern of black and pink and both mix together.

"Angel . . ." he moans as he meets my hips with damning thrusts, bucking into my clenching pussy. His face scrunches as his eyes glow bright gold beneath the lids. "Angel!" He grabs my hips and slams me down on his cock, hitting the back of me with both pain and pleasure. His wings lift us off the bed slightly as he fills me, his release slamming into me as he screams my name, his control a distant memory.

As we both come down from our high, my muscles relaxing and my mind coming back to me, Dea lowers us back to the bed.

"I am so sorry, Angel," Dea says when his wings vanish and his regular forms pops back into existence beneath me. His breath hiccups. "I am so sorry."

"Huh?" Why is he sorry?

"I did not want to have sex with you in that form so that you can always have free will. I am sorry I took that away from you."

"Oh." I lean over his body and place a delicate kiss to his lips. "No, Dea. I wanted that. More than anything."

He breathes in my kiss, hanging onto it like a lifeline, before he breaks away with a chuckle. "Fuck, Nine was right."

"Huh?"

Dea swears under his breath, and I get the feeling he wasn't supposed to have said that out loud. "Err . . . Sorry, it is just that Nine mentioned you were hot to watch when you come." He rushes out that last part, as though he's worried he might offend me.

I reach up and run a thumb over his cheek. "I'm not offended. If anything, it's hot as fuck that you guys talk about sleeping with me."

Dea breathes a sigh of relief, his usual, non-dirty-talking persona resting back in place.

"Thank you," I whisper just before falling to sleep.

"What for?" He wraps an arm around my waist and pulls me close to him.

"For letting me be myself."

"Ah, that. You are most welcome."

50

Back at the house, things are wild. No one is anywhere to be seen when we get there, so I change into my female form and use my Vampire hearing to discover they're all in my library; I left it open for them, given that it's the best place for research.

"Library."

Dea walks up with me, his fingers laced through mine. When we get there, however, papers fly everywhere, Nine is cursing in Chinese, Connie is yelling at Arrie in Danish, and Arrie is avoiding the book she's throwing at him.

"Hey!" I shout, using air magic to carry my voice to each of them. "What the fuck's going on?"

Nine sees us and relaxes, his eyes flicking to our hands and smiles; Connie runs up to me and squeezes me hard enough to hurt; and Arrie huffs and sits down among a pile of books.

"Thank fuck. These two are driving me insane," Connie says. "Please take back control. I'm dying here without you."

"How did you lot get anything done before me?" I giggle.

"Dea was in control."

Right. So with both of us gone, they return to being a band of squabbling children.

"Right, so someone give me an update so I can order you about like a badass."

Nine steps forward and wraps us both in a hug with a deep breath. "App marketing is going well, jobs are flowing in, and we already have a few profiles from our friends and allies around the world. Connie is mad at Arrie still over the interview week, which has been published by the way, and Arrie and I have been trying to organize the *Sheruta* Council to dedicate buildings for the embassies, but they're being difficult." He looks to Dea and pleads, "Please handle them. I might just drain all their accounts if I have to step foot in that building again."

Dea gathers Nine in a loving kiss before letting him go. "I will go down there this afternoon."

"Oh, and hon?" I look to Connie. "Mr. Compton is in a random guest room I asked the house to create. It's in the east wing."

Blowing out a breath through a tensed jaw, I head to the east wing, with a few helpful directions from Nine. It's above the cinema room on the same floor as our bedrooms, but it's opposite Dea's wing of the house. You know what, one day I'm going to draw a motherfucking map.

The door in front of me is so ordinary, so normal, so unlike the truths that lay beyond it. Am I scared? Hell yes. But will I let it defeat me? No fucking way.

Knock. Knock.

A gruff voice echoes from within, telling me to enter.

One deep breath at a time, I ease the door open and step into a pretty ordinary room. I'm not sure what I was expecting, but considering this moment feels like a milestone in my immortal life, the environmental expectation was set pretty high.

Seems not everything is like you read in books. Go figure.

"Taylor," Mr. Compton gasps when he notices me enter. "It's good to see you." His rugged frame looks exactly like it did before—regal, slightly graying, but still handsome in a weird, old uncle kind of way.

"Please," I say, "call me Magic." I smile and ask if I can take a seat in the lounge area.

"Please." He gestures to the two armchairs untouched by the window. "I hear you have questions and are ready to know the answers?"

I nod. "I was trying to avoid my past and carve a new future, but it's become impossible." I take a deep breath. "I want to more about who I was. Who my parents were. How come I can't access my Angel powers now, despite having accessed them in this immortal form once before? Who were my friends? I just want to know—"

Mr. Compton holds up a hand to stop me. "I get it, Tay—Magic. I really do. But I won't be able to tell you every aspect of your life. No one will. You'll have to be patient."

I huff. "Okay, well then let's start with my relationship to you and why I'm fluent in both Japanese and English."

"Ah, that I can answer."

I order some tea from the house, and we get started.

"You were born in Japan, and you lived there until your parents passed. But I brought you to the US with me when you needed protecting, which is why I placed you in a local Witch Coven. You used to visit Japan frequently as a teenager, though I was never sure why. Eventually, you enrolled in a Japanese high school that offered a boarding option when you were fifteen, and you never came back to the US unless it was on a job or seeing me."

"So I basically lived bilingually, linguistically and culturally, hence the language thing."

He nods. "What would you like to know next?"

"Who killed my parents?"

He flinches. Everything in him tenses up and he avoids my eyes. "It's not a nice answer, Magic." Looking into my determined eyes, he sighs. "The SC. They put the original hit out on your parents. I tried to stop them. I did everything I could."

He works for the people who killed my parents? That's . . . "They trusted you, didn't they?"

He nods. "I spearhead the supernatural-human relations department, so I have access to sensitive information about difficult supes and humans. I use that info to broker peace. But not everyone in the SC wants that. Some of them, mostly humans, think it's about time the supernatural community backed off and left humanity alone."

It's my turn to flinch. "Get me a meeting with the Supernatural Council."

He looks at me and laughs. Like, actually laughs. "They don't meet like that. Not all at once anyway. What would you have me do?"

"They're ignoring our calls; they won't agree to a meeting. I can't help if I don't know their issues."

Mr. Compton sighs. "You're right about that. The issue is they don't want your help." He looks about, as if trying to determine if there're enemies nearby. "There are some within the SC that want to use your public outing and paint you as the figurehead of the enemy. The figurehead of supernaturals."

"They want us to be evil."

He nods.

I sink my head into my hands. "I should never have staged that coup. It was all fake." Tears rim my eyes. "I've made a tentative situation a whole lot worse."

"Hey," Mr. Compton soothes. "We'll get through this. You'll get through this."

"How?" I look at him in complete despair, my hands shaking and my voice quavering. "How am I supposed to save the world? I don't even remember your name! And when they find out what I did for a living when I was mortal, both the supes and the humans will hate me." Tears crawl from the corners of my eyes to my chin in small rivulets, and until now, I didn't realize how much this was getting to me. "I just feel so helpless."

Mr. Compton gets off his seat and yanks me to my feet, wrapping solid arms around my frame and providing me with a safe space to cry. "My name is Nigel. And I'm still your godfather. You might be immortal now, and strong enough to seriously kick my ass, but I'm still here for you."

I try my best not to get snot and spit all over my godfather's fancy blue shirt. Goddess, I'm so pathetic.

"Want me to stay for a while? I can call in for a couple weeks' holiday?"

I nod, not trying to speak or do more than I'm capable of in my diminutive form.

He pulls me off him and looks me in the eyes. "It's okay to fuck up—it's okay to fuck up so badly you think the world might end—but it's not okay to quit. We need you, Horseman of Magic. No matter how long that takes."

51

The garden is beautiful and sunny today, and I can't help but feel refreshed and at peace with the morning sun edging the chill off the air. Arrie threw my workout clothes at me this morning and walked off, trusting that I'll meet him at our usual time and place.

Progress.

Maybe he'll actually speak to me so I can yell at him?

One could hope.

I'm just stretching my male form as I warm down from my beginner's yoga session (ugh, beginner) when I notice a movement in the trees slightly too big to be an animal.

Who's there?

Changing into my female form, I zoom my Vampire vision in, and his white-blond hair glistens in the sun speckling through the tree branches. He's too big to hide behind a copse of trees, and I can see the outline of his arms in the shadow.

Sighing, I jog to where he stands and glare at him with my arms folded over my chest in distaste.

Arrie just wipes an embarrassed hand over his face and grabs my arm and drags me to his usual clearing kicking and screaming.

Once he's deposited me onto the forest floor, I stand and place a fake smile on my face. "Hello, friend." Oh yeah, I'm in full bitch mode. With feet stood hip-width apart, I prepare to block Arrie's oncoming punch.

But it never comes.

He stands facing me, mouth slightly open, eyes downcast. Is he about to . . . apologize? His mouth closes into a grim line as he throws a left hook. Then a right hook. Then a jab.

Guess not.

Sighing, I block his simple attacks with ease. I've come far since we first started, even learning to counter his attacks with some of my own. The issue is I've become used to his fighting style and strength. When punching other people, I'm too overpowering. I need to learn how to rein it in, lest I hurt someone without intending to.

I block Arrie's oncoming series of jabs and send a flurry of my own, my rage and frustration at Arrie's recent assholeishness (totally a word) brewing over the edge of my restraint.

Fire tingles across my skin before I can stop it, and it lurches toward him, causing him to stumble back with wide eyes.

Arrie's eyes look hurt; not physically, because the idea that I could actually harm him is ridiculous, but emotionally. As though he can sense where my mind is at. Or it's written all over my face. Yeah, it's probably the latter, right?

"Killer, I . . ."

The use of my old nickname in that warm, affectionate tone has tears forming in the corners of my eyes, and goddess damn it, I'm not crying over this asshole. Nope. Never. "Save it."

I try to turn around to leave, but Arrie catches my arm and spins me back around. "No. Wait!"

My patience is truly running out, and something inside me flips. Something dark and disturbing. An anger that's more than just him—it's everything I've been pushing down, every frustration, every internal scream. "What do you want from me!" My voice is a shrill scream that surprises even me. "You hated me, then you liked me, then I thought maybe you . . . But now you just want to be friends?" I can't keep the hurt out of my voice as I throw the words at him.

"Magic, stop." His command has my words halting and my mouth hanging open.

He's never used my new name before.

"Just calm down before you do something you'll regret." His hands are out in front of him, and I don't miss the slight tremble in his knees. He's afraid of me. "Just take deep breaths."

"What are you—?"

That's when I notice it. The dark bubble of dust surrounding me like a cloud. The death magic from my mortal life . . . It surrounds me like a cocoon. Suffocating me. And it's growing stronger.

Hands wave through it, like washing through the ocean but colder, darker, and I realize that I can touch it, connect with it. I can shape it.

Muffled voices penetrate the bubble, but Arrie's is the closest. "You need to calm down."

"Calm down? Then how about you shut the fuck up!"

Taking a deep breath, I place my mind elsewhere, somewhere calmer, brighter. Warmer. I block out all the noise, frustration, and anger in a few deep breaths and snap into my male form with the kind of efficiency I wish to have on an everyday basis.

I look to Arrie, who looks like he's just had his soul played with, and turn away. I walk past Connie, Dea, Nine, and Nigel, who are all stood on the edge of the clearing with wide eyes and shocked expressions, and go to pour myself the world's largest cup of coffee. I also may or may not have asked the house for a giant pile of candy.

I'm going to practice my magic, something I have come to associate with calm placidity, like an internal version of yoga, and I'm going to forget Arrie exists.

. . .

"STUPID FUCKING ASSHOLE," I MUTTER AN HOUR LATER AS I FAIL YET ANOTHER ATTEMPT AT A simple Fae spell intended to flip a single page of a book. "Would it have been so hard to apologize like a normal person?"

Yep. I'm well and truly failing at my attempt to forget Arrie's existence. "Arrgh!" He's such a . . . There isn't a word strong enough.

The plasmascreen next to me pings, and I look over to find a new job has been posted on the app. Opening it up, I read the job and recoil, a pitying sadness washing over me. HEALER NEEDED FOR THREE-YEAR-OLD DAUGHTER: $65,000.

I scan through the description, and the more I read, the more I feel for this family. Their daughter has picked up some rare magical disease while on holiday that no doctor knows what to make of. She's dying. And there's nothing her parents can do about it.

Nine?

Yeah?

Send Dea on the new job. Film it with permission.

On it. And Sweetie?

Yes?

You should really talk to him.

Ugh. I shut out Nine's mental probing for a while, ignoring his persistence. They can all go shove themselves into the nearest broom closet. I'm not being the one to go to him; he's the asshole here (right?), he can come to me.

Two days later, I send Nine and Connie to the Bahamas on some conflict resolution job between two Shifter packs, Arrie to Greece to defeat some kind of weird magical sea monster no one has ever heard of, and I'm left on my own—well, Nigel is still here. Luckily for us, all agreed to have their jobs filmed to help with promotion in exchange for the price being wavered. This whole marketing malarkey is a nightmare, but at least I have Connie spearheading it.

"So, with everyone gone, what are you going to do?"

I shrug over the breakfast table as we eat some fancy French toast thing Nigel asked the house for. "Dunno," I say around a mouthful. Swallowing, I take a breath. "More training probably. Dea and Nine have been handling the *Sheruta* Council for the embassy inclusion here in-realm, we're mid-campaign for the app, and there's been no insane, war-level threats recently."

"I got a call from the SC this morning, and they've passed the motion to section off New Orleans."

"What?" I choke for a minute before getting my bearings. "But if they helped instead, we could clear the area, increase blood supplies, and re-establish the neighborhood."

"I know." Nigel looks downcast by the entire ordeal. "But what can I do? I'm not even on the Council."

"I have to talk to them. This is getting out of hand. If they stop pressuring the magical community, everything will ease up. The Fae and rogue Vampires will likely stop being so damn stupid."

"They won't hear you out," he mumbles. "They don't want to be affiliated with you at all. They see you as a threat, would be my guess. They know you've created peace among the Vampire Council, that you're allied with the Shifters, that you've created this new fancy app to combat their Hunter Society. They see your potential."

See, that's all well and complimentary, but it does make my job harder. How can I get them to listen if I can't even see them?

Think, Magic, think.

"Don't do anything stupid, Tay—Magic."

"Me? Do something stupid? I don't what you're talking it." I plead innocent with wide eyes and play with my pink hair like I used to when I would visit him as a child.

He chuckles, then turns serious for a moment. "Don't start a war with the Supernatural Council."

Goddess, he's right, isn't he? I can't do anything brash, like go on live TV and accuse them of everything they've probably done and air it to the masses. That would cause a riot, only steering humans toward war, not away from it. No. Whatever I do, it has to be something smart and underhanded.

Just as we're washing up, I have an idea. "Nigel? Where does the SC keep their plans and records?"

His eyes go wide. "What are you thinking?"

"Well, I can't really do anything about what they've already done, but I can prevent them from doing more. If only I know what that is."

He smiles. "Breaking into the most secure server in the world? Should be a piece of cake, right?"

We both break into a fit of laughter and start planning a heist with more gusto than I thought possible from this straightlaced man.

A few hours later, we've detailed every inch, every negative possibility, and have a strategy. The plan is, in its foundations, simple: break into the Chinese SC headquarters, get to the server room, plant one of Nine's little hidden bugs he once showed me, activate it, download the data, and leave. The question is whether to leave the bug in place to gain future data or remove it and not risk getting caught. On the one hand, we'd know all their plans—past, present, and future—but on the other, we could start a more damaging war if they figure out who that bug belongs to. The last thing the world needs right now is a fight between the Supernatural Council and the Horsemen of the Apocalypse.

I don't want to sit on the opposite side to the SC, but what choice do I have? They won't even sit down and let me introduce myself. How can I work with that?

At least this way we could prevent further damage. I just hope this plan doesn't backfire like the last one.

53

"You should commercialize these crystals. It would be of real benefit to the world."

I scoff while we walk to the hotel we're staying in before our mission this evening. "That would require the Witches working with the Fae, unless you wanted me to make every piece of technology for the entire world?"

"Ah. Witches."

"Yup."

We walk down brightly colored streets with gray backgrounds, like a wonderful mixture of the past and present, in silence, other than the occasional question from Nigel.

I haven't bothered waiting for the others, and I instead just left them each a message saying I have a plan and am going to the Chinese Supernatural Council with Nigel. I know I should wait for them, but I don't want them talking me out of my plan; they love working with the SC. But it's time to do something about those tyrants.

Arriving at the rundown hotel, we check in and wait out the evening while going over the plan. "Nigel, we're not going to get caught, are we?"

I have my doubts. Serious ones. But I'm not too worried about being caught myself—it's Nigel being captured that bothers me. Would they execute him? Shit. I can't risk his life. He isn't breaking into the building with me, but he is still waiting at the drop point. He's still in danger.

"You don't have to come with me. You can stay here."

Nigel places a gentle hand on my shoulder. "Can't do that, kiddo. You need me."

He's right of course, I do need him. Only he knows the layout, since maps of SC buildings are not public, so he has to guide me on the comm systems.

"But—"

"No buts." He grabs a towel before heading into the shower. "You're still my goddaughter, and I won't stand on the side lines while you risk everything for this war."

I nod, vaguely aware he believes in this all-out war that's coming. Maybe it's already here, and all of this mess is the war. Goddess knows. Can't Fate give us a hint every now and then.

We powerwalk down the street, avoiding busy sidewalks and large groups of people, mostly sticking to back alleys and underground walkways. In a couple of miles, there's an old bus station that's been cornered off for reconstruction; that's the drop point. Just one mile from the building, free of people, few cameras . . . It's perfect. We don't talk as we walk, but we occasionally give each other sideways glances of concern and confidence-inducing smiles; well, I guess his are supposed to be confidence inducing, but they come out more of a grimace.

He doesn't like this plan.

I don't care.

This is a necessary risk. And if all goes to plan, I'll be in and out before anyone notices. You know, assuming I don't accidentally burn down the building or fly into a stranger or Vamp out at the smell of blood or suddenly need to shift or a hundred other issues associated with my volatile magic.

Deep breaths, Magic. Deep breaths.

"Okay," Nigel says, "we're here."

The fence in front of us is easy enough for me to airlift us over, even with the barbed wire curling around the top. Feet on the ground, we both exhale.

"Find a good place to hide, preferably away from any cameras."

Nigel looks me in the eyes. "You got this, kiddo."

"I know."

I take off in the opposite direction, heading to the back of the construction site, where there should be a concrete wall. On the other side of that concrete wall should be an alley that leads onto the main street heading toward our target building.

A few more air-sped steps around various corners and over fallen-down walls, and bingo. A concrete wall. I leap over it and land silently on the empty other side, where garbage cans are stacked with rotting garbage and a black cat streaks through the shadows.

Between my Vampire strength and speed and my air magic, I'm as silent as Dea.

The main street is littered with people—just as we suspected. While we avoided people on the way here, from here on out, it'll be useful to blend with the crowds.

I have my hair tied back and a black cap on, hopefully hiding my identity. We aren't massively well-known yet, but I don't want to risk the chances of someone recognizing me from that viral video because of my long pink hair. (I know, it's a travesty hiding it under a damn cap.)

Goddess, I'm really doing this.

Shaking the crazy, unconfident thoughts from my head, I walk down the street with a smile and pep to my walk. I want to look like a normal tourist, so I've dressed the part. Another bonus to having two genders: the ability to work two different outfits. In my female form I'm all touristed out, magicam dangling around my neck; but, in my male form, I'm wearing all black in the hopes of blending with the shadows when I sneak through the building's upper window.

Three blocks of shops, stalls, and color, and I'm ready to gauge my eyes out. So many people, so many colors, so much noise. Ugh. With shops' closing times being midnight in most countries, late-night tourism is a real issue for inner-city dwellers, but alas, I have no issues there. *Sheruta* is perfect.

There's a tall, gray, official-looking building up ahead, and one zoomed-in look at the sign on the front revolving doors tells me it's my target. The Chinese Supernatural Council.

There are at least twenty floors to this monstrosity, but Nigel said the records are kept on floor fifteen, so I need to enter as close to that as possible. I checked online maps before leaving, and there should be an alleyway toward the back, so I head that way.

From there, I can find the nearest open window.

This alleyway, much like the last, has garbage cans strewn everywhere, garbage over-flowing, and the repugnant smell brings an eye-watering sting to my nostrils.

Looking around, I notice an open window three floors up from ground level with a light off. Hopefully those windows aren't safety locked, or I'll have to break in, and that could trigger an alarm. If I try a window too high, someone might notice me, so I can't really go higher than floor five.

I airlift myself up to the open window and pull, trying to edge it open wider, and to my surprise, it isn't safety locked. I fly in and land silently on the carpeted floor. The room in question looks like a regular office, so I take a moment and relax.

Switching on my comms and camera, I bring Nigel into the picture. "Nigel? Can you hear me?"

"Loud and clear, kiddo. You got in I see?"

"Without a hitch." I pace the room and calm my nerves enough to switch forms—and then turn the second comm on. "Did the comms and camera switch okay?"

"Yep. Like a cock-a-doo."

"Like a what?"

He sighs. "Never mind."

Okay, Magic, time to go. Yanking the door knob, however, I realize I'm locked in. Shit. I didn't think about that.

First time heist and whatnot.

Err . . . quick way to unlock a door with my powers?

Aha!

Switching to my female form, I use air magic to carefully move each pin and tumbler (waaaay more tricky than it sounds, by the way) and, after fumbling and messing up a dozen times, I finally manage it with a silent fist pump.

"If you can find a way in the doors of each room, that would be great, but I wouldn't be surprised if they used electronic door locks. You got lucky whoever's office that is is old-fashioned."

"Got it."

I move through the corridor in my male form as silently as possible and find the stairs pretty quickly. Taking a deep breath, and grumbling somewhat about how I'm about to run up twelve flights of stairs, I sprint forward.

The quicker I get up there, the quicker I can fucking leave. This place is a death trap, and finding me here would start an even bigger war.

By the time I'm ten floors up, my breathing starts to labor and my muscles scream. Shit. This is harder than I thought it'd be.

"C'mon, Magic. You're a Horseman of the Apocalypse for fuck's sake. Get up those damn stairs!"

Fucking prick. "Like to . . . see . . . you . . . try."

He laughs on the other end, and I grimace at him while sticking him the middle finger over the camera.

Just five more floors to go. You can do it, Magic. And when you get back, we'll work on your male fitness, promise. I have it easy with my female form because of my Vampire strength, but Shifters are only a bit stronger than the average human; they rely on their animal strength. And the Fae are not made for physical activity outside of long-range attack physiques.

Floor thirteen . . .

Floor fourteen . . .

Floor fifteen . . .

"Phew!" I wipe sweat from my forehead and stand in front of the door whose edges glow pale blue from the digital lock system. "Shit."

"Know how to hack digital locks?"

"Not in my immortal life. Reckon I could do it as a hunter?"

I hear Nigel shuffle on the other end. "I'm not sure, kiddo. Maybe. If anyone could, it was you."

Okay, past-life memories, now's your time to shine. C'mon, c'mon, c'mon. I try to think back to the many nightmares I've had about my previous mortal job, to a few of the buildings I've broken into, but nothing specific about picking digital locks comes to mind.

Staring at the panel on the right side of the door, the one you usually scan your datachip through, I raise my hand as though to swipe a chip across, and . . .

Come on, Taylor, you can do this, I mentally chant to myself. It's just a simple digital lock. All you have to do is rewire the thing to open. And then, bingo, you're in.

I yank the bottom of the pad open and see thousands of crisscrossing wires threading throughout the system. All I have to do is determine which one opens and closes the door, and then rewire it to the connectors.

It crosses my mind that this is fucking insane; I'm breaking into a secure building to handcuff someone and drag them to the SC.

Using a nimble finger to follow various wire paths, I eventually find the right one and swap the connectors, watching as the blue sheen around the door switches to green.

So all I have to do is swap the connectors on the right wires. Sounds easy enough. Assuming no one has updated the system since that memory.

"Magic, you okay?"

"Oh, yeah. Sorry Nigel. Flashback."

"Okay."

Yanking the bottom of the panel open, I see a familiar set of wires and get to work. It takes me much longer to determine the right ones without memory of the theory behind this movie-level BS, but I manage it, and eventually the light turns green,

"Wow. Color me impressed. You're like a real-life assassin." He hisses and mumbles, "Sorry."

I wave him off, and then remember he can't see that. "It's okay. Let's just get this done."

The corridor itself is much like the others, only this one has people stationed every few hundred meters.

"Shit," I whisper. I'm gonna have to take them out. But I don't really want to kill them. They're just doing their jobs after all—that's not a moral sin or a crime.

Okay, I can do this.

I sprint down the corridor, my feet padding along the tiles in silence, and stop around the first corner. Two night guards stand ten feet from me, and by the looks of it, they're human. I sniff the air. Yup. Definitely human.

Gathering my wits, I connect to my Fae magic and whisper an air-connection spell, which essentially connects my magic to the air around me, and use it to manipulate the air around the guards' heads.

I slowly seep the air away from them, creating two small pockets of vacuous space around each of their heads, and watch them suffocate.

Just enough to knock them out . . .

They slump their shoulders as their heads fall, their necks no longer able to keep them up.

I whoosh the air back to them and run up to either side, whacking my hands against their necks, eager to ensure they're still alive.

A faint pulse meets my fingers, and I sigh in relief. "They're alive." I just hope they stay down long enough to not pull the alarm while I'm here.

They'd organize a sweep of the entire building the moment the alarm activates, so I have to make sure my little bug and I are out of there before then.

Two more corridors, two more sets of night guards.

Damn, this floor is heavily guarded for some simple records. It makes me wonder what else is here. But I don't have time to check every locked room.

"The door to the server should be around the next corner."

I put a thumbs up in front of the camera attached to my chest and move on. Rounding the next corner with ease, two more guards meet my eyes, but I snuff out their oxygen and watch them faint.

"That is damn effective, kid."

"Are you going to call me kid even when I'm sixty?"

"Yup."

Sighing, I unlock the door—finding my digital hacking skills speed up the more I practice—and step inside.

It's a room filled with many banks of computers, all glowing that familiar blue of magical tech light that permeates every technological invention in the last century (been doing a lot of reading, don't judge my inner nerd).

Where the fuck am I supposed to stick the bug?

"Does it matter where you stick it?" Nigel asks in my ear.

I hesitate and mumble, "No idea."

"Great," he whispers.

"Don't be a dick. I didn't think the server would look like this."

"All right, all right, don't get your panties in a twist. I'm looking up server blueprints now."

In the meantime, I switch to my female form, who has the bug in her back pocket, and wander around, getting the layout of the room. I don't have to exit the room because I'm going to use a crystal to get back home straight from here, but it'll be good in the event security is alerted and I have to fight.

The room itself is filled with black and glowing-blue machinery—row upon row of plasma-filled metal banks that I assume make up the computer—that has my head spinning as I try to navigate the maze of technology. Walls of plasma-filled metal tower above me, and I quickly find myself lost the more I try to navigate.

"Okay, you need to find a good, accessible point and place the cyberbug into the system, attach it to the wire, and go."

"It's that simple?"

"It's that simple with Nine's cybermagic tech."

Goddess bless that sexy nerd of mine. I'll thank him later, but right now, I'm sure I'm running out of time.

I open a few panels and try to find some kind of wiring, any; so long as we get in, it should be fine. Well, according to Nine and Nigel. But I'm running out of luck for the evening it seems, because the universe is giving me nothing.

"C'mon, Fate, work with me here," I whisper to myself. And just as the last syllable comes out of my mouth, I open up the nearest section and find some wiring. "Okay . . ."

I attach the wires just like Nine explained back when I was merely curious—never thinking it would come in useful—and open the app on my plasmascreen that it connects to.

"Yes!" I shout, but a little too loudly because the door to the server room opens in the exact moment. "Shit."

54

The bug is still doing its thing, so I can't leave now. I still have data to trawl through. I want everything: plans, names, money trails, communications. Anything and everything I can get my hands on.

"Change into your male form, kiddo."

Right. The only form the general public know is my female one—I haven't publicly shown my male form yet.

I switch with effortless ease and continue watching the download progress. It's 54% complete, but I'm not sure there's enough time to get to 100%.

"Stop! Put down the bug and put your hands in the air!"

I sigh, hoping this guy is just some dumb human, and turn. The more time I can give the bug, the better off we'll be. I have to keep this man busy.

The man in front of me has mousy-brown hair, a small stature, and holds a magigun in his shaking hands. Taking a whiff of the air, I note he isn't human.

Looks like I'm shit out of luck.

But what he is exactly is a mystery. He smells kind of like a Witch, but this is a strange place to bump into one of their kind. Why would any Witch work for the SC? Moreover, why would the Witch Coven allow it?

They know more than they're letting on when I last visited, clearly, but that's a problem for later.

"What do you want?" I ask. "Money, power, a fight?"

His eyes flicker to mine for a moment as surprise etches onto his face and his hands lower. But only for a moment. He's quick to raise it again and make me lose my opportunity. "You ain't gonna buy me off, hacker. I'll drag you in just like everyone else."

His weedy voice grates my Shifter ears, and I can't help but wince at the timbre.

Seems he wants to do this the hard way. Without wanting to give away my dual nature in this form, I blast him back around the corner with a quick Fae spell I mastered for basic defense.

"A Fae. Bloody typical," I hear him moan as he crawls back around the corner and comes straight for me. "Your kind are always causing problems, you sick fuck!"

Nigel has gone quiet in my ear, and I don't want to give him away by asking if he's okay, so I keep his cover.

I don't bother responding to the strange man in front of me; I agree, the Fae are a bunch of sickos. Instead, I hurl more basic defense spells at him, hoping one will stick enough to check my bug's progress.

Eventually, after a few failed attempts, I manage to knock the magigun out of his hands and use it to knock him out with. (I know, it's a little clichéd, but what's a gir—guy to do?)

Yanking the plasmascreen from my pocket, I watch the download tick to 87%. Damn. It still isn't done. I really don't want to wait for this guy to wake up, but it looks like I have no choice.

I sit on the floor for a bit, watching the man's chest in front of me rise and fall with his even breaths; like this, he's more peaceful, less harsh, and I wonder if I can just knock him out a bit longer with that Fae spell I used on the night guards. But I decide against it—I don't want to kill him.

That isn't who I am anymore.

91%

93%

94%

Time ticks on as I watch the download complete itself.

A sigh and a groan comes from the direction my new weird friend is lying, and I curse my eternal bad luck.

"Can you just stay down for another five damn minutes?"

He smirks. "Nope. Sorry." He aims his magigun at me and fires.

But being the quick-thinking bitch I am, I duck and move out of the way just in time.

The look on his face is priceless. Yes, asshole, I just dodged a magical bullet. (Cue audience round of applause.) Thank you. Thank you very much.

"How did you—?"

I cut him off with a hand in the air, informing him to stop. "You're not very good at this, are you, kid? Let me give you a pro tip: train harder."

100%

I rip the bug from the wires, slam the container closed, and grip my Earth-to-*Sheruta* crystal hard in my back pocket.

It lays in the palm of my hand as I smile at my would-be murderer (you know, if he was any good at his job and if I could actually die) and say, "Bye bye." Waving, I smash the crystal on the ground and think of home.

But just as the swirling vortex of ether sweeps into nothingness, I feel a sweaty palm on my arm. Opening my eyes, I witness, in horror, the sight of the young man's hand gripping my arm as we travel home together.

55

"You little fucking shit!" I scream the moment I land in a heap in the middle of my library. "What the fuck do you think you're doing, asshole?" I whirl on the young man from earlier with a clenched fist and a spell at the ready.

"Stop!" he screams. "Who are you? What are you?" He stammers most of the words out before pleading, "Please don't kill me."

Sighing, I unclench my fist. "I'm not going to kill you, idiot. But you have caused me a significant number of problems. You can't be here."

Nigel pops out of the air with a look of abject horror on his face, and for a moment, I forget about the weedy little nobody who hijacked a ride on my teleporting crystal—which I didn't know was possible—and wrap my arms around Nigel's neck.

Thank the goddess he's okay.

"Nigel?" the young man asks. "Is that you?"

Nigel unwraps my arms and tears an exhausted hand through his hair and down his face. "Hey, kid."

Kid? He's practically a man. One, I hasten to point out, who tried to kill me not two minutes earlier. How the fuck do they know each other?

Before I can ask that very question, thundering footsteps echo across my bedroom and library before the rest of the team sprint into our tense space with different questions.

"Where have you been?" Dea shouts.

"What mess did you make this time, hon?" Connie winks and smiles, but it falls off her face when she notices our latest intruder.

"Sweetie, do you want to explain what the fuck you think you were doing!" Nine shouts both mentally and physically. Nine's rage explodes beside me in a ball of red-haired fury I haven't seen before. "You could have caused a massive problem for us! You could have been seriously injured! You could have messed everything up!"

"Silence!" Dea roars. "Now is not the time for this." He looks to the young man and asks, "Who is that?"

The question is aimed at me, but since I don't have an answer, Nigel answers for me. "That is Aki Angelis." He turns to me and grimaces. "Your brother."
  "W-What?"

VOLUME 3

My brother? I have a brother. Had? Is it still a relation if you're technically the walking dead? Shaking my head, I take a few steps backward, away from the boy across the room, from the lying douche canoe of a godfather, Nigel, and from the team.

I have a brother. A twin brother.

An actual relation.

I'm not alone.

"Now, Taylor," Nigel begins. "Don't be mad—"

"Magic," I whisper without lifting my gaze from the floor. "My name is Magic."

But if he's my brother, then why didn't he come find me when we announced ourselves to the world? We must not have been close then. Just another person who abandoned me.

The team have all shut their complaints up for now, all staring at me with those same pitying eyes; everyone, that is, except Arrie, who just stands with his arms crossed over his chest with not a care in the world. As usual.

Will he ever care?

He does care. That's the point.

I ignore Nine's cryptic nonsense with a headshake and walk up to Nigel. "How?"

The boy, Aki—my brother—has grown silent in the face of all these revelations, but his look of bewilderment whenever he faces me says it all.

"You didn't know, did you?" I ask him.

He shakes his head. He opens his mouth to speak, but nothing comes out, so he closes it again.

I turn back toward Nigel and repeat my earlier question. "How?" My fists clench, my control slipping, and I quickly change into my male form lest I burn my library to the ground. And I guess I don't really want to hurt anyone. Well, many of them anyway. Nigel might be the exception right now.

He shakes his head and sighs. "It's a bit . . . complicated."

Aki stands beside me and says, "Then explain it," through clenched teeth.

Nigel looks from me to Aki, then back at me, and then back at Aki, until he sighs and runs a hand through his hair. "This is insane." He shakes his head. "Seeing you two together is . . . Wow."

"Here," Nine says, "take a seat." He asks the house for a chair beneath Nigel.

Nigel plonks himself down with a look of bewilderment and utter exhaustion.

He did just help me break into a Supernatural Council HQ building. Maybe I should cut him some slack? That's the reasonable thing to do, right? "We can chat about this tomorrow, if you'd like?" See, I can make adult decisions.

Nigel goes to nod, but Aki cuts him off. "No fucking way. This asshole is gonna explain how I have a twin sister when I didn't even know my own parents because they abandoned me when I was born." His face slackens. "They kept her? But gave me away?" Grief chokes him. "Why?"

I place a hand on his shoulder, trying to comfort my . . . brother. Jesus. That's ridiculous.

"Because two Angel-descended Witches growing up with little-to-no control over their death magic in the same place would have put an even larger target on your heads." Nigel shakes his head. "There was no rhyme or reason why it was you, Aki. It just was."

"But," I interrupt, "I thought it took time for the Angel-descended powers to manifest into death magic? How did they know?"

Nigel looks to Aki with pity, his usually cheerful eyes turning solemn. "Because Aki killed the delivery nurse upon arrival. His powers manifested the second he was born." He looks at me. "You took the usual number of years."

I look to Aki, surprise etched onto my face, no doubt. He's strong. Really strong.

"I see," Aki whispers. "So, what happened then?"

Nigel looks to Aki and says, "They placed you with me, until I found you a suitable home in Japan, where you grew up with Witches who knew of your powers and could help train you." He looks at me. "And they left you in the care of your parents."

"Who died when I was six," I finish. "Then you placed me with Witches in the US." My eyes widen. "That's why, isn't it? Because the Witch Coven in Japan was already looking after Aki. And there are so few Witches in the world."

Nigel nods. "The next best place was with the Witches near me."

I spin to face Aki. So this guy, who nearly arrested me and took me to the enemy, is my twin brother? And then he hijacked my teleporting crystal—which I didn't even know was possible—and stumbled upon an unknown-to-most realm? I turn to Nine in befuddlement. "Well now what the fuck do I do?"

Nine rests two hands on my shoulders, looks me in the eyes, and says, "I have no idea." He smirks. "But this was your plan, so you deal with the fallout, Sweetie." He gives me an I-told-you-so smile and winks.

"Seriously?" I ask. "Fucking seriously?"

"Well, Angel," Dea starts, and I sigh, "you did sneak into a secure building, steal all their data, nearly get Nigel in a lot of trouble, and then had a fight in a server room with your twin brother." He shrugs. "This is very much your mess."

"What were you even thinking?" Arrie grumbles.

I swear, I'm gonna throw a fireball at that stupid asshole's face one of these days. He's such a fucking *deku*. "Well"—I turn to him with a big stupid grin on my face—"I was thinking that if I know what the SC are planning to do next, I can intercept or reduce the damage to the supernatural communities at risk."

"So you're taking a side?" Aki asks.

I spin to face him. "What?"

"By standing against the SC, you're taking a side." He shrugs, as though that's obvious.

"Well . . ." It is, isn't it? "How am I supposed to protect humans and supernaturals if I can't actually protect them?" I groan. "And maybe the SC needs to be taken down a peg or two? They are kind of a bunch of controlling a-holes."

Connie shrugs. "They're just trying to protect their people."

I spin to face her—I'm getting dizzy with all this spinning—in shock. "By threatening the lives of other species? Are you fucking serious?"

She walks up to me and wraps me in a hug. "I know." She breathes me in as I wrap my arms around her waist. "But they believe supernaturals are a threat to humankind. They're trying to separate them so that humans can go back to normal."

"But supernaturals were always around." I gesture around us. "This is normal. Now everyone can see it."

"Angel is correct," Dea says, looking at me. "This is how it has always been."

I ponder for a moment, hand scratching my chin in thought. "Maybe we just need to reduce the risk to humans and get them to see the benefits of supernaturals . . ."

There is so much going on right now that I have to think to myself for a moment about my top priorities. I look to my brother, who is still in a realm he doesn't understand talking about shit he knows nothing about. "Right, Aki."

He snaps his face toward me.

"You're staying in a guest room until I know what to do with you."

"What?" he squeaks. "What do you mean 'do with me'?"

"Hey," I say, poking him in the chest, "you're the one who hijacked my teleporting crystal and came here without permission. I don't know what to do about that right now." I ask the house for a room besides Nigel's and am greeted by a quiet grumble. "Nigel, please take Aki to the room next to yours."

Nigel nods while Aki protests, but Nigel grabs him by the upper arm and steers him out of my library, saying, "You're the damn idiot who came here illegally. Be thankful you still have your head attached to your damn body, kid."

A sigh escapes my lips. "Fuck me." That was exhausting. "I need a list, or maybe a mega board."

Connie snickers. "What for?"

"All the fucking issues I have to solve."

She places a gentle hand on my chest. "We have to solve."

"Right." I smile. "We."

The next morning, I wake up with Dea and Nine snuggling into me and Connie hovering above me, where she stands on my bed, handing me a piece of paper.

"The list you asked for." She climbs off the bed and walks back into my library.

Are they all gonna hang out here forever now?

Not if you don't want us to.

Eh, it's fine. I'm just feeling a bit overworked and crowded.

I wince.

Sorry.

You're allowed to need alone time, Sweetie. He places a sweet kiss on my temple and gets out of bed.

"Where is mine?" Dea asks, a lazy morning smirk on his face aimed at Nine.

Nine blushes and crawls over me to get to Dea, who grabs both sides of his face and plunges his tongue past his lips, drinking him in as though he's the last drop of water left.

I'm just enjoying the show.

Perv.

Dea runs his hands under Nine's sleep tee and sticks out a bare wrist for me. And I dig in for breakfast, just slightly weirded out that this has become my normal. The piece of paper in my hand crumples as Dea moans into Nine's kiss.

Fuck. Bro, you're hard as steel, Nine sends to us both.

I take one last pull, and Dea grinds into Nine, who's straddling his waist with lust filling his gaze, before I pull away with a smile. "Thank you."

Dea snaps his gaze to me, heat filling those now-golden irises. "You are most welcome." Nine tries to get off, but Dea's firm hand on his waist keeps him in place. A beautiful hand wanders down Nine's waist to his underwear, and my breath hitches.

A good morning threesome sounds like a great way to wake up.

Nine groans. *I knew you'd be hot as fuck after we snapped that restrictive band you placed around yourself.*

Dea chuckles. "If that is what you want, Angel."

He's offering me two dicks on a silver platter and asking if I want that? Who the fuck doesn't want that? I couldn't be happier about the direction my relationship has gone in.

But the bedroom door slams open as Arrie grumbles his way in, takes one look at us, and storms into the library.

Right. Everything isn't quite perfect yet.

"It will be," Nine says. "I promise." He kisses my forehead and gets out of bed, the lust spell broken.

I straighten the piece of paper and read Connie's list:

- App advertisement
- Nigel and Aki
- New Orleans
- Rogue Vampire faction
- Fae Queen
- Blood supply
- Embassy creation
- SC data

"Wow. That's a lot."

Nine snatches the paper out of my hands and glances over it. "Divide and conquer, Sweetie."

Dea reads over Nine's shoulder and agrees, his eyes lancing mine, saying we'll definitely be coming back to that threesome conversation later. "Well, let us make some plans over breakfast."

I BRING MY CLENCHED FIST UP TO THE WHITE DOOR AND HOLD MY BREATH. TERRIFIED.

Knock, knock, knock

A soft shuffle on the other side of the door sounds, and then the click of the lock, before a Japanese man who looks similar to my reflection stands before me. Bewilderment on his face, surprise in his eyes. "Please don't arrest me. Or kill me."

"I . . ." Wait a minute. "You think I'm here to kill you?"

His brows shoot to his hairline as he gasps. "You're not?"

I shake my head. "Jesus Christ, no. What kind of monster do you think I am?"

He shrugs, clearly not wanting to answer the question. "Well, I saw the viral video, so . . ."

Ugh. Of course he has.

Couldn't I have gotten a long-lost twin brother who is anti-social media?

But alas, my karma meter is still running on empty.

"I'm not going to kill you. Or have you arrested. I'm actually here to offer you breakfast. And maybe a chat?"

"Oh." He freezes for a moment, not sure what to do with himself, before he opens the door all the way and gestures me inside. "Then come in, I guess."

I walk into the room with some trepidation. "Wow. A twin brother." My head spins as the realization hits me like a freight train. "This is insane."

He gestures to a round armchair that swivels. "Maybe you should sit down. You kinda look like you're gonna pass out."

"I feel like it."

"It's been a rough couple of days." His hand rubs the back of his back. "So I know how you feel." Aki sits next to me, perching on the edge of the large armchair. "I . . . I'm sorry I hijacked your teleporting crystal. I-I-I didn't know."

I smile. His face is so cute when it's flushed. "It's okay. I mean, it's not, but since you're my brother, I guess you get family privileges."

"Family privileges, huh?" His worry turns to a smile. "Does that also mean I get to use this magical house?" He looks around, awe-stricken. "Because it's sooo cool."

"She is pretty cool. And yes, feel free to ask her for whatever you like."

"Really?"

"Yeah. Really." I ask the house for a cupcake and a glass of water, then settle in to devour both. "These are great cupcakes."

After a moment of us eating cupcakes together, I swallow my last mouthful and sigh. "So, I guess my question is: what now?" He doesn't answer, so I make an offer. "If you wanna stay here, you can. If you wanna grab a place nearby, I can help. If you wanna walk away and pretend this isn't a thing, return to your normal life, you can do that too. I'm happy to support any decision you make." My voice trails off, fear seeping through the cracks. "But I'd love for you to stay."

I don't have much family. And yeah, I was pissed yesterday, but today I realize he was doing his job. "Though, only if you don't report me." I jab a finger at him. "I was doing something important yesterday. Illegal, but important."

"Yeah, I was thinking about that. And I get it."

"You do?" Wow. That was easy. I thought I was going to have to use facts and figures and seven-point slides to persuade him. "Really?"

"I've been researching more about you and the Horsemen last night, and what the SC have done to New Orleans. I guess before, I just didn't really think about it, you know. I was just following orders. But I get it. You're trying to help." He grabs my hand and smiles. "I'm your brother. It's my job to keep you safe."

"That might be a tall order. We're at war. I'm gonna be fighting armies sooner or later."

"Then I'll be there to cheer you on. Or bandage your wounds. Or whatever it is a brother does for an immortal sister at war."

We all sit around the breakfast table an hour later, including Nigel and Aki, and discuss how we're going to conquer all the items on Connie's list.

"We should divide things by priority," Nine says. "That way we can focus more energy on important things and less energy on things that can wait."

Dea chimes in with, "Right. And I think the embassies should be in the top three, since that will help us tick off other things as we will ask for assistance."

"And you," Connie says with a smile, "will have more troops to order around."

"Therefore," Nine says, "making you less stressed."

I'm uncomfortable talking about our plans in front of Aki. I want to trust him, but I don't really know him all that well. Most of my adult memories have come back by this point, and my nightmares ended weeks ago, but I still don't have most of my childhood memories, other than flashes, and I don't want to trust anyone in vain.

What if he betrays us?

"Well, the blood supply, the embassies, and New Orleans should be our key priorities, right?" I ask the team. "That way we're helping as many people as possible. I'd include the app stuff in that, but it's all working itself out."

Connie nods over a bite of egg. "I'm hiring a manager for that, so they can deal with all the advertisement, running, and managing of it all." She looks at me. "That okay?"

"Absolutely. But we still own it, right?"

"Of course."

"Good." I don't want someone else owning something so important when I don't even know who is on our side.

I look at Aki and sigh. What do I do about him?

"Err," Aki says, "I'm thinking about finding a place in town. Sticking around a little?" He scratches the back of his neck while avoiding my eyes.

He phrased it like a question, but is he actually asking permission?

I look to Dea, who shrugs and nods.

"Sure," I say. "That would be . . . nice."

He looks at me with shy, hopeful eyes. "Maybe I could help you out?"

"Yeah," I mumble. "Maybe."

"C'mon," Nine says to Aki, "I'll take you to the housing office to see what's available. Or I can take you to a few hotels?"

Aki smiles and nods. "Thank you." He bows his head. "That would be wonderful."

Nine offers him a hand up and guides him toward the front door with a smile, his arm around his shoulder.

When did they get all buddy-buddy?

"Hon?"

"Huh?" I spin back toward Connie. "Sorry, what?"

"I asked, what did you want us to do?" She gestures to herself, Arrie, and Dea. "And," she leans in and whispers, "don't worry, he's crazy about you."

I shake off the paranoia. "Right." I look at Dea while I attempt a smile. "Can you please handle the embassy? If possible, I'd love everything set up in a couple of weeks. Possible?"

"Absolutely, Angel."

He gets up to leave, but I jump to my feet and spin him around at the last minute and yank him into my arms. "I love you," I whisper up at him.

He smiles down at me and tucks my hair behind my ear. "I love you, too." Dea then leans down and places a light kiss to my lips, but nips my lower lip hard before pulling away. "Do not overwork yourself today."

"Yes, sir."

He shakes his head and turns to leave.

Turning back to Connie, Nigel, and Arrie, I blush a little before shaking it out. No need to be embarrassed in front my girlfriend and . . . Arrie. But looking around, I notice Arrie isn't there anymore. Where'd he go?

Sighing, Connie gets up and wraps me in a hug. "Just ignore him." She smiles and asks, "What about me?"

Right. "I need you to hire someone for the app, see the advertisement through, and make sure everything goes perfectly." I peck her on the cheek and smile. "You are the team's official manager."

Her face lights up. "Really?"

I nod. "Yup. You're great at it, Connie."

She blushes. "But that's a . . . normal job." She can't stop smiling, and it's adorable.

"It is. Is that okay?"

She picks me up by the waist and circles me around the room. "It's more than okay. It's . . . awesome!" She squeals in my ear. "I have to go!" She runs out of the kitchen with a spare piece of toast hanging out of her mouth. "Got shit to do."

"See you later," I say as she sprints up the stairs.

Nigel sits at the kitchen table still, having stayed silent throughout the entire breakfast ordeal, but he gets out of his chair and looks at me. "So," he starts, "you and the Horsemen?" He gives me that fatherly 'is everything okay with your boyfriend?' look.

I groan. "I'm . . . happy." I look to the back door, where I assume Arrie went. "Nearly."

Nigel sighs. "Well, it's not exactly what I had planned for you, but if you're happy . . . then . . ." He wraps me in a hug. "Who am I to argue?"

"You'd have to fight me, old man."

"Old man?" He laughs. "I'm not old."

I shrug. "Not yet."

He laughs, and I release a breath. I'm still mad. He should have told me about Aki. But he was only trying his best. We're all only human. Well, most of us anyway.

"Wanna help?" I ask as I raise the flash drive that holds all the gathered data from the SC into the light.

He flinches. "Are you sure the rest of the team will be okay with that?"

I shrug. "The damage has already been done, right? What harm will looking do?"

"Okay. If you're sure?"

"Nothing to lose." I hope.

Nine is out with Aki, Dea is dealing with the embassy and the *Sheruta* Council, Connie is off dealing with press stuff and the app, and Arrie is somewhere being his moody self; all the while, Nigel and I are sitting behind my desk, about to plug in the flash drive.

It's time to see what the SC is planning.

"I really hope we gain something useful from this." I sigh. "It'll suck if this was for nothing."

"Yup." Nigel put a hand on my shoulder. "There'll be something we can use. I'm sure of it."

Taking a deep breath, I open the folder and take a quick browse through.

There's a lot on here. And I mean a lot. Hundreds, possibly thousands, of files. Some are labeled—things like financial, taxation, and importation and exportation records—but other things are numbered, lettered, or use some other nonsense system.

"Ugh," I groan, "it'll take ages to trawl through all this."

"Maybe search for keywords, like blood, Vampires, Fae, pixie dust, or something?"

"Not a terrible suggestion, old man." I smirk while trying to find something—anything —on the Vampire blood supply and New Orleans lockdown.

A file pops up labeled AREA 50 PLANS.

Well, that sounds ominous, at best.

Opening up various maps, plans, and details, Nigel and I gasp in unison.

"Is that . . .?" he asks.

"I think so . . ." I hiccup as I scroll through. "But that's so . . ."

"Evil?"

"Yeah."

He sulks back into his chair and rakes a hand through his hair and slams a fist on the desk. "That's it."

"Huh?"

"I can't do it anymore." He looks haggard, his eyes worn out from years of hardship.

"Taylor . . . I mean, Magic, they're planning on locking down every Vampire city in the world! I can't stand by and silently work for a company who does that shit!"

I watch with sympathy as he struggles with the idea of his employer being so evil. "Move here." I look to him with a serious expression. "If you'd like, you can move here to *Sheruta*." I shrug. "You don't have to, but it would be nice to have you around, I guess."

He looks to me with a smile, curious. "Any werepanther packs around?"

"The were packs here in *Sheruta* are mixed, and then they have their own individual families. But it shouldn't be too hard to find a nice place in the pack."

He sighs. "I guess I'll hand in my resignation then."

Wait. Do we need him? Like, if he were a part of the SC, does that help us in any way? No. I can't ask that of him. He's risked too much already. It wouldn't be fair.

"What is it?" he looks at me and asks.

"Well . . ." I sigh. "I was just thinking that if you leave the SC, we can't use that connection anymore. But it's okay. I don't want you to have to do something you're uncomfortable with."

He looks to me from his seat. "What kind of things?"

I shrug. "No clue. But we wouldn't have that for the future, just in case." I place a hand on his shoulder. "But it's okay, Nigel. Honestly."

He nods, and I turn back to the screen, scrolling through the paperwork, maps, and more that detail the plan. I need to put a stop to this. It's not okay to single out an entire species like this. And, if anything, the Fae are the most trouble to humans, so why pick on the Vampires? It doesn't make sense.

"I'm going for a walk," Nigel mutters.

I watch him leave with a heavy heart, genuine concern flooding my face for a moment, before I continue reading the files. I'll need help. There are five cities in the world, after New Orleans, that are the biggest Vampire hotspots, and they're all home to feeding clubs, light-protected housing for turned Vampires, and are a general safe space for them to be. It isn't fair to take that away from them.

There's only one person who can help strategize a solution to something this complicated, and it's the one person I don't want to deal with. Arrie.

I find Arrie outside in the horse paddock, giving their unused steeds a bit of attention. I wonder why I don't have one? Eh. I guess I don't really need one. Arrie's is the biggest, with black coat, a long flowing mane, and strong legs; but the others are also huge, much bigger than regular horses, with Dea's being spindly and a weird translucent white color.

I don't really want to disturb his peace, given that he's actually not frowning right now, with his hair tied back and his jaw relaxed, not a frown line in sight, but I don't have a choice. I need him. The world needs him. And I know how pissed I'd be if someone waited, like Dea did with the New Orleans thing, to tell me I was needed.

Clearing my throat, I yell, "Arrie!"

He looks over his shoulder and sighs, a frown now marring his beautiful face.

"Please," I say, hearing the whimper in my voice and wincing. Goddess, I sound so pathetic. "I need your help."

"What do you need me for?" he grumbles. He's still stroking the horses, one hand on Dea's and his own. "You have three slaves all ready."

I wince. Again. "Well, I need your strategy ability."

"Sure you do."

"Arrie!" My anger slips through, and I snap. "I don't have time for your sulking. The Vampires need your help. The Supernatural Council are planning their first big move: they're going to shut down the five major Vampire cities."

Arrie spins around with a concerned look on his face, his ice blue eyes piercing mine, trying to see if I'm being serious. "Really?" He walks closer, his voice now easier to hear. "You're being serious?"

"Would I fucking be here talking to you if I wasn't?"

He smiles at me for the first time in days, and my heart feels like it's about to burst. That smile . . . It's beautiful. Full of wonder and magic and hope. Like I can breathe again just at the sight of his lips curling and his laughter bubbling. Maybe I can save whatever we have?

"Fine," he grumbles. "I'll help."

"Thank you." Relief washes over me. "C'mon, I need you to help me with this now."

He nods and follows me back to the study, where I print a physical copy of the main map out and lay it on the desk.

"This"—I point to the five marked areas—"is where they'll shut the cities down: New York City, Delhi, Shang Hai, Cairo, and Dhaka."

"That's a lot of ground," Arrie grumbles. "Across large expanses of Earth." He rakes a hand through his hair. "This won't be easy."

"I know." I place a comforting hand on his arm and smile. "But we have Earth-Earth teleporting crystals now, so that'll make the travel easier, right?"

He looks relieved by that fact. "Right. If you make enough of them, we can just hop back and forth between each other."

I look at him questioningly.

"Oh, the best way to deal with this is to divide and conquer, like Nine said this morning. Each take a different city and defend it."

That's a good plan. "But we'd be alone . . ."

"Not if Dea can get the embassy up and running in time."

"Then we'll have help from at least two pillar communities!" Maybe more . . . "But there are other species," I mumble to myself.

"Huh?"

"Nothing." I spin around and head into the middle of the library to do some deep research. "Just come up with the best strategy for me, okay?"

"But what if it's not enough?" I hear him whisper to himself.

Pretty sure I wasn't supposed to hear that.

I turn back around to face him with a smile. "I believe in your powers, Arrie. Even if you don't."

He nods and takes a deep breath before delving into the files open on my computer.

Meanwhile, I head into the section of my library that holds the books on magical species. See, there are lots of different species in the world—not just the main four and humans—so what if I asked for help from them, too? They might be small, but together, they could be powerful.

Really powerful.

But I know little about them. I know Fae farm dust from pixies, so maybe we can help there. And I know fairies are in danger from deforestation and losing green spaces and gardens. And Nine mentioned something about a few Demon species still existing? Argh! I need a lesser supernatural expert.

Well, Nine answers, *all you had to do was ask.* He turns the corner from where I'm sat and smiles.

"Did you find somewhere for Aki to stay?" I inquire, trying not to seem too interested. "You know, that he likes?"

Nine chuckles. "Yes. He's renting a small apartment near to here. He'll be close by when you're ready." Nine settles on the floor next to me and rests his head on my shoulder.

"There's so much to do."

"There's five of us." He entwines his fingers through mine, and I smile.

"You're right." I am not doing this alone. I have an entire team to help.

You have an entire family to help you. "Now how about we start crossing things off that list?"

By the time I'm done chatting with Nine, Arrie comes to join us with a smile on his face. "I did it," he says. "I know the best strategy in each city and who to use for each one's defense based on the information I found on the flash drive."

"Good job."

But at the sight of my proud smile, he frowns and huffs to the floor.

Seriously? Can I do nothing right anymore?

Sighing, I growl. "Just write it all up for me."

He rolls his eyes at me but nods.

At least he can follow instructions, which is an improvement from earlier.

"Then we're going to take back New Orleans for the Vampire Royal Council."

Nine and Arrie swivel their heads my way with equal shocked expression on their faces.

"Seriously?" Nine asks. "That's your plan?"

"Yes." They still look shocked, so I flop to the floor on my back and explain. "The Vampires need their hometown. New Orleans is their capital. It would be like France without Paris."

Connie runs down the library out of nowhere and spins toward me. "I've had the best day!"

"Yeah?" I grab her arms to steady her. "Wanna tell me all about it?"

"Hell yeah I do." She turns to Nine and Arrie and smiles. "She made me Team Manager. And in doing so"—she spins back around to me—"I am going to help you plan all of this workload and suggest who you should use for what tasks. Helpful?"

"Fuck yes." I sigh in relief. It's all so daunting to me. Like a pile of rocks I have to somehow turn into a mountain but with no plans, no knowledge of how, and no skills to do so with. "That sounds great."

"Good. Because the first thing on my list is to stop us training you."

Wait. "Huh? But—"

She holds a finger to interrupt my interrupting. "I know. But you need us elsewhere.

And we can't do our jobs if we're too busy training you. So I'm going to look for other people to help. Maybe a Fae magic expert to help you delve into your spellwork better. And there's bound to be a bo staff fighter around somewhere, right?" Her thoughts trail off for a moment before she shakes her head and comes back to us. "So for now, the only training you'll have is with me and Arrie in the mornings for combat."

I internally grown. Of fucking course the only bit to stay is the bit with the grouchy asshole who'd rather punch me than train me.

"Dea is handling the embassies with the *Sheruta* Council, so all of that will have to wait until he's done. We're guaranteed the Shifters and Vampires, which just leaves the Witches and Fae."

Connie's hand rests in her hair, and I can't help but stare in wonder at her for a moment while she goes to work. She's amazing when she's being herself.

"And the lesser species," Nine chimes in.

"Huh?" Arrie and Connie ask at the same time.

Nine fills them in on my plan to get as many species involved as possible, and Connie breathes a sigh of audible relief at the plan.

"That helps."

"It does?" I ask.

"Well, yeah," she replies, as though it's the most obvious thing in the world. But at my confused expression, she explains, "Because now it won't be two against two. It'll be hundreds against two."

"And who knows where the humans will side," Nine says. "Not all of them are going to blindly follow the SC. They're not known for their unity."

I listen to them chat about the state of the world for a bit while I mentally check out. It's been a tiring day, and it isn't even lunch yet. This leadership thing is harder than I thought it would be.

All we need now is the date of the SC's Area 50 Plans. The plans make it look like it'll all be simultaneous, so as to dissuade the Vampires from rallying against them, but the actual date is a mystery.

Dea's still out dealing with the embassy by the time my training session with Connie comes around, but the rest of us have had a successful afternoon: Nine and I researched as many lower supes as possible, Connie handled the app advertising and hired a management company, Arrie continued with plans for stopping Area 50, while Nigel continued looking through the data we got from the SC.

All in all, it's looking successful.

"So," I ask Connie for a second time, "everything with the app management is handled?"

"Yup." She dodges my fire attack and rolls back. "And the interviews and press releases from our PR stunt went okay, too." She shoots an arrow at me from across the room. "You can search it all up if you like."

Right. The PR guy. "The guy from the SC?" I stop fighting for a moment and take a deep breath. "That went well?" I guess I just thought the SC would do anything to smudge our name. "Really?"

"I know," she breathes. "I'm shocked too." She lunges at me from across the room and tries swinging her sword toward my face. "But we do have one or two more things to be released."

"I don't understand." I pin her to the floor with a foot swipe that knocks her off balance. "If they don't like us, then why are they helping us?"

Connie shrugs from her place on the floor before grabbing a fistful of my sports bra and yanking me on top of her. "No clue." Her lips part as her eyes gaze at me with a familiar glint to them. "But your official manager is ordering you to stop worrying and kiss me."

"I could get used to these orders." I lean down to drag my lips against hers in a teasing whisper of a kiss.

She groans in impatience beneath me while trying to yank me closer.

But I just laugh under my breath and kiss her again—hard. Without holding back, I press my body against hers and tangle our lips together in a growing need I find myself struggling to satiate with a single kiss.

Just as I'm undoing the first button on Connie's gym shirt, the door opens and someone coughs to announce themselves. "Maybe, Angel, you should take that upstairs?"

"Pfft." Connie raises her head from the floor. "As if you'd have a problem walking in on us . . ."

"I would not, no, but others might. And I might remind you we have a guest."

Nigel, right.

Sighing, I stand up and move to help Connie to her feet. "Dea's right."

"Guess so." She leans in and kisses me gently, leaving a trail of fire everywhere she touches. "But we will return to this." With a wink, she exits the gym and leaves me alone with Dea.

"Soooo . . ." Dea smirks. "You and Con have been getting pretty serious recently?"

"Yeah." I cough. "Ummm . . . We, you know, have made things more official."

Dea smiles down at me. "I am happy for you, Angel." He places a gentle kiss to my forehead. "And very proud of how far you have come."

"I feel like there's a but coming."

"But—"

"Why is there always a but?"

He places a finger to my lips, silencing me, and whispers, "Remember what we talked about in Tokyo?"

I look at him in confusion, my brows furrowing.

"I suggested you spend more time in your male form so that you can get used to it." He wraps me in his arms as I freeze, not wanting to have this conversation. "I know you are scared, I know you have been staying in your female form to avoid the issue, and I know you do not want to talk about it, but both forms are an important part of who you are." He pulls back and holds me at arm's length. "Even if you decide that your female form is your go-to, that you identify as a woman, you should not feel uncomfortable using your male form." He brushes a hair from my face. "You are going to need it, after all."

The scary thing is, I don't think of my male form as strange, weird, or not a part of me. It's become an important part of who I am, like the second side of myself I never knew I needed. And that terrifies me. I know it's weird. I know it doesn't fit in. And I know by now that I should be used to feeling like a freak, but I'm not. And I don't think I ever will be.

6

I spend the following day mostly alone with my thoughts; I do my best thinking alone, so I ask everyone to leave me be while I mull things over. Because sometimes, the best plans come from isolated thinking. And this plan is definitely a winner.

But I'll need a big brainiac to pull it off.

Luckily, I know just the guy.

"Nine?" I yell in the middle of my library. I swear he's around here somewhere.

Yeah?

I could use some of your sexy brains over here, if you're free?

I'm always free for you.

Then get your ass over to the comfy teal-blue couch by the window in the northwest corner of my library.

After a few minutes, Nine rounds the corner with a big smile and wraps himself up in my arms and between my legs for a giant cuddle. "What kind of fancy thinking you been doing, then, Sweetie?"

"Well, I was just thinking that fixing the blood supply problem would go a long way right now."

"It would."

I hand Nine a mini chocolate cupcake I asked the house for earlier and watch him eat with glee.

"So, would it be possible to create a synthetic type of blood that could sustain a Vampire, even temporarily?" I sigh, knowing how stupid my thoughts are. "It's just, if we could take the pressure off the blood supply, make sure the cities are protected, and win back New Orleans, then the Vampires should be able to live happily without the SC controlling the blood supply."

"It's a lovely thought, but I've tried a few times over the centuries to create synthetic blood that could sustain a Vampire, but with no good results."

Poo. That sucks.

Nine shoots up and jumps to his feet. "Wait . . . what did you say?"

"Say what when?"

"Earlier . . ." He runs a hand through his hair as his eyes glaze over and that perky smile crosses his face. "You said it didn't have to sustain them permanently, just enough to remove some of the pressure off the blood supplies."

"Well, yeah, permanently would be great, but it's not realistic, and the primary goal is to get the Vampires of New Orleans up and running again."

"Right, right, right." He paces in front of the couch, mumbling words I barely understand to form sentences I can't follow. "So if I were to reduce the number of white blood cells and remove that problem from the equation, then I might be able to solve Armen's Gap."

"Armen's Gap?"

Nine turns to me with a smile and says, "The problem with creating a blood supply for Vampires is that creating so many moving components to a living cell is difficult. One of the more difficult parts to make is the white blood cell. It's tricky, and its function is vital. I can't just miss it." He flicks his eyes to mine with a grin wider than the ocean. "But what if I could?"

"If you're not creating a type of blood as a permanent form of sustenance, then it's okay if something is lacking."

"Yes!" Nine yells and drags me into a tight hug. "Because they'll still be getting that from the other part of their diet." He puts me on the floor and runs away, off to some lab somewhere, I assume. Just before he leaves my line of sight, he says, *Thank you. I love you.*

I love you too.

I don't think I'll ever get used to saying I love you.

One day, it'll be the first and last thing you say every day.

After a quick search of the house at Vampire speed, I find Connie and Dea doing lengths in the pool.

"Hey guys!" I run over to the edge. "Mind if I join you?"

Connie swims up to me and says, "Not in that form." She leans up and kisses my cheek. "You'd out-swim us in a heartbeat."

Right. Fair enough.

Dea gives me a look of concerned warmth, but I shake my head. It's okay. He's right. I need to start being more me. No more being afraid of the world's judgement. No more stupid freak outs over the littlest things. And no more fear of being myself. So, with an instance of magic, I change forms, and then I put some swim shorts on.

Doing lengths in my male form is hard. Like, seriously hard. Shifters are supposed to be naturally fit, but it's like swimming up a mountain against an ocean current. And Connie is making the effort look easy, as usual, but even Dea is having an easier time of it than me.

Connie swims up behind me as I gasp for breath at the edge of the pool. "We need to get this form fitter." She wraps her hands around my waist and curls around my back, her hot skin pressing against the warmth of the water. "You rely too much on your female form."

"Is everyone going to have an opinion about that? Am I seriously going to have to listen to that four times over?"

"Who . . .?" She looks over to Dea with her famous stink eye, and he shrivels. "Stop making Magic feel bad." She whispers in my ear, "I can cheer you up, hon, if you like?" She edges her hands to the rim of my shorts, her nails teasing along the sensitive skin there.

I tense, not really sure what to do or how I feel.

"It's okay," she whispers. "We don't have to do anything you're uncomfortable with."

She spins to swim away, but I grab her hand last minute and twirl her back to me. Her lips are so soft beneath mine, I take a moment to simply breathe her in and watch her shudder beneath my touch as I skim a hand beneath the material of her bikini top. When we part, momentarily breathless, I whisper, "I just need some time to get used to this form." I grab both her hands in mine and trace kisses across her knuckles. "Go slow with me?"

She nods, her gaze more than a little hazy. But she eventually snaps out of it and swims away with a small smile on her face.

"We are all more than a little taken with you, Angel," Dea says from behind me, making me jump.

"Christ, Dea!" My hand jumps to my chest and rubs soothing circles over my frantically beating heart. "You scared the shit outta me."

He chuckles and places a warming hand on my shoulder. "Sorry. It was not intended."

Spinning around to face him, I hover in place as I take in the glowing galaxies that are his eyes. "So beautiful," I whisper. I shake my head when I realize I said that out loud. "Err . . . Your e-eyes, I mean."

Those golden irises glow brighter as he laughs at my fumbling. "Oh, Angel, you are a delight."

"Aaaaaand now your head won't fit through the door."

"Anything you want to do now?"

"I'd like to know how the embassies are doing, but Connie forbids me from talking work in the evenings, so that'll have to wait." I swim closer and let his arms fold around me as I take in his tattoo up close. "I . . . I'm scared," I admit.

"Of what?"

"Of not being good enough. Of being too weird. Of never fitting in. Of failing." Taking a deep breath, I whisper, "Of everything."

Dea lifts my chin with a single finger, forcing me to meet his steely gaze. "It is okay to be afraid, but you must never let that fear defeat you, or scared is all you will be." He smiles, his lip piercings glinting in the gym lights. "How about we start with afraid and happy? And go from there."

"I think I can manage that."

7

Everyone sits at the table the following morning, and I take charge with ease. For a change. "Nine, you're still working on our idea?"

He nods with a mouthful of eggs, which he swallows before saying, "Gonna have to call some friends and colleagues and work on it together, though. It's a big job."

"What is Nine working on?" Dea asks.

"A blood supplement for Vampires."

All four heads snap Nine's way—with Nigel looking more impressed than the others —and everyone speaks at once.

I cut them off with a wave of my hand. "Yes, we think it can work, but no, we're nowhere near ready to talk about it." I look back toward Nine. "ETA?"

"A few months?"

"Dea, where are we with the embassies?"

"A few days out, at most."

"Wow," I breathe. "That was quick. How?"

He shrugs. "A friend on the *Sheruta* Council owed me a favor, and with Nine's new communication technology, I contacted all the councils, covens, and whatnot with ease. They are sending their chosen representatives in three days' time. They are just waiting on ours." He looks at me expectantly.

Thinking about it, I do have a preference. "Prince Lucien. But you guys can pick everyone else. I don't know enough about the other pillar communities to make a choice."

"I think Pansy would make an excellent choice for the Shifter seat," Connie chimes in. "Having a smaller, respected Shifter within the community would help balance out all that testosterone-driven power in the endless meetings." Connie looks to me with a smile. "She's a rabbit Shifter, but she's fearless."

"And maybe one of the Coven's relatives for the Witches?" Arrie suggested. "Might help us win back some of their favor."

I look to Dea. "The Witches actually agreed to send a representative?" I expected them to tell us to go to hell.

He grins in that devilish way of his. "I persuaded them to put it to a vote among their people. Seems lots of Witches agree with you, Angel."

"Good." I pour myself some OJ. "That should shake them up a bit."

"The Fae, on the other hand," Dea says, "are refusing to send anyone, wanting no part in our world."

Connie snorts. "There's a surprise." When everyone looks to her, she continues, "Well, what did you expect?"

"She's right," I chime in. "They'll hopefully play ball one day. But right now, we need to do the best we can."

Nigel coughs to get our attention and looks at me with a serious expression. "On top of moving in with Aki this afternoon, I've decided to stay on with the Supernatural Council for now. You're right, Magic. We might need an inside pair of eyes."

Anguish tears through me. "You don't have to—"

"I know," he interrupts. "But I want to." He gestures to all of us. "You're putting everything on the line for this war that I've helped create." His eyes sweep to his lap. "The least I can do is help fix it. Plus, maybe I can get you a meeting with the SC."

"If you're sure?"

He nods.

"Then, I have a task for you."

He looks up at me with pure determination.

"I need to know the date for their Area 50 plans." He looks concerned for a moment, but I shake my head. "Nothing that will get you into trouble. Do not risk your life over this. You hear me?"

He nods, but I get the feeling his heart isn't in the agreement. He'll risk everything if it comes down to it, I just know it.

"I will not come break you out of prison." I stab a fork in his general direction. "No matter how much you plead and beg."

Everyone laughs, knowing I'm joking. I'd move Earth itself to keep Nigel safe. He's the only family I have left after all. Well, not anymore.

Connie gets my attention. "No more news about us for now, the app is doing well with over a thousand jobs being posted and accepted every day, and I've arranged for a Fae to help you with your spellwork. She lives here in *Sheruta* so should be free from any influence from the Fae Queen. I've also found a bo specialist in Tokyo. She's actually on the Shifter Council, so it wouldn't hurt for you to strengthen our ties there."

"Good. I'm happy to start training again."

"One more thing," she says with a wince.

I'm not going to like this, am I?

"I've asked Aki to help you with your death magic."

Silence grounds me as no one speaks.

"I know you're going to be mad, but it'll help you learn to control it."

"Since you nearly killed me the other day," Arrie grumbles.

My hands clench into fists seconds before reaching the table. "Would you shut the fuck up for once in your damn immortal life?" Tears brim my eyes. I snap my attention to

Connie. "Why?" I try to ask, but it comes out as more of a whine. I will not cry right now. I will not cry. Nope. Not happening.

Connie's expression softens as she reaches a hand to me and squeezes my arm. "Because I get the feeling you'll need it."

Dea moves to stand behind me and rests his hands on my shoulders. "There is someone out there pulling the strings, Angel. Someone cloaked in shadow."

"They'll come out," Arrie says. "Eventually." He shrugs when I look at him confused. "They'll want their moment in the spotlight. Their big hurrah."

"I know I would." Connie laughs, but it doesn't eviscerate the tense silence permeating the air.

Someone pulling the strings, huh?

Someone with a death wish, clearly.

CHAPTER 8

Connie arranged for me to meet my new Fae spellwork trainer this morning, so I sit in my favorite little café, eat cake (it's never too early for cake), and drink coffee until eleven am comes around and a tall, blue-haired, green-skinned Fae woman walks through the door, her hips swaying beneath a small ruffled skirt and a scowl crossing her otherwise beautiful face.

She scans the small number of people in various seats and settles on me with a smirk.

I jump to my feet and smile. "You must be my new trainer." I bow deep. "Magic. It's lovely to meet you."

I haven't spent a lot of time in my male form, so I'm surprised when that smirk turns into a smile. "Yeah, I know." She rolls her eyes. "Come on." Her head nods toward the door beyond before she spins on her heel and exits.

Eyeing my half a cup of coffee with disappointment, I sigh. Great. Another bossy trainer. Can I not just for once get a kind-hearted trainer who wants to joke and gently guide me in the right direction?

Just once?

The Fae lady leads me out of town, past all the shops and nice buildings, across a few fields filled with various produce (from wheat to cotton to potatoes), over a rickety bridge passing over a stream that hops and jumps around jagged rocks, and down a small path through a copse of trees. She stops, waves a hand through the air, touches a magical rune, and reveals a hidden village of Fae.

"Wow!" My eyes don't know where to look; from the modern cottages to the small rainbow gardens outside each, and from the magic barrier that turns the sun purple to the green-skinned Fae children playing in the stream running through the village center, my eyes drink everything in. "This is . . . beautiful."

I trudge through the barrier, running my hand along its spellwork and marveling at the complexity with a jaw-dropping mark of surprise. I didn't know Fae spells could be this amazing.

I creep around the edges of the village, observing. The sun shines down on the Fae, who watch me curiously but continue with their tasks. Everyone is doing something, from looking after children to harvesting vegetables to tending gardens to fixing holes in various houses. It's like a little self-contained community.

The Fae who led me here grabs my hand and pulls me to the edge of the village, where a small cottage sits away from the others. "This is where you'll be training every other afternoon."

I think I whisper an acknowledgement, but my breath catches and my eyes can't stop wandering. I think I'm in some form of beauty shock. Is that a thing? It absolutely should be.

"Are you going to just stare all day, or would you like to get to work?"

"Oh, right." I shake my head out of its glow and face her. "May I ask your name?"

"No." She sits cross-legged in the center of the garden that surrounds the small cottage and closes her eyes. "Sit in front of me."

I follow her instructions.

How does Connie know this Fae? Where did all these people come from? Why do they live separate to the rest of *Sheruta*? Why is she my trainer?

The Fae sighs and opens her eyes. "Fine. I will answer three of your questions if we can begin straight after."

"Deal."

She looks at me expectantly and waves her hand, indicating I can ask away.

"Who are you and your people?"

"We are Fae. Nothing more. Nothing less. But we live in our own world, of sorts. We prefer to remain unconnected to others, where can thrive in peace."

"I see." So they're like the Witches, then? Here's to hoping our relationship doesn't end the same way. "Why do you all live separately to the rest of *Sheruta*?"

"It has always been that way. When our first found her way here, she preferred the company of nature and decided to live in the forest. Eventually a few people joined her, and our numbers have grown since. We just want our own piece of peace. We live off the land."

I look to this strange lady with the green skin, blue hair, and purple tattoos inked down her arms and frown. "Who are you?"

"I do not take kindly to people nosing their way into my business. But if you must know, I joined my people thirty years ago, where I have been ever since. I prefer solitude over the company of others. But I also happen to be one of the strongest spellcasters in *Sheruta*, so Connie asked for my help."

I bow my head. "And I thank you for it." Taking a deep breath, I relax my shoulders. "If I'm being honest, Fae spellwork concerns me because it takes time to learn. It's one of the least intuitive forms of magic. But I don't have forever."

"Yes, Connie explained the time-sensitive nature. But you must be patient or you will not master Fae magic. You are right to be concerned regarding its complexity, for Fae magic contains many aspects and moving parts that create a whole."

"Right," I reply. "There're runes, ingredients, incantations, and other things that make up Fae magic, right?"

She nods.

"And getting a handle on all of them just seems so . . . daunting."

She purses her lips and frowns. "Look, Magic, I'm here because Connie asked me to be, and I owe her. But if you're not in this with both feet on the ground running, then feel free to leave."

Shock plasters me to the spot. She thinks I should leave? Fuck that. "To hell with that. I have Fae magic to learn and a world to save, so stop being a mysterious piece of shit and start teaching me."

For the first time since I've met her, she smiles. A genuine, heartfelt smile. "Well then, I guess I'll train you." She coughs to clear her throat and then forms a ball of plasma between her two hands in mid-air. "This is a form of energy known as plasma. It is Fae created. It is the substance our spells are made from. And what we use to create plasmascreens and other such technologies. It's easiest to see when in the form of a barrier spell, like the one surrounding our village."

She throws it at me, and I catch it between my hands.

"You should be able to feel it, latch onto it, and shape it in any way you see fit." She watches me create shapes with the already-created spell with a harsh scowl on her face. "If you explore the plasma enough, you'll start to feel the spellwork that makes it and keeps it steady."

I've done this already when in the Andes Mountains, when I took down that cloaking spell, so I easily find the runes, incantations, and ingredients that make up this one. But it's different. I've never seen a more complicated piece of spellwork. It's like she's taken an emotion and crafted it into a spell. "Incredible," I whisper. "It's like you've woven the incantations into the runes."

She looks at me a little impressed for a moment before saying, "It is a small piece of what makes up our barrier." She stands, hands on hips, and orders, "Your task for today is to get out of the barrier."

"Wait. What?"

"Must I repeat myself?"

"Err . . . yes."

She sighs and walks up to me. (Will she ever stop sighing?) "Today's exercise is to break through the barrier. If you can do that, I'll continue training you." She walks into what I assume is her own cottage and slams the door.

The barrier? I have to get myself through the barrier. Somehow. Okay. Deep breath. I can do this.

I sooooo can't do this. I've been standing beside the barrier that sits a few meters from my new trainer's cottage with a frustrated frown on my face for the last few hours. No matter what way I rewrite the runes or what incantations I use, nothing is working. The stubborn barrier remains in place.

"Ugh. Couldn't we have started simpler?" I complain to myself under my breath.

"No," she says from behind me. Making me jump. "If you want to go home today, you'll have to break through the barrier."

"Wait. You're kidnapping me?"

She scoffs. "I'm training you." She places a hand on my shoulder and whispers, "Break through the barrier."

My fists clench as my breath comes out in ragged, uneven huffs. "Any further instructions you wanna give, or are you going to stand there repeating yourself all afternoon?"

"You know the incantations are tied up in the runes, but what about the ingredients?"

"The ingredients?" Right. This spell uses more than just runes and words. "I don't know much about spell ingredients," I admit sheepishly.

"You've been relying on runes and incantations until now?"

I nod. "I've only really used Fae magic when needed, so it's all been on-the-go kind of spells, which don't tend to use ingredients."

"You're correct." She places a hand on either shoulder and squeezes. "But Fae magic can be useful for multiple purposes, including defense, which many believe to be its primary and original purpose. Learning complex spellwork will help you overall, even if you mostly use your magic for fighting."

I don't want to use my magic just to hurt people. I want to use my magic to make people's lives better. "Okay." I turn my attention to the spellwork at hand and analyze what effects are being placed upon the runes and incantations. "Well," I say, "there's something stabilizing this flower-looking rune here and something else kind of . . . gluing this incantation to this spirally rune over here."

"Well done," she says. "That's a stergi root stabilizing a compulsion rune, otherwise it wouldn't wear off and people who come near the barrier would simply be under our thrall forever, since the barrier spell never deactivates." She moves to stand next to me and grabs a tendril of the barrier and pulls. "And that glue you spoke of is a combination of mint, volcanic earth, and blessed flowers that have been spelled to form a rune adhesive that helps some incantations bind themselves around more repellent runes. That rune creates the barrier's shape, so it tends to not like being stable. The incantation helps the rune stay in the shape we want, which is a sphere."

Wow. It's so complex. A lot of work has gone into this. "I'm impressed. Most spells I see are just simple runes and words, sometimes with an ingredient in or two. But nothing that winds and weaves together like this." I stop to take a breath and wipe the sweat from my brow. "Whoever designed it is a truly skilled Fae."

"Thank you."

"Wait a minute." I spin on my heel to face her. "You designed this barrier spell?" I try to hide my surprise, but I ultimately fail. "Really?"

She nods, her pastel green skin tinting a vague shade of pink under the afternoon sun. "They had something else before, a weaker spell. So I offered to replace it in exchange for a place among their village."

She must be hiding from someone; otherwise, why would she live here and not among other people? And why fight to create something so complex that clearly took her some time and effort if the needs of doing so weren't dire?

I wonder what her story is.

"So," she continues, snapping us out of our moment, "you should be able to see a few ways around this spell now I've basically spoon-fed you the answers."

I cough and splutter. "I should?"

She smiles for a moment—I'm pretty sure it's the first time I've ever seen her do so—and walks away. Again.

"Great," I mumble.

Okay, so we have a rune adhesive, but that would be impossible to remove since it's a form of glue. There must be an easier way to break the barrier. The stergi root would be easy to remove, but that wouldn't help me; it would just destabilize the compulsion rune —which would have no effect on me anyway, I don't think.

Think, Magic, think.

I need to get out of here, dammit!

That's it!

I need to get out of here. I need to be on the other side of the barrier. But that doesn't mean I need to break the barrier. That would take ages and probably more knowledge than I currently possess about its makeup. But maybe I could create a hole or write myself into the spell. After all, these Fae can come and go as they please. All my new trainer did was put her handprint on the barrier.

Maybe there's a rune or an incantation that creates a kind of ID chip in the spell? And if I find out what that is and how it works, maybe I can magically hot-wire myself into the spell.

I weave through incantation after rune after effect for a full hour before I come across the little bundle of spellwork at the center of the barrier's alignment runes that allows for the people of the village to pass through with ease.

But I've seen nothing look like this in any textbook or spell before.

"What are you?" I whisper to myself.

It seems to be a joining of four different runes—a storage rune used to store their identities, a detection rune used to identify their magical signature, a separation rune that creates a ripple in the barrier, and a time rune that shuts the entire process off after thirty seconds—but there's also an ingredient here that links the separation rune to the detection rune, otherwise it would just separate the barrier anytime it wanted.

"What is that ingredient?"

Taking a step back, I look around me. It looks like there's nothing where the barrier should be, but that's not the case. There's a circle of weeds every few feet going all the way around, if I'm not mistaken.

"Wow."

They look just like forest foliage. Completely camouflaged.

I bend down to take a peek and a sniff, then it hits me. I recognize this plant. It's the gugi plant. The same one I use for directional intent when making the teleporting crystals. I would know its green, heart-shaped leaves anywhere.

But how is a weed, used for directional intent, helping link the detection and separation runes?

Oh, I get it.

Direction isn't just one-dimensional; it's all over the place. The weed is telling the separation rune how big to be and what shape to be and where to situate itself in relation to the habitant's data stored in the storage rune detected by the detection rune.

"That's truly brilliant."

I might have a hard-on for this Fae's mind.

That's a bit weird, isn't it? Oh well.

But how do I write myself into the spell?

I sit in a huff on the forest floor for a while, thinking around everything I've learned and experienced while pulling apart the barrier spell and seeing how it has been created.

I could just add my magical signature to the storage rune. Could it really be that simple? That easy?

It's like how the magical signatures on my library doors work—not that we shut my library door.

I stand against the barrier and bring up the storage rune, where I place my magical essence inside, watch it get added to the few dozen already there, and step back.

"That should do it."

Holding my breath, I place my hand against the barrier, watch it glow like it did for my trainer earlier, and step through.

"I did it!" My fist pumps into the air and jump up and down. "I did it."

"That you did, Magic." My trainer stands on the other side of the barrier with a wide smile. "Well done."

"How long were you watching me?"

She shrugs. "The entire time." She walks back to her cottage and shuts the door. "It wasn't a hard task, but finding the solution was challenging. You navigated a complex spell and pieced everything together. I would be happy to train you, Magic."

Guess it's time to go home.

10

Night falls by the time I get home, and I'm exhausted. All that puzzling everything out was hard work. But the magic itself was simple to accomplish. Guess that's the difficulty with Fae magic—it's more of a science than a magic. Once you know all the moving parts, it's easy, but learning those parts well enough to recognize them on the fly . . .

A lifetime of work.

Everyone's doing their own thing when I get in, so I grab a book and head to my bathroom for some me time to unwind. I love Connie and the guys, but sometimes I just need a conversationless moment so I can breathe again.

By the time I'm clean, my legs are like warm Jell-O, my skin is wrinkly, and my mind is a relaxed mush, Nine, Dea, and Connie are already in my bed—which I swear gets larger every time I see it—and I smile to myself for a moment.

"I could get used to this."

"You already have." I hear a familiar grumbling voice echo from the doorway.

I spin to face Arrie with a sour look on my face, but he seems calm tonight. Less agitated. Maybe some mental space away from me helped him think? He did once tell me he struggles to communicate with people and that he talks best when driving.

"Yeah, I guess I have."

"I've been working on the plan, if you wanted—"

I walk up to him and place my finger on his lips. "Not right now," I whisper. "I'm exhausted. That Fae Connie has teaching me magic is grueling, at best."

His face lights up with a smile for the briefest of seconds, and for a moment, I remember what it's like being happy with this man. He's unique, and I miss him. And it hurts that he wants to label us as friends after we've spent so much time together.

But I don't push for answers.

Instead, I turn around and head to bed. "There's always a free space to join us, if you wish," I whisper over my shoulder.

He moves a foot over the threshold to my rooms, but he scowls and steps back. "I don't think that's a good idea."

Oh. "The offer's always open, in case you change your mind." I shrug and clamber into the pile of heat under my duvet.

THE NEXT MORNING, I FIND MYSELF BEING ESCORTED TO TOKYO BY CONNIE AND NINE TO MEET my bo staff trainer. After yesterday, though, I'm a bit nervous. My Fae magic trainer is . . . hard. Is that how this is going to go, too?

Chin up, Sweetie. I don't think this'll be the same as yesterday.

How do you know?

Because unlike yesterday, you're with the Shifters. And they're pretty cool and chilled.

Promise?

I promise.

Nine rubs his thumb over mine, where our hands are entwined, and looks at me. "You're going to be fine."

"Of course you are, hon." Connie, holding my other hand, yanks me into her for a quick, reassuring hug. "This'll be great. But if you're really nervous, I can stay?"

I think about it for a moment but shake my head. "Thanks, but I think this is something I have to do on my own."

"If you're sure?" Connie asks, mother-henning me, as usual. "If she gives you a hard time, though, just come get me." She punches a fist into her other hand and smirks. "I'll defend you."

"But not against my Fae trainer?"

Connie shivers. "I like you, Magic. I really do. But that woman terrifies me."

Nine laughs. "Only cos she put you on your ass when you first met."

Connie sulks, but I drag us along to the nearest entrance to the Shifter Underground. "C'mon," I whine. "I might be nervous, but I don't wanna be late."

"Right," Nine says. "My appointment is five minutes after yours. I can't be late for that."

Nine's only tagging along to meet with a fellow scientist who wants to help on the blood supplement project. And if Nine needs help, then it's clearly some serious juju.

The Shifter Underground is a series of networking tunnels, hideouts, rooms, and underground houses that permeate the beneath of Tokyo, just underneath the subway network. It's just as large as Tokyo and just as impressive. There's space for every Shifter possible, from large open parks for wolf packs to small networks of hidey-holes for hibernating Shifters. It's one of my favorite places on Earth.

Connie leads us down a series of tunnels and into a gym arena, where a woman sits with two bo staffs in the middle of a cordoned off area.

"Right," Nine says and grabs my hand, "I'm off, Sweetie." He places a gentle kiss to my knuckles and spins me into his arms. *Try not to worry too much. I promise I'll come pick you up in a few hours.*

I nod and watch him leave, his red hair remaining in my vision until he turns the corner and is out of sight.

"Hon, over here!" Connie yells.

I run over as fast as possible, not able to manage Vampire speed in my male form, and smile as politely as possible at the lady beside Connie. "Hey! I'm Magic." I offer her my hand.

She shakes with a firm grip and smiles. "Korby."

Connie smiles at me and nods reassuringly. "I'm not staying, Korby, but I'm sure you two will get along just fine. Basically cut from the same cloth." She waves me off as she leaves, leaving me to my fate.

"So, you wanna know how to use the bo staff, right?"

I nod. "Yeah. We're stretched a bit thin right now, so we thought some outside expertise might be useful."

"What drew you to the bo staff in the first place?" she asks as she hands me one of the bo staffs from the floor.

"Well, it was Connie's idea at first, but I wanted something less brutal." I shrug. "Something more me."

"Bo staffs are pretty brutal when used right, you know. But I get what you're saying."

"Plus," I add, "we can really utilize this with my magic when the time comes."

Her eyes glow bright for a moment, as all Shifters do when they get emotional, but she settles back down and faces me. "You can't use magic while training with me. Just your Shifter side. Otherwise I can't help."

Sounds fair. "Sure. No problem."

"Besides, that way you can master the bo properly before getting all fancy and tailoring your style to you." She eyes my body up and down, and her eyes glow a bright gold color.

I suddenly realize the problem. "I know this form can be difficult for some, but I need this to be professional. Besides, I'm already involved." I just wanted to get that out in the air. "Sorry. Awkward, I know."

Her cheeks blister a bright red color, and I'm floored by the stuttering and stumbling and flailing she does for a moment. "It's . . . err . . . n-no problem. S-Sorry."

"Hey, stop that." I wave a hand in her direction. "I get it." I think back to Dea and how I can still barely look at him without getting my panties in a twist. "Trust me."

"Sure." She gets into a stance ready to fight me. "Sorry, again."

"Don't mention it." I mimic her stance and try my best to parry her oncoming blow, but it's like all my usual natural talent with this weapon has flown out the damn window. "Ah!"

"Thought Connie said you had some basic skills?" she taunts.

"I do!" I yell as I parry another blow to the head. "Usually."

"Well"—she stops—"you're holding the bo wrong." She puts her bo down and comes to help me. "You want to place your hands so you're dividing the bo into thirds, like this." She places one hand one third of the way down the bo, and the next another third of the way down. "Your left hand should face down while your right hand should face up. That way you have maximum control."

"Right."

"Your stance is good."

I look down to my feet and smile. Yes, go feet!

"I'll go through some basic bo staff maneuvers with you, and then we'll put them into practise. Okay?" She smiles at me, and it feels good to be smiled at after yesterday.

"Okay. Let's do this!"

Korby takes me through ten different maneuvers and then has me put them into practise in all kinds of combinations, defending her attacks and defending myself. And I can already see the possibilities of how to use my magic. My elemental Witch magic in particular will go well with this type of weapon. And if I carve some runes into the wood and maybe add some charms, I can really vary it up.

After three hours of the most grueling workout possible, I'm done. My body is about to collapse in on itself, and I can't lift my arms above my head. But it doesn't look like Korby is doing any better.

"You alright?" she asks as she slumps beside me.

I nod, barely able to move. "Think . . . so."

"That was intense."

"Yeah . . ." I chuckle. "I've had more chilled workouts with Connie."

"Sooo . . ." Korby starts, and I internally cringe. "You and Connie?" She coughs to clear her throat. "Is that a thing?"

"Uh-huh." I sit up and look over at Korby, who's still flush-faced and struggling to sit up. "I'm kinda in a relationship with Nine and Dea too."

Once she sits up, her eyes go wide. "Like, all of them?"

I nod, my eyes shooting to the ground in embarrassment.

"Hey, no." Korby grabs my hand and helps me to my feet. "Sorry, I didn't mean to embarrass you. It's cool you've found your family." She smiles up at me. "Genuinely."

Looking around, I don't spot Nine, so I turn to Korby and ask, "Wanna hang out for a bit?" I shrug when she looks at me in surprise. "I've got time to kill before Nine picks me up."

"Sure." Her eyes brighten at the suggestion. "That'd be great."

"Well, the where is on you. I barely know my way back up top." I point to the ceiling and laugh. "But," I start, "would you be more comfortable if I were in my female form?"

She looks to me and frowns. "I don't want you to be uncomfortable on my account." She looks to the floor. "It's okay, honestly."

I shrug and switch to my female form. "Then I'll go like this."

Korby looks up to me and smiles with relief. "Thank you."

She takes me to a bar a few tunnels down, and it's drowning in Shifters.

"Maybe I should have stayed in my male form . . ."

"Why?" she asks, genuinely perplexed. I flash my fangs, but she laughs. "Don't be stupid. We used to war with Vampires, but that was a long time ago. We've coexisted in peace for hundreds of years now. There're even some living down here in the Shifter Underground."

"Oh, I thought there was still some . . . tension."

Korby shakes her head. "Even the councils are friendly with each other. The Vampire King is an amazing ruler. He really helped bring us all together."

"Really?" I ask as we sit at two stools up at the bar and order some cocktails. "How so?"

She sips her bright blue cocktail and turns to me with a smile. "Well, for starters, he pulled all of his forces back to Vampire-controlled states the day after he took his place on the throne. His decision to do so pretty much ended the war. They signed a peace treaty soon after, and the rest is history."

"Wow," I exclaim. "That's amazing."

"Uh-huh."

Looking Korby over, I'm surprised someone so young is on the Shifter Council. Her dark brown eyes smile every time she looks at me while her flawless skin glows under every light. She couldn't be older than twenty, surely?

"Magic?"

I shake my head out of my thoughts. "Sorry. What were you saying?"

Korby laughs but shakes her head. "It's okay. I get that a lot." She takes another sip of her drink. "I'm older than I look."

"Really?"

She raises her eyebrows. "Asking for my age, Magic?"

"Maybe." I gesture with my fingers. "Just a little."

Korby laughs. "I'm thirty-two."

"No fucking way!"

A few people near us scowl at my loud exclamation, but that just makes us laugh louder.

Korby places a warm hand on my shoulder. "Sorry. Didn't mean to embarrass you further."

"It's okay." I wave her off. "I do a good enough job on my own usually, anyway."

Ready to go?

Sure. I'm in the bar a few tunnels down from where you left me.

I know.

My head snaps up and looks around, landing on a familiar red-head standing in the doorway. "Nine!" I run over to him and wrap my arms around his neck. "I missed you."

He giggles at my antics. "I missed you too, Sweetie."

Korby walks from behind us. "Hello, Famine."

He waves a dismissing hand at her and says, "Call me Nine. No need for formalities."

"If you're sure."

"Positive." He smiles at her, and I watch her blush in that cute way of hers. "So," Nine asks, "when's the next training session?"

I look to Korby in question.

"Oh, I was thinking three times a week? If that's good?"

"Sounds perfect," I say as I wrap my arm through hers. "Don't think I could do that every day, anyway."

"Soooo," Nine asks on the way home, "how'd it go? You seemed to like Korby . . ."

"She's great." I change into my male form, stretch my arms, and wince. "But seriously, though . . . That was a workout from hell!"

Nine wraps an arm around my waist and yanks me closer. "Connie went home earlier, so it's just us. Wanna grab something to eat before we head back?"

Just the two of us?

Yup.

Sounds great. I've missed everyone over the last few days. I'm so used to having you all around so much, I guess.

He rubs circles on my waist, where his hand sits, and says, *Yeah, it's been tough on everyone. Dea the most, I think.*

Really?

Yeah, he's been a bit . . . depressed.

"Maybe we should all go out tomorrow? Like a date?" I hesitate a moment. "But won't that upset Arrie?" Ugh. Why am I even thinking about that asshole?

Have you talked to him yet?

I shake my head.

You should.

Maybe Nine's right. Maybe I need to be a little more proactive with Arrie, rather than wait for him to be ready and come to me. I just don't wanna force his hand or make him uncomfortable or anything.

Maybe he needs a little uncomfortable nudge in the right direction.

I look into Nine's brown eyes and smile. "Maybe."

"C'mon"—Nine drags me down the next turning—"I know a great *izakaya* near here."

"Really?"

Yeah, you'll love it.

Nine guides me down the street and into an *izakaya*, which is like a tavern or pub, and we sit at a small table in the corner. It must be a good place because it's packed. But then, it is straight after Tokyo's work day.

"Ohhhh, look, Nine! They serve *umaki* here." Nine looks at me like I'm crazy, but the eel wrapped in omelet is sooooo good. Goddess, I'm drooling just thinking about it. "Oh, and look at that sushi platter!" I point to the menu and smile.

"How about we get the sushi platter to share, and then we'll each have our own sides?" Nine suggests.

"Sounds perfect!"

We order, and when Nine looks at me like I'm his whole world, I stop and ask, "How has your day been?"

"Mine?" He chuffs. "Not nearly as exciting as yours, Sweetie. I met with some scientists here, and some specialists and contacts thanks to Alpha Cal. I think I got them all onboard."

"That's great."

Nine's face splits into a grin as he spins into an excited stream of nerd talk I can barely follow. But watching his eyes light up will always be worth it. "And when I told them about the idea to forgo the white blood cell creation altogether, they balked. But I talked some reason into them."

I can imagine Nine standing in front of some lecture theater full of people just like him —though, maybe not as hot—talking their ears off about this brilliant new idea he needs help with. In fact, I kinda wish I skipped out on Korby and went with him. Maybe one day I can persuade him into some lecture theater sex.

I might even wear some glasses.

I nearly spill my drink.

You'd do that for me?

I'd do anything for you. Especially if it turns you on.

He brushes his foot up against my leg and sears me with a heated gaze as I lean in for a kiss.

Our food arrives, and we both drink Hoppys and chat shit until it gets dark and we decide to head home.

"Thank you," I whisper.

What for?

"For taking me out and forcing me to relax. I'm not very good at it on my own."

Nine laughs, his smile lighting up insides until I'm a gooey pile of mush. "No, you're not. But that's okay." He grabs my hand. "You've got us."

We walk through the front door just as Connie and Dea spring on me, yanking me away from Nine.

"We missed you, Angel," Dea whispers in my ear, his voice a little more sullen than usual.

"Wanna snuggle and watch a movie?" Connie asks. "All of us?" She gestures to Dea and Nine as well as me and herself.

"That sounds perfect."

We all snuggle under blankets on one of the corner sofas in the cinema room, and even Arrie joins us, though he sits apart from our snuggle huggle.

And for the first time in a really long time, things are looking up. Two nights in a row I fall asleep peacefully in the arms of the people I love. And I feel loved too.

12

Nine cuddles into my side the next morning and nuzzles my neck. *I told Dea that we're taking you on a date today. All four of us.*

You did?

Uh-huh. Figured we could go on that holiday to Paris you mentioned, but then I thought maybe not, since that's Fae central.

Yeah. Maybe it's best we don't antagonize them further. Before we go, I want an update from everybody. Make sure there's nothing we need to do.

Nine puts his finger on my lips. *Shhhh. Everything is fine, Sweetie. Promise. But yeah, okay. If it'll make you feel better.*

It will.

Dea mumbles something as he stirs on my other side. "Wha are you two talking about?"

"I didn't think our mental chat would wake you." I wince when I realize how tired he looks. "Sorry."

"No problem, Angel. I was waking up anyway."

You look exhausted, bro. We can lie in if you like?

"Yeah, it's cool to lounge for a bit. I don't mind what we do."

"Mmmmm . . ." Dea mumbles before closing his eyes and rolling into my side for another hug. "But then we will have less time together."

But it'll be time better spent.

"Maybe just another hour." He snuggles further into my arm, and I can't help but lean down and press a kiss to his head.

He's so adorable like this. All peaceful and not in control.

He is, isn't he?

I look to my left to find Nine staring lovingly at Dea and sighing in that loved-up puppy dog way of his, and I smile. "You're both amazing," I whisper.

Dea grumbles something that sounds like shut the fuck up, but I can't be sure.

He said he's an Angel of Death, not adorable.

"Well, our Angel of Death is definitely adorable."

Yup. Definitely.

Dea rolls back over. "Ugh." He smiles. "How does this Angel of Death go back to sleep with all of this audible loving going on?"

Nine and I get up after that, not wanting to wake Dea—again—who has been working immensely hard on the embassies over the past couple of days. Just the thought of all that politics makes me shudder.

Breakfast is a grand affair this morning: French toast, strawberries, something called crumpets, and croissants.

We wanted to start your day off with a foodie bang.

It's gorgeous, thank you.

I take a bite out of my French toast that I topped with strawberries and groan.

And delicious, too.

"So, Arrie," I start with a wince. Those piercing ice blue eyes still hurt to look at when he stares at me with that much animosity. "Where are we with the war plans?"

He rolls his eyes. "This isn't a fantasy movie." He takes a deep breath. "I can't do much else until the ambassadors arrive, which isn't until tomorrow." He shrugs. "Anything else you need?"

I do not miss the sarcasm in his voice. "If you're going to a bitch about everything, then yes, I'm sure I can find something for you to do." I look to Connie. "What about you?"

Connie looks sheepishly to the floor. "Well, I . . ." She looks to Nine and then back to me, a small blush forming on her cheeks. "I can't come today. I'm sorry."

"Why not?" I ask, trying my best to hide the disappointment but failing miserably.

She grabs my hand and rubs circles over space between my thumb and forefinger. "Because there's still loads to do. I haven't picked a manager for the app, I need to get hold of the SC's PR manager to ask when the rest of the interviews and stuff are going live, I need to somehow get a meeting with the SC for you, which we're still working on by the way, there's still a ton of data to trawl through on the flash drive . . ." She takes a deep breath and then makes an annoyed face. "And shit, I haven't sorted out temporary accommodation for the ambassadors yet." A string of less-than-lady-like curses leaves her mouth. "I'm sorry, I'm really busy doing all the backend work here."

I get up off my chair and go to stand behind her, massaging the stress out of her shoulders. "It's okay." I place a light kiss on the top of her head. "How about we do something just the two of us on Earth this Friday? Our usual dates, but more . . ."

"Date like?" she offers.

"Yeah."

She jumps to her feet and beams at me. "I'd love that!"

Maybe she prefers dating me alone, rather than making it a group thing? I'll ask on Friday. "Then it's a date."

She slams her lips against mine suddenly, causing me to stumble into the wall, but she holds us both up with a powerful arm around my waist. At first, we don't move, just smile against each other as we stifle our laughs, but eventually she moves our lips in a rhythm I pick up with ease, and the world melts away.

Warm hands snake up my top and settle on my chest, as though she can't kiss me without touching my skin, caressing some intimate part of me that burns with her every touch. A delicious sizzle of need that sets my body alight and makes me gasp into her mouth.

I go to pull away, diving left, but she pins me to the wall and captures my lips again. My eyes snap open and see the need in her closed-eye gaze, the lines of want highlighting her brows as her hair flies behind her.

Fuck.

Seeing the need on her face and feeling the desperation in the way her hips move against mine causes a low growl in the back of my throat to slip free.

I need her, too.

My mouth trails kisses down her jawline, past her neck and onto her collarbone, and her giggles send a thrill through me. I want to delve below her top and pepper kisses across her chest, play with her nipples until she is no longer holding back, and see where it takes us.

But she takes a deep breath and places a solid hand on my chest, pushing me away. She looks at me with swollen lips and a gleam in her eye. "You have a date with your boyfriends."

"Pretty sure they won't mind me starting my day off with a piece of my girlfriend."

She groans into my mouth once more for a small, deep kiss, but she pulls away. "Friday we'll have all the time in the world. I promise."

"Friday."

She walks away, and I watch her ass sway across the kitchen in that seductive rhythm of hers.

When I turn back to the table, both Nine and Arrie have disappeared. Arrie probably left in a huff. But where's Nine?

In my bedroom with Dea.

Oh, cool.

Dea's voice echoes into my mind. *We have been arranging our date. We will come and get you in half an hour. Wear something for hot weather.*

Hot weather. Got it.

13

Hot sun blasts my skin as a gentle breeze breathes life back into my sweat-soaked nape. I shoved my hair up this morning in expectation of the hot weather, and I'm thankful I did.

Mid-October in Borneo is hot.

But beautiful.

"This morning," Dea starts, "we will be checking in to our private villa. Then we will go snorkeling with the turtles and have a beach lunch before going . . ." Dea's dramatic pause is of note this morning. "Orangutan trekking."

"Orangutans? Wow. Really?"

Dea nods but looks a little nervous, while Nine smiles at me and loops his arm through mine.

"That's amazing!"

"Then," Nine adds, "we'll be having an amazing dinner and then spending the night here in the villa."

"But," Dea adds, looping his arm through my free one, "we do not have to do anything sexual this evening if you do not want to. We can just spend time together."

I giggle. "Yeaaaah, cos I'm going to be able to keep my hands off the pair of you in nothing but shorts." I roll my eyes.

Seriously, are these two mental?

They both chuckle.

You packed a bikini, right? Cos I'm okay with going nude. He winks at me.

Dea chuckles beside me. "You are terrible, bro."

As if you're really complaining.

"No. Never." Dea leans over and places a quick kiss to Nine's lips, but he pulls back in a red-flushed haze of embarrassment.

Seems they're still not really used to public displays of affection.

"You know, you guys can do things without me. I'm okay with you both having time to yourselves." I shrug.

They don't answer but drag me forward, hopefully toward somewhere I can sit down

—I'm sweating like a pig. Which, now that I think about it, is actually ridiculous because pigs don't sweat. Who even made up that phrase? What a moron. I'm sweating like a . . . horse. They sweat a lot, right?

Yeah, they do.

I look to Nine in a flourish of embarrassment that he heard my ridiculous inner monologue. Oh well, he's probably used to it.

Trust me, your mind is awesome.

Really?

Yup.

We continue up the road for a little while, until I pause in a breathless huff. "Can I not just fucking fly us there?"

Dea sighs. "Fine. If you must."

"I must." I change into my female form and gather us all into the air.

For a moment, I chuckle to myself that I'm making Dea fly when he has wings, but I mention nothing. He probably doesn't want to flare up our angel connection so soon after that night in the hotel.

"Ready?" I ask, not waiting for a proper answer as I shoot us forward. And in less than thirty seconds, I see a sprawling house that looks beautiful. All straw roofs, infinity pools, tiki bars, and loungers. "Is that it?"

"Yes," Dea answers and grabs hold of my hand. "Take us down to the gates. We should ask for entrance before terrifying the security team."

Right.

I set us down a few feet from the main gates.

The two security guards let us in with a few gasps and murmurs, one of them even pointing at me with a shaking hand. They weren't speaking English, but I'm not sure of the local language.

Bahasa Malaysian.

Ah. Okay. Nothing I can speak.

Shame.

The security guards continue to whisper to each other in feared, hushed tones, but there is nothing I can do about it.

Nine rips his arm away from mine and steps toward them, hands held above his head. I don't know what he says, but after a few minutes, they calm down and stop giving me weird looks. Instead, they just avoid eye contact and step away from us entirely.

"What did you say to them?"

Nine shrugs. "Just explained you weren't an enemy and we want to be left alone for the day."

"And they just agreed?" Dea asks.

"Sure." He looks at Dea as though it shouldn't surprise him. "I am the Horseman of Famine. A large part of dealing with food and resource scarcity is sharing it among people equally and creating decent economies, which requires talking and negotiating."

"Remind me again why you can't just deal with the Witches for me?" I sigh in exasperation. "Or why you didn't tell me the whole New Orleans thing would blow up in my face? Or why—"

"Okay, first, I'm not a fortune teller. I'm just me." He stops us in the middle of the driveway and turns me to face him with a hand on each shoulder. "Second, the Witches are annoying, and I've tried dealing with them before, but what they want is what they already have. They gain nothing from coming out of the supernatural closet."

"And third," Dea says from behind me, pressing his front up to my back, "Nine is good but not foolproof." His hands skate up my top and land in a firm position on my stomach as he blows kisses against my ear and down my neck.

A small moan escapes me, and then Nine captures my lips in a searing kiss that blows away any doubt in my mind that I'm not ready for these two.

"We . . . have . . . an . . . itinerary," I say between gasps and clashing lips. "I really do want to see the turtles and orangutans."

"I know," Dea whispers in my ear. "I was just reminding you that I love you."

"I was just looking for an excuse you kiss you," Nine chimes in.

"You never need an excuse." I run a hand down his face and cup his jaw. "You can kiss me anytime you wish."

Dea pulls us both away and turns us to the front door. "The world's perfect date awaits, Angel."

"I'll be the judge of that." I glare at him. "Besides, I have another date with Connie on Friday. Really gonna compete with her?"

Dea visibly shudders. "Not worth the pain of winning." He smirks at me to let me know he's joking, and then swings the door open.

Nine gives the grand tour: three bedrooms, two bathrooms, four reception rooms, two pools, and a minibar. "We could have gone grander," Nine says, "but we wanted intimate."

"I think it's perfect," I whisper as I hug them both. "Now, when do I get to see the turtles?"

Dea looks at his watch with wide eyes. "In twenty minutes. You might need to fly us there."

"No problem." I quickly change into my bathing suit in both forms, then run back out and grab both their hands, lift us into the air, through the front door, and up above the house. "Where to?"

"Over there." Nine points to a bit of coastline with some people dotted every few meters. "We're hiring the equipment from a shop near the beach."

"Pfft," I spit. "You're hiring equipment. I can shift into any animal I want, and I don't need to breathe under water in my female form."

Dea laughs. "I said she would laugh at the idea of using equipment, did I not?"

Nine scowls at him and throws a middle finger in his direction. "Know it all," he mutters under his breath.

I laugh. "Says the nerd."

We land a few minutes later on the sandy shores of the whitest beach I've ever seen, and the feel of it between my toes is like vacation running up my body in waves of relaxation. No world war on magic here. No sex-changing body issues confusing my gender here. No stupid boyfriend/not boyfriend pissing me off here. Nope. Not at all.

Nine grabs my hand and then Dea's—who has turned visible—and leads us to a small

hut-like store renting out all kinds of equipment: surfboards, beach stuff, and more importantly, snorkel equipment. For them.

No way am I not swimming with the fishes.

The straw hut shop blends seamlessly with the beach, weather, and endless ocean
waves in the distance as I take a deep breath and inhale the salty sea air, the sunshine, and
the warmth crackling against my skin. My bikini is a deep red that matches my skin tone
against the kissed sun and my tattoos.

But the guys are the real show.

Dea steps out in black shorts, his swirling golden tattoo glowing and his pale skin
almost as white as the sand beneath my toes. Nine holds his hand, his red and white
shorts falling longer than Dea's but suiting his slicked-back red hair and flirty smirk. With
both their bodies on display, it's definitely shaping up to be a good day.

"You two are totally going to mess your hair up and freak out about it, aren't you?"

They both chuckle, but it's Dea who says, "We brought hair gel with us, do not worry."

Of course they have.

THE WATER MOVES AROUND ME IN RIPPLES OF COOLNESS, WASHING AWAY THE SWEAT, RINSING
off the stress, and invigorating me with something akin to peace—though not quite, since
it's impossible to be at peace with so much on my shoulders.

I've stayed in my female form, letting the water trickle over my skin, drawing the
guys' gazes more often than I thought it would. And it feels good to have their attention.
So I let it roll around me, soak it in like a good breath of fresh air.

Turtles move beneath me as small fish swim between them, darting from one spot to
another. Some of the larger fish swim more slowly, like a mountain against the breeze, but
they're full of bright colors and sunshine nonetheless.

Focusing on the turtle beneath my face, I shift into my male form and then into a sea
turtle, and I watch the world change before me. Colors and ripples on the water all blare
across my vision, but the sounds of everything around me dull and flatten to a low vibration I can barely perceive.

Nine? Can you still hear my thoughts like this?

Yup.

Can you see through my eyes like this, too?

Yeah. It's pretty cool.

It is, isn't it . . .

I shift into something small and bright yellow so I can dart around everyone—much to
Dea and Nine's amusement. I brush up against their torsos and arms, letting Dea tickle
my dorsal fin. Next, I shift into a dolphin so I can jump around and act like a child in the
ocean for the first time. And after lots more shifting and exerting most of my energy, we
swim ashore and dry off under the sun while lying on the beach.

"That was so much fun," I say on an exhale.

It was amazing to watch everything through your eyes.

Dea rests a warm hand on my thigh, inches from my cock—and judging by the smug
smirk on his face, he knows it—and asks, "Do fish see in color?"

"Yup. They—"

"The composition of the color is different; brighter in some places and duller in others," Nine interrupts.

The know-it-all.

"Sorry."

"Sooooo," I start, "what are we doing for lunch?" I don't want to be picky, but I'm starving after that much shifting. Maybe I should have gone a little lighter?

Oh well.

"Oh," Dea says, "it is behind us."

I drag my head up off the beach floor and peer toward the treeline behind us, where a table with three chairs are set up. And on top of that table sits a spread of so much food my stomach grumbles loud enough for Nine to laugh.

"Stop laughing and help me . . . I'm dying," I dramatically groan.

"You're fine, you drama queen."

"But what if I never gain enough strength to move? Then how will I ever continue living?" I giggle under my breath and hold a hand out for either of them to help me up off the sand.

Dea's the one who obliges my drama and yanks me to my feet, but he spins me into his arms and places a gentle kiss to my cheek.

My cheeks burn a deep crimson as my brows rocket to my hairline on a sigh. "Mmmmm . . ."

C'mon, you two. Unless you want this food to go to waste. We've only got an hour before we need to be at the meeting point for the orangutan spotting.

Right. Food.

The only thing better than kissing. Maybe.

14

An hour later, Nine and I are trekking through an endless forest, with Dea invisibly walking behind us. He used up his visibility earlier, but we're alone with the guide anyway, so it isn't a problem.

"The forest is 140 million years old, making it the oldest forest in the world," the guide says. "And wild orangutans are only found here."

I'm glad I ate myself stupid earlier. I definitely needed the energy for this. Nine, remind me again why I can't just do this part in my female form? I'm getting used to my male form just fine, but this is torture.

Because Shifters are strong too, and you need a good workout in this form as well.

Between Korby and this, I'm sure I'll be ripped in no time.

"Sarcasm, huh?" Dea asks.

Yup.

Nine's gotten into the habit of projecting all internal conversations to everyone when it's the three of us, so no one misses out. Could he get any sweeter? Seriously, what did either of us do to deserve Nine?

Nine runs his finger between mine and grabs my hand, then strokes circles between my thumb and forefinger, sending shivers up my arm and down my spine. Dea, being invisible, wraps an arm around my hips and rests a thumb in my shorts.

The dense jungle around me sways with the barely there breeze, a cool stream on the nape of my neck that sends more shivers down my spine and air rushing out of my mouth in a relaxed gasp.

The guide treks us through various worn paths until we stop just off the side of a small trail and look up. Spots of dark orange leaping from tree to tree catch my eye, and I gaze in wonder at the strange animals living above us.

I look to the guide, then to Dea and Nine, and back at the orangutans. Yup. I'm gonna do it.

I study a still one for a moment, and then focus on its shape and features until I'm half the size I was and standing on Dea's feet.

"Wow," the guide gasps, "you're a . . . orangutan Shifter?"

Nine chuckles and Dea smiles. "Not quite," Nine says. "They're the Horseman of Magic."

His eyes widen as he takes a step back. "The . . . the one from the video?"

Ugh. That stupid viral video. What was I thinking? We need to take back New Orleans or do something. Something to pacify humans and the supe communities. Connie said the interviews are going well, but they're not as viral as that stupid video. Maybe we can do something else? Something more showy?

Stop spiraling. It's weird to watch in orangutan form.

Sorry. I am in Borneo with the orangutans, and I'm going to play with them. I will not be distracted by work right now. I'll fix all that when we get back.

But now, I need to figure out how to climb a tree.

After the third time of falling on my ass, I harrumph and crawl back to Dea's leg like a grumpy child.

Harder than it looks?

Yes.

Have you considered flying up as a bird and then changing when up there?

My eyes widen as I ooh my excitement.

You're a genius, Nine.

It's been known to happen.

Hardy-ha.

I shift into a crow and then fly up the trees until I'm a few feet away from the edges of the group. Then, balancing on a sturdy trunk I think will take my orangutan's weight, I shift. The tree creaks beneath me, and I use my arms to steady myself, but I end up whacking a thorny plant in the process and howling in pain.

Why are orangutans so hard to maneuver?

Nine and Dea are wetting themselves with laughter on the trail below me. I swear, when I get down there, I'm going to fly myself back to the villa and leave them behind.

No, you won't.

Oh, won't I?

No. How else will you get that delicious threesome you've been imagining all day?

Dea's voice echoes in my mind. *What kind of things do you imagine, Angel?*

Nope. Not right now. Trying to figure out how to be an orangutan without killing myself.

There's a tree branch I can swing from, and then I'll be closer to them. But I don't want to scare them. So I wait where I am situated until one notices me. And luck is favoring me today because a young orangutan looks my way and walks over, curiosity lingering in its eyes.

I hold out my hand, hoping it'll be okay if I touch it. I don't really know much about orangutan behavior. But how hard can it be?

Hard. Apparently.

When the youngster notices I'm not anything familiar, it immediately alerts mom, and then the entire group makes these guttural sounds and thrashes around until I'm so scared I fall to the floor and crash onto the path beneath me.

Shifting back into my male form, I groan, "Okay, never let me do that again." I wipe the jungle floor from my ass while Dea and Nine huddle over laughing, trying to catch their breaths.

"Oh god," Nine says, "that was hilarious."

"Yeah, yeah, yeah." I stalk myself and my bruised ego back down the trail and toward home.

"It's this way," the guide says as he corrects my direction.

Which only serves to crack Dea and Nine up again.

Fucking boyfriends.

WE TREK ALL THE WAY BACK WITH THE GUIDE, AND BY THE TIME I WALK THROUGH THAT FRONT door and let the AC suck all the hot air from my body, I'm exhausted. Bone tired.

"Wanna chill by the pool for a while?" Nine asks.

"It is cold," Dea adds.

They both offer their hands, and I take them, letting them lead me outside. Since I'm in my bikini in my female form, I shift and then cannonball into the deep end.

Fuck me, this water is kept cold somehow. But I am not complaining.

Nine and Dea jump in after me, and we bathe and fool around as the sun sets behind us, a perfect backdrop to a perfect date.

"You really think this has been perfect?" Nine asks as he floats next to me.

"Uh-huh. I got to be a fish, I ate great food, we all laughed and had fun, and I've not thought much about work the entire time."

"Or Arrie," Dea adds, then winces at Nine's accusatory glare.

I laugh at them both. "It's okay. I'm sure Arrie and I will be fine. Eventually." But there's something in the hesitation he showed the other night that has me doubting that. I'm not sure Arrie is ready for a serious relationship. Has he even had one since becoming a Horseman? Aside from his friends-with-benefits things with Connie. Which doesn't really count.

Now is not the time, Magic.

I shake my head, trying to shake the thoughts from my mind. I can always ask Arrie when I get home. Somehow.

Should go on a drive somewhere.

Right! Arrie talks more when he's driving.

You are a genius, Nine. And sorry, I'll stop thinking about Arrie while we're on a date.

Dea floats silently next to Nine, and part of me wonders if he's asleep, but then he flutters those beautiful eyes open and the question dies on my lips. He swims underneath Nine and comes up between us, settling me with a dark look, his pupils glowing gold. I've only ever seen that look that intensely once. In the hotel bedroom.

Fuck me sideways.

This man is going to kill me.

But you'll enjoy it.

If hell is a platter of Death, I'll happily spend the rest of eternity trying to die to get there.

"No need to die to taste this platter, Angel." He winks and grabs my chin in one hand before sweeping his lips against mine. Once. Twice. And on the third brush of a kiss so delicate I'm worried he'll break beneath me, his tongue delves into my mouth and tackles mine.

One point seven seconds.

That's how long it takes for my panties to soak through, Nine to grab my hips from behind, and Dea to groan as he leans into the kiss.

"Angel," he says between breaths. "You are perfect."

Exquisite.

Nine trails fiery kisses down my neck that leaves my skin tingling against the water and my arms shaking in Dea's hold. A nip here and a sucking lick there. And my legs wrap around Dea's waist, bringing us closer. So close I can feel the tremble in his hands as he strokes delicate fingers along my collarbones and down my shoulders. So close his cock is nudging my clit, and I can't breathe for how tense this atmosphere has gotten.

Like it'll swallow me whole one orgasm at a time.

But it turns out, I do not have a problem with that.

Nine delves his hands under the water and skims teasing fingers along the underneath of my bikini bra and up.

"Nine," I gasp.

"Yes?" he asks, fake innocence lacing his voice.

"Don't stop."

Dea groans in front of me, his eyes squeezing closed as he rolls his hips against me. "You two will be . . . the death of me." His voice a soft, husky whisper that sends delicious pleasure dancing down my spine. "Do you have anything you would like to do, Angel?"

"Or try?" Nine adds. He resumes his kisses, like his very existence relies on touching my skin. "You never know, we might play out one of your many fantasies."

I try for an indignant sort of sound, but Dea dips a hand into my bikini bra and flicks a harsh thumb over my nipple. "Do not play games with us, Angel," he warns, that familiar dominant edge returning to his voice. "Nine shares all kinds of things with me."

I go rigid for a moment, concern lacing my body, but then I relax. Who am I kidding? I love that they talk about me. Wonder if they compare notes?

Yup.

Dea snorts. "Nine told me all about how you love to beg, and I nearly orgasmed on the spot."

"It was hilarious."

"Did he do that thing like in the kitchen, where he pouted and screwed his eyes tight shut while trying not to go all dominant bear on you?"

Nine laughs, his hands gripping my hips. *Yup.*

Dea, on the other hand, swoops in with a dominating kiss that must take Nine by surprise, because his grip tightens on my hips as he rolls his cock into my ass.

And I think I just might know what I want.

I send the fantasy image to Nine, who breaks his kiss with Dea to give me a look of surprise, his eyebrows shooting to his hairline. "Really?"

"What? I can't be adventurous?"

He holds up his hands in defense. "Just assumed it would take longer to persuade you to lose those inhibitions."

"Pfft. I've already sampled both the goods, what's the point in holding back now?" Now I want both. Together.

I notice the moment Nine sends the image to Dea, because Dea's eyes glow a brilliant gold as he yanks on my wrapped legs to grind against me. "I will always find your mind fascinating. And I will forever be jealous that Nine gets to spend every second he can in that gorgeous head of yours."

15

We decide that to fulfill this particular fantasy, we really need Dea's bed and his box of goodies. I mean, how else will he tie us both up together?

I transport us straight into Dea's room, and Nine asks the house immediately for some refreshments while running his still-wet hands down my arms and nipping at my bottom lip until I grant him entry and he wraps his tongue around mine to distract me. Meanwhile, Dea steps up behind me and pulls me to the bed, yanking my thighs apart to straddle him as I face Nine, who stands between our legs and continues kissing the ever loving fuck out of me.

Dea's hands roam up my sides before he leans back and unties my bikini top with skilled hands and a sigh of relief when he has free access to my nipples.

Nine wastes no time in breaking our kiss and sinking to his knees, where he lavishes the nipple Dea leaves free for him.

And fuck if two pairs of hands and two mouths don't feel like I'm in some kind of heaven. A really good heaven. Filled with dick. And tongue. Maybe some boobs, too. Oh, and some chains and rope.

Yup. That's heaven.

Dea wiggles out from beneath me and pulls my hands together in a clasp behind my back, then yanks me backward. "Are you going to let me tie you up like a good sub, or are you going to be a brat?"

I wish I was the kind of person who could backchat and talk shit, but I just want to get fucked, so I say nothing and just let him tie my hands to each metal loop of the bed while I rest on bent knees.

Dea strokes gentle fingers down my arms as he goes, whispering, "Good girl."

His praise shoots straight up my body, setting it alight and dousing me in oil to fan the flames higher.

"Damn, bro. Magic looks good like that."

Dea takes a step back to admire his work and nods. "My Angel will always look good in restraints." He turns to watch Nine's eyes sparkle as he looks me up and down. "Just like you."

Nine turns to face him and wraps his arms around his neck. "I don't think I look quite as tasty as our little prize over there." He nods toward me. "But I can put on a show for you whenever you want."

"Do not sell yourself short, Famine." Dea grabs his chin and forces him to meet his gaze. "You look beautiful in restraints with that perfect scrunched-up look on your face just before I shove your dick down my throat."

A small whimper escapes my lips before I can catch it, and they both smirk in my direction. A predatory look in their eyes that sets my nipples on edge and reminds me I'm at their mercy tonight.

Totally at our mercy.

Nine creeps along the bed toward me and grabs my bikini bottoms in both hands before running them down my legs and throwing them off the bed. "And I want you screaming both our names before this evening is out."

Dea leans over and ties Nine's hands to the same loops as mine, smirking at us both the entire time. Then he kneels behind me before palming both ass cheeks and biting the sweet spot between my neck and my shoulder that always makes me shiver.

My head thrown back and my eyes closed, the guys revel me in warm kisses, nips and bites, firm hands, and gentle strokes. And just as I'm about to ask them to touch me somewhere better—anywhere with more nerve endings—Nine bends down, stretches his restraints as far as possible, and places a warm kiss to my clit.

My breath rushes out on a whisper as Dea rubs harsh thumbs over my nipples. "Yes. More, please." My hips rock into Nine's mouth of their own accord, and I can't help but moan as he takes me between his lips and sucks, flicking a quick tongue over the top.

"Harder, Nine," Dea orders.

And Nine submits to his demands and sucks harder, nipping his teeth with just the right amount of pressure to shoot stars across the backs of my eyelids as his tongue flicks quick, tense laps.

Dea delves a hand between my thighs and runs a finger up my slit. "Fuck. She is soaking wet."

Nine pops his head up in interest, and Dea pops his fingers into his mouth for him to lick clean. Nine's eyes close as a small moan escapes. "Fuck, Sweetie," he says once Dea returns his fingers to my teasing my slit. "You taste so good."

As Dea pumps one finger inside me, Nine secures his lips back to my clit and sucks hard enough to have me crying out and bucking into their hands and mouth. Nine's tongue travels farther south and tangles itself with Dea's fingers as they pump in and out of me.

I can feel the tension building just from their foreplay, and I briefly wonder if I'll survive this night with them teasing and dominating me in equal measure. But I still want them both inside me, so I can't put out just yet.

"She's holding on for later," Nine groans. "For when we're both inside of her."

Dea leans down and whispers in my ear, "You really want both our dicks at the same time, don't you?"

I nod, not trusting my words as Dea pushes another finger inside to match the first and Nine returns his attentions to my clit and nipples, his arms stretching wide behind him.

"Get undressed, Famine." Dea unties his restraints.

When Nine lets me go and steps off the bed, I groan as the ache for his tongue and teeth pound at me, causing my body to buck into nothing but Dea's fingers.

Nine strips his swim shorts off and sets his hard cock free with a swipe of his hand.

Dea leans around me and gets off the bed, joining Nine, then removes Nine's hand from his cock and replaces it with his own. "This is mine this evening. You will do with it as I say. Understand?"

Nine nods and looks at me.

"Yes," Dea confirms. "Stick that delicious cock of yours inside my sweet little Angel's pussy and make her moan so I can watch."

His words spin through me, searing through the lust haze they've both webbed over my mind that's left me speechless and right to the searing throb between my thighs making them shake.

Nine kneels in front of me, a playful smirk on Nine's face I wipe off with a kiss and a nip at his bottom lip. "Fuck me already. Please." I can't keep the whimper out of my voice.

But Nine seems to hear me because he lifts one leg over his hip and lines his cock up before easing himself home.

"Nine!" I gasp and whimper and moan as he stretches me, the friction shaking my thighs and throwing my head back. When he begins to move, I tug on my restraints and grab the rope hard. "Yes . . ."

"Harder," Dea instructs from where he's sat at the end of the bed, watching with eager eyes shining like gold. "And faster." His hand wraps around his shaft and tugs. "God, you two are so hot to watch like this." His breath ragged, his knuckles nearly white, and his eyes staring holes in our bodies.

Nine shuffles backward and leans me at an angle so he can bend his head to capture my nipple in his mouth, and I gasp.

"Dea . . ."

His gaze snaps to mine as his hand stops moving. "Yes, Angel?"

"I . . . help."

Nine snickers around my nipple as he pinches the other.

"Fuck!" A scream leaves my throat as my pussy convulses around Nine's dick, making him snap his hips and pound me harder.

My eyes still locked onto Dea's, I watch the moment that control snaps. The moment his desire wins out. "Fuck this." Dea crawls up the bed and kneels behind me. "Grab me the lube."

Nine gently pulls out of me—much to my disappointment—and reaches into the nightstand drawer. He throws a tube of it Dea's way.

"Good. Now get back inside of her."

Nine wraps my leg back around his hip and fills me tight, sending jolts of white-hot pleasure through me, while Dea runs his hands down my back. But he doesn't stop when he reaches the bottom, he continues, trailing gentle fingers down my ass, running tight circles around my ring, and continues down until he reaches the connection between me and Nine.

Nine suddenly moans, his eyes rolling and his lips parting. *Yes, that . . .* Seems words are lost on him, too.

I look down and see two of Dea's fingers and a thumb wrapped around the base of Nine's cock while he pistons into me. Just imagining myself in Nine's shoes has a different rage of desire infernoing around me.

Dea's hand on my cock . . .

Nine's mouth wrapping around the head . . .

Fuck, that's hot, Sweetie.

So hot.

Dea growls in my ear. "Is that what you want in the future?"

Nine must have sent the image his way.

I nod and thrust my ass backward, reminding him of what I want right now.

"Such a demanding little thing." Dea takes a moment, but then returns to my ass and runs a finger around the rim, pulsing gentle waves of pleasure through me every cycle.

"Dea, please . . . stop teasing."

He chuckles in my ear and presses a kiss to my neck. "Just making sure you are ready and relaxed enough, Angel. Trust me."

I nod. "I do trust you."

Just as Nine picks up his pace and slams into me at a new angle, Dea inserts one finger.

"Fuck!" Yes, I definitely want something bigger.

He doesn't move for a moment, so I thrust back and bury that finger to the hilt in eagerness, reveling in the slight sting that permeates my body. He adds a second finger, then a third, until I'm a whimpering, sobbing mess in their arms and the only thing keeping me up is the restraints and Nine's cooling hands on my ass cheeks.

Dea's hand runs up and down his shaft, spreading more lube, while his other hand remains buried in my ass. "Ready, Angel?"

My head nods of its own accord.

"She's more than ready, bro. Her pussy's been clenching for release for minutes now."

Dea grabs a fistful of my hair and turns me to face him. "Is that so?" He kisses me and pushes the head of his cock against my hole. "We will just have to do something about that."

Nine grabs my chin and forces my lips back to his as Dea slowly enters me. He's slow at first, not wanting to hurt me, but soon he's buried all the way in and they're both groaning at the tightness while I'm trying to keep it together.

But damn. I feel so full. They're touching every needy part of me, hitting every right spot, and I want—need—them to move. To—

"Shit, yes!" I scream as they both move at the same time. My head flops back onto Dea's shoulder and I'm gone. Lost in pleasure. My mouth is making all kinds of sounds I've never made before, and my desire shoots through the roof.

Dea wraps both my legs around Nine's waist and lifts me up and down onto their cocks like I'm their personal sex toy.

I can feel you, Dea. So good.

628

"I can feel you, too. You are so hard. Angel is so tight."

"Dea," I beg, "faster. Please."

His grip on my hips tightens as he slams me down faster, helping me chase the release that's just around the corner.

Fuck. I don't think I can hold on if Magic—

My world explodes in stars that shoot across the backs of my eyelids. "Goddess, yes!" The feral scream that escapes my throat makes it hoarse and dry, but I don't care.

Shit. Nine volleys a string of curse words into the air as his hands grab Dea's on my hips and yank me down. *Fuck.* He rides me through my orgasm as his crests and explodes into me.

I can't see Dea, but by the frantic pace and pounding into my ass as hard as he is, I know he's close. "You are both so . . ." He steals me from Nine's cock and buries his face into my neck as hot ropes of desire drown me.

We're all panting and heaving in silence, our breaths the only sound in the room.

"We're definitely doing that again," I whisper on a breathy exhale.

"Absolutely," Dea agrees. "That was some of the best sex of my existence."

Agreed.

Dea unties me and lays us on the bed, where he proceeds to clean me up with a fresh washcloth and warm, gentle hands.

Damn. I'm so in love with these nerds.

16

A pile of limbs, snores, and sweaty bodies wake me the next morning, all of us having passed out in Dea's bed the night before after the best orgasm of my life ended my ability to speak.

But I seem recovered this morning, if a little sore. A delicious kind of sore, though, that reminds me how it got there with every shift of my thighs.

Today's the day.

The chosen ambassadors are coming to *Sheruta* this morning to officially meet us and each other. It's a momentous occasion.

A knock at the door has me yanking the duvet up across my boobs while Nine and Dea groan themselves awake.

"Yes?"

"It's just me," a bright-sounding Connie says on the other side.

"Oh, come in." No longer concerned about my boobs being on show, I let go of the cover and smile at her. "What's up?"

Her blonde hair matches her bright smile as her brows raise in question at the pile of obviously naked bodies.

"Oh, shut up, Con," Dea groans. "It is too early to deal with your silent communication." A morning person he is not. "What do you need?"

"We only have thirty minutes before we need to be at the embassy to meet the ambassadors."

"Shit," I exclaim. "I have to get dressed." I rush to the door, give a quick kiss to Connie, and then Vampire speed to my bedroom just in time to see Arrie heading through the open door to my study.

Wonder what he's doing in there this early?

I don't have time to ask right now, though. I'll have to deal with Arrie later.

I get showered and dressed as quickly as possible. Twice. Then rush out to meet anyone else who's ready.

"Hey, hon!" Connie runs into me from behind and wraps her arms around my male form. "You okay?"

"Uh-huh. Kinda nervous about today, though." I spin to face her and am once again shocked at her beauty.

Surprise, surprise, she looks amazing. As usual. A short deep-green dress that stops mid-thigh, is clean cut, and shows off her figure perfectly. She's paired it with light makeup and long hair she left in soft waves down her back. After having cut her hair from floor-length to the bottom of her back-length, she's taken it well, but seeing it still makes me wince.

Maybe hair-growing spells are a thing?

I'll look into it.

"Don't be nervous," she whispers into my ear after leaning in. "You'll do great." Her hand brushes my chest as she steps closer and places a quick kiss to my lips. "I promise."

I nod, trying to big myself up into believing her, but I stop short of actually reaching that goal. I have no idea what I'm doing. I'm gonna mess it all up again, and then I'm gonna have to somehow fix my mistakes, and then I'll—

"Stop spiraling!" She takes a deep breath and looks me in the eye. "You're going to be fine because we'll be there with you."

My hands rest around her waist as I breathe in her mango-scented conditioner and let it fill me up. "You're right."

"There will be some press and journalists there today, but I've made it press-pass only."

"Okay, good."

We could handle some basic press, right?

Eh, I'm sure it'll be fine.

Just as we turn around to head downstairs, Arrie steps out of my room—clearly having come from the library—looking dashing in a dinner jacket, laid-back professional sort of style. And he's tied his hair up into a ponytail.

I itch to wrap my arms around him, tell him he looks hot, and sink my lips against his. To remind him he's loved. But I can't. He doesn't want that.

Arrie stares at me, those ice blue eyes drilling holes into my soul. He opens his mouth and then closes it again. And again. And again. Until eventually he grunts a hello and turns to walk away.

Damn him.

Connie sighs. "One day he'll pluck up the courage to speak to you."

"If I'm lucky."

We all stand together at the top of the winding path that leads to town, and as one, we take a deep breath.

"Everyone ready?" Dea asks.

No one answers, but we all stand united nonetheless.

"No matter what happens today," Connie starts, "no matter what drama the Vampires, Shifters, or Witches start, we stand as a united front."

Everyone nods at her, but Arrie does so with a grimace. "And who's leading this front?" he asks, sarcasm lacing his voice.

I clear my throat, and he sighs. "Dea."

The man in question looks surprised, but I shrug. "You've been dealing with this from day one. You know these people better than anyone. Usually, I'd ask Nine, but he'll be busy starting the blood replacement research tomorrow, so he can't. Connie's busy doing PR management and helping me not totally freak out. And Arrie will be busy with war plans. It's me or you, buddy."

"Okay, okay," Dea says with his hands in the air. "You are right, Angel." He places a solid, sturdy hand on my shoulder. "I will gladly lead today and tomorrow."

Arrie smirks at me.

But I ignore him. Which is my strategy for the entire day. "You're the best at politics, anyway."

Dea's head raises at the praise, and I smile. It feels good to make them feel good.

Yeah, love'll do that to you, Sweetie.

I chuckle and start walking, hoping I'll make it there without sweating too badly. No one talks on the way there, silence entering tense on the scale of atmospheric conversation. And I direly need to break it.

But for once, it's not me who does.

It's Arrie.

"So, what's the goal for today?" Everyone looks surprised he cares, and he huffs. "I'm still a part of this team, even though I'm the only one not fucking the captain." He shoots daggers at me.

Connie coughs. "I'll have you know, Magic and I are taking things slow. We have not yet slept together."

Arrie raises his brow at her. "You are going . . . slow? You?" He coughs to hide his laughter. "Sure."

Connie punches him in the arm hard enough to make him stagger, and now it's me who's hiding a laugh behind a cough.

"The plan," Dea intervenes before we all have a three-way fight. And not in a good way. "Is to welcome the new ambassadors, show them around the building, show them to their offices, and then brief everyone on the primary goals of the embassy."

"While cameras are there," Connie says. "There's a press conference after the briefing for our journalists to ask as many questions as they want."

Nine steps in. "I'll handle that."

I look him in the eyes with gratitude.

"It'll be easier, since I know what they're really thinking."

"Right," Connie says, "but I think Magic should at least open the press conference with some fancy words and explain our overall goal."

"Like a speech?" Nerves shoot through me.

"Yup," Connie says, "but I knew you'd hate that, so I prepared some words for you on key cards."

A sigh of relief escapes me. "Thank fuck."

The new building looms in front of us—seven stories of sea-green plasma-infused polymer, with plasmacsreens imbedded along the windows, night-time technology along the Vampire floor, and an impressive number of balconies, plant walls, and witchlights.

"Wow, Dea," I whisper, "you've really outdone yourself."

He chuckles. "I . . . had help."

"From who?"

"From us," a familiar voice echoes behind me.

I spin around and notice a familiar purple-haired Fae whose cakes never fail to make me smile. "Hey!" Various *Sheruta* residents surround him, all wearing the council pin on their breast pockets. "You're part of the *Sheruta* Council?"

He shakes his head. "Not quite, Miss."

An older Shifter with an impressively long beard steps forward with arms wide. "He volunteered to help us help you create the embassy."

"There were a hundred of us, Miss, who volunteered." He looks sheepishly to the floor. "You've inspired a lot o' people since your outin'."

Really? I don't think I have.

You stood up to the Fae Queen, attacked the rogue Vampires, and are not friends with the Supernatural Council. That last one alone has made you many friends.

Yeah, and many enemies.

You won't win 'em all, Sweetie.

I can damn well try.

I bow to café owner and say thank you before turning to the *Sheruta* Council. "Thank you for dealing with my request so quickly. It surprised me we could make a building in such a timeframe."

A man and woman behind the older Vampire both chuckle. "We have lots of united forces here on *Sheruta*. Including Witches and Fae willing to work together, Vampires willing to put in labor, and large Shifter packs. Plus, they all like you." Her dark hair and skin shine under the morning sun as she smiles.

"Well, I cannot thank your peace enough."

The older Vampire, who Nine informs me is called Derek, interrupts us. "We have new residents to greet and visitors to entertain, do we not?"

"Indeed, Councilman Derek. And again, thank you." Dea offers me his arm and swings us toward the portal building.

And for once, I'm heading there with a smile on my face, since it won't be me using that vomit contraption. Ever again.

Inside the building, we wait at the front desk for the various supernatural communities to arrive. And first to come through are the Shifters, who brought Alpha Cal, another woman from the council I just recognize, two other young men, and . . . Korby.

Korby runs at me with her arms outstretched and a smile wider than the sun plastered on her face.

"What are you doing here?" I ask, squeezing her tight.

"Well, you need to keep up your training, and Alpha Cal wanted to bring some friendly faces, so I volunteered. Figured I could stay in-realm for a few weeks to help you out."

"That's . . . Wow! Thank you so much." I shake my head. "I was happy to commute, you know."

She shrugs. "It's no big deal. Besides, now I know this place exists, I can't wait to explore it!" She bounces up and down on the spot, her short hair bouncing with her. "It'll be so much fun!"

"That it will."

I show her, Alpha Cal, and the others outside. "We'll be reconvening at the embassy once everyone arrives. Terrance here"—I gesture to a *Sheruta* volunteer—"will show you to your hotel rooms and personal lodgings in the meantime."

I thank them as they leave, giving Alpha Cal a personal handshake and an extra thank you, before turning back around and waiting for the next load of guests and residents.

"You think the Witches will still be angry with me?" I ask, my voice a gruff whisper. My eyes avoiding the team's.

"Yup," Arrie confirms. "Mad as the last rose of summer."

Connie scowls at him, then turns to me. "Probably, but this'll go a long way to mending things."

Dea adds his usual wisdom. "They will probably not be helpful to our overall cause, but they might offer assistance behind closed doors. And who knows, this might strengthen ties between them and the Vampires."

Speaking of, the Vampire King, Prince Lucien, and a familiar face walk through the doors next. Prince Phillipe's wife. The Vampire King chose her? That's so . . .

Generous. An inspiring move.

She's being abused by her husband, the next Vampire king, leader of the rogue Vampire faction, but by being here, she can't be touched.

I'm so shocked by this political move that it takes me a moment to realize I'm staring at the Vampire King with an open mouth. "I . . . I'm sorry, Your Majesty." I bow low. "Your choice surprised me for a moment."

He smiles. "I hope she will be a worthy asset to your goals, Horseman of Magic." He places his frail hands on my shoulders and whispers, "Keep her safe for me, would you?"

I nod. "I'll do my best."

"Soooo . . ." Lucien begins, "you picked me?" He smirks, all devilish and charming, as usual. "Really?"

If I'm not mistaken, there's an air of nonconfidence in that tone. He's not sure he can do this. But that's okay. Because I am.

"Yes, Prince Lucien. You are just the man for the job."

His eyebrows raise. "And how do you figure that?"

"Well, there are lots of benefits to the embassy plan, but we're pretty friendly with the Vampire Royal Council, so we don't need stronger ties there. What we need is unification. With your passion and charm, I'm hoping you can at least manage amicability with the Witch ambassadors."

He snorts and darts his gaze away. "Not bloody likely, love."

"I believe you'll be fantastic at this ordeal."

Prince Phillipe's wife walks up to me with a gentle smile and a little trepidation, which I don't blame her for. "I think that's a wonderful plan. And maybe seeing how united Witches and Vampires are here on *Sheruta* might give them the dose of reality they need."

634

"Precisely." I smile and offer my hand to shake. "I'd like to apologize for how I treated you before. I let anger get the best of me before looking at all the facts."

She waved me off. "Nonsense. I would have done the same thing in your shoes."

"Well, aren't we all peachy and making friends today," Lucien says, the sarcasm lacing his words stinging just a little.

"Don't be jealous, little prince. I'm sure we'll the best of friends before this war is over."

Mention of the war has everyone's faces sobering, the reality of why we're here sinking through the atmosphere like a stone.

"I'll try," Lucien says with more conviction than I've ever heard from his mouth. "I'll try my best."

Another volunteer shows them to their hotel rooms and personal lodgings while we wait for the third and most nerve-wracking visitors to arrive.

The Witches.

Fifteen minutes later, and I'm pacing the reception in frustration. They're late.

They're probably doing it on purpose as a political move.

Ugh. I swear, when all this politics is over, I'm never fucking dealing with it again.

I wish I could grant that request, Sweetie.

I know, I know. I'll be doing this for the rest of my existence. Which is immortal. So I should just suck it up with a smile.

And lots of internal sassing. Sassing is key.

That serves to make me chuckle, and the others look over at us with questions on their faces, but I wave them away. "It's nothing important."

Just at that moment, the doors to the spinning vomit room open, and the full Witch Coven and several other Witches arrive, all dressed in their typical garb.

And I start to shake and sweat.

The entire Coven. Why?

This is gonna be a pain, isn't it?

Probably. Have you considered apologizing?

Me apologize? They're being ridiculous!

You did insult their way of life, their culture, and disrespected their laws. And then assaulted one of the most important people in their world.

I grumble under my breath. But he's fucking right. As always. Guess it's time to suck it up.

I stroll up to the air Coven Witch and smile. "I'm glad to see you are well. I am . . . sorry for the way I behaved last time we met." I bow my head, a red blush blossoming across my cheeks, and say, "I hope that will not cause any problems with our goals at the embassy."

The seer Witch is smiling at me when I lift my head, and I get the feeling she likes me, though I have no idea why.

The air Witch simply nods her head at me and walks past, as though I'm an unimportant fly on her pristine wallpaper.

For fuck's sake.

They're not particularly forgiving, are they?

Nope.

17

A couple of hours later, when all our new residents and their guests have settled in and met us back at the embassy, we settle into the meeting room with an array of cakes, pastries, and tea—curtesy of our wonderful resident baker. The heads of all three councils and the council representatives of each main species here on *Sheruta* sit at a large round table with us. Everyone else sits around the edges of the room.

Dea turns visible for the first time today, and everyone turns their heads his way. "I will lead today's events." He coughs to clear his throat. "As you all know, communication between us Horsemen and the various supernatural councils has strained over the last few centuries. But with a new war brewing on the horizon, we feel it best to strengthen our ties. We hope that increased communication between the supernaturals present will also be of use."

The Witches shift uncomfortably in their seats while the Vampires do their best not to look their way. You could cut the tension with a knife.

"We have the four representative heads of the *Sheruta* Council with us today, so you know who they are. They will be designating a single individual per community to join each of your teams." Dea sips his tea and leans back. "But you all have chosen a member. As have we."

Alpha Cal bows his head in respect to Dea. "We Shifters feel proud and welcomed by our Horsemen, and we thank them for their generosity in allowing us a free choice during this troublesome time."

The Vampire King speaks up, adding his own gratitude. "We also would like to thank the Horsemen for inviting us to such a prestigious event and political movement." He looks at me. "It's truly a work of social art."

"Thank you, Your Majesty, Alpha Cal."

Everyone looks to me, but I keep my mouth shut and look back to Dea, not wanting to make any further mistakes.

Dea picks up the hint and takes over once more. "We hope to use this embassy to work together. To better connect the various councils and covens around the world by having one communication hub."

The head seer Witch clears her throat and looks to Dea with a question.

"Please," he says, "no need for permission to speak. We're equal here."

"Will we be joined by the Fae today? And what of the humans?"

Dea looks at her with a soft smile that borders on sad. "Unfortunately, the Fae Queen denied our request and is choosing not to participate."

Derek, the *Sheruta* Vampire representative, clears his throat. "And as a rule, we have no humans here on *Sheruta*."

"But does this not alienate them further?" Alpha Cal asks. "Would it not be best to extend a peaceful hand their way?"

"I agree," Connie says, "it would at least look good, if nothing else."

The four *Sheruta* Council representatives shift in their seats, but it's the Shifter representative—a mousy brown-haired man with a graying beard—who says, "I guess we can bring it up with the full *Sheruta* Council next meeting."

The head seer Witch nods in agreement along with the rest of the table, but I'm not so sure. "Where does that leave the SC? Should they not be involved? Do we directly oppose them?"

Someone from the back seats surrounding us coughs to get our attention, and Aki stands. "If I may interrupt?"

What the hell is Aki doing here in the first place?

Dea gestures for him to continue.

"Thank you." He bows in his direction. "I think Nigel has some good news on that front, but I'm uncertain."

"What news?" I ask.

"He mentioned this morning about maybe having persuaded the SC to meet with you."

Finally.

A sigh of relief escapes my entire team as we collapse into our seats.

"We will have to reconvene to discuss this further once we have had a conversation with them to see where they stand," Dea says.

Everyone seems in agreement, so Dea switches out with Connie for a bit to allow his visibility to recharge. I swear I'll look into making a visibility charm so he can use that before using his own energy stores soon. I really need to get on that.

Ooh, it might make a good Christmas present. That's just around the corner, right?

It is indeed. I promise I won't tell anyone what you're getting them.

Shoot. How do I keep things from you again?

Not a clue. You managed it once and then haven't done it again.

Fuck.

Connie goes through who's been picked for each species, starting with the Vampires. "For the Vampires, Prince Lucien was our pick, Princess Felicity was the king's pick, and Harrow was the *Sheruta* Council's pick."

One by one, they add themselves to the table, taking the place of the king himself.

"For the Shifters, Pansy was our choice, Leva was Alpha Cal's choice, while our very own Roofus was the *Sheruta* Council's choice."

I don't know any of them, but they all seemed friendly enough. Pretty sure I've seen Roofus around from time to time.

"For the Witches, Aki was our choice, Red was the Coven's choice, and Nana was the *Sheruta* Council's choice," Connie announces as, again, they join the table, taking the Coven's places.

What!

Why did no one tell me Aki is going to be on the council?

He said he'd tell you.

What?

Sorry, Sweetie, I've been a little busy recently.

Oh, Nine. I'm sorry. I didn't mean to shout at you. I'm mad at Aki. That conniving little toad.

"This is it." Connie gestures to everyone. "For now, this is the entire embassy representation. For us Horsemen, you'll likely interact with myself and Dea the most, but don't be afraid to ask any of us for assistance with anything you might need."

Everyone stands and claps, a few cheers whoop out, and the few journalists, who were making notes until now, congratulate us on this momentous occasion.

AFTER A FEW HOURS OF PLEASANTRIES, WHERE I HAD TO UNDERGO MORE SMALL TALK THAN I have ever used before—and hope to ever use again—we're stood outside the embassy's front doors, with all the members standing behind us and a massive audience in front. Including many journalists with cameras, notepads, and floating microphones to be heard over the crowd.

"This is your bit, hon," Connie whispers in my ear as she shoves the key cards into my hands.

I wish I had more time to prepare, but alas, I've been busy.

Looking to Nine and Dea beside me, Nine mentally adds, *Real busy.*

I sigh in my head and shake myself into a more professional mental position. I can do this. It's just a dumb speech. Nine'll take over halfway through, anyway.

Opening my mouth to start, I glance at the first card and smile. "Welcome, everyone, to the opening of the first multi-species embassy since the Supernatural Council opened its doors. We are very excited to introduce you to the new faces of Shifters, Vampires, and Witches here today." I gesture to the group of politicians behind me with a grand smile. "While we have a fair way to go, I'll admit, we will be stronger for having done this together. As a team."

The crowd cheers, and I hand over the microphone to Nine, who smiles at me and places a gentle kiss to my forehead. "You did great, Sweetie."

I finally exhale after stepping back into Dea's and Connie's waiting arms.

"Well done, hon."

"Yeah, Angel, you did great."

I don't think I did much of anything, but at least Nine can take over and do some real good.

He answers questions, smiles and diverts insults, hands over some questions to the relevant ambassador, and dodges tricky inquiries we don't have answers for yet. He truly shines.

"He's made for this," Dea whispers.

"Yeah, he should really do this full time."

Yeah, but Dea looks hotter doing so. And besides, I'm busy with the blood supplement plans. We start research in my lab tomorrow.

More visitors to *Sheruta*?

Yup. But I rented a building in town for them to stay in so we don't impose on the residents.

Sounds like you have everything covered. If you need anything, though, Connie can help with the minor details.

She's doing well with the management side of things.

Yeah, and she's enjoying it, I think.

She loves being this busy and doing something normal that isn't fighting related. But she misses you and is still hurting over Bandio Bontanos.

Just hearing that bastard's name whispered in my mind is enough to have my fists clenching and my breath hitching.

"You okay, hon?" Connie asks as she squeezes my hand.

"Yeah, yeah. I'm fine." I place a quick kiss to her temple and return my attention to Nine, who's wrapping things up for the day, it would seem.

"Thank you," he says, "to everyone who asked questions, will report on what we have done here today, and for supporting an important movement in these troubling times." He turns around and walks back into the building, gesturing for us to follow.

"Well," I say once the door closes, "that went well."

"Better than expected," Leva adds with a smile.

For a Witch, she's been pretty polite so far.

Maybe she's not aware of my troubling past with her Coven? Or maybe she cares little for all of that and wants peace?

Eh. I have no idea. But I'm determined to find out.

18

Dinner tonight at the house is a simple affair: we ask the house for pizza, eat, and go straight to sleep. But not before Arrie wishes us goodnight.

He actually says goodnight to me.

And I might have a little dance party in my chest as I lie between Dea and Nine while Connie's working out in the gym.

He said goodnight. To me.

Maybe he doesn't hate me after all. Maybe he's just dealing with some shit, and I should try to talk to him about it. Yeah, I'll talk to him in the morning. If he'll let me.

In the meantime, snoozy snooze.

But by morning, Arrie is nowhere to be seen, Connie leaves early to handle some embassy setup stuff, and Nine meets his colleagues to work on a Vampire blood substitute. Which leaves just me and Dea.

"So," I start, "I think we should give the embassy an update on what's going on. Tell them about the rogue Vampire faction and the Fae working together, and what we're going to do about it. I also think being 100% transparent will be the best course of action. Tell them about the SC's plans to take down the world's major Vampire cities."

"We should also give them hope, Angel. Tell them about Nine's blood substitute plans, about your plans to unite the lower supernatural world and ask for their help, and we will have to ask Arrie to work with them on defense plans."

"Sounds like a plan."

"Con said to meet her there at eight am."

Looking at the wall clock, I gasp and hurry. "That's fifteen minutes away!" Thank god we're already dressed. "Hurry up!"

Dea downs his fancy tea, I shove my coffee into a to-go cup, and we shoot out of the door faster than a jackrabbit. Haha. I can probably shift into a jackrabbit if I want to.

Now is not the time, Magic.

Dea grabs me around the waist and carries me in his arms, then fazes us the rest of the way. "There you go, Angel. Now we are early." He smiles a cheeky, charming grin at me.

And I can't help it. I bring my lips to his and wipe it off his face in a searing kiss. "I could have done that myself, you know."

He smiles against my lips. "I know, but then I would not have gotten to hold you."

What is with these guys? "None of you ever need to look for an excuse. You can just come right over to me, pick me up, and hug me."

"We know. But you're very busy, and you have four partners. We just like making the most out of the time we have."

Three. I have three partners. But now isn't the time to bring that up. "Okay. Well, feel free to steal me whenever you like."

Smirking up at that beautiful face, his grin spreads wide across that sharp jawline as his eyes glow gently beneath the sun.

"Hey, guys!" Connie yells from a distance as she runs toward us. "You made it!" She grabs me into a hug and then rests my hand in hers. "I'm so glad you're here. They're all asking for updates on things, and I didn't know what to do."

The fluster on her face mars her usually calm and excited features, and I want nothing more than to smooth those lines and make her laugh again.

So I guess I'm going to update the supernatural communities about the Fae and rogue Vampire faction's bullshit.

The drama that causes oughta make her smile plenty.

The glass walls, the plasmascreen walls, the plants hanging from every ceiling, and the regular break and game rooms every few meters make me smile. They thought of everything. A universally liked space.

The double door to the main meeting room looms in front of us, all beautifully decorated in plants and woodwork that makes it look inviting. How misleading. This room is anything but inviting. In there, I have to tell the Vampires that the SC is planning to shut down their main cities. In those comfortable as fuck chairs, I have to sit and ask the Witches for help. Through those doors, I have to prepare our world for war.

And I sure as shit don't want to.

"It is okay, Angel." Dea stops beside me, a friendly hand on my shoulder. "We will do this together."

"Yup," Connie says with a smile. "It's gonna suck, but we'll be there with you."

One deep breath later, I swing the doors open.

Lucien lounges on a sofa he's brought in while Pansy's blonde hair sits perfectly on top of her head in a neat bun as she straightens her back upon seeing us.

Dea, Connie, and I sit at random intervals around the table, trying not to sit at the head like some immortal dictators. My eyes swing to Aki, and for a brief moment, our gazes meet. He offers me a smile, and I try to return it, but something about him unrests me. Something I'm not sure I have a name for yet.

Maybe I'm just worried about having a brother?

"Do you have any updates for us?" Lera asks. She's one Shifter assigned by the Shifter Council, and her bubbly smile eases my concerns somewhat.

"Yes," Connie says, "though you'll have to forgive Magic. Uniting people is not really their strongest skill."

Prince Lucien snorts an agreement, and I would have glared at him, but Connie's use of their throws me for a loop. It's gender neutral.

I . . .

It's . . .

Fuck.

What's with these Horsemen always throwing my emotions under the bus when I need them to be on the sidewalk in step with me? Goddess dammit.

Dea coughs and looks at me expectantly.

Right. Vampires. The SC. War.

More important shit.

"A few days ago, I broke into the Supernatural Council's Chinese headquarters to steal as much data as possible. It was an intelligence gathering mission to help us prevent further destruction like what happened in New Orleans."

Prince Lucien's head crooks up, and he joins us at the table. "Do you have a plan for New Orleans? Because the king wants me to ask for your aid."

I bow my head. "We do. But we have a more pressing matter to deal with first."

Harrow looks astounded. "What could be more important than giving the Vampires back their kingdom?"

Both Vampire ambassadors look to him with small smiles of compassion and gratitude.

I glance at Dea, who nods and takes over, "Protecting the other five Vampire capitols." He coughs and takes a deep breath. "We believe the Supernatural Council is planning an attack on all Vampire capitols around the world."

All faces at the table look horrified, even the Witches look unsettled. Red looks like she wants to say something, but then holds back.

"Did you want to say something, Red?" I try to be gentle, but I'm still struggling with the idea that the Witches won't help.

Because they won't.

They never do.

"I . . . I just . . . I cannot believe the SC would do such a thing." She turns to the three Vampires in the room and grimaces. "I'm no fan of your kind. But you are a species, and you deserve to live. There's a reason Witch Hunters are no longer decreed in our Coven, because one of the early Coven Councils outlawed the practise. We don't like you, but we won't cause war by hunting you out either." She looks at Aki with a frown. "I have to wonder why the SC are suddenly picking up the mantel."

Aki coughs. "I handed in my resignation this morning, so I can stay here and help you." He looks to me when he says it, and I can tell he's trying to make a connection. To be a brother.

But I have no idea how to be a sister. Brother? Sibling.

"And what of Nigel?"

"I'm sorry," Lucien interjects, "but who is this Nigel guy?" He shrugs. "I'm not fluent in Horsemen Who's Who. Sorry."

Sighing, I explain that Nigel is my godfather, but that he works for the SC. "He wanted to quit. To work with us full time, but I mentioned that maybe we could use his connection, and now he's working undercover with us." I look to Aki to reiterate my earlier question.

"He's been going into the office from here, using some of your teleporting crystals."

"Ohhh," Connie says, "that reminds me. Magic combined Fae and Witch magic to make *Sheruta* to Earth teleporting crystals, as well as Earth to Earth. We'll get you all a supply." She looks to me, silently asking if that's okay.

I shrug. "They're easy to make now I know how. I can even show you how." Then I wince. "But I guess with no Fae in the embassy, it won't matter."

Roofus, the *Sheruta* Shifter representative, chooses that moment to add to my list of things to think about. "That reminds me. The *Sheruta* Council wants us to consider adding a *Sheruta* Fae to the embassy. Ready for when the Earth Fae join our ranks."

"But there's no guarantee they will."

He shrugs, as if to say he has no clue either. "They're pretty certain they will. That, or they believe in you a lot more than I do." He picks lint from his nails, and I have a deep desire to rip them off one by one.

Cool it, Magic. You need to get along with these people like a grown-ass adult. Internally groaning, I just about resist the urge to slam my head against the desk. Why is adulting so hard?

In my next life, I'm living as a fucking tree.

"So," Connie interrupts, "soon, Magic will be leaving to try and ask for help from the lower supernatural world."

Gasps and natters fill the room, with some looking at me in awe and others with confusion.

"We'd like any information you can give us regarding what's out there, their whereabouts, and anything else that might be useful. We'll reconvene soon to discuss. We understand it might be a little much to ask this of you from the off."

They all nod thankfully.

"Famine," Dea says with a nod toward Nine, "is creating a synthetic blood supply for the Vampires. He has tried working on this before, but he feels we have a new lead on how to solve a critical problem in its creation. Please offer all the support you can to help us with this, because once we take back New Orleans, getting up a fresh blood supply will be top on our list of priorities."

"War," Connie starts, "will be leading the defense plans for all five cities, and you'll all be required to help with that. Are there any problems?"

"Yeah," Roofus interrupts, "are we *Sherutans* obligated to help with Earth problems?"

Connie grinds her teeth. "No one is obligated to do anything. If you'd rather not help with the war plans, then feel free to leave." She gestures to the door.

Roofus looks at her like she's kicked his puppy, but he quickly recovers and smirks. "Noted."

"For now," Connie says, "we'll be meeting every day. At least me or Dea will be here in every meeting. We want to keep each other as updated as possible."

Everyone seems to understand the necessity. And surprisingly, everyone is more on board than I thought they'd be.

19

We get everyone on board: Vampires and Shifters. Both will need permission first, but they're pretty confident. But the Witches need to petition the full Coven Council first, otherwise the ambassadors will only be able to help from the sidelines.

Walking out of that meeting room is like a destressing massage.

"Hey, Magic!" Aki calls out from behind me. "Wait up!"

I spin on the spot and smile at my brother, who's running toward me. "I just wanted to say that as a Witch who isn't affiliated with the Coven Council, I'm with you." He places a steady hand on my shoulder. "To the end." His brown eyes meet mine, and for the first time, I'm glad I have a brother.

"Thank you, Aki."

"Say, d'you think maybe we could get a drink at the bar downtown?" He looks at his watch. "It is lunchtime."

The hope in his eyes is furious, burning like a flame that'll go out with even the slightest gust of wind. How can I say no? He's just offered his services—the strongest Angel-descended Witch in the world. We need him.

I need him.

"Sure. But I'm due for a Fae lesson in a couple of hours, and if I'm late, then I'll be legit worried for my life. That woman is terrifying." I shiver at the icy rage my tardiness would be met with.

"Okay, that's cool." He smiles. "I'm just glad to . . . meet you." He sighs. "You know, properly. Spend time with you and—"

I save him by laughing and shifting into my female form for lunch. "I get it. It'll be nice to get to know each other a bit better."

I say goodbye to Connie and Dea, who both look at me with proud smiles and kiss me in that deliciously possessive way of theirs that makes me flush, considering Aki is standing just a few meters away.

And then I'm off to lunch with my brother.

It's the same bar I went to with Connie that time, when we danced, got obscenely drunk, and then I flew us through the porch ceiling. The memory makes me chuckle under my breath.

"Something funny?" Aki asks, looking a little put out by my randomness.

"Just a memory of the last time I was here."

"What happened?"

We sit at a table in the corner, away from prying eyes and ears, and I regale him with the tale—leaving out the steaming hot kiss and wandering hands, of course—and when I get to the part about crashing through the ceiling, his laughs warms me.

"Right through the roof?"

"Uh-huh. Enough that Dea had to heal the shard of glass that shot straight through me."

He gasps. "You should be more careful!" His voice raises people's ears our way, and he shrinks back. "Oops. Sorry." He winces. "But you should be more careful."

"The glorious thing about being immortal is that careful means something different to us." I smile gently at him. "I can race at three hundred miles an hour and crash the car, and I'll be fine. I can get my head chopped off and it'll just grow back."

"Really? Like . . ." He gestures to his throat and lops his head to the side. "Like, clean off? Are you serious?"

"Yup." I smile, pride washing through me. Maybe it's cool that I'm immortal?

Aki beams at me just as our fries and beers arrive. "That's amazing!" He looks at the food with hungry eyes, but he turns his attention back to me. "What else can you do?"

"Well, I have two forms, each holding the different species' powers. Witch and Vampire in this form, Fae and Shifter in my male form."

"And you can shift into any animal, use all six types of Witch magic, and don't specialize in any specific form of Fae spellwork?" His eyes pierce mine with excitement.

"Yup. That's about it."

"Other than your dea—"

I throw my hand across his mouth. "Not here. But yeah, that too." I sigh. "I have no control whatsoever over it, but I'm kinda hoping that you'll help?" I meant it as a statement, but it came out as a question.

His eyes beam with pride as a smile takes over his face. "Yes. A million times yes!" He wiggles in his seat and looks like he wants to explode into rainbows.

It's cute.

"Need any help uniting the lower supe world?" Aki asks.

Do I? I'm not even sure when I'm leaving. "I need to make a plan first. See what supes we think we'd have a chance of helping in return for good favor. But yeah, maybe . . ." In truth, I'm still not sure I can trust him.

His face looks crest-fallen; his previously lit eyes now a dull shadow, his smile a frown, and a worrying crinkle in the center of his forehead.

For goddess' sake.

"Okay, okay, okay. You can help."

He looks at me like a child on Christmas morning.

Christmas! It's only two months away, and I want to get everyone a gift. A meaningful gift. Which means I need to work on Dea's invisibility charm and think about something for Connie and—

"Magic?" Aki waves a hand in front of my face, trying to get my attention.

Oops. Must have drifted off into another spiral. Damn. I've been doing so much better.

Okay, focus, Magic. Focus.

"Sorry, what were you saying?"

"I was saying how I can give you a few"—he looks around us with suspicion—"lessons before you leave, if you like." He looks to the table. "Not sure how helpful it'll be for your mission, but you know . . . Maybe it might come in useful."

The rest of my lunch with Aki was spent chatting about the world, our lives, and how great it would have been if we knew each other sooner. When I was mortal. I dodged the subject of me being an assassin for the Hunter's Society. But it'll come out eventually. And when it does, people won't want me interfering at all.

Which means I need to leave as soon as possible.

But I need to be better at Fae magic first if I have any hope of helping the pixies. And being better at death magic and more proficient with my bo staff won't be awful either. Who knows what kind of things I'll have to do to get their help.

Hopefully, if I can help them, they'll be more inclined to help me.

Getting through the barrier to the remote village is easy this time around, since I have already written my data into the storage rune, so I just press my palm against the detection rune, and bingo, I'm in. Just like my library door.

Right on time, too.

Phew.

Fae children play in small groups, laughter flitting through the air like hummingbirds while they run around and chase goddess knows what. They are all kinds of Fae, from green-skinned summer folk to blue-skinned winter folk, to pale-skinned fall and spring folk. No one argues, there is no tension. It's more peace than I can ever hope to create.

"Magic." A familiar grumbling female voice grates my ears. "You're here. Finally." Her arms crossed over chest and a frown on her otherwise beautiful face, she stalks over to me. "I've been waiting."

"You said two." I point to my watch. "It's two. Exactly." I cross my arms over my chest and smirk. "I'm on time."

"Humph." She turns and stalks off.

This time, I don't hesitate to follow.

She leads me not to her cottage, but to a small stream peddling through the center of the village. A few small children play along its banks here and there, but it's mostly raw and untouched.

"This is our main water supply." She gestures to a well a few meters away. "We collect the water from the underground stream that runs parallel to this one. It's our only source of clean water."

Seems a little risky, if you ask me.

"Today, I'm going to contaminate that supply with something unknown to you, and then you'll need to wash the stream clean so we may drink again."

Again, she's floored me. "You're going to risk your own water supply?"

She nods. "Of course." She taps me on the back. "You need proper motivation." She stares at me in confusion. "Can you do Fae magic in your female form?"

Oh, right. I change into my male form, still in the formal clothes I wore to the embassy, and smirk. "No, just this one."

"Strange." She wrinkles her nose in confusion, her pale green marred by the action. "So long as you can learn Fae magic, I guess."

My heart shrinks inside my chest as it hammers against its cage. My fingers clench into fists. I hate how much emotion lays beneath the anger, how much I want to break. Does she really find me that strange?

She turns around and places something green, slimy, and covered in mud into the stream, and I watch it pollute the stream as it creeps toward the well.

The entire water turns a dark green color, and as I run my fingers through it, I realize the texture has changed too. It no longer runs through my palms like water, but sticks to them like slime. What did she put in here?

Is it some kind of poisonous plant?

Or is there some spellwork at play?

Did she create it just for this purpose?

Ugh.

As usual, I know nothing.

Why am I always fighting blind?

Three deep breaths later, and I finally sit on the stream's bank to analyze any and all spellwork. If I want to know what's going on, I need to know the components in play and how they interact, otherwise I'll have no hope of getting home before nightfall.

First things first, this stream is spelled to be clean, which makes sense, but the water below is not. I wonder why until the answer hits me. There's no need for it to be. It's already clean. It must be, otherwise they wouldn't all still be alive and healthy. So why is this top one unclean to begin with? Maybe it's something in the topsoil? Or the plants?

Or maybe something in the above stream gets oxidized, and that causes a reaction . . . No, there's air below ground, too. So that doesn't make sense.

The clean rune is affecting some living component in the stream, so it's probably some kind of bacteria or fungi. A damn antifungal or antibacterial product would be more efficient, but whatever floats their boat, I guess. Besides, I get the feeling they don't use outside help much. Or at all.

But I don't really know the difference between antifungal and antibacterial spells, and I would probably need to google it to find out, which I don't have access to here—damn lack of a datachip—so it can't be that.

Can it?

All these questions are making my head spin.

I keep scanning the spellwork at play and pick up something interesting in the stream. A kind of plant with a rune attached. Could this be what she contaminated the stream with?

I hope so.

Analyzing further, it looks to a be a plant. Maybe some kind of weed. Damn, I need to get better with my botany if I have a hope of proceeding in these lessons.

Sure, I'll just add that to my list of shit to do. No problem.

The rune, on the other hand, is what's making the plant spread quickly and reproduce at such a rapid rate. Otherwise it would have taken a few weeks for the whole stream to be contaminated. But getting rid of that won't help me now.

I need to know how to get rid of the plant from the stream. I need to know what she meant by washing it clean. I know a couple of water spells if I want to get rid of all the water here and replace it with fresh stuff. Could that be the answer? Would be draining, though. There has to be an easier answer.

If I knew what the plant is, I might be able to know something about contradicting it— maybe a rune that cancels its effect or kills it entirely. Wait. There probably is a rune that kills fungi. An antifungal rune? Maybe a cleanliness rune? That's what's running through the stream already, though. If that works, then it would already be working.

So why isn't that rune doing something? If it's not cleaning the fungi or bacteria out of the stream, then what the fuck is it even doing in the first place?

I analyze that rune again, but this time, I look at what properties it looks for in the first place. What kind of things does it recognize as 'unclean?' This rune is only for non-living things, like acids, urine, and minerals the Fae don't want to be consuming. It does nothing for the living biomass around the stream. They mustn't be harmful. No point in wasting your energy topping up a rune every few weeks that doesn't even get triggered.

Okay, so do I know a rune that could work against living contaminants? No. Great. Helpful. Oh, maybe I could adjust the rune already in the water to include biological contaminants. That seems relatively quick.

Runes are lines, swirls, and patterns that form various magical bonds with the Fae's magic. Each line and swirl and pattern does something different until the whole creates the desired effect.

This rune looks like two swirls that meet each other in the middle. But how do I make that incorporate biological matter? Hmm. I really want a rune book right about now. "How am I supposed to know this off the top of my head?"

"Runes are intuitive to Fae," my trainer says. "That's how we discover new ones every few years. Reach inside yourself and see."

Reach inside myself . . .

She realizes how much 'myself' there is, right?

She realizes how chaotic I am, right?

Blowing out a frustrated breath, I concentrate on the Fae part of me, ignore the Shifter stuff, and try to focus on my internal reservoir of magic I get from the leyline below the house. It's topped full, like always. But how do I get it to search for a rune pattern?

Can I make the magic reach out and touch the rune already there?

Fae magic is a bit weird; it's the only time a supernatural deals with raw magical energy. Even Witches only deal with the plasma particles given off by the leylines. But because Fae can tap into the leylines directly, they have a direct link to magic. Or energy, as some scientists prefer to use.

So maybe that means I can direct the store inside of me toward the rune. Runes are made of this same energy, after all. I channel some of my stored plasma—or energy—toward the stream, where the rune is tethered. It wraps around the rune, analyzes it, and brings up an exact copy.

Hmm. "So that's what happens when you channel plasma around a rune."

My Fae trainer huffs in amusement from wherever she sits glaring at me. I closed my eyes a while ago so I can concentrate.

But how do I add to the rune to biological matter? She said it's intuitive. But do I add my thoughts and feelings to the plasma? Can I show my plasma the problem?

Don't be stupid, Magic, it's not alive.

I have to add the intent myself.

I wonder if it works like Witch charm magic? Intent is important there, too. And they do use the same source; albeit in different ways.

Using my own intentions, I guide more energy to the rune, but this time, I mentally will it to shape into a new rune that also cleans harmful biological contaminants.

Please work, please work, please work.

I really want to get back and make some plans for mine and Connie's date. A real date this time. Not just a friends thing.

The rune copies itself, like before, but this time it adds new swirls to the pattern, so it's four joining, rather than two. Could this be it?

Oh my goddess, this is it, isn't it?

Yes, yes, yes.

I finally let go of the intent when the rune finishes forming and place it into the stream, where it quickly turns the water from green to transparent again. And, just for good measure, I shift into my female form and touch the water, hoping to get some kind of sign that it's okay.

C'mon, c'mon, c'mon . . . Make me look cool in front of my trainer. Pleeeease.

The water ripples from my fingers all the way down the stream, and I can sense it rippling through the underground stream, too. Everything is clean.

Yes. Fae magic and Witch water magic.

Woo!

Nothing can break me now.

21

She cracked a smile. An actual smile! I got my Fae trainer to smile at me and say congratulations.

I sprint home in a flit of Vampire speed and race through the front door with a beaming smile on my face. "I did it!"

Connie rushes down the stairs to meet me at the same time Dea fazes to me from the kitchen. "Achieved what, hon?"

"Not only did I figure out her puzzle in record time, I used my Witch's water magic to send a ripple down a stream." Now I say it out loud, it sounds dumb.

I must have looked to the floor or something, because Dea grabs my chin and forces me to look at him in those beautiful galaxy eyes. "That is amazing, Angel. You are developing at a phenomenal rate."

"Yeah." Connie wraps her arms around my waist from behind. "It took us hundreds of years to develop as fast as you've managed in a few months."

"You're right." I pridefully turn around to face her and whisper, "Tonight's date is on me." Placing a gentle kiss to her cheek while not letting Dea run away, I whisper, "Thank you," to them both.

Connie smiles while Dea nuzzles my neck and says, "You are most welcome." He smoothes circles across my hips. "If I am not mistaken, you have a date to plan." He pulls away, and this time, I let him. "Have fun."

He sounds a little depressed, so I turn back around to face him with a question on my face.

"It is nothing important. It is just that Nine is busy and you are planning your date tonight." He waves away my concern. "It is okay. Maybe Arrie would be up for sparring and a movie marathon." He smiles at me.

"While you're spending time with Arrie, could you try to casually drop that I still like him," I mumble. "You know, if you don't mind."

Dea traces a thumb down my cheek and rests it on my lips. "Of course."

"Now c'mon," Connie nearly screams. "I wanna know what my date is!"

Yeah, me too. "Let's plan it together?"

She grabs my hand and yanks me upstairs. "You bet!"

EARLY THE FOLLOWING MORNING, WE TAKE A *SHERUTA*-EARTH TELEPORTING CRYSTAL STRAIGHT to the Bahamas. Bikini-clad, sun-lotioned skin free to breathe and smiles all around, because the date we planned together is an all-star luxurious cruise around the islands on a personal yacht. Staff, cocktails, an all-you-can-eat buffet, plenty of bedrooms to try out, water slides, movie theater, and star gazing all await us the moment we board.

I don't think I ever did anything like this as a mortal, and I'm excited to know how the other half live. Connie, of course, has done similar things, but she's never hired a private yacht for two. So bonus points to me.

And she's just as excited.

"C'mon, c'mon, c'mon . . ." She drags me up the yacht, and soon we're running around the deck, oohing and aahing over everything, from the view of the captain's cabin to the water slide curling around the side and ending up near the ocean.

"The slide descends whenever you wish, Horsemen." A tall, overly thin man with pinned-back black hair greets us. "And it is an honor to have you on board with us."

"Yes," a smaller gentleman with blonde hair and a wide grin says, "welcome. It's so exciting to have such important people join us."

The first man bows lightly and grimaces in the blonde's direction. "This is Lucy, you'll have to forgive her. She's a little excited about meeting you."

She . . .? I could have sworn . . . Oops.

I pretend like I didn't just assume someone's gender (me of all people) and smile. "It's lovely to meet you, Lucy." I bow to her.

And she giggles in that adorable way of hers. She's like a fluffy bunny. All sprinkles and rainbows. It's cute. She leans over and whispers, "Oh my god, Magic bowed to me," in the other man's ear.

I cough. "I'm half-Vampire in this form."

Lucy goes pale for a moment and then flushes a deep red. "I'm so sorry. Ohmygod. I didn't mean to offend you or anything. It's just so cool. You're like my hero. You can change forms, use both, be whoever you want at any moment of time. And I just wanted to—"

"Lucy," the other man groans, "please control yourself."

"Right." Lucy straightens and shakes her head. "Professional."

She really thinks I can be whoever I want? Like, whenever? I'm her . . . hero?

My face must have betrayed my shock, because Lucy whispers, "Not everyone hates you. Some of us think that standing up to those nasty Vampires was awesome!" Her voice ends in a squeak, but she straightens back up again and looks serious once more, side-eyeing Mr Serious next to her.

I see the headlines and I see the opinion polls, but I never really get to hear humans' points of view. Ever. It's nice to see they're not all blindly following the SC's propaganda.

"Would you like to be shown to your room for the evening?"

Connie shakes her head and grabs my hand, taking a longer-than-average perusal of my black bikini top that shows off my tattoo in all its skulled glory. Her eyes meet mine in a look I know. She wants some alone time in our room.

And this time we won't be interrupted.

"Yeah," she whispers, "definitely."

The black-haired man from before shows us to a luxury cabin with a bed that overlooks the sea in a window wall I'm jealous of. Like, I know I have a window wall of my own. But this one is curved, has an ocean view, and I want it. Can one steal a window?

"Like it, then?" Connie unpacks some of the clothes she brought for later, including the dress she plans on wearing to dinner tonight.

"It's beautiful."

I help her unpack, and soon we're hanging our evening dresses up together in the closet. They sit side-by-side, black against green. Like a couple. Like us.

Connie catches me staring and smiling. "They look good together, huh?" She wraps her arms around me from behind and rests her chin on my head, a warm presence reminding me she's part of my home. An important part of my life.

"Yeah, we do."

"I know we're on a date, but we can still do the Friday things, too. I know we've accomplished a lot this week, and I think it would be good for you to unpack it all. Emotionally speaking."

"You're probably right." But I don't want to talk about Arrie. Do I? Alright, maybe I do. Just a little. But it's our date night. I don't want to ruin it by bringing up other-man drama.

"What are you over-thinking now?"

I huff a laugh. "Am I that much of an open book?"

"Yup." She spins me around to face her. "It's all over your face." Light fingers trace the edges of my face in graceful slides of delicate fingers, and shivers run down my body. "The way your lips part and your brow furrows in concentration. You're like an emotional plasmascreen."

"Am not," I mutter under my breath.

"Are too," she whispers, lips inches away from mine. Her breath fans across them as her hands trail down my shoulders, arms, and eventually rub circles into my waist. "But I think it's beautiful. And besides, it makes my girlfriend duties easier."

"Girlfriend duties?"

"Yeah. It's part of my job to help you stay as stress free as possible, and to help you work through your emotions. The guys are rubbish at it." She looks away in thought for a moment. "Well, I guess Nine is pretty good at it, but that doesn't count."

"Eh. He mostly stays out of my relationships with the rest of the team, unless it involves Dea."

Her eyebrows waggle, and I giggle. "Sooooo . . ." She drags us onto the bed. "Spill!"

I eye her with a raised eyebrow, feigning innocence, but she shakes her bed. "I walked in on you completely naked between two very naked Nine and Dea. Soooo . . . tell me, what kinky threesome did you guys get up to?"

"Okay, okay . . ." I take a deep breath. "It started in the pool in the villa they rented for the day, but when Nine saw the fantasy floating through my mind, he showed Dea, and then we came back home to re-enact my imagination, which is surprisingly creative, apparently."

"Oh, do tell me." She grabs my hand and smiles. "C'mon, we might be a thing, but I'm still your best friend, right?"

The hint of uncertainty stabs me right in the feels, and I give in. Instantly. Damn this woman.

"Dea tied me and Nine up to the hooks on his bed, and then ordered us around, before they both . . . you know, had sex with me at the same time."

"Like, DP-ing in the same hole or one in the pussy and one in the ass?"

"You can fit two dicks inside your vagina?"

"Anyone can. It just takes patience, lots of lube, and lots of foreplay."

"Oh." I feel all weird and innocent. Which is odd considering I took two dicks not a few days ago. "That sounds . . . painful."

"Not if you do it right." She waves a hand in the air, dismissing our tangent. "So, two holes, then?"

I nod. "It was . . . amazing."

"And Dea ordered you both around?"

"Yeah, he ordered Nine to fuck me and then got impatient."

She flops onto the bed. "Wow."

Is that something she wants?

My concern must have flashed across my face, because she grabs my hand and whispers, "I'm just jealous I wasn't there to join in on the Magical fuckfest." She scrunches her nose in distaste. "I'm not sure I want something like that anymore."

"Really?"

She sighs. "I know it's hard to explain, but ever since you, everything's changed. I don't really even look at men anymore. It's just women." She shrugs. "Guess this means my sexuality's changing, huh?" She looks me in the eyes and smiles. "Don't get me wrong, I still want a threesome with you and Arrie one day. We're all so strong . . . It'll be great. And I still like men. But right now, the only person I want is you. Maybe that'll change some day, maybe I'll want to share the guys alongside you, but for now, all I desire is your legs wrapped around my face as you bury your head in that pillow over there."

A furious blush creeps up my face at her words, but I'm not embarrassed. Not with Connie. All her words do is send a thrill down my spine and a searing heat between my thighs.

She leaps from her spot on the bed and straddles my waist, pinning my hands to the soft fabric and sweeping a tongue across my closed lips. "But I'm enjoying this slow thing we're doing."

There's a look in her eyes I don't quite recognize on her, but it's all too familiar from the mirror. It's shyness. Going slow makes her shy.

I reach up and grip her bottom lip between my teeth, yanking her back to the bed with me. "I don't want slow." My hips grind into her on instinct as I take her mouth and make her mine.

Her hands wander up my body, grab the underneath of my bikini top, and move it aside. She breaks away from my kiss to travel down and then takes one of my nipples into her mouth.

Pleasure hisses through me, and I need something to grab onto, to ground me. So I slide my hands around her hips and yank them flush against mine.

Just as I'm about to pull her into another kiss, she rolls my other nipple between her fingers, and my body sparkles and aches all at the same time, like a firework about to explode.

"Connie . . ."

Our hips are a grinding dream as friction sears through me, and I know I'm close. Embarrassingly close. Our first time can't go out with me coming from just her mouth on my nipple.

But fuck, her tongue keeps doing that swirling thing in between sucking, and I can't think straight. Everything's hazy. My vision is blurring. And words aren't forming.

My back arches into her, and with a wicked smile and glee in her bright green eyes, she bites down on my nipple and pinches the other harder.

"Fuck, yes!" Tension soars through me in delicious waves and I scream her name and crash around her. "Shit."

I shoot up with a look of panic on my face. "Shit, I'm sorry. I didn't mean to finish so quickly."

Connie giggles for a moment before grabbing my face between both hands and forcing me to look her in the eyes. "There's a reason vaginas are better than penises, hon. We can go more than once." She looks me up and down. "And even if you can't, you have two forms. Might as well reap the benefits." She winks before lying beside me in a flustered heap. "Fuck, that was hot."

"So hot."

Shit. I can't just leave her unsatisfied, can I? That would be selfish. Besides, just imagining her screaming my name like that has a new fire lighting me up. I want to make her come on my tongue, I want to taste her, and I want to make her as chilled as me.

I flip her onto her back on the mattress and smile. "Your turn."

She laughs and pulls me into a sweet and gentle kiss. "We have all the time in the world for that, I promise."

"But—"

"I didn't do that just to make you return the favor. I did that because I wanted to, and because I wanted to make sure you're as satisfied as possible before the rest of our date."

"But—"

"No buts." She smiles and places a warm hand on my cheek. "Besides, I have plans for later that I want to be as horny as possible for."

"Plans, huh?"

"Oh, yeah. Big plans." She looks to my crotch and back to my face. "Huge ones."

She's talking about my cock, isn't she? Well, other me's cock. Wait. He's still me. Right? So, yeah, my cock. I think.

22

Nothing tastes better than a mimosa under the sun with a gorgeous as fuck woman lying between your legs, head rested on your stomach, as the world drifts away.

"I think this is the most relaxed I've ever been since waking up in the house."

"Yeah?"

"Mmmhhmmm . . ." The sun beats down in harsh waves of blissful warmth that have sweat beading on my forehead and a flush creeping across my chest. "I don't have to do anything right now."

Connie lifts her head and looks at me with a smirk. "Well, nothing except me."

"You are incorrigible." I laugh, shaking my head at her antics. "I fucking love it."

"I'm not being too much or anything?" she asks, her voice muffled by the fact she buried her head back into my stomach. "You're sure?"

I lift her head to meet her eyes with mine. "You're perfect just the way you are, Conquest. Trust me." From her bright green eyes to the sexy smirk playing across her face, she's all mine. And there's no way in hell I'm ever letting her think otherwise. Using my Vampire strength, I rip her across my body and force her legs to straddle my waist before slamming my lips against her. "Mine."

Her body's pliant in my arms as she lets me lift her and wrap her legs around my waist. I flit us to the nearest wall, causing her to screech a little bit—but one look at her excited face tells me she's loving every second—and slam her into the window.

The mewling whimper that escapes her lips has the dull throb between my thighs roaring like a bonfire in July, an inferno of need I *have* to quench lest I go down with the flames.

Her skin smells so sweet, and I nuzzle her neck as I trail licks, nips, and kisses along her collarbone and down her cleavage. "Mmmm . . . you're so beautiful."

Her legs squeeze around my waist as her hips shift against me, trying to quench her own thirst. I snap my gaze to hers, but she squeaks and throws me off, landing in a heap on the wooden deck. Hands shaking. Breaths coming quicker than they did a few moments ago.

"Connie?" What happened? Did I scare her somehow? I snap my attention to my reflection in the window and gasp. Shit. My fangs descended without me realizing, and my eyes burn a bright red. "I'm so sorry." I quickly gain my composure with a couple of breaths and bend down to grab her hand.

She flinches and pulls away.

We were doing so well with this, but her time in those caves probably undid all of that. Crap.

"I can give you some space, if you'd like?"

"I just . . . umm . . ."

I whistle and hope someone is nearby to help.

And low and behold, Lucy rushes to our side. "Is there something I can help you with?" She notices Connie on the floor and squeaks. "Conquest!" Lucy reaches down and helps her up off the floor.

"Can you take her back to our room for me, please? I'll be there shortly."

"Of course, Magic." Lucy wraps Connie in her arms and lifts her with ease. "C'mon, Conquest. Let's lay you down for a while, hmm?"

When they are out of sight, I let the flimsy control I have on my anger slip, and the rage flies through me. "Fuck!"

The boat rocks under gentle waves as I bend the ocean to my angered will.

She was doing so well, and now we're back to square one. And it's all his fault! I killed him far too quickly. "Connie," I whimper, the anger fading out of me as I remember how defeated she looked on her knees in front of me. Like the world had broken inside of her.

She needs me.

I race to our room, where she lies under the covers shaking and crying. Alone. Shit. I shouldn't have left her like this.

Lucy comes out of the bathroom with a glass of water and an extra blanket. "She really doesn't seem okay."

"She's not." My voice is a near growl, and the boat rocks some more. "Sorry." I take a calming breath, letting a meager attempt at calm flow through me.

At least the boat stops rocking. But my hands stay clenched into fists.

I take another deep breath and let all thoughts of that monster exit my brain as I shift into my male form. My shoes shrug off and land in a pile beside the bed before I crawl under the duvet behind Connie.

"Hey, Connie, it's just me."

I'm hoping my deeper voice might keep her calm. Let her know I can't Vamp out in this form.

I curl myself around her and wrap a firm arm around her waist, settling her body against my chest and burying my head in her neck. "You don't have to be okay for me. You can just breathe if that's all you can manage."

Her sobs wreck me. "I . . . can't get his face out of my head." Her voice is barely legible, her whispers gutting everything inside of me.

My anger is more manageable in this form, though. "I know," I whisper. Keeping my voice low. Nonthreatening. "But he's dead, Connie. I killed him myself."

"I know." Her breaths calm with that fact. And after what feels like hours, her sobs stop heaving and level out to an even stream of tears instead. "But my fear didn't just die with him. I wish . . . it did."

Lucy's disappeared by now, but she left a glass of water on the side and a warm blanket at the end of the bed. Grabbing both, I sit Connie up and make her rehydrate.

"I'm sorry," she says with a sigh. "This was supposed to be a date. A happy memory." Tear tracks run down her cheeks steadily, like the sadness is leaking from her, even as her body calms. "I just need a moment, and then—"

I grab her hands and shake my head. "Don't do that. Please." My voice breaks as she looks at me with a smile. How can she be smiling right now? "I know what it's like to feel broken, Connie. And it's not going to go away just because you wish it so. So if you need to be broken today, then I'll sit with your pieces with you."

Sobs overtake her for another moment before she falls into my arms and cries her pain into my chest. And that's where we lie for the rest of the afternoon, letting Connie have a safe space away from her duties and the team and the house and the war so she can just feel.

23

I offer to call room service for dinner, but Connie says no and that we should still make our reservation.

"Are you sure?" I grab her by the shoulders. "We can stay here, chat some more." We've been chatting about how she feels, letting her vent some of that fear and frustration and guilt. "We can stay here, if that's what you need."

Her fingers find my lips and shush me into silence. "That's a nice thought, but I'm doing better now. And I want this evening, too."

"Okay." I try to smile, but I'm worried about her. What if she breaks? What if she's frightened of me again? What if—?

"Whatever you're thinking," Connie calls from the bathroom, "stop."

"How the fuck could you tell from in there?"

"You haven't moved yet, so I figured you must be doing that spiraling thing."

"Ugh. I've been trying to stop, but it's so hard." I wipe a hand down my face as I shift into my female form. "Dea says I should focus on being happy and scared in equal measure. So I've been trying to make sure the happiness counts too."

"He's right." She exits the bathroom with a face full of gentle makeup. "And I think that's an excellent strategy."

I throw some dark makeup over my eyes, conceal some of my blemishes, throw on the dress hanging on the closet door, and look over myself in the mirror.

Not bad.

The dress hugs my curves until it reaches my knees, then it fans out in a netted black tail that drapes behind me as I walk. And the plunging neckline looks outstanding, showing off both my tattoo and boobs.

Once my hair is pinned in a half-up, half-down kind of attempt, I call it a day and walk out to meet Connie's smirk.

"You look . . . like a fucking meal in that dress." She swipes a tongue over those luscious lips, and I have the sudden urge the smudge that red lipstick.

Her dress trails to the floor in a sheath design but still hugs her curves—albeit in a gentler way than mine—and the entire ensemble makes her looks innocent and gentle. Which, of course, is ridiculous. She could snap this ship in half without breaking a sweat and then still have enough energy to battle an armada single-handed.

"You look radiant, Connie. Truly."

Something in my eyes must have flicked a switch in her brain, because she runs over to me and hugs me. "Thank you." She takes a deep, shaky breath and lifts her head off mine to look at me once more. "I needed that."

She's not talking about the compliment, is she?

"Anytime, babe." I take her arm and face us toward the door. "Shall we?"

"Definitely."

The night air blesses us with its breeze as we walk down the deck, arm-in-arm, with smiles on our faces. We asked for the staff to arrange a romantic, cozy dinner for the two of us, and to go all out on the food because, well, I'm a giant food whore. So we have no idea what everything's going to look like once we get inside.

Every moment spent with Connie doesn't feel like a date. It just feels like I'm in love with my best friend, who I get to do romantic, fun, sexy, and silly things with. And this feels just like that. No nerves. No worries. Just a calm sense of home that she always brings to my heart every time she's near.

The grand doors we've been told hold our surprise are just up ahead, and as we near, two ushers dressed to the nines in suits open the doors, and we proceed to be blown away by the setting that lay before us. White and gold sashes hang from an open-air dining room, the ceiling having been opened, letting the night in. A small table sits in the center of a decked awning, flowers trailing up the tresses, and comfy seats decorating one side.

"This is . . ."

"Amazing," Connie finishes for me. "Awe-inspiring. One of the most amazing things I've ever seen."

"Think we can get a photo of something to show the guys. I want Dea and Nine to know they'll always lose to you."

She giggles and grabs my hand. "I already asked the organizers for photographs, though they were a bit taken aback that I wanted them in physical form."

"You did?"

"Yeah, they've been photographing the entire day."

"Thank you." I want to remember this. In a thousand years' time, when I won't remember how I feel in this moment, I want to be reminded. "That was a good shout."

We sit in the love seat that sits to one side of the table, and the waiter brings out water, our choice of cocktails, and some mozzarella, sundried tomatoes, and olive mix as an entrée.

And obviously, I love everything they bring out, even the things I've never eaten before; but the best part of the dinner date is that Connie gets to sit right next to me, we get to feed each other, hold hands, wrap our arms around each other, and eat all at the same time.

Clearly, whoever created this dinner knows me or they got seriously lucky. Food and cuddles are the best. No competition.

Connie's left arm is wrapped around my right as she leans against me and breathes in deeply after helping me devour the last of a massive slice of caramel apple pie that actually made me salivate just at the sight and smell of it. That dessert could have given Arrie a run for his money.

In fact, if I didn't know for a fact that Arrie would never cook for me and Connie, I'd swear this was his talent on these plates.

"Wanna take a walk?" Connie whispers in my ear. "Digest all this awesome?"

"Definitely."

We say thank you to the servers and the chefs, and then leave, both of us struggling in these dresses with all that food. But with my hand resting peacefully in hers, nothing else really matters.

"Can I ask you a question?" I say just as we reach the top deck.

"Sure. It is Friday." She smiles at me, the starlight flashing across her eyes.

"Is there something about being with the guys that makes you uncomfortable?" She snaps her gaze away from me. "It's just, a few times now, I've noticed that you typically get a little shy of uncomfortable when interacting with me around all of them at once."

"I . . ." She turns away from me. "I'm scared." Her voice is barely a whisper. "I'm scared that you'll prefer to be with them on your own. That you'll decide I'm not good enough." She giggles, but I don't think it's intended to be a funny laugh. "It's not like I have a penis."

Now it's my turn to laugh. "You think I care what body parts you have?" I spin her around to face me. "Connie, you got me off with nothing more than nipple play and a bit of grinding earlier. I don't care that you don't have a dick." In fact, I quite like that about her. "But if you'd rather it be just us when it's us, for a while, then we can."

"But I know you want us to be a big family. Like, all together and stuff. And I want to give you what you want, but I look at them and I just feel so inferior."

"I don't know if you've noticed, but I'm immortal. We have all the time in the world to be together in whatever ways we choose. But right now, I want everyone to just be comfortable and happy."

She rests her head on top of mine and sighs. "I don't know what any of us did in our long lives to deserve someone like you, but I thank God every day that you exist."

"So, do you have any limits or hard nos when it's all of us together? Not just in a sexual way, either."

She grabs my hand, and we walk along the boardwalk together, gazing up into the night. "I think I'll be fine eventually. Before the caves, I wanted nothing more than to watch you with the guys and join in. For us to all be together. But I think Antonio brought all that old fear and unconfidence back."

I've noticed. Whenever she's not looking or paying attention or doing something, she's gazing off into space and looking a little hurt. She's still a bit thin. And even though her wounds have healed, it's like she still wears those scars.

"We can work on bringing you back to your normal self, or moving forwards in whatever direction you want, together."

We stroll back to our room together, my arm slung around her waist, kinda afraid she might break if I let her go. But the moment we're back behind that door, I realize her silence wasn't concern or sadness; she was planning for *this* moment.

I watch her eyes go from pleasant to needy in a split second, like she had it under a tight leash until now. Her blonde hair spills around her shoulders as she smiles at me in that flirty way of hers that makes her lips part and her breaths heave and my knees weak.

"Magic . . ." She pins me to the door with gentle hands that trace tingles down my arms. "I want you to fuck me with everything you have. I want you to make me fall apart beneath you. In either form."

I nod, not able to form words in the face of the beauty asking for my virginity. Just the thought of sliding my cock into her wet heat has me heaving oxygen into my lungs as though it's vital I take every next breath to douse the fire Connie ignited.

For once, I'm not afraid. I wouldn't pick anyone else to help me explore that side of myself with.

Connie grabs my arms and pulls me away from the door to face my back to her, where she sweeps the zipper down my back and helps me step out of my dress. Her breath hitches. "I forgot you aren't wearing a bra or pants in that dress," she says on a groan. "Fuck." She rakes needy fingers over my hips and traces butterfly fingertips over my clit and between my thighs on a breathy inhale.

"Do I get to make you come this evening, too? Or are you going to deny me?" I really need to repay the favor. It's gnawing at me that it was one-sided.

She giggles while walking around to face me. "I promise you'll get to watch me come with your dick buried deep inside me." She watches my face with caution, gauging my reaction with an expectant grin. "Please?" Her eyes beg mine, creases forming across her brow as she darts a tongue out to lick her lips. "You'll do that for me, right?"

I nod, all but a slave to her words.

"Perfect." She turns her back to me and asks, "Unzip me?"

My hands slide gently down her back, grazing her soft skin like petals falling to the ground beneath their rose god, and she steps out of the dress with delicate ease before turning to face me.

I've seen her naked before, but only in passing. This time, she's inviting me to stare. Inviting me to roam my eyes over her breasts, her hardened nipples, her flushed chest and neck, and the panty line edging down her hips as she slips them off. Now she's standing before me in nothing but her heels and jewelry.

I want to say something. To breathe her in and never let her go. But I'm rooted to the spot. Gravity has taken me captive, and I'm all but a slave to its nuances as I sway on the spot and reach a hand toward her creamy skin.

One painstakingly slow heel at a time, she inches forward, her lips getting closer to mine, her body mere touches from falling into my grasp.

"Connie, I . . ."

"Yes?" Her voice is like honey, syrup glazing my mind, making words difficult to form. "Something the matter?"

"Come . . . here."

Her body flushes hot against mine, her breasts pushing against my own as our lips meet in an unhurried frenzy that lights the matches to the heat pooling at my thighs.

And I groan, unaware of how my needy hands rake down her sides as our tongues dance.

"You don't . . . need to be . . . gentle . . . with me," Connie whispers between kisses, fitting the words in with every breath she can. "I'm more . . . than willing to . . . be yours . . . tonight."

If that's what she wants, then I'm happy to oblige. Just need to keep my fangs retracted and my eyes purple.

I grip each thigh in strong handholds and lift her up, wrapping each leg around my waist, before I lave strong strokes of my tongue against her nipples, making her cry out.

She grinds against me, out of her control, and I bite down, sending a wave of screaming pleasure through her body that has her rocking against me in a frenzy. "Magic, I . . . Please fuck me."

I chuckle, thrilled by her need and more than a little heated by her demands. I throw her onto the bed and crawl between her legs, settling between her thighs like I'm the cat who got the cream. High on her lust. "This what you want?" I ask, throwing my tongue at her heat and lapping a long line up to her clit.

"Yes!" Her fingers grip the duvet in a white-knuckled grip. And she cries out again as I trail my tongue back down and thrust myself inside.

She tastes like honeyed heaven. I grip her hips and lift her up to my face, providing a better angle to reach for that sweet spot that'll be sure to make her—

"Ah, there. Right there."

A tight fist yanks my hair and pushes my head down closer to her. And just as I leave her heat to trail kisses and nips and licks up to her clit, she uses her other hand to play with her breasts and pinch at her nipples in turn.

I seal my lips around her clit and flick my tongue against her with suction.

"Fuck. Harder!"

Following her command, I suck harder and lash my tongue harsher, no longer being careful. I'm not stopping until I taste her release. With one hand still holding her up off the bed, I reach the other to her tit and roll her nipple between my fingers in demanding strokes while she handles the other.

Her cries grow as she thrashes in my grip, grinding her heat against my lips as her sex drips down my chin and she screams. "Magic, yes, I'm gonna . . ." Connie bursts into my mouth with a cry as she comes.

I ride her through, not letting up the harsh strokes of my tongue as she moans and writhes in my grip, until her cries become mewls and whimpers. Then I set her back on the bed and crawl up between her legs to plant a kiss to her cheek.

Her chest heaves in ragged breaths as she calms and returns to earth, but when I lay my head on her chest, she yanks me back up and slams her mouth against mine, licking her sweetness off my tongue and my lips.

"That was . . . so good," she mumbles.

"So fucking good," I whisper. Every part of me aches, and I itch to reach my hands between my thighs and bury them there. To switch forms and bury my cock into her dripping heat. To hear her cries of pleasure in my ear as I ram her into headboard. "So . . . amazing."

"Struggling?" Connie asks, a hint of playfulness in her voice. "Want me to help?" She reaches down and sinks two fingers into me, thrusting up in slow and gentle strokes that do nothing but fan the flames. "Or is there something else you want?"

I want her lips wrapped around my clit, my cock, setting me on fire. I want to come on her face, on her fingers, inside of her, and watch her come alive beneath me again. "I . . . yes. Make me come. Please."

The urgent pleading in my voice has her eyes glowing brighter as they meet mine in a heated gaze that tells me she'll do anything I ask right now.

Anything at all.

Connie grabs my hands and flips us, pinning me to the bed and rolling her hips into mine. Friction. Glorious friction burns through me. "I'm happy to try anything with you," she says, seriousness entering her tone. "Seriously. No need to ask permission or anything."

"Okay." Relief flows through me. I can shift at any moment, and I don't have to check with her first. She's made her want for my cock clear either way. "Thank you."

She smirks and trails kisses down my neck, across my collarbone, and laves long licks against my nipples, sending thrills down my spine and causing my back to arch.

But she's soon going lower, slow enough to kill me with anticipation and have my hips rolling on their own, seeking her mouth. Her tongue. Her lips. But when she gets to my thighs, she ignores me and keeps going. All the way until she reaches my knees and I'm groaning with impatience.

"So impatient," she giggles.

"I watched you scream my name as you rode my mouth." She nips at my groin, and I gasped. "So yeah, I'm a little past needy."

She breathes a deep breath, her tongue lapping against my skin, until she's stroking a fiery wave of pleasure from my clit to my heat, and I'm moaning her name.

"Connie, yes . . . Please." I don't even know what I'm begging for at this point.

Her eyes meet mine from between my thighs, capturing my gaze in a trap I can't look away from. She buries her tongue between my lips and taps the tip of her tongue against my clit in a rapid beat that sends tingling pulses through my body. Before she seals her lips around me and sucks hard enough to have my hips arching off the bed and my cries shouting into the air.

My mind jumps from the here and now to the fantasy of those lips around my cock, sucking me deep down her throat, and I groan as I roll against her mouth.

Magic ripples across my skin as a familiar feeling tugs me into another form. My male form.

"Shit," I cry, "I'm sorry—" I snap my gaze to Connie, who's now got her lips wrapped around the tip of my dick with a smile on her face and her brows raised in question.

Challenging me.

She takes a breath through her nose and sinks lower, burying my cock in her hot mouth as her heat surrounds me.

"Shiiiit." I groan and thrust, inching my cock deeper, wishing she'd suck like she did earlier. "Harder."

She obediently grips my dick like a vice as she buries her nose in my groin and takes me down her throat.

Fuck, that's tight.

And then she hums.

Everything around my cock vibrates, and she pulls away slightly, hands gripping my hips and pushing me back into her mouth.

I don't need any further instruction. I throw my dick down her throat in sweet thrusts while she keeps humming and sucking. "Yes, like that." Stars sweep across my vision, and I'm just about to speed up and chase my pleasure when she pulls out.

"I want to ride it," she says in a haze as she glares at my dick standing to attention. "Please?" Her lip twists between her teeth as she bites down and looks at me under those lashes.

"Yes, please. I just need to . . . come." Need laces every word, and I want nothing more than to fuck her senseless.

She climbs up my body and settles her thighs on either side of my hips as she grabs me in her hand with firm strokes while she lines us up and sinks down.

I hiss, groaning and moaning loudly as she buries me to the hilt in her tight wetness. "Oh god, that's so . . . good."

Her hips wrestle in small circles as she throws her head back and enjoys me. She pulls her hips up and throws herself back down, causing her breasts to bounce and my hands to grip them in vices.

"Play with them," she begs, her hips continuing to bounce on my dick as she squeezes me.

Bolts of need shoot across my balls like lightning, and I pinch her nipples. Gently at first, but as her moans get louder and her cries more insistent, my fingers pinch harder and twist them.

"Fuck, yes." Her face is flushed as sweat drips down her forehead. "More . . ."

I move one hand to her pussy and pinch her clit, moving my fingers in small circles as she flutters around my dick.

She's close.

She's clenching around me tighter, making her harder than granite and my balls tighten.

"Fuck," I groan. "Yes." I grab her hips and flip us over.

Connie grabs her knees and lifts them to her chest, where I pin them. "Fuck me," she begs, "hard."

I drill into her, pounding her into the mattress as she screams my name. My fingers continue driving her orgasm closer, and soon she's gripping me like a vice, seconds away from exploding.

She holds her legs in place while I drive into her harder, fast strokes that have me nearly spilling inside her. But I want to feel her coming around my cock first.

"Come," I beg her, "please come."

I don't know how much longer I can hold on, but I don't need to worry, because as I pinch her clit harder and thrust faster, she cries out.

"Oh god, yes!"

"Yes, come for me."

Her pussy tenses around me, and pleasure shoots through my balls. But I don't stop. I pound into her while she screams, mewls, and cries, tears streaming down her face.

And a white-hot bolt of pleasure shoots through me as I shout her name. The strongest orgasm of my life flowing through me while I take it out on the amazing woman beneath me.

Catching my breath, I fall on top of her as her legs lower to the bed. "That was . . ."

"Amazing," she finishes.

And we both laugh.

24

Waking up tangled up in limbs will never get old. Connie's head lies on my chest, her leg hitched up over my hip, and her lips sigh softly as I stretch awake.

"Morning," she mumbles.

"Morning." She shoots up like the sunrise and sits on top of me, grinding into my stiff cock with a smile. "Did you enjoy yesterday?"

"Uh-huh." The groan that escapes my lips sets her eyes alight, and her smile turns wicked. She goes to grab my wrists and pin them in her favorite place—above my head—but I shake my head. "I'm sorry, hon, but I have training today."

She sighs, disappointment flickering across her beautiful face. "Yeah, and I have a bunch of shit to do, too."

We both look at each other with longing, but we eventually get up and dressed and head home, thanking Lucy and the rest of the team for a wonderful time.

Just as we land in the kitchen, something or someone glues themselves to my back and wraps their arms around my neck. *Sweetieeeee!*

Hey, Nine.

You're back.

I chuckle. "We are indeed." I spin around and grab him into a hug, then pull him off me.

His eyes have dark circles underneath them, are bloodshot, and his hair is falling in messy strands around his face, rather than being gelled back like usual.

"Oh my goddess, are you okay?" My hands rest on his shoulders as my brow creases in worry.

"Jees," he mumbles, "is everyone going to point out how shit I look today?" He throws an irritated glare at Dea, who's sitting comfortably at the breakfast table with a warm smile on his face, which is buried in a newspaper.

I swear he's the only person in existence to still read newspapers. The thought makes me laugh again. But then I turn back to Nine, who's looking to the floor and avoiding my eyes. "I'm sorry, Nine. I didn't mean to make you feel bad. It's just that you're usually so put together. You'd be worried about Dea if he came to breakfast in some thrown-together outfit, wouldn't you?"

"Yeah, I guess." He rubs a stressed hand over his neck. "I'm just a bit stressed from the research. It's not going as easily as I would have hoped."

Connie, Dea, and I all look at him in question, urging him to go on, but he just waves us away and wanders out the backdoor into the gardens.

"He has been like that since yesterday, Angel." Dea sighs. "He is working himself too hard."

Guilt slices through me. I'm the one who gave him that task, and he's putting himself through the ringer just to complete it. "I hope he knows he can take his time."

Connie wraps an arm around my waist and sighs. "There are Vampires dying in New Orleans, hon. I don't think the pressure is coming from you this time."

"But he should not have to shoulder that pressure alone," Dea says through clenched teeth after slamming the newspaper down on the table. "I have tried convincing him to take a break, but he will not listen."

"Maybe we can help him with the research instead?"

"I do not think any of us are qualified enough for that."

Dea's probably right. But I wish we could do something. Anything.

"I could always force him to take a break." I shrug. "Tie him up and make him watch a movie."

Dea's eyes light up for a moment, and I know instantly where his thoughts went, but then he looks at me with a serious expression and a frown on those delicious lips. "I think this is going to be one of those times where he has to do things alone. We should just stay by his side in case he needs anything."

Reluctantly, I agree with him. Besides, this isn't about me. It's about him.

"Well," Connie announces, "I have some things to organize, people to boss about." She wraps her arms around my neck, sending tingles throughout my entire body when her lips slant and meet mine. "You have bo practise in half an hour, then you're meeting Aki for lunch and are doing some death magic practise."

I wince.

Death magic, already?

"I know you're hesitant, but it could really help."

Sighing my defeat—because she's right, as usual—I say, "Okay. But I want to travel out to talk to as many of the lower supes as possible soon."

Dea rests his hands on my shoulders, making me jump slightly, and says softly, "Then we should meet with the embassy tomorrow, after our meeting with the SC, and discuss tactics, who is going, et cetera."

"Sounds like a plan," Connie yells as she runs up the stairs and waves goodbye. "I had fun riding you! We should do it again sometime!"

Heat blossoms across my cheeks, and Dea looks to me in surprise. "So, you and Connie . . . ?"

"Uh-huh. Both forms. It was great."

"Wow, um . . ." His hands run through his hair. A nervous habit, I've noticed. "I did not expect you to get so comfortable with your male form so quickly, Angel."

"I wasn't uncomfortable with my male form. I was uncomfortable with the staring, the talking, and the freakish nature of my existence. And I'm still not okay with that." I take a deep breath. "But that shouldn't mean I can't be myself. Especially in an environment like home, where I feel safe enough to exist."

Dea's galaxy eyes explode in gold, brighter than I've ever seen before, as he sweeps me off my feet and kisses me deeply, his tongue demanding entrance into my mouth like an ancient doorknocker you can't ignore, and I give in.

"I am so glad you find comfortability here at home and with us. It is good you feel you can be yourself."

KORBY JABS THE EDGE OF HER BO IN MY DIRECTION, BUT I SWEEP MY BO UPWARD AND KNOCK IT off course, so it jabs the air above my head. Making her smile.

"Nice!" She returns to her original stance a few feet away with an exhausted smile on her face. "Again."

Every muscle in my body protests. Every cell in my brain onboard to lie in a pool of sweaty exhaustion until tomorrow. But Korby's face is all determined lines and focus. And I can't let her down.

"Okay." You got this, Magic. Come on.

My feet a few inches apart, hands holding the bo staff above and below like she showed me, I root myself to the packed earth. Prepared for her attack.

But Korby is a strong Shifter, and she manages to throw me off balance nonetheless with a flurry of attacks too quick for me to process.

I lose my balance, my foot falling behind me so I don't fall on my ass.

She uses my split-second distraction to her advantage and rushes forward with a solid hit from the left, but my reflexes kick in and block.

"Good block!"

This time, I try attacking, but from the ground up in a side-stance. And yes, I manage to catch her leg and push her off balance, giving me an opening to catch her now-undefended side.

She falls to the ground in a huff and a groan, but then smiles at me—albeit with a grimace. "Well done."

I look at her with suspicion. "Did you let me have that hit?"

She shrugs. "Not really, but I have been going easy on you in general."

Oh. Well, I am just a newbie. "Care to have a go at me in my female form?"

"Vamp speed with elemental Witch magic?" She looks to the sky for a moment. "You're on. But you're paying my hospital bills."

"Deal."

In my female form, my fitness is better, my Vampire strength makes some of the moves easier, and my general senses are heightened. I don't use any Witch magic, though. I'll wait till I get to fight with Arrie or Connie before I try that out.

We spend the next hour testing my strength and abilities, Korby showing me some more advanced moves, and we make others up to work best with my skills. All in all, it's a good practise session, and the glass of cold water afterwards is some of the best liquid I've ever consumed.

"What's next on your training schedule?" Korby asks from her place on the garden floor.

"Training some Witch magic with Aki."

"Right, your twin brother?" She sounds as confused as I feel.

"Uh-huh. They separated us at birth, but we ran into each other recently. And then Nigel dropped the bomb on our shoulders."

"And since Witches are difficult to come by for training, you're using him?"

"Well, there are six different types of Witch magic, and most Witches can only specialize in one. But I can use all six."

"Ahhh, I see," she says, "so you need six different trainers in one of the hardest-to-find supernatural species. Bummer."

"Right." I don't correct her. I don't think it's wise people know about my death magic. Or the Angel-descended Witch part of my mortal DNA Fate decided to let me keep upon my immortal death. Yippee. "So Aki's helping out for now."

"You don't sound super enthused." She sits up and looks at me with curiosity. "Not really clicking with your brother?"

"He's . . . nice enough. He was grumpy for a bit, but we chatted and realized what happened was neither of our faults, so we decided to call it even and move on. But he's just so . . . normal."

Korby laughs, her eyes catching mine afterwards. "And that's a problem?" She gestures to herself. "I'm perfectly normal, and we get along just fine."

"But he's family, y'know. I'm surrounded by weirdoes every day, and it's odd to feel connected to someone so . . . mortal."

"He's gonna die one day, and then you'll be all alone." Korby looks sad for a moment before shaking her head. "I'm sorry, that was gloomy of me."

"You're right." I lie back on the grass and watch the clouds drift by. "All of my mortal friends will die one day. But I won't be alone." Thoughts of the team and home float through me. "I'll always have them." Even Arrie's grumpiness will at least be consistent.

"I can't believe you're all together. Like, together together." She looks at me with amusement, her lip curling upward. "Does that mean you all . . ." She raises her eyebrows and makes a crude gesture with her hands. "You know . . ."

I can't help it. I crack right the fuck up. I remember when it was me sat in her shoes finding their relationships strange. Not really getting it. But I do now. It's so normal and comforting. "It's not quite the orgy you're imagining."

"Oh . . ."

"Disappointed?"

"Yeah, a little."

"Well, Nine, Dea, and I are all together like that. But my relationship with Connie is separate."

"Oh, so it's more like you have your own harem, but two of them are into each other too." She lies back down on the grass and stares at the sky with me.

A brief moment of calm amid my training storm.

"Yeah, something like that."

"What about War?" She sighs. "Where does he fit into your harem?"

Tears prickle my eyes as a sense of loss overcomes me at the question. Where does he fit? At the moment, he's not even a friend. More just an unwilling colleague. I still haven't spoken to him yet—been a touch busy—but I want to. Maybe I'll do it after tomorrow's meeting.

"Magic?"

"Oh, sorry." I take a deep breath. "Arrie and I are just . . . friends."

25

Aki and I meet at my favorite café, and the owner greets me with his usual warm smile amid all that purple hair. "Welcome, Magic." He looks to Aki with a small frown before smiling. "An' . . . Aki, right?"

"That'll be me," he says with a charming smile as he offers his hand. If Aki was put off by his frown earlier, he doesn't show it. "You have a lovely place here, sir."

They've changed the wallpaper since I was last here; whereas before it was a deep red to match the deep purple chairs, now it's an ocean blue to match turquoise chairs. They even changed the décor to match the underwater feel.

"I like the new atmosphere." I walk up to the counter and place an order, then look at Aki.

"I'll let you order for me."

Okay. Sure. Cos I know him well enough order for him. I roll my eyes and order the same as me, hoping it'll be good enough.

"Yeah," the baker says, "I 'eard you were strugglin' with accessin' the water element in your Witch magic, so I thought maybe giving the right vibe somewhere you like to relax might 'elp." He looks sheepishly to the ground, but then pride smooths through his features as he lifts his head back up.

"You . . . did all of this"—I gesture to the café—"for me?"

"Indeed, Miss. Mr. Err . . . Magic." He stumbles over himself. "Sorry 'bout that."

"It's cool." I wave off his apology. "Just call me Magic."

"Right." He whisks himself into the kitchen out back, and I find us a cozy spot near the window.

"Does that not get a little . . . annoying?" Aki looks at me with tentative curiosity, as though he's unsure if he's allowed to ask about my male and female form conundrum.

A sigh breathes past my lips, and I find that I don't really know the answer. "Sometimes, I guess. It reminds me that I'm not exactly normal. But it's hard to switch to a new way of communicating with someone. It'll take time. And I need to be patient with everyone. I can see they're trying."

"Pfft. You're more patient than me." He smiles as our drinks arrive. "That's for sure."

"Remind me how you came to *Sheruta* again?" I laughed at his embarrassed face. "Maybe you could learn a little patience."

He looks at me with such reverence, I'm not sure how to hold his gaze. What does he even see when he looks at me like that? "I wonder which one of us is older?"

His mind works in such strange ways. "Must be what it's like to have a conversation with me," I mumble. Then shake my head. "I have no idea. Reckon Nigel will know?"

He shrugs. "Maybe. Haven't seen him in a few days."

"Wait. What?"

"Relax, sis." He looks at me with a charming smile that's supposed to put me at ease, but it doesn't. "He said he was going into work and will probably stay on Earth for a few days."

"Why the hell did no one tell me? I could have given him teleporting crystals so he could commute."

"Well, I think someone gave him one or something. Or he already had one. Because he said he'd use it if he needs to."

Must be one of the ones leftover from the mission to SC Chinese HQ. Weird to think that wasn't that long ago. Feels like months ago. But if he has one of those crystals, then he should be fine, right?

"Hey . . ." Aki grabs my hands. "He'll be all right. Promise."

"You can't promise something like that. We're at war," I whisper. "The SC are doing all kinds of weird things I don't know the motivation behind, and he's right there in the lion's den." My eyes heat with the tears brimming, but I hold them back. "And I'm leaving in a couple of days, so I won't be able to monitor him or help if he needs it."

"Wait, you're leaving?"

"Yeah," I confirm. "I'm hoping to plan a trip to some of the lower supes, to see if they'll help us." I look up to see his surprised face. "You know, even the playing field a bit."

"That's . . . pretty smart." He smirks, his lips twitching and his eyes gleaming. "Think I can come along? Or are you bringing your harem?"

"Ugh. Not you too." I huff. "I swear, everyone keeps calling the team that."

Just as he's about to take a bite out of his cake, he cracks up, laughing hard enough we get a few weird stares. "That's because it's true. They're all in love with you."

It is?

They are?

I mean, I know Nine and Dea are. We're in a good place. But the thing between Connie and I is new, and I don't even think Arrie and I are friends right now.

"Yeah, you're all so close. It's . . . weird."

"Wait. What about it is weird to you?" Frustration pours through me. "We're just there for each other. We're the only other immortal beings on the planet, and we work together all the time. We have each other's backs. And besides that, they're amazing people. They helped me when they didn't have to. They could have just kicked me out and told me to figure it out on my own, but they didn't. They—"

"Okay, okay." Aki holds his hands up in defeat. "I'm sorry. It's weird to me, but it's clear they're important to you." His smile doesn't quite touch his ears, but he tries. And he's only trying to for me.

"Okay." Taking a deep breath, I say the inevitable words of doom. "Might as well get this over with."

Twenty minutes later, we stand in a deep part of the forest, away from the popular unicorn sites and other animals. We face each other, Aki clear-headed and determined and at peace, by the looks of things, and me—in my female form, having switched a minute ago—shaking like a leaf in a hurricane.

I've been nervous before, sure. But not like this. I've pretty much spent the entire time since waking up in the house scared. But this is different. This is training me to kill. Not to harm or hone skills that could help me and others, but to train in a form of magic whose only purpose is to suck the life right out of anything I direct it at.

And we still have no idea if this magic is safe to use against another Horseman. I'm way too nervous to try that out. Plus the risk is too great.

"Our death magic is born out of survival. When we need it the most is when it's most active," Aki explains. "But we can train it to be used at will. It takes a lot of concentration, emotional control, and focus."

Emotional control. Great. Cos I excel at that.

"I saw that eye roll, Magic." He stifles a laugh and then goes back to his serious face. "What's got you worried?"

"Emotional control isn't my strongest skill, that's all." I think for a minute and then add, "And aren't emotions kinda important to Witch magic, anyway?"

"Yes. Emotional control doesn't mean taping your emotions down and being all stone-faced and emotionless. It means not letting them overtake you, being able to be sad when you're otherwise happy, and keeping them in check."

I don't see the difference, personally. That just sounds like a mediocre version of locking it all away.

"Maybe I'm not explaining myself well enough." He sighs and tries again. "It's not about controlling what you feel, but channeling it. You'll need to channel fear in order to access your death magic, but different Witches have different triggers for their elements. Some find water peaceful while others find it rageful."

"I explode into fire whenever I'm pissed off."

"Exactly!"

So I just need to channel the emotion that works best with my element. So then what does water work best with? I've used it twice now: once when I was angry at myself for hurting Connie and again when I was working with my Fae magic.

"Focus, Magic!"

Right. I'll think about that later.

"Fear controls death magic."

"For every Witch? But didn't you just say—?"

"This is an Angel-descended Witch power, so it works a little differently. It's always fear from what I've researched."

Okay, okay. He's better at this than me, so I'll concede.

"What scares you?"

Everything.

"But not just normal fear. Intense, life-threatening fear."

"But my life can't be threatened, Aki. I'm immortal."

He scratches his head. "Oh yeah. That might pose a problem." He sits with his legs crossed on the forest floor and closes his eyes.

"What are you doing?"

"Shh. I'm concentrating."

Okaaaay.

He's so weird.

But maybe his weird will be just what I need?

"Okay," he says suddenly, making me jump, "I've got nothing."

"Nothing? Really?"

"Yup." He walks over to me. "How am I supposed to help you channel life-threatening fear if you can't even die?" He raises his hands in the air and drops them to his thighs. "How am I supposed to work with that?"

But we can die.

We just have no idea where my seal is, and we got so busy with everything else, we forgot to continue searching.

"Okay," I start, "I might have an idea, but I'll need to chat to the team first and see what they think."

26

Since the training session with Aki went nowhere, I find Connie and see if she's free to help me brainstorm about my seal. There are still endless corridors and doors in my library I've not explored thoroughly yet. Maybe it's in one of those?

I find Connie in her room, on the bed, surrounded by various pieces of paper. I knock on the open door. "Hey!"

She looks up, the frown on her face turning instantly into a smile. "Hey yourself." She carefully gets off the bed, trying not to move any of the paperwork, and gives me a quick hug. "What's up?"

"Nothing much. Just wondering if you have a minute. But you look busy." I gesture to the pile of papers. "What is all that?"

"Everything I could find about various lower supernaturals and where they might be. Figured I could give you some good starting points."

"You're like three million steps ahead of me all the time." I shake my head. "How do you do it?"

"With two thousand years of practise!" She drags me into her room and slams the door behind us. "Now, what did you need me for?"

"My seal."

"Shit, yeah." She rubs a frustrated hand over her face. "We totally forgot."

"It's okay. We were all busy. And I forgot too."

"Well, what reminded you?"

"Aki. He said I needed to be scared for my life in order to access my death magic, but since I can't actually die, that's gonna be hard." I take a deep breath. "Then I remembered what Nine said when I first got here. About the seals being burned and then we can die."

Connie looks at me with pensive silence for a moment. "And you trust Aki messing with your seal?"

"I . . ." Wow. Good question. "I wasn't really thinking about that. It could be any of you, instead."

She leans her head from side to side. "I don't think messing around with your seal is a good idea. Not just to access a specific type of magic, anyway."

"But Connie. I have this magic for a reason. Fate allowed me to carry it over to immortality for a reason."

"Yeaaaah, or maybe Fate didn't care and just left it there."

My hands clench into fists as frustration boils beneath the surface. "You don't know that!"

"Neither do you!" Connie takes a deep breath. "Okay, okay. There's no point arguing over this."

Speak for yourself.

"But," Connie starts, "we're both right. You do need to explore your death magic. But I don't think playing around with your seal is the best way to do that."

"Well, how else do you expect me to fear for my life?"

"Use a memory." She looks at me like the answer's obvious, but I have no idea what she's talking about. "Use a memory of a time when your life *was* threatened. And then channel that emotion."

"That . . . might work."

Is everyone around here smarter than me? Or am I just a bit dumb? Eh. You can't have everything. I'm okay being a little stupid.

"Soooo, want some help with that?" I gesture to the paperwork scattered across her bed. A peace offering for yelling at her, I tell myself. But in reality, I just enjoy studying and research. All this active magic stuff is a pain in the ass. "Cos I'm pretty good with research."

"Sure. Could use a note taker."

"Then I'm your gal."

AFTER HOURS OF NOTING DOWN VARIOUS LOCATIONS, SCRAPS OF INFORMATION, AND CULTURAL references, Connie and I are officially done for the day. And when we meet the guys at the dining table, it's clear they're done too.

Nine's practically falling asleep, Dea looks like he's about to yell at someone if they come anywhere near him, and Arrie's bloodshot eyes and frowning face looks grumpier than usual.

I'm starting to see what Melissandre meant all those weeks ago. We're too busy and tired to manage housework for this monstrosity of a mansion.

"Any preferences?" Connie asks with a hand inches from the table.

"Sugar," Nine groans.

"Caffeine," Dea sighs.

"Meat," Arrie grumbles.

Connie looks at me, but I shrug my shoulders. "Something tasty."

Nine and Connie look to me with smirks, but it's Nine who says, *I can help with that.*

You are far too tired for sex right now. When was the last time you slept?

When was the last time you came to bed with us?

That was days ago! For goddess' sake. "We're all going to bed tonight. No fucking questions."

Connie raises a hand to argue, but I shush her. "Other than you. You slept like a log last night."

"It'll be a few days before I need to sleep again," she reminds us with a shrug. "One of the benefits of being me."

I point a finger at Arrie with a frown on my face. "That includes you." He opens his mouth to say something, but I interrupt. "I don't care how much you dislike it."

His face goes from tired and frustrated to genuinely angry in a blink, and everyone flinches. Well, other than Connie, who just sighs. "Who the fuck do you think you are?" He shoots to his feet with clenched fists. "You don't get to order me around." His booming voice didn't need him to shout; you could hear it from another realm.

"Watch your tone, Arrie," Dea warns.

"Sorry, I forgot you slaves seem to like taking orders." He goes to walk away from the table, trying to get past Connie, but she blocks him. "What now?" The exasperation in his voice breaks for just a second when he looks at me.

"You think you get to play asshole just because you won't man up and talk to Magic? You think we deserve your shitty moods just because you can't be a grown-ass adult?" Connie walks to the kitchen with her back to him while he just stares at her, dumbfounded.

I turn to face them, concerned about our kitchen's wellbeing for just a second. "Guys, I don't think this is the best time for—"

"I'm sick of him treating you like shit!" Connie yells. "It's all his fault in the first place."

"You think so?" Arrie asks. "You think this isn't at all on your shoulders? That all three of you haven't just become mindless slaves to one person's . . . *woman's*," he spits as he corrects himself, "will."

I tense in my seat at his words, my pink hair falling around my shoulders as an immediate tear falls from my eye in soundless silence.

But I'm not a woman.

Connie freezes, Dea stops drinking his tea, and Nine looks up from the table where his head was resting.

"Did you just—?" Dea starts.

"Use Magic's sex and gender against them?" Connie scoffs. "In an argument you started?" Connie's fists clench harder, her knuckles whitening and her eyes flashing with anger. "You absolute ass pig!" She grabs the nearest object to her, which happens to be a frying pan, and whacks him over the head.

A loud twang echoes across the kitchen, and we all stand in silence for a moment.

Arrie looks pissed but confused.

Dea looks like surprised.

Connie looks damn proud.

Nine looks like he's struggling not to laugh.

And I have no idea how I look, but I'm struggling to stick to a single emotion. They're on a pinwheel right now, and the ticker hasn't decided which one to land on.

It'll probably be anger.

Yup. It's anger.

"How can you do this to me?" I scream. "I know I'm being selfish expecting you all to be okay sharing me, and I know I'm not perfect. But I at least expected a reason. A short conversation at best. Heck, even a fucking letter would have sufficed, Arrie!" I turn to face him with angry tears slashing down my face. I try to hold on to that anger, but my voice breaks as I sob. "How could you?"

His face has a red welting mark from the frying pan, which I think was swung at him with Connie's full strength because he's bleeding. But it's his eyes that catch me off guard. They don't look angry anymore. They just look sad.

And for the first time, I realize that maybe there's more going on with Arrie than just him changing his mind. That maybe that sadness isn't aimed at me.

The following morning is awkward. Arrie walks to the embassy alone while the rest of us follow a few feet behind. We're supposed to meet the representatives there, and then we'll all meet Nigel, who will give us the location for the SC meeting.

We are all going. Contrary to my opinion that I should go alone so I could burn them all to the ground. That would solve all this quicker.

But no, Nine had to be the voice of reason. He said if there is someone pulling the strings behind all this, then we need to know who, otherwise they won't stop if we just destroy the Supernatural Council.

Wise words.

Annoying, but wise.

Just as we crest the hill that leads into the town center, Nigel runs up the path, panting, sweating, and looking a bit worse for wear. He dives past Arrie, who doesn't even look at him and keeps walking, then stops in front of us. Hands on knees. "Needed . . . to . . . make it . . . in time," he pants.

"Slow down." Nine rubs circles onto his back as I stuff my hands into my jean pockets. "Catch your breath."

Nigel nudges Nine's hands away and straightens. "There's no time for that." His face is beet red. "I ran from the other side of Colorado before I remembered I could have used the crystal." He looks irritated with himself, scowling at the fact he forgot. "The date. I have the date."

We all straighten, preparing ourselves.

"Two months."

"December, then?" Nine asks.

"Exactly one year after Angel showed up?"

"A coincidence, maybe?" Connie asks with a shrug.

"Pfft." Nine looks at us. "I'm starting to believe in Fate." He laughs at himself and then turns back to Nigel. "Do you have a date?"

Nigel nods. "December 25th."

"Christmas day?" Bewilderment strikes me until I suddenly get it. "They're attacking when people are probably going to be busy with their families. Lots of species celebrate Christmas across lots of countries."

Connie laughs, but we all scowl at her, so she explains, "Christmas was a pagan tradition that was adopted by Christianity, and then it kind of spread from the western world out to the east, and now the whole damn world celebrates it." She crosses her arms across her chest.

"You'll have to forgive Connie. She knew Jesus." Nine shoves her aside and looks to me. "You need to leave. Soon. We need as much help as we can, and you're our best bet of getting it."

I nod, knowing he's right. "Then let's get this meeting over with and call the embassy to action."

"They might have more information for us, hon," Connie suggests. And when I look at her confused, she explains, "About the lower supernatural species and where they might be."

"Right."

"Wait a minute," Nine says as we walk into the embassy building a few minutes later, "the meeting's here?"

Nigel rubs a nervous thumb over his index finger. "Well, they didn't want to give away any of their meeting places, since they're not public knowledge."

"Yeah, cos that screams trustworthy." I roll my eyes. "This is gonna suck, isn't it?"

A grunt comes from the front doors, and Arrie steps out. "Can you quit complaining for one second?" His bulging arms folded over his chest, he looks like a war chief. Like a political war chief. But a yawn escapes his otherwise tempered facade.

"Did you seriously stay up all night just to do the opposite of what Sweetie suggested?" Nine asks, incredulously.

Seriously, will this guy's stubbornness know any bounds? "Arrie, can we—"

"No," he grumps before moving on and up the stairs.

We all take the elevator.

"It's okay, Sweetie." Nine wraps his arms around my waist and rests his head on my chest. "He'll come around."

"You keep saying that, and I'm sick of it," I growl. "I can't even hold an amicable working partnership, let alone friends or anything else." I shrug Nine off, but his frown stabs at me. I rub the rising pressure out of my nose. "I'm sorry. That wasn't fair of me."

"Have I ever told you how good your ass looks in your male form?" Connie asks out of nowhere.

I look in the mirror of the elevator and catch her staring at my ass while licking her lips. "You done treating me like a piece of candy, babe?"

"Nope." Her flushed gaze meets mine, and she smiles at me. "Never."

The guys chuckle at us, and just as the elevator pings to the conference floor, Connie gently kisses my temple and grabs my hand while Dea grabs the other and follows Nine out.

I know Arrie's still annoying the crap out of me, but at least my life with these three is turning out amazingly.

Okay, however, goes out the window when I meet the Supernatural Council bigwigs. They're old. They're all men. And they're staring daggers at me so sharply it's a wonder I'm still alive.

Fuck me. This is gonna suck.

Just keep your cool.

Hence my male form. No Vampire craziness here.

Well, Vampires are known for their emotional outbursts.

I know, I know. I'm the poster child of emotional outbursts. But I got this. I will keep it down and buried at the center of the Earth.

Don't forget to lock its crypt.

I shoot him an incredulous look.

What? You get cranky and irrational and flamey when you're pissed.

By the smirk on Dea's face and the laugh Connie is so obviously trying to hold in, he projected that conversation to the team.

You can all quit fucking laughing at me now. Thanks.

That was it for Connie, apparently, because she burst out laughing. Getting the entire attention of the room, including all the ambassadors and the councilors.

"Sorry." She wipes her crying eyes. "Famine likes to send jokes to us using his telepathy."

"A bit of an inopportune time for jokes, is it not?" A man with gray hair, aging features, a long beard, and an angry scowl taps his fingers restlessly on the table. "Are you ready to proceed?"

We all look at each other with worried glances, and I catch Lucien's gaze across the room. He looks worried too. In fact, all the ambassadors do.

Nine, tell everyone to say nothing about knowing the Area 50 plans. Or anything about my trip to unite the lower supe world. I'm not giving these cunts any advantages. If we can make peace, then fine, but if not, I'm done.

Okay.

No one looks our way, so it seems to have gotten through to them how important this meeting is.

The Supernatural Council is made of twelve people: three humans, three Vampires, three Fae, and three Shifters. Our council follows a similar pattern, but where they have Fae on their side, we have Witches. Humans, however, are not with us. But Nine's pretty sure humans'll be divided, anyway.

They're not known for their unity.

The Supernatural Council dominates one side of the circular table while we Horsemen take the other, and smack in the middle of the two are the ambassadors.

The same old man as before—human, I now realize—coughs into his hand to get everyone's attention and starts what's probably going to be a long-ass meeting. "Now everyone is here," he says with a sneer, as though we were late, "we can begin."

Another old man sitting next to him, who's also human, takes the first offensive maneuver of the day. "All you ambassadors, you do realize that allying yourselves with the Horsemen appears as if you are no longer allying yourselves with the Supernatural Council?"

Red, the Witch Coven's ambassador, responds, "Are you suggesting that the Horsemen are your enemy, and that allying ourselves will lose us your support?"

Straight to it then.

The red flush on the old man's face is almost worth it. Almost. "Of course not," he grinds out. "We are simply asking where your loyalties lie."

Pansy, our Shifter ambassador, looks like she's about to burst already. "Our loyalties are to our people, and always will be. That's why we choose to work alongside you both. Otherwise, how can we best serve our communities?"

Harrow looks positively amused by all this to and fro, like a bad political milkshake, but then I guess this doesn't affect him, since he's a *Sheruta* Vampire. "If you both worked together, this wouldn't be a problem."

We stay silent, hoping beyond all hope that they'll choose to be allies. I doubt it. But you never know.

"Of course we," another old man, Fae this time, starts, "are working alongside the Horsemen. No one suggested otherwise, Mr . . ."

He shakes his head. "We don't have last names here on *Sheruta*. So it's just Harrow." His inky black hair almost smiles in the sunlight filtering through the partially shaded windows. "Pleasure to meet you."

The man nods.

"Now we have that settled," Nine starts, "we wanted to ask what your plans are for helping the Vampire blood supply issue and what your thoughts are of the Fae allying themselves with the rogue Vampire faction, who have shut down New Orleans, tried to kill me, and taken one of our own hostage."

The Fae councilman from earlier blusters and stutters before finding his words. "Those are some bold accusations, Famine." He takes a deep breath. "Our queen wishes to ally herself with the new Vampire King, when he eventually takes over." He slices his hands through the air. "That is all."

Nine, is he telling the truth?

Yes.

Then she's lying to her people about the truth behind the union.

It would appear so.

"You look troubled, Magic," Prince Lucien asks. "What is the matter?" He looks at me with meaningful eyes, trying to say something.

He says that you should stand up and speak up for everyone. To stop being, and I quote, a little Horseman.

Anger flares across my mind, but I tamper it down to something resembling frustration. Okay, Magic, you can do this. "It is difficult to communicate with the councilmen when even they aren't being given truths from their own species' councils and royalties."

"Are you suggesting our queen is lying to us?" another Fae councilman asks. "That's preposterous—"

I hold up a hand to silence them. "I'm suggesting that she's telling you what you want to hear. And that not a single member of your species is strong or brave enough to stand up to her to ask otherwise." Because that's what happens in a monarchy.

He leans back in his seat, flabbergasted. "We . . . will look into your claims."

Best you're gonna get, Sweetie.

I bow my head and smile through clenched teeth. "Thank you."

A Vampire councilman turns to Lucien with a smug smile. "So where does the king sit on this matter, then."

Lucien speaks softly but clearly. "Ah, yes. Well, I have news on that front. The Vampire King announced to the Vampire Royal Council this morning that he has renounced Prince Phillipe's title and claim to the throne."

The room collectively gasps before exploding into a flurry of questions and accusations.

Nine, have you taken a look into their minds yet?

Yes. The humans have all been compelled by a powerful Vampire. They're saying what they've been told to say. Two of the Fae councilmen genuinely don't know about the Fae Queen's alignment and what they're really up to. The other, the one who's stayed quiet until now, is in line with her and waiting to see how this plays out before making a move.

What of the Vampires and Shifters?

The Vampires are shocked. All three are already on Prince Phillipe's side. We're not winning any of them over.

You're telling me we've lost seven of the twelve council members?

Yes.

Brilliant.

For the next few hours, we throw snide insults back and forth while agreeing on nothing. There's no point, anyway; over half the council are already aligned with the enemy.

But we might sway the other six, if we're lucky.

Which could be good for the future if we play our cards right. Hence why I'm still sitting here taking jibe after jibe while smiling. Like an idiot.

A beautiful idiot.

Dea made himself visible about an hour ago, so he's good, though looking a little pained. Might be because of the current conversation, though, which has just switched onto Witches.

Guess it's their turn to take a few jibes.

Nine, can you remind them to keep their cool. And I'm totally with them, I want to burn their asses to the ground, too.

Red smiles beneath what I assume is supposed to be a frown, but she scowls at the councilman telling her Witches don't need to pick a side because they don't do anything, anyway.

(Yeah, ouch.)

"So," she begins, "let me see if I've got this right. You're saying we're not allowed an opinion because we're 'unaffected' by the current goings-on in the supernatural world due to not being out in the open?"

The pretty human councilman shifts in his seat without answering. Which means yes.

"There is a coven of Witches in every country in the world, sir. And even if we practise our magic in secret, we still come into contact with other supes on the regular, including Vampires. If Vampires start hunting us again, many of our kind will be left defenseless. And that's not taking into account the war we would be starting between Witches and Fae. We rely on your peace in order to maintain ours."

Yup. It's official. I like her.

The human councilman who talked first sighs. "What is it you want from us, Horsemen, ambassadors?" He looks around the room.

Nine looks to me, then to Dea, then to the ambassadors in the room, who all nod. "Nothing now." He gets up. "Thank you for your time." And walks away.

Follow.

We all get up and walk wordlessly out of the meeting room, following Nine up the stairs and into another meeting room.

For fuck's sake. How many meetings am I going to be stuck in today?

"As many as it takes," Nine responds out loud, a slight edge to his voice. "Sorry." He winces. He wraps an arm around my shoulders and kisses me softly, gently, and with as much tender love as he usually does. "Been a long week."

Dea curls behind him and whispers, "You need to get some sleep."

"I don't have time for that." The gruff edge to his voice is marred only by the tired yawn that escapes.

Everyone takes some time to breathe, get a glass of water, and chatter amongst themselves for a ten-minute break before we reconvene.

"Well," Red starts, "that was a disaster."

"Yup." I smile. "Pretty much how I thought it would go."

Dea shrugs. "At least we can say we tried. When everyone says we started this war, we have video footage of trying."

Arrie turns his head in our direction for the first time today. "You recorded that?"

Nine nods. "Yeah."

"Good," I say, "cos I wanna watch Red verbally kicking that asshole to the curb again."

Prince Lucien laughs, and then we're all giggling at the memory. "That was awesome, little Witch."

She scowls. "What part of me is little to you, Vampire?"

He holds his hands up in defense. "Don't get your magical knickers in a twist. I call everyone that."

"Correction," Nine adds, "he calls everyone he thinks is hot that. Including Magic."

I nod, confirming.

Is that jealousy I hear in your voice, Famine?

He doesn't answer.

Red smiles and blushes lightly and then shakes her head and takes a seat near the other Witch ambassadors, including Aki, who has remained silent today.

"You okay?" I ask him. "You've been a bit quiet."

He shrugs. "Just a little underqualified, that's all."

"No one is underqualified to speak about their own lives."

"Well, my life is defined by the fact that I have to hide my magic."

Red's eyes shoot our way, and I can only hope she thinks we're talking about Witch politics and not death magic.

Placing a comforting hand on his shoulder. "I know."

"Right," Nine calls everyone to attention, "we have some things to discuss, including what I read of everyone's minds while there and Magic's plans to leave tomorrow to unite the lower supe world."

Everyone looks to me in surprise.

But I stay silent and look to Nine, who explains what he already told me back in the meeting from hell numero uno. "The real issue," he says at the end, "is that they know we know all of that." He scowls. "They tried hard not to think about any of their plans, so I got nothing." Sighing, he slouches.

"Dude," Lucien says, "when was the last time you slept?"

Nine throws his arms up in exasperation. "I don't have the time, for fuck's sake. Will everyone just stop. I'm immortal. I'll be fine."

It's because we care.

I know. "Sorry," he apologizes. "I'm just a bit cranky."

"It is okay, Nine," Dea says, "I'll take over." He pulls him out of his seat and turns him to the couch in the corner. "Take a damn nap." Kissing the crook of his neck gently, he guides him to the couch and forces him to lie down.

Dea turns back to the table and sits down. "If I go invisible halfway through, I am sorry, but you will still be able to hear me."

"If it's uncomfortable," Harrow says, "then turn it off now. We're good."

Everyone nods, and Dea smiles. Thankful for the invisible relief, if that uncharacteristic slouch is anything to go by. And it's good to see two of my guys taking a break. They've worked so hard.

"Good," Dea says, "now Nine has updated everyone on where the councilmen were really at, we have something else to plan. Magic is leaving soon to try to get as many lower supes on our side as possible."

"But," Connie takes over, "this won't be easy. They've been largely ignored by all of us in the last few hundred, thousand years."

Everyone looks to the floor and ceiling and anywhere but us, unease spreading through the room like wildfire.

"What we need," she goes on, "is information."

"Like where the pixies are, for example," I chime in with an attempt at a smile. "Or if anyone knows of any Demons lurking about."

"Demons?" Lucien asks.

"Hey, I'll take help where I can fucking get it, little Vampire."

Lucien smirks and nods. "Fair enough."

Connie pulls out a bunch of paperwork I recognize. "We've got a few leads." They're the papers that were scattered on her bed last night. "But nothing concrete."

I wince, remembering something important. "The biggest hurdle is that I can only teleport to somewhere I've already been. Which is really fucking nowhere. So I'm gonna have to fly to a lot of these places."

On an airplane.

Ugh. Kill me now.

The world can die.

Arrie chuckles cruelly at me with a smirk on his face, and it takes some next level willpower not to wipe that shitty grin off his fucking gorgeous face. Why do I still want to jump his bones? He's being a cunt.

Focus, Magic. Focus.

"Well," Red's saying, "we Witches know where the fairies are."

Not quite pixies, but it's a good start.

"Where?" Connie asks, pen at the ready.

Red looks a little unsure, her eyes darting away from us.

"Hey," I whisper, "we're not going to cause any harm. I'm just going to ask for help. If they really don't want to, I won't force them."

Red nods, satisfied with that reassurance. "They're with the Witch Coven. But in a different part of the cavern structure."

Fuck me three ways to Sunday, I don't want to go back there. I'll probably be arrested if I even try.

Dea places a hand on my arm. "It might be a good time to make a public apology to the entire Coven. Maybe you can help them?"

"They are in need of some Fae lights," Red chimes in. "It gets awfully dark down there at night. And the witchlights are really dim."

I think I can work with that. "Thank you."

Red smiles, her red hair swaying as she brushes it back out of her way. "You're welcome."

"There's a Demon horde the Vampire Royal Council use to help with scaring newer Vampires into following the law," Prince Lucien offers with a shrug. "Could probably get you a meeting, at the least." When I look at him incredulously, he just smiles. "They don't hurt anyone, but try telling a newly turned Vampire not to drink from every human he walks past and see how much he listens." He sips his glass of water. "It's a good strategy because it works."

Well, it's better than I've managed so far.

"Okay, so fairies and a Demon horde." Taking a breath and a sip of water, I continue. "I think our best allies are going to be pixies, since they're so hunted by the Fae for their dust."

Everyone nods, seeing my point.

"But I have no idea where they are." Rubbing a hand down my face, I sigh in exasperation. "They've been seriously careful with their location."

Aki shifts uncomfortably in his seat and avoids my eyes. I throw him an accusatory glare, and he finally gives up. "They mostly live in the Amazon rainforest."

I give him a 'how do you know that' look, and he shakes his head while pointedly looking at the people in the room.

Okay, so he can't share how.

"Okay. Thank you."

Connie writes everything she can down, so hopefully we can make a plan later.

"Are you all going?" Prince Lucien asks. "Or are you going alone?"

I look at the team, but they all shake their heads. They're too busy right now. "I'm probably going to have to go alone—"

"I'm going with her," Aki interrupts, leveling his gaze my way, challenging me to say no.

Sighing, I give in. "Fine."

Now I have to make two batches of transport crystals.

29

My library has never looked so damn good. Can I marry books? Because I totally will if I can. The meeting lasted until dinner, with lots of people having random snippets of information we put together and ended up with an incomplete map to the lower supe world.

I have between now and Christmas to complete that map, visit all the supernaturals' homes, and convince them to join our cause. Which will probably involve me helping them first.

Oh, and I'll be doing so with my lost-lost twin brother, Aki. Sounds like a real vacation. I roll my eyes at my own internal snark and settle into a book about a hilarious cupid and her four beautiful mates.

I laugh and I cry and I choke on my own saliva more times than I care to admit for an immortal being, but by the time I'm done with book one, I'm feeling worlds better.

Who knew laughing was such mental medicine?

Literally everyone.

Nine, Dea, and Connie all round the corner of the nook I've found myself in with smiles and beauty. All lined up like this, I feel immensely lucky. They chose me. Me.

"We'll always choose you," Nine responds as he sits to my left.

Connie takes my right and wraps an arm around my shoulders. "Always."

While Dea sits on his ass in front of me, nudging my legs apart so he can sit between them. "Ah," he gasps, "I have an idea." He places his hand on the floor, and a few seconds later, a light rumbling noise alerts us that the house is creating something new.

And out of nowhere, a TV pops up in front of us.

"Want to watch a movie, Angel?"

"So long as I don't have to move."

Nine whispers into my ear, "No moving required."

We lie on the sofa together and watch two movies in a row, chatting, cuddling, laughing, and generally have a good evening before I leave for what could be a pretty long mission.

Hopefully it'll take a few weeks, and then I can come back home. But I might be gone the entire two months. That'll suck. But it is what it is.

"So," Connie starts, "Aki's going with you, huh?"

As we're walking back to my bedroom, I turn to face her question. "Yeah, I guess." I shrug.

"You are not worried about that?" Dea asks.

"Should I be?" I mean, I get he's my long-lost brother, but he's pretty nice. "Maybe it'll be a good opportunity to get to know each other a bit better."

Nine chuckles. "You really are working on being more positive, aren't you?"

"I'm trying," I whisper, embarrassment flooding me.

Hard.

"And you're doing wonderfully, hon." Connie walks us through the door and pops into my library, then comes back with a book in hand. "I don't wanna miss our last night together, but I'm not tired yet." So she shakes a book I saw her reading a few days ago in the air.

"Sounds good."

Just as I'm snuggling between Dea and Connie, a knock sounds on my door and Arrie enters, holding a familiar flash drive in hand. "I just wanted to tell you before you leave tomorrow that I've finished analyzing all the content. Most of it's just trade, tax, meeting records, employee information, et cetera." He shrugs, his voice robotic and devoid of emotion. "Anything you need while you're gone?"

My brain frazzles. Everything in me shrivels up and dies.

He's been going through that for me this entire time?

"Err . . . Maybe give Connie and Dea a hand if they need it, and make sure every-thing's ready for your plans at each city." I've not looked over them. I trust him.

On the day, I'll just be one of his soldiers. And I'm totally okay with that.

He nods and turns to walk away, but at the last minute he swings his head back around. "Good luck." There's something in his eyes—he wants to say more—but I think he's holding back.

Not wanting an argument right before my first solo (ish) mission, I decide not to engage. Sometimes, letting things simmer down is the best option. That way, I can chat to him once I've processed everything and not be a snarling mess.

Smart. He's still angry at himself.

Yeah, I got that.

Nine, Connie, Dea, and I snuggle into bed, Connie reading by a low lamplight (her enhanced senses helping immeasurably), and Nine and Dea sharing both me and each other. And I fall asleep easily, happily snuggled up between my partners. My family.

Aki smiles at me early the next morning at the breakfast table, where we're both sat—alone, because no one else is up yet—eating an English breakfast.

Dea would be so proud.

"You really made ten of those crystal things?" Aki asks.

"Each."

His eyes burst wide, surprise covering his face. "Wow. That's amazing."

"One to get to Earth, two Earth-*Sheruta* ones, just in case, and the rest are Earth-Earth." Laying my map down on the table, I use a cup to hold each corner in place. "We're starting in North and South America, and then we'll tackle things continent by continent."

He nods. "Prince Lucien said he managed to get us a meeting with the Demon horde the Vampire Royal Council use in one week's time in the New Orleans Bayou."

"Great." That's one ticked off our list. Which I also have laid out on the table. Between all the ambassadors, we have some serious intel. "And we might be able to ask Alpha Cal if he has any further leads if we pop into Tokyo when we get to Asia."

Aki looks at me in question.

"We're pretty friendly with the Shifters. Vampires too, but they have their own issues right now."

"Yeah, Prince Lucien's been going back and forth a lot and is pretty exhausted by the looks of things."

"He should have said something." I sigh. "I would have made him some *Sheruta*-Earth teleporting crystals. The moron."

"He's a little prideful, that one." He stifles a giggle. "Are all Vampires so . . . emotional?"

I laugh. "Yup." Since I had to make a hundred teleporting crystals last night and this morning, I'm in my female form. "We're a little testy. I think it's a blood thing." I shrug. "Not really sure."

"Leaving without saying goodbye, Angel?" Dea walks into the kitchen in his gym gear —sweats and no top—with a smirk. "I thought I would at least get a kiss goodbye."

"Aaaand, that's my cue to leave. I'll see you outside in an hour?"

I nod, barely paying attention, my eyes fixed on Dea's swirling tattoo and his abs, his Adonis belt, and the way his galaxy eyes pierce into me without holding back. "You're . . . beautiful."

I gasp when he fazes to me and picks me up—faster than my eyes can track without warning—and wraps my legs around his waist. Resting my arms on his shoulders, I lean down to grab his lower lip between mine and bite down. Hard. Then grab his gasp with my lips and throw it right back.

"Good enough?"

He shakes his head. "Nope." He smashes my back against the nearest wall and pins me there before plunging his tongue into my mouth.

His piercings graze against my lips, and I can't help but play with them. Their cold metal a complete contrast to Dea's warm mouth.

He rolls his hips into me and I groan.

"Fuck, Dea . . ."

"Yes, Angel?"

I moan in response, and instead of letting him dominate me, I let my fangs slip and bite down on his lower lip. Taking a few sips. He does make a tasty breakfast.

Dea's knees go weak, and I nearly slip from his grasp, but he pins me to the wall again with his hips and a growl.

His whimpers spur me on, and I take deeper pulls, letting his smoky lavender taste roll over my tongue in waves of sweet nectar that blur my vision and shoot silver swirls over the backs of my eyelids.

A cough breaks the moment, and I retract my fangs and peer over Dea's shoulder to see Arrie standing uncomfortably by the backdoor. "Can I have a moment, Magic?"

"She was in the middle of breakfast, dude," Dea whines.

But rather than be annoyed, Arrie smiles for a moment. "Well, I'm interrupting."

His growly voice vibrates through me, and my hips roll against without Dea thinking. Fuck. I slip from Dea's grasp—much to my Angel of Death's amusement—and rush to Arrie.

Is he ready to chat?

He nods to the backdoor, and I follow him out.

The cool morning air hits me like a freight train, and I take a deep calming breath before sitting beside Arrie on the porch.

He opens his mouth to speak, but then he closes it with a frown. "Argh. Why is talking to you so hard?" His hands clench around his knees as his shoulders hunch.

I smile, trying to be gentle. "It's okay if you're not ready, Arrie. I'm not in a rush."

He shakes his head, frustration edging into that beautiful smile. "I'm sorry." He takes a deep breath, and it all comes rushing out. "I'm sorry for yesterday. I shouldn't have used your sex and gender against you like that. It wasn't fair. I said it because I knew it would hurt you. But it's really me I'm angry at."

"I know." He looks surprised. "You're not as mysterious as you like to think you are, Mr Tall and Grumpy."

His laugh is music to my ears. Like a light in the fog I didn't know I needed because I thought I could see just fine.

"Why are you so angry at yourself?"

He groans as he wipes a frustrated hand down his face and clenches his jaw. "Argh!" His fist punches through the chair's arm, and he winces. "Why is this so hard?"

"It's okay." I rest a hand on his shoulder. "Thank you for the apology. Maybe we can chat some more when I get back?"

He nods. "I'd . . . like that."

I get up to leave, but he grabs my hands last minute and turns me around. "Here." He hands me over a dozen vials of blood. "For your mission." His ice blue eyes pierce mine, shattering me for a brief moment. "I know I need to do more than say sorry."

I give him a questioning look, confused.

"I want to earn your forgiveness, and then maybe we can work on being friends?"

His words shoot through me like a well-placed arrow. I thought that maybe he wanted to . . . get back together. But he still just wants to be friends?

The pain's written all over my face, apparently, because Arrie looks hurt for a moment. "Magic, I . . ."

"It's okay." My voice is quiet, a brush on the wind. "I'd like that."

My mind is lost to what I've dubbed "Arrie nonsense" when I meet Aki in the front gardens, where I find him quietly smelling the roses and letting the fairies hop from arm to arm as they take him in.

"I'm surprised they touch you like that," I whisper.

Making him jump. "Jeez, Magic." His hand wavers over his chest. "You scared the shit out of me."

"Sorry," I chuckle. "I'm serious, though. Usually they stay around their nests and fly straight back into them whenever one of us comes near them."

"Really?" Aki sounds surprised. "I've always found fairies to be pretty social."

"Maybe you were just born lucky."

He lets out an indignant snort, disagreeing with me. And to be honest, I disagree with myself. We were not born lucky in any sense of the word.

"Ready to go?"

He nods, grabbing the one *Sheruta*-Earth teleporting crystal he has on him. "Just think of the Washington monument, right?"

"That's what we agreed on." I grab my own crystal. "It should be night there at the moment."

Aki looks nervous, but after a quick breath, he smashes the crystal on the ground and disappears in a poof of smoke.

"So cliché," I mumble as I follow him.

The Washington monument glows bright white a few hundred meters from where I land, and I immediately snap my gaze around to find Aki.

"Where did he land?"

My Vampire eyesight allows me to see perfectly in the dark, and I quickly find him on the other side, sitting chill by the water. "There you are."

"Knew you'd find me, sis."

"Vampire eyesight comes in pretty handy."

It's chilly this time of year here, and I find myself needing the gloves in my backpack, so I throw them on and turn back around to Aki, who's staring at me.

He shakes his head in a huff of laughter. "Sorry, it's just a Vampire in gloves is hilarious."

"I'm also half-Witch, which means I get cold, *deku*."

"Ouch. Swearing in Japanese." He grabs my arm and yanks me into a hug. "I didn't even know you spoke Japanese."

I laugh, batting him on the arm. "Of course, you fucking idiot. It's my first language. I speak English because it's a common language between the team."

Though I'm pretty sure Nine can speak Japanese.

Actually, I bet most of them can. They've been around for two thousand years, for goddess' sake.

"So," he starts, "where to first?"

I grab the list and the map out of my backpack—feeling a little like a game character cliché—and see what's closest.

"Shell Beach, New Orleans."

"But the meeting isn't for another week?"

"Exactly. They're meeting us at Shell Beach, right?" He nods. "If we go there now, we can teleport back whenever we need to later."

"Riiiight. The crystals only take you to places you've already been."

"Uh-huh." I look around, wondering where the nearest airport is. "Which means we need an airport."

"Oh," Aki says, "that's this way."

THE FLIGHT TO LOUIS ARMSTRONG NEW ORLEANS INTERNATIONAL AIRPORT ONLY TAKES AN hour, but I still manage to throw up twice.

Uggh. Why didn't I make those anti-sickness charms?

The airport is only open to specific visitors, given the city-wide shutdown, but as a Horseman, I have clearance. Luckily I could persuade them into bringing an assistant with me, otherwise Aki would have had to go back home.

Alas, my powers of persuasion worked. For a change.

But the moment we step outside the airport, my relaxed demeanor changes. There's no cars, no people. Nothing. It's like a barren cityland out here.

"Wow," Aki breathes. "It's hard to believe this is New Orleans."

"Yeah."

Party central is officially asleep.

Aki taps his datachip and brings up a plasmascreen in the air, then hits maps. "Looks like Shell Beach is forty-three miles east, which'll take us fourteen hours to walk."

I snort. There's no way we're walking that far. "I can just fly us there. Probably take a couple hours."

"Can you fly two people for that long?"

I shrug. "Never tried before."

"Well, our flight to Manaus doesn't leave until this evening, so if there's anything you wanted to do while here, now's the time, right?"

"Right."

"Wonder how many shops are open at the moment?"

Aki laughs. "Shopping?"

I nod. "Yeah, Christmas is just round the corner, and I need to do some serious shopping." More December 25th preparations. "Though, we'll probably be celebrating a bit late this year."

"Maybe we should celebrate it early?" Aki hooks his arm through mine and starts our walk toward New Orleans central, though I'm pretty sure I'll have to fly us there, too. "Some people might not make it, and I just thought that maybe it would be nice to . . ."

Sighing, I agree with him. "Early might be best."

I eventually fly us to the center of New Orleans, lest we actually spend fourteen hours walking there.

"Well," I turn to Aki and say as we touch down in a park somewhere, "I could have made it, but not sure about your mortal feet."

He gasps in mock hurt. "My mortal feet can outmaneuver yours any day."

"Pfft. As if."

He punches me in the arm playfully, but he gasps when it's like punching stone. "*Chikushō*!" He waves his hand in pain, then clutches it to his chest. "What are you made of?"

I shrug. "Carbon." But inside I'm laughing. Hard.

"Top tip: don't punch Arrie or Connie, either."

He looks at me with raised brows and a small smile. "But Dea and Nine are fair game?"

"Pretty much." That makes him laugh, and we both have to take a few moments to compose ourselves. "But seriously, don't punch my harem." I point a finger at him and glare daggers.

He nods. "Wasn't planning to."

Nature pulses through me, like it usually does when I'm surrounded by its beauty, but the moment we step onto the street, harrow rips through my heart.

The streets are strewn with litter, buildings are boarded up, graffiti and vandalism run rife, and the Vampires in the shadows are looking at us like we're about to be the next zombie victim.

I grab Aki's arm. "We need to get out of here."

"Huh? Why?"

Right Vampire eyesight.

"Because there are hundreds of hungry Vamps around that want to kill us and eat us. Or, more precisely, you."

I watch his throat bob up and down as his hands tremble. "It's okay. We can teleport whenever we need to, and I can fly us up."

He nods with his eyes closed and gulps. "Okay, okay."

"Psst." A hiss sounds from behind us. "Hey, over here."

I turn, dragging Aki's line of sight with me, and scan the shadows.

"By the yellow graffiti under the broken stop sign."

I swing my vision in that direction and spot an old lady with a cane, her hands trembling and her eyes darting to the few Vampires within her vicinity.

I don't know what possesses me to go to her, but she looks like she needs help. Or at least someone to talk to. Living here must be rough.

"C'mon." I drag Aki with me, hastening our pace when we near the few Vampires looking at the old woman like she's prey. And that's when I realize she is.

She's human.

She leads us down the alleyway she has apparently come from, and then up the metal stairs on the side of the building. "We're going to the top." But her lungs heave with every step as her breath rattles.

"Here." I offer my hand, and she takes it. I walk us up the steps, not wanting to frighten her by Vampire speeding up and also not wanting to leave Aki alone. "There you go." I put her back on her feet.

She smiles at me gratefully. "You're the Horseman of Magic, right?"

I nod, not really sure if this is a good or bad direction of questioning.

"The one who created that app and the SC are talking smack about."

I laugh. "So they've started their smear campaign, have they?"

She grabs my hand and leads us to a bright rooftop garden, guarded by UV lights that make me wince as I pass them. "Sorry. They prevent regular Vampires from passing."

"S'okay." I rub the sore parts of my bare arms. "Just a little prickly." I shift into my male form, easing my time in this city. "That's better."

The old lady turns to face me and gasps. "Wow. You really can turn into a man." She chuckles. "Bet that's complicated."

"You have no idea," I mumble.

The garden is full of humans, a couple of Fae, and even a Witch. Everyone at risk from the Vampires. Some are sunbathing in fake lights, others are clustered together in groups, while others look frightened and huddled into a corner.

"You grabbed everyone you could find and gave them a safe haven?"

She chuckles and points to an old Shifter in the corner. "We did." She takes us to meet him and wraps an arm around his waist. "Hey, Tracker."

"Hey Lu." He splutters upon seeing me, and instead of saying hi, he stutters over a few different greetings and gives up, holding out his hand. "Tr-tr-tracker." He winces. "Sorry."

I wave him off. "Don't worry about it." I gesture to Aki. "My brother, Aki."

Aki holds out a hand. "Hi. I'm a Witch, if you need any immediate assistance." He bows and smiles at me.

I elbow Aki in the ribs. What the fuck is he doing? His magic is death. He can't just go around saying he's a Witch. For goddess' sake, I'm gonna have to watch out for him, aren't I?

"What?"

"I . . ." Oh, never mind. I wave him off.

"That's so kind of you," Lu interrupts. "Our only Witch has been having a hard time keeping up with all the charms and refueling them. The poor sod's exhausted."

"Oh," I say, "I can help with that."

Aki coughs. "Me too."

Wait, what? He can? But I thought Witches only had access to one type of magic? He can do more than one?

Aki looks at me with a small headshake, and then goes to greet the Witch in question, leaving me with Lu and Tracker.

Lu offers me a seat and a drink, which I gladly accept, happy to be off my feet. (Don't tell Aki, but my feet tend to get sore too. No amount of immortality will cure that.) "So," I ask, "is there a reason you wanted to chat with me?"

Lu glances at Tracker, who shifts in his seat. "We wanted to know if there was anything you planned to do about . . . this." She gestures all around her.

New Orleans.

"We have a plan."

She claps her hands together. "Oh, thank the gods. Is there anything we can—"

"But it's going to take time to get to." I'm not sure telling them about the SC's Area 50 plans is wise, but what the hell can they do from in here. "The SC plan to shut down all the major Vampire cities. We need to defend those, and that's taking some time to plan for."

"But after?" Tracker asks, his stutter nowhere to be found now. "Afterwards, you'll help us?"

"That's the plan."

They look like hope has just hit them in the face after forgetting what it felt like. And I guess that's probably true. These people need me. And I hate that I can't do anything right now. But it's okay. I'll come back, and when I do, I'll free them all.

32

After Aki and I refuel every charm the entire group are wearing, I fly us out of there and toward Shell Beach, where we'll touch down and look around, remembering specifics so we can teleport back in a week.

But halfway through the flight, Aki's stomach grumbles, and then mine follows, and soon we're both giggling mid-air as exhaustion takes us over.

"We'll see if there's something to eat near the beach, and then we'll fly back and refuel and sleep on the plane."

"Yeah, I know. My stomach's disagreeing, but I'm all onboard for the plan."

We spend a couple hours in the air, and the hardest part of flying for that long is the concentration required. But energy wise, I seem fine to make the trip there and back again.

Eventually, when I'm worried Aki might actually fall asleep mid-air, we touch down and breathe in matching sighs of relief.

"God, I've never been so relieved to have my feet on solid ground," Aki moans.

"Feel free to fly yourself back then," I grumble.

You know, assuming we weren't going to just teleport back.

"No hate, no hate. Just glad to be able to move of my own freewill again."

I take a look around, the water lapping at my heels as I jog to drier land. "Sorry about that." Aki's ringing water out of his shoe and I'm trying hard not to laugh. "But the meeting point's over there, by the harbor." I point in that direction.

"Yup." Aki looks around, smiling at the sun setting on the wet sand and the cliffs behind us. "Think you got everything?"

"Yeah, I can teleport back here." I grab a crystal out of my backpack and smash it at my feet, thinking of the airport. And the moment I open my eyes, the doors to the airport are before me while Aki stands beside me. "There."

"Time to take a nap," he says.

"We need to board the plane first, moron."

"You're pretty crabby for an immortal being, you know."

"Next time the world's fate is on your shoulders, let me know how well you're doing."

He smirks at me. "Well, I'd certainly be doing it with more of a smile. Especially since I can teleport to anywhere I've already been, meaning I can spend the afternoon in the sun and the evening in the city and the night with whomever I choose." He winks.

Ugh. "Yeah, yeah, alright."

"I'm just saying, you should live it up a little."

"You're just like Connie and Nine."

"Maybe you should listen to your boyfriend and girlfriend." He sighs. "That's still so weird to say."

"Huh?" Why is it weird?

"It's weird that you're in a polyamorous relationship. It's just . . . odd."

"It would be odder to only be with one of them." Trust me. I roll my eyes at his inability to understand something so natural. Most people have problems with my changing sex, my lack of a set species—heck, even my tattoos get more side-eye—but most people don't have a problem with my relationship choices. "Super odd."

He shrugs his shoulders. "Whatever makes you happy. I guess you're getting more than the rest of us at least."

I choke on air for a moment before calming myself. "Yeah, I guess." Should definitely not be talking about my sex life with my brother.

Fifteen hours on a plane makes your butt sore. Or, in my case, both my butts sore. I ate and napped twice, just to be sure—much to Aki's amusement—and now I'm cranky and in desperate need of a bath. And some coffee.

Manaus, Brazil in October is warm, but it's not stifling.

"C'mon," Aki says, "I booked us a hotel while you were napping." He sniggers. "Twice."

"Yeah, yeah, I probably didn't need to do that. I was just being cautious." I shrug. "I usually just feel refreshed after a night's sleep in both forms."

"Wonder why?" He has that curious look on his face Nine often dons when pondering my insanity. "Both forms are still you, of course, so I guess you have one pool of energy."

"Which would explain why using my Witch powers so much also makes this form tired."

"Strange you can only use that energy for specific types of magic, though."

We look at each, both puzzled, and shake our heads, leaving the question be. There's a lot about my nonconformity that doesn't make sense, and I'm learning not to dwell on that.

"What hotel did you book us?"

"Nothing fancy. Just an Ibis." He points to the tall building looming in the distance. "Only have so much money."

"You idiot," I mutter. "I have enough money to finance this trip." Nine's been teaching me investment. "So don't do that again. We're not going to have to scrimp while pulling off mission impossible."

"Right." He scratches the back of his neck, embarrassment flooding his features. "I'll try to remember that."

"I'll pay you back when we get back to *Sheruta*." Goddess, I miss home already. Shaking my head, I focus on the hotel now looming in front of me. Its blue doors and grass-green sides made of plants are beautiful, but then lots of buildings nowadays have greenery of some form on them, to decrease CO_2 emissions in our atmosphere. "This looks like a nice hotel." Better than that shitty motel Dea made us stay in, anyway.

"We'll check in, shake off the jetlag, and then check out your lead tomorrow, okay?" Exhaustion grips at my mind, and I'm pretty sure if I don't have a shower soon, I'm going to combust.

"Sure."

Aki walks up to the receptionist, who gives us a once over—eyes lingering a second too long on my chest—and then has us register our fingerprints to the rooms' online database.

Sophisticated. "Why don't they use datachips here?"

"They do, but I sent an email explaining who you are, and they said they'll use the old-fashioned way."

We get off the elevator and both turn right until we reach our rooms, positioned next to each other, and go our separate ways.

"See you tomorrow morning." Aki yawns. Seems he's just as tired as I am.

"Yeah, night."

We chuckle at the hilarity of saying goodnight at midday and vanish beyond our doors. The room beyond is clean, has a large window that lets in lots of light, and smells fresh. Plus, it has a large bed and a big tub.

AFTER A LONG SOAK IN THE BATH, ORDERING ROOM SERVICE, AND THEN TAKING A NAP UNTIL eight pm, I'm ready to do something for a few hours before going back to bed.

But what?

I'm too far away from my library to do any research, and I don't want to use all the crystals to go home every night just because I can, Aki is sleeping, and the team are probably busy.

But I guess I should check my phone. If I even remember how to use the old contraption. It's like over a hundred years old. Seriously. Why can't we just get chips already?

Yeah, yeah, yeah, I know. The SC controls all chip data, so it won't be smart. Even if we manage to sort out this mess, it'll still be a no.

But I'm pleasantly surprised to see messages from all members of the team, even Arrie.

CONNIE: HEY HON! HOPE YOU'RE DOING OKAY. REMEMBER TO GET ME A SOUVENIR.

NINE: IF YOU NEED ANYTHING RESEARCHED ON THE FLY, LET ME KNOW. I'LL HAPPILY SPEND time in your library while you're away. ;)

DEA: I CAN'T WAIT FOR YOU TO COME HOME. I MISS CUDDLING YOU AND HAVING YOU BETWEEN me and Nine.

. . .

ARRIE: STILL ALIVE?

I ROLL MY EYES AT ARRIE'S MESSAGE, COO OVER DEA'S, AND LAUGH AT EVERYONE ELSE'S. Typical team. Wonder if any of them are free for one of those holocalls?

I guess Connie would be the best person to call, since she's likely the least tired. Hope she's not busy. I have no idea what time it is over there.

Pulling the device out, I enter the code I know to be Connie's and wait, watching the flashing green light spin around the top.

Please be available. Please be available.

Then the light turns green, and Connie's voice screams over the speaker. "Magic! You're okay!" She sounds out of sorts, like I've caught her at a bad time.

"Is this a bad time?"

"No, not at all. I just ran around the house and gathered all the guys. Took me a minute."

"Oh. Hey Nine, Dea . . ." Is Arrie there?

Nine screeches out of the speakers. "Sweeetie! You're okay? All alive and happy?" Only Nine would ask if I'm happy like it's a casual greeting.

"Yes, Nine. I'm fine. Just checked into a hotel in Manaus, Brazil."

"Angel, I miss you."

An indignant snort sounds over the speaker, and there's only one person it belongs to.

"Hey, Arrie. Thanks for the blood supply."

"You supplied Magic with blood?" Connie asks. "Really?"

"How else are they gonna refuel when it's only our blood that does the trick?"

N'awww, he does care.

I think.

They don't have their holodisplay on, so I can't see them, but they're chatting, bickering, and it reminds me so much of home that my eyes mist over for a moment before I grab my emotions by the britches and haul them back into normal.

"Hey, everyone?"

They all stop talking.

"We're heading into the Amazon tomorrow to check out Aki's lead on the pixies, so I might not be able to recharge my devices for a while." Hence why I'm checking in. "But we managed to get to Shell Beach."

My silence punctures the air.

"What is it?" Dea asks. "What is wrong?"

"There are non-Vampires trapped in New Orleans."

"With a bunch of starving Vampires?" Nine asks. "Yeah, that's not good."

"There isn't enough of them to feed the Vampires, and it's like zombie town in there. I think we should send in a team to pick them up. Co-ordinate with the Vampire Royal Council."

"I'll arrange it," Connie says. "Everything's been quiet here, anyway."

"I'll help," Arrie says. "Give me something to do."

"If you're bored," Nine says, "you can always work on your groveling, since you'll need to do plenty to get between Magic's legs again."

I manage to blush, even though no one is here to witness—thank the goddess—but Connie knows me too well. "Stop blushing," she chastises. "We've all been between your legs at this point. Well," she corrects herself, "nearly all of us."

Arrie groans, and I distantly hear a door slam.

I laugh. "Stop frustrating him further. He's clearly having a hard time." I take a deep breath. "He wants to work on being . . . friends." The word slides out of my mouth like poison.

"Friends?" Connie asks. "But he—"

Someone must push her off whatever surface she was sitting on, because I hear a short scream and then an ouch as she punches the person in the arm. Probably Nine.

"Stop beating up Nine, Connie." My chest constricts as I picture them all huddled around a device just to speak to me. "He's probably still tired since he's probably still not sleeping."

Dea laughs. "You would be right about that. Though I managed to pull him into bed for a nap earlier, hence the chipper edge to his voice."

"Good. He needs to sleep."

"Stop fussing over me. I'm just as immortal as you two," Nine complains.

"Sooo," Connie asks, "how's everything going with Aki?"

"Err . . . fine, I think."

"Getting to know each other?" Dea asks.

"Yeah." Oh, Nine might know. "Nine, do you know of any Witches who can use more than one type of magic?"

"No, I don't think so. Why?"

"Because Aki can use charm magic, too."

"Really?" All three of them ask.

"Yeah. Saw it firsthand." I yank the duvet up to my chest and lay my head down. A yawn escapes me. "He helped the non-Vampires in New Orleans without batting an eyelid."

"That's weird," Nine confirms. "Maybe just ask him about it."

"Yeah . . . I guess." My eyes are starting to droop as my body slowly shuts down. "I miss you all."

"We miss you too, hon."

"Get some sleep, Sweetie."

"Have fun in the Amazon, Angel. Do not fall out of any more trees."

Nine bursts out laughing before someone turns the call off and I fall asleep.

33

The next morning we head to back to the airport, where we board a special helicopter I booked in advance to take us into the heart of the Amazon, away from all the usual tourist trails and things.

This will be my first helicopter ride, I think. And by the excited look on Aki's face, it's his first too.

"Do you think we'll see many cool animals?" he yells.

"Probably!" It becomes hard to talk when we lift into the air, so we stop trying to communicate.

As the world becomes smaller, I start to see the treeline up ahead, and we race toward it quicker than I expected. It's probably enhanced by Fae spells. Most of the transport industry is. But it's the beauty of the rainforest that leaves me truly speechless. The greenery goes on for miles.

After what happened in the 20th and 21st centuries, I'm surprised it's still so huge. But international laws came in to play, and large portions of the populace voted to stop cutting down the Amazon rainforest. As well as many other places. Companies were forced to look for alternatives, which then helped the job market. Prices went up, though. But it's worth it for the outcome.

Aki grabs my hand and yanks me to his side of the helicopter, where we're now low enough to see the treetops and the upper canopy without assistance. My female form could probably zoom in, but I'm in my male form. I get fewer weird looks this way, since I wasn't in this form when the video went viral.

The pilot looks nervous whenever I meet his gaze.

"There's a clearing up ahead," the pilot says through the headpiece we're now wearing. "I'm going to drop you off there, okay?"

"Yeah, that's fine."

As the helicopter places itself above the clearing, it descends, and soon we're on the ground and able to hear at regular volume again.

"That was awesome!" Aki jumps from the helicopter and lands on the flattened grass. "We're going back via helicopter, right?"

"Yup. But only because it was a two-way ticket. No one-way options."

"Hey," the pilot interrupts, "if I don't have to come back to get you, then I'm not." His gruff voice matches his stubble and wrinkled eyes. "I ain't associating myself with you." He points at me.

"Gee, thanks." I wave him off. "It's fine, we don't need your help getting back."

The relief on his face is evident, though insulting.

"I'm not some kind of monster, you know. Those Vampires I attacked were volunteers. The rogue Vampire faction are the ones working with the Fae and the SC to further divide people."

"Good." His arms crossed over his chest. "I don't want your kind anywhere near my family."

"My kind?" I take a deep breath, silencing him with a finger when he goes to interrupt. "Oh hunny, there ain't nobody in the world like me." I shift into my female form and bring a fireball to my hand, then blow it out with a strong gust of wind. I lower my fangs and think of all the tasty blood I'm missing out on by being here, and my eyes glow bright red.

"Fucking hell." The guy's face turns ashen, and he mumbles, "Freak," as he hops back into the helicopter and takes off.

"Fucking prejudiced asshole."

"There's just no persuading some people, is there?" Aki looks hurt, his eyes downcast and his lips frowning. "But maybe it might have been better not to threaten him with fire magic." He raises his eyebrows at me in question before turning away.

"Maybe," I mumble. "But he was being such a . . ."

"Bitch?"

I don't think I've ever heard Aki swear before. And the shock has me stifling a grin with one hand.

"Oh, lay off. You're as bad as Nigel. I swear sometimes." He rolls his eyes. "Speaking of Nigel, have you forgiven him yet?"

"Huh?" Oh, he's talking about keeping us a secret from each other. "Yeah, almost right away."

Aki turns to face me with another surprised look on his face. "Really? Why?" He pauses as he looks at the bright sky. "How?"

I grab Aki's hand and drag him into the forest on the edges of the clearing, starting us down some winding tracks. "He was trying to save our lives, Aki. If he had told us about each other, do you honestly think we wouldn't have sought each other out?"

He's silent. Pensive.

"Especially when I was mortal." I take a deep breath. "I could have really used a family member." I probably wouldn't have been half as evil if I did.

"Why do you say that?"

Do I tell him? Is he going to freak out and want nothing to do with me? Will he then go the press? So far they haven't published anything about my mortal life. Yet.

"Well, I . . ." I avoid his pestering gaze. "I wasn't a good person, that's all." Sweat boils across my palms and trails down my fingertips. "Fucking hell, it's hot." I wipe more sweat from my brow.

"Yeah." Aki's breath is shallow as he wipes sweat from his brow, too. "If you wanted to talk about it . . . About your mortal life, I'm happy to listen." He smiles. "It doesn't matter what it is." He opens his mouth to say something more, but then closes it again, deciding against it.

"Thanks."

An uncomfortable silence makes the air even denser than it already was, and I'm stifling beneath it, eager to shake it off and burn it to the ground.

"So, Aki, any girlfriends or boyfriends? Married? Children? Secret lovers?" I raise my eyebrows and wink. "C'mon, dish the dirt."

"You really wanna know?"

"Uh-huh. But first, where are we going?"

He rubs the back of his neck and groans. "Unsure. But I used to do security for this guy who had direct access to pixie dust. Straight from the source, apparently. Somewhere deep in the Amazon rainforest."

"You have got to be kidding me." Does he know how big the Amazon rainforest is? I wipe a frustrated hand down my face. "At least we have supplies."

"Yup. Kinda hoping we find some evidence of them or something."

I nod. I'll figure something out. "So, dish the dirt." He's not getting away with not telling me about his life.

"I've had a few girlfriends over the years. I once had a boyfriend, too. But nothing's stuck." He shrugs. "Guess none of them were meant to be."

"What about your career? Friends? Education? Places you've visited? C'mon, Aki . . . Share! It's what siblings do."

He chuckles and then sighs. "Fine, okay." He links his arm through mine, like he so often does, and regales me with his life's story while we look for evidence of pixies.

"I grew up in the Japanese Witch Coven in Shinjuku, Tokyo. They were . . . nice. Hard at times, but loving overall. I was never very good at school. I kept getting into trouble. All I wanted to do was practise my magic, but the Coven never allowed it. Said it was too dangerous." He sighs. "So I left when I was sixteen and never looked back.

"Spent some time alone in the mountains to practise my death magic, so I didn't harm any people, and eventually got good. Really good. Now I can take life at will, give it form, and use it to attack people."

"Like a living death shadow?" Kind of reminds me of the night I died. I shudder.

"Yeah . . . You've created one before?"

I nod, not sharing the story.

"So you're powerful then." He rubs his chin in thought. "Really powerful."

"I can't do it at will or anything. It was just a spur-of-the-moment thing."

He shrugs. "Shows you can, though. We just need to tap into those powers."

"Stop turning the conversation back onto me! I want to know about you. What happened after that?"

He shrugs but looks away. "I went back to Tokyo, apologized to the Witch Coven who raised me, and got a regular job. It's been pretty normal for me since then." He coughs.

"Well, until I hijacked my lost twin sister's teleporting crystal and learned I'm related to the Fifth Horseman of the Apocalypse, then became an ambassador for an important political embassy created for peace."

I laugh softly, realizing his life has been crazy over the past couple of weeks. "Yeah, sorry about that."

"Don't be. I could have left. You gave me the option."

"So, do you really think I could learn to access my death magic at will?"

Aki turns to me with a glare. "Yes." He stops us dead. "In fact, this is the perfect place to practise. We could not be farther away from other people."

"R-Right here? Right now?"

He dumps our backpacks onto the forest floor and looks at me with a smile. "Yes."

"Okay." I take a deep breath. "Connie suggested that I use a memory of a time I was threatened."

Aki bobs his head side to side. "That could work."

"Okay, let's try it." I can do this. Totally. For once, I'm not gonna fail. I bring the memory of my death to the forefront of my mind. It's honestly something I try not to think about, but today, I need to think about it. I need to let its fear flow through me. "Okay, c'mon, Magic."

The cold alleyway, the assassin's voice searing a permanent tattoo onto my brain, the fear pumping through my veins like ice. He shoots me. I flop to the ground and feel the life flare out of me like a volcano erupting its life onto the ground.

My hands tremble as my breathing hitches and something cold snakes around my hands.

"Yes!" Aki yells. "That's it! Right there!"

My eyes snap open and catch onto the dark mist swirling around my arms like poison clouds. "I did it."

"Okay," Aki says, "do you know how to get rid of it?"

I switch into my male form and smirk. "Perks of being me."

34

We walk for hours, well until sundown, and find no evidence of magic usage, pixie homes, or anyone else. This place is a barren forest. Empty of everything except the animals that belong here. So eventually we set up camp in a small area where we can hang hammocks from the trees to keep us off the forest floor.

It doesn't get cold at night here, so we don't bother with a large fire—just enough to cook some of our supplies with. And by supplies, I mean dried meat, canned vegetables, and oven-able potatoes that I'm pretty sure weren't okay.

Goddess, I miss Arrie's cooking.

My phone battery died sometime during the day, so I have no way to contact the team. In an emergency I can just go home, but I don't want to do that yet. I might be tired, but I want to see this mission through.

Though, given that I only have six blood vials left, I might have to go home for a pit stop eventually.

The night is filled with noises, dark as pitch because of the canopy covering any light, and Aki's snores mean I get not a damn wink before morning lights our way again.

For fuck's sake, I'm exhausted.

I am not Connie. I need sleep.

Aki, sensing my mood, asks what the matter is, but I'm grouchy as hell and don't answer him. It's only when he looks at me with that hurt expression that I soften and apologize.

"Sorry. I slept terribly."

"Really?" He frowns. "I slept just fine."

Yeah, I know. I nearly snap at him again, but there's no point. It's not his fault. "Can you remember anything else about where we're going? Anything at all?" I really don't feel like wandering the Amazon jungle for the next week.

Honestly sounds like a vacation planned by hell itself.

"Maybe . . . I don't know."

"Even if it seems pointless, it might not be."

He nods. "Okay. Well, he said something about underground tunnels."

"Underground tunnels?" Great, now I have to find an opening to something that's supposed to be hidden. What kind of shitty luck do I have? Do I have a sign on my cosmic back saying 'please, kick me continuously'? "Entrance?"

He shakes his head.

Goddess, damn it.

There must be some way to track pixies. Something to tell if they're nearby. If I had my earth magic unlocked, I could probably sense them. But all I have is air, water, and fire. None of which helps me now.

I know a few Fae tracking spells, but I'm not sure I have the right ingredients nearby. And I'm also not sure how to track specifically for pixies.

None of my enhanced senses in either form pick up anything weirder than jungle life, so I don't think they're nearby.

I'm going to have to figure out that tracking spell.

"Magic, maybe we should head ba—"

I hold up a finger to silence him. "Shh. Thinking."

We keep walking, and my mind keeps spinning. Trying to figure out a way to do a tracking spell and tailor it to pixies. Maybe an intention rune? I do know what pixies look like. If I knew their magical signature, I could use that with a detection rune, but I don't. Lower supes are less researched, less written about.

Guess I'll have to try an intention rune.

A bit of a shot in the dark, but oh well. It's the best I've got.

"I'm going to need some teedle weed, basal flower, and Witch's brew."

"Huh?" He looks puzzled, so I explain my plan.

"Wow. You can do that?"

"Not sure, but I'm going to try."

"Okay, well I know how to make Witch's brew, so I'll do that bit."

Right. Now I just need to find the other three plants, which I'm almost certain don't grow in the Amazon. I have some ingredients in a stash Nine gave me, but I haven't rifled through them yet. He said they're the basics.

At least teedle weed is pretty basic, so he might have included that.

Yanking my backpack off my back, I lift out the white container and flip the lid. There's more packed into here than I expected—like an herbalist's collection, they're all shoved into small bags and pots, some flowers suspended in small vials of water attached to their stems, and others are just seeds lying about.

I don't even know what they all are.

But one of the first bags I pull out is teedle weed.

"Thank the goddess for Nine."

"I've made the Witch's brew!" Aki shouts from where we settled down for lunch.

It's a brown sludge that doesn't look very appetizing, but thankfully I'm not drinking it.

"Thank you." I wave a hand at him. "I'll be right there."

Basal flowers . . . Basal flowers . . .

They're key to tracking spells, as they act like sniffer dogs, searching for their target. But is there something else I can use instead? Maybe a different plant?

What else did Nine provide?

Plants, weeds, seeds, flowers, and . . . a basal bulb. Wow. I'm surprised he had one just lying around. Here's hoping it'll work the same.

"Okay, Aki, I need you to dunk these ingredients in the Witch's brew for me."

He grabs the ingredients in my hands and places them in the sludge-filled bowl and looks to me expectantly.

Okay, now I need to draw three different runes: one for intention, one to bind the intention to the basal bulb, and one to connect the teedle weed so everything stays stable. Once that's done, I use an incantation I learned from one of my study sessions, but I recite it in Japanese. It basically forms a protective bubble around the rune and ingredients and slowly siphons my energy through, giving the magic some juice.

I pick up the bowl and watch it light up, magic sparking off it every which way. But with some reconfiguring of my intentions—an entrance to the pixie's lair—it sparks and fizzes once more before settling its light in one direction.

West.

"West it is," Aki confirms as he picks up our things and heads in that direction. "Neat spell, by the way."

"Thanks."

We follow the damn sparkling bowl for hours. My feet hurt, my arms ache, and my stomach is growling. "I need a break." The magic I'm using is exhausting, and we're nowhere near a leyline to recharge.

"Okay, but maybe stop the spell while we're resting?"

"Yeah, that's probably for the best." I stop right where I'm walking and sit on my backpack, the bowl at my feet. I stop siphoning my energy through the protective bubble and catch my breath. "Fuck . . . this . . . shit."

Aki laughs. "So, immortality does not cure all, hmm?"

"Oh, fuck off." I shove him to the floor and watch him shoot straight back up, brushing any critters and leaves and forest debris off his body. "Scared?"

He shivers. "Not a fan of bugs."

Now it's my turn to laugh. "But you're here in the Amazon with me?"

He shrugs. "Thought you might need a hand, and the others seemed busy. Besides, it's been nice getting to know you better, even if you are a grouch when you're tired and hungry."

"Who isn't?"

"Good point."

A rustling of leaves and faint footsteps my Shifter hearing can just pick up has me swiveling my head to the east.

"What's that?"

Aki guards himself, a fighting stance at the ready, and looks in the direction I'm pointing.

"Over there."

He gathers a familiar-looking ball of black magic in his joined palms and takes a deep breath. "I got this."

"We don't even know what this is," I hiss, frustration lacing my words. "It might not be an enemy."

Apparently, I spoke too soon, because something ethereal, white, glowing, and beautiful bounds toward us at the speed of light, knocking Aki to the forest floor and unconscious before I can even stand.

Large white wings shoot out of its back, and I'm floored. "An Angel?"

35

"You're an . . . Angel," I point out, shock keeping me rooted to the floor. "I didn't think you existed anymore."

She puffs out a breath and crosses her arms over her very naked torso. "Yes, well, things aren't always what they seem." Her voice is raspy and harsh, but she seems nonthreatening in her stance.

"Are you going to kill me?"

"Why bother? It's not like I can anyway, right?"

I nod. "Right." So, err . . . what now? "What are you doing here?" I gesture to the forest. "In the Amazon?"

She shrugs. "Got a good gig protecting the pixie population, and I stay out of the world's way." She eyes me up and down. "What are you doing here?"

"Looking for the pixies." I nod to Aki, who's still lying unconscious on the floor. "With my brother."

She winces slightly. "Ah, sorry about that. But that's death magic, gifted to him by an ancient bloodline, I assume."

"Yeah, we're Angel-descended Witches. Or, at least, I was, when I was mortal." She looks at me confused for a moment. "It's complicated."

"I can only imagine." She huffs a laugh before picking Aki up and hauling him over her chest. "You Horsemen are all so . . . complicated."

She can say that again.

"You coming?" She turns to walk west.

"Where?"

"To the pixies?"

I scramble to keep up, leaving the spell behind because it's not like I need it or anyone else can use it. "You're going to help? But why?"

"Because if I don't, you'll probably kill me. And because I can't really get rid of you. You kinda rule the world."

I flinch. What did the team do to this Angel? "I have no intention of hurting anyone. Especially not an Angel. I really do come in peace." Ugh. Could I be anymore cliché?

"The Horsemen of the Apocalypse never come in peace."

"Well, this one does. Since I'm the Horseman of Magic and all, I figured maybe I should respect the magic the world already has."

She laughs under her breath. "Yeah right." She looks behind her with a scowl. "Just try to keep up."

I shift into my female form so I can keep up easier, and when she next turns around, she looks at me bewildered for a moment before shrugging and turning back around.

Wow. No questions. That's a first.

"So, where are the pixies?"

"I'd prefer not to give that information out, if that's okay. Just follow me, and I'll take you to them."

"Okay." What the hell; I only need to chat with them, anyway. "How many are there?"

"A few hundred thousand, at best."

That's it? That's so few for a whole species. The Fae really have run them into the ground, haven't they?

"Surprised?"

"A little." I walk next to her, consciously checking on Aki now and then. "I knew they'd become endangered because of the Fae hunting them for their dust, but I didn't know how bad it was."

The angel nods. "Yeah, it's pretty bad. They have to run to a new base every time someone finds them. They're exhausted." She looks pointedly at me, expecting something.

"You want me to fix it?"

"Yeah, I do." She stops walking and faces me. "This is your job. You so-called Horsemen work toward peace, but all you really do is leave the world to its own devices so long as no wars are raging. That's not peace. That's just . . . not awful." She looks me in the eye. "And now look at you. Back into the fray because of yet another war."

"For an angel, you're pretty good at sarcasm."

"I can hide the wings and stop the glowing, if I want. So I often use it to hang with regular people whenever I can." She shrugs. "Unextraordinary people are some of the best I know."

I do not miss the snide in her voice. "Okay. Ouch."

"Just do your job, and I won't maim you."

"Pfft. Come on and try, Glowy."

She laughs, her resolve cracking for just a moment. "Glowy?"

"Yeah, well, you never introduced yourself, so I've nicknamed ya Glowy. Deal with it." I look around, not noticing a reason as to why we've stopped. "My name's Magic. That's Aki. And where are the pixies?"

Please don't let this have been a wild goose chase.

She snorts. "Through the vines on your right. Keep going straight, and you'll hit a wall. State your name and your business. If they let you in, they'll hear you out." She looks to Aki. "Would you like your brother back? I can keep him safe out here if you'd prefer?"

I weigh up my options, but there's no way in hell I'm leaving Aki to this murdering angelic psychopath. "I'll take my brother back, thank you very much." I hold out my arms, and she drops him into them without a semblance of grace.

Turning around, I take a deep breath and walk through the vines, trying not to think too hard about how many creepy crawlies are living in them.

Focus, Magic. Focus.

One more deep breath, and I keep going straight, noticing that I've somehow entered a cave and that I have no light to see by. Thank the goddess for night vision.

Aki's in my arms, still unconscious, but I manage to prevent any bumps to his head on the walls, only scraping his feet a teenie bit. He may have lost a shoe somewhere back there.

Oh well, he can grab it on the way out.

The moment we can, we're teleporting the fuck outta here. I really don't like the jungle.

The wall appears in no time, and I knock. A hollow echo knocks back. "I'm here to talk to the pixie race about potentially helping them relocate to somewhere not on Earth."

Hundreds of tiny whispers flood through the cave system, bouncing off the walls. But I can't make any of it out. Eventually, a tiny voice whispers, "Okay. You can come in."

The rock wall slides to the right, and I step through into a child's paradise. Seriously, Disney couldn't even make this shit up. Underground roots permeate the entire cave, and in every nook and cranny of them, little golden pixies have made small homes.

Pixie dust flies freely, and I find my nose itching, but I'm otherwise unaffected by it.

"Your home is beautiful."

A small pixie lands on my arm and looks me dead in the eye, his red eyes and sharp teeth looking as menacing as ever. "You are welcome here, Horseman, but only so long as you tell no one of our location."

I bow. "You have my word."

"Then you may meet Uzuki. Our leader."

"That's great. Thank you." I look to Aki and smile. "You don't happen to have somewhere safe I can leave my brother, do you? I did not trust Glowy out there." I nod back to the cave entrance.

The pixie does what I think is a smile, but he gestures to the small group of pixies who are busy making a human-sized cot for me to lay Aki on.

"Thank you," I whisper, remembering that their hearing is sensitive and you're supposed to whisper. "This is much appreciated."

After I lay Aki down, I follow the pixie with the red eyes and mean stare to a small hole in the wall at the end of the one of the cave tunnels I have to crouch to fit into.

"You must be Uzuki," I whisper, trying my best to bow in such small confines. "Thank you so much for meeting me."

A larger-than-average pixie, just slightly larger than male-me's forearm, steps out of the darkness and lights up the crevice like a fairylight, a short and stuffy smile on his face. "It's a pleasure, Horseman of Magic." He gets straight to the point. "I hear you want to help us?"

"Yes. I can offer you safe passage to *Sheruta,* our homeland. It's separate from Earth. You won't be hunted there."

"And in return for such generosity? I assume you want our allegiance in the upcoming war with the Fae, SC, and rogue Vampire faction?"

"You're awfully up to date for a pixie," I huff.

"We need to be. It's how we stay alive down here."

"Fair. I'm so sorry my fellow Horsemen haven't helped you sooner. But I'm here now, and I want to help, allegiance or not." I can't leave them like this, cowering for their lives. I'm sure we can find somewhere for them to call their own on *Sheruta.* "If you'll let me, of course."

"We have no room for pride in these troubled times."

"I guess not."

"Do you have a plan on how to transport us to your . . . realm?"

A plan. Right. Since I came up with the relocation offer on the fly, no, I don't. But they don't know that. I can't create portals, I don't have enough crystals, so they'll have to get to the main portal. But that'll be dangerous.

"Yeah, yeah I do." I look around. "You don't happen to have a plasma energy socket anywhere around, do you?" I hold up my dead holocaller in an eager smile.

Uzuki nods to the pixie who led me here with a smile. "Show Magic where she can plug that thing in and make her plans. We're with her." He turns to the few pixies around him and yells, "Tell everyone to get ready to fly out. We're moving tonight."

Pixies charge forth, getting ready, making plans, and something else blooms in the caverns that wasn't present when I entered. Hope.

36

Once my holophone is charged up enough, I dial the only person I trust to escort hundreds of thousands of pixies from Brazil to Colorado safely.

"Arrie?"

His gruff hello tells me it's the middle of the night there.

"Sorry, is it late?"

He grumbles something, then yawns. "Three am, but it's okay." His holodisplay looks tired, but he's awake, and that's all I need. "What do you need?"

"You."

His smile lights up the call. "Really?"

"Yup. Hundreds of pixies, and there's only one way to transport them to *Sheruta*. So I need a pixie escort I can trust."

He sighs. "You want me to babysit a species for you?"

The pixie from earlier huffed. "We do not need babysitting, War." His arms cross over his chest.

"Arrie, stop being an ass. I'm trying to do politics over here."

"Right, sorry. But you did wake me up."

"Yeaaah, sorry about that. I don't really understand how the time difference works across realms."

"Do yourself a favor," he replies, "and do not ask for an explanation from Nine."

I giggle, glad we're at the joking phase of our new . . . friendship. "Duly noted." I sigh. "Look, I know it's late, but how quickly can you get here?"

"I can be in Manaus in a few moments. But I'll need an escort to where you are."

"Yeaaah, even I don't know where I am."

"You don't know where you . . . Then how am I supposed to find you?"

"We'll have to meet you near Manaus somewhere."

The pixie chimes in, "We can get to River Negro through these tunnels. It comes out somewhere near Santa Maria."

"I can meet you there," Arrie grumbles. "I'll leave now." He ends the call, and I wince.

"I feel awful for waking him up."

"Well, he's a friendly one."

"Yeah, sorry about him. He's a bit of a grumpy gill. But he's the best fighter we have. If anyone can escort you to Colorado safely, it's him."

"If you say so." He hops back onto my arm as we make our way back to Uzuki to relay the plan. "So," I finalize, "if we can get to Santa Maria safely, then Arrie will take you the rest of the way."

A bright glowing light I recognize and shiver at lights up the back of me, and I turn with an uneasy smile. "Glowy, hi."

"Magic." She nods her head at me. "You're really escorting them out of here?"

"Yup." I look smugly at her. "And Arrie is escorting them from Santa Maria to Colorado, where the main portal to *Sheruta* is."

She looks troubled, and she spins on her heels and storms away. Well, she tries. She's a bit tall for the cave system.

"Is she okay?"

The pixie on my arm hums and laughs. "I don't think she's particularly keen to reacquaint herself with the person who destroyed most of her kind."

Right, the ancient war. The Horsemen killed most of the Demons and Angels so they'd stop preying on the other supernaturals. Seems a bit drastic, if you ask me. But then, I wasn't there.

I didn't exist yet.

Jesus Christ, my lovers are old. Talk about an age-gap romance. Oh well, age gaps are pretty on-trend right now, anyway.

I shake that thought from my head. Focus, Magic, focus. Now is not the time.

"Magic!" a familiar voice calls from the nearby tunnel.

"I'm down here, Aki. Come hear my plan."

He bounds toward my voice with a smile. "You found the pixies!"

"Well, we found the angel guarding the pixies, and then she beat me up—a lot—and eventually gave in and took me straight here."

"Ah." He gestures to my female body, which has sustained no damage, with a question. "You don't look beaten up . . ."

"You should see my male body. I ran out of Fae magic, and since we're nowhere near a leyline"—probably one reason the pixies settled here—"I'm exhausted." More than exhausted, actually, but it's not important right now.

"So, what's the plan?"

I tell Aki the plan, and he seems to approve, though he's a little worried about my exhaustion, which is apparently obvious to see.

"Maybe take a break?"

"No time for that. We need to meet Arrie in Santa Maria as soon as possible." I sigh, looking at the large number of pixies that have to travel a few miles. "I wish I could scout ahead and find Arrie and bring him back to the tunnel entrance on that side, but I can't leave them undefended."

That brilliant white glowing light is back, and this time, it comes with a pissed-off angel. "They are not undefended. Nor will they ever be. Nor do they need the Horseman of War to help them relocate." Her arms are crossed over her chest as she huffs at me and spits Arrie's name.

"Well, I wanted to be sure. Nothing wrong with a little backup." She looks like she disagrees with that statement, but I don't give her the chance to argue. "Fine," I say in place of whatever foul thing was about to come out of her mouth, "you and Aki can lead the pixies out. I'll scout ahead, make sure it's safe, and find Arrie so we don't have to wait around in an unsafe location."

She nods sternly and turns her back to me, her white glow diminishing ever so slightly because I can now look at her without getting eyestrain.

Getting her to work with Arrie is going to be a pain in the ass, isn't it?

37

Three lefts, two rights, another left, and I should be a few meters from the Santa Maria entrance. Apparently. So Uzuki says. But for all I know, he's led me on a wild goose chase for shits and giggles.

And believe me, these tunnels are not made for regular sized people. If I wasn't so drained in my male form, I would shift into a cat or something to make this easier. But alas, no can do.

I'm just about to turn the last left when I come to an abrupt halt. There's a river up ahead that's rushing faster than I can probably swim, even as a Vampire, but the exit is on the other side. I can see daylight throbbing through the small cat flap-like hole.

"Shit."

There's no room between the river and cave tunnel ceiling for me to fly, so I'm going to have to swim through.

If I die doing this, I'm so blaming Arrie.

It isn't really his fault, but I'm blaming him, anyway. He fucking deserves it.

The water is cold enough to make me scream when I dip my feet in, and shock holds my body hostage for a moment. Fuck. I won't make it across this without turning into an icicle.

And either way, Aki and the angel won't make it across. The pixies can probably fit in the gap between the water and ceiling, so they'll be fine. But I do rather need my brother alive. And I guess I need the stupid angel, too.

An idea flicks to mind, but I doubt myself. I've only done this once before, and not on this level. But it was a similar situation. I was puzzled. I needed a solution. Bonus: no Fae magic needed.

I scuttle away from the water's edge, place a hand on the ground, and feel for the water's energy. Just like with the air. After a few frustrating moments, I find it, but it's like catching flies with your bare hands. It's so slippery.

"C'mon, Magic . . ."

Just when I'm about to scream from frustration, I catch the water's energy and give it a good yank.

The river stops still.

Good. Now, what happens when I pull the energy apart?

The river slowly separates and forms a path along the riverbed.

Wow. This is like some Moses shit right here.

I can't keep it like this though, so I'm going to have to come back once I've found Arrie—who really should have given me a better meeting place.

Santa Maria is a municipality, not a city. A fact that becomes clear the moment I step out of the hole and into a park surrounded by a city.

"A city?" I grumble, "For fuck's sake."

"Gonna grumble the entire time, Killer?" Arrie says from somewhere behind me.

I jump out of my skin, screeching loud enough to wake the neighborhood. "Jesus fucking Christ, asshole!" I throw a fireball his way, but he just dodges, and I quickly put it out before it burns the grass. "What the fuck were you thinking?"

He laughs.

Arrie actually laughs.

And the sound delights me so much a tear trickles down my face as I stand there dumbfounded before my senses return. I run at Arrie, wrap my arms around his neck, and bury my nose in the crook of his neck, his pine needle scent washing through me. But then everything he's said and done rushes at me, and I jump away. "Sorry."

But damn it's good to have a member of the team by my side once more. Even if only momentarily.

"It's . . . okay." He sounds surprised, like he doesn't know what to do with me now. Which is probably how he feels, actually. "Where are they?"

I point behind me, to the hole in the base of a tree. "Through there. I'll need to help them cross the river below."

He walks to the hole, and watching him trying to fit through it is comical. Seriously, a seven-foot, made-of-muscle moron trying to squeeze through a hole that comes to my knee in height and is barely wider than me.

"Come on, big guy, you can do it."

He grumbles something under his breath. But after some wiggling and repositioning, he manages to fit through the hole and disappears beyond. "Wow. It's tiny in here," he echoes from below.

"Yeah," I say as I crouch through after him. "It really fucking is." I sit next to him on the other side, the river racing in front of us. "They're a few miles away."

"Sure." He leans against the dirt wall behind him, ducking his head.

Now there's nothing to do but wait. Alone. With Arrie. In silence, because anyone can hear us up top.

Great.

The need to break the silence with any sort of sound pinwheels through me, spinning and spinning and spinning until it fires out of control and sparks fly through my mind in the form of thoughts no one should really be thinking.

"Magic?" Arrie whispers. "I . . ." He hesitates. "I'm sorry."

I shrug and avoid his icy stare, full of expectations I'm not willing to fulfill. "It's—"

"Don't say it." He shakes his head. "It's not okay, Killer."

The familiar use of my old nickname whispered from his lips makes me shudder, and I can't hold back the tilt my lips curl into when they attempt to smile. "No, it's not." I finally lift my gaze from the floor and pierce his eyes with everything he's made me feel over the last few weeks: pain, confusion, frustration, anger, guilt, embarrassment . . .

The mask Arrie usually wears—the stone face he never sheds—melts like ice in the desert. His eyes water, tears threatening to spill over the edges, as a pained grimace slices through his face like a knife. And I watch as frustration ebbs and flows through him in equal measure.

Eventually, he swipes the tears away.

"You can talk to me, you know," I whisper.

He looks wide-eyed at me in surprise.

"I know there's more going on than just wanting to be friends." In truth, I don't think he wants to just be friends, but I don't mention that now. "I know there's something you're not saying. I won't force it out of you, though I'm sure I'd get great satisfaction from trying. But you can tell me, if you want."

I dodge his gaze again, but he forces my chin up and my gaze back to his with a harsh yet gentle finger. His eyes flit to my lips with a needy breath and wide eyes.

I lick my lips, my throat dry and my voice vanishing.

"I'm not . . . ready."

To tell me the truth or to kiss me?

Both?

"Maybe one day," he whispers as he leans forward and rests his forehead against mine. "One day . . ." More tears track down his face, but this time, he lets them be. A groan escapes his voice when he opens his lips next, but instead of pulling away and replacing his stone mask, his lips brush mine in the gentlest of touches that shoot sparks through me.

"Hey," I whisper, "we're immortal. We literally have all the time in the world."

He chuckles at that, and a sound of fluttering wings and an annoying female voice barking orders breaks the moment.

Just as they round the corner, the angel in the lead, Arrie swears under his breath in Norse. He grabs my wrist and yanks me into his arms. "What the fuck is she doing here?"

"Oh, so you're familiar?" He gives me an incredulous look. "Well, Glowy has been guarding the pixies, so you're helping her transport them safely."

"No I am fucking not." His arms curl across his chest as he stares daggers at me.

"Listen, asshole." I jab a finger into chest. "I do not have time for your attitude. It'll only be for a few hours." I do my best at begging him with my eyes.

And eventually—though it takes longer than I'm going to admit—he sighs and scrapes a hand through that luscious white hair. "Fine. But only because you asked."

I give myself a mental fist bump and crouch to the floor a few feet from the water's edge and repeat the same Moses shit from earlier.

I hear Arrie gasping in awe behind me, and I think another fist bump is in order. Maybe two. Who knows? I am on a roll tonight.

The angel leads the charge but stops dead in front of Arrie, and for a moment, I'm worried I'll have to break them up. Somehow. But she just glares at him and moves on, shoving him out of the way. The pixies follow her, and when we get to the end of the line, Aki is bringing up the rear.

"Hey, Magic." He smiles weakly at me, and it's clear he's exhausted.

"Hey." I clap him on the shoulder. "Don't worry," I whisper, "we're gonna rest up in a hotel soon. Preferably somewhere on a leyline."

"I'll look up a leyline map and grab a hotel for us."

I eye him gratefully. "Use this." I throw the payment chip at him after digging it out of my backpack's front pocket. "No more paying for shit."

38

It takes some doing to prepare Arrie for flight; I have to make him a flight charm—well, I make six, just to be safe—before sending them on their way. They didn't seem happy to be working together, but hopefully it'll be alright.

We also gave the pixies the go ahead to set up anywhere they want in *Sheruta,* so long as they work alongside the *Sheruta* Council. Which we assured them is nothing like the Supernatural Council.

"Hope they'll be alright," I whisper as we hop onto a train toward the nearest city on a leyline.

"I'm sure they will be." He places a gentle hand on my shoulder as he rests his head on the train window. "We should rest. It'll take a couple of hours to get there."

We agreed to take a couple of days to recuperate and replenish, and then we're heading to the Witches in South Africa. I shudder at the thought. I don't wanna play their dumb game. Not again.

We're there to find the fairies. Nothing else.

I stay awake through the night so Aki can sleep, and we eventually arrive at our hotel just as dawn breaks and I'm about to collapse from exhaustion.

"Go rest up." He practically shoves me through my hotel room door before heading off to his own down the hallway.

The bed beckons me home, and I flop down and lose myself in the soft sheets, the cool, crisp pillows, the snuggly duvet, and the blackout option I blink the windows to. I have just enough sense to shift into my male form before falling asleep.

Now I can recharge mostly in my sleep.

Yay for sleep mode.

A banging on my door wakes me up somewhere in the future, and I grumble to my feet and sweep it open with a growl. "What do you want?"

"Err . . . Magic?" Aki asks. "I've been trying to get in here all day!"

"Huh?"

He laughs as he barges in. "You've been asleep for eighteen hours!"

"Whaaa?" I flick the window back to normal and blink in the harsh daylight blazing into my retinas. I hiss and dim them to a more appropriate level.

"You must be starving? Wanna get dinner downstairs in the hotel restaurant?"

I nod, sleep still clouding my brain. "Shower. Food." I say each with a finger count, forcing the order of importance.

"Okay. I'll meet you down there. It's on floor five."

"Mmmhmmm." I zombie walk to the bathroom, where I mechanically step into the shower and wash two bodies, get out and dry two bodies, pee twice, and then clothe, style, and present two bodies. "This shit takes way too long," I mumble as the process wakes me up and my stomach forces me out of the door.

Turns out it's nearly sunset. And as I shove a forkful of whatever Aki ordered for me, I formulate a new plan. "We should leave as soon as possible." I sigh. "Not that I want to."

Aki looks at me in question. "They really hate you that much?"

I grimace. "I kinda air-blasted the air Witch last time I was there, got me, Dea, and Nine arrested, and then had to be rescued by Connie and Arrie, who killed a few of their soldiers in the process." I do not mention it's Arrie, specifically, who killed them. He suffers enough without my twin brother thinking he's evil.

Ugh. No, Magic. He hasn't suffered enough yet.

I'm gonna make him grovel hard enough he'll beg to be let up off his knees.

Aki winces. "That's . . . not so great."

I shake my head. "But they agreed to the embassy idea, so they can't completely hate us." A few more bites of what I later realize are tacos, and my male stomach is full. "They didn't try to kill me, at least." I shrug as I change into my female form, ready to fill up stomach number two.

"So, are you planning on making up with them?"

"I'll try, but I doubt it'll work." I meet Aki's purple eyes with a questioning gaze. "What's your relationship with them like?"

I didn't really see him having a friendly relationship with them back on *Sheruta*, but they didn't ignore him. They were civil.

"We're . . . friendly, I guess." He shrugs. "They don't really know me that well." Finishing his last bite, he coughs and stares at me. "What? I tried to stay off everybody's radar."

Makes sense. He wouldn't want anyone knowing about our death magic. Or our Angel-descended Witch magic. That could be a disaster.

"Okay, well, we need to leave. South Africa is five hours ahead of us right now, so it's getting late there."

We finish up dinner, gather our backpacks, check out of the hotel, and find an empty alley to teleport to South African from. A rush of fresh air, the scent of soil and trees, and the taste of open plains greet me, forcing a smile from my otherwise grim lips.

"Have you considered that maybe they'll be more receptive to your male form?"

Errr . . . "Right, yeah, probably." I shift forms, and while the beauty of my surroundings still brings me peace, it's different somehow. "Huh." It no longer feels like I'm breathing in the earth; it's just a pretty background.

Must be a Witch thing.

"Come on." Aki grabs my arm and yanks me down the side path that leads to the same entrance we used not a few months ago.

Déjà vu blares warning sirens through my mind, but I ignore them. It'll be okay. I can do this.

Just as we pass the waterfall and enter the cave beyond, something moves in the dark. I can sense it.

"Aki!" I yell. "Look out!"

A Witch storms toward us and grabs Aki by the scruff of the neck and lifts him off the ground. "You are not welcome here, Horseman of Magic."

"Oh, so you'll let Arrie back." I roll my eyes, hands on my cocked hip. "But I'm the problem."

"Arrie's magic is a plague, even to himself. We know this." He steps into the light, and I recognize him from before. The one with scars covering most of his face. "You caused the problem."

"Yeah, well, I cause a lot of problems, so you'll have to get to the back of the queue and wait your turn to air your grievances."

The male Witch stands in silence, waiting for my next move.

I sigh. "Look, I don't really want to be here either, but in case you haven't noticed, we have a war on our hands. A war that'll affect you lot, eventually."

"We're not even here for you," Aki chimes in. "We're here to visit the fairies."

The man's eyes widen. "How did you . . .?"

Aki tries to shrug, but he doesn't succeed. Instead, he ends up flopping like a fish on a hook out of water (I would have laughed if the situation didn't demand my focus). "Discovered them once when I was a child after I'd walked off when visiting with Nigel."

"You know Nigel?" the man asked, his shoulders relaxing.

I look to Aki, who nods his approval, and says, "He's our godfather."

"Our?" His face scrunches in confusion. "You two are related?"

"We're twins."

The man drops Aki to the dusty floor immediately and stands there, silently heaving slow breaths. "You're Asuka and Kame's children . . ."

39

Both Aki and I stare in disbelief at the man.

"You knew our parents?" I ask.

The man nods. "We knew where all the Angel-descended Witches were." He sighs and runs a hand down his face. "We didn't know there were any left." He spins on his heals and stalks off. "Follow!"

We stay on his heel, keeping up, though I occasionally have to tug Aki along as he falls behind. The snail. And as we enter the central cave, the witchlights creating a soft glow every few meters, I'm reminded of how much I really do love it here.

"Come along," the Witch says. "I'm taking you to the seer Witch."

"Err . . . why?" What the fuck can she do to help right now?

"Because she knows all."

"That's not really how seer magic works, but sure," I mumble.

We continue following him, Aki still struggling to keep up with the large man's pace, until we eventually come to a small home on the corner of the large cave. It's covered in leaves, flowers, and even has a small tree growing next to it.

"Please," he says, "stay here until called upon." He walks up the short garden path and knocks on the door.

We all wait with bated breath as she answers the door, a nightgown donning her body as a robe is wrapped around her shoulders. "What could you possibly want at this hour, Maxus?"

She sounds exhausted, and when two topless older men step up behind her, I realize why. We have interrupted something. Oops.

"I apologize, ma'am, but I have learned of some crucial information I think you'll be interested in." He gestures to us.

I give a little wave, hoping she'll remain as kind as she usually is to me. "Sorry for interrupting your night." I bow. "We're here to—"

"They're here for something unrelated, but it's important, so I thought . . ."

She sighs and stands aside, her men following suit. "Come on in then."

We all shuffle inside the small home. Witchlights hover at various intervals, illuminating the cluttered features, the dust-gathering items shoved onto every nearby surface as though they hold some sort of significance to the seer Witch.

"Make yourselves at home," she says. "We'll just be a moment." She and the two men trot off—probably to get dressed—and I resist the urge to use my Vampire hearing to listen to their conversation.

She has two men. Are they all together, like me and the team?

Aki and I sit on the few stools dotted around the room that are shaped into various animals. I sit on an elephant, while Aki takes the monkey. Maxus remains standing. A scowl upon his scarred face.

When she comes back, the men aren't with her, but she carries a pot of tea and four cups. Placing everything on the table, she pours out four cups of what smells like peppermint tea and sits on the couch, sighing after her first sip. "Help yourself." She gestures to the filled cups.

We all grab one, except Maxus, who clears his throat.

He opens his mouth then closes it again, opens, closes. It goes on like that at clunky intervals for a few minutes until the seer Witch says, "Just spit it out, Maxus."

"They're Angel-descended Witches. Ma'am." He lowers his gaze from her accusing eyes and fixes them firmly on the floor.

She rolls her eyes—a right sassy grandma, this one—and says, "Well, of course they are." She looks at me, then at Aki, and smiles. "I've known what you two are for quite some time. I left you alone because I figured if you needed someone or the Coven, you'd come to us."

Maxus stares at her in horror. "But, Ma'am, surely you should have said something—"

"There was nothing I *should* have done, Maxus. I do not share every piece of seer knowledge with the Coven, as you well know." They share a pointed look. "Besides, the Coven Council already knew. Nigel informed them."

"Wait," Aki interrupts, "Nigel told you?"

She nods. "You were there during that visit, I believe. The same visit that encourages your visit today."

Aki's eyes widen, understanding dawning behind his features. Filling in the gaps in our shared splotchy past. "I see." His voice threatens to break, his eyes closed.

I reach out and grab his hand. "It's okay. Nigel was just doing his best."

The seer Witch looks to our joined hands and smiles. "It's so lovely to see you both together again. Nigel informed us so we were kept in the loop, but he made sure to explain that he wanted you left alone. Which the Coven Council thought was for the best."

"They could have killed entire covens!" Maxus shouted, his frustration finally boiling over into anger. "They were just children with an enormous power, left in the hands of random coven families—"

She stands to her feet and scowls at him, a finger pointed at him in anger. "You think we didn't monitor them? That we left them unattended? Do you have no trust in your Coven Council, Maxus? We are, after all, the reason you are alive."

Maxus' face shines guilt through the night's witchlight. "Right. Of course, Amalie. I am sorry." He turns to face us, his scowl softening and a gentle smile returning. "Amalie will be able to answer your questions." He leaves, clicking the door shut behind him.

"Now," Amalie says, "what is it you came to talk about? I assume it's important if you are here, Horseman." She raises her eyebrows in my direction while drinking her tea. "After all, you did cause quite the turmoil when you were here last."

"I . . ." I take a deep breath. "I am so sorry." I bow deeply. "I should not have lost my temper, and I should not have caused any harm to your people."

"Yes, we lost seven Witches at the hands of the Horsemen of War that night. Many of their families are not fans of yours."

"I understand." I don't know what else to say. Will she kick us out before we've had a chance to—?

"But, that being said, you are an important person, and I will hear you out nonetheless." She looks to me, puts her cup of tea down, and adorns what I think might be her business face. "What can we do for you, Horseman of Magic?"

Hearing my title from the mouth of such an important person sends shivers down my spine. "The fairies."

"Ah, I see. You're hoping to get lower supernaturals on your side."

I nod. "Hopefully."

Aki steps in. "And I know they're here. Safe."

"Please," I say, "we mean them no harm. I won't even speak of this to the other Horsemen, if that's your wish." Though, there would be no hiding it from Nine, but I leave that piece of information out. Not like he would say anything, anyway. "Please."

Amalie's eyes glaze over a pale white as she gasps and grips the couch in a white-knuckled grip. But it's over quickly, and when she returns, she looks at me with a gentle smile. "I see you have moved the pixies to *Sheruta*? That is a good plan. I approve."

"Was that a . . .?" Aki asks.

"A vision, yes. The seer gets all kinds of visions. That one was just a snapshot." She raises an eyebrow. "And an Angel? Color me impressed."

"Well, she just looks after the pixies. Not sure if I'd count her as on our side."

"Don't discount her just yet." She winks at me, and I take that as a sign to mean our angel might come aboard if we give her time. "Well," she starts, "I need to consult the rest of the Coven Council, I'm afraid. This is not a decision I can make alone."

I wince. "Is that really . . . necessary?" The fire Witch is not my friend.

She laughs, a booming cackle that makes me flinch and then smile. "Relax. They do not hate you quite as much as they pretend. We Witches are on the precipice of drastic change, and they will have to adapt whether they like or not."

"Change?" Aki asks. "What kind of change?"

She winks and touches her nose.

Then, she gets up and grabs a glowing blue crystal on the side and sets it on the coffee table next to her tea. "The Coven Council, please."

The blue crystal glows a fan of plasma into the air, and before I know it, the rest of the Coven Council Witches' faces float in the glowy plasma air.

"Is that a . . ."

"It's a recent gift from the Fae Queen, actually," Amalie says. "You like?"

I don't say anything. A recent gift from the Fae Queen? That means they're trying to recruit the Witches. Shit. I don't want to go to war with two pillar communities. Shifters and Vampires versus Witches and Fae (plus the rogue Vampire faction). The results would be devastating.

Amalie grabs my attention and waves a hand in the air, as if to say don't worry. She turns to face the other Witches with an apologetic smile. "I am sorry for waking you all."

A series of grumbles follows.

The fire Witch scowls. "We are too old for this rubbish, Amalie."

Indeed.

Amalie smiles. "I know. But we have the Horseman of Magic and Aki here with me, and they have a small request of us."

"You expect us to personally help that cretin after what they did to our Witches?" She scowls—again.

Seriously, does this Witch know any other facial expression? Like, smile a bit, you know. Eesh.

"Yes, I am aware of Magic's . . . past." She throws me a pointed look. And I get the idea she knows *everything*. "But they're here to speak to the fairies. Ask them to join our side, probably in exchange for some kind of help with something they need, but we have their word they'll leave them be and not spill their location to anyone."

"Yes, but I'm going to need more assurance than that," the water Witch says. "While pixie dust stimulates a magical high, fairy dust temporarily boosts someone's magic power. We keep them safe for a reason."

"I know, sister," Amalie chimes in.

Are they really sisters? Wow. They look nothing alike.

"But," she continues, "this could be useful to the war, and we've all agreed that we can't just sit this one out. If you remember."

A few of the Witches bristle—fire and water mostly—but the rest nod, agreeing with Amalie.

"So, can I lead them there without committing treason?" Amalie manages to sound both sincere and sarcastic at the same time, and I realize that I might genuinely love her. Like a granny I never knew I needed.

A series of yeses follow, and I can only assume that means they're voting in our favor. What I don't understand is why.

40

An hour later, after Amalie said goodbye to her husbands—I know, I'm shocked too—we're heading down a series of cavernous passageways that are more winding than the pixie tunnels.

"Remind me not to get lost in here."

Amalie laughs. "You cannot get lost when in the earth, Horseman. You have all the Witch powers, do you not?"

"Yeeeeeah." I look sheepishly to the ground. "But I've only managed air, fire, water, and charm so far."

"No premonitions, then?" Aki asks.

I shake my head, no.

"They'll come," Amalie reassures.

"If you say so."

"I do."

She leads us down a final tunnel before coming to a clearing in the distance that glows a brighter shade of gold than the sun.

Fairy dust. So much fairy dust.

"Wow," Aki breathes. "That's insane."

"I thought you've been here before?" I ask.

"Well, yeah." He hesitates. "But I was young, and I only got a glimpse before I ran away." After a questioning look from Amalie, he answers with, "What? The Coven Council used to scare me as a child."

Amalie chuckles, and I laugh, too. "We don't hurt children." She places a firm hand on our shoulders. "I think you should go alone from here. I'll wait to guide you back."

"Thank you." I hope my honesty and sincerity shine through, because she's been a real help in a situation that could have ended vastly different. "You're a great Witch."

She pats my cheek. "I know, dear." Then she takes a seat on the floor and opens a plasmascreen from her pocket.

I grab Aki by the sleeve—he's still staring at Amalie—and drag us down the tunnel toward the glowing light.

Toward the fairies.

I've never seen a fairy on Earth before. They're so rare, some people regard them as myth. Decades before I was born, they went into hiding because people were using their dust for their own gain: boosting magic during wartime, greedy corporations gaining even more money, etc. But no one really knew where they went, just that they all vanished one day. Almost overnight.

The only reason I even know much about them is because we have fairy nests in the gardens at home, back on *Sheruta*. Otherwise, they'd be a complete mystery to me. Alongside everyone else.

The clearing is covered in specks of fairy dust, like glowing gold flakes waving through the air, and I take a moment to really appreciate what I'm about to do. There's nothing I can offer these fairies—they already live good lives thanks to the Witches—but we need them either way.

"They're never going to help us," I mumble.

"What makes you say that?" Aki asks.

"Someone is asking for help to win a war, Aki. After they went into hiding to avoid being used in such ways. It's disrespectful."

"Well, we're desperate." He wraps an arm through mine and pulls us forward into the clearing. "So let's go."

The bright smile he flashes my way makes me glad I brought Aki along. He's encouraging. Kinda like a ball of positive helpfulness.

Fairies are asleep in little nests that spiral up from the ground in spires of flower vines —various flowers growing on top—and with each exhale of their little breaths, fairy dust trickles into the air, adding to the cloud of it suffocating the atmosphere.

It's so cute. I might die of cuteness overload. Is that a thing? It's definitely a thing.

Aki chuckles. "Nothing is cuter than this."

Just as I take another step, twenty or so fairies whizz toward us, all armed with various weapons just bigger than their six-inch frames. Similar to pixies, they have wings that help them fly—though the myths say that they don't need them to levitate—but unlike pixies, fairies are gold in color and similar to the children's book version.

The one at the front with small horns and a green dress flies close to my face while the rest whisper amongst each other. "Horseman of Magic," a tiny voice whispers. "What is it you want?"

Seems my identity has become known even amongst the depths of society. Great. "I . . ." I look at Aki, not knowing what to say. "I apologize for disturbing you, but I would like to speak to whomever your leader is, please. If that's not too much trouble?"

The fairy's face scrunches as her grip tightens on her staff. "Our queen is resting."

"Then I'm happy to wait until she wakes."

A regular-volumed voice echoes across the cavern. "That will not be necessary." A four-foot fairy, as golden and glowing as the rest, glides forward, heading straight for us. "I am happy to speak with her now."

The twenty or so fairies who stood vigil fly to the edges of the cavern, allowing her to pass.

And when she reaches a spot not two feet from where Aki and I are standing, she stops with a cautionary smile and her hand in the air.

The whispers cease.

"Please, will you join me?" She gestures, with a wide open arm, toward the cavern that lies before us. "It would be an honor to host one of the Horsemen. Our kind has not done so in quite some time."

We follow her around the maze of vines and into a small cottage at the center, where the dust is thickest. "You've met the other Horsemen before?"

She chuckles. "No, not personally. But my mother, the previous fairy queen, did. She was most fond of Conquest. Rumor has it they partied for days."

Yeah, that sounds like Connie.

"But that was a long time ago. Much has changed."

"You're in hiding, for one. And the world is at war, for another."

The door unlocks with a wave of the queen's hand, and her childlike form floats through the doorway lined with salt and mushrooms.

After ducking low enough to pass through, Aki and I settle ourselves in the clean, open-plan lounge. Everything is lined with a fine layer of fairy dust, but other than that, there's not a thing out of place or even a speck of dirt to be seen. And with a plasmascreen hovering in the air, one of Nine's new holophones on the table, and various pieces of modern tech lying around, the fairy queen is more than up to date on the modernity of the world.

The queen coughs to grab my attention, and I snap my head in her direction. "Can I get either of you a drink?"

"I'd love a glass of water, if you don't mind," Aki says.

She looks at me, but I shake my head.

After a few beats of silence I'm not quite sure how to fill, she comes back with two glasses and places them on the stone coasters. "I assume," she begins, "you're here to ask for the fairies' help in the war."

It's not a question, but I feel the need to answer the silence nonetheless. "Yes, your majesty."

She waves a hand through the air. "Please, spare me the title. I have enough of that already. You may call me Seraphina, if you like."

"Seraphina, I . . ." I sigh. What the hell is the point? "I assume you know all the horrible things happening to the supernatural community, given the amount of technology in this room alone?"

"I do."

"Then," Aki interrupts, "you must know how vital your help would be?" He shoots me an apology with his eyes, but I shake my head. I don't mind. "With your help, the Horsemen can stop the rogue Vampire faction and the Fae and return the world to normal. To peace."

"Whose peace?" she asks. "Your peace? The human's peace? A Horseman's idea of peace is leaving the communities to squabble and pillage as they please. Is that the peace you'll be returning us to?"

"It'll be our peace, and no. I've already set up the embassy, and I'm happy to offer three representative seats per species, regardless of their standing in the supernatural world."

This clearly catches her by surprise, because her long lashes widen and her mouth forms an O before she can stop herself. She regains composure quickly. "I was not expecting that offer, I must say."

"The Fae and the rogue Vampire faction have all but infiltrated the SC, and they plan to bring down every main Vampire city on Christmas Day." I look to her pleadingly, hoping that'll shake some moral sense into her. "We're going to stop them, with or without your help. But we'll lose many fewer lives with you on our side."

She stands abruptly, her dress flowing around her ankles. "I'm sorry, but we cannot help you."

"Please," Aki pleads, "is there nothing we can offer to change your mind?"

Her eyes meet mine in a battle of wills, our opposing forces leaving me breathless and gasping for air.

"I'm sorry," she says finally, tears lining her eyes. "We lost millions of our kind to the outside wars before my mother took us to shelter with the Witches. I cannot let my people be used to fight other people's war. It would be an act of betrayal. And there's nothing you could give that would remove its sting." She gestures to the door. "If you would please leave."

"Well," Aki says in the hotel restaurant a few hours later, "that was a disaster."

"It went pretty much how I expected it to go."

"Really?" His surprised tone catches me off guard, like he really expected to get the fairy's help.

"Yup." The glass of cold water reaching my lips sends a pleasant chill down my spine. "It's not like their troubles happened all that long ago, Aki. I dislike the Witches outdated political moves because it's been centuries since their plight. But it was only a few decades ago the fairies were all but wiped out after having their dust harnessed for war." I take a few bites of the melktert in front of me. "Tell me, would you go against your people's wishes like that, just at the behest of a random person you don't even know?"

Maybe it would have been better had I brought all the Horsemen along with me. But then Arrie wouldn't be planning the war strategy and moving forces, Connie wouldn't be keeping everyone in line, Dea wouldn't be running the embassy, and Nine wouldn't be working on a blood supplement. This is the best way.

It was a good choice.

If I keep telling myself that, I might just believe it.

It's only been a week, but I miss them—even Arrie's assholery. And whenever I think about them, my chest hurts. There's so much I want to do with them: cuddle, watch more movies, sunbathe in the garden, beat Arrie to a pulp, research with Nine, learn how to get another tattoo . . .

One day, I'll be free enough to settle down. But for now, I might have to fight to get there.

"Hey, Magic? You okay?"

Aki's looking at me with a worried lip and a furrowed brow, that cute little wrinkle making me wince with guilt.

"Yeah, sorry. Just thinking . . ."

"About the team, right?"

"How . . .?"

He smiles. "You get this glowy sort of dazed look in your eye. It's totally gross." He grabs another glass of water before rejoining me at the table. "Guess it's time to go back to New Orleans and meet the Demons, right?"

"Yup." The silly straw I'm using with my smoothie slips from my mouth, and mango juice goes everywhere, making us both laugh. "Oops."

A server hands me some towels, and I use them to pat myself dry while she cleans the table.

"We'll leave in the morning," I say to Aki once the server has left. "Get a good night's sleep, because I've never met a Demon before and I'm not sure how this'll go." He looks nervous, but I rest my hand on top of his. "We'll be fine. I promise."

THE ROOM IS SMALL, BUT IT HAS A BED, A SHOWER, AND ROOM SERVICE, SO I'M HAPPY. AKI'S next door. For now, I have a call to make.

"Call Famine," I instruct the holophone.

It glows deep green for a few seconds. I wonder if he'll pick up or if he's asleep, but then Nine's face comes into view. "Sweetie!"

"Nine," I whisper, relief washing through me. "It's good to see you."

His glowing blue brows furrow in concern. "You okay?"

I shrug. "Politics is tedious. And I miss you all." Ugh. I'm so pathetic. I've become one of *those* girls. Guys. People. Definitely people.

I can't make too many details of Nine's face out, but he looks tired. Or maybe I'm just expecting him to look tired. "Are you okay? You look a bit . . ."

"Tired? Yeah, that's 'cos I am. But we've made fantastic progress on the blood supplement. We might be able to move into the trial phase soon."

"Wait. You did it? Really?" A smile looms across my face and his, and when he nods, I squeal. "That's fantastic! I'm so proud!"

Aki knocks on the thin wall separating our room in annoyance.

"Oops."

At Nine's questioning look, I explain, "Thin walls in this hotel."

"So," he starts, "how far have you got?"

"Is everyone else there?"

He holds up a finger, telling me to wait, and then nods. "Now we're all here."

Everyone says hi in turn, and hearing their voices soothes an on-edge part of me that feels like a long-held breath.

"Well, we didn't get the fairies on board, but I'm not surprised. They were lovely, though. Amazing species. Have you seen their nests? They're sooooo cute."

"Hon, never call a fairy cute to their face. They hate it," Connie said from somewhere in the background.

"Their little staff sticks really hurt when there's lots of them," Arrie chimes in. "Trust me."

Everyone chuckles, including me, and just the thought of Arrie getting beaten up by a bunch of six-inch fairies with pointy sticks is hilarious. Goddess, I've missed them.

Nine falls to the side with an oof, and Connie comes into view. "How's everything going with you and Aki?"

"It's . . . going great, actually. We've gotten to know each other more. But I still have so many questions." A thought flickers across my mind. "Have any of you heard from Nigel?"

"He's here at the house. Once he got the date for us, he quit and ran here as quickly as possible." She smiles. "He's safe."

Goddess, my godfather is living with my boyfriends and girlfriend. Alone. Without me. *Kuso.* What if they share embarrassing stories? What if Nigel grills them all father-style? What if the team gets annoyed with him?

"Stop spiraling!"

"Come on, Angel, we talked about this. Stop focusing on the anxiety. The more you focus on it, the worse it will be."

I nod. "I know, I know. And I've done so well on this mission. But you're living with my godfather. Without me." I snort a laugh. "Forgive me if I'm a little nervous."

"Relax," Nine says, clearly having recovered from Connie's shove. "He's been hanging out, training with Arrie a little and helping Dea with the embassy stuff."

"He's training with Arrie!? Are you insane? He's mortal!"

"I can hold back, Killer. Unless you've forgotten the weak-ass punches I threw at you when you first started training?" I can hear the smirk. "I can always remind you, if you like?"

Connie smiles at us, satisfied we've found some more common ground. Even if it's only as friends. Just the reminder sends a slash of pain through me, and my smile falters.

"I hope I didn't wake any of you."

She waves a hand. "Nah. It's midmorning here."

"Oh good. Arrie, did the pixies travel okay?"

Connie moves aside to make room for Arrie, who just about fits in the frame, though his shoulder cuts off. "Yeah. They're all settled in the northern part of the island, far away from other people."

"That's probably for the best. They don't trust easily."

"They seem to have no problem trusting an Angel," he grumbles.

"Ah, Glowy. How she's doing?"

"Still a grumpy asshole."

Look what pot is calling the kettle black.

I hold my tongue. Now is no time for an argument.

Arrie smiles and chuckles, and my heart flips, beating double time. Fuck. I'm in love with my . . . friend. That realization sends pangs of loneliness through me, as though three people aren't enough.

I'm such a whore. Can I not just be happy with three?

Dea's face fills the holoscreen, and one look into the blue-glowing version of his galaxy eyes, and I know I'm being stupid. It's not about the number. It's about the people. It's not that I want or need four—three is quite the handful as it is—it's that I need Arrie. And that need has nothing to do with my current relationship with Dea, Nine, and Connie.

"You doing okay, Angel?" The sincerity in his voice shakes me out of my head. "Really?"

I wiggle my head from side to side, unsure. "I'm . . . not doing awfully. But I . . ." I sigh. "I'm a little confused."

"About what?" I don't immediately answer, and he frowns. "Come on, you might as well tell us. Bottling it all up will not help."

"He's right, hon. You can always chat with us."

"The world needs me, but the only thing I care about is my own desires and needs. Doesn't that make me a little selfish?"

"Just normal," Dea says. "You think political leaders, kings and queens, MPs, and doctors do not worry about themselves all the time? That they are not still capable of worrying about both themselves and others simultaneously? We are all only a part of nature."

"And nature," Nine chimes in, "is pretty selfish."

"But you don't all have existential crises every other day? You're all so calm. You never need to chat or talk things through. It's just me. I'm so . . . needy." Ugh. And here I am, being needy about being needy. Shoot me now. This is an awful conversation.

Connie giggles, the echo making me want to hug and punch her at the same time. "We're a lot older than you. Like, a lot. But even so, I needed you to take care of me on our date, didn't I? I needed saving. I needed to chat about"—she gestures to the surrounding guys—"this."

"You did?" Dea asks. "Really?"

She nods, shyness overtaking my usually confident girlfriend. "It's dumb, but my relationship with Magic feels so . . . personal. It's not something I want to share on an emotional level." Her blonde hair waves as she looks to the floor.

"It's not stupid," I say. "It's okay to do things separately. Together. Or a bit of both. And it's okay to change your mind."

"And," Dea says with a hand on her shoulder, "it is okay to be uncertain."

"I'm not uncertain about my feelings for Magic. And I'm okay sharing. Really. It's just a little . . . overwhelming." She groans in frustration. "This is so unlike me."

"What is it that's making you uneasy?" Arrie places a hand on her shoulder, and she flinches.

"I'm not uneasy. Just feeling a little selfish. I want all of your time, hon. But I can't have it."

I wish I could jump through the holoscreen and wrap my arms around her. She's suffering. And I'm not there. I'd teleport back, but I don't want to leave Aki here alone. "You're still our badass Horseman of Conquest," I reaffirm. "Ain't nothing gonna change that. And I'll spend as much time with you as you need."

"Soooo," Nine says, "what was that I heard about your male form, Sweetie?" I can hear his eyebrows raising and his eyes darting to us both.

Connie's tears dry up with giggles, and she eventually bursts out laughing, holding her sides and trying to splutter an apology. "I'm . . . sorry." She gasps for air.

People do weird things in times of pain. I spiral out of control and forget to breathe, so who am I to judge?

"Well, we were . . . you know—"

"Fucking," Connie helpfully explains. "We were having sex, and I was about to give Magic the best orgasm she'll ever have in female form by someone's tongue, but then she burst into male form, and yes her dick just magically poofed into my mouth, and then we just continued." She shrugs.

Goddess, it's like a dagger to the soul. Like being grated against the flow—it doesn't fit anymore. I don't fit anymore.

I shrink. Connie didn't mean it. Connie didn't mean it. Connie didn't mean it. But tears threaten to burst forth nonetheless, and I can't help it as they rupture their banks and gush down my cheeks.

"Shit," Arrie swears. "Connie!" His rumbly voice takes on that angry, quiet, bitter quality it does when he's mad at me. "What were you thinking?"

"Quick," Nine says, "has anyone ever been to that hotel before? Maybe one of us can teleport there."

"I can just fly or faze," Dea chimes in.

Connie, meanwhile, freezes on her perch that is Dea's knee, her face a mixture of shock and hurt. "I'm so sorry," she whispers, her voice barely audible over the guys' panic. "I wasn't thinking, I . . ." Her eyes drop to the floor.

I'm pretty sure she's crying. Again.

Damn, we're a mess this evening.

I wipe my face and catch my breath. "This is ridiculous."

Everyone stops talking and returns to me.

"It's okay. I don't mind."

"Don't do that," Connie says. "I know you mind. We all know. We've tried to avoid using pronouns at all to avoid the issue, but it's hard. And we don't want to force you to do anything before you're ready."

"And," Nine says, "we don't want to make you take a new pronoun or anything, but it might be something to think about."

"A new . . . pronoun?" I haven't really thought about it. I guess I've stopped using my female form as default. I don't even really think about it anymore, I just exist in either form, regardless. "But what would I use?"

Connie shrugs. "No idea. But maybe have a think about it. If you like the idea, we can all brainstorm together, if you like?"

A smile widens across my face. "I'd like that. A lot."

"What about they?" Dea asks. "That's pretty popular, at least."

"In Chinese, we use *tā* for both men and women," Nine points out. "I think that's pretty cool."

"In Japanese, our language is tailored to who we are. So we can speak in a very feminine way or a very masculine way," I explain. "What pronouns we use not only depend on the gender of the person speaking but also on the social context of the situation and the social standing of the person we are communicating with."

"That sounds complicated," Arrie grumbles.

"A lot of it is something you just grow up with. It's normal." I shrug.

"So maybe not something linguistic, in that sense," Nine says. "Hmmm . . . we'll have a think about it. I'm sure we'll come up with something."

"Right." I shake my head. "It's not really something I'm focusing on right now. We're heading to the meeting with the Demons tomorrow. We headed to the meeting spot earlier in the week, so we can just teleport there."

"Good," Dea says. "Be careful."

"Don't worry. I'll kick their asses if I have to."

"Demons are known tricksters," Nine explains, "so make sure not to get played by them. Be specific about what you want from them. Include all exceptions and all inclusions you need, otherwise they *will* use that against you in the future."

"Demons are tricky assholes. Noted."

"And Magic," Connie says, her voice gentle and soft, "I am really sorry." She opens her mouth to say something else, but she must decide against it because she closes her mouth and smiles. "Be careful."

"And remember we love you, Angel."

"I love you all too."

I end the call, feeling lighter and more at ease than I have in days.

42

New Orleans isn't as calm as South Africa. Not by a long shot. And I'm missing the scenery almost as soon as we get there. Though my female form seems a little more achy —must be a Witch thing.

"So, do we have a plan?" Aki asks after he teleports beside me moments later. "I feel like we should have a plan for Demons."

"You're probably right, but I know as little about Demons as possible. They like to make deals, and the wording is vital. Nine says they like to play tricks on people."

"You plan to make a deal with Demons?"

"If it gets them on our side? Yes."

Aki mutters something under his breath, but without my Vampire hearing, I can't make it out. Which is probably a good thing. "I can't believe we're about to do this."

"So fighting an Angel is okay, dealing with Witches that probably want me dead is fine, but dealing with Demons is where you draw the line?"

"It sounds ridiculous when you put it like that," he mumbles.

"That's because it kinda is."

"Hey!" He punches me in the arm, but it does nothing but make him wince. Shifter strength and whatnot. "Wow, really, nothing?"

I shrug. "Sorry." I return my attention to the morning sky and take a deep breath. "We're due to take a boat from Shell Beach in half an hour."

"Right. Demons."

THE BOAT ARRIVES ON TIME, AND WE TAKE THE QUICK TRIP TO DEMON CENTRAL IN THE MIDDLE of the Bayou. We have teleporting crystals, weapons, and my ability to fly us the hell out of there if anything goes wrong. We'll be fine.

I hope.

"Magic?" Aki asks out of the blue. "What's your favorite color?"

"Orange. Yours?"

"White."

"That's . . . cool." Weird. That's weird. I just don't have the heart to tell my long-lost twin I find his favorite color strange.

"I know, it's odd. But it's like a blank canvas. I can make anything from white."

"Okay, I can understand that." I look at the sky once more and just breathe. "Orange reminds me of both the sunrise and sunset. Makes me feel all gooey."

"Gooey? That's what you're going with?"

"You know, when you're all melting on the inside because life has reminded you that it's beautiful after spending so long in the darkness. Gooey."

"Sometimes I like the darkness," he whispers, his voice a deep timber I don't think I've heard before. "It's like a familiar dream."

My hand rests on his shoulder, a hopefully comforting presence. "You're not alone anymore, Aki."

He looks at me like I've burst some kind of depression bubble like a reverent goddess. "You're a great sister. I'm glad we finally got to meet and spend some time together."

"Me too." I grab him into a hug and squeeze. Gently. "Okay, okay, my turn. What's your favorite thing to read? You do read, don't you?"

He shrugs. "Sometimes. When I do, I tend to stick to mysteries, thrillers, things with a little bit of darkness and a little bit of hope. Plus some action."

"You're pretty emotionally open, you know that?"

"Is that a bad thing?" The worry in his eyes that he might have disappointed me shoots straight to the heart.

"No, no, no. Not at all. Just an observation. I kinda like it."

"Really?"

I nod. "Uh-huh. It's refreshing. Most people stay closed off until you really know them, and even then, they only come out of their social shell when you prod them to. Otherwise they keep the emotions expected of them."

"You're not wrong. Okay, okay, my go." He flaps his hands in excitement a little. "Who was your first boyfriend/girlfriend? And how did it end?"

"Err . . . I might have to get back to you on that one. My mortal memories are pretty new, and while they're all there, it's like a file I have to flit through to find the right thing."

"Okay, then I'll go first." He takes a deep breath. "He was this really emo dude in high school. The kid at the back who's all quiet and moody but is actually really interesting and smart." He looks into the distance all wistful and gross like. "We had a summer fling end of senior year, but it ended when we both went off to college. I cried for three days when he left." He laughs, embarrassment coloring him pink. "Kinda cliché and ridiculous, huh?"

"Aren't most first loves?" My first relationship . . . "I'm pretty sure it was this asshole in tenth grade. He was Fae, but I didn't really understand that then. He tried to use this spell that would make me sleep with him, but it backfired and just made me irrationally pissed off at him for a week. I tripped him up in the hallways, punched him in the face— twice—and stuffed his locker full of expanding foam."

Our laughs echo in the Bayou's stillness, but the tears leaking from my eyes are loud as they spill off my jaw and onto my hands.

"That's . . . such a better . . . story," Aki says between heaveful breaths. "I feel sorry for that guy. Pissing you off is not a good idea."

"I wasn't a Horseman then, remember. So I wasn't nearly as badass."

"Right." He looks at me with confusion. "Because you're technically dead. And immortal."

"Yup. Difficult pill to swallow, huh?"

"A little."

The captain shouts, "We're here!"

And Aki and I disembark and wait by the port for the Demons to show us to their . . . lair?

43

What would a Demon lair look like? Would it be all dark and mysterious? Full of blood and the bones of their enemies? Yeah, somehow I doubt they live like they do in books. I've been pretty surprised by the species I've met so far, and this isn't going to be any different, is it?

Aki shifts from foot to foot beside me, hands clenching his sleeves and teeth chewing his bottom lip.

"Hey," I say, and he jumps a little, "we're gonna be fine. Promise."

He nods. Takes a deep breath, and then he grabs my hand and shoots me an apologetic look. "Sorry. Nerves."

His hand squeezes mine, and I squeeze back.

"Well, we can always teleport right out if something goes wrong. This isn't a video game. There's no no-teleporting zones. And Aki?" I look at him. "I'm immortal and much stronger than you, so please don't come rescue me and get yourself killed. Okay?"

"Right. Yeah." He looks away, his gaze dotting everywhere but at me. "So, there's no way to kill a Horseman? Like, at all?"

Everything in me freezes. Shit. Do I tell him? "Well, that's not strictly true. But it doesn't matter." I wave his question off. "It'd be fucking impossible to pull off." Especially given we still don't know where my seal is. It still hasn't turned up.

"Oh, okay." He looks disappointed.

And damn it. It really undoes me. "I'll tell you about it when we're back on *Sheruta*, alright?"

His smile brightens the fog we've found ourselves in, and I breathe an easy breath. I switch to my female form and use my Vampire vision to penetrate the thick low-hanging cloud, hoping for a sign. Anything. Red eyes glow in the distance, sitting atop bulky, mismatched forms I can't quite make out.

They must be farther away than we thought.

"Alright," I yell, "you can come out! We're not gonna hurt you."

A chorus of high-pitched giggles echo around the trees.

What are they, hyena Demons?

"Seriously, high-pitched giggles? Really?"

"What would you have suggested, Magic?" a deep, barely there voice sounds not seven feet from where we are. "A bunch of hisses? Demon whispers?"

Aki leans in close. "What's a Demon whisper?"

I shrug. Beats me.

"A Demon whisper, young Witch, is a spell unique to Demons that allows us to temporarily take control of another." He looks to me and adds, "Not that it works on Horsemen."

Relief sweeps through me.

Aki, on the other hand, tenses further. I didn't know that was even possible. But I still have hold of his hand, so I squeeze in reassurance, trying to remind him we can leave whenever we want. His shoulders drop. Minutely.

The Demon in front of us steps out of the fog, and I get my first look at an actual Demon. Bright green horns, skin as black as night, curling nails that have green tips, and a surprisingly beautiful face. You know, in an evil, Hades-decorated-this-guy kinda way. "My name," he says, his voice a more regular timber, "is Verity. Welcome to what we Demons call home."

I bow low. "Thank you for allowing us to visit." I look up at Aki, who is still staring at the Demon, eyes wide, and I cough. "Bow," I hiss.

He shakes himself out of his stupor and bows.

"Now we have the pleasantries out of the way," the Demon says, "we can retire to the mansion."

"Mansion?"

He leads us through dense fog and even denser trees, past winding bushes and creatures I don't know the name of, until we reach a fork in the road marked by an old-fashioned signpost you see in cartoons. Only the words marked on this sign post comprise letters I've never seen.

"Demon language?" I ask the Demon leading us.

"One of them, yes." At my questioning gaze, he explains, "we Demons once roamed Earth in the thousands. Millions, probably. We had many species across many lands, and therefore, we had many languages." He points to the signpost. "That one is Liggish. One of the many languages of the ancients. It's what we use in spells to help guard and protect our home." He waves his hand in the air. "And we also use it for signposts."

Aki's ears perk up, his eyes inquisitive. "Demons can perform spells?"

"Of course." A smile splits the Demon's face in two. "We were the original spellcasters."

"Is it like Fae magic?" I ask, all but forgetting my surroundings and that I'm talking to an actual Demon. "Ingredients, runes, and castings to make the magical essence that fuels their magic—fueled in turn by the leylines?"

"So you're a geek, too, hm? Just like that teammate of yours. Famine, wasn't it?"

As if he—it, they, something else?—doesn't know who Famine is. My eyes roll of their own accord. "Yes, Famine and I are . . . similar in that regard."

"A pair of geeks." The Demon giggles in that high-pitched way Demons seem to do, apparently. "How quaint."

The sarcasm is not lost on me.

This is gonna be a long day, isn't it?

Goddess, help me.

After a few more minutes, the fog clears, and a loamy mansion covered in moss and made of great cracked stones looms in front of us. Dim yellow lights illuminate the dense foliage every few meters, lighting up the cracks in the masonry and the deep green plants, shrubs, and bushes that make up the floor.

"Are they witchlights?" Aki asks, taking the words right out of my mouth.

The Demon turns to us and smiles. "Of course. They were kind enough to lend us their magic after The Great Purge." Venom drips from his lips at the reminder of their torturous past.

I've read about The Great Purge—when the team purged the Earth of most Demons and Angels, leaving small pockets left to lie in the rubble of their kind. The history books make it out to be all heroic, that the Horsemen were simply getting rid of evil. But I know better. They were ridding the world of creatures that preyed upon humans. The species and few Demons and Angels left behind were the ones causing no, or minimal, harm.

But to those Demons left behind, it must have seemed like a slaughter. When I asked Nine about it, he said they tried to negotiate and make peace, but no one was interested, bar a few.

I'm not sure where I stand on the issue, but it's supposedly where the Horsemen got the name Horsemen of the Apocalypse.

They're two thousand years old. I guess I can't expect them to always have made wonderful choices or to have been good people. Just like me, they grew into who they are today.

Despite the dark and gloomy outside, the mansion he leads us into is light, airy, and somehow welcoming. Looks like I was right. Demons don't pander to fictional stereotypes. The large open windows with fake landscapes and lighting brighten the entrance foyer, where white marble floors meet white marble walls. Trees, flowers, and other natural pieces of the Bayou trickle in now and then, but it's otherwise a whole different world from the outside.

"This place is incredible!" I exclaim, awe painting my every breath.

Aki can't stop looking at everything, running up to various plants and pieces of artwork to get a good look. Like a kid in a candy store.

I grab his arm and drag him down the hallway the Demon just turned onto. "C'mon."

"Oh, right." He drags behind me, his gaze catching on another one of the sculptures wrapped in vines. "But everything is so . . . pretty."

"Well, we might be here for a day or two, if they let us, so you'll have time to explore." I yank on his arm again. "But right now we're losing our Demon guide, and I don't want to get lost in a Demon mansion in the middle of the Bayou." I grind my teeth and clench my free fist.

"You make a good point." Aki reins in his amazement and walks beside me, only occasionally getting lost in the flowers and needing a gentle nudge. "But there's something about this place . . ."

"I know."

He's right. It's almost reverent. Like a goddess's home or some shit.

"Mr Demon!" I shout, trying to catch up with a slow as fuck Aki at my heels.

Just as we turn another corner, we run smack into a black back that smells like sulfur. "Mr Demon?" he asks, surprise etching his tone. "I don't think anyone's called me Mr Demon before."

I don't know if I've insulted, upset, or pleased him. It's kinda hard to tell. But he spins on his heels to face me, and the grin shooting from ear to ear answers my question. Seems he likes the moniker.

"We don't deal in things as corruptible as names here, darlin'." The smirk on his lips glints off the small dagger piercing his left ear. "But you can call me Sir anytime you like."

Aki coughs, stirring the air.

I flinch away from the Demon, who I am *not* calling Sir, and say, "If you don't mind leading the way, we really need to speak to your leader or king or . . ."

"Lord," he answers. "Our Demon Lord."

44

The Demon Lord, if you can really call him that, lounges across the throne, legs swinging over the armrest, some kind of handheld game console getting beaten under quick, punchy fingers while he laughs. "Ha! Suck it, Yoshi!" He looks up, meets my gaze with surprise, and jumps to his feet with a clearing of the throat. "Horseman of Magic!"

His four-foot stature barely reaches my chest, with red, yellow, and orange coloring firing along his black skin in waves. But it's the lack of scruff and mature bone structure that shocks me into a silence I don't know how to break.

The Demon Lord is a child?

I shoot a questioning look to the Demon who escorted us, who now leans against the wall near the door, cleaning lint from his claws.

He just smiles at me.

Swinging back around to the Demon Lord, I raise my hand in offer. He might be a child, but he's still of importance. Best be polite.

Aki bows low, staying quiet.

Thank goddess.

The Demon Lord edges forward, his eyes never leaving mine. "I've seen what you can do, so please forgive me my unease at being in your presence."

"I promise not to harm you, my lord." I look at Aki, who smiles softly. "I'm not really the type, anyway."

His eyebrows raise. "Really?" He presses the datachip in his wrist and brings up the datascreen, quickly types and presses a series of buttons, then swipes it around to face me. "Then how do you explain this?"

The this in question is the viral video of me attacking the Vampires in New Orleans a few weeks ago.

Remind me again why no one said anything about that plan? Not even a hint of forewarning. The fuckers.

"I was not really harming them. They volunteered to fake fight to draw out the rogue Vampire faction that harmed one of our own."

"Ah." His eyes grow understanding beneath the bright white irises. "A coup. Interesting." He skips back to his throne and smiles at me. "In that case, welcome to our home, Magic. I may call you Magic, yes?"

"Of course." I gesture to Aki. "And this is my brother, Aki."

"Brother?" He looks as confused as I felt when I found out. "Really?"

"Twin brother, actually. But he's mortal."

"So . . . he's your twin brother you left behind when you died and became the Fifth Horseman?"

"That about sums it up, yeah."

His faces relaxes into a stony expression, his back rigid on the throne. "What is it you have come to see us for?"

"Well"—I scratch the back of my neck—"we're trying to gain as much support as possible from the lower supernatural communities. And we thought that maybe—"

The Demon Lord laughs. A high-pitched screech that makes my hair stand on end and my hackles rise. He wipes his eyes and looks back up at me. "I'm sorry, but for a moment I thought you asked for our help."

"She did," Aki confirms. "The Fae are—"

The child holds up a hand. "I don't discuss politics without my advisors present. I'm just a child."

"A very well-spoken child." I was beginning to believe he's not as young as he seems, but I was wrong. "You seem almost old in nature, but inside a childlike body."

"I get that a lot. Thank you." He sighs, his face relaxing once again into that of a casual acquaintance. "My father, the previous Demon Lord, passed away six months ago. He had been the Demon Lord since The Great Purge, so it's caused some . . . teething issues."

Wow. His father was the Demon Lord for over a thousand years? Damn. These Demons can grow old.

"I see." A thought occurs to me. Out of the blue. "Well, maybe helping us can restore some of that broken peace. A show of strength, if you will."

He raises his hand, but I interrupt halfway.

"All I ask is that you hear us out. If you don't want to participate, we won't make you. We'll leave in peace."

"Oh, very well. But you'll have to wait until my advisors get here. They understand political complexities better than I."

"Thank you." I bow low once more, hoping to catch his good side. If he has one. "It's been an honor being in your presence."

WHILE WE WAIT FOR THE DEMON LORD AND HIS ADVISORS TO BE READY, WE'RE SHOWN ON A grand tour of the mansion by the first Demon we met. Verity. Or Mr Poison, as I've donned him in my head.

"And here we have the old pits, where we fight for societal standings, when making deals, and just for the hell of it." He laughs at a smaller Demon fighting in one of the pits with a large boulder of a Demon. "He tries to defeat Borl every day. One day he'll learn." He shakes his head.

The pits are a series of underground hollows made of stone, surrounded by crude stone seats leading up all sides, like an amphitheater.

"People watch these fights?" Aki asks.

"Of course. The betting fields are ripe for the taking, if you know who's been doing better in training." He winks at Aki. "Fortunes have been made here."

Aki looks disgusted, but thankfully for us both, he keeps his opinions to himself. That doesn't stop him from frowning at the Demon's back, however.

"So, how does one make a deal with a Demon?"

He stops in his tracks and spins to face me. "That's your plan? Bargain us into helping you? A bold move."

"Assuming you won't just help us outright, then yes. Hopefully." Looking back to the pits. "And I might know just how to do that."

"You think so, Magic?" His green-tipped claws tip my head up his towering frame. "Ever fought a Demon before?"

"Ever fought a Horseman of the Apocalypse before?"

Pain lances across his eyes, a memory rising to the surface if his far-off gaze has anything to say about it, but he shakes himself out and returns to the tour.

The lower levels of the mansion are older, more crude in their design that resembles the Bayou outside of the walls. But the farther up you go, the more grand the marbling, the more prestigious the Demons walking around the halls, and the grander the décor is. Demon hierarchy seems similar to the human hierarchy. Crude, perhaps, but at least it's something I'm familiar with.

We are just about to settle down to watch a movie in one of their theaters when a white-skinned being with large wings rushes into the room, heading straight for us.

I grab a dagger on instinct, prepared to fight with my second angel.

"Stand down, Magic," the Demon says. "It's just Sayal. He's here to carry a message for the Demon Lord." He looks at Sayal and smiles. "Word?"

"Yes, sir. They are ready for you both." He doesn't meet my gaze, but since I'm still holding a dagger in my hand, I don't blame him. "Maybe don't threaten the council, if you want them to cooperate." He looks to the floor. "Just a thought."

Right.

45

Back in the throne room, the Demon Lord sits in his usual seat, but this time he's surrounded by six older Demons—all clearly adults—who are spread out on either side of the throne.

The Demon Lord stands and clears his throat. "Thank you for allowing me time to gather my advisors. It is appreciated."

A Demon to his left—black-skinned with swirling gold patterns covering his body and gold-tipped horns adorning his head—clears his throat and shoots the young Demon Lord a withering look.

"Right." He sits back down. "You wanted the chance to be heard out. Well, here it is." He gestures the room. "Speak."

"Of course, my lord." I clear my throat and take a deep breath. "As you may or may not know, the Fae have been gathering their armies. They have joined with a rogue Vampire faction—not affiliated with the Vampire Royal Council—and are now threatening not just us, but the general Vampire population. They have the Supernatural Council under their thumbs, and they are doing everything in their power to suppress the general supernatural communities."

A few gasps litter the room, but the advisors remain stoic. The Demon Lord looks interested and concerned, but without the help of his council, I'm powerless here.

"They shut down New Orleans, and now they're planning to shut down the other main Vampire cities. They'll do this on Christmas Day morning."

"Turned Vampires cannot go out in the sun," one advisor clarifies. "But outside of New Orleans, there aren't many born Vampires." He smirks. "It's an excellent strategy."

"Indeed. You can see our concern."

"Of course," the Demon Lord says. "But why do Vampire politics matter to us?"

"They've been attacking the Shifters and Witches as well. Not to mention what they've been doing to the pixies for centuries. We believe they're trying to take over. A new Vampire-Fae rule. To do with the humans as they please. And they're starting with subduing the current Vampire system. They'll then likely move on to the Shifters and humans. It's unclear how they'll attack the rest of the populations, including the Witches, but they will eventually."

Everyone holds their breath.

No one speaks. No one moves.

And I think I may have stunned the Demons into silence.

The Demon Lord looks forlornly at the stone floor, a sadness on his face. "It will change everything if they succeed, won't it?"

The advisor who scorned him before answers, "Yes, my lord. But whether or not that will be in our favor is yet to be determined. If we allied ourselves with the Fae, we could join their new world."

This is what I was afraid of.

We offer nothing as an incentive. And not every species will do things out of the goodness of their hearts.

"We're prepared to make a deal," I offer. "Something you want or need that we can provide in exchange for your help." I smile, hoping to seem confident. "The morale you gain from appearing strong is just a freebie."

An old frail Demon with graying colors looks alarmed at me, his eyebrows raising toward his horns. "You are prepared to make a deal with the Demon Lord?"

"I know the risks." I think. "But they cannot be worse than letting the Fae, humans, and rogue Vampire faction take over."

The Demon Lord strides forward, his eyes glowing a fiery red as a deep, menacing smiles takes over his features. "Then what is it you offer me in return for our help, Horseman of Magic?"

"Best make it a good offer," one advisor says.

Think, Magic, think. What do they want? What do they need?

I look around, taking in their mansion in the middle of nowhere, and something clicks in my brain. "Support. The Horsemen will officially support you and whatever choices you make to further your species and help you grow. If you want to be an outed species and join the embassy, you can. If you want to stay hidden, we'll help protect your home with our own magic. Whatever your choice, if you help us, and so long as you do not cause any grievous harm to another species, we will help you."

"Really?" the Demon Lord asks, astonishment floundering across his face. "That's . . . quite an offer. But how can we trust you?"

Aki, silently stood beside me until now, steps forward. "I'll fight you for it. In the pits. You win, we'll walk away and never bother you again. I win, you take the deal and join our forces."

Laughter skitters across the room, bouncing off the marble walls, filling the flowers and vines with raucous hope. But it fills me with dread.

"Aki," I hiss. "What are you thinking?"

"Of saving the Vampires."

• • •

THE PITS FILL WITH DEMONS, A FEW ANGELS, AND THE ADVISORS WITHIN THE HOUR. WORD spreads fast down here, it seems. The Demon Lord is behind the left pit door, while Aki and I are standing behind the right pit door. Both open into the largest pit in the mansion.

"Aki, you can't kill him. And you must fight fair." I sigh, rubbing a hand through my short blonde hair. "You mustn't lose control of your death magic. We'll create more enemies that way."

"No shit, sis." Aki's bubbly exterior has vanished, and out of the ashes stands a stony expression, serious eyes, and pursed lips. "All I need to do is fight him in hand-to-hand combat, and we'll have the Demons on our side."

"But I should be fighting him!" It would have been easy with all the magic at my disposal. "This is ridiculous."

He places a firm hand on my shoulder and smiles. "I'll be okay. I'm a pretty good fighter."

"You are?"

"Yup." He's dressed in shorts that dangle to his knees and nothing else. "This should be a piece of cake. He's just a kid."

Yeah, something tells me that this will not be that simple. He might be a child, but he's still the Demon Lord.

The door opens, and our escort pokes his head through the door with a smirk. "It's time."

"Our first contestant is Aki, Witch, and brother of the Fifth Horseman of Magic."

Aki jogs into the pit, and I find a seat near the front.

"Aaaaand, fighting our guest today is none other than our very own Demon Lord, Lord Seraphety!"

His name is Lord Seraphety?

Verity whispers, "It's a placeholder name. Not his real one. Names are powerful things to us Demons. Knowing them can allow us to control you. So we withhold them to everyone bar those we truly trust."

Oh.

He struts into the pit, naked from the waist up, like Aki, and the fiery coloring on his horns and skin glowing brightly.

"The rules are simple," the announcer yells. "Hand-to-hand combat until someone draws first blood. No serious injuries or death here today, since the opponents are people of import. All forms of non-active magic are allowed, including mind control, telepathy, boosting charms, and things of the like."

Both Aki and Lord Seraphety circle each other as the announcer counts down.

"Five . . . Four . . . Three . . . Two . . . One!"

Lord Seraphety lunges at Aki quicker than I thought possible. And when Aki dodges and rolls to the left just as quickly, I change into my female form so I can follow. Aki swings a low punch, but Lord Seraphety blocks with a solid arm, absorbing the hit.

"Scared to take a hit, my lord?" Aki taunts. "Not very Demon-like of you."

He hisses at Aki, his eyes glowing brighter, and then charges. Horns first.

Aki's eyes widen, and just as those horns are centimeters from his gutting him, he jumps back, landing on two solid feet.

The Demons surrounding us boo and hiss. Disappointed.

"He nearly had him then," our escort shouts. "C'mon, he's just a silly Witch!"

I snort-laugh. If only they knew.

Luckily for everyone, Aki is holding back.

I do not want to be carrying his carcass back to *Sheruta* after he accidentally kills the lord of Demons. That'll be sure to get them to join the Fae.

Drums line the fence, all manned by Demons, and they pick up a single, thrumming beat when Aki recenters and aims for a throat punch.

It lands!

"Yes!"

The Demon Lord coughs and splutters for a split second, but he regains composure quicker than expected. Frustration ebbs. And he throws that anger out of him with a curved charge that catches Aki in the middle with the curve of his horns.

Aki flies across the pit and lands in a heap not far from me.

"Aki!" I Vampire speed to the fence, throwing the drummers out of my way, worry clouding my senses. "You okay?"

Aki stands, shoots a smile my way, and turns back to the fight. "Yeah." He's not bleeding yet.

How can a child throw a grown man so far across a room like that? Demon or not, that's insane.

Sitting back in my seat, confusion must rain clear across my face, because our escort whispers in my ear, "Impressed, huh?"

"How is he so strong?"

"Demons have Vampire-like strength."

Well, fuck. "Perfect."

"I know, right?"

"Sarcasm not a thing with Demons?"

He shrugs. "I choose to ignore such a stupid form of communication. Other Demons might engage. Idiots."

Aki lands a punch to Lord Seraphety's face, but he retaliates by throwing a rapid succession of knee strikes to Aki's gut.

Aki sputters and coughs, then throws himself out of the way with a spin. But he's off balance.

And Lord Seraphety notices. He takes advantage by charging, horns first, in Aki's direction.

This is it. It's over.

We've lost.

Aki reaches into his short's pocket and yanks out something small and black he smashes on the ground. Black smoke engulfs him seconds before those horns would have reached him.

A Witch charm!

When the smoke passes, Aki's a few feet off the ground, and Lord Seraphety charges into nothing, losing his footing and landing on his hands and knees.

Aki kicks him in the ass, sending him flying into the pit's wall.

The drums stop.

The announcer rings out, "First blood!"

The Demon Lord stands up and wipes his nose clean, a smear of blood on his hand, and I smile.

"Yes!" I stand up with a scream and punch a fist into the air. "Ha!"

"Alright, settle down," our escort says.

And that's when I look around and see everyone sitting in silence.

46

"A few bruises and scrapes, one broken rib, and a mild concussion," the doctor says. "You got off easy." She places her equipment back into their case and stalks off.

Leaving Aki with me.

He goes to stand up and stretch, but he winces and places a hand to his broken rib.

I grab a cup from the side and prick my finger with a single fang, dropping a small pool of blood into the bottom. Just a few drops. Nothing substantial. "There." I shove it under his nose.

His nose wrinkles in disgust.

I pull the cup back. "Fine. Deal with the broken rib yourself." And shrug.

He scowls at me but yanks the cup from my fingers and downs it in one. "There. Good as . . ." He wobbles on his feet and places a steadying hand on the nightstand. "*Uwa.*"

"Here." I help him sit back down. "How are you feeling?"

"Lightheaded. But strong." He twists one way, then the other, and then opens his eyes and smiles up at me. "Thank you. That's . . . amazing!"

"Yeah." I scratch the back of my neck. "Figured it out when Connie needed me." The memory sends a deep chill through my body. Seeing her like that . . . A mess of fear and depression. It was harrowing.

But she's getting better. Slowly. And one day she'll be okay with someone other than me touching her.

"Some real uses there."

"Huh?"

"For the war, I mean."

"Oh, right." I guess he's right. I could produce a bunch of blood pouches or test tubes or tablets or bubbles or something to each team for emergencies. "Probably couldn't produce enough for the whole army though."

"But enough to arm the higher-ups with a few cases in case they need them?"

I nod. "Certainly." Might get Nine on that when we return. Speaking of which . . . "I'm running out of blood. We'll have to return home soon."

Aki frowns. "Can you not just stay in male form?"

I shake my head. "Magical weakness affects all of me, regardless of my form. I can stay in male form without getting overly malnourished, but I'll be angry and annoyed and grouchy and generally a pain in the ass."

"Right." He places a smiling hand on my shoulder. "We kinda need you friendly when dealing with all these supes."

"Yup."

The doors to the infirmary burst open, and our escort Demon barges through and marches toward us. "So, you're both doing okay, then?" He looks us up and down. "Good. The Demon Lord will see you now."

"Huh?" Aki asks.

"For your deal." His eyebrows raise, and he chuckles at Aki's surprised face. "Yes, it wasn't just for the bro points of fighting the Demon Lord. Which you would have lost had he been fully aged and trained."

Aki chuckles, places a hand on the Demon's shoulder, and walks ahead of us, out of the infirmary. "I have no doubts about that."

IF I EVER SEE ANOTHER THRONE ROOM IN MY TIME, FEEL FREE TO JUST OFF ME. I SWEAR, THESE fucking supes and their superiority complexes. Though, is ruling the world as a Horseman really any different?

Damn, Magic, way to ask yourself the complex questions while staring at the Demon Lord.

"Our deal." The Demon Lord hands me a piece of paper ripped from an office-style notepaper and a pen. "Read, negotiate, and sign." He doesn't look at me when he talks.

"Are you really upset you were beaten?"

He shrugs and sinks back onto his throne, reminding me this Demon Lord is still a child.

"C'mon, you have loads of training to go. Think of all the strength you'll gain as you grow up."

He sighs. "Doesn't matter."

Before looking at the business in my hand, I walk up to the throne and kneel to I can look up at him and meet his gaze. "Hey, listen to me." I rest a hand on his knee. "Training's hard work. I was useless at magic a few months ago. I didn't know how to unlock my Witch abilities, I didn't know how to control my blood lust, I didn't know how to craft a Fae spell, and I certainly didn't know how to shift between forms or into an animal."

He meets my gaze, tears shining in his eyes. Unshed. "Really?"

"Uh-huh." I grip his hand and squeeze. "And, if you like, I'd be happy to donate some time to your training." I wince, thinking of my already insane list of things to do. "Maybe after I've dealt with the war. Sorry."

He waves a hand through the air, dismissing my apology. "I'd love to take training sessions from you or any of the Horsemen."

His advisors at the back of the room gasp and murmur.

But the Demon Lord is having none of it. He stands on top of his throne and turns his back to me, facing them. "I know they decimated our kind, but they had their reasons. The Great Purge was before my time. I can only lead our people into the future based on what we have now. Not what we had then." He shuffles back into his seat, then mumbles, "Always wanted to say that to those old crones."

I chuckle to myself and take an in-depth look at the words on the notepad in my hand. It all seems pretty standard to me. But I wish I had Nine here. He would know what seems fishy and what seems okay.

"So," I start, "you help us during the war, and we support you in whatever non-murderous endeavor you decide to take your species on in the future."

"That about sums it up, yes." He beams at me. "And I think I want to take our species out of the closet." Shocked gasps echo around the room. "So few know we exist, and there are many of us who wish to live in the outside world. I'm trapping my people here due to a centuries-old fear that isn't founded anymore."

"We'd be delighted to help with that."

"But maybe after things have settled back down."

Laughter flows from my mouth. "Yeah, that'll probably be best."

"Are there any other species you've gained help from?"

I look at him in surprise, his logic impressing me.

"I assume we're not the only lesser supernatural species to grace your presence in the last few weeks. The pixies were moved to *Sheruta* a few days ago. I assume that was your doing?"

"Yes. We thought it best to save them, regardless of their potential help." I take a deep breath. "But the fairies refused."

He stares into the distance, thoughtful, for a moment. "Well, as my first act of assistance, I want to advise you to take a trip to Switzerland. There are rumors flooding the Demon world that there might be a family of phoenixes living around the Jura Mountains."

My interest peaks, ears metaphorically flipping his way. "Phoenixes, really?"

"Indeed."

But I've never been to Switzerland.

Fuck, damn it.

I'm gonna have to fly.

47

We stayed with the Demons for another night, I gave the Demon Lord a few drops of Vampire blood to heal his battle wounds as a show of good faith, and Aki drank more alcohol than I thought possible by any living being.

We leave the next morning, Aki moaning and groaning beside me as we walk around the airport, picking up food from the few stalls open.

"Ugh," Aki groans for the hundredth time, "I don't think I can do it." He looks at the bacon roll in his hand with a slightly green tinge to his face. "It's like it's mocking me." His voice pitches higher, I assume, into his bacon voice. "Eat me, you're hungry." His voice pitches lower—into his stomach voice. "No, don't eat me, or I'll throw up what little contents I have all over the airport floor."

I can't help it, I laugh. His current pain is hilarious.

He scowls my way. "What's your problem?"

My laughter doesn't cease, but I manage to get a sentence out in between heaving gasps. "You shouldn't have drunk so much. You knew we were leaving in the morning."

"Why can't you heal me?!"

I shrug. "I can't heal a hangover, just injuries." I bite into my bacon roll and groan. Goddess, this shit is fantastic. "You're on your own."

"So much for sisterly love." He groans again as his head hits the table. "I shouldn't have had those last five shots."

"Five? Last?" I act shocked. "Just how much did you have to drink last night?"

"More than I've drunk in my entire life combined, and enough to drag that sexy Demon escort to bed." He smiles beneath his arm, I can feel it. "In fact, that might be worth this hangover." He raises his head and smiles, a wistful look brushing across his face. "Yeah, definitely worth it."

"Ew, ew, ew . . ." I bat my hands in the air. "I don't want to hear about my brother's sex life."

He swivels to face me. "But he was soooo good. Seriously, more than once, he got me off—"

I throw my hand over his mouth to shut him up. "Seriously, ew."

"Just because you're not getting any doesn't mean I can't have fun on our trip." He grins up at me, then winces and holds his stomach. "Besides, I bet your sex life is wild. Three—four?—partners? Orgy alert!"

"Oh my goddess, shut up," I hiss between clenched teeth. "Don't shout my sex life to the world . . ."

"Why? Trust me, you're getting more and better than the rest of us."

How has my life arrived at this moment?

"Because," I begin, then trail off. "Just because."

"Oh, what's that?" He cups his ear. "It's because you're a giant prude?"

I punch him—lightly—on the arm.

He flinches. "Hey! I'm ill!"

"It's self-inflicted, you giant douche canoe."

"Hey, I'm not a do—"

"Flight 201 now boarding," the lady over the tannoy echoes. "That's Flight 201 now boarding."

I grab Aki's hand and yank him behind me. "Come on, moron. And don't be sick on me on the plane."

The flight is long, Aki's sick a lot—but thankfully in the toilet—and I'm left to my own devices while he suffers. You know what that means? Reading time!

I load up my reading app on the plasmascreen, and there's a notification in the corner. A gift. Someone gifted me a digital book. Clicking on the icon and loading up the gift, I gasp. "Someone bought me a lot of books."

There's a note attached: To Killer, Some inspiration for your romance world. Love, Arrie.

He's gifted me one hundred romance books. And upon closer inspection, I realize they're all poly. Every. Single. One.

Rereading the note, my eyes can't look away from the signature. Love, Arrie. Is this some sort of an apology?

The first on the list is Not Quite Human by Kaye Draper, with another note from Arrie attached: Start here. So I dig in. And after several hours of wonder at reading a character similar to me, and many breaks to check on Aki, we land in Zurich Airport, Switzerland.

"I'm telling you, Aki," I say as we're clearing security, "Sam is just like me!" Then I think about it for a moment. "Well, maybe not exactly the same. I mean, I switch between man and woman while Sam is both always, but it's just . . . fuzzy."

"Fuzzy?" Aki asks as we're collecting our bags. "In what way?"

"Do you know what it's like to look in the mirror and never see yourself? No matter how hard you try, there's always a stranger staring back at you?" I wrap my arms around myself and try not to fall apart on the inside. "It's like not being able to recognize your own shadow. But seeing reflections like yours, even fictional ones, reminds you that maybe you're not as much of a stranger to yourself as you once thought." I smile, tears brimming. "So yeah, fuzzy."

Aki looks at me with a serious, deep, affectionate expression on his face, his eyes soaring into my soul and his heart beating alongside mine. He places firm hands on my shoulders and stops us walking. "Listen to me, sister. Just because your beauty isn't something you see on everyone else doesn't mean it isn't worth looking at, admiring, and being inspired by."

The brimming tears swim past their dam and pour over the edges in rivulets of warm pain spinning out of my body like a puppeteer emptying my vat of hurt and pouring it on the ground.

"Right." I sniff and enter his offering arms. "Thank you." My voice is barely a whisper, but being close enough to hug means I don't need to be brave enough to speak any louder.

He pulls away. "Now, shall we go find ourselves some phoenixes?"

"Yup." I wipe my face and compose myself before we exit the airport.

"How much do you know about phoenixes?" Aki asks as we grab a cab from the terminal and pay an exorbitant fee for the driver to take us to the Jura Mountains. Well, the nearest starting point, anyway. "I didn't even know they existed. I thought they were just legends, you know."

"Mmmm . . . It's kinda hard to know what's real and what's not when most of the supernatural community is still in hiding. Some things really are just legends, like dragons. But some things apparently exist."

"Like phoenixes?"

"Like phoenixes. But no, I've not ever met one. But I did know they existed. Nine mentioned their healing abilities once."

"They really have healing powers? That's rare. Even for the supernatural."

I nod. "Yeah, born Vampires have that power in their blood if offered, and some Witch charms have basic healing powers, but that's about it. I don't even really know what phoenix's healing abilities are like, if I'm honest. I didn't ask."

The truth is that we got a little distracted making out.

Oops.

But I'm not about to say that to my brother.

Not that he'd have a problem talking about my sex life.

Such a weirdo.

He seems to be in a better mood, less hungover, and more chatty now, so he takes the opportunity to pick up where we left off. "So, what's your earliest memory?"

Not the question I thought he would ask.

"Umm . . . Mom buying me one of those Hello Panda candy things. She took me took the park while we waited for Dad to finish work. We just . . . played. Nothing really grand. But I remember her beautiful smile as she pushed me high on the swing."

"Oh." Aki look at me with wonder and hurt in his eyes. "What were they like, Mom and Dad?"

"I don't have too many memories of them. I was pretty young when they passed. But the ones I do have always make me feel loved. They were kind-hearted. Good people. Dad used to do a cookout in the courtyard of our apartment building every month. He'd invite every neighbor in the building, and everyone would bring something, and we'd all eat, dance, play, and chat. He was always seeking the comfort of others—just being around them and absorbing their energy."

"They sound . . . wonderful."

"What were the Witches like in Japan? The ones who raised you?"

Aki shrugs. "I was raised by these two sisters who shared a house. They were . . . kind enough, I guess." He looks at my imploring eyes and sighs. "We just never clicked. They wanted me to just not use my magic, but I couldn't. It's . . . a part of me."

I nod. Understanding completely. "I can't not use that magic either. It just pops up when I'm in danger or seriously upset." Like when I tried to kill Arrie, for example. But I refrain from bringing that up. "My magic is like the air I breathe. I couldn't imagine giving it up."

I'm in my male form at the moment, given that my female form gets recognized too much, but the driver snort-laughs and tries to cover it up with a cough.

I side-eye him, doing my best to tell him to shut up without actually having to tell him.

He drops his eyes from the rearview mirror and refocuses on the road.

"Right," Aki agrees. "When I asked if they could just give up using theirs, it caused a huge argument and I left."

"How old were you?"

"Sixteen."

"I wish I knew you existed. I wish I were there to help."

He grabs my hand and squeezes. "I know. Me too."

48

The driver gets us to a small town not far from the Jura Mountains. I can see their huge mass looming in the distance—spanning 22,686 km^2 across more than just Switzerland.

"How in the world are we supposed to find phoenixes in there?" Aki asks the question on the precipice of my mind.

"I have no idea." I sigh, frustration gnawing. "I might need some help." I look to Aki. "We should teleport back to *Sheruta* so I can do some research with Nine. I'm running out of blood, anyway."

He nods. "Okay. Good plan."

Now we're in spitting distance of the Jura Mountains, we can teleport back whenever we need. So we grab our crystals, smash them at our feet, and think of home. And in fewer seconds than I can count, I'm standing in the kitchen with a mass of black feathers surrounding my entire body as harsh, demanding lips encompass mine.

Dea.

Some kisses are sweet, some remind you that you're loved, but some are all-consuming infernos; teeth, lips, groans, and hands all coming together in a wind tunnel of love and passion. That's what Dea's angel form is. A tornado of passion.

My mind turns that hazy shade of dizzy whenever I'm near his angel form, but I ignore it and rake my hands up his golden torso, meeting his kiss with equal amounts of force as I trace the outlines of his swirling tattoo and run gentle fingers across his lips before tugging on his piercings.

"I've missed you, Angel." His voice skitters across my skin, leaving a fiery path of goosebumps in its wake.

"Yeah," a rowdy voice echoes from somewhere on the other side of Dea's wings, "so have we, ass pig, so move out of my way!"

Dea spins around to face her and growls, his muscles tensing, his fists glowing red. "Mine."

"Dea," Nine's gentle voice pierces the tension, "come on, bro. Pull your mind back together." His hands run the length of Dea's jaw as their lips press together. But unlike the fiery volcano of our kiss, theirs is gentle—a lapping wave caressing the shore.

I run my hands up Dea's back, trying to soothe us both with some skin-on-skin contact. "We can snuggle later, if you like."

"Like this?" he asks, need and desire shooting through his voice.

A quiet chuckle escapes my lips. "I bet your wings'll make a great blanket."

Dea takes a deep breath and shudders at my hand wandering down the space between his wings. But after a few long seconds, his form shimmers and he changes back to himself. "I'm sorry," he pants, out of breath.

"Don't be," I reassure. "No harm done."

Connie huffs and pushes Nine and Dea out of the way, lifts me into her arms, where I wrap my legs around her waist, and peppers kisses up and down my neck. Shoving me to the nearest wall—which just so happens to be the fridge—her hands are free to roam my curves, my ass, and slip up my tank top . . .

A coughing sound echoes from the doorway, and Aki looks at me with an embarrassed smirk and a raised eyebrow.

"Err . . . right."

Connie puts me down, and I straighten my clothes out.

Hey, Nine. I missed you.

I missed you too, Sweetie.

Goddess, the silky soft voice inside my head is something I seriously missed. I never want to go without his voice in my head again.

No one loves my telepathy more than you, he chuckles.

Yeah, well, it has its uses.

I throw a sexy image of Dea in his birthday suit up in my mind and watch him close his eyes and smile. I wink in his direction and then clear my throat before addressing the room. "We're actually not done yet, but we've hit a bit of a knowledge gap. And I'm out of blood." Not to mention I'm thirsty as fuck for fresh blood. The chilled stuff Arrie provided is fine, but it's stale as shit.

"What knowledge gap?" Nine asks.

Arrie's still at the kitchen table, but he lifts his head from the newspaper and smiles at me.

Progress!

I spin back to Nine. "Phoenixes in the Jura Mountains, Switzerland."

His eyebrows shoot to his hairline. "Phoenixes? They exist?"

Aki finally enters the kitchen. "The Demon Lord seemed to think so. He's the one who gave us the tip."

"Ohhh," Connie says, "how'd the Demons go?"

"Good question." I face Aki with an accusatory glare. "Wanna answer that, Aki?"

His gaze shoots to the floor as a red flush blushes his features. "Well, I kinda maybe challenged the Demon Lord to a fight, won, then . . . slept with a first ranking Demon." He mumbles the last part, but I'm sure they all pick it up.

Heck, Connie has super hearing.

Aki was loud and proud with me, but with the rest of the team, he's all shy and whimpering. Why is that?

Maybe he's a little intimidated by us?

Is that what's in his mind?

Actually, I can't read his mind. Never have been able to. It's a bit like the shield you sometimes throw up when you don't want me hearing something.

Oh. That's a bit strange. Maybe it's an Angel-descended Witch thing?

Maybe.

Connie, Dea, and Arrie are all stifling giggles, but it's Connie who asks him, "Ohhh, sleeping with a Demon." She wraps an arm through his. "How was it?"

He looks at her with raised eyebrows, then smiles and delves into more detail than a sister ever wants to hear.

I shove hands over my ears. "La la la. Not listeniiiing!"

Connie drags him away, out of the kitchen, and I shift into my male form so I can't hear them anymore.

Galaxy eyes pierce me with a scolding gaze, and I remember how attracted to me Dea is in this form.

"Hey Dea," I whisper. "Hey Nine." I turn to the kitchen table to say hi to Arrie, but he's not there anymore. "Hey . . . Oh." Probably doesn't want all this PDA, anyway.

At the first sign of disappointment, Nine and Dea wrap their arms around me. Silent companionship. Love. I don't need anything else. Especially not someone who doesn't love me back.

"We're in the testing phase of an early prototype of the blood supplement, so I have a few days free," Nine offers. "I'm sure Connie's planning how to get away from management duties for the night, too."

"How about," Dea starts, "a night under the stars, a bonfire, some smores, drinks, laughter?"

"That sounds perfect." I hesitate, frustration bubbling to the surface. "I need to top up my blood supplies while I'm here and do some research into the Jura Mountains. Maybe something will pop up that hints to the phoenixes' location." I grab something from my bag. "Oh, and here's the deal I made with the Demons." I hand the contract over to Dea.

"I will give it a once over, but I am sure you did a splendid job, Angel."

"If you and Aki need some help, I'd be more than happy to spend some time in the library with you." Nine smirks. "We've yet to christen the stacks, after all."

"Nine," I groan. "We can't fuck in the library with my brother there. That's weird."

"Fair shout," he agrees. "I'll have to find another little slice of time to *slide* into your schedule."

Goddess, I've missed his bad puns.

"Glad I can be of service."

"I, too, can help, if you need it." Dea's arm wraps tighter around my waist as he grips my hip and places a soft kiss to my hairline. "We're all at your disposal."

"Okay, then let's grab Connie and Aki and make it a team effort!"

. . .

THE SCENT OF OLD BOOKS, NEW BOOKS, AND STACKS UPON STACKS OF MY OWN COLLECTION works better than any massage known to man. My shoulders unclench, days of travel wash away, and I breathe a deep breath of familiar, homely air. "Goddess, I've missed this place."

"I have missed seeing you in it, Angel."

"Yeah," Connie says from a nearby corner, "it's weird being here without you in it."

We round the corner, and I watch as Connie and Aki natter on a multi-colored couch, each of them curled up in either corner.

Aki smiles at me, big and bold. "Connie here was just telling me of your immortal journey so far. Seems it's been quite a ride."

I stare at Connie and point a finger her way. "No telling him the juicy bits! He might be your guys' friend, but he's my brother, and that's weird." And I don't trust her not to brag.

She salutes me, all serious-like. "Yes, sir." Before we both spill into giggles.

They both get up and walk over, my soldiers standing in a row, and Aki says, "What do you need from us?"

"Information. Phoenixes in the Jura Mountains, anything odd about the Jura Mountains, legends from French and Swiss mythology, etc."

"I'm going to start with the geography," Nine announces. "Maybe something'll bounce out at me." He wanders off, his face that gentle smile he gets when he's puzzling something out.

"And I'm going to look into mythology." Aki wanders off.

"I will join you," Dea says, "but I am sorry if you cannot see me."

Aki shrugs before they turn a corner. "S'okay."

Connie wraps an arm around my waist and smirks. "Guess that just leaves us, hon." She wraps both arms around my neck and snuggles her chin into my chest, inhaling deeply. "God, I've missed you."

Hands settling on her lower back and pulling her flush against me, I whisper, "I've missed you too." A sweet kiss to her head has her looking up at me with a twinkle in her eye and promises of things to come tonight. "I promise we'll spend time together this evening. Though, you're gonna have to share." I shrug. "Sorry."

"That's okay. You're worth sharing."

"C'mon," I say as I grab her hand, "guess we should get to my desk and ask my Seeing Stone."

A short walk around plenty of corners brings us to my desk, where papers are scattered everywhere, the flash drive rests next to my plasmascreen, and tucked away in my drawer lies the Seeing Stone.

This Seeing Stone works like a magical book finder. I just think the things I want to know the answers to, and poof, books appear on my desk that hold the answers. Today, I need answers regarding phoenixes in the Jura Mountains. Or just phoenixes in general. Either works for me.

Thud, thud, thud, thud . . .

A small mountain of books lands on my desk one by one, causing Connie and I to share a look.

"It's gonna be a long day, isn't it?"
She shrugs. "At least you got here in the morning."
"Guess there's that."

49

Five hours later, our three teams have all rejoined back at my desk, where Connie and I have been scouring the books—to little avail. Dea, Nine, and Aki have had some success, but not much.

"So, to recap"—I run a frustrated hand through my blonde hair—"our only lead is the Jura Mountains Region National Park, which hasn't been open to tourists in over two hundred years and is managed by a shell company whose real identity is wrapped up tighter than a virgin's asshole?"

Nine finds my joke funny, as does Connie, but Aki and Dea seem a little put off by the imagery. Which is rich coming from Dea, the guy who loves fucking Nine and me in the ass.

"Yeah," Nine says as he wipes the laughter from his eyes, "that about sums it up."

"Well," Aki chimes in, "that does narrow it down. 1,650 km^2 of space, rather than 22,686 km^2."

He has a point.

"If it comes to it, I can probably fly around that area and use my Vampire vision, but it hurt like a bitch last time."

"Well," Nine says, "according to history, there used to be border towns at the entrance that allowed admission, so maybe start there. It sounds to me like the phoenixes might be running their own community. But they'd need outside help for that."

"Right." Dea strokes comforting circles around my wrist. "And if they are keeping things this locked down, it seems only a natural jump there might be more species there than just phoenixes."

Aki's eyes widen. "You think they're running a commune or rescue center for lower supes?"

"We've seen weirder things in our time, kid," Connie answers. "This one even makes sense."

"Yeah," I say, "the lower supe world has been being exploited long before the pillar communities came out of the closet, so it makes sense they'd help each other out and create a safe haven."

"Maybe the humans there originally were helping?" Aki suggests. "Maybe they parted ways for a reason."

Dea and Nine share a look, and Nine explains, "They probably parted ways when we outed the supernatural world to humans. I imagine the lower supes wanted complete safety from humans."

"I wish we knew of all the supernaturals that exist," Dea says, "that way we will not leave so many out when we make a decision that affects them."

"You did the best you could." I rest a comforting hand on his shoulder and squeeze. "You can't work with what you don't have."

"It is our job to help everyone, Angel. But the more of the lower supernatural world you uncover, the less helpful I realize we have been." With creased brows and dull eyes, he storms off to some other—probably quieter—part of the library.

"Is he going to be okay?" Aki asks, worry ruining his usually smiling face.

Nine looks at him with a weak, reassuring smile. "Before Magic, Dea was in charge. Now they kinda co-lead, but everything was on his shoulders before."

Understanding dawns on Aki's face. "He feels guilty?"

He's surprised by that? "We're living, feeling beings, you know. Ones with a fair number of responsibilities resting on our shoulders. Of course he feels guilty. What the fuck did you expect? For us to be robots?" I storm off to find Dea, shifting into my female form so I can scent him out easier.

Just follow the smoky lavender scent.

When I see Dea on the floor, his head in his hands, I push my frustration at Aki away and wrap my arms around Dea's neck. "Heeey, it's okay."

"No, it is not," he grumbles. "The Demons we left alive hate us for good reason and have been living in isolation, the pixies are all but decimated because we did nothing to help, the fairies will not help us because we did not help them when they needed us, and now there might be a whole population of ragtag species we had no idea existed, all of whom have suffered and found their way to a safe haven we did not provide." His fists curl tighter, his knuckles whitening, and a growl escapes his lips. Only, it turns into a sob halfway through. "I should have done better."

"There are hundreds of species out there, Dea." I settle in front of him and force his chin up. "You have done amazingly without any guidance or help trying to lead a world that refuses to be anything more than broken pieces that refuse to glue back together." My hands rest on his wet cheeks, and I try for a smile. "You are an amazing person, Death, and I love you."

More tears spill, but a smile breaks out. "I love you, too, Angel."

"Where's my declaration of love?" Nine asks from a few meters away.

I didn't even know he was there.

Dea grabs his hand and yanks him down to where we're sitting and envelops him in a group hug. Looking him straight in the face with vulnerable eyes that are barely glowing and a weak smile, he whispers. "I love you, Famine. Do not forget it."

Nine's confident facade cracks as he rests his forehead to Dea's. "I love you, too. And I'm so sorry for not telling you sooner and letting us go so long apart—"

"Shhh . . ." Dea presses a finger to his lips. "There is no need for that."

Nine kisses Dea's finger, leans forward, and looks at us both. "Kiss me."

We both press our lips to his at the same time, our tongues tangling in an awkward, messy kiss that's somehow perfect. But with Dea's tears and Nine's cautionary vulnerability, I'm left feeling everything they're feeling, like an empathetic vat of emotions has just poured itself over me.

Connie's standing awkwardly off to the side, like she doesn't quite know what to do, so I break away and drag her to the floor with us, inviting her to bathe in the vat of gooey emotions.

Hey, there's plenty to go around.

She lays her head in my lap while Nine does the same on Dea's lap, and we bask in the simple act of being together after a long week apart.

"Where's Aki?" I ask, worried about abandoning him after snapping like that.

"Somewhere around the library," Connie answers. "Probably giving us all a moment alone."

I cringe. "I should apologize, huh?"

Nine chuckles. "Yeah, probably. But I like that you stand up for us." He grabs my hand. "It's very sweet."

"Pfft. I'm not sweet."

Connie laughs. "Yeah, you are."

And if she weren't in my lap, I'd punch her in the arm. Bitch.

Careful, she'll probably eat you for breakfast.

I can only hope.

Nine laughs in my head, and then out loud, and when Dea and Connie look at him in confusion, he repeats the conversation.

"Does sound like a good breakfast, to be fair," she confirms.

My cheeks burn hot, embarrassment flooding through me.

"Oh, come on," Connie says, "you've slept with all three of us. You can't possibly be embarrassed right now."

Apparently, though, I can. Which is weird because she's right. But oh well, whatever.

"Angel, do not make me prove you should not be embarrassed by us or yourself." He raises his brows, and his eyes glow brighter, some of that gold coloring brightening my smile.

If it makes him smile like that, I'll do whatever he wants.

Something smells amazing in the kitchen! Tomato-y, lemon-y, and fantastic. "What is that smell?" I wander my way into the kitchen in search of answers.

Arrie's standing at the stove in his frilly apron with a frying pan in hand that he's tossing cherry tomatoes in. "Tomato and garlic bruschetta, butternut squash risotto, and lemon tart with homemade cherry compote."

"Marry me." There's nothing I won't do to have a cook like this in my life forever. "You're amazing."

He laughs and the sound lights me up. "You're easy to please."

"Only when they want to be," Dea chimes in from the kitchen table.

They . . .

That doesn't sound too bad.

Maybe.

Realizing I'm standing in the kitchen doorway, gazing into thin air, I readjust my mind and shake myself toward the table. "Has anyone seen Aki? I tried to find him to apologize, but he's vanished."

"He left hours ago, Angel. Said something about giving us some privacy. Nigel's staying at his place, too. He left here a few days ago."

"Right." Guilt rocks through me. "I shouldn't have snapped."

"You are not perfect, Angel. Nor should you have to be."

Nine and Connie walk into the kitchen, both groaning at the smell of Arrie's cooking.

"Damn, you who tryna impress?" Nine asks, a smirk on his face. "I'm sure they'll love it."

"Get off," Arrie grumbles. "If you all settle down, I'll feed you." We all shut up, Nine takes his seat next to me, and Arrie laughs. Again. "It's like I've offered a bunch of toddlers an ice cream if they give me five minutes of peace."

"Puhlease . . ." I roll my eyes behind his back. "Your food is much better than ice cream."

"Especially the kind you give children," Nine agrees.

Arrie ignores our jaunting and serves the first course, placing my plate down with a smile.

You two seem friendlier?

Right. Friendlier.

I throw the conversation I had with Arrie while waiting for the pixies his way.

Nine just looks at me with a deep sadness. *I'm sorry.*

It's okay. I have to respect his decision. If he isn't ready, he isn't ready. There's nothing I can do about that. I just wish he would tell me why.

Maybe one day he will.

Here's to hoping that day is tomorrow. Or yesterday.

Give him time.

It's really all I can do.

"Soooo," I say to the group, trying to run away from that conversation, "what have I missed?"

"Well," Connie starts, "Arrie and Dea have been coordinating efforts to combine our forces for the upcoming defense of the five Vampire cities. The Vampire King is immensely grateful for everything we've been doing. Nine has been drowning in tests, science, and other nerd stuff, but he's pretty close to a workable blood substitute. Oh, and the pixies have taken the north forest as their own. The *Sherutan* residents welcomed them with open arms and are helping them set up home."

"Okay. That sounds great." They're doing better than me. "We should expect Demons soon, so you're probably going to need to prepare for that."

Connie nods. "Yeah. Since Demons prefer darker environments close to nature, we've been coordinating efforts with the Witches and Vampires here in *Sheruta* to brainstorm the best place to create a base for them."

"I assume Glowy is with the pixies?" I raise an eyebrow at Arrie.

He nods. "Wants nothing to do with us."

"Glowy?" Dea asks. He's been unusually quiet today.

I wonder what's bothering him?

"The Angel," Arrie confirms. "Magic didn't even try to fight her, so I assume you're a bit salty?" He looks at me.

I snarl. "I am not salty."

Connie and Nine chuckle at my obvious saltiness.

"Alright, I'm a little salty. But I was tired, nowhere near a leyline, and in the middle of the Amazon fucking jungle. I'm sure I'd have put her on her ass in any other environment."

"I didn't even know Angels still existed," Nine says. "Well, I assumed there were some still around, but I didn't realize we'd come across one."

"There are more with the Demons," I add. "I spoke to one, but there were some in the crowd watching Aki and the Demon Lord fight." I shrug. "You didn't kill them all, so of course they're still around. It's a small world."

"Getting smaller by the day," Dea mumbles.

The second and third courses are just as fantastic as the first, and with Arrie in his element, everyone is full, happy, and content.

"What does everyone want to do this evening?" I ask. "I promised Dea we'd cuddle, but other than that, is anyone free to hang out?" I know Connie, Dea, and Nine are. But is Arrie? I look to him. "Arrie?"

He shrugs. "Sure." But he doesn't look happy.

"You don't have to, if you'd prefer to do something else."

He sighs and meets my gaze. "I was going to leave you alone to spend time with your . . ." He looks at the others. "Partners. But if you want me there, I can hang out."

"I want you happy."

His gaze pierces mine, and the sad little smile on his face breaks some deep part of me.

Suddenly, I know exactly what to get Arrie for Christmas. And it'll for sure make him happy. Yay. That's two ideas down. Just two to go. Then everyone else.

FIRE CRACKLES INTO THE NIGHT SKY, SETTING THE STARS AFLAME AND OUR FACES ALIGHT. Connie's roasting smores with Nine while Dea lies in my lap, wings spread wide beneath us, and Arrie's chatting with Dea about a new car he wants.

"Will that engine not be a bit . . . loud?"

Arrie chuckles. "Dude, you're missing the point."

"Probably." He laughs. "I have never understood the point of cars and engines. Horses work well enough."

"Sure," Arrie counters, "if you want to get to your destination by the end of the year."

"I'm with Arrie on this one," I chime in. "Horses are slow. Cars can go up to three hundred mph nowadays."

Dea groans. "You young people are always trying to get places quickly. If you slow down, you might have less to moan and bitch about."

"Hey, who you callin' old?" Arrie asks.

Connie gasps. "He swore!" She grabs Nine's shirt sleeve and points to us. "Dea swore!"

"Outside of the bedroom?" Nine asks, acting shocked, as though he doesn't hear him swear every other night. "Well I never."

"Oh, lay off," Dea grumbles. "I am allowed to express myself."

I run soothing hands down his shoulders and brush his wings, and he shivers and sighs like he's been doing all night. Leaning down, I whisper, "I love you in both forms."

He leans his head back and reaches my lips, brushing them with the lightest of touches it feels like a feather blowing across them.

"Alrrriiiight!" Connie bounds over to us, carrying three bottles of tequila. "Who wants tequila shots?"

We all groan, but I laugh and ask the house for shot glasses. Five shot glasses pop onto the grass. One for each of us. Everyone grabs one, and Connie makes us wish we all didn't agree to her idea of a bonfire.

Twenty-three tequila shots are far too many, even for a Horseman. As evidenced by the fact Arrie is wobbling around with his head thrown back in laughter at Dea, who just dropped me out of the fucking sky.

My head hurts. I think I broke my ass. And if I don't get to a toilet soon, I'm gonna pee myself. "Need to pee! Need to pee! Need to pee!" I wobble to the toilet in the gym, not using Vampire speed or shifting, because both of those things seem like a bad idea given I can't walk in a straight line. We don't need another drunk flying incident.

Pretty sure my dick misses the bowl multiple times, and a realization hits me. Men don't poop when they pee. They might pee when they poop, but since they're standing up when they pee, they still have to control their bowels.

Wow. What a world.

So I sit down to poop.

And then stumble back out to the party, where Nine and Dea are making out by the fire, Nine grinding into Dea with drunken fervor; Connie is shouting at the stars for shining too brightly, and Arrie is picking a fight with the bonfire.

Connie downs another shot and trips over the log, falling into the edge of the flames. "Ahhh!" she shrieks. "Shit!"

Everyone stops what they're doing and worries over to Connie.

She's writhing on the grass, but her burn is already healing. "Someone just make it stop . . ." The sobbing comes next, and I know I need to get her to bed.

"You know," I say as I wrap my arms around her body, "it's usually you helping me."

"Well, it's my turn to be a mess for a change."

"Here"—Arrie offers his arms—"I'll take her. Stay and enjoy the night."

I hand her over and watch him stumble through the kitchen door, hoping they'll be okay.

"I'm sure Arrie will get her to her bed, Angel." Dea wraps an arm around my waist and leans on me, tucking his wing behind my back. "But if you like, you can go check on her. We'll be okay."

"It's okay. She's probably passed out now, anyway. I'll crawl in next to her later."

Nine tucks himself under Dea's wing and wraps an arm around my chest. "She'll like that."

"Join me when I do?"

"Of course."

Always.

51

Connie grumbles into my ear the next morning as Nine presses his backside into my dick and Dea lies on top of us all, wings still out. He stayed in his angel form all night? I don't think I've ever seen him do that.

Nine's sleepy voice echoes in my head. *I don't think he has. But he's been itchy since you left. His angel form's been popping out all over the place. He's been struggling.*

He's been struggling that much? Why didn't anyone tell me?

He didn't want us to. He wanted you to be able to be independent.

You've been helping him feel loved, right? In my place?

He chuckles inside my head. *Of course. But there's only so much I can do to soothe an angel mating bond.*

I need to spend some time with my angel when we get back. I'm hoping I won't be gone for more than a few days this time, anyway.

Connie groans again.

And I flip around to face her. "Hey, beautiful." I press a gentle kiss to her forehead, careful to give her space first thing in the morning. "You doing okay?"

"Mmmmm." She wraps an arm around my waist and snuggles into my neck. "Better now."

Dea shuffles on top of us, and we all groan.

"Bro, get off," Nine complains. "You're crushing me."

Dea rolls and weasels his way between me and Nine so he can grab me and yank me on top of him.

Connie and Nine rearrange themselves on top of Dea's wings, and now everyone is staring at my topless body, roaming their eyes over what little muscle I have.

You're hot. Don't be unconfident.

Thanks.

Dea offers me his wrist with a smile. "Breakfast?"

"Or you can drink from me instead, if you like?" Nine offers, holding his wrist out.

Connie stays silent, but I'll never force or expect her to feed me. Besides, I have three other . . . Two. I have two other partners for that.

I look at Connie, who smiles at me and takes a deep breath. "I'll be okay. Go ahead."

I shift into my female form and grab both their offered wrists, bend their hands back, sink one fang into each man, and drink from both at the same time. The rush of euphoric pleasure shoots across my body, and I instinctively grind down onto Dea's rapidly hardening cock.

The last time I was in this form, I was showering before slipping into Connie's bed, so I'm naked, and Dea's angel form makes it uncomfortable to wear clothes, so he's in nothing but his pants.

Connie gasps a little, and I feel her breathing rapidly and her heart throwing itself around, but she cautiously approaches and rests a hand on my face.

Nine and Dea are groaning beneath me, with Nine struggling to stop his hips thrusting into the air. But the moment I touch his cock through his pajama pants, that small amount of control snaps, and he meets my palm.

Still drinking from the guys, I look to Connie, my eyes blazing red and my face one that likely haunts her dreams.

But she doesn't seem scared anymore—the lust in her eyes pins my hand on Nine's cock and the way I'm riding Dea's in a haze I recognize from our time together. "Keep going."

I slow down my feeding because I don't want to take too much, but I'm not ready to lose the connection.

Connie straddles Dea's legs behind me and presses her breasts to my back in scorching heat that travels all the way through me. Her hand travels over my waist and down, meeting the wet heat below that's dripping onto Dea's pants. "God, you feel delicious, hon."

Nine's eyes snap open and focus on Connie's hands as she delves a finger into me and causes me to snap my jaw around their wrists harder as a moan escapes me.

I'm getting a little dizzy, Sweetie.

I let go of their wrists, but I still need them. Need what only they can offer.

As if sensing where my mind is at, they don't hesitate in shucking their clothes off.

Connie steals me to herself for a while, adding two, then three fingers and riding me into her soft mattress as my hips grind into her palm. Her kisses petal across my collarbone and up my neck, where she nips and sucks to the rhythm of her hand.

Dea's wings encompass us both when he returns to the bed, his dick on full show in front of me as I wet my lips.

"Wait," Nine says, "Dea, are you going to be okay sharing Magic in that form?"

I meet his eyes, questioning him, and he shrugs.

"I do not know for sure, but I am not feeling any murderous intentions right now. You are all making my angel happy, therefore you can all stay."

"Good," I say, "then get over here." I open my mouth and stick my tongue out flat against my chin.

"I think she wants your dick, bro."

"You do not say." Dea crawls over to me and teases my tastebuds with the tip, a smirk falling on his face when he looks into my eyes.

Connie crawls down my body, peppering kisses on her journey, and scores one swipe of her tongue up my heat, causing me to buck into her mouth and cry out.

"Don't stop," I moan.

Dea fills my mouth slowly with a single crawling thrust. "Yes, Angel."

I swirl my tongue around the head and encourage him to thrust, to use me and leave me in a puddle beneath him.

Connie thrusts two fingers back into me, and I cry out around Dea's dick. Curling them up and sucking my clit into that talented mouth of hers has me arching off the bed and crying her name.

Nine comes around to my side, avoiding Dea's wings, and leans his head to my chest before taking one of my nipples into his mouth.

Together, they're wrecking me in the best way. And I try to hold on, I really do, but they push me over the edge pretty quickly, and soon I'm screaming their names into Dea's dick and begging for more.

I remove Dea's cock and throw myself at Connie, pinning her to the bed with a flash of Vampire speed I know frightens her a little bit. But she calms when I nibble my way up her thighs and swirl my tongue through her wetness.

"Magic . . ." She grips tight fingers into my hair, pushing my head closer. Her head throws back onto the mattress as a rush of breath leaves her.

"They look so hot," Nine says. But Dea must shut him up, because he moans and loses his words.

The next thing I know, someone is entering me from behind and pushing me farther into Connie's pussy.

"You're so tight," Nine praises as he pounds me harder and then cries out. "Yes, Dea!"

Lifting my head to see what they're doing, Dea's wings are flapping in the air as he thrusts into Nine and controls all our actions from behind.

Connie whines beneath me, so I return my attention back to her and add a finger to the mix, hoping to feel her explode around me. "Yes, yes . . ."

Dea groans and slaps something hard—Nine's ass I assume, because he cries out and pushes into me faster, riding his pleasure through me. "I cannot hold back any . . ." Dea trails off as he explodes.

Goddess, this is the hottest way to start my day.

But right now, I want the beautiful goddess beneath me writhing in as much pleasure as possible, so I add two more fingers and suckle at her clit. Hard. Nipping gently here and there.

Her hand grips the sheets as she arches off the bed and cries out, spasming around my fingers and panting, out of breath.

Nine grabs my waist and yanks me around to face him, then throws his lips against mine in a passionate frenzy that has me riding his lap.

Use me.

He leans back on his hands and throws his head back.

I grab on tight to his shoulders and squeeze his dick and grind my clit against him.

Harder.

I follow his instructions and ride him harder, slamming down on his lap and lavishing the skin-on-skin sounds we're making. My body tightens, and I know I'm getting close.

Bite me.

When I hesitate, he yells, "Now, please!"

My fangs snap down and latch onto his exposed neck, sinking in deep. Blood rushes down my throat and I clench around Nine's cock as another orgasm rockets through me like I'm on fire.

But the scream that leaves Nine's mouth is one of pure pleasure, echoing through both the air and my mind. "Magic . . ." he moans as he comes down and caresses my sweaty body.

"That was . . ." Connie starts.

"Seriously attractive to watch."

"Fucking hot," she corrects.

Nine flops onto the bed in a haze, panting, drawing in desperate gulps of air.

"Are you okay?" I ask, making sure I didn't break him or something.

I'm . . . Fuck, that was the best orgasm of my life. You all need to try that. Trust me. He chuckles out loud. *Oops, sorry Arrie.*

He must have sent that to everyone, not just us three.

THE KITCHEN IS FILLED WITH BREAKFAST FOOD AND THE TABLE IS FILLED WITH FAMILY: CONNIE, Arrie, Dea, Nine, Aki, and Nigel. And I'm filled with smiles and rainbows. No surprises there then.

Arrie hands me a batch of vials filled with blood. "Here." And tries to smiles at me, but it's weak.

I smile in way of a thank you, then turn to Nigel. "So," I say, "you handed in your notice?"

"Yeah." He scratches his head, embarrassed. "The moment I found out the Area 50 date, I couldn't do it anymore. For years, I pretended to myself that I was doing the right thing, but I wasn't." He looks to the table. "I still can't believe the Supernatural Council are our enemies."

"I know," Aki says. "It's crazy."

"When we helped create them," Dea says, looking just as embarrassed as Nigel, "we thought we were doing the right thing. Uniting the pillar communities."

Nine strokes his hand on the table. "We were."

Aki looks at Dea, who's visible while we eat, seriousness lacing his stare. "You can't be held accountable for the actions of others, no matter how godlike you might be."

Dea sighs. "I know."

The defeat in his voice laces my mind, and I just know he doesn't believe a word Aki is saying.

Looking back to the rest of the table, I stuff more food into my mouth. "We shouldn't be gone long. We teleported here from near the Jura Mountains, so we're teleporting back and scouting the area until we find the phoenixes."

"So, a couple days, tops?" Aki asks.

"Uh-huh."

"Why?" Connie asks him. "Got something better to be doing?"

His face flushes. "Well, I kinda have a date on Saturday."

My head snaps up. "With who?" Moreover, when over the last week or so did he have time to arrange a fucking date?

"Verity." He avoids my eyes.

"Oh, him."

"I can steal one of those teleporting crystals, right?"

I wave my hand in the air. "Sure. I'll make you a batch of each type."

His smile stretches from ear to ear.

"In fact, I might just start making them in batches and leaving them in baskets outside my bedroom door. Free for anyone who needs them." That'll save me from fulfilling everyone's orders.

"Good plan," Connie says. "I'll ask the house to set something up. Hopefully. If it listens to me."

Nine and Arrie laugh.

"Am I missing something?"

Nine answers, "She asked for a ballroom a few hundred years ago, full of gold décor and other specific design features that took the house a little time to complete, and it's been a little stroppy with her ever since."

Laughter colors my voice. "Well, if you can't get her to cooperate, I'll do it when I get back."

"Her?" Arrie asks.

I shrug. "Feels right."

Arrie doesn't answer, just goes back to his breakfast plate.

"How do you plan to scout that large an area?" Connie asks. "It's kinda a big mountain range."

"I'm gonna fly around and look. Probably as an eagle. Maybe a falcon. Whichever's fastest."

"Peregrine Falcon," Nine answers. "Should be flying around 200 mph."

"Cool." Aki grabs a final piece of fried toast and tops it with strawberries. "That should make things quicker."

"It's possible they've got a spelled barrier, though. Who knows what kind of creatures are there if they really do have a sanctuary," Nine warns. "Might be worth going a little slower and feel for any spellwork."

"Noted." I swallow my mouthful. "And we're gonna start near the old villages and towns, see if they still have an entrance to the National Park."

"Need practise shifting into a falcon?" Nigel asks.

No, but I'll humor him. "Sure."

We go outside, and Nigel instructs me to stand feet apart. Ready. "Something every Shifter shares is the unique way in which we shift. It can be slow, but it's possible to be quick if you practise." He scowls. "And you don't put nearly enough practise into your shifting."

"That's because it's so natural to me."
"Just because you're talented, kid, doesn't mean you away with practising that talent."
Great. More training.
"Whatever complaint you just threw at me in your head, save it. This is important."
Damn. The man knows me. "Okay. Show me what you got, old man."

52

It's late evening in the Jura Mountains, but as I shift into my practised falcon, I realize that it's not an issue because falcons have fantastic night vision. I squawk at Aki, hoping to convey that everything is working out, and then take off.

He'll be fine.

Right?

Right.

The mountains span out in the distance below me, and I head in the direction the map on Aki's datachip outlined.

Rock. Rock. And more rock. What a surprise?

This is like the Andes Mountains all over again.

But, after about an hour of flying, I feel something. Something like a spell, but not quite. In fact, I don't think I've felt anything like it before. Maybe it's some kind of magic from a species I've not come across yet?

Hmm. Maybe.

But I have a bad feeling.

Something about this spell feels wrong.

I swoop down to get a better feel for the spell, but I'm stopped by a barrier. What the fuck? Who puts a barrier up this high? How rude.

Right. I take a deep breath. I need to fly around this thing and find its entrance.

After another half hour of flying, I come across some ruins to an old village and an end to the barrier spell. Upon landing, I shift back into human form and read the glowing sign swinging in the mountain wind: Welcome to Hurro Village.

Bits of old rock jut out of the ground in vague, house-like shapes every few meters, moss growing up the sides and infiltrating the cracks like its own personal battlefield. And it's winning. At the end of the village, the barrier spell stands, barring me entry. At first, I think it's a Fae barrier, like the one my trainer in *Sheruta* uses for the forest Fae, but upon closer inspection, I can't detect any leyline magic. Whatever energy is making this spell, it isn't what the Fae or Witches use. This is something new.

Excitement runs through me, bordering around my curiosity like an old friend, as I run my hand up and down the invisible barrier. I poke and I prod, but nothing changes. It doesn't budge.

"Damn." I'm impressed.

Even the grumpy Fae who refuses to give me her name would have a hard time dealing with this. Or she might not be able to at all, actually. Fae seem endlessly impressive, as though they can do anything. But that's not true. They can only use the energy they store from leylines.

If we could figure this out, or gain favor from whomever uses this magic, we might turn the tides of this war.

Magical energy reaches me from the other side. Not massive amounts, just slight tremors, like shaky breaths, pass through the barrier and surround me. Someone's there.

"Hi! My name is Magic. I'm the Fifth Horseman." I take a deep breath. "I know you've created a safe haven here, and I know you want it to be secret. I promise, no one outside of the Horsemen's primary team knows of your existence. If at all possible, I'd love an audience with your leader." I bow low, keeping my hands shown. "I am sorry for trespassing."

More magical energy surrounds me. It's not threatening, just examining, but given it doesn't feel like any magical energy I've ever felt, I don't have the power to push it away. And that leaves me feeling uneasy.

I'm too used to being the strongest in a room.

A blue-glowing light outlines a door shape in the barrier, and a beautiful lady stands there, a long-flowing skirt a bright ocean green that matches her hair and eyes blows in the breeze. "Magic." She bows her head slightly. "You are welcome to Hurro, but please do not use your magic offensively while you're staying."

I bow my head. "You have my word."

She turns and leaves, expecting me to follow, no doubt.

With no small amount of trepidation, I step through the door and gasp. Wonder fills me. There are creatures everywhere, some of whom I've never seen before, and they're all interacting as though they get along. There are also creatures I do know about: pixies, some fairies, lots of Witches, and even a few Fae. None of them explain the barrier, though.

The lady stands next to me, allowing me to take everything in with a smile on her face. "Beautiful, isn't it?"

Tears threaten to leak from my eyes, but I brush them away. "It's everything the world is supposed to be."

"And more." She places a gentle hand on my shoulder and guides me forward. "Come on. I'll show you to the people who act as leaders. But we don't really have leaders like other communities. It's more of a population-run community."

"That sounds nice."

We walk through fields, past houses of all shapes and sizes, through groups of children playing in the grass, past couples and groups of friends chatting, and I'm pretty sure my mouth is still hanging open.

"How many people live here?"

"Twelve thousand across the entire park, but only a few hundred here at the entrance.

Mostly it's the children and families of those of us who guard the barrier."

That makes sense. The National Park is an enormous area. They wouldn't want to commute if they couldn't travel quick.

Looking back at my guide and her unusual coloring, I'm struck by how odd her species identity is. She seems similar to a Shifter, but she's not. It's probably rude to ask, so I keep my trap shut for a change.

See. I'm learning.

"They're just through that door." She points to a stone building that reminds me of a hunting lodge, but more modern. "Heads up. They don't like guests."

Great.

The massive double doors open as I walk up the steps, and standing in them is a man as large as Arrie, with a frown just as grumpy, and hair just as long, sitting at his shoulders. In fact, I'd say this is his brother or son if I didn't know better. And the similarity has me instantly backing up a step.

He chuckles, a deep, boorish laugh that isn't at all like Arrie's. "Don't worry, Horseman. I'm not going to fight someone as strong as you. I value my life."

I ascend the final few steps and smile. "Wise choice."

"Please"—he gestures to the doorway—"come on in. We were all just having some food. Join us."

"I've eaten recently, but I'd like to join nonetheless."

We enter the modest-sized room, and again, I'm kinda impressed with how this place looks. "This is not what I expected." Plasma screens line the walls, showing news from all corners of the world, while banks of computers line the far wall, work benches litter the space, and bright open art décor and shiny wooden accents decorate the walls. Various people work at the various stations, some of whose species I recognize, some I don't.

"What were you expecting?" he asks. "Cozy fireplaces and bearskin rugs?"

Yeah, actually. "Something like that."

"We like to monitor outcasts and people who might need our help." He gestures to the room. "This is how we do that."

"You help people who need you?"

He nods. "As best we can."

"That's . . . amazing."

"I'm glad you approve." He guides us to a room off to the side, where a large round table sits with food dotted around and two smiling, cheerful faces adorning the seats. "Everyone, this is Magic."

Their eyes widen, coughs splutter, and faces drop their smiles.

"I'm not sure why he's here. But I'm sure there's a good reason."

An older woman scowls at me and points. "If you're here to draft us into your war, then you can leave. We want no part in any of the communities you claim to protect."

"Please," the large man from before says as he gestures to one of many empty chairs, "sit."

I take a seat away from the others, who are sitting at the other end of the table. "Thank you for allowing me to join you. I promise not to discuss your location outside of the Horsemen team. I understand the necessity of your discretion."

"We thank you for that," a young gentleman with brown hair and honey-colored eyes says. "My name is Eldry." He points to the large man and says, "This is Reetus." He then points to the scowling old lady from before and says, "And this is Wendy. You'll have to excuse her impoliteness."

I bow my head in each of their directions and grab a glass of water from the center of the table. "Before I begin, I was wondering if you could have someone fetch my brother from the eastern side of the mountains? I may have left him there as I searched for your location in falcon form."

Reetus howls with laughter. "The poor fella is probably freezing his butt off. I'll get Treelus to fetch him. He'll be here within the hour."

Within the hour? Just how fast can Treelus fly?

"We have a chopper," Eldry explains. Clearly, the confusion was written all over my face. "It's pretty fast."

"So now we have that out of the way," the old woman spits, "what is it you've come to ask of us, Horseman."

"Please, Mama," Eldry says, "be more polite. Magic is just here to help their people." He smiles at me.

"Thank you. And yes, I'm here to ask for your help. But I'm not naïve. I know you will not want to risk your people or the community you've worked hard to create. So I won't ask that of you." I'm not really sure where to start, so I guess the beginning will have to do. "The Fae have teamed up with a rogue Vampire faction the Vampires don't agree with, and they have the SC under their control. With that in mind, we created the embassy. Currently standing, it has representation for Vampires, Shifters, Witches, pixies, and Demons. We're happy to add any species, no matter how small their population."

Both men smile, but the old lady sticks to her scowl.

"We're trying to unite as many species as possible so we can usher in a new world. Yes, there's going to be fighting involved. It would be naïve of us to try otherwise. Peace treaties are off the table since all the enemy wants is to rule the world, kill humans whenever they want, and generally be a bunch of lawless assholes."

"Sounds very like the Fae Queen," the old lady agrees. "Same old, same old."

"What if that wasn't the case? What if we could make a difference? What if we could reform the Supernatural Council to care for every species, create laws that protect, not restrict?"

"A pipe dream. You are young." She frowns, but she relaxes somewhat. "Many have tried before you, and all have failed."

"They didn't have the Horsemen." I sigh, frustration bubbling. "Look, I don't mean to be rude or egotistical, but I was quite literally created for this purpose. That's how Horsemen work. We're plucked from the recently dead and reborn with a purpose whenever the world needs us."

"Is it true the original four purged the world of Demons and Angels to protect the supernatural and human world?" Eldry asks.

"Yes. Though we are trying to make peace with the few Angel and Demon populations left."

All three look impressed; even Wendy seems unable to prevent her satisfied smirk.

"So what is your plan?" Wendy asks.

"We have a short-term goal and a long-term goal," I begin. "To start with, we would like to protect the Vampire population from the SC's Area 50 plans. They're going to shut down all the main Vampire cities. If we want to stay united, then we have to protect our vulnerable. And they are indeed vulnerable during the day on Christmas Day."

"Not a bad strategy," Reetus says. "Not condoning, but it is a good strategy. While New Orleans might have a high population of born Vampires, the rest of the Vampire cities do not. And made Vampires cannot protect themselves during the day. So they rely on other species. But Christmas Day is celebrated by most species across many countries, so they'll be busy and ill prepared."

"Yup." I cross my arms over my chest. "It's a bloody good plan. The only hole? They have no idea we know."

Reetus's booming laugh penetrates the air. "Aww, c'mon, Mama! This would be the best action I've seen in years."

Wendy scowls at her son and whacks him across the head. "Always with the fighting!"

I smile at them, pleased that out of all the places I've visited and species I've interacted with, these seem like a family. "How about this: those who want to join our cause may, but it's not necessary. And there are plenty of non-fighting roles. Any help toward peace will be useful."

Wendy looks to her sons and sighs. "Fine. But only because these two have been begging me to get involved and help for the last few weeks."

Eldry stands with a smile. "It's our job to help the lost and lonely, and right now, the supernatural world is lost and lonely." He kisses his Mama on the head and heads over to me with a handout.

I shake it with a smile. "It's good to have help come so easily."

"Child?" Wendy asks. "I won't force my people to get involved, and this space we have here in the Jura Mountains is to remain a secret and not used in your war in any way. Do I make myself clear?"

"Perfectly." I offer my head. "Thank you for your help."

She shakes my hand with a small smile—the first I've seen—and asks, "What are your long-term plans?"

"Peace."

She shakes her head. "All these young people aiming for the same thing, you'd think they'd align."

Looking out the window at the community surrounding me, I take a deep breath and smile. "I have so many questions."

Eldry places a hand on my shoulder and smiles down at me. "I bet you do. When your brother arrives, I'll be happy to answer them."

His tan skin contrasts the moonlight sky out the window, and it strikes me how much this man reminds me of Nine. The easy-going playfulness, the way the light bounces off his skin . . .

Goddess, I miss them all.

I need more than a single night with my boyfriends . . . girlfriend . . . partners? Life buddies. Yup. Definitely life buddies.

Aki and I stay in a guest house at the entrance village that night, and we're both out like lights despite the time difference. Something about being here utterly drains me.

"Morning, sleepyhead," Aki grumbles at me sometime in the morning. "C'mon, get up." He kicks my bed from his across the small room.

"Alright, alright." I yawn and stretch and blink in the morning sunlight. "I'm up."

"Good, 'cos the big burly guy was just here, and he dropped breakfast off."

Ohhh, breakfast.

I sit up and sniff the air, immediately waking up.

"It's just toast," Aki says, his smile widening.

"Yeah, but it's food. And I'm hungry." In fact, both forms are hungry right now, but I'm gonna focus on male me first. "Ooh, and there's honey."

An hour later, when we're fed, showered, watered, and clothed, we arrive at the same house as yesterday to meet with Eldry, who is going to show us around and answer all my questions.

"Magic!" He gleams. "Aki!" He opens his arms wide and brings us both in for a hug. "Magic, you're in your female form today? How wonderful."

"Oh, yeah." Just how I feel today, but sure, let's roll with the compliments. They feel nice. "I can see best this way. Vampire vision."

"Cool." He steps into a small truck with plasma windows you can completely see through or choose to make opaque. "Hop in."

Aki and I sit in the back, gazing out the window.

"We don't do this very often," Eldry says, "usually only when a new resident arrives. But you're a bit special, so we're making an exception."

"I'm sorry," I say, "I don't mean to make your people feel like zoo animals."

He looks at me in the rearview mirror and smiles. "It's okay. They're going to be a bit of a spectacle today, anyway. News of your arrival has spread far. Mama sent out a message that anyone who wishes to assist in your cause may do so and are to meet us at the entrance village this evening at eight pm."

"Oh, that's so thoughtful of you."

"Nah, it's nothing." He drives us up a rocky path and over the hilltop, the sunrise lighting the distance. "Truthfully, Reetus and I 'av wanted to intervene for some time. Or at least to do something. You know? But Mama was against it." He shrugs and sighs, the weight of having done nothing sitting on his shoulders. "I think she was worried we wouldn't make it out alive, but with you and the Horsemen here, with the makings of an army, she feels a little more hopeful."

"She didn't look hopeful," I mumble.

Eldry bursts into laughter, shaking his head. "She's a grumbler, for sure."

Wonder if she and Arrie are related?

"Oh my god!" Aki shouts. "Look at that!" He points out the window to a field on our left in the distance. "Are they . . . unicorns?"

A gasp escapes my lips as I grip the edge of my seat and look to where he's pointing. And lo-and-behold, before my very eyes are unicorns on Earth. "You have a unicorn pack? Here on Earth? But Nine told me they were hunted to extinction."

Eldry looks at me, confused.

"Famine saved a small pack and relocated them to *Sheruta*. We have a large herd in the rainbow forest outside my bedroom window."

He blinks at me. "There're more of them?" He blinks some more. "That's . . . Wow."

"I think, Eldry," Aki says, "you'll like *Sheruta* and the Horsemen very much."

He chuckles. "Well, Reetus is already dying to go toe-to-toe with your Horseman of War. Says he wants to fight the strongest being to ever live."

"Pfft." I'm stronger. "Good luck to him."

Aki chimes in, "Aren't you technically stronger than Arrie?"

"Eh. It depends what you're measuring. I'm more versatile. I have lots of abilities and strengths, whereas the other Horsemen only have a select few. But Arrie's strength is unparalleled." I shrug. "I don't really know. I've never arm-wrestled the guy."

"Sounds like a fun afternoon," Eldry says. "Maybe you should run a carnival one weekend and put on some events. Would let the world see who you are more, too."

"That's . . . Not half bad an idea, Eldry." Surprise laces my voice.

He acts mock hurt. "Hey, I'm more than a pretty face, you know. I do run this place."

"With help," I counter.

He smiles. "With help."

"So," I say, preparing to start asking my questions. "We actually came to look for phoenixes. Demons told us they were here."

Eldry laughs. "Those fuckers."

"Huh?" Aki asks, leaning forward. "What?"

"They're forbidden from talking about this place. They helped us form it, actually."

"So they gave us a false tip leading us to the Jura Mountains so we'd find you?"

"Well, we do have phoenixes. They're intelligent and might listen, but they're like unicorns. They can't communicate with us using language."

"Ah, I see."

I fidget in my seat as we continue on our drive, passing all kinds of non-communicating species on our way.

"Go on, ask me all your burning questions. I promise you won't offend."

And before I can put my mind into coherent thoughts, my questions flood from my mouth like a landslide. "What makes the barrier? What kind of magic is that? The woman who met me at the barrier, who is she? What kinds of species are there here? When did you form? Why are you in hiding? Why did you not ask the Horsemen for help? *Sheruta* is safer than this barrier, regardless of how cool the magic is. What are you and your brother?" I look sheepishly to the car floor. "Err . . . sorry."

Aki and Eldry both laugh at me, but Eldry shakes his head. "It's okay. No apologies necessary. I'm actually surprised you kept all that locked away until now. Usually new residents list an endless stream of questions for days until they're left to process them."

"How do new residents come here?"

"We have agents who usually go out and save them, then return them to their new home. They have a choice, of course. If they want to stay out in the normal world, we usually help find them a temporary place and monitor them until things settle down. Sometimes they don't have a choice, like if a hunter is looking for them."

I wince.

The world still doesn't know about that. I've not even told Aki. It's going to come out soon, I can feel it on the edges of the upcoming disaster.

"Who are the agents?" Aki asks, as intrigued as me.

"Volunteers usually. Ones who have benefitted from our system and society who want to give back. We don't really have an economy here. Though we do have some money for outside of our little world."

"Wait, there's no money?" I ask. "How does that work?"

"Well, I guess we do have some basic form of an economy, but no. We don't have money here. Every household participates in this society in one way or another. And we work together to make resources that are shared amongst everyone." He looks at me in the rearview mirror and smiles. "It only works because our society is so small. You could never change the outside world's economy into something like that."

"No"—I shake my head—"I imagine not."

Aki looks out the window at the mountain next to us, awe leaking from his eyes. "Cool though."

I grab Aki's hand and squeeze, hoping his lack of chirp isn't because of me yesterday. "I'm sorry about yesterday."

Aki shakes his hand. "Don't bother. It's okay. I totally get it. You were right. I was being insensitive. I'm sorry." He smiles at me, but it's clear his heart isn't in it. He squeezes my hand back nonetheless, though.

"Err . . ." Eldry starts, "I have a question, if I may?"

I nod, telling him to go ahead.

"How are you related? Like, how does a Horseman have a brother."

"Twin brother, actually." I smile at his surprise. "I was born mortal, Eldry. Aki is my mortal brother. I died and was reborn a Horseman."

"Oh . . . oh." His tone changes halfway when he realizes I'll outlive him by thousands of years.

"It's okay," Aki says. "Magic has a great immortal family. She'll be just fine." The calm exuding his voice and the smile that accompanies it warms me.

"I'm glad you like them."

He scratches his head and leans toward me. "Yeah, sorry about the judgey asshole I was before. I just didn't . . . get it."

"It's cool." I shrug. "Many people don't get it."

"Hey," Eldry interrupts, "we're coming up to the first community I think you'll want to meet."

We reach a clearing in a valley surrounded by mountains on all sides, and in the center of the valley is a massive lake with bright-haired people playing, chatting, living.

"Welcome, Magic and Aki, to the mermaid community."

"Mermaids are real?" I squeal. "Really?"

Eldry laughs in my face. "Yeah. Not all of our communities are species-specific, but some who have specific requirements are."

"Like mermaids," Aki confirms. "Makes sense."

A familiar smiling face walks our way, her hand waving in the air, blue-green scales trailing up her arm and covering her shoulder.

"It's you," I exclaim. "You're a mermaid?"

She finds my surprise hilarious, her placid face from yesterday one of amusement today. "Yeah, guilty. Name's Lilly. Come on, meet some of my friends." She grabs our hands and drags us near the water.

Aki looks concerned. "You're not going to turn out to be those evil mermaids like in Peter Pan, are you?"

I shrug. "I can hold my breath indefinitely."

"I can't!"

"Sucks to be you."

Lilly looks at me with such reverence, I stand still for a moment. "You can really hold your breath indefinitely?"

"Yup. Vampire trait."

She looks at me, confused.

"Oh, I'm part Witch, part Vampire in this form."

"This form?"

Clearly, she doesn't keep up with the news. Oh well, I don't mind. "Yeah." I switch into my male form and smirk at her shriek. "I'm part Shifter, part Fae in this form." Then I switch back.

"You're . . . all," she gasps. "Now I understand."

"Kinda my shtick. Male, female. All species. Attracted to all genders. And . . ." I trail off, the words getting caught in my throat. "Nevermind."

She smiles gently at me. "I saw the notice on the board this morning." She nods to a plasmascreen floating in the air a little way from the lake. "You're looking for help to win your war. That's why you're here."

"Yes," Aki says, "but we're looking for more than just fighters. Healers, strategists, scholars, communication experts . . . Any skill that might be of use to us. Lives don't need to be put at risk in order to do the right thing."

"You know, Aki," I say as I look to him, "you're good at this whole talking thing."

"They're just words. It's not too hard."

Sure. Says the guy finding wording easy.

"Anyway," I say, "if there's anything we can offer in exchange, we're willing to help."

"Just you?" she asks. "Or all of the Horsemen?"

"All of us."

"So, the Horseman of War could come and . . . help?" Her eyes dart to the floor as a blush creeps along her pale skin.

She's interested in Arrie? But he's my . . . friend. He's your friend, Magic. And she's pretty hot. "I'm sure I can find *something* for him to do. Shirtless, of course."

Lilly's eyes light up as she shifts on the spot. "Wow . . ." She shakes her head. "Seriously, though, we could use his help. Or maybe you'd be a better option?"

"What is it you need from us?"

"Well, we've complained to the owners of the park many times, but no one can seem to defeat it." She walks us to the other side of the lake, where no mermaids are running around and the brush grows wild and free. "Down there is a naga." She points to the murky lake water—dark and mysterious compared to the mountain freshness of their side. "It kills us every time we swim too close, but it's taking more and more space, shutting us out of our own waters. Soon, we'll have to move. But this is the only lake large enough in the park."

They'll have to leave their sanctuary.

"The oceans are too dirty for our kind nowadays. And humans kill us on sight."

"So you want Arrie or me to kill this thing?"

"Just how big is it?" Aki asks, worry filtering through his tone.

"No one knows. We've never seen its whole body before."

"Any of us Horsemen could probably help, but I can send Arrie if you'd all like to ogle him at the same time?" The suggestion in my tone is a little bitter, but I try my best to hide it.

"I was just joking before. This is a serious problem for us. Whoever you think is best will do."

"I'll consult with the team and get back to you. I'm sure we can help, even without your help in the war."

"Really?" The worry in her eyes shoots straight through me.

"Yes. This is something we should have been helping with all along."

She waves a dismissive hand through the air and laughs. "The Horsemen aren't meant to help every little supernatural out with every issue. They're made to balance out the magical world."

"But we should be able to—"

"She's right," Aki interrupts. "You can't just help everyone. That isn't feasible. And you'll wear yourself out trying. Isn't that why you created that help board app to begin with? So you could rally the world to help each other."

I breathe deep, the mountain air scorching my lungs. "Yeah, you're right." I scan my surroundings, taking the view in. "But they can't use that app here. But I bet we could set up a local version, just for the park!"

"Really?" Lilly asks. "You can do that?"

"Well, I'm surprised they haven't already, but yeah, probably."

"They're more interested in keeping everyone safe and saving people from the outside world. They care, but that's their main mission. We're left to our own devices around here."

"You sound like maybe that's something you'd like to change?" Aki asks, curiosity dripping from every word.

"Perhaps. I'm just glad they saved my pod when they did. We would have died had they not protected us from those hunters."

Eldry hangs back by the car the entire time, but eventually we head back, both of us smiling the entire time. "So," Eldry says, "how did you like the mermaids?"

"They were amazing!" I clear my throat, trying to return to some semblance of professionalism. "But they're having problems with a naga. I can send a member of my team to them to have it removed, if that's okay with you?"

"You could kill a naga?"

"Well, I've never tried. And besides, I need to continue on, making friends and getting as much help as we can. But I'm sure War or Conquest could manage it just fine."

"Yeah, sure." He smiles, gratitude filling his face. "Send any of them over. I'll make sure we let them in."

"Thank you." I bow my head.

54

Eldry takes us to see all kinds of communities—from mixed villages to species-specific environments, like forests, treetops, underground cave systems, and large mountainous caverns. Every community welcomes us with open arms and are curious about my male-female shifting abilities and what I am. Meeting so many people in such a short space of time is tiring, but it's magical to watch how the communities integrate and communicate and work together. There's no politics, no arguing, no 'they only get along with them and not with them', no ancient wars and social nonsense . . . They're just people making the best of their home.

"Up that mountain," Eldry says a few hours before the sun is due to set, "is cave. You'll find the phoenixes there." He switches off the engine and stares intently at me. "But listen, Magic, the phoenixes aren't here because we rescued them. They've lived here for thousands of years. This is their home. Please be respectful. We do not want to make enemies of them."

"How many of them are there?" Aki asks.

"Thousands."

"I don't know much about phoenixes," I admit. "They're rumored to have healing abilities greater than Vampire blood, though."

Eldry shrugs, not knowing the answer. "We don't see them a lot. They tend to stick to the skies. Flying Shifters avoid them, say they give them 'fuck off or die' vibes."

I turn to Aki and smiles. "Ready to meet some phoenixes?"

"Why not."

"Good luck," Eldry says as I exit the car and shut the door. "I'll wait here for you."

I gather air around us both and lift us off the ground.

"Whoa," Aki exclaims. "I forgot how weird this feels." He waves his arms around, trying to balance himself in the air.

Not that he needs to.

"I've got you. Promise." I grip his hand and squeeze. "Up we go." I shoot us up fast enough that my hair whips behind me and Aki's ears tip red.

It takes a few minutes, but we eventually reach the pinnacle and both breathe a sigh of relief, our hands still squeezing onto each other's. In front of us is a large hole in the rock side, a dark cavern hollowing it out, going farther than even my Vampire vision will allow me to see.

Aki is the first to step onto the rock's ledge, settling his feet down with trepidation, worry clear in his eyes. "It seems . . . safe."

I settle myself onto the ledge, feet just tiptoeing onto the rock. My entire body is tense, locked up and ready to spring at the first sign of danger. Something about this place scares me. Puts me on edge.

"Do you feel that magic?" Aki asks as he grips my hand again.

"Yeah." It screams danger. And it's denser than anything I've felt before—even Dea's angel form. "You should stay here."

"Not a chance."

"But you're shaking." I squeeze his hand, trying to comfort my clearly frightened brother. "You don't have to do anything that scares you."

"But you're scared too."

And he's right, of course. I am scared. "But this is my job. And I can't die."

"And you're my sister I lived without my entire life. I'll be damned if I don't stand by your side now." His brows furrow in concentration, his stance ready for anything.

He's serious.

"Okay."

And we step into the cave.

55

The farther we walk, the darker it gets, but I don't notice at first. Until Aki stops and groans. "I can't see a thing."

"Oh, right." I light a flame in my palm, doing my best to control it. "There we go."

"That's better."

The flame flickers off the walls, bounces around the dark, and lights up the previously shadowy space. I imagine a movie moment, where my flame flickers onto some kind of monster, and judging by Aki's stance and gaze, so does he, but there's nothing in the darkness.

Nothing yet.

The path winds a bit, but it's nothing compared to the pixie tunnels, so I manage to keep track of where we've been in my mind.

"If there are thousands of them, then why haven't we come across any yet?" Aki asks.

"I have no idea."

Maybe this place will lead to somewhere special, like the Witches. Or maybe it'll lead to our deaths. I don't feel like regrowing limbs to bury my twin brother today. No thanks. But I keep moving forward. Keep hoping to spot a glimpse of a phoenix.

"Shhh," Aki hisses. "Do you hear that?"

Something rushing in the background pounds against my ears. Something that sounds a lot like . . .

I run, eager to see it for myself. But I stop when I reach the vertical tunnel running from the top of the mountain and down the center. And everywhere I look are thousands of bright gold birds set aflame.

"Wings."

Covering every square inch of the walls, phoenixes rest, glowing fiery reds and oranges and blues all the way up and as far down as I can see.

"Wow," Aki breathes.

"This is . . ."

In all our travels, I've never seen anything this magnificent. Nine'll freak out when he visits.

Before I can fully process everything, Aki dives off the edge, screaming, "Catch me!"

"Aki, no!" I dive after him, fear running through me. What if I don't catch him in time? "Wait!"

I push myself down the tunnel's hole quicker, using many bursts of air to increase my speed, and soon I've caught up with my idiot brother and grabbed his hand. "Are you fucking insane? *Kutabare*. You cunt bucket."

He snorts and laughs as I descend us the last few feet till we reach the floor. "Oh, your face was priceless!"

"What were you thinking?" My voice edges into a shriek as I grab him by the arms and yank him into me. Squeezing tight. I push him away again and look him up and down. He looks fine. A little wind-brushed, but otherwise fine. So I punch him on the arm. "What the fuck were you thinking?"

"Ouch!" He rubs his arm, flustered as he's had to take a step back. "What the hell?"

"You jump into a seamingly endless pit of phoenixes we know nothing about, and you're the one who's shocked?"

"Okay, okay." He holds his hands up in defense. "Not my finest moment. But I was excited and—"

A gust of foul-smelling wind howls over us, and the phoenixes this far down all hop off their rocks and fly up. Away. Silence follows.

Aki's eyes widen in shock, and I grab him toward me, gripping his sleeve tight. "Don't move."

There's something powerful near us, but I can't see it. Not even with my Vampire eyesight.

"What's going on?" he whispers in my ear.

"Shh!" I move in front of Aki and face the direction the power is coming from. "Don't move."

"Yeah, okay. Got it. You're great and I'm not," he mumbles.

"Seriously," I hiss between my teeth, "now is not the time."

A tumbling earthquake sound rumbles toward us, and we go still as statues. The ground shakes beneath our feet as we do our best not to completely freak out and run away. But something roots me to the spot.

Whatever is coming, I need to face it.

Out of the shadows, a clawed foot double the size of me pierces the rock in front of us, sending shards shooting in every direction. Then another lands several meters away.

I shield us with a wind barrier, the shards of rocks bouncing off it.

A snout leans toward us, entering the light, and before my judgement gets the better of me, a scream rips from my throat.

"Is that a . . ." Aki goes to ask, the words dying in his throat, "a dragon?"

56

Claw-tipped wings tuck onto its back, the lack of space in this mountain preventing it from flying, and its bright yellow eyes pierce my gaze, sending shivers down my spine.

"Aki, go!" I shove him farther behind me, signaling him to leave. "Leave now!"

"I'm not going anywhere." He steps up beside me and yanks two daggers off his waist, letting his death magic suffuse around them in waves of black mist. "I can help."

I smile at him, hoping it won't be the last time I get to do so for a while. Not really sure what happens to my body if it gets shredded by a dragon. "Alright, but don't die."

"Wasn't planning on it."

The dragon hovering over us roars, and the air vibrates hard enough to loosen shingle from the rock tunnel above.

With rocks raining down on us, a dragon leering over our lives, I arm myself with fireballs in each palm and spread my feet apart, keeping my balance. "You really wanna do this, dragon?"

It roars again, letting loose more shingle.

"I guess so," Aki confirms. He charges the dragon's foot, screaming the entire way.

I match him, Vampire sprinting to the other foot.

I throw the fire in my hands at the dragon's underbelly on my way, but they bounce right off. Okay. Lesson learned: dragons are impervious to fire attacks.

A deep whimper escapes its throat as it cradles its other foot underneath its body.

And Aki cheers and whoops.

"What did you do?"

"Cut off one of its claws!"

Hmm. Not a bad strategy. If it can't walk well, and it can't fly, then it can't really move to attack us.

"Keep going! Injure it until it can't move."

Aki nods, then dives into the dragon's underbelly and beneath its line of sight, dodging out of the way of its swipes and roars.

For a mortal, he's a pretty good fighter.

His death magic is doing damage, but it's not outright killing the creature. Briefly, I wonder why. Then I remember I'm being attacked by a mythical monster and shake my head. Get it together, Magic. Now is *seriously* not the time.

If we can just keep damaging it in small ways, we can wear it down long enough to land a serious blow.

Aki must do some damage somewhere because the beast roars and whines, rearing its head and stomping its feet to the floor.

I just manage to roll out of the way in time.

Goddess, this thing is strong. It's left indents in the floor where it stomped.

Rushing air around my body, I fly up to its head, careful to avoid its jaw, and land on its head. It tries to buck me off, but I'm careful. Gripping one of the many talons. Hard.

The dragon thrashes its head, and my body tries its best to fly off, but I hold steadfast.

I have a few knives on me, but not as many as usual. This was a diplomatic adventure, I didn't want to look dangerous. What a shit decision. Apparently, you never know when you might run into a dragon.

My knives don't even pierce its hide. "Dammit!"

"What's wrong?"

"Nothing I try is doing any damage. Its skin is too thick, and it's immune to fire."

Aki sounds out of breath, but he responds, "Use your death magic!"

That sounds like a terrible idea.

I shift form and change tactics. Maybe some of my Fae spells might be useful—when we get back, I'm going to study some more attack spells before we actually have to fight any Fae.

The dragon roars, and spittles of fire launch from its mouth.

I freeze.

So the myths are true. They can breathe fire.

Aki screams from somewhere, his voice sounding pained.

I rush to look around. "You okay?"

"Yeeaah . . ." He doesn't sound okay.

But I don't have time for that right now. He's alive. And that is some kind of miracle.

Using my magic reserves, I create some basic runes to start an entrapment spell. The incantation rushes from my lips, and I watch as a green glowing ball surrounds the dragon. I hop off and rush toward Aki, who's running away from the spell.

"How you doin'?" he asks.

"Eh."

The green glowing ball surrounds the dragon, but it rears its head and I know it's not going to hold.

"The spell isn't strong enough." I wring my hands and try to move my brain faster. C'mon, Magic, think.

Shifting into the largest bear I can think of, I wait until the dragon crashes its head into the spell and watch it crack and splinter. One more crash and it falls, crumbling to the ground.

Its eyes track its surroundings and lock onto us with a growl deep in its throat.

Before it can do any damage to us, I charge at the foot Aki injured earlier and let loose a roar of my own. I swipe at its foot, hoping to do something. But my claws barely do anything against this beast.

"Use your death magic!"

Goddess, he's right.

Sighing, I shift back to male, then back to female, and steady myself on the floor underneath the beast that is seriously ruining my . . . What day even is it? Well, it's ruining my fucking day. That's for sure.

I channel my emotions—frustration at this stupid dragon, loneliness at missing the team, and pain at Arrie wanting to just be friends. That familiar cold, achy tremble surrounds my hands, and I look down to see the same black mist I always see.

Panic trembles through me.

The mist grows, and I don't know what to do with it.

"Calm yourself!" Aki shouts from somewhere near me. "If you panic, it'll consume everything around you."

Calm. I can be calm.

I channel the usual empty calm I use when doing yoga, and the emotions numb as the mist stops roiling and sits on my arms. Ready to use.

"Now tell it what you want it to do."

Tell it what to do? So it's a living entity? Or something similar?

Eh, I'll ask Aki later.

I move out from under the dragon and face it, its maw dripping with fiery saliva and its teeth—all larger than me—glinting in what little light is filtering down the tunnel above us.

At my command, the mist moves, grows, and shapes itself around me, like a puppet in my control. It grows four legs with monstrous claws attached, two wings it pins to its back, and a monstrous set of teeth.

The dragon's eyes widen as it takes it in, and then it roars, frustrated. And then it does something weird. Unexpected. It submits. With its nose on the ground and tail wrapped around its back legs, it whines and growls. Reminding me that it might be submitting, but it isn't happy about it.

"Wow!" Aki shouts from somewhere behind me. "That was amazing!"

The mist is still surrounding me, still in its dragon form. I'm kinda afraid to put it away. But I'm growing tired.

"Yeah . . ." I cough and splutter, my body aching. "Now what?"

"Err . . ."

The dragon glows bright gold, a sun in the bottom of this pit. Its snout shrinks on its head as its feet also shrink and its body decreases to the size of a small iguana.

I take a deep breath and let the death magic go, returning to my previous level of awesome. Though not feeling too awesome right now.

"Death wizards . . ." A small, high-pitched voice echoes. "What do you want with me?"

I look to the dragon, small and cowering on the rock floor. "Are you speaking to me?"

"To you both, as it happens." I think it sighs, but it sounds more like a balloon deflating. "Are you going to kill me?"

Kill it? "No. You're the last of your kind, aren't you?"

"Indeed."

"Then definitely not," I confirm.

"Then what on Earth are you doing down here?"

"Good question." I stare daggers at Aki. "Wanna answer that?"

He shifts on the spot as he pierces his gaze to the floor.

The dragon laughs, a high-pitched child's giggle that has me struggling to hold back my own laugh. "I see. You should have just said something."

"Would you have let us go if I did?"

"Maybe." He looks up the hole. "What are you doing here at the park in the first place, wizards?"

"Wizards?" Aki asks.

At the same time, I answer his question. "Gaining as many followers as possible for the war."

"War? What have those Demons done now?"

Aki, ever the silent partner when I'm talking to a dragon—fair, to be honest—stands beside me and grabs my arm. "I'm not sure telling all our secrets to a dragon is a good idea. Who knows what side he's on." He flicks his gaze at the dragon. "You are a he, right?"

"Yes, young wizard, I am a male dragon. If I were a female, you two would not still be standing."

"So," I ask, "female dragons are stronger than the males?"

"Yes." He walks up to us and looks up at me. "Female dragons protect egg clutches, so they have to be. We males just like to fly around and look good."

I bend down and lay my hand flat on the floor.

He walks up and settles himself on my palm. "Well, we used to."

"What happened?" Aki asks. The tremble in his voice matches the one in my heart. Whatever happened to the dragons, it's going to be awful, isn't it? "I can't imagine anything strong enough to wipe out all dragons."

"Meteor."

"Oh," we say at the same time.

"It killed many of us instantly, but many more were left in a barren world, fending for themselves as they slowly starved to death. It was not a preferable way to die."

"I'm so sorry," I say, because I am. But the smile on my face probably says otherwise. "Sorry," I say again, "I just can't believe I'm talking to an actual dragon."

Aki points a thumb at me. "If you understood how many dragon books Magic here reads, you'll understand how much of a miracle it is they're not jumping up and down in squealing delight."

"As if you're not equally amazed!" I shift into my male form and smile at the dragon in my palm, who's looking at me like *I'm* amazing. "I have a shirt pocket in this form." I offer the small dragon my pocket and explain, "This way, other people won't know you exist."

"Ah. Yes. That is probably for the best." He looks to me with a question in his gaze. "Am I coming with you?"

I wave a hand around the cave. "Unless you'd like to continue living here, where you can't even fly?"

"Not particularly, no."

"Then you may come with us to our realm, and you can fly, make a home somewhere, and be free."

"Realm?" he asks from my pocket.

"It's . . . separate from Earth."

"How?"

I look to Aki, who shrugs. "I have no idea. But Nine might be able to answer your question. Actually, he's going to completely freak out when he meets you."

"Who is . . . Nine?"

Aki laughs. "Her boyfriend. Well, one of them?"

"Ah, so humans take multiple partners. I see."

"Well," I say. "Umm . . . Sometimes."

"My twin here is a little special," Aki says, and he shoots me a look I instantly want to wipe off his face.

"Yeah, well, you try bringing peace to this world. See how many boyfriends you need then."

Aki holds a finger up. "Let's not forget the girlfriend."

"Girlfriend?" the dragon asks. "That does not make sense to me."

"Well, love doesn't always make sense. You love who you love, you know." I shrug, trying to brush it off.

"I sense I have upset you in some way. I apologize. I have not seen humans in hundreds of years. But you are right. Whom we fall in love with is of little consequence. So long as they make you happy."

57

Eldry waits for us at the bottom of the mountain, and on our way down, the dragon—named Lo—tells us the phoenixes protect him. They usually don't let people travel down the hole, but they must have sensed something important or valuable in us and let us pass. We inform him about the park's current use, and it seems to please him.

"You are still alive, I see," Eldry says.

Lo flies out of my pocket and faces Eldry. "You are the leader of this . . . community?"

"Err . . ." To Eldry's credit, he composes himself pretty quickly and smiles. "I am one of three of us, yes. But we're a population-run community here. My mother, brother, and I just make sure everyone's needs and desires are met and run our outreach program."

"Outreach program?"

"They help lost and wayward supernaturals," Aki answers. "It's soooo cool."

Eldry smiles at him. "I'm glad you think so. Come on, we should get back. Mama's making a feast to see you off."

"Or celebrating that we're leaving," I mumble.

Eldry just looks at me with a smile in his eyes, suggesting I may be right.

Back at the entrance village, and after Reetus and Wendy have gotten over the shock of dragons existing and have asked their million and one questions to the poor dragon, we settle down and eat great food. Even Lo eats some steaks and char-grilled fish.

"So," Aki looks to me, "I made a list of all the residents' requests that we may be able to help with. I figured Connie would be the best person to send it to?"

I nod, shock filtering through me. "Err . . . Yeah."

"Cool." He fiddles with with some buttons on his datachip's screen. "All done."

Wendy frowns at Aki, and I realize that we probably should have cleared that first. I clear my throat and prepare for a verbal bashing. "Err . . . Lots of your residents are having problems you and they don't seem to be able to fix. Like the naga issue with the mermaids? So I sent a list to our team's manager, and she'll designate some of our time to helping your residents."

Wendy looks at us, calculating, before she forces a smile. "It pains me to know there are things we can't do for our people, but it pleases me that we have help."

I think that was a thank you?

"I still can't believe we've lived near a dragon this whole time and didn't know it," Reetus says. "Bloody crazy."

"Yes, well," Lo says, "I was trying to stay hidden."

"Is there a reason for that?" I ask, curiosity getting the better of me.

Lo crawls across the table and settles against my hand. "Humans have not been kind to the few of us who survived the meteor. I thought it best to hide for a while. But I fear time may have gotten the best of me." He stretches and flicks his tail into my palm. "I did not know quite how long had passed." His eyes slowly close as he yawns and falls peacefully asleep.

"We're taking him with us, don't worry."

Wendy blinks in surprise but looks secretly relieved.

"Even if he doesn't help us, he deserves freedom. He can have that on *Sheruta*. Hopefully."

"Hopefully?" Aki asks.

"Well, I've never brought a dragon home before. I don't really know what the residents will think. But they're usually kind people who like to provide homes to the magical." I look up at our hosts. "A bit like you guys, actually."

"We'll let any of the Horsemen through our border, but if they make trouble, I'll kick 'em out!" Wendy exclaims, fist in the air.

"They'll be respectful." I hope. "Oh, I forgot to ask a question. Where does your magical barrier come from? Who made it? What it is?"

Eldry looks at me with a curious smile. "I was waiting for you to ask that." He clears his throat and stands. "Follow me."

He leads me and Aki outside to a pillar that stands in the center of the village. "There are four of these at different locations around the park."

I run my hands along the wood, around the outlines of the runes etched into the surface, and smile. "Is this full of everyone's magical essence?"

"Yup." His arms across his chest, he smirks some more. "Everyone who agrees to live here has to agree to mark their magical signature on all four of them before settling. Then a Fae spell takes those and uses them to create the barrier."

"But I didn't detect a Fae spell?"

Aki looks like he doesn't even know what we're talking about, but he listens and smiles, anyway.

"It's hidden in a unique type of magic created by one of our founders. They were a special type of Witch using some kind of Angel magic."

Aki snaps his attention to me. "You don't think?"

"Maybe. Not sure I'd know it if I felt it."

Eldry looks puzzled. "What's going on?"

Aki raises one of his blades and activates his death magic. "This kind of magic?"

Eldry takes an instinctive step back. "Yeah, that's the one." His eyes widen as he looks at us both. "How can you . . .?"

Aki looks to me and nods, and then I turn to face Eldry. "Because we were born Angel-descended Witches. Just like our parents." I shrug, not really sure what this means. "If you ever need to fix the barrier for whatever reason, at least you know who to call."

Aki and I find that funny, but Eldry seems stunned. Rooted to the spot. "This isn't . . . possible. They all died out. I . . ."

Aki looks to the floor, a longing on his face I don't often see. "Our parents died when we were four. Hunters."

Eldry's face screws up in anger, and he spits on the floor. "Nasty people."

Aki agrees, but I take a step back, not knowing what to say or what part of the conversation to glob onto. How do you tell your brother you worked for the organization that killed your parents? I have to tell him.

But maybe not right now.

"We should probably get going," I say, breaking up their hate-fest. "It's late, and we have plans to make."

Eldry nods and shakes Aki's hand. "It was nice to meet you. I'll send you any sign-ups we have."

"Thank you. It's been a pleasure meeting you and your people. You have a wonderful community." I bow low and then grab my teleporting crystal and freeze. "Wait. Can I tele-port with a dragon?"

Aki raises his brows at me. "He's tiny. It'll be fine."

"Just because he's shrunk his size doesn't mean his power has also shrunk. He's still the monster we fought."

"Maybe take him through the main portal?"

"I don't want to turn the last dragon into magical ether particles, so yeah, the main portal it is. And we'll have to fly there." I whine, bitch, and moan, but in the end, I know it's for the best.

"Well," Eldry pipes in, "we have a jet you can use."

"Good. Because I don't know how to get a dragon through customs."

58

Placing Lo on one of the wooden seats in our Colorado portal, I cross my fingers and hope I'm not about to kill him.

"You should learn to relax, Magic," Lo says, smiling with all his teeth out. He's currently the size of a small dog, and the grin looks somewhat creepy. "You might give yourself a . . . What are they called? Those wars of the heart?"

"A heart attack?" Aki suggest.

"Yes! A heart attack."

I sigh. "I'm immortal, Lo. I can't die from a heart attack.

"Well, then maybe your heart could just spasm forever. I hear they are quite painful." He curls up on the chair and rests his head on his front claws. "Please activate the portal."

I relax into my seat, watch Aki do the same, and have one last second to panic before the whirling and hurling begins. When it stops and we're safely in *Sheruta,* I try my best not to vomit everywhere.

"For an all-powerful immortal being, who can add dragon tamer to their list, you have quite the weak constitution," Lo comments.

"Are you going to point out all my flaws or just the ones you find personally amusing?"

"All right, all right. Do not get your underthings knotted."

Aki snickers. "That would be panties in a twist."

"Oh, pfft." The dragon hops off the chair, walks toward me, and shrinks. "You humans have such a complicated language."

"This is just one of those languages, too," Aki informs. "Humans have a total of 6,500 languages across the globe."

Lo hops into my hand, and I tuck him into my breast pocket. "How on earth do you all communicate?"

"Badly." I pat my pocket and smirk. Nine is gonna freak. "Now hold still, I want to impress my boyfriend with our new pet dragon."

A heat envelops my nipple, and I look down to see my breast pocket on fire and a hole in my shirt.

"I am not tame enough to be a pet," Lo scowls, that high-pitched voice contradicting his powerful nature. "Do not suggest so again. You are my friend."

"Okay, okay." I hold my hands up in defense. "I want to impress my boyfriend with my new dragon friend."

"Better."

I transfer him to my trouser pocket and stalk as quickly as I can through town. I do not want to lose my trousers in public. And my female form is wearing a stupid long top and leggings so has no pockets to hide my new friend in.

Aki struggles to keep up, but he manages.

As I get within headshot, I mentally yell, Hey, Nine. Can you bring everyone out to the garden if they're in? I have a surpriiiiiise. Don't peek!

Hey Sweetie. If you don't want me to peek, then shut me out or think of different things.

Dea's massive cock.

Dea's massive cock.

Dea's massive cock.

Dea's massive cock.

I keep repeating that in my head, filling my mind with the rather pleasant image, as I get us into a large clearing in the garden and let Lo out.

He settles amongst the grass, almost invisible to the average eye.

The team rush out, all standing in a line before me.

"Wait right there!" I step in front of Lo and smile. "I present to you the last dragon!" I gesture behind me, where Lo is increasing his size and returning to normal.

The team stares at Lo with varying degrees of shock, but Nine is by far the most surprised.

"Wait a second . . . Dragons are real?"

"Yes," Lo says, his deep, booming voice penetrating the air. "We are indeed real."

Connie steps forward, inching toward Lo. "But you're the last of your kind?"

"I am not certain, but I have not seen another dragon in hundreds of years."

"So, Nine asks, "you live forever? Or are you just really old?"

Lo puffs smoke out of his snout and snarls. "Since dragons do not age, we cannot be what you humans refer to as old. But we do indeed live until someone or something kills us."

"So, you're born this size," Nine asks.

"We are born in our smaller forms, but we can shift to this size straight away. We also do not mature with age. We learn things as we go, but we can speak, fly, and converse from birth."

"Wow." Nine's jaw is still open, the shock still registered on his face. "You're free to make a home here on *Sheruta* wherever you like. If you'd like to see a map, I can show you where other species are."

"That would be most appreciated, thank you."

"My name is Famine."

"Ah. One of Magic's boyfriends."

My face heats slightly, but the team just look at me with adoration on their faces. Even Arrie.

"Where, then, is this girlfriend you spoke of?" Lo asks.

Connie giggles. "That would be me." She raises her hands. "We're all a little new in this relationship, so it's strange hearing someone talk about me being Magic's girlfriend."

"So you two"—his head shifts to Dea and Arrie—"must be her other boyfriends, then. It is nice to meet you."

"Oh, err . . ." I try to get Lo's attention. "Just Dea." I point to my sexy angel. "Arrie and I are . . . just friends." My voice comes out as a pained whisper, even though I try to make it sound normal and strong. Damn it. I don't want to look weak in front of him.

Lo shrinks to the size of a donkey and looks me in the eye. "Why would that be? Would it not be easier to romantically involved with the entire team?"

Arrie turns and walks away, clearly not wanting to deal with this conversation.

Connie rests a gentle hand on my shoulder. "It's complicated. How about I show you around our house and unload all the gossip?"

Lo shrinks further, fitting into the palm of Connie's hand. "I would like that."

"Con," Nine says, "if you bring him into Dea's study when you're done, I'll have an updated map for you both to look at."

"Kay." And they're off, making fast friends as usual.

"Guess that leaves you two to update me, huh?"

"Actually," Nine interrupts, "that leaves Dea. I need to do that map, and I'm in the middle of analyzing the trial data." The bags under his eyes suddenly look darker, and his tired skin and droopy eyes reminds me that he's been pushing himself.

"Okay." I wrap my arms around his waist and pull him to me. "But I want a cuddle later."

"Consider it a promise." He leans up and kisses me before kissing Dea on the cheek and returning to his nerd hole.

"Just us, then?" I look at Aki and Dea.

"I'm gonna chill out in your library for a bit," Aki says. "That okay?" He turns to leave without hearing my answer, the asshole. "I'll be gone by dinner, though!"

"Alright!"

Dea wraps a tight arm around my waist and smiles. "Just us, Angel."

The nickname sends shivers down my spine and forces a grin onto my face. "Perfect."

He pulls me along the beautiful garden path, and we walk in silence for a while, just soaking up each other's presence. "I will update you if you update me?"

"Deal." And so I explain about the details of the last two days, including our epic battle with a dragon and all the species we met along the way. Dea seems surprised by some but not others. For example, the team already knew mermaids exist—they've just never gone looking for the solitary creatures. "That about sums it up."

We've reached the *shinto* shrine, so we walk up the hill and sit, breathing in the beauty of the fairytale gardens we call our own.

"Beautiful, is it not?" Dea's eyes are closed as he breathes deeply. "But I confess, it has been lonely without you here."

"I'm sorry I had to go. Next time, maybe we can go together, like the good old days?"

Dea chuckles, his light laughter pulling my eyes to his. "I would like that." He opens them and locks gazes with me, the world fading away. "I did not know two people could come to mean so much to me. I cannot even imagine my life without you in it."

Tears prickle my eyes as I grab his hands.

He sweeps a piece of short blonde hair from my eyes and smiles. "It is okay to cry."

"I know, but I'd much rather kiss you instead."

"That I can help with." He leans in and brushes his soft lips against mine. Barely a whisper. "I love you." Before he delves his tongue past my lips and tangles it with mine, a war I will always willingly lose, and it's like I can feel his soul sighing in relief.

Passion is like a fiery red blaze beneath my skin, an itch I have to scratch, but this isn't like that. This reminds me of the ocean, lapping and rolling along the earth like it knows it belongs. It will always belong. And when it meets at the shore, those frothy tears spill over the edge because they both know they'll have to say goodbye for a while, but they'll always be there. A meeting of two suns.

And that's what kissing Dea is like in this moment. A meeting of two suns.

Breathless and unsteady, I pull back and lean on my elbows as I lie back on the stone. "I love you too."

He lies next to me and grabs my hand as we watch the clouds drift by. "The embassy is running smoothly. We are all moving supplies, gathering armies, running some extra training for those who have not fought a Fae or Vampire before. Arrie has been the busiest of us with the strategy preparations. Especially since there are five cities to defend. Each one has its own strategy given the layout of the city and location of the Vampires, et cetera."

"So he's not wallowing in self-pity anymore?"

"Not while he is kept busy, no."

"That's good."

"You are too kind for us, Angel." He rubs a thumb in circles over my hand. "He does not deserve your kindness."

"He's in pain. I'm not sure why, and I don't know how it relates to me, but I see it in his eyes. He's in burning agony and is keeping it all in."

Dea says nothing, practically confirming my theory. "Connie has been managing us and helping me with the embassy, though I think she is now going through your list of help requests from Jura Mountains Region National Park. Nine and the other scientists are all working diligently on the blood substitute, and he hopes we will have a working blood tablet by the time we have taken back New Orleans."

I shoot up. "Really?" My eyes widen in surprise as my heart beats like a drum in my chest.

"He is very good at what he does." Dea drags me back down and nestles me in his arms on the grass. "Just let me hold you." His voice rumbles halfway through, the tone changing slightly, so I know he's changed into his angel form.

Since we realized our Angel magics have mated, Dea's been clingier, needing more hugs and reassurances; but it's not affected my relationship with the others. Huh. So much for all those possessive fated mates stories. They're apparently a load of bullshit.

"What are you thinking?" he whispers in my ear.

"That all those fated mates stories are a load of possessive bullshit."

He laughs. "It would seem so. I could never cause you pain by holding you back. The thought hurts my soul."

"Are all angels such drama queens? Glowy is insanely dramatic, too."

"I am just expressive of myself," he grumbles.

"Uh-huh. Keep telling yourself that."

"Come on. We have something for you." Dea yanks me to my feet and guides me inside the kitchen, where a giant sign hangs from the doorway: VE's HOME!

Connie, Arrie, and Nine are all standing underneath it, smiling at me with love and adoration in their eyes—even Arrie.

"Ve?"

Nine looks at me with a smile. "It's a neopronoun. It's also a neutrally charged particle in chemistry, which I thought you'd like. You add a plus or a minus sign to make it positively or negatively charged."

"Oooooh, Nine." I wrap my arms around his neck. "Thank you so much. I love it."

"Actually, Sweetie. As much as I love taking credit and gaining boyfriend brownie points, this one was all Arrie."

Connie chuckles at my surprised face.

But when I turn to Arrie, the look of uncertain embarrassment floods me with something bubbly I'm trying my best to ignore. But I ultimately fail. I run at him and wrap my arms around his neck, bury my head into his shoulder, and whisper, "Thank you."

He wraps unsure arms around my back and hugs me close, breathing me in, letting himself have just one moment.

"C'mon, c'mon, c'mon," Connie jibes. "There's something else."

I untangle myself from Arrie and look at Connie. "What else?"

She grabs my hand and drags me down the hallway, up the stairs, and into my library, where she stops in front of a table.

Looking at that table makes me gasp. Because sat upon it is something we no one could find until now. My seal.

Aki runs around the corner. "Huh? Where's the fire? I heard running and gasping." He stops, slightly out of breath, beside me and stares at the scroll. "What's that manky old thing?"

"That," Nine says, having just joined us, "is a Horseman seal."

"And, and, and," Connie starts, "I have found the perfect place to store not just yours, but everyone's." She guides us around the corner and through a door I've not seen before. But the magic on the lock is powerful enough I might have to puzzle it out later. "I've already placed ours in here."

"I don't get it," Aki says. "What's a Horseman seal?"

I look to the team, who all nod their consent. "A Horseman seal is what binds our magic to us and keeps us alive. We couldn't find mine until now. It just never turned up with me."

Aki's eyes widen a fraction as he looks at the seal in my hands. "That . . . thing is keeping you alive?"

I nod. "If you burn it, my immortality will burn with it." I place it onto the table inside the room and lock the door, fiddling with the mechanism for a moment before I give up and promise to get to it later.

I'm tired.

59

The next month is spent training with Aki, Korby, and the mean Fae lady who still won't tell me her damn name. Meanwhile, Arrie, Dea, and Connie help collaborate our allies via the embassy and give embassy positions and *Sherutan* homes to all the lower supes we recruited; Nine runs more tests and trials for his new blood substitute, though he refuses to let me test it, saying that it won't work for a Horseman, anyway; and Lo can't find a place that's right for him, so he stays with me in the library. With a strict 'No Fire' rule, of course.

Everything is running smoothly, but with two days before the Area 50 plans, everyone is a little tense.

"C'mon," Connie whines, "it's Christmas Eve tomorrow. We should celebrate!"

"Con," Arrie grumbles. "We're going to war in two days. Now is not the time."

"That's why it's the perfect time. Besides, I got you all presents." Her eyes find mine at the breakfast table and beg and plead.

And goddess damn it, I cave. "Fine!" I throw my hands up in the air. "We can have Christmas Day on Christmas Eve and exchange presents. I also have bought everyone gifts, so . . ."

"You have?" Connie asks, the excitement clearly written all over her face.

"Yup."

"Eeeekkk!"

Dea smiles. "As have I."

"What?" Arrie grumbles. "No one told me we were doing gifts this year!"

"Do you not usually?" I ask the table.

Nine shakes his head. "We predate Christmas, Sweetie."

"Riiiight. Sometimes I forget how old you all are. You're all so . . . modern."

"Well," Dea says, "it would be awfully cliché of us to stay in our old tongues and attitudes. Of course we have evolved and grown over the centuries. That is normal."

"As normal as being immortal gods can be," I joke. "Sooo . . . how are we celebrating?"

"Errr . . ." Nine stumbles.

Dea looks like he might combust if he has to talk to one more person—bless him, all that talking with the embassy people while only having two hours of visibility a day.

Arrie doesn't even bother weighing in.

Connie, on the other hand, is practically vibrating in her seat. "Can I? Can I? Can I?" She bounces on her seat.

We all laugh at her. Even Lo chuckles from his seat next to Arrie, currently curled up on the chair the size of a Terrier dog. "I have not celebrated Christmas before."

Mwuhahahaha . . . I even have a gift for the dragon.

"Ohhhh . . ." Connie squeals. "We should open it up for anyone fighting for us. Like an open invitation to have a small Christmas celebration."

Arrie looks at her, confused. "You know we have armies in the thousands, right?"

She waves her hand at him, dismissing his concern. "Most will have their own plans, anyway. I bet the only ones to turn up will be the ones without loved ones and some of the higher-ups."

"It's a nice gesture," I suggest. "We are asking a lot of these people. Some of them have stayed in the shadows for years, and they're risking exposure for us." I furrow my brows and grab Connie's hand. "But I don't have thousands of gifts."

She snickered. "I don't expect everyone to exchange gifts. Just to chill and celebrate life before we ask them all to put theirs on the line."

"I think it is a swell idea," Dea says. "But I cannot stay visible all day." He looks uncomfortably to the floor.

I side-eye Nine with a smirk.

He's going to love it.

I know.

He's going to cry in public.

Would it be the world's best gift if it didn't?

Guess not.

Maybe we can wrap it with a pack of tissues.

Nine snorts his coffee by accident, and everyone looks at him strange. "It's nothing."

"I've actually missed that," Arrie grumbles. "Watching you both have internal conversations and laughing like children."

Everyone stares at him like he's grown a second head. Arrie? Being openly emotional?

"Wow. We really are going to war."

Arrie throws a strawberry at me. "Shut up."

I deflect with a small air shield, and it flies back at him and bursts on his head.

He wipes a finger through the splat of red on his forehead while everyone laughs, but he just smiles and shrugs as he wipes it off.

"You wanna organize, Connie? Or are you busy?" I ask her.

Dea chimes in, "Do you require help?"

"Yes, no, and yes," she answers in order. "All available hands on deck!"

Arrie groans, but Dea and I smile.

"I'm leaving the rest of the production to the rest of the team. I'm needed here at the moment," Nine explains. "It's just production paperwork, government approval nonsense, and stuff to deal with. But even without government approval, we'll find a way to distribute."

"Right, because why would the SC approve something that contradicts what they're trying to do?" I mock ask, then groan. I look to Connie. "Still no word as to that last interview?"

She shakes her head. "It's been over a month now."

"I know. I'm worried."

"I bet they're waiting on the outcome of Area 50," Nine suggests. "That way they'll have more information on where countries and the humans sit."

"Or they're waiting on us," I suggest. "See what we'll do in response, not knowing we already know their plans. Or maybe they do know that we know . . ."

"Nigel did not suggest that they knew," Dea says. "I feel he would have picked up on something."

"You're probably right." I shake my head. "I just have a bad feeling about something."

Connie claps her hands. "From this point on, we are celebrating. No shop talk at Christmas." She points to Nine. "Invite anyone and everyone you want, ensure to include all ambassadors and their families, Aki, Nigel, and some of our friends from around the kingdom."

"Yes, sir." Nine salutes her.

"Dea," Connie says as she points to him next, "you're on decoration duty. Find some space in the house where we can host my great plan. Plan for a few hundred."

He nods, but he looks confused. "You have not told us of your great plan yet, Con."

"Oh, right." She clears her throat and smiles at us. "We should have a chill-out party! You know, where we all watch movies, put on some music, open presents, eat food, and just relax before the big fight."

"So, nothing high maintenance, then?" I look into Connie's bright green eyes and plead with her to say no. That her idea is low maintenance enough I can get away with wearing my pajamas.

"No," she sighs, "nothing high maintenance." She looks like that's a big disappointment to her—her forlorn eyes shooting straight to my soul.

"Maybe our next date can be something extravagant?" I offer. "Something dramatic."

"Ohhhh, I'd like that. I still have to beat those two's snorkeling date yet." She thumbs Dea and Nine, who smirk at her.

"Yeah, well, we need to beat sex on a boat and stargazing," Nine offers, "so I guess we can call it even."

Arrie huffs. "If you really want a good date, you should come out with me. I'd beat any of these losers." He looks at me with a smirk, then realizes he's flirting and snaps his gaze away.

I sigh, hope lingering in a whisper. "I'd like that." Friends can go out on dates, right? You know, like meeting for coffee or getting lost in a giant bookstore . . . (Yeah, keep telling yourself that applies here.)

"One of my gifts involves me making something here at the house, at the very back of the garden, near the open fields. So no one go that way when the house rumbles. No one!"

They all agree, and by the time breakfast is finished, Connie is ordering everyone around—Dea to the great ballroom, Nine to his study to contact everyone we know, Arrie to town and Earth to buy presents—but she orders me to my library with her.

"We," she says, "are going to come up with an epic plan for the whole event." She bounces in her seat on the rainbow couch she first sat on when we came in here for the very first time.

That seems so long ago now.

"Well . . ." I sit next to her and wrap a short arm around her shoulders as I try to sit taller. But I get frustrated and switch forms, utilizing my taller male form. "Do you have any ideas?"

"I figured everyone is going to want the morning to themselves, so I was hoping you could have the house do a breakfast in every room?"

"I've never tried," I admit. "But I could probably pull that off. We're asking a lot of the house over the next couple of days . . ." Let's hope she doesn't hate me as much as she hates Connie. Apparently. Though I don't know how anyone could possibly hate Connie. "Does that mean we're preparing guest rooms today?"

"Yes. After this. And we'll drag Arrie and the house staff in to help."

"Aki and Nigel are in their apartments in town, so they might be able to help too."

"Yes!" She nestles against my side, a pad of paper and a pen in hand. "Then we'll let everyone celebrate with their own family and friends in the guest suites for a while. Besides, that gives us some morning time." She winks at me, and I instantly blush. She shoots up all of a sudden and asks, "Is he serious?"

"Huh?"

She shakes her head at me. "Nine says Arrie wants to cater Christmas dinner for all the guests."

"All of them? But that's . . . insane."

"Yeah." She sighs. "I bet he wants something to do to keep himself busy. He's not good with people."

"No shit." I roll my eyes. "But if that's what he wants, I'm sure we can lend a hand if he needs it. I can cook toast and pizza."

Connie laughs, and she smiles at me before nestling back into my side. "Okay, okay. Then we'll all gather for Christmas lunch, music, et cetera."

"Are we doing presents for the guests?"

"Maybe we can grab something last minute? Like a small gift bag from us all in their rooms to open in the morning. Not everyone will have gifts, after all." She jots everything down on paper, putting ticks next to some and circles next to others.

I leave her to her system.

"Then I figured we can all hang out and watch Christmas movies in the cinema room. Assuming it's big enough. I won't really know until Nine's finished." She looks frustrated by that, a wrinkle in her perfect brow.

"Hey." I turn to her and smile, running a thumb through the wrinkle, straightening it out. "No need to be stressed. This is a last-minute plan, and the house is handling most of it, anyway."

She takes a breath. "I know. It's a little more work than I thought it would be." She giggles. "Like always."

60

We spend all morning and afternoon doing up the guest suites—the ones we created temporarily for Aki and Nigel, but also some of the older wings we don't use anymore. Nine and Arrie both join us when they're done with their respective tasks.

"So," Nine says, "everyone wants to come. Even the Vampire King, his family, most of the Witch Coven, and some of the Shifters, including Alpha Cal."

"What?" Connie shrieks. "I didn't expect any of the bigwigs to come. That's . . . awesome."

"Nine?" I ask as I'm making a bed. "Did you invite my Fae trainer?"

"Yup." He tucks the sheet's corners in and smiles up at me. "I knew you'd want her here. You like her, even if you won't admit it to yourself."

"She's done a great deal for me over the last couple of months. I know all kinds of attack spells, and I've even mastered water magic in my Witch form thanks to her."

He smiles at me as we put the finishing pillows on the bed.

So far, we've managed 104 rooms with the staff's help. But we're about done and ready to send them home to celebrate Christmas with their families.

We all meet up at the end of the hallway and look exhausted.

Melisandre frowns at us. "Are you sure you do not need any more help?" Her brow furrows. "We can stay if you need us?"

I chuckle. "Don't be ridiculous. Go home and enjoy the holiday." Someone should. "We're done here, anyway. Only a couple of small things left to do."

The guests are due in a few hours, come nightfall.

"Okay, Magic." She bows lightly, though she doesn't have to. "And thank you for speaking to Death about my back. He healed me up good as new." She beams at me.

My heart flutters. "It was my pleasure." I'm so glad Dea spoke to her and helped.

She grabs the dozen staff behind her and signs them out for the day, all of them with relief and smiles on their faces.

"I had no idea we had so many staff members."

Nine chuckles. "We have a lot of money, so we wanted to give back a little. So we employ as many as reasonably possible. I think we have twenty staff members in total."

"Yeah," Connie chimes in. "We even have some chefs on standby to use if we ever need to." She turns to Arrie and scowls. "Do you need them for your stupid plans tomorrow?"

He runs a hand through his hair with a grumpy smile on his face. "It's just been a while since I've been able to cook for a crowd, and I wanted to give it a shot. Sorry."

"It's far too many—"

"Connie," I interrupt, "it's okay. We can help if he needs it. But there's nothing wrong with stretching your muscles every now and then." I punch Arrie in the arm. "Besides, it might take a few weeks to regrow these gorgeous arms if he loses them."

"Pfft." He grumbles under his breath. "It's been some time since I've lost a body part in battle. I'll be fine." He smirks, his beautiful face lighting up my insides. "You should be the one worried. You've never been in battle before. Be careful not to lose your big head."

My hands clench. "I do not have a big head!" Right? (Are there any exercises to shrink one's head?) Magic, concentrate, he was just joking.

He shakes his head. "You are too easy to tease." He turns to leave and walks away, but just before he turns the corner, he turns back around and smiles. "Well, are you coming with me to help Dea, or have you all forgotten him?"

Connie, Nine, and I run after him.

The great hall is looking unrecognizable from when I was last in it—the announcement ball. Holly garlands decorate the walls, the largest Christmas tree I've ever seen sits decorated in the corner, and five rows of tables divide the center of the room. And in the corner is Dea, with his golden skin and black wings, flying at the top of the Christmas tree to put the angel on top.

I snicker.

"Yes, yes," Dea shouts from across the room, "I know it is funny."

"Funny?" Nine asks. "Bro, it's hilarious."

"Fuck off," Dea swears.

And we all fake gasp.

"Oh, bugger off if you are not going to be of use. I am exhausted."

"I'm not surprised," Connie says. "I was not expecting you to have gotten this far. How did you manage all this?"

"Well, I did most of this in my angel form so I could fly around and do things quickly." He floats to the floor and turns around.

I switch forms, lift myself into the air using air Witch magic, and fly over to him.

He wraps his arms around me tight and takes a deep breath. "You smell like cherries." He sighs.

"It's my shampoo." He smells like smoky lavender, and I inhale his scent like an addict, never getting enough of his amazing this man smells. "You smell like smoky lavender."

"Lavender?" he asks, bemusement in his voice.

"Yeah." I take another deep breath. "It's the first thing I remember smelling when I woke up here, and it's always obsessed me."

Dea stretches an arm out, and Nine enters our cuddle, squeezing himself between us and stealing all the room with a wicked grin on his face. *Nothing I love more than being between you two.*

I can practically hear his wink.

"You are terrible," Dea whispers.

"Alright!" Connie shouts from across the room. "Cuddle time's over. Get back to work!"

We all turn around and salute her. "Yes, sir."

She scowls and throws a plate at us. "Fuck off!"

By the time our guests start to arrive, we're drained, exhausted, and utterly defeated by Connie's drill sergeant orders. We smile at them, make friendly conversation, and show them to their rooms.

"Here." I show the seer Witch and her two husbands. "I picked a room at the top of the house with a balcony, and you're close to the forest and gardens out here, so I'm hoping it's peaceful." The room itself is also nature-based.

"This is lovely, dear. Thank you." She settles onto the couch by the window and smiles as she takes in her surroundings. "I have to ask, but why did you invite everyone over for Christmas?"

I hold my hands up in surrender. "Not my idea. Just following my girlfriend's orders."

The men chuckle as they open the luggage and start to unpack. "We know that feeling."

"We just thought it would be nice to invite all our friends and family from around the supernatural community to celebrate with us. It might be the last time some of us see each other."

Her smiles turns solemn and she nods. "You are right, young Horseman." She looks me up and down with a laugh in her throat. "Though, you look like you need to nap for the next ten days, child."

"I feel like it." I sigh. "Connie thought this plan up this morning over the breakfast table."

The men choke with gasps. "You prepared all these rooms and got everything ready in under a day?"

"Yeah, but we do have staff who helped. Though, we've sent them home for the holidays now." I watch them all settle down and chat for a bit, staying to lend a hand if needed. "Breakfast will be brought to you in the morning, and feel free to lie in, spend time together, open presents, or whatever you would like to do. The house and grounds are yours for the next few days to explore. You may come across a few locked doors, but if the rooms are open, you're free to go in. I recommend taking a stroll through the rainbow forest. Lunch will be at one pm in the great hall tomorrow. And there's a full itinerary on the boudoir there." I point to where we left printed itineraries and information about the house and grounds. "If you'll excuse me, I have more guests to greet."

They thank me and settle down for the evening.

I greet Lucien, the Vampire King, some Shifters (including Korby), some of the pixies, and a few people I've never met in person before.

Nine, Arrie, Connie, Aki, Nigel, and Lo all also greet our guests and show them to their rooms. Everyone gasps at Lo, but no one is too surprised we own a dragon. Go figure. Dea sits it out, not wanting to be more energyless after using his visibility up. But by the time we're done and everyone is settled in for the night or exploring the house and grounds, we all head to my library and plonk ourselves down on the various couches.

"That was . . ." Nine sighs.

"Exhausting," Arrie finishes for him.

"Yeah, but did you see everyone's faces?" I ask. "They all loved the invitation and being here in general. Prince Lucien even asked if there was a way to do this every year."

"Maybe once every five years," Dea suggests.

Everyone laughs.

"What did you all want to do this evening?" Connie asks. "I hear the Witches are having a bonfire in the garden and some of the Vampires are watching movies in the cinema room."

"We should probably mingle," I suggest, "spend time with our friends. Isn't that the point of Christmas?"

Arrie stands and stretches. "Well, I'm going to start some early prep for the food. Got lots of vegetables to chop."

"Maybe it'll go faster if you use your axe," I say as he leaves the room.

I tune in my Vampire hearing and listen to him laugh as he exits my bedroom. Ahhh, that laugh. I'll never tire of it.

"You two seem friendly?" Connie asks, that suggestive tone she always uses when she wants information. The gossip kind.

I shrug. "He wants to be friends. I guess that involves being friends?"

Nine sighs. "I hate this." He groans and runs a hand through his hair. "I hate knowing you both and your desires and wants and not being able to do anything about it." His chest heaves, as though talking about this is painful by this point. "Especially Arrie. I want to knock some sense into that moron."

Connie groans, too. "I know. He's being an idiot."

I don't really follow their conversation, since I don't know Arrie as well as I know the others. But maybe one day that'll change. I found some time earlier to make Arrie's Christmas present at the end of the garden, and then I covered the entrance with a bow. I hope none of our guests think to use it. I did put up a sign.

"Where's Lo?"

"I think one of the Shifters wanted to fly with him, so he's out mingling with the guests," Dea says, wrapping his arm around Nine's shoulders.

"That'll be good for him. He's going to enjoy all this company after being alone for so long." I lay my head in Nine's lap, and Connie sits on the floor below me, her head by my belly as I stroke soft fingers through her luscious hair. "I'm glad we made more allies."

"Me too," Dea says. "It will help in the long run, but I also think it might help bring the world a little closer together."

"No shop talk," Connie says through a yawn. "I said . . . no shop talk."

"Okay, we're sorry." I run my hand back down her head and smile at her half-asleep eyes.

61

The next morning, Connie wakes first and bounces on my bed to wake us all up.

Dea groans, Nine complains, and I just smile, realizing that the rest of my life is going to be like this. It's going to be this perfect. Full of my favorite people in the world, all making concessions for each other so we can be happy and live our lives to the fullest.

"Presents! Breakfast!" Connie shouts. "It's Christmas Eve . . . Or our Christmas Day!"

Right. Breakfast. Let's get that out of the way first.

I step out of bed, wearing pajama shorts and a vest tee, my long pink hair flying around my face as I wipe the sleep from my eyes. With one hand on the wall, leaning to keep me in place, I ask the house for breakfast to be sent to every guest room, and ours, and for it to be a nice fancy spread.

Look, I know you've been worked ragged over the last couple of days, and I'm sorry. But we're going to war tomorrow, and this might be the last day we see some of these people. Help us make it one to remember?

The house is silent for a while, and then a series of intermittent grumbles follows, echoing around the house, followed by one of our very own on a silver cart at the end of the bed.

"There. Breakfast for our 123 guests."

Nine, Dea, and Connie blink at me, shock surprising them still. "Wow," Connie says, "I didn't think the house would listen."

"Yeah," Nine says, "the house never fulfills any request that large for me."

I shrug. "She must just like me."

"Or you're just full of magic," Connie suggests.

Nine looks at her like she's grown a second head.

"What?" she asks. "Magic is the Horseman of Magic. It makes sense."

"Yeah, I just didn't think of that before." Nine scratches his head. "What's happening to me?" He gestures to me. "First Magic helps fix the Armen's Gap." Then he points to Connie. "Now Con comes up with a good theory for why the house likes Magic." He sighs. "How come *I* didn't think of these things?"

He looks genuinely hurt and perplexed, so I sit in front of him, wrap my arms around his middle, and squeeze. "You're overworked. And you can't be expected to do *all* the thinking. You're just one person."

"Yeah, yeah . . . I know." He rests his weary head on my shoulder. "I'm just a bit tired."

A heavy knock sounds on the door, and Arrie pops his head round the corner. "Can I come in?"

I nod. "Of course. It's present time!" I squeal as I pop into my wardrobe and grab everyone's gifts. "I wrapped them all ages ago, and I've never been so excited."

Arrie pops his pile down on the end of the bed, his sleep tee riding up and showing off those delicious abs. "Does everyone have theirs? Because there's a giant pile outside your door."

Dea gets out of bed and fazes, but he's back in under thirty seconds with a heaving pile of gifts that he places next to mine and Arrie's at the end of the bed. "There."

"Guess it's just us, then?" Connie asks.

Nine nods and gets out of bed. "We'll be back in a minute."

They both leave to grab their presents, leaving Dea, Arrie, and I in my bedroom alone.

"Guess we should bring the other gifts in," I say. "Wonder who they're from?" We pile the gifts around my bed and smile. "That's ridiculous."

"You have stayed in your pajamas?" Dea asks, a smirk on his face.

"Figured you all would be." Arrie sits in the rocking chair by the fire, which he starts up. "Besides, I don't really want to get dressed on Christmas Day."

"When did you finally get to bed last night?" I sit on the stool beside him, warming my hands by the growing flames. "You didn't stay up too late, did you?"

He shakes his head. "Nah. But I did manage to chop all the vegetables." My gasping surprise takes him a moment to process, but when he does, he smiles. "I am a professional chef, you know."

"Yeah, yeah, yeah . . . No need to brag."

I'm back, Nine says. He places his presents on the growing pile, which is now looking a little silly.

Connie walks in moments later, her over-the-top pile taller than her head, and wobbles through the door. "Err . . . A little help?"

Dea laughs at her but grabs some of the gifts and unburies her face so she can see where she's going. "Just how many presents did you buy Magic?"

She blushes and tries to act cool. "A few."

Arrie snorts. "It's like you emptied out a mall."

"So what if I did? My partner deserves the best!"

Arrie surrenders, hands in the air, metaphorical white flag waving above his head.

We all sit on the various chairs, couches, and comfy spaces around the room, smiles on our faces.

"It's been so long since we've done this," Connie says, wonder filling her voice. "Why did we stop?"

"Because we had no one meaningful to buy gifts for," Nine answers while looking at me. "Besides, Magic is excited for Christmas."

"Of course I am!" I clear my throat, the admission on the tip of my tongue. "I had a few friends and Nigel, but I didn't really have a close-nit family before. This is kinda a first for me."

"Well, now I feel like an asspig for not arranging something more spectacular." Connie grabs a gift from the top of the pile and hands it to Arrie. "Here, asshole."

He reads the tag on top and smirks. "You tagged it 'To The Asshole'?" He scowls at Connie, but he's wearing a smile that shows he's not being serious. The oaf. He rattles the box that's just a little bigger than his hand and frowns. Unwrapping the paper, he smiles and looks at Connie with a little bit of pride. "How did you find some of this?"

Looking over to his hands, he's holding some kind of coffee, but the label's foreign so I can't read it. "What is it?"

Arrie holds it up and explains, "About 150 years ago, there was this small brand of coffee I loved, but they went out of business after twenty years. It was a shame."

Connie shrugs, pride filling her. "A woman never shares." She smiles at Arrie. "But I did find ten more boxes on my journey. They're in my room whenever you want them. But I'm pretty sure they're the last in existence, so you know, use them wisely and all that advice shit."

"Any you wish to open first, Angel?" Dea offers the entire pile my way.

But I'm at a loss. "Err . . . Maybe whoever is the recipient of that big box over there, toward the back?"

Arrie snickers. "Big boxes do it for you, huh?"

"Shut up." I whack him on the head, but he ducks out of the way.

Dea hands me the giant box.

"Ohhh," Connie squeals. "That one's from me. It's actually part of a set of gifts." She rummages through the pile and pulls out all of the relevant gifts from the matching set. "Here."

They tower by my feet. "Connie . . . You don't think this is a little much?"

"Pssh. Don't be stupid."

Box after box, gift after gift, I unwrap all her presents and am surprised each time. She's bought me an entire wardrobe. Hundreds of items of clothes, shoes, and accessories. Both male and female. "Connie, this is . . . insane."

"I knooow!" She's wiggling in her seat, excitement coursing through her.

"My gifts do not in any way rival this," I admit. Because they really don't.

The guys laugh, all of them looking at me with fondness—even Arrie.

Dea explains, "Everybody feels that way when receiving a gift from Con."

"Yeah," she says, "it's fine."

"If you say so."

We spend about an hour getting through random gifts from all our random friends around the world, including a bright pink dildo from Prince Lucien with a tag that says: IF THEY WON'T DO IT, THEN THIS WILL.

"I can't believe my first dildo is a gift from a Vampire Prince. One who I am not in a relationship with." A fit of giggles overcomes my good sense for a moment. "Okay, okay. I'm good." Phew. I grab my gifts for Connie and Nine off the small pile and hand them to them. "Here."

Connie rips hers open with gusto and then huffs when she has to open the unmarked box within. And when she finally gets at it, she smiles. "Hair growth serum?"

"Well," I look to the floor, "I feel kinda guilty that I had to cut your beautiful hair, so think of it as an apology. But there's more."

She dives back in and pulls out the tickets to Pour Moi, a new pop group she loves, and smiles. "I love these girls!"

"I know. I hear you listening to them when you're working."

"Yay! Now we have another date, right?"

"If that's what you want, but you can take anyone."

She nods. "Then I'll take you." She brings out the last gift, a felt box, and looks at it inquisitively. "What's this?" She opens it and gasps. "It's beautiful . . ." A silver and bronze dagger appears in her hand, carved with the goddess of Amaterasu-Ōmikami, the Japanese goddess of the sun. "I love it."

What girl doesn't love a knife as a Christmas present?

Nine, meanwhile, is opening his with more care while watching Connie open hers. He looks down and then back up at me confused. "It's a pad of paper?"

I chuckle. "It's a magical pad of paper. You talk and it writes it down in note form on the paper for you."

"That's super cool, Sweetie. Where did you find it?"

"You're kinda hard to buy for, you know. And goddess did I try to find something a little more unique. But I was struggling, so I went to a fancy tech company's website and bought a new piece of cool tech I thought you'd like." I shrug. "It's not the best gift in the world, but there are more—"

Nine flies at me, and we go sprawling onto the floor. "Thank you." There are tears in his eyes, and his cheeks can't stop smiling. "I always know what people are going to get me. This is the first time I've received a surprise gift, since you're the only person in the world who can block me out."

"Other than Aki."

"Right. Other than Aki." He sniffles and helps me to my feet. "Thank you. I love it." He opens the rest of his gifts—geeky pun t-shirts, the strongest coffee in the world, and a few other smaller things—and thanks me. "Should we give Dea's to him now?"

"Yes. Because we're going outside for Arrie's." Arrie looks at me with surprise, but I ignore him, focusing my attention on my boyfriend. I pull a small box out of my nightstand drawer and hand it carefully to Dea. "Here. It's from us both."

Dea looks at our serious faces and then back at the wrapped box. He carefully unwraps the layers of paper and flips open the box. "It is a charm bracelet . . .? It is lovely."

Nine snickers while I giggle. "No, you idiot," Nine scolds, "it's a Witch charm bracelet. Those charm beads are filled with visibility magic. You should be able to stay visible with it on for forty-eight hours."

"And we have a spare because you'll need to recharge them, so you can rotate . . ."

Tears leak down Dea's face. "How . . .? Why . . .?"

Nine smiles and grabs his hand. "Because we saw how much you were struggling. And because we love you."

"Damn it," Connie curses, "they gave the best present."

Everyone laughs, even Dea.

Connie scowls at us. "Next year, though, it's on."

"Bring it on, Conquest."

Arrie stands and grabs a gift from what's left of the pile. "Before we leave to see my outdoors gift, we should give you the rest of ours." He picks up a small box and hands it over. "Here."

He got me a gift?

I unwrap it and marvel at its beauty. In my hand sits a carved dragon statue, similar to the Fae doors all those months ago. Its wings are made of trellised roses while its body is made of vines. All carved out of some kind of rainbow wood.

"Arrie, it's beautiful." I looked up at him. "You made this?" But I thought he only did his shopping yesterday? Oh. He shopped for them yesterday, but he had a plan for me all along.

"You're welcome."

Nine and Dea hand over their gifts, and I open them, kinda giddy and excited but still in wonder over Arrie making me a gift weeks in advance. Before we even planned anything for the holiday.

The box in my hands opens, and laying inside is a book older than any I've ever seen.

"Here, Angel." Dea hands me a translational bookscreen. "This will help."

I place the screen over and wonder. Dragon Lore: Myths, Magicks, and Mayhems.

"It is the oldest book on dragon mythology and lore in existence. I bought it from a museum."

"Of course you did." I snicker. "I love it. Thank you." I'm going to need one of those fancy glass case thingies, aren't I?

Nine hands me a small gift first, soft and pliable. When I open it and look confused, Nine explains, "Unfold it."

So I unfold the piece of fabric and realize it's my very own nerd pun t-shirt. But this one says Error 404: Gender Not Found.

Nine's second gift is a box taller than me, but I manage to open it with a bit of spinning around and flexibility. The wooden box itself is a gift, with its intricate design of runes and other magical symbols. But when I open it, the world falls away. "Is this . . .?" My own bo staff.

Yep.

There's a large black crystal at the top, with various other multi-colored charms and crystals imbedded into the wood on the top third. In the center are runes littering the entire middle third, while the bottom third is blank except for a single rune. Fire proof.

"It should work well with your magic and shift with you. It should be flame proof and not erode after many water attacks. And the bottom third should be shiftable when you gain your Earth abilities. When you shift into an animal, it should shift with you into a small bead that should be easy to carry on this bracelet." He hands me a charm bracelet like Dea's. "This can mold to any size and should shift with you into any animal."

"Wow." I gape at the magnificence of it. "You really thought of everything."

"I have no idea how it'll hold against your death magic, so no, not quite everything."

"We can test it later." I look to Arrie. "Ready?"

62

Arrie's face is priceless.

Perfect.

Gorgeous.

Damn it, I'm getting distracted again.

"You made a racetrack?" He gestures to the loops and twists of road in front of us that used to be nothing but fields.

"With a new Axterix car." I cross my arms over my chest and puff with pride. I've stumped him.

"Wow," Connie says. "The house really does love you."

"Well." I look to the floor, avoiding everyone's eyes. "Since Arrie struggles to communicate with me, I thought that maybe we'd talk more often if we were driving."

Arrie sucks in a breath. "That . . . is . . . Umm . . ."

Nine chimes in with, "Thank you. He's trying to say thank you."

"Oh, I see." I jump at Arrie and wrap my arms around his shoulders. "You're welcome."

"Also, that is a seriously hot car," Connie says from where the car is parked. "Did you ask the house for it or actually buy it."

"I can't afford a car like that! I asked the house for it."

Arrie rests his hands on my shoulders and leans down. "I'm happy to drive you anywhere, Magic. Anytime."

Suddenly, a dragon as large as our house flies over my head and lands behind me, chuffing away.

"Hi, Lo." I pet his knee (which is as high as I can reach when he's this size) and smile. "Happy Christmas!"

Lo shrinks to the size of a large Labrador and growls in jest. "Happy Christmas."

"I have your gift for you in my room, if you want it?"

"You bought me a gift?" he asks, surprise lacing his voice.

"Of course we bought you gifts." Connie rubs her knuckles along his head. "You're our friend, aren't you?"

"Well, yes, but—"

"So then we bought you gifts."

"But I did not purchase such gifts for you to experience."

I chuckle and shake my head. "You don't give a gift in order to receive one. And besides, we knew you didn't. You can't exactly wander to Earth and buy one."

Sheruta has grown used to a flying dragon, and some have even been brave enough to come close when he lands somewhere public, but Lo still hasn't met any of the residents. He's a little wary.

"Arrie? Do you not have a hundred people to feed in a few hours?"

His face drops, his eyes widening in the closest to fear I've ever seen. "Shit, shit, shit!" He sprints off to the kitchen and leaves us be. "Happy Christmas!"

"I guess we should go and see our friends, then?" Dea asks, a hand on my shoulder.

"Yes. I have more presents to gift people." I grab Connie's hand, and Dea grabs Nine's, and with Lo beside us, we travel around the house and greet everyone, wish them a Happy Christmas, and provide some of our closest friends with gifts, such as my Fae trainer, Korby, and Prince Lucien.

Our last stop are the rooms Aki and Nigel are staying in for the night. I'm more than a little nervous about gifting my brother a Christmas present for the first time.

You'll be fine, I promise. If it makes you feel better, he's just as nervous.

Will he like my gift?

Yes, of course.

Good. Then I'll be okay.

I knock on the door and shout, "Happy Christmas!"

"Just a minute!" Aki shouts back. He shuffles around a second, and there's another voice in the room that he tells to be quiet, before he answers the door a crack. "Can you wait for me in Nigel's room down the hall?"

I try to be embarrassed for him, but I'm not. It's hilarious. "Sure. I'll just go visit our godfather while you finish with your Christmas hookup," I snicker.

"Says the person with three partners." He shuts the door and then laughs from beyond, probably forgetting about my Vampire hearing.

"C'mon." Connie drags us down the hall a little ways to Nigel's room. "Let's wait for him here."

"Happy Christmas!"

Nigel answers the door, his hair mussed, a pair of pajamas on, and sleep in his eyes.

"Sorry we woke you. We can come back later." I turn to leave, but Nigel grabs my arm and yanks me inside.

"Don't be silly, kid. I just drunk a little too much alcohol at the bonfire last night. Even for a Shifter."

Connie and Nine snicker as we all lounge in the sitting area.

"Where's Aki?" he asks.

Connie and Nine snicker some more.

"Indisposed," Dea explains.

Nigel rolls his eyes. "Was it that Demon he was with last night?"

"Demon?" I ask. "The same Demon from before?"

"They seemed to know each other."

"D'you think it's gonna be serious?" The idea of Aki with a Demon chills me slightly. Who knows the kind of trickery they'll pull over him.

Nigel shrugs. "Never seen him with a boyfriend before, but who knows."

"Wait," Nine says, "never?"

Nigel shakes his head, no. And smiles. "He's always been a bit private. It must be genetic because I had the same problem with you." His gaze sears me. "But you seem to have grown into yourself now you're immortal."

I offer Nigel my gift. "Here. I bought this for you."

"You got me a gift?" Surprise leeches from his eyes, those swirling grays a mixture of emotions I struggle to read. "You didn't need to do that." He pets Lo on the head, who, as I've learned, is more than content to watch and listen and learn.

"You're my godfather, I wanted to get you a gift."

He smiles as he pulls me into a hug. "As it turns out, I got you and Aki gifts too."

Ohhh . . . He did?

The door flings open and Aki stumbles through, still rushing to do up his shirt buttons. "I'm here. I'm here." He shoots me an embarrassed look. "Sorry."

"Don't be. You're allowed to enjoy yourself." I gesture to the empty seat next to us. "Come. Sit. Nigel is about to give us gifts."

"Ooooo." He laughs and rushes into the brown leather lounge chair. "What'd he get us?"

"No clue."

Nigel's booming laughter fills the room while Nine, Connie, and Dea watch with endearment filling their eyes. "Well, if you kids would sit still for five minutes, I might get around to giving them to you."

We all break into a fit of giggles, Aki and I lapping up the father-like attention like a pair of starved cats. We settle into our seats further and zip our lips.

"That's better." He reaches to the armoire beside the bed and grabs the two wrapped presents resting on top. "It's not much, but I hope it'll . . . help." His eyes turn serious, his lips in a straight line, and his gaze piercing ours in equal measure.

Aki and I grab the gifts from his hands—one each—and slowly tear into them as tension fills the air.

As I pull the last of the paper away, my eyes fall onto a picture frame that has tears brimming in my eyes and Aki's mouth falling open. "Is this . . .?"

"From the day you were both born," Nigel confirms. "I thought you both might like to have a copy."

The photo in the picture shows a young Mom and Dad sitting on a white hospital bed, smiling like their world wasn't about to fall from under them. Aki and I are wrapped in bundles in their arms, both of us crying.

"I'm sorry it's not much, but—"

I rugby tackle Nigel to the bed and wrap my arms around his neck, sobs leaving me. "It's perfect." I sniff, trying to not look too ridiculous. "Thank you."

Aki helps Nigel up, and they embrace, whispering words I ignore and tune out, giving them their moment.

Instead, I turn to my team and smile.

Connie pats her legs, asking me to sit on her lap, and I do so, letting her wrap her soft, strong arms around me and bury her nose in my hair. "Seems Nigel won the best gift title this year."

Nigel unwraps our gifts next, then Lo opens my chocolate coin maker and laughs, and Aki steals the show by squealing at the top of his lungs when he opens my charm bracelet gift. Now he can use all kinds of Witch magic and not be limited by only using death magic.

"C'mon," Nine says as he drags me to my feet. "We should help Arrie. He's stressing."

Connie stands and laughs. "Let's hope we have a kitchen left by the end of the day."

63

The rest of the day blows by in a breeze: we help Arrie finish the dinner, with Dea and I using our speed abilities to quicken the pace (you'd be surprised how fast you can whisk as a Vampire); we serve everything with the help of some of the other Vampires, including Prince Lucien and the king, who are more than happy to lend a hand; the Fae and air Witches move the plates up and down tables to help guests pile their plates with everything they want; and everyone gets along.

I'm just resisting the urge to pop a button when Korby smirks at me from across the table and throws a pea in my face. "Think fast!"

"Ah!" I don't manage to put up an air shield in time, and the pea lands on my forehead. "Hey!"

My Fae trainer shakes her head in disapproval and returns to her plate.

So I flick a pea at her and snicker.

But boy do I regret *that* decision.

She stares daggers at me and growls low in her throat. When she picks up a roast potato with her spoon and aims it my way, she smirks.

It flies across to me, but I duck and it keeps flying, until it misses and lands on the seer's head.

"Shit," my trainer swears.

"Crap," I say.

"Fuck," Korby cusses.

We all stare at the seer, apologies on our faces, but she bursts into laughter with the rest of the table.

Relief floods through me.

It's already slightly tense with Vampires and Witches in the same room, but with them helpfully ignoring each other and generally paying no attention, everything's been running smoothly.

Arrie scowls at us from a table over, his ice blue eyes stabbing mine across the distance.

He says no food fights with his food.

Fine, okay.

Arrie turns back to the guests near him, reuniting with our divide and conquer plan for this seating arrangement.

But I might throw a piece of cake at him later. Just for the laughs. Could you imagine the look on his face?

Don't rile the beast, Sweetie.

If I wanna poke the bear, I'll goddess damn poke it. After all, it's a pretty hot bear.

Nine laughs in my head. *You're on your own, then.*

Pfft. Fine.

I'm still gonna throw cake at him.

It really wouldn't be Christmas without the best gift.

"So," I turn to ask my Fae trainer the question burning a hole in my brain, "you joining the fight tomorrow?"

A few heads turn our way, including Prince Lucien and the Vampire King. Seems I'm not the only one wondering if this beast of a Fae will help us. Not that she hasn't already helped us, of course, by training me.

"Yes."

She says no more on the matter, but the wide eyes and gasps that echo from those who were listening in confuse me. Why is everyone so shocked that my Fae trainer is helping?

"Who are you?"

She sighs and places her silverware onto the table in exasperation. "I thought I told you not to ask that."

"Yes, but everyone else seems to—"

Prince Lucien leans over and smirks. "C'mon, Tally, put the poor little Horseman out of her misery."

She scowls at him, baring her teeth. "Magic prefers ve or they/their. Show some respect. Ve's about to save your entire species tomorrow."

My jaw drops, shock coursing through me.

Did she just . . . defend my pronouns?

I look her way, my eyes watering and blinking hard. "I . . . Thank you." I bow my head. "Tally."

Another sigh leaves her. "Great. Now ve knows my name. Now I can't ignore you when you're pestering me."

"Pfft. As if you could ignore me in the first place."

A few whispered words leave her mouth, and the wine in my glass flows out and lands in a heap in my lap.

"Hey!"

Everyone around me snickers.

Alright. Now it's on.

The water in the pitcher shakes, vibrating on the wooden table like a rattle. Threatening.

She looks at it with genuine concern in her eye. "No . . . wait."

The water streams out in a vortex and heads toward Tally, stopping just before her eyes. I let go of my hold.

But nothing happens.

It doesn't splash.

Tally remains dry. She smirks at me. "You really think I can't deflect some water?" Her hand is raised in the air, a glowing rune on her thumb alight with magic. "I thought I trained you better than that."

"Pfft." I return to my dinner, leaving my water fight firmly in the past. Besides, Arrie is right, this food took ages to make. I don't wanna ruin it. "Fine. You win."

HOURS LATER, THE SUN HAS SET, WITCHLIGHTS SET THE ROOM AGLOW, AND WE'VE MOVED THE tables out and replaced them with sofas. Everyone lounges, chats, meets new people, and tries their best to forget about what's coming tomorrow. The armies are all ready to go, having been moved the old-fashioned way, but we're all leaving by teleporting crystal in the morning. So until then, we might as well enjoy life.

After all, some of us might not have much life left.

"So, you're really fighting with us tomorrow? Against the SC?" Aki asks Nigel, both of whom are sitting next to me. "Seriously?"

"Yup." He looks proud, finally being able to take a stand. "I sure am."

"Magic," Aki asks, "have you seen Nigel fight in his panther form? It's amazing!"

I laugh, fully aware how awesome our godfather is. "Yup. Unfortunately so." I look to Nine, remembering his lifeless body and the hatred I have for the rogue Vampire faction. "He's pretty impressive."

Stop worrying about things we can't change. I'll be fine.

I know.

"He's huge!" Aki says, arms wide, a sloshing drink in one hand. "Like the largest pussy cat I've ever seen."

Nigel laughs, a red flush covering his cheeks. "Yeah, yeah. Alright."

Lo flies over and lands on the side table, facing Nigel. "You are a cat?"

"Yeah, a panther to be exact."

"Oh, I thought Aki was referring to one of those small cats."

Nigel scowls at Lo. "You thought I was a housecat?" Arms cross over his chest as a huff leaves his throat. "Really?"

"Well, it would be adorable."

"I am ferocious," Nigel snarls.

"Okay," I intervene, "you're all awesome. But please don't fight a dragon. Aki and I nearly died doing that once. Not really willing to repeat."

Lo turns to face me. "You cannot die."

I shrug. "Being torn into a million pieces by a dragon's talon . . . death. Don't really see the difference."

Arrie pats a large hand on my thigh. "You would come back."

I take a deep breath and look around the room.

He's right.

No matter what happens tomorrow, I'll heal. But they won't. They're risking it all for us.

Dea stands behind me, his visibility bracelet glowing faintly on his wrist, a beaming smile on his face. "Do not worry, Angel. We will make sure your loved ones stay safe."

I look to Lo, Nigel, and Aki, and concern rapids through me, my heart racing in my chest. How much protection can we give them when we'll be busy fighting an army? Not much.

"Hey," Aki says, punching my arm, "we can take care of ourselves. We don't need you." He gestures to Lo. "And don't worry about him. I doubt anyone could take out a dragon."

"While I thank you for your enthusiasm, I am not infallible. I am capable of being killed." He looks to me, warmth in his eyes. "But do not worry your pretty head over it, Magic. I doubt any modern-day army is strong enough to achieve such a feat."

"If you say so, Lo." But I can't stop my hands from clenching the edges of my sleeves. "If you say so."

The night ends too quickly. One minute I'm trying to persuade Prince Lucien to challenge his father to tippy cup, the next I'm waking up alone in a cold room with panic racing through me.

We decided to sleep alone last night so we all got as good a night's sleep as possible and Arrie didn't feel left out.

A knock sounds on my door.

"Come in." I jump out of bed and head to my bathroom.

"Hey, hon," Connie says from the bathroom doorway. "How are you holding up?"

I shrug, removing my pajamas. Then I shift into my male form and remove yesterday's clothes. "I'm okay, I guess. Just a bit nervous."

She snorts her disbelief. "Yeah, right. A bit?" She walks up to me and wraps her arms around my neck. "You're terrified, and you're wondering if we'll all make it out alive." She lays the gentlest kiss upon my lips as a hand rakes through my hair. A promise of more to come. "It's okay to be scared. War is scary. But we'll be fine. And by the end of the next few days, the Vampire cities will be protected and they'll have New Orleans back."

Her confidence seeps through, and my panic subsides.

I'm nervous still, but I can do this.

"Now go shower and get ready. Quickly. Arrie is like a drill sergeant downstairs already."

"Ugh."

Connie giggles and leaves.

Once I've showered twice and geared up into the combat armor Nine bought for me, strapping various weapons to both forms, charms, spell beads, and runes lighting me up like a magical Christmas tree. I look ridiculous, but I'm the best protected and prepared I could ever be.

My staff leans against my nightstand, and I grab it and toss it around a bit. I had the chance to ask Nine about some of the runes and charms imbedded into it yesterday, and

I'm pretty excited to put them to the test. I let go of the staff and shift into my male form, then grab it again. I practise that once or twice until I get the hang of it.

And boom, I'm good to go.

Downstairs is a veritable army of important people geared up in various armors and holding all kinds of weapons, everyone looking forlorn, wary, and like they would rather be doing anything else.

"Magic!" Aki runs at me and wraps his arms around me. "You okay?"

"Yeah, I'm just a bit—"

"Magic!" Arrie yells from across the garden. "Where have you been?" His angry face shoots straight through me, clenching in fear. "Get over here!"

"Sorry, I have to go and—"

"Now!"

I Vampire sprint to Arrie, arms crossed over my chest. "There. Happy now."

He holds a glass out to me with a twirly straw. "Drink up."

The pine wood scent of Arrie courses through me as I quickly down the glass and hand it back to him.

"Get in line."

I turn around and join Connie and the guys, all of us facing Arrie.

"Okay," he says, "now we're all here, I have a few announcements to make. First, all Vampires across the entire army have blood vials on them for healing. If you are injured then find a Vampire, or if you're a Vampire and see someone injured, please help them."

Mine are strapped to my male vest.

"Each Horseman will be in charge of a specific city's army, and they know the strategy they need to take. I will be in charge of the entire operation, and I will be leading the defense of New York. Conquest will be taking charge of Shang Hai. Magic will be taking charge of Dhaka. Death will be leading Delhi and Famine will be leading Cairo."

I already know the details of the plan for Dhaka, but Arrie didn't bother teaching us the strategy of each other's cities. We shouldn't need to know. I have Korby and a regiment of Shifters, Prince Lucien and an army of born Vampires and older turned Vampires, some pixies, Demons, and a Witch named Vicky and a small unit of Witches to use as support. Not all of the Witches can use offensive magic, so we've used them in cities where they're needed most. But with the largest Shifter army of the entire operation, we don't need as many.

Aki is with Nine's unit while Nigel is with Dea's unit.

Arrie says I'll be less distracted this way.

Connie called dibs on the dragon.

"You know where your teams will be placed and the general strategy for your area," Arrie continues. "Follow orders, stay safe, and do your best." He looks to the Vampires in our garden and nods. "There is no plan B here. There are no plans to pull back if things go wrong. We can't fail."

The Vampire King steps forward and smiles at us. "Thank you for your assistance in this matter. We will all forever be in your debt. I know there are those of you here today who disagree with helping Vampires, and I know we have a famously awry background with Witches. But I cannot thank you enough for putting that aside." He turns serious, his eyes piercing Lucien's. "Vampires, if any of you see Prince Phillipe, kill him on sight."

A few gasps filter through the air, and Prince Lucien looks to the ground as sadness fills his eyes for a moment. Then worry and confusion. But he quickly composes himself and meets his father's steely gaze.

Tally stands to my left, silent and tense, anxiety radiating off her like a tidal wave. Her fists clench into bundles beside her, her eyes darting around the group of people like we're supposed to be her enemies.

"Hey"—I place a warming hand on her shoulder—"everything's gonna be okay." My voice is barely a whisper, but the hard edge her shoulders lose tells me she heard.

Her fists unclench, and she grabs my hand and squeezes gently. She turns to face me. "Magic, I'm actually not who—"

"Alright," Arrie says, taking back control of the tittering whispers and chattering echoing around. "We'll each be in different time zones, but the SC have planned it so that each city will be attacked during daylight hours at the exact time around the world. That means the turned Vampires under one hundred years old cannot leave their buildings. This means our plans revolve solely around defense.

"The New York team with me will need to wait until sunrise before we see any action. But the Dhaka team with Magic have the opposite problem. You'll run out of daylight within the hour. I'm uncertain how the SC will react to that. But it's likely they'll be the largest force we face today. They'll want to get it over with as quickly as possible."

So Arrie placed "greatest warrior" in charge of that area. His words, not mine. I still think it should be Arrie.

But there's no time for that now.

This is the plan. I trust Arrie's battle strategy.

I have to.

65

I don't say goodbye. I don't have to. I'll see everyone I love first thing tomorrow. Prince Lucien, Korby, Verity, and I teleport to Dhaka, Prince Lucien leading the way (he's the only one who's been there before) and landing us in the center of a sordid room that smells of blood and sex.

"I apologize," Lucien cringes, "but it's one of the only places I've spent any amount of time in. I don't come here often." He leads us out of the Vampire lounge and onto the streets. "Our troops should be waiting just outside the border of the city—opposite to where we think the SC's troops will be waiting."

Nigel really came through with the info we need. He had their entire locational plans for all five cities. Mix that with the information on the thumb drive, and hey presto, you have a battle plan.

Arrie gave me strict instructions I must follow.

"Okay. We have two hours until the SC are due to attack, then one hour until we run out of daylight. Most of the Vampires in this city live in the same area, and we asked the local Vampire governors to discretely move all outlying Vampires to that location. This gives us a focal point."

"But not everyone will have followed, right?" Korby asks. "I mean, people don't like taking orders."

"Right," I confirm. "Which means we need street teams scouring Dhaka to confirm where the rest of the Vampires are to protect as many as possible." I turn to face Korby. "This is your job. Shifters can scent out Vampires from hundreds of miles away. Take the fastest few hundred and send them out in teams. When you know where one is, leave two-person teams as guards, then highlight them on the map on your datachip." That'll send the info straight to my plasmascreen. And in the next hour or so, we'll have a real-time locational map of every Vampire in the city.

Korby runs in the direction of our armies to follow orders, leaving just me and Lucien.

"What's next?" he asks.

The serious set of his face jars me into reality. "We need to move. Bring the remainder of our army to Baridhara and the surrounding areas."

He sprints at full Vampire speed in the same direction as Korby, retrieving the rest of our army. Meanwhile, I head to Baridhara, the center of Dhaka's supernatural district. The surrounding areas are also part of the supernatural district, but Arrie wants us to use a central strategy, spiraling out from the middle, therefore protecting the center as much as possible.

Plus, it's where all the city's important people are.

If I wanna get something done, I'm probably going to need them.

I sprint at full speed, getting there in ten minutes. And I'm floored by the busy beauty of this city. There are so many people, but it all seems to work in a continuous flow that has a kind of rhythmic pattern to it I can't help but admire. Like a well-oiled machine with smiling, happy cogs.

Of course, there are fewer people about on Christmas Day. Which doesn't make any sense considering the main religion here is Islam. But Nine said that Christmas is a public holiday still, with many people getting into the spirit, even if they don't follow all its religious traditions. Plus, there are Christians here in Bangladesh.

Either way, most of the city are celebrating in their own ways, with the young Vampires locked down for another—I check my plasmacreen's clock—two and a half hours.

Prince Lucien grinds to a halt on the street beside me, a little out of breath. "They're on their way."

"Okay." I bring up the defense positioning map Arrie made on the plasmascreen and start walking Lucien through who needs to go where, dividing out the Witches, Vampires, pixies, and Demons we have. "I'll need to walk Vicky through this as well. Send her my way if you see her?"

"Will do, little Horseman."

By the time Lucien has most of the army in the desired defense positions, Korby starts pinging me various locations on the map from around Dhaka, outlining where the Vampires are.

We're not sure what the SC are going to do with them, but we don't trust them not to round up the ones they can find. Especially if those Vampires can't fight back. We need to keep all of them safe.

Not a single one dies today.

Vicky runs up to me, exhaustion already setting across her features. "Magic, I've got the report for the number of enemy magic users. Over two thousand. Easy."

Shit.

A Shifter flies above me, his crow squawking before he shifts and lands next to me. "Four thousand soldiers, sir. Err . . . ma'am. Err . . ."

"Okay. Thank you." So we have four thousand soldiers heading our way, half of whom are magic users. Fae probably. We have an army of two thousand in total: 1,235 Shifters, 154 Witches, 38 Demons, 296 pixies, and 277 Vampire. I turn to face Vicky and the crow Shifter. "Shifter, go help Korby's team highlighting straggling Vampires."

He shifts and flies away, and soon he's out of sight.

I turn to Vicky and walk her through the defense positions, where we're using the Witches we have. "You're mostly defensive, so we want you in strategic positions around the perimeter of the central district. Any offensive magic users can join our teams."

She nods and turns, jogging away at a steady pace.

Looking to the sky, the sun is getting low on the horizon, so I air lift myself up, above the buildings, and sit on the highest skyscraper I can find. In a neat circle surrounding the central district is a series of glowing yellow dots marking our soldiers' positions.

Good.

Now I know where to place the barrier.

I shift into my male form and breathe in the fresh air. Okay, Magic, you can do this. I raise shaking hands and mutter a complicated incantation while drawing runes that link together to form a mini dome, and I watch as a light purple dome sparks from the floor up, growing, eeking forward, and eventually meets in the center a few meters above my head.

By this point, concerned citizens that aren't trapped by daylight have started noticing our activities, and the soldiers are doing their best to inform everyone to return to their homes and please remain cautious.

I asked Arrie if we were going to evacuate the cities, but he said that would help the SC and the Fae, not inhibit them. They want the Vampire hubs gone. So we need to protect them. However, by now the local government should have sent an update to everyone in the city with instructions to remain indoors. Good ol' datachips.

All we can do is hope we don't start a mass panic.

The dome won't stand against that many Fae, but it'll buy us some time. It won't let anyone in or out, regardless of species, other than me, so unfortunately, we can't let any Vampires who might seek a safe haven in either. Korby's on her own out there.

I hope she'll be okay.

I shift to a crow, securing my bo staff in its charm form around my wrist, and fly to the ground and land beside Lucien.

"Not long now," he huffs. "They're coming."

Shifting into man then woman, I hear what he does.

The soldiers are moving.

66

As I stand at the edge of the dome, listening to the soldiers' feet marching this way, I wonder how the other cities are doing. I bet Arrie's still waiting for sunrise, but Connie, Nine, and Dea are probably mid-fight right now. I hope none of them get hurt. And goddess, I hope Aki and Nigel are okay. They're the most vulnerable of my loved ones. I wish they stayed home.

But Aki was right. He's a good fighter. His use of death magic is far superior to mine. The Vampires need him.

Lucien and Vicky stand on either side of me, behind the dome, both stoic and silent, trying not to drown under the tension.

Just as I'm wondering what's taking the enemy so long, the first set of feet crest the horizon, and hundreds of Fae follow, a firm line set across all their faces.

Our soldiers outside the dome tense. A few Witches call balls of flame into their hands, Vampires prepare themselves to attack with their fangs descending, and the Shifters shift into their various forms.

I step through the spell, ready to join.

The leader of the enemy's army stops the procession, a snarl on his lips. "Seems we have encountered the same problem at every city we planned to attack."

I make my way to the front of our army and stand silently. I have no interest in talking.

Clicking on his datachip, he scowls and turns to his men. "We have been ordered to take the city under our control by any means necessary." He looks back at me, words on his lips, but instead, he raises an arm, hand splayed out, and closes his fist.

A few hundred Fae charge at us, spells hurling our way, while a line of long-range attacks rain down.

I shift to my female form and produce an air shield wide enough to cover the whole army.

The magical arrows and spells bounce off.

Fae swords clash with bear claws as jaws snap necks and lightning bolts shock bodies dead.

I keep the air shield in place and hurl fire bolts at the surrounding Fae. One catches an unsuspecting Fae in the face, but the other is dodged.

A scream rips from my left, and one our Vampires falls, clutching the side of their face.

I grab her by the scruff and shove a pricked finger into her mouth. "There."

She recovers and returns to fighting.

The battle wages around us, the sounds of death and fighting overwhelming my sense. But if I shift form, my air shield will come down.

Shit.

I don't have a choice.

I shift forms and watch the shield fall.

But I shift into a falcon and shoot to the long-range spellcasters, then shift in front of them and throw a magic-disabling spell at one half while trapping the rest in a magical barrier that'll feed off the magic around it.

Ripping my staff out of its charm bracelet, I slam the base into the ground and activate one of the runes.

The long-range spellcasters howl in pain as they cripple to the ground. "What is it doing?" many of them yell. Heads thrown back, bodies twitching on the ground, I leave them a pained mess.

Crack.

My head snaps around. "Shit. My dome!"

Cracks run up the side as it splinters into a thousand pieces.

I knew it wouldn't last forever, but I thought it would buy us more time than this. Fuck. I run back through the fighting army, dodging various attacks and healing a few people along the way, and I sprint through the breaking barrier.

Lucien and Vicky meet me, alongside Verity.

"Prepare our first and second lines of defense. We can't let them cut through us."

They spin on their heels and charge to their second-in-commands, all of whom follow the same actions. A few seconds later, lines upon lines of soldiers form rings around our perimeter—ten deep.

"When the dome falls, fall back!" I order the remaining soldiers still on the frontlines. "Fall to your commanders and follow their orders."

My plasmascreen pings, and I quickly glance to see several of the lights marking our Vampires blinking out.

Shit. They're dying out there.

One large crack pierces the dome's structure, and then it all falls apart, sprinkling ether dust into the wind. The soldiers fall back. The Fae and Vampire army facing us pause while I check how many we lost.

Too many.

But they don't pause for long; instead, they charge forward, meeting our swords with theirs. Some magiguns shoot off, incapacitating any supe in its snare.

I shift into my female form and stand with my soldiers. I whip my staff around to clonk a Fae in the head, then catch another in the stomach, preventing them from hurling whatever spells they were about to throw our way.

"Thanks," one of the soldiers says.

But I don't have time to turn and face him. A Vampire rushes me, so I send a tunnel flame to burn him alive, catching the two Fae behind him, and watch all three bubble and burn alive too quickly to even allow them to scream.

Suddenly, I'm surrounded by twenty or more enemies, and they're all looking at me like I'm an ant they need to crush under their boot.

Fuck that.

Using the water charm on my staff, I create a stream large enough to drown an elephant, and I send it hurtling along their faces like a whip.

"Shit. She's strong!"

I stamp my foot and send a barrel of flames at him, then spin on my feet and shift, hurling a bursting spell at the three on my left. Shifting back, I let the rain blood land on my tongue before racing along a line of six Vampires and ripping their throats out.

The enemies fall quicker than they can attack.

There are people everywhere, littering the distance for as far as even my Vampire eyesight can see. Shit. I need to get above everyone so I can see how we're doing. A bird's eye view.

I fly up, manipulating the air around me, and look around to see—

I'm yanked back to the ground. Hard. My head bouncing on the concrete. "Fuck!" My hand comes away from my head red and wet. I get my feet under me, wobble a bit, and—

Someone knocks me to the ground, straddling my waist, and my staff gets knocked aside. Raising his fist, he swings it down, fangs blaring, with a hiss. "Die, freak!"

I buck him off, twist his body around with my legs, and pin him to the floor. Thank fuck for all that training with Arrie. "Not today." I whip my head to his neck and drain him dry, his thrashing body slowly going pliant and limp.

The air around me shifts, and soon I'm flying high above the action, taking in how many of our men and women are alive vs theirs. The first ten lines of defense have been shattered, with many of them still fighting. But the last ten lines are standing strong. No one is getting through them.

Looking in the distance, though, where the other half of their army sits, waiting.

At this rate, we won't make it through this battle alive.

I need to do something big that'll wipe out a lot of soldiers at once without hurting our own forces. But what? I've spent the last month studying tactics, Fae spells, battle strategy, mastering my bo staff and Fae magic, helping Arrie with the five-city strategy, and trying to help Connie relay all the information to our allies. But at the end of the day, it all comes down to what happens when things go wrong.

It all comes down to what happens now.

I don't want to lose all our forces just to keep one city alive and pumping—how will we keep it defended once we've won if we have no one to defend it with?

I see Lucien surrounded by eight Fae by the river, one misstep from falling in, so I swoop down to help, throwing daggers at six of their heads while throwing a fireball at the other two.

"Thanks." The relief on his face is palpable. "What do you need?"

"Have everyone turn on their yellow lights."

He looks at me quizzically but sends the command out through his datachip. "There you go." He switches his on, too.

"Good." I slip down the river bank and wade in.

"What are you doing?"

"Saving our soldiers." Treading one foot carefully above the water's surface, I lift myself up and walk across the water. "And hopefully ending this battle's first half before we lose any more lives," I mutter to myself.

I get to the center and rise into the air, hair splaying out in the wind whipping around me, my breathing ragged after all the fighting and magic usage.

I've never lifted this much water before, but I'll be goddess damned if I don't manage it now. I have an audience, after all.

Hands raised with three charms and two runes glowing on my staff, enhancing my magic, the river water rises, swirling into a tornado beneath my feet. Straining, sweating, and panting, my limbs shake as my whole body aches and groans. We'll rest after we've won this battle. Promise. But for now, I need you to work with me.

A few of the soldiers near the river stop fighting, staring in awe, some of the Witches are cheering, chanting, and clapping, and the world around me stops.

Air. I need air.

I line the streets with a strong line of air to keep the water from touching the houses, then provide an air pocket for each yellow dot to keep them safe.

With a swish of my hands, I hurl the water over the battlefield, drowning the soldiers in a tidal wave. Screams pierce the air as bodies crush against the concrete walls, drown in trapped underwater areas, or simply get washed away with the tide. After five minutes of swishing the water around a giant loop on the streets, I pull it back into the river and look back at the results.

It's a mess. I've completely destroyed the city, save for the houses that I protected—and really, that was only because they have people inside. But trees are gone, debris from the river and streets litter the concrete, roads have been upturned, parks and areas of grass have been decimated. We're probably gonna get complaints about this, aren't we?

Fuck it.

That's a problem for tomorrow's me.

Right now, we have the other half of the army in the distance and something pinging on my plasmascreen. I yank it out and watch a bunch of lights huddle together in a cluster with next to none outside of it. Korby must have consolidated them to one area, worried they couldn't keep them safe on their own. Smart bunny.

I drop to the floor to catch my breath.

Lucien runs to my side with a smile larger than the Eiffel Tower. "That was amazing!" His arms widen and encompass me into a hug, where he tries to squeeze the life right out of me. You know, assuming he could.

"Thank you. If you could please . . . let me go."

"Oh, right." He drops me. "Sorry. Got a bit carried away." He offers me his wrist. "Here, if you need it."

"Err . . . thanks, but I'm fine." Prefer my team's blood, and I don't want that level of awkward.

"I'm good. Besides"—I shift into my male form—"I still have plenty of energy in this form."

"Good," Vicky says as she joins us, "because the other two thousand soldiers are coming our way."

67

"Resume the original defense positions," I order. "I want as many tight concentric rings around this area as possible." I turn to Vicky. "Take all the Witches and go to this location." I point to where Korby is on the map. "Help them."

She nods and runs off to collect the Witches.

"Lucien!" I spin to face him. "How are the Vampires doing?"

He looks uncertain. "They're tired and hungry, Magic. And they don't understand how to win this war."

"Neither do I." I look him straight in the eyes. "But Arrie does. And I trust him."

He takes a deep breath. "Then so do I." Lucien turns to his men and barks orders, sending them in the right direction.

Arrie said this would be the best strategy for them. Splitting their army into sections to see what lies ahead and test the waters. This next battle is going to be harder. And we have fewer men, less energy, and my female form is exhausted.

Switching back to my female form, I drink a few vials of blood Arrie prepared for me earlier and perk up a little. What I really need is sleep, but that'll have to wait. For now, the blood and my staff will have to do.

I fly up to a building not too far from ground level to get a better vantage point. I don't have the experience to really fight on the floor with spellwork, it seems, so I'll do it from above. Where I can see everyone.

The army march from the east, but it seems to not be all of them, simply half of what's left. So this will be the second wave, not the final wave. Balls. Now we'll have to last another battle before finally being near the end.

Looking down to the ground, I spot a commander near me. "Hey, Commander!"

He looks up at me with a smile. "Yes, Magic?"

"They're dragging this out, hoping to tire us. There'll be more waves of enemies in the future. We need to go easy, conserve energy. So tell Lucien to hold half our forces back. For now, have them check on the houses, the human governors, and see if everyone is okay."

"Yes, Magic." He salutes and strides away.

Arrie said this might happen. He also said if we only use half our forces, then we still have the other half for later when things get tiring. I hope he's right.

A wolf Shifter runs up to my building, shifts, and shouts, "Two minutes, Magic."

"Noted."

It's the moment of calm before the storm—the break in the chaos I don't know what to do with. It's the only one I'll get. How do I best use it to my advantage?

Aha.

I fly up to the large skyscraper from earlier and repeat my barrier spell. It didn't do a lot last time, but it did stagger the enemy's forces, giving us time to weed out the long-range soldiers and frontline heavy hitters. Maybe I can repeat that.

Plus, I'll be able to see their layout that way. It'll be naïve of me to assume that they'll use the same layout and strategy. I need to figure that out before I can adapt.

With the barrier spell forming the same purple dome from earlier, the first line of soldiers are stationed in front of it, all of them twitchy and nervous, their hearts pounding. But I'll stand with them.

I fly over to the front line, through the barrier, and land in front of them, meeting many of their gazes. "You soldiers holding up okay?"

They stand straight and salute. In silence. Like the trained soldiers they are.

"Good. Cos they're coming, and it's only half of what they've got over there. There's a good chance they could overwhelm us."

"We'll never give up!" a soldier shouts from somewhere down the procession line. "We'll die if that's what it takes."

Cheers shoot through the line of soldiers, pride lifting their frowns into smiles.

Silence hushing the air, stagnating our exhaustion and tempering our rage. We'll win. We'll win this because we have to.

68

Destruction rains around me, Vampires and Fae clashing in random flurries of fury so violent I can't make out the soldiers' uniforms well enough to tell enemy from foe. But none of it matters. This wave of enemies are stronger spellcasters. So the spells hurtling at us are causing damage—sometimes even lives.

I spin my staff and whack a Vampire over the head, then send a whip of water slashing through three Fae and a fireball barreling into five Vampires.

Shifting into my male form, I hurl a series of attack spells at anyone not in our uniform I can make out, sending each one to the ground. A few daggers later, and I'm putting my staff away and shifting into a panther.

Slashing claws across their faces is so satisfying. Better than hurling spells. The blood teasing my nostrils, even in this form, but I ignore the urge to shift and feed and use the rage it causes to fuel my shifting. Falcon—brown bear—horse—beetle—fly—wolf. I shift in and out of various forms, letting me weave through the clashing armies and cause damage where it'll hurt the most.

A fellow soldier's moaning on the ground, not quite dead. So I shift back into man, then woman, and prick my finger and shove it into their mouth.

Once their breath is back and they've healed and recovered, I help them up and toss them back into the fray.

There's no time for conversations on the battlefield. Everything moves faster than you can follow, and your only goal is to keep alive while downing as many enemies as possible. There's no time to think about the kill, mull over the ethics. It's kill or be killed out here. And I'd like to not regrow any limbs today.

"Magic!" someone shouts from in the distance.

I spin around and notice the barrier cracking, almost depleted. "Shit."

I shift into a falcon and fly back to ready our next line of defense.

Lucien meets me, evidently having been the one to call my name earlier. "Magic, they're getting slaughtered out there."

"I know." I meet his steely gaze. "That was the plan. Take as many of them down with them."

"That's . . ." He looks at a loss for words.

"That's war, prince. Arrie gave us many strategies to use depending on the situation. This was one of them. I won't hesitate here. Everyone with us today is prepared to die if that's what it takes."

He takes a deep breath and looks at the chaos behind what's left of the barrier. Then he looks back to his commanders and shouts, "Ready yourselves!"

The barrier finally fails against the Fae's attacks, and the next two lines of defense surge forward, joining the fray.

Lucien and I follow, Vampire sprinting to the center.

A few of the enemy at the rear stop fighting, our soldiers breaking with them, looking outwards as if confused.

"What's going on?" I storm through the crowd of soldiers, barging my way through. And when I get there, I stand stock still.

In front of me is a giant crowd of Dhaka's human population, facing with their backs to us. Because in front of them is the rest of the Fae army. And they all have arrows, guns, and spells aimed at the innocent lives bravely guarding us.

I run up to them and scream at them to run. "Please! You must leave!" They won't be safe here. They'll get hurt. Nothing will stand in the Fae's way. Whatever Prince Phillipe offered the Fae Queen, she wants it badly enough to murder entire populations, sway the SC to her side, and capture whole cities under her command. Whatever her end game is, it won't end with their deaths.

"Please! You'll get hurt!"

An elderly woman turns to face me with a smile. "We cannot stand by while you fight for us." Her accent is thick, but her English is nearly perfect.

"But this isn't your fight," I implore, trying to get her to see reason.

"They threaten the safety of our residents. Just because we are human does not mean the Vampires are not a part of us." She turns back around and walks to the front of the human crowd, arms raised in the air. A metaphorical white flag.

A Fae with a stupid orange hat on his head, white feather poking out, steps forward, magigun trained on the old lady. "You will step aside or you will die. We are following the Supernatural Council's orders."

Gasps and cries erupt from the human population—in the mob and those watching. Seems many people are seeing the truth for the first time.

"Step aside," he repeats.

None of them move.

"Please return to your homes, where you are safe," I encourage. "We can handle it from here."

Again, none of them move.

It doesn't matter what I say, does it? They're determined to play their part. Nine was right. Humans are unpredictable.

A loud crackle shoots through the air, and the old woman falls to the floor.

For a moment, the world stands still and the crowd are silent. But it only lasts a moment. It starts with a few shouts, then an ungodly scream as a young woman rushes forward and tries to shake the old woman awake. Her screams pierce the air, rumbling through everyone's fear and contempt. Shaking the earth to quake.

The Fae ready themselves, the Vampires among them descending their fangs. They're going to attack.

Without thinking, I shift into a falcon and fly into the air, zoom to the front of the crowd, and land with a thud. Quicker than I've ever managed, I shift into my female form and instinctively create a barrier of fiery water behind me. "Not a chance."

The leader snarls, his stupid feather hat bustling in the mild wind. "You will protect them? But not your own army?"

"My *trained* army *volunteered* to help defend the Vampire population from having their homes ripped from them. These are innocent people. They don't deserve to die by your ungodly hands."

Nothing is breaking through this barrier.

There's not a Fae spell strong enough.

The sounds of battle rage behind me while I handle the standoff in front of me. I'm not backing down.

Turning back around, I walk through my barrier and face the humans. "Please, I need you to return home."

Some of the people turn on a flickering light on their datachip—translators—and soon I'm facing dozens of flickering blue lights and eager eyes.

"I'm not willing to risk innocent casualties. I will protect this city. I promise. I wasn't there for New Orleans, but I'm here for this."

Some of them seem pacified, but none move.

"If you want to help, then record them, upload the videos, tell everyone what's happening. Tell the world the SC, the Fae, and a rogue group of Vampires are creating war. And it's humans that'll be caught in between." As fucking usual.

The group slowly dissipates, but they don't return to their houses; they stand on the sidelines, away from any fighting, all with their datachips set to record.

This could turn the tide of the war.

I remove my barrier and face the Fae in front of me. They're a thousand strong, and my army is busy dealing with the thousand or so behind me. It's me versus an army of Fae.

Great.

I open my staff from its bracelet and whack it on the ground, hard, then shoot of a few lightning spells as fast as I possibly can. Kinda want to catch them off guard.

Shifting, I hurl water at one half, fire at the other, and then fly into the air before soaring back down and tearing open a few necks.

All before they realize the fight has begun.

But when I land on the concrete, a thousand Fae shoot all kinds of spells at me, and dodging them is a bit like what I would imagine playing dodgeball with Connie and Arrie would be like. Like hide and seek in a minefield.

Block, counter, block, water shield, fire spray. Then I shift and quake the ground after cracking it with a pretty powerful group spell, and I watch a few Vampires and Fae fall through the crack. So I seal it back up.

Yup. I'm that kinda bitch today.

(Don't judge me, I'm fucking tired.)

They're edging closer, and one gets within arm's reach.

I yank the woman's hair and toss her away, drinking in those delicious screams as she hurtles into the distance.

I look around me, noticing the hundreds of enemies left for me to deal with and feeling the exhaustion burn my insides. This is taking too damn long. I shift into a fly and buzz my way above the horde of enemies, taking in the sheer ferocity we've dealt to this city.

Lucien and my army are still fighting, but no one looks overwhelmed. I can't see Korby and Vicky anywhere, and I don't have time to check my plasmascreen, so I just have to pray and hope they're okay. But below me is a writhing mass of shit I need to deal with.

In the distance, it's clear.

So this is the last of them.

Good.

I shift into my female form and call up a wave of fire, hold it as long as I can, then shift back and enhance it with Fae magic. It sprays to the ground, melting the skin of anyone it touches. I quickly put up a water barrier around the edges of the road, keeping the onlookers safe.

They gawk, they gasp, they take a step back. But they record everything like I've given them a mission they're willing to risk their lives over.

Returning my attention back, I look at what's left—the stragglers that might put up a fight. But when I lock onto the few twitching bodies, the few crawling Fae, I feel a sense of dread and guilt. I did that to them. To their entire people.

They were only following orders.

My feet touch the ground and I sigh, knowing I'll have nightmares about this for weeks. Months. Maybe years. But in the moment, the only thing I can do is help a few of the leftover bodies recover and let them go.

I bend down to deliver some blood to three people who missed most of the blast by hiding under an already dead body. "You can go."

They don't ask questions or talk shit. They run the moment they can away from this hellhole.

And I do that for every living body I come across, allowing those who are left to be unharmed. They don't need to die to accomplish my goal. Looking back at Lucien's success, we've already won.

The humans cheer, the soldiers chant, and in the distance, if I focus, I can hear Lucien barking orders over how to deal with the wounded, setting up a teleporting system back to the house, where a team are waiting to deal with injuries.

"Please," I say to the humans watching, "go home and wait for news. The city's governors should be ready to act and help as soon as possible."

A few translators blink at me, but otherwise they leave and go about their business, cheer on their faces that their city and its residents are protected.

I sprint to Lucien and meet him mid-order.

"No, we need all our functional soldiers here to protect the city. We'll need to reinforce our stance as much as possible."

The tired soldiers that are still standing groan and heave back to their positions, distaste and frustration ebbing at their frowns.

"Hey, little Horseman." He hugs me. "Guess you're not so little anymore, huh?" He looks around him with a sigh, the chaos grimacing. "Did you ever think to just take out the army yourself?"

I shrug. "Dea dismissed the idea pretty early on. He said that it wouldn't make political sense for us to just step in without uniting other supes. It would just look like we're fighting the SC or the Fae and everyone else is collateral."

"Yeah, I guess it wouldn't have gone as well." He wraps an arm around my shoulders. "Besides, we should be fighting our own wars. Thank you." He looks at me with sincerity in his blue eyes. "Seriously. We couldn't have done this without you."

"You're welcome."

Wonder how the others are doing?

Connie's probably won by now, but Arrie might take a little longer considering the SC were going to wait until sunrise. But what about Nine and Dea?

Lucien laughs at me, snapping me out of my worry. "Go."

"What?"

"Go on. Go check on your boyfriends and girlfriend. I can handle the cleanup."

"You sure?"

He shoves me. "Go!"

"Okay, okay. I'm going." I turn to shift, but then I turn back around at the last minute. "You need to check on Vicky and Korby." I hand him the plasmascreen. "This is where they are." I then shift into my male form and grab an Earth-Earth crystal from my one of my outfit's many pockets, then I pause. "Shit. I don't really know the other cities." Pretty sure I've been to New York before, but that's the one location I was going to leave until last, since Arrie will need another few hours.

A soldier with blonde hair and green eyes standing near me says, "I've been to Cairo before, if you need a guide. Th-that's how these crystal thingies work, right?"

I smile. "Perfect." Grabbing him by the scruff, I drag him to me and wrap an arm around his shoulders. "Get your Earth-Earth teleporting crystal out, smash it on the ground, and think of Cairo."

"Right." He follows my instructions, and I make sure to smash my crystal in time with his. The next thing I know, we're standing on a different street, in a different country, and he's wobbling beside me. "Whooooa."

"Here." I stabilize him a little and hand him another crystal from my pocket. "Use this to get back. Same technique."

He nods. "I'll need a minute, but you go on." He leans against a concrete wall to catch his breath. "I'll be fine."

I shift into my female form and listen for anything that sounds like a battle, but it's silent. There're no significant sounds coming from anywhere. Just general life stuff. That's weird. I fly up and over the buildings, hoping to spot something, and after flying for ten minutes at top speed, I notice a large group of people in the center of the city. None move, but there's a few bodies shouting in the middle of a large ring.

This does not look good.

I fly down and gasp. It's the team. They're all here.

I land behind them, and Connie, Dea, and Arrie all turn to me with equal looks of guilt, horror, and pity running across their faces.

"What's going on?" I ask. "Why are you all here? Where's Nine?"

Don't come any closer, Sweetie. I've got this.

Wait what?

Connie grabs me by the shoulders and meets my wandering gaze. "Did you know?"

Arrie stands next to her, a familiar scowl on his face. "Are you working with him?"

Dea fazes behind me and rips me away from them. "Of course ve's not. Look at their face!" He spins me around. "Erm . . . Something has happened. It is Aki . . . He is—"

I push him away and sprint past Arrie and Connie. "Where's Aki? Where's my brother?"

"Ahhh, there's my little sister," Aki's voice echoes my way.

I smile, walking toward it, until I notice him.

He's wearing all black, his death magic pouring from every surface, swirling around him. A menacing smile rips across his face at the sight of me.

"Stay right there!" Nine shouts from where he's standing in front of Aki, guns raised.

"Nine, what are you doing?"

Aki laughs, a high-pitched wail that grates on my ears. "As clueless as usual." He sighs at my confused face and holds up a scroll of ancient paper I've seen before. It's a Horseman seal. "He's trying to stop me. But it's futile."

"What are you . . .? I don't understand."

Behind Aki stands a small number of Fae and Vampires, including the Fae Queen and Prince Phillipe, who smile at him with adoration. But it's Aki himself that breaks me. He's looking at me like I'm an enemy—someone he needs to crush beneath his boot.

"Oh, sister," he coos. "I've spent a long two months with you, and I'll admit, I thought it would be harder to fool you than it was. I slipped up sometimes, but you never once suspected. Not even when I forgot to steal another teleporting crystal from your stash after returning to your home to plant your seal in your library."

It can't be . . .

He couldn't . . .

Could he?

"I don't . . . understand."

"Stop!" Nine screams. "This has nothing to do with Magic."

Aki scowls at him. "It has everything to do with *her*! It should have been me!" He rips his gaze back to mine, tutting at the tears streaming down my face. "But you went and died around the same time. The sister I didn't know I fucking had." He laughs. "And you are . . . so weak. If I had your powers, I wouldn't waste them on whoring myself out to the rest of the Horsemen, having panic attacks because 'oh no, poor me, I now have a penis.'" Aki wipes pretend tears away. "No! I'd use them to bring balance back to this forsaken world."

Arrie, now. Get him while he's talking.

No! I . . .

Magic, he's been running this show from day one. It's why I can't read his thoughts. It's why he went on the supe collection mission. He is holding your seal. If we don't fix this, you'll die.

But I . . .

"Did you really not see this coming?" Aki asks. "Wow, I must be more convincing than I thought. You didn't really believe all that spiel about just being yourself, did you?" He laughs at me, head thrown back. "Wow. I was just talking out of my ass."

Before I can even process what's happening, Aki brings a fireball to life using a charm on the bracelet I got him for Christmas. "Great gift, by the way. Thank you." And brings it to the parchment.

"Noooo!" Dea screams as he fazes forward and grabs the scroll right out of his hand.

Well, he nearly does.

Aki rushes back and flinches out of the way in time. "Nu-uh-uh." He smirks down at Dea's growling form. "We mustn't touch what doesn't belong to us."

"That's mine!" I scream, finally able to find my voice. "It belongs to me!"

"Well, you know what they say. Finders keepers, losers weepers." He chants the rhyme as though he stole my favorite toy, not the thing keeping me immortal. His laughs pierces the air.

Our army behind us is frozen, probably holding still on Nine's orders. But it seems they won their battle and Aki stepped into the limelight last minute.

I still can't believe it.

"Ohhhh, I wonder what the fierce Four Horsemen will do now I've got their whore's life on the line." He lights up his hand once again and raises it to the scroll.

Connie and Arrie rush in front of me, Connie with her bow and arrow, Arrie with his dual battle axes.

"Not a chance," Nine breathes through clenched teeth.

All four of them are standing in a line in front of me, protecting me with everything they have. But they can't. Not from this.

"Aki, please," I beg, "we can talk about this."

"Oh, I'm done talking to you. Listening to you whine and bitch about your perfect fucking life with your perfect harem and perfect world." He spits on the ground. "You're a terrible Horseman of the Apocalypse."

Aki raises the flame to the scroll.

Connie shoots arrow after arrow, Arrie throws a battleaxe at him, and Nine shoots, but they all bounce off the air shield he raises from his charm bracelet.

The scroll catches light, and Aki laughs as he drops it to the floor and watches it burn to nothing but ash. "Well, now all I have to do is kill you." He meets my gaze, murderous intent lingering in his eyes. "Shouldn't be too hard."

Arrie rushes me and carries me over his shoulders. "You need to leave. Now." He throws me into an alleyway with a dead-end. A defensible position. "Use your crystal to go back home."

"I . . ."

"Now!" Dea screams as he flies down from the roof.

Right. I shift forms and fumble through my pockets, looking for my crystal with shaking hands. Right.

Connie and Nine rush into the alley and stand in front of Arrie, weapons drawn.

You won't die here.

I finally manage to wrap my fingers around the right crystal and yank it out of my pocket.

But an explosion powers through the alley, and then everything slows down. Dea rushes me, eyes wide, and brushes his wings over us, as he tackles me to the ground. Silence ensues.

"Niiiiiine!" Connie screams. "Nine! Wait, no!"

Realization hits me, and I shove Dea off of me and race to the front of the alley. "Nine?"

My gorgeous red-haired Horseman of Famine is fading, his body crumbling into the wind. Dying.

"Famine!" Dea roars as he flies to him, struggling with his wings that have their feathers burnt to a crisp. "Nine . . ." The sob that leaves his throat is the last straw.

I grab Nine's face as both his arms have crumpled, leaving nothing but a limbless love of my life standing in an alleyway with shock plastered on his face. "Nine, no. You can't die." My lips slam to his, begging him to not leave.

"Nine, dammit, you ass pig. Don't you dare fucking die on me!"

But he fades and crumples until the last thing left—his lips—follow him.

I crumble to the floor, the life drained out of me, my heart pounding with a need to do something. Anything. But the only thing I can manage is a half scream, half sob that racks my body. "Niiiine!"

VOLUME 4

None of us move. Silence. Not just from us, but from the explosion's aftermath and the armies beyond. It's as though the world has come to a screeching halt and we're caught in its puppet strings, unable to move. To do anything.

I . . .

But . . .

"Nine," Dea whispers.

I still can't move. I want to go to him. To the Angel of Death crying at my feet.

But it seems Connie and Arrie are having the same problem because they're frozen behind me. Statues barely breathing. Barely moving.

Just when I thought I would be stuck in this frozen moment forever, Arrie moves and places a hand on my shoulder. "We can't stay here." He crouches to Dea and steals a shocked breath at his tear-soaked face. "Sorry, dude."

Dea stands, wipes his face despite the tears that continue to fall, and clenches a fist. "I know."

"But . . ." Connie behind me sobs, then growls. "I'm gonna kill him."

"No," I say, barely a whisper.

But they hear me because their heads all snap to mine at the same time.

"Hon, he needs to die."

My brother's face swims across my mind, flashing that sly grin, speaking those false words of comfort, and anger courses through me. White hot anger. "I'll be the one to kill him."

"It doesn't have to be you." She finally moves her feet in my direction and wraps an arm around my waist. "Any of us can do it for you."

Dea's still staring at the space where Nine was, where he faded, so I twine my fingers through his and squeeze. "Dea," I whisper, "we need to secure the city."

But he doesn't say anything. He just keeps staring into nothing. Into the space that used to hold our everything.

Arrie runs out of the alley and comes back five minutes later, dragging a Vampire I've not seen before. "Report."

The Vampire looks at us with a frown and then announces, "We secured the city. Then, when Aki, the Fae Queen, and Prince Phillipe teleported in, all hell broke loose. But they left the moment Aki burned the scroll."

"They left?" Arrie asks, frustration ebbing at his features. His fists clench, his knuckles white from strain, and I get the feeling he's holding it all back for us. "So the city is still secured?"

"Yes," the Vampire says. "We can move into the defensive strategy if you're ready?"

Arrie nods. "Oversee the defense of the city."

The Vampire nods and speeds away to carry out his orders.

Arrie looks at Dea not responding, at me, then at Connie, and sighs as a lone tear escapes his left eye. "Connie, take Dea home." He turns to Dea and places a hand on his shoulder. "Dude, if you can, please assist the healers and doctors stationed at the hospital. Many are wounded."

Dea nods in slow motion and then turns to Connie and grabs her hand.

Connie takes out two crystals and smashes them at their feet, holding my gaze the entire time. Anger. That's what flows through her bright green eyes. And I know exactly what she's trying to tell me: don't check out. We need you.

I know.

But I'm not sure I know how to deal with the swirling emotions inside of me. Fear. Guilt. Anger. Frustration. Rage. Grief. Overwhelming dark sadness. And it's all fighting for attention, each one wanting me to break down, lash out, crumple to the floor, launch headfirst into the next fight.

"Hey . . ." Arrie grabs me by the arms and yanks me into him. "Shh . . ."

And there, in the safety of the most confusing man I've ever met, guilt and grief take over as tears spill in rivers while sobs hack at me.

But it's the droplets falling onto my shoulders that have me snapping my head up to look at the man holding me. Streams of tears trace his angles and pour off his jaw. I can tell he's struggling to focus, struggling to stay afloat.

But we have to.

We can grieve later.

Right now, we have to make sure all the Vampire cities are safe.

"Arrie"—I reach up to stroke the tears off his face—"we need to go. This isn't the only city."

He shakes his head, clearing his focus, and stares those ice-blue eyes into mine. "Okay. Let's go." He grips my hand and grabs teleporting crystals from his pocket.

We visit each city together, ordering the start of the defensive strategy now that each city is safe, and we eventually land in Dhaka, where Lucien meets us immediately.

"The city is secure, the dead are being transported to their families, and we have already sent the wounded back to *Sheruta*. I've set up a perimeter and coordinated with local councils and law enforcement to keep your strategy in place, Arrie. And . . ." He looks at our blank expressions and grim faces and shivers. "What's wrong?" He turns to face me and frowns. "Magic?"

The words leave my lips in a desert emptiness, void of emotion and expression. The only way I know how to shove them off my tongue. "Nine's dead."

Lucien staggers back and catches himself on the nearby lamppost. "But . . . I thought . . . How?"

Arrie waves the question away. "It doesn't matter. He's gone." He steels a business-like expression and clenches his hand laced within mine. "Continue with the plan here. If you need one of us, you know where to find us."

Lucien looks at us with pity. "Go home. We can handle things from here."

We turn to teleport away, and just as we're about to vanish, Lucien looks at me with sad eyes. "I'm so sorry little Horseman."

I snap my eyes away from his just as we land in the house's garden, the weight of home wrapping around me like a blanket. But I can't fall down yet. "I'm going to help Dea at the hospital."

"Okay." But he doesn't let go of my hand. "I need to help co-ordinate what we do from here." He looks at me with this pained expression, like letting go of me is the same as removing the ground from under him.

And I just don't know what to do with that look. With the reverence in his eyes. "You need to find Connie. She can help with co-ordination efforts."

He nods then shakes his head. "How are your energy levels? Need any blood?"

I almost laugh. Because of course his focus is on making sure we're all fed. "I had plenty of enemy blood. It didn't really do much, but I'll be okay for a bit."

"I'll come to the hospital with you then. Maybe Connie's there."

She's probably not, but I think Arrie just doesn't want to leave my side. Who knows what's going through his head. I barely know what's going through it on a normal day. Much less after . . .

This.

2

The hospital is a small building; we built a special attachment unit for especially for this battle. Well, we politely asked the *Sherutan* residents for help. They were all happy to do their part—especially those who weren't fighting.

Its sprawling mass of buildings, wings, various levels, and wards could confuse the best cartographer, however, and we quickly find ourselves lost.

"Do you think he didn't make it? That he's at home?" My eyes find Arrie's in a frown.

"I don't know." His hand squeezes mine for what feels like the thousandth time as we walk down a series of corridors.

We started in the emergency department, thinking he would be there, and then wandered various wards, trying not to think about how Nine won't be here. Recovering.

Because he's already dead.

In the distance, my hearing picks up on a soothing voice with a lilt that always reminds me of home. "You will start feeling better soon."

"Dea!"

"Where?"

"This way." I drag him down a series of corridors, probably confusing the hell out of him, until we reach the Fae ward. "There you are."

Dea spins to face me and lifts the side of his lips. "Hi." He turns back to the room of Fae stretched out on various beds. "If you need anything, I will be onsite for the next few hours. But with your magical healing abilities and mine, you should recover before then."

The Fae smile at him and then continue nattering amongst themselves.

I grab Dea's hand while Arrie places a comforting hand on his shoulder. "Anything I can do to help?" My fangs descend, reminding him that my blood can heal at a miraculous rate.

"You will be most helpful in the emergency department, Angel."

He's on autopilot.

Just going through the motions expected of him.

"Okay. Then let's go." Arrie drags us both in that direction. "Err . . ." Then looks around confused, clearly lost.

Dea sighs. "It is this way." He guides us left, and we soon find ourselves in a busy ward with hundreds of different species, all moaning and groaning in pain, some at death's door, others not even conscious. "I did the best I can. But my healing abilities take time to work."

"How many patients?"

A nearby nurse answers me in his rush to see to all the patients. "2,167 total, ma'am. Sir." He rushes to apologize, but I wave him off. He doesn't have the time.

"That's a lot of wounded," Arrie grumbles.

"Yes, it is," Dea agrees. Exhaustion lining his eyes.

"You tended to all of them?" Surprise laces my voice. He nods. "Go lie down." Since it wasn't a suggestion, I shove him in the exit's direction, toward home. "I'll handle this."

Dea turns to leave, but Arrie says, "If you see Con, send her my way."

Dea nods and leaves—at a regular pace. Rather than his usual fazing.

A series of scary beeps echoes from my left as nurses shout orders and a doctor rushes over, shouting more orders. "He's going into cardiac arrest."

I yank a dagger out of my thigh holster and slice a two-inch cut into my palm, letting the blood flow. There's water in blood, right? Giving it a shot, I use my water Witch magic to stream some of my blood to the patient, whose mouth is covered by an oxygen mask. A nurse removes it, and I give two drops to the dying Fae and wait.

"His vitals are stabilizing."

Alright.

I wander my way into the center of the ward and cut my palm again, sending various streams of blood along all the beds, dropping small amounts into patients' mouths to speed up their healing.

It's not until I'm halfway through the emergency department that I start to get dizzy, a little light-headed, and a headache forms. "Shit."

"Here." Arrie shoves his wrist into my face.

And I bite down.

All the nurses and doctors are frozen in shock, some removing masks and others opening unconscious patients' mouths.

As I get to the last patient, I remove Arrie's wrist from my mouth and pull my blood back into my body.

"Wow," a blonde-haired nurse from beside me exclaims. "That was brilliant."

Light-headed, I smile. "Thank you."

But my body is fading, bright silver circles spotting my vision, and before I can find somewhere private, I pass out into powerful arms.

A flurry of activity bursts through my sleep-addled brain, coming in short bursts.

"Right, but we can't do that to the cities. They're some of the largest cities in the world, and not just for us Vamps." Lucien's voice. "They need to stay open."

"Then," a familiar grumbling from beneath me says, "we'll have to use resources to keep those defenses in place."

Connie chimes in next. "But we still need to take back New Orleans. We can't be stretched this thin."

"Whaa . . . ?" My eyes open to a familiar scene. A meeting. "What's going on?"

"Finally awake, little Horseman?"

"After saving over two thousand troops, yeah."

Lucien winces then smiles. "Heard about that. Not so little anymore, huh?"

"Ah," I wince, "my head feels like an army of horses have run it over with a thousand Arries on their backs."

"Here." Connie reaches over from my left with a tissue, then points to her mouth.

Oh. I wipe away the blood and let go of Dea's wrist, who sits to my right, his angel wings sitting behind us. Expression blank.

The Vampire king and Prince Lucien sit on the couch opposite, along with the Shifter and Witch representatives. But instead of a meeting room at the embassy, we're all sat in one of our lounges. For some reason.

"We were just discussing how to upkeep the defense of the five cities, hon."

"Ah, I see." Well, I'm gonna need a minute. Maybe five. "I'll be back momentarily." I jump to my feet and leave, clicking the door shut behind me.

Fuck.

Nine's dead.

I Vampire speed to the garden, where rain descends on *Sheruta* for the first time in a few weeks. Fitting. But no amount of rain washes away the pain lancing through me, filling my every pore and any available space.

Black wings wrap around me in the rain as hot breaths trail down my neck.

"Angel . . ." Voice strained, his arms wrap around my waist as hot tears collide with chilly rain on my shoulder. "I . . . I'm so sorry."

"No. I . . . I don't—"

"I know." He sighs into me. "I know."

"But we need to take back New Orleans. Somehow. How are we supposed to do that without him?"

"I am more worried about how I am supposed to breathe without him," he whispers.

Oh, Dea.

I turn in his arms to face him, slamming my lips to his, hoping to provide a little comfort. Even if it won't take the pain away.

"Angel," he mumbles between gasps. "I do not know what to do now."

"Me either."

But I know what we have to do. And that'll have to do for now. "C'mon, we should head back inside. I just needed a moment. Nine won't be the only loved one to die if we don't continue with the plan."

I guide us back inside, air dry us off, and drag us back to the lounge, where everyone awaits us. "Right, someone tell me the problem."

Korby smiles at me before saying, "Well, we'll use up eighty-five percent of our combined resources if we keep defending the cities this heavily. But we need to take back New Orleans."

"Korby!" I didn't notice her earlier. "You're okay." I rush to her side and grab her in a giant bear hug. "I was so worried." For just a moment, my smile is genuine.

"Yes," Lucien says, "well, I had to rescue her from a small army of Fae she couldn't handle by herself."

"Oh, bite me." She shoves a middle finger in Lucien's direction, then frowns when she looks at me again. "I'm so sorry."

The smile vanishes at those words. "Me too."

"We all are," Alpha Cal says. "If there's anything we can do." The offer seems genuine, but none of us know what to say. What to ask for.

My boyfriend is dead. What could they possibly do?

I clear my throat, pulling myself out of my thoughts. "For now, focus on holding the cities and recovering. Once all of your soldiers have recovered, we'll reconvene."

Arrie looks up from the floor. "I will consider the resource problem and come up with an appropriate strategy, then set the date for New Orleans."

Everyone gets up to leave, but Korby stays behind. "If you need a break from training, I understand. But I'm staying here in *Sheruta* indefinitely, so I'm available whenever you're ready." She shrugs. "Or just for coffee."

"Thank you." I need to wind down. I feel like I'm holding myself together with the thinnest of threads, and any minute now it'll shatter, emotions gushing like a river.

But it doesn't snap. And maybe that's the problem with grief. It feels like you're one step away from falling into your own grave, but instead, you're always holding on. Grasping for life out of some instinct to survive you didn't know you had. Forever doomed to walk on the edge.

Once everyone's left, we all collapse into a pile on the couch and breathe in silence.

Dea wraps his wings around us all, Arrie holds my hand in a death-like grip, and Connie rests her leg atop my lap, where I'm stroking warm hands up and down them.

"What now?" Connie asks, an empty curiosity in her voice.

Dea stays silent, and I don't have an answer, but Arrie shrugs. "I have no idea."

Wake up, eat breakfast, go for a walk, do some yoga, read, go to bed.

Wake up, eat breakfast, go for a walk, do some yoga, read, go to bed.

Wake up, eat breakfast, go for a walk, do some yoga, read, got to bed.

Like an empty shell, I walk around my life hollow, still waiting for that last thread to snap and for the tears to come, the screaming agony you see on the movie screen. But it's like I've forgotten how to breathe, only living because there isn't anything else to do.

I see the way Connie and Arrie look at me, waiting for the tears, for the moment when they can help, do something, mix my grief with theirs. Like the entire house is holding its breath, waiting for an emotional nuclear explosion.

We've been sleeping separately, all going about our days individually; though, I've noticed Arrie is always close. Somewhere nearby, ready to help. He's being . . . supportive, and I don't know what to think about that. I guess friends are supportive in times of grief. But he's grieving too. And I'm worried he's suppressing it to help the rest of us.

He loves by caring for others, but sometimes he needs to be cared for too.

With that thought in mind, I wander from my favorite couch in my library to the one around the corner that Arrie's curled up on. He's resting his head on the arm, a pillow wedged underneath, and his eyes are slipping shut as a blanket rests over his torso.

He's exhausted.

He's been cooking, caring for, and providing emotional support to the entire team without a second thought. As though that's where his instincts lie.

I don't care how much of an asshole he's been or what secret he's hiding or why he won't be with me; at the moment, all I care about is finding a slice of peace for us all to lie in. Arrie included.

There's no space on the couch, so I sit on the floor in front of him and open my book back up.

Eventually, after a few pages, he lays an arm over my shoulder, his hand dangling by my book. "Killer . . ." he mumbles in his sleep. "I miss you."

My breath hitches.

Looking over at the nearest clock, I realize it's four am and I should probably try to shut my brain off and get some sleep. The bedroom's not far, so I get up to leave.

But Arrie grabs the hem of my tee and frowns. "Where you going?" Sleep murmurs his voice.

"To bed. It's very late."

"Oh." He lets go of my tee with a sad smile. "Okay."

I sigh. "You can come with me, if you like?"

He looks up at me, his ice-blue eyes melting my purple ones into a puddle of goo. A furrow in his brow. "I . . ."

"We're friends, right?"

He nods.

"Then come sleep next to me so I get hugged by a bear while I attempt to sleep peacefully."

He nods, a smile creeping across his face. The first I've seen in weeks. And ever so slightly my heart warms, its frozen form thawing for just a moment.

The duvet wraps around us as Arrie grabs my waist and wraps me in the squishiest of hugs. "Go to sleep, Killer." Then he places a gentle kiss to the back of my head and nods back off.

He . . . kissed me.

But . . .

Why?

I ponder that question as sleep takes me, and I don't wake up once, I don't have a single nightmare, and for the first time since I slayed an army, sleep takes me in its arms and rocks me to peace.

THE SOFT AROMA OF MANGOES WASHES OVER ME IN THE MORNING, AND I PEEL MY EYES OPEN TO find Connie wrapped in my arms in front of me, her eyes fixed on the ceiling—or a memory that lies within, perhaps—as a few tears slip from her eyes.

I lean forward and kiss them away as more fall.

Arrie groans awake behind me and leans over. "Mornin'."

Connie sniffs but smiles—or tries to. "Morning." She turns to lie on her side, facing me, and grips my lips with hers, pulling me into her, breathing me in.

Usually, she'd be making some kind of advance or sexy remark by now, but I don't think that's her purpose today. I think she just needs me.

Arrie turns to leave, but I grab his hand and pull away from Connie. "Stay. Please?"

He looks at me, pain in his eyes, but nods.

So we stay in my bed, all cuddling under the duvet. There are some tears, some sobs, some smiles, and even a couple of light jokes. But the important thing is we're together.

"How's Dea doing?" Connie asks me, hope and concern drifting across her green eyes.

"I have no idea." I look up at the ceiling. "He won't let me into his room."

"Me either," she says.

"I've been leaving plates of food outside his room, but he hasn't touched them." Arrie strokes circles across my tummy while Connie lies in the crook of my neck. "He needs to be with us." He looks down at me. "At least with you. He shouldn't go so long without touching his mate."

"His Angel is probably needing you, hon."

"You think I should barge in there anyway, privacy be damned?" But isn't that a little . . . invasive?

My fingers worry themselves stupid, until Connie grabs them and wraps hers through mine. "Yeah, I do. Who the hell has privacy in a mating bond anyway?"

I chuckle. But she's right. Dea's always nosing his way into my emotional business for the better. Maybe it's time I do the same. "Okay, okay. I'll go see him."

"I'll bring you both breakfast," Arrie says.

"I'll come check on you both in a bit. I'm gonna take a walk."

I sit up and hug her, hoping to remind her that she's loved. But maybe actions aren't enough right now. "I love you."

She raises my chin with a finger so that our eyes meet. "I love you too. Never forget it. I'm just a little . . ."

"Empty?" I suggest.

She nods.

Arrie looks at us both and smiles. "Grief's empty, like a vase waiting for its flowers. It comes and goes in waves, never really disappearing but sometimes giving you breathing room."

I turn to face him. "But it doesn't mean you can't love. It's possible to be grieving and in love."

He frowns, as though he's never thought of it like that before, then gets up and heads out, probably to make breakfast.

"Go on," Connie says. "Go be with your Angel."

5

The black door in the corner with the giant hinges and the splintered wood stands as a gate in front of me. Locked.

"Dea, please let me in."

Silence.

"Dea, we need to let each other in. We can't just shut everyone out when we're hurting. You taught me that. You're my mate, and I need you, and I know that you need me too."

C'mon, come on, come on . . .

I don't know what else to say.

I'm not good with words like he is. I don't know what to say to make the pain go away, or if the words for that remedy even exist. And I want to respect his privacy, but sometimes people shut you out and you need to be a little forceful to get them to let you back in. Especially after trauma. And especially when you're angel mated to them and need regular touch.

"Dea, please. I—"

The door unlocks on silent hinges.

And I step through.

The room is pitch black, shadows in every inch of space, and the only light shines from two galaxy pinnacles huddled on the floor in the corner.

"Dea?" I close the door and kneel next to him, a hand gently raised and placed on his shoulder. "I . . . I'm here."

His body looks melted, like an ice cube that's met its temperature match, leaking the last of its endless water onto the floor. His eyes meet mine, and for the first time, I want to look away. I don't want to drown in their sadness. Because the only thing staring at me right now is a man on the brink of breaking in two with no way of stopping himself from falling over the edge.

Tears prick the edges of my vision. I don't have the right words, nor do I know what to do, but I lie next to him and yank Dea's head to my shoulder.

I don't think I can make this okay.

Because I'm just as broken, and I don't even know how to put back the pieces of myself—or even know who that is enough to grab a diagram. But I'm gonna try anyway, because he needs me. Because he's a part of my everything. And I can't lose another piece of my world.

Dea's fingers claw into my back as sobs wrack his chest and tears fall down my shoulder in waterfalls, gushing pain onto bare skin. "I . . . cannot . . . breathe."

"I know." My arms wrap his body in a tight hug, grabbing on with everything I have. "I know."

I can't even imagine how much pain must be wrecking him right now; they were lovers for hundreds of years. You don't just get over that. Whenever Dea entered a room, Nine would light up, like Dea was the switch to his happy. They connected in a way that I can only dream of understanding. Let alone achieving.

My feet stand of their own accord, and I grab Dea's hands in mine as our eyes connect. "Let's lie down."

With tears streaming down his face, a crease in his brow, and lips that won't stop trembling, he nods and allows me to pull him to his feet.

I guide him to the bed and sigh. The last time I was in his bed was between them both. Nine's absence cuts like a knife. Before settling us into bed, I strip the sheet and duvet cover and ask the house for something else. Anything else. Then I remake the bed and settle us under the black cotton sheets.

Dea sighs into my neck as he nuzzles close. "Nine hated cotton. It is why my sheets are always silk. He liked how they felt against his bare skin."

So many tiny details I didn't bother to learn and will never get to.

"I wanted to marry him." More tears slide down my cheeks. "Marry you all. Somehow. Someday." But that dream is fading, drifting into the impossible. It was always all or nothing with them, but I was naïve. There's still something in the nothingness, and right now, that something is the man listening to my pain while not knowing what to do with his own.

"I should have . . . married him centuries ago." More sobs escape his lips as the words fade into the empty air. "Should have said so many more words. Done more . . ."

I wrap my arms and legs around his torso and drag his head to my shoulder. "I know. He loved your words."

Connie and Arrie are outside the door, waiting. Listening. And when I concentrate, I can hear Connie's small hiccups and sobs and Arrie's hand brushing over her back.

"Arrie and Connie are outside. Want them to come in?"

Dea shrugs, words no longer able to escape past the tears.

"You can come in."

Arrie pushes the door open with a look of trepidation on his face. I don't think I've ever seen him scared before, but clearly the idea of Dea's pain terrifies him. Connie's tucked under his arm, shuddering. But when she meets my gaze and looks at Dea, she runs over to the bed and jumps under the sheet on Dea's other side, her arms wrapping tight around his torso.

Arrie climbs into the other side, settling behind me. I can sense his hesitation, but he eventually settles an arm around my waist and tucks his head into my neck. I don't draw attention to the pool of tears slowly forming on my neck, nor do I move an inch while his chest contracts into silent sobs.

I have no idea what happens next—what we are without Famine in our relationship—but I know one thing for certain: we will deal with this together.

DEA'S BED THE NEXT MORNING IS A PILE OF LIMBS, TEARS, AND SADNESS—A PUDDLE OF grieving people. Arrie is missing. I wonder where he went? I miss the warmth of his arms wrapped around my waist, even the slide of his tears on my shoulders was a comfort, knowing that we finally share something, even if it's pain.

Connie snores gently on Dea's other side, her arm still wrapped around his waist, her face scrunched up. I hope she's not having another nightmare—they've been getting more frequent of late.

"Arrie is going to get breakfast," Dea says, his voice raspy, as though all the tears have dried his throat. Though after a few days of crying, I guess it would. "He said he would bring it back to bed."

"Okay." I don't know what else to say. The dreaded silence of grief suffocates me, as though the world stopped turning the moment Nine died and we all stopped breathing. "Dea . . ."

"It is okay," he whispers. "You do not have to fill the silence; I think it is just going to have to hurt for a while."

Just as I open my mouth to respond, Arrie walks through the door, two trays in hand, the frilly apron he always uses tied around his waist. His usual grump of a smile plastered on his face. Pretty sure the man doesn't have a smile. "Breakfast."

Connie whines under her breath, a little whimper I would label cute if I didn't know she could spear me with an arrow from three hundred meters away. "Is it morning already?"

I rest my hand on hers on top of Dea's stomach, a grounding touch in the floating silence. "Afraid so. But Arrie brought breakfast."

"Hmmm?" She sniffs the air and smiles a beautiful smile I haven't seen since we laughed for the first time yesterday. It's weird what you notice, what you miss—the small things, the odd bits and pieces you never took notice of before. A smile is beautiful.

Arrie rests the two trays at the bottom of the bed and climbs back in beside me, scooting under the duvet. "It's not much, but it's . . . something."

I rest my spare hand on his knee and offer a weak smile, little more than a tremble, really. "It's perfect."

Connie brings the trays forward, digging in, but no one speaks. No one really knows what to say. Dea doesn't touch the food, he just looks at it with a sneering disdain written on his face, as though he completely forgot food was a concept and that its very existence insults him in some way.

"I wonder when Lo will be back?" He's been gone a while, and I'm not sure when he was due back, or if he'll return at all, but I miss my little library dragon. I miss my friend.

I miss my boyfriend.

Tears slide down my face, not entirely unexpected, but it's not as though I can stop them from falling. Cascading like small waterfalls. Like a flashing red light signaling where my thoughts have traveled.

Everyone looks to me, worry etched across their eyes with matching sad smiles. I think it's supposed to be sympathy. Pity. But I'm not sure.

Arrie's heavy, gentle hand rests on my shoulder as he whispers, "I'm right here."

My eyes meet his icy blue ones, and I don't know what to say. He's never been here before. Never gone out of his way to provide comfort or love or support. Why now?

The confusion is clearly written across my face, because his eyes dart away and return to the breakfast tray on our laps. After swallowing a mouthful of berries, he asks, "What now?"

Connie shrugs and whispers, "I don't know." She takes in a big breath, as though deciding finally that this is the moment she can speak something that's been on her mind for a while. "We need to tell the public."

I don't know what to say to that. She was somehow thinking of her job, thinking of all the little things that need to be done, like public announcements. I'm not sure I even have the energy to string a mental sentence together, much less focus on my job, which is probably a bad sign for the world, considering, you know, my job is to save it.

Connie jumps from bed, anxious energy running through her, and yawns. "I think . . . I think I need a distraction. Something to focus on. To give my attention to. To take my mind off . . ." She trails off, vocally gesturing to the painful elephant in the room that sits on top of our vocal chords, squashing us into silence.

No one seems able to say his name, his death, or anything remotely similar, as though just the very thought is a curse.

Is this when people are allowed to break down? I usually break down over the smallest of things, but right now I just feel numb.

Dea slides the tray down the bed and crawls back up to rest his head on the pillow and bury his face in the duvet. I don't think he's ready to face a world without Famine yet.

What is it people do now? Move on? Focus on something else? Drown in grief? I'm not sure which option I wish to land on yet.

"Anyone want to help run errands?" Connie rubs her hands together expectantly, her eyes begging mine, begging any of us to join her. "Please?" The hair stopping at the middle of her back, currently sticking out in all kinds of angles, reminds me just how much she's been through recently. How much she has been through in such a short space of time.

"Sure."

Dea whines gently beneath me, an almost silent breath I'm sure the others probably heard. I wash my hand beneath the duvet and rest it on his back, rubbing gentle circles, soothing his rugged breaths.

I don't know what to do. They both need me, but I can't be in two places at once, and Connie's right, she needs to expel her energy.

"I'll stay with him," Arrie suggests, his voice barely a whisper.

I look to him, surprised. And then a gentle smile washes over me. A genuine smile. One of relief and gratitude, and maybe, just maybe, my relationship with Arrie is on the mend.

6

The outside world is spinning on. I don't know what I expected, but a part of me wanted to see cities burning, people screaming, and my friends struggling—the world mirroring my mind. But, of course, it doesn't.

Connie doesn't let go of my hand as we walk to the embassy in companionable silence, each of us squeezing in thirty-second intervals. Reassurance. A team. That's what we are today.

"So," I start, breaking the silence, "we have an agenda today?"

Connie shrugs. "Nothing specific. We just need to check in with everyone, make sure the cleanup's gone to plan, that the wounded are doing okay, and nothing's gone to shit in the meantime."

"And I can ask about Lo."

Connie smiles sadly. "He's a dragon. He might have just taken off, hon."

I nod, the realization that I don't know Lo that well and he has no reason to return hitting me like a fresh wave of grief. "I know." My voice is quiet, barely a whisper. "But I just . . . want to know."

She squeezes my hand.

See, reassurance.

Teamwork.

And we have friends we need to check in with, like Prince Lucien, Korby, the Vampire king, my Fae trainer, and everyone else I've met on this journey. I want to make sure they're still doing okay.

We reach the embassy with somber expressions, our hands still grasping each other's, and walk to the offices upstairs, where we see Red.

Who looks at us with surprise. "Oh, umm . . . Hi." She smiles weakly as us. "I didn't know you'd be here so . . . soon."

So soon after Nine's death.

Because we should still be in mourning.

When I say nothing, Connie chimes in. "We're just wanting to make sure everything's okay. And we want a final report."

She nods, a business-like demeanor returning. "Right. We're collaborating on that report, hence why I'm here." She gestures to herself and the building. "And as for the Witches, we're doing okay. Minimal losses overall." Her gaze meets mine. "Which we have you to thank for. You kept our losses low, and for that I'm grateful." She bows her head low—respect.

I bow in return. "No need to thank me. I was just doing my job."

She looks at me with a small smile. "But your powers are something else, girl. Err . . . boy. I mean—"

I hold up a hand, stopping her ramble. "It's okay. Genuinely. But I prefer ve/they."

"Noted." She spins on her feet. "I'll take you to the Shifters and Vampires for a better update."

Red walks us into a large meeting room upstairs, but rather than step through into board meetings and paperwork, we step into chaos.

Voices hurl themselves across the room, a lion is growling in the corner, and five Vampires have their fangs out, including the king.

But despite all that, I smile, because on the table is a small Lo chasing a familiar rabbit. Korby.

"Lo!" Surprise and joy enter my voice, and I feel floaty for a minute, like the sun. "You're okay."

He leaves his rabbit conquest behind him as he flies over and lands in my hand. "Of course. I am a dragon."

Well, he's not wrong. "Yeah, but I worry anyway."

He smiles through sharp little teeth. "I am sorry. I should have checked in sooner, but when Lucien told me what happened, I thought it best to give you all privacy."

I poke a finger at his nose. "Well, next time interrupt my depression to let me know you're still breathing, please."

He lifts a wing and does his best salute. "Yes, Magic."

A panther in the corner shifts back into a man I recognize and immediately Vampire speed to. "Nigel!" I feel so guilty that I haven't really thought about anyone else over the last few days. Shit. I'm terrible goddaughter. "You're okay."

He wraps tight arms around me and squeezes, then breathes me in. "I'm here, kid. Right here." He takes a step back and gestures to the room. "Keeping your friends from murdering each other."

I chuckle, then look around the room. Frowning. "What the hell is going on?"

No one speaks, no one even breathes, but Connie smiles at me from the doorway with a thumb's up.

The lion in the corner shifts, and Alpha Cal looks at me with a scowl on his face. "We're trying to decide how best to split resources."

Seriously, it's been a few days, and they can't make a single decision on their own? Fuck my life.

"Well," I start, "what are the top priorities?"

"My Shifters are spread too thin. If the Fae attack, we can't protect our own."

Prince Lucien speaks up, frustration ebbing his tone. "We're sneaking blood supplies into New Orleans as best we can and keeping the defense system in place for the main Vampire cities."

Red, who's standing next to Connie, smirks at the room and meets my eyes. "We're monitoring the Fae, but there aren't enough Witches to go around."

I breathe. Deeply. And then breathe again. "Bring all our wounded from every city here. Fill up the hospital and bring all the medics, too. That'll free up some of the defenses and reduce pressure on the soldiers."

Prince Lucien smiles while Alpha Cal bows his head.

"That is a good plan, Magic," Rufus says. "But where do they go then?"

I rub a stressed hand through my pink hair. "Back to their respective homes. If they want to keep fighting with us, they can. But no one has to." But they're right. We are spread too thin. We simply don't have enough numbers to go around. But what if it isn't about numbers? "We're not using our soldiers most effectively," I mumble.

"What do you mean?" Alpha Cal asks.

"I mean, we've split everything up by species, but just like the battles, we're best when we utilize all our skills. Mix everyone up. Vampires would be great alongside Witches to monitor the Fae. They have better vision and senses, are quieter than mice when they want to be, and have night vision. Take some fairies with you if they don't mind. Vary up the species defending the cities, and then thin the numbers so we can also protect the Shifter strongholds. Biggest Shifter groupings take priority, Alpha." I turn to Connie. "In the meantime, we need to prepare to take back New Orleans."

She looks at me shocked. "Magic . . ." She sounds uncertain.

"I know." I take a deep breath, trying to remain calm. "I'm not ready either, but the world can't wait just because ours has stopped spinning." My voice lowers into a whisper. "Besides, Nine would hate that people are suffering because of him."

Everyone in the room falls silent—no one even breathes—and everyone bows their heads, avoiding looking at either of us. No one knows what to do.

I turn to the room with a brave face. "I know that it's difficult, and we've all lost people, but we can't take too long to recover. While we get stronger, so does the enemy. We can be ready to go in a few days if we use teleporting crystals."

"Are you sure?" Alpha Cal asks us. "We need you at your strongest for this." He turns to face Connie. "They need you."

I know that. I do.

But how I am supposed to retake an entire city guarded by the Fae army and the Supernatural Council without Famine?

"I need you," I whisper to the night sky, wishing he were here. He'd know what to do. "I don't know what to do now. Well, I guess I do know what to do, but I don't . . . I can't . . ." I sigh. "I just don't know."

"Spiraling out loud, Killer?"

"It's the only way he can hear me." I look to Arrie's ice-blue eyes that pierce the night and a tear slips free. "I could really use his advice right now."

He sits next to me and gazes up at the stars too. "I think he'd tell you to just be yourself. Trust your own judgement. Fate gave you to us for a reason." He moves my chin to face him and spears me with an expression I don't know how to interpret. "You are our greatest gift."

"Our?" It slipped free before I could stop it. Shit. "Sorry, forget I asked."

He stays silent, not answering. Thank the goddess.

But he lies beside me, staring into the night sky, his familiar, comforting presence flitting around me like a blanket on a cold winter's day. "I miss him."

I barely hear it, the confession slipping from his lips. But when I do, it burns hotter than fire, searing me with its flames.

"I wish I could just . . . forget," he whispers. "I wish I was never chosen."

I shoot up and curl my legs underneath me. "Don't say that. If you weren't chosen, I'd be left with some talkative shitty little twink of a Horseman of War. I already have two of those." I hitch a breath. "One. I have one of those." Tears fall from my eyes before I can stop them, slipping into needing comfort rather than giving comfort. "Everyone . . . needs me, and . . . I'm just . . . crying."

Arrie's arms wrap around me, his head resting atop mine. Our white hair mixing underneath the moonlight. "You don't need to be happy to comfort someone. Your tears are comforting too."

When I'm dry crying, no tears left, Arrie pulls me away from him and smirks. "Want to be the first to have a go on my Christmas present?"

I nod. Words not forming.

He pulls me to my feet and guides me to the back of the garden, where I asked the house for a racetrack and a new fancy car just a week ago.

We get in, strap ourselves with the seat belts (I don't have time to regrow limbs right now), and Arrie shoots us across asphalt.

"You know," he says, "I've never gotten such a splendid gift." His face shifts, sourness forming on his lips. "Not for a long time, anyway."

That's more than he usually says. So maybe he's getting closer to that something I can feel between us on the horizon. Maybe he's ready? No, I won't push him. I don't want to go backward.

"Magic?" He briefly meets my questioning gaze. "Do you think maybe I can start sleeping in your bed again?" He takes a deep breath. "It feels more lonely without Nine around."

I smile, something washing through me. Something that feels a little like love. "Always." I put a hand on his knee. "You never have to ask."

"If you need me to leave for any intimacy with Con and Dea, you can just say, and I'll—"

"We'll be fine, Arrie. We are not lacking for room options."

He laughs, and it vibrates through me like nothing I've ever felt before. It swirls around me and ignites everything inside me, pushing out the bad feelings, the grief, the guilt, and the anger. And for a moment in time, I'm so happy, I feel like I'm soaring through the skies.

"Besides, we're not exactly in the right headspace for sex right now."

Arrie frowns. "Sex can be a good healer. Besides, you have needs they should think about." He grins, a sly look crossing his lips. "We do not want to go down that road again."

Something tells me he'd do it on purpose and watch me suffer just to be the one I tear apart in a frenzy.

He swerves us around a corner with a sharp twist of the steering wheel, and I squeal, thrill soaring through me. "Ahh, Arrie!" My fist tightens on the passenger side door's handle.

"I'm just using the gift you gave me."

The smirk in his voice forces a smile to my lips.

"Besides, you'll live."

Assuming no one steals my seal and destroys it, sure. Ever since Nine, I feel more vulnerable, less immortal. Any of my team could be next, any of them could leave me, and I wouldn't be able to stop it.

The car slows to a halt, and Arrie rests a hand on my knee, a shadow of him touching me. He looks at me and brushes the tear out of my eye.

"What if the rest of you die, too? What if you all leave me?"

Arrie stops breathing and looks at me, a stolen breath held between us. "I'm never going to leave you, Magic." His giant hand cups my cheek as his fingers slide through my hair. "I'll fight beside you forever." He bows his head and screws his eyes tight shut without taking another breath, and before I know it, he's leaning in, eyes wide open and staring at my lips like they're the last ones on Earth he'll ever get to kiss. To feel against his skin.

He lights me up like electricity, an alive pulse racing through my veins that I'm too slow to do anything but feel. I'm at this man's mercy, too weak to do anything but experience him. I should push him away, have a conversation, maybe ask if this is what he really wants, but I don't. Can't. His lips are too glued to my soul.

His other hand slides up my thigh and grips my waist, then yanks me toward him. I straddle him in the driver's seat, his hardened arousal grinding into mine, all while not breaking contact, not taking a breath.

But when his hands run over my chest and starts to fiddle with my shirt buttons, I grab them. "Arrie . . ." I take a deep breath. "We're moving a little fast."

"Oh, right." A small groan slips from his tight lips as he grabs my hip and burns me with a fiery stare. "I've missed you."

I feather my lips across his, reminding him I'm always his. That I'm waiting for him. "I miss you too."

He presses his forehead to mine and breathes heavy. "Thank you."

"For what?"

"Going slow. Stopping me. Being patient. Forgiving me and—"

I shove a hand over his lips and smirk. "If you think you're off the hook that easily, then maybe you don't know me as well as you think you do." His eyes widen with worry. "If you want my forgiveness, then you'll have to earn it." I release my hand. "But I'm not going to punish you by being angry and avoiding you and treating you like shit. What you did hurt, even knowing there's a reason and things I don't know, but I love you too much to sit here and keep breaking you."

By the time we get to bed, Dea is already asleep, so we join him. Connie's doing her own thing, but I'm worried. She only sleeps every few days, which means she's alone for most of the nights. Alone in her grief.

"Maybe I should stay up with her," I whisper to Arrie, trying not to wake Dea. "She's gonna be alone."

Arrie rests a heavy hand on my chest. "Shh, Killer. Con will be fine. Just get some sleep."

"But she needs me too."

Dea rolls over and rests his head on my shoulder. "You cannot fix all of our pain. We are capable adults."

It's the first real sentence he's spoken since we got back home, and it's to give me wise old sage advice. I roll my eyes. Of fucking course it is.

The door opens slowly, silently, and Connie walks in with a small smile on her face. "I'm flattered. You're all talking about me." She crawls up the bed and sits in my lap. "Look at me." She meets my eyes. "I've been sleeping for less than these guys for a *very* long time, babe. I'm used to having my alone time." She leans in and swipes her lips briefly over mine—a quick burst of affection with all the power of a longer kiss. "Now, get some sleep."

I yawn but drag her down into bed with me, enjoying her warmth, her lying on top of me, a solid weight while I drift off.

"You know," Arrie grumbles, "if Nine were here, he'd be suggesting some kind of orgy."

"If Nine were here," Connie responds, "we'd already be having an orgy."

We all chuckle, but Dea slips back inside himself and buries his face in my neck.

I kiss his hair and whisper, "Do you want me to switch to my female form, so our angels can touch?"

Dea whines a little, clearly unsure, but eventually nods. "But it is not because I want you only as a female. I love both forms, and—"

"Shhhh," I whisper into his hair. "I know." I switch forms, and Connie squeals as I lose a few inches and move about on the bed some, but she holds steadfast nonetheless. "Besides, I have more holes for orgies this way."

Everyone chuckles, even Dea.

"Arrie?" I ask the dark room.

"Hmmm?"

"Can I tell them about earlier?"

"Tell us what?" Connie asks the room, suddenly alert. "You have to tell me now. Girl code."

Arrie nods against my shoulder, but his hand tightens into a fist against my leg.

"I don't have to, you know. When I ask a question, it's me giving you a genuine option."

"Oh," he says. "Well, okay then."

"Sooooo, that's a yes, then? Or a no?"

Connie groans from on top of me. "Listening to you two trying to have a conversation is painful."

Arrie punches Connie in the arm, who punches right back.

"Yes, you may tell them."

Dea is silent, but he's awake; I can feel his breathing. Connie, on the other hand, is leaning on her elbows, which are placed beside my shoulders, while she stares at me with childlike glee.

"Arrie kissed me tonight."

Connie's jaw drops, and Dea raises his head. Interest piqued. "Really?" he asks.

"Uh-huh." I nod, a smile forming on my lips. "We didn't chat about it or anything, but—"

"Magic reminded me to go slow."

"Wow, big guy"—Connie pats him on the head—"well done. Didn't know you had restraint in you."

He growls at her, and the deep vibration of his voice shoots right through me. My insides squeeze, and I do my best to not squirm, but apparently Connie notices anyway, since she just laughs at me."

"Well, well, well . . ." She looks at me, devilishly beautiful, and smirks. "I learn new things about you every day."

"Shut up." It comes out more as a mumble, and the guys look bewildered, but we both just giggle. They're used to us by now. Taking a deep breath, I force the words out of my mouth. "I'm scared."

"About what?" Arrie asks.

"Life without him." I sigh. "Sex without him. Thinking without him in my mind. It's so empty, it echoes. Like my thoughts are just shouting back at me." I look at everyone, a somber expression thrown across their features again. "Sorry, I turned everything sad again."

"It's okay, babe." Connie strokes my cheek with a soft thumb. "We're all allowed to just randomly be sad."

Arrie and Dea snuggle in on either shoulder, Connie curls up between my legs, and we all fall asleep together. Well, all minus one.

Connie, Arrie, and I sit at the embassy the next day, discussing specifics over strategy, how to retake New Orleans with the least number of casualties possible, and how to mingle our forces for maximum efficiency.

Arrie paces the room, his vision that shining, zoned-out look he gets when he's using his battle strategy mode. "Move half the fairies from New York unit four to Delhi unit eighty-seven. Schedule half the Vampire troops from all cities to support the Shifter cities, then move thirty-eight percent of the Shifter troops to the Vampire cities, remove Lo from active defense, and reinforce Cairo with the eighteen Witches from Dhaka."

Connie and I aren't much use right now. Arrie's in the limelight. And what a hot limelight it is. My jeans are getting a little strained over here. So I shift to my female form.

"Hot, isn't it?" Connie whispers into my ear.

Vampire eyes shoot our way, but I ignore them.

"Yup."

"Gonna tap that later?" she whispers back.

"Nope."

She frowns, huffs down a whine, and goes back to paying attention.

Dea's at home, still in bed. And I don't know what to do. He needs time. And in any other circumstance, I'd let him wallow for years until he's ready to poke his head back above water. But we need him in this war. There's no way we can do this with just the three of us. But I don't want to be the reason he's pushed before he's ready. I don't want to watch him snap.

"Stop spiraling," Connie whispers.

Arrie stops talking and looks my way, a question in his gaze. "You okay?"

I nod, but I don't smile.

The real answer is I'm not sure what okay feels like anymore. But that doesn't matter. I have to be there for Dea. For Connie, who was struggling before. And for Arrie, who needs me to remain by his side while he figures himself out.

I can't fall apart right now.

I look around, my gaze falling on the ambassadors in turn and then on the empty Witch seat. Blood boils in my veins.

I'm gonna kill him.

And I'm gonna enjoy it.

A few screams pierce my zoned-out hearing, and I look around. Shit. The couple of chairs around me are on fire. Shit, fuck, shit.

Water, Magic. Water.

Before I can generate a stream, one of the Witches, Nana, I think, puts them out with a scowl. "Watch your emotions next time."

I frown at her.

Then I frown at the empty chair again and point. "Someone fill that seat."

"We're working on that," Red says with a gentle look. She's a fire Witch. She gets it.

"Sorry everyone."

Everyone grabs new chairs, and the meeting rekindles with little fuss. Other than Lucien laughing at everyone's horror. But we all ignore his crazy.

By the time we're done, we have a plan. All that's left is a date. And for that, we're gonna need a little reconnaissance.

"Who's up for some spying on the SC?" I ask everyone while we're sat drinking cocktails in the sun, the balcony doors open. "I promise fun times ahead."

Everyone chuckles.

Red sticks her arm up. "You know I'm game."

Lucien shakes his head, a smile of affection on his face aimed toward Red. "I'll go with you."

My eyebrows reach the ceiling.

"What?" He shrugs. "Always up for spying on my big brother."

Something tells me that's not the reason he's going.

"Can I go with?" Nigel asks, having joined the drinks after our meeting was over. "I'm a bit bored doing not much right now."

"I thought Rufus was keeping you busy?" After he officially quit his job with the Supernatural Council, Rufus made him part of his right-hand team here on *Sheruta*. A way to look connected with Earth, I think.

Nigel shrugs. "It's just a little . . . stuffy."

Lucien grabs Nigel's hand and shakes it. "Happy to have you on board, Nige."

Nige? Since when is the little prince friends with all my people?

Connie's quiet next to me, her silence having fallen the moment the meeting was over. I wonder how she's really doing? Between Bandio Bontanos, our new relationship, and Nine, she's probably been through more than the rest of us recently. I hope she's doing okay. Well, as okay as she can.

I squeeze her hand and nestle hers in my palm.

She looks to me with a sad smile. And I know that look. That's the look she has when she's remembering Nine.

"Okay," I start, "we're gonna head home. Red, please lead the team. Be safe. Don't take stupid risks. We'll check in later." I help Connie out of her seat, and Arrie and I lead us back up the winding path to home.

This is the first day we've left Dea alone, and I won't lie, I'm scared what I'll find when we get back home. "I'm worried about Dea," I mumble.

"Me too." Arrie grabs my other hand. "This reminds me of what it was like when Haji died, but worse because there are more memories with Nine."

"And we're all sad too," Connie says, "so we can't . . . be as supportive."

I look to Arrie, then to Connie, and think of Dea . . . I need to help them through this. I need to be there for them. I can't let them fall.

"Well, at least we're one step closer to freeing New Orleans." Arrie speeds up, clearly wanting to get home. "It's awful reading all the news stories about how much those Vamps are suffering."

"The sooner we can free that city, the closer we are to dealing with this mess."

I snort. "Sorry, but we're a long way off peace. The SC need to be retired, the Fae need to adhere to the law or face consequences, the humans need to either get on board or shut up whining, and the Witches need to come out of the closet." I take a deep breath. "Anyone know how I'm supposed to fix any of that?"

Arrie looks at me with certified confidence. "You'll figure it out, Magic."

Connie tightens her grip on my hand. "You always do."

"Yeah, but I usually break something first."

10

Once we reach home, we're greeted with a whirlwind of magical pressure, and I drop Arrie's and Connie's hands and race to Dea's room at top Vampire speed.

I can hear Connie and Arrie following, equally worried.

"Dea?" I half yell through the popping feeling in my ears. "Dea!" The door to his room is half blown off its hinges and papers, potion bottles, and pillows fly around the room in a whirlwind of madness. And at the center of it all is a black ball of feathers huddled on the floor. Screaming. "Dea!"

I race to the center, dodging a pillow and smashing two glass bottles to the ground. The moment my hand finds its way beneath his wings he's using to protect himself and my skin makes contact, I breathe a sigh of relief.

And everything freezes.

There're pillows in the air, along with sheets of paper, books, and anything else previously stacked neatly in the room.

"Dea . . ." I yank on his arm and get him to a sitting position, wipe the tears from his face, and shove my arms around him. "I'm sorry. I won't leave again."

His usually golden skin burns red as painful magic pulses out of him. "No . . ." he groans. "Please, make it stop."

Arrie and Connie rush to my side, and Arrie growls. "Dea, stop being so stupid. Go and help whoever needs helping."

Connie's hand flattens on his shoulder. "The more you fight it, the more it'll hurt. Go."

And that's when I realize what's happening. Dea's being called to a lost soul. To help guide them to the otherworld gates. The gate Nine's currently waiting behind.

With a soft voice, and being as gentle as I can, I whisper, "This is your job. Without you, they'll be lost. They deserve happiness in death, Dea. We all do."

"No, I . . ." His skin glows red hot again. "Argh!" He grips his hair hard, yanking at it. "I do not want to carry another crying soul to their afterlife. To watch their loved ones cry and be the reason they are being left behind!"

Arrie grumbles something and then translates. "This is a really shitty time for a soul to get stuck."

It mustn't happen very often because I've not seen this before.

"Please, Dea. Go." I grab his hand and rub soothing circles on its palm. "I'll be right here for you when you get back, with tea, blankets, movies, books, and as many blowjobs as you like."

Arrie chuckles. "Hear that, dude? Unlimited access to Killer's mouth? Who'd turn that down?"

I look to him and blush. Then I return my attention to Dea. "In either form."

He snaps his attention to me and then looks sheepishly to the ground. "You do not have to do that just for me."

I lift his chin up. "Trust me, I'll be getting some too."

His lips tilt up ever so slightly, and a small breathy laugh escapes. "Tempting the Angel of Death with blowjobs and tea?" He sighs, clearly not wanting to go still. "Fine. Deal."

Everything in the room crashes down, and the moment he closes his eyes, he pops out of existence.

"Wait, what?"

Arrie laughs at me while Connie helps me to my feet. "Yeah, it usually teleports him to Earth, and then he can fly to the person at the speed of light like a homing pigeon."

"But faster." Connie gestures to the mess. "I think we should clean this up for him."

"I'll get started on some food." Arrie wraps a quick arm around my shoulders and squeezes, then he rushes off to make something no doubt delicious.

Connie and I are left to clean up Dea's room. We could call one of the maids, but we're funny about them being in our spaces. We still clean our own rooms. The maids just collect the washing.

Connie looks around the space and sighs. "He doesn't really like his job." She asks the house for trash bags and starts collecting things that flew out of the waste bin and picking up the broken glass.

"Why?" I grab the books and start re-shelving them. "I mean, he didn't kill them."

She runs a hand through her hair, and I once again feel guilty when it ends at her waist rather than her ass. "It's not that he feels guilty; he doesn't enjoy watching their loved ones crying and screaming or the emptiness of the soul. He says they're as blank as paper when passing."

I shudder. "Does that mean Nine's blank? Empty?"

Connie looks at me with a grimace. "That's probably why he doesn't want to go. He won't see him. He doesn't actually go through the gates—just guides them to the door and opens it."

"But just knowing that Nine's beyond them . . ." Alone. Without any of us. Blank and empty. While the world needs him. While we need him. While I need him.

Tears creep down my face as I shelve the last book.

"Sorry," she whispers as she wraps her arms around my chest.

My shoulders shake, and for a moment it feels as though my knees might not keep holding me up. "It's okay. I asked." I take a deep breath and turn in her arms. "You were just answering my questions." My lips meet hers, our gentle tears mixing between our teeth and lips. "I always want you to be honest with me."

She nods. Understanding. "Let's keep going. It'll be nice for this room to be clean for him. You know how he gets about his clean space."

I chuckle and wipe the tears away. "Yeah. He's a bit of neat freak."

"A bit?"

We both laugh as we do our best to return the room to its usual impossibly clean standards. We do okay, I think. But I'm sure Dea will move things around and readjust when he returns.

"Come on"—she grabs my hand—"let's go for a walk." She guides us outside into the bright and sunny weather of *Sheruta* and toward the rainbow forest, where I used to spend my mornings trying to punch Arrie in the face. Good times. "I'm sorry for being so checked out over the past few days."

She avoids my eyes, even when I try to meet them, so I squeeze her hand. "Stop apologizing for having emotions. You needed space and love, like being left to your walks and work but being consistently reminded that I'm here."

Her eyebrows raise. "Got me all figured out, huh?"

"Maybe a little of you." We pass the clearing I used to do hand-to-hand combat training in. "It's my job to understand you. To help you."

"Don't push yourself too hard, hon. You need space too."

But they need me. Changing the subject, I whisper, "I hope Dea's okay." He seems so broken, so unrelentingly upset. And I don't know how to fix it. Or make it even the slightest bit better, and I'm worried that there isn't a way to do that. "It's like I've lost them both."

I can hear the loud swallow of Connie's throat and feel the squeezing of my hand. She opens her mouth, then closes it again, then opens it, then closes it. Seems she doesn't know what to say either.

"It's okay," I reassure, "I don't need comforting words."

We walk all the way through the forest, enjoying the light filtering through rainbow-colored leaves pattering onto the floor in small bursts. We tiptoe past the unicorn herd toward the northern edge, and I stop to observe them. But they're as calm and placating as usual—all grace and no anger. As though they were plucked from a dandelion's heart and placed into the body of a silver cloud on a cloudless day.

I wish I were as peaceful.

There's this simmering rage deep inside me. One I can't seem to let go of. And just when I think I've gotten a handle on understanding it, of reining it in, it explodes into a million shards of glass. Like the fiery chair incident. And when I nearly choked Felicity to death.

Connie leads me up a familiar hill, past familiar rabbit holes, and we sit underneath a familiar *Shinto*. "It's peaceful up here."

"Yeah, I know. We can see everything: the forest, the town, the house, the fairy gardens." I take a deep, earth-scented breath and let it calm my soul. "It always reminds me that I'm home."

Connie rests her head on my lap and reaches up to twizzle the white strands of my hair through her fingers. "You're more comfortable with your male form now." It isn't a question.

"Yeah. Dea helped. But I also don't really want to grieve with Vampire emotions. Not if I have a choice to avoid it."

"Makes sense." Her palm lies flat against my cheek as she strokes my eyelid and smiles at me. "I know it hurts, and it'll continue hurting forever, but I'm so proud of how you've handled this." She leans up and places a gentle kiss as soft as rose petals against my lips. "The rest of us are falling apart, and while you're struggling, you're holding up for us." She whispers her lips against mine. "Thank you."

I smile against her, a sad smile I'm not sure could really signal happiness. "I'll always be here for you." I guide a gentle hand down her front, along the outline of her breasts, and then inch my fingers along her the edges of her tank.

She arches into my touch, a breath racing out of her mouth. Her hands reach out and grace their silken skin down my cheeks and round my neck, where she grips hard. Then pulls my face to hers. "Kiss me." Her voice needy, her eyes hazy.

I slide my tongue past her lips, caressing her mouth with a growing need, while my fingers play with the edges of her top and shorts, teasing.

Her hips arch into me, seeking, needing. "Magic . . ." she moans into my mouth.

"Hmm?" I say between kisses. I slide my mouth down her neck as my fingers slip up her top, her skin like silk, caressing every inch of my hand like rivers of scorching sand.

"Fuck me." She opens her eyes and pierces those earthy greens at me. "Please." Her mouth tipped open, her eyes begging, and her pink lips wet from my mouth, I lay her on the grass and straddle her waist.

"Anything in particular you'd like?" I whisper into her ear, my hands finding their way to her breasts once again and skimming beneath her bra.

"You." Her hands grip the sides of my head and yank me to her lips. "Inside . . . me," she gasps between breaths.

"I've been waiting for you to ask."

I've been purposefully gentle with all the team these last few days, not trying to pressure them or push them before they're ready, but now Connie lies before me, her tank top above her bra, her breathy moans caressing the air, and her legs parting beneath me. I sit between them and expose one nipple to the warm air.

Her chest arches toward me as a small whine slips from her mouth, so I take the nipple into my mouth and slide my tongue in soft circles while my hand exposes her other nipple for me to play with.

I want this to be perfect for her.

So I use my knees to widen her legs, to spread them in front of me, as I grind my rapidly hardening dick into her clit and hear her moan my name on the wind.

"Magic . . . please."

No way am I giving in that easily.

I seal my lips around her nipple and suck, continuing to use my tongue. My fingers on the other nipple pinch tighter, pulling slightly.

"Ahh, yes."

Her back arches off the ground as far as it can go as her legs wrap around my waist and pull me harder against her, increasing the friction.

The stiff material of my jeans feels more like a steal trap at this point, caging me in and squeezing the prisoner. But I continue on, not wanting to give Connie want she wants just yet. Wanting to relish every moan and sigh, capture them like falling stars.

I let go of her nipple with a pop, remove her tank top the rest of the way off, alongside her bra, then trail my lips south. Kissing every inch of skin along the way, paying attention to her pristine glow, to the way her hips slide beneath my hands, to the top hem of her shorts and how much I want them out of the fucking way. So I undo the button and gently wiggle them down her hips and throw them off.

Lying beneath me is a beautiful as sin woman in nothing but a pair of green lace panties, with golden blond hair trailing across lush green grass, looking at me as though I'm the most beautiful person she's ever seen. As though she's never looked in the mirror.

"You're beautiful," I whisper. I part her legs wide, placing a foot either side of my hips, and lick around the lace of her panties. Tickling, teasing.

My hands travel back to her breasts, rolling her nipples between my fingers in the same way Dea does to me. My dick aches to be free, to be slipping inside this woman, making her moan my name without a care for who hears us.

Connie squirms beneath me, trying to get my lips closer to her. "More," she demands.

And I oblige, sucking her clit through the material and tasting her. "So good." I lick my lips and swallow the taste, savoring the feel of her in my mouth.

Her fingers wrap around the edges of her panties, and yanks she them down her thighs, shoving my mouth away for a moment. Green eyes flash deviously at me, and a wicked grin to match.

She knows exactly what she's doing.

We pull her panties off the rest of the way and throw them to the floor, then I'm right back between her legs, eager for more. As my tongue darts out and wanders upward, past her opening and through her lips, to find its way to her clit.

"Shit," she curses and shoves her hips into my face. "Yes, please, more."

I've never been this turned on, this needy, this insistent about where I want my cock to be, but it's going into this woman soon, or I'm going to burst.

But first, I lick, suck, and nibble, enjoying the thrashing, moaning, and cursing slipping from Connie's lips as she loses control. Loses the battle of seduction.

My fingers find their way up her thigh, slipping through leaked wetness and gliding into her warmth, stretching her walls. And fuck, if I didn't want it to be me in there, her walls clenching my dick instead of my fingers. A groan slips from my lips as I suck a little harder and curve my fingers, looking for that perfect spot.

When I find it, she thrusts into my hand, chasing the rising tide.

"Don't stop."

"Don't plan to," I growl. My tongue and fingers work in tandem to keep her moans rising higher, her hips thrusting faster, and I follow her cues and speed.

Her hands grip my hair, keeping my face buried in her, riding her hips against my mouth like I'm her personal sex toy. "Yes, yes! Fuck, yes." Her walls spasm and clench hard around my fingers, but I don't stop moving them. And I don't let her clit go, continuing to suck.

Her legs tighten as her thighs clench and she shoves her hips into my mouth harder, faster. Riding the high as she moans.

As the orgasm subsides, her moans get slower, breathier, and her legs unclench as she gently pulls my head away and up toward her face. She smiles at me. "That was fantastic. I'm kind of jealous you made me come so hard your first time."

"Well, it is easier when you also own a vagina."

"True." Her lips slant against mine as our foreheads touch and our tongues dance in tandem to a relaxed, needy rhythm. She pulls away and smirks. "Now fuck me."

Jumping to my feet, I yank my jeans and underwear off.

"The t-shirt too," she commands. "I wanna feel those abs against me."

I shove it off and then bow. "As my lady commands."

We both giggle, the light shining in her eyes and bouncing off of me in a way that relieves the ache of grief and sadness.

Connie rises to her knees and crawls toward me, her mouth parting, her tongue licking those plump pink lips. And I know what she's going to do before she does it. Her lips kiss the head of my cock, licking the pre-cum and swallowing.

My eyes follow her bobbing throat as my balls tighten and my hand grips her lovely blonde hair, encouraging her to swallow me further. "More."

Her green eyes meet mine in a devious glare, and I watch as her lips descend, swallowing inch after inch, until my cock is touching the back of her throat and she's taking a deep breath in through her nose and swallowing.

"Damn." Her throat encloses around my dick, a tight channel constricting, wet, and then she starts to hum. "Shit." My hips buck, pulling out and then back in.

But she just continues to kneel, swallowing with each thrust. And I realize that she's had a lot of practise with this and used to fuck Arrie, and I can't imagine him holding back. She can take my weak-as-shit male form pounding her throat.

So I grip her hair tighter and keep her head in place, then pull most of the way out before diving back in. Pleasure rolls through me in waves, each tight, warm swallow filling me up and making me clench.

My thighs tremble.

And I thrust harder, faster, chasing the feeling that's rising on the horizon, biting at the heels of my sanity. Causing my knees to buckle and my breath to run in ragged gasps. "Connie . . . I'm gonna—"

She yanks my dick out of her mouth and jumps to her feet. "Not yet."

A low whine escapes my throat, my hips still wanting to buck. "Connie . . ."

"You want me?" she asks. I nod. "Then come get me." She takes a step back, her brows raised in defiance, and smiles. "Fuck me like you own me."

I grab her arm in a bruising grip and yank her back to me, her skin against mine, the air wrapping around us, the sun beating down on our backs. "Then c'mere."

She kisses me hard, her tongue plunging into my mouth and taking control, but I fight back, kiss harder, and shove her to the grass. The hiss that escapes her lips when I suck at her nipples in turn tells me just how oversensitive they are from earlier, but I don't care.

Her legs wrap around my waist and pull me in, lining my dick up against her dripping entrance, and I slam home.

We both moan, mine being muffled by the neck I'm nuzzling into, but hers echoing around us, her head flying back onto the grass.

"Yes, right there." Her thighs clench around me and encourage me to move.

So without breaking contact from her clit, I slide out and back in, relishing in the warmth now surrounding me.

The world seems to break away for a while as my focus pins itself to her, to our bodies connecting, to the pleasure rolling through me. To the moans she's screaming into my ear.

"Shit, you feel so good."

She tightens around me with a wicked smile.

And I moan. "So tight."

I rock my hips, trying to get that perfect angle for her and continue grinding, and I'm rewarded by a gasp and a shout.

"Magic!"

Her walls tighten slightly as her moans get louder, and I know she's close.

But I'm right behind. So close. I thrust into her harder, balls slapping against her ass, my dick slamming against the back of her.

"Fuck," she groans into my ear, "I'm gonna come again."

"Yes, come for me."

She spasms, tightens, clenches my dick like it's a lifeline as her hips grind against mine.

But it's her screams that send me over the edge, thrown like a cannonball, moaning louder than intended, as I pin her arms above her head and use her. Fill her up. And make her mine.

Just as she requested.

Arrie's laying the table when we walk in, hand-in-hand, red-faced, fully clothed, and he smiles when he sees us. A knowing smile.

Yeah, he probably heard us, but whatever. I don't care. That was some of the best sex I've ever had. And I didn't once worry about having a penis or being in my male form. I just enjoyed it.

I'll call that a brilliant win.

"Had a good time?"

Arrie lays the plates and some of the serving dishes out on the giant dining room table, but instead of the usual five, there's four. And suddenly, all the wind under my sail is gone. Deflated.

"Yeah," Connie says gently, "it was fun being railed by Magic's dick."

Oh my goddess, Connie. I just look at her, surprise in my eyes, hoping to convey that.

"What? It's not like ve doesn't have a dick."

Arrie coughs and focuses his look. "She's right. It's fine. Totally normal. Not even worth a conversation."

"Really?"

"Really." He smiles at me, but there's something there, lurking underneath, something he's not sharing.

I can tell.

"If you say so." I grab his arm as he goes to pick up a giant plate of crispy tacos. "Are you okay?"

He chuckles. "Yes."

I look at him dubiously, a question in my brows.

He sighs and runs a hand through his hair. The feeling is there, on the tip of his tongue, but he usually shrugs or swallows it and just says nothing.

"You can tell me, big guy." I rub his shoulder. "It's important to communicate, remember?"

"I'm just a little . . . jealous." He looks away as he says it and picks up the taco plate to place it on the table.

"Oh." Jealous? So he wants me? Well, of course he wants you, Magic. He kissed you with those 'come fuck me' lips in the car just the other night. "Sorry, I didn't mean to make you feel left out, I just—"

"It's okay." He looks at me with a smile. "Seriously."

If he says it's okay, then I'm going to choose to believe him. Because I think I'm beginning to understand that communication is always honest with this man, hence why he chooses to say nothing a lot.

Connie and I help him lay the table, and just when I'm about to ask where Dea is and wonder if he's okay, he pops into the kitchen on an exasperated breath.

"Dea!" I run to him and wrap my arms around his neck. Then shift into my female form and let him breathe me in at the crook of my neck, like he usually does. Besides, I like his Angel form touching me like this. "I love you."

A couple of silent tears slide down my shoulder, but he looks at me with a peaceful kind of sadness on his face and wipes them away. "I love you too, Angel." He lifts my knuckles to his lips and drops a light kiss. "Always."

"Good. Now come eat." Connie points to his share with a demand in her voice that brokers no argument.

He switches out of his Angel form and sits on his chair and stares at Nine's with a heart-breaking look of disappointment on his face, but I grab his hand and rub circles over his thumb, trying to distract him.

He needs to eat.

"I made tacos," Arrie says, clearly trying to help. "You like tacos."

Dea snaps his gaze to Arrie's with a small smile. "I do like tacos." And he grabs a tortilla, some meat, some salsa, and a couple of sides, and I breathe easy as my Angel of Death eats for the first time in days.

In a vague, bland voice, Dea whispers, "The soul was a woman in her twenties—Fae— who refused to leave Earth because the queen demanded she always stay by her side."

Connie looks like she's trying not to vomit, and Arrie looks pissed. I don't know what I am, though.

Connie explains, "The Fae Queen can order her people around, a little like how Nine's magic worked, but I've never seen it transcend death before."

"Me either." Dea shrugs. "Probably just a one off."

I file that potential problem away for later, maybe a question for my Fae trainer, and dig into the tacos. Arrie's tacos. Hehe, Arrie's tacos. Can tacos be butt cheeks or just frontal flaps?

Goddess, I'm tired.

Connie coughs after finishing her first taco and announces, "We are waiting on Red, Lucien, and Nigel to get back from scouting, which we think should take a few days, and when they do, we'll set the date for taking back New Orleans."

Dea looks at her. "So soon?"

She shrinks, following both Arrie and I shrinking, and looks at him with pity in her eyes. "I know, but they're suffering. They can't wait for us to get our shit together."

Dea nods, understanding, but clearly not wanting to follow through with that plan, anyway.

I grab his hand again, reassuring him everything's going to be okay. "If you like, you can stay here."

Arrie nods. "I can probably create a strategy without you, dude. If you're really not up for it."

Dea looks to me, to Arrie, and then to Connie, and then slumps in his chair. "I do not know." A worried hand rakes through his uncombed hair.

"Dea?" My hands shake slightly under the table. He looks at me. "Have you considered maybe seeing a grief counselor?"

His shock registers, then a small amount of anger, until eventually he looks at me and smiles a genuine smile. "If you think that is for the best, then I will give it a try."

"I think we'd all benefit from counseling, to be honest, but you're not coping. The Dea I know would never let other people suffer just because life's gotten a bit hard."

"A bit hard?"

Yeah, even I heard that one. For fuck's sake.

"He is dead, Magic. And he is not ever going to be undead. He's not coming back." He gets up and storms off, probably back to his room, the echo of his sliding chair the only thing I can still hear.

"Shit." Could I have said that better? Should I have not said it at all? What about different words?

"Shhh." Connie's hands are on my shoulder. "He's just upset because he knows you're right."

"And he hates that he's let himself fall so hard." Arrie gets up and sits next to me, in Nine's empty chair, and rests a hand on either knee. "That you're doing so much better than him, despite you being the emotional one."

"That's just because I don't feel anything."

Arrie and Connie both look at me with worried expressions.

"I feel numb. I cry sometimes, in bursts of sadness, and I have small moments with all of you, but overall, I feel nothing." I take a deep breath. "It's like I'm waiting for the tidal wave to hit."

"Oh, hon, I'm so sorry." She looks at me with guilt, nibbling on her bottom lip. "I just assumed you were holding up okay." She swears under her breath. "I'm so used to Nine telling me how everyone's doing when things get like this. I'm shit at doing it myself."

Arrie's low laughter filters through the air like a small rumble. "Sorry, it's just we're so shit at this without him."

Connie and I laugh too, and soon we're laughing and crying and falling apart and flying all at once. A cocktail mix of emotions we don't know how to navigate.

"Yeah, we are." I wipe my eyes and get up, stubborn pride soaring through me. "Now, if you'll excuse me, I've got an Angel of Death boyfriend I need to apologize to."

"Want us to join you?" Arrie asks. "Or do you want to be alone?"

"Errm . . ." I fidget my hands. "Can you both come with me?" I feel stronger as a unit.

12

That familiar black door with the old hinges—the ones we asked the house to fix for us after Dea's outburst—stands I front of me. In front of us. But this time, it stands open, like he expected us to follow. Or he's hoping for us to follow.

"Dea?" I enter the room, never really sure what I'll find these days, but I'm pleasantly surprised to find Dea rearranging things. Putting them back where they actually belong. I look to the bookshelf. "I see you didn't like the order I had going on?"

He looks at me with a small smile. "Sorry, Angel, no." He drops the duster he'd just picked up to start cleaning with and circles me with those strong arms. "Angel, I am so sorry for yelling."

Connie and Arrie stand near, both not looking too sure where they should be standing or sitting or looking. But Dea invites them into the hug, and soon I'm surrounded by all three of them. Their strength, their unity, their family. And something about it finally breaks me.

"I hate this!" My fists ball at my sides. "I don't have the energy to help any of you. But I need to because you need me." Heaving breaths wrack my body as the tears fall in sobbing waves. "Dea needs my Angel form to feel grounded, especially right now, and Connie needs me to be strong and keep touching her and flirting with her and being there for her, and Arrie is requiring so much patience that I just don't have right now. And I don't know what to do." All of their arms stay around me, strong and unyielding. "I just want Nine back. He'd know what to do."

My knees can't keep me up anymore, and I fall, my body finally cracking. But Arrie catches me. He wraps his arms around me and holds me tight as he carries me to the bed we've all been sharing, laying us down on the cotton sheets.

"I'm so sorry, Killer." His gruff voice is soothing, like a deep earthly rumble that grounds me to the present.

"We've been expecting too much of you." Connie lies on top of me, her weight a comforting presence on the anxiety boiling beneath my surface. "You have as much grief as we do."

I shake my head. "That's ridiculous. You knew him for two thousand years. I only had a few months." My hands grip the sheets. "Of course your grief hurts more."

Dea lies on my other side, his wings having come out, so he lays one over us all. "Grief does not work that way. It is not measured in years known or love felt. Just because we had him longer does not entitle us to more tears; you have every right to be grief stricken."

"But . . . but . . ." I swipe the tears away frustrated by them. "For fuck's sake, I thought I'd outgrown this emotional nonsense." I've been doing so well.

Connie giggles at me and places a hand on my cheek. "You'll never outgrow your emotions. They're made to be felt."

"And just because you feel them harder than most," Dea adds, "does not make you any less of an adult."

"You're allowed to fall apart, cry, and have breakdowns, Killer. We might be immortal, but we're only human."

I look to Arrie, unsure of how to reply. "So you're sounding like Dea now? Giving advice?"

He shrugs. "Maybe."

"Then you can lead the team," Dea adds, "since Magic and I seem to be incapable right now."

"Ve's doing a great job," Arrie argues. "We're just waiting on some intelligence and then we can plan the New Orleans take over."

Dea looks to the ceiling as he lies flat on his back. "I'll join you."

"Are you sure?" Connie asks, curling up between my legs. "You don't have to. Neither of you do. Arrie and I can do it alone."

Dea and I look to each other, then laugh.

"What?" she asks, genuine surprise lacing her words.

I grab her face between my hands and smile. "As much as I love you, I am not leaving New Orleans to the pair of you. The city won't even be standing by the time you're done."

"Pfft."

Arrie shrugs. "Could use some reconstruction."

"Not on our dime," Connie says. "With Nine . . . gone, our finances aren't refilling like they used to."

"Oh yeah." That was all Nine, too. "He did so much for us."

"Too much," Dea says.

"We don't have to change, though." I take a deep breath. "Sometimes having three partners is hard work, but I wouldn't change it for the world. I want you all to continue leaning on me."

"I don't want to be an inconvenience," Connie admits. "I know how much Dea needs you right now. I can take a step back, if you think that's—"

"No." I don't elaborate.

"Ooookay, I guess that's that."

Arrie stays silent, not offering anything, but I know that's because he isn't ready. And I will never push him.

Dea nuzzles into my neck. "I am going to rely on you all, rather than just you, Angel."

"That's acceptable." I chuckle to myself at a funny thought. "Do you think Nine's looking down on us somewhere and thinking finally, they have some communication without me."

Dea chuckles, and Connie and Arrie follow suit, and soon we're all laughing.

I know, it's weird for four grieving people to laugh, but the truth is that your other emotions don't switch off just because grief is taking the steering wheel. And that's okay. Laughter is meant to be heard in times of hardship. Otherwise, how are you supposed to come through the other side?

Today, I asked Connie if she could contact Korby and my Fae trainer, so I could do something instead of moping around. And with some luck, they both arrive first thing in the morning.

"Magic!" Korby throws her arms around me, my pink hair swaying with the weight. "It's so good to see you."

My Fae trainer smiles gently at me, but when I catch her doing so, she frowns and looks away.

"It's good to see you too, Mrs. No Name."

Korby raises her eyebrows. "Huh?"

"Oh, she won't tell me her name." I shrug. "Says it's unnecessary."

Korby also shrugs, but then she runs into the kitchen and puts her hand on the side and closes her eyes. In a few seconds, a steaming cup of Starbucks coffee enters her hand. "Ohmygod, ohmygod, it's true! Wow. The house is magical."

A familiar almighty thump echoes across the ground from outside, followed by a rush of tornado-level wind.

"Lo." I run out to great him. "Lo!"

He snorts, that gruffly thing he does when he laughs. "Hello, Magic."

Korby and my Fae trainer stand behind me, and I get the feeling something's happening.

"What's going on?"

"We have agreed," Lo says, "to train you together."

"All three of you?"

"Yup." Korby laces her arm through mine and drags us closer to Lo. "See, you need to start using your abilities together, rather than separately. So we brought as many people as we could to help."

Lo lowers his head. "Nigel is going to help you gain strength in your shift when he returns."

"Anyone available to help me with unlocking my earth powers?" I've managed to gather air, water, and fire, but no such luck with earth. It would seem it's as stubborn as a mountain.

"I can help with that," the earth Coven Witch says from behind us.

I turn around to face the older woman and her walking stick. "Hello." I bow low, respecting my Witch elder.

She waves a hand through the air, disregarding it. "No need for principle. We're here to help." She sits on a nearby tree stump near a fairy den and smiles. "But that was a long walk up that hill."

"In that case," Korby says, "go grab your staff."

I Vampire race to my room and grab the charm bracelet its sleeping form takes and then race back outside. I'm back before of them have taken a breath.

"Damn you're fast," my Fae trainer says.

"Have you not seen Magic's female form abilities before?"

She shrugs. "Sometimes. But never their Vampire stuff."

Korby looks to me in question.

"I've just never had a need for it during our sessions before. I've used some Witch magic though."

"C'mon." Korby drags me into a nearby empty space between a few fairy dens and the rainbow forest. "Let's begin."

Korby drills me for nearly an hour on all the various forms, footwork, and positions we've practised in both forms, and by the time we're done, my male form is panting and sweating in the morning sun.

"You can work harder than that," my Fae trainer says. "Put the same amount of discipline into this that you do my puzzles."

"Or engaging with your partners," Lo says.

I blush, but everyone chuckles, even Mrs. No Name.

"Wanna try this while flying?" Korby asks.

"What? How?"

Lo lowers his wing, and Korby climbs on. "C'mon," she says, "I wanna ride a dragon!"

Giving her this moment, I fly into the air and meet her bo staff's tip in the air as Lo gently rides through the clouds. I have to focus on keeping my balance in the air, directing myself, and dodging Korby's attacks. And that doesn't even consider going on the offensive.

Lo dives lightly, and Korby loses her footing, slipping near the wing. But just as I reach out with my air magic to save her, she finds her footing once more and is back to attacking me from the wing.

"Come on, Magic! You can do better than that!" The wind nearly steals her words from me at this altitude, but I rush the air toward me so I can hear her.

"Fuck off! This is hard work." Seriously, I'm doing a lot right now. Back off.

"We can go back to the ground if it's too hard." A hand on her hip and smirk across her lips, she knows what she's doing. Baiting me.

"Nope. Not gonna happen."

I fly over her, trying to attack from the higher ground, but she slides down Lo's wing and reaches up, spinning her staff and knocking mine out of my grip.

I race to catch it before it reaches the ground and then attack again, but this time from Lo's tail, trying to use the wind to my advantage. It flies me forward in a wind tunnel as I move the air into a tornado and spin my staff in a move that's designed to confuse Korby.

It works, because Korby takes a step back and looks at me with a moment of panic.

When my wind tunnel hits her, I grab her by the arm and lift her off of Lo as the dragon gets caught by the blast and it sent soaring through the air. Now Korby is dangling by the arm a hundred feet off the ground. Squirming in my grip.

"Don't make me drop you, Korby. Stop wiggling!" I lift her into my arms, where she feels safer, and fly us gently to the ground.

Korby's feet and hands reach the ground at the same time as she kisses the earth. "I'll never leave you again, I swear." She turns to face me with an angry scowl on her face. "What the hell were you thinking?"

"That I wanted to win?"

A smirk crosses her lips. "That was awesome! Terrifying but awesome."

My Fae trainer walks up to us and smiles. "You could just drop people from high in the air."

"Wouldn't work on everyone." I shrug. "Vampires won't die, flying Shifters can fly, air Witches can fly, and who knows what spells Fae can use to arrest their fall."

She weighs up my argument. "Fair points." She sits on the ground and starts weaving a spell around her, encircling herself in runes. "Your task today is to try to reach me."

I change forms and sit crossed legged outside her circle of complicated looking runes. "Okay."

"You can use any skills available to you. Your only clue is that I have used runes and only a single ingredient to create this defensive spell."

Only a single ingredient and runes? That isn't enough, surely? But analyzing her rune circle tells me one thing: this was designed to specifically keep me out.

Bullshit. That's what this is.

She sits inside, eyes closed, meditating or some shit. The perfect Fae. Little Mrs. No Name. I swear, when I find out who she is . . . I'm gonna kill her.

I get to work decoding the runes, finding out what they all do and how they all link together. What their purpose is. But there are a dozen runes here, and they're all complicated. I've never even seen some of them. But I don't have to have seen them before to figure out how they work.

Three of them contain the structure—a sphere—and ensuring it goes all the way around her and that no one can get in or out who isn't her. One of them is barring my DNA specifically from getting in (male and female). There are two runes linking the structural runes and one binding ingredient that's kind of holding them together, since there are so many. The other six are supporting runes, providing a metal-like resistance to the barrier, making it fireproof, waterproof, and earthquake-proof, amongst other things.

"I don't know how to dismantle this." If I know what the ingredient is, I can start to figure out how to deconstruct the entire thing, and it'll fall apart; which is one of the weaknesses of binding ingredients used in defensive spells. They rely on the attacker not knowing or understanding Fae spells. Which will work great against a different species, but not so much against your own.

"Think, Magic. The answer is sitting right in front of you."

"Huh?"

Okay, okay. Let's start over.

We have the structural runes, which I could attach the binding runes to and then it would change shape or start to deconstruct, but there's no real way to know how or in what way, so it feels like a dangerous thing to do. We have one rune that is barring me from getting in as a male or female, so shifting won't help.

Wait a minute.

Yes, shifting will help.

I shift into a falcon and fly through the barrier with ease, then shift back into a man. "Your spell doesn't keep my animal forms out, because my DNA changes when I shift, even if you take into account both my human forms."

She opens her eyes. "That did not take you as long as usual. It seems you are learning Fae logic." She dismantles the spell and everyone claps. "You cannot be contained by a regular barrier spell, since you can shift into any animal form at will and there's no Fae alive who can incorporate every animal's DNA into a barrier."

"Assuming I haven't drained my Fae energy, of course."

She looks at me confused for a moment.

"I struggle to shift and move and even really breathe when my energy is drained. The magical energy I experience in each form affects my form in total, not just my specific species. So a lack of blood in my female form affects my Witch magic, too."

"I see. So there's a limitation there, then." She mumbles something more to herself as she turns away and sits back where she was earlier.

"Earth magic?" I spin to face the resident Witch.

"Maybe after lunch?" Korby asks.

Lo hums his agreement.

"Okay, so lunch and then earth magic?"

The earth Witch smiles and nods. "At your own pace, Magic. It has been a trying time."

Indeed it has.

14

"Nothing—and I mean nothing—is better than ramen after a workout."

"You are absolutely right." I slurp my ramen soup at the bottom of the bowl, curtesy of Arrie, and lean back. Full. But still tired.

"How're you doin', hon?" Connie walks into the kitchen, her hair tied into two buns on top of her head and wearing nothing but a skimpy bikini.

"Err . . . fine," I drool. "Good, I mean, I'm doing great."

"Cute, huh?" She twirls. "Picked it up this morning on a shopping trip. Sounds stupid, but shopping makes me happy. And it felt good to have a slice of normal."

I hug her and give her a long kiss, trailing a hand I hope no one can see along her ass. "It's never stupid to do things that make you happy." I kiss her forehead and wink. "Besides, I like it."

"Of course you do, it's your favorite color."

The black material grazes along my hip as she walks out of the kitchen and goes to sunbathe—probably by the pool.

"You two are cozy," Korby taunts.

"Yeah, we are."

"How's the rest of your harem doing?" she asks, eating a second bowl of ramen.

"Arrie's okay, doing as best he can, and Dea is . . . struggling. But he's better than last week."

Korby puts her bowl down and smiles. "You included Arrie that time."

Huh? "Oh, yeah. Guess I did."

She waggles her eyebrows and laughs. "C'mon, dish the dirt."

I rejoin her at the table, finding the sight of an excited earth Witch and a bored Fae trainer hilarious. "He kissed me the other night. But we're taking things slow. There's something there still. Something . . . blocking him, I think."

"He's a man, child. He'll figure it out. You just have to give their brains a little longer to work." She smiles at me and grabs my hand. "Now, are we ready to try unlocking that earth magic?"

I sigh because no, I'm never ready to try unlocking a Witch magic. They're a pain in the ass. Every. Single. Time. But I smile gratefully and whisper, "Yes." As she guides me outside, I ask, "Where would you like to work?"

"Anywhere will do. It's all earth."

Right. Earth is like air—always around me. It's versatile like air, too. Unlike fire and water, which I can only summon through concentration because I have to create it most of the time.

There's a part of me that's excited to connect to the earth and learn its magic. Even as a mortal, I was fascinated by earth Witches. They're a life of the very fundamentals of Witch magic and what makes up their being. Lucky. I was stuck with death magic I somehow knew how to control; but that control is lost now. And relying on Aki's teachings seems a little foolish, even for me.

We sit on the ground, and she grabs my hands with a stern look. "You are a Witch, so you should be able to feel the magic all around you, the earth beneath your feet giving you stability."

I've always been quite attuned to the earth, finding peace within it whenever possible. I hope this is easier than the others.

"I associate earth with peace of mind, but then I used that for water, so maybe that's not quite right." I search myself, letting the feeling of my surroundings fill me up. "It's like this presence in my soul, making my chest expand and my brain relax. But I don't know what that feeling is."

"Love," my Fae trainer intervenes.

"Love?"

"That's an interesting association," she says, her hands on the ground beside me. "But I can see how the earth could mean love to someone who has been in search of it their whole life."

"Even as a child, I'd prefer to be outside when seeking happiness or peace, near hill-tops and rivers and mountains. Maybe that love has always been there, even before I was immortal. Is that possible?"

"I do not know, child. You Horsemen have your own magic that you guard closely."

With good reason. I broke that closeness and look what happened? Nine died.

"Now is not the time for pity parties!" Her scowl scolds hot, and I flinch. "Now is the time for focus."

Right. Focus.

In this form, I can hear everything: the trees swaying, the bugs titter-tattering, Connie sunbathing, Arrie doing his weird yoga dance routine in the forest's clearing, the fairies in their nests . . . It's all so beautiful. Like a whole world I'm connected to and can tune in to at will. "So why can't I just move a rock or rumble the ground?"

"Because you're trying too hard," she says. "Let it become you, not you become it."

Let it become me? What does that even mean?

I try to relax, set the will to sink into the ground aside, and just exist, waiting, hoping beyond hope, but nothing clicks into place. Nothing moves. I'm still just me.

No extra powers.

Yet.

. . .

WE KEEP TRYING FOR THE REST OF THE AFTERNOON, BREAKING IT UP WITH SOME BO PRACTISE and more Fae magic puzzles, Lo occasionally dropping in to cause mischief. But by the time the sun drops beyond the horizon, I've still not unlocked any kind of earth powers. But I have had a good day, perhaps the first full good day since Nine's passing.

Everyone says goodbye, and I find my way up to Dea's bedroom, expecting to find him in bed, but he's at his desk, furiously writing with a pencil that's barely long enough to call a pencil.

"Hello Angel," he whispers while he continues to work. "Come in."

"I can leave you be if you're busy."

He lifts his head and smiles at me. "It is okay. I was just working on an old project to pass the time, maybe distract myself a little."

"That's a good plan. Did it work?"

He shrugs. "It gave me some energy, but no, Nine is always on my mind."

I sit on his lap and let him play with my hair, slide his arms up my sides, entwine his fingers with mine, and just exist with me. "Do you want to watch a movie? Maybe have something to eat? Or do something else?"

"A movie sounds wonderful."

"Connie!" I listen out for her response, honing my ears in.

"Yeah?" She sounds out of breath.

Wonder what she's doing? "Movie night?"

"Always. I'll grab Arrie."

15

The next morning is a whirlwind of noise: Arrie makes us breakfast in bed with a complimentary glass of forest-tasting blood, Dea immediately works on his project, diving in headfirst, and Connie goes for a run. So I'm left alone with Arrie in Dea's bed while Dea sits at his desk, not really paying attention to the real world.

"Anything you wanted to do today?" I ask Arrie.

He looks sheepishly to the ground and runs a nervous hand through his hair. "Well, I was wondering if you'd like to go on a date with me?" His voice is barely a mumble, but it's there. "I know we're all a little emotionally frazzled, and I don't mean to rush you, but I'd like to start making things up to you. Apologize properly."

Dea stops what he's doing and turns to face us—more specifically, Arrie. A thunder rumbling across his face. "What are your intentions?"

Arrie looks at him in surprise, a wordless, open-mouthed shock dropping his jaw. "I . . . Well, err . . ." There's that nervous and frustrated hand traveling through his hair again. I can see the anger rising, his cheeks flushing, his fist curling.

But I grab it and thread my fingers through his.

"Because you cannot lead ve on again. If you go on a date, it has to be serious. It has to be because you want it to lead somewhere."

"I know that!" he snaps. "I'm not a fucking idiot, Dea."

The growl that escapes his lips has my thighs clenching and my mouth dropping open. "But it'll be slow." I grab Arrie's hand. "As slow as you need. Even if that means just dating for the next thirty years."

I'm done pushing this man. It needs to be his choice. I want to be his choice.

Arrie nods, a grateful blush creeping across his face. "I don't think I can go thirty years without touching you, Killer." He leans over me and pushes me back into the mattress. "So I'm gonna have to get my shit together." And he kisses me. But this isn't gentle or teasing, like Connie. This is demanding. A white-hot forge of pleasure crashing into my mouth, forcing my tongue to dance with the devil and never let go.

But when he does let go, I'm breathless, and I have to stop myself from rocking my hips into his. Because if we go down that road, we won't come back from its burning sands, and we'll never reach a good emotional place.

For once, I'm going to do this the emotionally healthy way. I'm going to date, kiss him at the front door, talk about our interests, go for long walks, and build something with this man who has very much stolen my heart.

"I would love to go on a date with you."

"Meet me at the front door at three pm. Wear warm clothes."

I nod, not really sure what to say, as he leaves the room.

I turn over and bury my head in a pillow, letting loose a squeal of excitement. Arrie is taking me on a date. A date!

I don't think I'm even mad at him anymore. I try to be, but he's really putting in some effort, apologizing, and trying to treat me better. But if he thinks for a second he's going to get away with not telling me what his deal is, he's got another thing coming.

"Excited, Angel?" The bed dips as Dea sits next to me.

I nod, my head still buried in the pillow and my legs fighting the urge to kick around.

He chuckles in my ear. "Good. You're allowed some good memories and happiness."

I lift my head and ask, "Even if Nine isn't here? Even if I'm supposed to be mourning him?"

"Even then. You can be happy and sad, just like you can be anxious and happy, at the same time? Remember that." He lies on his back and wraps me up in his arms. "And remember this." He slams his lips against mine, pushing me back into the bed, as his form changes and his wings burst over the sides.

My legs instinctively wrap around his hips, and I grind against him, need coursing through me. "Mine," I whisper as I nip at his lips and suck at his neck.

"Yours." Dea looks at me with all the reverence in the world, as though I'm the sun in his universe. "We don't have to have sex if you would rather wait?"

This team has unleashed something inside of me, and I'm no longer seeing the benefit of waiting to be okay. "So long as you're ready, I'm ready." I reach into his bedside drawer and pull out the birth control potions I know he keeps there—just in case. I down one and then return to his attention. "Sorry, I've not been taking them recently." I just forgot in all the emotional hysteria.

"Arrie told me you had fun with Connie the other day?" He traces light fingers along my collarbones and the edges of my bra. "Want to tell me about that?"

"We were just taking a romantic stroll through the garden, and we sat at the *Shinto* and things got a little out of hand. In my defense, though, she practically begged me to fuck her."

"Connie begged, huh?" He grips the lace of the bra with his teeth and tugs, revealing my nipples. "That is not like her."

"I know." I groan as he takes one into his mouth and teases and sucks. "She's usually so teasing and more of a leading lady, but she begged, so I licked her pussy, then she sucked my dick . . . And fuck, she sucked it all the way down her throat. She has some talent, that lady."

Dea's fingers delve between my thighs and stroke up my entrance, then back down, and back up, but never entering. "Tell me more."

"I was just about to come, but she pulled away and asked me to fuck her, so I pinned her legs to the garden floor and fucked her as hard as she'd let me."

Dea groans, a golden brightness in his eyes. "I want to see you fucking her one day."

"Really?"

"Really." He punctuates that with a sharp press of his fingers into me. "But right now, you are mine." His fingers delve in and out of me, caressing my insides with accurate strokes of silken goodness. "Say it."

My eyes shoot open and meet his golden galaxy ones. "I'm yours." He adds another finger, stretching me further, shooting pleasure through my entire body. "In whatever form you'd prefer."

His fingers stop, and he looks at me. Like, he really looks at me, and my breath catches in my throat and my body lights on fire, and I can't move. "I want you in whatever form you feel like being in today." But there's something in his eyes as he says it—something that sets me aflame.

I know what he wants. And now, when my whole world is falling apart and I'm treading the pieces trying to move forward, I just might be ready to give it to him.

I gently pull Dea's fingers out of me and then concentrate on my form, shifting it so that I'm lying on Dea's bed fully clothed in the last clothes I wore in this form, staring at him, silently begging him to fuck me.

His hand rests on the button to my jeans, a question in his gaze. "Are you sure?"

The vulnerability in his gaze gives me pause. "Dea?"

He looks up, meeting my sure expression.

"I wouldn't have offered if I wasn't sure." I slip my eyes to those lips, to the piercings on either side, and add, "But I like it when you order me to do something. It takes the indecisiveness out of the equation."

A wicked grin spreads across his face, and he snaps his hands onto my wrists quicker than lightning. "In that case, stay still for me, Angel." He pins my hands above my head and leans over me, his black hair dancing along the sides of my face. "Just let me know if you want me to stop."

I nod, words not wording, and spread my legs, letting him settle between them.

The smile fades from his lips and is replaced by something far more exciting—desire. It radiates off him like a flood I can taste in the back of my mouth, lingering even after I swallow every drop.

He rips his belt from his skinny jeans and wraps it around my joined wrists, then one of the bedposts, laying me out diagonally across the bed. "Now, be a good little angel and lie there quietly." Dea stands up and leans one hand on the canopy frame, staring at me. His eyes lick me up and down as he bites the corner of his lip, playing with the piercing there. "You look delicious."

But instead of doing something, he just stands there, looking beautiful, staring at me like I'm his next meal. But he doesn't do anything.

Just when I think he might stare at me all morning, he moves to grasp the bottom of his t-shirt and pulls it over his head. Revealing the delicious body beneath. Now it's my turn to stare—and maybe I try twisting on my bonds a bit. (Don't judge me, he's gorgeous.)

A small laugh escapes his lips, and I just know he's loving my struggles. I want to touch him. And the cocky bastard knows it. I want to run my hands over the lean muscles leading down beyond his jeans. To unbuckle the clasp and . . .

"Dea . . . I wanna—"

"I know. But you cannot right now," he says with a gleeful smile.

My cock is straining against my jeans, begging me to touch it, to give it some kind of attention. Begging anyone to. But I can't move my hands when they're tied up like this.

Dea slides his hands to his jean buttons and undoes all three at a time, one at a time, piece by piece, and I hate it. Love it. Can't stand it but don't want to look away. He bores holes into my eye sockets while sliding his jeans off his legs and tossing them aside.

"You okay there?" he asks as his fingers slide along the edges of his underwear.

I shake my head, no. I'm not okay. I need him to touch me.

"Whatever is the matter?"

I tug at my restraints again. "Touch me."

"Hmmm, maybe." His hand slips inside his underwear and grasps his dick. A groan escapes his lips as he leans on the canopy again, his naked body stretched out before me.

My mouth opens of its own accord, wanting nothing more than to swallow those moans. And maybe the cause of them.

As if reading my mind, Dea shucks off his underwear and straddles my waist. "Suck it." He presents his cock like a leaking gift on a silver platter.

And like the good little angel I am, I open my mouth with a moan and nod.

"Good Angel." He slides up closer to my head and rests the tip on my lips. "Now relax that tight little throat of yours." As I open my mouth wider, he slips the silky softness in, and we both groan at the same time. "Fuck, yes."

I raise my hips up, trying my best to find friction despite the clenching tightness of denim caging me in, and I meet Dea's hand.

"I've got you, do not worry." He massages my dick through my jeans.

And I'm so relieved, I forget that I'm supposed to be focusing on swallowing. On somehow taking this guy's dick all the way down without suffocating. But fuck, his hand feels so good.

Pleasure rolls through me, and I forget all about the cock in my mouth as I moan unashamedly.

"Take a deep breath."

I inhale.

Dea pushes further in, enough to tickle my gag reflex, and shit, I don't think I can do this. I'm gonna look like an idiot.

"Swallow."

My throat goes to constrict, spasm, and—

Dea grips my dick. Hard. Hard enough to hurt. Too hard. "Swallow."

Going against my throat's need to spasm, I swallow.

Dea pushes in further, and before I know it, he's pushing at the back of my throat and ordering me to swallow again.

I follow his orders, and Dea shoves his cock down my throat.

"Good, Angel. You're doing so well." His voice purrs. "Just lie there and keep taking my cock." He pulls out slightly, so that his dick is only just past the back of my throat, and then slides it back down.

The groan that escapes his mouth sets my body on fire. His head falls back as his hand grabs my hair in a punishing grip. "Yes, just like that." His hand tightens on my dick, and I moan. "God, yes."

My dick is leaking and my underwear is soaking, and I just want him to strip me naked and fuck me already.

But Dea just picks up the pace and fucks my face hard into the mattress. "Fuck, Angel . . . You are so tight." The pace is brutal, slamming down the back of my throat, but I stay relaxed, watching his face scrunch and his fists grip my hands tighter. But then his gaze meets mine, and he stops and pulls out. Gently. "You did so well." His hand caresses my cheek. "So well."

His hand roams down my t-shirt and buries itself underneath, where he travels across my smooth skin, setting tiny sparks alight every inch of the way. "Now, come here." He unzips my jeans and cups my balls around my underwear. "Let's get all this clothing off of you."

"Yes, please." I'm still breathless, but I manage to eek the words out in a small, breathless puff.

He slowly inches off my jeans, then my underwear, and stares in disbelief at my dick. As though he didn't fully believe it was really there before. "You're so big."

Oh. "I . . . err . . ." Is thank you the right phrase here? "Thanks?"

Dea chuckles. "It is definitely a compliment." He looks at me again and licks his lips. "Nine would have loved being fucked by you."

"Really?" Tears sting my eyes.

Dea looks at me and wipes the wetness away. "Oh yes. Remind me to tell you of the time I once fucked him with my dick and a dildo at the same time."

My eyes widen. "You can do that?"

Dea laughs. A full-on belly rumble that has my mouth smiling and my eyes watering again. "With enough prep and lube, yes." My dick twitches at the thought, and it does not go amiss by Dea, who smiles at me with raised eyebrows. "One day." Soft fingers trail across my jaw and trace my small smile.

His hand wraps around my cock with wonder, and he traces a thumb over the sticky head, making me buck and gasp. "One day, I'll persuade Arrie to fuck you in the ass at the same time as me. Really stretch you open."

My dick leaks more pre-cum at the thought, but my mind has a hard time imagining that. "Sounds like a lot of pain."

Dea rests his lips against mine and breathes, "I'll always make you feel good, Angel." His face lifts away with a golden glint in his eyes. "I'll only hurt you if you ask for it."

With a wink, he layers kisses across my jaw, nips at my neck, and licks lines of pleasure across my chest. Every touch is like lava in my veins, setting my body on fire and dousing my brain in fog.

I can't think.

I can't do anything but feel.

And fuck if this isn't the most relaxed I've been in days.

Dea takes a nipple into his mouth while his hand slowly jacks me up and down. His tongue flicks and circles as his hand twists and squeezes, and a series of long, unintelligible moans escape my lips while passionate fire torments me.

I edge closer, my body ready to explode, but I don't want to come like this. I want this gorgeous man to fuck me. And I want to watch as he comes undone while buried inside me. I want to feel what Nine felt every time he was with our Angel of Death.

"Dea . . ."

"Yes, Angel. Come for me."

"No, wait. I want it to be . . . you." Dea's hand stops moving, and despite it being what I want, the lack of movement and friction makes me frown and groan. "I want you to fuck me like you did Nine."

16

He looks at me with a curious and hurt expression, and shit, maybe that was insensitive.

"I'm sorry, I didn't mean to take away the privacy or important memory. I just wanted to know how he felt. I want it to be you, Dea. It was always meant to be you."

"It is okay." He takes a deep breath and looks at me. "I am not offended. It is just . . . hard." He grazes a soft finger down my cheek and smiles. "But I want to share him with you. You had so little time together. And it is unfair."

I wiggle my hips and grind my dick against his, letting our soft, velvety skin slide against each other.

And he groans, surprised. "I am definitely fucking that pretty ass of yours today."

My whole body clenches—in excitement, in fear, in anticipation—and I exhale a breathy sigh. "Yes, please."

A deep, throaty chuckle escapes Dea's mouth, and it vibrates through me. Everything in me aches. All I want is for this man to fuck me into oblivion and make me forget and remember.

"Now," he rumbles, his voice edging back into familiar, commanding territory, "spread your legs." He folds my knees up and then parts them, spreading me out before him.

Not only are my balls and dick right in front of him, but my ass is prime time right now, and I won't lie, it feels a little exposing. Cool air rushes along my hole, and my dick twitches in need.

Dea lowers his head to my groin and then travels lower, lower, until he's past my dick and licking stripes up my balls. "Just relax, Angel." His hands grip my thighs like vices and pin them apart, forcing them to give him more room. "I have got you."

He can have me for the rest of time if this is what follows.

He sucks a testicle into his mouth and hums, sending pleasure vibrating through my balls and straight up my cock like lightning. And I can't stop leaking, it seems, because it's starting to trail down my stomach in a small stream Dea runs a finger through.

He does the same thing with the other testicle, and I'm in heaven, moaning, writhing, tugging on my restraints with complete abandon, all traces of embarrassment and rational thought having flown out the window.

"Dea, oh my goddess." There's a growly edge to my voice as I say his name. "Don't stop."

Dea's mouth widens as he sucks both balls in at once, and my whole body tightens with need thrumming through me in waves that douse the edges of my sanity.

I can't think.

I can only feel what this man is doing to me.

But Dea stops, and I groan, until his hands release my thighs and gently spread my cheeks and his tongue is traveling another path. A very different, very new path.

Unexpected nerves shoot through me.

But Dea continues, licking up toward my exposed hole and flicking a quick circle.

"Mmm, yeah."

"You taste divine," he groans. His tongue laps at my hole, eager and hungry.

And the sparks that shoot are new, bright and golden, like fireworks, and I plant my feet firmly on the bedsheets, refusing to move them. Because I might just combust if he stops what he's doing.

His hands slide under my ass and yank me closer to him, so his nose is pressed against my ass crack and his tongue is piercing my hole.

And oh my goddess, the stretch is sooooo good. "Fuck."

Dea shoves his tongue deeper, as deep as it'll go, and I let out a tiny scream of pain and pleasure mixed—an echo of what's the come.

My hands grip my restraints, my toes curls around the messed-up sheets, and my eyes screw shut as the pleasure rockets up, builds, and needs somewhere to go. Anywhere.

Fuck, I wanna jack myself. I need to . . .

Dea wraps a hand around my dick, swirls his thumbs over the wet head and spreads it around, then jacks me in harsh thrusts. His tongue still buried inside my ass, licking every part of me I never thought I'd be comfortable enough to share.

"Mmmm . . . yes yes yes."

I can feel my balls start to tighten as my hips rock, seeking more friction, more speed. More something.

But Dea pulls his hand and tongue away.

"No, wait—"

"Shhhh, Angel." He places two fingers over my lips. "I will get you there. I promise."

"Please," I whine, looking straight into those golden eyes that are burning brighter than I've ever seen them.

Dea looks at me like I'm his next meal, his careful composure slipping like a landslide. He reaches over my head to the nightstand, where he pulls a bottle of lube I've not seen before. This one's blue, rather than the usual red.

My confused expression has him smiling as he explains, "Anal sex is best with gel-based lubricant." He holds up the bottle. "This is the same one I used that night with me and Nine."

That night flashes through my mind, Dea in my ass, Nine in front, and both hammering away at me like a personal sex toy. A whiny groan slips my lips.

"Yeah, I liked it too." Dea lathers two fingers in lube before returning to my spread legs. "I loved the sounds you made then, and how tightly you gripped me." He strokes a finger around the edge of my hole, and it quivers in response. "And I love how responsive you are."

A single finger pushes in, and it feels like he's stretching me beyond measure. There's no way he is going to fit. But we've done this before, and I trust him to do it again.

"Relax, Angel. Just bear down, it'll make it easier." I follow his instructions as he takes my dick in his other hand, no doubt distracting me. "Just think about how good it will feel to have my dick buried in your ass."

The image those words conjure up brings more pre-cum to the surface, spilling over. Dea leans down to lick it off, and I buck into his mouth.

He adds a second finger, slowly delving deeper, until he's gently lapping them in and out, fingering my ass. His grip on my dick tightens, and I rock my hips to the rhythm he's set, fucking myself on his fingers and into his fist.

"That's it, Angel. Such a good little boy."

His words take me aback. That's the second time he's said that, and I hum in response. Maybe I do like that?

"You are doing so well." He adds a third finger, then a fourth, and soon I'm throwing myself onto his hand, desperate for more. But he pulls his hands away and breathes a kiss across my starved lips.

I lean into him, but he's gone before I can get anything more.

He reaches for the lube again and spreads it over himself, and I watch as his hand rises and falls up his cock, twists and squeezes in the way he likes. His head falls back and his legs spread slightly. "Going to fuck you so good," he groans.

"Mmmm, yes," I whine, pulling against my restraints because it's mine. His cock is mine and I want it now. "Gimme."

Dea looks at me and smirks, that cocky grin telling me he knows exactly what he's doing. "You want it?"

I nod, words escaping me.

He grabs my thighs and pushes them to my chest, then lines his dick up and slowly pushes through my ring.

Blinding pleasure shoots through me, along with a slice of burning pain, but I bear down, and he pushes farther in.

"Fuck," he swears, "you are so tight."

"So good," I pant. "More."

He groans as slides the rest of his dick into me, his balls lying flat against my cheeks. His golden eyes meet mine in a wicked glare. "Hold on."

I grab the leather of my restraints, and he holds my thighs to my chest as I take a breath and steel myself.

The thrusts are harsh, punishing, like Dea can't bear to be soft and gentle right now. And as his hair flies around his face, his grip tightens on my thighs, and moans spill from his lips, he looks like a wild man, some wild thing whose humanity has long since left him.

He pushes my thighs against me tighter, causing my hips to shift higher off the bed, and something in me lights up like a Christmas tree. "Shit, yes." I throw my head back as a series of long, unintelligible words string my lips on a moan. "Don't stop."

His thrusts harden, becoming harsher by the second, until the only sounds in the room are skin slapping against skin and our combined moans as his balls slap my ass and my hole quivers in pleasure against his slick cock. Lips slam against mine as he breathes into me. "Never going to . . . stop."

"Ohh, mmmm, yes." My dick twitches uncontrollably between us as a stream of cum leaks and my balls tighten. "Oh goddess! Yes! Gonna . . ." My orgasm hits me like a freight train as my hips rock into his dick and my hole squeezes tight. Ropes and ropes of cum shoot across my chest.

"Oh fuck." Dea watches my face with rapture. "So fucking tight." His hips lose rhythm as a frenzy overtakes him, and he's slamming into me hard enough to have me gripping my restraints to hold on. "So close." Golden light shatters the dark room as he opens his eyes to meet mine. He holds that gaze as he shoots his orgasm into me and keeps on pumping, riding out his orgasm.

He eventually slows, and he slumps on top of me, spent.

"That was . . . amazing," I say on a breath.

"Yes. Yes, it was."

17

"Soooo," Connie says, her usual give-me-all-the-details voice coming in strong, "things with you and Arrie are going somewhere?" She holds up another outfit choice from the pile I had the house summon.

But I shake my head, no. Too pink. "Yeah, I think." I take a deep breath and rummage through the pile to find those cute jeans I had in my hands earlier. "I'm thinking of maybe bringing it up with him tonight. You know, just to make sure we're both on the same page. But I don't wanna scare him off or anything." I scratch my head, confused about the jeans and Arrie. "He's a bit skittish."

Her laugh bounces off my ears, and I look up to see her golden smile beaming my way. Her hair is in two long plaits today, tapered at her waist with two green bows that match the green of her eyes. And damn if her boobs don't look perfect in that tank top.

She laughs again. "My eyes are up here, babe." She points to her face, and I blush. "And you got enough sex from Dea earlier."

"Only in my male form," I whine. "My vagina is lacking said attention."

She snorts and then laughs, and I follow. But she looks at me with serious eyes. "Tell me everything."

What is with these people and making me recount my sex life? "Well, I was in my other form, but we talked about it, and I decided I wanted to finally take the plunge, so we had sex in my male form instead."

"And?"

"And . . . it was great."

"That's all the detail I get? Who topped who? Did he go all controlling on your ass?" She waggles her eyebrows. "Pun intended."

I laugh but sigh. I swear, these Horsemen. "Yes, he went all controlling on my ass. He also taught me to deep throat. It was great." I return my attention to the giant pile of clothes on the bed. "Now, I really really need something I can wear that'll be sexy but good for cold weather. How cold are we talking? Is he taking me to Scotland, Canada, Russia, or The Artic? Why is he never specific!"

"Because I did not want to give away the surprise, Killer." Arrie's standing in the door-way, leaning against the frame, looking phenomenal in a pair of low-rise jeans and nothing else.

"Oh, I didn't see you there." I cringe. "Sorry."

He moves to stand beside me, placing an arm around my shoulders, and glances at the pile. "What is it with you four and clothes?" He steals a breath. "Three, I guess."

The room falls silent. Just like it always does whenever one of us brings Nine up in conversation or forgets that we're now only Four Horsemen, not five.

It's the kind of silence that cuts like a knife through your sanity, where you wonder if you'll ever feel normal again and what normal even is now that a part of your foundation has come crumbling down.

I'm allowed to be sad and happy.

I'm allowed to be sad and happy.

I'm allowed to be sad and happy.

My eyes squeezing shut, I repeat Dea's advice in my head over and over again, my fists clenched and my body shaking.

"Heeey, shhh . . ." Connie rubs soothing hands over my shoulders while a firm, steady presence stands at my back, heavy hands silently on my waist. Grounding me. "It's gonna be okay," she whispers in my ear, like a gentle lapping of the ocean against my shore.

I need to . . . be there for them. Not crumble into the wind. I need to . . .

"Whoa, Killer." Arrie grumbles something under his breath. "Calm down."

Suddenly their comforting touches are gone and Connie is standing a few feet away nursing her hand. Arrie is behind me, but only by a couple of steps.

"You're flaming," he explains.

I look down at myself and see the flames licking my skin, and then I notice the heat, the slight sting, and I yelp. "Shit." I hiss, then work on calming myself, and empty the equivalent of a river over my head. When I'm left shivering, hands trying their best to warm me up, I curse. "Fuck's sake. Now I'm cold."

Arrie wraps strong arms around my shivering frame and lifts me into his arms, then throws a scowl Connie's way, and she's off, running into my bathroom. The sound of water pattering the tiles hits my eardrums.

"She's turned the shower on for you," Arrie whispers, his voice deep and rumbly and sending shivers rumbling through me. "You'll warm up in there. And you won't get a cold."

"But won't we b-b-be late?"

He laughs. "There's no timescale for our date. We'll be fine."

"Okay." I look up at him and smile—well, I try to. "Think you can pick out an outfit for me and then ask the house for something for my male form too?"

He frowns. "You want me to pick out clothes for you?"

"If it's not a problem. I'm not used to cold weather."

"I'll try." Arrie deposits me in the bathroom.

Where Connie helps my shivering hands disrobe and shoves me into the warm spray before leaving to help Arrie. The water warms my skin first, prickling along my edges, until the heat seeps deeper, warming my insides. And by the time I've shaved, washed my hair and body, and dried—twice—I step out of the bathroom to find Arrie holding up three pairs of boots with a frown.

"Need some help there, big guy?" I twizzle the towel around my long pink hair with a smile.

"I think I have a good outfit picked out . . ."

He sounds unsure, and goddess, if his frown and concentration isn't the cutest thing. "I'm sure I'll love whatever you've chosen." After all, I don't need to look perfect for this man. I can just exist.

"Well, I left the male one on the chair over there." He pointed to the chair next to the fireplace. "And I'm still finalizing the female one."

I walk up to the male one and smile. It's a lot of layers, a windbreaker, with a good hat and gloves. "Seriously, I have no idea in what order to wear all of this." I chuckle. "Your dates need to come with instructions."

Arrie looks at me with concern and frustration in his face.

"It's not a criticism. It's just a joke."

His face fades into a smile.

I switch into my male form. "But seriously, you'll need to tell me how to put all of this on."

"Oh. Right." He walks up to me and points out the first layer. "The layers better help keep the heat in, so start with underwear and thermals." Then he layers me up piece by piece until I'm standing in my bedroom looking like a human penguin. "Perfect."

"I feel like a marshmallow."

His laugh echoes across the room and licks candy up my insides. "Now, let's get you dressed into your female clothes. I had to ask Connie about the best bra options. I do not know how breasts work."

N'awww . . . Aaaaaaand now I'm melting like a marshmallow. "That's okay. I'm sure you figured it out."

Again, we start with underwear and thermals, and then shove a few layers on, including hat and gloves and a windbreaker.

"Remind me again where the hell we're going?"

Arrie looks at me with a smirk. "Nope."

I grumble, a groan slipping through. "Teleporting crystals, though, right?" Please, don't make me have to deal with portals. They're much, much worse.

"Of course." He grabs two from his pocket. "Ready?"

I grab hold of his arm with my gloved hands and nod. "Ready."

And soon we're swirling into the aether and I'm doing my best to not puke. But before I know it, we're landing on a snow-covered plain that's covered in white for as far as the eye can see. And my eyes can see pretty damn far.

"Wow." I step away from him and look around, startled. "Is this somewhere in the arctic circle?"

"Iceland." Arrie's own layers stare at me when I turn around. "It's my homeland." He wraps his arms around my waist and leans down to place a gentle kiss to my head. "I thought I would share my favorite places with you. That's what you do on a date, right? You share yourself with someone you want to connect with?"

"That's . . . right."
This is it. This is him opening up.
This is Arrie meeting me halfway.

The aurora borealis glimmers above us, and I'm mesmerized by its beauty, and for a second I forget the other beauty standing right next to me. "It's like a night rainbow sliding across a net of fireflies."

Arrie hums. "I've always loved how your mind works."

I turn to face him, his eyes lit in a midnight rainbow.

"I was always jealous that Nine got an instant all-access pass." He grits his teeth and steels his breath. "He always knew what you were thinking."

"Trust me, he often hated it."

Arrie raises a brow at me.

"He never said anything, but sometimes dealing with my inner turmoil hurt him. He often took walks or focused on something else to take a break. I was always feeling guilty."

Arrie rests his arms on my shoulder as we both stare up at the glowing night sky. "He loved you."

Loved. Past tense.

"And I love him."

Does he still love me in the afterlife? Does it still count if I'm alive and he's not? Can I still say he loves me? Or will it always be loved from here on out?

I guess I'll never know the answers to those questions.

"What are you thinking?"

He . . . wants to know what I'm thinking? "I was wondering if he still loves me in the afterlife."

Arrie stops breathing for a moment, then blows out a harsh breath. "Yeah, probably." A tear drops onto my hood. "He has to."

I spin in his arms and look up into his face. But the hurt I see on his face slashes me in two, cuts me into pieces and burns them at the stake. "This is about more than Nine, isn't it?"

He closes his eyes and nods. "I promise to try to open up. It's just . . . hard."

I nod, understanding. Well, I guess not. Not really. But I can see he's struggling. "What part is hard to you?"

He flinches, and the by the curling of his fist, I can tell I've offended him.

"Wait, sorry. That came out wrong. I didn't mean it spitefully. I was being genuine. What part are you struggling with? Is it trusting me? Thinking about the pain?"

Through clenched teeth, he whispers, "Getting the words out."

What has this man been through that even getting the words out hurts?

My hand reaches out to his cheek and lands there, like coming home. "I'm not going anywhere. My love isn't fragile."

The smile that cuts through the pain lights up brighter than the sky, and my knees go weak. But he keeps me on my feet. As always. "Then we best get going. We've got a trek to the hotel."

A trek? In this weather. Fuck that.

Air whips around us, settles into the familiar pattern it's used to when flying myself and Arrie, and we lift into the air.

"How about a lift?"

"I was hoping you'd say that." He points in the right direction, and I do the heavy lifting.

So we fly and cover the few miles in a few minutes, whereas it would have taken a good hour or so on foot. Thank fuck for magic. We fly past fjords, distant mountains, and I take us up high enough we can see the aurora more clearly.

"It's beautiful here."

I land us firmly on the ground at the front doors, where Arrie walks in, clearly comfortable, and smiles at the man at the check-in desk.

"Arrie, my man." He walks toward us with a smile and one-arm hugs Arrie. "How're you doin'?"

"Good." He shrugs, clearly blowing off the question. "Is our room ready?"

"It is. This way." He guides us to the elevators, where we rise on the middle floor and are guided to the room at the end of the corridor. "Here you are." He hands him the keychip and walks away. "Enjoy your night."

"Thanks." Arrie unlocks the door and strides in. "This is one of the safe houses I manage."

"But it's a hotel?"

"Sure. But it caters to specific clientele that pass my checks. Besides, this way, we can ask for room service if we're struggling."

That does make sense. And it runs itself, basically. So Arrie has very little management to actually do. Clever War.

"I'm impressed." Taking a gander around the room, it's all dark wood and faux fur throws, with a balcony against the wall full of windows on the far side. "Really impressed."

The bed, however, stands four poster in front of a wall with a mosaic of wooden carvings. An art style I recognize.

"You made this?"

"How can you tell?" His hand cups the back of his neck, a flushed embarrassment flooding his face. "It could have been anyone."

"No one carves like you." I throw my bag on the bed and sit on the edge, taking it all in. "It's so . . . warm." A little like home but not.

"Thank you."

Neither of us know what to say next. Or do. Because we're both looking at each other, then glancing around the room again, hoping we'll catch onto something we missed before.

"I have not . . . done this before."

"A date?"

He nods. "I'm not sure what to do now." He shrugs. "I have plans for us tomorrow, though."

"Okay. So how about we order some room service and watch a movie? That way, you don't have to struggle to hold a conversation if you don't want to." I look sheepishly to the ground.

He stands in front of me and redirects my gaze back to his with a single strong finger. "I like you. And I love listening to you talk. I even enjoy conversation with you. But . . . I dunno"—his shoulders bunch as he struggles to get the words out—"I've always enjoyed conversation-less socializing more."

"I know. And I'm okay with that. I like your silence. You don't have to force a conversation with me. I want you to just be yourself." I stand and place my hands on his chest. "And I want to learn who that is."

Something on his face shifts—he goes from uncertain to confident in half a second—and suddenly his face is above mine, leaning in, pressing me back onto the mattress. And when his lips meet mine, a pressure explodes in my chest. Rips me apart from the inside. And brings his weight crashing down upon me as we splay across the bed.

His hands shove my shoulders into the mattress with a huff as his thighs trap my legs together beneath him. His tongue plunges into my mouth like he can't breathe me in fast enough, can't get enough of me.

And I squirm beneath him, trying to move, to grab him or move against him or something. Anything.

But he pins my shoulders harder, his grip like iron, as he pulls away. His eyes are lust-shot, and a small whine slips from his silence as he stares at my lips with longing. "Fuck." He looks like he's going to tear in two. But eventually, with a groan of frustration, he pushes off of me and storms into the bathroom, slamming the door shut behind him.

A small laugh escapes me, understanding his mood for the first time. He's horny, but he's trying to go slow. Emotions first, sex later. Clearly, something he sucks at.

And I'm going to make it as hard as possible.

Time for your punishment, Arrie.

Luckily, Connie was in charge of packing my bag.

I pull out the pajamas and don them, making sure to forget the bra. Oops. So when Arrie comes out of the no-doubt cold shower, he notices me lying on the bed in a tank and shorts, nipples pebbling through the thin material, he wipes a frustrated hand down his face.

"Really?" He stands there, not daring to move.

"What?" I gesture to myself. "This is what Connie packed for me."

He mumbles something in Norse with clenched fists and storms over to me, crouching on the bed. "You really have it in for me, don't you?"

"What? You mean it's cruel to lead someone on while watching them suffer? Oh no." My hand covers my mouth in a mock gasp. "I wonder how that feels."

An actual, real life growl rumbles from deep in his chest. (I shit you not.)

And it does nothing but make me smile. "I'm sure you can keep it in your pants till morning."

He mumbles something else in a strange language—not Norse, English, or Japanese—and lies on the bed in a huff. Sulking.

"N'awww . . . You'll be alright. Promise." I place a small kiss to his cheek and switch on the plasmascreen. "What you wanna watch?"

Despite Arrie's sulking, we snuggle and watch some dorky romance I'm sure he hates, but he sits through and even laughs from time to time. And then we spend the night cuddling. (I swear, it was just cuddling.) And every time his arm shifted or his body moved, I was reminded of the fact that this was the first time we'd shared a bed alone.

Alone and, in Arrie's case, needy.

But today, apparently, he has a plan.

And I'd be lying if I said I didn't want to know what that plan is.

After I'm dressed in more layers and warmer than a dragon's ass, we exit the hotel and head to a place we can hire snowmobiles. Yes. An actual snowmobile. That I get to drive!

Yay.

"Ready?" Arrie asks, sat on a larger snowmobile next to me.

"Never been more ready for anything in my life."

He chuckles before shutting his visor and starting the engine and setting off.

And I follow.

Don't worry, I had a demonstration on how these things work. I'll be fine. And besides, the chance of me actually dying from a snowmobile crash? Slim to none. I'll be fine.

Arrie leads us across sheets of snow, up and down various hills, through a couple of copses of trees, and down into a valley where, at the very bottom, a group of ruins lays. He stops and hops off, then gestures for me to do the same. "You okay?"

"Uh-huh." I pull my helmet off and yank my hood up. "Just catching my breath. That was awesome."

"Maybe one day I'll take you rock climbing." He wraps an arm around my shoulder. "With our strength, we can probably scale Everest."

He's right, we probably could. "That would be great."

"I'll add it to the list."

I look around, trying to decipher why we're here. It's nothing but ruins and snow all around. "Arrie, where are we?"

He wanders over to a ragged stone jutting out of the ground. "This was my home."

His home? But . . . Oh, his home when he was mortal. This was where his wife and children played. Where they all slept. Where he watched them from a distance as they grew old and died while he remained the same.

"Houses were nothing more than wooden huts with fancy features back then. But it was home. For a while."

"What did the village look like?"

Arrie guides me to the edge. "This was the entrance. It used to be an archway." We walk through and along what I assume was once a path. "This was the main path, and we used to have merchants here. They'd have their wares outside their houses." We take a left. "The chief used to live up there. That's what the large circle of ruins is. I married his daughter."

"Of course you did." I sigh. I have to live up to the daughter of a Viking chief? Seriously?

"Well, she was very beautiful. And strong." He gazes into the distance, and for a minute, I lose him to memories. And I have a feeling those memories haven't diminished over time like most people's. "And behind us was just more houses, a few open houses for things like drinking and socializing."

He walks me through the rest of the village, reminiscing about where things were, what life was like, and how they celebrated, commiserated, married, and died.

"She was twelve when we married. I was fifteen."

"What?" I squeak. That's insane.

"Marriages were arranged back then from a young age, since there was no guarantee we'd live very long."

"Guess they didn't account for immortality, ey?" I meant it as a joke, but I don't think it landed like one. "I'm sorry, I didn't mean too—"

"It's okay."

But it kinda isn't, is it? Whatever this place is to him, whatever is haunting him from his past, it's wrapped up here. And it's clawing at him, holding him back. Holding us back. But I can't just wave my magic wand and wish it all away this time. All I can do is be here and hold his hand.

My fingers entwine with his in a tight grip. "Thank you for sharing."

"Maybe next time, you can take me somewhere important to you?"

Somewhere important to me? "I'm not sure I have anywhere that's important to me other than *Sheruta* and home." I shrug.

"Nothing at all from your mortal past?" He's standing right next to me, holding a conversation, but he's not really here. The words are empty—just something comforting to fill the space with. "There must be something."

"Arrie, all that stuff . . . My mortal life . . . It's not me anymore. It's like looking back on a whole different person. Yes, it happened, and I lost people, and I still have memories, but they're just that now. Memories. My life here as a Horseman is the only life I value." Actually, one person does spring to mind. "Well, I guess except Nigel."

"Hmm." I'm not even sure what that sound means, but by the look on his face, it seems to be a disagreement. "I'm not sure I can ever be like that."

"The past is a part of us, but it shouldn't be a part of our present. If it was meant to be here with us, it still would be."

He looks at me with these searing eyes, anger and fear and tears all intermingling into a maelstrom of emotion you'd miss if you weren't looking hard enough. But I do. And I don't miss. And it breaks a part of me I didn't know was beating.

"You really think that?"

My voice goes quiet and my body shudders. "I have to." Otherwise, I'm still just a killer.

He nods, understanding where I'm coming from. "It's different."

"How?" My hand rests on his shoulder as my other's thumb circles his hand I'm still holding. "What can't you let go?"

"Nothing," he mumbles.

"C'mon, that's not true, and we both—"

"All of it!" He throws his arms around us with an angry scowl. "Everything!" His breaths harshen as his fists clench, and I practically see the rage boiling beneath. "I should have been here, Magic! Here. With my tribe. My wife. My children. They were my whole world!" A heavy breath rushes out of him as he falls to the floor. "But I wasn't. So when invaders from the south ransacked the village, I couldn't do anything. I was one of the most powerful beings alive, and I couldn't even save my own family.

"Dea always said that it would get easier over time. That the pain would diminish—maybe not entirely, but enough to live with. But it's been over two thousand years, and it still feels like that first day I found them here, bodies mangled, raped, and beaten."

He stands and looks at me, fresh anger slicing my way, and whispers, "And every time I kiss you, every time I even look at you inappropriately, all I can feel is her. Her judgement, her hurt that I'm kissing someone else, her jealousy." He laughs harshly, like he hates me, but I just stand there. Silently. "She would have hated you."

I want to say something. But what? What do you say to someone in so much pain?

For a moment, I swear I can hear Nine's voice in my head. Telling me, *You tell him you love him.* But it's not Nine, because if it were, there'd have been an obviously tagged onto the end. Maybe even an eye roll.

"Probably, I am stealing her man." I look at him with vengeance in my eyes and a snarl on my lips. I grab his hands and shove his fingers through mine, forcing us together. "Look, I'm not going to patronize you by pretending to understand, but I'm not going anywhere. There's no fight to be had here. You already have me. You just need to embrace me."

"She loved these." He picks some purple flowers that are growing out of a crag between two rocks. "They're Artic Thyme flowers. Violet purple . . . Just like your eyes." He sighs. "I don't know what to do."

A frustrated hand runs through his hair, but I catch it and raise it to my lips. "Nothing." I shrug. "You don't have to do anything. You think I'm going to be annoyed that you aren't over your ex-wife? Arrie, it's okay that you've been in love before. And it's okay if that love was an epic for the ages. It's okay that you're broken and hurting. All you need to do is love me."

"You make it sound so easy."

"Because it is."

"But I . . . still love her."

I laugh, because this is actually a little funny if you think about it. "I'm literally fucking your ex casual hookup while telling her I love her every day. Do you really think I'm going to be jealous of a woman who's not with us anymore?"

"But I'm broken. I can't offer you what the rest of the team can. I can't be your one and only. There'll always be someone else who means just as much to me. Another woman."

"I. Don't. Care." I don't know how to get this across any clearer. "I just want the chance to love you." To hear him say it back. Just once.

"And if I'm thinking of her when I'm kissing you?" He steps closer, his fist clenched. "When I'm inside you? What then?"

"Then walk me through the memory so I can help you remember."

His hands grab my hood and yank it down, and then all of a sudden, his face is blocking the sun and his lips are cutting off my air supply and everything in me is singing as my hands grasp at the back of his windbreaker, trying to hold on. Trying not to get swept up in the waves of his emotion. With slashes of tongue and the sting of tears, he kisses me with everything in him. Laying it all out for me. And there's no way I'm letting go.

Call me a glutton for punishment, but I will happily continue being on the other end of this man's mood swings for the rest of time.

"Arrie," I gasp between breaths. "I'm sorry I made it so hard for you. That I didn't just ask sooner."

A raw, deep laugh interrupts the moment. "Sorry? You have nothing to be sorry for. I knew I was hurting you, and I just kept doing it. I should have stopped. Or at least just talked to you. But I'm shit at all that."

"You seem to be doing great today."

He pulls back and returns my hood up to my ears. "I am . . . trying for you."

And goddess dammit, if that doesn't turn my insides to mush and makes me want to kiss him again. "I know, but I didn't help. I just kept reacting instead of thinking."

"You were going through a hard time."

"Well, now we all are, so I can't just keep reacting anymore. I need to be more responsible than that."

His knuckles graze my cheek. "You don't need to do that for us. I love that you just react in whatever way you need to. It's beautiful."

"But I just cry all the time and get annoyed and frustrated with myself."

His head tips back and laughs. "Yeah, you do. It's great." He links his arm through mine with a smile, and together, we head back to our snowmobiles and leave about a million tons lighter than when we arrived. "Let's go."

About an hour later, we enter a town not far from the hotel, where Arrie takes me on a tour through the shopping district, past frozen ponds, and then treats me to the best lunch I've ever had. At one of his restaurants, of course.

We're sitting at the front at a small table next to the window, where I'm a little fixated on the beauty on the other side.

He's been quiet since we arrived at lunch, but it's a peaceful kind of quiet. Not the inner-turmoil he's trying to hide, kind. After the last bite of his toasted steak sandwich, he wipes his mouth with a cloth napkin and smiles at me. "I'm thinking of opening a bakery."

I blink in surprise. "A bakery?" I lick my lips. "You mean, I could have access to your brownies on tap?"

"I'll bake you a batch every morning, if you like?"

"Shut up and marry me now."

We both laugh, disturbing the couple behind us. Oops. (Not sorry.)

"But seriously, what kind of bakery? Got a theme yet?"

He shrugs. "Kinda. I'm thinking of opening a Vampire bakery. Mixing blood with baked goods so you can eat without feeling yuck."

He's designing a line of cakes and snacks for me? Awwww . . . That's so sweet.

"You look like you're going to melt all over my restaurant's floor."

Wiping the small tear from my eye, I take a deep breath. "I just might." Seriously, no one does big gestures like this man. The books—all of which had non-cisgendered characters—the Christmas present, the date, the conversations he's struggled through, and now this.

He really does care, doesn't he?

He was holding back because he wasn't ready to move on. And seeing him now, everything makes sense. He wants me, but he's been pushing me away because it hurts to feel like he's betraying her. But in doing so, he's hurt me.

The memory of his words, his insults, his leading me on and then shoving me away . . . It still stings. But he's trying. And right now, that's enough for me.

"Magic?" Arrie grabs my hand. "You okay? We can leave if you want to go home?"

I shake my head. "No, no. Sorry. I was just thinking about . . . us." Looking back to where we were a few months ago, I'm actually proud.

"The verdict?" He looks at me with tense anticipation.

But he doesn't need to.

I lean over and place a kiss to his cheek. "I'm proud of us."

"Me too." He leans forward and whispers in my ear, "Want to be my official taster?"

"Fuck yes." I lean back and look at him. "And Arrie? If you ever get frustrated and angry and you don't know what to do, just come find me and tap my shoulder."

He raises his eyebrows.

"I can handle you."

"You think so, hmm?"

I look him up and down. "Definitely."

We spent the rest of daylight hours in the hotel, cuddling, kissing, and watching terrible daytime TV. But when night fell, I raced onto the balcony in nothing but my shorts and strappy pajama top to see the aurora light up the sky.

But fuck, it's cold out here.

I light a fire in my hands and let it warm me up.

"Come here." Arrie wraps his arms around me from behind and rubs hands along my upper arms. "You're freezing for a Vampire."

"Still a Witch."

The lights shine above us, illuminating the world in a gentle, distant rainbow, and I'm floored. Again. Like it's thrumming through me and I'm coming alive.

"I should have taken you here sooner. Sorry."

"I'm here now. And we can always come back."

"I'll take you anywhere you want to go."

I turn in his arms. "Road trip? You know, the old-fashioned ones, by car."

He looks surprised for a moment and then softens his lips into a gentle smile before slanting them against my forehead. "That sounds beautiful."

"Really?"

"All your ideas are beautiful."

I hold a finger to his lips. "Not all of them. I shouldn't have faked our attack on the Vampires, and I shouldn't have just let you walk away." I look at those ice-blue eyes and fall more in love by the second. "Next time, I'll just pin you down and tie you up until you tell me what your deal is."

Arrie spins us around and slams me into the wall. "If anyone's going to be tied up, it'll be you." His hips pin mine in place as his hands travel up my waist and around my curves and land on my shoulders. "Trust me, I'm not the type to bottom."

Yeah, I kinda guessed that. "Guess you'll just have to be a little more flexible. Remember, I'm just as strong as you."

"The fuck you are," he growls. He yanks me up and into his arms before pinning back against the wall and holding up my ass with a single hand.

Our lips connect, messy, teeth clashing, groans echoing off the stone, and when his hand travels under my tank top, I arch into his touch.

A voice barges into the moment that I recognize. "Arrie? Magic?" Connie runs into the room and onto the balcony in a huff. "Sorry, but you need to come home." She takes one look at our embrace and waggles her eyebrows at me. "Dea this morning wasn't enough for you, huh?"

"That was in my other form," I explain as Arrie lets me down with a grumble. I gesture to my boobs and vagina and shrug. "This me is still horny."

Connie and Arrie both chuckle as I rush to get dressed and grab our crystals to take us home.

"I swear," I mumble, "this emergency best be important."

As we teleport into my bedroom, Dea shoots off my bed and looks at us with this serious expression I've come to fear. "The SC are going to bomb New Orleans."

"Wh-what?" I stumble, but Arrie catches me by the shoulder. "But why? How?"

"We do not know either of those things." Dea stands in front of me and places a reassuring hand on the other shoulder. "But Lucien and Red overheard the plans when they snuck into a meeting they absolutely should not have snuck into."

Connie's leaning against my doorframe, smirking at me and Arrie. "So we need to free New Orleans before that happens."

"Do we have a date?" Arrie asks, his no-nonsense tone back in full force.

"Three days." Dea's grim expression tells me we're not prepared for anything in three days.

But we don't have a choice. "Then we'll have to move our plan into action and free New Orleans in two days." I glance at Connie and smile. "But we'll need to stop the bomb, too."

"Otherwise they'll just bomb the city when it's free."

Realization dawns. "That's why they shut down the city." Everyone's eyebrows raise in question. "To limit the number of Vampire casualties. If any of the rogue Vampires got caught in the blast, the Fae Queen would lose her alliance."

"So she infiltrated the SC, probably with Aki's help, in order to have access to their forces." I sigh, guilt welling. "They're just as much a victim in this as we are."

"If only we could expose the bad eggs in the Supernatural Council . . ." Connie imagines, a slight wistfulness to her voice. "Then we could get rid of them and start fresh."

Arrie holds up his hand, stopping her thoughts. "One problem at a time. For now, we need to help New Orleans and give the Vampire king his kingdom back."

A*n hour later, we're sitting around a table with the entire embassy, delivering the* bad news. Everyone looks a little broken. But Lucien looks like he's going to yank his brother's brains out with a hook and eat them for breakfast.

"I'm gonna kill him," he growls. His knuckles glow white with clenched rage as his fangs descend (again) and his eyes radiate blood red violence. "They're our people! How could he be so evil?"

No one knows what to say, not even Dea.

"For now," I attempt, "we need to focus on evacuating the city. Just in case we fail." Everyone nods their agreement. "Which means we either need to infiltrate the city or take it back." I look to Arrie working in the corner, papers spread out before him, a frustrated hand working through his hair.

He doesn't look happy.

And that doesn't fill me with confidence.

"How we doing, big guy?"

Arrie looks over to me with a weak smile. "Not great. There's simply not enough of us while we're protecting the cities, even with a more even spread of power amongst our forces."

Connie turns to look at him. "So we do it covertly. We find an in and an out, and we evacuate the city quietly."

Dea sighs. "We have no way to know how many are stuck. We do not know if we will have enough time. It could be a few hundred or a few thousand."

Felicity chimes in with some helpful information. "Well, we had ninety-six thousand Vampire residents in New Orleans. Of them, only twenty-three thousand are accounted for outside of the Rogue Faction, which have thirty-one thousand Vampires. Which leaves forty-three thousand Vampires unaccounted for."

Arrie sighs. "That's too many to evacuate quietly. We'll never do it in two days."

"And," I chime in, "that doesn't account for the Witches, humans, and Shifters left behind."

Lucien slams his hands on the table. "Then we have to take back our city!"

I turn to Arrie. "We need to make it work. Somehow." I get up and sit beside him, running a hand down his stressed back. "Where are the problems?"

"There are too many entry points. We can't cover them all." He points to various points on the map. "There are two roads coming in north, water on the west and east sides, the rest of the urban area going south and southwest, and the bayou southeast. That's too much ground to cover. And we only have so many Witches and *Sherutan* Fae to cover the water, even with your help." He grips the map with frustration. "And water isn't your strongest element."

A shadow looms over the paper pile, and I look up to meet Lucien's stern eyes. "We don't need perfect, War. Just find us a solution that will result in as few casualties as possible."

We both look at him with a grimace.

"The best result I can find wipes a third of our army."

The room falls silent.

"That's twenty thousand people," Connie argues. "That's . . ."

"Yeah," Arrie agrees.

"But if we do nothing," Lucien argues, "then we lose over forty thousand people."

His math is right. Sucky, but right.

No one ever said this war would be easy.

I stand up, fists curled at my sides. "Arrie, tell everyone the plan."

Connie gasps. "But—"

"This is our job, Connie." I gesture to everyone in the room. "This is why we exist. This is why our armies exist. They're willing to sacrifice their lives for the greater good, but the innocent Vampires stuck in New Orleans didn't sign up for that. We have to get them out."

Dea clears his throat. "While you are all doing that, I will stop the bomb."

My eyes widen. "No. Not alone."

He rests a hand on my shoulder. "I am the best chance we have. I can find out where the bomb will be coming from, stay invisible, then stop it." He looks to Arrie in question.

And damn him, he just nods, agreeing with him. "You're our best chance, dude."

"Then it looks like we're going to war. Again." Rufus, the ever-knowing, ever-pissing-me-off Shifter, huffs. "Will *Sheruta* always have to help Earth's wars?"

I sigh, because I don't have the time for this. Or the patience. "Feel free to leave, Rufus. This is a voluntary position." I swing my arm toward the door and raise my eyebrows.

He remains seated, arms crossed, a huffy look on his face.

That's what I thought.

"What about Aki?" Connie asks, shooting me an apologetic look. "What's his goal?"

"Us." I look to the table. "I'm so sorry. He's moving all the pieces to start a war to lure us out so he can get to us." And to stop any of us from dying, I'm going to put as much protection on our seals as possible. No one is dying on me again. "I'm sorry you're all at war because of me."

"Don't give yourself all the credit, Magic," Red says. "Aki's just poking at already created holes."

"If it's anyone's fault, hon, it's ours." Connie looks to me with a soft, guilty expression. "We should have stepped in way earlier than we did. We should have been here for all species, including humans, from the get go."

"If anyone spots Aki in the battle at New Orleans, come find me." I look everyone in the eyes. "It's important you do not engage him." He wields death magic stronger than me, but I can at least defend myself. They can't. "He's more powerful than you know."

And I just happen to have given him more power for a Christmas present. What was I thinking? Now he knows all my spells and charms.

Connie gets to her feet and looks at everyone. "Get your armies ready. We move out tomorrow." She turns to Arrie. "We need that plan as soon as you're ready. Mobilize everyone the moment you can."

"Is there a spare office I can use?" Arrie asks Lucien.

Lucien nods and helps him carry all the paperwork out. Both men silent. But I get the feeling Lucien's silence will break soon, and it'll break like a tidal wave I'll have to contain somehow.

While everyone else is either preparing, helping Arrie or the embassy, or having some quiet time with family, I'm staring at the vault in my library. Inside are four seals—War, Death, Conquest, and Magic—that I've triple-checked are there and real, but I'm still trying to puzzle out a way of protecting them.

So I called for help.

I'm nervous to let anyone else know about the seals, but I need to make sure none of us die this time. If nothing else, so I can sleep soundly at night.

A knock on my study door has me sweating. Nervous doesn't begin to cover it. I shift into my female form and Vampire speed myself to the door, where I open it with a small smile.

"Come in."

My green-skinned Fae trainer looks at me, then at the library, then back at me. "Well, what in the world do you need me for? There's got to be more magic knowledge in this library than the rest of the world combined."

Despite the terror looming on the horizon, I laugh. "I know, but I don't have the time to study up. It's quicker with a teacher."

"I guess." She sighs. "What did you bring me here for?"

"Umm . . . Yeah, about that. I need your help, but it's a secret, and I can't tell you too much about it."

Her eyebrows raise. "I can't help if I don't know what I'm dealing with."

Fair. Annoying, but fair.

"I need a protection spell or some kind of Fae trickery to hide something from any prying eyes."

"Well, that shouldn't be too hard." She picks up a book on a shelf and huffs in amusement. "Do you know how much a copy of this is worth?"

I shrug. "Not really."

Lo flies toward us, his tiny dragon form carrying a stack of books on its back. My little dragon librarian. "Oh, hello." He puts the pile of books back where they belong and then turns to face me. "You did not tell me we were having visitors."

"Sorry, Lo." I cringe. "I just need her help with something important."

"Anything I can help with?" he asks.

"Nah, probably not. We won't be long." I guide us both back toward the vault deep in the library and gesture at its metal door. "I need to protect this and what's inside."

"I can build a protection spell for the room, but I can't do anything for what lies inside without knowing what it is." She shrugs. "Your choice."

"You don't understand how important this is. The last time I showed someone what's inside, Nine died."

"So what lies beyond this door is the key to your immortality?"

I nod, not daring to speak.

"You probably shouldn't have told me, but it's okay. I'll keep your secret." She grabs a chair from the corner and drags it to in front of the door. "I'll do my best to seal the door and lay some booby traps."

"Thank you." I place my hand on the door, and with a silent wave of stale air, it opens. "If you don't mind, I'm going to stay."

She nods, then gets straight to work, examining the material, the placement of everything, and getting a good feel for the space. Then she proceeds to spend all day layering various runes, ingredients, and words together, on top of each other, winding through each other. And by the time she's done, I'm exhausted just looking at her.

"I don't know anything in the world more protected." She steps back and takes a last look at her handiwork. "If anyone even touches it that isn't specifically you, you'll know."

"How does that work? Is it linked to my DNA or something else?"

"It's linked to your magical essence. Not just your death magic, not just your DNA, but everything that makes your magical signature yours." She looks me dead in the eyes and smiles. "No one can copy it, not even your evil twin."

I snort-laugh at the moniker. Evil twin. I guess he kinda is, isn't he?

"In fact, even your harem can't get in. You'll be notified the moment they try. Though I can add their signatures if they want me too."

"I'll ask them." I guess it'll probably be best. It's their immortality too. "Thank you."

She looks at me with pride in her eyes and a gratefulness I'm not used to coming from her. "Despite the fact I usually hate people, I've come to rather enjoy your company, Magic. Maybe some day, I'll let you know my name."

"That would be lovely."

"But I'm more than exhausted, so I'm going home to bed. Tomorrow's the big day, after all."

I walk her to the door in surprise. "You're fighting with us?"

Her hand lies on my shoulder. "Always."

A rustle and a creak of the floorboards behind me causes me to spin on the spot. Dea sits on a chair in the dark corner by my closet. "What was that about?"

"You okay?" I thumb point toward the door. "She was just working on a protection spell for the seal vault and laying some booby traps. No one can get in now, not even you lot. But she can add you to the spell, if you'd like." I huff out a sigh. "I watched her the whole time, assessing her work and making sure she didn't steal a seal."

Dea chuckles. "It's okay, Angel. I trust you."

"Well, I trusted Aki last time, and look how that turned out."

Dea wraps his arms around me and breathes me in. "It's okay. That wasn't your fault. None of us knew. Not even Nine."

He's finding it easier and easier to say his name, as though the pain is becoming more bearable. And I'm happy, but I'm also kind of sad. Nine's meant to be mourned forever. He's not someone who is ever meant to be gotten over.

"Soooo," he says, mystery and wistfulness edging his voice, "how did your date with Arrie go?"

I give him a questioning look.

"What? Curious boyfriends want to know."

I lie on the bed and breathe heavily, relaxing into my own bedsheets. "It went well. He took me to the village he lived in when he was mortal. He shared the story with me and told me why he's been struggling. He feels guilty. Like he's cheating on his dead wife." A small tear leaks down my cheek. "But I don't really think I got through to him. I just think he's tired of not letting himself love me."

"Maybe desperate want is something he needs to break through that barrier." Dea lies beside me and snuggles into my shoulder. "Maybe he just needs you."

"Uh." Tears flood my face. "This is . . . so much harder without Nine." I relied on him to nudge me in the right direction, like my sexy fairy godfather who also happened to enjoy making his family happy. "He . . ."

"Shh, Angel." He scoops me up and scoots us up to the top of the bed, where he sits me between his legs and lets me cry into his chest. "I know. It hurts. And you have been so focused on helping me through, helping Arrie through his problems, holding Connie's hands, fighting this war, you have not had time to grieve." Magic surrounds us for a second, and then black wings emerge beneath us and the chest I'm spilling tears onto glows gold. "But you can lean on us, too."

"But . . . I . . . don't want you to . . . break." Sobs interrupt each word, making my voice come out in hoarse breaths and hiccups.

His hands run under my t-shirt and sizzle across my bare skin, where our connection shoots up me like fireworks, and everything is cooler, softer, less intense. "I will not abandon you, Magic." His finger lifts my chin so our gazes meet. "I will not check out on you, no matter how bad things get or how broken I am. You are mine to protect."

Lo flies out of the library and lands on my shoulder, curling up and scorching small flames out of his nostrils as he breathes. Which is his way of saying I love you, I think. "Emotional control is not a strength. It's a weakness. It is a human way of saying 'I am not allowed to exist in this time and space, so I will tamper it down'. Showing emotion, acting, processing it, and then moving on is strength."

And I know that. But I cry so much. I'm sure everyone's annoyed with me, thinking I'm pathetic or maybe crazy. I do jump from crying to screaming to boiling in rage in the space of a single morning.

What would Nine say?

He'd probably spout some nerdy wisdom about how emotions work, and then Dea would chime in with some pearly words that would make me reconsider my entire emotional reasoning.

Yeah, that sounds about right.

Connie and Arrie wind up on the other side of the bed after coming home from their tasks for the day, and they both add to the cuddle pile, Arrie being the one on my right while Connie lays between my legs, like usual.

"Sooo . . ." Connie says the moment I stop crying, "what were you and Arrie getting up to when I interrupted?"

Lo snorts. "Uck. I'm gone." He returns to the library, probably to sort through more books and continue cataloging them. "Bye."

"What was that, Angel?"

"Hmm?" I look up to Dea, whose eyes are a sparkling night sky full of mischief and wonder.

"What were you two getting up to?"

"Leave ve be, dude," Arrie gruffs. "They don't have to announce every part of their sex life."

"Trust me, big guy"—I pat his leg— "Dea will not stop asking until I tell him. He's possessive like that."

Arrie just huffs, but the small smile tugging at the corners of his lips warms me. It's like he's back. The man that used to flirt with me, the one who pinned me to the rock that day we were rescuing Connie and kissed the ever-loving-fuck out of me. He's mine. Or, at least, he's going to be.

I proceed to tell both Connie and Dea every detail of our date, from the aurora to the hotel to the food to the trip to the village—which Arrie remains silent on, but he agrees to let me tell them everything he said—and when I'm finally done, a smile lights up my face. And I'm happy.

A part of me is still missing, and I'm not sure I'll ever recover from that, but I can be happy and lost at the same time. After all, I have three very good reasons to be happy right here.

22

Black gates surround me, as tall as the sky and as full of magic as I've ever felt. But it's strange magic. It's suffocating my senses, like a pressure forcing me to the spot that I can't shake off.

It's stealing my air, and I can't breathe.

Shit, why can't I breathe?

Panic grips me, but I take an imaginary breath, stabilizing myself, and try to think straight.

Where am I?

These gates look somewhat familiar, like I've seen them before. Maybe in a drawing. That's it! I've seen these in Dea's drawings in one of the textbooks in my library. These are the Black Gates to the Otherworld. Where Dea brings lost souls to help them cross over.

This is where Nine is.

But why am I here?

Magical pressure constricts like a snake, winding around me, and I still can't breathe. But the magic is . . . Fae. I think. It feels like something I know. Something I've felt before.

I wake up with a gasp, clawing at air as my lungs splutter, and all three of them surround me, touching me, calming me; and Arrie, ever the pragmatist, asks the house for a glass of water and a brownie.

The terror chases me, even as my eyes open and the nightmare subsides. Everything's so hazy.

"You alright?" Connie asks, sitting in front of me.

Dea rubs soothing circles on my bare back. "Would you like to talk about it?"

I shake my head. Words not wording. Thoughts not thinking. I'm just frazzled.

"How about some morning yoga?" Arrie asks, proving yet again that he has been paying attention.

But I shake my head again. Instead, I get up, throw on a nightgown, and head to my library. There's something I need to know.

Lo would be flying in the morning sun by now, so I'm alone for the moment.

Perfect.

I shift into my female form and sprint around the library, heading to the section I need.

Fae magic. I only have a couple of hours until I'm needed in New Orleans, so I have to be quick.

My eyes scan title after title, my Vampire speed helping, until I eventually land on the right volume. I was flicking through its contents page a few weeks ago, and right under section three lies THE AFTERLIFE'S BLACK GATE. I flick to the right page and scan the introductory paragraph, deciding this is what I'm looking for.

WHEN HEADING TO THE WORLD BEYOND THIS ONE, YOU'LL BE GREETED BY THE BLACK GATE —A PIECE OF FAE MAGIC FOLDED OVER A THOUSAND TIMES THAT WILL ONLY OPEN FOR THOSE WITHOUT A BODY—AND YOU WILL PASS THROUGH. DEATH SPOKE WORDS OF PEACE WHEN ASKED HOW SOULS COPE. THAT IT IS A NATURAL PROCESS WE INNATELY KNOW HOW TO DO.

Fae magic? The gate to the Otherworld is made of Fae magic? And what does this term mean here . . . folded? How can a spell be folded?

"Angel?" Dea fazes to my side, and I close the book in haste, placing it back on the shelf. "Are you okay?"

I shake the thoughts from my mind. "I'm fine. Sorry for scaring you."

Arrie and Connie walk from around the corner, frowns on their faces, arms crossed over their chests.

"I just wanted to look something up."

"And what would that be?" Dea asks, stern contemplation lacing his words. He saw the book. "What would Fae magic have to do with your bad dream?"

I look into those galaxy eyes and shudder. I can't tell him. Not yet. If I get his hopes up and it doesn't work, it'll crush him all over again. Besides, I have to deal with New Orleans first. "I need you to trust me." I look to Connie and Arrie. "All of you. It'll be best if I don't mention it until after we free New Orleans. We need our minds clear, and I need more time to research. Please. I just need time to process before sharing."

Connie nods, followed by Dea, but Arrie looks at me with a frown. He doesn't like this. Which makes sense. I hated it when he did it to me, too. But I watch his frown melt off his face and be replaced by a look of trust, his eyes meeting mine.

"Fine," he grumbles.

"We don't have time for this," Connie complains in a huff. "C'mon, I'm not going to war on an empty stomach." She marches toward the kitchen, dragging the rest of us with her. "But don't worry, Arrie. We'll just ask the house for food."

"I can cook."

"You are such a perfectionist," she whines, "it'll take way too long."

He huffs and throws himself into his usual chair in front of me. Dea on the left head, Connie on the right head, and an empty seat next to me where Nine used to sit. None of us have the heart to get rid of it.

The sheer number of slices of toast I eat should be illegal, but hey, I have two mouths to feed. I am, officially, eating for two. I chuckle to myself, and the team all look at me like I'm crazy, but I don't care. For the first time in days, I have hope. And that's enough for now.

"So," I turn to Arrie and ask, "what's the battle plan?"

"We're going to have to divide and conquer again, but across the same city, so we can swap and change as needed." He looks at Nine's empty seat. "We'll have to use a magicom system to communicate."

We all follow his sad gaze and realize at the same time that it's because Nine can't relay messages anymore. Because he's not here.

"Magic, you're taking the water fleet and protecting the east along with strong water Fae and Witches. I'm taking the northside with the two main roads while Connie will be taking the city to the west." He sighs, struggling with something. "We'll have to leave the southside to Lucien and the Demons. It's their territory anyway."

That does not fill me with confidence. No one but Lucien has heard from the Demons since the last battle, but he assures me he's been in contact. And I'll just have to trust him, I guess.

But I get why Arrie is worried: we're leaving an entire area of defense up to someone else. But I don't think Lucien will let anything happen to his city or his people.

I get up from the table and dust the toast crumbs off my hands. "Okay. Let's do this."

We all head to the armory to grab weapons and gear, setting ourselves up, and I shove the stuff on that I wore back in Dhaka. It's been mended. So it should hold up okay. And then we meet in the back garden by the firepit.

I'm the last one there, of course, because I had to change twice. But once I'm there, we teleport to the rendezvous point just outside the city, where the heads of our army await.

Lucien is the first one to notice us, followed by Red, then the Vampire king himself. Who I'm surprised to see.

"Your Majesty, you shouldn't be here." Shock laces my tone. "It's dangerous." And he's old, though I don't say that out loud.

"I appreciate your concern, Magic, but I am neither too royal nor too *old* to defend my city and my people." He gives me a pointed look, telling me he knows exactly what went through my mind. "These are my people. I want to help defend them."

Lucien chuckles at my shock. "Clearly, you've never seen Father in action. He's not Vampire king for nothing." His gaze bores into me, a look I know well. Lucien will protect his father. Regardless of the outcome of the battle.

Red looks at me with a serious expression. "All armies are in place and awaiting our orders."

The rest of the leaders teleport to their designated places in the battle plan while I look at Dea, Connie, and Arrie with no small level of trepidation. "I . . ."

"Shhh." Dea rests a hand on my face. "We are going to be fine."

Connie nods and wraps her arms around me, then dances her tongue with mine. "Don't get injured. I have celebratory plans for us." She winks at me and then teleports away, far too happy to be about to go to war.

Arrie lays a comforting, heavy hand on my shoulder. "You still need to plan our second date, Killer. Don't hold out on me."

"Don't do anything stupid," I try to tell him. "I need all of you alive."

He teleports away with a nod I don't quite believe, and then I'm left facing Dea, who has yet to leave my side.

"I will be back as soon as I can, Angel." He nuzzles my neck as he shifts, his Angel form exploding into the midday sun. "I promise, I will not get hurt and leave you behind."

"And I'll be here when you get back. Waiting."

I wasn't nervous before, but the butterfly storm has started churning in my gut, ready to burst forth from my mouth in a torrent of acid.

What if he dies too?

Shut up, Magic. He'll be fine.

Besides, we have a plan. Well, the start of one.

As he vanishes into thin air, I'm left alone staring up at the sun and taking a deep breath. "I can do this." The crystal smashes at my feet, and suddenly I'm spinning toward the ocean, falling fast.

I catch myself in the air and fly to the few ships floating in the water blockading the valley.

The first person I notice is my Fae trainer, who meets me right away. "We're ready whenever you are."

I nod, my head dizzy and my body shaky. "We'll wait here for now."

"Magic, can you hear me?" Arrie asks over the comm in my ear.

"Loud and clear, Arrie. How about you, Connie?"

"Coming in strong."

"Good luck." I take a deep breath and turn to my army. "It's gonna suck today. We're outnumbered and have a next-to-impossible task ahead of us. But water is the strongest element, and there's no option of breaking. No choice to lose. Everyone in that city is counting on us."

"Stand by for countdown," Arrie says.

"Formations!"

"Five, four, three, two, one. Go!"

"Charge!" I carry my voice on the air so it reaches the other six boats.

We all manipulate the water to carry our boats toward the port as quickly as possible. Everyone is holding on, trying not to fall into the water, staying brave and strong despite being terrified. And when the port comes into view, I step forward and raise all the boats, lifting the water into a tidal wave, and crash us onto the dock.

Water spills everywhere, crashing through buildings, hurtling down streets, but I set us down gently.

It wasn't enough to hurt any Vampires, but I'm hoping it'll get rid of a wave of Fae in one fell swoop.

One can hope.

We jump off the boats and charge the streets, disarming and knocking every guard unconscious that we see, clearing this entry point. But it's a few miles long, and we eventually have to spread out.

"Magic, don't hold back!" my Fae trainer yells as we head south with a small army of Witches and Fae behind us. "Now isn't the time for nice."

Not sure I know how to be nice to these assholes anymore.

There's a fence surrounding the city, and I pull it down as we go, yanking it to the floor at multiple points to gain us entry and everyone trapped inside an exit.

A small contingency of Fae and Vampires charge us, but my Fae trainer intercepts, hurtling them off their feet before they get within ten meters. Then she quickly draws a few rune circles on the ground in magical energy and rumbles the earth beneath us.

I use one of the spells on my staff and keep the enemies down while barging the nearest building with a ball of energy, sending it collapsing around us, crushing the enemy but dodging where we stand.

"Let's go." I run forward, waving everyone to follow me. "We have to reach Lucien before we can stop."

Easy for me to say, I'm a Vampire, but these Witches and Fae have human-like stamina. They can't run for miles without needing a breather. And eventually, we have to stop to let everyone catch their breaths.

"Magic, you should . . . go on," my trainer says. "We shouldn't hold you back."

I shake my head. "If Arrie thought that was the best strategy, then he would have suggested it. We stick to the plan."

She nods, understanding. Agreeing. Or, if neither of those, she's at least following orders. I don't really care which right now.

"We need to keep going."

The Witches condense water from the air for everyone, providing small balls for everyone to drink.

"Remind me to get one of you to teach me that trick."

"Still a Horseman in training?" one of them teases.

I rush air at her hair, sending it flying in all directions. Everyone laughs. "Seriously, I'm hundreds of years away from being anywhere close to the others."

"Pfft," a guy with pink hair says. "They're light-years from you."

Everyone nods, but I just stand there mentally aghast. They really think that? Not the time, Magic. Not the time.

"C'mon." I wave us farther south, following the fence. "We need to clear the perimeter. Then the real fight begins."

We jog as fast as we all can as a group, tearing down the fence and freeing the city. Physically speaking. We still have to remove the army from inside and get everyone to safety.

Eventually, my Vampire hearing picks up on a group of voices in front of us I recognize. Shouting. And sounds of a fight fluster through the air.

"They need help!"

We all run faster, but I get there first, throwing daggers at two Vampires ganging up on Lucien.

He looks our way with surprise and a fanged, red-eyed smile. "Good to see you, Magic." He pats my shoulder with a genuine display of affection. "Thank you."

The Witches and Fae take care of the other six enemies while I help the king to his feet. A little dirty, but none worse for wear. "You doing okay, Your Majesty?"

His red eyes greet me, and the amount of power leaking from this one man scares me to a standstill for a moment—alongside everyone else in my group. "Never been better."

The salacious glee dripping from those words reminds me that despite his diplomacy, he's a Vampire. A pissed off, tired, hungry Vampire.

Lucien barks at two of his men. "Head west to meet the two teams. Make sure they've succeeded and join their ranks."

Everyone is heading anti-clockwise, sending two Vampires to the next team. So while we wait for two Vampires to head our way, we refuel.

The king looks at his son with pride and surprise. I think he'll make an excellent king someday, but I don't say that out loud. It might be my plan, but I'll need to do some buttering up first. Something tells me he won't take up the mantle easily.

One of the blood vials from Arrie graces my lips with a delicious lavender scent trailing down my throat. Fuck, I didn't think I'd get anything from anyone but Arrie. He's a little possessive about feeding me, which I now realize is because he's jealous. Not just intentionally being a dick. But blood from any of them is phenomenal.

I wonder what Connie tastes like?

I shake that thought from my head, because there's no use fixating on something I'm never going to chase.

Lucien taps his datachip and smiles. "Thirty seconds till we storm the city."

This next part of the plan is gonna get messy. We need to take out the army and any opponents by any means necessary. As quickly as possible.

Tapping my comms, I ask, "How's everyone doing?"

"Clear and waiting," Connie says, a smirk to her voice.

"Getting . . ." A huff sounds through the earpiece. "There."

Connie chimes in, "Thirty seconds, Arrie."

"Fuck off, Con."

Their banter makes me chuckle, and when the king looks at me questioningly, I wave his concern away. "Arrie's still fighting."

Lucien laughs. "Really?"

I shrug. "Connie and I are waiting for him."

"Okay," Arrie says, "we're good on the north side."

I nod to Lucien. "Count us down, Prince."

He descends from fifteen, and when he reaches one, we sprint into the city, staying as a unit for the moment.

Vampires run around the outside of our group, defending our position, scouting ahead, while Witches, Fae, Demons, and some pixies stay in the center, throwing magic shields and spells around, protecting our position.

But after a mile or so with no encounters, we come to a standstill.

"Hey, Connie? Have you encountered anyone yet?"

"Nope."

Arrie hmmms. "Where is everyone?"

"I'll check it out." I turn to face my group. "Stay here. Lucien's in charge. I'm going to fly around and see what's going on."

Everyone nods, understanding, and Lucien looks a little surprised by his assignment, but he straightens and nods nonetheless.

I lift myself into the air and fly ahead, beneath the clouds so I can see everything, but nothing greets my eyes. Even when zoomed in. The city is totally empty.

"Guys," I say over comm, "there's nothing here. The city's empty."

"No," Arrie says, "there must be at least the trapped residents somewhere, even if they evacuated their people out."

I fly back to Lucien and turn to the king. "Is there any kind of underground tunnel system in New Orleans? Somewhere you could trap thousands of Vampires if needed?"

He thinks for a moment, then turns to Lucien. "The drainage system."

"With water in?" I ask.

He nods.

"Perfect." A smile grows across my face. "Take me to the nearest entrance."

Lucien stops his father when he takes a step, and he instead orders a random Vampire to run with me the few miles to a small maintenance door with a no entry sign.

I thank him, and he runs back.

My hand meets metal when I touch the handle, but a shot of energy zaps me like lightning. "Shit." I yank my hand back and switch forms. My hand hovers over the door, analyzing the spell, and I smile. "I know this spell." It's a defense spell aimed at keeping people out unless they have their DNA stored. It's similar to how my trainer's village barrier works, but with a fancy electrocution rune built in. And the great thing about this is that I know exactly how to get through it.

I add my magical DNA signature to the storage rune, and boom, I'm opening the door and jogging down the stairs beyond.

It's dank. It's dirty. And it's small.

And I hate it.

But it's all I've got right now. If the Vampires aren't here, then I don't know what to do.

After a few twists and turns, walking over piles of what I hope are snapping twigs, I gag at the stench now built up. Water trickles ahead of me, and I know I'm close. When a small opening with a metal grate greets me, I smile. Water.

I dip my hand in without thinking—well, trying not to think about it—and send my energy through the stream, taking note of anything and anyone the water touches.

C'mon, c'mon, c'mon . . .

"There!" Hundreds of people at what I think is the center of the city spreading out. No, thousands. "They're all here."

Well, at least we don't have to round them up.

"I've found them," I say over comms.

"Well done," Arrie praises, and I preen. "Where?"

I cringe. "In the underground sewage system spreading throughout the city. But there's a spell on the doors. I don't know how to get the Vampires out." I couldn't just add thousands of DNA signatures to the spell—that would take days. We don't have days. "I don't know what to do."

"Gosh, Magic," Connie says sarcastically, "if only there was an expert in Fae spells on your team."

Right! "Oh yeah, of course. Right. I'll be back. Hang tight."

I switch back to my female form and sprint back to Lucien and the team. "Found them."

The king's face lights up.

"Only, there's a problem." I turn to my Fae trainer. "There's a spell on the sewage maintenance doors, similar to the one on your village, but it zaps you every time you touch it."

She cringes, fear creeping across her face. "I . . ." She turns to the Vampires looking at her with such hope in their eyes and steals herself. "I'll take a look."

I fly us both there this time, trying to save time.

"Magic," she warns, "I'm not sure I can do this."

I look to her, utterly bewildered that she'd lose hope so quickly. "We can do this."

"No, you don't understand. I designed that spell so that you can't really break it. You can get a few people through it, but to break it, you'd need a team of Fae and several weeks of time to unweave everything."

"Oh." I place us on the floor in front of the door as my smile drops. "I see." I face her, resolve firming my feet to the ground. "Can we at least take a look?"

She rests a hand on my shoulder and looks at me with a worried expression, as though she's already made up her mind, but smiles anyway. "Maybe it's something different."

We both touch the spell over the door, weaving our hands through its intricacies, both of us looking worried, until she pulls her hand back and hangs her head.

"I really . . . I really am sorry." She lifts her head, a sad, lost expression in her features. "I designed that spell for the queen. I . . . It's all my fault."

"No, it's not." My hands rest on her shoulders. "It's hers. You are not responsible for the hatred of others."

There must be another way to get them out. Something that doesn't involve breaking the spell.

Think, Magic. Think.

"Argh!" My hands clench at my sides. "If only I could teleport them." I fiddle with the charm bracelet at my wrist that's hiding my staff and smile. "Maybe I can?"

She looks at me in surprise. "What do you mean?"

I snap my staff into existence. "Nine programmed these charms with all kinds of spells, but he left this one blank." I point to the purple crystal sitting in the cradle. "Told me to use it for whatever would be most useful to me."

"And you want to turn it into a teleporting crystal?" She looks the staff up and down, studying it. "I don't know. Maybe with some time and study, but on the fly . . ."

"Yeah, you'll be surprised the amount of shit I get done under pressure." Like creating a teleporting crystal that doesn't have to break and can transport anyone within its rune circle radius. I press the button on my comms. "Arrie, how much time do we have?"

"I'd say around four hours. Why?"

"Sweep the city clear, then get everyone together near me."

"Hear that, Connie?" I ask.

"Loud and clear."

I smile at my trainer, a wicked gleam of studious excitement. "What? We're gonna need some guinea pigs."

23

An hour later, after every team sweeping the entire city clear, we're gathered in the center, the army spread out around us in a protective circle.

"Sooo," Connie squeals, "what's the plan?"

I haven't seen her this excited in forever.

"Well, I can't break the spell on the door." I look to the floor, embarrassment flooding through me. "It'll take me years to get that good at Fae magic, and we don't have the time."

Lucien looks at me with worry, but the king smiles, asking, "But you have another plan, yes?"

"Of course." A deep breath. "I'm going to teleport them all out."

"At once?" Connie asks, looking impressed. "You can do that?"

I shrug. "No idea." I meet her gaze, then the king's, and exhale. "But I'm going to find out." I snap my staff into existence. "Nine built this for me with my powers in mind. This top crystal"—I point to the amethyst in the cradle—"can be whatever I want it to be. So I'm going to make it into a teleporting crystal I can reuse."

My Fae trainer beams at me. "If we make it produce an area radius, we can transport as many people as we can fit into the circle." She worries her bottom lip between nervous teeth. "With enough power."

"Let us worry about that." Arrie places a firm hand on her shoulder. "What do you need from us?"

"Time. And guinea pigs."

Arrie turns to the leaders of each group and yells, "Form a perimeter around the city. No one gets in or out without confirmation from me directly. Understood?"

Everyone nods an affirmative, and my knees go weak as a spark of something else shoots through my body. Damn, he's hot barking orders.

"Uh-huh," Connie agrees when she sees my flushed cheeks. "I know." She wraps an arm around me before giving me a quick kiss and setting off with her soldiers.

"Arrie?" Meeting his gaze, I lean into his embrace. "Can you contact Dea and see how he's doing? I'm worried."

A sympathetic grimace flashes across his otherwise stoic face, and he nods.

One by one, everyone leaves, and I'm left alone with the smartest Fae I know to figure out how to transport forty-three thousand people in as few trips as possible out of the city.

"So," she starts, "what first?"

"We need to figure out how to make a teleporting crystal that's activated without needing to be smashed on the ground. Once we've done that, we can figure out how to transport more than one person per crystal. Ask me again after that."

Her green skin glows under the warm sun, but her smile is anything but beautiful; it's cunning, like she's ready to flay the magical rules into pieces and refuse them to her will.

Between us, we can do this.

We have to.

Hunkering down on a nearby bench, I hand over my staff and allow her to analyze it. She whistles. "This is some magic." She looks to me with raised eyebrows. "Famine was amazing."

"Yeah," I sigh, "he was."

This would be the perfect time to ask her questions about the Black Gate. But I don't have time for that. It'll have to wait. C'mon, Magic, you can't be that selfish. The job has to come first.

"This is just an empty Witch's charm made from a powerful stone that looks like amethyst but isn't. It's boosting the magic somehow."

"Right," I say. "And here you can feel the threads tying it together." I grab a regular teleporting crystal out of my pocket and hand it over. "Smashing the crystal on the ground serves a purpose: it links the spell to the current location. But it doesn't have those linking tendrils because it's just a regular crystal."

"Maybe we can use them to spread outward to seal the location, kind of like a tracking spell."

I run my hand over the stone and grab onto the tendrils tight, then coax them outward, seeing what they do. But after a few seconds, they return to the stone and leak black ooze throughout the gem.

"It's relaying the information," she confirms. "Good. Now we just need to make it select location information only." She plays around with some runes, mutters a few spells, and eventually, something I've never heard of sticks. She hands the staff back. "There."

"You're making this look easy."

She shrugs. "It is so far." In answer to my incredulous face, she says, "When you've studied Fae magic as long as I have, you pick up a few things. You're still a baby."

"Well, this baby Fae needs more training." I analyze the staff, working my magical energy over her spellwork, wondering how it works. But I don't have forever, so I only get the basic gist. "Now, how to transport as many people around me as possible." I tie three runes together, then build two more on top of that, linking them with a basic linking spell and sitting them on top of the gem.

"Here." She rummages around in her cloak pocket and produces some glowing moss in a vial. "This will help."

I take it from her and hold it up to the light. "What is it?"

"Pretorium."

"It's kinda pretty."

She laughs, her voice a little strange with the unusual sound. "It's extremely rare, because it possesses the properties needed to magnify any spell tenfold, so it was farmed to basic nonexistence a long time ago."

"And you just happen to have some hidden in your cloak?"

She shrugs. "Never know when you might need a magical bomb. I keep a little of this and that on my person."

Of course she does.

"If you place this onto the rune circle you just made, it'll magnify it around you, allowing it to trap anyone in its circle."

"How big can it go? How many people can it catch?"

"No idea. Never put it with a signature circle before."

"Won't it use it up every spell?" That would be a nuisance. Especially if it's as rare as she says it is.

"Yeah, but I hear Witches have a natural way with earth and imbuing it into charms. Maybe there's a way to imbue the crystal itself with the pretorium, and then you can just link any spell you like to it."

"I . . ." She's just given a Horseman a magical power expander. "What were you thinking giving this to me?"

"You're a good egg, Magic. You're going to change the world. I can feel it. And I want to be one of the people in your team that made it happen." She punches me in the shoulder. "But don't waste that." She points to the vial. "It's all I have, and I can't get more for you right now."

"Right. Don't spill the glowing gogo juice. Got it."

I lift the crystal out of its cradle carefully and place some of the moss in the center, then the crystal on top of that. Now all I have to do is get the rune circle to draw power from the pretorium.

Once we're sat there staring at what we think is a teleporting crystal strong enough to transport an army anywhere in the world—Earth and *Sheruta*—I don't know what to say. It felt kinda . . . easy. But I don't want to say that out loud lest I jinx us. I guess without her it wouldn't have been easy, would it?

"Test it out?" She looks at me questioningly.

"Right."

I stand to my feet, prepared to teleport myself, but she stops me. "You should teleport me first. Just in case."

"Can't do that. It'll take me with it because I'll be at the center of the spell circle."

"Huh." She blinks at me, astonished. "Should have thought of that."

"It's okay. You just fried your brain trying to play 'guess that spellwork' with the Horseman of Magic. You're allowed to have senior moments."

I duck just in time to miss the punch she tries to land on me. Then I shift into my female form, ready to activate the charm and send power through it. Probably won't take much for just two people, but it'll be a good beta test.

"Ready?"

She nods.

And then we're glowing bright purple and hurtling through the aether. But it's taking too long. We're not even seeing any signs of the destination yet.

"Magic?!" she screams, pain lancing her voice.

I try to turn in the aether, and eventually manage it with a bit of air magic. A gasp slips through my lips.

She's slowly tearing into pieces in the aether, her form disassembling.

"Shit."

What's going wrong?

Why isn't it just teleporting one signature from one location to another.

"Reassemble the rune circle you made!"

I grab the gem with one hand and filter through the matrix of the rune circle with the other, checking everything. But everything's here. I double, triple check. Nothing's missing.

"You forgot the stability rune!" she screams into my ear.

I count the five runes and internally scream at myself for being so damn stupid. I quickly whip up a stability rune and attach it to the circle, then breathe more magic into the gem and fuel the alternation to the spell.

"There."

We hurtle toward the kitchen at home at record speed, but neither of us land on our feet.

In a heap on the kitchen floor, my Fae trainer looks at me with a face like thunder. "That hurt!" She huffs and takes a deep breath. "You can't make mistakes like. We're not all immortal like you."

"I know, I . . . I'm sorry." I avoid her gaze, scared of the disappointment I'll see if I raise my head. "I was so focused on getting it right, I didn't even think about keeping it all together."

She sighs a long, deep breath and grabs my hand. "I'm not dead, don't worry." She helps me to my feet. "And now we know it works. Let's get back."

The journey back goes off without a hitch, and we're suddenly back in the center of New Orleans with a tested plan.

"Arrie?"

"Yeah?" he rumbles in my ear.

"Any problems?"

"A few on Connie's end, but she's got it covered. I couldn't get through to Dea. I'm sorry."

My breath hitches. "Okay. Let's focus on the here for now." I take a deep breath and refocus. "Ask the king if he still wants us to teleport them all to the next city."

A few seconds later, Arrie reaffirms the plan.

I look to the Fae beside me and nod. "It's time."

We race to the nearest sewer entrance and steel ourselves. This is it. I'm saving a city.

The sewer is just as disgusting this time around as it was the first, and I have to hold my breath to wade through the water, trying my best to ignore what's floating around down here.

"This is the most disgusting thing I've ever done."

"Yep. Me too."

We eventually find our way to the edge of the group just as a fight breaks out.

"Well," I hear one of them say, "we have to do something!"

"Please," I try to shout, "I'm here to help."

Everyone turns to us with fear and surprise, but some with outright hostility, and I suddenly realize that there's a lot of nonsense circling about me right now, and it won't be an easy feat getting everyone on board.

"I can teleport everyone to safety."

"You're that new Horseman, right?"

"Why would you help us?"

I steel a breath and swallow my frustration. "Because it's my job."

"Ugh." My Fae trainer shoves past me and looks everyone in the eye. "Look, there's a bomb coming to wipe New Orleans off the map. Yes, we have someone trying to stop it, but in case they can't, we need to get you all out of here. Now. I know you cannot trust Magic, but you need to try, because without them, you're going to die."

I need to remember to ask her to write any future speeches. Straight to the point, not messing around, and everyone just magically listens.

"A bomb?"

Worried shouts echo down the chambers, where hundreds more Vampires are trapped.

"Please, let me help you."

They all stay silent as they begrudgingly nod their assent.

"Now, is everyone here, even the non-Vampires?"

Lu pushes through. "Magic? Is that you?" It's the human from before. "Are you really here?" Tears in her eyes and a wobbling lip, she falls toward me. "You came!"

"I promised I would. I'm sorry it took so long."

A few others come forward, thanking me, when I notice a familiar face from when Aki and I were last here. "You're the charm Witch, right?"

"Yeah, yeah I am. Got caught up in this mess again, as usual."

I grimace. "Yeah, sorry. But I'm here to get you all out."

"Then what are we waiting for, an invitation?"

"Well, I was trying to get everyone's consent, but it's—"

"Consent? Magic, we're trapped in the sewers with a bomb on the way. Quit being ridiculous and just teleport us already. They'll thank you later."

"Err, right." I shift forms and grip my staff tighter. "I need to be in the center as much as possible, so could you lead the way?"

He grabs my arm and drags me through the throngs of dirty people, desperate faces lit up in glimmers of hope, and goddess only knows what in the disgusting sewer water. "I don't know where the exact center is, but the crowds of people are thickest here."

"Okay, that'll do." I look to the surrounding Vampires and hope to the goddess that I don't disassemble them on the way. "I need everyone to pack themselves in as tightly as possible."

People shuffle to me, squashing me from all sides as a panicked kind of hope washes through the crowd. Questions of "what's going on?" and "are we really getting out of here?" fill my ears, but I ignore them. I need to concentrate.

I slam my staff on the ground and send my Fae magic into the crystal, encouraging those tendrils attached to the rare stone to seek out our location. "C'mon, c'mon." Then I shoot as much magic as possible into the staff and watch every rune on the side light up as the crystal spins in its cradle, the moss glows brighter, and the rune circle I created echoes around us in a large enough radius that we'll be taking hundreds at once.

And then we're gone, shooting through the aether. I try to remain concentrated on Baton Rouge. But fuck, it's hard directing more people than I can see, and my mind wants to wander and think about other things, but it can't. I can't. Right now, we need to help these Vampires. I can think about my own issues later.

I gather myself, take a mental breath, and concentrate on our goal location. I've been to Baton Rouge before, so it's not too hard, and before I know it, a vast green space opens up in front of me.

Yes!

We hurtle toward it, and the aether spits us out with more force than usual—I need to look into that—but we're safe. Hundreds of Vampires are safe.

Vampire officials come out of the nearest office building to meet us, and volunteers from all species start handing out blankets, water, synthetic blood tablets, and anything else they think will be useful.

They're in safe hands here.

I teleport myself back to the sewer, and do the same thing again forty-three times, each time dumping them onto the green that's managed to clear somewhat each time I come back. And when I teleport myself back for the final time, I land in my Fae trainer's arms in complete exhaustion.

"I can't believe you did that. So reckless." She half carries me out of the sewer system. "You shouldn't use all your magic like that."

"There's a leyline beneath us. Just need to . . . recharge."

"Magic, Connie, we have a problem," Arrie says in my ear. "The bomb is hurtling toward us."

I look up and see a giant magical ball of green light heading our way, still a few miles out. "Everyone's been evacuated."

"Okay, then send your armies home," Arrie commands everyone. Every soldier has a teleporting crystal, so I assume they use those. "Then meet in the center square."

I shift forms, so I have slightly more energy, and manage to drag us to the meeting point, where Connie, Arrie, Red, Lucien, and the king await us.

"What took you so long, little Horseman?"

I scowl at him. "I have just teleported thousands of Vampires in a mere forty-three trips, so if you could hold your judgement, little prince, that would be fantastic."

The surprise on everyone's faces hurts just a little.

"What? You didn't think we could do it? I'm hurt."

Connie wraps an arm around my shoulders, and I slump into her. "Always knew you had it in you, hon."

"Now," Arrie says, breaking the moment, "what to do about that bomb."

"It looks like Fae magic," my trainer says. "Powerful Fae magic."

Arrie looks to me with a grimace, then an idea lights up his eyes. "You share an energy source, yes?"

"Huh?"

He sighs. "Your forms share a single energy source? Didn't Nine say something like that a while ago?"

"Kinda. I'm tired and exhausted in this form too, but not as much."

"So if you fuel up, you can fly up there and help Dea?"

I look to the sky, to the glowing green ball, and watch Dea fly around it, trying to do something. But he's failing, because it's mere minutes from hitting us.

"I can try."

Arrie holds out his wrist expectantly, and without missing a beat, I sink my fangs in and drink my fill, letting the energy gained soothe me and the pleasure flood through me. Though I'm careful to let neither show in public.

Once finished, I shift forms and take a look. "I'm tired, and I don't have a lot of magic left, but I can certainly take a look and disable a few spells."

"It might not be that simple, Magic," my Fae trainer says. "Would you like me to come with you?"

"No. You should all leave." I look to the king. "Especially you, Your Majesty."

He goes to argue, but Lucien grabs two crystals and smiles at me. "Save our city, Magic."

"I'll do my best." I turn to my trainer and place a hand on her shoulder. "Get to Baton Rouge and see if you can help there. That way, you're within calling distance if I need any help."

She nods, then teleports herself away.

I'm just about to tell Connie and Arrie to leave when they look at me with raised eyebrows. Immortal, Magic. We're all immortal.

"Be careful," Connie says, worry trying her lip.

Arrie doesn't say anything; he just looks at me, and I know. I know he's worried. And he's feeling more than he knows how to communicate.

Without another word, and while trying not to cry (and failing, but shh, let's not spill those beans), I fly up, soaring myself faster than I'd previously managed. "Dea!"

Dea looks up and meets my gaze with relief. "Magic." He collapses into my arms and hugs me. "I have no idea what to do." He gestures to the bomb soaring next to us. "I was not expecting . . . this."

"Yeah, us either. But I'm here to help." I shift forms, and Dea catches me.

"I have got you, Angel." His voice caresses my ear and rushes straight to places that shouldn't be so thrilled I'm in my boyfriend's arms while next to a magical bomb. "Whatever you need, just tell me."

I analyze the bomb and exhale in frustration. There's so much here that I don't recognize, but I have to do something. Okay, Magic, start with the bits you do know.

There are plenty of explosion spells, of course, but there's also something that looks like a homing device, some kind of DNA recognition, and plenty of ingredients swimming around in various crystals and potions that I've never seen before.

I don't have the knowhow to break this.

There must be something else I can do.

I turn in Dea's arms and bite his neck, taking him by surprise. He falters, and we swoop low in the air for a minute before his wings catch us as he moans.

"Magic . . ."

Once done, I look up at him and smile. "Sorry. Just fueling up." I could really use Connie's blood too, but I'll just have to make do. I shift forms and untangle myself from Dea's grip. "I'm gonna smash it to pieces."

Dea's eye widen. "Magic, I am not sure that—"

I place a single finger over his lips. "I have neither the time nor the knowledge to do anything else. So this will have to do." I shrug. "I'm immortal. We'll be fine."

"There is no one left down there, I assume?" I nod my agreement. "We could just . . . let it go."

948

"This is their home. Their royal home. I can't let that happen. I promised Lucien I'd do everything I could."

He mumbles something that sounds like "that damn Vampire", but I can't be sure. He's gotten good at mumbling things beneath the volume my Vampire hearing can detect. The controlling asshole.

"Then I will get the others up here to help. We have a greater chance of pulling this off together." He flies to the ground at top speed and returns with both Connie and Arrie in his arms.

"Here." I create boards of air for them both, like the one I made for Connie that time at the Fae palace. "Use these."

Connie hops on like a surfer and quickly finds her balance, whereas Arrie takes a few seconds longer, his bulky weight making it harder.

"Are we really doing this?" she shouts.

"Yup."

Dea scowls at me, then sighs. "It appears so, yes."

Arrie laughs, like full-on belly laughs with shaking shoulders and a wicked grin. "Then let's go!" He draws his battle-axes and roars.

Connie grabs her short sword, Dea draws his daggers, and I call up two great fireballs and increase their density.

We're getting closer to the city, we're running out of time, and the pressure of the situation is crippling, but I can't crumble now.

Right now, I need to help save New Orleans.

"Now!"

All of us rush the bomb, throwing daggers, fireballs, strength, and swords at it, doing anything we can think of to break it apart to cause some damage. But nothing works.

Shit.

Calling up my Vampire strength, I charge through the air, faster than a bullet, and rush the structure. Crash. The impact dents the outer case, and it slows.

"I did something!"

Arrie gets ready next, and his eyes meet mine. He nods.

I rush the air around him and send him hurtling into the bomb. His battle-axes crack the dents, splitting the weird metal in half.

Connie and Dea are holding back, giving us space.

When we finally break the metal casing off, we get our first good look at the inside. It's made of some kind of light or white fire.

Maybe I could soak it dry?

Kill the fiery substance?

Let's try.

I turn toward the ocean to the east and drag a decent-sized ball of water, then throw it at the bomb.

Clouds of steam sizzle as the speed falters more.

"Do that again!" Arrie shouts.

"Yep." I'm sweating, panting, and unable to keep myself balanced in the air, but I take a deep breath and call water from the ocean in waves. Wave after wave, enough to drain the coast dry. "Hold on!"

Everyone moves out of the way, Dea dragging them both at maximum flight speed away from me.

I circle the water around me into a tornado and point the apex directly at the bomb.

It crashes around me, sizzling and sparking, angry and white. Hot fumes steam. Angry burning sounds spurt. But eventually, when I'm nearly out of water, the bomb is drowned and hurtling to the ground.

I catch it a few meters before it hits the ground—just in case. And I send all of the left-over water, including the now-flooded areas of New Orleans, back to the ocean.

"I hope that didn't affect the wildlife or the sea level too much." Oops. Didn't think of that.

Tiredness overwhelms me instantly, as though all the energy I had is slipping away with the adrenaline.

I'm suddenly looking up at the clouds. Why is the sky falling?

"Angel!"

25

"You think they'll be alright?" Connie asks.

An unfamiliar voice answers. "Yes. Magic will recover with time. They used all their magical energy. It would kill a mortal."

"Well, then we're lucky Killer here is immortal." Arrie laughs under his breath.

And I release a long exhale as my eyes begin to open. "Did we win?" I croak, my voice hoarse from disuse.

Arrie chuckles under his breath, a huff of a laugh filtering through the fog in my brain like a beacon. Clearing the muggy thoughts. "Yes, we won. New Orleans is safe."

"Safer than safe," Connie says. "Dea is helping oversee the rerunning of the city. The Vampires have their home city back. Congrats."

My eyes peel open and see Arrie run a stressed hand through his hair. "Yeah," his gruff voice meets my ears. "Dea got a little possessive and wouldn't let the doctor near you, so I had to send him back. Sorry." His eyes flash an apology, a look I'm not used to seeing on his gorgeous angles and ice-blue eyes.

"Oh." I could just imagine Dea doing that in his Angel form. All black wings and gold body protecting me from literally zero threats. The idiot. "Is he okay, d'you think?"

The doctor leaves just as Connie sits beside me and runs soothing hands down my bare neck and chest. "I think he's doing the best he can."

Arrie lies on my other side and runs a hand over my bare leg. "He'll be alright with you by his side."

"You think so?" I ask, eyeing him up. "You don't think he's just slowly dying alone in a corner of his mind?"

"Is that how he feels to you?" Connie asks. "As his mate."

I shrug. "I don't know. I think he can feel me a lot better than I can feel him. But yeah, it kind of feels like he's pushed everything into some dark corner of his mind and is just running on every emotion, ignoring his needs." A shiver runs through me. "I'm scared for him."

"Me too, hon." Connie lies down and snuggles into my side.

"What if . . . I could bring him back." The words tumble out of my mouth before I can catch them, and it's too late to shove them back in. They're out there.

"What?" Connie asks.

"What if I could bring Nine back?" I look to her, searching her eyes with mine, looking for an answer somewhere in those green depths. "What if I could fix everything?"

"No." Arrie doesn't offer up any more words or actions, just a tight squeeze of my thigh with his monster-sized hand.

"Why not?"

"Too many unknowns, hon. You'd be risking everything—and not just for us, but for the world, too. For a future you don't know you can achieve."

"But I could bring him back. I could . . . I could . . ."

"Shhh," Connie whispers. "Get some rest. We can talk about it later."

"Can you send Dea up when he gets back?"

They look at me like I've grown a second head. "Just to cuddle." Goddess. I wasn't going to give him false hope. I'm not the evil twin.

"Of course."

I drift off to sleep as they leave, and at some point during my nap, Dea snuggles into bed with me, one of his wings laying on top the duvet like a second blanket. "Shh, I am here, Angel."

My nose snuggles into his neck and inhales the smoky lavender scent I always associate with calm and tranquility.

"Did everything go okay?"

"Uh-huh." His head is rested on top of mine. "The king is back in his palace, Lucien is overseeing everything else, and I've made sure we have some of our forces protecting the city."

"We can't protect the cities forever."

"No, we cannot."

"So what now?"

His hands run over my bare skin, his touch sending a million little zings pinging across my body, as he whispers, "I do not know."

But I do.

I know.

Now, I want to get my boyfriend back.

It takes a couple of days to get my strength back, but once I do, I'm in my library researching the Black Gate and everything I can find on the Otherworld.

Lo helps, finally happy to be the one helping me for a change. "Are you sure this is what you want to do, Magic? It seems dangerous, even for an immortal . . . What's that word you taught me? Badass?"

I giggle, a little slip in my focus, before I return my attention to the task at hand. "Yes, I'm sure."

"Okay, then."

Lo now knows more about this library than I do, having had more time to explore. He's like my personal little librarian. Though, I guess he's only little because he's choosing to be—and because I threatened to drown him if he tried barging through these shelves in his regular size.

The book in front of me is a journal entry from Dea dated a thousand years ago. There is never a time when helping a soul cross to the other side is something I will not want to do. It is my greatest pleasure and yet my greatest burden. But I must admit to being poorly prepared at times to handle the immense emotional burden of being around a person's death scene. For that is where I am called. Nothing hurts more than watching a mother scream for their child or watching a lover crumple under the weight of impending loneliness, but bearing witness is within my duty.

Oh, Dea. It must be so hard for him to simply do his job. He really was handed the worst ability, wasn't he? Thank goddess Nine didn't need help passing. I think that would have killed him. It certainly would have killed me.

The book from earlier is spread out in front of me, and I've been trying to decipher what it means all damn morning but failing.

"What the hell is a folded spell?"

Ding, dong.

Someone's at the library door.

(Yes, I installed a doorbell.)

"I'll get it," Lo says, flying that way.

A few minutes later, Mrs. No Name Fae Trainer walks through the stacks toward me with a small, rare smile on her face.

"Anything I can help with?"

She opens her mouth, looks at the books I'm reading, and then closes her mouth, the smile falling from her face. "Or maybe there's something I can help you with?" She sits in the seat across from me. "Magic . . ." Her eyes meet mine, her warm green skin glowing in the daylight filtering through from outside. "The Black Gate? I know the legends. They're famous among my people. But if you're looking them up for the reason I think you are, then stop."

"So is it true? Did the Fae really create the gate to the Otherworld?"

She sighs. "No one knows. It happened before our history records began. But maybe." She drags one of the books and a translational bookscreen toward her and begins looking through the text with me.

"Hey," I ask, seeing it mentioned again, "what's a folded spell?"

"It's a type of concealment. You can fold parts of your spell away so other Fae can't read them. But it's a difficult technique few can master." Her head never rises from the pages, her eyes flicking back and forth over the lines of text.

"Hmmm . . ." I flick another page. "Can you do it?"

She looks to me with curiosity in her eyes. "Yes. And yes to your next question, too. I can teach you." She gestures for me to hand over the book I'm reading, and once she's flicked through the text herself, her head falls into her hands with a sigh. "Folded spellwork." Her head raises from her hands with slow movements. "Magic, I care about you. I didn't think I would, but you've become my friend. So I mean this with love: I'm not teaching you folded spellwork if the outcome is you risking your life to bring your dead boyfriend back."

"What?" a quiet, familiar voice echoes from behind me.

Fuck.

"You can bring him back?" Dea asks, still not stepping out from the bookcase I didn't even know he was hiding behind. "Really?"

"I . . ." I look to my trainer and scowl. "I don't know."

"But you think you can?" He steps out from his hiding place and walks toward me. "You think you can bring Nine back?"

"Dea . . . I . . ."

"Stop coddling me!" He flinches at his own raised voice. "Sorry, sorry." His hands run soothing lines down my arms in apologies not voiced. "Sorry. I just . . ."

"I didn't want to tell you because I don't know." I gesture to the books. "This is so complicated. And I don't even know how much of it is true or just fabricated legend." My eyes drift from his to the floor. "I didn't want to get your hopes up."

"But I want to help."

"If it doesn't work, it'll be like losing him all over again."

My Fae trainer interrupts, coughing. "Even if you do drag his soul out of the Otherworld, what then?"

"I honestly have no idea," I admit. "But something about that just feels right." Just like it did in my dream. "Arrie and Connie don't agree. They said it's too dangerous."

"They would," Dea gruffs. His hand strokes my cheek. "They just do not want to lose you after losing him. They are still hurting, like we are."

"But that doesn't mean it's not the right choice."

"Risking your life," my Fae trainer says, "for something you have no idea how to accomplish is never the right choice."

I turn to her. "Why do you think I'm here with a thousand books, trying my best to gather as much data about the Otherworld as possible?" Inhale. Exhale. "Just because I sometimes act like one does not mean I'm a child."

Her hands raise in surrender. "I never said you were."

"No, but everyone looooves treating me like one." My hands clench at my sides. "And it drives me fucking batty."

Dea snickers.

I spin, throwing an accusatory stare his way. "What is so funny?"

"Batty. You could turn into a bat if you really wanted."

For goddess' sake.

But the laughter spilling from his lips is like a dam breaking, and he can't stop, and then I can't help but join in. And even though we shouldn't be laughing, should be continuing this serious conversation, I shift into a bat and make everyone laugh, even stubborn old greenie over there.

I shift back to human and say, "Okay, okay."

They both slowly stop laughing, wiping tears from their eyes.

"So, I'm going to try. Whether everyone agrees or not. I couldn't live with myself knowing that I might have succeeded but was too scared to try." I turn to face Dea. "But you have to know that it might not work. In fact, it probably won't. We have to be prepared to fail."

He cups my jaw. "We are losing nothing if you fail. I will go with you and ensure you return safely." He turns to look her in the eyes and smile. "Does that satisfy you?"

She nods, clearly still unhappy.

"Good," I say, "then let's get to work."

27

All three of us spend hours pouring over textbooks, and I get the basic rundown on how folded spells work. Though I'm unsure I can actually create one. But it doesn't matter. I just need to know how to undo one or edit one or fiddle with it so I can remove a soul from inside to outside the door.

If I can manage that, then I can bring Nine home.

But what I do when I drag his soul back down to Earth is another question I don't have the answer to.

Will the teleporting crystal even work on a soul without a body? Can I even get him back to *Sheruta*?

What about Connie and Arrie? Will they hate me for doing exactly what they didn't want me to do?

This is insane.

Completely and utterly insane.

My craziest plan yet.

"Hey, Angel. Stop spiraling." Dea's gentle head rests atop mine. "We will be fine. We can do this."

"It's just . . . I have so many unanswered questions. Questions I'll never be able to answer. There are parts of this plan we'll have to make up as we go along."

"Uh-huh." He nods. "That is about the gist of it with you."

A scowl rips across my face.

"It really is," my Fae trainer says. "Your powers are basically limitless. I don't think you were created to be like the other Horsemen."

"In what way?" I ask, confused. I'm a part of the team. Just like the others.

"The others have specific powers designed to help specific problems. But yours are infinite. You can combine all types of magic to solve all kinds of problems. You've basically put them out of a job." She gestures to Dea. "The world doesn't need them anymore. It needs you."

"See, even grumpy agrees." Dea wraps his arms around my waist. "Look, even if we do not manage to bring him back, we tried. We owe him at least that much."

"Then you can be the one to tell Arrie."

Dea chuckles. "Yeah, he will not be happy." His fingers lace mine as he sighs a deep breath. "But we will tackle it together."

Another few hours, and we're all exhausted. So we head down for dinner, where Arrie and Connie are spreading out a lush evening spread of tacos and cheesecake. But it's Arrie's tacos and cheesecake, so it's elite. Not that tacos on their own (without the Arrie-level awesomeness) aren't great.

"I'm going to head back home for a few days. I need to rest." Her green skin does look duller than usual, and her bloodshot eyes echo how I feel.

"Are you sure?" Connie asks. "You're more than welcome to stay."

Lo flies into the kitchen. "Is that tacos I smell?" He settles into a spot on the table Arrie set for him.

"I'm sure. I'm exhausted." She says goodbye to everyone and leaves out the backdoor, heading home.

"So," Connie turns to me and asks, "what have you been doing all day cooped up in your study?"

I look to Dea and wince. "How about we eat first and then chat about that?" Because I'd like to get through dinner without Arrie throwing a fit.

"Because that's not ominous." Connie wraps an arm around my shoulder and places me in my seat. Next to Nine's seat. His empty seat. "Whatever it is, I'm sure it'll be fine."

Uh-huh. Absolutely. Fucking perfect.

The usual silence pervades dinner, the emptiness sitting next to me an all-consuming presence none of us can ignore.

"I found an interesting book today," Lo says, breaking the silence. "It was talking about how powerful Witch magic is when used together, combining their powers. Is that true?"

Dea looks to Lo and smiles. "Witches have a strong sense of community. They build entire homes out of mountains and caves and streams while weaving their magic together."

"Maybe we could ask for the local Witches help to create something more beautiful and permanent for the pixies in the northern forest?" Lo suggests. "They're just camping out there for now, waiting for someone to tell them to leave or to need to move."

"Oh, I should have checked in on everyone by now." Fuck. I've been so busy focusing on my team and New Orleans I forgot about everyone. "The Demons too. Glowy. Every-one. I'll check in on them all tomorrow."

"We can all go, if you like?" Connie suggests. "Though, I do have a few things at the embassy to take care of first."

Dea looks at me. "I'll continue with the research." Then he looks back to his plate and avoids the growing elephant in the room.

Arrie shrugs. "I can come along, if you'd like some company?"

"I don't mind."

"Okay." Connie slams her knife and fork down. "Out with it." At my eyebrow raise, she explains, "Whatever is ruining this dinner, whatever has you so worried and quiet, spill it."

I look to Dea, and together, we take a deep breath. "We're going to the Otherworld and bringing Nine back."

Everyone falls silent, no one even taking another bite—it's like I've stopped time.

"Okay." Connie takes a deep breath. "We should talk about this."

"It's not up for debate." Her eyes flinch, hurt, and I immediately regret my choice of words. "I'm sorry. I'm sorry that this means risking my life and that you're worried and that we don't agree. But I'd do the same for any of you. I have to at least try. Even if I fail, I owe him that much."

Connie clearly struggles, tears brimming her eyes, but she chokes it back. "I hate this." A shuddering breath exhales out of her, like defeat. "Like I have to choose between wanting you to be safe and saving him." She smashes her hand on the table, frustration rubbing tiredness into her beautiful eyes.

"I don't want you to go." Arrie looks me dead in the eyes as he says it, fists clenched. "If it means losing you, I don't want to save him."

Dea snaps, his wings popping into existence. "What do you mean you do not want to save him? Arrie! How fucking could you?"

"What do you want me to say, man? That I understand? That it hurts but I am okay sending my partner to their death? He's gone! But Magic is right here." He points at me, as if proving his point.

"He has been with us for two thousand years!"

"You think I don't know that?" His voice is quiet, deadly, on edge. As though he's going to explode at any moment. "I want him back too. But not at Magic's expense."

"It's not your choice," I tell him, because it isn't. "The only reason I'm talking it through with everyone is because last time I didn't, you all yelled at me."

"And brought back a murderous evil twin," Connie ever-so-unhelpfully points out.

Dea exhales. "I get it. You are scared. But Nine is scared too. Scared we might not come for him. Scared that we will give up and abandon him." Tears sting his eyes. "I need to go and get him, and I cannot do that without Magic."

But Arrie, ever the pissed-off Horseman of War, storms off, not wanting to listen to another word.

28

Knocking on that door is like standing on the edge of a cliff—unsure if I'm going to fall off or step back. But today is all about flying, and I can't do that if I don't leap first.

Knock, knock, knock.

"Arrie?" No answer. "Can I come in?"

The door swings open, and a tower of muscle stands between me and the other side.

"Are you just going to stand there, or are you going to let your partner into your bedroom so we can talk like grownups?"

Frustration slashes across his face like an unmovable iceberg. Frozen. But he steps aside and gestures a wide arm for me to enter. With a sigh. But I'll take it.

Baby steps, people. Baby steps.

Arrie thumps the door closed behind us and stands with his arms folded across his chest and that same frustrated scowl frozen on his face. He opens his mouth, then closes it. Opens, then closes.

He doesn't know what to say.

Okay, then I'll start.

"I'm sorry." Genuinely. "I'm so sorry I'm doing something I know will hurt you, and I'm sorry that there's nothing you can say or do that'll change my mind."

His eyes meet mine with an upheaval of emotion, like he can't quiet decide how he feels. Or maybe he feels more than one thing. (Seems unlikely.) Fists clenched, eyes screwed shut, he focuses on breathing. In, out. In, out.

But nothing he does makes his fingers uncurl or his eyes reopen, and I realize that maybe his anger is something he can't just breathe away. Maybe he needs some way to release it.

So I grab his curled fist and lift it to my mouth, biting down. Forest-scented blood trickles down my tongue in waves as a loud thump meets my ears, and I open my eyes to see Arrie's splayed hand on the wall and his eyes fixated on me with enraged fury and heat and lust.

And finally, when I'm nearly done, he uses purposefully gentle fingers to tuck a loose strand of hair behind my ear.

I unlatch my mouth from his skin and stare at him with a bloody smile. "Alright. Gimme your best shot, old man." I widen my stance, bring my fists to my center, and focus my weight onto the balls of my feet. "You wanna let out that energy, I'm all ready to go."

"Magic . . . I'm not going to—"

"I'm going to the Otherworld with Dea, regardless of how you feel, to save Nine. With or without your blessing," I remind him.

That stubborn face flits to one of rage and frustration in an instant, and his splayed hand forms a fist once again—one that comes swinging my way.

I meet it with crossed arms, but the force sends me skidding backward a few feet.

Ragged breaths meet my ears.

"That all you got?" He doesn't move, doesn't speak. Frozen. "Don't pretend like you haven't wanted to punch me in the face since the moment I got here."

Quick as lightning, his hand grips my throat and squeezes, cutting off my oxygen supply. "You're just going to leave us? To leave me? For Nine? For someone who's already dead that you have no idea if you can bring back!" His voice edges louder the more he speaks. "Why is he more important than us?"

He's not. I would do the same for any of them. But I can't say that because he's lifting me off the ground by my throat—thank goddess I don't need to breathe—and my dangling feet squirm.

I kick outward, landing a foot to his steel abs.

But he doesn't move.

Of course he doesn't.

So I flail and kick upward, landing a blow to his chin that knocks his head back and loosens his grip enough for me to unwind his fingers and fall to the floor.

His eyes snap back to mine, furious. "Since when did Nine become top in the relationship."

"He isn't. Wasn't." I take a breath and back up. "Isn't."

"Then why risk us losing you for him?"

I don't say anything. Because there's nothing I can say to that. I'll risk it all because I love him, just like I love all the rest of them. Just like they love me.

So even if the world burns, I'll make the choice to risk it all.

"Why?" He throws a fist my way, but I block. Then another that I dodge. "Why can't you just be happy with the three of us? Or at least try." Tears brim his eyes. "Are we not good enough for you?"

That question catches me off guard, and he swings his grip to my shirt, which he catches and uses to yank me toward him. He snarls in my face, a growl escaping that vibrates through me.

I wrap my legs around his torso and squeeze.

But he unravels them and throws me across the room.

I fly through the air, too fast and too sudden for me to think about catching myself, and I land in the wall next to the door. Half in, half out. "Owww . . ."

Arrie charges at me, a seven-foot tower of ice-cold fury, and I brace for impact. But he stops in front of me and grabs my legs, ripping them open. He pins my knees to the wall, resting his hands underneath, holding me in place.

Oh, fuck.

His icy blue eyes meet mine, and I swear they're a shade darker, more teal ocean than ice cold. But the look he gives me is half feral anger and half uncontrolled lust, and a full-body shiver racks me head to toe.

"Why?" he asks.

Again, I don't answer.

I don't know how.

A growl rips from his teeth, vibrating through his lips. And before I can protest or try to get out of his grip, he buries his head up my skirt and grabs my panties between his teeth.

The sound of ripping fabric and snarling fills the air as my breath hitches and my brain freezes. This is not where I thought this would go. But it doesn't matter, because without preamble or foreplay, he's spearing me with his tongue, parting my lips with practised skill.

A small sound of protest escapes before Arrie curls his tongue and flicks the tip across all the good nerves. And that protest turns into a moan as I curl my fingers into fists at the wall, trying to hold on to something—anything. But I'm suspended against a wall with nothing but his palms flat behind my knees keeping me up.

"Arrie . . ."

"Shut up," he growls. His tongue pulls out and slashes upward, lashing at my clit in harsh strokes that are too much too quick.

I try to wiggle free, to move away, but I can't. He's got me pinned.

His wicked gaze flies up to me, and the salacious smile that meets my eyes makes me tense and my body quiver. "Sit there and fucking take it."

Nothing prepares me for the way he dives back up the fabric of my skirt and wraps his lips around my clit and sucks, his tongue circling and my moans and growls vibrating.

Oversensitive sharpness soon turns to waves of molten pleasure as my back arches. "Arrie . . ." His name leaves my lips on a sigh as I push myself into his mouth further.

He grips my thighs and pushes them higher, splitting me open further.

As he sucks harder, soaring my body higher, my legs growing shakier by the minute, my fingers thread through his hair. "Arrie, harder."

The rugged groan that escapes his lips sends a thrill through me like nothing else, and he moves his hands to my ass for a minute while he undoes his jeans. Lips never leaving my pussy.

His tongue circles faster as I clench around nothing. Emptiness filling me.

"Arrie, fuck me." I squirm, trying to move to his rhythm, but it's hopeless pinned to the wall like this. "Please fuck me."

He rips his mouth from me and meets my eyes again. "No." And then he returns to licking my slit, spearing his tongue into me like it's the last thing he'll ever get to do.

I'm dripping down his chin, but he doesn't care.

He just continues to stab his tongue in and out of me, and when he curls the tip, sparks shoot through me.

"Fffuck," I stutter, my body tensing as my legs shake. "Oh goddess."

He pulls out and licks a stripe up, swirling his tongue around my clit, making me cry out. He finds his way under my hood and stays there, forcing pleasure through me in tidal waves.

My legs try to tighten, yanking against his arms, but he keeps me firmly pressed into the wall.

His lips suck as his tongue flicks, and it's all I can do to hold on as my pleasure crests and I'm thrashing in his arms as the dickhead fucking laughs at me.

"Arrie!"

He lashes his tongue harder, sucking tighter, and I'm gone. Flying off the handle as uncontrolled screams leave my throat. He holds me through, slowing his mouth down as the wave ebbs, prolonging the orgasm as long as possible.

But when I'm done, he looks up at me, his chin coated in my cum and his smile gone, he asks, "Why?"

"Because I love him just as much as I love you. And if it were me up there, and there was a way you might save me, you'd give everything you had to at least try."

Arrie looks at me like he finally sees me, as though something has clicked into place that wasn't there before. And he lets go of my knees and helps me to my feet, steadying my wobbly legs. "You good?" I meet his gaze with a heated, lazy one of my own, and he laughs. "Yeah, I guess you are."

I grab his hand and yank it to my face, where I rest my head and keep his gaze locked in mine. "Arrie?"

"Yeah?"

"Fuck me before I go."

His eyes widen, and it's clear he gets my meaning. If I don't come back and something goes horribly wrong, I want to have good memories, and I want to revel in them forever.

He brushes a palm across my cheek and whispers, "I'll do more than that. I'll make love to you."

29

Arrie turns me around, and we pass through the Zen garden that is his main bedroom—past the trees, the ponds, the koi fish, and across the wooden bridge—to the bed by the window wall.

"I can close the blinds," Arrie offers.

It's still light out, and while I don't relish the idea of any of the housekeepers seeing me dick deep, the way the sunlight dapples across the gardens and the atmosphere it creates brings me more peace than I knew a bedroom could.

"I'm good, unless you'd prefer to."

He shrugs. "I don't care about things like that." He sits on the edge of the bed and gestures me to follow, then places me on my feet between his open knees. "I'm okay to do this in whatever form you'd prefer."

He'd be okay with that? Really?

"I want you to be comfortable, Killer." He looks up at me, his eyes shining with something more than lust. "Always."

"Except when you're pissing me off. Then you want me angry."

He looks sheepishly to the floor, embarrassment flushing his features. "I like it when you're passionate. It lights you up."

My fingers angle his chin back up to re-catch his eyes, and I'm floored by the emotion I see in them. He looks almost tearful.

"I do not want you to go, but I am willing to respect the reason behind your decision to leave." His fingers thread through mine in a tight grip. "It is not about me."

I place one knee beside him on the bed, then straddle him with the other. "You don't have to be good at sharing." A harsh puff of air escapes me. "Maybe I kinda like it when you're possessive." Something in me likes how close we are, how many words are pouring out of his mouth to meet mine. "Passionate," I correct.

"Yeah?" His strong grip wraps around both my wrists. And he flips me onto my back on the bed, then drags me up toward the headboard, where he deposits me in a heap with a smirk I'm beginning to become addicted to. "Still think you want me in your harem?"

My knees fall to the mattress either side of me, an open invitation. "It wasn't complete without you."

He shucks his jeans all the way off, leaving him in just his underwear standing at the foot of the bed. Staring at me like I'm his next meal. "I like that skirt."

It's a plaid black and white one I paired with a black bralette and knee-highs—a look I know Connie likes. Pretty sure Dea would prefer I walk around the house naked. But it's good to know Arrie likes me in a skirt. Maybe I'll have to wear them more often.

He crawls up the bed and strokes a hand up my leg, dipping underneath the skirt. "Easy access."

A laugh escapes me. "Of course that's what you like about it."

"Maybe one day I'll show you why." The mischievous look in his eyes promises dirty secrets in public places, and goddess am I here for it. "But right now, I want that top off." His jaw snaps shut, his teeth clenching. "Now."

I rush to obey, thrill shooting through me.

It's not the first time he's seen me naked, but it's the first time he's been allowed to adore me in such a state. And while I'm unclipping my bralette at the back, slipping it off slowly, teasingly, he roves his eyes over my breasts. Landing on the hard points of my nipples he worked up earlier.

His underwear grows tighter the more he looks at me, and the outline of his erection has my mouth watering. He follows my gaze and huffs a laugh. "Later. Right now, I want to bury myself in you."

"Leave the skirt on?"

He nods, words lost on him. But he crawls overtop of me, his fists landing either side of my face as that hard bulge I was staring at moments ago nuzzles between my legs.

A small gasp, and he's swallowing my sounds like a dying man breathing his last breath, dancing our tongues together, our teeth clashing, my lips numb and plump.

My hands roam down chiseled pecs, abs made of steel, and settle on hips I drive toward me like I'm high on this man. "Take your underwear off."

Instead of listening to me (because goddess forbid he does that), he grinds his hard cock into me, lighting me up and rewarding himself with a moan. He swivels his hips, not stopping, and drops his head to my nipple. And that talented tongue from earlier reminds me just how much practise he has pressing all the right buttons.

"Arrie," I gasp, out of breath and clenching the sheets beneath us. "Arrie, yes. More."

A growl leaves his lips and rumbles across my skin. "I love how you sound." He bites my nipples between gentle teeth just harsh enough to hurt. And my hiss turns into a moan when the pain turns into pleasure. "And it's finally for me. I've been listening to you moan for them for far too long."

"You've been listening, huh?"

"All the goddamn time." Another bite, then a swirl of his tongue as his hips continue to grind against me. "Like a fucking pervert with my dick in hand." He grabs my hands and shoves them into the mattress. "You're infuriating."

All he had to do was be nice to me. Wow. Imagine that. A guy cock-blocking himself.

He lets one of my hands go and pinches the other nipple, setting fire to my body in the best way.

"Ffffuck . . ."

He groans as he grinds faster, picking up the pace with his tongue and fingers. "Yeah, I love the way you sound."

"Then get in me and make me scream already." My voice half sobs, half begs.

And by the way he chuckles around my nipple and pins me to the bed with his hips, he loves it. Which is good news for me, because I'm one of those pathetic people who naturally beg, it would seem. (Don't roll your eyes at me.)

But so far, I've had zero complaints from my lovers.

Eventually, Arrie lifts himself off of me and shucks his underwear off, releasing the hard dick that's been grinding into me for the last fifteen minutes.

Everything in me wants me to wrap my lips around the head and see how long it would take for him to explode down my throat. Or to squeeze around it while he pounds into me.

"Would you like to use a condom?"

"Oh, err . . . If you'd prefer to? I haven't been using them so far." I look away, suddenly unsure of myself. "I'm on birth control and only sleeping with the team, who have only been sleeping with me, so . . ."

"Right. No, that's okay." He shrugs. "I don't mind."

He leans back over me, carrying his weight on his knees and wrists, then nudges my opening with his dick, grazing it up my entrance like a damn tease.

Instead of begging this time, though, I reach down and grab it, squeeze hard, and watch his eyes roll into the back of his head. Then I line myself up and roll my hips up into him, sinking in a few inches.

Both of us moan, his louder and gruffer than mine. He leans down, resting on top of me, and buries his face in my neck as he slowly enters me further, inch by glorious inch. The stretch burns me alive, flexing my muscles further than before, and soon he's nudging the back of me, a gentle caress that promises more.

"You good?" I ask, after he lies there for a solid few seconds, breathing hard. "Because I really want you to use that strength on me."

His laughter reaches my ears, and I melt in his arms. He places his wrist to my mouth and sighs in relief when I grip it hard. "Best fuel up then."

And I do. I take what I need from him in slow pulls, relishing in the sounds leaving his mouth, the small, slow thrusts he's making inside me. My lips latch on, and I suck harder, leaving us both high.

"God, that's . . . Fuck, don't stop."

So I don't. I keep pulling harsh, long pulls of his blood, leaving plenty of room between each so he won't pass out. "Fuck me."

He nods, then drags his hips all the way back, before slamming them into me, forcing the bed to close the small gap between it and the window wall. Again and again he slams into me, hitting that delicious spot at the back of me that sings with every point of contact.

But I have to stop drinking from him or he'll lose too much blood, so I lower his wrist and grab his chin in firm fingers and swivel his gaze to mine. "Don't hold back."

He shakes his head. "Never planned to." A growl rips from his lips as he clamps harsh fingers around my hips and lifts them off the bed.

I throw my hips onto him, sinking him into me. His hard dick throbbing against my walls. His uneven breaths mixing with mine.

Skin slaps against skin, fingers grip into hips and sheets, and moans echo throughout the room—and if the others didn't know what we were doing in here before, they definitely do now.

With every thrust of his hips, he grinds against my clit, soaring me to new heights, and when he takes my nipple into his mouth once again, I convulse around him.

"Argh . . . Do that again."

I clench around him, tightening myself.

"Oh, oh god." He yanks me off him and flips me around so I'm on all fours. Then he grabs my hip with one hand and wraps my hair around the other, holding me in place while he fucks me ragged.

My back arches, his cock hitting just the right spot, and I release my hands from where they were clenched in the sheets and let him hold me up. Use me. Take his fill of me.

"Let me choke you."

I do my best to nod, but I can't—he's yanking my head back too hard. "Yeess," I hiss. "Please."

He yanks on my hair so my back is to his chest and I'm sat above his lap as he rocks into me.

A thick, callused hand wraps around my throat and squeezes, cutting off my air supply. Then a second hand joins it so he's strangling me.

And I can't breathe.

He picks up the pace, ramming into me hard enough so that I can't move. And my back arches deep, deep enough to hurt a little, but the pain spurs me on.

I try to moan, to scream, to make some kind of noise, but my throat is straining against his grip, and all that comes out is pathetic gurgle.

My head goes heavy, dizziness spinning through me, and my head lolls.

"Yeah, that's it. Right there."

He releases his grip, one hand delving to my clit, which he pinches in hard squeezes. His head lowers to mine, the hand around my throat squeezes again, threatening. "C'mon, Killer. Come for me."

He fucks me faster, harder, the wet sound of our bodies joining and our skin slicking and slapping against one another all I hear as my body shatters.

Arrie's fingers pinch harder, enough to send pain spiraling through me. And his hand chokes me again.

Oh goddess. Oh fffuck. A torrid scream leaks from my throat—raw and ragged—as I spasm around him.

"Yes, yes, yes." Arrie buries my head into the mattress and grips my hips, pummeling into me fast. "Oh god. Fuck!" he shouts as he comes, filling me.

He flops against me, his hips coming to a stop. "Fuck . . ."

I'm too stunned and exhausted to respond, my breaths coming in ragged heaves as he rolls off of me and tucks me into his arms.

Gentle fingers run along my neck with a wince. "That's gonna leave a bruise. Sorry."

My throat is sore, but I manage to croak, "It'll heal."

I spend the night in Arrie's room, plus the following morning, and he dotes on me like I'm his one true love; he cleans me up, puts some cream on my nipples, gives me a throat sweet and some numbing spray for the pain, and keeps me wrapped in a tight ball of blankets and soothing arms forever.

Well, it feels like forever.

But eventually I do have to get out of bed and back to my office.

As I'm getting dressed, Arrie is quiet. Actually, he's been quiet ever since we finished fucking. "Killer?"

"Hmm?" I turn around as I'm trying to find my bralette. "Yeah?"

"Sex is a good communicator."

I laugh, he laughs, and we both stare at each other with loved-up eyes and wonky smiles. "Yeah, it is. But we should try communicating outside of it, too. Maybe next time we can go for a drive. Just meet me by the track out back."

He nods. "I will try."

I run my hand up his arm and smile. "It's okay. We have all the time in the world to learn communication skills." I thumb gesture to the door. "Gonna come help me so I don't kill myself trying to undo a folded spell keeping the Black Gate shut?"

"It's a Fae spell?"

"Yeah. Kinda came to me in a dream."

"A premonition, maybe?"

"Like, Seer magic?"

"Maybe." He shrugs. "You are supposed to have all the Witch abilities."

I guess. "But it's the first I've had if so." Thinking back to some of my nightmares, the possibility that they might not all be from the past sends shivers up my spine. "I hope."

Arrie throws on a pair of jeans and a t-shirt, then joins me as I'm leaving the room. "Let's get you saving your other boyfriend." He still looks hurt, still looks like letting me leave is the last thing he wants to do, but he's encouraging me, anyway.

Because he . . . loves me?

He didn't say it back.

But he might not be ready yet. And that's okay. At his own pace is the pace I want to be at.

We walk into my study early afternoon to find Dea and Connie already pouring themselves over books and printed web pages, not even noticing us enter.

When we sit down to join them, Connie snaps her head up with a smirk. She waggles her eyebrows.

"Yes, Connie." I sigh. "Just . . . yes."

"Eeeeek!" She launches herself at me with arms wrapping around my neck. "Yay!" Her lips meet mine in a slanted kiss that tastes of cherries and coconut (her favorite smoothie). Her tongue tangles with mine in a mess of teasing heat and tingles. She pulls away, breathless, and whispers, "I need you next." She turns around to the guys and shouts. "Bagsy Magic tonight."

"I am not some car you can call shotgun over." I harrumph but smile at her. She's so adorable. "I am a grown-ass person."

"Fine." She looks at me with a serious expression upon her face. "Can we go on a date tonight?"

"Y-Yeah. Sure."

She rolls her eyes. "There. Same thing achieved." She shrugs and moves back to her seat.

Dea looks at Arrie still holding my hand with a small smile on his face before burying his nose back into his book. "Good morning."

"No Fae trainer today?" I ask Connie.

"No. She messaged to say she'll be here tomorrow if we need her. But she needs a rest."

Oops. I may have been overusing her. "Yeah, that's cool. She can take as long as she wants. She's not an employee." I feel guilty. She didn't really have time to rest after the shit in New Orleans. "Maybe I should send a fruit basket or something."

"A fruit basket?" Arrie asks, confused. He slumps into a chair and analyzes the white board of key notes we started to take yesterday but they've added to this morning. "What is a fruit basket?"

"A basket of fruit?" Was that not obvious?

"And what does the fruit basket do?"

Err . . . "It makes her feel appreciated and not taken for granted?"

"You do not sound sure, Killer." He lifts the nearest book into his hand and delves into reading.

I . . . What?

THREE HOURS LATER, I'M STARVING AND NO CLOSER TO WORKING OUT HOW TO GET MY ASS through the gate. "I still think Dea could just drag any of us through."

Dea's fingers massage his temples. Frustrated. "I. Do. Not. Know. If that. Will. Work." He lifts his gaze to mine. "I have never taken anyone but dead mortals through the Otherworld Gate."

I shrug. "Guess I'll be the guinea pig."

Arrie growls from beside me. "Just because you fucked me into submission does not mean I am going to let you go off with half a plan and a pile of pointless hope." He points the papers in his hand. "We'll figure this out before you leave, not as you go."

"Wow." I breathe in amazement. "That's like the longest paragraph I've ever heard from you."

He squeezes my wrists together in a nod to the position he had me in against the wall, and I flush.

Connie laughs to herself. "Might as well have added a "Yes, Daddy" for good measure."

I wrinkle my nose. "I'm not *that* submissive." I look to Dea. "Am I?"

He wraps an arm around my shoulder and places a soft kiss to my forehead. "There is nothing wrong with being naturally submissive." He gestures go himself and Arrie. "Especially with us as boyfriends."

Arrie's hand lands heavy on my thigh.

I look to Connie, who's looking at the three of us with some kind of look I can't interpret. "Ready to go on our date?"

She looks at me with wide eyes and a giant smile. "Yes, yes, yes!" Then jumps to her feet. "What do you want to do tonight?"

"Did you have anything in mind?" She usually does, and I'm happy to go along with the plan.

"Ohhh, the tickets!" She runs out of the library and comes back a couple of minutes later with the concert tickets I got her for Christmas waving in the air. "They're for tonight. I totally forgot."

"Then what are we waiting for?"

She looks at what we're both wearing and scowls. "Better clothes for a start."

I sigh, then giggle. "I'm going to get to see you naked before we leave, aren't I?"

She slaps me on the butt as she grabs my hand and yanks me along behind her. "Babe, you're gonna get a round two before we leave."

Arrie and Dea snicker as we leave, promising to keep up the research while we're gone. And I give a silent look to Arrie, telling him to keep an eye on Dea. He's doing better than before, but grief is fickle—it rises and falls as often as the sun.

"So," Connie starts, "what you thinking?" She rifles through my wardrobe and drawers until she's gotten a few options for me to try out. "Something more shorts and knee-highs or something more dress and tights."

"As long as there's a choker, I'm down." My words flash Arrie's hands gripping my neck across my mind, and I absently rub the bruise that's basically faded.

"Is that . . .?" My flush meets her gaze, and she squeals. "Tell me everything!" She chucks the tights she had in her hands onto the bed and drags me to the chairs in the corner. "Now."

"Well, I went up to talk about things, to at least try some communication. But he was too angry, and he was struggling to feel anything else. So I drank his blood and punched him in the face."

Connie's eyes go wide as she gasps. "You . . . punched him in the face?"

"I tried to. He blocked. But we fought for a little bit, letting some of his anger out, but then he changed the game and . . . threw me into a wall, pinned me there, and went down on me."

"That does not explain the bruise on your neck, hon."

"It didn't really end there."

Her hands ball into excited fists that she calms down with a few breaths, her braids bouncing everywhere. "There's more. There's more. Okay, okay. There's more."

I giggle, because she's being ridiculous, but I carry on with the story, anyway. "When we were done, and he finally understood why I'm leaving to get Nine back, I asked him to fuck me." I'm just leave out the part where he said he'd make love to me and then utterly destroyed my vagina. "So he did."

"How? In what way?"

"You are very into my sex life."

Her hands throw themselves into the air in exasperation. "I am your sex life."

True.

"Well, first we were just having sex normally, with him on top, but then he flipped me over onto all fours and . . ."

"Oh my god, he pulled you to him by the throat, didn't he?"

I just nod, embarrassment flooding me, my eyes wanting to look anywhere but at Connie. Which is stupid. She's seen me in all kinds of positions.

She squeals again. "Does that mean he'll be with us sometimes when we're all together together?"

I shrug. "I dunno. We haven't talked about it. But assuming he wants to, yeah."

Connie's eye light up like Christmas Day morning, but she looks over to the clock on the wall and to the clothes on the bed, then sighs. "We need to get a move on."

So I try on a few outfits in both forms, test them out, and settle on a pair of shorts with a long skirt flowing down the back of them that I've wanted an excuse to wear for weeks. Paired with a black tee, a harness, a choker (obviously), and my hair wavy down my back.

"Maybe I should change my hair color soon?" I suggest as we head to Connie's room to pick out something for her.

"Ohh, what you thinking?"

"Maybe something like the midnight sky or galaxy kind of colors?"

Her room looms ahead, and when we enter, Connie darts straight for her wardrobe and pulls out a short dress on a hanger. "I've had it picked out for weeks."

It's strappy, short enough I'm sure I'll see plenty of ass tonight, and a kind of burgundy color I wouldn't pick out for someone else. But on Connie, it'll look amazing.

She's amazing.

When she's pulling the tight dress down her body—one I can't stop staring at (and maybe there's a little drool, but shh)—she asks, "When you getting your hair done? Can I come with? Ohh, maybe I should change my hair color too?"

"What kind of color?"

"I don't know. I've never dyed it before."

Now it's my turn to choke in surprise. "Really? Like, never? Not in two thousand years?"

She shrugs. "I really like my hair. It's beautiful. But maybe changing it up might be fun. Besides, it'll just grow back out."

"There are color removing spells nowadays, anyway. If you hate it, I can just make one and change it back."

"Sold!" She laces up her boots and finishes her lipstick, then turns around to me. "Okay, I'm ready."

My charm bracelet snaps into my staff as I wrap an arm around her waist and teleport us to Madison Square Garden. Thankfully, I've been here before. Otherwise we would have had to fly here from somewhere and ruin our hair.

The normally blue lights up the side of the building flash different colors—pink, blue, green, orange, then red—in sequence as the queues move slowly in through the doors.

The queue takes ages to get through, but eventually we're buying drinks from the bar and fighting our way through to the front of the crowd, where we cradle our two beers each like they're our lifeline. But one look at Connie downing one of hers, and I guess I have to get rid of one.

Oh well, bottom's up.

Beer is gross by the way—0/10 don't recommend—but it does the job. And by the time the warmup acts are done and I've found a new all-girl rock group to listen to in the future, the main act lights up the stage, and I get to watch as Connie loses her shit.

She sings along, dances as best she can in the space, and screams and shouts at all the right moments—or whenever she damn pleases, it would seem. She wraps her arms around me from behind, pushing me into the railing, and shouts into my ear, "This is the best Christmas present ever! I'll say thank you when we get home! Or sooner if you're lucky."

I only just caught that last bit, but the words lick flames up my neck and melt me into a pile of goo. Public sex? Hell yes.

I think.

Maybe.

Oh, what the hell. Connie'll persuade me and I'll love every second of it. That seems to be how this goes with the team. And I'm happy to just be along for the ride.

The two Fae members of the band fly through the air while singing all the high notes, the skirts flowing in the wind. The rune circle on the floor lights up, changing the color of all their outfits simultaneously, and the crows roar.

But as the song continues and the chorus repeats for the second time, Connie slips a hand up my skirt and layers kisses down my neck.

Wait, here?

Like, right here, right now?

But before I can overthink things, her fingers are sliding past the edges of my thong and delving low, cupping, and sliding into me with a gasp. She latches her lips onto my neck, clearly trying to match Arrie's bruise that's since faded, and sucks and nips and licks as her fingers curl and the palm of her hand grinds.

I look up onto the stage and find none of the women are looking our way anyway— and around us are only other adults. So I stop worrying and rock my hips into her hand, chasing the feeling now pumping through my body in time to the music.

She tries to whisper something in my ear, but I can't catch it, as the music changes and they play another of their songs I've heard Connie listening to.

Music pounds through me as notes hit my ears and Connie's fingers play me like an expert, her fingers pressing firmer and her hand grinding faster. My gasps get lost in a sea of voices.

Connie pulls my head back to meet hers, and her gaze catches me on fire as her lips suck mine in a frenzied passion I have no struggles meeting.

Oh, shit.

My body drowns as my head falls back onto her shoulder, the guitar solo ripping through the air, rendering my screams unheard. Pointless. But Connie laps them up, and when I've stopping convulsing around her, she grabs both sides of my panties and tears them in half, removing them from my body and tucking them into her pocket with a wink.

She then leans into my ear and shout-whispers, "Don't worry, I'm not done yet."

Crowds of people disperse as the concert ends, and while we take ages to exit the arena, we hold hands and chat all things music.

"Soooo . . ." Connie squeals. "Who are we seeing next time?"

I laugh, because only Connie would ask that. "Well, we could see that Fae band you like?" Their show is supposed to be full of magic as well as music. "That sounds like fun."

"Ohmygod, yes. Seeing 'In Flight' live would be a dream!" Her giddiness is infectious. She looks to me and asks, "Remind me why we're not just teleporting ourselves outside?"

"Because I'd drag everyone within the spell circle's radius with us." I gesture to the crowds of people around us. "And I don't wanna scare them."

She chuckles to herself, probably finding the idea of teleporting a bunch of random strangers without telling them hilarious. I am not such a demon. Well, I might do that to Arrie—but he's an asshole, so that doesn't count.

"What are you chuckling at?" She nudges my shoulder.

"Just thinking about teleporting Arrie to Alaska without telling him."

"Have you been before?"

I shake my head. "Be worth the trip, though."

"Even better if you make sure he's not got any teleporting crystals on him. He'd have to fly back to the main portal."

"Oooh, you're evil." I lean in and kiss her forehead. "I love it."

I picked the hotel this time, and knowing Connie, I went extravagant. Exclusive. If I were with Arrie, I might have picked somewhere we could camp, but I'm not. Connie likes finer things, so I'm going to provide the finest.

We weave out of crowds and find ourselves in a street with a large enough space that I can teleport us to the hotel doors, then I collapse my staff back into a charm bracelet and wrap my arm through hers.

"Well, that's easier."

"Yup." I gesture to the grand revolving door of the Highlight Hotel. "Your chamber awaits, my lady." I gesture her in as she giggles.

The bellhop notices us straight away and guides us to reception, where we're given a room key and a smile; we don't even have to provide our names.

"Seems you're well known now," Connie suggests. "Well, I guess after our interviews and all the video footage, people just know us." She looks to the floor, her eyes floating with something definitely not positive while her smile vanishes for a second. "We'll never get back to being anonymous, will we?"

We both enter the elevator, guided by our silent bellhop.

"I don't think we should be, but if we stay out of the way for a few hundred years, we'll just be a piece of history." I wrap an arm around her shoulders and guide her eyes to mine. "If that's what we want."

I'd do anything for the team. For my family.

The bellhop clears his throat as the elevator dings. "Follow me, please." He guides us to a room at the end of a winding hallway, the doors to which are double, made of aged wood, and have an endless plating of gold swirling all around them. "Your rooms, Magic." He nods to me, then to Connie. "Conquest." And turns away on his heels.

Unlocking the door with the fancy keychip covered in artwork made of vines, we step inside.

There are vines in the ceiling, weaving through the beams like they were carved from a tree, and the vines drape in some places, with the occasional piece hanging all the way to the floor.

"Ohhh, now that's a nice bed," Connie says as she jumps on the four-poster opposite the window. She spreads her arms wide but doesn't manage to touch the edges. The brown and gold bedsheets beneath her crumple as she rolls to standing and rejoins me. "You okay?"

"I don't think I'll ever get used to staying in places this amazing. It feels like I have a rich sugar daddy."

"Or four." Connie exhales slowly. "Three."

Both of our eyes crumple as they close, inhaling our breaths together. I tangle my fingers with hers.

"C'mon," I say on a sigh. "Let's check out the bathroom." I drag her through the door behind us and breathe another sigh of relief when I see a claw foot tub big enough for the both of us.

As Connie stands in front of the mirror, I run the hot water and put in all the bubbles, salts, and silky goodness I can find in the caddy provided by the hotel. I slowly take off her dress, remove her bra and panties, then grab a makeup wipe out of my purse and wipe her face clean. All the while her mind is somewhere else; Nine, Bandio Bontanas, or somewhere else in her past, I don't know. But I'm going to stay here.

Her eyes refocus on the present, exiting their distant gazing, and she looks down to find me wiping the last of her foundation off. "Sorry."

My hand cups her cheek. "You never have to apologize for existing, Conquest."

"I know. I just feel I ruin our dates sometimes. When I can't pull my thoughts in and I just . . ." Her words trail off, probably unsure how to complete the sentence.

"You could never ruin our dates. I love you even when you're sad." I grab her hand

and walk her toward the bathtub that's now full and appropriately bubbly. "Maybe even more so because that's when you need my love the most."

Connie doesn't say anything as I help her step into the tub, and when I follow, I nest her between my legs and let her head fall back onto my chest, her hair spreading out in the bubbles next to us. I wander my hands over her chest, through her hair, across her forehead, and lie with her in the water, relaxing. Allowing the heat to light the chill on fire and set the grief aflame.

"You know, I used to be a badass."

I laugh, because that's ridiculous. "You're still a badass."

"Maybe the badassery is taking a break."

"Breaks are good," I mumble against her forehead before placing gentle kisses there. "They let you know who you are."

"Maybe," she says as she turns around to face me, hovering her naked body inches above mine, her breasts pressed against mine, "I want to be more of a lover than a fighter for a while."

"Yeah?" I push her hair back so I can see her beautiful face better. "And who will I have to compete with for all this loving attention?"

She smiles, and goddess, it lights up the room. "No one. I'm all yours. Always."

"Then let me love you," I whisper across her lips before letting them brush together in a hint of passion. "Let me make you feel like you're on top of the world."

A small laugh escapes her lips on a sigh. "You've been spending too much time around Dea." Her knees kick open my legs as far as they'll go, before she grabs them and throws them over the side of the bath and her hands grope my breasts before mumbling, "Been learning all the good words."

"I'll say whatever it takes to make you smile and get you in my bed, Connie." I sigh as she takes my lips in hers again. "I'll wax poetic or talk dir—"

Her fingers pinch my nipples, then roll them around, and a moan slips free as my hips shift forward, seeking friction.

"That sound is all the motivation I need." One hand slips beneath the water and cups my pussy, a finger resting teasingly on my entrance. "I'll let you love me, but only once I'm done with you."

My head falls back onto the bath's rim, and she sinks a single finger into me, hooking it just right, and slowly rubs circles as she presses her palm into my clit. It's slow—so slow it's barely there—but it's doing things to my head, making it spin with its arms out as music dances in my ears.

She bends her head to my neck and laces kisses up to my ear, shivers traveling down my body. "I want you to eat me after I'm done with you. I want you to bury your tongue in me while you get yourself off. And I want to watch you do it."

She adds a second finger, slowly, and speeds up ever so slightly, almost unnoticeable, but she grinds her palm harder—short, fast circles.

My bent knees start to shake as they clench the sides of the tub, and she grins, delight filling her face.

"That's it, babe." Her forehead rests on mine, her nose toughing my own. "Take it."

My hips grind into her hand, picking up enough speed to slosh some of the water over the sides of the bath. "S-s-shit."

Connie squeezes my nipple before rolling it around between her fingers, then she bends her head over my arched chest and sucks the other into her mouth. Her teeth grazing my nipple slightly.

My hips buck as her fingers move fast, sending lightning through me, and my legs squeeze the sides of the bath. "Connie . . ." I spasm around her fingers, gushing into the water, as my whole body lights on fire. My hips thrash, chasing the orgasm as my screams echo off the tiles.

"Fuck yes," Connie mumbles around my nipple.

I grind and buck and thrust until the sensation subsides and I'm nothing more than a wet, panting mess in a bathtub only half filled with water. No bubbles left.

32

She carries my dripping body to the bed, where she throws me onto the covers and stands at the end. Lording over me. "I'm not done with you." She crawls between my legs and peppers kisses to my knees, up my thighs, and stops at the junction between them and my throbbing pussy. "You can play with me all you want another day, but tonight, I want you to myself before I have to hand you back to the guys and share."

I can't manage a single coherent word, so I just nod my head and let it fall to the mattress. All I can do is feel the heat of her hands on my thighs and the wet, firm tongue that's licking the outside of me, cleaning me up.

Her tongue dips in, then out, then back in, but not far enough. Just enough to tease.

"Connie . . ." I groan, hands grabbing her hair and pulling her back to me.

"Such a needy Vampire," she chuckles. And as she says that, my fangs slip free from my control. "I love that you can't control it. That I'm making you wild." Her mouth returns to its mission, teasing my lips, running her tongue up past my slit and to my clit, where she rubs quick, harsh circles that make my eyelids flash silver and my fists clutch the bedsheets.

Too much. Too much, too quickly. I hiss with oversensitivity, but she doesn't care.

She wraps her lips around my clit and sucks, her tongue flicking quick flicks.

My hips come off the bed as I moan, thrusting into her face, and she slips her hands beneath my ass and holds me to her, not allowing me to pull back.

Pulling one hand away, she hooks three fingers inside me and yanks them back out, then shoves them in. Hard. Fast. As though she can tell I want it rougher than the bathroom.

"Ah, goddess. Yes!"

My hips shift in what little room Connie allows them to have, holding me to her as she sucks my clit between her teeth.

The room spins as my eyes clench shut, my fangs and pussy throbbing in tandem. The obscene sounds coming from her working me spur me on, and before I know it, another orgasm crests. "Fuckfuckfuck," I hiss between clenched teeth. My hips buck in her hand as she continues pumping me, riding me through.

As the orgasm subsides, she sets me down on the bed and lays her head on my stomach her hips shifting into a grind on the bed every now and then.

Fuck. No.

I'm never leaving this woman wanting.

She's mine.

I flip her off me and pin her to the bed, our eyes meeting. I'm sure mine are red, and when I realize this, I look away, shutting them.

"No, don't look away."

"Connie, it's okay if you'd prefer—"

"Shh. It's okay. I want you to look at me."

And so I meet her green eyes, her perfect smile, and her flushed cheeks, and I kiss her, tasting myself on her lips as I grind into her.

Her tongue licks up and down my fangs, re-stoking the fire, but I take back control and pin her hips against the bed to match her arms. She can't move. Or escape.

And while I can see a flicker of fear pass her eyes every now and then, the roaring lust I see in them surpasses any concerns I might have.

She bites her lip, and my eyes track the movement. "Just . . . don't bite me."

"I won't." I layer a kiss to her neck, allowing her to writhe beneath me, trying to gain some kind of friction between us, to please herself. But I stay just out of reach.

"Magic . . . Babe?"

I lift my head, concern filling me.

She laughs and flips us over so I'm beneath her again. "You really fell for that?"

"That was a dirty trick."

Her legs split mine apart, then her knee presses hard onto me, and I shameless grind, seeking friction. Pleasure. Her.

"Don't worry," she whispers. "I'll get you off again." She straddles me and crawls her way up my body so she's kneeling over my breasts. "But first you're gonna open up."

My mouth slips open, my tongue shamelessly seeking her out, wanting her taste to mark it.

She parts her knees farther open, lowering herself onto my face, and the moment my tongue can reach her, I lick a stripe from top to bottom as she grabs hold of the pole in the center of the bed top. She uses it to rub herself over my mouth, her skin over my fangs, her juices coating my tongue. "Get yourself off," she groans. "Please."

I reach my hand around her, finding myself still dripping, and shove as many fingers as I can inside me, desperate to feel that high.

Connie looks over her shoulder and moans. "Yeah, like that." She grinds against me, using me like a personal sex toy.

But I do my best to keep up, to spear my tongue inside her, to suck on her clitoris like she did mine, to avoid piercing her with my fangs that are running through her folds with every grind of her hips. I seal my lips over her clitoris, not letting go, even as she tries to pull away.

And her moans inch toward screams as my name slips from her lips. "Magic . . ." She slams her hips back down and rides me, grinding against my mouth as I flick my tongue around, inside, and across.

Her sounds shoot through me, making me convulse, as my fingers pierce into me harder, faster. As I remember her mouth on me, my legs wrapped around the side of the bathtub, my dick buried inside her while we laid naked in the gardens.

"Magic, shit, yes," she groans as her moans reach fever pitch and her juices explode into my mouth.

My hand moves faster as she uses me, and my legs shake as I moan, not able to hold it back, which only seems to heighten her orgasm, the vibrations sending her wild as she slams her pussy into my mouth and I suck and lick as hard and fast I can.

"MMMMMagic!"

Her screams send me over the edge, and before I know it, I'm grinding and thrusting onto my hand, my hips bending off the bed. Fuck, fuck, fuck.

Her grinding slows to a halt, and my hand stills as my butt falls back onto the bed.

"Fuck yeah," she says on a sigh as she flops next to me. "We're doing that again."

"Uh-huh," I manage before sleep exhaustion takes me.

CHAPTER 33

Arrie's arms wrap tight around my waist, his nose nestled into my neck. "Don't die, Killer." His heart pounds against my back, rapid, thrusting beats that unsteady me and halt my breath. "Just come back alive."

Connie wraps her arms around the front of me, meeting Arrie's torso at my back, and she breathes me in. "I'm scared. But I know you have to go. I'm just sorry I can't be there with you."

Dea stands next to us, his wings folding around us all, then dropping to the ground. Silent. He doesn't need to say anything.

Connie looks up at me and runs her hand through my white hair. "Bring him back."

I smile, my tongue stuck in my throat.

"We will." Dea hugs us with his wings and then backs off, dragging me with him. "Come on."

I untangle myself from Connie and Arrie and let Dea drag me out the back door, where I portal us to Earth and reform my staff into its charm bracelet form.

Dea sweeps me onto his feet and wraps a golden arm around my waist for security. "Ready?"

"Ready."

He shoots us into the sky, high enough to be soaring near the clouds, and everything below looks so insignificant, but it's mine to protect. Ours. It's a world that's ours to protect.

But we can't do it without Famine.

"It is going to get hard to breathe."

Right.

I write a rune pattern on my throat, then swallow a bayus leaf, and mutter a small incantation. As I breathe my next breath, an air bubble forms around my head. A pocket of air that recycles my exhales into oxygen for me to inhale.

We spend a good hour flying in what seems like a random direction, but Dea knows where he's going. He has been doing this for two thousand years. I trust him.

Eventually, after boredom passed long ago, a black dot grows in the distance. It looms ever closer. Bigger and bigger. Until I'm breathless from its magnificence and wide-eyed from its beauty.

The spell wraps around its entirety, forming a black shimmer over a pair of gates made from something that looks like plasma, something equally made from the leyline energy.

"Get me closer. I need to touch them."

Dea's breath hitches, fear no doubt coursing through him. But he obeys.

And soon I'm touching the energy that makes up the Black Gates to the Otherworld. Beyond this is the land of the dead. And the severity of what I'm about to do settles on my heart like a lead weight.

A complex, almost unreadable spell graces my fingertips. I could spend years and never finish unraveling it. Multiple generations of Fae created this from a time long before records began—from a time before myth.

I try to file through the basics, see the building blocks, but they're buried beneath tangled webs of interweaving spellwork I can't decipher. "It's really old. I can't really read much of it." I sigh, defeat washing over me. I don't know if I can do this. "Even the runes are foreign."

"Breathe, Angel." He rubs my shoulder and places a gentle kiss to my neck. "I know you can do this."

He's right. I can do this.

I was made for this.

Or remade.

Whatever.

After a few deep breaths, I shove all the tangled network of spells aside to see if there's anything underneath; and there, beneath centuries of spellwork, is a single, seemingly innocent rune.

I graze a single finger of it, and glowing blue lines upon lines shoot out from the gate, scattering in all directions, beyond what the eye can see.

"What are they?" Dea asks.

I spin us around a little, getting a better look, and gasp. "They're the leylines. The Black Gate is powering the leylines."

"But that is . . . impossible."

"Well, they had to come from somewhere."

Dea wraps both arms around me tighter and spins us back to the gate. "I just assumed they were natural, like the Earth."

"Even the Earth was made from something, Dea."

"I guess so."

I shrug. "We just don't think about it because it happened so long ago." Grazing my hand along the rune, I take a deep breath. "Right, Magic. Focus."

The rune seems innocent enough, but upon closer inspection, it seems like it's one rune made of many, as though someone just took various parts of many runes and glued them together to create some kind of rune hybrid. The level of knowledge and skill this one aspect of the spell took is simply insurmountable.

I'll never be this good.

At least not right now.

And that's not me being pessimistic; that's me knowing my current limits. I can't rewrite this rune or rub it out or replace parts of it. It's simply beyond me. So I'll have to do something else. But I do take a mental picture of what it looks like, because I'm gonna study the shit out of this piece of orgasmic beauty later.

"You okay there, Angel?"

"Huh?" I whip my head around to look at Dea's smiling face. "Oh, yeah. I'm fine. Just concentrating."

"Uh-huh."

Weaving out from that single monster-mash rune are three lines of spells—all different —formed of various smaller runes, some of which I recognize, some of which rings some bells, and some of which I've never seen before. There's also a green glow around them, which I've come to notice is what happens when an incantation is used. Usually I can kinda feel it, like an echo, when I run my hands through it, and when doing it to this one, it's like a loud shout. Like it hasn't been heard in years and it's excited to finally see me.

It vibrates around my hand.

"Hey, little fella. Wanna tell me what your incantation is? You'd be being super helpful."

"What the hell are you doing?" Dea whispers in my ear.

I ignore him. I don't have the brain space right now to explain how this spell feels alive, and how it feels like it's communicating to me. And I don't know how to say that without sounding insane.

Ergo, I'm saying nothing.

The spell vibrates harder, tickling my hand and sending vibrations up to my elbow.

"You like it when I talk to you, huh?"

It vibrates harder, sending further tingles up to my elbow. It tickles, and I want to yank my hand away, but I don't want to offend the spell. Maybe if I can find a way of getting it to answer yes or no, I can narrow down the spell somehow?

"Ready to help?"

The vibration tickles my hand again.

"Okay, vibrate for yes, do nothing for no. Understand?"

More vibrations.

"Alright. I'm trying to find out what you do. How you affect the spells around the three threads. Do you bind them in some way?"

Nothing happens.

"Okay. Do you enhance them?"

Again, nothing.

Maybe . . . "Are you the spell, and the runes are supporting you?"

The vibration starts up, getting faster, and I have to fight the urge to yank my hand away as a giggle escapes my lips.

"Ohh, yay. Okay. Okay." I run my other hand through my white hair and take a deep breath. I file through the three strands, seeing what runes are there, seeing what ones I recognize and what they could possibly mean. "I think this one stabilizes you in some way."

A light vibration tickles my palm.

The other two are trickier to read, focusing on runes that I don't recognize and that look like some kind of older runic language, almost similar to the scribbles I've seen Arrie make from time to time.

"These are like Norse?"

The vibrations start up again.

"But they're not quite the same. They're curvier."

Dea leans in. "But that means they are at least two centuries old, if not older."

"So they predate you?"

"It would seem that way, yes." His wings flap gently, keeping us in the air.

"So the Black Gate existed before you, along with whatever you want to call the land that lies beyond it?"

"Yes." He tightens his grip on my waist. "I simply opened them before. I did not create or destroy them. But they were locked, and no one could figure out how to open them. And there was kind of an army of angels guarding them."

"So you killed the angels and opened the gate, allowing everyone to pass on?"

"Humans were already passing on, but supernaturals were not. So I opened the gate, and then they seemed to be able to open and close at will."

"Can you open it again?"

Dea nods. He flies us up higher, to the center of the gates, and grabs the knocker bigger than his head. "Ready?"

"Ready." I grab his arms tight, my teeth clenched hard, my knuckles white. "Let's go."

He grabs the knocker and lifts it, then throws it back down. The loud knock that follows shakes the air, sending a gust of wind through us so strong, Dea has to flap to keep us from being blown away. Then he lifts it again. And again.

And the Black Gates, the entrance to the afterlife, opens.

"Remember," he says close to my ear, "you cannot pull a soul back out. And I do not know if I can pull you in."

"I know." I place my hands on the spell the entire time, mapping what changes, looking at the runes that activate and logging what each one does. "But now I have more pieces to this puzzle."

"Huh. That was clever of you."

His praise shoots through me, lighting me up.

And I place my hand again on the three strands shooting out of the monster-mash rune, but something's different. The incantation that seemed alive is now subdued in some way. I look up, winding my way through the tangle of spells that follow those three, and gasp.

Light bulb moment.

It's not subdued, it's spread. The tangled spells are now also green, glowing from the spread of the incantation.

"The knock!" I breathe in, my bubble still keeping me oxygenated. "The knock is the incantation. Because it doesn't have to be words. It can be any sound."

Dea listens silently for a change, taking it all in.

The gates, on the other hand, continue to open as light spills from beyond. Light that blinds and clarifies simultaneously. Light that, without, would make life feel cold and empty. It's a feeling I've had before, but I can't place. Like a long-lost emotion that reverberates through every life, that one thing that makes us all vibrate with power but no one has ever come up with a word for before.

"What is that feeling?" I mumble.

"It is the feeling of life keeping us alive, the energy that makes our heart beat even when we do not want it to. It is soul-deep love."

"Has anyone else ever felt this besides you?"

"Every soul that passes feels like this and continues to feel like this for all of eternity. It is what we miss out on being immortal."

That's . . . "Is pulling Nine back not selfish, then? If this is how happy he is, how content, then are we doing the right thing?"

Dea chuckles behind me, his chest vibrating against my back. "I am done doing the right thing for the benefit of everyone else. For once, I want to do the selfish thing. Even if that is the wrong thing."

"Okay then, but if I break the world, this is also your fault."

"I am happy to share blame."

"Good."

Dea flies us forward, to the edge of the gate's border, and tries to push us across, but an invisible barrier prevents us.

"*Kutabare.* I can't cross." I run my hands up the spellwork again, seeing if there's some kind of database or barrier spell I recognize. "But I don't know what I'm looking for." I'm hoping to just add myself to whatever spell mojo it has going on, but what prevents living beings from entering a space?

"Maybe it is like an if statement."

"A what?"

"A piece of logic that lets the spell make decisions based on certain information, like your status of being alive or dead."

"Okay, so I'm looking for more of a scanner, then." I run my hands through the threads, and notice a vibration pulling one of the original three. The second one that I couldn't identify earlier. "This one?"

The vibration tickles my hand again.

"Hmm." A concentrating hand strokes through my hair. "Okay." The runes seem to be scanning something, or trying to gather information from an external source. It's like they're pulling our essence inwards, toward themselves, and analyzing it. "So, this is what's scanning us?"

I wish I had a camera or something on me. I'm never gonna remember all this to study later.

But where does it store the information? That's what I need to alter. That's what I need to change.

I trace the information, follow it along the thread, and find it somewhere in the tangle, in a small bundle of knots made of various runes so complicated reading them makes me dizzy.

But I have to read them.

If I don't, I'll never rescue Nine.

So I begin at a random point, running along the runes like I would a sentence, but then I realize that's wrong. This isn't a linear rune construction. It's a Norse one. Or something similar. And in Norse, when you put the runes together, it forms a picture that symbolizes a specific meaning. Like hieroglyphics.

I pull back and look at the small knot within the larger tangle in a more generic way, like zooming out to see the bigger picture.

"It's me." I'm the rune. They align and shift to an image of the person—well, to an image of the person's face. And next to me is Dea, only more a more accurate depiction than it's created of me. Probably due to having created it before. "The runes create an image of us."

"I see it. It is . . . fascinating."

"Insane. This is insane. I can't imagine inventing this."

"Seems it would take more than a single generation, so it is likely the brain of many."

But I still don't know how to adjust this. How is it analyzing that I'm alive? Where in the image does it state I'm alive? And how? I'm technically dead. But maybe it doesn't read life that way. Maybe it simply reads if I'm a body.

But Dea's a body. Which means it makes an exception.

So instead of looking at me, I look at Dea and try to trace a difference, try to spot what his has that mine doesn't. I mean, it glows a fainter green, and it's a clearer picture, plus his eyes look all huge and weird, but they're otherwise the same.

I inspect those eyes, and that's when I notice it. The runes are different. His contain a rune in each eye, while mine are empty. So if I just copy them over to my eyes, it should just . . . let me pass.

As I do that, my hand slips through the barrier, and I gasp, inhaling the clean, crisp air of beyond.

"You did it!" Dea lifts me up and spins me around like a princess. "You found a way to get a living soul beyond the Black Gate." He crashes me back to him and smashes his lips to mine. "You. Are. Amazing," he says between kisses.

"Well, I try." I shrug. "But I still don't know how to get Nine out."

"I have never tried pulling a soul out before, so I do not know for certain if I can just . . . pull."

"Just like that?"

"Just like that."

"That probably won't work."

"No, but it is worth trying the simple thing before you have to deal with that spell again."

"I'm calling it the monster spell."

"Monster spell? Good name."

"I thought so." I step off my feet and look around me, marveling at the simplicity of . . . heaven? The afterlife? A soul's home? Whatever you want to call it, it's . . . kind of empty. "Where are all the souls?"

"Wherever they want to be. This space isn't physical, so it has no space limit."

I look around the empty space, pacing along the stones of the courtyard beneath my feet, and eventually happen upon a fountain; and sat upon that fountain, in a nerd pun t-shirt that reads 'I am Schrodinger's Cat' with clever alive/dead wording underneath, is Nine.

My boyfriend.

He looks up at me, then down at the hand entwined in Dea's, and smiles. *I've been waiting for you.*

34

"Nine," I whisper. My voice is barely audible, barely edging into existence. But it's there. Meeting his ears.

Dea doesn't move. His hand stays laced with mine, his lips part but no sound comes out, and his body trembles, like an emotional earthquake rumbles through him. "I . . ."

"Oh god," Nine says, standing up, "did you have a massive breakdown?"

Dea lets go of my hand and jumps into Nine's waiting arms. "Nine." His sobs echo around the empty space, joining mine.

Nine looks at me and smiles. *You gonna come here or stand there gawking?*

I didn't think I could do it. I didn't think I could be here.

I know.

I wrap my arms around them both, sandwiching Dea between us, and breathe in the bonfire, lavender, paper smell that is them both together. Both halves of my triad.

"You know," Nine says, "it's been boring as hell waiting for you, bro." He lets Dea hug him for as long as he wants, saying nothing about the snot and tears running down his shoulder or the tighter-than-Earth grip he's squeezing him with. But he looks at me, and those orange-brown eyes bore into mine with the intensity of the sun. "I didn't think I'd get to see you, Sweetie."

"You'd not believe the lock on that gate," I say while wiping my tears away and composing myself. "The spell of the century, that one."

His brows dip in confusion. "Spell?"

"Oh, yeah. The Black Gate is a Fae spell, and it powers the leylines."

His eyes widen, his breath stopping short. "Really?" *That's awesome. You could switch off the leylines and render the Fae powerless.*

Yeeeah, maybe in another hundred years, when I've untangled that spell.

Oh, right.

Are you two done geeking out? Dea asks in our heads, I assume projected by Nine. *Because my eyeliner has never looked this bad.*

I switch forms—

Only, my body doesn't switch.

"Why can't I switch?"

They both turn to me, looking confusing.

"I can't shift back into my female form."

At all?

"Nope." I sigh. "For goddess' sake, I left my handbag with my other form."

Dea raises an eyebrow.

"It had eyeliner in."

Here. Nine grabs the bottom of his shirt and uses it to wipe away the black-stained tears smearing over Dea's cheeks and around his eyes. And when he's done, they just stare at each other.

At the same time, they stretch out their hands to me, and I grab them. They yank me to them.

"It is not complete without you, Angel." Dea looks down at me and smiles in relief, in genuine, heart-throbbing happiness. "It is not a competition."

No, but if it were, I'd win best t-shirt.

Have you seen some of my crop tops? They are works of art!

"This." He points to his t-shirt. "This is something I made up. You can just ask for anything your mind conjures, and it'll pop out at you. Like the house but an upgrade." He gestures to the left (well, I think it's left. Is it left when all around you is white emptiness?), and a house pops up.

A small house with cottage windows and a cute red door, like it popped out of a fairy-tale book for children and said hello in a cute Disney voice.

Nine, still holding onto our hands, drags us that way with a small smile. "Welcome to my home."

"Home?" Dea asks. "Your home is on Earth, with us."

I run a frustrated hand through my hair. "Yeah, we've come to take you back."

He rushes us to the door and shoves us through, then slams it shut behind us. "I know why you're here." He turns to face us, a solemn expression on his face. "But you can't take me back."

"Well, not yet." I shake my head. "I haven't figured out how to get you past the spell, but with enough time, I can—"

"No, no, no. You don't understand. I can't leave." Nine walks to a small living room and slumps onto the couch. "Angels guard this place. And like the Angels on Earth, they're strong, ruthless, and are numerous enough to form an army."

Dea sits beside Nine and places a hand on his shoulder. "You do not seriously expect us to just turn around and leave, do you?"

I sit on his other side, my hand on his knee. "We came to take you home, and we're not leaving until you do." Nothing will stand in our way. "And we don't have all the time in the world, because we left Earth in the hands of Connie and Arrie."

Nine sighs and lets his head fall into his hands. "They're more likely to kill the entire Fae Court than fix anything. You know that, right?"

Dea smirks at me. "Well, Magic may have mellowed Arrie out a little recently, so maybe not."

"Dea," I groan.

Nine swivels his head my way and smiles. "So you got my message, then?"

Message? Huh? "Oh, when we were at the old village ruins?"

He nods.

"Yeah, I got it."

Figured a little dead boyfriend energy might give you a boost.

"Nine!" Dea slaps his arm. "Do not joke about that."

Too soon, buddy. He turns to me and asks, "Do you have a plan for my body, or are you expecting me to be a ghost in your harem?"

"I am not fucking a ghost for the rest of time, so yes, I have a plan." I try my best to block out the image of me being witchy and hoping for the best, but I don't think I succeed, because he looks at me all stern like.

"That's your plan?"

I shrug. "I'll deal with it later, okay. For now, let's just work on getting you out of here." I look to Dea. "I need you to lead. This is far too precarious to leave up to my stupid brain."

"Agreed." He stands to his feet and starts pacing. "So we need to sneak you out of here, avoid the Angels, and do so without really knowing if we can move you past the barrier?"

"Yup."

That about sums it up, yeah.

"Okay, Magic." He turns to me. "You need to go back to the gate with Nine and see what happens. I will distract the Angels and meet you there."

"That's the best you can come up with?" I ask, incredulous.

"Do I look like Arrie to you?" He crosses his arms over his chest. "He is the one with the fancy battle strategy ability. I am not."

I sigh, running a hand through my hair and along my neck, where it rests as I look up to Nine's living room ceiling. "How many?" I swivel my eyes to Nine.

"Too many to count."

35

"You're the Angel of Death, Dea!" My hands ball into fists, my voice stretches thin. "They should just let you do what you want."

"That is not how it works," he hisses through clenched teeth.

"How do you know that?" I jump to my feet and yell. "How do you know what will happen?"

"I don't!" He faces me as he stops pacing the length of the living room. A stressed hand runs across his neck. "But I am not risking either of your lives trying." His golden eyes pin me to the floor. "I cannot lose you too."

"Err . . . guys?"

"Then don't." I take a deep breath. "Fight to keep us both."

"I do not know how to do that, Angel."

"Guys?"

Dea wraps a wing around me, shooting warmth and comfort through my body. "It is an unknown."

"Everything we do is unknown." My hands firmly on his chest, I push him away an inch. "I never know what I'm doing, everything is on a whim. I just have to trust that Fate knows what it's doing."

Guys! Nine snaps.

"What?" Dea and I yell simultaneously.

Nine just points out the window, which is no longer white nothingness. A white forest with shimmery blue layered over top flicks into existence, trees taller than I can see, with grass and ferns trailing a forest longer than I can possibly imagine.

They're coming.

Dea looks to me, a panicked look on his face, and asks, "What do we do?"

"Soldier up, Horsemen."

Dea grabs one of his daggers out of his belt and throws it to Nine, who catches it with a smirk. He looks at me with a question, but I shake my head.

Instead, I get my hands ready to create some Angel-kicking spells. Not that I know any. But this is a great time to try.

Never know when that might come in handy.

Outside, air circulates in waves of fresh breezes I didn't know were missing, and the grass beneath my feet wavers as I inhale deeply.

Then, on the edge of the forest's horizon, a line of white soldiers appears, armor the same color as their skin, power the same intensity as Glowy's.

"Dea," I whisper. "Get ready to grab Nine and fly."

He looks to me with panic in his eyes, the golden irises swirling in worry.

"I need you to trust me."

He nods.

"Just try to see if you can pass him through the barrier." I turn to Nine. "Let me know if he can or not."

Nine nods, then offers me his daggers.

I shake my head. "I don't need them. But thanks."

"Remember," Dea warns, "you cannot shift form here. Fae and Shifter abilities only."

"Yup. Well aware of that limitation."

Really?

Yup. But I don't have time to puzzle it out right now. There's kinda an army of Angels heading my way.

"Focus," Dea warns.

One soldier breaks rank and walks forward, heading our way. He storms across the forest floor, his wide strides larger than his body, making his legs look like Blu Tack being stretched. "You cannot leave with the dead, Death." His ethereal voice booms around the space, reminding me that it's actually an empty chasm. "You may only arrive with them."

"He's not supposed to be dead." I step forward, in front of Dea and Nine. "He's a Horseman of the Apocalypse. He was chosen by Fate to help Earth."

"Never the less, he's dead. He is in our charge now." His face is mere inches from mine, the expressionless look turning my stomach and sending goosebumps through my bones. "He no longer belongs to the world of the living."

"He will always belong to the world of the living. He is immortal."

"No one is truly immortal." His hand raises above his head, and the line of Angels draw their swords.

Go. Go now.

The whoosh of Dea's wings crackles through my hair as I smile, a relieved breath releasing from my lungs. I'm positive Dea can just drag a soul out. But if not, I'll do my best to alter the monster spell. Somehow.

The soldier's hand clenches into a fist, and the army charge forward on silent feet, all stretching their legs across the forest floor like creepy weirdos.

The soldier in front of me draws his sword, and I take a step back, conjuring an air spell between my fingers. My staff is in charm bracelet form, but I can grab it if needed. For now, I'd rather use what spells I have available.

I don't want them knowing all my tricks too soon.

His sword swings at me as he takes a step, but just before it meets my head, I breathe into the spell. "*Kūki.*"

A rage of wind slams into the sword and arcs down, swirls around his body, and picks him up. He flies into the air with a shout. "Put me down, Magic!"

"Gonna let me and my boyfriends go?"

"I cannot."

"Then no. I don't think I will." I get another air spell ready, but this time, I direct it into a tunnel. "*Tatsumaki.*"

I haven't moved from my spot, but soon, the entire army is stuck in a tornado that rips the trees up from their soil-less ground and rages leaves through the air.

Nine's house falls to pieces behind me, the roof flying off and joining the fray.

I wish I could say I feel bad, but I don't.

Nine's home is with us at the house, not here in some cottage all by himself. He waited for us. In a white world with no one else to call a friend—for months—all by himself. He never has to see that house again.

The Angels spinning in a wind vortex are all screaming, struggling to breathe properly, and begging me to let them down. And I will. Eventually. But right now, I need to catch up to Nine and Dea and see how they're doing.

I run in the direction Dea flew, hoping to find the gates. And I keep running. And running. And running. Until I have to stop and catch my breath so hard I hunch over, hands on knees, heaving in gulpfuls of air.

"Shit." Where is the gate?

I look up, breaths still ragged, and see a black dot in the distance. Everything else is white nothingness. So much white, I can't tell which way is up. But I head toward that dot, keeping my eyes on it, staring it down. I will reach it.

After taking more steps than I care to guess, I reach the looming Black Gates, but Dea and Nine are nowhere to be seen.

Nine?

Can you hear me?

Nothing.

I hope that means they're on the other side and not trapped in some kind of magicless box guarded by more Angels.

Yup. Definitely option number one.

Because I don't know what I'd do if it were option number two.

So I put my hand on the gate and push, and to my surprise, it opens. Just like that.

And just like that, red hair rushes me as wings engulf me.

"You made it," Dea breathes into my ear.

"Yeah, piece of cake."

Nine chuckles. *You got lost?*

Shut up.

They both chuckle as their arms surround me, but Nine's are becoming translucent, his touch fading.

"Nine?" Dea asks, worry etched into his frowning brow. "What's happening?"

I'm returning to soul form.

Dea touches his body, but I can't. Why can't I touch him? Why can't I just hug my boyfriend? Why is this happening?

"Shhh," Nine comforts. "You knew this would happen."

"We did," Dea confirms. "You said you would know what to do when it does." He stares me down, one eyebrow raised, his lips quirked into an I-told-you-so expression. "Do you?"

"You damn well know I don't!"

I switch forms, enjoying the fact that I now can. I missed the freedom of being myself —someone I've come to realize is persistent, emotional, a little selfish, but full of determination and love.

You finally found yourself, huh?

Maybe I'm still finding myself, but I've certainly found some important pieces.

Dea rests a gentle hand on my cheek, his wings brushing my back. "You will always be finding yourself. Changing. Moving with the times. It is what makes us human." He smiles. "You do not need to continuously look for who you are. All you need to do is live."

36

For now, we take Nine home. Maybe there's something, or someone, there that can help. He's alive.

He's actually alive.

I watch as Dea and Nine walk side-by-side up the hilly lane that leads to our home, fingers entwined, telepathically conversing the entire time.

They both look back at me expectantly.

And I run to them both, tears finally leaking from my eyes, my own emotion finally coursing through me. "I was so scared . . ."

Dea wraps his arms around my middle, his chest to my back, as Nine looks at me help-lessly. His hands ghosting over my skin with frustration.

"I didn't know what to do." Breaths escape my lips in ragged heaves as tears flood my cheeks and drip off my skin. "Everyone needed me to be strong, to lean on. And I didn't know . . . what to do." Exhaustion washes over me, and a half-cry, half-yawn escapes. "I'm so tired."

Nine smiles, a gentle caress of a grin I've missed. *You've done so much for everyone else, all while being too scared to lean on them. You can relax now. I'm home.*

"I am so sorry, Angel." Dea's lips touch my neck and breathe me in. "I was so lost. I knew you needed me, and I was not there."

A warm splash lands on my shoulder, and I laugh. A hearty, belly-deep laugh. "We're such a mess."

"Wanna go add to that mess?" Nine asks, gesturing to the house. "They're waiting."

Connie and Arrie stand at the door, smiles on their faces, Arrie's arm around the back of Connie's shoulders.

"You're back!" she shouts, then runs over. "You brought him back." Her hand covers her trembling mouth, tears escaping her, and she goes to jump at him, but stops. "You're still just a soul?"

For now.

Nine looks at me with all the confidence in the world, but fuck, I really don't know how to give him a solid form.

Arrie stomps over, his usual frown in place of a grin. "So, you're back?"

"As good as new." Nine gestures to himself, his dirty clothes still worn and ripped from the battle he died in. "Well, soon to be."

"It's good to have you back, dude." Arrie places the hand he wanted to place on Nine on me, steadying my body to the ground. "You done rescuing boyfriends?" He looks down at me, a quiet smirk on his stony face.

"Assuming none of you die again, yes."

Connie laughs. "So do us a favor, and start protecting your lives. I don't wanna be without pussy again."

My cheeks burn bright as I shoot my gaze to the floor.

"Oh, come on," she whines. "You've fucked us all. You can't possibly still be embarrassed by me liking how good you taste."

"Well . . ." Maybe I can? Maybe we're still a few hundred years from me being openly crude with the team.

Don't worry. Fuck us all at the same time, and you'll be well over it.

At the same . . . time?

THE DINNER TABLE THAT NIGHT CONSISTS OF THE TEAM, NIGEL, MY FAE TRAINER, KORBY, Prince Lucien, and Red. All wanting to celebrate the return of Nine.

Albeit, they have questions. Lots of questions.

"So, does that mean you can bring anyone back?" Lucien asks.

I shrug. "I have no idea. Probably not." I turn to Dea. "How did you get him through the gates?"

Dea looks at Nine, who looks to me and then everyone else. "I think it was because I'm a Horseman. I'm not really mortal in the same way you all are."

Is that true?

I don't know. But I don't want them all thinking we can bring whoever we want back.

That would be a dangerous piece of knowledge, indeed.

"How do you intend to give him a body then?" the green Fae asks. "Because he cannot be a ghost for all eternity."

"Well, that is a good question . . ." She stares me down, and I sigh. "I don't know."

Red splutters her drink. "What do you mean you don't know? You did this without knowing?"

"Look," I snap a little too harshly. "I do a lot of things without really knowing how they work. Okay? It's par for the course around here. I was kinda hoping I would just know. But I don't yet." I look at everyone around the table and smile. "But I will try. Even if it takes me a hundred years."

I sincerely hope not. That is a long time to go without sex for.

Oh goddess, how I've missed your mind.

It is a beauty.

You're beautiful alright. Beautiful and smart and funny and you smell amazing.

He looks to the ground, his pasty cheeks slightly reddening. And it's then I remember he doesn't get compliments often, and I enjoy showering him in them.

Nigel raises his glass. "Regardless of the road ahead, here's to Famine. It's really really good to have you back, buddy."

Nine looks to him. "Thanks."

Everyone raises their glasses and cheers.

And we eat a series of amazing small plates served to us with food from one of Arrie's restaurants that we ask the house for—the poor guy needs a break—and everyone agrees it's the most delicious ever.

To Arrie's grumbling dismay.

He likes to be the one to cook the food we gawk at.

And technically this was made by someone else, even if it is his own recipe. And that's not good enough. Apparently.

I rest my hand on his knee on the couch we're snuggling on in the cinema. "It's still your food. But if you really want to impress me, I wouldn't mind brownies for breakfast." I grin up at him, and he cracks a smile.

"Brownies for breakfast it is."

Connie lies between my legs while I rest on Arrie's shoulder. Dea's wings hang behind the couch as Nine lies on him, the only person he can touch right now, and only if Dea's in his Angel form.

But it doesn't matter because we're here. All of us. Home. And for the first time in forever, I breathe an easy breath.

That night, Connie snuggles into my left, both of us lying on Dea's wing, his other curled around Nine, as Arrie lies behind us all, myself and Dea in his lap. All of us together. And I sleep better than I've slept since before Aki turned into a murdering, raging psychopath and my boyfriend died.

Wow.

It really has been an insane few weeks.

Arrie leaves at the ass-crack of dawn, like usual, and wakes us all up a few hours later with brownies in bed.

"Aww, dude, you didn't have to," Nine jokes.

"Shut up." Arrie chucks a pillow at his head, but it sails right through. "Err . . . sorry."

Nine shrugs but goes silent. "Thanks for the brownies, but I can't eat them yet. I will, however, take a mountain of them the moment I have a corporeal form with which to eat them."

"Ugh." My head hits the pillow as I lie back down, the weight of that task throwing back into bed. "Thanks for the reminder."

"Well, I made the brownies for Magic." He shoves the plate under my nose, and I rise back up.

Risen back from the dead by brownies.

Not a bad way to become a zombie, if you ask me.

God, I've missed your brain, Sweetie.

I grab one off the towering pile and shove it into my mouth with gusto, groaning at the chocolaty goodness now coating my tongue. "Fuck, they're good," I mumble with my mouth full.

Fully refreshed, I hop out of bed, much to the chagrin of the rest of the team, and stand in front of the mirror. What kind of day is it gonna be today?

I grab a dress out of the closet, hold it up in front of me, and frown. Nope. Not a dress day. Maybe shorts and tights? Nope. Not that either. Shoving some sweatpants on, I relax a little but it still doesn't feel right. So I switch forms and get undressed again, then put my male sweatpants on that fit this height. Then look back in the mirror again, the weird uncomfortable feeling in my chest lightening.

"There."

"Is that really how you decide what form to be in for the day?" Arrie asks, amused.

"Well, sometimes I just know. I wake up knowing how I feel." I shrug, then grab a comb and run it through my hair. "Other times, it's not so clear, so I try a few things on, see how I feel in them, and that usually lets me know where the wheel of gender identity has fallen today."

"Is it always certain?" he asks, sitting on the edge of the bed.

"No. Some days, no matter how hard I try, I can't seem to settle how I feel. Like something is always a little off." I gel my hair into place and then grab some sneakers. "On those days, I just do my best to be as comfortable as possible with looking as close to how I feel as I can."

Dressed, I turn to the team. "I am going for a run. Then I'm doing some yoga, and then I'll get to work on trying to fix my boyfriend." I kiss everyone on the forehead, wave to Nine, trying to not to let the fact that I can't kiss him get to me, and leave.

The mid-morning air is crisp today, a cold wind settling over *Sheruta* for the first time since I've lived here. And the breeze cools my aching lungs when I run harder than my stupid weaker male body allows, squeezing out sharp breaths.

Arrie runs past me, taking the same route, and smiles as he goes. The asshole. Whoever said smiling was the appropriate social interaction while running had obviously never been on a run. Or was a god with already Vampire-like stamina.

I pick myself back up and continue. Just one more lap of the forest, and then I can start yoga. At least that's on my ass. For the most part.

Just a few more minutes. Nothing too intense.

And when I finally finish, climb the stupid hill, and sit in my *Shinto* shrine, I thank the goddess for the Earth for providing something for me to sit on. Because goddess knows I'm not getting back up for the next century.

Okay. So running isn't fun.

Not even for a Shifter.

But yoga? That's fun.

Big, deep breaths calm my racing heart as I stretch high into the sky and then bend low to the grass, clearing my mind. As I breathe out, a rustle in the nearby trees makes me peek open an eyelid.

"You can come out, Arrie. I know it's you."

He always watches.

But now we're together, he can watch freely and not sneak around like a yoga perv. So he exits the tree he was standing behind, brushing off the foliage from his undershirt and cargo pants, and climbs the hill to sit beside me in silence.

I, on the other hand, continue with my yoga routine, adding in a whole new standing position: the eagle pose.

"I've not seen that one before," Arrie comments.

"It's a garudasana, also known as an eagle pose," I say on a breathy exhale. "I'm getting a little better in my male form," I explain as I move into a warrior pose, "so I thought I'd add some new positions this morning."

"You'll have to teach me one day." His eyes are still closed, hands resting atop crossed knees. "My flexibility isn't great for a warrior."

"Always happy to help make you more flexible," I suggest, sneaking a look at him.

He chuckles, and the deep vibrato of the laugh makes me lose balance in my tree pose and stumble onto my ass, where I land heavy with an oof. "Damn you and your sexy-as-fuck laugh."

I dust myself off and try to recenter, but it's pointless. My mind is drifting too much. Besides, I need to head in and grab an update from Connie. "How long have I been gone?"

Arrie looks up at me, all blue eyes and chiseled chin, and says, "Two weeks."

CONNIE AND I CATCH UP WITH A WORKING BREAKFAST IN MY LIBRARY AN HOUR LATER, AFTER A shower, a brownie, and a hot make-out session with Mr. Muscular and Charming.

"I've really been gone two weeks?"

She nods, her hand laced in mine.

"It feels like it's been a few hours."

"Well, it was an awful two weeks with just Arrie to keep me company. He was grump as hell without you around."

I flip through a couple of textbooks on magical theory I'd grabbed from the shelves on my way over. "Get up to anything fun while I was gone?" I ask, suggestion lacing my tone. My eyebrows wiggle, and goddess damn it, I'm bad at this. Sighing at her laughter, I put the book down. "Just tell me the details. I want the juicy details."

She coughs, looking around at anywhere but me, and finally says, "I haven't slept with Arrie since our first date in my bedroom that night."

Wait. "What?" I stumble over her words, tripping up on their meaning. "Why not?"

She shrugs and bites into an apple. Upon swallowing, she wipes her mouth and says, "Just didn't feel right to be using him for dick while dating you for actual feelings. Felt like I should be at least exclusive to emotional connections, even if that was with more members of the team than just you." She shrugs again. "No hate to anyone else, it just didn't feel right for me. So I broke things off with him."

"For me?"

"Hon, I love you. I do. But I wouldn't break things off with another member of the team just for you. At least not without serious pressure from yourself. I love them too. But it's a different kind of love right now. And I think I'm comfortable with that. I broke things off with Arrie for me."

"Soooo . . . group sex is off the table?"

She puts down her apple and looks offended. "Not on your life. I wanna watch you come alive with one of the guys. And besides, group sex is still with you."

"You are a complicated person, Conquest."

"I'm a woman. We're all complicated."

"That you are."

"What you talking about?" Nine asks, floating over the table, a giant grin on his face.

"Whether I'd be up for group sex with everyone."

Nine mimes spluttering a shocked cough, and we all laugh. "Group sex, huh?"

"We've done group stuff before, just not with everyone."

"You're seeing where we all stand with comfortability, aren't you?" He floats into a seat he doesn't quite sit in and places his hands behind his head. "Well, you know I'm game, Sweetie. As long as you and Dea are okay, I'll fuck any of them with you."

"Manwhore," Connie accuses.

"Says the girl who's caused more middle-aged orgies than cupid himself."

"Hey. I was a repressed woman living an immortal life, give me a break."

"And now I'm a ghost."

"Yeah, about that . . ." I look to Nine, apprehension in my eyes, I'm sure. "I have no idea how to give you a physical form."

"I know," he confirms. "But I'll help you try." He looks at the book pages I have open and scratches his chin. "Might need to call for backup, though. I also have no idea what I'm doing."

"In the meantime, I'll update you on where we are with things," Connie says. "The Vampires are returning to New Orleans with help from the embassy, the new artificial blood pill is being distributed for free at the moment while the Vampires get back on their feet." She looks to both of us. "We're footing the cost, but we won't be able to forever. I have offered embassy seats to the pixies and Demons, who graciously accepted, so we're getting those set up."

"What about Glowy?"

"The Angel? I didn't think to since we don't know any other Angels, but I can if you'd like?"

"Just because we don't know any, doesn't mean she doesn't. Besides, there were a couple at the Demon hideout in the bayou."

"Done." She adds it to her list, then places her head in her hands and sighs before announcing, "We have no idea where the Fae Queen and her army are. Nor Aki or the Rogue Vampire Faction. They've vanished."

"Great news," I moan, my face also hitting my hands. "Any chance of scouts finding anything?"

"Already sent out," Connie says, "but so far, no news."

"Great," Nine interrupts, "now we're all caught up, can we please call for magical backup and get me a corporeal form? Not being able to fuck you or eat Arrie's brownies is a damn crime."

Arrie find us just as Nine says that, and he smiles. "Nice to know my brownies are as good as my partner." For just half a second, he stumbles over what to call me, and I can't believe he even put more than a moment of thought into his words.

"That's what I want when I get a body," he says, an idea coming to him, "brownies, sex, and being bitten." He looks at me, all the confidence in the world on his face. "All three at the same time."

I chuckle, finally feeling a little less embarrassed by conversations of sex with the entire team. "Consider it done." I turn to Connie and smile. "Please make sure everyone is still preparing for whatever is coming next while we think of next steps. I'll consult Arrie and Dea and get back to you. If you could consult the embassy, that would also be of help."

"Consider it done," she says, mimicking me. Just as she gets up and goes to leave, she turns back around. "And I wanna be there to watch Nine's coming home present." Her tongue snakes into my mouth as she fists my hair in her hand and my neck in her other, her heat shooting straight through me. "Don't forget me."

"I could never forget you." Images of me in the bathtub, my legs dangling either side, as she brings me to bliss, sear across my head.

Much to Nine's delight, apparently, as he blows out a breath.

Arrie chuckles in the corner and eyes Nine, who he shares a look with him.

Don't send my sexy to everyone!

Why not? You're fucking us all, anyway.

Well, because . . .

Oh, forget it. Just ask Connie too.

I don't mind, Connie's voice echoes into my head a few moments later. *Not like they haven't seen me naked before.*

Good, Nine says. *Now I can turn everyone on!*

Goddess, I've missed his meddling.

Another hour of pouring through research books, of which Nine can't even touch, and help arrives in the form of Dea, Lucien, Red, Nigel, and my Fae trainer. Between us all, we should be able to at least brainstorm some ideas of where to look next.

"Everyone, grab a seat," I order. "I need your help."

"What with, little Horseman?"

I point to Nine. "He needs a body, and I have no idea what I'm doing." They look at me as though I've just popped my head off my shoulders. "Do I look like the grim reaper's polar twin to you?"

I wonder where the grim reaper came from? Did Dea have a death goth phase?

Phase? Have you seen him?

I look to our boyfriend, whose head of black hair is in a book with a translational bookscreen overtop, and sigh. Yeah, I have.

Uck. You two are disgusting. He looks at me with a smile and clearly holds back his laughter at my face. *Don't worry*, he says with an eye roll, *I find you both lovingly adorable.*

I love you too.

Now, can we please get back to finding you a body?

"Can I reanimate a body and tie his consciousness to it, somehow?" I ask the group.

Again, they look at me with utter astonishment.

"I can't even believe I'm here," Red says. "Seriously, reanimating corpses? What are you, Frankenstein?"

"I am not a monster, thank you," Nine chides as he floats above us. "Does anyone know anything about death magic?"

No one says anything, but Red shifts uncomfortably.

I look to her and ask, "What it is?"

"Well, there's a rumor—more like a legend—in the Witch Coven that earth magic has energy-restoring properties, with legends of famous Witches bringing all manner of things back to life, from plants to whole forests, and sometimes . . . people." She looks at everyone, who is looking at incredulously. "They're just legends. Things we tell children to amaze them before bed."

"But maybe there's something more to them," I suggest, my brain running away from me.

38

Three hours later, after everyone had gone to lunch, the seer and earth Witches of the Coven sit before me in my library, an opposing smile and scowl on each of their faces.

Nine flies over and hovers in front of them.

Each of them scowls, shock and appall plastering their faces in equal measure.

The earth Witch stands up, her cane jamming into the floor. "What have you done?"

The seer joins her, pity and frustration flashing in her eyes. "Magic, this isn't how things are supposed to be."

"Spare me." My eyes roll of their own accord. "I know you aren't going to agree with my decision, but we Horsemen are hardly natural. I did not bring you here to lecture me."

"Then why are we here, child?" the seer asks. "My magic cannot help you here. I cannot foresee the dead."

"Really?" But that dream felt so real, and it was of the realm of the dead. Does that not count? Is it a Horseman thing? "But . . ." I turn to the other Witch in the room, who has so far remained silent. "How true are the legends of your people?"

"I see Red has been speaking of matters she should not. Again." The earth Witch sits back down with a heavy sigh, defeated. "I know not of the past, but I do know that every living being has earth magic running through them. It is the very basis for what we earth Witches use. The energy given off of the leylines that give sustenance to life."

"The leylines power life?"

She rocks her head from side to side. "Not quite. But it flows through life. You Horsemen do not have that thread."

"Makes senses," Nine confirms. "We're basically the walking dead."

"What flows through you five is something else entirely. Something linked to earth magic but not quite. Almost like its polar opposite from the same source." She looks around her in wonder and asks, "Do you have a copy of THE ORIGIN OF WITCH MAGIC?"

I hold up a finger and grab the seeing stone from my desk around the corner, then come back. After a few seconds, I ask it, and the book pops into her lap.

"That is quite handy."

Well, I know what's going on the 'making the world like me again' Christmas list.

She flicks through the book and places it open on a page with a giant diagram on the table. "This"—she points to the large circle in the center of the page—"is the origin of the leyline's power. We know not what it actually is."

The Black Gate.

But I don't think she'll take that very well. So I elect to stay silent.

See, politics.

Improvement!

"And these"—she follows the various lines snaking from the black circle—"are all the various types of magic the leylines produce. Each one is a different type of magic that every Witch can access." She points to each one in turn. "Earth, air, fire, water, charm, and seer."

There are two dotted lines circling the others coming from the very center. "What are those?" Nine asks.

She looks to the seer Witch, who nods. "Those are life and death magic. It's something Angel-descended Witches could do when they used to rule our Coven."

"Angel-descended Witches used to rule? Why?"

"Because they had the power to unite people," the seer Witch explains, "to bring us great power and prestige. Their powers were revered by most of the magical community."

"That was over a thousand years ago, when Angels and Demons used to rule this Earth," the earth Witch scowls. She points to the dots coming off those lines. "But this is what flows through everyone. Everyone, that is, but you five. And even if you could tap into this power somehow to bring someone's physical form back—which I don't know that you could—that form would be mortal."

Which would put Nine's life at risk in any battle. And I'd have to reform it every time it died.

Not to mention how much trouble Dea would get into having to continuously drag my soul back.

"So, what you're saying is . . . ?"

"You're asking the impossible, dear." The seer Witch stands and places a hand on my shoulder, then looks to Nine. "I'm sorry, but I don't think it can be done."

"You've both given me plenty to think on. If you'd like, I can teleport you both back to wherever you'd like on Earth."

"That would be splendid," she says, a smile on her face. "I'm so sorry we couldn't be of more use."

After sending the seer Witch back to her husbands and the earth Witch back to a mall she was shopping in—which totally explains her bad mood, I'd be angry if I was interrupted while shopping—I settle back into the library with my head resting on a pillow.

It aches.

It really, really aches.

Can Horsemen even get headaches?

Yeah, if we're overstressing. Like now.

"I just don't know what to do. I'm not overworked here. I have two problems, but no solutions to either of them." Unlike before, where I had lots of problems, but not enough time to deal with them all.

"How many people know about your death magic?"

"Aki, you four, Nigel, the Witches might . . . I've lost track." My arm rests over my eyes as my feet kick off their shoes and rest on the couch. "Even if it has to do with my death magic. Nine, I can't use that on you. Even if I wanted to. I know so little about it. Let alone combining it with earth magic—which I still haven't unlocked yet by the way—to create a form for you. And even then, I don't know how to make that form immortal."

Arrie walks up to me and wraps his arms around my middle. "Just kill it."

"What?"

"Kill the mortal form, right?"

I turn in his arms to face him, confused.

"Sometimes you nerds are dumb." He takes a deep breath. "Our mortal forms die before we're made into Horsemen, then Fate takes over. It'll probably just make you immortal again. And if it doesn't, then we know we can drag your soul back and try something else." He shrugs. "No big deal."

"So I just have to make a body. Any body."

"Preferably *my* body, Sweetie," Nine corrects. "I'm rather fond of my dick."

Sighing, I look at him with stern resignation. "Any other requests to make an already impossible job that much harder?"

"Could you make me taller? Just by a few inches?"

A stressed hand runs down my face just as they come back from lunch, Lucien with his arm wrapped around Red's shoulders, an achieved smirk on his face.

Those two are getting closer and closer every time I see them. I wonder what would happen if a royal Vampire and a Coven Witch got married?

Nigel is laughing with my Fae trainer, who has a brilliant smile plastered across her usually harsh face, and I smile in response. Happy she's settling in, making friends. Maybe she gains something from being part of my training circle after all.

They all gather around, chit-chatting, Red with a brownie in her hand, and Nigel picking up where he left off with the open book on the table.

Red is the one to ask, "What did Aunt Sasha say?" My look of confusion must encourage her to explain, "The earth Witch."

"So your grandma is the fire Witch and your aunt is the earth Witch?" I ask, trying to wrap my head around their family dynamics.

"Yep." She pops the last bit of brownie into her mouth and swallows. "They're twins. My mom is Musa, daughter of the fire Witch."

"Your Coven is complicated."

"We're old." She shrugs, not seeing the big deal.

Getting back to the point, I answer her actual question. "I just sent her and the seer home, actually. They were . . . informative, if not all that helpful."

Nine floats over the table, not even blocking the light. "Actually, they were most helpful. I think the answer might lie in your earth and Angel magic."

My head falls into my hands. "It couldn't rely on a type of magic I have some skill in?"

"Fate's a bitch like that," Arrie mumbles from behind me, settling into a comfy armchair with a . . . Is that the romance book I was reading last week? "She likes to challenge us, to push us past our boundaries and see what happens."

"Well," Nine says, "I'm more of a 'know what's going to happen before you try it' kind of a guy." He sighs, papers flittering over the table. "But I guess I'll have to concede to Magic's usual 'figure it out as you go' method."

"Hey! That's gotten us out of many a bind in the past."

"Like dragging you out of the Otherworld," Arrie remarks.

Finally. A good use for his snark.

Finally using it for you instead of against you. Hey, by the way, you need to show me what happened between you two.

Later.

But just as I say that, images of him fucking me from behind while grabbing my throat flash across my mind in vivid detail.

Fuuuck.

I ignore the annoying voice of my boyfriend in my head and stick my eyes back into the book the Coven Witches had made me grab. Maybe more answers will be given.

39

A few hours later, and no closer to an answer, Connie and Dea walk in, side-by-side, smiles on their faces.

What have they done?

"We have done it," Dea says. "We have come up with a plan for how to at least weaken Aki and the enemy."

"Really?" Nine asks. "That's what you've been doing all day?"

"Well, as much as I want you to have a body," Connie says. "We need to keep doing our job, too. So we thought we'd help Magic out by solutionizing a different problem." She shoves a giant sheet of A1 paper into my hands with a proud smile on her beautiful face. "Check it out. Meanwhile, we'll check out what you've done and see if we can add to it."

Nine, Arrie, and I pour ourselves over the sheet of paper with Dea's beautiful handwriting on and check their notes. Lucien and Red leaning over our shoulders.

"They want to tackle the SC first?" I ask.

"It makes sense," Arrie adds. "It'll weaken their defenses because they won't have the legal power they once did."

"And most of the SC are being blackmailed or brainwashed, so if we can fix those members, they won't have the majority vote anymore." Nine flies around the table I've laid the piece of paper on, excited. "It's not a bad plan."

Connie calls from a few feet away, "We don't know where Aki is, or what the Fae Queen and the Rogue Vampire Faction have planned, but we do know where the houses and locations of the various council members are."

Dea's got his head in the various notes I made, cross-referencing them with the Fae trainer's, who has found the project as perplexing as everyone else. But we're certain the answer to Nine's corporeal form is by mixing different types of magic.

"This looks promising," Dea says after putting the papers down. "You have clearly used the knowledge at your disposal." He thinks for a minute, then looks at me with a gleam in his golden galaxy eyes. "Have you considered using your death magic to direct the earth magic into a soul and seeing the effect?"

"If we knew more about the effects of that, we would be able to create a better solution," my Fae trainer adds. Agreeing with Dea.

"Wouldn't that be dangerous?" I ask, curious.

Dea shrugs. "To be honest, Angel, I think souls are impervious to most damage. They are not alive. You cannot do much to them." His eyes drift to Nine, who's silently staring at us all, tears in his eyes.

You okay?

I don't want to be the reason you're all in pain. He floats away to somewhere else in the library.

Dea goes to follow, but I grab his hand. "I think he needs some time alone."

Connie hugs me, her arms wrapping around my middle, and Arrie stands beside us, a worried look on his face.

"But what if he wants to go back?" Dea asks.

"He won't," Arrie says, looking confident in his answer.

Lucien, Red, and my Fae trainer all leave, leaving us just with Nigel—who looks sheepishly to the ground. "Listen, Magic . . . I—"

"Don't." I hold up a hand, stopping him. "Don't apologize for something that isn't your fault. He's clearly got issues."

"But—"

"There are no buts." I place both hands on his shoulders and take a deep breath. "You are not to blame for a kid you didn't raise. It was unfair of our parents to place so much on your shoulders."

"If I had taken you both in, maybe he would have turned out better."

"And maybe we wouldn't have turned out at all. Two Angel-descended Witches so close together? It's what killed Mom and Dad." Patting his back, I smile. "You did the best with what you had."

"When this is all over, we should go to Japan and visit them."

"I'd like that."

Nigel hugs me goodbye and leaves, leaving me alone with all four of the team for the first time in forever. And when I turn around and notice them all smiling at me, tears roll down my cheeks.

Dea's shifted into his Angel form so he can hold Nine's hand—who has come back after taking a breather—Arrie leans an elbow on Connie's shoulder, and I just stand there like a lemon leaking juice all over my cheeks with a smile on my face.

"I'm just so happy you're all here." I turn to face Nine, sincerity entering my voice. "I'll find a way. I promise."

He shakes his head with a small smile. "We should prioritize dealing with the SC for now, Sweetie."

Dea looks to him sharply. "But—"

"It's the right move," Nine interrupts. "And you all know it. I can wait."

"But you shouldn't have to," Connie whispers, then grits her teeth. "You've done nothing but serve the people, and we can't even take a couple of weeks to focus on giving you a corporeal form?"

"Afraid not, Con." Nine floats in front of her and raises an open hand. "I'll be here still. Always."

She meets his hand mid-air, not able to actually touch it, and exhales a frustrated breath.

Dea's hand rests on Nine's shoulder and he nuzzles his neck with his nose. "We will fix you."

Nine's hand reaches back and rests on Dea's neck. "I know."

40

The following day, the embassy meets, including our new additions—our fellow Demon Verity and a pixie named Carter. Since their populations are each solely in one place right now, there's no need for more than one representative. But we can change that over time as needed.

Now our embassy is up to twelve members.

I have a feeling that the more members we have, the more species that are represented, the more difficult our discussions are going to be.

Connie slaps a hand on the table, grabbing everyone's attention, and clears her throat. "We would like to extend an invitation to our resident Angel and chat about adding an Angel division to the embassy."

"It's getting a little crowded," Rufus mutters.

"The point of the embassy," I clarify, "is to represent every species on the planet. But it'll take time to grow into that. We're lucky we have most of the pillar communities leading the way."

Our single Fae representative from *Sheruta* we've since added to the embassy holds back a lot, I've noticed, and now is no exception. So I make a point to ask him, "How are the Fae doing?"

He clears his throat and looks around the room, everyone's eyes fixed on him. "Well, I think." He looks to the floor, his hands fidgeting in his lap. "They're a little angsty from what their kin are doing on Earth."

Red holds in a laugh and Lucien squeezes her knee.

"They're also nervous how it is going to make them look in the long run. People are becoming afraid and on edge around us Fae, and it's making it hard to feel a part of the community."

Connie and Dea nod (his charm bracelet working wonders). "We understand," Connie says. "Hopefully things won't remain this way. We have every intention of removing the issue."

Everyone snaps their gazes our way.

"And how, Horsemen," Lucien starts, "do you plan on achieving that."

Arrie taps on the wall behind us, and up flashes Connie's diagram and list. "With this."

On this piece of paper turned plasmascreen wall art is a step-by-step process of how we're going to deal with the SC.

"So we have twelve council members. Of which, the three humans are being compelled, two of the Fae were not aware of the queen's real motives, and all three Vampires are aligned with Prince Phillipe."

"The obvious first start," Dea begins, "is to undo the compelling of the humans."

Nine is float-sitting in the chair with a smile on his face. "I would be happy to offer my assistance. Gotta love wiping away compulsion."

You can do that?

Yup. Centuries of Vampires with compulsion talents equals centuries of practise.

"We will follow this by communicating with the two Fae councilmen and try to reason with them," Dea adds, "which I will be doing myself." He looks to Prince Lucien with a worried look, unsure if this next step will even work. "Then we need to implore the Vampire king to see reason and request a Vampire seat vote. He needs to take a public stance against the SC."

Lucien puts his head into his hands, his long blonde hair falling around himself like a curtain. With a heavy breath, he says, "I will try, but I cannot make any promises."

"Then try hard, Prince," Red says, "because without the Vampire councilmen on our side, what way discussions go with regards to removing support from the Fae Queen's efforts will depend solely on the Shifter councilmen."

The three Shifter ambassadors shake their heads. "We do not like to show open support for any singular movement. We try to remain an open vessel of refuge for all. Defend when necessary, but otherwise remain passive."

"I know," I start, "and I respect your way of life and beliefs, but if it comes down it, people will die if you choose to remain neutral. Your own people are dying, and will continue to do so unless we act."

They do nothing but nod their heads, silently taking on board my words. Hopefully.

Addressing the whole room, I ask for an update on our scouting efforts. "They can't have just vanished! They're an entire fucking army."

Lucien speaks up, reporting on Vampire efforts. "We've scoured the whole of France by this point, offered payment for any information, and nothing."

Dea, hand on chin, at peace with a new puzzle to solve. "All it would take is one charm Witch, and he will have all he needs to create teleporting crystals as often as he likes."

"So they could be anywhere," Red mumbles. "Great."

I flick my gaze to her, asking, "Any charm Witches missing?"

"Not in the Coven, no." She shakes her head. "If there are Witches helping them, then they're from out in the world."

"Have any way of checking on each coven, doing a headcount?"

"Sure. I'll bring it to Coven tonight." She looks to the window, thinking for a minute, then swivels back around. "Should have an answer within a few days, maybe a week."

"So quick?" one of the Shifter ambassadors asks, incredulously.

"There aren't many of us to count."

Nine, we need to find a way to help the Witches after all this is over. See if there's anything they need.

I'll get Connie to write it down.

A few seconds later, she brings out a different notepad and makes a note, then smiles at me, nodding.

"Okay then," I say. "Arrie, go with Nine and keep him safe while he wipes away the compulsion. Take as many teleporting crystals as you need." I look to Dea, then to some of the ambassadors in the room. "I'll need volunteers to go with Dea and I to speak to the Fae. We'll need to go prepared with evidence and a full plan, so only those of you who like the Fae please."

Our *Sheruta* Fae ambassador nods his head "I will join you as a show of Fae strength." A few others join, and soon we have an ambassador envoy ready to go.

"Okay, so Dea, I'll need you here with me working with everyone to create a solid plan. Persuading a Fae is not an easy task." An idea takes root. "Oh, and take Nigel. He might be able to help you."

"Actually," Lucien interrupts, "I need you with me, Magic." He shrugs. "Father likes you. That might help."

"Okay, then Dea, you'll be handling the Fae without me. That okay?"

"I am a Horseman, Angel." He smiles, his dimples melting my insides into goo. Like always. "We will be fine."

"Then, Red and Nana, could you please help the Witches do a headcount?"

Sheruta's Witch ambassador shakes her head. "I've never left *Sheruta*, but I will do a headcount here. You never know."

41

It's our first mission since New Orleans, and tensions are running high. The entire embassy is splitting up, dividing ourselves.

"Connie?" I pull her aside once everyone else has left. "I need you to make sure some of our army are here, protecting the embassy. With so many of us gone, we're open to attack. Too open."

"Already on it," she reassures, her hands tapping away at a plasmascreen balanced on her fingertips. "Helpfully, it's kinda hard to get here, even with teleporting crystals."

"Right. You'd need one for every soldier to pull it off. That's unlikely." I breathe a sigh of relief. "Even I'd have a hard time producing that many."

"We could get datachips and reroute it to a private network. It would allow us easy access to the internet on the go, messaging and calling each other as we go, rather than having to schedule it every time, and eventually we could discuss using it as regular citizens."

Dea scowls. "We have always tried not to do that."

"But that was before we were out in the open, public knowledge," Connie adds. "I think I'm with these two on this. Sorry Dea."

Everyone looks to Nine, who shrugs. "I can't get one, anyway."

"You're still a member of the team, ass rat. You still get a vote."

"Then, I guess it's about time we treat ourselves the same as we treat everyone else, and not like we're on some societal pedestal."

Dea sighs, head in hand, looking tired. "I need to go home and change my charm bracelet out before I start planning with everyone else."

"And lunch," I say. "I'm starving."

"I have a new batch of brownies for you to try," Arrie says, a suspicious look in his eyes.

"I'm all up for trying brownies."

"Me too," Connie says.

But Arrie replies, "These are just for Magic. Sorry."

"Oh, I see how it is. Just for the girlfriend brownies?" Connie jokes.

Arrie laces his fingers through mine, a small but perceivable smile on his usually grumpy face. "Yes."

"You've done it," Connie whispers beside me. "You've melted him."

"Only took a year, too. I was prepared to spend the next century slowly chiseling away at him."

We all leave, taking the walk back to the house for lunch before we have to divide and conquer.

"You know, just once I'd like to have a mission with all five of us."

Dea shakes his head. "No, you do not." He wraps his hand through the one Arrie isn't holding. "If something requires all five of us, the world is either ending or warring so bad that the human population is at risk."

"Dea's right," Nine says. "We should never have a single problem so bad that we need all of us. But problems like this, that are complex, often require us to split up and conquer together."

"There's gonna be a battle, isn't there?" Connie asks hesitantly. "I can feel it."

"Me too," Arrie rumbles. "It's what Aki is waiting for."

"That will need all five of us," Dea adds. His thumb rubs circles over my hand, reassuring me that they'll be here.

"Maybe it's a good thing I'm not corporeal right now." At our confused faces, he explains, "I can use my powers and take zero damage. I'm unbeatable like this."

"I promise I'll fix you." My hands squeeze Arrie's and Dea's. "I promise I won't just leave you like this, unable to touch or feel or interact."

Nine hovers in front of me, floating backward. "I know you will. Sweetie. I believe in you."

"It's just less logical science and more hocus-y pocus."

Once home, Lo flies into the kitchen and lands on my head, smiling, purring away.

"Haven't seen you in a while, Lo. I missed you."

"Mmmmm, been exploring *Sheruta*."

"Everyone want cake and pizza from the pizzeria in town?" Connie asks, the ordering menu on the plasmascreen in her hand.

Everyone agrees, thanking Fate for the opportunity to chill on the couch and not focus on anything.

"Oh," Lo says, interrupting, "I let that Fae lady into the library. The one teaching you spells."

"Oh, she's here?"

"Upstairs. Said she needed your library for some research."

Connie shrugs when I look to her. "Guess I'll go ask if she wants pizza." She walks up the stairs, as exhausted by all the planning, researching and politics as the rest of us.

I carry Lo on my head to the living room, the guys trailing behind me. All of us sit in silence; even Nine floats near the ceiling in complete silence, not mentally chatting to anyone I don't think.

"How long do you think we'll be gone for?" I ask.

"Won't take me long to undo the compulsion. Don't even need to speak to them, just be within eyesight." Nine shrugs, confident his mission will be easy.

"Mine might take a few days," Dea says. "Fae are not known for being easy to reason with. But at least they live within the same part of Paris, so I will not have to do everything twice."

"I don't know how long it'll take me to convince the Vampire king to cast a revote on the Vampire councilmen."

Arrie places a hand on my shoulder. "We will come to you when we're done if you like?"

"Yes, please." Something about going back to New Orleans puts me on edge. Lots has happened to me in that city in the last year; I'll be happy to see the back of it. "I don't really do a lot of missions solo."

Connie comes downstairs, shaking her head. "She's deep in some Fae nonsense up there. I'm just gonna deliver her pizza when it arrives." She crashes into the spare armchair by the window in a huff. "Fuck, I'm exhausted."

"Mmhhmm," I agree. "I need a damn shopping trip."

Dea smiles while Connie grabs the edge of the couch with glee. "Yes. Yup. We're doing that!" She turns to Dea, elated. "Wanna join?"

"Sure."

"It's a date, then." Connie writes something down on an old-fashioned notepad with a pencil.

Using a little air magic, I blow it over to me and grab it out of the air.

"Hey! No fair . . ."

I flick through the pages and feel my cheeks burn a little hot. She's been keeping note of everything I say I want. In a bullet-point list. Like some kind of ideas book.

Ideas for dates. Gifts. Loving things to say.

"This is why you're so good at gift giving?" I float it back to her with an apology on my face. "You keep track."

Just as she opens her mouth to scold me, the doorbell rings. "Ooh, pizza." She sprints to the door, somehow finding the energy—then again, she's probably not low on physical energy. A pile of pizza boxes towering over her head walk back through the doorway, and everyone laughs.

"How much pizza did you order, Con?" Arrie asks, amazed.

"Enough so that you don't steal any of mine!" she shouts from somewhere behind the boxes.

I help her out with a bit of air magic, spreading them across the floor, looking at all the labels. After a few moments, I find mine—pepperoni with extra chili—and grab it and sit back down.

Connie grabs the two she ordered for the Fae upstairs in my library and delivers them, leaving the guys alone to fight for the rest.

Dea goes to grab the biggest box labeled Meaty Champion, but Arrie growls. Like, legit growls. Like some kind of animal. "Touch it and spend six months growing back your head."

Dea lets it go with a worried glance my way and instead picks up the Hawaiian.

"Ugh," Nine groans. "You seriously need a better palate."

"Considering you are a part of my palette, I would say it is just fine." He shifts into his Angel form and pats his lap. "Come here."

Nine floats down from where he was on the ceiling with a sheepish look on his face, but the moment he settles on Dea's lap, he breathes a sigh of relief. Eyes rolling into the back of his head. Lips parted.

I want to give him that look.

I want to touch my boyfriend.

Connie comes back and settles back onto the armchair with her chosen pizza and cake from the army-sized pile on the floor.

"I . . . I'm so sorry." Tears roll down my cheeks before I can stop them, uncontrollable rivers of grief. The weight of the world pushing them off my chin. "This is all my fault. I trusted Aki. I trusted him. And look what's it done!" Hands shaking, breaths ragged, words spill. "You're floating in Death's lap, deprived of touch, of life. Of pizza! Because I didn't think to be more cautious about who I trust."

None of them move. Connie puts another bite of pizza in her mouth, content to listen and watch until she's needed.

Nine, on the other hand, leaves Dea's lap and settles above me with his legs crossed, inches from my open pizza box. "Now you listen here. And listen good. Because I'm only going to say this once." He waves a hand through my face, and a cold shiver floats slowly through me like a lazy wave. "You are not responsible for the actions of others. Not even if those actions could have been prevented. The responsibility of others falls on them, not you. No matter how much you believe otherwise." He takes a deep breath, despite the fact I'm certain he doesn't need to. "You are simply wrong." Then he smiles and floats back to Dea. *Besides, Dea will just have to get us both off while all tied up.*

Sniffling, trying my best not to look too pathetic, I shove another bite of pizza in my mouth and huff.

Why is he always right?

Lucien walks into my bedroom the next morning—well, he more swaggers into my bedroom, but still, you get the point—and sits on the couch near the fireplace. "So, persuading my father to take a stand against the SC. A public stand."

"Tall order?" I ask, fluffing my skirt out and removing the last curler from my hair. "Shouldn't he want to support his people?"

"I know you weren't around for when Vampires came out of the closet, little Horseman, but I was. And let me tell you, it was hard. The SC did a lot to smooth things over for us. In fact, the only reason we weren't hunted with pitchforks was because of the years of campaigning the SC did for us."

"So you owe them?"

"Yeah, basically."

Grabbing my charm bracelet and tying it around my wrist, I ask, "Do you believe in holding grudges to a community's detriment, Prince Lucien?"

"No?"

"Good. Then you shouldn't believe in holding an IOU to a community's detriment either. This is silly." Arrie and Nine have already left, and Dea is at the embassy, so I call to my Fae trainer and Lo, "I'm off. Enjoy my library."

"Bye!" I hear them both call, both sounding distracted or otherwise engaged.

I switch my charm bracelet into my staff and bang it on the floor. "Time to go home, Prince Lucien."

Magic swirls around us, the pressure of teleporting overcoming my senses, and I have to hold in the vomit threatening to expel all over Lucien. But once we land, the hedge next to me is not so lucky.

"Magic! That is *my* hedge."

Looking around, I realize I have once again teleported into Lucien's front garden. "Oops. Sorry. Weak stomach."

"You couldn't have teleported us to the Vampire Council building?"

I shrug. "I could have, but it seems rude to just poof into a government building, and I can't be bothered to get arrested again by another pillar community. And I couldn't really remember what the outside looks like, then I panicked because I had already banged the magic stick, so I thought of the awful parties you used to run here, and poof. Here we are."

Lucien sighs, heavy, and rolls his eyes, and then grabs my hand and drags me down the street. "I cannot believe the future of my species is in your hands."

"Hey!" I yank my hand out of his and walk in step beside him. "I will have you know I have come a long way."

His fangs drop when he lowers a salacious grin at me and winks. "You think so, little Horseman? Keep up then." He sprints at full Vampire speed down the street.

And I follow, keeping up with ease while using air magic to boost my already faster-than-most-people-can-see speed. Until I'm overtaking him and seconds from the Vampire Royal Council building and laughing at his out-of-breath wheezing.

"Keep up then."

We screech to a halt in front of the building I now remember as being as big a disappointment as when I found out the moon isn't made of cheese. Corporate building with plasmascreen ads on the windows.

"Beat you."

"You cheated." He catches his breath for a quick second, then places a hand on my shoulder. "Don't think I didn't miss the air magic."

"Pfft. Don't know what you're talking about."

Lucien laughs as we walk through the front door and head on up to the same floor as before, where large meetings are held. But unlike last time, I have full control of my Vampire senses and know that human blood is meh.

I have much tastier morsels at home.

"Ready?" he asks.

Fluffing out my skirt, ensuring my boobs are placed to effect, and dragging my hair back in front of my shoulders, I look to him with confidence. "Yes."

The door swings open on silent hinges and we're greeted by the full weight of the council watching us as we make our way past the couches and seats and human blood volunteers and settle up on the stage.

Now I just need to make one hell of a speech.

Lucien looks my way, but I gesture for him to start. It'll be best that way. Lure them in with someone they know and trust, then hit them with the cold hard truth.

He steps just in front of me and looks his father dead in the eyes, not afraid, not backing down, and for the first time I've seen, really taking his place amongst his people. "You are not going to like the conversation at hand today, but I implore you"—he gestures to the room, meeting a few eyes—"all of you to simply listen."

His father places the human woman on his lap aside and leans in, listening. "Continue."

"We have three enemies collaborating—the Fae Queen and her army, Prince Phillipe and his delusions, and the SC causing mayhem with every decision made—and we need to start eliminating the threats one by one, weakening the opposition. We don't know where the Fae Queen's armies are, and we suspect that Phillipe has joined her, which leaves the Supernatural Council."

He looks to me, wide eyes subtly asking me to join in.

I step forward, wondering what the fuck I'm supposed to say to these people. "I know you're scared, and I know that playing politics is the job of the council, but if we don't loosen the hold the SC has on our magical communities, we won't win this war. They're too strong with their alliance."

Grabbing the plasmascreen rod out of my bag, I place it into the air and turn it on, watching as the screen rises in front of us, showing the plan from earlier. "We are dealing with the human and Fae council members as we speak, undoing the damage done to them. But this still leaves two species, splitting the council in half. I don't know about you, but that's not good enough for me. I don't want to leave the fate of the world up to a 50/50 chance. Either you command a revote of the Vampire councilmen, or we leave the fate of the Vampire community up to the Shifters."

A deep breath leaves my lungs.

They don't like it. I can see it in their eyes. The king is shaking his head, as though the very thought repulses him. "You ask too much this time, Magic." He looks around the room and asks, "Anyone who opposes this plan, raise your hand."

Every hand in the room goes up collectively.

"You see," he starts, "if we have another vote, we cannot have another for a decade. And this council does not think the SC are as big a threat as you make them out to be."

"Not as big a threat?" Lucien asks, rage slowly rising in his voice. "They have the biggest collection of armies in the world. If they choose to back the Fae Queen, or let themselves be manipulated and controlled by her, we will have a world war on our hands." His hair falls out of their perfect braids, falling around his face. "And you're just going to sit by and risk not only our people, but the people of every other species in existence? And why? Because you're a coward!"

"Watch your tongue!" the king booms. "Do not forget who you speak to."

"I speak to my future council. I look to the faces of those who will lead my people under my reign, in my stead when I am ill, who will be by my side when I make decisions for the benefit of Vampires as a whole, and not just for the ease and comfort of myself."

It's definitely going to be him, then? Lucien will be the next king?

The current king looks to me with a simple smile, answering my question. Then he turns back to his son with pondering eyes and a small smile hidden beneath contemplating lips. "We will discuss this further and reconvene tomorrow."

The breath Lucien releases is full of seething rage and frustration, but the voice in which he speaks is null, empty of emotion. "Thank you for your time and consideration, Father, council." He nods to the room and turns to me, gesturing me down the center aisle ahead of himself.

43

"He's so . . . Argh!" Lucien stomps back to his house, where he slams the door behind him. "I mean, does he not understand how important this is?" The fridge door slams shut him, and he carries various ingredients to the chopping board. "Is he that dense?"

"I don't think—"

"What does he think's going to happen? The Horsemen will ride to the rescue so he doesn't have to do anything?" Lots of chopped fruit later, and he's blending it all and adding it to a large glass jug. "You're not all powerful. You can't just snap your fingers and make shit happen."

"Maybe he just—"

Then he screws the cap off the vodka and triple sec and pours copious amounts in, before topping it all off with cranberry juice and ice. "It's like he doesn't want this shit to end." Grabbing two cocktail glasses, he pours us one each and hands me mine. "Like he's content to just sit there and do nothing."

The first sip is fruity, but with a sharp twist of alcohol that rolls around my taste buds. "This is really good."

Lucien stops ranting for a second to smile at me. "Might not be as good a cook as your brick wall of a boyfriend, but I can make a damn good summer cocktail."

"That you can." I raise my glass at him and wander out to the garden, where the large pools bring back memories of a previous life, of hate and violence. "They're all gonna find out one day, and it's like I'm sitting on edge, waiting for it to happen."

Lucien stands next to me, both of us basking in the heat. "Your past is yours and yours alone to bear. You don't need to tell anyone." He shrugs as he knocks back the rest of the glass. "You're still a person entitled to privacy, you know."

A small chuckle escapes my lips at the absurdity. "Have you seen the news headlines? The chatter online? The smear campaigns?" Taking another sip and a deep breath, I say, "Privacy is the very reason the Horsemen were in hiding for as long as they were."

"Really?"

"Uh-huh. They wanted their own lives, to be able to walk down the street without being hounded, to not be judged on every action." I take my boots and tights off, rolling them into a pile beside me, and dangle my feet in the pool. "I kinda ruined their lives."

Joining me, he ruffles my hair. "Yeah, but I bet you make up for it in orgasms." He turns to me, fangs descended, a glint in his eyes. "Seriously, how do you keep up with all four of them?"

I shrug. "Connie's the only demanding one. Nine and Dea are together, and Arrie and I are a new thing. Besides, it's not like they're not friends. They get it." The cool water and the iced cocktail are heaven in the beating sun, and I'm going to have to remember what Lucien did to make this drink. "And, you know, group sex."

Lucien splutters on nothing. "Group sex? You?"

"What?"

"Just never thought I'd see the day when a prude like you would be chatting about group sex with me."

My eyebrows raise in question. "What, Red not satisfying you enough?"

An actual blush creeps across his face. A blush! The satisfaction that gives me races through me.

"We haven't . . . We're not really . . . together."

"Why not?"

"Sometimes," he says with a laugh, "I forget that you weren't always as up-to-date with supernatural politics. Vampires and Witches. A Vampire prince and a Coven Witch, no less?" He grabs the rest of my drink and downs it in one. "Never gonna happen."

"You're my choice, Lucien." When he looks at me in question. "When the king inevitably asks for my opinion on how to replace him, I choose you. Not because you're the next oldest or the prettiest—"

"You think I'm pretty?" he preens, running a hand through his hair.

"You know you're pretty, stop fishing." We both laugh, knowing I'm right. "But I choose you because you're the most capable of running a species, of inciting change, of standing strong. And I think that if Red is really someone you want, you'd chase her until the sun burned down the world, consequences be damned." I get up to grab another drink from in the kitchen, but I turn back around. "And who knows? Maybe a Vampire prince and a Coven Witch is just what you all need."

Just as I enter the kitchen and grab the jug to pour myself another glass, a small pop sounds, and Nine and Arrie stumble into the kitchen. "You were quick."

"I told you," Nine says. "Easy peasy. Did all three in less than two hours and even had time to explain what's going on."

"Briefly," Arrie mutters. The scowl on his face is my first clue, but the frustration lacing those eyes is the second.

Rather than boil in his mood, I push him up against the counter and lean into his neck, where I pepper kisses and tease sharp teeth along his most sensitive spots.

After a few seconds, he nestles his nose into my neck and wraps a large hand around my waist. "Magic . . ."

"Hey," I hear Lucien call as he walks into the kitchen, "no threesomes in my house unless I'm invited."

I snicker, but apparently Arrie doesn't find it as funny, because he snarls. "I'm not sharing with you."

"Stop being snarly. Lucien's just angry that I'm getting more than him."

"I can get whatever I want whenever I want."

"Yeah, but none of that is Red, so you don't want to."

"Red?" Nine asks, hovering near. "Really?"

Lucien shrugs, wanting the argument to end if his scrunched up porcelain face is anything to go by. "Probably not."

"Why not?" Nine asks, ever the gossip. "I mean, I know why." He taps his head. "But I wanna chat about it, anyway."

"Stupid Vampire Witch thing," I say, waving my hand through the air.

"Vampires live an awfully long time, Lucien. For a mortal, anyway. And let me tell you, in a hundred years, you're going to regret letting society tell you who to love."

"I am not letting soc—"

"Yeah you are, but it's okay." I pat him on the back, smiling. "I get it. You're scared. So you're choosing the easy road."

Arrie smirks at me, Nine smiles, and I just internally preen.

"I am not!" He slams a glass on the counter and it shatters into pieces, so he forces a breath out through his nose. "God, you're annoying."

"Yup."

"Fine!" He looks into the mirror in the corner of the room and sighs, then re-braids his hair. "I'll back by morning." Grabbing a teleporting crystal out of his pocket, he vanishes as quickly as it breaks on the floor.

"Guess I'll clean up, then." I use some air woo-woo to shove the glass pieces into the bin and brush my hands off. "So, what now?"

"Well, Dea and Connie are busy," Nine says, "so it's just us three for a while. Where are you with the Vampire king?"

"He's thinking about it. Thanks to Lucien." I walk back out into the sunshine and breathe in the warm air. "He'll make a great king one day."

"That he will, Killer." Arrie rests his hands on my shoulders, standing behind me, while Nine flies around the garden for a bit.

"You know," he shouts, "I will miss being able to fly."

"I'll make you a flying charm or something one day."

Yay!

Arrie chuckles under his breath, a smile peeking through—it's becoming more common hearing his laugh and smile.

"How are you doing?" I ask, looking up at him with my head tilted back. "I know how much you're struggling with moving on."

He shrugs, wordless. "I . . ." Then he sighs, running a hand down his face. "I am managing."

Nine stands next to us, floating down to the ground. "He is focusing on how happy you make him and enjoying your new relationship, but when things are quiet and everyone is busy, he can't stop feeling guilty."

"What he said," Arrie mumbles.

I wrap my hands over his on my waist and take a deep breath, organizing my thoughts. "When you're feeling that way, you should seek one of us out. It doesn't have to be me—I get why I might not be the best person to lean on—but it should be someone. You've been suffering alone for a really long time, so I think it's time to start trying something else."

"Ve's right, dude. You can't just suffer for another thousand years, and burying it all so you can be happy with Magic also isn't the answer."

"Then what is?" His hands clench into fists as his body goes rigid. "What else am I supposed to do? Our relationship is both the best and worst thing in the world for me. And I don't know what to do with that."

I turn in his arms and grab his face, yanking it to me. "You just have to feel. There is nothing wrong with love, hate, guilt, happiness, or anything else. All you have to do is feel." My nose meets his as our foreheads touch. "That is the healthy choice. To express emotion and let it flow through you. Doing anything else is immature and unhealthy."

Nine smiles at us in the corner of my eye. "Just don't aim your emotions at people."

"Okay." I pull away, thinking about the best use of our time, then look to Nine, who's a ghost. Riiiight, so we can't really go too far afield. "Want to order in? Think of all the tasty takeouts they'll do here in New Orleans."

Takeout consisted of sugar—beignets, pastries, a whole nine-inch cake, and a sample of every ice cream flavor on the menu—and we popped the excess on the kitchen counter at home for Connie. With all the politics and organizing she's doing, she could sure use the sugar rush.

We're watching some lame horror movies on the screen when Arrie's hand lands on my thigh, brushing under the hem of my skirt and dangerously close to the "touch me and fuck me" zone.

"Arrie, wait, I—"

"Can I watch?" Nine asks, a wicked glint in his eye. "Pleeeease?"

"I was just about to say no to Arrie."

"Why?" Arrie asks. "Did I do something wrong? Is this about earlier?"

"Shhh." I put a finger to his lips, silencing him. "It's not you. I don't want Nine to feel left out considering neither of us can touch him."

"Oh." Something tells me he didn't think of that. But that's okay. It's my job to think of my boyfriends, not his. "Okay."

"No, wait," Nine says. "I maaaay have peaked on your first time a little." My raised eyebrows and Arrie's scowl make Nine sigh. "Heaven does have *some* perks, you know. But I missed loads cos it's hard to focus on Earth up there, and I really wanted to see." He pouts, lip sticking out and everything, like a child.

Arrie doesn't seem to mind, as he smiles and leans in to me, his kiss suddenly plundering my lips, his tongue suddenly slipping past my teeth, and his desire for me suddenly pressing into my stomach as he climbs on top and pins my wrists to the couch. He turns to face Nine with a smirk. "Any requests?"

"What am I, a porn star on demand, taking requests like a damn DJ?"

Yes, Nine says at the same time as Arrie says, "Tonight you are, yeah."

Fucking typical men.

44

"Hmmmm," Nine ponders. "What to ask for . . ." After a few more moments—a few moments of Arrie kissing down my neck and brushing lips against my cleavage—Nine says, *I wanna see ve on their knees, sucking dick like a pro.*

If he thinks I'm taking Arrie's dick like a pro, he's gonna be disappointed.

He trails kisses up the side of my neck and whispers into my ear, "Just do your best."

Apparently Nine is translating thoughts like he does when he's with Dea.

I want to say I'm not into this, that I don't have any bodily response to Nine watching us like we're starring in a porno, but I am into this. My body is responding. And if my boyfriend wants a show after being dead, then a show it is.

Arrie straddles my lap, leaning over me as he kisses me everywhere he can reach, my hands still unable to move from where they're pinned. His foresty scent washes over me, his neck exposed as his teeth rake over my shoulder, pain and pleasure shooting through me.

My fangs slide free, and they're sinking into Arrie's artery before I even think to ask. But it's Arrie. He likes it. And predictably, the moment I drink, he groans and grinds into my stomach, seeking friction.

Everything lights up when he kisses my neck again, and now it's not just him seeking friction, moaning.

I want more. Need more. But I let him go, slipping free, and shifting us so he's the one pinned beneath me. Weaker than me. And now his rock-hard dick is mine for the taking.

Take his pants off.

Following orders, I sink onto the floor on my knees and undo his belt, whipping it off, then I unbutton his jeans and slide them off, leaving him on Lucien's couch in nothing but his underwear and a t-shirt.

The imprint his dick leaves in his underwear has my mouth watering and my body pulsing. My hand reaches out to run a finger from bottom to top, then dipping into the waistband.

His breath hitches.

Nine watches with rapt attention, eyes pinning my hand under his glare.

"Nine?" I whisper. "Are you able to take your clothes off?"

His nods. "Yeah, they're just ghost clothes."

"Good." My fingers wrap around Arrie through the fabric, his length hot in my hand as a groan slips free from his lips uncontrolled. "I want a show too."

Arrie scowls, impatient. "Just suck my dick, Magic." When I don't move my hand or go to undress him, he grabs a fistful of my hair and yanks his underwear off, then smirks. "Open up."

The sting of the pull on my hair zaps through me, lighting me on fire. And I can't help it, my mouth opens on a gasp.

Arrie takes advantage of the reaction and shoves the head of his dick in my mouth. "Yeah, like that."

My pants are flooded, and fuck I wish Nine weren't a ghost, because being filled from both ends sounds like a great way to defile Lucien's house.

I wish I could fuck you too. He settles beside Arrie, totally naked, dick in hand. *I really do.*

"Watching me fuck her will have to do," Arrie says between clenched teeth just as I slide my lips further down his length. "Fffuuck." His hand on my hair fists tighter, and he pushes me down further.

So far that I'm not sure I can take much more without gagging.

"Breathe in," Nine says. "And swallow the moment it hits your gag reflex."

Okaaaay.

(Cue doubt.)

I take a deep breath in through my nose, and Arrie slowly pushes my head further down toward his pelvis. He's trying to go slow, I can feel it, but he's pushing up against the back of my throat and I'm panicking. I know I did this with Dea, but it's different. So different.

Following Nine's instructions, I swallow, and Arrie sinks his length down my throat with a moan so wild I can't help but flit my gaze up his torso and watch his eyes roll back and his head hit the back of the couch.

Nine's watching too, his hand slowly moving up and down his cock—too slowly if you ask me, but hey, it's his orgasm.

Experimentally slowly I raise my head back up, Arrie's grip loosening, and swallow him back down. Again. Again. And again. Until I find a rhythm that's comfortable and has pre-cum leaking down my throat and Arrie's moans gradually getting louder.

Shit, dude, you look good. I want my dick sucked like that.

I'll give you all the dick sucking you want when I can. Promise.

For now, I do my best to suck and swallow at an even pace that increases incrementally. But when Arrie growls and tightens his hand, his hips rising up to meet my mouth, I don't focus on what I'm doing anymore and instead bounce my head in rhythm to his hips, letting him use me.

Letting him light a fire inside me so hot, I'd need all four of my partners to extinguish it properly. Or Connie and a bathtub, it would seem.

Shit, Nine groans. *When was that?*

Arrie moans louder, his eyes widening as they meet mine. "Fuck, one day I'll . . . I'll be there to watch that."

On our last date. Came so hard and so many times I passed out and woke up the next morning forgetting time had even passed.

I send Nine images of the various things I've done since he's not been with us, and by the sounds Arrie's making, he's sharing them.

Both of their heads roll back as they rock their hips at the same pace, Nine mimicking Arrie's, I assume.

I go to speed up, but Arrie pulls out of me and grabs me by the shoulders and shoves my skirt off, rips the tights and panties off, and shoves me on the couch, ass up.

He has enough sanity to slam two fingers inside me first, furiously ramming me apart, preparing me as best he can in whatever state his mind's in.

Not wanting that state of mind to end, I send more images—things we've done, things I want to do, and things I've read about—and Arrie's eyes glaze over as Nine chuckles at us both, his dick leaking.

There's preamble here, and I realize that he went easy on me before, afraid I'd break or some shit. But he knows better now. So he lines up and buries himself in me in one motion, not caring if I'm ready for him. He wants me.

"Something tells me he's getting you."

Arrie moans as he moves back out and slams back in. "So fucking wet." Then he says something in Norse, but I don't catch it.

He said you're tight and wanted something to shove into your ass.

Caught between heat and horror that anything more will fit, Arrie grabs my throat and squeezes so my head rushes. But I can still breathe.

I send more snippets Nine's way, and he shares them one at a time, slowly working Arrie into a frenzy I'm not sure my vagina will survive.

"Ffuuck," he groans. His fingers reach to my clit and pinch hard enough to hurt, rubbing between his thumb and forefinger. A growl whispers against my ear, "Come. Fucking come now."

And goddess damn it, my body explodes, fire spreading, moans leaking from my lips on the end of curses.

"Shit," Nine swears. "That's fucking hot."

"Ffuuck, yes. That." Arrie slams into me, his skin slapping against my ass, leaving bright red marks, no doubt. "Arrghh!" His fingers close around my throat so tight it hurts and I can't breathe as he comes, pounding me harder than anything I've felt before.

"Shit, shit shit." I watch as cum spills across Nine's stomach, his hips riding his hand in rapid movements until he's stopped leaking.

Arrie comes to a stop, his hand loosening around my neck, and he grabs my waist and pulls me back against him. "I'm not done with you." He pulls out and slides his fingers in place instead, his thumb softly circling my clit.

It's in such contrast to the rough pounding he just gave me, I don't know what to do with it. But it's nice, like a massage and a thank you.

And I know in this moment that I'd marry this man if he asked. I'll never let him pull away again. He can have his space and be with me at the same time.

He shoves his knee between my legs, separating them, and the cum he filled me with leaks down his fingers and onto the couch. "Anything you want?" he asks.

"Ummm . . ." Aside from Nine inside me now? "I'm not sure."

He keeps up his movements, but he settles me in his lap and drapes my legs over the sides of his, pinning me apart. "Anything you wanna see, dude?"

I look back over to Nine, who's working his still-hard dick, but slower than before. His eyes are watching us, tracing Arrie's fingers and watching my pussy like someone who'd give anything to have their face down there.

Nine groans inside my head. *I'd give every tomorrow for a taste of you. Just a drop.*

"I want you. So much." A sob leaves me, and Arrie stops and pulls out, but I shove his fingers back inside me. "Don't stop."

"You don't have to," he says in my ear.

"But I want to. I want to have you fuck me and be as close to Nine as possible." Tears leak down my face. "Please."

He kisses my cheek. "Anything for you, Killer." He looks to Nine, their gazes meeting. "Anything."

Nine moves to the front of me, watching Arrie's every movement.

Arrie tweaks my nipple with his other hand, and I arch into him, moans slipping freely, legs tense but like jelly at the same time.

"Curl your fingers and use the heel of your palm on her clit," Nine orders.

Arrie follows his instructions, placing a kiss on my neck at the same time.

And after a few seconds, the heat inside me rachets up, soaring through me like fireworks. "Nine . . ."

"I'm right here." He holds up his spare hand, a tear rolling down his cheek, as his hand speeds up. "I'm right here enjoying the show."

I can feel myself leaking all over Arrie's hand, a mixture of himself and me, but he doesn't seem to mind. He speeds up ever so slightly, increasing the pressure, and my body screams.

I'm so close.

"Don't stop."

"I won't," Arrie whispers, then peppers kisses up my neck and along my cheek bone.

My legs shake as my knees clench against Arrie's, and the moans slipping from my mouth border on screams as I clench around his fingers. Tighter than ever. "Ah! Yes, yes, yes." My hands grip Arrie's elbows, nails digging in. "Niiine!"

"Oh god," Nine curses. "Yeah, Sweetie. You look so fucking good." He's staring directly at me, watching me orgasm on Arrie's fingers and drip onto the carpet, listening to me scream his name.

"Want you . . . inside me," I manage just as the orgasm peaks, lasting longer than usual.

Nine's knees buckle, hitting the floor, as more cum shoots from his dick. *Want to fuck you till you pass out,* he says as he screams my name.

We all just stay where we are, motionless. Nine hovers while Arrie holds me, and I'm still crying. I just want my boyfriend to hold me. I want them both.

I know, Sweetie. I'm so sorry.

"Not your fault."

Arrie sniffs behind me, and it's then I realize that he cried watching us. "I know this isn't the right time, but dude, even your cum is ghostly."

"Shut the fuck up," Nine groans.

Lucien knows. I can tell by the stink eye he's sending us. We're walking to the Vampire Royal Council building early in the morning, getting some fresh air.

I look at him—really look at him—and realize that maybe it isn't me he's annoyed at. His hands haven't unclenched all morning, and I didn't hear him come home last night. He's also still wearing the same clothes.

"Sooo," I ask, "how did things go with Red?" Terrified of the answer.

He stops. He sighs. And for a moment, he looks like a man with a broken heart. "She said no."

We all stop, looking at him with sadness.

"Don't do that!" He waves his hands at our faces. "Don't look at me like I'm some kicked puppy. I'm not. I'm a Vampire prince." He straightens his shirt and replaces his braids. "It's time I fixed this stupidity."

With Lucien marching the way, the Vampire Council building soon looms, but today there are no ads or announcements on the plasmascreen windows; instead, there's a regal-looking picture of the king with the caption CHANGE IS COMING. We all look at each other with raised eyebrows, and Lucien brings up the interface to his datachip, scrolling through emails, messages, and other communications, looking for any inkling of an answer.

By the look on his face, he finds nothing.

Great.

We're going in blind. As usual.

Here's to hoping the king still likes me enough to keep me in the loop.

The council chamber is tense, with hushed whispers bouncing across the room like a playground fair, but we take our seats near the front and wait for the king to arrive. We're thirty minutes early for a change, so no dramatic entrances for me.

Lucien looks me up and down with a small smile. "You know, you're kinda hotter as a guy." He gestures to my jeans, shirt and waistcoat look I'm sporting today, stolen from his own wardrobe. "Especially when I get to dress you."

Should take Dea and go shopping together. Probably make a great pair.

Lucien's eyes light up for a second, but then he steals himself and takes a small inhale. "I would be honored." Which is Lucien code for he'd shit himself for the opportunity.

Shopping it is. Besides, I could use a better guy wardrobe. All I have are jeans and t-shirts.

Thirty minutes later on the dot, the doors swing open and the king storms in, followed by an entourage of guards and other personnel. His crown sits atop his head, and he's wearing what looks to be a very official robe.

I look to Lucien, who's sitting there with nervous hands clasped in his lap. Nine and Arrie smirk between them, clearly knowing something I don't.

Guess I'll just have to pay attention and find out.

"Good morning, everyone," he starts, sounding louder than I've ever heard him sound. "Yesterday we were asked a very important question, a request from the Horsemen and the embassy that has taken our council a great deal of time to discuss." He looks around the room, his gaze softening. "Many of us have not had the chance to go home yet, and for that I am grateful."

They haven't gone home? I look around the room, and sure enough, lots are looking tired and ragged, paler than usual.

"We came to a decision last night that we feel will have great effects for the community at large, as well as the world." He looks to me with a knowing look and smiles. "We have agreed to allow a revote for the Vampire Supernatural Council representative seats. We have already informed the SC, and the announcement is due to go public in a matter of hours. This is a lengthy process that will take time to organize, time I am sure the Horsemen do not have. It is therefore our choice to suspend our seats on the SC in the meantime. This will remove us from any position of international power."

He looks to me as he says those words, his meaning clear. He's putting himself and his people at risk for me. This could end badly for them if I don't protect the king's choice. If I don't help protect his people.

Clearly I've gained prominent clout with the Vampires.

Yay.

Lucien rises and joins his father on the small stage, a smile on his face. "We will bounce back from this stronger than ever, and no one will be left behind once we've dealt with this problem." He looks to me, trying to ask something, but I trust him. He can say what-ever he wants. "The embassy already has pixie and Demon representatives in our efforts to share our position and world with supernaturals in politically lower stations. Hope-fully, we can create a world where all species are equal and everyone's lives and cultures are protected."

A few clap, a few scowl, and a few don't seem to know what to think.

So I step up and join them both on stage. "I know this is scary. I do. And I know a change of this magnitude is a challenging path to walk as a community. But I promise to stand for you. For all of you. Once the threat has been removed, we will work to improve the Supernatural Council and rebuild it to what its original purpose was aiming for: peace between the magical and non-magical communities."

I think generally settled but uneasy is the best I'm going to get today. At least Nine will know how they're thinking and feeling. I hope.

 the ass ever, but I have to do it. It's my job. And you don't always get the luxury of loving your job.

We're sat in a café not far from the council building, when Lucien turns to Nine and asks, "How are the council feeling?"

"Everyone is stunned," he says from his floating seat next to me. "They haven't processed how insane it is to leave the SC. But there are quite a few councilmen who are happy to finally be challenging their rule."

Arrie sips his coffee in silence, happy to simply absorb the conversation, but his hand is on my knee, a comforting weight.

"Well, they have caused havoc for Vampires everywhere, and if not for Nine's blood supplement, they'd all be starving right now. It makes sense some of them are angry and seeking to fix things."

"Hopefully that anger helps us maintain control." Lucien stresses a hand over his wrinkled forehead. "I hope Father is up to taking control of this. He's not as . . . mentally there as he used to be."

"You're next in line, right?" I ask.

Lucien nods. "But I can't step up until he steps down or passes on."

"Could you not stand beside him, helping where he needs it? Like a united front?"

Nine smiles at me, then turns to Lucien. "I think he'd like that."

He looks at us with a gracious yet thoughtful look on his face. "I'll suggest it to him."

"Sooooo," I ask, getting to the good stuff, "what happened with Red?"

A huff of frustration leaves his down-turned lips. "Exactly what you're imagining. A humiliated Vampire prince on his knees begging a stubborn future Coven Witch to admit her feelings and work together to create a world where we can be happy."

"And she didn't go for that?" That sounds unlikely. Red might be stubborn, but she's an idealist, always thinking for herself and not just for her people. "That doesn't sound like Red."

"Well, then you go talk to her." He throws his hands up in the air in defeat. "Because I am done trying to persuade her to give us a chance. If she wants this, she can come and get it herself."

Ohhh, grumpy Vampire prince. Was this what I was like with Arrie? Ugh. No wonder no one wanted to hang out with me.

A little taste of your own medicine never hurt anyone.

Shut up.

I go to smack him in the arm, but lower my hand at the last minute when I remember that it'll go right through him. For fuck's sake. I need to sort him out a body.

You will.

I'd certainly rather be figuring that out than dealing with all this political bullshit. It's exhausting.

Yes. Yes, it is.

"I wonder how Dea and the ambassadors are doing with the Fae councilmen?" I ask, wanting to change the subject. "Maybe they could use our help in the meantime?"

Lucien looks up, a little surprised.

"All we can do right now is wait. Besides, I can teleport us back in no time."

Lucien waves a hand at me. "Go. Be free." His hand sinks into his other hand. "Come back for the announcement of the councilmen electives tomorrow. Father wants to do this as quickly as possible."

I wrap a single arm around Lucien's shoulder and change my charm bracelet into its staff form and leave, letting Arrie and Nine follow behind me. Once clear of other people, I teleport us to Rue de Rivoli, Paris.

Our scenery changes, and I'm suddenly standing on a street lined with old yellowish-brick buildings bustled together in a neat row, a wide road wedged between them.

"Does anyone know where Dea and the ambassadors are?"

Arrie says, "The two Fae councilmen are staying not far from the Fae palace."

"We've been there before," Nine says, floating away. "Follow me."

Here's to hoping it's not too far. Walking was not on my agenda today when I selected this outfit. Nor was Paris, which is a little colder than New Orleans. But oh well, live and learn. Dress for all the places you're going in a day.

After twenty minutes of fast-paced walking (more like light-paced jogging), we round a familiar corner near the Fae palace, which is just a few left turns away.

"We don't actually have to go to the Fae Court, do we?"

"No," Nine says while laughing. "We wouldn't have sent most of our ambassadors into the Fae Court, Sweetie."

"Right." Of course. That would have been silly. "It's, what, six pm here?"

Arrie nods, checking his fancy time zone watch.

"Then they're probably at dinner somewhere."

Arrie pulls out his mobile phone—which, yes, we still use from time to time, and yes, I'll be grabbing us datachips the first moment I can—and phones who I assume is Dea, because after a few moments, we're changing direction and heading toward a nearby street with restaurants and plasmascreens lining the buildings with ads, and old-fashioned streetlights that curve at the top. Good old Paris' old and new mishmash never fails to make me gape in awe.

"They're in here." Arrie opens the door and speaks to the greeter, who guides us past tables seating couples, families, get-togethers, and business meetings, until we pass a curtain at the back, which leads to an exclusive area cut off from the main restaurant. And there, sat with six ambassadors, is my Angel of Death in a suit I've not yet seen with a placating smile on his gorgeous face.

He looks up when the curtain falls back into place and lifts a genuine smile the moment he sees us. He makes his excuses to the table and gets up to greet us. "I was not expecting you, Angel." He wraps an arm around my waist and tucks a thumb into my belt loop. "You look amazing."

"Thanks." A small blush creeps over my face. "Lucien dressed me."

Nine floats through us, making us shiver, and shoves his face into Dea's. "I'm here too."

Dea shifts into his Angel form and chuckles. "I know, Famine. You are impossible not to notice." He runs a hand down Nine's cheek, and I get to watch his shiver as his eyes close and his head falls ever so slightly back. "I could never forget you."

"Well," Arrie says, breaking the moment, "we've come to be help, if you need it."

"I will always take my team's help."

Nine grabs one hand while I grab his other, and Arrie rests a hand on my shoulder, as we make our way over to the table where servers are setting us seats and moving things around to accommodate our sudden arrival.

Red sits on the other side of Arrie, with two of our Shifter ambassadors on her right. And on the other side of Nine, who kindly hovers above his seat, sit our two Vampire ambassadors and our single Fae ambassador.

We have the full entourage today, it seems. A round house.

The two Fae sitting in front of us look stressed, if their sweating foreheads are anything to go by. But they pour over the paperwork and the videos and the rest of the evidence presented to them with fervor nonetheless. Enraptured by our experiences.

"This is all real?" one asks, his blue skin mildly white in the low twinkling lights of the green-and-brown-colored restaurant. "How do we know it's not all fabricated?"

"Oui," the other says. "Why should we believe you over our beloved queen?"

Red stifles a frustrated groan as the table goes rigid on our side.

"Because," Dea says, "we have no reason to lie. We are going to war with the Fae with or without you. All we are trying to achieve here is to the neutralize the threat the Supernatural Council produce."

"We are not asking for the SC's help," Red reaffirms. "We are asking that they stand neutral."

"I just . . ." The blue-skinned Fae frowns at the paper in his hand, his fingers shaking. "This is . . . unbelievable."

"One of our own got kidnapped under the Fae Queen's orders simply because she doesn't like us." I shrug. "I'm sorry, but she's not who she says she is."

"Magic is right," Nine agrees. "She's manipulative. She's purposefully blocking information to you and your people, even through your datachips, to make you see the world in the way she wants you to see it."

Maybe we could undo that for the Fae datachips, and then they'll see for themselves.

Not a bad idea, but a risky one. We won't know the outcome of that.

We cannot control what the Fae would do with such information, Dea echoes inside my head.

Don't they deserve informational freedom? Don't they deserve to make a decision for themselves, rather than have everything decided for them by a tyrannical ruler who wants to be placed above every other species?

No one says anything, and everything around us is clearly waiting for one of us to say something. Anything.

"Then undo it," the Fae with the blue skin says. "If you're so certain she's doing all of"—he gestures to the piles of papers—"this, then undo the block on our datachips."

Dea turns to Nine, who sighs. "I'd need access to the network to do that. Every species runs their own, as a way to segment people's information and control what gets shared, so she'll have that stored somewhere safe. Probably in the castle itself."

The two Fae look to each other, then nod. Serious expressions on their faces. "We are willing to let you into our datachip networks, so long as we can come with you and see everything you're doing."

Dea looks to everyone, who nod in turn. Then he turns back to the two Fae and agrees to their terms. "I wish to leave as soon as possible. As you can imagine, time is of the essence."

"It is not far from here, but getting you in might be a problem. It is heavily secured, and no unauthorized personnel are permitted past the doors."

Dea smirks, then takes his charm bracelet off, removing the permanent visibility spell. "That will not be a problem." He puts it back on in time to see the two Fae reattach their jaws to their faces. Dea turns to me and Arrie, then to Nine, and tells us, "Stay here."

"May I come with?" our Fae ambassador asks. "I've always wanted to see Earth's Fae Court."

"Of course." Dea whisks all four of them away, and we're left to eat dinner.

Well, Nine won't be eating, but the rest of us are.

"At least the food's nice," Arrie grumbles.

"Not as nice as yours." I turn to look at Red, who meets my eyes and then quickly darts them away again.

But I keep staring, and it must annoy her, because she turns to me and asks, "Do you have something you need to say?"

"Yes, actually."

"Magic," Arrie warns. "You shouldn't get involved in other people's affairs."

He's right. For once.

"Oh, pfft. Shut up the pair of you. Lucien is my friend." I give them both a withering stare, and they leave me alone. "You really hurt his feelings."

"He's a Vampire prince, I'm sure he'll be fine," Red scoffs, shoving a piece of her roasted duck in her mouth.

"He's still a person, Red. Being someone important doesn't mean you don't deserve happiness."

"Maybe if you're a Horseman," she snarls. "The rest of us aren't so lucky."

I get the feeling she's not talking about Lucien anymore. She's talking about herself.

"I can't officially date a Vampire, okay. It's against Coven law."

"It's . . . what?"

"I'll be kicked out, disowned. I won't have a home anymore. Or a people. He knows this. But he's asking it of me, anyway." I can hear the sob in her words, the emotion that maybe I shouldn't have started out in the open.

I reach over and lay my hand on hers. "No matter what you decide, you'll always have a home in *Sheruta* and friends in us. And you'll keep your ambassador position on our side."

She looks to me with a thoughtful smile, a single tear running down her face. "Thank you."

"How long do you think they'll be?" Felicity asks, her gentle voice gracing my ears. "It's just . . ." She looks around, fidgeting. "I haven't been to Earth since . . . you know."

Oh, goddess. How stupid of me. "I can send you home if you like?"

She looks to the table and nods, a small gesture. "Yes, please."

"Here." Arrie hands her a teleporting crystal from his pocket. "Take this."

One day, I need to set up a production warehouse in *Sheruta* for those damn crystals. Witches and Fae can make them together. Easy peasy.

Not a bad plan. Should get Connie to help. You know, afterwards.

Guess it's one more thing for the list, I think to myself as Felicity heads home.

Nine's hand goes to rest on my knee, but it hovers just above as he realizes he can't actually touch me.

"Okay people, if anyone has any ideas on how to make a corporeal form for my boyfriend, I am all ears," I address the room. "I am sick of not being able to hold his hand."

Everyone remains silent as not a single person offers a suggestion. Well, it was worth a try.

"Have you considered looking into death magic?" one of the Vampires asks.

And I have to hold in my audible groan.

How the fuck am I supposed to use that to create life?

"It's just that when I was Thailand, there was a Witch who claimed it could bring and take life at will."

I snap my head to him, eyes boring holes. "Bring *and* take life?"

He nods.

"Thank you. That's actually helpful."

He bows his head and returns to the conversation he was having with the Vampires next to him.

Death magic can give life, too? But how? It's called death magic, for fuck's sake. How can it give life? Aki never mentioned anything about it giving life. So maybe he doesn't know? Or maybe he knows and didn't want to tell me because he's a manipulative little shit with a god complex.

I'm so gonna kill him.

I'm gonna drive a dagger through his black heart, carve it out of his chest, and make him eat it. And then I'm going to ask Dea to find the gates to hell and make him drag him there.

Nine looks mildly horrified, but I wave off his concern.

Arrie's phone rings, and he answers, listens, and his eyes go wide for a moment before he schools his features and says, "We'll be right there." He looks to me, Red, and the others. "We have to go. They've run into some trouble."

Everyone runs from their seat, Red swiping her datachip on the way out to pay for everything, and come to a halt outside the doors.

"Does anyone know where they are?"

No one says anything.

"Sweetie," Nine says, "you can probably track Dea if you focus hard enough."

Track him?

Angel mated, Sweetie.

Oh, right.

I shift into my female form and focus on Dea, allowing the memory of him to fill me, the scent of smoky lavender and the feel of his Angel feathers running over my bare skin. And something in me sets alight and joins him to me. He's scared, alone, and panicking, and I need to get to him.

"Follow!"

I sprint toward him, but I slow down when I realize that not everyone can keep up with my Vampire speed.

Please be okay. Please be okay. Please be okay.

We jog down alleyways and speed across roads we should probably be more careful crossing, but it doesn't matter. Dea's scared. He's panicking, and I don't know why. And I'm not there.

Briefly I can hear Nine telling Arrie to just leave me be and let me do my thing, and I appreciate that. I don't want to hurt one boyfriend while trying to save another.

"We're close." A couple of more turns, and we're here. Somewhere. But it's just an empty plaza. Where are they? "Why aren't they here?"

One of the Vampires squints and gasps. "We're on top of them."

I look to the floor and roll my sleeve back. "Get out of the way." Air magic soars me high into the sky and hovers me a hundred feet above the plaza, and then I'm shooting down to the ground with my fist out in front of me.

The earth shatters beneath me as stone cracks and the plaza caves in, opening whatever is beneath us.

The others rush forward, craning around the dust to see the damage, and when it finally settles, a large hole has opened up beneath us. And in the hole is a shaking Angel on his knees surrounded by rows upon rows of computers glowing bright blue.

"Dea!" Nine is the first down, flying through the pieces of rubble without issue. "Dea?"

"Nine?" Dea doesn't look at him, but looks at the something in the distance that's not there. "Nine? Where are you?" Tears track down his face as his puffy eyes weep. "Why can I not see you?"

"I don't know."

I soon join them, but I can't touch him. He's surrounded by an impenetrable shield made of some kind of glowing green plasma. A Fae spell. "Just hold on, Dea."

"Magic?"

"I'm right here."

"Why can I not touch you?" He's reaching his hands out, but they're coming to a stop at the barrier. "What is that? I cannot see beyond the nightmare behind my eyelids."

"Nightmare?" I ask, shifting forms. I run my hands through the spell, feel for the key points and how they interlink and weave together. "What nightmare?"

"That day in the bedroom, when I could not feel anything, not even you."

"After Nine died?" I ask, still analyzing the spell. It seems to be some kind of mental illusion spell. Luckily, they're easily broken with a counterspell.

He sobs, his body shaking.

"Okay, just hold on a second. I'm going to break the spell." I raise my hands and trace several runes, joining them together in bundles that act at central nodes, and then slipping in an incantation. "That should just about do it."

The green glow blows away on the breeze, and Dea releases a heaving breath, hands slamming onto the concrete beneath us. Upon opening his eyes, he runs into us and slams both Nine and I against his body. "Do not get caught in one of those spells."

Everyone around us laughs a little, letting us have our moment. Even Arrie. Who is standing vigil in front of us, blocking us from everyone else, including the three Fae who accompanied Dea.

The one from our embassy is shaking like a leaf, his eyes shocked and the hair on his head singed off, leaving him bald.

"You okay?" I ask, not stepping out of Dea's hold.

"I've just . . . never seen a Horsemen fall before."

Dea stands up straight. "It was more of a trip." He shakes his shoulders out and looks to the other two Fae, who so far have done and said nothing. "Tell me where the damn thing is."

Everyone scrambles out of his way as he waves his wings, flapping the dust off them, and standing tall. My Angel of Death.

They rush to the other side of the room and point to a plasmascreen, where they scan their chips and enter their identities into the computer.

Nine hovers over them and orders, "Click on the button on the bottom right."

Dea follows his instructions, since Nine can't touch anything—he just goes straight through it—and after twenty minutes of trying to figure it out, they finally have the block removed from their datachips.

Seriously, I kind of daze out through most of it, since it's like they're speaking another language, but I trust they can do it. Especially Nine, he's a genius.

I try.

The ambassadors stand around, not quite sure what to do, but they at least have the sense to set up a perimeter so the general public leave us alone.

Red is coordinating with the local police officers who have arrived on the scene. And if I'm not careful, by the heat of their tones, I'm going to have to get us all out of here before we're arrested.

I shift forms so I can listen to their conversation better, but it's over by the time I manage to blink, let alone shift.

"Racaille," the officer mutters under his breath, his hand resting on his magigun at his hip.

We need to leave.

I Vampire speed toward everyone, carrying them into the center of the room, where Nine, Dea, Arrie, and the Fae are, and my staff pops into existence and soon we're hurtling through the aether toward *Sheruta*.

I didn't really think about it when I made the decision, but I may have brought the Fae councilmen with us. Oops.

I turn to them and apologize. "Sorry, fellas. But they were going to open fire in a few moments." I gesture to the ambassadors. "I might be immortal, but they're not."

Neither of them knows what to say, but our Fae ambassador says, "Maybe you should stay in *Sheruta* for a few days. See how we do things here."

"That's a good idea," I agree. "We can set you up in a hotel, and you're free to work, chat to other people, etc. You're not a hostage."

"Also," Dea adds, "it might be a good idea to go back after everything has died down."

They look to each other, frustration and unease on their faces, but they turn back to us and nod. Remaining silent.

We're in the main meeting room, and Connie and Felicity rush in, looking at us all with a mild amount of surprise on her face, probably wondering what we're all doing together. But she doesn't have time. "We have a problem."

47

"She's here," Connie says. "All three of them are here."

"Connie," Nine starts, "you're going to have be more specific."

"Aki, the Fae Queen, and Prince Phillipe are here."

Oh, for fuck's sake. I don't have time for this. I need to get back to Lucien.

Everyone looks to me expectantly, looking for guidance. Instructions. Something.

"Okay." I turn to the Fae ambassador. "Take these two to the hotel around the corner and put it on the embassy's tab. Then come back." Felicity is leaning against the wall with a worried look on her face. "Could you please contact Lucien and give him an update?" Then, without missing a beat, I ask Connie, "Where are they now?"

"Being held at the portal in the guildhall, but I don't think they'll stay there for long."

I turn to Rufus and the other *Sheruta* ambassadors. "Evacuate the center."

They look shocked, but I'm not taking any chances. Connie didn't mention an army, but even alone, those three are pieces of work. Not a single *Sherutan* is dying because my twin brother is a psycho.

"Nine, could you please fly high over the guildhall and see what they're thinking. Do not get caught. They still don't know you're alive."

He floats through the wall, gone, while everyone else gets to it.

"Red, Arrie, have our army on standby."

They march out the room, a feral pair if I ever saw one. Remind me not to mess with the two of them together.

"Dea, Connie, and I will go meet them," I say to the one Witch and two Shifters left in the room. "You alert the various councils and stay here, ready to step in if necessary."

OUTSIDE IS CHAOS, PEOPLE LEAVING THEIR HOUSES AND BUSINESSES, AND THE GUILDHALL IS even worse. Employees are panicking, not knowing what to do. Everyone running around as though they have no heads.

"Everyone," I shout, "please leave and follow the evacuation procedure."

Everyone starts leaving, and soon I've found the fire alarm setting and pull it. The ringing echoes through my head like a siren, but I ignore it. Instead, I march to the portal room, where the doors are closed and six security guards stand watch, fear and determination on their faces. But relief floats through them when they see us.

"You're relieved." I wave my arm, dismissing them. "Leave with the rest of the evacuees."

"We've shut the portal down," one of them says on his way out. "No one can get in or out of *Sheruta* without a teleporting crystal."

I sprawl my senses out, drowning out the fire alarm, and check to make sure no one else is in the building. "Building's clear."

"Ready?" Connie asks.

Dea and I both look at her and smile. "Ready."

The doors swing open with a gust of wind, and we march forward. My staff is still out, gripped tightly in my hand, ready for use.

Stood in the middle of the portal building are three of my least favorite people, being led by Aki. And I'm about ready to roll heads when Nine says, *The Fae Queen and Prince Phillipe are here for peace. I still can't get inside Aki's head.*

Connie and Dea probably heard that, too.

Dea is the first one to say something. "Leave. You are not welcome in our home."

The Fae Queen smiles gently, her beauty gracing my senses. "Now, now. You own an entire realm. There must be space for us to chat somewhere."

"If you think we're listening to a thing you've got to say—"

"You will," Phillipe says, "when you learn what we have to say."

"You are a Horseman of peace, aren't you?" Aki says. Even his words sound false, dripping in poison. How did I ever believe a word that came out of his mouth? "I know you don't want war, sister."

The hiss that leaves my lips sounds feral, even to my ears. "You're no brother of mine. Leave!" I slam my staff into the ground and light my other hand on fire. "Or suffer."

Aki smirks, confident, annoying as hell. "So hostile."

"You tried to wipe out the main Vampire cities, created hostility between the magical and human communities, lied to and manipulated me, and killed my boyfriend among thousands of others." One of the charms in my staff spreads around the room, creating a smoke screen that covers everyone else, so thick you couldn't possibly see through it. "If you think you're anything but a villain, then you're as psychotic as I thought you were."

His smirk vanishes as rage contorts his mouth into a snarl, and his eyes flash daggers. "I am not psychotic! It's this world that's insane. Everyone just acting as though the Fae couldn't wipe them out whenever they chose or as though Vampires aren't draining everyone dry. Disgusting!"

"What are you talking about?"

"You're that cut off from society, you don't even see it, do you? How much everyone is struggling? Well, I can change that. I can put a real power in charge. Real control. Real safety."

His hands move into position, and I'm ready for him. His fingers twist and contort into waves of different stances, and a black sandy mist fills the room, sweeping beneath my fog like a disease.

"Aki, stop. You could hurt everyone using that."

"Don't worry, it won't kill your precious Horsemen. I already tried that."

"Then why?"

He doesn't answer; instead, he gathers the mist into a ball in front of him, sucking up every last drop, and he hurls it at me.

Like a boulder, I go flying, hitting the wall, and the spell creating the fog dissipates, leaving the room. Vanishing.

"Magic!" Connie yells, running at me.

"No. Stay where you are!" I hold out a hand and use air magic to push her back into place. "I can't fight more than one."

She reluctantly turns back around and comes face to face with a smiling Fae Queen.

"I thought you liked me," she coos. "I thought we were friends."

"We were, but my job is more important than any single friendship." She sighs, taking a deep breath. "And Magic is right. What you're doing is wrong. Misguided."

"Is that your official opinion or just the one that's mirroring your girlfriend?"

Connie laughs a little, a small chuckle that snaps everyone's attention her way. "Sorry, it's just I'm not known for letting Magic think whatever they want. I'm always the one to put them in their place when they're being dramatic or just wrong." She places a strong hand on the Fae Queen's shoulder and looks her dead in the eye. "So yeah, it's my official opinion, Your Majesty."

Before I can even blink, she rams one of her daggers into her side, and blood spatters.

Aki cringes, a flicker of fear crossing his face. But he turns back to me, concentrating on his own fight. "You really have got them wrapped around your pathetic little finger, haven't you?"

"That's kinda how love works, Aki." I teleport myself to right in front of him, and blast fire at his face.

He skids backward, pain leeching from his screams.

But he steadies himself and forms a small dragon with his death magic, copying what I did in the cave where we found Lo. "Neat little trick, huh? Thank you for that."

I grab a ball of water and encompass his dragon, drowning it in salty water. "If all you're gonna do is copy me, then I guess this'll be easier than I thought."

Aki grabs a fistful of my hair and yanks, catching me off guard, making me scream. He brings my face inches from his and breathes, "You're nothing but a rat. It should never have been you."

"I know." Tears leak down my face as my hands shake. "But it was."

"You're not strong enough." He yanks my hair again, pulling my body flat against his. Threatening.

"I know."

"You can't possibly hope to rule the world."

"I don't."

He throws me to the floor, a heaping pile of tears and shaking limbs. But I stand back up nonetheless. And I face him. I put my staff back on my wrist and produce fire in one hand and water in the other, dropping my fangs.

My hair sprawls out behind me as magical pressure surges.

Connie is kneeling on the Fae Queen's shoulder, keeping her down, and Dea has somehow pinned Phillipe to the wall, immobile and eyes closed.

"I am neither strong enough nor good enough for the position bestowed upon me, but I will stand up and fight, anyway. Because that is my job. My duty. And you are threatening the lives of an entire species. Threatening the way of life for millions, billions of people."

All at once, I hurl a fiery waterspout, sweeping him up and spinning him around the room. Aki's hair flails as he screams, tears leaking down his face when I zoom my vision in.

Nine, tell someone to turn the portal back on.

Already on it.

Thirty seconds later, the portal starts to whirl, and I drop the magic, dumping Aki's unconscious body on one of the chairs. Connie and Dea doing the same thing. And we turn around and leave.

"That went . . . unexpected," Dea says.

"What were they trying to do?" Connie asks.

"Aki had a camera on his coat. I couldn't break it. Some kind of spell has protected it. I couldn't break it without giving away that I knew what he was trying to do."

"Which was?" Connie asks.

"He's trying to frame us."

"It's been a long ass day, I'm going for a nap." I look to the clock on the kitchen wall and frown. "I have to be back in New Orleans in a few hours."

"I've got a list of shit to get through," Connie groans. "Then I might go shopping." She turns to me and leaves a lingering kiss on my lips that tastes like peppermint tea. "Anything you'd like?"

"Cake."

She looks to everyone else. "Yeah, I guess if there's anything you guys need, I can pick it up."

Everyone lists off one or two items, and then we all head to bed, exhausted. And since I still haven't fixed Nine's body issue, he sleeps on Dea's other side, who stays in his Angel form, which is actually quite nice, because Angel mated cuddles are legit the best. Arrie is on my other side, asleep in seconds.

The poor thing. I think I socialized him too much today.

It's soooo weird that Nine needs to sleep. He's a soul. Why in the world does he need to sleep?

That's a great question, he says sleepily. *Maybe when we say we're bone-tired, what we mean is soul-deep tired. Maybe our souls can get burned out and need resting, too.*

Kind of like when we're more than exhausted. When it's not sleep we need, it's rest and recuperation and special interests and things that make us happy and comfortable.

Yeah, like that.

Sleep comes easily, and soon I'm drifting away into whatever recess of my brain controls my dumb dreams. Well, they've been alright recently, but it still puts me on edge.

Just as I'm dreaming about whose dick I get to suck next, the scene changes, and it's not a gorgeously naked Nine lying on my bed anymore, it's a blank space. Completely white. Kind of like what the Otherworld looks like. But also not.

There's something in the air in the Otherworld. Like it's nothing but not nothing. Nothing in the physical form. It's still something. But this feels like genuine nothing. Bone-deep emptiness. There's not even air around me.

And I realize I can't breathe.

Wait a minute, I'm dead. I don't need to breathe.

A figure shimmers in the distance, and I walk toward it, casually, confident that I can't actually be hurt here.

Where am I?

Who is that?

As I get closer, the answer to the second question becomes obvious. It's Aki. Only, he can't see me. Which is a good thing because Aki is crying on his knees in front of a tamaya *with our parents' pictures on and a charm bead I've not seen in a while—one of Dea's invisibility charms.*

"Aki . . ." I whisper.

He turns his head from side to side and frowns. "No, no, no . . ." His hands clasp at his head. "Go away, go away. Leave us alone!"

I back off, giving him some space.

He bows low to the floor and says a prayer, his tears staining the carpet below his knees.

That's when the rest of the room fills in, and I find myself in a rural home with sliding doors and chabudai tables, with bamboo mats set to four place settings.

This must be Aki's home.

But why am I here?

Aki gets up and stretches, then wipes the tears from his eyes, before he grabs a plate of sashimi from the fridge and sits to the table. "Itadakimasu," he whispers.

He's really traditional in his ethnicity. Then again, I guess you would be if you grew up here. But I was moved to the US as a young child, so I'm less Japanese and more American. Maybe I should consider spending some time in Japan, getting to know my roots better?

Focus, Magic. Focus. You're here now for a reason. What is that reason?

Well, color me stupid, 'cos I don't fucking know. This seer shit is hard work. I don't know how the Coven seer does this all the fucking time.

This is the present, I think. Since Aki's got a bruise on his temple that I put there earlier. That also means he is indeed creating his own teleporting crystals. We need to find out which Witch is helping them.

But it's not until Aki has finished his meal and washed up, taken a shower, and then gone into his bedroom that I see it.

He's wearing something. Something that's glowing a faint blue. Something I didn't give him. It's hanging around his neck on a piece of rope. It looks like a piece of stone? As my hand hovers near, it glows brighter.

Aki gasps, then looks around the room. "You're here, aren't you?"

"Yup." Not that he can hear me.

He grabs the necklace and unties it, then dangles it in front of the mirror he's standing in front of. "It's nothing special, really."

There's a symbol on it. A symbol I've seen before. Of a horse holding a scroll in its mouth while standing on its hind legs.

That's the Horsemen symbol.

I wake up gasping, sweating, drinking in lungfuls of fresh air.

And the guys are around me in an instant, touching me, soothing me. Dea wraps his wings around us all as he places a hand on my stomach, all the while Arrie is running a hand up and down my back.

I replay the vision/dream/seer thing in my head, rolling that necklace around my mind like a puzzle piece. I look to Nine, who's floating next to Dea with a shocked look on his face. "What is that?"

"It's part of the original Horseman seal he broke."

49

Connie's not in the house right now—probably still running errands—but Arrie, Dea, Nine, and I go check out the vault with our seals in.

"See," Nine says, "these appear after a seal is broken, but the actual seals that get broken are stone tablets." He picks up one of the scroll seals and unravels it. "These are hidden inside the stone tablets."

"So he kept a piece of the stone seal?" Dea asks. "Why?"

"It explains why I couldn't read his mind. And why our powers are weaker against him."

"I don't think that's why he's wearing it, though." I grab the seal from Nine and roll it back up, placing it back onto the magically protected pedestal. "I think he just kept it because he didn't know what else to do."

Arrie scoffed. "He's an egotistical asshole." At my questioning eyebrows, he explains, "He assumed he was the strongest being on the planet when he broke the fifth seal. He's arrogant. There are all kinds of powerful Fae, Vampire abilities, and not to mention a fucking dragon."

"Lo wouldn't have counted," Nine says. "He's not magical in the same way we are. He uses a power older than Angels and Demons, and therefore older than our magical system." Nine leads us out, floating through the closed door. "I mean, he was around with the dinosaurs."

"Still, Aki's an asshole." He wraps an arm around my shoulder and squeezes. "He made Magic cry."

"That makes someone an asshole?" I ask, trying to hide my smile but failing.

"Yes."

"Dea's made me cry. Is he an asshole?"

Arrie shrugs. "He gets a free pass because he's your mate. He can soothe whatever part of you he breaks."

"Including the parts you break," Dea comments.

Arrie's hand balls into a fist, but I grab it, stretch it out, and thread my fingers through his. "It's okay. I forgive him."

Arrie stands stock still, like a statue, and turns to me. "Really?"

I wrap my tiny arms around his huge waist. "Of course." And I place a soft kiss on his chest, where my head rests. "I don't condone what you did, nor am I going to say it was the right thing, but I get it. You're struggling. I still see it in the way you mistake me for her first thing in the morning or when you notice me from a distance or when your kiss changes to something more hesitant." My hands rest on his shoulders. "But partners struggle together. And it's okay to be grieving, even after two thousand years." I gesture to Dea. "Do you see me hating Dea's gorgeous tattoo? No. Because Haji was important to him. Why would I take that away or fight it? I'm okay with you loving us both. But since I'm the one alive, we come first. Our feelings matter more than you pushing me away. They matter more than your guilt. You hear me?"

I point a demanding finger into his chest, but he grabs it and twirls me around, then lifts me up and wraps my legs around his waist. "We come first."

Dea coughs to get our attention. "If you two do not mind, we have a world falling apart. And Magic needs to get back to Lucien."

"Lucien! Shit." I climb down from Arrie, kiss him and Dea goodbye, wave to Nine, and then teleport to the reception of the council building, where Lucien stands waiting for me. "Lucien, hi."

"You're late."

"Sorry. Had to break into the Fae datachip center, fight Aki, eat, nap, then work out a seer dream. Been a busy twenty-four hours."

"You and me both." Lucien, I notice, is wearing a suit. A business suit made to tailor with diamonds in the pick stitching and a shirt that's as white as his hair with a black tie and a pocket cloth. "Cannot tell you how much had to be done to get ready for the presentation of the candidates." He pulls a watch out of his suit pocket and mutters "shit" under his breath.

"Is that a pocket watch?"

"No time for fashion tips, we're late." He grabs me by the hand and drags me to a room somewhere on the first floor. He turns to look at me as we stand outside. "Tell me you have something better than that to wear?"

I shift back into my male form, who is still wearing the awesome clothes I borrowed from Lucien, if a bit dustier. I dust myself off, straighten things out, and then smile at him, smug.

"Looking good. Now, are you ready?"

"Thank you. And yes, I think so." I have no idea what a candidate presentation entails, but I can handle anything these Vampires throw at me.

We enter the room, and I'm met with dozens of cameras, the king, a backdrop that looks like a window over NYC, and three Vampires I don't know sat in seats beside him.

Okay, I'm so not ready.

"Stand over there, behind the cameras, and just watch," Lucien says. "The king wanted you here in support, so do as he says."

I shuffle into place as Lucien straightens his suit jacket for the hundredth time and settles into the spare chair on the other side of the king. Who also looks handsome in a suit with diamonds in the pick stitching.

The director films, and we're off. Starting with the king himself.

"Hello, communities. Today we're going to introduce our candidates for the first round of the Vampire Supernatural Council seats. Each round will have three candidates, and one will be chosen each time by public polls. There are three seats available, so there will be three rounds."

Lucien chimes in with a smile and a dashing charm. "Remember, if you want to see change or you care about how your communities are governed, then you need vote. Without doing so, you might not see who you want in power."

"Let's have a look at our first candidate, Mr. Victor Hesham," the king says, gesturing to the man on his right. "He's been active in the political community right here in New Orleans for the past twenty-three years after being a turned Vampire abandoned by his sire."

Victor Hesham smiles gently at the king and nods. "That's right. I didn't know what to do, so I got a night flight from North Carolina to New Orleans and walked up to the council building and said 'hey, I'm a new Vampire, please help me.'" Everyone laughs, finding the idea hilarious, but I just find it sad. "But everyone here has been so generous, including the king himself, who took his time to walk me to the nearby turning clinic, who set me up with a job, a stand-in sire, and even an apartment."

Wow. What a clinic. They must really help their communities. I wonder who runs them or who created them.

"What kind of changes would you like to see?" Lucien asks.

"I'd like to see more laws protecting Vampires. I'd like to push for a law that makes it illegal to abandon a Vampire you turned. It was unfair what happened to me, but it happens to lots of people, even children." He smiles gently at the camera, then turns to the king. "I want to protect consensual Vampire feeding spots, make them legal, and I want to create more Vampire-friendly housing in non-Vampire cities, so those of us who don't have lots of money can choose to live wherever we like, just like everyone else."

Him. I'd vote for him.

The other two also get a chance to speak, but neither hold people's attention like Victor or feel as passionately or as strongly about Vampire freedoms. He'll get the seat.

Just when I think things are about to end, the king stands from his seat and gestures me forward. "Here today, in support of this part of our journey as a community, Magic, the Fifth Horseman."

Lucien and the candidates clap, straighten themselves in their seats, and smile as I sit down, taking the king's seat. Now the king stands behind the camera, watching me. And I have to say something.

I have no idea what to say.

I swear, I'll kill Lucien when this is over. He could have fucking warned me, the piece of shit.

"We, the five Horsemen, are happy to support the Vampire community during this time. And we wish the candidates the best of luck in their ventures—I'm sure you will serve your communities with strong yet kind leaderships."

Victor turns to me and shakes my hand, asking, "Tell me, how is the war going?"

Connie is usually in charge of this stuff. I never do it without a script or Nine's help. Shit. I don't know what to say.

"It's . . . umm . . ." Deep breaths, Magic. In, out. "We are doing our best to restore order, to spread truth to the world, and to bring peace between non-magical and magical communities."

It's a political answer, but it's the best I've got. I can't just go around telling them details and potentially ruining plans.

I shake the others' hands, and each ask me questions, and I do my best to answer, but it's the last question that catches me off guard.

The third candidate with the dusty blonde hair and the expensive suit looks at me with interest. "Is it true you can switch between a male and a female form? And that you identify as genderfluid?"

"I'm not sure what label would best fit someone like me. And I don't want to intrude on a community. But yes, I have a female and a male form." I switch and then switch back, demonstrating. "And I like the pronouns ve and they."

"How intriguing." He looks genuinely impressed for a minute before he schools his face and sits back down. "It seems like you're an interesting person, Magic."

"Well, I try."

Everyone laughs, and we get to work wrapping things up, where I hand things back over to the king, who I am also going to fucking murder later. But it's good to feel wanted. For a community to want me to be a part of it. I hope I eventually feel this way with the other pillar communities.

50

"I'm going to murder you both," I groan as we walk back to a different room. "I swear, a little heads up next time. I would have prepared something." Well, I would have gotten Connie to do it.

The king laughs, his booming voice bouncing off the walls. "If I told you, you would not have been yourself."

Sighing, I shift into my female form, who's wearing a cute little black dress for the day. "Then one of you fuckers best buy me a donut, 'cos I'm starving."

Lucien, the darling that he is, buys me a dozen. Delivered. Ohhhh, how I love Vampires. They actually love me. Lucien tries to steal a donut, but I slap his hand. "Mine."

The king, however, I allow to take one.

Lucien whines. "But . . . but . . ."

"He's the king, little prince. He gets a donut."

"So when I'm king, will you share your donuts then?"

I just laugh. As if. "Nope. You'll always be a little prince to me, even with a dumb crown on your head."

The king laughs again—more times in one day than I've ever heard—before coughing to clear his throat. He looks tired. Less pristine. Old, almost. For a Vampire. They don't really do the whole "old and gray" thing. "Speaking of crowning princes, Lucien." He turns to his son. "I want to name you crowned prince. Officially."

Lucien looks to his father with stunned silence. "I wasn't expecting it so quickly. Is everything okay?"

The king laughs and shakes his head. "Such a pessimist. Everything is fine, but we don't know what will happen during this war. I want to secure our people's future."

Lucien doesn't look happy—in fact, he looks about ready to have his final emotion snap—so I grab his hand and say, "It's the right thing to do. It's always good to have a backup plan. Even if the first failing is unthinkable." I smile at his scowling face. "Trust me, you don't want to be in a position where there is no backup plan."

"Fair point, I guess," he says on a sigh. "We have to win this war, don't we?"

"If we don't, Aki and the Fae Queen will take over the Supernatural Council and govern the entire supernatural world. Humans will be their next target." The pressure on my shoulders is starting to wear me down. I'm ready to say fuck it and go on a month-long cruise somewhere. The world can save itself.

The king settles a hand on mine and smiles gently. "I know you're scared, but so were they when they fought in the first war. You're so much like them, and you don't even see it. You are doing well by the magical communities and the humans."

"Lucien? Do you mind giving me a moment alone with your father?"

He scowls but obliges, heading out of the room. "I'll be at home if you need me. I need a damn nap."

With him gone, I turn back to the king and ask the question that's been burning on my mind for the last few hours. "If a Vampire marries a Witch, what happens?"

He looks surprised. "That is not the question I was expecting from you." He thinks for a moment, lips down-turned. "While there are no legal ramifications, nor would we kick anyone out of the community, I'm afraid it would be difficult for the communities at large. And god only knows what kind of weird rules the Witches have." His eyes search mine. "Why do you ask?"

"I'm not going to tell you someone else's secret. Not even if you're royal." The smirk behind my smile makes him laugh again, and I realize that I just enjoy making people laugh. "Besides, I'm not sure he's ready for people to know yet."

The king's eyes go wide, a smile behind them, but caution lies there too. "A Witch, huh? How . . . of the times."

I can see the wheels in his head turning, connecting the dots. Here's hoping he doesn't bring it up with Lucien, because he might try to murder me, and I really don't have the time to grow back limbs right now.

"When is the next thing you need me for?"

"The community has two days to vote, then the announcement is made and the second round starts."

"Then I will be back in two days."

"I'll have lunch ready. Brownies, I hear?"

"Always."

Back home, I'm ready to sleep. For, like, a decade. Maybe I could create some kind of Sleeping Beauty spell that would actually allow me enough time to recharge for a change. A hundred years sounds like enough time.

But just as my eyes start to drift close, Arrie walks into my room and asks, "You're back?"

"That's it! I'm done." I get up, throw on my lounge pants, and shove my hand to the wall. If you wouldn't mind creating a couple of doors for me, that would be great? One into and out of my study that isn't through my bedroom.

A smaller than usual rumble vibrates the house, and I go to inspect the house's handiwork. Perfect. A door leading into my study that's a few feet from my bedroom door and a door that leads to the garden on the other side. Complete with a path that leads to the outside of the property and joins up with the main path to town.

"There." I turn to Arrie. "I am dead tired. I'm sorry I yelled at you." I throw a quick kiss to his lips so he knows that it genuinely wasn't anything personal. "Is this an emergency?"

He shakes his head.

"Then if you're not joining me for a nap, please, respectfully, fuck off."

He chuckles as I remove my lounge pants once more and climb back into bed. He closes the door to my study that everyone usually uses and locks my bedroom door so I can't be disturbed, then climbs in behind me.

"Mmmmm, much better."

He wraps his strong arms around my waist and nestles his nose into my neck. "Sleep tight, Killer."

51

"I did it!" my Fae trainer shouts. "I found a way to combine your death magic with Fae magic and Witch earth magic to give Nine a body." She heaves large gulpfuls of air into her lungs, catching her breath. "I swear, when I die, they best make a fucking statue out of me."

"I promise I'll build a giant statue in your honor." I roll my eyes at my grumpy trainer, her green skin looking more sallow than usual. "Now, are you going to share, or did you have some plan to use all of those pieces of magic on your own?"

She hands over the piece of paper she was waving in the air just a minute ago with a frown. On it, crudely drawn, is a diagram like the ones I often see in magical theory books. Not unlike the one in The Origin of Witch Magic.

In the center is a dark circle penciled in—and I'm assuming that's my death magic—but cutting through it are wavy lines in black pen that form a cross. What are those? But looking to the top right, I notice she's made a key. Wavy lines are Fae spells. Okay, so a Fae spell intersects the death magic. Got it. Then surrounding the edges of those spell lines is a circle in red pen which means . . . Quickly looking to the key. Aha! Earth magic. "So it's encased in earth magic?"

"No, it's laid on top of earth magic. You'll need to do that first."

"You want me to lay some earth magic down (which I can't yet do, by the way), then manage death magic while keeping multiple Fae spells alive, which are probably complex nonsense?"

"That summarizes it, yes."

I turn to her and politely, in my best customer service voice, say, "Your order has been processed and will arrive to you in three to four business days." She rolls her eyes at my sass. But I just flop into the chair beneath me. "Seriously, I have no idea how to do this. I love that you worked so hard on something that has no bearing on you, but this feels years away in skill."

"Maybe we can do it together instead?" she offers. "I can do the Fae spells, you can do the death magic, and then we just need to find an earth Witch."

"Collaborate?"

"Yes, then you can practise doing it together over the next few years until you master it. You'll have time to practise in a way that doesn't keep your boyfriend a ghost."

But that would mean exposing people—mortal people—to my death magic. Wouldn't that be dangerous? A stupid idea?

Nine floats over, having been browsing my book collection all morning, discovering new titles, and asks, "Can you grab a book for me and turn the pages?" He goes beet red, ashamed for having to ask.

"Sure." I go over to the shelf he directs me to and drag PORTAL MAGIC off the shelf with raised eyebrows.

He waves a hand through air as he floats over to the table and hovers in the chair next to mine. "Nothing important. Just curiosity."

I open the book's content page and watch him browse through. "Page 348, please."

I flick to the page, and turn when he asks, go back to the content page when he asks, and realize that I can't let him live like this. He'll need help with absolutely everything. So I turn back to my Fae trainer, who's watching us with sad eyes, and whisper, "Alright, let's do it."

TWO HOURS LATER, WE'RE OUTSIDE IN A RANDOM FIELD NO ONE USES, JUST THE FAE, A FRIEND of Red's, Nine and I hanging in a field, doing complicated, "should totally be forbidden" magic. And I would be lying if I said I wasn't scared.

Scared of hurting my friends. Scared of not being good enough. But mostly, I'm scared of failing.

The hope and anticipation on Nine's face is impossible not to see. But it might not work. It might be something that takes years to figure out. We might not even manage it in their lifetime. Which . . . fuck. We need to figure it out before the smart Fae lady dies. I don't know if I can do it without her.

"You were an interesting conundrum, Famine," she praises, happy as a cow, apparently. "Giving someone a physical body shouldn't be possible, but you're immortal already, which gave me an edge." She looks to us both with a wince, lowering her voice. "And I might have taken a sneaky peak at your scrolls, sorry."

I frown, scowl, and blister at her.

"Don't be too mad. I needed to see what made you immortal to begin with."

"And you just, what, analyzed an ancient spell, read ancient script, and figured that out?" Nine asks, clearly as annoyed as me.

"Yes," she says with a shrug.

Well, damn. Alright then.

Nine huffs but sighs. "Let's get this over with."

I think he's just annoyed that someone is better at magic than him. Which is adorable to see.

"If you're all done being hush-hush, I'd like to get this over with. I have a family dinner to return to." The earth Witch in question is stood a little ways over from us, her small stature almost comical if she wasn't slated to be a part of the next Coven. "Mom said I had to be back by six."

Oh, she's twelve. Did I forget to mention that?

Yeah, I'm putting a child at risk. Yeah, I know that's evil. No, I don't regret it. Well, I hope I won't, anyway.

We get into position, Nine and I at one end of the field, the others at the other end.

I can see them chatting for a minute, then the earth Witch, Zara, waves circles through the air, determination flowing through her. She stomps a single foot forward, and the grass uproots itself and floats into the air, forming a circle. Some dirt floats with it, gravel and bits of worms and beetles.

The Fae gives a lovely smile she never gives to me and then proceeds to encapsulate an energizing spell that pulls the earth's energy out of the floating earth pieces and forms a green bubble in the middle of the field.

Zara is straining, shaking, struggling to hold the ball of energy in its raw state. Something Witches have no experience with since they never work with Fae.

You can do it, Zara. You were made for this.

You'll be a great Mom one day.

He breaks my concentration with that sentence, and I flick my gaze to him and scowl. Now is not the time to be dropping the conversation of children, Nine. I snap my attention back to Zara, who seems to be doing better, the ball steadier.

She nods to us, and Nine floats as I walk into the energy. And it hits me like a truck. This energy is like coming home. Like a steady rhythm beating my heart like a drum, keeping me grounded. This is why I can't do this yet, because I'm not steady or at peace. I'm as uncertain as the wind.

Maybe once the war is over, I can work on unlocking this power, but I don't think I'll be able to achieve it before then.

My green-skinned friend nods to me, letting me know it's ready for the next stage.

I face Nine, terrified and on edge. "I'm sorry if I kill you."

"Sweetie, I'm already dead."

Right. Of course.

I can do this.

I hope.

My hands rise into the air as I dig deep, into anger and uncertainty, into the stress of the role that's been thrust at me without a single care for whether it's what I fucking want. To the terror at losing Nine, the grief, the heartbreak of watching Dea fall apart.

C'mon, c'mon, c'mon . . .

Black sand seeps from my feet, filling the floor around us in like a black hole to hell. I gather it up and swirl it around us, mimicking the ball of energy. It flows through Nine, leaving him unharmed, thank the goddess, and I release my held breath.

Now it's time for the mystery step.

I can do this.

I swirl the black sand mist through the earth energy, pushing it through the aether molecules, splitting them up, then I grab their pieces and sew them back together, knitting them into something else. Something more.

Sweat drips down my brow, my nose, and off my chin. My clothes are soaked through. I've never held death magic for this long before. My limbs shake like leaves on a tree in a storm, only this time, I'm the storm.

Okay, Nine echoes the Fae's voice in my head. *You're doing well. Keep that in position. I'm going to thread the spells through one at a time. Don't worry about what they are, just trust me. I'll teach it to you another day.*

Okay. Go.

Nine is a mixture of black sand mist, green earth energy, and the weird reconnected energy that's dark swirly green. He reaches out a hand, and rather than pushing the magic through him, it bounces off him. And the smile he radiates fills me with so much joy, I nearly lose the death magic.

Steady.

I refill the magic, steadying it. And then breathe again.

Somewhere in the distance, I can just about hear Connie, Arrie, and Dea breathing, shaking. And I wrap their scents around me, allow them to fill me up, to fuel my senses with calmness.

The aether particles in the ball of magic stop moving. Frozen. And I can suddenly see outside. Everyone's face is frozen in shock, not understanding what's going on. But Zara is still struggling. So we have to continue.

Okay, I'm threading the first spell through. Magic, stand out of Nine's way.

I move to the side of the magic, out of Nine's way, while holding the magic in place, still shaking, still struggling. It's like all the energy in me is being zapped out. Sucking me dry.

I could never have done all three of these things together. (Heck, I'm not even sure I can keep Witch magic alive while in my male form, or vice versa.)

Straining my hearing, I can just pick up on Arrie whispering, "You've got this, Killer."

Dea is silent, shaking, his hand laced in Connie's, who's also muttering under her breath. "I love you. You can do this."

The first spell breaks through the magic, passing straight through Nine, who's now tethered to the magical ball and spinning on the floor. She weaves the second one through the magic and then through Nine. But this time it ties itself to the new sewn-together aether particles, linking them all together, weaving the ball into a mesh.

The spell pops. Like a bubble. And my connection to the magic is lost. I look to Zara, and she's as confused as me, having lost the connection. Did something go wrong?

Nine gasps. *Magic!*

I snap my gaze back to him and gasp. The magic is flowing into him, lighting him up like a human Christmas tree, but it's clearly painful because he's wincing. "Nine?"

It's fine. I'm fine.

But he's gasping in pain, panting, and finally, when the last of the magic snaps into his form, he screams, flying high into the sky.

Not wanting him to be alone, I follow, lifting myself into the air with sheer momentum and using what little magical resource I have left. He leads me to the upper atmosphere, where we're still as statues, not breathing, not moving.

His eyes lock onto mine and hold on to them, scared. *I don't want to die again. I don't want to leave you and Dea alone again.*

Shhhh, it's going to be okay. I'm not going to let that happen.

His body is glowing, pain racing through him, and the screams he shouts leave my body pierced, scared. Guilty.

He's in pain, and it's all my fault. Because I was in too much pain to let him go. Because I wanted him back.

No. That's not true. He waited for me. He knew I'd come for him. He trusted me so much, he waited in the Otherworld for me to come get him, and I'm not letting him down now.

I throw myself at him, grabbing onto his shoulders and wrapping myself around him, giving him something real to hold on to.

His tears run back down my neck and back as his hands clench my t-shirt. "Magic . . . It's . . . working."

What? I pull my head back and gasp. I can touch him. He's . . . real. My hands land on his cheeks and force his eyes to meet mine. "You're real?"

"Real enough to do this." He throws his lips against mine, devouring them. One of those kisses that reminds you why you're alive, that fuels your heart and sets your soul alight. "And this." He smacks my ass and laughs. "I'm alive."

We fly down, the magic still glowing lightly under Nine's skin, but it's slowly dying out, and we land on the grass, hand-in-hand, smiling.

The team rush over, but it's Dea who reaches us first, having fazed over. And he collides into Nine headfirst, pinning him to the ground with an oof. Arrie and Connie kneel beside them, both eager to touch Nine, to cement his skin to memory and reunite with a two-thousand-year-old friend.

But I turn to someone else standing just beside me. Someone I run to and wrap my arms around, squeezing the life out of. "Thank you." Tears stream down my face. "Thank you."

"Okay, that is quite enough." She untangles me from her and stands in front of me, pride shining in her eyes. "You are welcome, Magic."

Zara is standing just behind her, mouth agape, not having believed what she just helped do.

"And thank you," I say as I wrap her in a hug. "You did something amazing today. If there's anything you need or want, just let me know. We are forever in your debt."

She thinks for a moment, then asks, "Do you have an earth teacher yet?"

I shake my head, no.

"Then I'd like to train you." She looks to herself with doubt for a moment, then shakes herself out of it. "I know I'm only twelve, but I'm bright for my age, and I can do lots of things, and I—"

"I'd love that."

"Day after tomorrow at the Coven. Eleven am sharp."

I salute her as she grabs her teleporting crystal and smashes it to the ground. "Yes, ma'am."

52

He smells like paper and ink and bonfires. Like reading a book on Halloween curled up next to the fireplace drinking hot cocoa and eating brownies.

"I'm grateful for my body and all, but you could not have brought my muscles back with me?" he complains when he's looking in the mirror. "Two thousand years' worth of work."

"I'm sorry the impossible spell didn't work quite as you'd hoped while I gave you a body."

Everyone laughs, the smiles never leaving their faces.

I wrap my arms around Nine's waist and rest my thumbs in his waistband. "I missed you." And then breathe him in like he's my addiction and I can't quite get down off the high.

Dea wraps his longer arm around us both, and we stare at ourselves in the mirror. Pride shoots through me and fills me up, leaving me happier than I ever remember feeling. Mortal or otherwise.

"So, Nine," Connie asks as he snuggles into the cuddle beside me, "what do you want to do first?"

"Anything you want?" Arrie asks.

Nine wiggles his eyebrows at us in the mirror. *A blowjob, please.*

He's just joking, but I'm dying to finally have Dea and Nine together. It's been empty without them both.

"So, umm . . . how does this work now?"

Nine chuckles, but the rest of them look at me like I'm a headless chicken. *Ve's trying to ask for group sex but doesn't want to upset anyone.*

I turn to Arrie. "I know we haven't talked about it, and we're still finding our feet, but—"

He silences me by throwing me onto the bed and asking, "Female or male?"

I'm not sure. "Both?"

Connie lies next to me, scraping my hair behind my ear. "Yes, please." She peppers kisses down my neck as Arrie grabs my hands and pins them above me.

Dea and Nine are making out by the mirror, their tongues sliding together as belts snap out of belt loops and t-shirts come off of heads.

Connie watches too, her eager hands sliding up my sweat-soaked vest top alongside Arrie's, who is pressing strong hands to my hips while he undoes my shorts.

Dea and Nine are in their underwear when Dea spins Nine in front of him and bends him over so his hands are flat on the bed by our feet. "Dea," he moans as Dea sits on his knees while yanking Nine's underwear down and palming his ass.

As Connie finds her way underneath my sports bra, she tweaks my nipple and nips my bottom lip. "I love your little gasps and moans," she says.

"I liked it when you screamed my name," Arrie croons in my ear.

But Connie hears, because super hearing, and she groans. "I want a movie of that night."

I play it in my head, starting from the beginning. "Care to help out, Nine?"

He tries to say yes, but Dea circles his hole with his tongue, so it comes out as a gasp instead. But he sends the memory to everyone. Which I only know because Connie's hips grind into my thigh as she says, "That's so hot."

I keep the memory playing, remembering how he pinned me to the wall and licked me like an ice cream in a world devoid of sugar.

Arrie's breathing heavy in my ear, gasping at the memory, his body shaking slightly. "Is that really how you remember that?"

"It was one of the best moments of my life." I unbuckle his belt and shove his jeans down his hips, freeing his cock. "And I want more."

He throws the rest of his clothes off, then proceeds to get rid of mine with the help of Connie, and their rushed hands and lips and teeth seem to want nothing more than to get at me. To touch me. To smother me with pleasure.

On my knees, Connie bends down onto her elbows and kisses my hips, thighs, and doesn't let up, rushing to me with a stiff tongue that licks a stripe from bottom to top and sends my head back onto Arrie's chest.

Nine is still bent over, his fingers fisting the sheets as he muffles his cries into the duvet. Whatever Dea is doing to him is pulling him apart as he leaks pre-cum onto the floor as it drips from his dick. "Dea," he cries, "just . . . please."

"Shhh," he whispers. "Just lift your head and enjoy the show."

He does as he's told and looks up at me, orange-brown eyes on fire as they bore holes into mine. *You look like a goddess.*

Connie raises my leg and rests it on her shoulder to get better access as Arrie pinches harsh fingers on my nipples and twists and pulls. Connie puts her lips around my clit and sucks, sending my hips barreling into her face as I grind, seeking movement, friction, and she doesn't let up.

"Shit . . ."

Arrie growls above me, and I can feel the tension in his rigid body, waiting. Like a lion allowing his lionesses to get their fill first. But his patience will snap sooner or later. He does not seem like the sharing type.

Dea shoves two fingers into Nine's ass, stretching him, pumping him full, and Nine cries out. Connie's teeth graze my clit, and I'm moaning with him, struggling to compose myself.

Arrie's fingers seek me, stroking my wet lips as I try my best to spear them into me, but he has me pinned against him. Unable to move. Fangs out, eyes burning red, I hiss as he shoves a one inside roughly.

Connie's tongue works overtime as she flicks pleasure and licks circles around me, playing my body like a personal violin. And Arrie adds another finger, stretching me, and I can feel my body cresting over the hill, just needing one final push.

Dea sinks his rock-hard dick into Nine's ass, moving him up the bed slightly, closer to Connie, and he screams his name. "Dea!"

His body takes the pounding Dea gives, relentless. His wings pop into existence, his golden body lighting me up. "You left me," he growls. "You left me, and I couldn't do anything about it." His eyes are in pain, but his body is in heaven, and the mixture plays out across his face, twisted into some pain-filled pleasure that he takes out on Nine. "You're mine."

"Yours," Nine sobs. He keeps his head up, watching me ride Arrie's fingers and Connie's mouth as my hips piston between them. "Yours," he whispers.

Dea smacks his ass, the sound ringing out.

And I'm shooting over the edge, screaming Arrie's name as he lifts me off the bed with his fingers, Connie fighting to stay with me by gripping onto my hips and sealing her lips around my clit.

"Oh god," Nine moans. "Fffuck."

Dea watches me, taking a minute to stop owning Nine and watch his mate, his eyes blasting golden light around the room.

As Arrie sets me down on the bed, he rips Connie's head by the hair off of me and bends me over, shoving my face into Nine's dick. "He wanted a blowjob." Arrie lines his dick up with my hole and thrusts in, groaning in relief. "Fuck, yes."

I suck Nine's dick as Arrie throws me up and down it with rough hands on my hips.

Nine's cries reach a fever pitch, but he takes the double pounding, as I hear Dea's skin slapping against Nine's.

"Fuck, just look at you, Magic," Connie whispers from beside me, her fingers deep inside herself. "Taking two dicks at once."

I don't like that she's left out, and it puts me off for a second until I get an idea. I throw the image Nine's way, hoping he's lucid enough to send it to everyone else.

"Are you . . . sure?" she asks. "I don't want to overstep anyone's boundary."

"Sharing within the group is fine, Con," Dea says. "Especially when we are all together. It does not mean you want a relationship with everyone."

With that, she climbs onto my back, rests her head on Nine's shoulders as she plants her feet either side of me, spreading herself wide for Arrie.

"Get us both off," I say, holding Nine's dick in my hand. None of us are moving at this point, waiting to make sure everyone is okay. "I don't want my girlfriend left out while you're busy. So keep her busy for me."

Arrie doesn't hesitate (thank goddesses for his directness), and I feel him dive for her as she leaks all over my back while her fingers are still fucking herself with rough, harsh movements. He moves inside me again, picking up the pace slowly this time, tentatively finding the right rhythm for us all.

And I move the angle of my hips, allowing him to hit the back of me, slipping moans from my lips like curses on a sailor's ship. And I swallow Nine's dick back down my throat, swallowing when he reaches my gag reflex.

Fuuuck, Sweetie.

Connie moans as she moves her fingers faster, her knuckles grazing my back as I hold her up with ease. "Shiiit."

Nine turns his head and shuts her up, swallowing her next moan with his lips. "Shhh, I'm trying to listen to Magic's screams."

Just as he says that, both Arrie and Dea speed up, grabbing our hips and pounding, shutting us both up for a blinding second as pleasure shoots up my body, making it shake and somehow swallow Nine deeper so my nose meets his skin.

I'm gagging on Nine's dick, no one caring that I can't breathe, my moans sounding more like choked wet gasps as I gurgle, drool dripping down my chin.

Arrie's fingernails dig into my hip as Connie's legs shake beside me, her moans delving into screams as Arrie brings her to release, gushing onto my back.

He races, thrusting harder, smacking my ass as he tries his best to break me. His hand once again finds its way to my neck, yanking me back onto his dick, but this time Nine's cock is in there, so when he screams louder and Dea swears, Arrie chuckles.

"Fuuuck, yeah," Nine groans. "Don't stop."

Arrie grips harder as I swallow faster while holding my breath, and from the sounds of things Dea rams into him harder than ever, flapping his wings to give himself more momentum.

I can hear Connie fucking herself beside me again, enjoying the show, getting what she's always wanted: to watch us. And I can hear Dea whispering into Nine's ear, "You are mine. And my mate and I will continue to own your body until you're begging us to stop. Never. Leave. Me. Again." He punches each word with a thrust of his hips. "Mine!" he shouts, punishing him.

Nine's sobbing, moaning, crying, and screaming all at once, and I have no idea if he's okay or if he needs to stop.

Don't fucking stop.

"Shit," Arrie swears. "Not gonna last." He grips my hip and throat tighter, bruising me, as he moans quietly in my ear, whispering my name. "Magic, fuck." His thrusts become erratic, and he's coming, filling me, releasing himself.

Nine swells in my mouth, slumped on top of my back, just taking it. Not being able to do anything else. But he swells, shaking, his knees buckling. Dea grabs him, continues fucking him but holds him up. "Dea . . . fuck. I need to come," he whines. "Please."

"Shit," Connie swears from beside me. "Nine, are you okay?"

I look up, and tears are streaming down his face as his eyes squint shut.

"Not stopping," Dea grinds out from behind clenched teeth, "unless he safe words out."

I hollow out my cheeks, sucking harder, doing my best to work his body, give him what he needs. But my own is singing, pulsating between my thighs in a needy ache that's starting to hurt. So I delve down, using my own fingers.

But Arrie bats them away, shoves three fingers inside me. "I'll do it." He shoves me onto Nine's dick. "I know you like my roughness."

I really fucking do.

Dea smacks Nine's ass loud enough I wince, and he screams out as Dea grabs his balls and squeezes lightly, his fingers grazing my chin. "Come for me." He's pounding him faster this time, a familiar pace I've seen before. Hard and fast. Just how Nine likes it.

"Yes, yes, yes," Nine cries. "Don't stop. Fuuck." He thrusts down my throat as Arrie thrusts fingers into me, slamming into the back of me. And then Nine's coming, screaming into the air and into our minds, coming down my throat that I have no choice but to swallow.

He falls fully onto my back, giving up hope of keeping himself upright, as Dea wraps his arms around his waist and pulls himself out and Nine out of me, then lies him down on the bed.

Arrie stops and goes to lie next to him, wrapping his arms around Nine's shoulders, comforting him. "I got it."

Connie is looking at Dea and I, eagerness in her eyes. But fuck, I just want to get some of her.

"Go," Dea says. "Go have your dessert."

So, being the good partner I am, I do as I'm told and bury myself between Connie's thighs. "Sorry, I didn't mean to leave you out or anything."

"You didn't. But I'll pretend you did if it makes you get up here."

I don't need to be told twice. I climb up her body and kiss her, but she shoves her tongue into my mouth without hesitation, groaning at the taste of Nine on my tongue.

Yanking her legs up, I bend them and pin her knees to the bed, opening her up for all to see.

"What do you have in mind?" she asks suspiciously, her eyes gleaming with mischief.

I shift into my male form and grin. "But with Dea in me, of course."

"Oh." She blushes.

"This okay?"

She nods. "I've never done it before, though."

I silence her concerns with a gentle kiss. "Me either, don't worry." I look behind me at Dea, who has his cock in his hand, watching us with rapt attention.

"Do not let me stop you, Angel. I am happy to enjoy the show."

"Or you could get in one of us and be a part of the show."

Connie grabs my breasts, tweaking my nipples and making me gasp. "Ve's done so much for everyone else today. Get in Magic, and we'll work them together."

Dea doesn't hesitate—doesn't even respond. My mate settles in behind me and lines himself up, ready to do what he loves. Take control.

"Now he gets to make us both scream." I giggle.

"Bet he'll be thinking about this for a few days."

Instead of responding, he smacks my ass, then Connie's, and we gasp. Laughing.

"Fucking you is always something I think about, Angel." And he slides in, filling me up. "But hearing you scream with your girlfriend will be a hot memory in the making, for sure."

We struggle to find the right rhythm for a while, something that pleases all three of us, but we figure it out, and soon we're all panting while Arrie watches and Nine sleeps.

Dea smirks over at Arrie. "Wishing you had not tapped out so soon, huh?"

"Shut up and get them off."

Connie's sliding against me, setting me alight, and Dea's pounding into me, stretching me. And I'm pretty sure this is going to be the quickest orgasm in the world on my behalf. But I want to last. I want to come with them.

"Come on," Dea groans. "You have no idea how hard it was holding back with Nine." He grabs a fistful of my hair and uses it to shove my lips against Connie's. "Kiss and come."

He speeds up, grinding us faster, and I angle my hips further, increasing the pressure.

"Shit," Connie curses. "Can't last."

"Fuck yeah." I pin her hands to the bed and let Dea work us both. "Come on. I saw how many orgasms you gave yourself earlier. You can manage one more for us, right?"

She nods and whimpers, bucking her hips into me. "Oooh, yeah." Connie grinds and moves her hips faster as Dea fucks me through it, his wings brushing all of us with delicate feathers. "Gonna . . . come." She moans into the air, her head tilted back on the pillow as she clenches around me.

And Dea's hips stutter as he's finally nearly there, but I think it's more intense than he thought it would be, because he drags me off of Connie and shoves my face into the mattress as he uses me. Pounding into me from behind as he bends over my hunched form. "Come for me again, Angel. For me. Please."

And fuck, I didn't know you could come from words alone. But this man is a work of art. I pulsate around him as he slams into me, and I sob into the mattress because it's too much too soon. Overstimulated. Overwhelmed.

But Dea's coming in me, leaking out, muffling his cries in my shoulder. And with one last slap on my ass he empties himself and flops on top of me. "Fuck, that was good."

"So good," Connie confirms.

I whimper, more than done. And rather sore from all the rough pounding from Arrie and Dea.

Arrie chuckles, still holding onto Nine.

"Is Nine okay?" I ask from beneath Dea. "He was full-on crying while you fucked the life out of him earlier."

Dea laughs and pulls out of me. "He is okay. He would have told me to stop if he wanted me to. I would not actually force myself on any of you."

He sounds kind of offended, and I realize that maybe I phrased that badly. "Sorry, I didn't mean it like that." I get us up and wrap my arms around him. "I know you wouldn't."

Dea rests his face in the crook of my neck, comforting himself, as he shifts forms, putting his wings and golden skin away. "He will be okay. Especially after cuddles." He turns to Arrie. "Thank you for the aftercare help."

"No problem. I missed him too." And looking at Arrie cuddling into Nine, holding him so gently, I remember that while it's not the same, they love each other too.

The next morning Arrie, being the early bird that he is, brings us waffles in bed. Yes, we were all served breakfast in bed by my boyfriend. How cool is that?

Living the dream.

"I don't really know what to do now. I mean, I'm on standby to help the Vampire king, but where is everything else?"

It's Connie's time to shine because she jumps in with, "Well, the community heads have been made aware of the situation with regular updates, the embassy are keeping their armies and the armies of those in support of us on their toes with regular training drills, and we're now fully equipped with magicomms for the entire army on a hierarchical network."

"So we either wait for them to come to us or look like the bad guys by going to them?"

"That is probably what they are waiting for, Angel."

"To make us look evil to get the support of the public at large?"

"It won't work," Connie says around a bite of her waffle. "We've done too much press. We've saved too many cities and people and changed too many lives—on camera."

"Then what else?" I ask, turning to Arrie. "If you were in their shoes, what would you do?"

"I'd remove public support. Isolate you. Force you to have fewer allies." He grabs a waffle, adds some strawberries, cream, and honey, and eats what looks like heaven on a lattice.

I want one of those. And so Nine proceeds to make me one.

"You don't have to—"

"You suck my dick, you get waffles." He hands me a heaping mountain version of what Arrie just made himself.

Connie gets a call on her holo, and she quickly shucks on some clothes and takes it in the study. But a few minutes later, she rushes back in with a frustrated frown on her face. "Aki released a really cut and edited video of the fight. It looks bad, Magic. Really bad."

I sigh. "I saw this coming." Turning to Nine, I ask, "Any chance the portal has CCTV?"

"Of course it does. We like to be able to keep track of who comes and goes." He also jumps out of bed and throws some clothes on. "I'll get right on that."

"I should probably call our PR manager and get things rolling," Connie says. She kisses me on the cheek on her way out.

"Just us three, then?"

Arrie corrects me. "Just the two of you. I have army stuff to deal with. Be back in time for dinner, though."

And he leaves.

"Are you busy today?" Dea asks me.

I shake my head, no. "Not until eleven, when I have an earth magic lesson with Zara at the Witch's Coven."

"So until then you are all mine, is what you are saying?" He drags me on top of him so I'm straddling his thighs. "We have hours before you need to be anywhere, and no one else in the house."

A few hours later, I'm dragging my butt to the Witch Coven in South Africa with only a few seconds to spare. I did not want to explain to my new teacher why I was late had I actually been late.

I teleport into the center of the Coven dead on eleven, and I'm met with a sassy yet happy twelve-year-old Witch. She might look small, but she's mighty. And the future of the Coven.

"You're right on time."

"I try." I look around in wonder, remembering how beautiful this place is. "Where are we training today?"

"In one of the caverns off the center. They have a few purposefully empty to allow for magical training. It's where I spend most of my time these days." She guides us that way, past houses made of earth and trees that have been coaxed from the ground by talented earth Witches.

"They're just trying to prepare you. The world is changing, and you'll help lead them during it."

"I know. It's just I don't have many friends." We climb up a rugged staircase that leads into an open hole in the wall next to some a sign that says Training Caverns.

"Then I'm happy to be your friend and pupil, Zara."

"Let's just get training." She guides us down several winding paths until we reach a dead end, where we take a left into the biggest cave I've ever seen.

In fact, the only reason I can see the end is because I can zoom in with my Vampire vision.

"I've brought us to the cavern at the end because it's the farthest away so you can't hurt anyone if you do anything stupid. So don't hold back."

"Right. Good plan."

"Three rules: be as emotional as you can be; listen to every instruction, even if you don't understand them; and don't hit me with any death magic. I don't want to die."

I chuckle, finding her last rule hilarious. "Don't worry, it's hard to wield magic, so it won't just pop out by accident." Well, it's unlikely to.

She nods. "Then let's get started. First, tell me how connected to the earth you are. Remember rule number one."

Be emotional. So she wants the truth. Not just some wishy-washy answer. "I like the forest, and I love meditating and doing yoga outside. I even keep my curtains open because I like the moon shining on my face. It's peaceful, like I'm home and can never be alone because the earth is always there."

"Good news, you're definitely an earth Witch. But we already knew that. Accessing earth magic is harder than the other three. That's because it takes more energy and concentration. Some people theorize that it's because it's the most dangerous, so it's magic's natural barrier."

"More dangerous than fire?"

"Yes. You can bring down mountains if you so choose." My eyes widen, and she laughs. "With your level of power, you could reshape the Earth. Drown enter countries and raise land anew from the bottom of the ocean. You're mother nature reincarnate."

Is this really how some people view me?

"It doesn't feel that way. It just feels like I'm never enough for the challenges the world throws at me."

"That's because it's all boring politics. But when you have to use your magic, you'll be the answer everyone needs." She leans in closer to me. "Besides, you're pretty good at the politics stuff."

"You think so?"

"You've made such a difference around here. The energy is changing. More people want to come out, share our gifts with the world. It'll happen with the next council, we think."

"Not if the fire Witch has anything to say about it. She'll outlive me if she gets her way."

We both laugh. "Martha is such a hardass. Don't worry, you're not the first Witch to be caught by her hard views. And you won't be the last."

"That makes me feel better." I shake my limbs free from tension. "Right, so how do I access it?"

"You meditate until you get it right."

"Get what right?"

"The connection. It's different from other elements. You can really speak to the earth. It kind of vibrates back at you."

I gasp, looking at her with wide eyes. "What did you just say?"

"It communicates back at you. Like it's alive."

That's why the no one has seen anything like the Otherworld Gate! Because it's Witch and Fae magic together, and they haven't worked together since before the original Horsemen's time. It's earth magic I was feeling that day at the Black Gate.

"I think I've done that before, but it was a bit different then."

"Let's try repeating yourself, then. What were you doing back then?"

I'm not sure telling this child is a good idea. "I'm not sure I can say. I was dealing with a very old, very complex piece of magic, and as I was trying to figure it out, it vibrated back at me, guided me through the puzzle."

"Definitely earth magic of some type. Let's try to do that again." She sits on the earth cross-legged and closes her eyes, breathing in deeply. "Just try to feel your surroundings. Allow yourself to be open and let the magic come to you, rather than reaching out for it."

I follow her, also sitting cross-legged and closing my eyes. An open mind. "But my mind is always busy. How do I also keep it open?"

She laughs to herself. "Sorry, I just remember when I asked that question. My trainer told me to think through all my thoughts, all the possible combinations I can, and then live in the echoing emptiness that follows."

Think all my thoughts? "You're aware the entire world is on my shoulders and I'm a mess, right?"

"Yeah, I think this will take a while for you, but it's worth trying, anyway."

"Alright." Think all my thoughts. Well, there's the elections that are coming up for the Vampires, and I hope Victor wins. He's a decent Vampire with a great view of the world. And then there's Lucien and Red, who I really want to see happy but who are getting in their own way. Aki, the Fae Queen, Felicity, Arrie's insistence on working on our communication, Connie's hesitation last night with Arrie . . . And the list goes. But I allow every single one of them to pass through me. To think about them and move past them. Not let them hold sway over me. To not get stuck with them. I can always think about them tomorrow.

And when all the thoughts were done, when my brain had finally thought about everything on its to-think list, it was a little emptier. I'm not sure my worries will ever go, nor the pain and the bad memories. But it's roomier in here now. There's space to grow.

"Okay, I think it's emptier."

"Good. Now feel the surrounding earth. That feeling you get when you're walking through the forest or when you're breathing in the morning air . . . find that here's version of that."

It's just earth. There's nothing here.

But I reach my senses out, anyway. I heighten my hearing and my touch and my smell, and before I know it, my senses are filling with earth. The smell of the minerals, the organic matter, the worms tracing tunnels beneath me, the beetles scurrying across the ground, the spiders making homes in the crevices.

And something larger scurrying across the surface.

I hone in on it, traveling behind it, seeing where it goes, mapping the surface of the cavern out in my mind. It's like I can see, but I can't. My eyes are closed. But the entire cavern is before me in feelings, senses, and maps—all in my head. "This is amazing."

"Yeah, it is." She gasps, then instructs, "Open your eyes."

I snap my eyes open and see dirt and gravel floating all around us, frozen in place. "Are you doing that?"

"Nope."

"I'm doing that?" I ask tentatively as I stand and reach out for a small stone.

"Yup." She's smiling. "You're brilliant. It takes most Witches months to get this far. To connect. But it's like the connection is already there, ready for the taking."

"I can't believe I'm doing this." I jump a little, excited that I finally unlocked my earth powers. But the rocks around us fall, and I quickly zap up an air barrier above our heads, letting the stones roll off and onto the floor. "Sorry."

"And you can change between elements pretty quickly, too."

I grab a fireball in my left hand as I conjure a ball of water in my right, then send them zooming around the space.

"Both at the same time?"

"Uh-huh. I made a waterspout the other day by combining air and water. Famine reckons that the reason I was given so many individual powers is not simply so that I can fit in with multiple species but so that I can use them together and adapt to whatever situation I'm in."

"Flexibility," she confirms. "It's a power in itself. And this is just Witch abilities. You have Fae spells and Vampire strength and the ability to turn into any animal you wish."

"Don't forget the death magic." I laugh. "But seriously, maybe forget about it. I don't like people knowing that I have that ability. The world is already unsure of me."

"You're like marmite, Magic." She looks up at me with reverence and fondness. "You divide people. But it's an honor to have such an important role in your growth."

"You are a very wise twelve-year-old, you know."

She shrugs. "People say I'm old for my age because I'm an orphan who has to look after her two younger siblings."

"Didn't you say Mom yesterday?"

"Grandma. She's Mom. But she's old. She can't really run around after Eli and Ferra."

"I understand your pain. I was an orphan, too. Though I only had myself to look out for, and I grew up with the Witches in the US."

"What happened to your parents?"

"Hunters. Angel-descended Witches are sought after and killed by the SC because of the power of their magic."

"Yeah, it sucks. They used to be the most powerful among us. Revered for their power. Well, that's what the ancient archives say."

"How far back do the archives go?"

She shrugs. "Not a clue, but at least a thousand years because I was reading about the Horsemen in the Middle Ages just yesterday."

"Hmmm, interesting. Thank you."

"If you want access to them, you'll have to petition the Coven Council."

A groan slips from my mouth before I can catch it, and we both laugh.

"If you were nicer to them originally, they wouldn't be so hard on you."

"Hey! Some of them like me."

She holds up a single finger. "One. The seer likes you. For some reason." She gathers some dirt in her fingers and places it into the palm of my hand. "Let's try something else. Try the same thing you did earlier, but with this pile of earth specifically. Homing in the sensory connection is a skill. It might take time."

"Okay. Let's go." I had great success with the first task, I'm hoping that I'll be a natural with this.

Alas, I was wrong. I am shit at this.

Every time I try to hone in on the pile of stupid dirt, my focus snaps and I zoom out again. "It's like an elastic band."

"Right, but this elastic band can be trained to stretch further. Your homework for this lesson is to keep practising this. You can't really do much to topple the mountain without being able to ignore the earth around it first. Otherwise, pop goes the forest. The river. The land. The—"

"Yup. Get the picture. Pop goes Magic and their team, too."

"Speaking of team . . . Are you in a relationship with Famine?"

"Yes. And the rest of them too. We're a polycule."

"Like the seer and her two husbands?"

"Yeah, like that. But Death and Famine have a relationship together too."

"Oh, I see." She shoos me home, saying she has her own training to get to.

Which makes sense, she's a child. She probably has some kind of formal education to get to.

But when I get home, it's darker than expected. "It's night?"

How the fuck does this time zone thing work across the realms?

54

Looking at the clock in the kitchen, I realize it's only seven pm, it's just getting dark a little early right now. Apparently. "I swear, this realm is as strange as me." Looking at the counter, there's a steaming pile of tacos and a note. Dinner can be reheated for five minutes in the microwave on full power. We're chilling in the theater – Arrie

Awww, he made me dinner.

I reheat the tacos, following the instructions to the T, and then find my way down the dark stairs and into the theater, where they're watching some cartoon about a talking dog.

Must have been Nine's turn to choose.

They're all lounging on the couch that's hovering in the air, so I shoot myself and my tacos up there to join them, and settle on the other side of Arrie, who snakes an arm around my shoulders.

"Thanks for dinner."

He kisses my temple and says, "You're welcome."

"Shhh," Nine complains, "you'll miss the best joke!"

Yup. It's his pick.

Comfort films are allowed in this house.

No judgement here. Cartoons are fun.

Knew there was a reason I fell in love with you.

Do the others not like them very much?

Eh. I think they put up with them for me.

Well, no putting up here. I'll watch them with you whenever you like.

We watch another film after that one but on the bed, and somehow, we fall asleep there, in our clothes, all of us exhausted. And I notice that all of us are touching Nine somehow; whether it be a finger or a foot or an arm, none of us let him go.

Something tells me going to war again is going to be tough. He's getting the easiest jobs.

But in the morning, I'm the first one awake for a change. So I take advantage of the morning silence and go for a run through the forest, then start my regular yoga routine, where I attempt to do my homework, but I quickly get frustrated and have to do breathing exercises to calm down.

Eventually, I call it a day and head to the shower. The nice, refreshing cool water dripping down my back and legs, cooling me off.

Maybe I could see Korby today and work on my bo stuff. I haven't seen her in ages. Or maybe just see her in general.

Breakfast is on the table by the time I reach the kitchen, and I gobble it up with vigor and then run off, kissing them all on the lips, lingering a little longer on Nine's. "Going to see Korby! Be back later." And I run out the door.

Korby is staying in an apartment above the pub, where she works most nights. I offered to buy her a place (or make her one), but she said she prefers living a modest life, where work keeps her busy and life keeps her entertained.

I knock on her door at nine-thirty, which I didn't think through, because she opens it with a scowl and growls, "What are you doing here at this stupid hour?"

"Oops. Thought I'd pop in to see how you're doing?"

"I've only been asleep for five hours, Magic!"

"I can come back later?" But I'm peering into her apartment, seeing what it looks like, being nosey, and she sighs.

"No, it's okay. But you're putting up with my bad mood until I'm fully awake."

"Deal. I'll even buy us breakfast."

"Done."

She lets me enter, and I'm seeing myself around, having a nosey, when someone steps out of the bedroom. Someone distinctly male. "Oh my goddess, I didn't know you had company. I'm sorry. I'll meet you in the café and—"

Korby laughs, flustering at my embarrassment. "That's what you get for coming knocking at such an ungodly hour."

She did this on purpose!

Korby and the guy have a quiet conversation that I don't listen to, at all, and then he leaves.

"He's just . . . a repetitive one-night stand. Nothing too big. Well . . ."

I snort over the glass of water I poured myself. "A repetitive one-night stand is a sort-of relationship, you know."

"Yeah, but he's a Fae. And I always wanted to settle down with another bunny. Create more bunnies."

I almost gag at the normalcy with which she says that.

"It's a Shifter thing. We do interbreed, but it's not common."

Curiosity peaked, I ask, "Why not?"

She shrugs. "We're just more attracted to our own breed, I guess. It's not a hate thing. Wolves especially stick to their own. In fact, most predators do."

"So being with a Fae is especially unusual."

"Precisely." She makes us coffee, and I just about go weak at the knees. "Want a cup?"

"Yes, please. And I'd marry you for some creamer. Seriously, they don't have that here, and I've been meaning to ask the house, but I keep forgetting."

Korby drags a carton out of the fridge and shakes it at me. "You Americans are good for two things: coffee and tacos."

"Just two?"

She shrugs. "Culinarily speaking, yes. But I'm Japanese. I don't put a lot of stock into non-fresh food." She holds up a finger. "Except tacos. You rule the taco world."

As we drink our cups of coffee, I once again apologize for waking her up and disturbing her morning after. "You know, you should consider keeping the Fae. They're super handy with spells and technology, and they dance great."

She frowns at her coffee mug.

"You're here, in *Sheruta*, and I don't think Shifters are so familiar here."

"No, they're not. I already asked. Nobody thinks me being with a Fae would be weird. In fact, there are other Shifter-Fae couples here in town."

"Then, what's the problem?"

"I like you. I do. But I didn't plan to stay here indefinitely, just as long as you need me."

I wrap her in my arms and breathe in her orangey scent. "You're my friend, I'll always need you. But you are just one teleport away. I'll be happy with wherever you're happy."

"And when I figure that out, you'll be the first to know."

"Come on, there's loads to *Sheruta* I haven't had the time to see, like the mall. Wanna go exploring?"

"Fuck yeah. But breakfast first, right?"

"Absolutely."

Shifters and their appetites always surprise me, but with constantly shifting back and forth, it's not a surprise. It takes serious energy. Maybe I should eat more and I'd be less tired.

Shopping with Korby is loads of fun—she has the enthusiasm and the stamina to keep up. We go into all sorts of shops on the way to the mall: tea, clothes, chocolate, various technology establishments, magical bits and pieces, including a hair dye and removal spell for Connie.

But when we get to the mall, my tiny little mind explodes into oohs and aahs as I look up at the ten floors you navigate by floating platforms that have plants spilling over the edges. Advertisement plasmascreens are everywhere, trying to sell you everything from certain Shifter scents to love potions.

"Love potions are bogus, by the way," I say to Korby. "Not possible."

"Yeah, most people assume as much. Wanna get lunch? I'm starving."

"We only just had breakfast . . ." I look to the clock on the tower in the center of the mall and gasp. "Four hours ago?"

"We've been shopping for a while," Korby says with a laugh. "Besides, don't you feed with your meals?"

Feed? "Oh, that. No, I typically just have some in the morning and then whenever I'm hungry."

"Well, we can order whatever we want from any of the restaurants from the food portals."

"Food portals?"

Korby points to the queues lining up in front of a row plasmascreens. "You order from any of the restaurants, and the food comes down the shoots." She points to the crowd of people awaiting their orders.

"That's clever." I assume it's not actual portal magic, but whatever, still cool. "Reckon they sell noodles here?"

"They have a pretty good ramen stall, actually. Not quite as good as home, but it still tastes great."

"Then let's go!" I grab her hand and yank her to the back of the line, which manages to go down pretty quickly despite its length. I shifted forms an hour ago when we bought me some more masculine clothes, trying out different styles until we found something that works. "Thanks for the help with the guy shopping. I hadn't been yet."

"Putting it off?"

"Yeah," I nod. "I'm more comfortable with who I am now, but it was shaky for a while there. And shopping for the part of yourself you're still scared of is kinda . . . unnerving."

"That reminds me of how some Shifters feel," Korby says as we reach the screen and she places her order. "Some Shifters have a hard time feeling comfortable with their shifted forms, like it's some kind of demon inside them." She shrugs. "It's more common with predatory species."

"I don't spend a lot of time in my Shifter forms either, to be honest." I place my own order. "I just spend so much time mastering my other forms. Their magic is harder, more complicated. My Shifter stuff gets left behind."

"The predators go for a run through the northern woods every morning, if you wanted to join them. Even Nigel goes."

"What about you?"

Korby smiles as she picks up our orders from the shoot. "We prey species live together. The apartment I'm in above the pub is connected to the ones behind me. It allows us to feel safe and connected, and to have giant cuddle piles whenever we like."

After we sat and ate lunch, we started hitting some of the magic shops, because some of the best ones are here at the mall.

"Thinking of getting some of those air shoes that've just come out," Korby says. "Then I could hover around the bar and be quicker." So she picks up a pair and adds it to her basket. "It took me ages to get used to not being able to use my datachip here."

"Right. Everyone on Earth just scans the items and leaves. I forget about that." We don't have datachips, so we just take them up to the cashier. "One day, I'm getting a fucking chip. Fuck the others." I turn to the makeup behind me and oooh at a color-changing lipstick that I can't not pick up. You just squeeze your lips together and cycle through until you land on the right shade. Like a color wheel.

"I'm glad we went shopping today," Korby says as we head into a bakery on our way home. "You've been training too much."

"Agreed. But it's hard to take breaks knowing you could miss an important lesson that would save an entire species."

"Fair point." She takes a bite out of her pecan twist. "But counter point: you can't save the world unless you're the best you you can be, and you can't be that without taking breaks."

"So you're saying that shopping and pastries are me saving the world?" A laugh slips free as I also dig into my pecan twist. "I could get on board with that."

Magic? Emergency. Come home!

"Shit." I whip my staff out and teleport us to the kitchen, where Arrie is bleeding out on the tiles, looking like death. "Arrie!"

55

"Arrie!" I drop my shopping bags and rush to his side, where Dea's healing him. "What happened?"

Lo is circling above us, the size of my head. "We were attacked during training."

"So that's where you've been lately?"

"Been . . . training . . . in . . . Jura Mountains."

"Magic," Lo cautions, "they need help."

Okay. Okay, okay, okay. "First things first, Dea, stay here and help Arrie into bed and heal him." I look to Connie and Nine, both of whom have never been to the Jura Mountains and shake my head. Connie's the better fighter. "Connie, hand your plasmascreen to Nine and go grab your shit." I turn to Lo. "Go with Nine, help him update the embassy and grab the rest of our army, then teleport to me. I'll teleport back and take everyone to the Jura Mountains. Korby, you don't have to do anything—"

"I'm coming with you." She grabs our bags and places them on the dining room table. "But I need to get changed, so I'll be with Nine when you come and get us." She runs out of the house, faster than a regular human, but slow for a Shifter.

Everyone else disperses, Dea carrying Arrie up the stairs, Connie getting changed and grabbing her weapons, and Nine and Lo running out of the door.

After two dress changes—one in each form—and making sure I have my charms set to what I want on my staff, throwing knives strapped to my thighs and daggers to my hips, I'm ready to go.

Connie runs into me as I'm coming out of my room and grabs my arm before we teleport to the Jura Mountains.

The mountains loom in the distance, but I barely notice them behind the chaos exploding in front of me. Our army is spread thin, struggling to hold on, while the enemy decimate us blow after blow. Pushing us back.

We're losing.

And without Arrie, I don't know any of our defense strategies. Much less formations or attack combinations or anything like that. "I need the next in command."

Connie looks around and spots Red throwing fireballs, then drags my gaze that way. "There."

I fly us over and we land next to her. Three daggers fell the two soldiers at Red's back while a couple of arrows handle the two at her front.

"Red!"

"Yeah?" she shouts from a few feet away, out of breath.

"Arrie's down. We need you to take charge. Nine and the rest of our army are on their way, but it'll be a few minutes."

"I don't think we have a few minutes." She grunts as a knife scratches her arm and she flinches away. Then she spins and hurls a small fire tornado at the attacking group to her left. "We're outnumbered, and they took us by surprise."

"Shit." I look behind us and realize there are villages there. Innocent people. "We can't let them get through us. There are innocent civilians in those villages."

"I know that. I was hoping you'd swoop in and do your godly magic shit!"

"Err, right." I turn to Connie, use a spell to trip up the two soldiers trying their best to get anywhere near her, and watch as she takes them out with a single arrow to the head each. "Work with Red to retreat our soldiers to beyond the hill behind us. I'll cover us."

"Got it!"

I shift forms and fly into the sky, looking down from above, seeing if there's anything I missed. There are more of their soldiers coming through the mountains. Far more. We need to put a stop to that. Now.

Flying myself over there, I know what I need to do. Only, I'm not sure I can do it. I settle on top of the rock on one side of the pass, kneeling on the rugged stone, taking ragged breaths of icy air.

My hands fall onto the stone, and I seek it out. The essence of the mountain. But I can't find it. Every time I go anywhere near it, it slips away like air in the desert. What did Zara say? To clear my mind and let it come to me.

Okay. Alright.

I block out the background thumping of the soldiers marching through the pass below me, the screams of the dying behind me, and the grunts and pants of our soldiers fighting for their lives. I simply focus on the surrounding earth. The rock beneath me, the little tufts of resistant grass poking through the cracks and the moss and lichen starting new life atop a mountain that clearly doesn't want it here. I reach out my magic and hold it out, inviting the earth in. And I wait patiently.

Okay, maybe not so patiently. But there is a war going on behind me.

Something lands on my shoulder, and the magical essence is familiar. "Lo. Hi."

"Hello, Magic. We are ready whenever you are."

"Be riiiight there." I breathe in through my mouth and out through my nostrils and wait in silence.

And I wait. And I wait.

Until eventually something touches the edges of my aether. Something strong and foreboding yet gentle and lenient in its giving. Hello mountain.

It vibrates under my hand, tickling my magic.

I need a favor from you. Would you mind breaking and blocking the path? If you would like me to fix you back up again later, I can, but for now, we need to block those footsteps from getting any closer to the valley.

And again I wait until it's ready to answer me.

Eventually, it links itself to me, and all of a sudden, I can push and pull, move the rock. Like it's joined forces with me. Wrapped its fingers through mine. I push on the edges of the mountain, and when it doesn't move, I push harder.

I push so hard that I can feel blood dripping from my nose and air huffing out of my mouth. But it crumples piece by piece, until it's falling down, the crash and echo of stone upon stone piercing the valley.

Thank you.

And I un-tether the connection, reminding myself to come back and fix it, if that's what it wants.

"Join the fight, Lo." I stamp my staff on the mountain top. "I'll be back with an army."

The army in question is in the field behind our house, I find out after flying over *Sheruta* to find it. Probably should have asked Lo where they were. Lesson learned.

Right now, I have to get them all to the Jura Mountains as quickly as possible. So I enlarge the spell's radius like I did in the tunnel in New Orleans and take a deep breath. Okay.

"Time to go," I make the wind carry to every soldier.

They take deep breaths and ready themselves, some holding knives and guns in their grips.

And I teleport four thousand soldiers into a battlefield in a single swoop.

56

Chaos reigns. The sounds of gunfire, swords clashing, and fiery explosions ricochet off the mountainous rock around us, creating a valley of noise. The villages start a mile to the east, and we can't let them get that far.

But so far, our retreat hasn't helped.

A badass she may be, but Red is not a trained commander.

Nine?

Yeah? he asks, sounding out of breath.

We're splitting the battlefield into nine sections, I say as I fly high above, looking down on everything. Like a grid. And I'm going to maneuver you all around like chess pieces. I need you to relay messages to each section, so buckle up.

Buckle up? For whaaaaa?

I swoop down and grab him by the underarms, yanking him into the sky. "See this?" I think up a mental image of grid lines across the battlefield, dividing everyone up. "I want to use it."

Okay. What first?

See those two fire Witches in A2? Have them move to A1 and dispatch the Fae throwing water whips everywhere. Then move the bear Shifter in B3 over to B2. They're the biggest area with the most number of enemies, so they need heavier fighters.

Then let's move Cas and Dan from C2 up as well. They're the strongest Fae we have.

No, split them up. One to B2 and one to A2.

Done.

I watch the soldiers we picked move around the battlefield, barreling through enemies along the way, dodging others, until they're where they can do the most damage.

Once the fire Witches now in A1 have helped thin the water specializing Fae, I send them to B1 to help dispose of some highborn Vampires causing havoc with their stupidly good natural defense. Some unfriendly fire out to sort them out.

What next?

B2 are still struggling, but I don't see another move we can make.

Okay, send us to B2.

I fly us down there and drop us onto the field. It's more chaotic down here amidst the fighting, where I can't see the grid lines and I can't tell where section B2 ends and begins.

But there are three Vampires and a terrifying number of crows coming at me, so I can't afford to get confused.

I blow the crows into the nearest mountain rock with enough force to splatter blood over the surrounding tufts of grass.

The three Vampires charge at full speed and circle me before I have the time to react. Shit. I'm cornered.

Their menacing grins dagger at my insides as they hiss, hands in fists at their sides.

My best move right now is to counter.

The one on my left charges at me, fingernails the length of claws (and probably just as strong too), but it's the green liquid oozing off them that forces me to dodge him first swing. They're poison, I'll bet. He swings again, and I duck then roll out of the way. But when he swings again, I grab his arm and twist it behind him, then yank.

A sickening pop sounds. Followed by his screams.

The other two are in front of me now, but I have more room to maneuver, so I light them up, controlling the flames, not allowing them to travel farther than I say so. And upon my exhale, I extinguish them.

I'm starting to find all this fighting surprisingly calm.

I'm pretty sure that's not a good sign.

We can get you therapy later, Nine says as I turn around to find him straddling a Fae with an explosion rune in his palm.

"Nine, look out!"

Instinctually, I hurl a knife at the Fae's head and watch it sink to the floor with a thud.

Nine looks at me in surprise, his eyes wide and his mouth parted. *I knew that rune was there, Sweetie.*

Right. Of course he did. Telepathy, Magic.

But thank you for the assist.

One of Connie's arrows flies past my head, the fletching brushing my face. A shout behind me follows, then a curse. And I spin to find Phillipe crouching in the grass, his knee felled by an arrow.

She meant to hit him there.

Why?

Because the king requested him alive.

Oh, right.

I shift, and a binding spell slips from my fingertips like a breath of wind on a morning breeze. Easy. Effortless.

But Phillipe thuds to the ground, his limbs bound. "I'll gut you like the worm you are, Magic!"

"Yeah, yeah." I grab my staff and point the teleporting crystal at him, hoping my plan will work. "Get in line." And I send him to the embassy's holding cells I briefly remember from the tour everyone gave me upon opening. "I really hope he made it there."

Shrugging, I decide that I don't really care if he did or didn't. A happy accident in the making if there ever was one.

Nothing like an old Vampire prince to torture and maim. Well, alright, I'll probably not torture and maim him, but the idea still makes me smile. A person can dream.

Turning back to the battle, I blast air in several directions, hoping they'll smash against more rocks. But once I've cleared the surrounding area, I realize we're just getting rid of the last drudges.

"It's over."

"Yup," Connie says, putting an arm around me. "Wasn't that hard."

I eye her up and down—not a speck of a dirt on the woman—and laugh. "Only because I brought in reinforcements and sealed off the only path the enemy could use to get here."

"Oh, was that you?" she asks, sarcasm lacing her words. "Never would have guessed."

Red laughs besides her, then checks the wounded, including the enemies, and sets up a makeshift infirmary for us to use.

And I help. Because I injured a lot of these people. And guilt is gnawing its way into my heart.

57

I send Nine home to check on Dea and Arrie, see how the embassy is doing. Many aren't fighters. And they need to be updated. Not to mention many of them relay information back to different species' councils and other bodies of important people.

In the meantime, Connie gets stuck in helping gently carry some of the wounded to the nearby village alongside some Vampire, Shifter, and air Witch helpers. All using their magic for good.

"Isn't it weird?" I ask Connie as she places another wounded down on the grass, this one missing a leg. "To be going from violent murder to gentle healer in the space of a few minutes?"

"This is what war is like, Magic. It's why we like to avoid it."

"She's right," a village healer called Kiara says. "You saved us today. And part of that meant defending against people who would do you harm if they could. But this"—she gestures to the rows upon rows of wounded soldiers, ours and theirs—"is a great mercy. It shows compassion."

Connie leaves, going back to continue carrying the wounded over.

The Witches and Fae have started helping us, creating fresh water, sterilizing needles and other equipment, getting a cooking fire going, cooling patients down with a cold wind, and creating comfier beds of grass and moss on slightly raised platforms.

I've been using my Vampire blood to save the most critical patients, and the few healers have been listing their injuries as I've gone. It's good system. But I need Dea. Only my blood can heal; I can't do anything for broken bones or non-critical things with the number of wounded in the thousands.

As if on cue, Nine teleports back in with a tired-looking Dea in tow. He fazes over and Nine teleports back. "What do you need?"

"Help. I'm helping the most critical patients, but some are in agony with broken bones and cracked skulls and missing limbs."

"I can heal the less major wounds, but I cannot do anything for missing limbs other than seal the wound and keep it clean."

Kiara steps in, putting her bowl of water down. "Then heal the broken bones so we can send those patients on their way. In the meantime, I will continue to help those missing limbs or organs."

"Use some of the fire Witches to help you cauterize the wounds in the field."

She nods once, the stern lady that she is, and rushes off. I have no idea what species she is, but she's a . . . to-the-point old woman.

Dea and I get to work, and by the time we've gotten through the soldiers already here, Connie and her small army of strong helpers bring in the next batch. So the moment there's a makeshift bed free for them or a new set made, they're laid down and we get to work.

This goes on for hours. And before we know it, darkness is setting in and the Witches are setting up witchlights along with Fae who are creating illuminating spell bead clusters that I desperately want the spell to. They're so pretty. (Or would be if, you know, they weren't illuminating the dying or critically wounded.)

Nothing, and I seriously mean nothing, feels better than the comfy patch of grass I find to sprawl out and nap in. The healers and makeshift nurses have been tagging in and out, using a nearby space they've fashioned into a sort of rest area.

I grab a large bowl of broth off the tray someone is handing out, and when he asks if I'd rather have something better from the nearby village kitchen, I decline and say this will be fine.

Then I tag back in and spread some more drops of blood around the most critically wounded and watch as their skin knits back together and their bones snap back into place. It looks painful, but they do nothing more than sigh a breath of relief. It might block their pain receptors at the same time as heal them. I don't know.

A familiar grumpy face storms over the hill carrying three bodies lain on top one another, his ragged hair in clumps over his shoulders. He places them gently into spare beds near me and forces me to spin around and look at him. "You're okay?" he asks, checking my head, shoulders, torso, then limbs. "Shift."

I shift into my male form so he can repeat the same process.

And I watch his face go from on edge to relaxed in a matter of seconds. "You're okay."

I nod, but I feel a little shaky, if I'm honest. "Just a little light-headed." I let another drop of blood fall in the Shifter lion's snout and watch its ribs crack back into place and its skin and muscle stitch back together. "There's many people to heal."

"How long have you been at this?"

"Well, it was light when I started. But I did nap and eat earlier."

Arrie growls low in his throat, clearly unhappy with my personal caretaking skills. He picks me up bridal style and carries me over to the edge of the makeshift hospital, then further to a rocky outcropping, where he places me on my butt. "Feed." He holds out his wrist. "Now."

"You've just recovered, Arrie. I don't want to—"

His snarl cuts me off. "Feed."

"Okay, okay." I snatch his wrist and sink my fangs in, letting his forest-tasting blood hit my tongue and trail a path of beauty down my throat.

The only sign this is having any effect on him is the slight heaviness to his breathing and the hand running through his hair and settling on his neck.

The moment I feel better, I stop. Pulling back.

"Better?"

I fold my arms over my chest and stand back up, heading back to work. "Yes."

Which makes Arrie laugh. "You are too stubborn for your own good."

I turn back around just before I hit the first line of beds. "Then it's a good job I have such a caring boyfriend."

Smugness radiates off him in waves, and I walk back to where I was with a pep in my step as I heal the next dying man, a Vampire I remember flying into a rock. He doesn't even notice it's me as I fix him up. But when he comes to, his leaking throat having stopped bleeding and sewn itself shut, he screams at the sight of me.

"Hey, hey, shhh . . ." I try to calm. "I'm not going to hurt you. I just healed you."

But there's no consoling him.

"Oi!" the wolf next to him whacks him on the shoulder. "Quit your hollerin'. She could have left you for dead out there, but she organized an army to help all wounded, regardless of side."

His eyes finally lay upon mine, widened shock in them. A short, gruff, "Thanks," rips from his lips. Then he turns over in his bed.

"You're welcome. Someone will be along with food in a moment. Blood pills are on hand, too." I move onto the next patient, trying to put his screams out of my mind.

This sucks.

And there's nothing I can do about it.

Aki is forcing my hand. I have to be the bad guy. But I so desperately wish I didn't have to be. Though, I guess I could have gone easier on the opposing soldiers—I even flew some of them into mush against the mountain—but I was so focused on the battle, on protecting our people, on keeping the villages safe, that I couldn't think of anything else.

Damn, this sucks.

I drop five drops of my blood into a wounded Witch's mouth and watch seven broken bones mend, a half fallen-off leg sew itself back together, and a sigh of relief leave his mouth.

"Thank you, Magic," he whispers before falling asleep.

"You're welcome."

Connie leads the charge once more, bringing more wounded through, but half of her soldiers come over the hill empty handed. Could it be?

"That's the last of them," she informs us. "The field is empty of survivors."

A sigh of relief escapes my mouth for the first time tonight. "Could you set something up for the dead? Organize them to be teleported back to their families in coffins?"

"Sure, but it'll take a while."

Brutus claps me on the back. "Some fighting there, Magic. Ma says we'll handle the teleporting and finding of the families if you supply the teleporting crystals and coffins."

"Done." Connie shakes his hand. "I'll have those to you in a few days."

"There's a batch of a hundred teleporting crystals in the baskets outside my room."

Connie nods that she's heard, but she's off, organizing food, supplies, and rejoining our army's hierarchy. Re-solidifying our defense. She was the best choice.

Yeah, she was. I spin on my heels to find Nine sat upon a rock at the edge of the last line of wounded soldiers. *C'mere.*

I seek him out and end up in his arms, breathing in his bonfire and ink and paper smell, letting it fill me up. "I missed you."

"I've not been gone long," he chuckles.

"I don't think I'll ever not miss you again."

"Dea says the same thing." We watch our Angel of Death make his way on unsteady feet through the final line of wounded, nearly collapsing. "We should probably . . ."

"Yup." We both get to our feet and walk his way, and just as his eyelids flutter and his knees give way, I catch him. "I'm going to take him home. I've done everything I can do here, anyway."

"Okay. Need anything from here?"

"Don't think so. Could you check in with Connie and ask when she's coming home? Sorry, don't mean to treat you like a relationship PA."

It's okay. I'll go check in with your girlfriend.

Thank you.

Arrie's standing behind me and grabs Dea for me, hauling his passed-out form over his shoulder. "Ready to go home?"

"Yeah, I've done everything I can do. And I need like three days' worth of sleep." We walk to an empty area, wait for Nine to return, and then I teleport us back to my bed.

"No sex. No food. No showering. Just sleep."

"Sleep," Arrie agrees. "We can shower and fuck in the morning." He lays Dea down on the edge of the bed and snuggles in on the other side, leaving the duvet open for us. "Ready?"

I yank all my clothes off and fall into bed beside Arrie, Nine joining me on the other side, snuggles between myself and Dea.

"What did Connie say?"

"That she wants to make sure everyone is well and the villages are okay before she leaves. And to remind you that she doesn't need as much sleep as us."

"Right. Never ending stamina. Forgot."

58

I want to sleep in the next day, to join Arrie in my shower, to lie in bed with Dea and Nine, who are cuddled up under my duvet making out. But a little annoying prince is waiting for me in the kitchen. Like a dickhead.

"Best get going, Sweetie. You don't want to keep his highness waiting."

"Shut up." I squeeze my butt into the suit trousers, zipping up, and then I'm out the door without a second to spare. "Love you all!" I call behind me as I rush down the stairs.

Lucien does not look happy with how late I'm making us. His arms folded, a scowl on his face, his foot tapping away impatiently on the floor. "You're late."

"I don't know if you heard, but there was a fucking war at the Jura Mountains. I've only been back for, like, five hours. Back off."

He flinches. "Sorry. I'm still annoyed with Red."

"She fought well. And she's alive with nothing more than a few scratches."

You could practically see the panic and tension leech out of him. "That's . . . good. That's good."

"C'mon." I grab his arm and teleport to the Vampire Council building. "We're already late."

The king waits for us in the same room as earlier. And instead of the rude, impatient greeting I got from his son, he's standing there with nothing but a smile. "Magic, Lucien. You've managed to join us." He greets me with a kiss on the cheek (yes, even in male form, which is weird and endearing and wrong all mixed into one). "I was worried you wouldn't make it given recent developments."

"Everyone is doing okay, but we lost many."

"Magic is doing well on five hours of sleep," Prince Lucien comments.

"Only in this form," I joke. "My other form is still stuck in pajamas as I ran out of time to get both forms ready."

Everyone laughs, both of them finding my two form antics hilarious, apparently.

One of the Vampires running in the election chips in. "So, you can only switch into whatever clothes you were wearing in that form last?"

"Yeah. It's a bit of a pain really." I take a seat in the same place as before. "Thank goddess both forms share an energy source, or I'd have to eat twice, too."

"Wow. You're, like, one of the most interesting people I've ever met."

Interesting good? Or interesting bad? Eh. Never mind. Interesting good because I'm fantastic.

After five minutes of prep, the cameras roll, and the Vampire king announces to the world that the winner, by a landslide, is Victor Hesham. We all clap, even the losers, and everyone enjoys those fancy triangle sandwiches and blood that's been decanted into wine glasses. Which I pass on, naturally.

Once the cameras have stopped rolling, the other two candidates make their excuses and leave, but the four of us gather around and have a drink to Victor's success.

"Good luck, Victor. And I hope you make all the differences you dream of."

He shakes my hand with a warm smile. "I look forward to working with you."

A few minutes later, three new Vampires take their seats, all of whom I haven't met before, and we start the process all over again. I try to pay attention. I really do. But my mind is racing. And everything rushes around me like blurry cars on the highway.

When will the next attack be? Where will it be? How many people will die?

I know Aki's in Tokyo, so maybe I could find him and deal with him there, instead of waiting and always being on the defensive. But that would make me the bad guy, right? We're only supposed to help, to guide. Not to act out of our own opinions and biases. But he's my brother. He killed my boyfriend. How am I supposed to not hate him?

And what about the Fae Queen? What do I do with her? She's trying to take over the SC and put her species on top of the others, to rule with a Fae fist, as it were. But she can't. That defeats the point of the pillar communities and the Supernatural Council's very existence.

And Phillipe is in the embassy's cells awaiting whatever the hell I'm supposed to do with him. I've been meaning to tell Lucien and the king, but I haven't found the right time. I guess without all these ears around. Maybe after we're done.

Will taking Phillipe out of the fight even remove the Rogue Vampire Faction? Won't they just employ someone else? Or is he the only thing holding them together?

Pretty sure if we remove Aki and the Fae Queen, we can smooth things over and put someone else on the Fae throne. So that's something. At least.

Checking back in with my surroundings, the third Vampire is talking about creating a new blood supply to remove the need for the blood pills. And anger simmers beneath the surface. Nine worked himself stupid creating those. Stop being such an ungrateful ass.

Unbiased, Magic. Unbiased.

Goddess, I'm bad at this.

But it's over before I know it, and they're leaving to go back to whatever political candidates do in their spare time and I'm finally alone with Lucien and the king.

"We have Phillipe in a cell in the embassy," I say the moment the door closes. "What do you want me to do with him?"

The king gestures us to sit and releases a held breath. "It has been a long twenty-four hours. Let us have some more blood and food, and then we can update each other."

Nodding, we all agree.

"And, Magic, if you would like to switch forms, I care not for your pajama'd look."

Laughing, I politely decline. No need to tell him I'm naked and still aching from last night. I think I'll stick to this form.

A few moments later, a servant arrives with a trolley of more food and blood, which I obviously decline. But the muffins look good, so I help myself to yet more food.

"Stress eating, great. That's all I need," I mumble.

"If anyone has a good excuse for stress eating, little Horseman, it's you." Lucien smirks at me. "Do you have an update on how many we lost?"

I nod, not liking the figure Connie gave me. "Too many. 876, of which, 239 were Vampires."

Lucien and the king are both silent, their gazes to the floor.

"I'm sorry."

"It is not your fault. We would have lost far more if you were not there." He reframes his face and says, "The Supernatural Council messaged all the pillar communities this morning saying they're disbanding any military actions and removing themselves from the Fae Queen's side. They wish to remain impartial during this trying time."

I can't help it, I smile. "I'll take that. Impartial is good enough."

"And you caught Phillipe yesterday?" Prince Lucien asks. After I nod confirming, he continues. "So now it's just Aki and the Fae Queen."

"I know where Aki is, but I don't think a battle in the biggest city in the world between the two of us is a good idea. And if I lure him anywhere, he'll bring the entire army."

"You can't avoid the war that's coming," Lucien says, his wisdom voice turned all the way up. "Even if you manage to deal with your evil twin, we still have to deal with the Fae Queen and her army."

"Lucien is right," the king says. "We've had many battles over the past few months, but the one coming will be what we have been preparing for."

"I just wish I knew where it would be. That way we could plan accordingly."

The king smiles at me, a plan forming in his mind. "If you draw him out, and he brings an army, then you do not need to know. You picked the place."

"That is . . . right."

"I am not king for nothing, Magic." He laughs, lighthearted and amused. "There's juice in this old goat yet."

Which sounds ridiculous because he doesn't look a day over twenty-five. But he's really, really old. Like, close to nine hundred, I think.

I turn to Lucien, curious. "How old are you?"

Lucien chokes on his wine glass of blood and smirks. "Checking out a guy's age are we, Horseman?"

I shrug. "Yeah. Guess so."

"Well, I'm 251."

"Goddess, everyone I know is so old."

"You are literally fucking people two thousand years old," Lucien remarks.

"Yeah, but they're technically dead, so that doesn't count."

"That's worse."

"Says the Vampire."

"Okay, children," the king interrupts. "Enough bickering. I think Magic deserves to go home and finish getting rest."

"Right, yeah. I'm exhausted." I turn to Lucien. "Check back in with the embassy soon, because there will probably be a meeting for future plans."

"Will do." He mock salutes me before I stand back and teleport myself back to bed.

As my eyes peel open from the perfect nap, I hear voices coming from across the room.

"A test?" Arrie asks.

"Yes. I think we should give their powers a final test." There's a smile to his voice, a hint of amusement.

Connie laughs, picking up on whatever Dea is hinting. But I don't hear Nine.

I'm lying on the other side of your bed, also tired.

Ah. What kind of test are they talking about?

He scoffs into my mind, clearly not on board with said plan, but answers anyway. *War games. We each get a flag and the first person to hold all five wins. We usually play around the house's grounds.*

Why do they want to test my powers in the first place?

Dea wants to push them. You don't find many opponents difficult because your magic is so adaptable, but fighting us might be harder.

Plus, seeing Arrie put me on my ass will make Dea and Connie laugh.

That too. Don't worry, Sweetie. I think you'll do better than they think.

"I'm up for war games," I say out loud. "But I think it would be more fun with teams from the embassy. Make it a real strategy test."

"Niiine," Connie moans. "I wanted to tell them."

"You are finally awake," Dea says with a beautiful smile. "You have been sleeping for ten hours."

I shoot up out of bed. "Ten hours? I don't have ten hours. Why didn't one of you wake me!" I try to hop into the jeans I left on the floor but stumble and shift into a crow, fly, and land on Dea's armrest instead. Then I shift back, groaning. "I don't have ten hours to waste on sleep."

Connie coughs to get my attention. "Remember when we talked about not running yourself into the ground?"

"I vaguely remember it . . ." I avoid her accusing eyes like they're darts on fire. "But war is coming soon. I don't have time."

"We are basically already in a war," Arrie grumbles. "This is what they look like. Many battles, much stress."

"They are not," Dea says, "like they are portrayed in the movies, where it is all one big final, organized battle that determines the fate of the earth."

"Oh." I guess he's right. That is a little naïve to think. "Then . . . can I have brownies?" I look to Arrie before I go and sit on his lap, wiggling into place. "Pleeeeeease?"

He rolls his eyes, but the corners of his lips lift in amusement. "I'll go make another batch." He shoves me off him. "A large one, since you eat so many of them."

"They are like orgasms on a plate, Mr. Grumpy," I say as I head into the bathroom to shower. "Don't you dare take that away from me!"

After showering both forms and feeling cleaner than I've ever felt—more refreshed too —I follow my Vampire's nose into the kitchen, where I see a stack of the best thing known to mankind (or specieskind, I guess). Brownies.

"Yay!" But before I can snatch one from the stack cooling by the open window, Arrie hands me a plate with one on. "Okaaay, guess I'll eat this one." He also hands me a fork, but I'm not that posh. So I just shove half into my mouth.

And everything in me explodes. It sets my senses alight, draws my fangs forth, and has my eyes burning red before I can stop them. After I swallow, I turn to him and ask, "Is this the first prototype?"

"Uh-huh." He looks to the floor, almost nervous. And is that embarrassment?

"It's fantastic!"

He looks up and meets my eyes. "Really?"

I jump into his arms and wrap my legs around his torso, smiling down at him. "Best thing I've ever tasted."

A breath leaves him, and I realize he was worried. About my opinion and what I thought of something he loves. "That's good. I'm going to try a few other things, too."

"Ohhh, like muffins and lemon drizzle cake and those cute little apple pastries you sometimes make? What about—"

He shuts me up by kissing me. Lips press against mine in haste, but eventually the kiss slows down, deepens, and soon his tongue is dancing with mine and I'm remembering all the ways he's fucked me lately. All the eyes that watched us. All the amazing ways he sets my body aflame.

And if the small, under-his-breath groan is anything to go by, he's thinking the same thing. But he breaks for air instead, putting me back on my feet. "I have a few things to do today. Sorry."

He looks genuinely sorry. Like he doesn't know how to reject me. Or if he should. So I lean up to his face and pull him in for a kiss, a quick reminder that I still love him. "It's okay. I get it. You're allowed to say no." And then go for a stroll through the garden, managing to walk past the unicorns and a few fairy dens.

Everything is beautiful today. Even the sun shining is more beautiful than it usually is. It's amazing how much good sex, friends, and brownies can make you see the same world differently.

Remind me to fuck you with everyone else again in the future. You're basically glowing.

If a little tired still, but yeah. I feel great.

Nine laughs, but I don't know where he is in order to punch him in the arm.

If you really must, I'm with the horses.

Yes. I must. So I fly over to him, wanting to get to him quickly, and watch as he straddles a leg over his horse and grabs the reins. Then he flies across the field, jumping the fence, and gallops beyond.

His red hair flies in the wind as his legs hold on to the horse's sides (he's riding without a saddle, because of course he is).

You had to know how to do this in the Chinese army. They didn't like paying extra for saddles if they could avoid it.

So, not too dissimilar to most modern governments, then?

Not really, no.

I zoom down beside him and fly alongside the horse, keeping up with its speed easily. This is probably why I don't have a horse. That and I can just shift into one. Though, Dea could just faze or, so why does he get a horse?

His energy reserves aren't able to be topped up like yours, and he runs out quicker.

Well, at least he can control his visibility now.

Two thousand years of having to schedule everything around his visibility limit outside of the house. Just solved in one afternoon by our new partner.

I was thinking . . . When all of this is over, I'd love to spend more time in Japan. There's so much to my culture I don't know because I was raised American, and I'd like to experience more of it. Could we do that? Just live in Tokyo or somewhere more rural for a few years?

We could. Nothing saying we can't.

Would be like an extended vacation.

Want me to buy you a house there? Then you can stay whenever you like for however long you like. In fact, we have a safe house there already. You can have that. Or I could buy you something better. Something that's totally yours, and—

Nine! I would love a house there. Thank you. But you don't have to do that. Houses are expensive.

You deserve everything you get from us. You were totally torn out of your world and shoved into an identity you had no idea how to navigate. And you still manage to focus on other people more than yourself.

And here I thought I was quite self-centered.

Everyone who goes through an identity crisis thinks about themselves a lot; it's part of the process. But that doesn't make you a bad person. It just makes you human.

I guess so. I would like to do more for all of you. Take you on dates, buy you gifts, shower you with love. You all need it. And I don't do it enough.

We haven't had the time, Sweetie. I promise that after this is all over, you can dote on our every whim.

I shift into my male form, then into a stallion, and I gallop alongside him, taking all the turns he does, jumping all the fences he does. Nine has to slow down a bit, since I'm not as large as their horses, but we still have fun.

I'm so glad you're home.

Me too.

. . .

LATER THAT DAY, WE HAVE A MEETING AT THE EMBASSY TO DISCUSS POTENTIAL PLANS FOR drawing Aki and the Fae Queen out with their armies.

Rufus, our Shifter representative from here on *Sheruta* is sternly against the idea of us using *Sheruta* as a battlefield. "We would need to evacuate the entire town. Something that's never been done. We wouldn't have a home if things went wrong."

"But I can't evacuate other countries or cities, and I can this one. It's at least a possibility."

"One we cannot ignore," Dea says. "*Sheruta* was here when we were made. It is either as old as we are, or it predates us. It exists for a reason, just like we do."

I turn to him, surprised by his theory. "You think Fate created it for this purpose?" Then I turn to Nine and Connie, who usually have an opinion on such things.

"I always used to think that *Sheruta* was Fate's apology," Nine says. "That we might have gotten dealt a shitty hand, but here's an entire realm to yourself to do with as you please. But Fate is never that kind." He shrugs. "Maybe Dea's right."

Rufus scoffs. "You get to live forever. How is that a bad hand?"

Arrie scowls, meeting his gaze. "When you've watched every friend and family member and lover die for two thousand years, come back and tell me you'd still choose immortality. We will outlive everyone in this room. We will attend all eleven of your funerals."

At least Rufus has the dignity to look sheepishly to the floor.

Lucien's gaze softens as he takes us in, ending his pitying look at me. As though he's seeing us for the first time.

"We should lure the army to Margalla Hills National Park," Nine says after looking something up on the plasmascreen in his hand. "It's in Pakistan, and it's one of the largest open areas in the world. But it's not too near a city if we head to the north of the area."

No one seems to disagree, though they're still staring at us like we're dying puppies.

"Okay," I say, "enough. You can pity us later. We have a final battle to plan." At least I hope it'll be the final battle.

Lucien raises his gaze again, looking directly at me. "Father has made a choice about Phillipe." Well, that sounds dramatic. "Execute him."

The table gasps.

Red looks at him disapprovingly. "Execute him? You mean, his own father wants him dead?"

"Red, he killed hundreds of Vampires, wants to see the Fae Queen and himself sitting at the top of the world, and, might I remind you, he supports Aki and his ridiculous ideals."

"But he's your brother!" She seems genuinely horrified by the idea, but everyone doesn't seem that bothered.

Our single Fae seems on the fence, like he has something to say but doesn't feel like he can speak up.

I nod to him, encouraging him to speak. He's here for that reason, after all.

"While I don't wish to condone murder, it would send a message. Maybe the Rogue Vampire Faction will disband afterward."

"Or maybe they'll fight back harder," Red retaliates. "Maybe they might try to grow their ranks. Maybe it'll send discourse through the entire Vampire community and cause even more problems."

"We could just keep him locked up until everything has died down, then decide what to do with him," I suggest. Maybe everyone might be a little more inclined to show mercy when their people are no longer at risk.

Lucien is suspiciously quiet regarding his own feelings, which is unlike him, so I look to him. Really look at him. And it's clear as day on his face. He doesn't want his brother to die, but he has to respect his father's wishes. "I think we should interrogate him. See what he knows. Maybe he knows where the Fae Queen is."

Dea looks in agreement, along with everyone else.

"But who is going to interrogate him?" My hands wring in my lap, scared they'll ask me to do it. I don't ever want to do that again. Not after last time. Felicity meets my gaze and nods. She understands.

"That would be me," Nine says on a sigh. "I can extract information the easiest. And if I don't get what we need, and I can just force him to tell the truth."

I settle my hand on his leg and squeeze. "You don't have to do that. You never have to use your powers in a way that doesn't feel right for you."

"If you have fight and kill and do things you hate, then so do we. We can't just expect you to do all the hard stuff."

Connie agrees, nodding. "He's right. We have to step up and help you do the shit stuff. Or it's not a team effort."

Lucien pipes up, happy to help. "I'll help you, Nine. He might respond better if I'm there, or it might piss him off and make him slip up. Either way, it'll probably be of use."

"Thanks, dude."

"So," Arrie says, plasmascreen in hand, "the Margalla Hills National Park is owned by a council, controlled by the SC, so we should give them a head's up, try working with them better. It's also a completely open area with some buildings nearby, so perhaps evacuating those houses would be a good plan. But quietly, otherwise Aki and the Fae Queen will have time to plan ahead, and we want to draw them out suddenly, so they don't have time to strategize. That way we can capitalize on the time they have to spend communicating a defense. Just like they did with us at Jura Mountains."

Everyone nods, but I'm just proud. He's really come out of his shell these last few months, becoming more confident in his abilities and helping the team with them. He let us handle the decision around Phillipe, and while we were doing that, he spent time planning a strategy and the basic building blocks of a battle plan.

He's more intelligent than he looks.

Gah. I'm already disgusted by your newfound admiration for Arrie. It's gross.

Just because I'm not fawning over your brain this time. Jealous?

A little.

Oh, really? I'm sorry.

Don't be. Jealousy is normal.

Well, I'll make sure to tell you how smart you are and make you feel special this evening.

Thank you. I look forward to seeing this special interest. Will it involve your dick?

Maybe. If you ask nicely.

Please, may I have your dick? The snicker behind his mental voice is all too clear, and we both have to concentrate on not laughing while everyone discusses battle plans and numbers and defense systems with Arrie.

Yes, you may.

Maybe leave the domming to Dea, Sweetie.

Yeah, probably. Besides, he'd be furious if you subbed for anyone else. Trust me. He was so broken when he lost you. I show him the image of Dea crying on the floor, breaking apart.

But he goes silent, his face downcast, hands fiddling in his lap. *I hate that I caused so much pain.*

You didn't. Aki did. And I'll kill him for it.

60

The cells in the basement are not what I expected. They're bright, with a small book collection, a TV every cell can see, and a menu ordering system (albeit limited and simple options) for the three meals a day.

At my surprised expression, Connie explains, "We're not running a prison. We just have this here in case we needed to hold anyone before we hand them over to whatever council they're represented by."

"*Sheruta* doesn't have a prison," Dea explains, waving a hand through the air.

Lucien, mildly shocked by this notion, looks at Dea quizzically. "Really?"

"We do not have a lot of crime here."

"Maybe the world can learn from *Sheruta*," he muses out loud, mostly to himself, with a small smile on his face.

I think he'll miss this place when he becomes king. He'll have to stay in New Orleans then. Maybe he'll turn the job down. He does have other siblings, I think. But he's the next strongest in the family line, and that's how succession works.

Phillipe is wearing the same dirty, blood-stained clothes I sent him here in—a black sleeveless tunic top with delicate embroidery and matching pants. His muscles flex in the natural lighting filtering in through the small window at the back of his cell. And he smirks from beneath heavy lids as we walk up to him.

"Ah, yes. I was wondering when you'd get around to interrogating me." His face is confident as he continues to lie on the bed, arms folded beneath his head, legs crossed. "Want to pilfer through my brain, Famine?"

"Yes." He's like stone, not a single emotion showing. "We need information to save the world from your friends."

"Pfft." He sits up, laughing. "Save the world? You act so justly, so righteous. It's just an opinion. And opinions can be wrong."

I wave his words away. "We're not here to chat. Sorry." Nine, don't let him get you talking. You don't want to accidentally send him information. If he escapes—"

I know.

Okay.

Lucien walks through the swinging doors, a mess of emotions on his face, lips downturned.

Phillipe changes, his posture going rigid. "Lucien." The words like poison spilling from his lips.

"Phillipe. You comfortable?"

"Sure. This is actually quite a nice mattress."

I bet Connie'll be happy to know her choices are liked, even by this asshole.

"So, how does this work?" Phillipe asks. "You enter my mind like Father does, then I spill the beans?"

Nine shrugs. "Something like that." He steps forward, hands on the bars and frowns. He concentrates, his brows furrowing, but nothing happens.

Everything okay?

I can't read his mind.

Lucien sighs. "For fuck's sake. What have you done now?" He stands just behind Nine, arms crossed, hair slightly out of place.

But Phillipe just shrugs. "I dunno, but it's probably nothing the great Horsemen can't fix."

Silver Leaf, maybe?

Perhaps. But this feels a little different. Like Aki and his mind barrier.

Of course he protected his allies. Why didn't I think of that sooner? I have no idea how he does that, though, so I can't undo it, even I wanted to. But it's safe to assume it's something like Silver Leaf; maybe even a spell that uses it.

But spells aren't a Witch thing.

So maybe it's not Aki's doing. Maybe the Fae Queen is behind this.

That is the most likely option, yes.

But wouldn't you have to continuously take Silver Leaf for the spell to remain active? So, logically, we just wait.

We don't have time to wait. Aki knows we have him, so he'll march before his time is up.

Lucien's voice echoes around us. "Really? You are the worst brother in existence." He storms to the cell's bars and stretches the metal, stepping through the hole he made. "Fucking stop being a dickhead."

"Lucien?" I warn.

"Relax, he cannot hurt me. Father used mind control on us siblings as children so we would stop hurting each other in fights and to better train us."

But doesn't that mean Lucien also can't hurt Phillipe?

As if to prove me wrong, he flings him across the room, and Phillipe flops to the ground, confused and in pain, bleeding from a bash to the head. "How . . . ?"

Lucien smirks. "Father removed the spell from me so I could help deal with you."

Phillipe snarls, anger flashing across his eyes. "That fucking ass."

Lucien slaps his brother across the face, forcing his head to snap back farther than it should logically go. Then he grabs him by the ankle and dangles him upside down. "Anyone got any spelled rope?"

"Sending for some," Nine says.

A few seconds later, a guard comes running in with some spelled rope in his hand.

Nine goes to take it, but I stop him and grab it instead. "Thank you. Please lock the door on your way out."

He nods and silently walks away, not even a flicker of emotion on his face.

I walk through the hole Lucien made in the cell's bars and grab Phillipe's ankles, fly myself into the air and tie his feet to the upper bars. "There."

"Good work. Makes him look lovely and pretty."

"Thanks." I have no idea what Lucien is going to do, but I know him. He won't kill his brother, not when we need him alive. And especially not like this. He'd leave it for his father to do. Which I don't blame him for. "I've been working on my villainy."

Then, in the speed in takes to blink, Lucien slashes his nails across Phillipe's neck, puncturing his artery. And blood spurts all over the cell walls and Lucien's white shirt.

Or maybe I was wrong.

Maybe he would kill him.

A highborn Vampire can't die this way. He's draining him dry.

Why? Ohhh, to get rid of any Silver Leaf Vain in his system.

And to weaken him. Vampires need circulating blood. It hurts being without.

Proving Nine's explanation correct, Phillipe tries to scream, but it just bleeds him dry quicker. A gargling sound escapes his throat, and I want to puke, but I hold it in. Lucien and Nine need me strong right now. They need pissed-off me. The me who doesn't care about flinging Vampires into mountains.

But apparently, I can't turn that on on cue, because I'm struggling with this.

Phillipe thrashes around, trying to escape the ropes binding his feet to the upper bars, but they dampen someone's strength, leaving them weak and without supernaturally powered muscles. So he gets nowhere. He just continues to struggle. Gurgling. Blood pouring everywhere, spattering the cell walls in dark red ichor that drips to the floor.

Lucien just stands there, immobile, watching his brother writhe in agony. Unable to even scream. "Anything yet?"

"Nearly." *I can read emotions, surface thoughts, but I can't dig deeper yet.*

"Then we'll keep going."

They're ruthless.

How are they . . .

Because we have to. You can leave. You don't need to be here for this.

If you have to do something you hate, then I'll stand by your side while you do it. This job can suck. But it's easier together.

A small smile creeps onto Nine's face, just a slight up tilt of the corner of his lips. A sliver of a smile. But it's all I need to know that he feels supported.

Phillipe continues to struggle, but to no avail, and eventually his movements weaken, his arms flop to the floor, and the blood slows to a trickle that rivers down his neck and off his chin.

"He's out cold," I say.

"Yup," Lucien confirms. "His mind should be free of influence now." He steps out of the cell and washes his hands in the sink of a different cell, patting a towel over his face. "You're welcome."

Nine's brow furrows, concentration lining his face, and he breathes out. "I'm in." *I can see everything.*

"Good. Can you—" Lucien begins to ask, but I shut him up.

"Don't distract him. Just let him do his thing."

"Right." He takes a seat on a cell's bed, head heavy in his hands. "God, this sucks."

Snickering, I sit beside him. "Still find Vampires saying things suck hilarious, sorry." A hand on his shoulder finds tense muscles and the weight of the world sat there. And I happen to know a thing or two about that. "The world will always be in danger, little prince. All we can do is help fix the pieces that fall our way. You're doing great."

"I just didn't expect to have to do that to my own brother. We used to spar as kids. Throwing each other around, not a scratch to be gained with the help of Father. He was always teaching me new things, sneaking me out to bars as we got older. But he changed once he married Felicity."

"Sometimes people do change. And there's nothing we can do but sit there and help them when they ask for it."

"He'll never ask for help. It's not his style. But he'll get it anyway, because I won't let Father execute him. I can't."

"You might not get a choice, but I'll stand by you either way." He looks to me, surprised. "Whatever you think is best, I'll support it."

"You trust me that much?"

"I trust that you want what is best for people. That you make choices to the benefit of you, your family, your friends, and your people. I can't ask more of someone than that."

Nine gasps as his eyes fly open, and he spins around to face us. "We need to stop the battle plan meeting. Now."

61

"Wait, wait," I plead as we're running up the staircase. "Stop!"

They both stop and stare at me, frustration looming on their eyes.

"Nine, you need to explain. We need to think this through. Everything is delicate right now."

"But the longer we wait, the worse it gets."

"The worse what gets?"

"The Demons are working for Aki. They're going to betray us. And the one we put on the council is going to feed all of the information back to him."

"Okay." Shit. Fuck. "But if we rush in there, magic a-blazing, we out ourselves. They'll know we know."

"Yeeeah," Lucien says, clearly confused.

"But if we feed them false information, it can work to our advantage."

Nine looks stumped. "I can't believe I didn't think of that. Wow, I need a nap." He runs a frustrated, tired hand down his face, his eyes closed. "That is, of course, the plan."

"Okay, so what information do we feed him, because he knows what Phillipe knows?" Lucien asks, which is a valid question.

"We'll have to use real information," Nine says. "But give him false information about what we're going to do about it."

"Then reconvene with everyone else secretly and make a different plan."

Nine shakes his head. "That risks the Demons finding out. No, it'll be better if we Horsemen make the new plan and then send a secret message to the rest of the council. Messages are easier to keep secret than entire meetings."

"Right."

Everyone seemingly on board, we continue heading up the stairs, this time not in a rush. I think Nine needs time to think. He's the only one with all of their information and knowledge, so it'll be up to him to come up with the specifics.

The doors to the meeting room loom in front of us. Once light and welcoming, now they stand there all dark and foreboding, despite the white color and the plants and the plasmascreens that act as windows. But it doesn't matter, we have to go in anyway.

All Lucien and I have to do is act like we know nothing.

All I have to do is sell an entire set up.

Right.

I pat him on the back, sending him on his way.

You'll do great.

I sweep the doors open in a blast of air magic that makes us seem dramatic and in haste, and Nine rushes in, Lucien and I following at his heels.

"Wait!" He feigns being out of breath, holding up a hold while he leans on his knees. "Wait. We need to change . . . plan."

Arrie scowls, having already started to write the plan down, if the giant plasmascreen wall with diagrams and notes is anything to go by. "What's wrong?"

"The Fae Queen has more than one Witch. She has a small regiment of them from all over the world, promising them a home in her court where they can practise their magic openly away from the public's prying eyes."

"What kind of Witches?" Connie asks, worrying clouding her eyes.

"Fire and earth, as well as a few charm Witches. It's the charm ones I'm worried about. We have the upper hand by being able to mix Fae and Witch magic, but if they can do it too, Aki will use that to his advantage."

"Right," Arrie says, taking it all in stride. "We need to plan a defense strategy around the fact that different types of magic will be used, including teleporting crystals, charm spells, and mixed spells on the field."

Red looks worried. "Very few of us have faced that kind of magic before. Our armies aren't trained to handle that."

"Then we best get training them. Fast," Arrie says. "Take this strategy—I'll send a copy to you all—and Magic will work on best defenses for such attacks and hand you a diagrammatic list." He looks pointedly my way, letting me know he expects that of me post-haste.

"On it."

"Anything else?" Dea asks, suspiciously looking at Nine.

"Nothing I think will be of use to us. But the Fae Queen and her army are hiding under the ocean, which is why we couldn't find them."

"Under the . . . ocean?" our resident Fae asks, surprise lacing his words. "I've heard of rumors of an old palace under the Atlantic Ocean, but I thought it was just a legend."

"Apparently not," Nine scorns. "They are there, but the defenses are many. It's built like a fortress. I think it's best we stick to the plan of drawing them out."

Arrie shakes his head. "They won't send the whole army. At least, I wouldn't. It'll be best if we have a small team infiltrate the ocean palace once half the army are gone. We have no way of knowing where the Fae Queen herself will be, but my bet is on the palace."

Everyone looks at him expectantly.

"I'll probably send a few Horsemen and elite soldiers, leaving our main armies in place for the actual battle. It'll be a stealth operation anyway, so splitting the army in half is just sure to make us lose the half we send to the palace."

His eyes come back into focus, and he looks at me with a smile. I wish I could tell you what that smile means, but it could be anything from 'I'm horny' to 'Look, I bought you a pet penguin'. Either way, I'm happy he's happy.

We end the meeting, and we Horsemen greet everyone as they leave, Lucien saying goodbye for a day as he helps deal with the election campaigns. Though he promises to come back for Phillipe in an hour or so. He's transferring him to their dungeons at the Vampire Royal Council building.

But the Fae hangs back, looking nervously at the five of us.

"Is there anything wrong?" Connie asks.

"Well, it's just . . . earlier, when you rushed in, I sensed something. Something magical happening in the room. But I couldn't tell from whom. So I thought I would ask if it were you?"

Connie looks to us with a question on her face.

"Not me."

Everyone else shakes their head.

"Shit," I curse. I quickly shift forms and scan the room, looking for Fae magic or tech that's out of place. And bingo, I found it. Hiding underneath the desk. I yank it out and throw it on the table, then set it on fire. "Listening device."

Everyone looks confused, but Nine and I just share a conspiratorial gaze.

"What's going on?" Connie asks.

"The Demon ambassador is working for Aki. All the Demons are, I say on a sigh. "It's why we forced Arrie to change his plans." Facing him, I add, "Do not actually change those plans."

"A false lead?" Dea asks. "Clever."

"Thank you." Pride rings through.

But the Fae looks at us concerned. "If the Demons are going to betray us, then that's . . . bad."

"Yes and no," Nine explains. "They don't know we know, so technically they've just handed us the advantage."

His eyes light up, understanding dawning. "I see. I will keep quiet, then."

"I will be personally informing everyone of the right plan the moment we have it finalized," Nine explains. "It's the only surefire way to keep it private."

"Then I best get practising some defense magic. I will see you all later." He leaves in haste, worry peppering his step.

"He's a little . . . odd," Arrie says.

"Jesus, Arrie," Connie scorns. "You can't just go around calling people odd."

"Why not? I waited until he was out of earshot." Frowning, he leads the way home, a little sour after being told off by Connie.

62

"Where's Arrie?" I ask Connie once I come in from my morning yoga session the next day. "He wasn't watching me like usual."

She shrugs.

But Nine looks up from the plasmascreen he's holding with a sad smile. *He's out by the fairy garden that leaves off the left of the house.* He sends me a mental image so I know how to get there. *Be gentle.* "I'm off to deliver the messages to the ambassadors." He turns to me. "Good luck."

Gentle? Good luck?

This part of the house is where the older rooms sit, and the gardens here have been left unattended, left to grow wild and free. But there's a small archway off what I think used to be a pathway, the stones since cracked and mostly sunken into the ground.

"Arrie?" I gently ask, hoping he's nearby.

But no one answers me. Shifting into my female form, I strain my hearing and try to find out where he is, and when I hear sobs coming from beyond the archway, I rush in, not expecting the image in front of me.

Arrie's kneeling at the back of the garden, his hands clenching the grass beneath them, straining for control. For something to hold on to. There's a gravestone in front of him, followed by smaller gravestones either side.

This is . . .

I don't say anything. All I do is kneel beside him, place a hand on his knee and the other on the ground. And a second later purple flowers shoot up around their graves, curling into the stone and around our feet.

Arrie looks to me with tears pooling down his cheeks, his chest heaving, struggling to take in breaths. It's like he's stuck in the past, still as raw as he was two thousand years ago. "Just feeling the emotions . . . sucks."

He did this for me?

I wrap tight arms around him, grounding him. "You don't have to push yourself. But it's lovely that you came to visit her. I'd be so mad if you didn't visit me."

He wipes his eyes as he pulls out of my hold, a gentle yet sad smile on his face. "Thank you for the flowers. She loved them so much, she would decorate the whole house with them. Used to drive me crazy."

"You do not strike me as the flower type."

He shakes his head with a laugh. "I didn't used to be. But I like my Zen garden bedroom the house provided. Always felt like a gift from her, telling me to let nature calm me."

"She sounds wise, like Dea."

"But strong. She'd wield a battle-axe like no other woman I've ever seen."

And that's how we sit for the rest of the morning, me listening to his memories as he shares them, talking about his wife, his children, and a whole life I wish I could have seen.

63

"So, the goal is to catch everyone's flag and not lose them. You have the entirety of the grounds, but not beyond. We don't want to be destroying buildings we don't own," Nine explains, excitement in his eyes instead of the unsteady somber from earlier. "As per Connie's request, there are plasmacams everywhere, so try not to destroy them."

Dea, Arrie, and Con are ready to go, geared up, and eager to get started.

"You have one hour before the horn will sound and you will have to start your strategy." He looks to me. "Understand, Sweetie?"

"Set up my strategy, and when the horn sounds, the game starts. Whoever has all flags at the end wins. What happens if we're knocked out and no one has all the flags?"

"The winner will be whoever is holding the most," Dea answers.

"Everything clear?" Nine says, who is also dressed in strong cloth-like material acting as armor, but he also has a layer of carefully placed chain mail. "Just remember, try not to remove anyone's head. Take far too long to regrow."

"And it's horrifying," Arrie grumbles.

"Remember that time you got your head blown off by a rhino Shifter, Nine?" Connie laughs, unable to stop for a moment.

"Yes, yes. I'm sure it was hilarious." He does not look impressed. "Can we get started?" He looks to the time on the clock of the kitchen and smiles. "We have forty seconds before the cameras start rolling and we have to get going."

I'm a little nervous. This is like a final test of my abilities, but instead of facing regular opponents, I have to face them. Two-thousand-year-old beings with more practice in battle than I can ever hope to have. Also, the idea of facing Connie or Arrie in hand-to-hand combat leaves my knees knocking a little.

You know, just a tad.

And what about Nine?

He could make me do whatever he wanted. While he might not like to do so with other people, it would be okay with us. How do I combat that?

"Ten," Nine counts down, "nine, eight, seven . . ."

We step outside onto the porch and get ready to run. Well, they do, I just lift myself into the air and ready myself to fly.

"Five, four, three, two, one!"

Dea fazes instantly, blurring into the forest, whereas Arrie and Connie sprint at full speed into the distance, both heading north. But Nine and I stay still.

I have no idea what Nine is doing, but I'm flying.

We've had a whole twenty-four hours to prepare, and Connie prepared a live stream of the game so the public can be entertained and we can gain some more brownie press points. But it means I've had a full twenty-four hours to strategize and plan and prepare spells and charms that'll do some impact to my team.

None of us saw each other until dinner, where we sat in silence and stared each other down. But it was when Arrie strapped his dual battle-axes to his back that it started to feel real.

I have to actually fight them.

For real.

No holding back, which I'm pretty they've been doing with me until now.

I fly over the gardens, seeing if I can spot any of them, but the only person I know where they are is Dea, whom I can sense. He's somewhere near the forest. And while, yes, it seems like an advantage, I have to remember that if I can sense him, he can sense me, too.

Nine is still by the house, staring out into the garden, unmoving. But Connie and Arrie are nowhere to be found.

Hmmm . . .

Time to start laying my traps, then.

They're Fae spells I've rigged to alert me when tripped. Which will come in handy when trying to find everyone. Plus, they don't drain my magic here because we're on a leyline, so my biggest advantage over the others is that my Fae magic won't tire.

But I bet they've already thought of that.

Oh well, doesn't mean I can't use them.

I place three dozen traps all over the gardens, including in the forests, fields, fairy dens, and on the general pathways; though, I've avoided over-placing on the pathways because who will use those. Some are placed in trees, bushes, and under rocks, whereas others are placed just in the way but hidden with an invisibility spell I may or may not have stolen from Dea while sucking his dick.

Hey, don't judge me. Use what you got.

And I've got dick-sucking skills I can use to distract.

We've spent twenty-three minutes of our prep time so far, so I have seven minutes to set my final trap. And this one is specific to Arrie. I'm hoping it won't catch anyone else, but I'm not sure if that aspect of the magic will work. I bury it in the ground near the house and use my newfound earth magic to make it look like nothing has been disturbed.

"That just about does it." Now I just have to prepare my defenses.

I fly back into the air and head to the very back of the garden by the outer border fence, where there's nothing but a couple of fairy dens and fields. But behind the fence is the northern forest. And that's the point of being here.

There's magic in that forest. Magic I can tap into with enough concentration.

We are not, to my dismay, allowed to hide our flags. They have to be on show. And did I mention they glow, like dazzling pieces of shit giving away my location, even if I wanted to hide? So, instead of wrapping it around my bra strap (which was my original plan), I tie it to my belt loop just behind my dagger.

I'm armed to the teeth today: knives, daggers, my staff in charm bracelet form, and so many charms and spells in my bum bag that I'm genuinely worried they'll all spill out the moment I open it.

Fifteen minutes left.

Time to set up basic defenses.

I don't actually think anyone will struggle with these, but they'll stop them for a short pause, and that's long enough for me to see who I'm dealing with and choose my defense strategy.

I'm betting they'll be gunning for me.

And I don't have a clue what Nine is playing at, because as far as I can tell, he's still by the house.

Oh well, I don't have time to worry about him. I have to lay some spells and traps down this end, and after doing that, I raise a wall of earth around me, then a ring of fire blowing high into the sky around that.

Without Nine playing yet, Connie and Dea are most likely to find me first. I'm hoping Dea will play fair and not tap into our mate connection, but I don't count on it, which would, hopefully, leave Connie as gunning for first place.

She's good, but she can't just walk through fire. Not to mention the wall.

But there's sound on the other side of the wall, and before I know it, blonde hair sails down from the sky in two plaits and a wicked smile. "Nice try."

Shit. She jumped the wall?

I push the wall outward, giving myself more room. But I don't take it down. The last thing I need is a two-on-one battle. She's enough on her own. Throwing all my strength against Connie might work, but I'll be too tired out to fight the others, so I have to find another way.

Luckily, I thought she might be first. Truthfully, I thought she would be second, but hey ho. Work with what you've got.

I throw a couple of testing knives her way and watch her dodge them with ease, as expected. But when I throw a torrent of fireballs her way, she whooshes toward me instead of dodging.

Slam.

I'm on the ground before I can even take a breath and prepare myself.

"Never gonna beat me with that weak defense, hon."

That's what she thinks.

I slam the flat of my foot on the ground and am rewarded with a rumble getting closer. Louder. Closer still. And soon a chunk of earth slices toward her, throwing her off me with a screech.

She jumps to her feet and smashes a charm bead quickly at her feet, floating her into the air. And she flies at me. Dagger in hand, she slices at my face.

But I fall to the ground, then shoot myself into the air as quickly as possible. Quicker than that spell allows her to follow. As soon as I'm above her, I zoom to the ground head-first, gaining speed.

Her eyes flicker in fear for a quick second, but Connie stands her ground—steadfast, unmoving. She doesn't flinch. Until I'm literally three seconds from her face, when she rolls out of the way, and I smash my fist into the ground.

Pain lances through me, shooting up my arm. "Shit," I curse. My fingers break on impact and I can barely move them.

I switch forms and shift into a falcon, racing her around the sky, until she shoots an arrow at my wing. Piercing right through it. I fall to the ground. The pain is preventing me from shifting back to man, but I can shift into something else with a wingspan.

I try an eagle, and luck be with me, the injury doesn't transfer. That's some magical blessing right there. Fuck yeah.

"Well, that's just bullshit," Connie shouts.

I shift into a man and smile. "For you!" I grab my staff, flashing it into my hand. "For me it's perfect." Then I activate one of the crystals in the wood I'd spelled just for this occasion.

As I stamp the wood on the charred ground, Connie's legs sink into the dirt with a yelp. "What are you doing?"

One of her best assets is her stamina. I can't remove her perfect aim, but I can keep her in place while I knock her unconscious.

And so I shift back into my female form, fingers having healed—thank fuck for Vampire healing speeds—and I hurl a ball of water larger than her at her body.

She screams before I plunge her under. But the smile on her face as she's holding her breath tells me she's not really scared. She's just a drama queen.

I yank the water this way and that until I have a grasp on her bow, which I yank off her back.

Her eyes widen in surprise as she accidentally breathes in water.

Oops. I pull the water down to the ground, allowing it to rehydrate the burned areas. But I keep her pinned in place. "Don't panic, babe. I'll heal you later."

"Wha—?"

A bubble of air circles around her head, and then I pull the air out, leaving her without breath. And she quickly falls asleep, her oxygen limit reached.

I un-stick her from the ground and remove the air bubble, then lay her unconscious body on the floor, tucking a strand of hair behind her ear before grabbing her green flag and tying it to my purple one at my waist. "Sorry."

A loud crash in the distance has my head swiveling that way. Two of the guys are fighting. I resist the urge to check on Dea, and instead lower my defenses so I can see better. Once the walls of earth and fire are down, I zoom my vision east and see three trees being felled as Dea falls into them wings first.

That would be Arrie.

I leave them to it and sprint back to the house to find Nine, but he's not there. I can't see him.

But I know he knows where I am. So finding him is going to be a bitch. But maybe I can figure it out. I'm smart too. Okay, maybe not Nine smart, but smart enough.

Don't sell yourself short, Sweetie. You're very smart.

Don't patronize me.

He laughs in my head, echoing around my skull.

Instead, I push thoughts of his voice in my head aside and look at the surrounding ground. Maybe I can find tracks. It's not like he has any earth magic, so he can't just magically erase them (which is a very cool way I'm going to figure out how to use my powers later).

My mental list is getting out of hand.

Tracks, Magic. Tracks.

I scour the area, flying just above the ground so as not to create footprints while looking. There! Just by the first fairy den is a lone set of footprints. Nothing leading up to them, nothing going ahead of them. They just stand there facing the fairy den like he vanished into it or something.

He wouldn't . . .

More trees crash behind me, echoing around the garden, so I know Dea is putting up a fight against Arrie. Unless Connie got free. That's a terrifying thought.

Crouching low to the ground, I hover in front of the fairy den, watching small, glowing little creatures whiz around the bush, traversing their home. "Hi there."

They all turn to face me, blank expressions. But one of them comes forward, standing in front of everyone else. "He said you would come looking for him here." Despite being so tiny, their voice is loud and clear.

"So he came through here?"

Their head bobs side to side, as if they don't know. "Not quite through here, no."

A grumbling groan escapes me. "If not here, then where?"

"I did not say not here, I said not through here."

What?

Not through here?

I look to the footprints below me once again and grin. "Not through here!" Not through, but under. I look to the fairy and smile. "Thank you. If there's anything you need or want, I'd be happy to help."

"More dens that lead to our sister dens farther south would be nice."

"I'll get right on that when I have a free minute."

They bow, and the rest of the fairies behind them bow too. Then they fly away, leaving me alone.

Below me. Right, well. Time to dig.

My hand rests firmly on the ground. Earth isn't my strongest element right now, but I should be able to sense what's below me and maybe make an opening. I managed to move a fucking mountain earlier.

Hands run through grass as I cross my legs and settle on the ground, stretching my senses out. I block out the crashing from the others fighting and focus solely on the what's close to me. Like the fairies flitting across their bushes, flying around their home, the ants scurrying behind me and the beetle pushing dirt around his home. But below me, below the maze of the animals and the insects' networks, is an empty space followed by a series of tunnels.

He carved out the ground so he could travel anywhere in the garden.

The fucking asshole.

I think you misspoke genius.

Genius, asshole. I don't see the difference.

Taking a deep breath, I open a small entrance just large enough for me to fit through.

Either way, Nine. I'm coming for you.

64

It's dark down here, surrounded by nothing but dirt. Even with a small fire in my hand, I can't see more than a few feet in front of me.

Where are you?

Somewhere around.

He's going to be an asshole to find. If only I knew how to turn on the block in my mind that blocks him out. I've done it a handful of times, and Aki has it perfected (because of course he does), but I don't know how to control it. I usually like Nine in my head, but right now, I wished I had put more effort into learning how to keep him out.

But I have other senses he doesn't.

Yanking my boots off, I walk barefoot through the maze of tunnels, trying to sense the surrounding earth through my feet. I search for what must be around at least ten minutes. Maybe longer. But I can't feel anything other than insects.

Until for a split second, nothing longer than a blink, I feel a vibrating rustle coming from the tunnel to my left. The one on my right is empty, I think. But there's something down this one.

So I turn my fireballed hand left and follow it.

Well done.

I turn a corner, and there he is, feet on either side of the tunnel, split like a spider.

"Can't believe you found me so easily. Damn those new earth powers."

"Right? Aren't they amazing?"

"They are something." He hops to the floor, hand on his holster, eyes on me. "But then you are incredible."

"Thanks." Hands filling up with knives, I prepare myself to fight. He might not be as strong as Arrie or as perfect as Connie, but he's smart and can read my every move. Out fighting him is going to be hard. "Maybe I might be as great as you one day."

"Stick around long enough, and maybe the genius might rub off."

"Let's hope so." I grip the two knives in my hands and chuck them his way, testing the waters. "Or this whole immortality thing will get old fast."

He dodges them, ducking to the floor, but I bring them flying back, soaring through the air like bullets.

But this time, he turns and shoots them down, knocking them out of the air like leaves.

"Damn." I've never seen him shoot properly. Not really. "Didn't realize you were so handy with those."

He snuffs, seemingly offended.

"You'll have to give me a lesson one day."

"Stop distracting me." He shoots a couple of magibullets my way, but I block with a body-sized slab of earth.

A shield.

So he sprints at it, crashing through the earth like paper, and then shoots again.

But this time, I crash the earth on top of him, opening the tunnel up to the sunlight that pours in. I hop to the ground, waiting for him to join me.

He pops out of the rubble like a daisy, hopping to the grass as well. A wicked smile on his face.

Something tells me out in the open wasn't the right move. But why else would he have been down there?

So I could get to you without walking into Arrie or Connie.

Why is everyone gunning for me? That seems unfair.

Instead of answering, he grabs his second gun and shoots round after round of bullets at me.

I deflect them with whooshes of air, more earth shields, and more tornadoes of air, which seemed a bit overkill, even for me. But whatever.

He doesn't give up.

More bullets rain around me.

And I'm spinning in the air, dodging, deflecting, without time to even think.

So when an arrow lodges into my arm, I scream in pain and whiz around to see a furious Connie behind me.

Great. Two on one.

I yank the arrow out, then shift form. Shifting into a bear, I barrel toward her, swiping a sharp clawed paw at her face.

She jumps over me, landing gracefully on her feet behind me. Nine's now in front of me, having run around us. And now I'm caught between a bow and two magiguns pointed at me, not sure how to deflect them both at the same time.

Until something glints in the corner of my eye.

One of my traps.

If I can get one of them over there, I could take out one of them without having to deal with them both. But shit, now Nine knows the plan. Connie it is.

I kinda feel bad catching her in so many traps.

But it is the game.

Before he has time to communicate my plans with her and team up, I throw him into the field on our right, hoping to throw him out of the fight for a minute. "Sorry!" I scream behind his flying body and waving limbs.

Connie unhooks her fingers slowly, releasing another arrow, but I dodge at the last second, shift back into my female form, and use air to funnel it back to her.

She looks surprised, a wicked grin on her face. Pride floating through her eyes. "Nice."

I use that second to sprint to the other side of the trap, which should be invisible to her, encouraging her to chase me.

She barrels after me, not breaking a sweat.

My arm is healed, so I'm not in pain anymore, but I know she can outlast me in a fight. Never-ending stamina has its perks, but this is definitely one of the downsides.

Her feet plant into the ground as she pulls back the string, her gaze steady on me.

C'mon, just one foot. Just one foot forward.

I step back, edging away, hands up ready to blow the arrow out its trajectory.

And she steps into the trap and instantly screams—screams that pierce my ears and tear my eyes from her burning body.

Fire rages up in a storm around her, her hair burning to nothing instantly.

Shit, shit shit.

Too far.

Placing my hand to the ground, I disable the trap and watch her body collapse to the ground in horror. Her skin is pealing in places, charred in others.

"Connie?" I whisper. "Shit. I'm sorry."

Nine finally runs up beside me, having recovered from being thrown into a field. "Teleport her to the hospital." He looks for her flag but smiles at me when he notices it on my belt.

The makeshift hospital is just on the outside of the grounds, so I teleport her there, leaving just four of us left. I think. Then I spin to face Nine, who's out of breath and struggling to focus, his arm broken and shoulder ripped out of place.

He puts his hands up, admitting defeat. He hands me his orange flag with a smile. "I'm going to make sure she's okay."

He's letting me win.

I hate fighting.

I nod, turning to face Dea and Arrie, who are still going at it in the forest. I fly myself into the air, carrying myself on the wind with gentle caution, assessing the situation from afar. They're both skilled fighters, but one is my mate, and I'm not sure we can hurt each other in any real way. Not even for a game.

And then there's Arrie.

I find them in the forest. Dea's wings are broken, and he's on the ground, tears falling to his chin, as Arrie stands above him, both axes in hand. His eyes are burning, focusing on the battle.

"Dea!" I fly to his side, landing heavily on the floor. "Are you okay?"

"Fine, Angel. Just fighting Arrie." He looks to Arrie's burning eyes and watches him take a step back, focusing his attention on me. "Be careful."

Arrie has one blue and one black flag, having already taken Dea's flag.

I teleport him to the hospital with the others and face Arrie, gearing up for the real battle.

I don't have a plan for this. No matter what I thought of or came up with, it wasn't good enough. His battle strategy ability basically makes it impossible to plan because he'll outmaneuver me.

So instead I face him. Hands armed with throwing knives and fire magic, mind taking in my surroundings and minding his stance.

"Arrie."

"Magic." His voice is empty, devoid of emotion.

65

Nothing prepares me for the brute strength with which he punches me. The searing pain in the side of my head thrums as I'm thrown back into the tree, doing something awful to my spine. I can't move my legs. Can't wiggle my toes. I can't even breathe.

So I shift.

Using my male form to at least be able to run.

Using everything I have, I run. I use the wind rune in my staff to put some breeze behind me, giving me a small advantage. I'm faster than Arrie in both forms.

But he's thundering behind me. He might be big, but he's not slow. All that muscle is designed to carry him and his weapons, not falter and be slow.

There are cameras at all angles, flying above us, below us, and beside us, but we ignore them. The world wants to see us.

"Stop running, coward."

Coward? I grind to a halt, spinning to meet a face of thunder, battle-axes flying through the air. "Ah!" I shift into my eagle form, not trusting my falcon to be healed yet without speedy Vampire healing. I soar into the canopy, banking and spinning back around to face Arrie.

I can't believe he threw both battle-axes at me.

How fucking rude.

But rather than pick them up, he faces me with fists instead, punching my eagle in the face.

I sprawl behind, trying desperately to use my wings to bring me back to level. But I hit a tree trunk and slide to the ground, where roots cradle my cracked wing.

Shifting back into a man, I stand and grab my staff, ensuring I remember the words to the spell. When Arrie tumbles close, within range, I yell the spell.

And he grinds to a stop. Frowning. "What did you do?"

I'm not going to answer that. Arming him with more information to strategize with is not wise. I'm not the smartest, but I'm not dumb. Instead, I use a trapping spell to tangle his feet into the ground and watch his now-weak form try to get out.

"Why can't I . . . break free?"

Because you're weak, I want to say, but I refrain from doing so.

I edge closer, trying to be cautious yet fast. The trap spell won't hold him long, and I have no idea how long a weakening spell will last on Arrie. My hand is inches from the two flags at his waist. Nearly there—

Snap.

Arrie's arm grabs my throat and yanks me off the floor just as his feet are finally free. "I don't need super strength to beat you." He pins me to a nearby tree, where his hips pin mine to the bark as his hand closes around my throat. "You're mine."

Oh, I know.

I press my hips into his, showing him just how much his I am.

And his eyes focus out a bit, losing control over his battle focus mode, and I use it to my advantage to wrap legs around his waist and flip us onto the ground.

I shift to my female form, but the pain is still too great, so I shift back. For fuck's sake. I have no idea how to beat Arrie in my male form. I need my Vampire strength.

His fist meets my face in a riotous roar as my head pounds and my ears ring.

I don't know if I can do this. If I can beat him.

Not like this. Not without access to my Witch magic or my Vampire strength. Fae magic is all about strategy, but with his strategy ability, he'll just out maneuver me. The only skill that leaves me is my Shifter stuff.

But how do I beat the Horseman of War as a Shifter?

Wait a minute. I don't need to beat him. I just need the flags. Then it's game over.

I've got this.

I shift into a blue tit and fly high above his head until he's standing, then I shoot to the ground, shifting into a bear as I land heavily on the ground. Clawing at his face, I growl.

But he takes the swipe as he's pushed back a few paces, arms protecting his face.

So I shift into a panther and leap at him, knocking him to floor.

He lands with a whoosh, the breath knocked out of him. "Oof."

A chuff sounds from my throat as I claw at his arms, leaving gouges in his forearms the length of his radius.

The growl that sounds from him is half pain, half frustration, and eventually he throws me off, jumping to his feet. "Stop!"

Nope.

I shift into a rat next, so I can crawl up his pant leg and grab the flags, but he grabs me by the stomach, his hand engulfing my entire body, before I can make it above his knee.

So I shift into a beetle this time, something smaller and less easily thrown off. I scurry up his leg, underneath his pants, and make it out of his belt with ease. Now to grab the flags.

Keeping them tight between my mandibles and hoping for the best, I shift into a wolf. Please transfer the flags to my teeth. For the love of magic, please work in my favor.

Apparently karma is all out of favors, though, because I shift an inch from the flags, and Arrie digs a dagger into my shoulder the moment I appear.

I whelp and pounce backward.

Arrie looks at me, a snarl on his face, his eyes still glowing and his hair having long since fallen out of his braids. "Stop messing around."

I shift back into a blue tit and fly to his face.

Maybe if I blind him, I can just grab them sneakily.

(Don't judge me, I can just heal him later.)

I fly fast at his face, but he puts his arms up before I can get there. Taking advantage of the distraction, I change tactics and go for the flags. My talon snags one, and I chirp. Yes! I shift back into a man and yank, then look down at my hand. A black flag lies in my palm.

"Shit," Arrie growls. He tries to snatch it back, but I sprint as fast as I can away from him, using the air rune to give me a boost.

It gives me time to tie it to my belt.

One down, just Arrie's to go.

The light blue flag flows at his waist, and I eye it with greedy determination. I can do this.

I shift into my female form and sprint faster—faster than Arrie can possibly keep up with. And I laugh.

Turning, I stand with my feet firmly on the ground, ready to face him. Pain gone, I won't be caught off guard by him again.

Arrie nears, murder in his eyes and a smile on his face. He's going to beat me to a pulp, and he's going to enjoy it. The psycho. But I won't let him. He charges me, battle-axes somehow returned to his grip.

I dodge his charge, letting him tumble to the floor and roll back up to standing. Fireball in one hand and a boulder the size of my head in the other, I'm ready.

When he lifts his gaze to mine, I hurl both at him in succession. One. Two. Then hurl two more fireballs. And I keep going, hurling different elements at him, seeing how much he can handle.

He crushes the boulders with his axes, so I quit with those and instead focus on spinning him off step with various small tornadoes, his feet struggling to stay on the ground. Then I light him up.

Blazing him like the trap did to Connie.

But he races away, dodging in a zigzag, avoiding my aim like a pro.

So I stop that and instead chuck a tidal wave at him. But I'm out of breath, struggling to keep up the pace. And all of a sudden my heart is racing, sweat drips off my brow, and my breath comes out in pants as I'm forced to curl over, hands on knees. "Shit."

Arrie swings one of his axes at me, and I don't dodge in time.

I fly to the side, bracing myself for impact with the ground. I protect my face with my arms, and my legs come out fully intact, somehow, but my arms are crushed, bruised, and basically useless. So I can't cast or attack in this form for a few minutes.

Usually, that wouldn't be a problem, but a few minutes could cost me the game right now.

So I shift back to my male form and stand my ground, reminding myself that I have all kinda of spells, charms, and runes in my staff.

Time to use some.

"Come on, then!" I scream at him.

He smiles, his eyes still focusing, his breathing still even, but he's covered in scrapes, cuts, and bruises. And I'm pretty sure he's just ignoring the pain of a broken ankle.

The brightness of his eyes stuns me for a second, but it's the thud of his ax on the floor that widens my eyes in genuine surprise. He walks up to me slowly, arms out, feet in a fighting stance. And smiles.

I return the stance, ready for an even fight.

No magic.

Just a fist fight to the . . . incapacitated. Though I'm pretty sure Arrie could punch someone into the afterlife if he so desired, but maybe not someone who's also immortal.

He swings for me, but I duck and swing my leg out, catching his broken ankle and forcing him to the floor.

He grunts as his ass lands on the forest floor.

I swing my legs over him and pin him to the floor. I shift forms and use my Vampire strength to actually keep him down, my fangs dropping free and his arteries pulsing beneath me.

I can hear the rush of blood. I'm tired. Weak.

It's only Arrie.

So I go for it, refueling.

And when I feel his answering response, his hips rising into mine, I relax, my grip loosening. Blood floods my mouth, trickles down the back of my throat and heals my bruises, cuts, and broken bones. And I'm so grateful, because I'm going to—

Arrie throws me off him and shouts into the air, his fist pumping into the air carrying five flags. Including mine.

I lost.

66

He's here.

I grab Arrie's hand and teleport us to the makeshift hospital, which is nothing more than a tent with a couple of beds in. Everyone's there, Dea and Connie in beds next to each other. Connie's skin has started growing back, but it's not quick enough.

"Angel?" Dea asks, gesturing to my lips. "You still have blood on your face."

Oh. I wipe my face clean and then sit next to Connie. "Sorry babe. I didn't think it would affect you that much. I promise not to burn you alive again." I take a fang to my index finger and make a small tear, then shove the finger in her mouth, which she opens diligently. "There you go."

I let her take as much as she likes, needing her to be on top of the world, before turning to Dea.

He takes a different bleeding finger, licking stripes across the pad and sending shivers down my spine.

"You won, bro!" Nine exclaims. "Well done!"

"Didn't think I was gonna for a minute there."

Nine turns to me with an amused smile on his face. "Better luck next time, Sweetie."

"I don't have time for that," I curse. "Where is he?"

"He's stood next to a Vampire I don't know by the embassy building. His army is coming through."

Connie shoots up out of bed, looking surprised and ready to go, her usual beauty back again with full force. "It worked?"

Arrie grumbles, "My plans always work."

"We drew him out," Dea confirmed. Then turns to Connie.

"Right. *We* have evacuated *Sheruta* to New Orleans, your traps are active and should funnel them away from the town, and our armies are in place."

Everyone nods, but I turn to Arrie. "You good? Not too exhausted?"

He shakes his head and grabs his battle-axes he somehow always manages to recover.

"I'm good, Killer." He wraps an arm around my shoulder before handing me three vials of his blood I shove into the pouch hanging at my waist.

Dea and Nine do the same thing, arming me with special go-go juice in case I need it, but when Connie hands me her three, I hesitate.

"Are you sure?" I don't want her to do something she'll regret or be uncomfortable with.

"It's the right thing to do." He green eyes land on me, shooting me with confidence in her decision. "You're going to need it fighting Aki."

"And remember," Nine says, "you need to remove that necklace if you can. He's more powerful with it." His eyes close for a moment as he concentrates. "He's looking for us. We need to move."

Everyone gets up, makes sure they have all their weaponry, and moves in separate directions to their designated positions.

We planned this. This is going to work.

Use the televised game to lure Aki in after evacuating *Sheruta*. Done. Prepare our armies and get into position. Done. Win the war. I guess we'll see.

I materialize in front of Lucien, Red, and the team of thirteen, preparing to traverse the town without being seen to lure Aki and the army away from the town and through our traps. And our secret weapon is currently curled up quietly in Lucien's pocket.

"You okay there, Lo?"

"I am well. Resting before the fight."

"Good."

Red smiles at me. "Saw you taking on Arrie on the plasmascreen. You were amazing!"

Lucien chuckles and then scolds, "Till you got distracted."

"Shut up."

The rest of the team are a mix of Shifters, Fae, Witches, Vampires, and a few pixies, just in case we need another method of communicating with the other teams. Every team has a few.

"Ready?" I ask.

Everyone stands and looks at me with determination on their faces.

"Good. C'mon." I lead them through the forest, down a few winding paths, and into the town center, where Aki is standing with a few Vampires, a smirk on his face. "Aki."

"Sister! Hello."

My illusion spell is working (well, it was a group effort), and not-really-people people are walking about, chatting, looking alive. But if you look closely, you'll notice they aren't interacting with anything but each other. Hopefully Aki hasn't noticed that.

"Leave. You are not welcome here."

"But I thought we were having a battle for strongest Horseman. Where was my invite? Surely I'm at least in the running."

I snarl, my fists curling. "You're not a Horseman."

His face changes from smirking to frowning in an instant, his eyes darkening. "More a Horseman than you." His team of Vampires are ready, preparing to charge, but he holds up a hand, stopping them.

"Leave, and you can just live your life. Free."

"Free? You think living as a mortal is freedom?" His voice breaks, and for a moment, I feel sorry for him. His mind is so warped with power, he can't see the real world anymore. "You think I can just leave the world in your stupid hands?"

I'm a few steps from him now, within grabbing distance; all I have to do is grab my staff and teleport us. But I don't want him stealing it from me—that would be devastating. And I don't trust him not to do exactly that. I throw it into my hand and quickly activate the sticking rune, then teleport us to the first stop.

Predictably, his hand wraps around the wood with a smile. "Dumb sister." But he can't grab it from me.

"Predictable brother." I yank it from his grip and walk back a few steps, putting some space between us.

We're on the beach, close to the water. There are a bunch of water Witches and Fae behind the cliff, ready to intervene if we need it. But the important thing is that there are no buildings here.

Our army isn't far from here, just over the other side of the hill, ready to charge on my command. Nine and Arrie are with them. Connie is elsewhere, taking care of the backup plans.

Dea, on the other hand, is getting the rest of the second squad ready. I'll join them when I can. For now, I need to help make a dent in this stupid war.

"Our army is on the way, Taylor," he snarls. "You won't win. Not this time."

"Eh. I like our chances." I raise two fingers behind my back, and a few dozen Witches and Fae materialize behind us, a tidal wave in the making. I'm helping them slightly, giving it a little more stability and oomph. "We're not built on hate like you. We're unified."

"Unity?" Aki laughs. "Just a societal concept, nothing more."

Ugh. I can't with this asshole. I flick a third finger. "Now."

The tidal wave rushes over our heads and dives toward Aki and his team, throwing them over the hill. "Ahhh!" His screams are music to my ears.

Lucien gets Lo out of his pocket and chucks him into the air. "Go get 'em." He grows into his large form, circling the battlefield over the other side of the hill, waiting.

And there, in the distance, coming eastward, is the thundering sound of thousands of boots on the ground. An army. Made mostly of Vampires or Fae, but the Demons will join them, and then there are a few Witches they've collected too.

It'll be hell.

But I will win.

67

We teleport to the cliff, looking on from a distance, out of reach of Aki and his impending army.

Swords clash, magic is thrown in every direction, and our friends are fighting for their lives, blood staining the sandy grass.

The Vampire king amongst them, he speeds around the battlefield removing heads like candy, and Lucien looks on with worry.

"He'll be fine," Red reassures, her hand on his arm.

"I just wish I could be there."

I look at Nine, my gut clenching. "Me too." But we have a more important job to do right now. "When they need it, they have the second half of our army waiting. Connie won't let them lose."

Everyone nods, solemn faces. Silent.

I have to trust that Arrie, Connie, and Nine can handle this without us. That Arrie can lead us to victory. We were always meant to work as a team, and part of that is trusting that they can do what they've been doing for two thousand years. In the meantime, I have a Fae Queen to deal with.

Dea teleports in with his team a moment later, bringing our team's total to twenty. It's not much, but then that's the point. "Ready?" he asks, his eyes on one figure in the distance.

"As I'll ever be."

I'll be fine. I promise. I love you both.

I love you too.

His eyes meet ours for a second, before some Vampire clambers onto his back, and he has to yank her off, sticking a knife in her heart, then cutting her head off.

I turn to face the team of twenty, Red, Lucien, Dea, my Fae trainer, our Fae ambassador, and I included. "Is everyone ready?"

They all nod.

"Then get ready, because this will be a little scary." I teleport us to the Atlantic Ocean, a memory I have of looking out a plane window, and many of them scream as we plummet to the ground, not really able to breathe.

Okay, air bubble. I gather the surrounding air, moving it into a bubble that will gradually lower us to the floor and give us oxygen.

"No one panic," Dea orders.

Lucien shakes his head, fear gripping him. "Your lives are fucking crazy."

"Yup."

But he's spinning in place, grasping for a surface that's not there. "Shit shit shit."

Red grabs his hands and spins him to face her. "Stop panicking. Just take deep breaths."

And Lucien isn't the only one listening to her, as I notice lots of people with their eyes closed following her instructions. Calmness slowly washes over everyone at her words.

I look to Dea, matching his gentle smile.

"Okay, we need to find the entrance."

The water Witches with us all turn and face the ocean, but one of them says, "We need to be a little closer. I can't get a read from this high up."

"Okay. Lowering us."

I can't read the water yet, my magical limits becoming more and more obvious the further complications I face. But I can glide us over it.

Nine's voice washes over me: *there's nothing wrong with help. Working with the world was your idea after all.*

He was right, of course. He's always fucking right. The genius asshole.

"There," the Witch from earlier says. "I can read from here."

And the other two agree, so I keep us at this height, trying to cover us with clouds and keep us out of sight, lest we do stumble onto some underwater Fae kingdom unexpectedly.

"Lots of fish, some sunken ships, but no underwater Fae kingdom. You sure it exists?"

"Yes," the only Fae with us says. "It's legendary among our people, even us on *Sheruta* have heard of it."

"We scoured old books and legends for days," I say, "it should be around this part of the ocean. I hope."

Red and Lucien remain patient, silently observing the work. Not really able to help.

A couple of hours later, and more frustration than I thought possible, and one of the Witches exclaims, "Wait! There!"

They all turn to where she's facing and analyze the water below. "That could be something. It's like an underground tunnel running beneath the ocean. But it's really deep."

"Nothing to worry about," I say with false confidence. I lower the bubble at speed so we're on top of the water, then I sink us.

The light quickly fades, and soon everyone who isn't a Vampire cannot see, but given the night vision thing, I'm good. "No one panic. I can still see."

"Me too," Lucien says.

A few of the other Vampires agree.

And everyone seems to take a collective breath, let it out, and then grab onto their own clothing, shivering.

"It is quite cold down here, Angel," Dea says.

"Oh, right. Huddle together for now. If I light a fire, we have nowhere for the smoke to go." I rush everyone into the center of the bubble, allowing them to share body warmth, and I do not miss how Lucien curls around the back of Red, keeping her closer to the others. "We're nearly to the floor, I think."

"Let's hope there's no anglerfish, like in Finding Nemo," Red says.

"Why?" I ask. "Why would you put that thought into my head?"

"Sorry," she winces. "Bad habit."

Lucien chuckles.

The other Vampires are also on the outside, along with Dea, who cannot die from hypothermia but who does have wings, allowing everyone else to have an extra layer of heat as he wraps them around the group.

Slowly, I rest our bubble on the bottom of the ocean floor, which is surprisingly empty. "Okay, we're here." I pop the bubble at the bottom, allowing my feet to find the floor and see what's down there. "It is a tunnel. No guarantee it's the one we're looking for."

An earth Witch nods and crouches low to the ground, helping us by creating a hole in the ocean floor. "Alright, I'm about to break through."

Two of the water Witches kneel beside her and curl their hands into tight fists. "We can't hold this for very long."

As the hole widens and light spills into the ocean, everyone rushes through, quickly and efficiently lowering themselves onto whatever lies beyond. My Fae trainer goes first, taking it upon herself to deal with whatever might be lurking in mysterious tunnel number one.

Once everyone is through, including Dea, who had to shift back in order to fit, I crouch near to the floor and grab the water they're holding back. "Go," I say through clenched teeth.

Shit. I have to make it through this hole, but I'm holding up the fucking ocean here. It's kinda hard work. Soon I'm panting, and eventually, I lower myself through the hole and look to the earth Witch with us. "Any time, babe."

"Right." She plugs the hole back up, and I release the water, hearing it roar overhead.

I release a panting breath, hands on knees. "Fuck, that was hard." But looking around me, I realize the hard part might be to come. "Where are we?"

68

Hanging lanterns light the way at every few hundred meters, the metal gratings under our feet illuminating ominously in the partial dark.

"Sooo, left or right?" I ask the group while looking around, having raced both directions for a mile or two. "It's the same for a while in both directions, I'm afraid."

"Well," Lucien says, "that way is land, right?"

Dea nods, agreeing.

"So that way, farther out to sea." He does not look sure, but it's the best plan we have.

So left it is.

We head that way, various Vampires racing ahead every mile or so, giving us instructions and choices as to what is coming up. But it's seemingly miles and miles of tunnels.

"How did the Fae Queen lead an entire army down here?" I mumble. "Seems inefficient."

"You'd be surprised what a community can do and how quickly when motivated," Red responds.

I hang back a bit, standing next to my Fae trainer, who has been remarkably quiet on this venture. "You okay?"

She looks to me with curious eyes. "Of course." But there's something there. Something strange I don't understand, and I get the feeling there's something she's not telling me.

But I trust her.

She'll tell me in her own time.

"Well, if you want to chat, I'm right here."

She looks at me fondly, if slightly irritated (which, on second thought, might just be her face), and smiles. "Thank you."

"We must be nearly there by now," one of the water Witches complains. "We've been walking for hours. And it was a few hours before that."

She's right. Connie, Nine, and Arrie are taking care of everything back on *Sheruta*, and they might not be okay. What if they're all dying and stuck at the bottom of the ocean?

"They are fine," Dea says. "I think we're nearly there. The lights are getting more frequent."

Lucien, who's up front, raises his fist, and we all stop. "I can hear voices," he whispers.

I walk up to him and strain my hearing, zooming in on the sounds coming from somewhere in front of us. "They're talking about dinner and their husbands."

"Guards," Dea says. "We should take them out and hide their corpses somewhere."

"I wasn't going to kill them," I scold. "Just throw them unconscious."

"It's too risky," Red says. "They could sound an alarm if they wake up, and we don't know how long this will take us to complete."

"I'll do it," Lucien says. He races forward before anyone can stop him, light footsteps making his almost as soundless as Dea, but if I strain, I can hear him. A small, almost unperceivable gasp echoes across the grates, and then Lucien races back. "Done. Just need to find somewhere to put their bodies."

We all move forward hesitantly, all of us on edge. But the corpses look merely asleep, no blood in sight. As I notice the small pinpricks in their necks, I realize he drained them dry.

A raised eyebrow is all I throw at him.

"Quickest and cleanest way to kill someone," he says with a shrug.

"See if this grating comes up," Red says. "Quickly."

Everyone manages to lift one of the panels that line up to form the walkway we're on, and we dump their bodies in the small space beneath, thankful for a Fae's lithe form.

"Okay. Moving on." I point forward. "Thank goddess we picked the right direction."

"I'm not just a pretty face," Lucien jokes.

Everyone chuckles.

Another Vampire runs ahead, quiet and swift, and when he returns, he says, "Another hundred meters and there's a locked door."

"Locked how?" I ask.

"Digitally."

I crack my knuckles and smile. "Bring it on."

Everyone looks to me with surprise on their faces, but Lucien and Dea smirk, knowing my mortal past.

"I can have non-magical skills. Secret ones."

"If you say so," the earth Witch says.

We eventually get to the door, which is heavy, seemingly to keep out water if needed, and digitally locked with a pad on the left-hand side. I check it out, yanking off the cover, and nod.

I've done one of these before, when breaking into the Chinese SC HQ. Good job they used SC technology, or this might have been a bitch. Pushing all the right buttons and cutting all the right cables, and we're in.

"What were you, a burglar in a past life?" someone asks.

"Something like that," I mumble.

"Not to worry, little Horseman." Lucien pats me on the shoulder. "You'll always be the hero to me."

"Thanks." I remove his hand and open the doors. "Here goes nothing."

We don't know what's beyond this door. There could be an army waiting for us—or it could be empty. For all we know, the queen could be sitting on her throne right behind this door. Though I doubt it.

But when I swing it open, it's just an empty room with elevator doors on the other side. It's a squish to get us all in, but we manage.

"What button?" Red asks.

"What are the options?"

"One through five."

I think for a minute. "We're probably on one, so go to five. She'll most likely be there, at the top. Hardest to get to."

"Or she could on the bottom, which is hardest to reach to from the surface," Dea suggests.

"There's like a million tons of water above us, I doubt she's worried about that."

"I'm with Magic," Lucien says, and most people agree. "Level five it is."

Red presses the button and the doors close behind us, then we're sailing up, all facing the other entrance, ready for whatever it throws at us.

But it once again opens to emptiness.

"Where the fuck is everyone?" I whisper. "I'm starting to think we've been duped."

"Maybe they're hiding somewhere, knowing the other half of their army are fighting," Lucien suggests.

"They did not take their whole army, did they?" Dea asks.

"They wouldn't be so stupid," I respond. "He might be evil, my brother, but he's not an idiot." I take a deep breath, entering the atrium made of glass, the black, swirling ocean lying beyond the room like a terrifying ghost. "Onward, I guess."

There are a set of stairs to the left, another to the right, and a small door at the back. All of which might lead to her.

I check the door at the back quickly, but it's just storage, so that leaves the two small staircases. "Probably the spiraling one on the left, right?"

So Red goes right, checks what is that way, and comes back and nods. "Just empty bedrooms that way."

We all creep up the stairs, but something doesn't feel right. This has been too easy. Something is off. The air in here feels untouched, like it's been days, maybe weeks, since someone's been here.

"I don't think this is—"

"Shh," Lucien scolds.

"But something isn't—"

"Shut. Up." He strains forward at the top of the stairs and looks around, confused. "What is that sound?"

I can't hear anything, but then, his hearing is better than mine. Maybe he has super-sonic senses, like Connie. Could that be his Vampire ability? I still have seen nothing in action from him.

The group dissipates, checking all the doors up on the stone platform quietly, quickly. And without stumbling. They were chosen for their stealth, this team, and Dea did not disappoint with that.

There is one door at the back, almost hidden, like it's tucked away, and we go for it, turning the doorknob against my better judgement, and are sucked in. Like it gobbled us whole.

Some of them scream, but some of us remain silent. But we're falling. Like, really, really, falling. Into pitch-dark blackness with zero windows or sources of light, and I don't know what to do.

Breathe, Magic. Breathe.

After a few ins and outs, I light a small ball of fire in my hand, keeping it close to me so as not to light the tunnel on fire; Red follows suit, keeping hers tight to herself too. And when it lights up, I realize we're falling beneath the ocean floor.

Dea shifts and gets his wings out, grabbing some of the others, while I get rid of the fireball and use air to bring us to a stop. "Where are we?" he asks.

"I have no idea, but we must be beneath the ocean floor? How much further until it's just magma or whatever is beneath the surface?"

No one answers—probably because no one knows—but I slowly rise us up to the top again, giving Dea's wings a rest.

"Thank heavens it's you," Red says. "Imagine if we did this without you?"

Once we're back on solid ground and we silently all agree to stay the fuck away from that door, Lucien says, "Booby traps, then?"

"Would seem so." I stand in the center of the glass-domed room and raise my hands. "I need silence to concentrate," I tell everyone, lest they get the clever idea to talk. I shift to my male form and use my Fae magic to highlight any and all traps and magical circles, runes, and other spells in the room.

My Fae trainer looks around, taking it all in. "Seems this room is filled with traps, but there's a secret door over there." She points next to the door I went into earlier. "Might be something."

We all creep up to it, this time being a little more cautious. But I'm the one who opens the door and steps through. "I'll go first. Wait here."

Even Dea seems to think this is a good idea, as he says nothing, but he's feeling apprehensive. I look to him before stepping over the barrier with a smile. I'll be fine, I try to convey with my eyes.

He smiles back, nodding.

But before I can turn around, as I'm stepping over the edge, my surroundings change, and I can no longer see them behind me. In fact, there's not even a door behind me anymore.

It's an empty stone room with metal bars along one side and a small window on the other. "Fuck." That door teleported me to a prison.

69

As far as I can tell, there's nothing around me. The outside of the bars is black nothingness, the outside of the small window is pure white, and there are no stones, sticks, or anything pointy I can use to get out of here.

So that leaves me with what I brought with me myself.

But even if I manage to open the bars somehow or crawl through the window, I don't think it would help.

Pressing my face through the giant mental bars, I peer into the blackness. "Where am I?"

If I don't get out of here quickly, the others are going to come after me, and we're all going to be stuck here.

I grab my staff and try teleporting myself out—no use.

I analyze the surrounding spells, trying to see if I can de-puzzle them—they're too complicated.

I throw my female self against the bars, trying to break them—I'm apparently not strong enough. But that throws me for a second because I can probably lift a forest, and somehow I can't break through basic metal?

"What the fuck is going on here?"

I have my powers, but I can't seem to use them. Testing that theory, I try to shift into any kind of animal, but I can't. Something is stopping me.

Dick on a stick, I'm fucking stuck here.

Think, Magic, think. There must be a way out of here. I can't shift, so Shifter magic is out. I'm not strong enough to do any damage, so Vampire stuff is out. I could scan the Fae magic, so I seem to still have access, which makes sense, because otherwise how would they maintain the spells. What about Witch magic? I shift into my female form and try lighting up a fireball or conjuring water. I can't seem to shift any of the dirt on the floor, either. Dammit.

Okay, so just Fae magic.

I'm going to have to science my way out of here. Magic is just science with extra woo woo.

I sit cross-legged in the center of the small room, just a few feet either side of me where I can place my hands on the floor and feel the magic. It pulses through me. I can feel the intricate spellwork, the knots and tangles, where the runes affect the spell, where incantations have been replaced, and where certain ingredients have been combined into potions and used to impact the spell.

It's complicated.

Not quite as complicated as the Otherworld Gate, which I'll still be trying to decipher in two thousand years, but complicated enough that I'm worried about the time it will take. We've been here too long.

Connie, Arrie, and Nine have been fighting for hours, and we're no closer to the queen. Maybe we should have left earlier.

Putting those worries to the back of my mind for now, I focus on finding out what the spell does. It seems to mostly be a holding spell, but I can't really find out where I'm supposed to be being held. Or how to send me back.

I reach through the magic, following various rune circles and spell lines, until I reach a familiar presence. Someone whose spellwork I've felt before. She's there, searching for me.

So I grab on, tying my magic to hers, and then tying myself to my magic, and soon I'm dematerializing, vanishing from the weird room.

"Oh my God, Magic," Red says, exacerbated. "What the hell happened?"

"Do not go in there," I say, out of breath. "Teleports you to a room that blocks non-Fae magic."

My green-skinned Fae trainer helps me up, plopping me back onto my feet.

"Thank you."

"You're welcome."

I look around, not noticing anything else, and then look to Dea. "Maybe you were right. Maybe floor one is where she is."

"It is the next logical place to look." He wraps an arm around my shoulder. "Just try not to get caught in too many more traps, Angel."

"Better me than the rest of you." I shut the door before everyone turns around—because falling through that—and then something in the room clicks.

Barely audible, but it's there. A faint clicking.

Someone gasps. "What's that?"

I look toward where the earth Witch is looking and frown. There's a shimmer in the air. As though there's an invisible barrier surrounding us. Walking up to it, I reach my hand out. But I squeal when it zaps me. "Don't touch that."

The Fae trainer sighs and raises her hands, feeling out the room. And in a few seconds blue-glowing runes fill the air in a dome shape, interlinking in a complex weave that leaves my jaw dropping. "It's a trap," she says.

The elevator doors open, and the Fae Queen walks in with a few soldiers behind her, smiling. "That it is."

I slam my hands against the barrier, testing its strength, but it stays standing. Lucien swears, Red looks furious, and Dea's worried face makes my stomach roil. If I ever get stuck in a Fae spell again, it'll be an immortal lifetime too soon.

The Fae Queen looks us over, but her eyes widen in surprise as her mouth is rendered speechless when she lands upon a particular someone. "You." Her fists clench, her soldiers pull their weapons out, and the room's domed glass goes stormy, lightning striking and thunder sounding. "What are you doing with them?"

My Fae trainer, whose name I was never given, steps forward, solemn emptiness on her face. "Helping."

"Against your own people?"

"You have not been my people for a long time, assuming you ever were."

"Do you know how long I have been looking for you? Get over here. Now." Her tone brokers no argument, her eyes furious as her earlier smirk is now a thin grimace. "Ophelia."

Ophelia looks to me, sad eyes meeting mine, and says, "I'll take the spell down, but when I do, I need you to fulfill the rest of the plan no matter what."

I don't understand what she's talking about, but I nod anyway. Agreeing to anything my friend needs of me.

With a simple wave of her hand, she removes the complex spell and grimaces in pain.

"Ophelia," the Fae Queen whispers, an eerie, almost supernatural sound coming from her mouth, "come here."

Ophelia's feet take her to the Fae Queen, but her face tells me she doesn't want to go there. "Yes, Mother."

70

Mother? Wait. She's the missing Fae princess the news has been on about for the last few years? That's why she wouldn't give me her name. Did she not trust me?

Fulfill the rest of the plan no matter what, she said. Even if it means hurting her to get to her mother.

Goddess, I don't like this.

Our eyes meet, and I can feel the sadness coming off of her in waves of grief. She really doesn't want to be over there. And I'm going to make sure she doesn't have to be for much longer.

I switch forms and brace myself, trusting that she'll take the spell down.

The Fae Queen smiles as she takes her daughter's hand and goes to turn around, but Ophelia smirks at the last minute and jumps forward, slamming her hand against the barrier with a high-pitched scream that shoots through me.

But a second later, the barrier is down and we're free.

The Fae Queen drags Ophelia back, behind her contingent of soldiers, and sighs at her. "Really, Ophelia? When will you learn to behave?"

"When you stop being such a bitch."

"Stay there and don't move, Ophelia," she says in the same voice as before, that eerie, echoing magical voice I don't understand.

The Fae Queen stands in front of her daughter but behind her guards, like a coward.

Red and Lucien are upfront, ready to go, fire in hand, fangs lowered, and for a brief moment, I think to myself that yeah, they'd make a great future for our world. But my smile drops when one soldier charges Red and punches her in the face hard enough to swerve her head at a weird angle. And Lucien roars, fury consuming him.

His eyes burn a violent red as his fingernails grow into claws and his fangs descend further, his hair blowing back from the magical pressure in waves of white-hot anger. A single swipe of those claws is all it takes to have the soldier screaming in agony—drowning out every other sound in the room.

The soldier's face melts, burning and charring in places, as his eyeballs melt from his eyes. "Wha . . . What did you do to me?"

Lucien smirks at him. "Poisoned claws." He lifts his hand and stares at those very claws, admiration on his face. "Never really liked using them until now."

Red just looks at him with wonder and shock, matching my expression. But Dea doesn't look surprised at all. He just stands there in silence, a small smile on his face.

And then chaos breaks out as our team charges the other, not a one of them holding back. Itching for violence.

Dea flies overhead, picking off the soldiers one by one, then dropping them from the ceiling, sometimes charging them into the ground headfirst.

A Fae comes at me, a rune circle on his palm that I don't recognize, but I don't give him time to use it and find out its function. I grab him by the collar and throw him into the nearest wall. His head bashes inward, blood and brain matter spattering over the wall.

Then I rush the next attacker, a Vampire with muscles that might rival Arrie's. I duck under his first swing, then kick him in the balls before slamming his head to the tiled floor.

Thankfully, we don't have an entire army to deal with. But the smile on the Fae Queen's face tells me they're near. I need to get to her. To shove teleport her into one of our cells in the embassy. Then it'll break whatever hold she has on Ophelia.

I rush past one-on-one fights, two-on-one fights, and plain chaos as Red lights up the room. Until I'm face-to-face with Queen Bitch, who has a tight grip on Ophelia, a snarl on her face, and eyes the color of thunder.

I swear, she looks like an angry snake.

One I'm gonna poke with an angry stick and see if she's really poisonous.

"Magic."

"Hi, Your Majesty." I smile gently, sincerely, for just a moment. "Sorry, but I'm going to require my friend back. I've grown rather fond of her, you see, and she's an important part of my inner circle. Not to mention badass."

She scoffs. "The only reason she's as 'badass' as you say is because she received a royal education provided for her because she's my daughter."

I groan, a hand wiping down my face. "You're one of *those* parents. Spare me. You feel like because you spread your legs and ripped your pussy giving birth to her that you in some way own her. As though she owes you blind loyalty and love simply by existing." My hands crumble into fists. "Hate you break it to you, but love and loyalty are earned, even by those with whom we share blood." I clap my hands, congratulating her with as much sarcasm as I can muster. "Congrats, you provided the bare necessities to your child that qualify you to be a parent. You want a gold medal?"

Ophelia is holding back laughter, though not moving. Her eyes meet mine again, and I can see the thanks behind her irises.

But the Fae Queen is stewing in seething anger in front of me, clearly in disagreement with me. "See, the problem with you Americans is that you lack basic respect for other cultures. Here in the Fae Court we remain loyal to our parents no matter what."

"You have a culture of abuse? Seems like something, as a queen, you have the power to change."

No more words are exchanged as she steps forward and throws a rune at me, but I swipe it away, not even paying attention to what it was. And then I dodge her attempts to throw various spell beads from her necklace at me—again, not knowing what they are.

"Rusty?"

The shrill scream out of her mouth sends unpleasant shivers down my spine, but she manages to get a weak punch in before I'm grabbing her wrists and teleporting her to our prison.

But before I can do that, Ophelia yells, "Wait!" I stop and turn to her, but all she does is yank the crown off of her mother's head and smiles. "Okay, I'm good."

And I finally teleport her to the prison, where her magic should be fully dampened. "That was easier than expected."

Ophelia shrugs. "Queens aren't trained in combat."

I raise an eyebrow at her in question. Then why is she?

"Usually."

We turn to the last remnants of the fighting, just a few more pairs of magicuffs being placed onto wrists, and we're panting but free. "Move out of the way," I say to everyone, including myself. And I teleport them to the same prison.

I turn to Ophelia with a scowl. "So, what now, Your Majesty?"

The matching scowl she sends me withers me on the spot, and maybe I'm not ready to take her on scowl for scowl.

"There's something I need to do, but I'll meet you on the battlefield."

So I teleport everyone back to *Sheruta* as Ophelia goes somewhere else, probably to do some Fae royal nonsense, and the sight we're greeted with turns my blood to stone.

71

The battlefield is basically a graveyard. We're on top of the cliff, where we were before we left. And looking down on all our friends lying dead or injured has us all silenced in the space of a breath.

Dea flies off, probably in search of Nine, making sure he's okay.

I can't believe I abandoned them to this. I could have gotten anyone else to go—Nine would probably have managed that okay.

You didn't know what you'd face.

Nine?

Alive and well, Sweetie. But Arrie's pretty badly hurt. He's in the makeshift hospital with the other wounded that teleported out.

I turn to the team. "I'm going to heal the wounded, get them back out in the field. Nine and Connie are fighting at two separate locations: the north forest and the field in front of us. Divide yourselves between them."

Nobody asks questions. They just leave. And I teleport to the hospital, adrenaline and fear running hot through my veins. Arrie's easy to spot, groaning on a bed while trying to stand back on his feet.

Predictably.

"Arrie, if I see you get back up again," a nurse says, "I'll drop a building on your head."

I smile, standing at the edge of the bed. "Don't worry, I'll help."

Arrie's gaze snaps to me, and I swear I see a breath of relief flow through him. "You're okay?"

"Yup. Our operation was a success and easier than expected." I grab his chin in my grip and drip some blood from my finger into his mouth. "Now rest for a few minutes until that's done healing you, and you can go back out there."

Spinning, I turn to face everyone else and project my voice on the air. "You're not required to return to fighting, but I'm going to heal you all so you're free to do so. There are other jobs available, such as collecting the dead from the edges of the battlefields, helping the nurses here, and patrolling *Sheruta* to ensure they don't disturb the residences." Blood pours in a steady stream from my fingertips into everyone's mouths. "It takes a few minutes to fully work."

I turn to the nurse. "I'll come back as often as I can to help. In the meantime, keep up the great work." Then I teleport out of there to find Connie, who's in the forest somewhere, having engaged our backup plan a while ago, it seems.

More dead lie strewn across the forest floor, a mixture of ours and there's—the sight disgusts me. So many dead, and for what. So he can have more power. What a waste.

"Magic?" Connie screams from across the field before running through fights to get to me. "You're back? Did it work?"

"A raving success. What can I do?"

"You have to get to Lo. He's over there." She points westward. "Magic." She looks at me with serious eyes for a second before lowering her gaze. "I think he might be . . . dead."

Those words shock me to my core. And I'm teleporting farther down the forest in visual increments, trying not to teleport myself into a tree or a corpse, until I eventually find Lo's body on the forest floor, lying still. If you ignored the odd feeling in the air, you could almost pretend he was sleeping.

"Lo!"

I screech to a stop beside his body, anxiety and worry coursing through me.

"Maaagic . . ." It's so faint, his voice, but it's there. "I'm . . . sorry."

I fly over to his face and watch giant tears fall into a small puddle on the strewn leaves. "Hey, hey. It's okay. You're going to be okay." I slice my wrist open, anticipating lots of blood being needed.

"No, Magic." His eyes meet mine. "It'll take far too much blood to cure a being like me, and then you'll be out of commission until you've slept it off. They need you." His eyelids droop. "The world needs you."

"I can't let the last dragon die, Lo. Even if it weren't you, I couldn't do it."

"Ah, there she is. My sister." His voice pierces through me.

This is all his voice. His plan. His violence. None of it had to happen. "How could you do all of this?"

"Me? This was your plan." Hand on heart, he smiles at me, blood covering his torso.

"Because we didn't have another choice. It was the only way to keep you from terrorizing the other species, and eventually the humans." Because let's not forget that he cares nothing about them and would have tried to mess with them, eventually. "You forced my hand."

Tears leak down my face as I gesture to Lo. "He's the last dragon in existence! What were you thinking?"

"Took a lot of magic, for sure. Nearly gutted me dead. But I managed it. Solo." He smirks. "Something you couldn't manage on Jura Mountains."

This is just a pissing contest to this asshole, isn't it? He just wants to be me. Though, why anyone would want my life is beyond me. All I want is a small apartment in Tokyo to live out a regular lifetime with those I love. But he wants the world at his feet.

I'm done with this.

I'm done holding back, letting him get away with shit just because I'm too afraid to hurt my own brother. He killed Nine. Lo is on his last legs—if he's not dead already. And he wants the world to serve him.

Shifting into my male form, I put my staff away and shift, moving my body into a new shape, forming something I've not shifted into before. And before I know it, I'm growing in size, growing wings large enough I have to be careful of the trees, and my feet with talons the size of people.

Aki's smirk wipes off his face as horror dawns.

And a dragon's roar rips from my snout as fire engulfs the air above the trees.

I shrink my size to maneuver around the trees, mimicking the various sizes I've seen Lo in before, and I chase Aki, who's using teleporting crystals to jump a few hundred meters in front of him each time.

He won't be able to keep that up. He can't have that many teleporting crystals left. Eventually, he'll run out, and when he does, I'll pin him to the floor.

Arrows bounce off my wings and stick into my thick hide, fireballs the size of heads aim at my face, but I just open my mouth and swallow them.

If I weren't about to eat my brother (or maybe I'll torch him, I haven't decided yet), I'd totally be loving this moment, but the dead bodies beneath my wings and the smell of blood up my nostrils and the sound of Aki's breaths ragged and his whimpers, his sniveling grate my senses to shreds, and it's all I can focus on.

Aki.

Aki.

Aki.

I chant his name over and over again in my head, so afraid that if I stop, the rage will dissipate and I'll go easy on him. Right now, I need that anger to burn through me like a flame raging against the night. Right now, I can't be peaceful. Because if I am, the world loses.

So I'll sacrifice it all—my brother, my sanity, my innocence—so the world will forever beat on.

Aki's feet stumble as he pats at his empty pockets and scatters his limbs across the forest floor. "Wait, wait, wait. Please, don't—"

I grab him by the arm and toss him into the air, the open my mouth below him. Waiting.

He's inches from my teeth, seconds from being destroyed, and he's suddenly hit by a flying person sailing through the sky.

I spin around and roar, fire burning my throat, but I swallow it. I don't want to burn the forest down.

It's a stupid Demon that saves him. And not just any Demon, but Verity. I know he made the deal, but did he have to save his life? Couldn't he have just stayed by the sidelines and watched?

"What are you doing?" I roared.

"My job!" He shrugs. "Sorry." He plops Aki back onto his feet, and then races away, clashing with one of our Witches farther up field.

Aki uses those few seconds to adjust himself and raise his hands into the air. Black sand pours from them in streams until it floods the area around us and everyone, even his own people, die instantly.

"Wait, Aki, no—" He throws it at me, and I have to shift back to male, then to female, and catch it. "What are you doing? This is so dangerous!"

"Stop being so afraid and fight me already! The last one standing can be the Fifth Horseman."

Ugh. He doesn't get it, does he?

"It will always be me, Aki. Even if I die, it will have always been me. You can't change what Fate has decided." I hold the magic in my shaking hands, unsure what to do with it, but eventually I let it go, let it travel back to him at speed, like a death bullet.

He catches it, adds to it, and slowly seeps it toward me like a fog, and out of that fog sprouts a tiger made from the same stuff. It pounces at me, and I blow it away with air, making sure it doesn't seep beyond the boundary of bodies already dead.

"Stop this," I plead. "Please."

He gathers all the death magic into a ball and lets it fester, growing in size and power until it's so big, I do not know how I'll possibly be able to stop it. He says nothing. Just looks at me with salacious glee and dangerous intentions. Before lobbing it my way.

I scramble to catch it, widening my arms as far as possible, but it engulfs me. I can't breathe for a second, until I remember I don't need to in this form, and then I let out the oxygen in my lungs and relax.

Calm, Magic. Stay calm.

Black sand is in my eyes, up my nose, and in places it has no business being. But I have to stay calm. I can find a way to remove it all.

I light a fire in my palm, seeing if it will burn, but it's no use. It's not flammable. Then I try dousing it in water, shoving it away with earth, and blowing it away, but it comes back every time. So I grab my staff and activate the protection rune, drawing a shield around me. And like it was made for this circumstance, it removes all the sand from my body and keeps it out like I'm wrapped in plastic wrap. But it doesn't do anything else. The sand still surrounds my shielded body.

But now I can think.

I start siphoning it away, placing it behind me and storing it in a hill of black sand I'm keeping for later, until finally I can see my brother watching me. Assessing me.

He looks impressed, but I'm not.

I'm pissed. So I charge at him when he's not expecting it, and pin him up against the nearest tree. "This is ridiculous. You're being a child." I yank a look down at his neck and see the rope. I just need to grab it. Then he'll be weaker, like the normal version of himself.

But if it doesn't work, then he'll know I know, and my only piece of information leverage will be gone.

He struggles in my grip, not strong enough to break it, but his kicking feet are annoying, so I use a foot to pin his ankle to the tree also, keeping him still.

"Going to kill me, sister?"

"Hush. I'm thinking. And it's sibling."

"Pfft, you're a woman who can grow a dick. Doesn't make you a man."

My eyes bleed red as my fangs descend, frustration ebbing at my self-control, and instead of overthinking it, I just use my free hand to rip the cord from around his neck with all my strength.

"Nooooo!"

And it comes free, dangling in my grip.

I don't know how to destroy it, but I let Aki go, jump back several hundred feet, and snap it in two. Stone crumbles in my fingers. It's just stone. "Huh." Thought it would be spelled or made of something stronger, but it's not. It's fragile. So I hold it in a small ball of water and wash it with small waves and twists and turns, essentially eroding it until it's nothing but crumbled wet dust in the palm of my hand.

"What have you done?" Aki screeches once he's finally caught up to me. "How did you? Why?"

I shrug, not really caring to tell him about my badly trained seer abilities. He's weaker now, and I should have no problems killing him.

So I grab the largest chunk of earth I can manage with my newly found earth magic and slam it against his body, sending him spiraling into the air. Where I grab him in a tornado that I do my best not to destroy trees and people with, and throw him into the sky. I meet him up there, not really understanding why he's screaming quite so pathetically.

"It's just air, Aki. Surely you can magic your way out?" I put a finger to my lips. "Oh, that's right, you're a useless mortal with regular magic now."

"Regular magic? Even as a mortal I'm stronger than you." His hands form a complex series of gestures, twists, and turns, and soon his death magic has taken on a life of its own as it swirls and twirls through the air.

Before I can predict what it's going to do, and as we're falling quickly to the ground, it strikes out like a snake, jabbing me in the side. Then again. And again. And again. Until I'm hurting all over and my skin is turning black as my skin rots.

"Shit." I lower myself to the ground, letting Aki simply fall. (Who cares?) "What is this?" I rip my t-shirt off and look at the damage, and it's like my skin is slowly blackening, charred like roast meat left in the oven too long. How do I fix it?

I don't know death magic enough to reverse the damage, other than to try siphoning out of myself—but a quick try of that tells me it won't work.

I have daggers, knives, my staff, and my pouch with . . . I have Horsemen blood! But when I go into the pouch, there's nothing there but a pile of broken glass.

Aki lands on the floor on the back of a unicorn made of death magic.

"Shit!" I teleport back across the forest, away from Aki, who looked about ready to throw that unicorn at me.

"Magic," Connie says, almost sounding out of breath, "how's Lo?"

"I don't know—" A scream leaves my lips as the death magic spreads through me farther.

Connie notices me holding my side. "What's wrong?" She drags us away from three Vampires fighting and ducks behind a rock. "Let me look." I take my hand away, and she gasps. "What is that?"

"Death magic."

"He did this?"

"Yeah. Not sure it can kill me, but it fucking hurts, and I can feel my magic weakening."

She reaches into my pouch and sighs, coming to the same conclusion I did. "Fuck balls."

"Yup." Another scream rents the air, stealing my breath and forcing me to lie down. "Can't ask Nine, or it'll remove one of the guys from their position. The field already took too much damage while Arrie was down." Connie looks concerned for a minute, but I wipe it away with, "I healed him, don't worry."

Relief washes through her. But then she looks to me, brows furrowed, and a tear slips free. "Use me."

"No, Connie. I can't do that to you. Not after . . ."

"It's okay. I'm asking you to feed from me." She leans her head to one side, exposing her neck.

"But—"

"Magic. Enough. We need you. And right now, you're infected with something we have no cure for. No one in the world will have a cure to that. I don't have time to grab one of the guys and bring them here, and even if I did, doing so would kill too many people where they are. This is the best way."

Even so, her hands are shaking.

She's scared.

But she's right, I don't have a choice.

I'll never forgive myself for this, but I let my fangs slip and my eyes turn red. I push her head to the side so she can't see me feeding, and I sink in.

The rush of blood fills my senses, and her beautiful, powerful taste floods my tongue. It's like a summer's breeze, with exotic fruit and sunscreen and sand. Like a cocktail of sun.

The blood rushes over the death magic, allowing my body to have enough energy to fight it. It fizzles in my veins. Sending my torso white hot with pain until it fades. And then I don't feel anything. Not even the death magic.

Connie fists my hip, gripping tight, and I pull back a little, listening to her, but she groans. "No, don't stop."

So I take a little more and let her yank me on top of her. But we're in a battlefield and this isn't the time or place. So I pull back and quickly tuck away my fangs and calm down before I look at her. "If you ever want more, we can resume at a later date, but we do have a world to save right now."

"Right." She coughs, then touches the wound at her neck. But she shakes it off. "Go kill him. Then save our dragon."

She runs off before I can think to ask how she's doing, but I guess I can give her more time later. Afterward.

Right now, I have to fight to make sure we have an afterward.

73

Aki's doing something near Lo with a vial, so I smash more earth into his face, sending him flying, hopefully smashing the vial while I'm at it.

I'm done with this asshole.

I sprint at him, slamming him into the ground the second he gets up. But I don't let him move an inch, with several punches to his face that dent his cheek bone.

And when he finally stands after I let him, he stumbles back to the floor. "Magic . . ."

"No!" I roar. "You killed him! One of few people I care about more than the world, and you murdered him trying to get to me." I throw him onto a lone sword sticking out from the ground, his shoulder pierced. "What did you think I would do after that? Let you walk around freely?"

I walk up to him, bend down to his dying body, and whisper, "I'll rip you apart piece by piece." I yank him off the sword and sink my fangs into his neck, drinking more deeply than I usually would. And when I rip myself from his neck, I rip an arm from his torso and throw it away.

Just as I'm about to take a deep breath, he grabs my sleeve with his only hand and tries to pull me toward him, so I lean over. "You'll never be good enough for this job."

"No, I won't. But perfection isn't the point. All I need to do is try." And I rip his head from his shoulders, then set the pieces alight. And I watch as he dies. Never having to deal with him again puts a smile on my face and sends peace rolling through me.

Nine, sends out the message that it's time for stage four.

Okay.

A second later, I get the mental message: *Stage three complete. All soldiers move to stage four.*

A cheer goes up from around us as everyone knows what that means. We have all three enemies dealt with, two in custody and one dead.

Phase four is tricky, but with Nine, it'll be easier. He gathers mental images from everyone he needs and sends them out to all soldiers, including the one of me ripping

Aki's head from his body, which makes him wince. And then he announces, *You are free to leave with zero consequences. Go home to your people. Anyone still fighting will be eliminated.*

After that, I expected teleportation crystals smashing everywhere, but most remain, choosing their beliefs over their own life.

That still leaves half an army who are still fighting, swords and magics clashing around me.

Shit. Now what?

We keep going. We outnumber them.

I teleport over to the front field, spotting Arrie straight away. Nine's not far. And Dea's in the air, leading the part of the battle that's air born.

Just as I'm about to teleport Nine over to Connie, splitting us up a little more fairly, someone stands over the edge of the cliff we were on earlier. Someone whose figure I'd recognize anywhere.

"Ophelia?"

Zooming my vision in, I notice the crown on her head and a similar set of bracelets wrapping around her arms as her mother had. She looks . . .

She looks like a queen.

Her voice rings out loud and clear, "Fae, you are commanded to return home and wait until further instruction greets you."

As one, they drop their spells and weapons, and the ones air born fall to the floor. They do not look happy about it, but they retreat, poofing out of existence as they use their teleporting crystals.

She flies down to us, spotting me and standing beside me. "Sorry, I needed to do an important spell to gain the ability to do that."

Arrie smacks her on the back. "Well done, Your Majesty."

Dea also descends, standing with us.

No one moves. Not even the enemy. They're down to simply the Vampires and the few Witches that remain. Fae made up most of their army.

Nine, sends out the message again.

A second later, he repeats the same message, and most vanish this time, not wanting to lose, it seems. They're all smarter than I gave them credit for.

"And the rest?" Arrie asks, an evil glee in his eye.

I gesture my arm wide, letting him have at it. "Be my guest."

74

An hour later, I'm at the hospital, helping with the cleanup efforts and healing patients when the guys stumble over the ridge as the sun starts to set. Nine's hobbling on one leg, half propped up by Dea, Arrie's grinning, and Dea looks relieved to see me.

Grabbing Connie's hand, I speed us over there and hug everyone. "We did it!"

"You did it," Dea corrects.

"I nearly lost a leg out there," Nine complains, "we did it."

"If you wanted to keep your leg, you should not have walked into that Fae's trap."

"Well, I couldn't be bothered to keep fighting him," he explained with a wave of his hand.

As he does so, I drop a few drops of blood into his mouth. "Might take a couple of minutes. Seems to heal bones slower." I turn to everyone else. "Anyone else have cuts, scrapes, et cetera?"

Arrie holds out an arm as Dea lifts his wings with a wince.

Sighing, I heal them both before ordering them all to help with the effort. "How does the city look?" I ask Connie.

"Good. We managed to keep most of the fighting contained. Somehow."

"Good. Start allowing the residents to come back and send the ambassadors and their generals the signal to start sending people home."

She nods, going off, seemingly relieved to have something non-violent to do.

"Arrie, Dea, please help carry people to the hospital. We're starting them off here, then moving them to the regular hospital if they need to stay. Nine?" I turn to him, giving him an extra hug. "I'm so glad you're alive."

"Me too, Sweetie." *I love you.*

I love you too.

Breaking the moment, Lucien Vampire speeds over, concern flittering across his face. "Has anyone seen my father?"

No one says anything, but Arrie steps forward. "Lucien, I'm so sorry, but a lightning spell struck him a few hours ago. He's dead."

The look of horror on his face breaks my heart.

The Vampire king is dead.

I turn to him. "What about Red, Korby, and the others?"

Lucien looks to the ground, speechless. "I have not seen them." He looks up at us with sad eyes, tears staining his cheeks. "Excuse me, but I have to find his body."

Grabbing his hand, I squeeze. "I'll help. And we can look for Red and Korby while we're at it." I teleport us to the battlefield Arrie was commanding. "I'm so sorry, Lucien. He was a great man."

"And a great father."

We search the area, and eventually, after following the lightning patches that charred the ground, we find his crown lying next to his body. "Is it him?"

Lucien leans down and licks a little of his blood, then bursts into tears.

Not knowing what to do, I kneel next to him hand on his back, letting him say goodbye to his father.

An hour later, someone familiar runs over. "Lucien!"

He shoots his head up, looking at her with tears in his eyes and lets her come to him. "Red." He grabs her around the waist and hugs her tightly to him, not letting her go.

"Lucien . . ." Sobs rack her as relief courses through her. "I'm so sorry. Yes. Yes, I'll marry you."

Taken aback, I just sit there, not sure whether to congratulate or not, given the Vampire king's dead body lying next to me.

She looks to me, then to crown in my hands and the body beside me. "Wait, is that . . . ?"

I just nod, not having it in me to say the words yet. "I hate to ask, but have you seen Korby and Nigel?"

"Oh, yeah, they're helping with the cleanup effort, I think. Nigel's missing an arm though."

"What?" He's missing an arm?

"Go," Lucien says. "I'll be okay."

Red wraps her hand through his with a gentle smile as they both kneel at the king's side.

So I teleport back to the hospital, where I see Nigel helping to hand out supplies with his one remaining arm. "What are you doing up and about, old man?"

He looks to me and smiles. "Magic! I knew you were alright, but . . . you know, an old man's going to worry."

"Sit down right this instant." I point to a spare spot on the grassy floor. "I'll heal up the wound. If you had the arm, I could try to reattach?"

"Burned to a crisp, I'm afraid."

I unwrap his bloody stump, amazed at how quickly it's already healed, but with a drop of blood, it heals completely in no time. "There."

"I hate to ask, but is he . . . dead?"

I nod.

He looks sadly at the floor for a minute. "I knew it was needed, but he's still my godson."

"We can have a funeral, if you'd like?"

"I'd like that."

Before I can say anything else, someone rushes me from behind, and I'm so overwhelmed and tired that I genuinely don't hear or sense them coming. But Nigel smiles gently at me.

"You're okay," I hear Korby say in my ear. "I trained you well enough that you're okay." She spins me around to face her. "I was worried you'd be injured or something and it would be all my fault."

She's rambling, and I let her. It's so good to see Korby alive and well. And without a scratch on her, by the looks of things. She fought well.

"I can't believe it's over. I watched what happened to Aki. I'm sorry it had to be you."

I think there will always be a part of me that'll be haunted by the memory of me killing my own brother, but it was for the best. And I don't regret it. Not for a second.

"Well, I'm going to help cook food for the whole army. We'll catch up after, right?"

"I still have training to do, so of course. And shopping." And with that, I continue helping heal people, using my magic for good, like I'm cleansing my soul. Trying to outweigh all the murder with lifesaving Vampire blood. Other Vampires join in and help me. Their blood isn't as effective, but it does the trick.

As it gets dark, I sit on top of the hill where my *Shinto* shrine sits, still intact, and a few deep breaths has tears coming to my eyes. They're all dead. The king, Aki, and all of those people who have friends and family who love them.

If only I could have . . . found another way.

We tried. He gave us no choice. Their deaths are on him. Nine walks up to me, sits cross-legged beside me, and puts a hand on my knee.

"You never know what the future holds, so you cannot judge past actions with today's knowledge. It is not fair to yourself," Dea says, joining Nine's other side, his wing wrapping around us both.

"More words of wisdom?" Connie asks. "How predictable." She lays her head in my lap, looking up at me. "I'm okay."

The image of her scared face as I had to feed from her will forever haunt me. And that's one war wound I don't think I'll heal from.

Arrie sits on my other side, as silent as ever. But he tucks his arm under Dea's feathers and rests his hand on my shoulder. Then he breaks his silence to whisper three simple words that send my body flying high into the sky. "I love you."

"I love you all."

EPILOGUE

A year later, we're somewhere I never thought we'd be. At Ophelia's coronation in the Fae Court. They have spared no expense in the celebration, invited the media so the world can feel a little more at peace with a new, less tyrannical ruler on the throne, and we're front and center with those cameras right on our faces.

Orange and green drapes decorate the dais in front, with many steps leading up to the top, where Ophelia sits, her gaze resting on mine nervously.

You can do this, I mouth. She has to.

She never wanted the throne, but she gave up her right to abstain when she took her mother's crown. She gave up her future to save the world.

And so I promised to give her one holiday every year at my personal expense, anywhere in the world. Until the day she dies. As a thank you. But right now, she's staring daggers at me, fiddling with a piece of paper in her lap, and looking like she might throw up.

Sighing, I rub my hand over the blue rune on my wrist and teleport to behind the throne, making sure to remain unseen. "You okay?"

"No. This is terrifying. And it's all your fault."

"Hey, I tried my best. This was my best." Taking a deep breath, I ignore the insult and remind her, "We're right here. You have a whole council by your side. You are not ruling your people alone. You were educated and trained for this day. You can do this."

I hear her taking deep breaths, matching my rhythm. "I know. I just imagined my life turning out differently. When I was a kid, I used to dream of falling in love with a suitor, taking the throne, and ruling my people. But then I saw what she really was, and I didn't want any part of it. So I ran. I abandoned my people."

"You saved them. And I think that running away gave you the skills to do so. I don't think you would have been as helpful to us if you hadn't. We wouldn't have won the war without you, and you wouldn't have helped us if you didn't run away. It is all as it is meant to be."

"So you believe in Fate, then?"

"Yeah, I think I do. Fate chose me, the only Witch alive who can wield death magic, to save the world from a tyrant who can also wield such magic. Does that sound random to you?"

"No, I guess not."

"Then stop being a little whiny bitch and be a queen."

"Thank you," she whispers. "Now get back to your seat."

I teleport back, having successfully told off the future Fae Queen. She's been queen for the past year, really, but this is making it official. She reunited her people, though things are still rocky, and things are starting to look up.

Lots has changed with the SC, as King Lucien is keeping an eye on things, pushing harder than his father but ruling with a softer hand. Blood restrictions have fully lifted and the Vampires are once again free.

Connie grabs my hand as Dea's knee rests against mine, comfort flooding through the mate bond we've grown and focused on making stronger over the last year.

She okay? Connie asks.

Yeah, just a little nervous.

I bet.

The little lump in my handbag wiggles, his heat seeping through to my leg, and he climbs out of the bag and soars into the air, his form no bigger than the size of my palm. My little dragon friend flies through the decorations, jumps off a hanging flower pot, and settle down in my lap.

"Doing okay there, Lo?"

"I'm okay. My wing is still sore, but I'm slowly getting back to flying."

It took both mine and Dea's powers to heal Lo over a grueling couple of months. Healing baths, learning dragon anatomy, and some fancy spellwork did the trick, and I didn't lose my friend. Thank the goddess.

Everyone stands as the crown is placed on her head and a spell I haven't cared to analyze is spoken by the entire Fae audience, and then runes glow on her green skin, lighting up the room as the matching engraved runes in the walls also light blue. Everyone claps and cheers as she walks down the center aisle a queen.

Red says from behind me, "You think she'll be okay?"

"Yeah, she'll muddle through." I look to a heavily pregnant Red, the ring on her finger glinting in the rune light. "I'm sure she'll keep badgering me with things she wants for the rest of her life as payment."

Lucien shrugs. "I would." His hand on his pregnant wife's belly, he kisses her on the cheek.

Their wedding was wonderful, full of a mixture of Witch culture and Vampire parties —charms, blood, and alcohol. And the Witches coming out the closet caused a whole hoo-ha with the humans, who started asking what else existed, so the Demons followed, with our begrudging support. But Red and Lucien's unborn baby that's caused the biggest stir post-war. Since The Treaty of Magical Inbreeding prevents hybridization between species, it's technically an illegal being, but Lucien is pushing hard for the change.

"C'mon," Connie says, "let's go party with the Fae."

Still her favorite of the pillar communities, she leads all of us to the atrium being used for the after party, a part of the ceremony the media are banned from. No need for the world to see us drunk.

The Fae garden attached is beautiful, and that's where I find myself as the sun goes down and the stars glitter across the sky. Connie has her arms wrapped around me as Dea's wings encircle us both.

Flowers bloom under the pond in front of us as starlight reflects off the reflective surface of the glassy grass, lighting up the entire garden.

"No one's here but us. We could do whatever we wanted," Nine teases, a finger trailing along my collarbone.

Connie's hand sneaks under my dress beneath my panties. "Any requests?"

"That thing we did while in New York City for that boring conference sounds good?"

Arrie chuckles. "I think I can handle that, Killer." His voice growls against my ear, sending shivers down my spine.

"But right now, we have something else in mind," Dea says.

Nine, Connie, and Arrie move aside, revealing Dea on one knee in front of me, a smile on his face. They all join him, lining up in front of me, each with a ring box in hand.

Wait. They're going to . . .

Dea smiles, his wings almost glowing in this light, despite their black color. "You gave the entire world a future, so let us give you one."

Together, as though they practised, they ask, "Will you marry us?"

The End

EXTENDED EPILOGUE

1

Water drips up toward the ceiling as my hand shakes with concentration, the leaf's edge tipping also, as though the hapelio plant has forgotten how gravity works.

"Why is it doing this?" I whine, my free hand clenching the wooden desk I work at.

"Wow, hon. You've managed to defeat gravity. Congrats." Connie's arms wrap loosely around my shoulders as her nose buries itself into my neck. "But you should be getting ready. It's kind of a big day."

"I know." I sigh, and the water droplets fall back to the desk. Shoving the plant aside, I spin in my seat and grab her hips. "And I promise I'll relax and enjoy it. I just wanted to care for my plant."

"I know, it's special. But so are you." She laces her fingers through mine, her gold hair glowing despite the lack of light in my hole-in-the-wall office. "So are we."

"You're right. You're right." I look up at her green eyes and her small smile and reach my lips her hers. "I'm sorry."

"It's okay. I was just making sure you left yourself enough time to get ready in both forms." She pulls away and helps me up. "Because a wedding is kind of a big event, and you're the star of the show."

"We, babe." I spin her back into my arms. "We are the star of the show." I didn't make her plan for a double bride entrance for nothing; I will give my wife-to-be the wedding she's been waiting two thousand years for.

The bell to the front door rings, and Arrie steps inside, brushing off the blossom leaves from his shoulders with a rare smile on his otherwise stony face. He looks from me to Connie with a surprised smile. "I was just coming to get her," he says to Connie, "to make sure she made it on time."

The dark brown floor gleams under the low dusty lighting of the shop as potion bottles line the shelves in every color, glow, and glitter imaginable while charm beads huddle in baskets underneath. It took some work, but I eventually got my shop open and my business off the ground with some help from Connie and Nine. I even ship to Earth using *Sheruta's* new delivery system—teleportation crystals, it seems, were my biggest money-making idea during the Great Magic War.

The flour on Arrie's hands tells me exactly what he's been doing, and I'm not the only one who notices.

Connie crosses her arms and frowns. "Have you *both* been working on your wedding day?"

We look to the floor together, small smiles on our faces.

"I swear," she says to me, "one day, I'll whisk you away for a full year and force you to take a break." She points a finger at Arrie and steps closer to him. "And you. Don't encourage her."

He takes a wise step back, his large frame knocking into the door's bell. "Well, we're ready to get going now."

"Damn right you are," she mutters under her breath. Grabbing us both by the arm, she drags us out of my shop and pauses. "I guess you can lock up."

"Not that anyone would be dumb enough to steal from you," Arrie grumbles but laughs.

"We still have people who don't like us." Connie sighs. "The embassy works hard to make friends and allies, to help people all around the world, regardless of where they stood in the war, but it's impossible to please everyone."

"Besides, it's only been three years," I add. "People will forget eventually, but it won't be that quick." I shift form, scan a quick hand over the lock and activate the spell, then turn back around. Taking a few steps back, I stare back at WITCHEVER, FAEVER and smile. So much hard work went into this place. It was something I did just for me—not for the world, not for my partners or relationship, not for my friends or allies—I did it for me.

I wanted it.

And next door, nestled right next to my brown brick building, is another brown brick building with a display in the window that still takes my breath away. The wedding cake is eight layers of artistry, all decorated with different memorable moments of our lives (both before and after me), each a different flavour. Including a blood-flavoured layer for our Vampire guests.

I turn to face Arrie and Connie and smile. "Let's start getting ready."

Connie squeals in delight. "For our wedding day."

MY BEDROOM HAS BECOME A FLURRY OF ACTIVITY, WITH TWO HAIR STYLISTS, ONE MAKEUP artist, a breakfast platter, and Ophelia, Nigel, Kat, Lucien, Red, and their two-year-old little angel, Taylor. Who is running around in her vest and underwear while Red tries her best to get her wiley little child into a dress appropriate for a wedding.

"C'mon, Taylor, it's just for as few hours, and then you can go back to jeans and a t-shirt for the reception, I promise." Red looks ready to burn Taylor at the stake, but Lucien places a cooling hand on her shoulder and smiles at the two of them.

"Taylor," he says gently, getting down on the floor to meet her eyes, "this is a very important day for your godparent. Magic is getting married. And you're the flower girl, so that means you need to scatter flower petals down the aisle so it looks magical. You can't scatter flowers in jeans, can you?"

"Fairy, fairy!" she squeals, flapping her arms like wings.

Ophelia laughs and raises her hand, pressing a rune on her finger and making Taylor fly.

The little girl laughs and squeals in delight, flying around the room with the biggest grin on her face, her one red eye lighting up. The other, a green eye to match her mom's, shines gently.

"C'mon," Nigel says, "let's get you in your dress and then suit."

"Ohhh, yes," Red says, dragging Ophelia into the closet with us. "This is going to be great."

"It was a beautiful dress," Ophelia says. They both came dress shopping with me, along with Lucien, given that my usual shopping partners couldn't. "It would be great to see it with the hair and the makeup and the whole look."

Red grabs the hanger from the hook that holds my dress, the train carefully laid out over the floor to avoid it crinkling. Carefully, and with more time than I ever thought it would take to get a dress on, we wrapped me up in expensive fabric, locked me into a corset, and placed my boobs just right into the padding. And then I looked in the mirror.

"It looks . . ." I do not have the words. The black tulle fell to the floor with silver stars trailing down it as the netted train sat behind me. But it's the neckline that shows off my tattoo that I love the most. It sits low, and the skull on my chest matches my wedding dress (my single requirement). "Beautiful."

Ophelia looks at me and smiles. "Are you going to turn off your runes for today?" She grabs my arm and looks at the glowing blue runes running up the outside. "Or do you have some fantastic piece of magic I don't know about that makes them change color?"

"I did think about it—but no, I'm going to just switch them off. I don't need them."

Red slaps her hand to my back. "You have the most powerful wedding party in existence. You'll be fine."

"That, and no one will get past the defences," Ophelia says with such pride, determination, and inner strength, it's hard to argue with her.

I run a hand down the runes on one arm, then the other, and let out a calming breath as I remove them. They're easy enough to switch on and off, but being so used to them on now, it's hard to feel this unprotected. With them on, all I have to do is wave my hand a specific way, and lots of complicated spells will ensue, regardless of what form I am in. But with them off, I have to do the spell manually.

Ophelia, on the other hand, chose a blue dress to match her runes, so at least one of us is still armoured.

I've waited a long time for this. Persuaded a lot of stuck-in-their-ways men to change their lives for this. Saved the world for this. I'll be damned if I let even one protestor or negative sentence get in my way. This is my happily ever after, and I'm going to live it.

"Aaaand, the suit." Red hands it over, and I shift forms and get undressed. "It's an odd suit."

Ophelia laughs but nods. "Yes, it is. It's worn by Fae noblemen when they marry, but this one has been modified a bit to include some Shifter traditions."

Red looks at me with awe and wonder in her eyes. "Is that why you're wearing lilacs and lavender in your hair? To mimic our sacred flowers?"

I nod, the shrug. "You've all given me a piece of your home, so I wanted to make sure I wore something from every home I have." I look myself up and down in the mirror once more as I explain, "Apparently Lucien has something for me that will represent the Vampires, too."

"Ahh, yeah, he does." Red looks to the floor, flustered. "It's a bit personal, though."

Furrowing my brows, I ask, "What is he going to give me, some ornate royal dildo?"

Red bursts out laughing, and even Ophelia joins in once she's stopped blushing and rolling her eyes. "No, I promise it's not *that* personal."

After doing up all the strings, buttons, and weird metal clasps on this suit, I leave the walk-in closet we makeshifted into a dressing room to a room full of eyes and smiles.

"You're wearing something of the Fae?" Lucien asks, surprised. "On your wedding day you're still playing politics?"

Ophelia scowls at him and opens her mouth to no doubt say something rude, but I beat her to it.

"It's an honor to wear such a gift on my wedding day. Besides, it can be my something borrowed."

"And the dress is new," Nigel chimes in.

Zo walks through the library door with a beaming smile. "Shift back?"

I do as she asks.

"And now"—she says with a smile—"you have blue roses in your hair to match the lilac flowers and lavender stems."

I twirl in front of the mirror, marvelling at how beautiful the pastel flowers work in my black hair, which has been braided all the way down my back.

Lucien hands a squirming Taylor off to Red, who sits on my bed and watches some child program on a plasmascreen with her. Lucien, however, turns to me with a box. "Since everyone has given you something from your various homes, it is my turn to gift you something."

The red box he hands me is just larger than my hand and laid with gold around the edges that match the old look of the clasp at the bottom. Carefully opening it, I catch a familiar red ruby before I can even look at the rest. The ruby is as large as my thumbnail and is set into a choker made from the most vibrant silver I've ever seen, and that would be because it once belonged to a man who was old enough to collect such treasures.

"It was my father's," Lucien explains.

"I know. I remember seeing it on his crown. Why would you . . .?"

Lucien looks at me with a smirk, then places a hand on my shoulder. "Because you saved my people, little Horseman, and you gave me a life I never thought I would want, much less have." He looks over to Red and Taylor on the bed, who are both engrossed in whatever TV show they're watching. Though I get the feeling Red is watching out of the corner of her eye, the occasional glance our way a dead giveaway.

"I'm sorry I couldn't save him. That I wasn't strong to protect him when he needed it the most."

Nigel places a calming hand on my other shoulder. "He was a good man."

"He would have been honoured to be here today," Lucien says, "so I guess I thought I would give him a way to be."

Tears sting my eyes, and Lucien hands me a tissue quickly, so I don't bleed perfect makeup all down my face. "I'm sorry it doesn't match your color scheme."

Ophelia looks to me, then to Zo, and smiles. "We can probably change that if you'd like, right?"

Zo also smiles. "Changing flower colours? Easy. Can't do anything about ties and materials, though." She shrugs and looks to the floor apologetically.

"I can," Ophelia confirms.

Zo stands behind me and waves a hand over the flowers in my hair, changing the colors but not the flowers themselves, so they're now orange, yellow, and red lilacs and lavender stems. She does the same for everyone else's, then makes me shift form and changes the colors of the one in the breast pocket of my suit. "I'll go change them throughout the ceremony and then get started on Connie and the guys." She grabs her bouquet and leaves in haste.

Ophelia, on the other hand, stands and runs a thumb over one of the runes on her wrist, and everyone's colors in the room changes from purples and pinks and blues to oranges, reds, and yellows. "There. Easy."

"You have a color changing rune?" Red asks, having stood up to watch the Fae magic. "Really?"

Ophelia shrugs. "You never know when you need an outfit change. Running a kingdom is tough sometimes."

Lucien runs a hand down his face, his crown staying perfectly in place. "Don't have to remind me."

Red's aunt stepped down as fire Witch a few weeks after the war ended, and Red stepped up, taking her place and leading her people into a new era, so she also agrees.

A knock on the door swivels all our heads, and Nigel opens it. "It's Korby."

"Are you ready? Connie is waiting for you."

Ophelia bows out, heading toward Connie, and Lucien leaves after kissing Taylor on the forehead. That leaves just Nigel, Red, Taylor, and Zo, when she returns.

The room I waited in exits onto the top of a giant curved stairway, and while I thought this would be easy, nerves were beginning to set in. Everyone I know is down there, along with a few cameras and people of import, and I have to marry the people I love in front of all of them.

"You'll be fine." Red places a warm, comforting hand on my shoulder. "They're perfect for you."

I know that. But what if they don't think so in three thousand years? What if they want a break? What if they grow to hate me?

I could never hate you. And I think Arrie would rather give up his immortality than be parted from you. And, in case you've forgotten, Dea is mated to you. We love you.

I love you all too.

Tapping into my mate connection, I circle around Dea's feelings, nosing. Well, technically I've been invited for life, but it still feels a little intrusive to me. He's nervous, too. But excited. And totally loving standing at the front with Nine beside him.

Despite my protests, those two aren't getting married today. Maybe someday, were the exact words used when I asked. Today, they wanted to marry me.

"It's time," Red says, having been given the mental signal from Nine, I assume. "You ready?"

I nod, looking to the door that opens.

Red lets Taylor out, who walks in front of her, and at the same time, Ophelia and Korby exit the door across from us. Then Zo follows, along with another earth Witch, and between them they float rose petals around the room, twirling them in the air as instructed.

But it's the woman dressed in white with the long blonde hair in front of me that freezes me in my place. Orange and red rose petals floats across my vision as her lace dress falls to the floor in waves, her plaited hair following down her back.

Her green eyes meet mine, and she smiles. "You ready?" she mouths.

"Yes," I mouth back.

Nigel takes my arm as Ophelia takes Connie's, and one step at a time we exit the doors and walk down the few steps to the landing, meeting each other in the middle. Her hand meets mine, and she places a delicate, gentle kiss upon the top, her lips whispering across my skin.

"I love you." The words leave my lips with ease, the anxiety long since having fizzled from my heart. "I'm so ready to marry you."

Her laugh graces my ears. "I love you too."

Hands entwined, our other arms still resting on Nigel and Ophelia, we turn to face the three men at the altar.

Nigel looks at me with a soft smile, then to Connie, and then to the guys with a little less of a smile (he's still on the fence about the whole "being with three penises thing"), but he grips my arm tightly nonetheless. "I'm so proud of you, Magic."

"Thank you."

The stairs are shallow, so there's no chance either of us are falling down them, but the aisle is long, and my black dress floats behind us, next to Connie's white one, a smattering of fire-colored petals lying on the train.

Lucien has Taylor on his lap, who's squirming and struggling to stay still, Lucien looking more than a little stressed by this. So I wave a finger, and a thorn-less rose falls into her lap.

She looks at me with mismatched eyes and smiles so wide, I'm sure her face hurts.

Lucien, on the other hand, looks relieved and thankful.

As Taylor plays with petals, picking them off and humming to herself, the string quartet plays in the corner and petals continue to snow from the ceiling that I spent a lot of time spelling to look like the galaxy sky at night. But by the daylight, it looks almost pastel in color, and I smile at my handiwork.

I look up finally, straight ahead of myself, and see Dea's galaxy eyes shining gold as he looks at me. His elaborate black suit has embroidered flowers down the lapel that are now orange and yellow, while his shirt does that fluffy thing the old fashioned ones often do, and I'm once again astounded that anyone can pull off that look, but he does it so well.

Nine, on the other hand, stands at the altar looking more normal, but his red hair, which he refused to dye back to his natural black, has an orange flower tucked behind his ear. *Dea placed it there.*

Arrie's looking uncomfortable in his suit, tottering side to side in the lace-up shoes, which I expected, but he looks happy to see me. His ice blue eyes boring into mine like icicles. His voice echoes through Nine's telepathy: *You get me in this suit for one day, Killer. Then I'm never wearing it again.*

Nigel turns me to face him when we reach the front. "You ready?"

"I've been ready for three years."

His smile beams ear to ear, and then he kisses my fingers and joins Lucien in the front row as Ophelia does the same with Connie, having said something to her that makes her smile glow.

Mine and Connie's entwined finger leads us the couple of steps it takes to reach the guys, who smile at us both.

"You're beautiful," Dea says, then turns to Connie and says the same, adding, "Not that you need us to tell you that."

"It's nice to hear it from others, too." I get the feeling she would have punched him in the arm had it been any other day.

You made everything look as amazing as you, Sweetie. Congrats.

Arrie twirls me into him and whispers in my ear, "I can't wait to whisk you away this evening and it be just the five of us." He leans back and looks me over, his heated gaze setting me on fire. "*Utusukushii*." Beautiful.

The familiar woman standing behind them smiles at us, then turns to the room. "Thank you for joining us today and for celebrating this historic and beautiful union." The seer, using a volume spell Ophelia created for her, addresses the room. "I know that we have moved a long way in society over the last couple of years, and a lot of us feel like we're on a rollercoaster, but this—these people right here—deserve every thanks we can possibly give them. They deserve all the happiness their long life offers."

Connie steps up to join the guys, placing herself in between Nine and Arrie, forming an arc in front of me. The bridesmaids help place her train neatly around us all and then stand in a line to our left and right.

"This type of ceremony isn't common—one where we have four people all marrying the same person—but since the Polyamory Right to Marry Act passed two hundred years ago, we've been free to consensually marry whom we wish." She looks to her two husbands, and they smile gently at her, their gray hair shining pastel in the light from the ceiling. "Today, we have personal vows from all four of the people in front of Magic, and then a joint vow for everyone."

Personal vows?

I do not have personal vows, because they told me not to.

I'm going to kill them.

At least wait until after tonight. I've been rather looking forward to fucking my wife.

If you're lucky, I'll let you live long enough to orgasm.

The other three grimace as Nine clearly projects that to them.

Don't be too harsh on the guys, hon. It was my idea.

I'm going to fucking murder you.

Dea clears his throat, unwraps a piece of paper from his pocket, and looks at me as he says, "I never really wanted to marry anyone, let alone fall in love. I always thought it was best for the world if we never had someone in our lives that was more important than our duties. So I isolated us for two millennia. I hurt us. On purpose. And I have never been more sorry for my actions. Or more wrong. But three years ago, some random pink-haired person showed up with a Horseman symbol hovering above their dying body, and I knew things were about to change. Not just the world we fight so hard to keep turning, but our world that we used to fight to keep empty. A world that is now filled with so much love and happiness and emotion that taught me it is okay to have emotions—that it does not make me a bad person if I feel something negative. That, actually, feeling emotions is what makes us human. It is what makes us understand you all. With Magic, I am not only better at my job, but I am a better person. And I have never been happier to have been wrong."

I can feel how much of that was true. How much he meant every word. It resonates across the bond, making it glow and preen and shine between us.

Nine goes next, but he doesn't bring out a piece of paper, because he, apparently, has memorised his vows (of course he has). *Magic, I didn't know what to write when I stared at the piece of paper. It was blank for weeks. The first assignment of my life that I very nearly failed.* The room laughs, and Dea grabs his hand. *But then Dea reminded me that it doesn't have to be perfect or meet some set of requirements, it just has to be honest, like you. Beautiful, like you. Emotional, like you. Because Dea's right. Our lives are so much brighter with you in them. I just want to marry you, show you the world, and cuddle you. I don't care about anything else, like speeches or sounding perfect. I just care about you.*

The room awes, and Connie rolls her eyes, clearly wanting to have the best speech.

"So, after those sappy speeches, I bet you're all tired of hearing how much we love this person." She turns to me and spins a finger around in a circle, asking me to shift. I follow her instructions, of course, because I'm not ruining her moment. I might not live to regret it. "Magic is, of course, a unique person. They have skills and features that others could only dream of, and while it's been a blessing to watch you come into yourself and learn that you're perfect, regardless of your gender or labels or anxiety, you did not always think that. So this is my promise to you: I promise to love you not only when you understand yourself and in moments when you're happy and comfortable, but when you're unsure of who you are. I promise to love you when you can't look in the mirror and love yourself, when you're so unsure of who you are that you don't even have a name. I promise to love the pieces of you for as long as it takes for you to find out where they fit, and then I'll continue loving your whole being."

Something in me snaps, and tears run down my eyes as the meaning of her words hit something deep inside me. She doesn't care if I'm confident or if I know who I am, she'll love in whatever shape I come in, even if that's in pieces.

Arrie mumbles under his breath, "How am I supposed to follow that?"

And Connie laughs, whispering, "I told you so."

What does the winner win?

A solo date with you on our honeymoon.

Arrie coughs, clearing his throat, and looks to me in panic. This is not his strongest skill. His eyes worry, and his hands shake, and we all look to him in panic for a moment, before I step into his arms and wrap him up.

"You don't need to wax poetic at me. I know how much you love me. And I know how hard this is for you."

He shakes his head and pulls me off of him. "I prepared something." Determination courses through him as his fists clench and his eyes dart to the paper in his hands. "I am not good with words. It is why I am more of a fighter and strategy man. I'm also not good with friends or people or family. When I first became a Horseman, two thousand years ago, I lost everything. I was the only one of the four of us to have a family before Fate chose me. But we also didn't have the portal for a while, so I couldn't go and see them, even if I wanted to. And by the time we figured that out, my wife was old and my children fully grown. I was hurting for a long time. My . . . anger drove me."

He didn't have to tell the world this.

He wants to. He wants them to know how much you mean to him.

"Until Magic came along, and then my anger got worse."

The room laughed.

"Lots of people find Magic endearing and emotional and caring, but I found them annoying, overreactive, and full of so. Many. Emotions." His jaw hardens, and I laugh under my breath. My emotional nonsense still pisses him off. It's adorable. "But I've found that those very qualities that once angered me also embolden me. They teach me that my anger is valid. My grief is valid. My existence is valid. And I've never felt more free after letting you in. You free me, Magic. And I'm so grateful that you exist and piss me off every day."

Everyone laughs, including myself, but the laughter is mixed with tears and shaky legs, and I'm not sure how to get through the planned group vows now. "I love you all." I also hate you all.

They smirk at me, but the seer just smiles at us, wiping a tear from her eye. "Now, are you all ready?"

We nod, and they grab a box each from their pockets. I, on the other hand, grab a box from Lucien while he waits next to me, holding the other three. "That was, quite frankly, disgusting," he says while still wiping tears from his eyes.

Dea places the first piece of the ring on my finger—a beautiful black sapphire in a gold ring that has a gap waiting for the next piece—while repeating the words, "I promise to love into eternity and to protect and cherish for as long as I hold breath." Then Nine, whose gold band holds an emerald as green as the grass on a summer's day, links his between Dea's, leaving space for Connie. Connie's holds an amber crystal, and I'm so caught on fire by its appearance that I miss her repeating the words and Arrie stepping up with a blue diamond to finish off the interlocking rings. "I promise to love into eternity and to protect and cherish for as long as I hold breath."

I place the individual rings on their fingers, each gemstone matching the one they placed on me, as I repeat the words slowly, giving myself enough time to get to each of them.

"I now pronounce you bound for eternity, together until the stars fall from the sky."

"That's some cake," Korby says, an impressed smile on her face.

"Yeah. Arrie made it."

"What?" Her eyes widen, pupils blown. "Really?"

"Mmmhmmm. The bottom few tiers are memories from the early days, in the first two thousand years of their life, the middle tiers are when I first became a Horseman, and the final few tiers are when we were all together."

"With you showering magic from the top, of course."

She's referring to the two figures on top, both of whom are me in each form, bringing magic vines from the bottom up to wrap around the cake and showering magic sparks down the cake. Beside that are a falcon, panther, and housecat, my preferred Shifter forms.

Luckily, Arrie is a fantastic baker, and he made the little fondant versions of me very flattering, looking badass as I make the cake magical.

"Did he cater the whole wedding?" Nigel asks from my other side.

Laughing, I shake my head. "No, but only because we persuaded him not to. He wanted to."

The man in question steps up behind me and wraps an arm around my waist. "I would have. It being my wedding and all. But ve wouldn't let me."

"That," Nine chimes in from beside Nigel, "is because you would have gotten stressed and taken it all upon yourself, refusing to work with a team, and then been a giant pain in the ass for a couple of weeks."

Arrie huffs, resting his head atop mine. He spins me in his arms and kisses my lips gently, like a whisper. "I like the suit."

"Yeah?" My arms snake around his waist as I lean up to kiss him back.

Instead of saying anything back, he kisses me. Not the whispering kiss like before or the gentle kisses he sometimes gives me when saying goodbye, but the scorching kind he only gives me in bed when the lights are low and we're alone. Leaning closer to him, his palm rests around the back of my neck, pulling me closer. His tongue sneaks past my open lips, and I let him. Not caring the world is watching or that Nine is smirking or that Nigel promptly left, not wanting to watch his goddaughter sucking face.

Did you know there's an empty cupboard around the corner behind the cake?

His question doesn't require an answer, but I pull away from Arrie nonetheless and raise my eyebrows.

All he does, however, is grab my waist and guide me gently behind the table the cake is hovering over, Nine quickly on our heels.

I assume I'm invited, given it was my idea?

Sure, Arrie responds through the mental link.

I've had plenty of threesomes with these two over the past couple of years since our first at Lucien's place, and something about the rough way Arrie's hands work in tandem with Nine's playful exploration just works.

Nine flicks the lock, shutting us in, a light switch nowhere to be seen. And then Arrie's on me, pushing me against the wall and unbuckling the belt holding my trousers up. Out of Nine's inner jacket pocket comes lube (because of course that's what he packed to his wedding), and then his hands are joining Arrie's, unzipping my trousers and yanking them and my underwear to the floor so I'm stood half naked in a store cupboard meters from the nearest wedding guest.

You'll have to be quiet, Sweetie.

"You too," Arrie whispers at Nine, a smirk on his face.

Not in here I don't.

Arrie skims rough fingers over my cock, whispering touches along the base, flicking heat through me like sparks. "How do you want to do this?"

I brought lube.

"Of course you did," Arrie mumbles.

Maybe like . . . this. I send an image to Nine, who then sends it to Arrie, I assume, because his fingers wrap around my length with a small groan under his breath.

"That . . . that looks good." He pulls me off the wall and stands where I was, pulling my back against his front, never taking his wrapped fingers off my dick. "Gimme that packet." He holds out his hand for Nine. "We don't have long before we have to get back."

Dea is already looking for us.

Sneaking his free hand down, his undoes his own pants and yanks them down, freeing himself. Then rips the lube packet open, spreading some over his fingers before reaching down and teasing my hole.

Nine unwraps Arrie's fingers and replaces them with his own smaller, delicate ones that expertly wrap around the base and squeeze. A few strokes, and his tongue is flicking over the head as Arrie buries the first finger in my ass and my head lolls back onto his shoulder.

Having done this many times before, Arrie knows exactly the angle I like most, and soon he's working me over in rhythm with Nine's tongue lapping up the evidence of my arousal. My fingers clench Nine's hair, keeping him there. Begging him to swallow me down.

Don't worry, Sweetie. I'll get you there.

It's not until Arrie's three fingers deep and spearing me open that Nine finally wraps his lips around the head and sucks gently.

"Ready?" Arrie asks in a whisper.

I don't have the words, so I nod, a small moan slipping free as I do.

Yup.

Nine pulls back, leaving my dick bare in the warm air as Arrie lifts me up by the knees, spreading me open, and Nine guides Arrie's dick home. And gently, with more care than he usually shows, Arrie lowers me onto him.

"You don't have to be that careful, Arrie. This isn't my first time."

Nine stands and cups my cheek. *It's our wedding day. He wants to be gentle for a change.*

"I promise to rail you on our honeymoon, if you'd like." He continues bouncing me gently up and down, prying me open careful centimeter by centimeter, and the pleasure that slowly builds has me grabbing Nine's shoulders.

When Arrie finally bottoms out, Nine gets on his knees and returns to laving my dick with his tongue.

Nine, for the love of Christ, just suck my dick already.

So impatient.

Yeah, so maybe I haven't grown that *much.*

If you were in my position, you'd be impatient, too.

Arrie, strong as he is, has no problem holding me a little away from him and pulling all the way out before burying himself back in with the smallest of groans that sends shivers down my spine and across the rest of my skin. "Fuck," he whispers. "So good."

It took a while for Arrie and I to have sex in my male form, but when we did (with many a nudge from Nine), we'd not stopped. Both finding it fantastic.

Picking up the pace slightly, Nine swallows my dick down his throat in one move I'm still impressed by.

And the only thing preventing the shout that wanted to leave my mouth was the reminder that everyone out there are people I love, and goddess, I cannot have that conversation with even one of them.

Dea's close by.

A smirk leaves my lips as Arrie's pace picks up and he yanks me back onto him. *Feel free to let him in.*

Nine chuckles, sending waves of pleasure straight to my balls, and Arrie follows when Dea's groan enters our minds.

Really? he asks. Now?

I don't know if Nine answers, but Arrie and I are too busy enjoying each other to bother holding a conversation.

"Can't hold on," I whisper as I can feel my orgasm creeping up on me.

And Arrie, ever the performer when it comes to my pleasure, picks up his pace and starts fucking me harder, at the same time as Nine sucks a little faster, and soon I'm careening over the edge, holding in the expletive and doing my best to slam back onto Arrie's cock.

Arrie groans in my ear, slightly breathless as his hips stutter and the rhythm stops while he buries himself deep my ass.

We all stop as Nine pulls off and swallows while staring straight at me, eyeing me in Arrie's arms. *Fuck, that was awesome.* Shoving his hand down his pants, he pulls himself out and tugs on his dick hard.

Neither off us take our eyes off of him as he wraps those delicate fingers around his cock and moves quickly, stepping closer to where I'm still speared on Arrie.

I love watching you with us.

He shoves image after image my way, of Arrie riding me from behind as he rails my female form, my head buried in Connie. Of Dea pinning me to his bed by my throat as my hands are tied to the post with his belt. Of my head bobbing up and down on Nine's dick while I'm on my knees.

A knock on the door has us all turning toward it in the door. "Come on, hurry up," Dea whispers. "People are asking for you."

Nine's face scrunches, the heat of the moment overtaking him as he jerks back, exploding on the floor to avoid dirtying my suit with a small, breathless scream that sounded more like a whisper.

"Fuck," Dea says on the other side of the door, clearly close enough to have heard that. "Seriously? You three are incorrigible."

The music dances through the air as Dea steps in front of me, taking me from Arrie's arms and wrapping his own arm around my waist. My long hair flows behind me as he whisks me around the room with a smile on his face. "I cannot believe you three," he admonishes. "They got you first."

"Jealous?"

"Yes," he growls. "I should have gone first."

"You are all equal, and you know that." I pull my head up from his shoulder and look him in the eyes. "I love you. I promise to show you after our guests have left."

His grip on my waists tightens and his eyes glow brighter as they bore down on me. "Yes, you will."

He's extra growly and possessive today, it would seem. I want to reel back and tell him where to shove his nonsense, but the Angel magic sings through me, pulsing along my nerves, lighting me up from the inside out.

His shifts, and his wings unfold on an exhale as his gold hands skim along my bare arms. "Fly with me?"

Our guests are on the floor below us, but I pay them no mind as I lift myself into the air, flowing my black dress behind me while Dea places me on his feet.

"That's better."

He's needed more and more skin-on-skin contact since the war, along with plenty of rest and emotional comfort since I brought Nine back form the dead. It's like the moment the war ended, everything in him just melted out of his brain. So while we've been working and exploring the new world, he's been resting and recuperating.

"So much better," he praises as his wing tips trace the lines of my arms and shoulders. "I cannot wait for the honeymoon."

"Still not gonna tell me where we're going?"

"No."

One thing he did do, however, was plan the honeymoon, with the help of the rest of my family, who pitched ideas and helped plan the details. Or so I hear. Nine might have let a couple of details slip in our mental conversations, but none of the main details. I know we're going somewhere I want to go, and I know there are plenty of foodie things and even something to do with knives.

As Dea lowers us to the floor, Connie basically yanks me from his arms with a smirk. "My turn."

She turns to me with a gorgeous smile and whisks us around the room with equal skill.

"Seriously, I'm never going to be as good as you lot at dancing." My feet fumble after hers as I try to look like I know what I'm doing.

"Don't worry. It'll barely come up. No need to get good at something this useless."

For something that isn't supposed to come up very often, I sure find myself doing it annually. And I sure as fuck am not doing it annually for the rest of my existence.

My harrumph amuses her, because her laugh lights me up, and I guess I'll continue dancing if it means I get to be in her arms as she makes me feel like a princess.

"I hear you got up to some fun earlier?" She leans in and whispers, "When's my turn?"

"After the guests have gone."

She looks around the room and eyes the many tables and chairs. "Ohhh, can I feed you cake and fuck you on the tables? That sounds fun?"

Since the war ended, Connie's been happier, more stable, and her antics have already gotten us into a world of trouble in many countries, including the small weekend trip we took to India where the only reason we weren't arrested for what she did to me against a tree was because I teleported us out before anyone recognised us.

"Ready to cut the cake?" she asks as the music comes to a stop.

"Absolutely ready to eat it, so yes." It's an Arrie cake. I can't fucking wait.

She laughs and drags me in that direction, through the circle of people, and then looks up for the guys, who are all coming our way, seemingly having cottoned on to her plan. She looks at them and asks, "Ready?"

Arrie steps up and says, "Each tier is a different flavour, so we should cut pieces off each tier."

"That makes things easier." I grab his hand tightly in mine. "That means I can cut a piece with each of you." But since Arrie made the cake, I want to start with him. "Wanna do the top one with me?"

"Actually, I want to do the bottom one with you." He looks at me and seems to emotionally backtrack. "If that's okay?"

"Whatever you want is fine. You're the only one who knows what's inside this cake."

He takes my hand and then the largest knife, and we cut into what I can only describe as a really, really dense cake. But it's not until we pull the slice out and place it onto the plate that I realise it's not a cake. It's a brownie.

"Is that one giant brownie?" Connie asks.

Arrie nods. "It's Magic's favorite. Plus, it's blood infused, so the Vampire guests will love it, too."

"Who's blood did you use?"

He shrugs. "A mixture from various species." He pulls a vial of blood from his pocket. "Pour this over your slice."

Following his directions, I pour the blood icing over the slice of brownie, and then he feeds me a small forkful, moving closer to me as he does so. The flavour that hits my tongue makes my head fall to his shoulder as my body explodes and my magic is set on fire. "Fuck. Is that . . . ?"

"It's everyone's blood. I thought you should get to try it."

I've never really had everyone's blood at once before, and the way it lights me up is like nothing I've ever felt, like the blood in my veins sings and the life in my body buzzes with pleasure.

"The next layer is another favorite flavour combination of yours, if you wanted to cut it with Dea and Nine?" he asks.

But I'm not sure I can move my body just yet. "Just one sec." C'mon, Magic, pull yourself together. I will the magic in my veins to stop buzzing, but when I can't seem to do that, I shift forms. "I'll enjoy that later." Kissing Arrie on the cheek, I turn to Dea and Nine and grab their hands. "Ready?"

"Yes," they say together.

Dea says, "We do not know what the flavors are either. He would not tell us."

I look to Nine, and he confirms with a shake of his head. "Dying to know the rest."

We all hold the knife handle and cut into the second tier, revealing a red cake with cream in the center. "Ohhh, strawberry and cream." The words leave my mouth before I can stop them, and I realize that everyone is still listening to us, most watching us.

It tastes as good as it looks as we all take a bite.

"My turn." Connie hands me a box as she turns me toward her. "Here."

Opening the purple ornate marble box reveals a gift. "You got me a new knife?" Its turquoise handle is also made of marble as the silver blade has the words INTO ETERNITY engraved down both sides. "It's beautiful."

She pulls it out of the box and points it at the top tier of the cake. "Wanna use it to cut our tier?"

I grab the handle with and reveal and beautiful slice of green cake I recognise anywhere. Arrie made it for me once a year or so ago, and now I ask for it whenever I can. Many cake breakfasts have been filled with matcha green tea cake. "Matcha green tea cake. Of course it is."

I share the slice with Connie, and then offer the last few mouthfuls to the guys, who all agree that it's one of the best flavors of cake. Especially when made by Arrie.

"Thank you," I whisper in his ear as I give him the biggest hug in existence. Turning to the staff member behind the table, I say, "We can slice it for guests now. The bottom tier is for Vampires only."

He nods, his purple beard still amazing me as he walks away with the top tier and brings it back a few minutes later all sliced up and ready for people to eat.

The rest of the night flies by in a whirlwind of dancing, talking, joking, and everyone telling me how amazing the day has been. And I swear, the next person to tell me how beautiful I look is getting a lecture about how typically feminine that word is. Usually, I'd just shrug and move past it, but it's been a day of beautifuls and handsomes and pretties and charmings depending on what form I'm in.

People aren't going to understand. And it's going to suck. But they're trying.

I know. It's just hard to feel so out of place by a simple descriptor. And then I feel guilty that it's my wedding day and I should be having less whiney thoughts and more happy, having the time of my life thoughts.

Connie wraps her arms around me and rests her head on my shoulder. "People love you. I'm sure if you asked them to stop, then probably would."

"I'm just being silly. It's fine."

"Anything making you uncomfortable is not fine," Dea chimes in, his hand tucking a piece of hair behind my ear. "You have told me I am beautiful many times, and I am a man. It does not have to be a gendered term."

Maybe over time the world will use descriptors for everyone, and the problem will resolve itself.

And we'll be here to watch it happen.

"Yes, we will." Dea stands next to Arrie, leaning against him in all his beauty and self-imposed import.

"You know what I can't wait for?" I ask the team. "I can't wait to see what the next big technological advancement is. Like the internet or the telephone or electricity. What's next? I can't wait to be around to see the evolve."

Lucien and Red walk up to the table, but a sad smile crosses Lucien's face. I wonder what that's about?

He's mortal.

He won't be here to see the world evolve, and I'll have to say goodbye. One day. But that's a lifetime away, and it doesn't mean I shouldn't enjoy his friendship in the meantime.

"The event ends in a half hour," Lucien says. "Is there anything else you need or want before we head off?" Taylor is asleep in Red's arms, and gosh she must be tired.

"No. Go home." Tucking a piece of white hair behind Taylor's ear, I kiss her on the forehead and smile. "I'll let you know when we get back from our honeymoon."

Slowly, the room filters out until there's just a few left, Nigel among them.

"It's been a great day, kiddo. And you've been an amazing bride and groom." He smiles brightly, his hands tucked into his trouser pockets. "And when you get back from your travels, I have a gift for you. So make sure you don't forget about me and stop by."

He lives in town, running with a mixed pack he's come to love, and it's been amazing to watch him grow. I think he might even be in love with a local meerkat Shifter, but I haven't yet told him I know that—men are sensitive.

The moment the last person leaves and we dismiss the staff, we have our house back to ourselves. And Dea, never one to miss an opportunity to be his controlling self, grabs me around the waist and yanks me into him. "Now it is my turn."

Arrie huffs while Nine laughs. Connie just rolls her eyes at him. "Seriously, I don't know how you put up with those three." Her arms fold over her chest. "If it were me, I'd take myself and maybe Nine, then just run away."

Laughing, I understand what she means. "Because you think you're both easy, but in actuality, you're harder because you wear your emotions so tightly to your chests that I have to pry them out of you. I spend much more time wondering how you and Nine are really feeling than I do worrying about Dea and Arrie, who's emotions I usually know already."

She falters, splutters for a moment, and then huffs before yanking me out of Dea's arms. "Doesn't matter, my speech was best, so I get the solo date on our honeymoon." She looks into my eyes and asks, "Right?"

"Yeah, but only if the others really don't mind. Our honeymoon is supposed to be an us thing, not a "take in turns thing"."

Dea wraps his arms around my middle while Connie remains in front of me. "I am not actually mad. I am thankful you make my family as happy as you make me."

"Same," Nine says at the same time as Arrie.

Connie sits on the table behind her, spreading her legs as she eyes Dea, who shoves me between them. Her hands skim up my chest and undo the buttons one at a time. "So I get you all to myself for one night." She licks up my chest, flicking her tongue along the pulse in my neck. "Delicious."

Dea's hands fall to my belt, which is quickly undone and thrown aside, then he makes quick work of the zip and buttons, slowly pulling my pants down to the floor. "Step out of them, please."

I follow his instructions, caught in the green gaze of Connie's eyes as she continues her kisses lower, undoing the bottom buttons.

My shirt comes off, pulled by someone, and then I'm standing there in my wedding reception room in nothing but my underwear before my three husbands and wife, all of whom are looking at me like they want to devour every inch of me, revel in every sound, flinch, and arch of my body.

"So, wife," Connie says, "want me to remove your dress too?"

Nodding, I shift and spin around so I'm facing Dea.

She undoes the corset lacing one crisscross at a time and then removes the buttons at the top, all the while placing kisses along my neck and down my shoulders.

Dea looks down at me, his galaxy eyes spinning into mine as our emotions collide along the bond, his happiness and excitement flooding me. "You are beautiful in both forms. In fact, I would say your male form is more beautiful with all the Fae magic running through your veins." He smirks, his lip rings glinting in the low lighting of the enchanted ceiling. "And it is all mine." He looks to Connie, Nine, and then Arrie, and sighs. "Ours. It is all ours."

"Damn straight it is," Connie confirms just as she's pulling the top part of the dress down my body and revealing the underwear I put on especially for them. "Damn. That's . . ."

Dea looks at the black corset wrapped around my waist and cupping my breasts and rakes his hand down my collarbones, fiddling with the lace on the edges of the material.

"Wait till you all see Connie's," Nine chimes in. "I may have gotten bored this morning and spent time peaking on you both getting dressed." He shrugs, as though that's totally okay. And I guess it is.

Of course it's okay. You're my wife.

You're always invited, no invitation necessary.

Connie finishes taking down the rest of the dress material, but takes a second to spread it out across a table near us so it doesn't get creased or wrinkled. Which leaves me in my suspenders and underwear and corset and choker with the red ruby set in place.

"Lucien gave it to you?" Dea asks, a thumb gracing over the king's jewel.

"It was from the king's crown. He said this way he gets to still be a part of my day."

"So that's why you changed the color scheme last minute," Connie confirm. "To match the jewel." She spins me around so she can see it, examine it, and a tear falls from her eye. "We've seen many Vampire kings in our time, but he was different. Special in some way."

"He wanted peace, despite his nature," Arrie says, sounding a little like Nine, if I'm honest. "It was a brave thing to do in his time."

Connie goes to unbuckle it, but I pause her hand before it undoes the clasp. "Leave it on. I like it."

Dea turns to Nine and smiles, gracing his lips with a kiss. "You can just watch for a bit."

Nine furrows his brows and goes to protest.

But Dea grabs his wrists and yanks him to him. "You had your fill earlier in a closet without me. You can watch while I am forced to take third place."

Nine does nothing but smile, enjoying Dea's more dominant nature, which has shone through since Nine came back from the dead and hasn't left yet. But we're all enjoying it, so no one has said anything.

That's because you're all watching it with horny eyes.

"Kind of hard not to," Connie says as her hand delves beneath the material of my underwear and cups me. "And the way it sets Magic on fire is worth every second." Her fingers graze just above my clit, pressing downward and gently whispering in my ear, "Happy to watch with you."

While I love watching Dea and Nine, and I'm sure I'll do just that many times in the upcoming weeks, tonight, I want to make everyone feel loved and special. "That's okay. There's plenty of time for that."

Nine smiles at me, nodding, and then sits next to Connie with his eyes closed. *Gonna sit in your head for a bit.*

Okay.

We've done this before, where I can feel Nine's presence in my head as he feels what I feel, and it always makes me feel watched, observed, treasured, and sexy.

Connie's legs dangle either side of me, my ass pressed against her waist as her hands graze gentle fingers up and down my skin. Dea's in front, shrugging off his jacket and undoing his tie as everyone eyes his every move. Everyone, that is, except for Arrie, who's ice blue gaze is fixed on the bra and suspenders like someone who's found the best brownie in the world.

You are a great brownie.

Two buttons undone, shirt untucked, Dea plunges a forceful tongue down my throat as he steps forward, pressing his body into my mine.

Connie catches me, steadying me with firm hands on my waist as Nine gasps, his own hands trailing down his pants.

Arrie climbs across the table and sits behind Connie, his legs dangling outside of hers as he gently moves her hair to one side, leaving space for kisses and nips up her neck.

But it's Dea I'm focused on. Hyperfixated on the man in front of me barging through the door with ragged breaths and golden eyes as his hands grab my hips with bruising force. "Mine." As he exhales, his wings pop out and his skin glitters as his nails dig into my skin. "Finally mine."

"Yours."

He smiles against my lips, the corners passing mine as his piercings run over my lower lip in that familiar cold metallic way that I always associate with Dea.

Connie gasps behind me, and Nine shows me why: Arrie's fingers delving deep under her underwear with an ever-increasing tempo that has her whining in my ear and shifting her hips, rocking into his hand. Her teeth dig into my neck, and my fangs descend.

Dea chuckles, then leans his head to one side, baring his neck. "Dig in."

I pierce his skin with practised gentleness, and he feels no pain, only pleasure, as I drink deeply, setting myself on fire in the process. Every nerve ending alight as I arch my back, rubbing my clit on the underwear seam to gain some kind of friction—any amount of pressure.

Dea presses me into Connie's front until her breasts are pressed against the bare skin of my back and my ass is sitting in her lap. She sneaks her fingers back under my underwear and slides smooth skin across my clit in slow, circling motions.

A sigh of relief leaves my lips. "Goddess, that's better."

She giggles. "You're welcom . . . ahh . . ."

Dea undoes all the buttons on his shirt until he's stood in nothing but dress pants and an open shirt, his golden tattoo swirling on his shoulder. Then he spins me around and presses me to his back, the skin contact singing through me as I now face Connie, who I lean down and kiss while she continues to ride Arrie's fingers.

My fangs graze her lips, and she wraps the tip of tongue around one, laving it, and a moan slips from my mouth unbidden.

Nine's hand moves in rhythm to Connie's tongue under his pants as his closed eyes squint tight and a small moan echoes mine. "Damn," he whispers. "They're really that sensitive?"

"Uh-huh," I manage as Dea delves two fingers into me and I brace my hands on Connie's shoulders, trying to stay upright. His hard length presses against my back. Needy. Insistent.

"Get up on the table." He picks me up by the waist and dangles me above Connie, who closes her legs slightly. And I straddle her, my knees landing either side Arrie's legs, splitting myself wide open. "Good, Angel."

His fingers return to behind me, but instead of touching me, they're undoing his pants buckle and shoving them to his knees. "Now, stay still." In a few seconds, the head of his cock is nudging my entrance and slowly sliding home, and I'm doing my best to hold onto Connie's shoulders and stay still.

But when Arrie grabs my knees and yanks me closer to Connie's body so we're pressed against each other and my clit can feel every inch of her lace panties, I can't. I lose the battle against my body and start shifting my hips, grazing my clit against her underwear.

"I said still," Dea whispers gently in my ear but no less demanding.

My body stops, but my mouth slips a whimper.

And then he's delving his hand around me, slipping it beneath my underwear he nudged aside earlier and pinching my clit between two fingers, grinding in harsh movements.

The back of his hand is clearly doing something to Connie, because she bounces lightly beneath me, riding both hands as her fingers guide my nipple into my mouth and pinch the other.

"Shit." Dea hasn't moved, but I don't think he'll need to. His cock is pressed against the back of me, grinding the sweet spot I found with a little practise and my hips move of their own accord.

Connie's moans match mine, and soon Nine's join us as his hand speeds up under his pants. "Fuck her already," Nine says out loud, unable to focus long enough to say anything inside our heads.

With a deep chuckle, Dea pulls out, looking directly at Nine, who meets his gaze, and slams back in.

Holy goddess, fuck.

Nine falls back onto the table with a deep moan that has his hips arching off the table.

Behind Connie's shoulder, Arrie's length is standing strong in his hand, roughly pumping up and down as his breaths labor in harsh pants. Connie's still riding his hand and Dea's as she focuses on my nipple, swirling her tongue in tight circles, but it's Dea who's taking me apart thrust by thrust.

He's angled me deep, so his cock is reaching the back of me, and he drags against every good spot on the way in, so instead of finding friction I'm having to hold back a tidal wave. Because I can't finish this quickly. Not on my wedding night.

We're not done with you yet. Just let go.

Dea doesn't let up, lowly growling in my ear, "I am not going to stop until I am done, regardless of how many or few times you finish."

"So just enjoy it," Arrie grits between his teeth.

Connie pinches both nipples harder and slams her lips into mine as I topple over the edge with her, our screams mixing into each others' as our tongues entwine, Nine exploding beside us as my orgasm crashes through him.

But Dea doesn't let up; if anything, he moves faster, his hips stuttering as the small moans slipping from his lips indicate that he's holding back.

"Let me help," Arrie says gruffly.

Connie slips from between us and helps Nine out of his pants before falling to her knees and wrapping her mouth around his spent cock.

Dea, on the other hand, spins me around so my back's facing Arrie as his fingers find my ass and begin to stretch me open. "Do we have any lube?" he asks.

Nine grabs his jacket from the chair beside him and throws it our way while he throws his head back in a whine.

Dea fishes the packet out and hands it to Arrie, who is quick to rip it open with his teeth and finish prepping me with quick precision until I'm stretched, lubed, and ready.

Just as he's about to enter, Connie pulls off Nine's now hard cock with a pop and smirks at me. "It's my turn next."

Arrie sinks in inch by inch, pulling out each time, and gradually going deeper with each gentle thrust, but it's not until he's seated all the way in that Dea smiles at him and nods.

"Hold on tight, Angel." He holds my legs open as I hover over Arrie's lap, and Arrie's hands soon join his, propping me up so they can both reach.

Connie and Nine both stop what they're doing to watch, both smiling and both of their eyes blown wide and hazy with lust.

Dea spears into me with agonizing force, and Arrie pulls out, only to follow him home. "Fuck, ve's so tight like this," Arrie groans.

Dea's scrunched-up face clearly agrees as his grip on my knees tightens and his lips part with effort, a breathless groan escaping.

Arrie leans back onto his hands and matches Dea's rhythm, both working tandem to force me to fall apart.

Nine falls into my head, gasping and squirming beside Connie, who takes his cock in hand and slowly keeps him calm while never taking her eyes off me.

"You look . . . amazing," she whispers, awe dripping from her voice.

Arrie's firm hands on my thighs tighten, his breaths coming in ragged, harsh puffs that graze my ear.

Dea's scrunched-up face bends to kiss mine, his tongue snaking around mine before he pullks away and asks, "Are you okay, Angel?"

"F-Fine." The word barely comes out as they thrust in together, stretching me wide and making me fuller than I've ever been before. "Don't stop."

Together, they pick up the pace, pounding into me harder and more frantically, until they're not matching each other's paces anymore; they're just enjoying me.

"Argh!" Arrie's hips stutter then come to a full stop as his growls grace my ears and his fingers bruise my thighs.

But Dea doesn't stop. He goes hard enough that it feels like a punishment I'll never stop enjoying. As Arrie slips away, Dea lays me on the table and pins my knees to my chest, fucking me deeper. His unusual eyes meet mine in a smile, our connection pulsing between us, his feelings of love, cherishment, and admiration burning in me somewhere deep.

Fuck, this man loves me, and it feels so good.

I briefly notice Nine removing Connie's hand from his dick and just staring at us, tears falling down his face.

Something soft works its way beneath me, but I don't take heed. I'm too lost in this man making my every nerve ending burst into flames and my legs shakes and my throat hoarse. And eventually, after what feels like a lifetime of intensity, I spiral over the edge, dragging Dea with me as he moans my name in the pulsing air.

5

My body is wrecked—in the best way—so Arrie carries me up to bed after I wobble on my feet for all of two steps and my knees buckle. His strong arms wrap around me, and it reminds me of the night he carried me to bed after movie night my first week here. I felt safe then, too.

"I'll always keep you safe, Killer."

We all get in to my bed, which has grown in size even further in the last couple of years, and we all snuggle in with room to spare. But Connie has other ideas.

She crawls up my body and rests her hips on mine. "It's my turn."

Nine snorts as Dea chuckles. "I'm not sure Sweetie has anything left in them."

"Well, they might have wrecked your vagina, but your dick is still good, right?" The devilish light in her eyes makes me swoon and flutter, and without missing a beat, I shift. "Perrrfect," she purrs, then looks around at the guys and mockingly asks, "C'mon, you can't be beat already? We have all night left."

Arrie, never one to back down from a challenge, sits up and kisses my neck, a low purr vibrating across my skin like fire.

Dea, on the other hand, genuinely looks exhausted, and he looks at us as though we might be on our own here, but he takes one look at me on top of the duvet, his eyes roaming over my chest and down toward my hardening cock, and licks his lips. "I am happy for Connie to take the reins."

"Good, because I wasn't looking for your permission."

His eyes dig into her soul, and I swear, I watch it shiver beneath her skin.

But Nine just laughs as he climbs atop Dea's lap and places a placating kiss to his lips, silently asking them to open. And Dea lets him, of course, because he could never say no to either of us.

"Can I give ve the tickets now?" Connie asks, shooting her question at all three of them as she takes her tongue to my inner thigh, skating it across the skin in small circles. "I want Magic to go to bed happy."

"I think I'll be happy regardless, what with all the orgasms I've gotten today." I look to Dea and Arrie, knowing it's them who want to wait. "But yes please." I bat my lashes at them both.

They look at each other and sigh, Arrie dragging a hand through his hair and Dea resting a frustrated one around his neck. "Fine, Angel."

"But," Arrie adds, "I want to keep the activites and plan a secret, so we can take you everywhere and show you a good time without you worrying about all the times and shows and restaurant bookings."

"Deal." As Connie's ministrations turned hotter and higher, the word came out more of a breathless sigh.

But it's Arrie who grabs the envelope on the dresser by the door, where I was supposed to open it first thing in the morning, as planned. He presents it to me just as Connie wraps her lips around me, and a hiss escapes my lips as I break the wax seal. I gently pull out bright pink tickets to a hotel in Paris.

"It's Paris?"

"Just like we talked about," Arrie whispered.

Connie looks up at me as she takes me deeper, swallowing me down her throat in one practised move I still can't do as well as her.

"F-Fuck." I nearly scrunch the tickets, but then I remember that I might want to keep them, so Nine takes them from me with his spare hand and places them on the nightstand before returning to the soft strokes he glides gently up and down Dea's lubed cock.

Dea's head is thrown back onto the headboard, a mixture of oversensitive pain and pleasure upon his face.

Arrie returns to my neck, where he kisses up in a line toward my lips, which he takes between his in a surprisingly tender kiss.

My hand wraps around Connie's hair, fingers threading through the silky strands as my hips arch up into her mouth. My other hand wraps strong fingers around Arrie's dick and strokes it back to life after what happened downstairs.

He looks at me as if to say "More?", and I don't have the words while Connie licks a circle around my head, so I just nod and manage a small, "Always."

I pull Connie off my dick by her hair and pull us both to our knees, where I plunge into her mouth with a searing kiss I hope leaves nothing to the imagination, our tongues battling it out to see who tops, but when I nip her lower lip and draw blood, she withdraws, hissing.

"You bit me?"

"Well, technically, I'm not a Vampire right now, so it's allowed. Right?" I smirk, enjoying my little technicality—if mildly apprehensive regarding her answer.

She looks at me with a smile. "It's always allowed, in any form. Just warn me first." Her hands skim up my chest and rest on her shoulders. "How'd you want me?"

"On your knees."

Nine turns to face me at my words, his brows raised in question. I send him the image I have in mind, and he squirms in delight. *Ohhh, yes. That'll be fun.*

Connie bends over in front of me, her ass at my groin, and I grab her hips, forcing her lower so I'm lined up ready, then edge my fingers in inch by inch until they're buried deep and stroking that familiar spot that drives her wild, my fingers not otherwise moving.

Nine's head bobs up and down Dea, swallowing him to the hilt as Dea's head throws back, a silent moan on his face.

Connie buries her head in the pillow beneath her, her moans muffled and caught before reaching my ears, but the bucking of her hips into my hand and the wetness coating my fingers is all I need to know that she would be begging if she could.

So I grab her hips with firm hands and bury myself to the hilt in one swift move, filling her to the brim. She squeezes me tight, strangling my dick and causing me to stop to take a deep breath.

"Struggling, Angel?" Dea's eyes meet mine with a smirk.

"Not at all," I grit through a tight jaw.

Arrie's lubed fingers trail down my ass and around my hole in teasing circles, causing me to buck into Connie, who groans out loud, having lifted her head from the pillow.

"Fuck, Magic, just . . . please."

I don't think I've heard her whimper quite this much before.

You've spent all evening making her watch, making her wait. She's dying.

Oh. Oops. Yeeeah, I'm not at all sorry. When Arrie delves two fingers in and scissors me, spearing me apart, I thrust into Connie a little harder, my hips stuttering. "Fffuck." But rather than wait for Arrie, I keep going, Connie's heat wrapping around me like an addiction I never want to come up from.

"Faster," she moans.

And, not wanting to disappoint, I speed up, noticing Nine following her instruction too, having sped up his lips that are sealed tight around Dea's cock.

Arrie pokes the head of his cock into my ass, stilling my hips for a moment—which makes Connie whine—and he slowly enters me, inch by glorious inch. "Shit. I don't have forever here, Killer."

He sounds apologetic, but I might be in the same boat because Connie's spasming around me like she's ready to come and Nine is lowering himself onto Dea's cock like he's been waiting all evening for the chance.

Either one of your cocks would have done, but yours is busy.

"Wait your turn," Connie groans, bucking her hips backward, causing me to buck back into Arrie, who is now bottomed out.

We all groan at once, but Connie laughs, finding her minimal control funny.

My fingers roll around to her front and grip her clit between two fingers, pinching hard. Her hiss music to my ears.

Arrie grabs my hips and starts slow, teasing thrusts, until he's speeding up and controlling not only my pleasure, but Connie's too. Knowing my ass a little too well, he nails my prostate with a surprising level of accuracy, and I'm soon struggling to hold on.

Fucking let go, Nine huffs at all of us.

But I'm the first to go because Connie tightens around me, seconds from bursting; my hips frantically thrust into her and back onto Arrie, seeking pleasure, trying to make it last as long as possible, and soon Connie follows, screaming into the pillow in front of her. Arrie bites my shoulder while he fills me, and I totally miss Nine and Dea's, because they're already cleaning up by the time I pull out of a totally spent Connie.

When we're all showered and curled up in bed, I whisper into the night, "We're going to Paris."

Arrie's Brownies

1. Preheat oven to 180 degrees Celsius (350 degrees Fahrenheit or gas mark four)
2. Melt 170g (3/4 cup) butter and 100g of chocolate.
3. Transfer the mixture into a mixing bowl and add a pinch of salt, one teaspoon of vanilla extract, 50g (1/4 cup) of white sugar, 50g (1/4 cup) of brown sugar, and 50g (1/2 cup) of cocoa powder. Stir until combined.
4. In a small bowl, add two teaspoons of flaxseed and two teaspoons of water. Mix until well combined, then add to the main mixing bowl and stir.
5. Sift 125g (1 cup) of self-raising flour into the mixing bowl and stir until combined.
6. Pour mixture into square roasting dish that is lined with greaseproof paper (not greased with butter). Break 50g of chocolate into squares and sprinkle on top, pushing each square into the mixture slightly. Bake for twenty-five minutes.

www.ingramcontent.com/pod-product-compliance
Lightning Source LLC
Chambersburg PA
CBHW060540310726
48982CB00009B/1325/J

9781999347291